the as

John Grisham is tl
one work of non-
and a novel for you
of Directors of tl
York and is the Chairman of the Board of Directors of the Mississippi Innocence Project at the University of Mississippi School of Law. He lives in Virginia and Mississippi.

Also available by John Grisham

Fiction

A Time to Kill
The Firm
The Pelican Brief
The Client
The Chamber
The Rainmaker
The Runaway Jury
The Partner
The Street Lawyer
The Testament
The Brethren
A Painted House
Skipping Christmas
The Summons
The King of Torts
Bleachers
The Last Juror
The Broker
Playing for Pizza
The Appeal
Ford County
Theodore Boone: Young Lawyer
The Confession

Non-fiction

The Innocent Man

john grisham

the associate

arrow books

Reissued in the United Kingdom by Arrow Books in 2011

14

First published in the United Kingdom in 2009 by Century
First published in paperback in 2009 by Arrow books

Arrow Books
The Random House Group Limited
20 Vauxhall Bridge Road, London, SW1V 2SA

www.randomhouse.co.uk

Addresses for companies within The Random House Group Limited can be found at: www.randomhouse.co.uk/offices.htm

The Random House Group Limited Reg. No. 954009

A CIP catalogue record for this book
is available from the British Library

Printed and bound in Great Britain by Clays Ltd, Elcograf S.p.A.

Typeset by SX Composing DTP, Rayleigh, Essex

TO
Steve Rubin, Suzanne Herz, John Pitts,
Alison Rich, Rebecca Holland, John Fontana,
and the rest of the gang at Doubleday

Chapter 1

The rules of the New Haven Youth League required that each kid play at least ten minutes in each game. Exceptions were allowed for players who had upset their coaches by skipping practice or violating other rules. In such cases, a coach could file a report before the game and inform the scorekeeper that so-and-so wouldn't play much, if at all, because of some infraction. This was frowned on by the league; it was, after all, much more recreational than competitive.

With four minutes left in the game, Coach Kyle looked down the bench, nodded at a somber and pouting little boy named Marquis, and said, 'Do you want to play?' Without responding, Marquis walked to the scorers' table and waited for a whistle. His violations were numerous – skipping practice, skipping school, bad grades, losing his uniform, foul language. In fact, after ten weeks and fifteen games, Marquis had broken every one of the few rules his coach tried to enforce. Coach Kyle had long since realized that any new rule would be immediately violated by his star, and for that reason he trimmed his list and fought the temptation to add new regulations. It wasn't working. Trying to control ten inner-city kids with a soft touch had put the Red Knights in last place in the 12 and Under division of the winter league.

Marquis was only eleven, but clearly the best player on the court. He preferred shooting and scoring over passing and defending, and within two minutes he'd slashed through the lane, around and through and over much larger players, and scored six points. His average was fourteen, and if allowed to play more than half a game, he could probably score thirty. In his own young opinion, he really didn't need to practice.

In spite of the one-man show, the game was out of reach. Kyle McAvoy sat quietly on the bench, watching the game and waiting for the clock to wind down. One game to go and the season would be over, his last as a basketball coach. In two years he'd won a dozen, lost two dozen, and asked himself how any person in his right mind would willingly coach at any level. He was doing it for the kids, he'd said to himself a thousand times, kids with no fathers, kids from bad homes, kids in need of a positive male influence. And he still believed it, but after two years of babysitting, and arguing with parents when they bothered to show up, and hassling with other coaches who were not above cheating, and trying to ignore teenage referees who didn't know a block from a charge, he was fed up. He'd done his community service, in this town anyway.

He watched the game and waited, yelling occasionally because that's what coaches are supposed to do. He looked around the empty gym, an old brick building in downtown New Haven, home to the youth league for fifty years. A handful of parents were scattered through the bleachers, all waiting for the final horn. Marquis scored again. No one applauded. The Red Knights were down by twelve with two minutes to go.

At the far end of the court, just under the ancient scoreboard, a man in a dark suit walked through the door and leaned against the retractable bleachers. He was noticeable because he was white. There were no white players on either team. He stood out because he wore a suit that was either black or navy, with a white shirt and a burgundy tie, all under a trench coat that announced the presence of an agent or a cop of some variety.

Coach Kyle happened to see the man when he entered the gym, and he thought to himself that the guy was out of place. Probably a detective of some sort, maybe a narc looking for a dealer. It would not be the first arrest in or around the gym.

After the agent/cop leaned against the bleachers, he cast a long suspicious look at the

Red Knights' bench, and his eyes seemed to settle on Coach Kyle, who returned the stare for a second before it became uncomfortable. Marquis let one fly from near mid-court, air ball, and Coach Kyle jumped to his feet, spread his hands wide, shook his head as if to ask, 'Why?' Marquis ignored him as he loafed back on defense. A dumb foul stopped the clock and prolonged the misery. While looking at the free-throw shooter, Kyle glanced beyond him, and in the background was the agent/cop, still staring, not at the action but at the coach.

For a twenty-five-year-old law student with no criminal record and no illegal habits or proclivities, the presence and the attention of a man who gave all indications of being employed by some branch of law enforcement should have caused no concern whatsoever. But it never worked that way with Kyle McAvoy. Street cops and state troopers didn't particularly bother him. They were paid to simply react. But the guys in dark suits, the investigators and agents, the ones trained to dig deep and discover secrets – those types still unnerved him.

Thirty seconds to go and Marquis was arguing with a referee. He'd thrown an F-bomb at a ref two weeks earlier and was suspended for a game. Coach Kyle yelled at his star, who never listened. He quickly scanned the gym to see if agent/cop No. 1 was alone or was now accompanied by agent/cop No. 2. No, he was not.

Another dumb foul, and Kyle yelled at the

referee to just let it slide. He sat down and ran his finger over the side of his neck, then flicked off the perspiration. It was early February, and the gym was, as always, quite chilly.

Why was he sweating?

The agent/cop hadn't moved an inch; in fact he seemed to enjoy staring at Kyle.

The decrepit old horn finally squawked. The game was mercifully over. One team cheered, and one team really didn't care. Both lined up for the obligatory high fives and 'Good game, good game,' as meaningless to twelve-year-olds as it is to college players. As Kyle congratulated the opposing coach, he glanced down the court. The white man was gone.

What were the odds he was waiting outside? Of course it was paranoia, but paranoia had settled into Kyle's life so long ago that he now simply acknowledged it, coped with it, and moved on.

The Red Knights regrouped in the visitors' locker room, a cramped little space under the sagging and permanent stands on the home side. There Coach Kyle said all the right things – nice effort, good hustle, our game is improving in certain areas, let's finish on a high note this Saturday. The boys were changing clothes and hardly listening. They were tired of basketball because they were tired of losing, and of course all blame was heaped upon the coach. He was too young, too white, too much of an Ivy Leaguer.

The few parents who were there waited outside the locker room, and it was those tense moments when the team came out that Kyle hated most about his community service. There would be the usual complaints about playing time. Marquis had an uncle, a twenty-two-year-old former all-state player with a big mouth and a fondness for bitching about Coach Kyle's unfair treatment of the 'best player in the league.'

From the locker room, there was another door that led to a dark narrow hallway that ran behind the home stands and finally gave way to an outside door that opened into an alley. Kyle was not the first coach to discover this escape route, and on this night he wanted to avoid not only the families and their complaints but also the agent/cop. He said a quick goodbye to his boys, and as they fled the locker room, he made his escape. In a matter of seconds he was outside, in the alley, then walking quickly along a frozen sidewalk. Heavy snow had been plowed, and the sidewalk was icy and barely passable. The temperature was somewhere far below freezing. It was 8:30 on a Wednesday, and he was headed for the law journal offices at the Yale Law School, where he would work until midnight at least.

He didn't make it.

The agent was leaning against the fender of a red Jeep Cherokee that was parked parallel on the street. The vehicle was titled to one John

McAvoy of York, Pennsylvania, but for the past six years it had been the reliable companion of his son, Kyle, the true owner.

Though his feet suddenly felt like bricks and his knees were weak, Kyle managed to trudge on as if nothing were wrong. Not only did they find me, he said to himself as he tried to think clearly, but they've done their homework and found my Jeep. Not exactly high-level research. I have done nothing wrong, he said again and again.

'Tough game, Coach,' the agent said when Kyle was ten feet away and slowing down.

Kyle stopped and took in the thick young man with red cheeks and red bangs who'd been watching him in the gym. 'Can I help you?' he said, and immediately saw the shadow of No. 2 dart across the street. They always worked in pairs.

No. 1 reached into a pocket, and as he said 'That's exactly what you can do,' he pulled out a leather wallet and flipped it open. 'Bob Plant, FBI.'

'A real pleasure,' Kyle said as all the blood left his brain and he couldn't help but flinch.

No. 2 wedged himself into the frame. He was much thinner and ten years older with gray around the temples. He, too, had a pocketful, and he performed the well-rehearsed badge presentation with ease. 'Nelson Ginyard, FBI,' he said.

Bob and Nelson. Both Irish. Both northeastern.

‘Anybody else?’ Kyle asked.

‘No. Got a minute to talk?’

‘Not really.’

‘You might want to,’ Ginyard said. ‘It could be very productive.’

‘I doubt that.’

‘If you leave, we’ll just follow,’ Plant said as he stood from his slouch position and took a step closer. ‘You don’t want us on campus, do you?’

‘Are you threatening me?’ Kyle asked. The sweat was back, now in the pits of his arms, and despite the arctic air a bead or two ran down his ribs.

‘Not yet,’ Plant said with a smirk.

‘Look, let’s spend ten minutes together, over coffee,’ Ginyard was saying. ‘There’s a sandwich shop just around the corner. I’m sure it’s warmer there.’

‘Do I need a lawyer?’

‘No.’

‘That’s what you always say. My father is a lawyer and I grew up in his office. I know your tricks.’

‘No tricks, Kyle, I swear,’ Ginyard said, and he at least sounded genuine. ‘Just give us ten minutes. I promise you won’t regret it.’

‘What’s on the agenda?’

‘Ten minutes. That’s all we ask.’

‘Give me a clue or the answer is no.’

Bob and Nelson looked at each other. Both shrugged. Why not? We’ll have to tell him sooner or later. Ginyard turned and looked down the street and spoke into the wind. 'Duquesne University. Five years ago. Drunk frat boys and a girl.'

Kyle's body and mind had different reactions. His body conceded – a quick slump of the shoulders, a slight gasp, a noticeable jerk in the legs. But his mind fought back instantly. 'That's bullshit!' he said, then spat on the sidewalk. 'I've already been through this. Nothing happened and you know it.'

There was a long pause as Ginyard continued to stare down the street while Plant watched their subject's every move. Kyle's mind was spinning. Why was the FBI involved in an alleged state crime? In second-year Criminal Procedure they had studied the new laws regarding FBI interrogation. It was now an indictable offense to simply lie to an agent in this very situation. Should he shut up? Should he call his father? No, under no circumstances would he call his father.

Ginyard turned, took three steps closer, clenched his jaw like a bad actor, and tried to hiss his tough-guy words. 'Let's cut to the chase, Mr. McAvoy, because I'm freezing. There's an indictment out of Pittsburgh, okay. Rape. If you want to play the hard-ass smart-ass brilliant law student and run get a lawyer, or even call your old man, then the indictment comes down tomorrow and the life you have planned is pretty much shot to shit. However, if you give us ten minutes of your valuable time, right now, in the sandwich shop around the corner, then the indictment will be put on hold, if not forgotten altogether.'

'You can walk away from it,' Plant said from the side. 'Without a word.'

'Why should I trust you?' Kyle managed to say with a very dry mouth.

'Ten minutes.'

'You got a tape recorder?'

'Sure.'

'I want it on the table, okay? I want every word recorded because I don't trust you.'

'Fair enough.'

They jammed their hands deep into the pockets of their matching trench coats and stomped away. Kyle unlocked his Jeep and got inside. He started the engine, turned the heat on high, and thought about driving away.

Chapter 2

Buster's Deli was long and narrow with red vinyl booths along the wall to the right. To the left was a bar and a grill behind a counter, and a row of pinball machines. All manner of Yale memorabilia was tacked haphazardly on the walls. Kyle had eaten there a few times during his first year in law school, many months ago.

The last two booths were properly secured by the federal government. Yet another trench coat stood at the last table, chatting with Plant and Ginyard, waiting. When Kyle made his slow approach, the agent glanced at him, then offered the standard smirk before sitting in the next booth. No. 4 was waiting there, sipping coffee. Plant and Ginyard had ordered sandwich platters with subs and fries and pickles, all of it untouched. The table was covered with food and cups of coffee. Plant climbed to his feet and moved around to the other side so that both agents could watch their victim. They were shoulder to shoulder, still in trench coats. Kyle slid into the booth.

The lighting was old and bad; the back corner was dark. Pinball racket mixed with a loud game on ESPN from the bartender's flat screen.

'It takes four?' Kyle asked, nodding over his shoulder at the booth behind him.

'That's just what you can see,' Ginyard said.

'Would you like a sandwich?' Plant asked.

'No.' An hour earlier he had been famished. Now his digestive system and his excretory system and his nervous system were on the verge of a meltdown. He was struggling to breathe normally as he desperately tried to appear unfazed. He removed a disposable pen and a note card, and with all the nerve he could summon, he said, 'I'd like to see those badges again.'

The responses were identical – disbelief, insulted, then oh-what-the-hell as they slowly reached into their pockets and extracted their most prized possessions. They laid them on the table, and Kyle selected Ginyard's first. He wrote down the full name – Nelson Edward Ginyard – then his agent number. He squeezed the pen hard and recorded the information carefully. His hand shook, but he thought it wasn't noticeable. He rubbed the brass emblem carefully, not sure what he was looking for but still taking his time. 'Could I see a photo ID?' he asked.

'What the hell?' Ginyard growled.

'Photo ID, please.'

'No.'

'I'm not talking until I finish the preliminaries. Just show me your driver's license. I'll show you mine.'

'We already have a copy of yours.'

'Whatever. Let's have it.'

Ginyard rolled his eyes as he reached for his back pocket. From a battered billfold he produced a Connecticut license with an ominous snapshot of himself. Kyle examined it and jotted down the birth date and license data. 'That's worse than a passport photo,' he said.

'You wanna see my wife and kids?' Ginyard said as he removed a color photo and tossed it on the table.

'No, thanks. Which office are you guys from?'

'Hartford,' Ginyard said. He nodded at the next booth and said, 'They're from Pittsburgh.'

'Nice.'

Kyle then examined Plant's badge and driver's license, and when he had finished, he pulled out his cell phone and began pecking.

'What are you doing?' Ginyard asked.

'I'm going online to check you out.'

'You think we're posted on some nice little FBI Web site?' Plant said with a flash of anger. Both found it humorous. Neither seemed concerned.

'I know which site to check,' Kyle said as he entered the address of a little-known federal directory.

'You won't find us,' Ginyard said.

'This will take a minute. Where's that tape recorder?'

Plant produced a slender digital recorder the size of an electric toothbrush and flipped it on.

'Please give the date, time, and place,' Kyle said with an air of confidence that surprised even him. 'And please state that the interrogation has yet to begin and that no statements have been made before now.'

'Yes, sir. I love law students,' Plant said.

'You watch too much television,' Ginyard said.

'Go ahead.'

Plant situated the recorder in the center of the table, a pastrami and cheddar on one side and a smoked tuna on the other. He aimed his words at it and announced the preliminaries. Kyle was watching his phone, and when the Web site appeared, he entered the name of Nelson Edward Ginyard. A few seconds passed, and to the surprise of no one Agent Ginyard was confirmed as a field agent, FBI, Hartford. 'You wanna see it?' Kyle asked, holding up the tiny screen.

'Congratulations,' Ginyard shot back. 'Are you satisfied now?'

'No. I'd prefer not to be here.'

'You can leave anytime you want,' Plant said.

'You asked for ten minutes.' Kyle glanced at his wristwatch.

Both agents leaned forward, all four elbows in a row, the booth suddenly smaller. 'You remember a guy named Bennie Wright, chief investigator, sex crimes, Pittsburgh PD?' Ginyard was talking, both were staring, watching every nervous twitch of Kyle's eyelids.

'No.'

'You didn't meet him five years ago during the investigation?'

'I don't remember meeting a Bennie Wright. Could have, but I don't remember that name. It has been, after all, five years since the nonevent did not happen.'

They absorbed this, mulled it over slowly while maintaining eye contact. It appeared to Kyle as if both wanted to say, 'You're lying.'

Instead, Ginyard said, 'Well, Detective Wright is here in town, and he'd like to meet with you in about an hour.'

'Another meeting?'

'If you don't mind. It won't take long, and there's a good chance you can head off the indictment.'

'Indictment for what, exactly?'

'Rape.'

'There was no rape. The Pittsburgh police made that decision five years ago.'

'Well, it looks like the girl is back,' Ginyard said. 'She's put her life back together, gone through some extensive therapy, and, best of all, she's got herself a lawyer now.'

Since Ginyard stopped without a question, there was no need for a response. Kyle couldn't help but sink an inch or two. He glanced over at the counter, at the empty stools. He glanced over at the flat-screen television. It was a college game, the stands full of screaming students, and he asked himself why he was sitting where he was sitting.

Keep talking, he said to himself, but don't say anything.

'Can I ask a question?' he asked.

'Sure.'

'If the indictment has been issued, how can it be stopped? Why are we talking?'

'It's under seal, by court order,' Ginyard said. 'According to Detective Wright, the prosecutor has a deal for you, one that the victim's lawyer cooked up, one that will allow you to walk away from this mess. You play ball, and the indictment against you will never see the light of day.'

'I'm still confused. Maybe I should call my father.'

'That's up to you, but if you're smart, you'll wait until you chat with Detective Wright.'

'You guys didn't advise me of my *Miranda* rights.'

'This is not an interrogation,' Plant finally said. 'It's not an investigation.' Then he reached into the smoked-tuna basket and pulled out a greasy fry.

'What the hell is it?'

'A meeting.'

Ginyard cleared his throat, leaned back a few inches, and proceeded. 'It's a state crime, Kyle, we all know that. Normally we wouldn't be involved, but since you're here in Connecticut and the indictment is in Pennsylvania, the boys in Pittsburgh asked us to help arrange the next meeting. After that, we'll step aside.'

'I'm still confused.'

'Come on. Bright legal mind like you. Surely you're not that thick.'

There was a long pause as all three considered the next move. Plant chomped on his second fry, but his eyes never left Kyle. Ginyard took a sip of coffee, frowned at the taste, and continued staring. The pinball machines were silent. The deli was empty except for the four FBI agents, a bartender absorbed in the game, and Kyle.

Finally, Kyle leaned forward on his elbows, and with the recorder just inches away he said, 'There was no rape, no crime. I did nothing wrong.'

'Fine, talk to Wright.'

'And where is he?'

'At ten o'clock, he'll be at the Holiday Inn on Saw Mill Road, room 222.'

'This is a bad idea. I need a lawyer.'

'Maybe you do, maybe you don't,' Ginyard said, leaning in so that their heads were a foot apart. 'Look, I know you don't trust us, but please believe it when we say you should talk to Wright before you talk to anyone else. Hell, you can call a lawyer, or your father, at midnight. Or tomorrow. If you overreact now, the outcome could be a disaster.'

‘I’m leaving. Conversation over. Turn off the recorder.’

Neither made any move toward the recorder. Kyle looked at it, then leaned down and said, very clearly, ‘This is Kyle McAvoy. The time is 8:50 p.m. I have nothing else to say. I have made no statements, and I am leaving Buster’s Deli right now.’ He scooted off the bench and was almost out of the booth when Plant blurted, ‘He’s got the video.’

A horse kick to the groin could not have hit harder. Kyle clutched the red vinyl and looked as though he might faint. Slowly, he sat down again. Slowly, he reached for a plastic cup and took a long sip of water. His lips and tongue were parched, and the water did little to help.

The video. A fraternity brother, one of the drunks at the little party, had allegedly recorded something with his cell phone. Supposedly, there were images of the girl, naked on a sofa, too drunk to move, and admiring her were three or four or five Beta brothers, all naked, too, or in the process of undressing. Kyle vaguely remembered the scene, but he’d never seen the video. It had been destroyed, according to Beta legend. The cops in Pittsburgh had searched but never found it. It was gone, forgotten, buried deep in the secrecy of Beta brotherhood.

Plant and Ginyard were elbow to elbow again, all four eyes focused and unblinking.

‘What video?’ Kyle managed to ask, but it was

so lame and so unconvincing that he didn't believe himself.

'The one you boys hid from the cops,' Plant said, barely moving his lips. 'The one that places you at the scene of the crime. The one that will destroy your life and send you away for twenty years.'

Oh, that video.

'I don't know what you're talking about,' Kyle said, then drank some more water. Waves of nausea crashed through his stomach and head, and he thought about vomiting.

'Oh, I think you do,' Ginyard said.

'Have you seen this video?' Kyle asked.

Both nodded.

'Then you know I didn't touch the girl.'

'Maybe, maybe not. But you were there,' Ginyard said. 'You were an accessory.'

To keep from throwing up, Kyle closed his eyes and began rubbing his temples. The girl was a wild little thing who'd spent more time in the Beta house than in her dorm room. A groupie, a clinger, a party animal with an abundant supply of Daddy's cash. The brothers of Beta passed her around. When she cried rape, the brothers had instantly gone mute and solidified into an impenetrable wall of denial and innocence. The cops eventually gave up when she proved too unreliable with the details. No charges were filed. She later left Duquesne and mercifully disappeared. The great miracle of the ugly little episode was that it had been kept quiet. No additional lives were ruined.

'The indictment names you and three others,' Ginyard said.

'There was no rape,' Kyle said as he continued to rub his temples. 'If she had sex, I promise you it was by consent.'

'Not if she blacked out,' Ginyard said.

'We're not here to argue, Kyle,' Plant said. 'That's what lawyers are for. We're here to help cut a deal. If you'll cooperate, then this will all go away, at least your part of it.'

'What kind of deal?'

'Detective Wright will handle that.'

Kyle slowly sat back and tapped his head on the red vinyl bench behind him. He wanted to plead, to beg, to explain that this wasn't fair, that he was about to graduate and pass the bar and start a career. His future held so much promise. His past was unblemished. Almost.

But they already knew that, didn't they? He glanced at the tape recorder and decided to give them nothing. 'All right, all right,' he said. 'I'll be there.'

Ginyard leaned even closer and said, 'You have one hour. If you make a phone call, we'll know it. If you try to run, we'll follow, okay? No funny stuff, Kyle. You're making the right decision here, I swear it. Just keep it up, and this will all go away.'

'I don't believe you.'

'You'll see.'

Kyle left them there with their cold

sandwiches and bitter coffee. He made it to his Jeep, then drove to his apartment three blocks from campus. He rummaged through his roommate's bathroom, found a Valium, then locked his bedroom door, turned off the light, and stretched out on the floor.

Chapter 3

It was an old Holiday Inn, built in the 1960s, when motels and fast-food chains raced to build along the highways and frontage roads. Kyle had passed it a hundred times and never seen it. Behind it was a pancake house, and next door was a large discount appliance store.

The parking lot was dark and one-third full when he backed the red Jeep into a space next to a minivan from Indiana. He turned off the lights but left the engine running and the heater on. A light snow was falling. Why couldn't there be a blizzard, or a flood or earthquake, an invasion, anything to interrupt this awful scenario? Why, exactly, was he sleepwalking through their little plan?

The video.

In the past hour he'd thought of calling his father, but that conversation would take far too long. John McAvoy would provide sound legal advice, and quickly, but the backstory had many complications. He'd thought of calling Professor Bart Mallory, his adviser, his friend, his brilliant teacher of criminal procedure, a former judge who would know exactly what to do. But again, there were too many blanks to fill in and not enough time. He'd thought of calling two of his Beta brothers from Duquesne, but why bother? Any advice they might give would be as unsound as the strategies racing through his mind. No sense ruining their lives. And in the horror of the moment he'd thought of the various schemes he could use to disappear. A mad dash to the airport. A clandestine car ride to the bus station. A long jump off a tall bridge.

But they were watching, weren't they? And probably listening, too, so all phone calls would be shared. Someone was watching at that very moment, he was certain. Perhaps in the minivan from Indiana there were a couple of goons with headsets and night-vision gear, getting their jollies as they monitored him and burned taxpayer money.

If the Valium was working, he couldn't tell.

When the digital clock on the radio hit 9:58, he turned off the engine and stepped into the snow. He walked bravely across the asphalt, each step leaving footprints. Could this be his last moment of freedom? He'd read so many cases of criminal defendants freely walking into the police station for a few quick questions, only to be charged, handcuffed, jailed, railroaded by the system. He could still run, to somewhere.

When the glass doors slammed behind him, he paused for a second in the deserted lobby and thought he heard the clanging of cell-block iron at his back. He was hearing things, seeing things, imagining things. Apparently, the Valium had reversed itself and had him ready to jump out of his skin. He nodded at the decrepit clerk behind the front counter, but there was no audible response. As he rode the musty elevator to the second floor, he asked himself what kind of fool would voluntarily enter a motel room filled with cops and agents all hell-bent on accusing him of something that never happened? Why was he doing this?

The video.

He had never seen it. He did not know anyone who had seen it. In the secret world of Beta there were rumors and denials and threats, but no one had even known for sure if the 'Elaine thing' had actually been recorded. The reality that it had, and that the evidence was now in the possession of the Pittsburgh police and the FBI, made him ponder the bridge scenario.

Wait a minute. I did nothing wrong. I did not touch that girl, not that night anyway.

No one touched her. At least that was the sworn and battle-tested version within the Beta fraternity. But what if the video proved otherwise? He would never know until he saw it.

The noxious smell of fresh paint hit him as he stepped into the hallway on the second floor. He stopped at room 222 and glanced at his watch to make sure he was not a minute too early. He knocked three times, then heard movement and muffled voices. The lock chain rattled, the door was jerked open, and Special Agent Nelson Edward Ginyard said, 'Glad you could make it.' Kyle stepped inside, leaving the old world behind. The new one was suddenly terrifying.

Ginyard had his jacket off, and strapped over his white shirt was a shoulder harness, with a fairly large black pistol in a black holster snug under his left arm. Agent Plant and the two others from Buster's were staring, and all three were also coatless so that young Kyle could get the full measure of their arsenal. Identical nine-millimeter Berettas, with matching holsters and black leather harnesses. Seriously armed men, all with the same scowl as if they'd be more than happy to shoot the rapist.

'Good move,' Plant said, nodding now.

Actually, Kyle thought in the haze of the moment, coming here was a very stupid move.

Room 222 had been converted into a makeshift field office. The king-sized bed had been pushed into a corner. The curtains were tightly closed. Two folding tables had been hauled in and were covered with the evidence of busy work – files and thick envelopes and notepads. Three laptops were open and on, and in the one nearest the door Kyle caught a glimpse of himself, from his high school yearbook. Central York High School, class of 2001. Tacked to the bare wall behind the folding tables were eight-by-ten color photos of three of his Beta brothers. At the far end, almost to the curtains, was one of Elaine Keenan.

The room adjoined another, and the door between them was open. Agent No. 5 walked through it – same gun, same holster – and glared at Kyle. Five agents? Two rooms. A ton of paperwork. All this effort, all this work, all these men, just to nail me? Kyle felt light-headed as he observed the power of his government in action.

'Do you mind emptying your pockets?' Ginyard said as he offered a small cardboard box.

'Why?'

'Please.'

'You think I'm armed? You think I might pull out a knife and attack you guys?'

Agent No. 5 saw the humor and broke the ice with a good laugh. Kyle pulled out his key ring, jangled its collection for Ginyard to see, then put it back in his pocket.

'How about a pat down?' Plant said, already moving toward Kyle.

'Oh, sure,' he said, then raised his arms. 'All Yale students are heavily armed.'

Plant began a very soft and quick frisk. He finished just seconds after he started, then disappeared into the other room.

'Detective Wright is across the hall,' Ginyard said. Yet another room.

Kyle followed him out of the room, into the stuffy hallway, then waited as he tapped gently on the door to room 225. When it opened, Kyle entered alone.

Bennie Wright displayed no weaponry. He offered a quick handshake while spitting out, 'Detective Wright, Pittsburgh PD.'

A real pleasure, Kyle thought but said nothing. What am I doing here?

Wright was in his late forties, short, trim, bald with a few strands of black hair slicked back just above his ears. His eyes were also black and partially concealed behind a pair of tiny reading glasses perched halfway down his narrow nose. He closed the door behind Kyle, then waved at the appointed spot and said, 'Why don't you have a seat?'

'What do you have in mind?' Kyle asked without moving.

Wright walked past the bed and stopped beside yet another folding table, this one with two cheap metal chairs facing each other. 'Let's talk, Kyle,' he said pleasantly, and Kyle realized he had a slight accent. English was not his first language, though there was almost no trace of his native tongue. But it was odd. A man named Bennie Wright from Pittsburgh should not have a foreign accent.

There was a small video camera mounted on a tripod in one corner. Wires ran to the table, to a laptop with a twelve-inch screen. 'Please,' Wright said, waving at one chair as he settled himself into the other.

'I want all of this recorded,' Kyle said.

Wright glanced over his shoulder at the camera and said, 'No problem.'

Slowly, Kyle walked to the other chair and sat down. Wright was rolling up the sleeves of his white shirt. His necktie was already loose.

To Kyle's right was the laptop with a blank screen. To his left a thick, unopened file. In the center of the table was a fresh legal pad, white, with a black pen on it, waiting. 'Turn on the camera,' Kyle said. Wright punched the laptop, and Kyle's face appeared on the screen. He looked at himself and saw nothing but fear.

Wright went efficiently into the file, retrieving the necessary paperwork as if young Kyle here were simply applying for a student credit card. When the proper sheets were found, he placed them in the center and said, 'First, we need to cover your *Miranda* rights.'

'No,' Kyle said softly. 'First we need to see your badge and some identification.'

This irritated the detective, but only for a few seconds. Without a word, he fished out a brown leather wallet from a rear pocket, opened it, and said, 'Had this for twenty-two years now.'

Kyle examined the bronze badge, and it did indeed show signs of age. Benjamin J. Wright, Pittsburgh Police Department, officer number 6658. 'How about a driver's license?'

Wright yanked back his wallet, opened another compartment, fingered through some cards, and then flung down a Pennsylvania photo license. 'Satisfied now?' he snapped.

Kyle handed it back and said, 'Why is the FBI involved in this?'

'Can we finish up with *Miranda*?' Wright was readjusting the paperwork.

'Sure. I understand *Miranda*.'

'I'm sure you do. A top law student at one of our most prestigious law schools. A very smart young man.' Kyle was reading as Wright was talking. 'You have the right to remain silent. Anything you say can and will be used against you in court. You have the right to an attorney. If you can't afford one, then the state will provide one. Any questions?'

'No.' He signed his name on two forms and slid them back to Wright.

'Why is the FBI involved?' He repeated the question.

'Believe me, Kyle, the FBI is the least of your problems.' Wright's hands were hairy, still, calm, and his fingers were laced together on top of the legal pad. He spoke slowly, with authority. There was no doubt this meeting belonged to him. 'Here is my suggestion, Kyle. We have so much ground to cover, and time is slipping by. Did you ever play football?'

'Yes.'

'Then let's say this table is a football field. Not a great analogy, but one that will work. You are here, at this goal line.' With his left hand he striped an imaginary line in front of the laptop. 'You have a hundred yards to go, to score, to win, to walk out of here in one piece.' With his right hand, he laid down the other goal line, next to the heavy file. His hands were four feet apart. 'A hundred yards, Kyle, bear with me, okay?'

'Okay.'

He pulled his hands together and tapped the legal pad. 'Somewhere in here, at about the fifty, I'll show you the video that is the source of this conflict. You won't like it, Kyle. It will make you ill. Nauseous. Sick to your stomach. But, if we are able, then we will continue your little march to the goal line, and when we get there, you will be quite relieved. You will once again see yourself as the golden boy, the handsome young man with an unlimited future and an unblemished past. Stick with me, Kyle, allow me to be the boss, the coach, the man calling the plays, and together we'll make it to the promised land.' His right hand tapped the goal line.

'What about the indictment?'

Wright touched the file and said, 'It's here.'

'When do I see it?'

'Stop asking questions, Kyle. I have the questions. Hopefully, you have the answers.'

The accent wasn't Spanish. Eastern European maybe, and at times it was so slight it almost disappeared.

Wright's left hand touched the goal line in front of the laptop. 'Now, Kyle, we need to start with the basics. Just some background, okay?'

'Whatever.'

Wright pulled some papers from the file, studied them for a second, then picked up his pen. 'You were born on February 4, 1983, in York, Pennsylvania, third child and only son of John and Patty McAvoy. They divorced in 1989, when you were six years old, neither has remarried, correct?'

'Correct.'

Wright made a check mark, then launched into a series of quick questions about family members, their birth dates, education, jobs, addresses, hobbies, church affiliations, even politics. As the list grew longer, Wright shuffled papers and the check marks multiplied. He had his facts straight, every one of them. He knew the date and place of the birth of Kyle's two-year-old nephew in Santa Monica. When he finished with the family, he pulled out more papers. Kyle felt the first signs of fatigue. And they were just warming up.

'Would you like something to drink?' Wright asked.

'No.'

'Your father is a general practice lawyer in York?' It was a statement, but more of a question.

Kyle only nodded. Then a barrage about his father, his life and career and interests. After every fourth or fifth question, Kyle wanted to ask, 'Is this really relevant?' But he held his tongue. Wright had all the data. Kyle was simply affirming what someone else had found.

'Your mother is an artist of some variety?' Kyle heard him say.

'Yes, and where is the football right now?'

'You've gained about ten yards. What kind of artist?'

'She's a painter.'

They probed the life of Patty McAvoy for ten minutes.

Finally, the detective finished with the family and settled on the suspect. He served up a few easy ones about his childhood, but didn't dwell on the details. He already knows it all, Kyle told himself.

'Honors from Central York High, star athlete, Eagle Scout. Why did you select Duquesne University?'

'They offered me a basketball scholarship.'

'Were there other offers?'

'A couple, from smaller schools.'

'But you didn't play much at Duquesne.'

'I played thirteen minutes as a freshman, then tore an ACL in the final minute of the final game.'

'Surgery?'

'Yes, but the knee was gone. I quit basketball and joined a fraternity.'

'We'll get to the fraternity later. Were you invited back to the basketball team?'

'Sort of. Didn't matter. The knee was shot.'

'You majored in economics and made near-perfect grades. What happened in Spanish your second year? You didn't make an A?'

'I should've taken German, I guess.'

'One B in four years is not bad.' Wright

flipped a page, made a note about something. Kyle glanced at his face on the laptop and told himself to relax.

'High honors, a dozen or so student organizations, intramural softball champs, fraternity secretary then president. Your academic record is impressive, yet you managed to also maintain a pretty active social life. Tell me about your first arrest.'

'I'm sure you have the records in your file there.'

'Your first arrest, Kyle.'

'Only one. A first, not a second. Not until now, I guess.'

'What happened?'

'Typical frat stuff. A loud party that didn't stop until the cops showed up. I got caught with an open container, a bottle of beer. Nitpicking stuff. Misdemeanor. I paid a fine of three hundred bucks and got six months' probation. After that, the record was expunged and Yale never knew about it.'

'Did your father handle it?'

'He was involved, but I had a lawyer in Pittsburgh.'

'Who?'

'A lady named Sylvia Marks.'

'I've heard of her. Doesn't she specialize in stupid fraternity stunts?'

'That's her. But she knows her stuff.'

'I thought there was a second arrest.'

'No. I was stopped by the cops once on

campus, but there was no arrest. Just a warning.'

'What were you doing?'

'Nothing.'

'Then why were you stopped?'

'A couple of fraternities were shooting bottle rockets at each other. Smart boys. I was not involved. Nothing went in my file, so I'm wondering how you heard about it.'

Wright ignored this and wrote something on his legal pad. When he finished scribbling, he said, 'Why did you decide to go to law school?'

'I made that decision when I was twelve years old. I always wanted to be a lawyer. My first job was running the copier in my father's office. I sort of grew up there.'

'Where did you apply to law school?'

'Penn, Yale, Cornell, and Stanford.'

'Where were you accepted?'

'All four.'

'Why Yale?'

'It was always my first choice.'

'Did Yale offer scholarship money?'

'Financial incentives, yes. So did the others.'

'Have you borrowed money?'

'Yes.'

'How much?'

'Do you really need to know?'

'I wouldn't ask the question if I didn't need to know. You think I'm talking just to hear myself talk?'

'I can't answer that.'

'Back to the student loans.'

'When I graduate in May, I'll owe about sixty thousand.'

Wright nodded as if he agreed that this was the correct amount. He flipped another page, and Kyle could see that it, too, was covered with questions.

'And you write for the law journal?'

'I'm the editor in chief of the *Yale Law Journal*.'

'That's the most prestigious honor in the school?'

'According to some.'

'You clerked last summer in New York. Tell me about it.'

'It was one of those huge Wall Street firms, Scully & Pershing, a typical summer clerkship. We were wined and dined and given easy hours, the same seduction routine all the big firms use. They pamper the clerks, then kill them when they become associates.'

'Did Scully & Pershing offer you a position after graduation?'

'Yes.'

'Did you accept or decline?'

'Neither. I have not made a decision. The firm has given me some additional time to decide.'

'What's taking so long?'

'I have a few options. One is a clerkship for a federal judge, but he might get a promotion. Things are in limbo there.'

'Do you have other job offers?'

'I had other offers, yes.'

'Tell me about them.'

'Is this really relevant?'

'Everything I say is relevant, Kyle.'

'Do you have any water?'

'I'm sure there's some in the bathroom.'

Kyle jumped to his feet, walked between the king-sized bed and the credenza, switched on the light in the cramped bathroom, and ran tap water into a flimsy plastic cup. He gulped it, then refilled. When he returned to the table, he placed the cup somewhere around his own twenty-yard line, then checked himself on the monitor. 'Just curious,' he said. 'Where's the football right now?'

'Third and long. Tell me about the other job offers, the other firms.'

'Why don't you just show me the video so we can skip all this bullshit? If it really exists, and if it implicates me, then I'll walk out of here and go hire a lawyer.'

Wright leaned forward, adjusted his elbows on the table, and began gently tapping his fingertips together. The lower half of his face eased into a smile while the upper half remained noncommittal. Very coolly, he said, 'Losing your temper, Kyle, could cost you your life.'

Life as in dead body? Or life as in brilliant future? Kyle wasn't so sure. He took a deep breath, then another gulp of the water. The flash of anger was gone, replaced by the crush of confusion and fear.

The fake smile widened, and Wright said,

'Please, Kyle, you're doing fine here. Just a few more questions and we'll move into rougher territory. The other firms?'

'I was offered a job by Logan & Kupec in New York, Baker Potts in San Francisco, and Garton in London. I said no to all three. I'm still kicking around a public-interest job.'

'Doing what? Where?'

'It's down in Virginia, a legal aid position helping migrant workers.'

'And how long would you do this?'

'Couple of years, maybe, I'm not sure. It's just an option.'

'At a much lower salary?'

'Oh, yes. Much.'

'How will you pay back your student loans?'

'I'll figure that out.'

Wright didn't like the smart-ass answer, but decided to let it slide. He glanced at his notes, though a quick review wasn't necessary. He knew that young Kyle here owed $61,000 in student loans, all of which would be forgiven by Yale if he spent the next three years working for minimum wage protecting the poor, the oppressed, the abused, or the environment. Kyle's offer had been extended by Piedmont Legal Aid, and the clerkship was funded by a grant from a mammoth law firm in Chicago. According to Wright's sources, Kyle had verbally accepted the position, which paid $32,000 a year. Wall Street could wait. It would always be there. His father had encouraged him to spend a few years out in the trenches, getting his hands dirty, far away from the corporate style of law that he, John McAvoy, despised.

According to the file, Scully & Pershing was offering a base salary of $200,000 plus the usual extras. The other firms' offers were similar.

'When will you select a job?' Wright asked.

'Very soon.'

'Which way are you leaning?'

'I'm not.'

'Are you sure?'

'Of course I'm sure.'

Wright reached for the file, shaking his head grimly and frowning as if he'd been insulted. He retrieved more papers, flipped through them, then glared at Kyle. 'You haven't made a verbal commitment to accept a position with an outfit called Piedmont Legal Aid, in Winchester, Virginia, beginning September the second of this year?'

A rush of warm air escaped through Kyle's dry lips. As he absorbed this, he instinctively glanced at the monitor, and, yes, he looked as weak as he felt. He almost blurted, 'How the hell do you know this?' but to do so would be to admit the truth. Nor could he deny the truth. Wright already knew.

As he was lurching toward some lame response, his adversary moved in for the kill. 'Let's call this Lie Number One, okay, Kyle?' Wright said with a sneer. 'Should we somehow arrive at Lie Number Two, then we turn off the camera, say good night, and meet again tomorrow for the arrest. Handcuffs, perp walk, mug shot, maybe a reporter or two. You won't be thinking about protecting illegal immigrants, and you won't be thinking about Wall Street. Don't lie to me, Kyle. I know too much.'

Kyle almost said, 'Yes, sir,' but instead managed only a slight affirmative nod.

'So you plan to do some charitable work for a couple of years?'

'Yes.'

'Then what?'

'I don't know. I'm sure I'll join a firm somewhere, start a career.'

'What do you think of Scully & Pershing?'

'Big, powerful, rich. I think it's the largest law firm in the world, depending on who got merged or swallowed yesterday. Offices in thirty cities on five continents. Some really smart folks who work very hard and put enormous pressure on each other, especially on their young associates.'

'Your kind of work?'

'It's hard to say. The money is great. The work is brutal. But it's the big leagues. I'll probably end up there.'

'In what section did you work last summer?'

'I moved around, but most of my time was spent in litigation.'

'Do you like litigation?'

'Not especially. May I ask what these questions can possibly have to do with that matter back in Pittsburgh?'

Wright took his elbows off the table and tried to relax a little deeper into the folding chair. He crossed his legs and placed the legal pad on his left thigh. He chewed the end of his pen for a moment, staring at Kyle as if he were now a psychiatrist, analyzing the patient. 'Let's talk about your fraternity at Duquesne.'

'Whatever.'

'There were about ten members of your pledge class, right?'

'Nine.'

'Do you keep in touch with all of them?'

'To some degree.'

'The indictment names you and three others, so let's talk about the other three. Where is Alan Strock?'

The indictment. Somewhere in that damned file less than three feet away was the indictment. How could his name be listed as a defendant? He had not touched the girl. He had not witnessed a rape. He had not seen anyone having sex. He vaguely recalled being present in the room, but he had blacked out at some point during the night, during the episode. How could he be an accomplice if he wasn't conscious? That would be his defense at trial, and a solid defense it would be, but the specter of a trial was too awful to imagine. A trial would come long after the arrest, the publicity, the horror of seeing his photo in print. Kyle closed his eyes and rubbed his temples, and he thought about the phone calls home, first to his father and then to his mother. Other phone calls would follow: one each to the recruiting directors who'd offered him jobs; one to each of his sisters. He would proclaim his innocence and all that, but he knew he would never shake the suspicion of rape.

At that moment, Kyle had no confidence in Detective Wright and whatever deal he had in mind. If there was indeed an indictment, then no miracle could keep it buried.

'Alan Strock?' Wright asked.

'He's in med school at Ohio State.'

'Any recent correspondence?'

'An e-mail a couple of days ago.'

'And Joey Bernardo?'

'He's still in Pittsburgh, working for a brokerage firm.'

'Recent contact?'

'By phone, a few days ago.'

'Any mention of Elaine Keenan with Alan or Joey?'

'No.'

'You boys have tried to forget about Elaine, haven't you?'

'Yes.'

'Well, she's back.'

'Evidently.'

Wright readjusted himself in the chair, uncrossed his legs, stretched his back, and returned to the most comfortable position with both elbows stuck on the table. 'Elaine left Duquesne after her freshman year,' he began in a softer voice, as if he had a long tale to tell. 'She was troubled. Her grades were a mess. She now claims that the rape brought on severe emotional distress. She lived with her parents for a year or so in Erie, then began drifting. A lot of self-medication, booze and drugs. She saw some therapists, but nothing helped. Have you heard any of this?'

'No. After she left school, there was not a word.'

'Anyway, she has an older sister in Scranton who took her in, got her some help, paid for rehab. Then they found a shrink who, evidently, has done a nice job of putting Elaine back together. She's clean, sober, feels great, and her memory has improved dramatically. She's also found herself a lawyer, and of course she is demanding justice.'

'You sound skeptical.'

'I'm a cop, Kyle. I'm skeptical of everything, but I have this young woman who is credible and who says she was raped, and I have a video that is pretty powerful evidence. And on top of that, there's this lawyer who's out for blood.'

'This is a shakedown, isn't it? All about money?'

'What do you mean, Kyle?'

'The fourth defendant is Baxter Tate, and of course we know what that's all about. The Tate family is very rich. Old Pittsburgh money. Baxter was born with trust funds. How much does she want?'

'I'll ask the questions. Did you ever have sex—'

'Yes, I had sex with Elaine Keenan, as did most of my pledge class. She was wild as hell, spent more time in the Beta house than most Betas, could drink any three of us under the table, and always had a purse full of pills. Her problems began long before she arrived at Duquesne. Believe me, she does not want to go to trial.'

'How many times did you have sex with her?'

'Once, about a month before the alleged rape.'

'Do you know if Baxter Tate had sexual relations with Elaine Keenan on the night in question?'

Kyle paused, took a deep breath, and said, 'No, I do not. I blacked out.'

'Did Baxter Tate admit to having sex with her that night?'

'Not to me.'

Wright finished writing a long sentence on his legal pad as the air cleared. Kyle could almost hear the camera running. He glanced at it and saw the little red light still staring at him.

'Where is Baxter?' Wright asked after a long, heavy pause.

'Somewhere in L.A. He barely graduated, then went to Hollywood to become an actor. He's not too stable.'

'Meaning?'

'He comes from a wealthy family that's even more dysfunctional than most wealthy families. He's a hard partyer, lots of booze and drugs and girls. And he shows no signs of outgrowing it.

His goal in life is to become a great actor and drink himself to death. He wants to die young, sort of like James Dean.'

'Has he been in any films?'

'Not a single one. Lots of bars, though.'

Wright suddenly seemed bored with the questions. He had stopped his scribbling. His hard stare began to drift. He stuffed some papers back into the file, then tapped a finger at the center of the table. 'We've made progress, Kyle, thank you. The ball is at midfield. You want to see the video?'

Chapter 4

Wright stood for the first time, stretched, and stepped to a corner where a small cardboard box was waiting. It was white, and in a neat hand someone had printed, with a black marker, the words 'IN RE: KYLE L. McAVOY et al.' Kyle McAvoy and others. Wright fetched something from the box, and with the steady purpose of an executioner preparing to pull the switch, he removed a disc from its sleeve, slid it into the drive on the laptop, punched a couple of keys, then took his seat. Kyle could barely breathe.

As the computer clicked and hummed, Wright began talking. 'The phone was a Nokia 6000 smartphone, manufactured in 2003, with ETI Camcorder software installed, one-gigabyte memory card that holds about three hundred minutes of compressed video, megapixel quality at fifteen FPS, voice commands, voice activated, state of the art for the time. A really nice cell phone.'

'Owned by?'

Wright shot him a smart-ass grin and said, 'Sorry, Kyle.'

For some reason, Wright thought it would be helpful to show the phone itself. He punched a key, and a still photo of the Nokia appeared on the screen. 'Ever see this?' he asked.

'No.'

'Didn't think so. Here's the scene, Kyle, in case you're a little fuzzy on the details. It's April 25, 2003, last day of classes, final exams start in a week. It's a Friday, unseasonably warm for Pittsburgh, high of eighty-five that day, almost set a record, and the kids at Duquesne decide to do what all good college kids do everywhere. They start drinking in the afternoon and have big plans to drink all night. A crowd gathers at the apartment complex where you rent a place with three others. A party materializes by the pool. It's mostly Beta brothers and a few girls. You go for a swim, get some rays, drink some beer, listen to Phish. The girls are in bikinis. Life is good. Sometime after dark, the party moves inside, to your apartment. Pizza is ordered. The music, Widespread Panic by this time, is loud. More beer. Somebody shows up with two bottles of tequila, and of course this is consumed as fast as possible. Remember any of this?'

'Most of it.'

'You're twenty years old, just finishing your sophomore year—'

'Got that.'

‘The tequila gets mixed with Red Bull, and you and the gang start doing shots. I’m sure you’ve had a few shots.’

Kyle nodded, his eyes never leaving the screen.

‘At some point, clothes start coming off, and the owner of the cell phone decides to secretly record this. Guess he wanted his own little video of the girls without their tops. Do you remember the apartment, Kyle?’

‘Yes, I lived there for a year.’

‘We’ve examined the place. It’s a dump, of course, like a lot of college housing, but, according to the landlord, hasn’t changed. Our best guess is that the guy with the cell phone placed it on the narrow counter that separates the small kitchen from the den. The counter seems to be a catchall for textbooks, phone books, empty beer bottles, pretty much everything that passed through the apartment at one time or another.’

‘That’s correct.’

‘So our man pulls out his cell phone and sneaks over to the counter, and in the midst of a wild party he turns it on and hides it next to a book. The opening scene is pretty wild. We’ve studied it carefully, and there are six girls and nine boys, all dancing and in various stages of undress. Ring a bell, Kyle?’

‘Some of it, yes.’

‘We know all the names.’

‘You gonna show it to me or just talk about it?’

‘Don’t be so anxious to see it.’ With that, Wright punched another key. ‘It’s 11:14 p.m. when the video begins,’ he said, then hit another key. The screen suddenly exploded into a frenzy of loud music – Widespread Panic playing ‘Aunt Avis’ from *Bombs and Butterflies* – and gyrating bodies. Somewhere in the back of his brain Kyle had hoped for a dim, grainy, fuzzy clip of a bunch of Beta idiots drinking in the dark. Instead, he gawked at a remarkably clear video shot from a tiny phone camera. The angle chosen by the unknown owner of the phone provided a view of almost the entire den at 4880 East Chase, apartment 6B.

All fifteen hell-raisers appeared to be very drunk. All six girls were indeed topless, as were most of the guys. The dance was a group grope with no two partners moving together for more than a few seconds. Everyone held a drink in one hand; half had a cigarette or a joint in the other. All twelve bouncing breasts were fair game for the guys. In fact, all exposed flesh, male or female, was available to everyone. Touching and clutching were encouraged. Bodies came together, hunching and lurching, then parted and moved to the next one. Some of the guests were loud and rowdy, while others appeared to be fading under the flood of alcohol and chemicals. Most appeared to be singing along with the band. Several locked lips in long kisses while their free hands searched for even more intimate places.

'I believe that's you with the sunglasses,' Wright said smugly.

'Thank you.'

Sunglasses, yellow Pirates cap, off-white gym shorts drooping low, a lean body with pale winter skin in need of sunshine. A plastic cup in one hand, a cigarette in the other. Mouth open to sing along. A drunken fool. A twenty-year-old lunatic on the verge of another blackout.

Now, five years later, there was no nostalgia, no longing for those rowdy and carefree college days. He didn't miss the hell-raising, the hangovers, the late-morning wake-ups in strange beds. But at the same time, there was no remorse. Kyle felt a little embarrassed that he'd been caught on tape, but it was a long time ago. His college days had been pretty typical, hadn't they? He'd partied no more and certainly no less than virtually everyone he knew.

The music stopped for a moment, between songs, and more shots were prepared and passed around. One of the girls fell into a chair and appeared to be done for the night. Then another song began.

'This goes for about eight more minutes,' Wright said, glancing at his notes. Kyle had no doubt that Wright and his gang had analyzed and memorized every second, every frame. 'As you will note, Elaine Keenan is not present. She says she was next door, drinking with some friends.'

'So she's changed her story again.'

Wright ignored this and said, 'If you don't

mind, I'll fast-forward a little, to the point where the police show up. Remember the cops, Kyle?'

'Yes.'

The video scrambled forward for a minute or so, until Wright pressed a key. 'At 11:25, the party comes to an abrupt halt. Listen.'

In mid-song, and with most of the fifteen still in view, dancing and drinking and yelling, someone off camera clearly yelled, 'Cops! Cops!' Kyle watched himself as he grabbed a girl and disappeared from view. The music stopped. The lights were out. The screen was almost completely dark.

Wright continued: 'According to our records, the police were called to your apartment three times that spring. This was the third time. A young man by the name of Alan Strock, one of your roommates, answered the door and chatted up the officers. He swore that there was no underage drinking. Everything was fine. He'd be happy to turn off the music and keep things quiet. The cops gave him a break and left with a warning. They assumed everybody else was hiding in the bedrooms.'

'Most of them fled through the back door,' Kyle said.

'Whatever. The cell phone video was on voice activation, so it clicked off after sixty seconds of near silence. It was at least twenty feet from the front door. Its owner ran off in the panic, forgot about it, and in the melee someone knocked things around on the counter, the cell phone got bumped, so the picture got adjusted. We can't see as much as we could before. About twenty minutes pass and all is quiet. At 11:48, there are voices and the lights come on.' Kyle moved closer to the screen. About one-third of the view was blocked by something yellow. 'Probably a phone book, the yellow pages,' Wright said. The music started again, but at a much lower volume.

The four roommates – Kyle, Alan Strock, Baxter Tate, and Joey Bernardo – were walking around the den, in shorts and T-shirts, and holding drinks again. Elaine Keenan walked through the den, talking nonstop, then sat on the edge of the sofa, smoking what appeared to be a joint. Only half of the sofa was visible. A television, unseen, was turned on. Baxter Tate walked over to Elaine, said something, then put his drink down and yanked off his T-shirt. He and Elaine fell into a pile on the sofa, obviously making out while the other three watched television and milled about. They were talking, but the music and TV drowned out their words. Alan Strock walked in front of the camera, pulling off his T-shirt and saying something to Baxter, whose view was blocked. There were no sounds from Elaine. Less than half of the sofa was visible now, but a tangle of bare legs could be seen.

Then the lights were turned off, and for a second the room was dark. Slowly, the glare from the television focused and bounced off the walls to provide some illumination. Joey

Bernardo came into view, also pulling off his shirt. He stopped and stared at the sofa, where some manner of frenzied activity was under way.

'Listen,' Wright hissed.

Joey said something that Kyle could not understand.

'Did you get that?' Wright asked.

'No.'

Wright stopped the video and said, 'Our experts have studied the audio. Joey Bernardo says to Baxter Tate, "Is she awake?" Tate is obviously having sex with Elaine, who's passed out drunk, and Bernardo stops by, takes it all in, and wonders if the girl is actually conscious. You want to hear it again?'

'Yes.'

Wright reset the video, then replayed it. Kyle leaned down, and with his nose six inches from the screen he watched hard, listened even harder, and heard the word 'awake.' The detective shook his head gravely.

The action continued, with the music and the television as a backdrop, and though the den of their apartment was dark, figures could be seen in the shadows. Baxter Tate finally got off the sofa, stood, appeared to be completely nude, and walked away. Another figure, Joey Bernardo, quickly took Baxter's place. Some of the sounds could barely be heard.

A steady clicking arose from the scene. 'We think that's the sofa,' Wright said. 'Don't suppose you could help on that one?'

'No.'

And before long there was a high-pitched heaving sound, and the clicking stopped. Joey moved from the sofa and disappeared. 'That's pretty much the end of the movie,' Wright said. 'The video goes on for another twelve minutes, but nothing happens. If the girl, Elaine, ever moved or got off the sofa, then it's not on the video. We're almost certain that Baxter Tate and Joey Bernardo had sex with her. There's no evidence that either you or Alan Strock did.'

'I did not. I can assure you of that.'

'Any idea where you were during the rapes, Kyle?' Wright asked the question, then pressed a key and the screen went blank.

'I'm sure you have a theory.'

'Okay.' Wright was again armed with his pen and legal pad. 'Elaine says she woke up several hours later, around three in the morning, naked, still on the sofa, and suddenly had a vague recollection of being raped. She panicked, wasn't sure where she was, admits she was still very drunk, eventually finds her clothes, gets dressed, sees you fast asleep in a recliner facing the television. When she sees you, she realizes where she is and remembers more of what happened to her. There's no sign of Strock, Tate, or Bernardo. She speaks to you, shakes your shoulder, but you do not respond, so she hurries from the apartment, goes next door, and eventually falls asleep.'

'And doesn't mention rape for four days, right, Detective, or has she changed her story again?'

'Four days is correct.'

'Thank you. Not a word to anyone for four days. Not to her roommates, her friends, parents, no one. Then suddenly she decided she was raped. The police were very suspicious of her story, right? They finally showed up at our apartment, and at the Beta house, and they asked questions and got very few answers. Why? Because there was no rape. Everything was consensual. Believe me, Detective, that girl would consent to anything.'

'How could she consent if she was unconscious, Kyle?'

'If she was unconscious, how could she remember being raped? There was no medical exam. No rape kit. No evidence whatsoever. Just the blacked-out memory of a very confused young woman. The cops dropped the case five years ago, and it should be dropped now.'

'But it's not. It's here. The grand jury believed the video proves there was a rape.'

'That's bullshit and you know it. This isn't about rape; this is about money. Baxter Tate's family is filthy rich. Elaine has found herself a greedy lawyer. The indictment is nothing but a shakedown.'

'So you're willing to risk the spectacle of a trial, and a conviction? You want the jury to see that video? You and your three roomies drunk out of your minds while a young woman is taken advantage of?'

'I didn't touch her.'

'No, but you were there, very close by, less than ten feet away. Come on.'

'I don't remember it.'

'How convenient.'

Kyle slowly got to his feet and walked to the bathroom. He filled another plastic cup with tap water, drained it, refilled it, and drank it. Then he sat on the edge of the bed and buried his head in his hands. No, he did not want the jury to see the video. He had just seen it for the first time and prayed it would be the last. He had a visual of himself and his three pals sitting in a crowded courtroom, lights dimmed, judge frowning, jurors gaping, Elaine crying, his parents stoic in the front row as the video is played to a rapt audience. The scene made him sick.

He felt innocent, but he wasn't convinced the jurors would agree.

Wright ejected the disc and placed it carefully back into a plastic case.

Kyle stared at the industrial-grade carpet for a long time. There were sounds in the hallway, muffled voices, feet shuffling, maybe the Fibbies were getting restless. He really didn't care. His ears were ringing and he wasn't sure why.

Each fleeting thought was chased away by the next, and he found it impossible to concentrate, to think rationally, to focus on what should and should not be said. Decisions made at this ugly moment could reverberate forever. For a moment he settled on the three Duke lacrosse players who were falsely accused of raping a stripper. They were eventually cleared of everything, but only after an excruciating trip to hell and back. And there was no video, no link whatsoever to the victim.

'Is she awake?' Joey says to Baxter. How many times would that question echo around the courtroom? Frame by frame. Word by word. The jurors would have the video memorized by the time they retired to consider the verdicts.

Wright sat patiently at the table, hairy hands folded again and motionless on his legal pad. Time meant nothing. He could wait forever.

'Are we at midfield?' Kyle asked, breaking the silence.

'Past midfield, around the forty and driving.'

'I'd like to see the indictment.'

'Sure.'

Kyle stood and looked down at the folding table. The detective began a series of movements that were immediately confusing. First, he pulled his wallet out of his rear left pocket, removed his driver's license, and placed it on the table. He produced his Pittsburgh PD badge and laid it on the table. From a box on the floor he pulled other cards and other badges and began arranging them in line on the table. He reached for a file, handed it to Kyle, and said, 'Happy reading.'

The file was labeled 'INFORMATION.' Kyle opened it and removed a stack of papers stapled together. The top one looked official. A bold title read: 'Commonwealth of Pennsylvania, Allegheny County, Court of Common Pleas.' A smaller heading read: 'Commonwealth versus Baxter F. Tate, Joseph N. Bernardo, Kyle L. McAvoy, and Alan B. Strock.' There was a docket number, file number, and other official markings.

Wright produced a pair of kitchen scissors and methodically cut his driver's license into two perfect squares.

The first paragraph read: 'This prosecution is in the name of and by the authority of the Commonwealth of Pennsylvania against the above-named defendants—'

Wright was cutting some of the other plastic cards, all of which appeared to be either driver's licenses or credit cards.

'Who, within the jurisdiction of this court—'

Wright ripped his bronze badge from its leather wallet and bounced it on the table. 'What are you doing?' Kyle finally asked.

'Destroying the evidence.'

'What evidence?'

'Read page two.'

Kyle, who was at the bottom of page one, flipped to page two. It was blank, not a word, letter, period, anything. He flipped to page three, then four, then five. All blank. Wright was busy removing other badges. Kyle held the bogus indictment and gawked at the detective.

'Have a seat, Kyle,' Wright said with a smile as he waved at the empty folding chair.

In an effort to say something, Kyle managed only a dying whimper. Then he sat down.

'There is no indictment, Kyle,' Wright proceeded as if it all made sense now. 'No grand jury, no cops, no arrest, no trial. Nothing but a video.'

'No cops?'

'Oh, no. This stuff is all fake.' He waved his hands over the pile of destroyed identification. 'I'm not a cop. Those boys across the hall are not FBI agents.'

Kyle rolled his head back like a wounded boxer, then rubbed his eyes. The indictment fell to the floor. 'Who are you?' he managed to grunt.

'That's a very good question, Kyle, one that will take a long time to answer.'

In disbelief, Kyle picked up one of the badges – Ginyard's, FBI. He rubbed it and said, 'But I checked this guy out online. He really works for the FBI.'

'Yes, these are real names. We just borrowed them for the night.'

'So, you're impersonating an officer?'

'Certainly, but it's just a small offense. Not worth your trouble.'

'But why?'

'To get your attention, Kyle. To convince you to come here and have this little meeting with me. Otherwise, you might have run away. Plus, we wanted to impress you with our resources.'

'We?'

'Yes, my firm. You see, Kyle, I work for a contractor, a private one, and we've been hired to do a job. We need you, and this is how we recruit people.'

Kyle blew out a chestful of nervous laughter. His cheeks were getting warm, the blood was beginning to circulate. There was a rising thrill at the relief of not being prosecuted, of having been rescued from the firing squad. But the anger was beginning to boil.

'You recruit by blackmail?' he asked.

'If necessary. We have the video. We know where the girl is. She does indeed have a lawyer.'

'Does she know about the video?'

'No, but if she saw it, your life could get very complicated.'

'I'm not sure I follow you.'

'Come on, Kyle. Rape has a twelve-year statute of limitations in Pennsylvania. You have seven years to go. If Elaine and her lawyer knew about the video, they would threaten criminal prosecution to force a civil settlement. It would be, as you say, nothing but a shakedown, but it would work. Your life will go much smoother if you play along with us and we keep the video buried.'

'So you're recruiting me?'

'Yes.'

'To do what?'

'To be a lawyer.'

Chapter 5

With a crushing weight suddenly lifted from his shoulders, and with his breathing somewhat normal again, Kyle glanced at his watch. It was after midnight. He looked at Wright, or whatever the hell his name really was, and he wanted to smile and even hug the man because he wasn't a cop from Pittsburgh and he didn't deliver an indictment. There would be no arrest, no prosecution, no humiliation, and for this Kyle was euphoric. But at the same time he wanted to bolt across the table and punch Wright's face with as much violence as he could generate, then knock him to the floor and kick him until he didn't move.

He vetoed both ideas. Wright was fit and probably trained and could take care of himself. And he certainly wasn't the type anyone would want to hug. Kyle leaned back in his chair, placed his right ankle on his left knee, and relaxed for the first time in hours.

'So what's your real name?' he asked.

Wright was preparing a new legal pad for a fresh round of note taking. He entered the date in the top left corner. 'We're not going to waste time with frivolous questions, Kyle.'

'Oh, why not? You can't even tell me your name?'

'Let's stick with Bennie Wright for now. It doesn't really matter, because you'll never know the real name.'

'I like this. Real cloak-and-dagger shit. You guys are good. Really had me going there for about four hours. Had a knot in my colon as big as a pumpkin. Already thinking about finding a nice bridge to wing it from. I hate your guts and don't ever forget it.'

'When you shut up, we can get down to business.'

'Can I walk out right now?'

'Sure.'

'And no one will grab me? No more fake badges and phony FBI agents?'

'None. Go. You're a free man.'

'Oh, thank you.'

A minute passed without a word. Wright's fierce little eyes never left Kyle's face, while Kyle, hard as he tried, could not return the stare. His foot twitched and his eyes darted and he drummed his fingers on the table. His mind raced through a hundred scenarios, but he never once thought of leaving the room.

'Let's talk about your future, Kyle,' Wright finally said.

'Sure. Now that I won't be arrested, the future has certainly improved.'

'This job you're planning to take. Piedmont Legal Aid. Why do you want to waste a couple of years saving the world?'

'Don't really see it that way. There are a lot of migrant workers in Virginia, many of whom are illegal, and they're subjected to all sorts of abuse. They live in cardboard boxes, eat rice twice a day, work for two bucks an hour, often don't get paid for backbreaking work, and so on. I figure they could use some help.'

'But why?'

'It's public-interest law, okay? Obviously you don't get it. It's lawyers giving their time to help others. They still teach this in law school. Some of us believe in it.'

Wright was not impressed. 'Let's talk about Scully & Pershing.'

'What about them? I'm sure you've done your research.'

'They offered you a job?'

'Correct.'

'Beginning when?'

'September 2 of this year. I take the bar in July, and would start working in September.'

'As an associate?'

'No, as a full-fledged partner. Or how about a secretary, or a copy clerk? Come on, Bennie, you know the routine.'

'Don't get angry, Kyle. We have a long way to go.'

'I see. And we should cooperate now, and be pals, because we're striving for a common purpose. Just you and me, right, Bennie? A couple of old friends. Where the hell is this going?'

'It's going to Scully & Pershing.'

'What if I don't want to work there?'

'You have little choice.'

Kyle leaned on his elbows and rubbed his eyes. The folding table was narrow, their faces were two feet apart.

'Have you said no to Scully & Pershing?' Wright asked.

'I'm assuming you already know the answer to that question. I'm assuming you've been listening to my phone conversations for some time.'

'Not all of them.'

'You're a thug.'

'Thugs break legs, Kyle. We're much too smart for that.'

'No, I have not said no to Scully & Pershing. I've informed them that I'm giving serious thought to public-interest law for a couple of years, and we've even discussed a deferment. They've given me extra time, but I need to make a decision.'

'So they still want you?'

'Yes.'

'At a starting salary of $200,000?'

'Something like that. You know the numbers.'

'One of the largest and most prestigious law firms in the world.'

'The largest, at least that's what they tell everybody.'

'Big firm, important clients, wealthy partners with contacts everywhere. Come on, Kyle, it's an offer most law students would kill for. Why not take it?'

Kyle jumped to his feet and paced to the door and back. He glared down at Wright and said, 'Let me make sure I follow you. You want me to take the job at Scully & Pershing, for reasons that I'm sure will be against my best interests, and if I say no, then you'll blackmail me with the video and the rape allegations. Right? Is this where we're headed, Bennie?'

'More or less. "Blackmail" is such an ugly word.'

'Wouldn't want to offend anyone, Bennie. I'm sure you're very sensitive. But it's blackmail, or extortion, or whatever you'd like to call it. It's a crime, Bennie. And you're a thug.'

'Shut up and stop calling me a thug!'

'I could go to the cops tomorrow and bust your ass. Impersonating an officer, attempted blackmail.'

'It won't happen.'

'I can make it happen.'

Wright slowly stood and for one horrible second made a motion as if he were about to throw a nasty punch. Then he casually pointed a finger at Kyle and in a firm and steady voice said, 'You're a kid with a snoot full of law. You want to run to the cops, go ahead. Work up your little textbook theories about who's right and who's wrong, and you know what will happen, Kyle? I'll tell you what will happen. You'll never see me again. The boys across the hall, the FBI agents, are already gone. No trace whatsoever. Vanished, forever. Before long, I'll have a visit with the attorney for Elaine Keenan, show her the video, look once again at the net worth of Baxter Tate, provide her with the current addresses and phone numbers and e-mails for you, Alan Strock, and Joey Bernardo, prod her to have a chat with the prosecutor in Pittsburgh, and before you know it things are out of your control. Maybe charges will be filed, maybe not. But, trust me, I will destroy you.'

'Where's Elaine? You got her in a bunker somewhere?'

'It doesn't matter. We have reason to believe she feels strongly that she was raped in your apartment.'

'Please.'

'She's a ticking bomb, Kyle, and the video would set her off. You have seven more years to worry about it.' With that, Wright returned to his chair and made some notes. Kyle sat on the edge of the bed, facing the mirror.

'It could get really ugly,' Wright continued. 'Think about it, Kyle. Yale Law's brightest student arrested on rape charges. The women's groups screaming for all eight testicles. The video leaked onto the Internet. A brutal trial. Chance of conviction, prison. A career ruined.'

'Shut up!'

'No. So if you think I'm worried about your two-bit threats, please rest assured that I am not. Let's talk business. Let's take the video and lock it away so that no one will ever see it. How does that sound, Kyle?'

It sounded pretty damned good at the moment. Kyle scratched his stubble as he said, 'What do you want?'

'I want you to take the job at Scully & Pershing.'

'Why?'

'Now we're getting somewhere, Kyle. Now we can talk business. I thought you'd never ask why.'

'Why? Why? Why?'

'Because I need information.'

'Great. That really explains things. Thank you so much.'

'Bear with me for a few minutes, Kyle. You need a little background here. There are two gigantic corporations who compete with each other. Both are ruthless competitors, both are worth billions, and they really despise each other. There have been lawsuits, nasty ones, big public spectacles with no clear winner or loser. So, over the years, they have tried to avoid the courtroom. Until now. Now they're about to square off in the mother of all lawsuits. It will be filed in a few weeks in federal court in New York City. At stake is something in the neighborhood of $800 billion, and the loser might not survive.

Nasty, vicious litigation. A bonanza for the attorneys. Each uses a huge Wall Street law firm, and guess what? The two law firms hate each other.'

'I can't wait to get in the middle of that.'

'That's where you're headed. One firm is Scully & Pershing. The other is Agee, Poe & Epps.'

'Otherwise known as APE.'

'Yes.'

'I interviewed there.'

'Did they offer a job?'

'I thought you knew everything.'

'Only what I need to know.'

'I didn't like the firm.'

'Attaboy. Now you can really dislike them.'

Kyle walked into the bathroom, ran cold water in the sink, splashed it on his face and down his neck, and for a long time stared at himself in the mirror. Don't get tired, he told himself. Ignore the fatigue and the fear. Try to anticipate what's coming. Try to throw him a curve, mess with his timing, knock him off course.

He sat down across the table from Wright. 'Where'd you find the video?' Kyle asked.

'Kyle, Kyle, such a waste of time.'

'If the video is used in court, then the owner of the cell phone camera will have to testify. You can't protect his identity at that point. Does he know this? Did you explain it to him? He's one of my fraternity brothers, and I'll bet he'll refuse to testify at trial.'

‘A trial? You’re willing to go to trial? A trial holds the possibility of a conviction, which means prison, and prison for cute little white boys convicted of rape is not pretty.’

‘I’ll bet she won’t press charges.’

‘You have nothing to bet with. She needs money. If she can squeeze it out of Mr. Tate, and a few bucks from you and the other two, she’ll do it. Trust me.’

‘I wouldn’t trust you with my dirty laundry.’

‘Enough of the insults. We’ll go to her lawyer and show her exactly how to do it. Or, maybe we won’t. Maybe we’ll just release an edited version of the video on the Internet tonight. Cut out the rape and let everyone see the party scene. We’ll e-mail it to all your friends, family, prospective employers, the whole world, Kyle. See how it plays. Then maybe we’ll edit it some more, maybe include some of the rape, post it again. When Elaine sees it, your face is in the newspaper.’

Kyle’s mouth actually dropped open, and his shoulders slumped. He could think of no quick response, but the one thought that hit him hard was that of being shot. Mr. Wright here was a ruthless little cutthroat who worked for some group with unlimited resources and great determination. They would ruin him. They might even kill him.

As if reading his mind, Wright leaned in a little closer and said, ‘Kyle, we’re not Boy Scouts. And I’m tired of this bantering back and forth.

I'm not here to negotiate. I'm here to give orders. Either you follow my orders, or I call the office and tell my pals to destroy you.'

'I despise you.'

'So be it. I'm just doing my job.'

'What a miserable job.'

'Can we talk about your new one?'

'I didn't go to law school to become a spy.'

'Let's not call it spying, Kyle.'

'Then give it a name, Bennie.'

'Transferring information.'

'Oh, bullshit. It's nothing but spying.'

'I really don't care what you call it.'

'What kind of information?'

'Once the lawsuit gets cranked up, there will be a million documents. Maybe ten million, who knows? Lots of documents and lots of secrets. We expect each of the two law firms to commit fifty lawyers to the case – maybe as many as ten partners, the rest associates. You'll be in the litigation section of Scully & Pershing, so you'll have access to a lot of material.'

'Security at these firms is extremely tight.'

'We know that. Our security experts are better than theirs. We wrote the book, Kyle.'

'I'm sure you did. May I ask what these two big companies are fighting over?'

'Secrets. Technology.'

'Great. Thanks. Do these companies have names?'

'Fortune 500. I'll give you more information as we progress.'

‘So you’re going to be part of my life for a while?’

‘I’m your official handler. You and I will spend a lot of time together.’

‘Then I quit. Go ahead and shoot me. I’m not spying and I’m not stealing. The moment I walk out of Scully & Pershing with a document or a disc I’m not supposed to have and give it to you or anybody else, I’ve broken the law and violated half the canons of ethics. I will be disbarred and convicted of something.’

‘Only if you get caught.’

‘I’ll get caught.’

‘No. We’re much too smart, Kyle. We’ve done this before. It’s our business.’

‘Your firm specializes in stealing documents?’

‘Let’s call it corporate espionage. We do it all the time and we’re very good at it.’

‘Then go blackmail someone else.’

‘No. It’s all you, Kyle. Think about it. You take the job you’ve always wanted, at an obscene salary, living the fast life in the big city. They try to work you to death for a few years, but they reward you. By the time you’re thirty, you’re a senior associate making four hundred grand a year. Nice apartment in SoHo. A share of a weekend house in the Hamptons. A Porsche. A circle of friends who are all smart and rich and moving up as fast as you are. Then one day the lawsuit is settled. We disappear. The statute runs out in Pittsburgh. The video is finally forgotten, and at the age of thirty-two or thirty-three you're asked to join Scully & Pershing as a full equity partner. A million or two per year. The pinnacle of success. A great career ahead of you. Life is great. And no one there will ever know about the transferring of information.'

A headache that had been smoldering for the past hour finally matured and hit hard in the middle of his forehead. Kyle stretched out on the bed and massaged his temples. He closed his eyes, but in the blackness managed to keep talking. 'Look, Bennie, I know you don't care about morals or ethics and such things, but I do. How, exactly, am I supposed to live with myself if I betray the confidences of my firm and its clients? Trust is the most important thing a lawyer has. I learned that from my father when I was a teenager.'

'All we care about is getting the information. We don't spend too much time pondering morality.'

'That's about what I figured.'

'I need a commitment, Kyle. I need your word.'

'Do you have any Tylenol?'

'No. Do we have an agreement, Kyle?'

'Do you have anything for a headache?'

'No.'

'Do you have a gun?'

'In my jacket.'

'Let me have it.'

A minute passed without a sound. Wright's eyes never left Kyle, who was motionless except for his fingers pressing gently on his forehead. Then Kyle slowly sat up and asked in a whisper, 'How much longer are you planning to stay here?'

'Oh, I have lots of questions.'

'I was afraid of that. I can't keep going. My head is splitting.'

'Whatever, Kyle. It's up to you. But I need an answer. Do we have an agreement, a deal, an understanding?'

'Do I really have a choice?'

'I don't see one.'

'Neither do I.'

'So?'

'If I have no choice, then I have no choice.'

'Excellent. A wise decision, Kyle.'

'Oh, thank you so much.'

Wright stood and stretched as if a long day at the office were finally over. He reshuffled some papers, fiddled with the video camera, closed the laptop. 'Would you like to rest, Kyle?'

'Yes.'

'We have several rooms. You're welcome to take a nap if you'd like, or we can continue tomorrow.'

'It's already tomorrow.'

Wright was at the door. He opened it and Kyle followed him out of the room, across the hall, and into room 222. What had once been an FBI command center had now been converted back to a regular $89-a-night motel room. Ginyard and Plant and the other fake agents were long gone, and they had taken everything – files, computers, enlarged photos, tripods, briefcases, boxes, folding tables. The bed was back in the center of the room, perfectly made up.

'Shall I wake you in a few hours?' Wright asked pleasantly.

'No. Just leave me alone.'

'I'll be across the hall.'

When Kyle was alone, he pulled back the bedspread, turned off the lights, and soon fell asleep.

Chapter 6

Contrary to his best intentions, Kyle awoke several hours later. He desperately wanted to sleep forever, to simply drift away and be forgotten. He awoke in a warm, dark room on a hard bed, and for a second wasn't sure where he was or how he had managed to get there. His head was still hurting and his mouth was dry. Soon, though, the nightmare returned, and he had the urgent desire to get away, to get outside, where he could look back at the motel and convince himself that the meeting with Detective Wright had not really happened. He needed fresh air, and maybe someone to talk to.

He eased from the room and tiptoed down the hall, down the stairs. In the lobby some salesmen were gulping coffee and talking rapidly, anxious for the day to start. The sun was up, the snow had stopped. Outside the air was cold and sharp, and he inhaled as if he'd been suffocating. He made it to his Jeep, started the engine, turned on the heater, and waited for the defrost to melt the snow on the windshield.

The shock was wearing off, but the reality was even worse.

He checked his cell phone messages. His girlfriend had called six times, his roommate three. They were worried. He had class at 9:00 a.m. and a pile of work at the law journal. And nothing – girlfriend, roommate, law school, or work – held the slightest interest at the moment. He left the Holiday Inn and drove east on Highway 1 for a few miles until New Haven was behind him. He ran up behind a snowplow and was content to putter along at thirty miles an hour. Other cars lined up behind him, and for the first time he wondered if someone might be following. He began glancing at the rearview mirror.

At the small town of Guilford, he stopped at a convenience store and finally found some Tylenol. He washed it down with a soft drink and was about to drive back to New Haven when he noticed a diner across the street. He had not eaten since lunch the day before and was suddenly famished. He could almost smell the bacon grease.

The diner was packed with the local breakfast crowd. Kyle found a seat at the counter and ordered scrambled eggs, bacon, hash browns, toast, coffee, and orange juice. He ate in silence as the laughter and town gossip roared around him. The headache was fading fast, and he began plotting the rest of his day. His girlfriend might be a problem: no contact in twelve hours, a night spent away from his apartment – highly unusual behavior for someone as disciplined as Kyle. He certainly couldn't tell her the truth, could he? No, the truth was a thing of the past. The present and the future would be a life of lies, cover-ups, thievery, espionage, and more lies.

Olivia was a first-year law student at Yale, a Californian, UCLA graduate, extremely bright and ambitious and not looking for a serious commitment. They had been dating for four months, and the relationship was far more casual than romantic. Still, he did not look forward to some stuttering tale of a night that simply vanished.

A body closed in from behind. A hand appeared with a white business card. Kyle glanced to his right and came face-to-face with the man he had once known as Special Agent Ginyard, now wearing a camel hair sport coat and jeans. 'Mr. Wright would like to see you at 3:00 p.m., after class, same room,' he said, then disappeared before Kyle could speak. He picked up the card. It was blank except for the handwritten message: '3:00 p.m., today, room 225, Holiday Inn.' He stared at it for a few minutes as he quickly lost interest in the remaining food in front of him.

Is this my future? he asked himself. Someone always watching, following, waiting in the shadows, stalking, listening?

A crowd was waiting by the door for seating.

The waitress slipped his bill under his coffee cup and gave him a quick smile that said 'Time's up.' He paid at the cash register and, outside, refused to scan the other vehicles for signs of stalkers. He called Olivia, who was sleeping.

'Are you all right?' she asked.

'Yes, I'm fine.'

'I don't want to know anything else, just tell me you're not hurt.'

'I'm not hurt. I'm fine, and I'm sorry.'

'Don't apologize.'

'I'm apologizing, okay. I should have called.'

'I don't want to know.'

'Yes you do. Do you accept my apology?'

'I don't know.'

'That's better. I expect some anger here.'

'Don't get me started.'

'How about lunch?'

'No.'

'Why not?'

'I'm busy.'

'You can't skip lunch.'

'Where are you?'

'Guilford.'

'And where might that be?'

'Just down the road from New Haven. There's a great little place for breakfast. I'll bring you here sometime.'

'Can't wait.'

'Meet me at The Grill at noon. Please.'

'I'll think about it.'

He drove back to New Haven, refusing every

half mile to glance at his mirror. He slipped quietly into his apartment and took a shower. Mitch, his roommate, could sleep through an earthquake, and when he finally staggered out of his bedroom, Kyle was sipping coffee at the kitchen counter and reading a newspaper online. Mitch asked a few vague questions about last night, but Kyle deflected them nicely and gave the impression that he had bumped into a different girl and things went extremely well. Mitch went back to bed.

Complete fidelity had been agreed to months earlier, and once Olivia was convinced Kyle had not cheated, her attitude thawed a little. The story he'd been working on for several hours went like this: He'd been struggling with his decision to pursue public-interest law instead of taking a big job with a big firm. He had no plans to make public-interest law a career, so why go there to begin with? He would eventually work in New York, so why delay the inevitable? And so on. And last night, after his basketball game, he decided he had to make a final decision. He turned off his phone and took a long drive, east for some unknown reason, on Highway 1, past New London and into Rhode Island. He lost track of time. After midnight, the snow picked up and he found a cheap motel where he slept for a few hours.

He had changed his mind. He was going to New York, to Scully & Pershing.

He spilled this over lunch, over a sandwich at The Grill. Olivia listened with skepticism but did not interrupt. She seemed to believe the story about last night, but she was not buying the sudden change in career plans. 'You must be kidding,' she blurted when he hit the punch line.

'It's not easy,' he said, already on the defensive. He knew this would not be pleasant.

'You, Mr. Pro Bono, Mr. Public Interest Law?'

'I know. I know. I feel like a turncoat.'

'You are a turncoat. You're selling out, just like every other third-year law student.'

'Lower your voice, please,' Kyle said as he glanced around. 'Let's not have a scene.'

She lowered her voice but not her eyebrows. 'You've said it yourself a hundred times, Kyle. We all get to law school with big ideas of doing good, helping others, fighting injustice, but along the way we sell out. Seduced by big money. We turn into corporate whores. Those are your words, Kyle.'

'They do sound familiar.'

'I can't believe this.'

They took a couple of bites, but the food was not important.

'We have thirty years to make money,' she said. 'Why can't we spend a few years helping others?' Kyle was on the ropes and bleeding.

'I know, I know,' he mumbled lamely. 'But timing is important. I'm not sure Scully & Pershing will defer.' Another lie, but what the hell. Once you start, why quit? They were multiplying.

'Oh, please. You can get a job with any firm in the country, now or five years from now.'

'I'm not so sure about that. The job market is tightening up. Some of the big firms are threatening layoffs.'

She shoved her food away, crossed her arms, and slowly shook her head. 'I don't believe this,' she said.

And at that moment Kyle couldn't believe it either, but it was important, now and forever more, to give the impression that he'd carefully weighed the issues and had arrived at this decision. In other words, Kyle had to sell it. Olivia was the first test. His friends would be next, then his favorite professors. After he'd practiced the routine a few times and the lying was finely tuned, he would somehow muster the courage to visit his father and deliver the news that would lead to an ugly fight. John McAvoy detested the idea of his son working for a corporate firm on Wall Street.

Kyle's selling job, though, did little to convince Olivia. They traded barbs for a few minutes, then forgot about lunch and went their separate ways. There was no goodbye peck on the cheek, no hug, no promise to call each other later. He spent an hour in his office at the law journal, then reluctantly left and drove back to the motel.

*

The room had changed little. The video camera and laptop were gone, no sign of electronics anywhere, though Kyle was certain every word would be recorded in some fashion. The folding table was still ground zero, but it had been moved closer to the windows. Same two folding chairs. The setting was as stark as a police interrogation room somewhere deep in the basement.

The headache was back.

Kyle flipped the card Ginyard left behind onto the table and began with a pleasant 'Please tell this son of a bitch to stop following me.'

'We're just a little curious, that's all, Kyle.'

'I'm not going to be followed, Bennie, do you understand?'

Bennie gave a smart-ass smile.

'The deal's off, Bennie. I'm not going to live my life with a bunch of goons watching everything I do. Forget the surveillance, forget the wiretaps and hidden mikes and e-mail snooping, Bennie. Are you listening? I'm not walking down the streets of New York wondering who's behind me. I'm not chatting on the phone while thinking some bozo might be listening. You've just wrecked my life, Bennie, the least you can do is allow me some degree of privacy.'

'We have no plans—'

'That's a lie and you know it. Here's the new deal, Bennie. We agree right now that you and your goons stay out of my life. You don't eavesdrop, you don't follow, you don't hide in the shadows or stalk or play your little cat-and-mouse games. I'll do what you want me to do, whatever the hell that is, but you have got to leave me alone.'

'Otherwise?'

'Oh, otherwise. Otherwise, I'll take my chances with Elaine and her bogus rape charge. Look, Bennie, if my life is going to be ruined, then what the hell? I get to pick my poison. I have Elaine on the one hand, and I have your goons on the other.'

Bennie exhaled slowly, cleared his throat, and said, 'Yes, Kyle, but it is important for us to keep up with you. That is the nature of our work. That is what we do.'

'It's blackmail, pure and simple.'

'Kyle, Kyle, none of that now. That doesn't move the ball.'

'Please, can we forget about the ball? That's so tiring now.'

'We can't just turn you loose in New York.'

'Here's my bottom line – I will not be stalked or watched or followed. Do you understand this, Bennie?'

'This could pose a problem.'

'It's already a problem. What do you want? You'll know where I live and where I work – they're basically the same place for the next five years anyway. I'll be at the office eighteen hours a day, if not more. Why, exactly, will it be necessary to keep me under surveillance?'

'There are procedures we follow.'

'Then change them. It's not negotiable.' Kyle jumped to his feet and headed for the door. 'When do we meet again?'

'Where are you going?' Bennie asked as he stood.

'None of your business, and don't follow me. Do not follow me.' Kyle had his hand on the doorknob.

'Okay, okay. Look, Kyle, we can be flexible here. I see your point.'

'When and where?'

'Now.'

'No, I have things to do, without being watched.'

'But we have so much to talk about, Kyle.'

'When?'

'How about six, tonight?'

'I'll be here at eight, and for only one hour. And I'm not coming back tomorrow.'

Chapter 7

At the New Haven train station, Kyle boarded the 7:22 for Grand Central. He wore the better of his two suits, a plain white shirt with an utterly boring tie, and black wing tips, and he carried a handsome leather attaché case his father had given him last Christmas. He also carried the morning's editions of the *New York Times* and the *Wall Street Journal*, and he was indistinguishable from the other sleepy-eyed executives hustling off to the office.

As the frozen countryside blurred by, he ignored the papers and let his mind wander. He asked himself if he would one day live in the suburbs and be forced to ride a train three hours a day so his children could attend fine schools and ride their bikes down leafy streets. At the age of twenty-five, that was not very appealing. But now most of his thoughts about the future were complicated and dreary. He'd be lucky if he didn't get himself indicted and/or disbarred. Life in the big firms was brutal enough, and now he would have the impossible chore of grinding through the first years while stealing confidential information and praying daily that he didn't get caught.

Maybe commuting wasn't such a bad deal after all.

After three days and many hours of talking, haggling, bitching, and threatening, Bennie Wright had finally left town. He had receded into the shadows but, of course, would soon materialize again. Kyle hated his voice, his face, his mannerisms, his calm hairy hands, his slick head, his confident, pressing manner. He hated everything about Bennie Wright and his company or firm or whatever it was, and many times during the past week he had changed his mind in the middle of the night and told them all to go to hell.

Then, in the darkness, as always, he could feel the handcuffs, see his mug shot in the newspapers, see the looks on the faces of his parents, and worst of all he could see himself afraid to glance at the jurors when the video was played to a hushed courtroom.

'Is she awake?' Joey Bernardo asks while Baxter Tate has Elaine down on the sofa.

Is she awake? The words echo around the courtroom.

The countryside vanished as the train sped through suburbs and towns, then it went underground, at some point dipped under the East

River and entered Manhattan. Kyle strolled through Grand Central and hailed a cab at the corner of Lex and Forty-fourth. Not once had he looked over his shoulder.

Scully & Pershing leased the top half of a building named 110 Broad, a sleek glass edifice with forty-four floors, in the heart of the financial district. Kyle had spent ten weeks there the previous summer as an intern – the typical big-firm seduction routine of socializing, lunching, barhopping, watching the Yankees, and putting in a few light hours of work. It was a joke of a job and everybody involved knew it. If the wining and dining worked, and it almost always did, the interns became associates upon graduation and their lives were basically over.

It was almost 10:00 a.m., and the elevator was empty. The lawyers had been at their desks for hours. He stopped at the thirtieth floor, the firm's main lobby, and paused for a second to admire the massive bronze lettering that informed all visitors that they were now on the hallowed turf of Scully & Pershing. Attorneys-at-law, all twenty-one hundred of them, the largest law firm the world had ever known. The first and still the only firm to boast of more than two thousand lawyers. Counsel to more Fortune 500 companies than any other firm in the history of American law. Offices in ten U.S. cities and twenty foreign ones. A hundred and thirty years of hidebound tradition. Magnet to the best legal talent money can buy. Power, money, prestige.

He already felt like a trespasser.

The walls were covered with abstract art, the furniture was rich and contemporary. Some Asian whiz had done the decorating, magazine quality, and there was a brochure on a table that went into details. As if anyone who worked there had the time to stop and ponder the interior design schemes. A gorgeous little receptionist in stiletto heels took his name and asked him to please wait. Kyle turned his back on everything and became entranced in a work of art so bizarre he had no idea what he was looking at. After a few minutes of mindless gazing, he heard the receptionist call, 'Mr. Peckham is waiting. Two floors up.' Kyle took the stairs.

Like many Manhattan law firms, Scully & Pershing spent money on the elevators, reception areas, and conference rooms – the places clients and other visitors might actually see – but back in the bowels of the firm where the grunts worked, efficiency ruled. The halls were lined with file cabinets. The secretaries and typists – all women – worked in tight cubicles within reach of each other. The copyboys and other gofers worked on their feet; New York real estate was simply too expensive to provide them a spot or a nook of any significance. The senior associates and junior partners were awarded small offices on the outer walls, with a view of similar buildings.

The rookie associates were stuffed in tight windowless spaces; three or four of them wedged together in cramped cubicles, nicknamed 'cubes.' These 'offices' were tucked away and kept out of sight. Lousy accommodations, brutal hours, sadistic bosses, unbearable pressure – it was all part of the blue-chip law firm experience, and Kyle had heard the horror tales before he finished his first year at Yale. Scully & Pershing was no better and certainly no worse than the other mega-firms that threw money at the brightest students, then burned them up.

At the corners of each floor, in the largest offices, the real partners anchored things and had some say in the decor. One was Doug Peckham, a forty-one-year-old litigation partner, a Yale man who had supervised Kyle during his internship. They had become somewhat friendly.

Kyle was shown into Peckham's office a few minutes after 10:00 a.m., just as a pair of associates were leaving. Whatever the meeting was, it had not gone well. The associates looked rattled, and Peckham was trying to calm down.

They exchanged greetings and pleasantries, the usual banter about good old Yale. Kyle knew that Peckham billed $800 an hour, at least ten hours a day, and therefore the time that Kyle was now wasting was quite valuable. 'I'm not sure I want to spend a couple of years doing legal aid,' Kyle said, not too deep into the meeting.

'Don't really blame you there, Kyle,' Peckham said in a quick, clipped voice. 'You have too much potential in the real world. This is your future.' He spread his arms to take in his vast empire. It was a nice office, large by comparison, but not a kingdom.

'I really would like to work in litigation.'

'I see no problem there. You had a great summer here. We were all impressed. I'll make the request myself. You know, though, that litigation is not for everyone.'

That's what they all said. The average career of a litigator is twenty-five years. The work is high pressure, high stress. Peckham may have been forty-one, but he could easily pass for fifty. Completely gray, dark circles, too much bulk in the jowls and around the waist. Probably hadn't exercised in years.

'My deadline has passed,' Kyle said.

'When?'

'A week ago.'

'No problem. Come on, Kyle, editor in chief of the *Yale Law Journal.* We'll be happy to cut you some slack. I'll talk to Woody in personnel and clear it. Our recruiting has gone very well. You're joining the best freshman class in years.'

The same was said about every freshman class at every major firm.

'Thanks. And I'd love to work in the litigation practice group.'

'Got it, Kyle. Consider it done.' And with that Peckham glanced at his watch – meeting over. His phone was ringing, there were hushed voices just outside his door. As Kyle shook his hand and said goodbye, he decided he did not want to become another Doug Peckham. He had no idea what he wanted to become, or if he would in fact become anything other than a disbarred lawyer, but selling his soul to become a partner was not in the plans.

Associates were waiting at the door, sharply dressed young men not much older than Kyle. Smug, harried, nervous, they stepped into the lion's den, and as the door closed, Doug was raising his voice. What a life. And this was an easy day in litigation. The real pressure was in the courtroom.

On the elevator down, Kyle was struck by the absurdity of what he was expected to do. Upon leaving the offices of Scully & Pershing, and riding the elevator like hundreds of others, he was expected to have hidden somewhere upon his person or within his effects top secret information that belonged not to him but to the firm and especially to its client. And he would give this valuable data to Bennie with the hairy hands, or whatever his real name was, who would then use it against the firm and its client.

Who am I kidding? he said to himself. There were four others on the elevator. Sweat popped out above his eyebrows.

So this is what my life boils down to. A chance of prison for rape in Pennsylvania or a chance of prison in New York for stealing secrets. Why not a third option? Four years of college, three years of law school, seven rather successful years, all the potential in the world, and I'll become a highly paid thief.

And there was no one to talk to.

He wanted out. Out of the elevator, the building, the city. Out of this predicament. He closed his eyes and talked to himself.

But there was evidence in Pennsylvania, and none in New York. Yet. He was certain he would get caught, though. Months before any crime was committed, he knew he would get caught.

Two blocks away, he found a coffee shop. He sat on a bar stool in the window and for a long time looked rather forlornly at 110 Broad, at the tower that would soon become his home, or his prison. He knew the numbers, the statistics. Scully & Pershing would hire 150 new associates worldwide, 100 in the New York office alone. They would pay them a nice salary that would amount to about $100 an hour, and the firm would in turn bill their well-heeled clients several times that rate for the associates' work. Kyle, like all rookie grunts on Wall Street, would be expected to bill a minimum of two thousand hours a year, though more would be required to make an impression. Hundred-hour workweeks would not be uncommon. After two years, the associates would begin dropping out and looking for more sensible work. Half would be gone in four years. Ten percent of his freshman class would survive, claw their way to the top, and be awarded with a partnership after seven or eight years. Those who didn't drop out along the way would be squeezed out by the firm if they were not deemed partnership material.

The work had become so awful that the trend was for firms to market themselves as 'quality of life' firms. The associates were expected to bill fewer hours, have more vacation, and so on. More often than not, though, it was simply a recruiting gimmick. In the workaholic culture of every big firm, the greenest associates were expected to bill almost as much as the partners, regardless of what the recruiters mentioned over lunch months earlier.

Sure the money was great. At least $200,000 to start with. Double that in five years as a senior associate. Double it again in seven years as a junior partner. Well over a million bucks a year at the age of thirty-five as a full partner with a future filled with even higher earnings.

Numbers, numbers. Kyle was sick of the numbers. He longed for the Blue Ridge Mountains and a nonprofit's salary of $32,000 without the stress and pressure and hassle of life in the city. He yearned for freedom.

Instead, he had another meeting with Bennie Wright. The cab stopped in front of the Millenium Hilton on Church Street. Kyle paid the driver, nodded at the doorman, then took the elevator four floors up to a room where his handler was waiting. Bennie motioned to a round table with a bowl of bright green apples in the center, but Kyle refused to sit or remove his jacket.

'The offer is still good,' he said. 'I'll start in September with the other associates.'

'Good. I'm not surprised. And you'll be in litigation?'

'Peckham thinks so.'

Bennie had a file on Doug Peckham, as well as files on all of the litigation partners and many of the firm's other lawyers.

'But there's no guarantee,' Kyle added.

'You can make it happen.'

'We'll see.'

'Have you thought about an apartment here in Manhattan?'

'No, not yet.'

'Well, we've done some homework, looked around.'

'Funny, I don't recall asking for your help.'

'And we've found a couple of places that will be ideal.'

'Ideal for who?'

'For you, of course. Both places are in Tribeca, fairly close to the office.'

'What makes you think I would even remotely consider living where you want me to live?'

'And we'll cover the rent. Pretty pricey real estate.'

'Oh, I see. You'll find an apartment for me, and pay for it, so I won't need a roommate. Is that it, Bennie? One less person for you to worry about. Helps to keep me isolated. Plus the rent means that we're financially joined at the hip. You pay me, I give you secrets, just a couple of shrewd businessmen, right, Bennie?'

'Apartment hunting is a bitch in this city. I'm just trying to help.'

'Thanks so much. No doubt these are places that can easily be watched, maybe even wired or bugged or compromised in ways I can't even imagine. Nice try, Bennie.'

'The rent is five thousand bucks a month.'

'Keep it. I can't be bought. Evidently I can be blackmailed, but not bought.'

'Where are you planning to live?'

'Wherever I choose. I'll figure it out, and I'll do so without any involvement on your part.'

'As you wish.'

'Damned right. What else do you want to talk about?'

Bennie walked to the table, picked up a legal pad, and studied it as if he didn't know what he'd already written on it. 'Have you ever seen a psychiatrist?' he asked.

'No.'

'A psychologist?'

'No.'

'A counselor or therapist of any type?'

'Yes.'

'Details please.'

'It was nothing.'

'Then let's talk about nothing. What happened?'

Kyle leaned against the wall and folded both arms across his chest. There was little doubt in his mind that Bennie knew most of what he was about to explain. He knew far too much. 'After the incident with Elaine, and after the police finished their investigation, I talked to a counselor in student health services. She referred me to a Dr. Thorp, a specialist in drug and alcohol addiction. He roughed me up, got under my skin, forced me to take a long hard look in the mirror, and he convinced me the drinking would only get worse.'

'Were you an alcoholic?'

'No. Dr. Thorp didn't think so. I certainly didn't either. But there was too much drinking, especially of the binge variety. I seldom smoked pot.'

'You're still sober?'

'I quit drinking. I grew up, found some different roommates, and have never been tempted. I've yet to miss the hangovers.'

'Not even an occasional beer?'

'Nope. I never think about it.'

Bennie nodded as if he approved of this. 'What about the girl?' he asked.

'What about her?'

'How serious is the relationship?'

'Not sure where you figure into this, Bennie. Can you help me here?'

'Your life will be complicated enough without a romance. A serious relationship could pose problems. It's best if you postpone it for a few years.'

Kyle laughed in frustration and disbelief. He shook his head and tried to think of an appropriate retort, but nothing came to mind. Sadly, he agreed with his tormentor. And the relationship with Olivia was going nowhere fast. 'What else, Bennie? Can I have some friends? Can I visit my parents occasionally?'

'You won't have the time.'

Kyle suddenly headed for the door, yanked it open, then slammed it as he left.

Chapter 8

There is a student lounge on the first floor of the Yale Law School, and on the walls outside its door are posters and notices advertising internships and even careers in public-interest law. The students are encouraged to consider spending a few years helping battered women, neglected children, death row inmates, immigrants, runaway teens, indigent defendants, the homeless, asylum seekers, Haitian boat refugees, Americans sitting in foreign jails and foreigners sitting in American jails, First Amendment projects, innocence projects, conservation groups, environmental activists, and on and on.

A belief in public service runs deep at Yale Law. Admission is often determined by the applicant's record of volunteerism and his or her written thoughts about using a law degree to benefit the world. First-year students are inundated with the virtues of public-interest law and are expected to get involved as soon as possible.

And most do. Around 80 percent of all freshmen claim that they are attracted to the law by a desire to help others. At some point, though, usually about halfway through the second year, things begin to change. The big firms arrive on campus to interview and begin their selection process. They offer summer internships, with nice salaries and the prospect of ten weeks of fun and games in New York, Washington, or San Francisco. Most important, they hold the keys to the lucrative careers. A divide occurs at Yale Law, as it does at all prestigious schools. Many of those so enamored with righteous dreams of aiding the downtrodden suddenly switch gears and begin dreaming of making it to the major leagues of American law, while many are turned off by this seduction and cling to their idyllic notions of public service. The divide is clear, but civilized.

When an editor of the *Yale Law Journal* takes a low-paying job with legal services, he is a hero to those on his side and to most of the faculty. And when he suddenly caves in to Wall Street, he is viewed less favorably by the same people.

Kyle's life became miserable. His friends on the public-interest side were in disbelief. Those on the corporate side were too busy to care. His relationship with Olivia was reduced to sex once a week and only because they needed it. She said he had changed. He was moodier, gloomier, preoccupied with something, and whatever it was he couldn't tell her.

If you only knew, he thought.

She had accepted a summer internship with an anti-death-penalty group in Texas; thus she was full of zeal and big plans to change things down there. They saw less and less of each other but somehow managed to bicker more.

One of Kyle's favorite professors was an old radical who'd spent most of the 1960s marching for or against something, and he was still the first one to organize a petition against whatever he perceived to be the latest injustice on campus. When he heard the news that Kyle had flipped, he called and demanded lunch. Over enchiladas at a taco bar just off campus, they argued for an hour. Kyle pretended to resent the intrusion, but in his heart he knew he was wrong. The professor railed and hammered and got nowhere. He left Kyle with a disheartening 'I'm very disappointed in you.'

'Thanks,' Kyle retorted, then cursed himself as he walked to campus. Then he cursed Bennie Wright and Elaine Keenan and Scully & Pershing and everything else in his life at that moment. He was mumbling and cursing a lot these days.

After a few rounds of ugly encounters with his friends, Kyle finally found the courage to go home.

The McAvoys drifted into eastern Pennsylvania in the late eighteenth century, along with thousands of other Scottish settlers. They farmed for a few generations, then moved on, down to Virginia, the Carolinas, and even farther south. Some stayed behind, including Kyle's grandfather, a Presbyterian minister who died before Kyle was born. Reverend McAvoy led several churches on the outskirts of Philadelphia before being transferred to York in 1960. His only son, John, finished high school there and returned home after college, Vietnam, and law school.

In 1975, John McAvoy quit his job as a lowly paid pencil pusher in a small real estate law firm in York. He marched across Market Street, rented a two-room 'suite' in a converted row house, hung out his shingle, and declared himself ready to sue. Real estate law was too boring. John wanted conflict, courtrooms, drama, verdicts. Life in York was uneventful enough. He, an ex-Marine, was looking for a fight.

He worked very hard and treated everyone fairly. Clients were free to call him at home, and he would meet them on Sunday afternoons if necessary. He made house calls, hospital calls, jail calls. He called himself a street lawyer, an advocate for clients who worked in factories, who got injured or discriminated against, or who ran afoul of the law. His clients were not banks or insurance companies or real estate agencies or corporations. His clients were not billed by the hour. Often, they were not billed at all. Fees were sometimes delivered in the form of firewood, eggs and poultry, steaks, and free labor around the house. The office grew, sprawled upstairs and down, and John eventually bought the row house. Younger lawyers came and went, none staying more than three years. Mr. McAvoy was demanding of his associates. He was kinder to his secretaries. One, a young divorcée named Patty, married the boss after a two-month courtship and was soon pregnant.

The Law Offices of John L. McAvoy had no specialty, other than representing low-paying clients. Anyone could walk in, with an appointment or without, and see John as soon as he was available. He handled wills and estates, divorces, injuries, petty criminal cases, and a hundred other matters that found their way to his office on Market Street. The traffic was constant, the doors opened early and closed late, and the reception area was seldom empty. Through sheer volume, and an innate Presbyterian frugality, the office covered its expenses and provided the McAvoy family with an income that was in the upper-middle class for York. Had he been greedier, or more selective, or even a bit firmer with his billing, John could have doubled his income and joined the country club. But he hated golf and didn't like the wealthier folks in town. More important, he viewed the practice of law as a calling, a mission to help the less fortunate.

Patty had twin girls in 1980. In 1983, Kyle was born, and before he started kindergarten, he was hanging around his father's office. After his parents divorced, he preferred the stability of the law office to the strains of joint custody, and each day after school he parked himself in a small room upstairs and finished his homework. At the age of ten he was running the copier, making coffee, and tidying up the small library. He was paid $1 an hour in cash. By the age of fifteen he had mastered legal research and could hammer out memos on basic subjects. During high school, when he wasn't playing basketball, he was at the office or in court with his father.

Kyle loved the law office. He chatted up the clients as they waited to see Mr. McAvoy. He flirted with the secretaries and pestered the associates. He cracked jokes when things were tense, especially when Mr. McAvoy was angry with a subordinate, and he pulled pranks on visiting lawyers. Every lawyer and every judge in York knew Kyle, and it was not unusual for him to slip into an empty courtroom, present a motion to a judge, argue its merits if necessary, then leave with a signed order. The court clerks treated him as if he were one of the lawyers.

Before college, he was always around the office at five on Tuesday afternoons when Mr. Randolph Weeks stopped by with a delivery of food – fruits and vegetables from his garden in the spring and summer and pork, poultry, or wild game in the fall and winter. Every Tuesday at 5:00 p.m. for at least the past ten years, Mr. Weeks came to pay a portion of his fee. No one knew exactly how much was owed or how much had been paid, but Mr. Weeks certainly felt as though he was still in debt to Mr. McAvoy. He had explained to Kyle many years earlier that his father, a great lawyer, had pulled a miracle and kept Mr. Weeks's oldest son out of prison.

And Kyle, though only a teenager, had been the unofficial lawyer for Miss Brily, a crazy old woman who'd been run out of every law office in York. She trudged the streets of the town with a wooden file cabinet on wheels, boxes of papers which she claimed proved clearly that her father, who had died at the age of ninety-six (and she still suspected foul play), was the rightful heir to a huge tract of rich coal deposits in eastern Pennsylvania. Kyle had read most of her 'documents' and had quickly concluded that she was even nuttier than most lawyers suspected. But he engaged her and listened to her conspiracies. By then he was earning $4 an hour and worth every penny of it. His father often parked him in the reception area to screen those new clients who at first glance showed the potential to waste a lot of his time.

Except for the usual adolescent dreams of playing professional sports, Kyle always knew he would be a lawyer. He wasn't sure what kind of lawyer, or where he would practice, but by the time he left York for Duquesne, he doubted if he would return. John McAvoy doubted it, too, though, like any father, he often thought of the pride he would have if the firm name became McAvoy & McAvoy. He demanded hard work and excellent grades, but even he was a little surprised at Kyle's academic success in college and at Yale Law School. When Kyle began his interviews with the big corporate law firms, John had plenty to say on the matter.

Kyle had called and told his father he would arrive in York late Friday afternoon. They had agreed on dinner. As usual, the office was busy at 5:30, when he arrived. Most law firms closed early on Friday, and most lawyers were either in bars or at the country club. John McAvoy worked late because many of his clients got paid at the end of the week, and a few stopped by to write small checks or see about their cases. Kyle had not been home in six weeks, since Christmas, and the office looked even shabbier. The carpet needed replacing. The bookshelves sagged even more. His father couldn't stop smoking; therefore smoking was permitted, and a thick haze floated near the ceiling late in the day.

Sybil, the ranking secretary, abruptly hung up the phone when Kyle walked through the door. She jumped to her feet, squealed, grabbed him, and thrust her gigantic breasts at him. They pecked on the cheeks and enjoyed the physical greeting. His father had handled at least two divorces for Sybil, and the current husband would soon be on the street. Kyle had heard the details during the Christmas break. The firm currently had three secretaries and two associates, and he went from room to room, downstairs first, then upstairs, where the young lawyers were kept, speaking to the employees as they packed their briefcases and purses and tidied up their desks. The boss might enjoy staying late on Fridays, but the rest of the firm was tired.

Kyle drank a diet soda in the coffee room and listened to the voices and sounds of the office as it wound down. The contrasts were startling. Here, in York, the firm was filled with co-workers who were friends who could be trusted. The pace was busy at times, but never frantic. The boss was a good guy, someone you would want as your lawyer. The clients had faces and names. The lawyers across the street were old pals. It was a different world from the hard streets of New York City.

Not for the first time he asked himself why he didn't tell his father everything. Just spill it all. Start with Elaine, her allegations, the cops and their questions. Five years earlier he had come within minutes of hustling home and asking his father for help. But then it passed, and then it went away, and John McAvoy was never burdened with the ugly episode. None of the four – Kyle, Joey Bernardo, Alan Strock, and Baxter Tate – had told their parents. The investigation ran out of steam before they were forced to.

If he told his father now, the first question would be, 'Why didn't you tell me then?' And Kyle wasn't prepared to face it. Many tougher questions would follow, a regular cross-examination by a courtroom brawler who'd interrogated his son since he was an infant. It was much easier for Kyle to keep his secrets and hope for the best.

What he was about to tell his father was difficult enough.

After the last client left and Sybil said goodbye and locked the front door, father and son relaxed in the big office and talked about college basketball and hockey. Then family, the twin sisters first, as always, then Patty.

'Does your mother know you're in town?' John asked.

'No. I'll call her tomorrow. She's okay?'

'Nothing's changed. She's fine.' Patty lived and worked in the loft of an old warehouse in York. It was a large space with lots of windows that provided the light she needed to pursue her painting. John paid the rent, utilities, and everything else she needed through a monthly stipend of $3,000. It wasn't alimony, and it certainly wasn't child support, but simply a gift he felt compelled to pass along for her upkeep because she could not support herself. If she had sold a painting or a sculpture in the past nineteen years, no one in the family knew about it.

'I call her every Tuesday night,' Kyle said.

'I know you do.'

Patty had no use for computers or cell phones. She was severely bipolar, and the mood swings were, at times, astonishing. John still loved her and had never remarried, though he'd enjoyed a few girlfriends. Patty had been through at least two ruinous affairs, both with fellow artists, much younger men, and John had been there to pick up the pieces. Their relationship was complicated, to say the least.

'So how's school?' John asked.

'Downhill. I graduate in three months.'

'That's hard to believe.'

Kyle swallowed hard and decided to get it over with. 'I've changed my mind about employment. I'm going to Wall Street. Scully & Pershing.'

John slowly lit another cigarette. He was sixty-two, thick but not fat, with a head full of wavy gray hair that began no more than three inches above his eyebrows. Kyle, at twenty-five, had lost more hair than his father.

John took a long drag from his Winston and studied his son from behind wire-rimmed reading glasses perched on his nose. 'Any particular reason?'

The list of reasons had been memorized, but Kyle knew they would sound flat regardless of how smoothly they were delivered. 'The legal services gig is a waste of time. I'll end up on Wall Street eventually, so why not get the career started?'

'I don't believe this.'

'I know, I know. It's an about-face.'

'It's a sellout. There's nothing that requires you to pursue a career in a corporate firm.'

'It's the big leagues, Dad.'

'In terms of what? Money?'

'That's a start.'

'No way. There are trial lawyers who make ten times more each year than the biggest partners in New York.'

'Yes, and for every big trial lawyer there are five thousand starving sole practitioners. On the average, the money is much better in a big firm.'

'You'll hate every minute of a big firm.'

'Maybe not.'

'Of course you will. You grew up here, around people and real clients. You won't see a client for ten years in New York.'

'It's a nice firm, Dad. One of the best.'

John yanked a pen from his pocket. 'Let me write this down, so a year from now I can read it back to you.'

'Go ahead. I said, "It's a nice firm. One of the best." '

John took notes and said, 'You're gonna hate this firm and its lawyers and cases, and you'll probably even hate the secretaries and the other rookie associates. You're gonna hate the grind, the routine, the sheer drudgery of all the mindless crap they dump on you. Response?'

'I disagree.'

'Great,' John said, still writing. Then he pulled on the cigarette and blew out an impressive cloud of smoke. He put down the pen. 'I thought you wanted to try something different and help people in the process. Did I not hear these words from you just a few weeks ago?'

'I've changed my mind.'

'Well, change it back. It's not too late.'

'No.'

'But why? There must be a reason.'

'I just don't want to spend three years in rural Virginia trying to learn enough Spanish so I can listen to the problems of people who are here illegally in the first place.'

'I'm sorry, but that sounds like a great way to spend the next three years. I don't buy it. Give me another reason.' With that, John shoved his leather swivel chair back and jumped to his feet. Kyle had seen this a million times. His father preferred to pace and toss his hands about when he was agitated and firing questions. It was an old habit from the courtroom, and it was not unexpected.

'I'd like to make some money.'

'For what? To buy things, some new toys? You won't have the time to play with them.'

'I plan to save—'

'Of course you will. Living in Manhattan is so cheap you'll save a fortune.' He was walking in front of his Ego Wall, framed certificates and photos almost to the ceiling. 'I don't buy it, and I don't like it.' His cheeks were turning colors. The Scottish temper was warming up.

Speak softly, Kyle reminded himself. A sharp word or two would make things much worse. He would survive this little clash, as he had survived the others, and one day soon all the harsh words would be over and Kyle would be off to New York.

'It's all about the money, isn't it, Kyle?' John said. 'You were raised better.'

'I'm not here to be insulted, Dad. I've made my decision. I ask you to respect it. A lot of fathers would be thrilled with such a job.'

John McAvoy stopped pacing and stopped smoking, and he looked across his office at the handsome face of his only son, a twenty-five-year-old who was quite mature and unbelievably bright, and he decided to back off. The decision was made. He'd said enough. Any more and he might say too much. 'Okay,' he said. 'Okay. It's all you. You're smart enough to know what you want, but I'm your father and I'll have some opinions about your next big decision, and the next. That's what I'm here for. If you screw up again, I'll damned sure let you know it.'

'I'm not screwing up, Dad.'

'I will not bicker.'

'Can we go to dinner? I'm starving.'

'I need a drink.'

They rode together to Victor's Italian Restaurant, John's Friday night ritual for as long as Kyle could remember. John had his usual end-of-the-week martini. Kyle had his standard drink – club soda with a twist of lime. They ordered pasta with meatballs, and after the second martini John began to mellow. Having his son at the largest and most prestigious law firm in the country did have a nice ring to it.

But he was still puzzled by the abrupt change in plans.

If you only knew, Kyle kept saying to himself. And he ached because he couldn't tell his father the truth.

Chapter 9

Kyle was relieved when his mother did not answer the phone. He waited until almost eleven on Saturday morning before calling. He left a pleasant little message about popping in for a quick hello as he was passing through York for some vague reason. She was either asleep or medicated, or if it was a good day, she was in her studio thoroughly absorbed in creating some of the most dreadful art never seen in a gallery or an exhibition. Visits with his mother were painful. She rarely left her loft, for any reason, so the suggestion that they meet for coffee or lunch was always dismissed. If the meds were in sync, she talked incessantly while forcing Kyle to admire her latest masterpieces. If the meds were out of order, she would lie on the sofa with her eyes closed, unbathed, unkempt, often inconsolable in her gloom and misery. She seldom asked about his life – college, law school, girlfriends, plans for the future. She was much too absorbed in her own sad little world. Kyle's twin sisters stayed far away from York.

He left the message on her recorder as he was hustling out of town and hoped she didn't return the call anytime soon. She did not; in fact, the call was never returned, which was not unusual. Four hours later he was in Pittsburgh. Joey Bernardo had tickets for the Penguins–Senators hockey game Saturday night. Three tickets, not two.

They met at Boomerang's, a favorite watering hole from their college days. After Kyle quit drinking (Joey did not), he avoided most bars. Driving to Pittsburgh, he had hoped for some quiet time with his old roommate, but it wasn't to be.

The third ticket was for Blair, Joey's soon-to-be-announced fiancée. By the time the three of them settled into a tight booth and ordered drinks, Joey was gushing with the news that they had just become engaged and were looking at wedding dates. Both were glowing with love and romance and seemed oblivious to everything else. They held hands, sat close, even giggled at each other, and after five minutes Kyle felt uncomfortable. What had happened to his friend? Where was the old Joey – the tough kid from South Pittsburgh, son of a fire captain, accomplished boxer, all-conference high school fullback, tremendous appetite for girls, a cynical, smart-ass wisecracker who believed women were disposable, the guy who'd vowed he wouldn't marry until he was at least forty?

Blair had turned him to mush. Kyle was astonished at the transformation.

They eventually tired of their wedding plans and potential honeymoon destinations, and the talk turned to careers. Blair, a chatterbox who began every sentence with either 'I' or 'me' or 'my,' worked for an advertising agency and spent far too much time detailing some of their latest marketing maneuvers. Joey hung on every word while Kyle began glancing at the clock behind them, high above a row of windows. As she prattled on, Kyle worked hard at maintaining enough eye contact to feign interest, but his mind drifted to the video.

'Is she awake?' Joey asks as Baxter has sex with a dangerously intoxicated Elaine Keenan.

'Blair travels to Montreal quite often,' Joey said, then Blair ricocheted onto the subject of Montreal and its beauty. She was learning French!

Is she awake? Joey, sitting there with his hand under the table no doubt rubbing some flesh, had no earthly idea that such a video existed. When was the last time Joey even thought about the incident? Ever? Had he forgotten it completely? And what good would it do for Kyle to bring it up now?

After the Pittsburgh police quietly closed the file on Elaine and her rape, the brothers of Beta buried it, too. During his last two years of college, Kyle could not remember a single instance when the episode was discussed. Elaine disappeared and was quickly forgotten.

If Bennie Wright and his operatives had been snooping around Duquesne and Pittsburgh in recent weeks, Kyle wanted to know about it. Perhaps Joey might have seen or heard something. Perhaps not. Joey wasn't noticing much these days except for Blair.

'Have you talked to Baxter?' Joey asked when Blair finally stopped for air.

'Not in a month or so.'

Joey was grinning as if a joke was on the way. 'He finally got in a movie, you know.'

'No kidding. He didn't tell me.'

Blair giggled like a first grader because she undoubtedly knew the rest of the story.

'That's because he doesn't want you to know,' Joey went on.

'Must be a great movie.'

'Yep, he got drunk one night – and by the way, the drinking is now in no-man's-land – so he called and told me he'd made his debut. It was a cheap cable flick about a young girl who finds a human leg washed up on a beach, and for the rest of the movie she has nightmares about being chased by a one-legged killer.'

'Where does the great Baxter Tate fit in?'

'Well, you have to watch real close or you'll miss him. There's a scene on a boat where the cops are gazing at the ocean, presumably looking for the rest of the body, though this is never clear. The movie has a lot of uncertainties. One of the deputies walks over to the sheriff and says, "Sir, we're low on fuel." That's our movie star.'

'Baxter is a deputy?'

'And a bad one. He has only that one line and delivers it like a frightened sophomore in the school play.'

'Was he sober?'

'Who knows, but I would say yes. If he'd been drunk, as usual, he would've nailed the line.'

'I can't wait to see it.'

'Don't, and don't tell him I mentioned it. He called the next morning, begging me not to watch it and threatening me if I told anyone. He's a mess.'

And that reminded Blair of one of her friends who knew someone 'out there' who landed a role in a new sitcom, and away she went. Kyle smiled and nodded as his brain switched compartments. Of the three roommates, Joey was the only one who could possibly help, if indeed help was possible. Baxter Tate was in dire need of intensive rehab. Alan Strock was thoroughly consumed with medical school at Ohio State and, of the four, was clearly the least likely to get involved.

For Joey, the stakes were high. He was on the tape, wondering aloud if Elaine was awake and conscious while Baxter did the deed, then Joey himself took a turn. He was currently handling accounts at a regional brokerage firm in Pittsburgh and had two promotions under his belt. He was goofy in love with Air Blair here, and any hint of an old rape charge would upset their perfect lives.

On the one hand, Kyle felt as though he was taking the fall for Joey. He hadn't touched Elaine that night, yet it was his life and career now getting hijacked by Bennie Wright and his dirty little video. Shouldn't Joey at least know about it?

And on the other hand, Kyle couldn't convince himself that he should drop the bomb on Joey at this point. If he, Kyle, took the Scully & Pershing job and met the demands of Bennie Wright, and didn't get caught, there was a decent chance the video would eventually be forgotten.

Hours later, during a break in the game, with Blair off in the ladies' room, Kyle suggested they meet Sunday for breakfast. He needed to leave town early, he said, and might it be possible to get together without Blair for an hour or so? Let her sleep in, maybe?

They met for bagels at a shop owned by a chain, a place that had not existed when Kyle was at Duquesne. Blair was still asleep somewhere, and Joey admitted to needing a break. 'Sweet girl,' Kyle said more than once, and each time felt guilty for lying. He could not imagine a life with such a windbag. She had great legs, though, the type Joey had always coveted.

They talked about New York for a long time – life in a big firm, the grind of the city, the sports teams, other friends who were there, and so on.

Kyle eventually brought the conversation around to the old Beta gang, and they played catch-up for a while. They laughed at pranks and hazing and parties and stupid stunts pulled by themselves and others. They were twenty-five now, far removed from the craziness of their early college days, and the nostalgia was fun for a few minutes. Several times, the 'Elaine thing' was at the surface, waiting for a comment or a question, but Joey did not mention it. It was forgotten.

When they said goodbye, Kyle was convinced Joey had buried the episode forever, and, more important, no one had brought it to his attention recently.

He drove north to Interstate 80, then headed east. New York was not far away, neither in time nor in distance. A few more weeks in the cozy world of academia, then two months prepping for the bar exam, and in early September he would report for duty at the largest law firm in the world. There would be a hundred associates in his class, all bright kids from the finest schools, all polished and decked out in their newest clothes, all anxious to jump-start their brilliant legal careers.

Kyle felt lonelier each day.

But he wasn't exactly isolated, not even close. His movements to, in, and around York and Pittsburgh were closely monitored by Bennie Wright and his gang. A small magnetic transmitter, the size of a man's wallet, was tucked away under some mud and dirt in the rear bumper of Kyle's red Cherokee. It was hot-wired from the left taillight and emitted a constant GPS signal that kept track of the vehicle anywhere it went. From his office in lower Manhattan, Bennie knew precisely where the Jeep was located. He was not surprised by Kyle's visit home, but the trip to see Joey Bernardo was far more interesting.

Bennie had no shortage of gadgets – some high-tech, some low-tech, and all very effective because he tracked simple civilians and not real spies. Corporate espionage was far easier than that of the military or national security variety.

Kyle's cell phone had long since been compromised, and they listened to every conversation. The kid had yet to mention his predicament to anyone on the phone. They were also listening to Olivia's chatter, as well as that of Mitch, his roommate. So far, nothing.

They were reading Kyle's e-mails. He averaged twenty-seven a day, and almost all were law school related.

Other efforts to listen were far more difficult. An agent had eaten at Victor's in York, at a table twenty feet from Kyle and his father, but heard almost nothing. Another had managed to land a seat two rows away at the Penguins game, but it was a wasted effort. At Boomerang's, though, one of Bennie's stars, a twenty-six-year-old blonde in tight jeans, managed to secure the booth next to Kyle, Joey, and Blair. She sipped one beer for two hours, read a paperback, and reported that the girl talked nonstop, and about nothing.

Bennie was generally pleased with the progress. Kyle had abruptly declined the legal services job in Virginia. He had hustled over to New York and cleared things with Scully & Pershing. He was seeing less of Olivia, and it was obvious, at least to Bennie, that the relationship was going nowhere.

But the sudden trip to Pittsburgh was bothersome. Had he planned to confide in Joey? Had he in fact done so? Was Alan Strock next? Would Kyle attempt to contact him and/or Baxter Tate?

Bennie was listening in all the right places, and waiting. He had leased two thousand square feet of office space in a building across Broad Street and two blocks down from Scully & Pershing. The tenant's name was Fancher Group, a financial services start-up domiciled in Bermuda. Its registered agent in New York was Aaron Kurtz, also known as Bennie Wright, also known as a dozen other men, with perfect identification to prove any alias he chose. From his new perch, Bennie could glance out his window and gaze down Broad Street, and in a few short months he'd be able to actually see their boy Kyle enter and leave his place of employment.

Chapter 10

The lawsuit was filed in federal court in the Southern District of New York, Manhattan Division, at ten minutes before five on a Friday afternoon, a time chosen so that the filing would attract as little attention as possible from the press. A 'late Friday dump.' The lawyer who signed it was a noted litigator named Wilson Rush, a senior partner with Scully & Pershing, and throughout the day he had telephoned the clerk to make sure it would be properly received and docketed before the court closed for the week. Like all cases, it was filed electronically. No one from the firm was required to walk into the Daniel Patrick Moynihan U.S. Courthouse on Pearl Street and hand over a thick pile of papers to commence the action. Of the forty or so civil lawsuits filed that day in the Southern District, it was by far the most serious, most complex, and most anticipated. The parties involved had been feuding for years, and while much of their bickering had been well reported, most of the issues were too sensitive to bare in public. The Pentagon, many senior members of Congress, and even the White House had worked diligently to prevent litigation, but all efforts had failed. The next battle in the war had begun, and no one expected a quick resolution. The parties and their lawyers would fight with bare knuckles for years as the dispute crept its way through the federal judiciary and eventually landed at the Supreme Court for a final ruling.

The clerk, upon receiving the complaint, quickly rerouted it to a secure bin to prevent its contents from being exposed. This procedure was extremely rare and had been ordered by the chief district judge. A bare-bones summary of the lawsuit was ready and available to the press. It had been prepared under the direction of Mr. Rush, and it, too, had been approved by the judge.

The plaintiff was Trylon Aeronautics, a well-known defense contractor based in New York, a privately held company that had been designing and building military aircraft for four decades. The defendant was Bartin Dynamics, a publicly held defense contractor based in Bethesda, Maryland. Bartin averaged about $15 billion a year in government contracts, a sum that represented 95 percent of its annual revenue. Bartin used different lawyers for its different needs, but for the biggest fights it was protected by the Wall Street firm of Agee, Poe & Epps.

Scully & Pershing currently had twenty-one hundred lawyers and claimed to be the largest firm in the world. Agee, Poe & Epps had two hundred fewer lawyers but boasted of more offices around the world; thus, it claimed to be the largest. Each firm spent far too much time jockeying with the other and boasting of its size, power, prestige, billings, partner profiles, and anything else that might jack up its rankings.

The core of the dispute was the latest Pentagon boondoggle to build the B-10 HyperSonic Bomber, a space-age aircraft that had been dreamed about for decades and was now closer to becoming a reality. Five years earlier, the Air Force had launched a contest among its top contractors to design the B-10, a sleek bomber that would replace the aging fleet of B-52s and B-22s and serve the military through the year 2060. Lockheed, the largest defense contractor, was the expected front-runner in the competition, but it was quickly outpaced by a joint venture put together by Trylon and Bartin. A consortium of foreign companies – British, French, and Israeli – had smaller roles in the joint venture.

The prize was enormous. The Air Force would pay the winner $10 billion up front to develop the advanced technologies and build a prototype, and then contract for the procurement of 250 to 450 B-10s over the next thirty years. At an estimated $800 billion, the contract would be the richest in the Pentagon's history.

The anticipated cost overruns were beyond calculation.

The Trylon-Bartin design was astounding. Their B-10 could take off from a base in the United States with a payload the same size as a B-52, fly at seventy-six hundred miles per hour, or Mach 10, and deliver its payload on the other side of the world in an hour, at a speed and from an altitude that would defy all current and foreseen defensive measures. After delivery of whatever it happened to be hauling, the B-10 could return to its home base without refueling either in flight or on the ground. The aircraft would literally skip along the edge of the atmosphere. After ascending to an altitude of 130,000 feet, just outside the stratosphere, the B-10 would turn off its engines and float back to the surface of the atmosphere. Once there, its air-breathing engines would kick on and lift the plane back to 130,000 feet. This procedure, a skipping motion much like that of a flat rock bouncing across still water, would be repeated until the aircraft arrived at its target. A bombing run that originated in Arizona and ended in Asia would require about thirty skips with the B-10 popping through the atmosphere once every ninety seconds. Because the engines would be used intermittently, significantly smaller amounts of fuel would be required. And, by leaving the atmosphere and venturing into cold space, the heat buildup would be dissipated.

After three years of intense and often frantic research and design, the Air Force announced that it had selected the Trylon-Bartin design. This was done with as little fanfare as possible since the dollar amounts were staggering, the country was fighting two wars, and the Pentagon decided it would not be wise to broadcast such an ambitious procurement plan. The Air Force tried its best to downplay the B-10 program, but it was a waste of time. As soon as the winner was announced, fighting erupted on all fronts.

Lockheed roared back with its senators and lobbyists and lawyers. Trylon and Bartin, historically fierce competitors, began sniping almost immediately. The prospect of that much money splintered any notion of cooperation. Each corralled its politicians and lobbyists and joined the fight for a bigger piece of the pork. The British, French, and Israelis eased to the sidelines but certainly did not go away.

Both Trylon and Bartin claimed ownership of the design and the technologies. Efforts to mediate succeeded, then failed. Lockheed loomed in the background, waiting. The Pentagon threatened to yank the contract and have another contest. Congressmen held hearings. Governors wanted jobs and economic development. Journalists wrote long pieces in magazines. Waste and watchdog groups railed against the B-10 as if it were a shuttle to Mars.

And the lawyers quietly prepared for litigation.

★

Two hours after the lawsuit was filed, Kyle saw it posted on the federal court's Web site. He was at his desk in his office at the *Yale Law Journal*, editing a lengthy article on his computer. For three weeks now he had been checking the filings in all the federal courts in New York, as well as the state courts. During their first wretched session, Bennie had mentioned the upcoming filing of a massive lawsuit in New York, the one that Kyle was now expected to infiltrate. In meetings since then, Kyle had repeatedly prodded Bennie for information about the lawsuit, but each inquiry had been met with a dismissive 'We'll talk about it later.'

Oddly, the online posting of the lawsuit revealed nothing but its title and the name, address, law firm, and bar certification number of Wilson Rush. The word 'SECURE' was inserted after the title, and Kyle was unable to access the contents of the complaint. In the Southern District of New York, no other case filed in the past three weeks had been locked away in such a manner.

Red flags began to wave.

He searched Agee, Poe & Epps and studied their exhaustive list of corporate clients. The firm had represented Bartin Dynamics since the 1980s.

Kyle forgot about the law journal work piled on his desk and around his chair, and lost himself on the Internet. A search of Trylon soon revealed its B-10 HyperSonic Bomber project and all the problems it had caused, and, evidently, was still creating.

Kyle closed the door of his small office and checked the printer for paper. It was almost eight on Friday night, and though the law journal types were known for their odd hours, the crew had cleared out for spring break. He printed all available corporate info on Trylon and Bartin, then added more paper. There were several dozen newspaper and magazine articles on the B-10 fiasco. He printed them all and began reading the most serious ones.

He found a hundred defense and military Web sites, and on one for futuristic warfare there were pages of background on the B-10. He checked prior court filings to see how often Scully & Pershing had sued on behalf of or defended Trylon, and did the same for Agee, Poe & Epps and Bartin. On into the night he dug and dug, and the thicker his file became, the worse he felt.

There was a chance he was chasing the wrong lawsuit. He couldn't know for sure until Bennie confirmed it. But there was little doubt. The timing was on schedule. The law firms were in place. Billions were at stake, just as Bennie had said. Two corporations that were old competitors. Two law firms that hated each other.

Military secrets. Stolen technology. Corporate espionage. Foreign intelligence. Threats of litigation and even criminal prosecution. It was one monumental, sordid mess, and now he, Kyle

McAvoy, was expected to insert himself into the fray.

In recent weeks, he had often speculated about what type of case was worth the high cost of such elaborate espionage. Two corporate rivals fighting over a pot of gold could describe any number of disputes. Perhaps it was an anti-trust case, or a patent dispute, or a couple of drug companies brawling over the latest obesity pill. The worst-case scenario was the one he had just been handed – a gold-plated Pentagon procurement program complete with secret technologies, warring politicians, ruthless executives, and so on. The list was long and disheartening.

Why couldn't he just go back to York and practice law with his father?

At 1:00 a.m., he stuffed his notebooks into his backpack and for a few seconds went through the fruitless ritual of straightening his desk. He looked around, turned off the light, locked his door, and again realized that any decent operative could intrude whenever he wanted. He felt certain Bennie and his thugs had been there, probably with bugs and wires and mikes and other crap that Kyle tried not to think about.

And he was sure they were watching. In spite of his demands that Bennie leave him alone, Kyle knew they were following him. He'd seen them several times. They were good, but they had made a few mistakes. The challenge, he told himself repeatedly, was to act as though he had no clue that they were watching. Just play the role of a naive, unconcerned college kid hauling a backpack around campus and looking at girls. He never changed his routines, or his routes, or parking lots. Same spot for lunch almost every day. Same coffee shop where he met Olivia occasionally after class. He was either at the law school or at his apartment, with few diversions along the way. And because his habits remained the same, so did those of his shadows. They became lazy because he was such an easy target. Kyle, the innocent, lulled them to sleep, and when they nodded off, he caught them. One face he'd seen three times already, a young ruddy face with different eyeglasses and a mustache that came and went.

At a used bookstore near the campus, Kyle began buying old paperback spy novels for a dollar each. He bought them one at a time, kept the current one in his backpack, and when he finished, he tossed it in the wastebasket at the law school and bought another.

He assumed that none of his communications were confidential. His cell phone and laptop were compromised, he was certain. He increased, slightly, his e-mails to Joey Bernardo, Alan Strock, and Baxter Tate, but all messages were quick howdies with almost no substance. He did the same for other Beta brothers, all under the guise of encouraging his buddies to do a better job of keeping in touch. He called each of them once a week and talked sports and school and careers.

If Bennie was in fact listening, he heard not one word to indicate Kyle was even remotely suspicious.

Kyle convinced himself that to survive the next seven years, he must learn to think and act like his adversaries. There was a way out. Somewhere.

Bennie was back in town. They met for a sandwich on Saturday at a pita place north of town, away from campus. He had promised to drop in every other week or so throughout the spring, until Kyle graduated in May. Kyle had asked why this was necessary. Bennie had offered some meaningless blather about maintaining contact.

In each of their subsequent meetings, Bennie's personality had softened slightly. He would always be the no-nonsense hard-ass handler with a mission, but he was acting as though he wanted their time together to be somewhat pleasant. After all, they would spend hours together, he said, and this always evoked a frown from Kyle, who wanted no part of any pleasant chitchat.

'Any plans for spring break?' Bennie asked as they unwrapped their sandwiches.

'Work,' Kyle said. The break had started the day before, and half of Yale was now somewhere in southern Florida.

'Come on. Your last spring break and you're not headed for the beach?'

'Nope. I'll be in New York next week looking for an apartment.'

Bennie looked surprised and said, 'We can help.'

'We've had this conversation, Bennie. I don't need your help.'

Both took enormous bites and chewed in silence. Finally, Kyle asked, 'Any news on the lawsuit?'

A quick dismissive nod. Nothing.

'Has it been filed yet?' Kyle asked. 'Why can't you tell me about it?'

Bennie cleared his throat and sipped his water. 'Next week. Let's meet next week when you're in New York, and I'll walk you through the lawsuit.'

'Can't wait.'

Another hefty bite and they chewed for a while.

'When do you take the bar exam?' Bennie asked.

'July.'

'Where?'

'New York. Somewhere in Manhattan. It's not something I'm looking forward to.'

'You'll do fine. When do you get the results?'

Bennie knew the dates and places the exam was given in New York. He knew when the results were posted online. He knew what happened to young associates if they flunked the bar. He knew everything.

'Early November. Did you go to law school?'

A smile, almost a chuckle. 'Oh, no. I've always tried to avoid lawyers. Sometimes, though, well, that's what the job requires.'

Kyle listened carefully for the accent. It tended to come and go. He thought of the Israelis and their talent for languages, especially among the Mossad and the military.

Not for the first time, he wondered whom he would be spying for and against.

They met five days later at the Ritz-Carlton in lower Manhattan. Kyle asked Bennie if he had an office in the city, or whether he did all of his work in hotel suites. There was no response. Before the meeting, Kyle had looked at four apartments, all in SoHo and Tribeca. The cheapest was $4,200 a month for an eight-hundred-square-foot walk-up, and the most expensive was $6,500 a month for a thousand square feet in a renovated warehouse. Whatever the rent, Kyle would be handling it himself because he did not want a roommate. His life would be complicated enough without the strains of living with someone else. And besides, Bennie did not like the idea of a roommate.

Bennie and company had followed Kyle and the broker around lower Manhattan and knew precisely where the apartments were located. By the time Kyle arrived at the hotel, operatives were calling the same realtor, inquiring about the apartments, and making plans to visit them. Kyle would indeed live where he chose, but the place would be infested by the time he moved in.

Bennie had some thick files on the small table in the suite. 'The lawsuit was filed last Friday,' he began, 'in federal court here in Manhattan. The plaintiff is a company called Trylon Aeronautics. The defendant is a company called Bartin Dynamics.'

Kyle absorbed this with no expression. His file on the case and the litigants now comprised three four-inch spiral notebooks, over two thousand pages, and was growing by the day. He was sure he didn't know as much as his pal Bennie here, but he already knew a hell of a lot.

And Bennie knew he knew. From his comfortable office on Broad Street, Bennie and his tech guys kept close tabs on Kyle's laptop and his desk computer in his office at the law journal. They monitored nonstop, and when Kyle opened his laptop in his apartment to send a note to a professor, Bennie knew it. When he was working and editing a case note, Bennie knew it. And when he was monitoring the court filings in New York and digging through the dirt on Trylon and Bartin, Bennie knew it.

Sit there and play dumb, son. I'll play along, too. You're smart as hell, but you're too stupid to realize you're in way over your head.

Chapter 11

As springtime reluctantly arrived in New England, the campus came to life and shook off the lingering chill and gloom of winter. Plants bloomed, the grass showed some color, and as the days grew longer, the students found more reasons to stay outside. Frisbees flew by the hundreds. Long lunches and even picnics materialized when the sun was out. Professors became lazier; classes grew shorter.

For his last semester on campus, Kyle chose to ignore the festivities. He kept himself in his office, working feverishly to finish the details for the June edition of the *Yale Law Journal*. It would be his last and he wanted it to be his best. Work provided the perfect excuse to ignore virtually everyone else. Olivia finally got fed up, and they parted amicably. His friends, all of them third-year students and about to graduate, fell into two groups. The first concentrated on drinking and partying and trying to savor every last moment of life on campus before being evicted and sent into the real world. The second group was already thinking about their careers, studying for the bar exam, and looking for apartments in large cities. Kyle found it easy to avoid both.

On May 1, he sent a letter to Joey Bernardo that read:

> Dear Joey: I graduate from law school on May 25. Any chance you could be here? Alan can't do it and I'm afraid to ask Baxter. It would be great fun to hang out for a couple of days. No girlfriend, please. Correspond by regular mail at this address. No e-mails, no phones. I'll explain later.
>
> Best, Kyle

The letter was handwritten and mailed from the law journal office. A week later, the reply arrived:

> Hey, Kyle: What's with the snail mail? Your handwriting really sucks. But it's probably better than mine. I'll be there for graduation, should be fun. What the hell is so secretive that we can't talk on the phone or use e-mail? Are you cracking up? Baxter is. He's gone. He'll be dead in a year if we don't do something. Oh, well, my hand is aching and I feel like such an old fart

writing with ink. Can't wait to get your next sweet little note.

Love, Joey

Kyle's reply was longer and filled with details. Joey's response was just as sarcastic and filled with even more questions. Kyle threw it away as soon as he read it. They swapped letters once more, and the weekend was planned.

Patty McAvoy could not be coaxed from her loft for her son's graduation, not that any real effort was made. Indeed, both John McAvoy and Kyle were pleased with her decision to stay at home, because her presence at Yale would complicate things. She had skipped the diploma service at Duquesne three years earlier just as she had skipped the commencements for both of her daughters. In short, Patty didn't do graduations, regardless of how important they might be. She had managed to attend both daughters' weddings, but had been unable to take part in the planning of either. John simply wrote the checks, and somehow the family survived both ordeals.

Joey Bernardo arrived in New Haven Saturday afternoon, the day before the law school's ceremonies, and, as directed by the written word carried by the U.S. Postal Service, he proceeded to a dark and cavernous pizza parlor called Santo's, a mile from campus. At precisely 3:00 p.m. on Saturday, May 24, he slid into a booth in the far-right corner of Santo's, and began to wait. He was amused and quite curious, and he was still wondering if his friend was losing his mind. One minute later, Kyle appeared from the back and sat across from him. They shook hands, then Kyle glanced at the front door, far away and to the right. The restaurant was almost empty, and Bruce Springsteen was rocking through the sound system.

'Start talking,' Joey said, now only slightly amused.

'I'm being followed.'

'You're cracking up. The pressure is getting to you.'

'Shut up and listen.'

A teenage waitress paused at the table just long enough to see if they wanted anything. Both asked for diet colas, and Kyle ordered a large pepperoni pizza.

'Wasn't really that hungry,' Joey said when she was gone.

'We're in a pizza place, and so we need to order a pizza. Otherwise, we'll look suspicious. In a few minutes, a thug wearing faded jeans, a dark green rugby shirt, and a khaki golf cap will walk through the door, completely ignore us, and probably go to the bar. He'll hang around for less than ten minutes, then he'll leave. Though he'll never look at us, he'll see everything. When you leave, either he or one of his teammates will follow you and check your license plates, and within minutes they'll know that I had a semisecret meeting with my old pal Joey Bernardo.'

'These guys are friends of yours?'

'No. They are professional operatives, but because I'm just me and not some highly trained thug myself, they're assuming that I have no clue that they're following me.'

'Great. That clears things up. Why, old buddy, are they following you?'

'It's a very long story.'

'You're not drinking again, are you? Not back on the smack?'

'I never did smack and you know it. No, I'm not drinking and I'm not losing my marbles. I'm dead serious and I need your help.'

'You need a shrink, Kyle. You're spooky, man. There's a glow in your eyes.'

The door opened and the thug walked in. He was dressed precisely as Kyle had said, but with the addition of a pair of round tortoise-shell eyeglasses. 'Don't stare,' Kyle whispered as Joey's jaw dropped. The diet colas arrived, and they took a drink.

The thug went to the bar, ordered a draft beer, and from his stool could see their table in the long mirrors behind the racks of booze, but he could not possibly hear what they were saying.

'He just put on the eyeglasses,' Kyle said with a large smile as if they were telling jokes. 'Sunglasses would be too conspicuous in here. He added the big round ones so he can look around and not get caught. Please smile. Please laugh. We're just two old chums reminiscing here. Nothing serious.'

Joey was flabbergasted and could manage neither a smile nor a laugh. So Kyle erupted in a loud cackle, then pulled off a slice of thin pizza as soon as it arrived. He was animated and smiling, and with his mouth full he said, 'Eat, Joey, and smile and please utter a few words.'

'What have you done? Is that guy a cop or something?'

'Or something. I've done nothing wrong, but it's still a complicated story. You're involved in it. Let's talk about the Pirates.'

'The Pirates are in last place, and they'll be in last place come September. Pick another subject, or another team.' Joey finally took a slice and bit off half of it. 'I need a beer. I can't eat pizza without a beer.'

Kyle flagged down the lazy little waitress and ordered one beer.

There was a large screen in one corner. ESPN was running baseball highlights. For a few minutes, they ate pizza and watched the footage. The guy in the rugby shirt was working on a twelve-ounce draft, and after about ten minutes it was gone. He paid in cash and left. When the door closed behind him, Joey said, 'What the hell is going on?'

'That's a conversation the two of us must have, but not here. It'll take an hour or two, and then the first conversation will lead to another and another. If we do it here this weekend, we'll get caught. The bad guys are watching, and if they see us engaged in serious talk, they'll know. It's important for us to finish the pizza, walk out the front door, and not be seen together alone, until you leave town tomorrow.'

'Thanks for inviting me up.'

'I didn't invite you for the graduation, Joey. Sorry about that. The reason you're here is to give you this.' Kyle slid across a folded sheet of paper. 'Put it in your pocket, and quick.'

Joey grabbed it, glanced around as if assassins were moving in, and shoved it in a jeans pocket. 'What is it, Kyle?'

'Trust me, Joey, please. I'm in trouble and I need help. There's no one else but you.'

'And I'm involved, too?'

'Maybe. Let's finish the pizza and get out of here. Here's the plan. The Fourth of July is just around the corner. You come up with this wonderful idea for a rafting trip down the New River in West Virginia, three days on the river, two nights camping out. Me and you and some of the old gang from Duquesne. A boys' weekend while we can still do it. The list there has ten names and e-mails, stuff you already have. It also has the name of an outfitter in Beckley, West Virginia. I've done all the homework.'

Joey nodded as if nothing made sense.

Kyle pressed on. 'The purpose of the trip is to shake the surveillance. Once we're on the river and in the mountains, there's no way they can follow me. We can talk and talk and not have to worry about being watched.'

'This is crazy. You're crazy.'

'Shut up, Joey. I'm not crazy. I'm dead serious. They watch me around the clock. They listen to my phone calls, and they've bugged my laptop.'

'And they're not cops?'

'No, they're much scarier than cops. If we spend too much time together now, they'll become suspicious, and your life will get complicated. Eat some pizza.'

'I'm not hungry.'

There was a long gap in the conversation. Kyle kept eating. Joey kept watching the ESPN highlights. Springsteen kept singing.

After a few minutes, Kyle said, 'Look, we need to go. I have a lot to tell you, but I can't do it now. If you'll plan the rafting trip, we can have some fun and I'll give you the full story.'

'You ever been rafting?'

'Sure. You?'

'No. I don't like the water.'

'They provide life jackets. Come on, Joey, have some fun. A year from now you'll be married and your life will be over.'

'Thanks, pal.'

'It's just a boys' trip down the river, a bunch of old friends from college. Shoot the e-mails and put it all together. Whatta you say?'

'Sure, Kyle. Whatever.'

'But when you e-mail me, use the diversion.'

'The diversion?'

'Yes, it's written down. In your e-mails to me we're headed for the Potomac River in western Maryland. We can't give these thugs too much notice.'

'What are they gonna do, follow us down the river in a speedboat?'

'No. It's just a precaution. I don't want them anywhere around me.'

'This is real strange, Kyle.'

'It gets stranger.'

Joey suddenly slid the pizza aside and leaned forward on his elbows. He glared at Kyle and said, 'I'll do it, but you gotta give me a clue.'

'Elaine's back, with her rape scenario.'

Just as quickly as he had leaned forward, Joey shrunk back to his side of the booth and limply recoiled. Elaine who? He'd forgotten her last name, if in fact he'd ever known it. That was five, maybe six years ago, and the cops had not only closed the file but slammed the damned thing shut. And why? Because nothing happened. There was no rape. Intercourse maybe, but with that girl everything was consensual. He had a December wedding planned with the woman of his dreams, and nothing, absolutely nothing could screw it up. He had a career, a future, a good name. How could this nightmare be alive?

With so much to say, he managed to say nothing. He stared at Kyle, who couldn't help but feel sorry for him.

Is she awake? Joey asks.

No response from Baxter Tate. No response from the girl.

'This is something we can deal with, Joey. It's frightening, but we can handle it. We need to talk, for hours, but not here, not now. Let's get away.'

'Sure. Whatever you say.'

That night, Kyle met his father for dinner at a Greek place called the Athenian. They were joined by Joey Bernardo, who'd had a few drinks in preparation for the evening and was so mellow he was quite dull. Or maybe he was just stunned or scared or something else, but he was certainly preoccupied. John McAvoy downed two martinis before he touched a menu and was soon telling war stories about old trials and old cases. Joey matched him martini for martini, and the gin thickened his tongue but did not lighten his mood.

Kyle had invited him because he did not want his father to launch into a last-ditch effort to persuade him to resist the evils of corporate law and do something productive with his life. But after the second martini, and with Joey barely coherent, John McAvoy made such an effort. Kyle chose not to argue. He ate garlic crackers and hummus and listened. Red wine arrived, and his father told another story about representing some poor soul with a good case but no money, and of course he won, as is true with the vast majority of lawyers' tales. John McAvoy was the hero of all of his stories. The poor were saved. The weak were protected.

Kyle almost missed his mother.

Late that night, long after dinner, Kyle walked the Yale campus for the last time as a student. He was stunned at the speed at which the last three years had gone by, yet he was also tired of law school. He was tired of lectures and classrooms and exams and the meager existence on a student's budget. At twenty-five, he was now a fully grown man, nicely educated and all in one piece with no bad habits, no permanent damage.

At this point, the future should hold great promise and excitement.

Instead, he felt nothing but fear and apprehension. Seven years of school, great success as a student, and it was all coming down to this – the miserable life of an unwilling spy.

Chapter 12

Of the two apartments Kyle was considering, Bennie preferred the one in the old meatpacking district, near the Gansevoort Hotel, in a building that was 120 years old and had been built for the sole purpose of slaughtering hogs and cows. But the carnage was now history, and the developer had done a splendid job of gutting the place and renovating it into a collection of boutiques on the first floor, hip offices on the second, and modern apartments from there upward. Bennie cared nothing about being hip or modern, and could not have cared less about the location. What impressed him was the fact that the apartment directly above 5D was also available as a sublet. Bennie grabbed it, 6D, at $5,200 a month for six months, then he waited for Kyle to lease 5D.

Kyle, though, was leaning toward a second-story walk-up on Beekman Street, near City Hall and the Brooklyn Bridge. It was smaller and cheaper at $3,800, still an obscene amount for the square footage. In New Haven, Kyle had been splitting $1,000 a month for a dump, but one that was three times as large as anything he'd seen in Manhattan.

Scully & Pershing had paid him a signing bonus of $25,000, and he was thinking of using it to secure a nice apartment early in the summer when more were available. He would lock himself away in his new digs, study nonstop for six weeks, and take the New York bar exam in late July.

When it became obvious to Bennie that Kyle was ready to lease the Beekman apartment, he arranged for one of his operatives to suddenly appear, badger the real estate agent, and offer more money. It worked, and Kyle was headed for the meatpacking district. When he verbally agreed to take 5D, for $5,100 a month for a year, beginning on June 15, Bennie dispatched a team of technicians to 'decorate' the place two weeks before Kyle was scheduled to move in. Listening devices were planted in the walls of every room. The telephone and Internet lines were tapped and wired to receivers in computers located directly above in 6D. Four hidden cameras were installed – one each in the den, the kitchen, and the two bedrooms. Each could be withdrawn immediately in the event Kyle or someone else started poking around. They, too, were connected to computers in 6D, so Bennie and his boys could watch Kyle do everything except shower, shave, brush his teeth, and use the toilet. Some things should be kept private.

On June 2, Kyle loaded everything he owned into his Jeep Cherokee and left Yale and New Haven. For a few miles, he went through the usual nostalgia of saying goodbye to his student days, but by the time he passed through Bridgeport, he was thinking about the bar exam and what was waiting beyond it. He drove to Manhattan where he planned to spend a few days with friends, then move into his apartment on the fifteenth. He had yet to sign a lease, and the real estate agent was becoming irritated. He was ignoring her phone calls.

As scheduled, on June 3 he took a cab to the Peninsula hotel in midtown and found Bennie Wright in a tenth-floor suite. His handler was dressed in customary drab attire – dark suit, white shirt, boring tie, black shoes – but on June 3 he had an additional article or two. His suit coat was off, and Bennie had strapped around his shirt a shiny black leather holster with a nine-millimeter Beretta snug just below his left armpit. A quick move with the right hand, and the pistol was in play. Kyle ran through all the sarcastic remarks he might make in the presence of such weaponry, but decided at the last second to simply ignore it. It was obvious that Bennie wanted his Beretta to be noticed, maybe even mentioned.

Just ignore it.

Kyle sat as he always sat with Bennie – right

ankle on his left knee, arms folded across his chest, wearing a look of complete contempt.

'Congratulations on your graduation,' Bennie said, sipping coffee from a paper cup and standing by the window that overlooked Fifth Avenue. 'Did things go well?'

You were there, you asshole. Your boys watched me and Joey eat a pizza. You know what my father had for dinner and how many martinis he knocked back. You saw Joey stagger out of the Greek place drunk as a skunk. When they took my photo in cap and gown, your goons were probably snapping away, too.

'Swell,' Kyle said.

'That's great. Have you found an apartment?'

'I think so.'

'Where?'

'Why do you care? I thought we agreed that you would stay away from me.'

'Just trying to be polite, Kyle, that's all.'

'Why? It really pisses me off when we get together and you start this happy horseshit like we're a couple of old pals. I'm not here because I want to be. I'm not chitchatting with you because I choose to. I'd rather be anywhere else in the world right now. I'm here because you're blackmailing me. I despise you, okay. Don't ever forget that. And stop trying to be polite. It goes against your personality.'

'Oh, I can be a prick.'

'You are a prick!'

Bennie sipped his coffee and kept smiling.

'Well, moving right along. May I ask when you take the bar exam?'

'No, because you know precisely when I take the bar exam. What am I here for, Bennie? What's the purpose of this meeting?'

'Just a friendly hello. Welcome to New York. Congrats on finishing law school. How's the family? That kind of stuff.'

'I'm touched.'

Bennie set down his coffee cup and picked up a thick notebook. He handed it to Kyle. 'These are the latest filings in the Trylon-Bartin lawsuit. Motion to dismiss, supporting affidavits, supporting exhibits, briefs in support of, and briefs in opposition to. Order overruling said motion. Answer filed by the defendant, Bartin, and so on. As you know, the file is sealed, so what you're holding there is unauthorized.'

'How'd you get it?' Kyle asked.

Bennie responded with the same silly smirk he always gave when Kyle asked a question that could not be answered. 'When you're not studying for the bar exam, you can bone up on the lawsuit.'

'A question. It seems to me that it's a long shot for Scully & Pershing to assign me to the litigation section that happens to be handling this case, and it's even more of a stretch to believe they would allow a green associate to get anywhere near it. I'm sure you've thought about this.'

'And the question is . . . ?'

'What happens if I'm nowhere near this case?'

'Your class will have about a hundred rookie associates, same as last year and the year before. Roughly 10 percent will be assigned to litigation. The others will go into everything else – mergers, acquisitions, tax, antitrust, transactions, securities, finance, estates, and all the other wonderful services the firm provides. You'll be the star of the litigation rookies because you're the brightest and you'll work eighteen hours a day, seven days a week, and you'll suck up and kiss ass and backstab and do all the right things it takes to succeed in a big law firm. You'll want to work on this case, you'll demand it, and because it's the biggest lawsuit in the firm, you'll eventually be assigned to it.'

'Sorry I asked.'

'And while you're worming your way onto this case, you'll be providing us with other valuable information.'

'Like what?'

'It's too early to discuss. Right now you need to concentrate on the bar exam.'

'Bless you. I hadn't thought about it.'

They sniped for another ten minutes, then Kyle left in a huff, as usual. From the backseat of a taxi, he called the realtor and said he'd changed his mind about living in the meatpacking district. The realtor was upset but managed to keep her cool. Kyle had signed nothing, and she had no legal ammo to launch. He promised to give her a call in a few days, and they would resume their search, for something smaller and cheaper.

Kyle moved his junk into a spare room in the SoHo apartment of Charles and Charles, two Yale Law grads who'd finished a year earlier and were now working for different mega-firms. They had played lacrosse at Hopkins, and were probably a couple, though they'd kept things quiet, at least at Yale. Kyle had no interest in their relationship. He needed a bed for a while and a place to store his possessions. And he needed to keep Bennie honest, if that was possible. The Charleses offered him their junk room for free, but Kyle insisted on paying $200 a week. The apartment would be a great place to study because the Charleses were seldom there. Both were being thrashed by hundred-hour workweeks.

When it became clear that Bennie's operation had just been stiffed for six months' rent at $5,200 per, for apartment 6D in the slaughterhouse, plus the costly 'decoration' of 5D below it, plus $4,100 a month for a year for the apartment on Beekman, Bennie fumed but did not panic. The wasted money was not a factor. What bothered him was the unpredictability of it. For the past four months, Kyle had done little to surprise them. The surveillance had been effortless. The trip to Pittsburgh in February had been dissected and no longer concerned them. But now Kyle was in the city, where watching him was more challenging. A civilian subject is usually easy because of predictable thoughts and patterns. Why would he try to shake surveillance if he didn't know it was there? But how much did Kyle know or suspect? How predictable was he?

Bennie licked his wounds for an hour, then began planning his next project – research on Charles and Charles and a quick inspection of their apartment.

The second detoxification of Baxter Tate began with a knock on his front door. Then another. He had not answered his cell phone. He had been driven home by a cab at four in the morning from a trendy nightclub in Beverly Hills. The driver helped him into his condo.

After the fourth knock, the door was quietly opened with no effort because Baxter hadn't bothered to lock it. The two men, specialists in retrieving wayward family members with addiction problems, found Baxter on his bed, still dressed in last night's getup – white linen shirt stained with some strain of liquor, black linen Zegna sport coat, bleached designer jeans, Bragano loafers, no socks over his very tanned ankles. He was comatose, breathing heavy but not snoring. Still alive but not for long, not at the rate he was going.

They quickly searched the bedroom and adjoining bathroom for weapons. Both men were armed, but their handguns were hidden under their jackets. Then they radioed to a waiting car, and another man entered the condo. He was

Baxter's uncle, a man named Walter Tate. Uncle Wally, brother to Baxter's father, the only one of five siblings who had accomplished anything in life. The family banking fortune was now three generations old and declining at a steady, but not alarming, rate. The last time Walter had seen his nephew he was in a lawyer's office in Pittsburgh cleaning up after another drunk-driving episode.

Because his four siblings were unable to make even the most basic decisions in life, Walter had long since assumed the role of the family boss. He watched the investments, met with the lawyers, handled the press when necessary, and reluctantly intervened when one of his nieces or nephews flamed out. His own son had been killed hang gliding.

This was his second intervention with Baxter, and it would be the last. The first had been two years earlier, also in L.A., and they had shipped the boy off to a ranch in Montana where he sobered up, rode horses, made new friends, saw the light. Sobriety lasted all of two weeks after he returned to his worthless career in Hollywood. Walter's limit was two rehabs. After that, they could kill themselves for all he cared.

Baxter had been dead to the world for about nine hours when Uncle Wally shook his leg long enough and hard enough to rouse him from his drunkenness. The sight of three strange men standing by his bed startled him. He backed away from them, scrambling to the other end of the bed, then he recognized Uncle Wally. He'd lost some hair, put on a few pounds. How long had it been? The family never got together; in fact, the family strove mightily to avoid one another.

Baxter rubbed his eyes, then his temples. A skull-cracking headache arrived suddenly. He looked at Uncle Wally, then at the two strangers. 'Well, well,' he said. 'How's Aunt Rochelle?'

Rochelle had been the first of Walter's wives, but she was the only one Baxter ever remembered. She had terrified him as a child, and he would always despise her.

'She died last year,' Walter said.

'That's just awful. What brings you to L.A.?' He kicked off his loafers and wrapped his arms around a pillow. It was now obvious where this was going.

'We're taking a trip, Baxter. The four of us. We're gonna check you into another clinic, sober you up, then see if they can put you back together.'

'So this is an intervention?'

'Yes.'

'Groovy. Happens all the time out here. It's a miracle a single movie ever gets made with all the damned intervening that goes on in Hollywood. Everybody's always getting asked to help with an intervention. I mean, look, you're not going to believe this, but two months ago I took part in an intervention. A link, that's what I was called, but I guess you guys know all about that. Can you imagine? I'm sitting in a hotel room with these other links, some I know, some I don't, and poor Jimmy walks in, beer in hand, and gets absolutely ambushed. His brother sits him down, then we go around the room and tell the poor boy what a miserable piece of shit he is. Made him cry, but then they always cry, don't they? I cried, didn't I? Now I remember. You should've heard me lecturing Jimmy about the evils of vodka and cocaine. If he hadn't been crying so hard, he would've come after me. Could I have a glass of water? Who are you?'

'They're with me,' Uncle Wally said.

'I figured.'

One of the specialists handed Baxter a bottle of water. He drained it in one long, noisy slurp with water splashing down his chin. 'Got any painkillers?' he said desperately. They handed over some pills and another bottle of water. When he had consumed it all, he said, 'Where we going this time?'

'Nevada. There's a clinic near Reno, in the mountains, spectacular country.'

'It's not a dude ranch, is it? I can't take another thirty days on a horse. My ass is still raw from the last detox.'

Uncle Wally was still standing at the foot of the bed. He had not moved a step. 'No horses this time. It's a different kind of place.'

'Oh, really. I hear they're all the same. Folks here are always talking about their latest rehab. Always comparing notes. Great way to pick up girls in a bar.' He spoke with his eyes closed tightly as the pain rippled through his head.

'No, this is different.'

'How so?'

'It's a bit tougher, and you'll be there longer.'

'Do tell. How long?'

'As long as it takes.'

'Can I just promise to stop drinking right now and skip the whole damned thing?'

'No.'

'And I'm assuming that since you're here and since you're the big chief of this sorry little tribe my participation is not exactly voluntary?'

'Right.'

'Because if I say go to hell, get out of my house, I'm calling the police because the three of you broke in, and that there's no way I'm taking a trip with you – if I say all that, then you'll simply bring up the trust funds. Right?'

'Right.'

The nausea hit like lightning. Baxter bolted from the bed, shedding his sport coat as he stumbled through the door to the bathroom. The vomiting was loud and long and mixed with waves of profanities. He washed his face, looked at his swollen red eyes in the mirror, and admitted that a few days of sobriety was not a bad idea. But he couldn't imagine a whole lifetime with no booze and no drugs.

The trust funds had been established by a great-grandfather who had no idea what he was doing. In the days before private jets and luxury yachts and cocaine and countless other ways to burn the family fortune, the prudent thing to do was to preserve the money for future generations. But Baxter's grandfather had seen the warning signs. He hired the lawyers and changed the trusts so that a board of advisers could exercise a measure of discretion. Some of the money arrived each month and allowed Baxter to survive quite comfortably without working. But the serious money could be turned off like a spigot, and Uncle Wally controlled it with an iron fist.

If Uncle Wally said you were going to rehab, then you were about to dry out.

Baxter stood in the bathroom door, leaning on the facing, and looked at the three. They had not budged. He looked at the specialist nearest to him and said, 'You guys here to break my thumbs if I put up a fight?'

'No,' came the reply.

'Let's go, Baxter,' Walter said.

'Do I pack?'

'No.'

'Your jet?'

'Yes.'

'Last time I was allowed to get hammered.'

'The clinic says you can drink all you want on the ride in. The bar is stocked.'

'How long's the flight?'

'Ninety minutes.'

'I'll have to drink fast.'

'I'm sure you can handle that.'

Baxter waved his arms and looked around his bedroom. 'What about my place? The bills, the maid, the mail?'

'I'll take care of everything. Let's go.'

Baxter brushed his teeth, combed his hair, changed his shirt, then followed Uncle Wally and the other two outside and into a black van. They rode in silence for a few minutes, but the tension was finally broken by the sounds of Baxter crying in the rear seat.

Chapter 13

The bar review course was offered at Fordham University on Sixty-second Street, in a vast lecture hall that was filled with anxious former law students. From 9:30 until 1:30 each weekday, various professors from nearby law schools covered the intricacies of constitutional law, corporations, criminal law, property, evidence, contracts, and many other subjects. Since virtually every person in the room had just finished law school, the material was familiar and easily digested. But the volume was overwhelming. Three years of intense study would be reduced to a nightmare of an exam that ran for sixteen hours over a two-day period. Thirty percent of those taking it for the first time would not pass, and because of this there was little hesitation in forking over the $3,000 for the review course. Scully & Pershing picked up the bill for Kyle and its other new recruits.

The pressure was palpable the first time Kyle

walked into the room at Fordham, and it never went away. By the third day he was sitting with a group of friends from Yale, and they soon formed a study group that met every afternoon and often worked into the night. During three years of law school, they had dreaded the day they would be forced to revisit the murky world of federal taxation or the tedium of the Uniform Commercial Code, but the day was at hand. The bar exam consumed them.

Scully & Pershing was typical in that it forgave the first flunking of the exam, but not the second. Two bad tests, and you're out. A few of the crueler firms had a one-strike policy, and there were a handful of more reasonable firms that would forgive twice if the associate was showing promise on all other fronts. Regardless, the fear of failure boiled just under the surface and often made it difficult to sleep.

Kyle found himself taking long walks around the city, at all hours, to break the monotony and clear his head. The walks were informative, and at times fascinating. He learned the streets, the subways, the bus system, the rules of the sidewalks. He knew which coffee shops stayed open all night and which bakeries had warm baguettes at 5:00 a.m. He found a wonderful old bookstore in the Village and resumed his rabid new interest in spy and espionage novels.

After three weeks in the city, he finally found a suitable apartment. At daybreak one morning, he was sitting on a stool in the window of a coffee shop on Seventh Avenue in Chelsea, sipping a double espresso and reading the *Times*, when he saw two men wrestle a sofa out of a door across the street. The men were obviously not professional movers, and they showed little patience with the sofa. They practically threw it into the back of a van, then disappeared through the door. A few minutes later they were back with a bulky leather chair that received the same treatment. The men were in a hurry, and the move did not appear to be a happy one. The door was next to a health food store, and two floors above it a sign in a window advertised an apartment available for a sublet. Kyle quickly crossed the street, stopped one of the men, then followed him upstairs for a look around. The apartment was one of four on the third floor. It had three small rooms and a narrow kitchen, and as he talked to the man, Steve somebody, he learned that Steve had the lease but was leaving town in a hurry. They shook hands on an eight-month sub at $2,500 per. That afternoon, they met again at the apartment to sign the paperwork and transfer the keys.

Kyle thanked Charles and Charles, reloaded his meager assets in his Jeep, and drove twenty minutes uptown to the corner of Seventh and West Twenty-sixth. His first purchase was a well-used bed and night table from a flea market. His second was a fifty-inch flat-screen television. There was no urgency in furnishing or decorating. Kyle doubted he would live there beyond the eight months and could not imagine having guests. It was an adequate place to start, then he would find something nicer.

Before leaving for West Virginia, he carefully set the traps. He cut several four-inch pieces of brown sewing thread, and with a dab of Vaseline stuck the threads to the bottoms of three interior doors. Standing and looking down, he could barely see the thread against the oak stain, but if anyone entered the apartment and opened the doors, they would leave a trail by displacing the threads. Along one wall in the den he had stacked textbooks, notebooks, files for this and that, generally useless stuff that he wasn't ready to part with. It was a haphazard pile, but Kyle arranged everything in careful order and photographed it all with a digital camera. Anyone looking through it would be tempted to toss things back into the collection, and if that happened, Kyle would know it. He informed his new neighbor, an elderly lady from Thailand, that he would be gone for four days and was not expecting any visitors. If she heard anything, call the cops. She agreed, but Kyle was not at all confident she understood a word he said.

His counterintelligence tactics were rudimentary, but the basics often worked just fine, according to the spy novels.

The New River runs through the Allegheny Mountains in southern West Virginia. It's fast in some places, slower in others, but on any stretch of it the scenery is beautiful. With Class IV rapids in some areas, it has long been a favorite of serious kayakers. And with miles and miles of slower water, it attracts thousands of rafters each year. Because of its popularity, there are several established outfitters. Kyle had found one near the town of Beckley.

They met there at a motel the first night. Joey, Kyle, and four other Beta brothers. They drank two cases of beer to celebrate the Fourth of July, and woke up with hangovers. Kyle, of course, stayed with diet soda and woke up pondering the mysteries of the bankruptcy code. One look at his five friends and he was proud of his sobriety.

Their guide was a rather rustic local named Clem, and Clem had a few rules for the twenty-four-foot rubber raft that was his livelihood. Helmets and life vests were mandatory. No smoking, period. No drinking was allowed in the 'boat' while it was moving down the river. When it stopped, for lunch or for the night, they could drink all they wanted. Clem counted ten cases of beer and realized what he was facing. The first morning was uneventful. The sun was hot, and the crew was subdued, even suffering. By late afternoon, they were splashing water and began jumping in. By 5:00 p.m., they were parched, and Clem found a sandbar to settle into for the first night. After a couple of beers each, and one for Clem himself, they pitched four tents and set up camp. Clem cooked T-bones on a grill, and after dinner the crew ventured off to explore.

Kyle and Joey followed the river for half a mile, and when they were certain they could not be seen, they sat on a log with their feet in the backwater. 'Let's have it,' Joey said, cutting to the chase.

For weeks, even months, Kyle had struggled with the conversation they were about to have. He loathed the idea of upsetting his friend's life, but he had decided that he had no choice but to tell the story. All of it. He justified his decision by convincing himself that he would certainly want to know if things were reversed. If Joey had been the first to see the video and knew of its dangers, he, Kyle, would want to know. But the bigger reason, and one that made him feel selfish, was that Kyle needed help. He had worked on a rough draft of a plan, and it was more than he could handle himself, especially with Bennie lurking in the shadows. The plan could easily lead nowhere, and it could just as easily lead to something dangerous. It could be aborted at any time. It could also be rejected outright by Joey Bernardo. The first step involved Elaine Keenan.

Joey listened in rapt silence to Kyle's detailed replaying of the initial encounter with a man known as Bennie. He was sufficiently stunned by the existence of the video. He was thoroughly bewildered by the blackmail. He was terrified by the thought of some forgotten girl accusing him of rape and producing the evidence to back it up.

Kyle unloaded everything but the background on the lawsuit. He had not yet passed the bar and received a license to practice, but he had signed a contract with Scully & Pershing and felt an ethical obligation to protect firm business. This was silly in light of what he would be forced to do, but for the moment his career was unblemished and he felt rather ethical.

Joey's first reaction was a halfhearted attempt to deny any contact with Elaine, but Kyle waved him off. 'You're on the video,' Kyle said as sympathetically as possible. 'You're having sex with a girl who's probably floating in and out of consciousness. In our apartment. Baxter goes first, then you. And I saw it on a twelve-inch laptop screen. If it's ever seen in court, it'll be on a big screen, a massive one. It'll be like sitting in the cinema with the images and sounds enhanced so that everybody there, especially the jurors, will have no doubt that it's you. I'm sorry, Joey, but you're there.'

'Totally nude?'

'Not a stitch. Do you remember it?'

'It was five years ago, Kyle. I've worked hard to forget it.'

'But you do remember?'

With great reluctance, Joey said, 'Yeah, sure, but there was no rape. Hell, the sex was her idea.'

'That's not real clear on the video.'

'Well, the video is missing several important details. First, when the cops showed up that night, we scattered. Baxter and I ran next door and ducked into Thelo's apartment where there was a smaller and quieter party. Elaine was there, bombed as usual and having a good time. We hung around for a few minutes, waited for the cops to clear out, then Elaine tells me she wants to leave, wants to go back to our place for a 'session,' as she liked to call it. With Baxter and me. That's the way she was, Kyle, always on the prowl. She was the easiest lay at Duquesne. Everybody knew it. She was very cute and very easy.'

'I remember well.'

'I never saw a girl so promiscuous and so aggressive. That's why we were stunned when she cried rape.'

'And it's why the police lost interest.'

'Exactly. And there's something else, another little detail not on the video. The night before the party, you and Alan and some others went to a Pirates game, right?'

'Yes.'

'Elaine was in the apartment, which was nothing new. And we had a three-way. Me, Baxter, and Elaine. Twenty-four hours later, same apartment, same guys, same everything, she passes out, wakes up, decides she was raped.'

'I don't remember this.'

'It was no big deal until she cried rape. Baxter and I talked about it and decided to keep it quiet because she might claim we raped her twice. So we buried it. When the police started squeezing us, we finally told them. That's when they packed up and went home. Case closed. No rape.'

A small turtle stopped swimming by a log and seemed to stare at them. They stared back, and for a long time nothing was said.

'Do Baxter and Alan know about this?' Joey finally asked.

'No, not yet. It was hard enough telling you.'

'Thanks for nothing.'

'I'm sorry. I need a friend.'

'To do what?'

'I don't know. Right now I just need someone to talk to.'

'What do these guys want from you?'

'It's very simple. The scheme is to plant me as a spy in my law firm, where I can extract all sorts of secrets that the other side can use to win a big lawsuit.'

'Simple enough. What happens if you get caught?'

'Disbarred, indicted, convicted, sentenced to five years in prison – state, not federal.'

'Is that all?'

'Bankrupted, humiliated, it's a long list.'

'You need more than friends.'

The turtle crawled onto the sand and disappeared into the roots of a dead tree. 'We'd better get back,' Kyle said.

'We gotta talk some more. Let me think about this.'

'We'll sneak away later.'

They followed the river to the campsite. The sun had dropped below the mountains, and night was approaching quickly. Clem stoked the coals and added wood to the fire. The crew gathered around and opened beers, and the chatter began. Kyle asked if anyone had heard from Baxter. There was a rumor the family had locked him away in a high-security rehab unit, but this had not been confirmed. No one had heard from him in three weeks. They told Baxter stories for far too long.

Joey was notably quiet, obviously preoccupied. 'You got girl trouble?' Clem asked at one point.

'Naw, just sleepy, that's all.'

By 9:30 they were all sleepy. The beer and sun and red meat finally caught up with them. When Clem finished his third long joke in a row with a lame punch line, they were all ready for their sleeping bags. Kyle and Joey shared a tent, and as they were arranging two rather thin air mattresses, Clem yelled across the campsite, 'Be sure and check for snakes.' Then he laughed, and they assumed it was another attempt at humor. Ten minutes later they heard him snore. The sound of the river soon put them all to sleep.

At 3:20 a.m., Kyle checked his watch and saw the time. After three rough weeks of bar review, his nights were erratic. The fact that he was essentially sleeping on the ground didn't help matters.

'You awake?' Joey whispered.

'Yes. I assume you are too.'

'I can't sleep. Let's go talk.'

They quietly unzipped the front tent fly and

eased away from the campsite. Kyle led with a flashlight, moving carefully, watching for snakes. The path led up to a rocky trail, and after a few minutes of tentative hiking they stopped near a huge boulder. Kyle turned off the flashlight, and their eyes began to focus in the darkness.

'One more time,' Joey said. 'Describe the video.'

Since it was seared into Kyle's memory, he had no trouble replaying it – exact times, camera location, angle, the people involved, the arrival of the police, and the presence of Elaine Keenan. Joey absorbed it again without a word.

'Okay, Kyle,' he said finally. 'You've lived with this since February. You've had plenty of time to think. Right now I ain't thinking real clear. Tell me what we should do.'

'The big decision has been made. I'm officially employed by Scully & Pershing, and at some point I'll get around to the dirty work. But there are two things I want to know. The first concerns Elaine. I know where she is, but I'd like to know who she is now. Is she capable of dragging this up again, or has she moved on? Does she have a life, or is she living in the past? According to Bennie, she has a lawyer and she still wants justice. Maybe so, maybe not, but I'd like to know the truth.'

'Why?'

'Because Bennie is a liar by trade. If she's still angry, or if she's dreaming of squeezing money out of us, especially Baxter, it's important to know. It could impact what I do at the law firm.'

'Where is she?'

'She lives in Scranton, but that's all I know. For about two thousand bucks we can hire a private investigator to do a background on her. I'll pay it, but I can't arrange it myself, because they're watching and listening.'

'So you want me to do it?'

'Yes. But you have to be careful. No phones or e-mails. There's a reputable investigator in Pittsburgh, not too far from your office. I give you the cash, you give it to him, he does the snooping, gives us the report, and nobody will know about it.'

'Then what?'

'I want to know who Bennie is and who he works for.'

'Good luck.'

'It's a long shot. He might work for an opposing law firm, or a client involved in a big lawsuit, or he might work for some intelligence operation, domestic or foreign. If I'm being forced to spy, I would like to know who I'm spying for.'

'That's too dangerous.'

'It's very dangerous, but it can be done.'

'How?'

'I haven't got that far yet.'

'Great. And I'm guessing that I'll be involved in this plan that has yet to be created.'

'I need help, Joey. There's no one else.'

'I got a better idea. Why don't you just go to the FBI and tell them everything? Tell them this creep is trying to blackmail you into stealing secrets from your law firm?'

'Oh, I've thought of that, believe me. I've spent hours upon hours walking through that scenario, but it's a bad idea. There's no doubt whatsoever that Bennie will use the video. He'll send a copy to the Pittsburgh police, a copy to Elaine, and a copy to her lawyer with clear instructions on how to use it to inflict as much misery as possible on me, you, Alan, and especially Baxter. He'll put it on the Internet. The video will become a big part of our lives. You want Blair to know about it?'

'No.'

'This guy is ruthless, Joey. He's a professional, a corporate spy with an unlimited budget and plenty of manpower to do whatever he wants. He would watch us burn and have a good laugh, probably from someplace where the FBI can't touch him.'

'A real prince. You'd better leave him alone.'

'I'm not doing anything stupid. Look, Joey, there's an even chance that I can survive this. I'll do the dirty work for a few years, and when I'm no longer useful, Bennie will disappear. By then, I've violated every ethic in the book, and I've broken laws too numerous to mention, but I haven't been caught.'

'That sounds awful.'

And indeed it did. Kyle listened to his own

words and was hit again by the folly of it all, and by the bleakness of his future.

They talked for two hours, until the sky began to change, and never once thought about returning to the tent. It was cooler on the ridge.

The old Joey would have jumped in with both feet, looking for a fight. This later version was much more cautious. He had a wedding to think about, a future with Blair. They had already bought a new condo together, and Joey, without the slightest trace of embarrassment, claimed that he was enjoying the decorating. Joey Bernardo, decorating?

Breakfast was scrambled eggs with hot sauce and bacon with onions. Clem cooked over the fire while his crew broke camp and loaded the raft. By eight o'clock, they were off, floating leisurely on the New River, headed nowhere in particular.

After a month in the city, Kyle savored the fresh air and open spaces. He envied Clem, a good ole boy from the mountains who earned little and needed even less. Clem had worked 'these rivers' for twenty years and loved every minute of it. Such an uncomplicated life. Kyle would trade with him in an instant.

The thought of returning to New York made him ill. It was July 6. The bar exam was in three weeks. Scully & Pershing was two months away.

Chapter 14

Tuesday morning, September 2, 8:00 sharp. A hundred and three nicely dressed and quite apprehensive new associates congregated on the law firm's forty-fourth-floor mezzanine for coffee and juice. After signing in and receiving name tags, they chatted nervously, introduced themselves, and looked for friendly faces. At 8:15 they began to file into the large meeting room, and on the way in each was handed a four-inch-thick notebook with the bold Scully & Pershing Gothic logo printed on the front. It was filled with the usual information – a history of the firm, a directory, pages and pages on firm policies, health insurance forms, and so on. In the 'Diversity' section there was a breakdown of their class: Male, 71, Female, 32; Caucasian, 75, African-American, 13, Hispanic, 7, Asian, 5, Other, 3; Protestant, 58, Catholic, 22, Jewish, 9, Muslim, 2, Undeclared, 12. Each member had a small black-and-white photo with a one-paragraph bio. The Ivy League dominated, but there was fair representation from other top schools such as NYU, Georgetown, Stanford, Michigan, Texas, Chicago, North Carolina, Virginia, and Duke. There was no one from a second-tier school.

Kyle sat with a group from Yale and played with the numbers. Fourteen from Harvard, and though they were indistinguishable at the moment, it would not be long before the rest of the class knew who they were. Five from Yale. None from Princeton because Princeton had never established a law school. Nine from Columbia.

With 103 associates at a starting salary of $200,000, there was now more than $20 million in fresh legal talent sitting in the room. A lot of money, but over the next twelve months each would bill at least two thousand hours at $300–$400 an hour. The hours would vary, but it was safe to say that the rookie class would generate at least $75 million for the firm in the coming year. These numbers were not in the binder, but the math was easy.

Other numbers were missing, too. Of the 103, 15 percent would leave after the second year. Only 10 percent would survive and make partner in seven or eight years. The attrition was brutal, but Scully & Pershing did not care. There was an endless supply of disposable labor, even that of the Harvard and Yale variety.

At 8:30, several older men entered the room and sat in chairs along the narrow stage. The managing partner, Howard Meezer, stepped to the podium and began an elaborate welcoming speech, one he had no doubt memorized from years of use. After telling them how carefully they'd been chosen, he spent a few minutes touting the greatness of the firm. Then he outlined the rest of the week. The next two days would be spent in that room listening to various talks about all aspects of their new careers and life at good old Scully & Pershing. On Wednesday, they would spend a full day in computer and technology training. On Thursday, they would break down into smaller groups and begin brief orientations in specialized fields. The tedium was rapidly approaching.

The next speaker talked about compensation and benefits. Next was the firm's librarian, who spent a long hour on legal research. A psychologist talked about stress and pressure and in a nice way told them to remain single as long as possible. For those who were already married, the top ten law firms in New York currently had a 72 percent divorce rate among associates under the age of thirty. The monotony of the lectures was broken by the 'tech team' when they handed out shiny new laptops for everyone. A lengthy tutorial followed. Once the laptops were warmed up, the next technical adviser handed out the dreaded FirmFone. It was similar to most of the current smartphones on the market, but it had been designed especially for the hardworking lawyers at Scully & Pershing – designed and built by a software and gadget company that the firm had taken public with great success a decade earlier. It came with contact and biographical information for every lawyer in the firm, in all thirty offices, plus every paralegal and secretary, almost five thousand people in New York alone. The database included detailed summaries of all S&P clients, a small library of the most commonly used research, recent state and federal appellate decisions, and a registry of all New York and New Jersey judges and court clerks. The phone was equipped with high-speed Internet access and a dizzying assortment of bells and whistles. It was valuable and invaluable, and if one was lost, stolen, or otherwise misplaced, bad things would happen to its owner. It was to be kept at hand twenty-four hours a day, seven days a week until further notice.

In other words, the fancy little FirmFone now controlled their lives. Mega-firm lore was replete with outrageous tales of cell phone and e-mail abuse.

There were snide comments and soft groans from the crowd, but nothing too loud. None of the class clowns wanted to get too cute.

Lunch was a quick buffet on the mezzanine. The afternoon dragged on, but interest remained high. These were not boring law school lectures. These were important. The orientation ended at six, and as they hurried out, there was a lot of chatter about heading to the nearby bars.

⋆

On Wednesday, Kyle passed his first test. He and eleven others were assigned to the litigation practice group and led to a conference room on the thirty-first floor. They were greeted by Wilson Rush, the firm's leading litigator and attorney of record for Trylon Aeronautics in its case against Bartin Dynamics, though that lawsuit was not mentioned. Kyle had read so much background on Mr. Rush he felt as though he'd already met him. The great man told a few war stories, great trials from his illustrious career, then hurried away, no doubt off to sue another large corporation. More thick notebooks were passed out, and the next lecture was on the nuts and bolts of preparing lawsuits, responses, motions, and other filings that either pushed litigation along or tried to bog it down forever.

The first gunner appeared. There is at least one in every class, whether it's first-year contracts in law school or a group of fresh recruits on Wall Street. A gunner sits in the front row, asks complicated questions, sucks up to whoever happens to be at the podium, works every angle, cuts throats for better grades, stabs backs to make law review, interviews only at the top-rated firms regardless of how bad their reputations might be, and arrives at the firm with every intention of making partner before anyone else in his class. Gunners succeed magnificently; most make partner.

His name was Jeff Tabor, and they immediately knew where he was from because in the midst of his first question he managed to say, 'Well, at Harvard, we were taught that not all known facts should be included in the initial lawsuit.'

To which the fifth-year associate handling the lecture quickly retorted, 'This ain't Kansas, Toto. It's our way or the highway.' Everyone laughed but the gunner.

At 9:00 p.m. on Wednesday, the twelve new litigation associates met at a three-star restaurant in midtown for what was supposed to be a nice dinner with Doug Peckham, the partner who had supervised Kyle the previous summer. They waited in the bar and had a drink, and at 9:15 the first comment was made regarding Doug and his tardiness. All twelve had their FirmFones in their pockets. In fact, each had two phones. Kyle's old one was in the right pants pocket, the FirmFone was in the left. At 9:30, they began to debate the idea of calling Mr. Peckham, but decided against it. Then, at 9:40, he called Kyle with a quick apology. He'd been in trial, things had run late, and he was now back at the office tending to some urgent matter. The associates were to proceed with dinner and not worry about the bill.

The fact that a partner was working until 10:00 p.m. on a Wednesday night throttled the enthusiasm for a fine meal. It also set the tone of the conversation. As the wine flowed, they began telling the worst associate-abuse stories they'd heard. The contest was won by Tabor the

Gunner, who when lubricated with alcohol was not the same asshole he'd been throughout the day. During a recruiting visit a year earlier, Tabor had dropped in on a friend he'd known in college. The friend was a second-year associate with another mega-firm and was perfectly miserable in his new profession. His office was tiny, and while they were chatting, Tabor's friend tried to shove a sleeping bag under his desk, out of view. Tabor, ever curious, had asked, 'What's that for?' And as soon as he asked the question, he knew the answer. His friend sheepishly explained that he often found it necessary to catch a few hours of sleep during the night when he was overworked. Tabor pressed on and extracted the truth. The firm was a lousy place to work. Most of the rookies were on the same floor, and it was nicknamed 'the Campsite.'

On the ninetieth day of Baxter's recovery at Washoe Retreat, Walter Tate entered the small conference room and shook hands with his nephew. Then he shook hands with Dr. Boone, Baxter's chief therapist. Walter had spoken with Boone several times by phone, but the two had not met.

Baxter was tanned, fit, and in relatively good spirits. He had gone ninety days with no booze or drugs, the longest stretch in at least ten years. Under the direction of Uncle Wally, he had reluctantly signed the paperwork that allowed the clinic to keep him locked away for up to six months. Now he was ready to leave. Uncle Wally, though, was not so sure.

The meeting belonged to Dr. Boone, and he went through a rather wordy summary of Baxter's progress. Once properly dried out, Baxter had proceeded nicely through the initial stages of therapy. He was aware of his problem. On day 23, he admitted he was an alcoholic and an abuser of drugs. However, he still would not admit to being physically addicted to cocaine, his favorite. At all times, he had been cooperative with his counselors, even helpful to other patients. He exercised strenuously each day and became fanatical about his diet. No coffee, tea, or sugar. In short, Baxter had been a model of good behavior. His rehab had been successful, so far.

'Is he ready to be released?' Uncle Wally asked.

Dr. Boone paused and stared at Baxter. 'Are you?' he asked.

'Of course I am. I feel great. I'm enjoying the sober life.'

'I've heard this before, Baxter,' Walter said. 'The last time you stayed clean for, what, two weeks?'

'Most addicts need more than one rehab,' Dr. Boone added.

'That was different,' Baxter said. 'It was only thirty days, and I knew when I left that I'd start drinking again.'

'You can't stay clean in L.A.,' Walter said.

'I can stay clean anywhere.'

'I doubt that.'

'You doubt me?'

'Yes. I doubt you. You have a lot to prove, son.'

Each took a breath and looked at Dr. Boone. It was time for judgment, for the sentencing, for a final word in this horribly expensive facility. 'I want your frank opinion,' Walter said.

Dr. Boone nodded, and without taking his eyes off Baxter, he began, 'You're not ready. You're not ready, because you're not angry, Baxter. You must reach a point where you're angry at your old self, your old life, your addictions. You have to hate the way you were, and when this hatred and anger consumes you, then you'll have the determination not to go back there. I can see it in your eyes. You're not a believer. You'll go back to L.A., back to the same friends, and then parties, and then you'll take a drink. You'll tell yourself that one drink is okay. You can handle it, no problem. That's what happened before. You start with a couple of beers, then three or four, and then it spirals down. Booze at first, but the coke quickly follows. If you're lucky, you'll come back here and we'll try again. If you're unlucky, you'll kill yourself.'

'I don't believe this,' Baxter said.

'I've talked to the other counselors. We're all in agreement. If you leave now, there's a good chance you'll screw up again.'

'There's no way.'

'Then how much longer?' Walter asked.

'That depends on Baxter. We haven't broken through yet, because he's not angry at his old self.' Dr. Boone's eyes met Baxter's. 'You still have this fantasy of making it big in Hollywood. You want to be famous, a star, lots of girls, parties, magazine covers, big movies. Until you get that out of your system, you cannot stay clean.'

'I'll find you a real job,' Walter said.

'I don't want a real job.'

'See what I mean?' Dr. Boone said, pouncing. 'You're sitting here now, trying to talk your way out so you can hustle back to L.A. and take up where you left off. You're not the first Hollywood casualty I've seen, Baxter. I've been around the block a few times. If you go back there, you'll be at a party within a week.'

'What if he goes somewhere else?' Walter asked.

'When he's finally discharged, we'll certainly recommend a new place of residence, away from his old friends. Of course there's booze everywhere, but it's the lifestyle that has to change.'

'What about Pittsburgh?' Walter asked.

'Oh, hell no!' Baxter said. 'My family's in Pittsburgh, and look at them. I'd rather die on skid row.'

'Let's work here for another thirty days,' Dr. Boone said. 'Then we'll reevaluate.'

At $1,500 a day, Walter had his limits. 'What will you do for the next thirty days?' he asked.

'More intensive counseling. The longer Baxter stays here, the better his chances of success when he reenters.'

'"Reentry." I love the term,' Baxter said. 'I can't believe you're doing this.'

'Trust me, Baxter. We've spent hours together, and I know that you're not ready.'

'I'm so ready. You don't know how ready I am.'

'Trust me.'

'All right then, let's meet again in thirty days,' Walter said.

Chapter 15

The orientation dragged on through Thursday and became as dull as most of the litigation files the new associates would soon be assigned to. On Friday, they finally got around to the issue that had been conspicuously ignored the entire week – office assignments. Real estate. There was little doubt that their space would be cramped, sparsely furnished, and hidden from view, and so the real question was, how bad will it be?

Litigation was concentrated on floors 32, 33, and 34, and somewhere in there, far away from the windows, were cubicles with the new names mounted on small plates and stuck to the movable walls. Kyle was shown to his on the thirty-third floor. His cube was divided into four equal shares by canvas partitions so that it was possible for him to sit at his desk, talk quietly on the phone, and use his laptop with some small measure of privacy. No one could actually see him; however, if Tabor to his right and Dr. Dale Armstrong to his left rolled their chairs back no more than two feet, then they could see Kyle and he could see them.

His desk had enough surface area for his laptop, a legal pad, the office phone, and not much else. A few shelves finished off the design scheme. He noted that there was barely enough room for a man to unroll his sleeping bag. By Friday afternoon, Kyle was already tired of the firm.

Dr. Dale was a female mathematics whiz who'd taught at the college level before deciding for some reason to become a lawyer. She was thirty, single, attractive, unsmiling, and frosty enough to be left alone. Tabor was the gunner from Harvard. The fourth member of their little cube was Tim Reynolds, a Penn man who'd been eyeing Dr. Dale since Wednesday. She did not seem at all interested. Among the torrent of firm policies and dos and don'ts that had been carped on all week, the one that rang loudest was a strict prohibition against interoffice romances. If a love affair blossomed, then one of the two had to go. If a casual affair was discovered, there would be punishment, though its exact nature was not spelled out in the handbook. There was already a hot rumor that a year earlier an unmarried associate had been fired while the married partner who'd been hounding her got sent to the office in Hong Kong.

A secretary was assigned to the four. Her

name was Sandra, and she had been with the firm for eighteen long and stressful years. She had once made it to the major leagues as an executive secretary for a senior partner, but the pressure proved too much, and she had slowly been demoted down through the minors, all the way down to the rookie league, where she spent most of her time holding the hands of kids who were just students four months earlier.

Week one was finished. Kyle had not billed a single hour, though that would change come Monday. He found a cab and headed for the Mercer Hotel in SoHo. The traffic was slow, so he opened his briefcase and pulled out the FedEx envelope sent from a brokerage house in Pittsburgh. Joey's handwritten note read: 'Here's the report. Not sure what it means. Drop me a line.'

Kyle found it impossible to believe that Bennie could monitor the avalanche of mail in and out of Scully & Pershing every day – fifteen hundred lawyers cranking out paperwork because that's what they were supposed to do. The mail room was larger than a small-town post office. He and Joey had decided to play it safe with snail mail and overnight delivery.

The report had been prepared by a private security firm in Pittsburgh. It was eight pages long and cost $2,000. Its subject was Elaine Keenan, now age twenty-three, who currently lived in an apartment in Scranton, Pennsylvania, with another female. The first two pages covered her family, education, and employment history. She attended Duquesne for only one year, and a quick check of her birth date confirmed that she was not quite eighteen when the episode occurred. After Duquesne, she attended classes off and on at a couple of schools around Erie and Scranton, but had yet to finish her degree. During the previous spring semester she had taken some classes at the University of Scranton. She was a registered Democrat with two campaign stickers on the rear bumper of her 2004 Nissan, which was titled in her name. According to the available records, she did not own any real estate, firearms, or stock in foreign banks. There were two minor incidents with the law, both involving underage drinking and both handled expeditiously by the courts. The second scrape required counseling for alcohol and drug use. Her attorney had been a local female named Michelin Chiz, better known as Mike. This was notable since Elaine worked part-time in the law offices of Michelin Chiz & Associates. Ms. Mike Chiz had a reputation as a fierce divorce lawyer, always on the side of the wives, and always ready to castrate wayward husbands.

Elaine's full-time job was with the City of Scranton as an assistant director of parks and recreation. Salary, $24,000. She had been employed there for almost two years. Before that, she had bounced from one part-time job to another.

Her living arrangement was not clear. Her

roommate was a twenty-eight-year-old female who worked in a hospital, also took classes at a local college, had never been married, and had no criminal record. Elaine was observed off and on for thirty-six hours. After work the first day, she met her roommate in the parking lot near a bar favored by the alternative crowd. Upon meeting, the two roommates held hands briefly as they walked to the bar. Inside, they joined three other women at a table. Elaine had a diet soda, nothing stronger. She smoked skinny brown cigarettes. The women were very affectionate with each other, and, well, the obvious became more obvious.

Scranton had a women's shelter called Haven, and it advertised itself as a refuge and resource center for victims of domestic abuse and sexual assault. It was nonprofit, privately funded, and staffed by volunteers, many of whom claimed to have been victims.

Elaine Keenan was listed as a 'counselor' on Haven's monthly newsletter. A female employee of the security firm used a pay phone in downtown Scranton, called Elaine at home, claimed to be the victim of a rape, and said she needed someone to talk to. She was afraid to come forward for all sorts of reasons. Someone at Haven had told her to call Elaine. They talked for almost thirty minutes, during which time Elaine admitted that she, too, was the victim of a rape and that the rapists (more than one) had never been brought to justice. She was eager to help, and they agreed to meet the following day at Haven's office. The entire conversation was recorded, and, of course, no meeting occurred the next day.

'Still the victim,' Kyle mumbled to himself in the back of the cab. The night Kyle had sex with her, about a month before the alleged rape, he'd been in his own bed, sound asleep, when she crawled under the sheets naked and quickly got what she wanted.

The cab was at the Mercer. He returned the report to an inside pocket of his briefcase, paid the driver, and entered the hotel. Bennie was in a room on the fourth floor, waiting as usual with his customary purpose and appearing to have been there for hours. They did not exchange pleasantries.

'So how was the first week?' Bennie asked.

'Great. A lot of orientation. I got assigned to litigation,' Kyle said as if he'd done something to be proud of. He had succeeded already.

'Very good news. Excellent. Any sign of the Trylon case?'

'No, we haven't been near a real case. We start work Monday. This week was just the warm-up.'

'Of course. They give you a laptop?' Bennie asked.

'Yes.'

'What kind?'

'I'm sure you already know.'

'No, I do not. The technology changes every six months. I'd like to see it.'

'I didn't bring it.'

'Bring it next time.'

'I'll think about it.'

'What about a phone? A BlackBerry?'

'Something like that.'

'I'd like to see it.'

'I didn't bring it.'

'But the firm requires you to keep it on at all times, is this not true?'

'True.'

'Then why don't you have it?'

'For the same reason I didn't bring the laptop. Because you want to see them, and you're not going to see them until I'm ready. They are of no value to you at this point, and so the only reason you want them is to make sure I'm compromised, right, Bennie? As soon as I give something to you, then I've broken the law, violated the ethics, and you own me. I'm not stupid, Bennie. We're going slow here.'

'We reached an agreement many months ago, Kyle. Have you forgotten? You have already agreed to break the law, violate the ethics, do whatever I want you to do. You will find the information and give it to me. And if I want something from the firm, then it's your job to get it. Now, I want the phone and I want the laptop.'

'No. Not yet.'

Bennie walked back to the window. After a long pause, he said, 'Baxter Tate is in rehab, you know?'

'I know.'

'For some time now.'

'That's what I hear. Maybe he'll clean up and get a life.'

Bennie turned and walked to within striking distance. 'You need a reminder, Kyle, of who is in charge here. If you don't follow my orders, then I'll provide a little reminder. Right now I'm giving serious consideration to releasing the first half of the video. Plaster it around the Internet, notify all the folks who might find it interesting, have some fun with it.'

Kyle shrugged. 'It's just a bunch of drunk college kids.'

'Right, no big deal. But do you really want it out there, Kyle, for the whole world to see? What would your new colleagues think at Scully & Pershing?'

'They'll probably think I was just another stupid drunk college kid, like many of them when they were younger.'

'We'll see.' Bennie picked up a thin file from the credenza, opened it, and pulled out a sheet of paper with a face on it. 'You know this guy?' he asked, handing it to Kyle, who glanced at it and shook his head. No. White male, age thirty, coat and tie, at least from the shoulders up.

'Name's Gavin Meade, four years now at Scully & Pershing, litigation, one of about thirty associates toiling away on the case of Trylon versus Bartin. In the normal course of things you'd probably meet him in a few weeks, but Mr. Meade is about to be sacked.'

Kyle was holding the sheet of paper, looking into the handsome face of Gavin Meade, and wondering what sin he'd committed.

'Seems he, too, has a little problem from the past,' Bennie was saying, relishing the role of executioner. 'Seems he, too, liked to get rough with the girls. Not rape, though.'

'I didn't rape anybody and you know it.'

'Maybe not.'

'Got another video, Bennie? Been crawling through the gutter again, looking for someone else to ruin?'

'Nope, no video. Just some affidavits. Mr. Meade doesn't rape women; he just beats them. In college, ten years ago, he had a girlfriend who had a problem with bruises. One night he put her in the hospital. The police were finally invited in, things unraveled for Mr. Meade. He was arrested, jailed, formally charged, and facing trial. Then there was a settlement, money changed hands, the girl wanted no part of a trial, and everything was dropped. Meade walked away, but he's got this record now. No problem, he just lied about it. When he applied to law school at Michigan, he lied on his application. When he went through the background check at Scully, he lied again. Automatic termination.'

'I'm so happy for you, Bennie. I know how much these little stories mean to you. Go get him. Ruin him. Attaboy.'

'Everybody has secrets, Kyle. I can ruin anyone.'

'You're the man.' Kyle slammed the door and left the hotel.

At noon on Saturday, three charter buses pulled away from the Scully & Pershing office building and left the city. They carried all 103 members of the first-year associate class. On board each bus was a full bar and plenty of snacks, and the drinking was fast and serious. Three hours later, they arrived at a yacht club in the Hamptons. The first party was under a tent near Montauk Beach. Dinner was under another tent on the hotel grounds. The second and last party was at the mansion of one of the Scully descendants. A reggae band played by the pool.

The 'retreat' was designed to break the ice and make the recruits happy they'd come on board. Many of the firm's partners were there, and they got as drunk as the associates. The night went long, and the morning was not pleasant. After an early brunch, with gallons of coffee, they settled in a small ballroom to listen to the wise old men offer their secrets to a successful career. Several retired partners, legends at the firm, told war stories and cracked jokes and offered advice. The floor was open, and any question could be asked.

After the old goats were gone, a very diverse panel went to the front and continued with the storytelling. A black man, a white woman, a Hispanic, and a Korean – all partners – talked about the firm's commitment to tolerance and equal rights and so on.

Later in the day, they ate shrimp and oysters on a private beach, then the buses were reloaded and headed back to Manhattan. They arrived after dark, and the weary young lawyers headed home for a short night.

For them, the concept of exhaustion was about to be redefined.

Chapter 16

Any hope of pursuing meaningful work was promptly crushed at 7:30 Monday morning when all twelve new litigation associates were sent into the abyss of Document Review. As far back as the first year of law school, Kyle had heard horror stories of bright and eager young associates being marched into some dreary basement, chained to a desk, and given a mountain of densely worded documents to read. And while he'd known that his first year would include a generous dose of this punishment, he simply wasn't prepared for it. He and Dale, who was looking better by the day but showing no signs of a personality, were assigned to a case involving a client that was being hammered in the financial press.

Their new boss for the day, a senior associate named Karleen, called them into her office and explained things. For the next few days they would review some crucial documents, billing at least eight hours a day at $300 an hour. That would be their rate until the bar results were made known in November, and, assuming they passed, their hourly rate would jump to $400.

There was no thought given to a quick word about what might happen if they did not pass the bar exam. Scully & Pershing associates posted a pass rate of 92 percent the previous year, and it was simply assumed that everyone had passed.

Eight hours was the minimum, at least for now, and with lunch and coffee thrown in, that meant, roughly, a ten-hour day. Start no later than 8:00 a.m., and nobody ever thought about leaving before 7:00 p.m.

In case they were curious, Karleen billed twenty-four hundred hours last year. She had been with the firm for five years and acted as though she were a lifer. A future partner. Kyle glanced around her well-appointed office and noticed a diploma from Columbia Law School. There was a photo of a younger Karleen on a horse, but none of her with a husband, boyfriend, or children.

She was explaining that there was a chance that a partner might need Kyle or Dale for a quick project, so be prepared. Document Review was certainly not glamorous, but it was the safety net for all new associates. 'You can always go there and find work that can be billed,' Karleen said. 'Eight hours minimum, but there is no max.'

How delightful, thought Kyle. If for some

reason ten hours a day were not enough, the door to Document Review was always wide open for more.

Their first case involved a client with the slightly ludicrous name of Placid Mortgage – ludicrous in Kyle's opinion, but he kept his mouth shut as Karleen rattled off the more salient facts of the case. Starting in 2001, when a new wave of government regulators took over and adopted a less intrusive attitude, Placid and other huge home mortgage companies became aggressive in their pursuit of new loans. They advertised heavily, especially on the Internet, and convinced millions of lower- and middle-class Americans that they could indeed afford to buy homes that they actually could not afford. The bait was the old adjustable-rate mortgage, and in the hands of crooks like Placid it was adjusted in ways never before imagined. Placid sucked them in, went light on the paperwork, collected nice fees up front, then sold the crap in the secondary markets. The company was not holding the paper when the overheated real estate market finally crashed, home values plummeted, and foreclosures became rampant.

Karleen used much softer language in her summary, but Kyle had known for some time that his firm was representing Placid. He'd read a dozen stories about the mortgage meltdown and seen the name Scully & Pershing mentioned often, always in defense of Placid's latest setback.

Now the lawyers were trying to clean up the mess. Placid had been battered by lawsuits, but the worst one was a class action involving thirty-five thousand of its former borrowers. It had been filed in New York a year earlier.

Karleen led them to a long, dungeonlike room with no windows, a concrete floor, poor lighting, and neat stacks of white cardboard boxes with the words 'Placid Mortgage' stamped on the end. It was the mountain Kyle had heard so much about. The boxes, as Karleen explained, contained the files of all thirty-five thousand plaintiffs. Each file had to be reviewed.

'You're not alone,' Karleen said with a fake laugh, just as both Kyle and Dale were about to resign. 'We have other associates and even some paralegals on this review.' She opened a box, pulled out a file about an inch thick, and went through a quick summary of what the litigation team was looking for.

'Someday in court,' she said gravely, 'it will be crucial for our litigators to be able to tell the judge that we have examined *every* document in this case.'

Kyle assumed it was also crucial for the firm to have clients who could pay through the nose for such useless work. He was suddenly dizzy with the realization that in just a few short minutes, he would punch in and begin charging $300 an hour for his time. He was worth nothing close to that. He wasn't even a lawyer.

Karleen left them there, her heels clicking on

the polished concrete as she hustled out of the room. Kyle gawked at the boxes, then at Dale, who looked as stunned as he did. 'You gotta be kidding,' he said. But Dale was determined to prove something, so she grabbed a box, dropped it on the table, and yanked out some files. Kyle walked to the other end of the room, as far away as possible, and found himself some files.

He opened one and glanced at his watch – it was 7:50. Scully lawyers billed by tenths. A tenth of an hour is six minutes. Two-tenths is twelve, and so on. One point six hours is an hour and thirty-six minutes. Should he roll back the clock two minutes, to 7:48, and therefore be able to bill two-tenths before the hour of eight? Or should he stretch his arms, take a sip of coffee, get more situated, and wait until 7:54 to begin his first billable minute as a lawyer? It was a no-brainer. This was Wall Street, where everything was done with aggression. When in doubt, bill aggressively. If not, the next guy will, and then you won't catch him.

It took an hour to read every word in the file. One point two hours to be exact, and suddenly he had no reluctance in billing Placid for 1.2 hours, or $360 for the review. Not long ago, say about ninety minutes, he found it hard to believe he was worth $300 an hour. He hadn't even passed the bar! Now, though, he had been converted. Placid owed him the money because their sleaze had gotten them sued. Someone had to plow through their debris. He would aggressively bill the company out of revenge. Down the table, Dale worked diligently without any distraction.

Somewhere in the midst of the third file, Kyle paused long enough to ponder a few things. Still on the clock, he wondered where the Trylon-Bartin room was. Where were the highly classified documents, and how were they protected? What kind of vault were they stored in? This dungeon appeared to be security-free, but then who would spend money to protect a bunch of mortgage files gone bad? If Placid had dirty laundry, you could bet it wasn't buried where Kyle might find it.

He thought about his life. Here, in the third hour of his professional career, he was already questioning his sanity. What manner of man could sit here and pore over these meaningless pages for hours and days without going bonkers? What did he expect the life of a first-year associate to be? Would it be any better at another firm?

Dale left for ten minutes and returned. Probably a bathroom break. He bet she kept the meter running.

Lunch was in the firm cafeteria on the forty-third floor. Much had been made about the high quality of the food. Great chefs consulted, the freshest ingredients used, a dazzling menu of light dishes, and so on. They were free to leave the building and go to a restaurant, but few associates dared. The firm's policies were prominently published and distributed, but there were many unwritten rules; one was that the rookies ate in-house unless a client could be billed for a real lunch. Many of the partners used the cafeteria as well. It was important for them to be seen by their underlings, and to brag about the great food, and, most important, to eat in thirty minutes as an example of efficiency. The decor was art deco and nicely done, but the ambience was still reminiscent of a prison mess hall.

There was a clock on every wall, and you could almost hear them ticking.

Kyle and Dale joined Tim Reynolds at a small table near a vast window with a spectacular view of other tall buildings. Tim appeared to be shell-shocked – glazed eyes, vapid stare, weak voice. They swapped stories of the horrors of Document Review and began joking about their departures from the legal profession. The food was good, though lunch was not about eating. Lunch was now an excuse to get away from the documents.

But it didn't last long. They agreed to meet after work for a drink, Dale's first sign of life, then headed back to their respective dungeons. Two hours later, Kyle was hallucinating and flashing back to the glory days at Yale when he edited the prestigious law journal from his own office and managed dozens of other very bright students. His long hours led to a product, an important journal that was published eight times a year and read widely by lawyers and judges and scholars. His name was first on the masthead as editor in chief. Few students were so honored with such a title. For one year, he was the Man.

How had he fallen so fast and so hard?

It's just part of the boot camp, he kept telling himself. Basic training.

But what a waste! Placid, its shareholders, its creditors, and probably the American taxpayers would get stuck with the legal fees, fees being racked up in part by the now-halfhearted efforts of one Kyle McAvoy, who, after reviewing nine of the thirty-five thousand files, was convinced that his firm's client should be locked away in prison. The CEO, the managers, the board of directors – all of them. You can't jail a corporation, but an exception should be made for every employee who ever worked at Placid Mortgage.

What would John McAvoy think if he could see his son? Kyle laughed and shuddered at the thought. The verbal abuse would be funny and cruel, and at that moment Kyle would accept it without firing back. At that moment, his father was either in his office counseling a client through a problem or in a courtroom mixing it up with another lawyer. Regardless, he was with real people in real conversations, and life was anything but dull.

Dale was seated fifty feet away with her back to him. It was a nice back, as far as he could tell, trim and curvy. He could see nothing else at the moment but had already examined the other parts – slim legs, narrow waist, not much of a chest, but then you can't have everything. What would happen, he reckoned, if (1) he slowly, over the next few days and weeks, put the move on her, (2) he was successful, and (3) he made sure they got caught? He'd be bounced from the firm, which at that moment seemed like a great idea. What would Bennie say about that? An ugly, involuntary dismissal from Scully & Pershing? Every young man has the right to chase women, and if you get caught, well, so what? At least you got fired for something worthwhile.

Bennie would lose his spy. His spy would get the boot without getting disbarred.

Interesting.

Of course, with his luck, there would probably be another video, this one of Kyle and Dale, and Bennie would get his dirty hands on it, and, well, who knows?

Kyle mulled these things over at $300 an hour. He didn't think about turning off the meter, because he wanted Placid to bleed.

He had learned that Dale earned a Ph.D. in mathematics at the age of twenty-five, from MIT no less, and that she had taught for a few years before deciding that the classroom was boring. She studied law at Cornell. Why she thought she could make the transition from the classroom to the courtroom was not clear, at least not to Kyle. Right now a class of struggling geometry students would seem like a parade. She was thirty years old, never married, and he had just begun the task of trying to unravel her withdrawn and complicated personality.

He stood to go for a walk, something to get the blood pumping into his stultified brain. 'You want some coffee?' he asked Dale.

'No, thanks,' she said, and actually smiled.

Two cups of strong coffee did little to stimulate his mind, and by late afternoon Kyle began to worry about permanent brain damage. To be on the safe side, he and Dale decided to wait until 7:00 p.m. before checking out. They left together, rode the elevator down without a word, both thinking the same thought – they were violating another of the unwritten rules by leaving so early. But they shook it off and walked four blocks to an Irish pub where Tim Reynolds had secured a booth and was almost finished with his first pint. He was with Everett, a first-year from NYU who'd been assigned to the commercial real estate practice group. After they sat down and got themselves situated, they pulled out their FirmFones. All four were on the table, much like loaded guns.

Dale ordered a martini. Kyle ordered a club soda, and when the waiter disappeared, Tim said, 'You don't drink?'

'No. I had to quit in college.' It was Kyle's standard line, and he knew all of the follow-ups it would provoke.

'You had to quit?'

'Yep. I was drinking too much, so I quit.'

'Rehab, AA, all that stuff?' Everett asked.

'No. I saw a counselor, and he convinced me that the drinking would only get worse. I went cold turkey and have never looked back.'

'That's awesome,' Tim said as he drained the pint of ale.

'I don't drink either,' Dale said. 'But after today, I'm hitting the bottle.' From someone with absolutely no sense of humor, this declaration was quite funny. After a good laugh, they settled into a rehash of their first day. Tim had billed 8.6 hours reading the legislative history of an old New York law aimed at discouraging class action lawsuits. Everett had billed 9 hours reading leases. But Kyle and Dale won the game with their descriptions of the dungeon and its thirty-five thousand files.

When their drinks arrived, they toasted Placid Mortgage and the 400,000 foreclosures it had precipitated. They toasted Tabor, who had vowed to stay at his desk until midnight. They toasted Scully & Pershing and its wonderful beginning salaries. Halfway through the martini, the gin hit Dale's mushy brain and she began giggling. When she ordered a second, Kyle excused himself and walked home.

At 5:30 on Tuesday, Kyle was wrapping up his second day in the dungeon and mentally drafting his letter of resignation. He would happily tell Bennie to go to hell, and he would happily face Elaine and her rape claim in a courtroom in

Pittsburgh. Anything would be better than what he was enduring.

He had survived the day by continually repeating the mantra 'But they're paying me $200,000 a year.'

But by 5:30, he didn't care what they were paying him. His FirmFone pinged with an e-mail, from Doug Peckham, and it read, 'Kyle, need some help. My office. Now if possible.'

He forgot his letter of resignation, jumped to his feet, and bolted for the door. To Dale he said as he dashed by, 'Gotta run see Doug Peckham, a litigation partner. He's got a project.' If this sounded cruel, then so be it. If it was boasting, he didn't care. She looked shocked and wounded, but he left her there, all alone in the Placid dungeon. He ran down two flights of stairs and was out of breath when he walked through Peckham's open door. The partner was on the phone, standing, fidgeting, and he waved Kyle into a fine leather chair across from his desk. When he signed off with a 'You're a moron, Slade, a true moron,' he looked at Kyle, forced a smile, and said, 'So how's it going so far?'

'Document Review.' Nothing else needed to be said.

'Sorry about that, but we all suffered through it. Look, I need a hand here. You up to it?' Peckham fell violently into his chair and began rocking, thrusting himself back and forth without taking his eyes off Kyle.

'Anything. Right now I'll shine your shoes.'

'They're shined. Gotta case here in the Southern District of New York, a big one. We're defending Barx in a class action filed by some folks who took their heartworm pills and eventually croaked. Big, messy, complicated case that's raging in a number of states. We go before Judge Cafferty on Thursday morning. You know him?'

I've been here two days, Kyle almost blurted. I don't know anybody. 'No.'

'Caffeine Cafferty. He's got some chemical imbalance that keeps him up all night and all day, and when he's off his meds, he calls up lawyers and screams at them because the cases are moving so slowly. When he's on his meds, he yells, too, but doesn't swear as much. Anyway, his schedule is called the Rocket Docket because he moves things along. Good judge, but a real pain in the ass. Anyway, this case has dragged on, and now he's threatening to send it to another jurisdiction.'

Kyle was scribbling notes as fast as possible. At the first break in the narrative, he said, 'Heartworms?'

'Actually, it's a drug that eats away plaque in the major blood vessels, including the left and right ventricles. From a medical point of view, it's complicated and nothing you should worry about. We have two partners with medical degrees handling that aspect of the case. Four partners total, as well as ten associates. I'm lead counsel.' He said this with far too much smugness. Then he jumped to his feet and lumbered over to the window for a quick look at the city. His white starched shirt was oversized and did a nice job of hiding his bulbous physique.

Bennie's summary had been typically to the point. Peckham's first marriage broke up thirteen months after he joined Scully & Pershing fresh out of Yale. His current wife was a lawyer who was a partner in a firm down the street. She, too, worked long hours. There were two small children. Their apartment on the Upper West Side was appraised for $3.5 million, and they owned the obligatory house in the Hamptons. Last year Doug earned $1.3 million; his wife, $1.2 million. He was regarded as a top litigator whose specialty was defending big pharmaceuticals, though he rarely went to trial. Six years earlier he was on the losing end of a major case involving a painkiller that caused suicides, at least in the opinion of the jury. Scully & Pershing sent him to a spa in Italy for a two-week treatment.

'Cafferty wants to get rid of the case,' he said, stretching a sore back. 'We, of course, will fight that. But, truthfully, I would rather see it in another jurisdiction. There are four possibilities – Duval County, Florida; downtown Memphis; a rural county in Nebraska called Fillmore; or Des Plaines, Illinois. Your mission, should you choose to accept it, is to research these four jurisdictions.' He fell into his chair again and began rocking. 'I need to know what juries do there. What are the verdicts? How do big companies fare in these places? Now, there are several jury research outfits that sell their data, and we subscribe to all of it, but it's not always accurate. Lots of numbers but not a lot of useful info. You gotta dig and dig. You gotta call lawyers in these four places and find the dirt. Are you in, Kyle?'

As if he had a choice. 'Sure. Sounds great.'

'I wouldn't call it great. I need this by 7:30 Thursday morning. Have you pulled an all-nighter yet?'

'No. I've only been here for—'

'Right, right. Well, get to work. Memo form, but nothing fancy. We'll meet here at 7:30 on Thursday with two other associates. You'll have ten minutes to do your summary. Anything else?'

'Not right now.'

'I'll be here until ten tonight, so zip me a note if you need something.'

'Thanks, and thanks for getting me out of Document Review.'

'What a waste.'

The desk phone was ringing as Kyle hustled out of the office. He went straight to the cube, grabbed his laptop, and raced off to the firm's cavernous main library on the thirty-ninth floor. There were at least four smaller libraries scattered throughout, but Kyle had yet to find them.

He could not remember being so excited over

a research project. It was a real case, with deadlines and an angry judge and strategic decisions in the air. The memo he was about to prepare would be read and relied on by real lawyers in the heat of battle.

Kyle almost felt sorry for the poor rookies left behind in Document Review. But he knew he'd be back there soon enough. He forgot dinner until almost 10:00 p.m., when he ate a cold sandwich from a machine while reading jury research. With no sleeping bag at hand, he left the library at midnight – there were at least twenty associates still there – and took a cab to his apartment. He slept four hours, then made the thirty-minute walk back to Broad Street in only twenty-two minutes. He was not about to start gaining weight. The firm's private gym on the fortieth floor was a joke because it was eternally empty. A few of the secretaries used it during lunch, but no lawyer would be caught dead there.

His meter began promptly at 5:00 a.m. By 9:00, he was calling trial lawyers and defense lawyers in Duval County, Florida, in and around Jacksonville. He had a long list of cases that had gone to trial, and he planned to talk to every lawyer he could get on the phone.

The more calls he made, the longer the list became. Lawyers in Florida, Memphis and western Tennessee, Lincoln and Omaha, and dozens in the Chicago area. He found more cases and more trials, and called more lawyers.

He tracked every Barx trial in the past twenty years and compared their verdicts.

There was no word from Doug Peckham, no text message or e-mail on the FirmFone always lying on the table next to the legal pad. Kyle was delighted to be given such free rein, such discretion. Dale sent an e-mail and asked about lunch. He met her in the cafeteria for a quick salad at 1:00 p.m. She was still imprisoned in the Placid tomb, but mercifully three other rookies had been sent in to help with the grunt work. All three were thinking about quitting. She seemed genuinely pleased that someone she knew had been given a real task.

'Save me some Placid files,' Kyle said as they left the cafeteria. 'I'll be back tomorrow.'

He left the library at midnight on Wednesday, after billing Barx for eighteen hours. Six the day before. He added two more early Thursday morning as he polished up the fifteen-page memo and rehearsed his ten-minute presentation to Peckham and a team of senior associates. At precisely 7:30, he approached the partner's door and saw that it was closed.

'He's expecting me at seven thirty,' he said politely to a secretary.

'I'll let him know,' she said without making a move toward the phone.

Five minutes passed as Kyle tried to settle his nerves and appear calm. He had a knot in his stomach, and there was sweat around his collar. Why? he kept asking himself. It's just a brief presentation before a friendly audience. We're on the same team, right? Ten minutes, fifteen. He could hear voices in Peckham's office. Finally, the door was opened by one of the associates, and Kyle walked in.

Peckham appeared surprised to see him. 'Oh, yes, Kyle, I forgot,' he said, snapping his fingers and frowning. 'I should've e-mailed. The hearing's been postponed. You're off the hook. Keep the memo. I might need it later.'

Kyle's mouth fell open and he glanced around. Two associates were huddled over a small worktable, papers everywhere. And two more were seated near the desk. All four seemed to be amused.

The False Deadline.

Kyle, of course, had heard of this little maneuver. The hapless associate is run through the grinder to produce a useless memo or brief that is time sensitive but will never be used. But the client will nonetheless get billed, and will pay, so even though the research is not needed, it is at least profitable.

Kyle had heard of the False Deadline, but didn't see this one coming. 'Uh, sure, no problem,' he said, backtracking.

'Thanks,' Peckham said as he flipped the page of another document. 'See you later.'

'Sure.'

Kyle was at the door when Peckham asked, 'Say, Kyle, where's the best place for Barx to try the case?'

'Nebraska, Fillmore County,' Kyle said eagerly.

Two of the associates laughed out loud, and the other two were highly entertained. One of them said, 'Nebraska? No one tries cases in Nebraska.'

'Thanks, Kyle,' Peckham said, patronizing. 'Nice work.' And please get out of here.

For $200,000 a year, plus treats, the job would naturally have its moments of humiliation. You're getting paid for this, Kyle kept repeating as he slowly made his way up the stairs. Take it in stride. Be tough. Happens to everyone.

Back in the dungeon, he managed to smile. When Dale asked 'How did it go?' he said, 'It's hard to say.' At the far end of the room two associates were plowing through mortgage files. Kyle nodded at them, then parked himself near Dale, arranged his pen, legal pad, and FirmFone. He opened a box, removed a file, and reentered the world of Placid Mortgage. It was known territory, and he felt oddly safe there. He would not be harmed or humiliated. A long career as a document reviewer would no doubt be dull, but it would also be much less hazardous than that of a litigator.

Chapter 17

When Kyle left the office late Friday afternoon, he considered his first week to be a success, though a dismal one. He billed Placid thirty hours and Barx Biomed twenty-six, and though virtually all of this valuable time would eventually mean little to either client, he wasn't paid to worry about such things. He was there to do one thing – bill. If he kept up the pace and managed only fifty hours a week, he would hit twenty-five hundred for the year, a high number for a first-year and one that would catch the attention of the higher-ups.

For the week, Tabor the Gunner billed fifty hours. Dale, forty-four. Tim Reynolds, forty-three.

It was amazing how consumed they were with the clock after only five days on the job.

He walked to his apartment, changed into jeans, stuffed a phone in each pocket, and headed for the ballpark. The Mets were at home against the Pirates, who were already guaranteed another losing season. With seventeen games to go, the Mets were in first place, two games ahead of the Phillies, and primed for another choke in the stretch.

Kyle had paid cash for two tickets sold by a broker recommended by a paralegal at the firm. As he made his way to Shea Stadium, he picked up his surveillance as it was picking up him.

His seat was fifteen rows behind the third-base dugout. The night was hot; the Mets were in first; the place was packed. He timed his entrance perfectly and sat down just as the first pitch was thrown in the bottom of the first. To his right was a young boy holding a baseball glove and eating ice cream. To his left was a real fan with a Mets cap, Mets jersey, blue and orange sweatbands, even goofy Mets eyeglasses. Under the cap and behind the glasses was Joey Bernardo, who had spent his entire life in Pittsburgh and hated the Mets almost as much as he hated the Phillies.

'Do not acknowledge me,' Kyle said as he watched the field.

'Don't worry. Right now I hate your guts. And I hate the Mets almost as much as I hate you.'

'Thanks. I like the glasses.'

'Can I take them off? I can't see a damned thing.'

'No.'

They were talking out of the corners of their mouths, just loud enough to hear each other.

Shea was alive with every pitch, and there was little chance of being overheard.

Joey took a sip of a tall beer. 'Are they really following you?'

'Oh, yes. Every day, everywhere.'

'Do they know that you know?'

'I don't think so.'

'But why?'

'Basic espionage tradecraft.'

'Of course.'

'Information is crucial. The more they watch and listen, the more they know about me. If they know what I eat, drink, wear, watch, listen to, and who I talk to and hang out with and where I like to shop and browse and sneak away to, then they might one day be able to use it all to their advantage. Sounds pretty dull to you and me, but not to these guys.'

More beer as Joey absorbed this.

A ball bounced off the left-field wall, scoring a run, and the crowd was on its feet. Kyle and Joey acted like all the other fans. When things had settled down, Kyle continued: 'For example, I've found this wonderful little store in midtown that sells all sorts of spy gadgets. Tiny cameras, hidden mikes, phone-tapping devices, and some high-tech stuff that the military has left behind. It's run by a couple of misfits who claim to be ex-CIA, but then people who are really ex-CIA don't talk about it. I found the store online, at the office, not at the apartment, and I've been there twice when I was able to shake surveillance. I might need the store one day, but if the goons knew I had discovered the place, they would really be interested.'

'This is too weird.'

A lady in front of Joey turned around and offered a curious glance. They did not speak for the rest of the first inning.

'How about the report on Elaine?' Joey whispered.

'It worries me.'

'So what's next?'

'I think you should go see her.'

'No way.'

'It's easy. Just bump into her and see what happens.'

'Right! Drive to Scranton, a town I can't recall seeing in the past ten years, somehow find her, recognize her, assume she'll recognize me, then what? Have a friendly little chat about the last time we were together? Have a laugh for old times' sake? Hell, Kyle, she accused me of rape.'

'Shhhh,' Kyle hissed softly. The word 'rape' sort of hung in the thick air, but no one reacted to it.

'Sorry,' Joey whispered, and they watched the game for a long time.

A ferocious argument erupted at first base after a close call, and all fifty thousand fans had an opinion. In the roar, Kyle said, 'It would be an interesting meeting. To see how she reacts. Will she talk to you? Is she bitter, angry, full of vengeance? You take the high road and say that the encounter has always troubled you, that you want to talk about it. See if she'll meet you for a drink and a serious conversation. You're not going to admit anything, you just want to see how she feels. Maybe you want closure. What's there to lose?'

'What if she recognizes me, pulls out a gun, and bam!?'

'I'll take care of Blair.' Kyle managed this with a grin, though the thought of spending any more time with Joey's girl was not pleasant.

'Thanks. She's pregnant, you know. Thanks for asking.'

'Why is she pregnant?'

'Basic biology. But we're both surprised.'

'Congratulations, Daddy.'

'Getting married is one thing, but I'm not so sure about this fatherhood business.'

'I thought her career was at full throttle.'

'Yep. Me too. She said she was on the pill, but I don't know.'

This was not a topic Kyle wanted to explore. The more they talked, the easier conversation became, and that was not wise. 'I'm going to the restroom,' Kyle said.

'Bring me a beer.'

'No. I don't know you, remember?'

'Come on, Kyle. You think someone here is watching you?'

'With binoculars. At least two of them. They followed me here, probably bought tickets from a scalper outside the gates, and now they're watching.'

'But why?'

'Basic surveillance, Joey. I'm a valuable asset, yet they don't trust me. You should read some spy novels.'

'That's your problem. Too much fiction.'

Kyle took his time between innings. He visited the men's room, then bought a diet soda and peanuts. When he returned to his seat, he struck up a conversation with the kid on his right, a loyal Met fan who knew every player and all their stats. His father was in advertising, and Kyle managed to seem intrigued with that career. He cracked peanuts, scattered the hulls at his feet, and ignored Joey for a long time.

Joey, still half-blinded by the oversized Mets eyeglasses, suffered in silence. The Pirates were down four runs after four innings, and he was ready to leave. Kyle eventually re-shifted, and began studying the scoreboard in center field. 'Any word from Baxter?' he said without moving his jaws.

'Nothing. I think they've locked him in a cave.'

'I know the feeling. I've been in a dungeon all week.'

'I don't want to hear it. For the money they're paying you, no complaints.'

'Okay, okay. They know that he's in rehab, and they probably know where he is,' Kyle said as a long fly ball was caught on the warning track.

'They?'

'The goons. Their leader told me last week that he's in rehab.'

'How often do you meet with this guy?'

'Too often.'

'Have you handed over any secrets?'

'Nope. I have not been compromised.'

Joey sipped his beer, swallowed slowly, and with the cup in front of his mouth said, 'If they know about Baxter, are they keeping tabs on me?'

'It's possible. Play it safe. Vary your movements. Be careful with all correspondence.'

'Oh, this is just great.'

'My apartment is full of cameras and mikes. They come and go when they wish. I don't have an alarm system, don't want one, but I know when they've been there. Everything I do in my apartment is subject to being watched and recorded. But they don't know that I know, so I give them nothing of consequence.'

'So you're outsmarting these professional intelligence agents?'

'I think so.'

Another long pause in the conversation as the Pirates changed pitchers again.

'What's the endgame, Kyle?'

'I don't have one. I'm taking small, safe steps. Next, we make contact with the girl and see how bad things are there.'

'Pretty bad, I'd guess.'

'Let's see.'

Kyle reached for his vibrating pocket and yanked out the FirmFone. He scrolled down, found the message, and felt like cursing. 'What is it?' Joey asked, trying not to look at the phone.

'It's a partner. He's got a project. Wants me at the office at seven in the morning.'

'Tomorrow's Saturday, Kyle.'

'Just another day at the office.'

'Are these guys crazy?'

'No, just greedy.'

During the seventh-inning stretch, Kyle eased out of his seat and made his way to the gates. Joey stayed until the eighth, and finally he left as his beloved Pirates were losing their ninetieth game.

Jeans were allowed on Saturdays and Sundays. The fact that there was a dress code for the weekend, however relaxed, said much about the practice of corporate law on Wall Street.

Why were they even there?

Kyle wore jeans, as did Dale, who looked spectacular in a pair of tight ones. Tim Reynolds wore starched khakis. All three were dazed at the reality of being in a small conference room on the thirty-fourth floor at 7:00 a.m. on the second Saturday of their fledgling careers. They joined four older associates, four young men Kyle had not had the pleasure of meeting or even seeing during his first two weeks on the job. Passing introductions were made, but only because they were expected.

The partner who had called the meeting was nowhere to be seen. His name was Tobias Roland, Toby behind his back, and of all the sizzling gossip Kyle had heard so far, the worst had been about Toby. Toby stories were abundant, and very few were even remotely flattering. Yale undergrad, Columbia Law, poor kid from a rough neighborhood with a gigantic chip on his shoulder. Brilliant, ruthless, conniving, he'd made partner in only five years, primarily because he worked harder than the rest of the workaholics and never relaxed. His idea of time off was a ten-minute tryst with a secretary on the sofa in his office. Most secretaries were terrified of him, too frightened to complain or file suit. Some, though, found him sexy enough for a quick romp. For fun he berated young associates, often cursing them in the foulest of language for the smallest of infractions. He intimidated the other partners because he was smarter and always better prepared. At the age of forty-four, he was the top-producing (billing) litigator in the firm and had not lost a jury trial in eight years. Toby was in demand by the in-house lawyers of many major corporations. A year earlier, Kyle had read and clipped an article in *Fortune* touting the greatness of Scully & Pershing's 'fanciest litigator.'

When Toby beckoned, you went running, albeit with a great deal of trepidation.

In his place that morning was a senior associate named Bronson, who, as he explained without a trace of enthusiasm, was standing in for Mr. Roland, who was just down the hall working on another aspect of the lawsuit at hand. He might pop in at any moment, and this prospect kept everyone wide awake.

Their client was a major oil company that was about to be sued by a Dutch firm over some disputed reserves in the Gulf of Mexico. The lawsuit was expected to be filed in New Orleans, but Mr. Roland had decided to file a preemptive lawsuit in New York. The plan was to file it first thing Monday morning. It was an ambush, a daring tactic that could backfire, the type of risky maneuver that Toby was famous for.

After a few minutes of listening to a lawsuit described in terms reminiscent of the D-day invasion, Kyle realized that his Saturday and Sunday were shot to hell and would be spent researching jurisdictional issues in the law library. He glanced at his FirmFone, scrolled down through the e-mails, and something caught his eye. At 7:30 on a Saturday morning, the firm was sending an e-mail to all lawyers announcing the resignation of Gavin Meade, a fourth-year associate in litigation. No details. No comments. Nothing but a quiet and quick exit.

Everybody has secrets, Bennie said. How did he do it? Perhaps an anonymous package mailed to someone in Human Resources. Affidavits, police records, the works. Poor Meade, ten years removed from his crime and hustling through the grind at $400,000 a year, when suddenly he gets a summons to a meeting with closed doors.

Bronson was rattling on about being the hub of a wooden wheel, with spokes running down and out to the seven associates below him, and several running upward to Mr. Roland and the other litigation partners. At the hub, he, Bronson, would direct traffic between the big boys and the rookies. He would organize the work, supervise the research, and handle correspondence with the partners. Everything crossed his desk.

Time was crucial. If word leaked, the Dutch firm and its lawyers might do all sorts of evil things. The nation's oil supply hung in the balance, perhaps even Western civilization.

Off they went to the library.

Chapter 18

After a series of phone calls that became more and more tense, a deal was finally reached. Dr. Boone and Uncle Wally acquiesced, but managed to keep one string attached. Baxter would leave early, but spend three nights in a halfway house in Reno before 'reentry' into the real world. A hundred and five days after arriving sloppy drunk, with a blood alcohol content of 0.28, and with significant residues of cocaine in his system, Baxter rode through the gates and left behind the safety of the Washoe Retreat. He was squeaky-clean and ten pounds lighter, and not only had he kicked booze and drugs, he had also quit smoking. He was fit, tanned, and clear-headed and thoroughly believed he had conquered his demons and would henceforth live the sober life. He was armed for battle with the teachings of Dr. Boone and the other counselors. He had confessed his sins and surrendered to a higher power, whatever and whoever that was.

At the age of twenty-five, he was beginning a new life, and Baxter was both proud and apprehensive, even frightened. As the miles passed, he found himself more uncomfortable. His confidence was rapidly disappearing.

He had failed so many times in so many ways. It was a family tradition. Was it in his DNA?

An orderly drove him from the clinic in the Nightingale Mountains into Reno, a two-hour drive in which little was said. As they approached the city, they passed a splashy billboard advertising an imported beer in a cold green bottle. The slinky young woman holding it could entice any man to do almost anything. Fear hit Baxter harder. It consumed him, and beads of sweat lined his forehead. He wanted to turn around, to run back to the clinic, where there was no alcohol and no temptations. But he said nothing.

Hope Village was in a run-down section of Reno – abandoned buildings, cheap casinos, and bars. It was the domain of Brother Manny, the founder, pastor, and leader of Hope Village. He was waiting at the curb outside the church's front door when Baxter stepped onto the hot sidewalk. He grabbed Baxter's hand and shook it violently. 'Mr. Tate, may I call you Baxter?'

The question suggested its own answer. He was Baxter, not Mr. Tate.

'Sure,' Baxter said, his spine stiffened from this physical assault.

'I'm Brother Manny,' he said, placing his

thick left arm on Baxter's shoulder, completing a rather rough howdy do. 'Welcome to Hope Village.'

He was about fifty, Hispanic, bronze skin, gray hair pulled back tightly into a long ponytail that fell to his waist, warm eyes, big toothy smile, a small scar beside his left nostril and a larger one on his right cheek. His face was adorned with a soft white goatee that had been pampered for many years.

'Another escapee from Washoe Retreat,' he said with a deep, melodious voice. 'How is the good Dr. Boone doing up there?'

'Fine,' Baxter said. Brother Manny's nose was about five inches from his. Close contact obviously did not bother him, but it made Baxter uncomfortable. 'He sends his regards.'

'A fine man. Come, I'll show you around. We have you for just three nights, as I understand.'

'That's right.'

They began walking slowly. Brother Manny kept one arm across Baxter's shoulders. He was a large man, with a thick barrel chest, and he wore dungarees and a white linen shirt – top two buttons open – with a long tail left out so that it swept behind him. Sandals, no socks.

The church had once belonged to an affluent white congregation that fled to the suburbs. As Baxter shuffled through the tour, he also got the backstory. Manny Lucera had found the Lord during his second term in prison – armed robbery, the proceeds from which were meant to buy drugs for personal consumption – and upon his parole he was led by the Spirit to Reno to start his ministry. Seventeen years ago, and the Lord had blessed him mightily. The church had grown and now housed a shelter for the homeless in the basement, a soup kitchen that fed anyone who showed up, a community center for the poor kids in the neighborhood, an intake center for women and children fleeing abusive men, and there were plans for an orphanage. The old buildings next door had been purchased and renovated. The complex was crawling with people – employees, volunteers, street people – and they almost bowed in deference when they saw Brother Manny.

They parked themselves on a picnic table in the shade and sipped canned lemonade. 'What's your drug?' Manny asked.

'Coke, booze, but I didn't say no to anything,' Baxter admitted. After fifteen weeks of baring his soul to people who already knew everything, he did not hesitate to tell the truth.

'For how long?'

'Started slow when I was about fourteen. Picked up steam as I got older. I'm twenty-five now, so eleven years.'

'Where are you from?'

'Pittsburgh, originally.'

'Background?'

'Privileged.'

Brother Manny issued the questions and absorbed the answers with such ease that after fifteen minutes together, Baxter felt as though he could chat for hours and tell him everything.

'First rehab?'

'Second.'

'I did every drug you can imagine, and some you've never heard of, for twenty years. I bought, sold, smuggled, and manufactured drugs. I got knifed four times, shot three, and went to prison twice for drugs. I lost my first wife and two children because of drugs and alcohol. I lost my chance for an education. I lost eight years because of prison. I almost lost my life. I know all about addictions because I've been there. I'm a certified drug and alcohol counselor, and I work with addicts every day. Are you an addict?'

'Yes.'

'Bless you, brother. Do you know Christ?'

'I guess. My mother took me to church every Christmas.'

Brother Manny smiled and slowly wiggled his large rear end off the table. 'Let me show you your room. It's not the Ritz, but it'll do.' The homeless shelter was a large basement room with a temporary partition dividing it – women on one side, men on the other. It was open, with rows of Army surplus cots in neat lines. 'Most of these people work during the day. They're not bums,' Brother Manny was saying. 'They'll start drifting in around 6:00 p.m. Here's your room.'

Near the showers, there were two small private rooms with nicer cots and portable fans. Brother Manny opened the door to one and said,

'You can have this one. It's for a supervisor. To get a private room, you must have a job, so you'll help with the dinner preparation, then later, when everybody's tucked in, you'll help with security.' He uttered these definitive statements in such a way that any thought of protest was immediately cut off and out of the question.

Baxter's world was spinning. He'd begun the day in the cushy confines of a four-star rehab ranch, and done so with giddy thoughts of finally leaving. Now he was in the hot basement of an old church that was home to fifty-two of the poorest souls in America, and he was expected to live with them for the next three days. And to cook their meals and break up their fights.

Baxter Tate, of the Pittsburgh Tate dynasty. Bankers, blue bloods who lived in mansions handed down from one miserable generation to the next, proud and arrogant people who married into other, similar clans, thus producing even shallower gene pools.

How had he reached this point in his young life?

Legally, he could leave anytime he wanted. Hit the door, find a cab, never look back. There was no court order restraining him. Uncle Wally might be disappointed, but that would be the extent of Baxter's worries if he fled.

'Are you okay?' Brother Manny asked.

'No.' It was refreshing to be so honest.

'Take a nap. You look pale.'

⋆

He couldn't sleep because of the heat. After an hour, he sneaked away and found himself roaming downtown Reno. He had a late lunch in a diner – his first burger and fries in months. He had the money to get a hotel room for a day or two, and that plan consumed him as he zig-zagged through the streets. He passed and repassed the casinos. He'd never been a gambler, but every casino had a bar, didn't it? Of course the bars were off-limits, but he couldn't stomach the thought of returning to Hope Village, at least not now.

At a blackjack table he pulled out five $20 bills, got some green chips, and played the $5 game for a few minutes. An aging cocktail waitress swept by, asked what he wanted to drink. 'A bottle of water,' he said without hesitation, then patted himself on the back. The only other player at the table was a cowboy, black hat and all, with a bottle of beer in front of him. Baxter drank his water, played his hands, and occasionally glanced at the bottle of beer. It looked so harmless. So beautiful.

When his chips had been taken by the dealer, he left the table and wandered around the casino floor. It was a dreadful place, sparsely filled with people who had no business being there, gambling with money they could not afford to lose. He walked by a sports bar, with wide screens showing old football games. The weekend's point spreads were posted. The bar was empty. He settled onto a stool and ordered water.

What would Dr. Boone say about this? Not six hours into 'reentry' and he was already at a bar. Relax, Dr. Boone. It's just water. If I can resist the urge here at ground zero, then the next place will be easy. He sipped water and occasionally glanced at the rows of liquor bottles. Why were there so many different shapes and sizes? So many different types of spirits? One entire row was taken by flavored vodkas, delicious liquids he had consumed by the barrel back in the days when he was a drunk.

Thank God those days were over.

In the distance, across the floor somewhere, a siren squealed and bells erupted. A lucky slot player had hit a jackpot, and the racket was to remind everyone just how easy it was to win. The bartender filled a glass with a draft beer, then slammed it in front of Baxter. 'On the house!' he proclaimed. 'Super Slot Jackpot!'

Free drinks for everyone at the bar, which was nobody but Baxter. He almost said, 'Hey, pal, take it away. I don't drink anymore.' But the bartender was gone, plus it would sound silly. How many nondrinkers sidle up to a casino bar at three o'clock in the afternoon?

The glass was frosty, the beer ice-cold. It was darker in color, and Baxter looked at the tap. Nevada Pale Ale. One he'd never tried. His mouth was dry, so he sipped water. For 105 days he'd been hammered by Dr. Boone and the other pros at Washoe Retreat into believing that another drink would eventually lead him back to his addictions. He'd watched and listened as other patients, or guests as they were called, struggled through detox and told their stories of repeated failures. Don't ever be fooled, they warned repeatedly, you cannot handle a single drink. Total abstinence is required.

Maybe so.

Small bubbles of water formed on the glass, then began to run down to the napkin under it.

He was twenty-five years old, and he never truly believed, not even in his purest moment back at Washoe, that he would live the rest of his life without a drink. Somewhere deep down in his soul he knew he could find the willpower to have a drink, maybe a couple, then stop for the night before things got out of hand. If he planned to drink, why not start now? The last time he tortured himself for fourteen days before breaking down. For two weeks he lied to himself and especially to his friends about loving the life of sobriety, and every single moment he craved a drink. Why go through the misery again?

The beer was getting warm.

He heard the voices of his counselors. He remembered the tears and confessions of the other guests. He heard himself proclaim the gospel of the sober – 'I am an alcoholic, weak and powerless, in need of strength from a higher being.'

And they were weak, those other losers back at Washoe Retreat. But not Baxter. He could handle a few drinks because he was stronger. He rationalized that he would, under no circumstances, succumb to the romance and horror of cocaine. Nor would he indulge in hard liquor. Just a little beer, occasionally, and he might get serious about wine.

No big deal.

Still, he could not make himself reach forward and touch the glass. It was eighteen inches away, well within his grasp, just standing there like a coiled rattler ready to kill. Then it was a luscious treat that delivered a pleasant buzz. Back and forth, back and forth. Evil versus good.

'You need to make new friends,' Dr. Boone had said repeatedly. 'And you can't go back to your old haunts. Find some new places, new friends, new challenges, a different place to live.'

Well, how about this, Dr. Boone? Sitting here for the very first time in a run-down Reno casino he couldn't remember the name of? Never been here before? Ha-ha.

Both hands were free, and at some point Baxter realized his right hand was shaking slightly. And his breathing was labored and heavy.

'You okay, buddy?' the bartender asked as he walked by.

Yes, no. Baxter nodded something but couldn't speak. His eyes were locked on the glass of beer. Where was he? What was he doing? Six hours after leaving rehab he was in a bar brawling with himself over whether he should take another drink. He was already a loser. Look where he was.

With his left hand, he reached forward, touched the glass, then slid it slowly toward him. He stopped when it was six inches away. He could smell the barley and hops. The glass was still cold, or cold enough.

The war shifted from good versus evil to run versus stay. He almost managed to shove himself away from the bar and sprint back through the slots to the front door. Almost. Oddly, it was Keefe who helped him make the decision. Keefe was his best friend at Washoe, and Keefe was from a wealthy family that was paying for the third rehab. The first two tanked when Keefe convinced himself that a little pot was harmless.

Baxter whispered to himself, 'If I drink this beer now, and if things turn out badly, I can always go back to Washoe, and with two failures, I'll be convinced that total abstinence is required. Just like Keefe. But right now I really want this beer.' With both hands he clasped the glass, raised it slowly, sniffing as it grew closer. He smiled when the cold glass touched his lips. The first sip of Nevada Pale Ale was the most magnificent nectar he'd ever tasted. He savored it, eyes closed, face serene.

From over his right shoulder someone yelled loudly, 'There you are, Baxter!'

He almost choked and he almost dropped the glass. He jerked around and there was Brother Manny, closing fast and obviously not happy. 'What are you doing?' he demanded as he lowered a heavy hand on Baxter's shoulder and seemed ready to trade punches.

Baxter wasn't sure what he was doing. He was drinking a beer, one that was definitely off-limits, but he was so horrified at the moment he couldn't speak. Brother Manny delicately took the glass and slid it down the bar. 'Get rid of this,' he growled at the bartender, then he sat on the stool next to Baxter and moved in low until his nose was once again five inches away. 'Listen to me, son,' he said in a soft voice. 'I cannot make you leave this place right now. That is your decision. But if you want me to help you, then say so. I'll get you out of here, take you back to my church, make some coffee, and we'll tell some stories.'

Baxter's shoulders sagged and his chin dropped. The ale was still attacking his taste buds.

'This could be the most important decision of your life,' Brother Manny said. 'Right now, at this moment. Stay or go. If you stay, you'll be dead in five years. If you want to go, then say so and we'll leave together.'

Baxter closed his eyes and said, 'I'm so weak.'

'Yes, but I'm not. Let me get you out of here.'

'Please.'

Brother Manny practically lifted him off the stool, then put a thick arm around his shoulders. They slowly made their way past the slot machines and empty roulette wheels, and they were almost to the front door when Brother Manny realized that Baxter was crying. The tears made him smile. An addict must hit the bottom before he starts his climb.

The pastor's office was a large cluttered room next to the sanctuary. The secretary, Brother Manny's wife, brought them a pot of strong coffee and two mismatched mugs. Baxter sat low in an old leather sofa and sipped furiously, as if he could rinse away the taste of the beer. The tears had stopped, for now.

Brother Manny sat close by on a wooden rocker, and as he talked, he moved slowly back and forth. 'I was in prison in California,' he was saying. 'The second time around, in a gang, doing worse stuff on the inside than we did on the streets. I got careless one day, got away from my turf, and the rival gang jumped me. Woke up in the prison hospital with broken bones and cuts and such. Cracked skull. Terrible pain. I remember thinking death would be welcome. I was so sick of living, sick of my life, sick of the miserable person I was. I knew that if I survived and one day got paroled again, I'd end up on the streets, playing the same game. Where I grew up, you either went to prison or you died young. Sounds very different from the way you grew up, doesn't it, Baxter?'

He shrugged.

'In many ways it is, in many ways it is not. My life was all about myself, much like yours. I loved the bad things, just like you. Pleasure, selfishness, pride – that was my life, and it's been yours, I suppose.'

'Oh, yes.'

'It's all sin, and it all leads to the same end – misery, pain, destruction, ruin, then death. That's where you're headed, son, and you're in a hurry to get there.'

Baxter nodded slightly. 'So what happened?'

'I got lucky and lived, and not long afterward I met an inmate, a career criminal who would never be eligible for parole, and he was the gentlest, sweetest, happiest person I'd ever talked to. Had no worries, every day was beautiful, life was grand, and this from a man who'd spent fifteen years in max security. Through a prison ministry, he'd been exposed to the gospel of Christ, and he became a believer. He said he was praying for me, as he prayed for a lot of the bad guys in prison. He invited me to a Bible study one night, and I listened to other inmates tell their stories and praise God for his forgiveness and love and strength and promise of eternal salvation. Imagine, a bunch of hardened criminals locked away in a rotten prison singing songs of praise to their Lord. Pretty powerful stuff, and I needed some of it. I needed forgiveness, because there were lots of sins in my past. I needed peace, because I'd been at war my entire life. I needed love, because I hated everybody. I needed strength, because deep inside I knew how weak I was. I needed happiness, because I'd been miserable for so long. So we prayed together, me and those bad boys who were like little lambs, and I confessed to God that I was a sinner, and that I wanted salvation through Jesus Christ. My life changed in an instant, Baxter, a change so overwhelming I still can't believe it. The Holy Spirit entered my soul, and the old Manny Lucera died. A new one was born, one whose past was forgiven and his eternity secured.'

'What about the drugs?'

'Forgotten. The power of the Holy Spirit is far greater than human desire. I've seen it a thousand times with addicts who try everything to quit – rehab clinics, state facilities, shrinks and doctors, fancy meds sold as substitutes. When you're an addict, you're powerless in the face of booze and drugs. Strength comes from somewhere else. For me, it comes from the power of the Holy Spirit.'

'I don't feel very strong right now.'

'You're not. Look at yourself. From Washoe Retreat to a cheap bar in a run-down casino in a few hours. That might be a record, Baxter.'

'I didn't want to go to that bar.'

'Of course not. But you did.'

'Why?' His voice was soft, fading.

'Because you've never said no.'

A tear rolled down Baxter's cheek, and he wiped it with the back of his hand. 'I don't want to go back to L.A.'

'You can't, son.'

'Can you help me? I'm pretty shaky here, okay? I mean, I'm really scared.'

'Let's pray together, Baxter.'

'I'll try.'

Chapter 19

Six months after the Trylon-Bartin dispute went public with the filing of the lawsuit, the battleground had been defined and the troops were in place. Both sides had filed ponderous motions designed to capture the higher ground, but so far no advantage had been gained. They were of course haggling over deadlines, schedules, issues, discovery, and who got to see what documents, and when.

With the waves of lawyers working in sync, the case was plodding along. A trial was nowhere in sight, but then it was far too early. With monthly billings to Trylon averaging $5.5 million, why push the case to a conclusion?

On the other side, Bartin Dynamics was paying just as much for a vigorous and gold-plated defense coordinated by the bare-knuckle litigators at Agee, Poe & Epps. APE had committed forty lawyers to the case and, like Scully, had such a deep bench that it could send in another wave whenever necessary.

The hottest issue so far was no surprise to either set of litigators. When the forced marriage of Trylon and Bartin unraveled, when their clumsy joint venture blew up, there had been a virtual slugfest for the documents. Hundreds of thousands, perhaps millions of documents had been generated during the development of the B-10 HyperSonic Bomber. Researchers employed by Trylon grabbed all the documents they could. Researchers for Bartin did the same. Software was routed and rerouted, and some of it was destroyed. Hardware controlled by one company found its way to the other. Thousands of secured files disappeared. Crates of printed documents were hoarded and hidden. And throughout the melee each company accused the other of lying, espionage, outright thievery. When the dust settled, neither knew exactly what the other possessed.

Because of the supersensitive nature of the research, the Pentagon watched in horror as the two companies behaved outrageously. The Pentagon, as well as several intelligence agencies, leaned heavily on Trylon and Bartin to keep their dirty laundry private, but they were ultimately not successful. The fight was now controlled by the lawyers and the courts.

A major task for Mr. Wilson Rush and his Scully & Pershing team was to accumulate, index, copy, and store all documents in the possession of Trylon. A warehouse was leased in

Wilmington, North Carolina, about a mile from the Trylon testing facility where most of the B-10 research had taken place. After it was leased, it was completely renovated and made fire-, wind-, and waterproof. All windows were removed and replaced with a six-inch cinder-block wall. A Washington security firm wired the warehouse with twenty closed-circuit cameras. The four large doors were equipped with infrared alarms and metal detectors. Armed guards patrolled the empty warehouse long before any of the documents arrived.

When they did arrive, they came in unmarked tractor-trailer rigs, complete with more armed guards. Dozens of deliveries were made over a two-week period in mid-September. The warehouse, nicknamed Fort Rush, came to life as ton after ton of paperwork was stacked neatly in white cardboard boxes, all waiting to be organized into a system understood only by the lawyers up in New York.

The warehouse was leased by Scully & Pershing. Every contract was signed by Wilson Rush – contracts for the renovations, security operations, transporting of documents, everything. Once the documents entered the warehouse, they were deemed AWP – Attorneys' Work Product – and thus subject to a different set of rules regarding disclosure to the other side.

Mr. Rush selected ten associates from his litigation team, ten of the brightest and most trusted. These unlucky souls were shipped to

Wilmington and introduced to Fort Rush, a long, windowless hangar of a building with shiny concrete floors and a pungent industrial smell to it. In the center was the mountain of boxes. Along both sides were rows of empty folding tables, and beyond the tables were ten large, fierce-looking copy machines, with wires and cables running everywhere. The copiers were, of course, state-of-the-art color and capable of instant scanning, collating, even stapling.

Far away from their New York offices, the associates were allowed to wear jeans and running shoes, and they were promised bigger bonuses and other goodies. But nothing could compensate them for the dismal job of physically copying and scanning a million documents. And in Wilmington! Most were married, with spouses and children back home, though of the ten, four had already suffered through a divorce. And it was quite likely that Fort Rush would be the cause of even more marital problems.

They began their forbidding task under the direction of Mr. Rush himself. Every document was copied twice, in a split second, and instantly scanned into the firm's virtual library. Several weeks down the road, when the task was complete, the library would be accessible by a secured code, and once inside, a lawyer could locate any document in a matter of seconds. The firm's computer experts designed the library and were supremely confident that its security was impenetrable.

To impress upon the associates the gravity of their seemingly mindless work, Mr. Rush stayed for three days and was involved in the unpacking, sorting, scanning, copying, and repacking. When he left, two other litigation partners remained and directed traffic. Such mundane work was normally contracted out to a copying service and supervised by the firm's litigation support staff, but that was far too risky with these documents. They had to be handled by real lawyers who appreciated their importance. The real lawyers manning the copiers averaged about $400,000 in salary, and most had at least one degree from an Ivy League school. At no point in their graduate or postgraduate studies could they have pictured themselves running copiers, but after four or five years with Scully & Pershing they were shockproof.

The rotation began after the first week. Eight days in the warehouse, then four days in New York, then back to Wilmington. The assignments were staggered, and a total of fifteen associates were eventually used. All were forbidden to discuss any aspect of Fort Rush with anyone in New York. Security and confidentiality were paramount.

The first project took six weeks. Two point two million documents were copied, indexed, and added to the library. The associates were freed from Fort Rush and flown back to New York on a chartered jet.

By then, Bennie knew exactly where the

warehouse was located and had a general idea of its security features, but his interest in these matters was only passing. What Bennie wanted, of course, was access to the virtual library, access only his spy could deliver.

Chapter 20

For another $1,000, the security firm in Pittsburgh watched Elaine Keenan long enough to determine her daily routine. She usually had lunch with some co-workers at a sandwich shop not far from the parks and recreation complex where she worked.

A chance encounter would have to be believable, and Joey couldn't sell the idea of bumping into her in the lesbian bar she and her roommate occasionally frequented. He wasn't sure he could sell any encounter with Elaine. Aside from the casual sex five and a half years earlier, he'd never really known her. She had been one of several groupies around the Beta fraternity, and he'd tried to forget all of them.

The security firm provided three color photos. Joey had studied them for hours and was not convinced he'd ever met the girl. Kyle, however, had studied them and claimed to recall her vividly.

Now, at the age of twenty-three, her dark hair was tinted a deep red and worn very short. There was no makeup, no lipstick, nothing but matching tattoos around her forearms. If she had any interest in being attractive, it was not apparent. Somewhere under all the attitude was a cute girl, but sex appeal was unimportant.

Joey swallowed hard, cursed Kyle again, and entered the sandwich shop. He eased behind her as she waited in line to order, and after a few minutes, as the line moved slowly forward, managed to bump into her. 'Sorry,' he quickly said with a wide fake smile.

She smiled back, but said nothing. He moved a step closer and said, 'Hey, you were at Duquesne a few years ago, weren't you?' Her two co-workers glanced back but were not interested.

'Briefly,' she said, eyeing him carefully, searching for any clue.

He snapped his fingers as if trying to recall something. 'Elaine? Right? Can't think of the last name.'

'That's right. And who are you?'

'Joey Bernardo. I was in Beta.'

A look of horror swept over her face, and she dropped her gaze to the floor. For a moment she was frozen, unable to speak, ready, it seemed, to erupt. Then she shuffled a step to keep pace in line. She turned her back on the man who once raped her, a man who walked away from the crime not only unpunished but completely vindicated. Joey watched her from the corner of an eye and felt uneasy for several reasons. First, she was obviously frightened by him, but since she considered herself the victim and him the rapist, this was not surprising. It was also uncomfortable being this close to someone he'd once had sex with, regardless of how casual or how uneventful it now seemed.

She turned halfway to him and hissed, 'What are you doing here?'

'I'm eating lunch, same as you.'

'Would you please leave?' Her voice was barely audible, but one of her co-workers turned around and glared at Joey.

'No. I'm just getting a sandwich.'

Nothing else was said as they ordered and moved down to the pickup counter. Elaine hurried off to a distant table and ate quickly with her two friends. Joey ate alone at a small table near the front door. The note was already prepared. It read: 'Elaine: I'd like to talk to you about what happened. Please call my cell at 412-866-0940. I'll be in Scranton until 9:00 tomorrow. Joey Bernardo.' He hauled his tray back to the counter, then walked to her table, handed her the note without a word, and disappeared.

Two hours later, she called.

At 5:00 p.m. sharp, as agreed, Joey returned to the sandwich shop. He found Elaine at the same table she'd used for lunch, but instead of sitting with a couple of friends, she was accompanied by her attorney. Icy introductions were made, and Joey sat down across from them with a knot in his throat and a strong desire to maim Kyle McAvoy. Where the hell was Kyle anyway? He was the lawyer.

Elaine's lawyer was an attractive middle-aged woman. Everything was black – pantsuit, thick coral necklace, boots, eye shadow, and, worst of all, her mood. This woman went for the throat. The business card Joey was holding and glancing at proclaimed her to be Michelin 'Mike' Chiz, Attorney & Counselor at Law. She began matter-of-factly: 'My first question for you, Mr. Bernardo, is, what are you doing here?'

'How many questions do you have?' Joey asked in his finest smart-ass manner. He had been assured time after time by his psuedo-lawyer and near co-defendant, one Kyle McAvoy, that there was no danger in this chance meeting with Elaine Keenan. Any legal action she wanted to initiate could have been commenced long ago. Five and a half years had passed.

'Well, Mr. Bernardo, may I call you Joey?'

There was almost no chance that she would allow him to call her Mike, so he abruptly said no.

'Very well, Mr. Bernardo, I have just a few questions. I have represented Ms. Keenan here for some time now. She actually works part-time in my office, a fine paralegal, and I'm familiar with her story. Now, what are you doing here?'

'First of all, I don't have to explain a damned

thing to you. But I'll try to be nice, at least for the next sixty seconds. I work for a brokerage firm in Pittsburgh, and we have some clients in Scranton. I'm here to see these clients. I got hungry around noon today. I chose this four-star restaurant at random, walked in, saw Ms. Keenan here, said hello, she freaked, I wanted to chat, and now I'm taking questions from her lawyer. Why, exactly, do you need a lawyer, Elaine?'

'You raped me, Joey,' Elaine blurted. 'You and Baxter Tate, and maybe Kyle McAvoy.' By the time she finished, her eyes were moist. Her breathing was heavy, almost heaving, as if she might lunge at him at any moment.

'Maybe this, maybe that. You never got your story straight.'

'Why did you want to talk to my client?' Ms. Chiz demanded.

'Because it was a misunderstanding, and I wanted to apologize for the misunderstanding. That's all. After she cried rape, we never saw her again. The cops investigated, found nothing because nothing happened, and by then Elaine had disappeared.'

'You raped me, Joey, and you know it.'

'There was no rape, Elaine. We had sex – me and you, you and Baxter, you and most of the other boys at Beta – but it was all very consensual.'

Elaine closed her eyes and began shaking as if chills swept her body.

'Why does she need a lawyer?' Joey asked Ms. Chiz.

'She's suffered greatly.'

'I don't know how much she's suffered, Ms. Chiz, but I do know that she suffered very little during her days at Duquesne. She was too busy partying to spend time suffering. Lots of booze, drugs, and sex, and there are lots of boys and girls perfectly capable of refreshing her memory. You'd better get to know your client before you pursue some bogus legal action. There's a lot of bad stuff back there.'

'Shut up!' Elaine snarled.

'You want to apologize to her?' the lawyer said.

'Yes. Elaine, I apologize for the misunderstanding, whatever the hell it was. And I think you should apologize for accusing us of something that did not happen. And right now, I want to apologize for even being here.' Joey sprang to his feet. 'This was not a good idea. So long.'

He walked quickly out of the deli, strolled to his car, and left Scranton. Driving back to Pittsburgh, when he wasn't cursing Kyle McAvoy, he was hearing her voice again and again. 'You raped me, Joey.' Her words were painful and free of doubt. She may not have known precisely what happened in their apartment five-and-a-half years earlier, but she certainly knew now.

He hadn't raped anyone. What began as consensual sex, at her suggestion nonetheless, had now been transformed into something far different, at least in her mind.

If a girl consents to sex, can she change her mind once things are under way? Or if she consents to sex, then blacks out halfway through the act, how can she later claim she'd changed her mind? Difficult questions, and Joey wrestled with them as he drove.

'You raped me, Joey.'

The mere accusation carried a heavy dose of suspicion, and for the first time Joey questioned himself. Had he and Baxter taken advantage of her?

Four days later, Kyle stopped by the mail room at Scully & Pershing and picked up a letter from Joey. It was a detailed summary of the encounter, complete with their choice of sandwiches and a description of Elaine's hair color and matching tattoos. After setting out the facts, Joey offered his opinions:

> EK has definitely convinced herself that she was raped by several of us, JB and BT for sure and 'maybe' KM. She is weak, fragile, emotionally unstable, haunted, but at the same time carries a certain smugness in her victimhood. She has chosen the right attorney, a tough broad who believes in her and would not hesitate to start legal trouble if she could find any evidence. Her finger is on the trigger. If that little video is half as

damaging as you say it is, then by all human means keep it locked away from these people. Elaine and her lawyer are two cobras, pissed and coiled and ready to strike.

He finished with: 'I'm not sure what my next little project might be, but I'd rather not go near Elaine again. I don't like being called a rapist. The entire episode was unnerving, plus I had to lie to Blair to get out of town. I have two tickets to the Steelers–Giants game on October 26. Shall I call you with this news so your goons will know about it? I really think we should go to the game and hash out our next moves. Your faithful servant, Joey.'

Kyle read the letter and summary in the main library while hiding between shelves of ancient law books. It confirmed his worst fears, but he had little time to dwell on it. He quietly tore the sheets of paper into a hundred pieces, then dropped them in a wastebasket as he left the library. Immediately destroy all written correspondence, he'd instructed Joey.

The hotel nearest his apartment was the Chelsea Garden, a fifteen-minute walk. At eleven that night, Kyle dragged himself along Seventh Avenue, looking for the hotel. Had he not been so exhausted, he might have enjoyed the cool autumn night with leaves sweeping across the sidewalk and half the city still awake and going somewhere. But Kyle was numb with fatigue and capable of only one thought at a time, and that was often too much.

Bennie was in a suite on the third floor, where he'd been waiting for two hours because his 'asset' couldn't get away from the office. But Bennie didn't mind. His asset belonged at the office, and the more time he spent there, the quicker Bennie could get on with his work.

Regardless, though, Bennie opened up with a nasty 'You're two hours late.'

'Sue me.' Kyle stretched out on the bed. This was their fourth meeting in New York since Kyle had moved there, and he had yet to hand over anything that Bennie wasn't supposed to have. His ethics were still intact. No laws had been broken.

So why did he feel like such a traitor?

Bennie was tapping a large white poster board mounted on an easel. 'If I could have your attention, please,' he said. 'This won't take long. I have some coffee if you'd like.'

Kyle wasn't about to concede an inch. He jumped to his feet, poured coffee in a paper cup, and sat on the edge of the bed. 'Go.'

'This is the Trylon team as it is now assembled. At the top here is Wilson Rush, and below him are eight litigation partners – Mason, Bradley, Weems, Cochran, Green, Abbott, Etheridge, and Wittenberg. How many have you met?'

Kyle studied the eight squares with the names scrawled inside them, and thought for a second.

'Wilson Rush spoke to us during orientation, but I haven't seen him since. I did a memo for Abbott on a securities case, met him briefly, and I had lunch one day in the cafeteria with Wittenberg. I've seen Bradley, Weems, maybe Etheridge, but I can't say I've met them. It's a big firm.' Kyle was still amazed at the unknown faces he encountered every day in the halls and elevators, the cafeteria and libraries and coffee rooms. He tried to socialize and at least say hello, but the clock was always ticking and billing was much more important.

His supervising partner was Doug Peckham, and he was relieved Peckham's name was not on the board.

There were a bunch of smaller squares under the partners. Bennie tapped an index finger near them. 'There are sixteen senior associates, and under them another sixteen younger ones. The names are in that binder over there. You need to memorize them.'

'Sure, Bennie.' Kyle glanced at the binder, this one a two-inch blue one. The last three were black and thicker. Then he studied the names on the board.

'How many of these associates have you worked with?'

'Five, six, maybe seven,' he said with no effort at being accurate. How would Bennie know whom he'd worked with? And how Bennie knew the names of all forty-one lawyers assigned to the Trylon case was a question Kyle didn't even want to consider. A few of the names would appear in the court file, but only the big boys. How many sources did he have?

He pointed to a smaller box. 'This is a senior associate named Sherry Abney. You met her?'

'No.'

'A rising star, fast track to partnership. Two degrees from Harvard and a federal clerkship. She reports to Partner Mason, who's in charge of discovery. Under her is a second-year associate by the name of Jack McDougle. McDougle has a cocaine problem. No one at the firm knows it, but he's about to get busted, so everybody will know it. His departure will be quick.'

Kyle stared at the box with McDougle's name and thought of so many questions he didn't know where to start. How did Bennie know this?

'And you want me to take his place?'

'I want you to schmooze it up with Sherry Abney. Check her out, get to know her. She's thirty years old, single but committed to an investment banker at Chase who works as many hours as she does, so they have no time for any fun. No wedding date, as of now, at least nothing that has been announced. She likes to play squash, when she can find the time, and as you know, the firm has two courts on the fortieth floor beside the gym. You play squash?'

'I guess I do now.' Kyle had played several times at Yale. 'Not sure when I'll find the time.'

'You figure it out. She just might be your entrée onto the Trylon team.'

Go, team, go. Kyle planned to avoid Trylon and its litigation team as diligently as possible. 'Small problem here, Bennie,' Kyle said. 'Nice homework, but you're missing the obvious. There are no first-year grunts anywhere near this case. A couple of reasons. First, we don't know anything – five months ago we were still in law school – and, second, the smart boys at Trylon probably told their lawyers to keep the rookies away from this case. That happens, you know. Not all of our clients are stupid enough to pay $300 an hour for a bunch of kids to stick it to them. So, Bennie, where is plan B?'

'It takes patience, Kyle. And politics. You start angling for the Trylon case, networking with the upper associates, kissing the right asses, and we might get a lucky break.'

Kyle wasn't finished with the discussion about McDougle. He was determined to pursue it, when another man suddenly appeared from the sitting room adjacent to the bedroom. Kyle was so startled he almost dropped the half-filled cup of coffee. 'This is Nigel,' Bennie was saying. 'He'll spend a few minutes on systems.' Nigel was in his face, thrusting forward a hand to shake. 'A pleasure,' he sang in a cheery British way. He then moved to the tripod and mounted his own display.

The sitting room was twelve by twelve. Kyle looked through the open double doors into it. Nigel had been hiding in there and listening to every word.

'Scully & Pershing uses a litigation support system called Jury Box,' he began quickly. All movements were rapid and precise. British, but with a strange accent. Forty years old. Five feet ten inches, 150 pounds. Short dark hair, half gray. Eyes, brown. No remarkable features but slightly elevated cheekbones. Thin lips. No eyeglasses.

'How much have they taught you about Jury Box?' Nigel wanted to know.

'The basics. I've used it on several occasions.' Kyle was still reeling from Nigel's unexpected appearance.

'It's your typical litigation support system. All discovery is scanned into a virtual library that can be accessed by all lawyers working on the case. Quick retrieval of documents. Super-quick search of keywords, phrases, contract language, anything, really. You're up to speed?'

'Yes.'

'It's fairly secure, pretty standard stuff these days. And like all smart law firms, Scully also uses a more secure system for sensitive files and cases. It's called Barrister. You in on this one?'

'No.'

'Not surprised. They keep it quiet. Works pretty much like Jury Box, but much harder to access, or to hack into. Keep your ears open for it.'

Kyle nodded as if he would do precisely as he was being told. Since February, on that awful night when he'd been ambushed after a youth-league basketball game on the cold streets of

New Haven, he had met only with Bennie Wright. Or whoever he really was. He had assumed, without really thinking about it, that Bennie, as his handler, would be the only face of the operation. There were other faces, to be sure; in particular, a couple of the street pounders who followed him night and day and who'd made enough mistakes so that Kyle could now spot them. But it had not occurred to him that he would actually be introduced to someone else with a bogus name who worked for the operation.

And why was he? Bennie was certainly capable of handling Nigel's little presentation.

'And then you have the Trylon case,' Nigel was singing. 'A completely different matter, I'm afraid. Much more complicated and secure. Whole different batch of software, really. Probably written just for this one lawsuit. Got the docs locked up in a warehouse down south with Uzis at every door. But we've made progress.' He stopped long enough to allow himself a quick approving smile at Bennie.

Aren't we clever?

'We know that the program is code-named Sonic, as in B-10 HyperSonic Bomber, not very creative if you ask me, but then they didn't, did they? Ha-ha. Sonic cannot be accessed by the nice little laptop they gave you greenies on day one, no sir. No laptop can have a peek at Sonic.'

Nigel bounced to the other side of the tripod. 'There is a secret room on the eighteenth floor of your building, heavily secured, mind you, with a bank of desktop computers, some really fancy stuff, and there is where you will find Sonic. Pass codes change every week. Passwords every day, sometimes twice a day. Must have the proper ID before logging in, and if you log out without quitting to a tee, they'll write you up and maybe show you the door.'

Show me the door, Kyle almost said.

'Sonic is probably a bastardized version of Barrister, so it will be incumbent upon you to master Barrister as soon as you're given the opportunity.'

Can't wait, Kyle almost said.

Slowly, through the shock and the fatigue, it was sinking in that Kyle was crossing the line, and doing it in a way he had not envisioned. His nightmare was to walk out of Scully & Pershing with secrets he was not supposed to have, and deliver them like Judas to Bennie for thirty pieces of silver. Now, though, he was receiving firm secrets from an outside source. He had yet to steal anything, but he damned sure wasn't supposed to know about Sonic and the hidden room on the eighteenth floor. Perhaps it wasn't criminal and maybe it wasn't a violation of the canons of ethics, but it certainly felt wrong.

'That's enough for now,' Bennie was saying. 'You look exhausted. Get some rest.'

'Oh, thank you.'

Back on Seventh Avenue, Kyle glanced at his watch. It was almost midnight.

Chapter 21

At 5:00 a.m., the usual hour now, the alarm clock exploded at full volume and Kyle slapped it twice before it shut off. He hurried through the shower and the shave, and fifteen minutes later he was on the sidewalk, fashionably dressed because he could certainly afford fine clothes. His life had quickly become a harried, fatigued mess, but he was determined to look nice as he stumbled through the day. He bought a coffee, a bagel, and a copy of the *Times* at his favorite all-night deli, then caught a cab at the corner of Twenty-fourth and Seventh. Ten minutes later, he'd finished breakfast, scanned the newspaper, and gulped half the coffee. He walked into the Broad Street entrance of his office building at 6:00, on schedule. Regardless of the hour, he was never alone during the elevator ride up. There were usually two or three other bleary-eyed and gaunt-faced associates, all sleep deprived, all avoiding eye contact as the elevator hummed and rocked gently upward and they asked themselves several questions.

What was I thinking when I chose law school?

How long will I last in this meat grinder?

What fool designed this method of practicing law?

There was seldom a word because there was nothing to say. Like prisoners riding to the gallows, they chose to meditate and put things in perspective.

At the cube, Kyle was not surprised to see another young lawyer. Tim Reynolds had been the first to sneak in a sleeping bag – a new, thermally insulated Eddie Bauer special that he claimed he'd owned for years and taken all over the country. But it had a new smell to it. Tim – without shoes, tie, shirt, or jacket, and wearing an old T-shirt – was partially curled under his small desk, inside the sleeping bag, dead to the world. Kyle kicked his feet, woke him up, and began with a pleasant 'You look like crap.'

'Good morning,' Tim said, scrambling to his feet and reaching for his shoes. 'What time is it?'

'Almost five. What time did you go to sleep?'

'I don't remember. Sometime after two.' He was pulling on his shirt quickly, as if a dreaded partner might appear any second and issue demerits. 'I have a memo due for Toby Roland at seven and I have no idea what I'm doing.'

'Just keep billing,' Kyle said without a trace of sympathy as he unpacked his briefcase and pulled out his laptop. Tim finished dressing and grabbed a file. 'I'll be in the library,' he said, already a wreck.

'Don't forget to brush your teeth,' Kyle said.

When Reynolds was gone, Kyle went online, to a Web site called QuickFace.com. There were several sites that allowed amateur sleuths to put together composite sketches of faces, and Kyle had studied them all. QuickFace was by far the most detailed and accurate. He began with Nigel's eyes, always the most important feature. Get the eyes right, and half the identification is over. The site offered over two hundred different types of eyes – every race, color, origin, and blend. Kyle went through them quickly, found the closest set, and began his face. Nose, thin and pointed. Eyebrows, moderately thick and a bit long down the sides. Lips, very thin. Cheekbones, higher and wider. Chin, not long but very flat, no dimple. Ears, oval and stuck close to the skull. After he added the hair, he went back to the eyes, tried another pair, then another. The ears were too high, so he lowered them. He tinkered and sculpted until 6:30 – a half hour unbilled and wasted unless he chose to pad a bit during the day – and when Nigel was properly put together and easily identified from forty feet away, Kyle printed the face and hustled off to the library, carrying a thick file because everyone carried a thick file into the library. His private spot was a dead end in a dark corner on the third level of stacked tiers, a lonesome place where they stored thick tomes of annotations no one had used in decades. On the second shelf from the bottom, he lifted three of the books and removed an unmarked manila envelope, letter-sized. He opened it and pulled out three other composites – a splendid rendering of his archenemy, Bennie, and two others of the goons who were stalking him around New York City. To his knowledge, he had not been within fifty feet of them, and had never made eye contact, but he'd seen both on several occasions and was confident that his artwork was at least a decent starting point. The addition of Nigel's dreadful face to the collection did nothing to improve its overall attractiveness.

He hid the envelope and returned to the cube, where Tabor the Gunner was busy making his usual noisy preparations for the day. The issue of whose career held the most promise had been settled weeks earlier. Tabor was the man, the star, the fast-tracked partner-to-be, and everyone else could get out of the way. He'd proven his talents by billing twenty-one hours in a single day. He'd shown his skill by billing more the first month than all other litigation rookies, though Kyle was only four hours behind. He volunteered for projects and worked the cafeteria like an old Irish ward boss.

'Slept in the library last night,' he said as soon as he saw Kyle.

'Good morning, Tabor.'

'The carpet in the main library is thinner than the carpet in the twenty-third library, did you know that, Kyle? I much prefer sleeping on the twenty-third, but it does have more noise. Which do you prefer?'

'We're all cracking up, Tabor.'

'Yes, we are.'

'Tim used his sleeping bag last night.'

'For what? He and Dr. Dale finally getting it on?'

'Don't know about that. I woke him up an hour ago.'

'So you went home? Slept in your own bed?'

'Oh, yes.'

'Well, I have two projects due at noon today, both extremely important and urgent, and I can't afford the luxury of sleep.'

'You're the greatest, Tabor. Go, Superman.'

And with that Tabor was gone.

Dale Armstrong arrived promptly at seven, her usual time, and though she looked a bit sleepy, she was put together as always. Evidently, the bulk of her fat salary was being spent on designer clothing, and Kyle, along with Tim and Tabor, looked forward to the daily fashion statement.

'You look great today,' Kyle said with a smile.

'Thank you.'

'Prada?'

'Dolce & Gabbana.'

'Killer shoes. Blahniks?'

'Jimmy Choo.'

'Five hundred bucks?'

'Don't ask.'

Admiring her each day, Kyle was quickly learning the names of the high priests of female clothing. It was one of the few topics she cared to discuss. After six weeks of shared space in the cube, he still knew very little about her. When she talked, which was not very often, it was always about law firm business and the miserable life of a first-year associate. If there was a boyfriend, he had yet to be mentioned. She had dropped her guard twice and agreed to drinks after work, but she usually declined. And while every rookie was openly grousing about the hours and the pressure, Dale Armstrong seemed to be feeling the strain more than most.

'What are you doing for lunch?' Kyle asked.

'I haven't had breakfast yet,' she replied coolly and withdrew into her little section of the cube.

Chapter 22

The lights in the shelter came on each morning at six, and most of the homeless awoke and began making preparations for another day. The rules did not allow them to stay past eight o'clock. Many had jobs, but those who didn't were expected to be on the streets looking for employment. Brother Manny and his staff were very successful in placing their 'friends,' even if the work was often part-time and minimum wage.

Breakfast was served upstairs in the fellowship hall, where volunteers manned the small kitchen and prepared eggs, toast, oatmeal, and cereal. And it was served with a smile, a warm 'Good morning' for everyone, and a quick prayer of thanks once they were all seated. Brother Manny, a notorious late sleeper, preferred to delegate the early-morning duties at his compound. For the past month, the kitchen had been organized and supervised by Baxter Tate, a smiling young man who'd never boiled water in his previous life. Baxter scrambled eggs by the dozen, toasted loaves of white bread, prepared the oatmeal – real, not instant – and also restocked the supplies, washed the dishes, and he, Baxter Tate, often said the prayer. He encouraged the other volunteers, had a kind word for everyone, and knew the names of most of the homeless he graciously served. After they had eaten, he loaded them into three old church vans, drove one himself, and delivered them to their various jobs around Reno. He picked them up late in the afternoon.

Alcoholics Anonymous met three times each week at Hope Village – Monday and Thursday nights and at noon on Wednesday. Baxter never missed a meeting. He was warmly received by his fellow addicts, and quietly marveled at the groups' compositions. All races, ages, male and female, professionals and homeless, rich and poor. Alcoholism cut a wide, jagged path through every class, every segment. There were old, confident drunks who boasted of being sober for decades, and new ones like himself who freely admitted that they were still afraid. They were comforted, though, by the veterans. Baxter had made a mess of his life, but his history was a cakewalk compared to that of some of the others. Their stories were compelling, often shocking, especially those of the ex-convicts.

During his third AA meeting, with Brother Manny watching from the rear, he walked to the front of the group, cleared his throat, and said, 'My name is Baxter Tate, and I'm an alcoholic from Pittsburgh.' After he uttered those words, he wiped tears from his cheeks and listened to the applause.

Following the Twelve Steps to recovery, he made a list of all the people he had harmed and then made plans to make amends. It wasn't a long list and was heavily focused on his family. He did not, however, look forward to a return to Pittsburgh. He'd talked to Uncle Wally. The family knew he was still sober, and that was all that mattered.

After a month, he began to grow restless. He did not relish the thought of leaving the safety of Hope Village, but he knew the time was coming. Brother Manny encouraged him to make his plans. He was too young and smart and gifted to spend his life in a homeless shelter. 'God has big plans for you,' Brother Manny said. 'Just trust him and they will be revealed.'

When it looked as if they might escape at a decent hour on Friday night, Tim Reynolds and others quickly organized a drinking party and hurried out of the building. Saturday was to be a rare day off. No member of the litigation group at Scully & Pershing could be seen at work on Saturday because it was the annual family picnic in Central Park. Thus, Friday night was cleared for serious drinking.

Kyle declined, as did Dale. Around 7:00 p.m.,

as they were both wrapping up the last details of an endless week, and with no one else around, she leaned around the canvas partition that separated their tight cubicles and said, 'What about dinner?'

'Great idea,' Kyle said without hesitation. 'Any place in particular?'

'My place. We can relax and talk and do whatever. You like Chinese?'

'Love it.' The word 'whatever' was bouncing around his addled brain. Dale was thirty, single, attractive, apparently straight, a pretty lady alone in the big city. At some point, she had to think about sex, though Kyle was depressed at how little he thought about it.

Was she picking him up? It was a startling idea. Dale was so shy and reserved it was hard to believe she would put the move on anyone.

'Why don't you pick up some Chinese and bring it over?' she said.

'Great idea.'

She lived alone in Greenwich Village, in a fourth-floor walk-up. They discussed various take-out restaurants in the neighborhood, then left the office together. An hour later, Kyle climbed the stairs with a sack of shrimp-and-chicken fried rice and knocked on the door. Dale opened it, with a smile, and welcomed him to her apartment. Two rooms, a den-kitchen combo, and one bedroom. It was small but nicely decorated, a minimalist theme with leather and chrome and black-and-white photos on the wall. She, too, was well-appointed and pursuing the less-is-more approach. Her white cotton skirt was extremely short and revealed more of the slender legs Kyle and the other vultures had been admiring. Her shoes were short heels, open toe, no straps, red leather, high-class-tart stuff. Kyle glanced at them and said, 'Jimmy Choos?'

'Prada.'

The black cotton sweater was tight, without a bra under it. For the first time in far too many weeks, Kyle began to feel the excitement of sexual arousal.

'Nice place,' he said, looking at a photograph.

'Four thousand a month, can you believe it?' She was opening the fridge, one about the size of a large desktop computer. She removed a bottle of white wine.

'Yes, I can believe it. It's New York. But no one made us come here.'

She was holding the bottle of chardonnay. 'I'm sorry, but I don't have any club soda. It's either wine or water.'

'I'll have some wine,' he said, with only a slight hesitation. And he decided on the spot that he would not torment himself by arguing back and forth about whether he should take a drink after five and a half years of sobriety. He'd never been to rehab, never been forced to detox, never considered himself an alcoholic. He had simply stopped drinking because he was drinking too much, and now he wanted a glass of wine.

They ate on a small square table, their knees almost touching. Even at home and completely relaxed, conversation did not come easily for Dale, the mathematician. He could not imagine her in a classroom in front of fifty students. And he certainly couldn't picture her in a courtroom in front of a jury.

'Let's agree that we will not talk about work,' Kyle said, taking the lead. He took his fourth sip of wine.

'Agreed, but first there's some great gossip.'

'Let's have it.'

'Have you heard about the split?'

'No.'

'There's a rumor, I heard it twice today, that Toby Roland and four other partners, all in litigation, are about to split and open their own firm. They may take as many as twenty associates.'

'Why?'

'A fee dispute. The usual.' Law firms are famous for exploding, imploding, merging, and spinning off in all directions. The fact that some unhappy partners wanted their own show was no surprise, either at Scully or at any other firm.

'Does that mean more work for the rest of us?' he asked.

'I sure hope so.'

'Have you met Toby?'

'Yes. And I hope the rumor is true.'

'Who's the biggest prick you've met so far?'

She took a sip of wine and thought about the

question. 'That's a tough one. So many contenders.'

'Too many. Let's talk about something else.'

Kyle managed to shift the conversation around to her. Background, education, childhood, family, college. She had never been married. One bad romance still stung. After one glass of wine she poured another, and the alcohol loosened her up. He noticed that she ate almost nothing. He, though, devoured everything in sight. She pushed the topics back to his side of the table, and he talked about Duquesne and Yale. Occasionally, the law firm would get mentioned, and they would find themselves wrapped up in it.

When the wine and food were gone, she said, 'Let's watch a movie.'

'Great idea,' Kyle said. As she looked through her DVDs, he glanced at his watch. Ten twenty. In the past six days he'd pulled two all-nighters – he now owned a sleeping bag – and averaged four hours of sleep each night. He was physically and mentally exhausted, and the two and a half glasses of quite delicious wine he'd just consumed were thoroughly soaking whatever brain he had left.

'Romance, action, comedy?' she called out as she flipped through what appeared to be an extensive collection. She was on her knees, the skirt barely covering her rear. Kyle stretched out on the sofa because he didn't like the looks of either chair.

'Anything but a chick flick.'

'How about *Beetlejuice*?'

'Perfect.'

She inserted the disc, then kicked off her heels, grabbed a quilt, and joined Kyle on the sofa. She wedged and wiggled and snuggled and pulled the quilt over them, and when she was finally situated, there was a lot of contact. And then there was touching. Kyle sniffed her hair and thought how easy this was.

'Doesn't the firm have a rule against this sort of thing?' he said.

'We're just watching a movie.'

And they watched it. Warmed by the quilt, the wine, and each other's bodies, they watched the movie for all of ten minutes. Later, they could not determine who fell asleep first. Dale woke up long after the movie was over. She spread the quilt over him, then went to bed. Kyle woke up at 9:30 on Saturday morning to an empty apartment. There was a note saying she was around the corner at a coffee shop reading the newspapers, so stop by if he was hungry.

They rode the subway together to Central Park, arriving around noon. The litigation section of the firm threw a family picnic on the third Saturday of each October, near the boathouse. The main event was a softball tournament, but there were also horseshoes, croquet, bocce, and games for the kids. A caterer barbecued ribs and chicken. A rap band made its noise. There was an entire row of iced kegs of Heineken.

The picnic was to promote camaraderie and to prove that the firm did indeed believe in having fun. Attendance was mandatory. No phones allowed. For most associates, though, the time could've been better spent sleeping. At least they were not subject to being dragged into the office for another all-nighter. Only Christmas, New Year's, Thanksgiving, Rosh Hashanah, and Yom Kippur afforded the same protection.

The day was clear, the weather perfect, and the weary lawyers shook off their fatigue and were soon playing hard and drinking even harder. Kyle and Dale, anxious to avoid even the possibility of gossip, soon separated and got lost in the crowd.

Within minutes, Kyle heard the news that Jack McDougle, a second-year associate from Duke, had been arrested the night before when a narc team kicked in the door of his apartment in SoHo and found a substantial stash of cocaine. He was still in jail and likely to remain there over the weekend until bail could be arranged on Monday. The firm was pulling strings to get him out, but the firm's involvement on his behalf would only go so far. Scully & Pershing took a hard line on such behavior. McDougle would be laid off pending the charges. If the gossip turned out to be true, he would find himself unemployed in a few weeks.

Kyle paused for a few minutes and thought about Bennie. His chilling prediction had come true.

*

Litigation had 28 partners and 130 associates. Two-thirds were married, and there was no shortage of young, well-dressed children running around. The softball tournament began with Mr. Wilson Rush, senior of all seniors, announcing the brackets and the rules and declaring himself the acting commissioner. Several lawyers had the guts to boo him, but then anything was permitted on this fine day. Kyle had elected to play – it was optional – and he found himself on a ragtag team with two people he'd met and seven he had not. Their coach was a partner named Cecil Abbott (of Team Trylon), who was wearing a Yankees cap and a Derek Jeter jersey, and it was soon evident that Coach Abbott had never run to first base in his life. With a cold Heineken in hand, he prepared a lineup that couldn't beat a decent T-ball team, but then who cared? Kyle, easily the best athlete, was stuck in right field. In center was Sherry Abney, the fifth-year associate Bennie was stalking as Kyle's entrée into the Trylon-Bartin case. As they came to bat in the first inning, Kyle introduced himself and chatted her up. She was visibly upset by the McDougle arrest. They had worked together for two years. No, she had no idea he had a drug problem.

Mingling was encouraged, and after Coach Abbott's team was finally saved by the mercy rule in the fourth inning, Kyle plunged into the crowd and said hello to every strange face he encountered. Many of the names were familiar. He had, after all, been studying the bios for six weeks. A notorious partner, Birch Mason, also clad in Yankee garb and half-drunk by 2:00 p.m., grabbed Kyle like an old friend and introduced him to his wife and two teenage children. Doug Peckham took him around to meet some of the partners. The conversations were all the same – where'd you go to school, how's it going so far, bet you're worried about the bar exam results, life gets better after the first year, and so on.

And, 'Can you believe McDougle?'

The tournament was double elimination, and Kyle's team distinguished itself by becoming the first to lose two games. He found Dale playing bocce, and they headed for the food tent. With plates of barbecue and bottles of water, they joined Tabor and his rather homely girlfriend at a table under a shade tree. Tabor, of course, was on a team that was undefeated, and he'd driven in the most runs so far. He had urgent work at the office and planned to be there at six the following morning.

You win, Kyle wanted to say. You win. Why don't they just go ahead and declare you a partner?

Late in the afternoon, with the sun fading behind the towering apartment buildings on Central Park West, Kyle eased away from the party and found a park bench on a knoll under an oak. Golden leaves dropped around him. He watched the game in the distance, listened to the happy voices, smelled the last of the smoke from the grills. If he really tried, he could almost convince himself that he belonged at that party, that he was just another of the many successful lawyers taking a quick break from their hectic lives.

But reality was never far away. If he got lucky, he would commit a heinous crime against the firm and not get caught. But if luck went against him, then one day during this family picnic they would be talking about him the way they were talking now about McDougle.

Chapter 23

Sunday, with most of the litigators nursing hangovers, Kyle was up early with a clear head, a tall coffee, walking shoes, and five hours to do nothing but hike the city. The FirmFone was in his pocket, but the FirmFone would not be ringing, because the Sunday after the picnic was a day off as well. A few of the gunners and diehards would be at the office, but most of the firm's litigators would savor another beautiful autumn day without billing an hour.

He worked his way south, through the Village and into Tribeca, then east into the frenzy of Chinatown. In SoHo, he managed to get a seat at the bar at Balthazar, a popular restaurant modeled after a Parisian bistro and raved about in all the guides. He had eggs Benedict and tomato juice, and was thoroughly entertained by the rowdy crowd. Then he found the Brooklyn Bridge, climbed to the top, to the promenade, and hiked across the East River to Brooklyn. It took forty minutes, and then forty minutes back into Manhattan, where he made his way to Broadway and followed it through the garment district, the theater district, Times Square, and on to Columbus Circle.

Brunch was at 11:30, at the Upper West Side apartment of Doug and Shelly Peckham. It was an old building on Sixty-third, two blocks off Central Park, and as Kyle rode the stuffy elevator to the third floor, he caught himself doing what most New Yorkers do in their spare time and even while they're working. He pondered real estate. Doug Peckham, as a forty-one-year-old full equity partner in the firm, earned $1.3 million the previous year. His income was no secret. Scully & Pershing, like most mega-firms, published their numbers. Peckham could expect to earn at least that much for the rest of his career, so he could afford a nice place. But $1.3 million a year in New York was not exactly in the big leagues. Not even close. The heavy hitters were the investment bankers, hedge fund whizzes, high-tech entrepreneurs, and corporate executives who were worth billions and thought nothing of dropping $20 million for a midtown apartment. And of course each had the obligatory weekend home in the Hamptons for the summer and one in Palm Beach for weekends in the winter.

The Peckhams had a place in East Hampton. Kyle hoped Shelly and the kids enjoyed the summer house because he knew Doug certainly did not. He was at the office most Saturdays and often on Sundays.

Shelly greeted him with a hug, another old friend now, and welcomed him into their open and unpretentious apartment. Doug was in jeans, sockless, unshaven, and pushing Bloody Marys on his guests. Four other associates were present, all under the supervision of Partner Peckham. The brunch was another effort by him and the firm to soften the edges and make Scully seem like a humane place after all. The goal of the get-together was to talk. Doug wanted to hear their problems and concerns, their ideas and plans, their impressions, and their goals. He also wanted to hurry up and finish brunch so they could watch the Giants versus the 49ers and drink beer, kickoff at 1:00.

Shelly did the cooking herself, and Doug helped serve and pour the wine. After an hour of useless chatter about the same boring lawsuits they'd slaved over all last week, it was time for the Giants. Kyle, the only first-year associate at the table, contributed less than anyone. Halfway through brunch he was already planning his return hike downtown. After dessert, they gathered in the den, where a small fire made things cozy and Doug fiddled with the controls to his high-def, flat-screen TV. In an effort to liven up a dying party, Kyle claimed to be an avid 49ers fan, a hater of the Giants, and this succeeded in generating some trash talk. Two of the older associates were asleep by the end of the first quarter. Doug began to nod off, too, and at halftime Kyle made a clumsy exit and hit the streets.

At five on Monday morning, he was at the office, digging in for another long week.

The Giants' next game was on the road, at Pittsburgh, and two hours before game time Kyle and Joey Bernardo settled into their seats at the forty-yard line and tried to stay warm. A cold front had chased away autumn and a freezing mist hovered above the new stadium. It didn't matter. As diehard Steelers fans, they had shivered through many games at Three Rivers Stadium, the old place that was gone now. They welcomed the cold. This was real football weather.

Mercifully, Blair had little interest in football. Now five months pregnant, she had gained an enormous amount of weight and was not handling prospective motherhood too well. Joey was having second thoughts about marriage, but for some reason felt trapped. Kyle had little useful advice. If she wasn't pregnant, he would tell his friend to run. But you can't abandon a pregnant fiancée, can you? It just didn't seem right. What did he know about such matters?

As the crowd settled in and the teams warmed up, Kyle was ready to talk. 'Speak softly, and tell me about Elaine Keenan,' he said.

Joey had a flask filled with vodka, his anti-freeze. He took a swig, grimaced as if it tasted awful, and said, 'Nothing but trouble.'

Their only correspondence about Elaine had been Joey's written summary of his encounter. Kyle needed all the details, and they needed a plan.

'She is one bitter young woman,' Joey said. 'But she's not nearly as mean as her lawyer.'

'Start at the beginning, and tell me everything as it happened.'

Another swig, a good smacking of the lips, a glance around to make sure no one cared, and then Joey launched into a slow, thoughtful, detailed reenactment of his trip to Scranton. Kyle interrupted with questions, but the narrative moved along. Just before the coin toss, with the stadium packed and rocking, Joey finally finished with the admonition, 'If they have the slightest opening, they'll attack us with a fury. Don't give them the opening. Let's just bury this little episode.'

They watched the game for a while and talked about nothing but football. During a time-out, Joey said, 'So what's the plan?'

'Can you come to New York next weekend? Steelers–Jets. Four o'clock Sunday at the Meadowlands. I'll get tickets.'

'Oh, boy. I don't know.' The problem was Blair, with money also a concern. Joey made a nice salary with commissions, but he wasn't getting rich. Now he had a baby on the way and a wife sometime after that, or vice versa, they couldn't decide. One day Blair wanted to postpone the wedding until the baby arrived so she could regain her figure. The next day she wanted to hurry up and get married so the birth wouldn't be out of wedlock. Joey was just straddling the fence, hanging on by his fingernails, and getting whipsawed from both sides. They were now paying for an expensive new condo. He couldn't afford to spend too much watching football.

'Why do you want me in New York?' he asked.

'Because I want to try to get a photo of Bennie.'

'And why do you want a photo of this guy? These people are dangerous, right?'

'Oh, yes. Lethal.'

'So why are we messing with them?'

'I want to know who they are.'

Joey shook his head and looked away, toward the scoreboard, then he took a sip and leaned close to Kyle. 'I say we leave them alone. I say you do what they want you to do, play their games, don't get caught, keep the damned video buried, and life will be good for all of us.'

'Maybe. Can you come to New York?'

'I don't know. I'll have to figure it out.'

'It's very important. Please.'

'How, old buddy, do you plan to get a picture of this guy Bennie? He's a professional operative, right?'

'Something like that.'

'You're a lawyer, I'm a stockbroker. We have no idea what we're doing, and we could easily get ourselves in trouble.'

'Yes, we could.'

Kyle took a small package from a pocket of his bulky black and gold Steelers parka. 'Take this,' he said, keeping it low so that no one could see it. Joey took it and stuffed it into a pocket of his own black and gold Steelers parka. 'What is it?'

'It's a video camera.'

'Doesn't feel like a video camera.'

'It's a video camera, but not one you're likely to see in a store window.'

The Steelers scored on a long pass, the game's first touchdown, and the crowd celebrated for five minutes. During the ensuing time-out, Kyle continued: 'It's not much larger than an ink pen. It goes in the pocket of either a shirt or a jacket, with a thin wire running to a control switch in your left hand. You can talk to someone face-to-face and video the conversation without their knowledge.'

'So I just walk up to Bennie, who's probably heavily armed and has several other heavily armed pals nearby, and introduce myself and ask him to smile.'

'No. There's a better way. But this week you need to practice with it.'

'Does it have a name?'

'It's all there in the paperwork – specs, instructions, all that stuff. Just bone up on it this week and learn how to use it. If things go perfectly, you'll have about three seconds to video Bennie.'

'And if they don't go perfectly?'

'I'll rescue you.'

'Great.' A long, nervous swig from the flask. 'So, Kyle, let's say we get Bennie on video. How do you, not me, but you, go about identifying him?'

'I haven't figured that out.'

'There's a lot you haven't figured out.'

'I'll e-mail you Tuesday, tell you I've got tickets, the usual drill. Are you in, Joey, old pal?'

'I don't know. I think you're crazy, and you're making me crazy.'

'Come on. You need to have some fun while you can.'

Kyle was hard at work in the main library when the FirmFone rattled softly at four on Thursday afternoon. The e-mail described itself as urgent and commanded the first-year associates to congregate immediately on the forty-fourth-floor mezzanine, the largest gathering place at Scully & Pershing. The message meant only one thing – the bar exam results were in. And the fact that Kyle was being summoned meant that he had passed.

For weeks they had labored against the clock and suffered the often unbearable pressure of adjusting to life in the big firm, and added to that misery was the bar exam hanging over them like a dark cloud. It was always there, seldom discussed because the exam was over and talking about it only made life worse. But it woke them up when they desperately needed sleep. It followed them to the table and could ruin a meal in an instant. The bar exam. What if they flunked the bar exam?

The ritual varied from firm to firm, but Scully & Pershing had a rather pleasant way of breaking the news. They gathered the lucky ones together and threw a party. Though it was supposed to be a surprise, by the second week of September every new associate knew the drill. The cruel part of the festivities was that the unlucky ones were simply not invited. They were left to retreat, to sneak out of the building and go wander the streets for the rest of the day.

As Kyle ran up the stairs and raced along the hallways, he searched for his friends. There were high fives, yelps for joy, people running in shoes that were not meant for running. He saw Dale and gave her a hug, and they walked quickly together. Once on the mezzanine, the crowd was already in a raucous mood before Mr. Howard Meezer, the firm's managing partner, stepped to a small podium and said, 'Congratulations. Let's have a party. Not another hour can be billed today.'

Champagne corks were soon flying. Bartenders were busy, and waiters began passing delicious antipasto. The general feeling was one of euphoria, even giddiness, because the nightmare was over and they were now lawyers forever.

Kyle was enjoying a glass of champagne with Dale and a few others when the conversation shifted to their less fortunate colleagues. 'Does anybody see Garwood?' And they began searching the party for Garwood, who was unaccounted for and soon presumed to be on the other list.

Tim Reynolds approached them with a nasty smile, a drink in one hand and a printout in the other. 'Tabor flunked,' he announced proudly. 'Can you believe it? A Harvard casualty.' Kyle wasn't as pleased. Sure, Tabor was obnoxious and opportunistic, but he was their cube mate, and flunking the bar would kill him. He wasn't a bad guy.

Word spread; the body count rose. In all, there were 8 failures out of 103, a pass rate of 92 percent, an excellent number for any class at any firm. Once again it was clear that they were the brightest stars and were now destined for even greater things.

They got as drunk as possible, then rode home in private sedans arranged by the firm. Kyle had only two drinks and walked to Chelsea. Along the way, he called his father with the wonderful news.

Chapter 24

His appointment at noon Friday with Doug Peckham was described as a working lunch to review some discovery, but when Kyle arrived ten minutes early, the partner said, 'Let's celebrate.' They left the building and crawled into the back of a Lincoln sedan, one of the innumerable 'black cars' that roam the city and keep the professionals out of the yellow cabs. The firm had a fleet of black cars on call.

'Been to Eleven Madison Park?' Doug asked.

'No. I don't get out much these days, Doug, because I'm a first-year associate and I'm either usually too tired to eat, or I don't have time, or I simply forget.'

'Whining, are we?'

'Of course not.'

'Congrats on passing the bar.'

'Thank you.'

'You'll like this place. Great food, beautiful dining room. Let's have a long lunch, with some wine. I know just the client we can stick it to.'

Kyle nodded. Two months in, and he was still uncomfortable with the notion of sticking it to clients. Padding the file. Overbilling. Racking up expenses. He wanted to ask what, exactly, the client was about to get stuck for. Just the lunch, which was a certainty, or would the client also get billed for two hours of his time and two hours of Peckham's? But he didn't ask.

The restaurant was in the lobby of the old Metropolitan Life Building, with views of Madison Square Park. The decor was contemporary, with high ceilings and wide windows. Doug, of course, claimed to know the chef and the maître d' and the sommelier, and Kyle was not surprised when they were seated at a choice table looking at the park.

'Let's get your evaluation out of the way,' Doug said, snapping a bread stick and sending crumbs across the pristine white tablecloth.

'Evaluation?'

'Yes, it's my job as your supervising partner to evaluate you after the bar results. Obviously, if you'd flunked, we wouldn't be here, and I wouldn't have nice things to say. We'd probably be stopping by one of those carts pushed by a street vendor, selecting a greasy kielbasa, taking a walk, and having a bad conversation. But you passed, so I'm going to be nice.'

'Thank you.'

The waiter presented menus while the water was poured. Doug chomped on a bread stick, more crumbs flying across the table. 'Your billing is above average; in fact, it's very impressive.'

'Thanks.' No surprise that any evaluation at Scully & Pershing would begin with how much money one was raking in.

'I've had nothing but positive comments from other partners and senior associates.'

'Drinks? Something to start with?' the waiter asked.

'We'll order some wine with lunch,' Doug said, almost rudely, and the waiter disappeared.

'At times, though, you seem to lack commitment, as if you're not fully on board. Fair?'

Kyle shook his head and thought about a response. Doug was a no-nonsense type, so why not level with him? 'I live, eat, and sleep at the firm, like every other first-year associate, because that's the business model some guy came up with years ago. The same way medical residents go twenty hours a day to prove their mettle. Thank God we're not treating sick people. I don't know what else I can do to prove my commitment.'

'Good point,' Doug said, suddenly much more concerned with the menu. The waiter hovered, waiting.

'You ready?' Doug said. 'I'm starving.'

Kyle had yet to look at the menu and was still stinging from the criticism of his commitment. 'Sure,' he said. Everything looked delicious. They ordered, the waiter approved, and the sommelier appeared. At some point during the serious wine discussion that followed, Doug mentioned a 'first bottle' and a 'second bottle.'

The first was a white burgundy. 'You'll love it,' Doug said. 'One of my favorites.'

'I'm sure.'

'Any problems, complaints?' Doug asked, as if he were clicking off the items on the evaluation checklist.

With perfect timing, Kyle's FirmFone vibrated. 'Funny you should mention it,' he said as he pulled it from his coat pocket and looked at the e-mail. 'It's Karleen Sanborn, looking for a few hours of light lifting in the Placid Mortgage mess. What shall I tell her?'

'You're having lunch with me.'

Kyle typed the e-mail, sent it, then asked, 'Can I turn this off?'

'Of course.' The wine was being presented. Doug sampled it and rolled his eyes, and two glasses were poured.

Kyle pressed on. 'My complaint is this damned phone. It has become my life. When you were an associate fifteen years ago, they didn't have cell phones and smartphones and FirmFones, and so—'

'We worked just as hard,' Doug interrupted with a wave of dismissal. Stop complaining. Get tough. With his other hand he was raising his wineglass to inspect its contents. He finally took a sip, then nodded his approval.

'Well, my complaint is this phone.'

'Okay, anything else?' Another check mark in another box.

'No, just the usual complaints of associate abuse. You've heard them before, and you don't want to hear them now.'

'You're right, Kyle, I don't want to hear it. Look, as partners we know what's going on. We're not oblivious. We survived it, and now we reap the rewards. It's a bad business model because everybody's miserable. You think I want to push myself out of bed at five every morning so I can spend twelve crazy hours at the office so, at the end of the year, we can divide the spoils and be at the top of the rankings? Last year APE's partners averaged $1.4 million. We were at $1.3 million, and everybody panicked. We gotta cut costs! We gotta bill more! We gotta hire more associates and grind them into the concrete because we're the biggest! It's crazy. No one ever stops and says, "Hey, you know, I can live on a million bucks a year and spend more time with my kids, or more time at the beach." No sir. We gotta be No. 1.'

'I'll take a million bucks a year.'

'You'll get there. Evaluation's over.'

'One quick question.'

'Shoot.'

'There's a cute first-year associate, and I'm growing rather fond of her. How big a deal is it?'

'Strict prohibition. How cute?'

'Getting cuter by the day.'

'Name?'

‘Sorry.’

‘You gonna do it at the office?’

‘Haven’t got that far yet. There are plenty of sleeping bags.’

Doug took a breath and leaned forward on his elbows. ‘There’s a lot of sex around the place. Come on, it’s an office. You put five thousand men and women together and it happens. The unwritten rule is this: Don’t screw around with the employees. Secretaries, paralegals, support staff, clerks, those who are considered somewhat below us. We call them the nonlawyers. As for your fellow associates, or partners for that matter, no one really cares as long as you don’t get caught.’

‘I’ve heard some great stories.’

‘They’re probably true. Careers have been ruined. Last year two partners, both married to other people, started a hot affair, got caught, and were kicked out. They’re still looking for jobs.’

‘But for two unmarried associates, come on.’

‘Just don’t get caught.’

The first courses arrived and sex was forgotten. Kyle had a leek and cheese tart. Doug went a bit heavier with a salad of Maine lobster with fennel and black trumpet mushrooms. Kyle drank less wine and more water. Doug was determined to polish off the first bottle and get to the second.

‘A bit of a shake-up is coming down,’ Doug said between bites. ‘I’m sure you’ve heard.’

Kyle nodded with a mouth full.

'It's probably going to happen. Five of our litigation partners are leaving with a bunch of associates and several clients. The mutiny is being led by Toby Roland, and it's not pretty.'

'How many associates?' Kyle asked.

'Twenty-six as of this morning. It's a free-for-all. They're waving money and twisting arms and no one knows how many will eventually leave, but it will knock a hole in litigation. We'll survive.'

'How do we fill the gap?'

'We'll probably raid another firm. They didn't teach you this in law school?'

They both laughed and returned to their food for a moment.

'Will this increase the workload for those left behind?' Kyle asked between bites.

Doug shrugged as if to say yes. 'Maybe. It's too early to tell. They're taking some big clients with some big lawsuits. In fact, that's why they're leaving.'

'Is Trylon leaving or staying?'

'Trylon is an old client, and it's firmly within the protective custody of Mr. Wilson Rush. What do you know about Trylon?' Doug was eyeing him closely, as if they were moving into territory that was off-limits.

'Just what I've read in the newspapers and magazines. You ever worked for them?'

'Sure, several times.'

Kyle decided to push on, just a little. A waiter removed their plates. Another poured more wine.

'What's this Bartin dispute all about? The *Journal* said the court file is locked away because the issues are so sensitive.'

'Military secrets. Huge sums of money involved. The Pentagon is all over it. They tried like hell to stop the companies from fighting, but it blew up anyway. There's a lot of technology involved, not to mention a few hundred billion dollars.'

'Are you working on it?'

'No. I passed. There's quite a team, though.'

Fresh bread arrived to cleanse the palate. The first bottle was empty, and Doug ordered a second. Kyle was carefully pacing himself.

'The partners and associates who are leaving,' Kyle said, 'how many are working on the Bartin lawsuit?'

'I don't know. Why are you so interested?'

'Because I don't want to work on it.'

'Why not?'

'Because I think Trylon is a rogue defense contractor with a rotten history of making cheap products, screwing the government and the taxpayers, dumping dirty weapons around the world, killing innocent people, promoting war, and propping up nasty little dictators, all in an effort to increase the bottom line and have something to show the shareholders.'

'Anything else?'

'Lots.'

'You don't like Trylon?'

'No.'

'The company is an extremely valuable client.'

'Good. Let someone else work for them.'

'Associates are not allowed to choose who they work for.'

'I know. I'm just sharing my opinion.'

'Well, keep it to yourself, okay. That kind of language will get you a lousy reputation.'

'Don't worry. I'll do the work that's assigned to me. But as a favor, as my supervising partner, I'm asking that you keep me busy elsewhere.'

'I'll see what I can do, but Mr. Rush makes the final decisions.'

The second wine was a pinot noir from South Africa, and it, too, caused Doug's eyes to roll around. Their entrées – braised pork shoulder and aged prime rib of beef – were not far behind, and they got serious about eating.

'You know your rate now goes to four hundred an hour,' Doug said, chewing.

'Are you still at eight hundred?'

'Yes.'

Kyle was not sure he had the spine to bill a client, regardless of how large the corporation might be, $400 for an hour of his inexperienced legal work. Not that he had a choice.

'On the subject of billing,' Doug said. 'For the month of October, I need you to estimate my hours on the Ontario Bank case. I got busy and lost track.'

Kyle managed to keep chewing a small bite of braised pork, but he almost choked. Did he say 'Estimate my hours'? He certainly did, and this was something new. There had been nothing at orientation, nothing in the handbook, nothing anywhere about 'estimating' hours. Just the opposite. They had been trained to treat billing as the most important aspect of their practice. Pick up a file, look at the clock. Make a phone call, record the time. Sit through a meeting, count the minutes. Every hour had to be accounted for, and the billing was done on the spot. It was never to be delayed, and it had to be precise.

'How does one estimate hours?' Kyle asked carefully.

'Look at the file. Check the hours you billed on it. Look at my work, then estimate my time for the month of October. It's no big deal.'

At $800 an hour it was indeed a big deal.

'And don't underestimate,' Doug said, swirling his wine in the goblet.

Of course not. If we're going to guess here, let's be damned sure we land on the high side. 'Is this a common practice?' Kyle asked.

Doug snorted in disbelief and swallowed a hunk of beef. Don't be stupid, boy. It happens all the time. 'And since we're now talking about Ontario Bank,' he said, meat visible between his teeth, 'bill 'em for this lunch.'

'I was planning on getting the check,' Kyle said, a lame effort at humor.

'Of course not. I'll put it on a credit card and bill the bank. I'm talking about our time. Two hours for you, now at four hundred, and two for me. The bank had record earnings last year.'

That was nice to hear. They would need healthy earnings to continue their relationship with Scully & Pershing. Twenty-four hundred dollars for lunch, and that did not include food, wine, or tip.

'And now that you've passed the bar,' Doug said as he took another bite, 'you are entitled to use the black cars and bill clients for dinner. The rule goes like this: If you work until eight o'clock at night, then call a car. I'll give you the number and code, and be sure the client gets billed for the car. And if you choose, you can go to a restaurant, spend no more than a hundred bucks on yourself, and also bill the client.'

'You gotta be kidding.'

'Why?'

'Because I'm at the office almost every night until eight, and if somebody else is buying dinner, then I'll be damned sure I stay until eight.'

'Attaboy.'

'Seems kinda rich, doesn't it?'

'What?'

'Billing the client for expensive dinners and lunches and cars.'

A swirl of the pinot, a thoughtful stare at the red liquid, a long pull. 'Kyle, my boy, look at it this way. Our biggest client is BXL, the seventh-largest company in the world, sales last year of $200 billion. Very smart businessmen who have a budget for everything. They live by budgets.

They are fanatics about budgets. Last year their budget for legal fees was one percent of their total sales, or about $2 billion. We didn't get all of that, because they use twenty different law firms around the world, but we got our share. Guess what happens if they don't spend the amount they budget, if their legal fees fall short? Their in-house lawyers monitor our billings, and if our numbers are low, they call up and raise hell. What are we, the lawyers, doing wrong? Aren't we properly protecting them? The point is, they expect to spend the money. If we don't take it, then it screws up their budgets, they get worried, and maybe they start looking around for another firm, one that will work harder at billing them. You follow?'

Yes, Kyle followed. It was beginning to make sense. Expensive meals were necessary not only to keep the hungry lawyers going but also to properly balance their clients' financial statements. Now it seemed almost prudent.

'Yes,' Kyle said, and for the first time the wine warmed his brain and made him relax.

Doug spread his arms and looked around. 'And look at where we are, Kyle. Wall Street. The absolute pinnacle of success in America. We're here, we're on top, we're smart and tough and talented, and we make a boatload of money to prove it. We are entitled, Kyle, and don't forget it. Our clients pay us because they need us and we offer the best legal advice money can buy. Never forget that.'

John McAvoy had lunch every day at the same table at an old café on Queen Street in York, and from the time Kyle was ten years old and hanging around the office, he loved having lunch with his father. The café's special was a vegetable plate that varied each day and cost little, with homemade rolls and iced tea, no sugar. The café attracted lawyers, bankers, and judges, but there were also mechanics and bricklayers. The gossip roared and the bantering was nonstop. The lawyers always joked, 'Who's paying for lunch?' and boasted of wealthy clients who they'd stick with a $3.99 check.

Kyle doubted that his father ever gave a passing thought to billing a client for lunch.

Doug insisted on dessert. Two hours after entering the restaurant, they pushed themselves out the door and into the black car. Both nodded off during the fifteen-minute ride back to the office.

Chapter 25

For the first time in the nine-month life of the operation, Kyle contacted Bennie and suggested they meet. All prior meetings had been prompted by the handler, not the asset. Kyle gave no reason for wanting to meet, but then none was necessary. It was assumed that Kyle finally had something valuable to pass along. It was almost 6:00 p.m. on Friday, and Kyle was working in the main library on the thirty-ninth floor. By e-mail, Bennie suggested the hotel 60 Thompson in SoHo, and Kyle agreed. Kyle always agreed because he was not allowed to disagree or suggest another meeting place. It didn't matter; he had no intention of showing up, not that Friday night. Joey wasn't in town yet.

Four hours later, Kyle was hiding in the Placid Mortgage tomb mindlessly flipping through foreclosure files – now at $400 an hour – when he e-mailed Bennie with the sad news that he wouldn't be leaving the office anytime soon. Could be an all-nighter. Although he loathed the work and hated the tomb, and found it hard to believe he was still at the office so late on a Friday night, he was slightly amused at the image of Bennie waiting impatiently in the hotel room for a meeting that would not take place because his asset was holed up in the office and wouldn't come out. The handler couldn't complain if the asset was hard at work.

Kyle suggested a meeting late Saturday afternoon, and Bennie took the bait. Within minutes he e-mailed the instructions: 7:00 p.m., Saturday, room 42, Wooster Hotel in SoHo. So far, a different hotel had been used for each meeting.

On a desk phone, Kyle called Joey's new cell number and passed along the details. His flight from Pittsburgh would arrive at LaGuardia at 2:30 on Saturday afternoon. He would take a cab to the Mercer Hotel, check into his room, and kill time while his friend practiced law. He would roam the streets, walk in the front doors of bars and out the back, browse through bookstores, dart here and there in cabs, and when he was certain he was not being followed, he would drop in at the Wooster Hotel and mill around the lobby. He had in his pocket a copy of the Bennie Wright composite Kyle had been perfecting for weeks. Joey had studied it for hours and was confident he could spot the man anywhere. Now Kyle wanted Bennie in complete digital color.

At 7:30, Kyle walked through the hotel lobby and took the elevator to the fourth floor. Bennie had a small room, no suite this time. As Kyle tossed his trench coat and briefcase on the bed, he glanced into the bathroom. 'Just looking for Nigel, or perhaps another surprise,' he said as he flipped on a light switch.

'Just me this time,' Bennie said. He was relaxing in a velvet chair. 'You passed the bar. Congratulations.'

'Thanks.' The inspection over, Kyle sat on the edge of the bed. The inspection had revealed no one but Bennie, but it had also revealed no luggage, no shaving kit, nothing to indicate Bennie would stay in the room after Kyle left.

'You're putting in the hours,' Bennie said, again making an attempt at small talk.

'I'm a full-blown lawyer now, so evidently I'm expected to work even more.' He noted the shirt – light blue cotton, no pattern, no buttons on the collar, no necktie. The slacks were dark brown, wool, pleated. The jacket was evidently in the closet next to the bathroom, and Kyle cursed himself for not noticing it. Dark socks, no distinguishable color. Black scuffed shoes, quite ugly.

'Here's the scoop,' Kyle said. 'Five litigation partners are splitting off – Abraham, DeVere, Hanrahan, Roland, and Bradley. They're opening up their own shop and stealing at least three clients in the process. As of last count, twenty-six associates are jumping with them. Of the partners, Bradley is the only one working on the Trylon-Bartin case. However, at least seven of the associates are assigned to the lawsuit.'

'I'm sure you have a memo.'

Kyle pulled out a single sheet of paper, tri-folded, and handed it over. It was a summary of the names of all the Scully & Pershing lawyers who were leaving. He knew Bennie would want it in writing, something to preserve in the file and keep as evidence of his treachery. There. He'd finally done it. He'd handed over firm secrets, and now there was no turning back.

Except that it was not exactly accurate. The gossip was changing by the hour, and no one seemed to know precisely who was planning to leave. Kyle had taken a few liberties with the names, especially those of the associates. Nor was it highly confidential information that he was passing along. The *New York Lawyer*, the trade daily, had carried at least two brief stories about the spin-off in the litigation section of Scully & Pershing. Given the ever-shifting nature of law firm personnel, it was not headline news. And besides, Bennie already knew as much as Kyle. And Kyle knew he knew.

The memo gave no details about the business of any client. In fact, it did not mention a client by name. While it appeared to have been put together in a hurry, Kyle had spent time on it and was convinced it was not a violation of ethics.

Bennie unfolded the sheet of paper and

studied it carefully. Kyle watched him for a moment, then said, 'I need to use the bathroom.'

'In there,' Bennie said, pointing without looking.

As Kyle walked to the bathroom, he passed the closet, its door half-open, and hanging on a rack was a cheap navy sport coat and a dark gray trench coat.

'I'm not sure this means anything,' Kyle said when he returned. 'Trylon's in-house attorneys are hands-on, and they prefer the more experienced associates. Those who are leaving will likely be replaced with third- and fourth-year people. I'm still a long shot.'

'Who'll take Bradley's place?'

'Not a clue. There are a lot of rumors.'

'Have you met Sherry Abney?'

'Yes, we played softball together at the picnic in Central Park. We hit it off, but she's not in charge of which associates are assigned to the case. That decision rests with Mr. Wilson Rush.'

'Patience, Kyle, patience. Good intelligence is based on long-term placement and relationships. You'll get there.'

'I'm sure I will, especially if you keep picking off the associates ahead of me. How'd you get rid of McDougle? Plant the drugs in his apartment?'

'Come on, Kyle. The young man had a serious problem with cocaine.'

'He didn't need your help.'

'He's on the road to recovery.'

'You asshole! He's on the road to prison.'

'He was dealing coke, Kyle. A menace to society.'

'What do you care about society?'

Kyle stood and began gathering his things. 'Gotta run. My old pal Joey Bernardo is in from Pittsburgh for the Jets game tomorrow.'

'How nice,' Bennie said, getting to his feet. He knew Joey's flight numbers, coming and going, and he knew their section and seat numbers for tomorrow's game.

'You remember Joey? The second one in your little video?'

'It's not my video, Kyle. I didn't take it. I just found it.'

'But you couldn't leave it alone, could you? Later.' Kyle slammed the door behind him and hurried down the hallway. He ran down four flights of stairs and entered the lobby not far from the elevators. He made eye contact with Joey, then went straight to the men's room around the corner. There were three urinals to the right. He straddled the center one, waited about ten seconds, then was joined by Joey on the left. There was no one else in the men's room.

'Light blue shirt, no tie, navy sport coat, all under a dark gray trench coat. Black-rimmed reading glasses that come and go, probably will not be wearing them when he comes down. No sign of a briefcase, hat, umbrella, or anything else. He should be alone. He is not staying for the night, so I expect him to be down shortly. Good luck.' Kyle pulled the flush handle, left the room, and left the hotel. Joey waited two minutes, then returned to the lobby, where he picked up his newspaper from a chair and sat down. His dark hair had been cut short the day before and was almost entirely gray. He wore fake eyeglasses with thick black frames. The camera, slightly larger than a disposable pen but practically indistinguishable from one, was in the pocket of his brown corduroy jacket, next to a red pocket square.

A hotel security agent in a smart black suit watched him closely, though his curiosity had more to do with the relative inactivity of the lobby than with any real suspicion. Thirty minutes earlier, Joey had explained to the agent that he was waiting on a friend who was upstairs. Two clerks behind the reception desk went about their business with their heads down, seeing nothing but missing little.

Ten minutes passed, then fifteen. Each time an elevator door opened, Joey tensed slightly. He kept the newspaper low, on his knees, so that he could appear to be reading while the camera had a clear shot at the target.

A bell, the door to the elevator on the left opened, and Bennie the Handler was there all by himself in a long gray trench coat. The composite of his face was remarkably accurate – slick bald head, a few strands of black hair greased down about the ears, long narrow nose, square jaw, heavy eyebrows over dark eyes. Joey swallowed hard, his head down, and squeezed the 'on' button in his left hand. For eight steps, Bennie walked directly toward him, then veered with the marble walkway toward the front door and was gone. Joey twisted his upper body slightly so the camera could follow, then he switched it off, breathed deeply, and became engrossed in his newspaper. He looked up each time the elevator opened, and after ten long minutes stood and walked back to the men's room. After lingering for half an hour, he feigned frustration with his tardy friend upstairs and stomped out of the hotel. No one followed.

Joey plunged into the Saturday night chaos of lower Manhattan, strolling aimlessly with the thick foot traffic, window-shopping, ducking into music stores and coffee shops. He was convinced he'd lost his tail two hours earlier, but he took no chances. He hurried around corners and cut through narrow streets. At a used bookshop he'd scoped out late in the afternoon, he locked himself in the tiny toilet and washed his hair with a cleansing rinse that took out much of the gray. What was left was covered with a black Steelers cap. He dropped the fake eyeglasses in the wastebasket. The video recorder was stuck deep in his right front pocket.

Kyle waited nervously at the bar in the Gotham Bar and Grill on Twelfth Street. He sipped a glass of white wine and chatted occasionally with the bartender. Their reservation was for 9:00 p.m.

The worst-case scenario, indeed the only way they could screw up the operation, was for Bennie to recognize Joey and confront him in the lobby of the Wooster Hotel. It was a long shot, though. Bennie knew Joey was in the city, but he would not recognize him in disguise, nor would he expect him to be anywhere near the hotel. Kyle was assuming that since it was Saturday night, and since he had done little if anything in two months to arouse suspicions, Bennie would be traveling light with a skeleton crew on the streets.

Joey arrived promptly at nine. His hair was almost natural; in fact, as he walked through the front door, Kyle could not see a hint of gray. He had somehow exchanged the well-used brown corduroy jacket for a more stylish black one. His smile told the story. 'Got him,' he said as he took a stool and began looking for a drink.

'So?' Kyle said softly as he watched the door for anything suspicious.

'Double Absolut on the rocks,' Joey said to the bartender. Then to Kyle, much lower, he said, 'I think I nailed him. He waited sixteen minutes, used the elevator, and I shot him for at least five seconds before he passed by me.'

'Did he look at you?'

'I don't know. I was reading the newspaper. No eye contact, remember. But he never slowed down.'

'No trouble recognizing him?'

'No. Your composite is terrific.'

They drank for a few moments as Kyle continued to watch the front door and as much of the sidewalk as he could see without being obvious. The maître d' fetched them and led them to a table in the rear of the restaurant. After the menus were presented, Joey handed over the camera. 'When can we see it?' he asked.

'A few days. I'll use a computer at the office.'

'Don't e-mail me the video,' Joey said.

'Don't worry. I'll make a copy and send it snail mail.'

'Now what?'

'Good work, pal. Now we enjoy a fine meal, with wine, as you'll notice—'

'Proud of you.'

'And tomorrow we watch the Steelers kill the Jets.'

They clinked glasses and savored their triumph.

Bennie yelled at the three operatives who'd lost Joey after his arrival in the city. They had first lost him late in the afternoon, not long after he had checked in at the Mercer and hit the streets. They'd found him in the Village before dark, then lost him again. Now he was having dinner with Kyle at the Gotham Bar and Grill, but that was exactly where he was supposed to be. The operatives swore he moved as if he knew he was being followed. He had deliberately tried to shake them. 'And did a damned fine job, didn't he?' Bennie yelled.

Two straight football games, one in Pittsburgh, now one in New York. More e-mail chatter between the two. Joey was the only friend from college Kyle was now regularly in touch with. The warning signs were there. Something was being planned.

Bennie decided to beef up surveillance on Mr. Joey Bernardo.

They were also watching Baxter Tate and his remarkable transformation.

Chapter 26

At 4:30 on Monday morning, Kyle hurried off the elevator, alone, on the thirty-third floor and walked to his cube. As usual, lights were on, doors were open, coffee was brewed, someone was working. Someone was always working, regardless of the day or hour. The receptionists, secretaries, and clerks weren't due until 9:00, but then they only worked a forty-hour week. The partners averaged around seventy. It was not unusual for an associate occasionally to hit a hundred.

'Good morning, Mr. McAvoy.' It was Alfredo, one of the plainclothes security agents who roamed the hallways during the weird hours.

'Good morning, Alfredo,' Kyle said as he wadded his trench coat and tossed it in a corner, next to his sleeping bag.

'How 'bout those Jets?' Alfredo asked.

'I'd rather not discuss it,' Kyle shot back. Twelve hours earlier, the Jets had drubbed the

Steelers by three touchdowns in heavy rain.

'Have a nice day,' Alfredo said happily as he walked away, his day obviously made better because his team had slaughtered the Steelers and, more important, he'd found a place to rub it in. New York sports fans, Kyle mumbled as he unlocked his drawer and pulled out his laptop. As he waited for it to power up, he glanced around to make sure he was alone. Dale refused to punch in before 6:00. Tim Reynolds hated mornings and preferred to arrive around 8:00 and make up for it at midnight. Poor Tabor. The gunner had flunked the bar exam and had not been seen since. He'd called in sick last Friday, the day after the results were published, and evidently his sickness had continued throughout the weekend. But there was no time to worry about Tabor. He could take care of himself.

Working quickly, Kyle slid the tiny T-Klip from the video camera into an adapter, which he plugged into his laptop. He waited a few seconds, clicked twice, then froze as the image appeared: Bennie in perfect color, standing at the elevator door, waiting patiently for it to open completely, then walking forward, the steady, confident walk of a man with no fears, no hurries, four steps over the marble floor, then a long glance down at Joey but no connection; five more steps and he disappeared from view. Screen blank. Rewind, watch it again and again, slower and slower. After the fourth step, when Bennie looked casually at Joey, Kyle stopped the action and studied Bennie's face. The shot was clear, the best of the video. He clicked on 'print' and quickly made five copies.

He had his man, at least on tape. How about this little video, Bennie? Guess you're not the only one who can play games with hidden cameras. Kyle quickly fetched the copies from the printer beside Sandra's desk. All printing was supposed to be logged in and charged to a client, but no questions were asked by the secretary if a few pages were used for personal reasons. Kyle held the five copies and patted himself on the back. He stared at the face of his tormentor, his blackmailer, the rotten little son of a bitch who was currently in charge of his life.

He thanked Joey for such a superb job. A master of disguise, too quick for the bloodhounds behind him, and a brilliant cameraman.

There was a voice somewhere nearby, and Kyle put away his laptop, hid the T-Klip, and walked up six flights to the main library on the thirty-ninth floor. There, lost among the stacked tiers, he added four of the prints to his hidden file. The fifth he would mail to Joey with a note of congratulations.

From an upper-level balcony, he looked down at the central floor of the library. Rows of tables and study carrels, piles of books scattered around urgent projects. He counted eight associates hard at work, lost in a world of research for memos and briefs and motions that were past due. Five o'clock on a Monday morning in early November. What a way to start the week.

The next step in his scheme had not yet been determined. He wasn't certain there was a next step. But for the moment, Kyle was content to take a breath, savor a small victory, and tell himself there was a way out.

Just minutes after the markets opened Monday, Joey was chatting with a client who wanted to dump some more oil stocks when his second desk phone rang. He routinely carried on more than one phone conversation at the same time, but when the second caller said, 'Hey, Joey, it's Baxter. How are you?' Joey got rid of the client.

'Where are you?' Joey asked. Baxter had left Pittsburgh three years earlier, after they graduated from Duquesne, and he seldom returned. When he did, though, he rounded up the old gang, those who could not avoid him, and threw some wild drunken party that killed a weekend. The longer he stayed in L.A. and pursued his acting career, the more insufferable he became when he was back home.

'Here, in Pittsburgh,' he said. 'Clean and sober for 160 days now.'

'That's great, Baxter. Wonderful. I knew you were in rehab.'

'Yes, Uncle Wally again. God bless him. You got time for a quick lunch? I need to talk to you about something.'

They had never had lunch, not since college.

Lunch was too civilized for Baxter. When he met friends, it was always at a bar with a long night ahead of them.

'Sure. What's up?'

'Nothing much. Just want to say hello. Grab a sandwich and meet me down at Point State Park. I'd like to sit outdoors and watch the boats.'

'Sure, Baxter.' Since it was all so obviously planned, Joey was becoming suspicious.

'Noon okay?'

'See you then.'

At noon, Baxter showed up with nothing to eat, nothing but a bottle of water. He was thinner and dressed in old dungarees, a faded navy sweater, and a pair of black combat boots, all selected from the secondhand shop above Brother Manny's shelter for the homeless. Long gone were the designer jeans, Armani jackets, and crocodile loafers. The old Baxter was history.

They embraced and swapped insults, and found an empty bench near the point where the Allegheny and Monongahela rivers merge. A large fountain spewed water behind them.

'You're not eating,' Joey said.

'Not hungry. Go ahead.'

Joey set aside his deli sandwich and studied the combat boots.

'You seen Kyle?' Baxter asked, and they spent a few minutes catching up about Kyle, Alan Strock, and a few of the other fraternity brothers. When Baxter spoke, he did so softly and slowly and he gazed across the rivers, as if his tongue were working but his mind were engaged elsewhere. When Joey spoke, Baxter listened but did not really hear.

'You seem detached,' Joey said, blunt as ever.

'It's just weird being back, you know. Plus, it's so different now that I'm sober. I'm an alcoholic, Joey, a full-blown raging alcoholic, and now that I've stopped drinking and all of that poison is out of my system, I look at things differently. I'm never going to drink again, Joey.'

'If you say so.'

'I'm no longer the Baxter Tate you once knew.'

'Good for you, but the old Baxter wasn't such a bad guy.'

'The old Baxter was a selfish, pompous, egotistical, drunken pig, and you know it.'

'True.'

'He would've been dead in five years.'

An old barge inched along the river, and they watched it for a few minutes. Joey slowly unwrapped his turkey on rye and began eating.

'I'm working my way through recovery,' Baxter announced quietly. 'Are you familiar with the process in Alcoholics Anonymous?'

'Sort of. I had an uncle who sobered up a few years ago and is still active in AA. It's a great program.'

'My counselor and pastor is an ex-con known affectionately as Brother Manny. He found me in a bar in a Reno casino six hours after I left the rehab clinic.'

'Now that's the old Baxter.'

'Indeed. He's led me through the Twelve Steps recovery process. Under his direction, I've made a list of all the people I harmed along the way. Talk about frightening. I had to sit at a table and think of all the people I've hurt because I was drunk.'

'And I'm on the list?'

'No, you didn't make it. Sorry.'

'Darn.'

'It's mainly family members. They're on my list, and I'd probably be on their lists if they ever got serious about life. Now that I've made the list, the next step is to make amends. That's even more frightening. Brother Manny beat his first wife before he went to prison. She divorced him, and years later when he sobered up, he tracked her down to say he was sorry. She had a scar above her lip, thanks to him, and when she finally agreed to meet with him, he begged for forgiveness. She kept pointing to the scar. She was crying, he was crying, sounds horrible, doesn't it?'

'It does.'

'I assaulted a girl one time. She's on my list.'

The turkey on rye froze halfway down the esophagus. Joey kept chewing, but the food wasn't moving. 'You don't say.'

'Elaine Keenan, remember her? She claimed we raped her at a party in our apartment.'

'How could I forget?'

'Do you ever think about her, Joey? She went to the police. Scared the hell out of us. We almost hired lawyers. I tried my best to forget about it, and I almost did. But now that I'm sober and my mind is clear, I'm remembering things better. We took advantage of that girl, Joey.'

Joey placed the sandwich aside. 'Maybe your memory is not as sharp as you think. What I remember is a wild girl who loved to party, loved to drink and snort coke, but what she loved the most was random sex. We did not take advantage of anyone. At least I did not. If you want to revise history, then go ahead, but don't include me.'

'She passed out. I went first, and while I was doing it, I realized she'd blacked out. Then I remember you walked up to the sofa and you said something like "Is she awake?" Do you remember any of this, Joey?'

'No.' Portions of it were familiar, but Joey wasn't sure anymore. He'd worked so hard to forget the episode, then he'd been shocked back to reality when Kyle described the video.

'She claimed she was raped. Maybe she was right.'

'No way, Baxter. Allow me to refresh your memory. You and I had sex with her the night before. Evidently she liked it, because on the night in question we bumped into her again and she said, "Let's go." She consented before we got back to our apartment.'

Another long pause as each tried to anticipate what was next.

'You thinking about having a little chat with Elaine?' Joey asked.

'Maybe. I need to do something, Joey. I don't feel right about what happened.'

'Come on, Baxter, we were all drunk out of our minds. The whole night was a blur.'

'Oh, the wonders of alcohol. We do things we don't remember. We hurt others because of our selfishness. And when we finally sober up, we are compelled to at least apologize.'

'Apologize? Let me tell you a quick story, Brother Baxter. I bumped into Elaine a few weeks ago. She lives in Scranton. I was passing through on business, saw her in a deli during lunch. I tried to be civil, she freaked out on me, called me a rapist. I suggested we get together a few hours later for a polite cup of coffee. She showed up with her lawyer, a real tough broad who thinks all men are scum. So let's say you go over to Scranton, find her, and tell her you're sorry because there's a good chance she was telling the truth after all, and you want to feel better about yourself because now you're sober and you have this desire to be a good little alcoholic. Know what'll happen, Baxter? Indictments, arrests, trials, lawsuits, prison – all of the above. And not just for you, Brother Baxter, but for some of your friends as well.'

A brief gap as Joey caught his breath. He had Baxter on the ropes, time to finish him off. 'Her lawyer explained that the statute of limitations on rape is twelve years in Pennsylvania, so time has not expired. We got a long way to go. You get near her with some half-baked, feel-good apology and you'll find out what rape is all about when they lock you away.'

Joey jumped to his feet, walked across the boardwalk, and spat at the rivers. He returned to the bench but didn't sit down. Baxter hadn't moved, but he was shaking his head.

'She wanted the sex, Baxter, and we were happy to accommodate her. You're blowing this way out of proportion.'

'I've got to talk to her.'

'Hell no! You're not going near her until the four of us – me, you, Kyle, and Alan – have a long discussion. That'll be ugly, won't it?'

'I need to talk to Kyle. He has more sense than the rest of us.'

'Yes, he does, but he has a crushing workload. Tremendous stress.' Joey tried to imagine such a meeting between the two. Kyle, thinking about the video, while Baxter and his amazing new memory confirm the details. It would be a disaster.

'I'll go to New York,' Baxter said.

'Don't do it.'

'Why not? I'd like to see Kyle.'

'Okay, but if you talk to Kyle, then talk to Alan, too. Everybody talks for a good long time before you go blundering into Scranton and screw up our lives. I'm telling you, Baxter, this girl is out for blood and her lawyer has a nose for it.'

Another long gap in the conversation. Joey finally sat down and thumped his pal on the knee. Just a couple of old frat brothers who still cared for each other. 'You can't do this, Baxter,' Joey said with as much conviction as he could muster. At the moment, he was thinking about his own skin. How would he tell Blair, who was now five months pregnant? *'Hey, babes, just got a phone call. Seems they want me downtown, something about a rape charge. Could be serious. Might not be home for dinner. Someone said reporters are waiting. Catch it on Channel 4. Later. Hugs and kisses.'*

'I'm not sure about what happened, Joey,' Baxter said, softly and slowly as ever. 'But I know what I did was wrong.'

'My uncle, the alcoholic, when he went through AA, he made a list, too. He had stolen a rifle from my father, and he saved his money until he could buy another one. Brought it to the house one night, big surprise, big scene. But if I remember correctly, you, as the alcoholic working your way through the Twelve Steps process, cannot make amends if doing so will harm others. Isn't that right?'

'That's correct.'

'Then there's your answer. If you approach her and beg forgiveness, she and her lawyer will go nuts and drag in me and probably Kyle and Alan as well. You can't do it, because it will harm us.'

'If you did nothing wrong, you have nothing to worry about. I'm confronting what I did, and what I did was wrong.'

'This is crazy, Baxter. Look, you're clean and sober and full of the gospel, good for you. I'm very proud of you. The future looks great, yet you're willing to throw it all away and risk twenty years in prison. Come on! This is madness.'

'Then what should I do?'

'Get your ass back to Reno or somewhere far away and forget about this. Go live a great life out there. Just leave us alone.'

Two policemen walked by, laughing, and Joey stared at the handcuffs on their belts.

'You can't do this, Baxter,' he said. 'Give it some time. Pray about it. Talk to your minister.'

'I have already.'

'And what did he say?'

'He said to be cautious.'

'Smart guy. Look, you're in a state of transition right now. Everything is unsettled. You're out of L.A., you're clean and sober. All good stuff. Again, I'm proud of you. But it's a mistake to rush off and do something foolish.'

'Let's walk,' Baxter said and slowly rose to his feet. They strolled along the river, saying little, watching the boats.

'I really want to see Kyle,' Baxter finally said.

Chapter 27

In the four and a half months Kyle had lived in his grim little apartment, he had managed to avoid having guests. Dale had asked about it a few times, then let the matter drop. Kyle described his place as a dump with almost no furnishings, lukewarm water, bugs, and uninsulated walls. He claimed to be looking for something much nicer, but then what first-year associate had time to look for an apartment? The truth was that he wanted a dump for that very reason – he could keep guests away, and in doing so avoid the risks of having their conversations listened to and recorded. Though he had not attempted to rid the place of mikes and electronic bugs, he knew they were there. He suspected there were cameras, always watching, and since he had lulled them into believing that he was clueless about their surveillance, he went through the motions each day of living pretty much like a hermit. Intruders came and went, at least one per week, but there were no invited guests.

Dale was content to meet at her place. She had a fear of bugs. If you only knew, thought Kyle. My apartment has every kind of bug known to the covert world.

They eventually managed to sleep together without actually falling asleep beforehand. Both collapsed shortly afterward. They had violated firm policy on at least four occasions and had no plans to stop.

When Baxter called and asked if he could crash at Kyle's for a few days, Kyle was ready with a string of lies that were mildly convincing. Joey had sent a Mayday call from his desk phone to Kyle's just minutes after he'd said goodbye to Baxter. 'We gotta do something,' Joey said over and over until Kyle told him to shut up.

The idea of Baxter lounging around his apartment and talking at length about the Elaine episode was almost too much to imagine. Kyle could see Bennie with his technicians, clutching his headphones, listening to Baxter preach about the need to confront the past, admit everything, and so on. If the Elaine episode blew up back in Pittsburgh, Kyle would be dragged into it at some level, and Bennie would risk losing his leverage in New York.

'Sorry, Bax,' Kyle said happily on his cell phone. 'I have only one bedroom, if you can call it that, and my cousin has been sleeping on the sofa for a month. She's in New York looking for a job, and, well, I gotta say, the place is cramped.'

Baxter checked into the Soho Grand. They met for a late pizza at an all-night joint on Bleecker Street in the Village. Kyle picked the place because he'd been there before and, as always, had taken notes on its suitability for future use. One door in and out, large front windows that faced the sidewalk, lots of noise, and it was too small for one of the bloodhounds to enter without being noticed. Kyle arrived at 9:45, fifteen minutes early so he could secure a booth and sit facing the door. He pretended to be engrossed in a thick document, the tireless associate ever dedicated to his work.

Baxter was wearing the same dungarees, sweater, and combat boots Joey had described. They embraced, then fell into the booth talking nonstop. They ordered soft drinks, and Kyle said, 'I talked to Joey. Congrats on the rehab. You look great.'

'Thanks. I've thought about you a lot in the past few months. You quit drinking during our sophomore year, right?'

'Right.'

'I can't remember why.'

'A counselor told me that the drinking would only get worse. I didn't have a serious problem, but one was definitely foreseeable. So I quit. Didn't touch a drop until a few weeks ago, when I had some wine. So far, so good. If I get worried, I'll quit again.'

'I had three bleeding ulcers when they took me in. I thought about suicide, but I didn't really want to do it because I'd miss the vodka and cocaine. I was a mess.'

They ordered a pizza and talked for a long time about the past, primarily Baxter's. He unloaded story after story about the last three years in L.A. – trying to break into the movie business, the parties, the drug scene, the gorgeous young girls from every small town in America doing everything physically possible to either get a break or marry rich. Kyle listened intently while keeping an eye on the front door and the front windows. Nothing.

They talked about their old friends, Kyle's new job, Baxter's new life. After an hour, when the pizza was gone, they eventually got around to more pressing matters. 'I guess Joey told you about Elaine,' Baxter said.

'Of course he did. It's a bad idea, Baxter. I understand the law, and you don't. You're walking into quicksand and you could take us with you.'

'But you did nothing. Why are you worried?'

'Here's a scenario,' Kyle said, leaning closer, eager to unveil a narrative he'd thought about for hours. 'You go see Elaine, looking for some type of redemption, forgiveness, whatever you think you might find there. You apologize to someone you once hurt. Maybe she turns the other cheek and accepts your apology, and you two have a nice hug and say goodbye. That probably will not happen. What is much more likely to happen is that she chooses not to take the Christian approach, doesn't give a rip about this cheek-turning business, and decides, with the advice of a pretty nasty lawyer, that what she really wants is justice. She wants vindication. She cried rape once and nobody listened. You, with the best intentions, will vindicate her with your awkward apology. She feels violated now, and she likes being the victim. Her lawyer starts to push, and things unravel quickly. There's a prosecutor in Pittsburgh who, not surprisingly, likes to see his face on the front page. Like all prosecutors, he's tired of the mundane, the gang shootings, the daily street crime. Suddenly he has a chance to go after four white boys from Duquesne, and one just happens to be a Tate. Not only a Great White Defendant, but four of them! Talk about headlines, press conferences, interviews. He'll be the hero, and we'll be the criminals. Of course we are entitled to a trial, but that's a year away, a year of absolutely terrifying hell. You can't do it, Baxter. You'll hurt too many people.'

'What if I offer her money? A deal with only two parties, me and her?'

'It might work. I'm sure she and her lawyer would enjoy those discussions. But offering money implies guilt, an admission of some sort. I don't know Elaine, and neither do you, but given Joey's encounter, it's safe to say she is not too stable. We can't predict how she will react. It's too risky.'

'I can't live with myself until I talk to her, Kyle. I feel like I harmed her in some way.'

'Got that. It sounds great in the AA handbook, but it's a different matter when other people are involved. You have to forget about this and put it behind you.'

'I'm not sure I can.'

'There's an element of selfishness here, Baxter. You want to do something that you think will make you feel better. Well, good for you. What about the rest of us? Your life will be more complete, our lives could be ruined. You're dead wrong here. Leave this girl alone.'

'I can apologize to Elaine without admitting I committed a crime. I'll just say that I was wrong and want to apologize.'

'Her lawyer is not stupid, and her lawyer will be sitting there with a tape recorder, probably a video camera.' Kyle took a sip of a diet soda and had a quick flashback to the first video. If Baxter saw it now, saw himself tag-teaming with Joey while Elaine was motionless, his guilt would crush him.

'I have to do something.'

'No, you don't,' Kyle said, raising his voice for the first time. He was surprised at the stubbornness across the table. 'You don't have the right to ruin our lives.'

'I'm not ruining your life, Kyle. You did nothing wrong.'

Is she awake? Joey asks. The words rattle around the courtroom. The jurors scowl at the four defendants. Maybe they feel compassion for Kyle and Alan because there is no evidence that they violated the girl, and find them not guilty. Maybe they're sick of the whole bunch and send them all to prison.

'I'll take all the blame,' Baxter said.

'Why are you so determined to get yourself into more trouble than you can imagine? You're toying with prison here, Baxter. Wake up, man!'

'I'll take the blame,' he repeated, very much the martyr now. 'You guys will walk.'

'You're not listening to me, Baxter. This is far more complicated than you realize.'

A shrug. 'Maybe so.'

'Listen to me, dammit!'

'I'm listening to you, Kyle, but I'm also listening to the Lord.'

'Well, I can't compete—'

'And he's leading me to Elaine. To forgiveness. And I believe she will listen, and she will forgive, and she will forget.' He was firm, and pious, and Kyle realized he had little else to throw at Baxter.

'Let it sit for a month,' Kyle said. 'Don't do anything hasty. Joey, Alan, and I should have a say in the matter.'

'Let's go. I'm tired of sitting here.'

They roamed the Village for half an hour before Kyle, exhausted, finally said good night.

He was dead to the world when his cell phone rang three hours later. It was Baxter. 'I talked to Elaine,' he announced proudly.

'Tracked her down, called her, woke her up, and we talked for a few minutes.'

'You idiot,' Kyle blurted before he could stop himself.

'It went pretty well, actually.'

'What did you say?' Kyle was in the bathroom, splashing water on his face with one hand and holding his phone with the other.

'Told her I've never felt right about what happened. I didn't admit to anything other than some misgivings.'

Thank God for that. 'What did she say?'

'She thanked me for calling, then she cried and said no one has ever believed her. She still feels like she was raped. She's always known it was Joey and me, with you and Alan somewhere close by watching the action.'

'That's not true.'

'We're gonna meet in a couple of days, have lunch, just the two of us, in Scranton.'

'Don't do it, Baxter, please don't do it. You will regret it forever.'

'I know what I'm doing, Kyle. I've prayed about this for hours, and I'm trusting God to get me through it. She promised not to tell her lawyer. You gotta have faith.'

'She works for her lawyer, part-time, did she tell you that, Baxter? No, she did not. You'll walk into a trap and your life will be over.'

'My life is just beginning, old pal. Faith, Kyle, faith. Good night.' The phone snapped shut; the connection was dead.

*

Baxter flew back to Pittsburgh the following morning, retrieved his car – a Porsche he planned to sell – from the long-term parking area, and checked into a motel by the airport. Credit card records revealed that he spent two nights in the motel and never checked out. His cell phone records showed numerous incoming calls and text messages from both Joey Bernardo and Kyle McAvoy, with no outgoing calls in return. He had two long conversations with Brother Manny in Reno, and some short ones with his parents and his brother in Pittsburgh. There were two calls to Elaine Keenan.

On the last day of his life, he left Pittsburgh before sunrise, headed for Scranton, a drive that would cover three hundred miles in about five hours. According to the credit card trail, he stopped for gas at a Shell station near the intersection of I-79 and I-80, about ninety minutes north of Pittsburgh. He then headed due east on I-80 and traveled two hours until his journey came to an end. Near the small town of Snow Shoe, he stopped at a rest area and went to the men's room. It was approximately 10:40 a.m. on a Friday in mid-November. Traffic was light, and there were only a few other vehicles at the rest area.

Mr. Dwight Nowoski, a retiree from Dayton who was traveling to Vermont with his wife, who was already in the ladies' room, discovered Baxter not long after he had been shot. He was still alive but dying quickly from a gunshot to the head. Mr. Nowoski found him on the floor by the urinals, his jeans unzipped, the floor covered with blood and urine. The young man was gasping and whimpering and thrashing about like a deer hit by a car. There was no one else in the men's room when Mr. Nowoski walked in and stumbled upon the horrible scene.

Evidently, the murderer followed Baxter into the toilet, took a look around to make sure they were alone, then quickly placed a nine-millimeter pistol, a Beretta according to the lab, at the base of Baxter's skull and fired once. A silencer muffled the gunshot. The rest area was not equipped with surveillance cameras.

The Pennsylvania State Police closed the rest stop and sealed the area around it. Six travelers, including Mr. and Mrs. Nowoski, were questioned at length at the crime scene. One gentleman remembered a yellow Penske rental truck coming and going, but he had no idea how long it was there. The group estimated that another four or five vehicles had left the rest area after the body was discovered but before the police arrived. No one could recall seeing Baxter enter the men's room, nor did anyone see the murderer follow him in. A lady from Rhode Island recalled noticing a man standing by the door to the men's room when she entered the ladies', and upon further reflection she agreed that it was possible he might have been a lookout. He was not going in, nor was he coming out. Regardless, he was long gone, and her description was limited to: male white, somewhere between the ages of thirty and forty-five, at least five feet eight but no more than six feet four, wearing a dark jacket that could have been leather, linen, wool, cotton, anything. Along with the lab reports and autopsy, her description was the extent of the physical evidence.

Baxter's wallet, cash fold, and watch were untouched. The police inventoried his pockets and found nothing but a few coins, his car keys, and a tube of lip balm. The lab would later report that there was no trace of alcohol or illegal drugs in his system, on his clothing, or in his car.

The pathologist did note a remarkable degree of liver damage for a twenty-five-year-old.

Robbery was immediately ruled out for the obvious reasons – nothing was taken, unless the victim was carrying something valuable that no one knew about. But why would an armed thief leave behind $513 in cash and eight credit cards? Wouldn't a thief consider stealing the Porsche while he had the chance? There was no evidence that the crime had anything to do with sex. It could've been a drug hit, but that seemed unlikely. Those were usually much messier.

With sex, robbery, and drugs ruled out, the investigators began scratching their heads. They watched the bagged body disappear into the rear of an ambulance for the ride back to Pittsburgh, and they knew they had a problem. The apparent randomness of the act, plus the silent gunshot and the clean getaway, led them to conclude, at least at the scene, that they were dealing with professionals.

The confirmation that a member of such a noted family had met such a strange and brutal end brightened up a dull news day in Pittsburgh. Television crews scampered to the Tate estate in Shadyside, only to be met by private security personnel. For generations the Tate family had offered 'No comment' to every inquiry, and this tragedy was no different. A family lawyer issued a terse response and asked for prayers, consideration, and respect for privacy. Uncle Wally once again took charge and issued orders.

Kyle was at his cube, chatting with Dale about their plans for the evening, when the call came from Joey. It was almost 5:00 p.m. on Friday. He had eaten a pizza with Baxter late on Tuesday night, then chatted with him a few hours later, but had not spoken to him since. As far as he and Joey could tell, Baxter had disappeared, or at least he was ignoring his phone.

'What's the matter?' Dale asked as she noticed the look of shock. But Kyle did not respond. He kept the phone to his ear and began walking away, down the hall, past the front desk, listening as Joey unloaded all the details now being splashed across the television. He lost him in the elevator, and once outside the building he called Joey back and kept listening. The sidewalks along Broad were packed with the late-afternoon rush. Kyle plodded along, without a coat to layer against the chill, without a clue as to where he might be going.

'They killed him,' he finally said to Joey.

'Who?'

'I think you know.'

Chapter 28

'A funeral lasts for two hours,' Doug Peckham was saying as he glared at Kyle. 'I don't understand why you need to take two days off.'

'The funeral is in Pittsburgh. I have to fly there, then fly back. He was a fraternity brother. I'm a pallbearer. I'll need to see the family. Come on, Doug.'

'I've done funerals!'

'For a twenty-five-year-old roommate shot in the head?'

'I get all that, but two days?'

'Yes. Call it vacation. Call it personal time. Don't we get a few personal days a year?'

'Sure, it's somewhere in the handbook, but no one takes them.'

'Then I'm taking them. Fire me, I don't give a damn.'

A deep breath on both sides of the desk, and Doug said calmly, 'Okay, okay. When is the funeral?'

'Two o'clock, Wednesday afternoon.'

'Then leave late tomorrow afternoon, and meet me here at five thirty Thursday morning. I gotta tell you, Kyle, this place is a powder keg. This Toby Roland split is getting nastier, and larger, and those of us who stay behind are about to get dumped on.'

'He was my roommate.'

'And I'm sorry.'

'Oh, thank you.'

Doug waved off the last comment, picked up a thick file, and thrust it across the desk. 'Can you read this on the airplane?' While phrased like a question, it was an outright command.

Kyle took the file and locked his jaws to keep from saying, Sure, Doug, I'll give it a look on the plane and I'll sneak a peek at the wake and I'll analyze the damned thing during the service and review my thoughts at the burial when they lower Baxter into his grave, and then, when I'm flying back to LaGuardia, I'll flip through it again, and for every minute I'm even remotely thinking about this file, I'll bill, or double bill, or maybe even triple bill the poor client who made the mistake of selecting this full-service sweatshop for its legal needs.

'You okay?' Doug asked.

'No.'

'Look, I'm sorry. I don't know what else to say.'

'There's nothing to say.'

'Any clue as to who pulled the trigger?' Doug

shifted his weight as he attempted a bit of small talk. He feigned, badly, interest in what had happened.

'No.' If you only knew, Kyle thought.

'I'm sorry,' Doug said again, and his effort at showing interest was gone.

Kyle started for the door, but stopped when he heard, 'I asked you to estimate my hours for the Ontario Bank case, didn't I? Over lunch, remember? I need the hours.'

Estimate your own damned hours, Kyle ached to say, or, better yet, Just keep up with your time like everybody else.

'Almost done,' Kyle said and made it through the door without further abuse.

The interment of Baxter Farnsworth Tate took place on a damp and overcast day at the family burial plot in Homewood Cemetery, in central Pittsburgh. It followed a staid and by-the-book Episcopal service that was closed to the public and especially closed to the media. Baxter left a brother, who attended the service, and a sister, who did not. Over the weekend the brother made a gallant effort to restructure the funeral into a 'celebration' of Baxter's life, an idea that fell flat with the ultimate realization that there was so little to celebrate. The brother yielded to the rector, who led them through the standard rituals of remembering someone whom he, the rector, had never met. Ollie Guice, a Beta from Cleveland who had lived with Baxter for two of their years at Duquesne, struggled through a eulogy that evoked a few smiles. Of the eight surviving members of their pledge class, seven were present. There was also a respectable showing from old Pittsburgh – some childhood friends and those required to attend because they came from the upper crust. There were four long-forgotten pals from the second-tier boarding school the Tates had shipped Baxter to when he was fourteen years old.

Unknown to Kyle and the others, Elaine Keenan had attempted to enter the church but was turned away because her name was not on the list.

No one from Hollywood made it to the funeral. Not a single soul from L.A. Baxter's C-list agent sent flowers. A former female roommate e-mailed the rector a brief eulogy that she insisted be read by someone in attendance. She was 'on the set' and couldn't get away. Her eulogy made references to the Buddha and Tibet and was not well received in Pittsburgh. The rector tossed it without a word to the family.

Brother Manny managed to talk his way into the church, but only after Joey Bernardo convinced the family that Baxter had spoken highly of his pastor in Reno. The family, along with all the other mourners, eyed Brother Manny with some suspicion. He wore his standard white uniform – baggy bleached dungarees and flowing shirttail – and layered it with a garment that was probably a robe of some variety but looked more like a white bedsheet. His only concession to the solemnity of the occasion was a black leather beret that adorned his tumbling gray locks and gave him an odd resemblance to an aging Che Guevara. He wept throughout the service, shedding more tears than the rest of the hidebound and stoic collection combined.

Kyle shed no tears, though he was deeply saddened by such a wasted life. As he stood next to the grave and stared at the oak casket, he was unable to dwell on the good times they had shared. He was too consumed with the raging internal debate over what he should have done differently. In particular, should he have told Baxter about the video, about Bennie and the boys, about everything? If he had done so, would Baxter have appreciated the danger and behaved differently? Maybe. Maybe not. In his zeal to clean up his past, Baxter might have gone nuts if he knew he'd actually been filmed doing whatever he did to Elaine. He might have confessed under oath and said to hell with everybody else. It was impossible to predict because Baxter was not thinking rationally. And it was impossible to second-guess now, because Kyle did not foresee the extent of the danger.

But he certainly saw it now.

There were about a hundred mourners huddled around the grave site, all pressing close together to hear the final words from the rector. A few cold raindrops hurried things along. A crimson tent provided shelter for the casket and the family seated near it. Kyle glanced away, at the rows of tombstones where the old money was buried, and beyond them to the stone gate at the cemetery's entrance. On the other side of the entrance was a large pack of media types, waiting like vultures for a glimpse of something newsworthy. Ready with cameras, lights, and microphones, they had been kept away from the church by the police and private guards, but they had dogged the procession like kids at a parade, and now they were desperate for a shot of the casket or the mother collapsing as she said goodbye. Somewhere in their midst was at least one of Bennie's boys, maybe two or three. Kyle wondered if they had a camera, not for a shot of the casket but to record which of Baxter's friends had bothered to attend. Useless information, really, but then so much of what they did made no sense.

They knew how to kill, though. There was little doubt about that. The state police had nothing to say so far, and as the days passed, it was becoming evident that their silence was not necessarily of their choosing. There was simply no evidence. A clean hit, a silent bullet, a quick getaway, and no motive whatsoever.

Brother Manny wailed loudly from the edge of the tent, and this rattled everyone else. The rector missed a beat, then droned on.

Kyle stared at the horde in the distance, too far away for any one face to be recognized. He knew they were there, watching, waiting, curious about his movements and those of Joey and Alan Strock, who'd driven in from med school at Ohio State. The four roommates, now reduced to three.

As the rector wound down, a few sobs could be heard. Then the crowd began backing away from the crimson tent, inching away from the grave site. The burial was over, and Baxter's parents and brother wasted no time in leaving. Kyle and Joey held back, and for a moment stood near the tombstone of another Tate.

'This will be our last conversation for a long time,' Joey said softly but firmly. 'You're messing around with the wrong people, Kyle. Just leave me out of it.'

Kyle looked at the pile of fresh dirt about to be packed on top of Baxter.

Joey kept on, his lips barely moving as if bugs were close by. 'Count me out, okay? I've got my hands full here. I've got a life with a wedding and a baby in the future. No more of your silly spy games. You keep playing if you want, but not me.'

'Sure, Joey.'

'No more e-mails, packages, phone calls. No more trips to New York. I can't keep you out of Pittsburgh, but if you visit here, don't call me. One of us will be next, Kyle, and it won't be you. You're too valuable. You're the one they need. So for our next mistake, guess who gets the bullet.'

'We didn't cause his death.'

'Are you sure about that?'

'No.'

'These guys are around for a reason, and that reason is you.'

'Thanks, Joey.'

'Don't mention it. I'm going now. Please keep me out of it, Kyle. And be damned sure nobody sees that video. So long.'

Kyle allowed him to walk ahead, then he followed.

Chapter 29

At 6:30 on Thursday morning, Kyle walked into Doug Peckham's office and reported for duty. Doug was standing at his desk, which resembled, as always, a landfill. 'How was the funeral?' he asked without looking up from whatever he was holding.

'It was a funeral,' Kyle said. He handed over a single sheet of paper. 'Here is an estimate of your hours on the Ontario Bank case.' Doug snatched it, scanned it, disapproved of it, and said, 'Only thirty hours?'

'At the most.'

'You're way off. Double it and let's call it sixty.'

Kyle shrugged. Call it whatever you want. You're the partner. If the client could pay $24,000 for work that wasn't performed, then the client could certainly pay another $24,000 on top of that.

'We have a hearing in federal court at nine.

We'll leave here at eight thirty. Finish the Rule 10 memo and be here at eight.'

The prospect of a litigation associate getting near a courtroom during his or her first year was unheard-of, and for Kyle a gloomy day suddenly improved. Of the twelve in his class, no one, at least to his knowledge, had seen live action. He hurried to his cube and was checking e-mails when Tabor appeared with a tall coffee and a haggard look. Since flunking the bar, he had slowly managed to put himself back together, and though he was initially humbled, the cockiness was returning.

'Sorry about your friend,' he said, flinging his overcoat and briefcase.

'Thanks,' Kyle said. Tabor was still standing, slurping coffee and anxious to talk.

'Have you met H. W. Prewitt, litigation partner two floors up?' he asked.

'No,' Kyle answered, still pecking away.

'He's about fifty, big Texan. They call him Harvey Wayne behind his back. Get it? Harvey Wayne, from Texas, double first name?'

'Got it.'

'They also call him Texas Slim because he weighs about four hundred pounds. Mean as hell. Went to a community college, then A&M, then Texas Law and hates anybody from Harvard. He's been stalking me, caught me two days ago and gave me a project that any part-time secretary could handle. I spent six hours Tuesday night taking apart exhibit binders for a big deposition yesterday. Took them apart, then reconfigured them just the way Harvey Wayne wanted. There were a dozen binders, couple of hundred pages each, a ton of paperwork. At nine yesterday morning I put them on a cart, raced them down to a conference room where about a hundred lawyers are gathering for this depo, and what did Harvey Wayne do?'

'What?'

'There's this door that leads to another conference room and it won't stay shut, sort of swings back and forth, and so Harvey Wayne, fat ass, tells me to stack the binders on the floor and use them as a doorstop. I do what he tells me, and as I'm leaving the room, I hear him say something like "Those Harvard boys make the best paralegals." '

'How much coffee have you had?'

'Second cup.'

'I'm on my first, and I really need to crank out this memo.'

'Sorry. Look, have you seen Dale?'

'No. I left Tuesday afternoon for the funeral yesterday. Something the matter?'

'She got nailed with some heinous project Tuesday night, and I don't think she's slept at all. Let's keep an eye on her.'

'Will do.'

At 8:30, Kyle left the office with Doug Peckham and a senior associate named Noel Bard. They walked hurriedly to a parking garage a few blocks away, and when the attendant pulled up in Bard's late-model Jaguar, Peckham said, 'Kyle, you drive. We're going to Foley Square.'

Kyle wanted to protest but said nothing. Bard and Peckham climbed into the rear seat, leaving Kyle, the chauffeur, alone in the front.

'I'm not sure of the best route,' Kyle admitted, with a flash of fear at what would happen if he got lost and the two big shots in the back were late for court.

'Stay on Broad until it becomes Nassau. Take it all the way to Foley Square,' Bard said, as if he made the drive every day. 'And be careful. This little baby is brand-new and cost me a hundred grand. It's my wife's.'

Kyle could not remember being so nervous behind the wheel. He finally found the mirror-adjustment scheme and eased into traffic, cutting his eyes in all directions. To make matters worse, Peckham wanted to talk. 'Kyle, a couple of names, all first-years. Darren Bartkowski?'

Without glancing at Peckham in the rearview mirror, Kyle waited and finally said, 'So?'

'You know him?'

'Sure. I know all of the first-year litigation associates.'

'What about him? Have you worked with him? Good, bad, talk to me, Kyle. How would you evaluate him?'

'Uh, well, nice guy, I knew him at Yale.'

'His work, Kyle, his work?'

'I haven't worked with him yet.'

'The word is he's a slacker. Ducks the partners, late with projects, lazy with the billing.'

I wonder if he estimates his hours, Kyle thought but kept his concentration on the yellow cabs passing, darting, turning abruptly, violating every known rule of the road.

'Have you heard he's a slacker, Kyle?'

'Yes,' Kyle said reluctantly. It was the truth.

Bard decided to help thrash poor Bartkowski. 'He's billed the fewest hours so far of anyone in your class.'

Talking about colleagues was a contact sport at the firm, and the partners were as bad as the associates. An associate who cut corners or ducked projects was labeled a slacker, and the tag was permanent. Most slackers didn't mind. They worked less, got the same salary, and ran almost no risk of being fired unless they stole money from a client or got caught in a sex scandal. Their bonuses were small, but who needs a bonus when you have a fat paycheck? Career slackers could slide for six or seven years at a firm before being informed they would not make partner and shown the door.

'What about Jeff Tabor?' Doug asked.

'I know him well. Definitely not a slacker.'

'He has the reputation of being a gunner,' Doug said.

'Yes, and that's accurate. He's competitive, but he's not a cutthroat.'

'You like him, Kyle?'

'Yes. Tabor's a good guy. Smart as hell.'

'Evidently not smart enough,' Bard said. 'That bar exam problem.'

Kyle had no comment, and no comment was necessary because a yellow cab swerved in front of them, cutting off the Jaguar and forcing Kyle to slam on the brakes and hit the horn at the same time. A fist shot out from the driver's window, then an angry middle finger, and Kyle received his first bird. Be cool, he said to himself.

'You gotta watch these idiots,' Doug said.

The sound of important papers being extracted crackled from the backseat, and Kyle knew something was being reviewed. 'Will we get Judge Hennessy or his magistrate?' Doug asked Bard. Kyle was shut out of the conversation, which was fine with him. He preferred to concentrate on the street in front of him, and he had no interest in assessing the performance of his colleagues.

After ten minutes of downtown traffic, Kyle was wet under the collar and breathing heavy. 'There's a lot at the corner of Nassau and Chambers, two blocks from the courthouse,' Bard announced. Kyle nodded nervously. He found the lot but it was full, and this caused all manner of cursing in the rear seat.

Peckham took charge. 'Look, Kyle, we're in a hurry. Just drop us off in front of the courthouse at Foley Square, then circle the block until you find a spot on the street.'

'A spot on which street?'

Doug was stuffing papers back into his briefcase. Bard suddenly had business on the phone. 'I don't care. Any street, and if you can't find a spot, then just keep making the block. Let us out here.'

Kyle cut to the curb, and a horn erupted somewhere behind them. Both lawyers scrambled out of the rear seat. Peckham's final words were 'Just keep moving, okay. You'll find something.'

Bard managed to tear himself away from his phone conversation long enough to say, 'And be careful. It's my wife's.'

Alone, Kyle eased away and tried to relax. He headed north on Centre Street, drove four blocks, then turned left on Leonard and headed west. Every inch of available space was packed with vehicles and motorbikes. An amazing abundance of signs warned against parking anywhere near a potential space. Kyle had never noticed so many threatening signs. He passed no parking garages, but he did pass several traffic cops working the streets, slapping tickets on windshields. After a long, slow block, he turned left on Broadway, and the traffic was even heavier. He inched along for six blocks, then turned left onto Chambers. Two blocks later he was back at the courthouse in which he was supposed to be making his debut as a litigator, if only as a reserve.

Left on Centre, left on Leonard, left on Broadway, left on Chambers, back at the courthouse. Ever concerned about billing, he noted the time. The second loop ate seventeen minutes of the clock, and along the way Kyle again saw nowhere to park. He saw the same signs, same traffic cops, same street bums, same drug dealer sitting on a bench working his cell phone.

Nine o'clock came and went without a call from Peckham, not even a quick 'Where the hell are you?' The hearing was under way, but without Kyle the litigator. Kyle the chauffeur, though, was hard at work. After three loops, he was bored with the route and added extra blocks to the north and west. He thought about stopping for a coffee to go, but decided against it out of fear of spilling something onto the fine beige leather of Bard's wife's new Jaguar. He had settled into the leather and was comfortable behind the wheel. It was a very nice car. A hundred thousand dollars and no doubt worth every penny. The gas tank was half-full, and this was worrying him. The stop-and-go driving was a strain on such a large engine. The hearing that he was missing was an important one, no doubt requiring the presence of many high-powered lawyers, all anxious to plead their positions, and things might drag on for a long time. It was obvious that every legal parking spot in lower Manhattan was taken, and with clear instructions to 'just keep moving,' Kyle accepted the fact that he had no choice but to burn fuel. He began to look for a gas station. He'd fill the tank, bill the client, and score a few points with Bard.

Once the tank was full, he began to ponder other ways to score points. A quick car wash? A quick lube job? When he passed the courthouse for the seventh or eighth time, a street vendor selling soft pretzels looked at him, spread his arms, and said something like 'Are you crazy, man?' But Kyle was unperturbed. He decided against a wash or oil change.

Now confident in traffic, he picked up his phone and called Dale. She answered on the third ring and in a hushed voice said, 'I'm in the library.'

'Are you okay?'

'Yes.'

'That's not what I hear.'

A pause. 'I haven't slept in two nights. I think I'm delirious.'

'You sound terrible.'

'Where are you?'

'Right now I'm on Leonard Street, driving Noel Bard's wife's new Jaguar. What do you think I'm doing?'

'Sorry I asked. How was the funeral?'

'Terrible. Let's do dinner tonight. I need to unload on someone.'

'I'm going home tonight, to bed, to sleep.'

'You have to eat. I'll grab some Chinese, we'll have a glass of wine, then sleep together. No sex whatsoever. We've done it before.'

'We'll see. I gotta get out of here. Later.'

'Are you gonna make it?'

'I doubt it.'

At 11:00 a.m., Kyle congratulated himself because he could now bill the client $800 for driving in circles. Then he laughed at himself. Editor in chief of the *Yale Law Journal* behind the wheel here, making perfect turns, clean stops and goes, taking in the sights, dodging the cabs, ah, the life of a big-time Wall Street lawyer.

If his father could see him now.

The call came at 11:40. Bard said, 'We're leaving the courtroom. What happened to you?'

'I couldn't find a parking space.'

'Where are you?'

'Two blocks from the courthouse.'

'Pick us up where you dropped us off.'

'My pleasure.'

Minutes later, Kyle wheeled to the curb like a veteran driver, and his two passengers jumped into the rear seat. He pulled away and said, 'Where to?'

'The office,' came the terse reply from Peckham, and for several minutes nothing was said. Kyle expected to be grilled about what he'd been doing for the past few hours. Where were you, Kyle? Why did you miss the hearing, Kyle? But nothing. Sadly, he began to realize that he had not been missed at all. To create some noise, he finally asked, 'So how'd the hearing go?'

'It didn't,' said Peckham.

'What hearing?' said Bard.

'What have you been doing since 9:00 a.m.?' Kyle asked.

'Waiting for the Honorable Theodore Hennessy to shake off his hangover and grace us with his presence,' Bard said.

'It was postponed for two weeks,' Peckham said.

As they stepped off the elevator on the thirty-second floor, Kyle's phone vibrated. A text message from Tabor read: 'Hurry to cube. Problem.'

Tabor met him at the stairs. 'So how was court?'

'Great. I love litigation. What's the problem?' They were walking quickly through the hall, past Sandra the secretary.

'It's Dale,' Tabor whispered. 'She fainted, collapsed, passed out, something.'

'Where is she?'

'I've hidden the body.'

At the cube, Dale was lying peacefully on a sleeping bag partially hidden under Tabor's desk. Her eyes were open, she seemed alert, but her face was very pale.

'She woke up at five Tuesday morning, and she hasn't slept since. That's about fifty-five hours, which might be a record.'

Kyle knelt beside her, gently took her wrist, and said, 'You okay?'

She nodded yes, but was not convincing.

Tabor, the lookout, glanced around and kept

talking: 'She doesn't want anyone to know, okay. I say we call the nurse. She says no. What do you say, Kyle?'

'Don't tell anyone,' Dale said, her voice low and raspy. 'I fainted, that's all. I'm fine.'

'Your pulse is good,' Kyle said. 'Can you walk?'

'I think so.'

'Then the three of us will slip out for a quick lunch,' Kyle said. 'I'll take you home, and you're going to rest. Tabor, call a car.'

With a hand under each arm, they slowly pulled her up. She stood, took deep breaths, and said, 'I can walk.'

'We're right beside you,' Kyle said.

They caught a curious glance or two as they left the building – one petite, well-dressed young associate, with very pale skin, arm in arm with two of her colleagues, off for a quick lunch, no doubt, but no one cared. Tabor helped her into the car, then returned to the cube to cover their trails if necessary.

Kyle half-carried her up the three flights to her apartment, then helped her undress and tucked her in. He kissed her forehead, turned off the lights, and closed the door. She did not move for hours.

In the den, he took off his coat, tie, and shoes. He covered the small kitchen table with his laptop, FirmFone, and a file full of research for a memo he'd been neglecting. Once he was fully situated, his eyelids became heavier and heavier until he walked to the sofa for a quick nap. Tabor called an hour later and woke him up. Kyle assured him Dale was sleeping well and would be fine after a long rest.

'There's an announcement coming at 4:00 p.m.,' Tabor said. 'Big news about the split. Watch your e-mails.'

At exactly 4:00 p.m., Scully & Pershing sent an e-mail to all of its lawyers announcing the departure of six partners and thirty-one associates from its litigation practice group. The names were listed. The departures were effective as of 5:00 p.m. that day. The bulletin then proceeded with the standard drivel touting the greatness of the firm and assuring everyone that the split would have no impact on the firm's ability to fully service the needs of its many wonderful and valuable clients.

Kyle peeked through the bedroom door. The patient was breathing nicely and had not changed positions.

He dimmed the lights in the den and stretched out on the sofa. Forget the memo, forget the billing. To hell with the firm, at least for a few stolen moments. How often would he have the chance to relax like this on a Thursday afternoon? The funeral seemed like a month ago. Pittsburgh was in another galaxy. Baxter was gone but not forgotten. He needed Joey, but Joey was gone, too.

The vibration of the phone woke him again. The e-mail was from Doug Peckham, and it read: ‘Kyle: Major realignment in litigation. I’ve been added to the Trylon case. So have you. Office of Wilson Rush, 7:00 a.m. sharp tomorrow.’

Chapter 30

For the senior litigation partner, and member of the firm's management committee, the cost of square footage was not a concern. Wilson Rush's office was spread over a large corner on the thirty-first floor, an area at least four times larger than any Kyle had yet seen. Mr. Rush evidently liked boats. His polished and gleaming oak desk was mounted on four rudders from old sailing yachts. A long credenza behind it held a collection of intricate models of sleek clippers and schooners. Every painting depicted a grand vessel at sea. As Kyle walked in and did a quick scan, he caught himself almost waiting for the floor to rock and the salt water to splash across his feet. But he forgot about the decor when Mr. Rush said, 'Good morning, Kyle. Over here.'

The great man was rising from a large conference table at the far end of his office. A crowd had already gathered there and heavy lifting was under way. Kyle sat next to Doug

Peckham. Quick introductions were made. There were nine others present, excluding Mr. Rush and Mr. Peckham, and Kyle recognized most of the faces, including that of Sherry Abney, the senior associate Bennie had been shadowing. She smiled. Kyle smiled back.

Mr. Rush, seated at the head of the table, launched into a quick review of the current upheaval. Two of the partners who'd mutinied with Toby Roland, and seven of the thirty-one associates, had been assigned to the Trylon versus Bartin case – 'much more about that in a minute' – and it was imperative that the firm's manpower be shuffled immediately because the client, Trylon, was important and demanding. Therefore, two partners, Doug Peckham and a woman named Isabelle Gaffney, were entering the fray, along with eight associates.

Mr. Rush was explaining how uneasy the in-house boys at Trylon were with the defections and how necessary it was to shore up the troops, to literally throw more lawyers at APE and Bartin Dynamics.

Isabelle, or Izzy behind her back, was somewhat notorious because she had once required two associates to wait in the delivery room while she was temporarily sidetracked giving birth to a child. Firm lore held that no one had ever seen her smile. And she wasn't about to smile as Mr. Rush went on about the reshuffling and realigning and deft maneuvering of the unlimited legal talent at his disposal.

Two first-year associates were being added, Kyle and a mysterious young man from Penn named Atwater. Of the twelve litigation rookies, Atwater was by far the quietest and loneliest. Dale was a distant second, but she had warmed up nicely, at least in Kyle's opinion. He'd spent the night on her sofa again, alone, while she was dead to the world. He'd slept little. There was too much to consider. The shock of being assigned to the Trylon case caused him to stare at the ceiling and mumble to himself. The horror of Baxter's murder, the images of the funeral and burial, the harsh words of Joey Bernardo – who could sleep with such nightmares rattling around?

Late that night, Kyle had called Peckham and picked and probed to find out why he had been selected to a case he had been rather vocal in trying to avoid. Peckham had no sympathy and was not in the mood to talk. The decision had been made by Wilson Rush. End of conversation.

Mr. Rush was now going through the basics of the lawsuit, material Kyle had committed to memory weeks and months earlier. Binders were passed around. A half hour dragged by and Kyle began to wonder how a person as dull and methodical as Wilson Rush could be so successful in the courtroom. Discovery was under way, with both parties at war over the documents. At least twenty depositions had been scheduled.

Kyle took notes because everyone else was taking notes, but he was thinking about Bennie. Did Bennie already know that Kyle had landed the prize position? Bennie had known every member of the Trylon team. He knew that Sherry Abney supervised Jack McDougle. Was there another spy in the firm? Another victim of Bennie and his blackmail? If so, was this person watching Kyle and reporting to Bennie?

Though he hated every meeting with Bennie, their next encounter would be the biggest challenge. Kyle would go through the motions and engage in somewhat civilized conversation with the man responsible for the murder of Baxter Tate, and he would be forced to do so without a hint that he was remotely suspicious.

'Any questions?' Mr. Rush asked.

Sure, Kyle thought, more questions than you can possibly answer.

After a full hour of update and review, Kyle, Atwater, and the other six new associates were led by Sherry Abney to the secret room on the eighteenth floor. Secret to some, but Bennie and Nigel certainly knew about it. Along the way they were introduced to a nonlawyer named Gant, a security expert of some variety. Gant stopped them at the door and explained that it was the only door. One way in and one way out and a coded plastic strip smaller than a credit card was required for entry and exit. Each lawyer was given a card, and every time the lawyer came or went, it was recorded. Gant nodded at the ceiling and informed them that there were video cameras watching everything.

Inside, the room was about the size of Wilson Rush's office. No windows, bare walls, drab olive carpet. There was nothing in the room but ten square tables with a large computer on each one.

Sherry Abney took charge. 'This case now has over four million documents, and they're all right here in our virtual warehouse,' she said, patting a computer like a proud mother. 'The actual paperwork is in secured storage in a facility in Wilmington, but you can access it all from one of these. The main server is locked up in a room next door.' She kept patting. 'These are pretty fancy computers, custom made by a company you've never heard of and never will. Do not, under any circumstances, attempt to repair, examine, or just plain fiddle with the hardware.

'The software is called Sonic, and it, too, is customized for this case. It's really just some home brew that our computer folks put together, a variation of Barrister with some bells and whistles added for security reasons. Pass code changes every week. Password changes every day, sometimes twice a day. When it changes, you will receive a coded e-mail. If you try to access with the wrong code or password, then all manner of hell breaks loose. You could be fired.'

She looked around with as much menace as possible, then continued, 'This system is self-contained and cannot be accessed anywhere else within the firm, or outside the firm. It's online, you just can't get to it. This is the only place, the only room in which you are able to access the documents, and this room is closed from 10:00 p.m. until 6:00 a.m. Sorry, no all-nighters in here, but it is open seven days a week.'

At her direction, each associate sat down before a computer and was given a pass code and password. There was nothing on the screen to indicate who manufactured the computer or who wrote the software.

Sherry walked from lawyer to lawyer, looking at the monitors and chatting like a college professor. 'There's an extensive tutorial at the beginning, and I strongly suggest you go through it today. Pull up the index. The documents are classified in three basic groups, with a hundred subgroups. Category A contains all the harmless junk that Bartin has already been given – letters, e-mails, office memos, the list is endless. Category B has important materials that are discoverable, though we have not handed all of them over. Category R, for "Restricted," is where you'll find the good stuff, about a million documents dealing with the technological research that is the heart of this little dispute. It's top secret, classified, and no one but the judge knows if it will ever be shown to Bartin. Mr. Rush thinks not. Category R is privileged, confidential, Attorneys' Work Product. When you enter Category R, a record of your entry automatically registers with Mr. Gant's computer right next door. Any questions?'

All eight associates stared at their monitors, all thinking the same thing – there are four million documents in there, and someone has to examine them.

'Sonic is amazing,' Sherry said. 'Once you master it, you will be able to find a document or group of documents within seconds. I'll be here for the rest of the day for a workshop. The sooner you learn your way around our virtual library, the easier your life will be.'

At 4:20 on Friday afternoon, Kyle received an e-mail from Bennie. It read: 'Let's meet tonight at 9:00. Details to follow. BW.'

Kyle responded: 'I can't.'

Bennie responded: 'Tomorrow afternoon, say 5:00 or 6:00?'

Kyle: 'I can't.'

Bennie: 'Sunday night, 10:00 p.m.?'

Kyle: 'I can't.'

Kyle was sleeping when someone rapped on the door of his apartment at ten minutes after seven on Saturday morning. 'Who is it?' he yelled as he stumbled through his cluttered den.

'Bennie,' came the reply.

'What do you want?' Kyle demanded at the door.

'I've brought you some coffee.'

Kyle unlocked and unchained the door, and Bennie walked by him quickly. He was holding two tall paper cups of coffee. He placed them on the counter and looked around. 'What a dump,' he said. 'I thought you were making some money.'

'What do you want?' Kyle snapped.

'I don't like being ignored,' Bennie snapped back as he jerked around, ready to pounce. His face was taut and his eyes were hot. He pointed a finger that came within inches of Kyle's face. 'You do not ignore me, understand?' he hissed. It was the first real display of temper Kyle had seen from him.

'Be cool.'

Kyle brushed by him, their shoulders touching solidly, and walked to the bedroom, where he found a T-shirt. When he returned to the den, Bennie was removing the tops from the cups. 'I want an update.'

The nearest weapon was a cheap ceramic table lamp Kyle had found at a secondhand store. He took the coffee without saying thanks. He glanced at the lamp and thought how nicely it would crack over Bennie's bald head, how wonderful it would be to hear them break into pieces, both lamp and skull, and how easily he could pound away until the little bastard was dead but still bleeding on the cheap rug. Greetings from my old pal Baxter. Kyle took a sip, then took a breath. Both men were still standing. Bennie was wearing his gray trench coat. Kyle was decked out in red boxers and a wrinkled T-shirt.

'I got assigned to the Trylon case yesterday.

Big news, huh, or did you already know this?'

Bennie's eyes revealed nothing. He took a sip, then said, 'And the secret room on the eighteenth floor? Tell me about it.'

Kyle described it.

'What about the computers?'

'Manufacturer unknown. Basic desktop models but supposedly custom built for the project, all linked to a server locked away next door. Lots of memory, all the bells and whistles. Video cameras everywhere and a security expert next door monitoring everything. It's a dead end if you ask me. There's no way to steal anything.'

To which Bennie offered a grunt and a smart-ass smirk. 'We've cracked much bigger vaults, I assure you of that. Everything can be stolen. Let us worry about that. Sonic is the software?'

'Yes.'

'Have you mastered it?'

'Not yet. I'll go in later this morning for another lesson.'

'How many documents?'

'Over four million.'

That brought the only smile of the morning. 'What about access to the room?'

'Open seven days a week but closed from ten at night until six in the morning. There's only one door, and there are at least three cameras watching it.'

'Does someone check you in?'

'I don't think so. But the key leaves a record of each entry and exit.'

'Let me see the key.'

Kyle reluctantly got the key from his room and handed it over. Bennie examined it like a surgeon, then gave it back. 'I want you to visit the room as often as possible over the next few days, but don't arouse any suspicions. Go at different hours, watch everything. We'll meet at ten on Tuesday night, room 1780, Four Seasons Hotel on Fifty-seventh. Got it?'

'Sure.'

'No surprises.'

'Yes, sir.'

Chapter 31

With seventy-eight thousand lawyers in Manhattan, the selection of one should not have been so difficult. Kyle narrowed his list, did more research, added names, and deleted names. He had begun the secret project not long after he arrived in the city, and had abandoned it several times. He was never sure he would actually hire a lawyer, but wanted the name of a good one just in case. Baxter's murder changed everything. Kyle not only wanted protection; now he wanted justice.

Roy Benedict was a criminal defense lawyer with a two-hundred-man firm located in a tall building one block east of Scully & Pershing. The location of the chosen lawyer was crucial, given the attention paid to Kyle's movements. Benedict measured up in other important areas as well. He had worked for the FBI before law school at NYU and after graduation spent six years with the Department of Justice. He had contacts, old friends, people on the other side of the street now, but people he could trust. Crime was his specialty. He was ranked in the top one hundred of the city's white-collar defense specialists, but not in the top ten. Kyle needed solid advice, but he couldn't afford an ego. Benedict's firm was often listed as opposing counsel in lawsuits involving Scully & Pershing. The icing on the cake was his basketball career at Duquesne some twenty-five years earlier. On the phone, he seemed to have little time for small talk and said he wasn't taking any new cases, but the basketball angle opened the door.

The appointment was at 2:00 p.m. on Monday, and Kyle arrived early. He found it impossible to walk through the law firm without comparing it with his. It was smaller, and it spent less trying to impress visitors with abstract art and designer furniture. The receptionists were not as cute.

In his briefcase he had a file on Roy Benedict – old stats and photos from Duquesne, bios from legal directories, newspaper stories about two of his more notorious cases. He was forty-seven, six feet six, and appeared to be in great shape, ready for a pickup game. His office was busy, smaller than most of the partners' at Scully, but nicely appointed. Benedict was cordial and genuinely pleased to meet another New York lawyer who'd played for the Dukes.

Kyle explained that he didn't play much. The

basketball talk dragged on, and Kyle cut things off by saying, 'Look, Mr. Benedict—'

'It's Roy.'

'Okay, Roy, I can't spend too much time here because I'm being followed.'

A few seconds passed as Roy allowed this to sink in. 'And why is a first-year associate at the biggest law firm in the world being followed?'

'I have a few problems. It's complicated, and I think I need a lawyer.'

'I do nothing but white-collar crime, Kyle. Have you screwed up in that area?'

'Not yet. But I'm being pressured to commit a whole list of crimes.'

Roy bounced a pencil on his desk, tried to think of how to proceed.

'I really need a lawyer,' Kyle said.

'My initial retainer is fifty grand,' Roy said and watched carefully for a response. He knew within $10,000 how much Kyle was earning as a first-year associate. His firm didn't try to compete with Scully & Pershing, but it came close.

'I can't pay that much. I have five thousand in cash.' Kyle yanked an envelope from his pocket and tossed it on the desk. 'Give me some time, and I'll get the rest.'

'What does this case involve?'

'Rape, murder, theft, wiretapping, extortion, blackmail, and a few others. I can't give you the details until we reach an agreement.'

Roy nodded, then smiled. 'There's someone following you now?'

'Oh, yes. I've been under surveillance since early February, back at Yale.'

'Is your life in danger?'

Kyle thought for a moment. 'Yes, I believe so.'

The air was thick with unanswered questions, and Roy's curiosity got the best of him. He opened a drawer and withdrew some papers. He scanned them quickly – three sheets stapled together – added some notes with a pen, then slid them across. 'This is a contract for legal services.'

Kyle read it hurriedly. The initial retainer had been reduced to $5,000. The hourly rate cut in half, from $800 to $400. Kyle had just recently accepted the fact that he charged $400 an hour. Now he would be the client paying that much. He signed his name and said, 'Thanks.'

Roy took the envelope and placed it in the drawer. 'Where do we begin?' he asked, and Kyle sank deeper into his chair. A huge weight was leaving him. He wasn't sure if the nightmare was coming to an end or if he was digging a deeper hole, but the fact that he had someone to talk to was beyond comforting.

Kyle closed his eyes and said, 'I don't know. There's so much ground to cover.'

'Who's following you? Government agents of some sort?'

'No. Private thugs. Very good ones. And I have no idea who they are.'

'Why don't we start at the beginning?'

'Okay.'

Kyle began with Elaine, the party, the accusations of rape, the investigation. He introduced Bennie and his boys, his blackmail, the video, his covert mission to steal documents from Scully & Pershing. He produced a file and spread out the photos of Bennie, along with the composites of Nigel and two of the street thugs who'd been following him.

'Bennie Wright is just an alias. The guy probably has twenty names. He speaks with a slight accent that's probably eastern European. Just a guess.'

Roy studied the photo of Bennie.

'Is there a way to identify him?' Kyle asked.

'I don't know. Do you know where he is?'

'Here, in New York. I saw him on Saturday, and I'll meet him again tomorrow night. He's my handler. I'm his asset.'

'Keep talking.'

Kyle removed another file and went through the basics of the Trylon-Bartin war, and in doing so discussed only the facts that had been published in news stories. Even though Roy was his lawyer and sworn to confidentiality, Kyle was a lawyer, too, and his client expected the same. 'It's the largest Pentagon contract in history, so it's potentially the biggest lawsuit ever filed.'

Roy spent a few minutes scanning the articles, then said, 'I've heard of it. Keep talking.'

Kyle described the surveillance and eaves-dropping, and Roy forgot about Trylon and

Bartin. 'Wiretapping carries five years, federal,' he said.

'Wiretapping is nothing. What about murder?'

'Who got murdered?'

Kyle raced through Joey's involvement, then the surprising arrival of Baxter and his desire to reach out to the girl. He handed over a dozen newspaper reports on the random shooting of Baxter Tate.

'I saw something about this in the news,' Roy said.

'I was a pallbearer at his funeral last Wednesday,' Kyle said.

'I'm sorry.'

'Thanks. The cops have no clue. I'm sure Bennie ordered the hit, but the killers have vanished.'

'Why would Bennie kill Baxter Tate?' Roy alternated between scribbling notes, looking at the face of Bennie Wright, and picking through the file, but for the most part he just shook his head in confusion and disbelief.

'He had no choice,' Kyle said. 'If Baxter succeeded in making some harebrained confession to Elaine, which certainly appeared likely, then the events that follow are out of control. I think the girl goes nuts, cries rape again, and I'm dragged back to Pittsburgh along with Joey and Alan Strock. My life is derailed. I leave the firm, leave New York, and Bennie loses his asset.'

'But with Baxter dead, doesn't the rape case lose some steam?'

'Yes, but the video is still out there. And believe me, we want no part of it. It's brutal.'

'But it doesn't implicate you?'

'Only for being a drunken idiot. When the sex begins, I'm nowhere to be seen. I don't even remember it.'

'And you have no idea how Bennie got the video?'

'That's the greatest question of all, one that I've asked myself every hour for the past nine months. The fact that he somehow heard of the video, then stole it or bought it, is something I cannot comprehend. I don't know which is more terrifying – the video itself or the fact that Bennie got his hands on it.'

Roy was shaking his head again. He stood and unfolded his gangly frame. He stretched and kept shaking his head. 'How many interns did Scully & Pershing hire the summer before last?'

'Around a hundred.'

'So Bennie and his group get the names of a hundred summer interns, and they investigate them, looking for an Achilles' heel. When they get to your name on the list, they snoop around Pittsburgh and Duquesne. They probably hear about the rape, lean on someone in the police department, get the rape file, and decide to dig even deeper. The file is closed, so the cops talk more than they should. There was the rumor about a video, but the cops could never find it. Somehow, Bennie does.'

'Yep.'

'He's got plenty of money and plenty of people.'

'Obviously, so who's he working for?'

Roy glanced at his watch, frowned, and said, 'I have a meeting at three.' He grabbed his desk phone, waited, then barked, 'Cancel my three o'clock. And no interruptions.' He fell into his chair and rubbed his chin with his knuckles.

'I doubt if he works for APE. I cannot believe that a rival law firm would spend this kind of money to break so many laws. It's inconceivable.'

'Bartin?'

'Much more probable. Plenty of money, plenty of motive. I'm sure Bartin is convinced the documents were stolen from them, so why not steal them back?'

'Any other suspects?'

'Oh, please, Kyle. We're talking about military technology. The Chinese and the Russians prefer to steal what they can't develop. That's the nature of the game. We dazzle with the research, they just steal it.'

'But using a law firm?'

'The law firm is probably just one piece of the puzzle. They have spies in other places, and there are more people like Bennie, who have no name and no home and ten passports. He's probably a well-trained former intelligence pro who now hires himself out for a zillion dollars to do exactly what he's doing.'

'He killed Baxter.'

Roy shrugged. 'Killing doesn't bother this guy.'

'Great. Just when I was starting to feel better.'

Roy smiled, but the wrinkles never left his forehead. 'Look, give me a few days to digest this.'

'We need to move fast. I now have access to the documents, and Bennie's much more excited.'

'You'll see him tomorrow night?'

'Yes. At the Four Seasons Hotel on Fifty-seventh. Care to join the party?'

'Thanks. How long do these little meetings last?'

'Ten minutes if I'm lucky. We bitch and bark, and then I slam the door on the way out. I act tough, but the whole time I'm scared to death. I need help, Roy.'

'You've come to the right place.'

'Thanks. I gotta go. Doofus is waiting.'

'Doofus?'

Kyle stood and reached across the desk. He picked out a composite and laid it on top of the pile. 'Meet Doofus, probably the worst of the street crawlers who've shadowed me for the past nine months. His buddy there is Rufus. He's bad, too, but not as bad as Doofus. I have become so adept at appearing to be so clueless that these clowns think they can follow me in their sleep. They make a lot of mistakes.'

They shook hands and said goodbye, and long after Kyle was gone, Roy stared at his window and tried to absorb it all. A twenty-five-year-old former editor in chief of the *Yale Law Journal* being stalked on the streets of New York City by a deadly group of professional operatives who are blackmailing him into spying on his own law firm.

Roy was awestruck by the scenario. He smiled and reminded himself of how much he loved his job.

There were a few bright spots in the ugly split among the firm's litigators. More partners would be needed, and sooner. Advancement opportunities were created with all those gaps to fill. And, most crucial to the first-year associates, offices had been emptied. The jockeying began as soon as the malcontents fled. Over the weekend, Tabor nailed down a place of his own and had moved his junk by Sunday night.

Kyle gave little thought to a move. He'd grown accustomed to his little cubicle, and he enjoyed having Dale close by. They groped occasionally when they were completely safe. He looked forward to her daily appearance and expected a full rundown on what she was wearing and who designed it. Discussing her clothes was almost as much fun as removing them.

He was surprised when Sherry Abney dropped by late Monday afternoon and asked him to follow her. They took the stairs one floor up to the thirty-fourth, and, after walking past a dozen doors, she stopped, stepped in, and said, 'This is yours.'

It was a twelve-by-twelve square room, with a glass desk, leather chairs, handsome rug, and a window that faced south and allowed real sunlight to pass through. Kyle was overwhelmed. Why me? he wanted to ask. But he pretended to take it in stride.

'Compliments of Wilson Rush,' she said.

'Nice,' Kyle said, stepping to the window.

'You share a secretary with Cunningham next door. I'm just down the hall if you need anything. I'd get myself moved in because Mr. Rush might stop by for a quick inspection.'

Moving took fifteen minutes. Kyle made four trips back and forth, and during his last one Dale carried his sleeping bag and laptop. She was genuinely happy for him, and even passed along a few decorating ideas. 'Too bad you don't have a sofa,' she said.

'Not at the office, dear.'

'Then where and when?'

'I take it you're in the mood.'

'I need to be loved, or at least lusted after.'

'How about dinner, then a quickie?'

'How about a marathon, then a quick dinner?'

'Oh, boy.'

They sneaked out of the building at 7:00 p.m. and took a cab to her apartment. Kyle was unbuttoning his shirt when his FirmFone buzzed with an e-mail sent by an unknown partner to about a dozen grunts. All hands were needed on deck immediately for an urgent orgy of work that was absolutely critical to the future of the firm. Kyle ignored it and turned off the lights.

Chapter 32

For no reason other than sheer obstinacy, Kyle arrived forty-five minutes late for the Tuesday night meeting at the Four Seasons. He expected to see Nigel, so he was not surprised when Bennie's sidekick met him at the door and pretended to be pleased to see him. 'Kyle, old boy, how have you been?' he chirped with a fake smile.

'Marvelous. And your name is?'

'Nigel.'

'Oh, yeah, I forgot. Last name?'

'Sorry, old boy.'

'Do you have a last name, or do you have so many you can't remember which one fits right now?'

'Good evening, Kyle,' Bennie said, rising to his feet, folding a newspaper.

'So nice to see you, Bennie.' Kyle placed his briefcase on the bed but did not remove his trench coat. 'Now, who called this meeting?' he asked.

'Tell us about the room on the eighteenth floor,' Bennie said, abandoning any more preliminaries.

'I've already described it.'

Nigel fired away: 'Ten monitors on ten tables, right, Kyle?'

'Yes.'

'And where are the computers themselves?'

'On the tables, next to the monitors.'

'The computers, Kyle, tall and thin, short and fat? Give us a hint here!'

'More of a square box, to the right of each monitor.'

On the dresser next to the television there was a thin notebook, already opened. Nigel lunged for it and said, 'Take a look at these computers, Kyle. All shapes and sizes, various makes from around the world. See anything remotely similar?'

Kyle methodically flipped through it. Each page had color photos of eight computers, ten pages in all, eighty machines that varied wildly in design and construction. He settled on one that looked more like a color jet printer than a computer.

'Yes, rather square,' Nigel observed. 'How many disc drives?'

'None.'

'None? Are you certain, Kyle?'

'Yes. These were custom built for maximum security. There are no disc drives, no ports, no way to transfer the data.'

'Control panel? Switches, buttons, lights, anything, Kyle?'

'Nothing. Plain-vanilla box.'

'And the server?'

'Locked up next door. Out of sight.'

'Interesting. And the monitors, Kyle?'

'Basic LCD flat screens.'

'Let's take a peek,' Nigel said as he opened the notebook to another section, this one filled with an assortment of monitors. 'Size, Kyle?'

'Fourteen inches.'

'Full-color display I'm sure?'

'Yes.' Kyle stopped on the third page and pointed. 'This one is very close.'

'Excellent, Kyle.'

'And printers?'

'None.'

'Nowhere in the room? Not a single printer?'

'None.'

Nigel paused to scratch his face and ponder this. 'Suppose you're working on a brief or a memo. When it's time to produce it, what happens?'

'You notify your supervisor, who then enters the room, pulls it up, reviews it, and so on. If it is to be submitted to the court, or to the opposing attorneys, it's printed.'

'Where? I thought there were no printers.'

'There's a machine in a room next door with a paralegal who monitors the printing. Every sheet of paper that's printed is coded and duplicated.

It's impossible to print anything without leaving a trail.'

'Quite nice, really.' With that, Nigel took a sharp step back and relaxed. Bennie took over. 'Kyle, how many times have you entered the room?'

'Once a day for the last five days.'

'And how many people are normally in the room?'

'It varies. Sunday afternoon I was alone for about an hour. This morning there were five or six others.'

'Have you been there late at night when they close the room?'

'No, not yet.'

'Do it, okay. Be there at ten one night.'

'I can't go there just to hang out, Bennie. It's not a coffee room. Surveillance is constant, cameras watching and all that. There has to be a reason to be there, other than casing the joint.'

'Does anyone notice when you come and go?'

'There's not a guard at the door. The key makes a record of each entry and exit, and I'm sure it's all recorded by closed circuit.'

'Do you take your briefcase in with you?'

'No.'

'Are briefcases forbidden?'

'No.'

'Do you wear your jacket?'

'No. Jackets are not required around the office.'

Bennie and Nigel studied each other for a minute or so, both minds hard at work.

'Will you go there tomorrow?' Bennie asked.

'Maybe. I'm not sure right now. It depends on what I'm asked to do in the morning.'

'I want you to enter the room tomorrow, carrying your briefcase and wearing your jacket. As soon as you're settled in, take off your jacket. Keep the briefcase under the table.'

'Will this work, Kyle?' Nigel piled on quickly.

'Oh, sure. Why not? Anything else? And what if I haul in a box of tacos and drop cheddar crumbs on the keyboard? Where is this going?'

'Just trust us here, Kyle,' Nigel said gently. 'We know what we're doing.'

'You're the last person I'd trust.'

'Now, Kyle.'

'Look, I'm tired. I'd really like to go—'

'What are your plans for the next few days?' Bennie asked.

'I'll work tomorrow, leave the office around five, take the train to Philly, rent a car, and drive to York. I'm having Thanksgiving dinner with my father on Thursday. I'll be back in the city late Friday afternoon, and back at the office early Saturday. Good enough?'

'We'll meet Sunday night,' Bennie said.

'Your place or mine?'

'I'll pass along the details.'

'Happy Thanksgiving, boys,' Kyle said as he left the room.

*

On his new office door, Kyle hung two waterproof, all-purpose trench coats, one black and the other one a light brown. The black one he wore every day, to and from work and when moving around the city. The brown one was used rarely, only on those occasions when Kyle really didn't want to be followed. At 2:30 on Wednesday, he draped it over his arm and rode the elevator to the second floor. From there, he took a service elevator to the basement, put on the trench coat, and ducked through the rows of thick plumbing pipes and electrical cables and heating units until he came to a metal stairway. He spoke to a technician, one he'd spoken to on several occasions. He saw daylight in a narrow alley that barely separated his building from the fifty story edifice next door. Ten minutes later, he walked into the office of Roy Benedict.

They had chatted briefly on the phone, and Kyle was uneasy about the plan.

Roy was not at all uneasy. He had studied the file, analyzed the facts and issues, weighed the predicament, and was ready to move. 'I have a friend with the FBI,' he began. 'A friend I trust completely. We worked together years ago before I became a lawyer, and even though we are now on opposite sides of the street, I trust him even more. He's a heavyweight here in the New York office.'

Kyle flashed back to his last encounter with the FBI. Fake names, fake badges, a long night in a hotel room with Bennie. 'I'm listening,' Kyle said with skepticism.

'I want to meet with him and lay everything on the table. Everything.'

'What will he do?'

'Crimes have been committed. Crimes are in process. Crimes are being planned. And not small crimes. I suspect he will be as shocked as I am. I suspect the FBI will get involved.'

'So Bennie gets nabbed by the feds?'

'Sure. Don't you want him locked up?'

'For life. But he has a vast network out there in the shadows.'

'The FBI knows how to lay its traps. They screw up occasionally, but their record is very good. I deal with them all the time, Kyle. I know how smart these guys are. If I talk to them now, they'll move in quietly and lay the groundwork. When they want to, they can throw a whole army at the enemy. Right now you need an army.'

'Thanks.'

'I need your permission to talk to the FBI.'

'Is there a chance they'll take a look and let it pass?'

'Yes, but I doubt it.'

'When will you talk to your friend?'

'Maybe as early as this afternoon.'

Kyle barely hesitated. 'Let's do it,' he said.

Chapter 33

It was almost midnight when Kyle quietly slipped through the unlocked kitchen door of his family home in York. All lights were off. His father knew he would be arriving late, but John McAvoy let nothing interfere with a night's sleep. Zack, the ancient border collie who'd never met an intruder he didn't like, managed to rouse himself from his pillow in the breakfast nook and say hello. Kyle rubbed his head, thankful to see the dog one more time. Zack's age and exact lineage had never been clear. He was a gift from a client, partial payment on a fee, and he liked to spend his days under the desk of John McAvoy, sleeping through all sorts of legal problems. He usually ate lunch in the firm's kitchen with one of the secretaries.

Kyle kicked off his loafers, sneaked up the stairs to his bedroom, and within minutes was under the covers and dreaming.

Less than five hours later, John practically

kicked in the door and boomed, 'Let's go, knucklehead. You can sleep when you're dead.'

In a drawer, Kyle found an old set of his thermal underwear and a pair of wool socks, and in the closet, among a collection of dusty old clothes that dated back to high school, he pulled out his hunting overalls. Without a woman in the house, the dust and spiderwebs and unused garments were accumulating. His boots were precisely where he'd left them a year earlier, last Thanksgiving.

John was at the kitchen table preparing for war. Three rifles with scopes were laid out, next to several boxes of ammo. Kyle, who'd learned the art and rules of hunting as a child, knew his father had thoroughly cleaned the rifles the night before.

'Good morning,' John said. 'You ready?'

'Yep. Where's the coffee?'

'In the thermos. What time did you get in?'

'Just a few hours ago.'

'You're young. Let's go.'

They loaded the gear into the late-model Ford pickup, four-wheel drive, John's preferred means of transportation in and around York. Fifteen minutes after crawling out of bed, Kyle was riding through the darkness of a frigid Thanksgiving morning, sipping black coffee and nibbling on a granola bar. The town was soon behind them. The roads became narrower.

John was working a cigarette, the smoke

drifting through a small crack in the driver's window. He usually said little in the mornings. For a man whose day was spent in the midst of a busy small-town law office, with phones ringing and clients waiting and secretaries scurrying about, John needed the solitude of the early hours.

Kyle, though still sleepy, was almost numb with the shock of open spaces, empty roads, no people, the great outdoors. What, exactly, had been the attraction of a big city? They stopped at a gate. Kyle opened it and John drove through, then they continued deeper into the hills. There was still no trace of sun in the east.

'So how's the romance?' Kyle said, finally attempting conversation. His father had mentioned a new girlfriend, a serious one.

'Off and on. She's cooking dinner tonight.'

'And her name is?'

'Zoe.'

'Zoe?'

'Zoe. It's Greek.'

'Is she Greek?'

'Her mother is Greek. Her father is an Anglo mix. She's a mutt, like the rest of us.'

'Is she cute?'

John thumped ashes out the window. 'You think I'd date her if she wasn't cute?'

'Yes. I remember Rhoda. What a dog.'

'Rhoda was hot. You just didn't appreciate her beauty.' The truck hit a rough section of gravel road and bounced them around.

'Where's Zoe from?'

'Reading. Why all the questions?'

'How old is she?'

'Forty-nine, and hot.'

'You gonna marry her?'

'I don't know. We've talked about it.'

The road went from gravel to dirt. At the edge of a field, John parked and turned off the lights. 'Whose property is this?' Kyle asked softly as they gathered their rifles.

'It used to be owned by Zoe's ex-husband's family. She got it in the divorce. Two hundred acres, crawling with deer.'

'Come on.'

'True. All legal and aboveboard.'

'And you handled the divorce?'

'Five years ago. But I didn't start dating her until last year. Maybe it was the year before, I really can't remember.'

'We're hunting on Zoe's property?'

'Yes, but she doesn't care.'

Ah, the small-town practice of law, Kyle thought to himself. For twenty minutes they hiked along the edge of the woods, without a word. They stopped under an elm tree just as the first hint of light fell across the small valley before them.

'Bill Henry killed an eight-point last week just over that ridge there,' John said, pointing. 'There are some big bucks in here. If he can get one, anybody can.'

A deer stand had been built in the elm, twenty

feet up, with a rickety ladder leading to it. 'You take this stand,' John said. 'I'll be a hundred yards that way in another one. Nothing but bucks, okay?'

'Got it.'

'Is your hunting license current?'

'I don't think so.'

'No big deal. Lester's still the game warden. I kept his son out of jail last month. A drug head. Meth.'

John walked away, and as he disappeared into the darkness, he said, 'You stay awake, now.'

Kyle tucked the rifle over his shoulder and crawled up the ladder. The deer stand was a small platform made of planks and two-by-fours anchored into the elm, and like all deer stands it was constructed with little thought to comfort. He twisted one way, then another, and finally situated himself with his rear on the planks, his back to the bark, his feet dangling. He'd been in deer stands since he was five years old, and had learned the lessons of complete stillness. A soft breeze rustled a few leaves. The sun was rising fast. The deer would soon quietly ease from the woods to the edge of the field in search of fescue and field corn.

The rifle was a Remington 30.06, a gift for his fourteenth birthday. He tucked it firmly across his chest and promptly dozed off.

The crack of a gunshot jolted him from his nap, and he swung the rifle around, ready to fire. He glanced at his watch – a forty-minute nap. To his left, in the direction of his father, he saw several white tails bouncing in a rapid getaway. Ten minutes passed with no word from John. He'd obviously missed with his first shot and was still in the stand.

An hour passed without a sighting, and Kyle fought to stay awake.

Thanksgiving Day. The offices of Scully & Pershing were officially closed, but he knew that a few of the gunners were there, casually dressed in jeans and boots and billing away. There were a few partners hard at work, all with deadlines screaming at them. He shook his head.

Sounds were approaching, footsteps unconcerned with making noise. John was soon near the elm. 'Let's go,' he said. 'There's a creek just beyond the field, a favorite watering hole.'

Kyle lowered himself carefully, and when his feet were on the ground, John said, 'You didn't see that buck?'

'Nope.'

'I don't know how you missed it. It ran right in front of you.'

'The one you shot at?'

'Yeah, at least a ten-pointer.'

'I guess you missed it, too.'

They returned to the truck and went for the thermos. As they sat on the tailgate, sipping strong coffee from paper cups and finishing the last of the granola bars, Kyle said, 'Dad, I don't want to hunt anymore. We need to talk.'

*

His father listend calmly at first, then lit a cigarette. As Kyle plowed through the rape investigation, he expected an eruption, a series of sharp and painful questions about why he had not called his father. But John listened intently without a word, as if he knew this story and had been expecting the confession.

The first flash of anger came when Bennie entered the narrative. 'They blackmailed you,' he said, then lit another cigarette. 'Son of a bitch.'

'Just listen, okay,' Kyle pleaded and went full speed ahead. The details came in torrents, and several times he raised his hand to keep from being interrupted. After a while, John became stoic, absorbing it all in disbelief but saying nothing. The video, Joey, Baxter, the murder, Trylon and Bartin and the secret room on the eighteenth floor. The meetings with Bennie, Nigel, the plan to filch the documents and hand them to the enemy. And finally, the hiring of Roy Benedict and the appearance of the FBI.

Kyle apologized repeatedly for not trusting his father. He admitted his mistakes, too numerous to recall at that moment. He laid open his soul, and when he finished, hours later it seemed, the sun was well into the sky, the coffee was long gone, the deer long forgotten.

'I think I need some help,' Kyle said.

'You need your ass kicked for not telling me.'

'Yes, I do.'

'Good Lord, son. What a mess.'

'I had no choice. I was terrified of the video, and the thought of another rape investigation was just too much. If you saw the video, you'd understand.'

They left the rifles in the truck and went for a long hike along a narrow trail through the woods.

The feast of turkey, dressing, and all the trimmings had been prepared by a deli that sold the whole package to those who preferred not to be troubled. As John set the dining room table, Kyle left to fetch his mother.

Patty answered her door with a smile and a long hug. She was up, and properly medicated. She escorted Kyle through her apartment and couldn't wait to show off her latest masterpieces. He eventually led her back to the door and down to his rental car, and they enjoyed a quick drive through York. She was wearing lipstick, makeup, and a pretty orange dress that Kyle remembered from his teenage years, and her hair was clean, neat, and almost white. She chattered nonstop with news about locals she'd known years ago, bouncing from one subject to another with a randomness that would have been comical under other circumstances.

Kyle was relieved. There'd been an even chance she would be off her meds and out of her mind. His parents greeted each other with a polite hug, and the small struggling family worked its way through the gossip about the twin daughters, neither of whom had been back to

York in over a year. One was in Santa Monica, the other in Portland. They called both and passed around the phone. The television was on in the den, muted, a football game waiting to be watched. At the dining table, Kyle poured three glasses of wine, though his mother wouldn't touch it.

'You're drinking wine these days,' John said to Kyle as he sat the small turkey on the table.

'Not much.'

The two men served Patty, fussed over her, worked hard to make her comfortable. She prattled on about her art and about events in York that happened years earlier. She managed to ask a few questions about Kyle and his career in New York, and he made his life sound enviable. The strain from events in New York was palpable, but Patty did not notice. She ate almost nothing, but her son and ex-husband devoured the lunch as quickly as possible. After pecan pie and coffee, she announced she wanted to go home, to her work. She was tired, she said, and Kyle wasted no time loading her up for the ten-minute drive.

One football game blurred into another. Kyle, on the sofa, and John, in a recliner, watched the games between naps, and said little. The air was heavy with things unsaid, questions that came and went, plans that needed to be discussed. The father wanted to lecture and yell, but the son was too vulnerable, too dependent at that moment.

'Let's go for a walk,' Kyle said when it was almost dark.

'Walk where?'

'Around the block. I need to talk.'

'Can't we talk here?'

'Let's walk.'

They bundled up and put Zack on a leash. They were on the sidewalk when Kyle said, 'I'm sorry, but I don't like to have serious conversations indoors.'

John lit a cigarette with the ease of a longtime smoker, perfect coordination without missing a step. 'I'm almost afraid to ask why not.'

'Bugs, mikes, nasty little twerps listening to conversations.'

'Let me get this straight. You think that my house might be bugged by these thugs?'

They were strolling along the street Kyle had roamed as a child. He knew the owner of every home, at least the owners back then, and every home had a story. He nodded at one and asked, 'Whatever happened to Mr. Polk?'

'Dead, finally. Lived in a wheelchair for almost fifty years. Very sad. Back to my question. We're not walking down memory lane here, okay?'

'No, I don't think your house is bugged, nor your office, but there's a chance. These guys believe in surveillance and have an unlimited budget. Bugging is easy. Ask me, I'm an expert. I could make a homemade listening device in half an hour with a few items from RadioShack.'

'And how did you acquire such knowledge?'

'Books. Manuals. There's a great little spy store in Manhattan and I drop in occasionally, when I'm able to lose my tail.'

'This is unbelievable, Kyle. If I didn't know better, I'd say you're cracking up. You sound schizophrenic, like a few of my clients.'

'I'm not crazy yet, but I've learned to play it safe and have the serious conversations outdoors.'

'Your apartment is bugged?'

'Oh, yes. I know of at least three listening devices hidden in the place. One is in the AC vent above the sofa in the den. There's one hidden in the bedroom wall, just above the chest of drawers, and there's one in the kitchen in a door facing. I can't really examine them, because there are also three tiny cameras, at least three, that watch me continuously when I'm in the apartment, which is not very often. I've managed to locate these devices by pretending to do all sorts of routine chores around the place, cleaning vents, washing windows, scrubbing floors. The place is a dump, but it's pretty clean.'

'And your phone?'

'I still have the old one from law school, and they're listening. That's why I haven't switched. I know they're listening, and so I give them enough harmless crap to make them happy. I installed a landline in the apartment, and I'm sure it's bugged. I haven't been able to inspect it, though, because the cameras are watching. I use it just for harmless stuff – ordering a pizza, bitching at my landlord, calling a car service.' Kyle pulled out the FirmFone and glanced at it. 'This is one the firm gave us on day one. I'm pretty sure this one is bug-free.'

'The question is, why is it in your pocket on Thanksgiving Day?'

'Habit. It's turned off. For serious stuff I use the desk phone in my office. I figure that if they can bug the office phones, then we're all really screwed.'

'Oh, you're screwed, there's no doubt about that. You should've told me months ago.'

'I know. I should've done a lot of things differently, but I didn't have the benefit of hindsight. I was scared. Still am.'

Zack stopped at a fire hydrant. John needed another smoke. The wind had picked up and leaves were blowing and landing around them. It was dark, and they still had dinner at Zoe's.

They made the block and talked about the future.

Chapter 34

The associates who'd dared to slack off by leaving for the short holiday break returned with a vengeance early Saturday morning. The time away was refreshing, though the strain of frenzied travel left them even more exhausted. And time off also meant no billing.

Kyle punched his clock at 8:00 a.m. sharp when he entered the secret room on the eighteenth floor and settled himself at one of the workstations. Four other members of Team Trylon were there, lost in a virtual world of endless research. He nodded to a couple, but no one spoke. He wore jeans and a wool sport coat, and he hauled in his black Bally briefcase, six inches thick and showing some wear. He'd bought it at a shop on Fifth Avenue a week before orientation. All briefcases at the firm were black.

He placed it on the floor beside him, partially under the table, directly under the plain-vanilla computer that had so captivated dear Nigel. He withdrew a legal pad, then a file, and before long his workstation looked authentic. After a few minutes, he took off his jacket, hung it on the back of his chair, and rolled up his sleeves. Trylon was now paying old Scully an additional four hundred bucks an hour.

A quick look around the room revealed one other briefcase. All other jackets and coats had been left upstairs in the offices. The hours began to drag by as Kyle lost himself in the futuristic world of the B-10 HyperSonic Bomber and the people who designed it.

The only good thing about the secret room was the prohibition against cell phones. After a few hours, Kyle needed a break, and he wanted to check his messages. Specifically, he was waiting to hear from Dale, who hadn't bothered to show up on such a beautiful morning. He walked to his office, closed the door, which was a minor violation of firm policy, and called her private cell phone. As a refuge from the much-hated FirmFone, every associate carried a private one as well.

'Yes,' she answered.

'Where are you?'

'I'm still in Providence.'

'Are you coming back to New York?'

'I'm not sure.'

'Need I remind you, young lady, that this is the third consecutive day in which you have not billed a single hour.'

'I take it you're at the office.'

'Yes, racking up hours along with every other first-year grunt. Everyone's here but you.'

'Fire me. Sue me. I don't care.'

'You'll never make partner with that attitude.'

'Promise?'

'I was thinking about dinner tonight. There's a new restaurant in the East Village that just got two stars from Frank Bruni.'

'Are you asking me out for a date?'

'Please. We can split the check since we work for a gender-neutral firm.'

'You're so romantic.'

'We could do the romance later.'

'So that's what you're really after.'

'Always.'

'I get in around seven. I'll call you then.'

Kyle clipped Trylon twelve hours, then called a sedan for the ride to dinner. The restaurant had twenty tables, a Turkish menu, and no dress requirement, though jeans were preferred. After the two-star review by the *Times* the place was crowded. Kyle got a table only because there had been a cancellation.

Dale was at the bar sipping white wine and looking almost serene. They kissed, a peck on each cheek, then squeezed together and started talking about their Thanksgiving holidays as if they'd just had a month at the beach. Both of her parents taught mathematics at Providence College, and, though wonderful people, they had a rather dull existence. Dale's gift for math led to a relatively quick Ph.D., but she began to fear she'd wind up much like her parents. The law beckoned her. The law, as portrayed in film and on television as nonstop excitement. The law, as the cornerstone of democracy and the front lines for so many social conflicts. She had excelled at law school, received offers from the top firms, and now, after three months of practice, she sorely missed mathematics.

Later, at their table and still sipping wine, she was quick to confess some exciting news. 'I had a job interview this morning.'

'I thought you had a job.'

'Yes, but it sucks. There's a boutique firm in Providence, downtown in a beautiful old building. I got a job there one summer when I was in college, making copies and coffee and doing the general gofer routine. About twenty lawyers, half women, a general practice. I talked them into an interview on a Saturday morning.'

'But you have a cherished associate's position with the largest firm in the world. What more could you want?'

'A life. The same thing you want.'

'I want to be a partner so I can sleep until 5:00 a.m. every day until I die at fifty. That's what I want.'

'Look around, Kyle. Very few stay more than three years. The smart ones are gone after two. The crazy ones make a career out of it.'

'So you're leaving?'

'I'm not cut out for this. I thought I was pretty tough, but you can have it.'

The waiter took their orders and poured more wine. They were side by side, in a narrow half booth with a view of the restaurant. Kyle's hand was between her knees under the table.

'When are you leaving?' he asked.

'As soon as humanly possible. I practically begged for a job this morning. If I don't get an offer, I'll keep knocking. This is madness, Kyle, and I'm checking out.'

'Congratulations. You'll be the envy of our class.'

'What about you?'

'I have no idea. I feel as though I just got here. We're all in shock, but it'll wear off. It's boot camp, and we're still sore from the initial bruising.'

'No more bruises for me. I've collapsed once. It won't happen again. I'm slacking off to fifty hours a week and I dare them to say something.'

'Go, girl.'

A platter of olives and goat cheese arrived, and they toyed with it. 'How was York?' she asked.

'The same. I had lunch with my real mother and dinner with my next one, a quick deer hunt that killed nothing, and some long talks with my dad.'

'About what?'

'The usual. Life. The past. The future.'

*

Nigel was present for the second meeting in a row, and long before Kyle arrived in the hotel suite, preparations had been under way. On a small desk, Nigel had set up a computer that looked very similar to those on the eighteenth floor. Next to it was a monitor that was identical to the one Kyle had stared at for twelve hours the day before.

'Are we close here, Kyle?' Nigel was singing away as he proudly revealed his copycat workstation. 'Please have a seat.'

Kyle sat at the desk, with Bennie and Nigel watching every move.

'It looks very similar,' Kyle said.

'Just the hardware here, Kyle, as you know. Not crucial, but we're trying to pinpoint the manufacturer, that's all. Only the software matters, we know that. Are we off the mark?'

Neither the computer nor the monitor had markings or names or models or makers. They were as blandly generic as the ones they were trying to imitate.

'These are very close,' Kyle said.

'Look hard, man, and find something different,' Nigel pressed. He was beside Kyle, bent and staring at the screen.

'The computer is slightly darker in color, almost a gray, and it's sixteen inches wide and twenty inches tall.'

'You measured, Kyle?'

'Obviously. I used a fifteen-inch legal pad.'

'Bloody brilliant,' Nigel exclaimed and

seemed ready to hug Kyle. Bennie couldn't hide a smile.

'It has to be a Fargo,' Nigel said.

'A what?'

'Fargo, Kyle, a specialty computer company in San Diego, big on government and military machines, tons of work for the CIA, big stout computers with more security and more gadgets than you can believe, I assure you of that. You won't see one at the local mall, no sir. And Fargo is owned by Deene, a client of you know who. Old Scully protects its ass at a thousand bucks an hour.'

As Nigel chirped away, he hit a button on the keyboard. The screen became a page unlike any Kyle had ever seen. Nothing from Microsoft or Apple.

'Now, Kyle, tell me what the first page looks like. Anything remotely similar here?'

'No, not even close. The home page has one icon for the tutorial, but that's it – no other icons, message boards, edit bands, format options, nothing but an index to the documents. You turn the computer on, get through the pass codes and passwords, then wait about ten seconds, and, presto, you're into the library. No system profiles, no spec sheets, no home page.'

'Fascinating,' Nigel said, still staring at the monitor. 'And the index, Kyle?'

'The index is a real challenge. It starts with broad divisions of documents, then it breaks down into subcategories and subgroups and sub-this and sub-that. It takes some work to find the batch of documents you're looking for.'

Nigel took a step back and stretched. Bennie moved closer and said, 'Suppose you wanted to locate the research materials relating to the B-10's air-breathing engines and the various types of hydrogen fuel that were tested. How would you get there?'

'I don't know. I haven't been there yet. I've seen nothing about air-breathing engines.' The statement was true, but Kyle decided to draw a line at this point. With over four million documents in play, he could easily claim he had not seen whatever they were curious about.

'But you could find these materials?'

'I could find them quickly, once I knew where to look. The Sonic program is pretty fast, but there's a ton of paper to sift through.'

Bennie's movements were quick, his words a little more urgent than usual. Nigel was downright giddy with Kyle's information. It was obvious that his progress had them agitated.

'You were in the room yesterday?' Bennie asked.

'Yes, all day.'

'With a briefcase and a jacket?'

'Yes, both, no problem. There was one other briefcase. No one checks them.'

'When will you return to the room?' Bennie asked.

'The team meets in the morning, and there's a

good chance I'll get another assignment. Monday or Tuesday for sure.'

'Let's meet Tuesday night.'

'Can't wait.'

Chapter 35

Now that he was an official member of Team Trylon, Kyle had the honor of beginning each week with a 7:00 a.m. Monday chalk talk in a huge conference room he'd never seen before. After three months in the building, he still marveled at the meeting areas and balconies and tucked-away mezzanines and small libraries he was stumbling upon for the first time. The firm needed its own guidebook.

The room was on the forty-first floor and large enough to house many smaller law firms. The table in the center seemed as long as a bowling alley. Forty lawyers, give or take a few, crowded around it, gulping coffee and settling in for another long week. Wilson Rush stood at the far end and cleared his throat, and everyone shut up and froze. 'Good morning. We'll have our weekly session. Keep your comments brief. This meeting will last for one hour only.'

There was no doubt that they would leave at exactly 8:00 a.m.

Kyle was as far from Rush as possible. He kept his head low and took furious notes that no one, not even himself, could have read afterward. Each of the eight partners stood in turn and gave succinct updates on such gripping topics as the latest motions filed in the case, the latest haggling over documents and experts, the latest moves by APE and Bartin. Doug Peckham presented his first report on a complicated discovery motion. It almost put Kyle and the others to sleep.

But Kyle stayed awake, and while scribbling on a legal pad, he kept telling himself not to smile at the absurdity of the moment. He was a spy, perfectly planted by his handler, and now within reach of secrets that were so important he could not comprehend their value. They were certainly valuable enough to cause men to commit murder.

Kyle glanced up as Isabelle Gaffney took her turn on the floor, and ignoring her words, he looked at the far end of the bowling lane, where Wilson Rush seemed to be glaring at him. Maybe not, there was so much distance between them, and the old man was wearing reading glasses, so it was hard to tell exactly whom he was frowning at.

What would Mr. Rush do if he knew the truth? What would Team Trylon and the hundreds of other Scully partners and associates do when they learned the truth about young Kyle McAvoy, former editor in chief of the *Yale Law Journal*?

The consequences were horrifying. The magnitude of the conspiracy caused Kyle's heart to hammer away. His mouth became dry and he sipped lukewarm coffee. He wanted to leap for the door, sprint down forty-one flights of stairs, and run through the streets of New York like a madman.

During lunch he used the basement exit ploy and hustled over to the office of Roy Benedict. They chatted for a minute or two, then Roy said there were two people Kyle should meet. The first was his contact in the FBI, the second was a senior lawyer in the Department of Justice. Kyle nervously agreed, and they walked next door to a meeting room.

The FBI supervisor was Joe Bullington, an affable sort with a big toothy smile and hearty handshake. The man from Justice was Drew Wingate, a sour-faced sort who acted as though he preferred not to shake hands at all. The four sat at a small conference table, Kyle and Roy on one side, the government guys on the other.

It was Roy's meeting, and he took charge. 'First of all, Kyle, how much time do you have?'

'About an hour.'

'I've laid it all on the table. I've had a dozen conversations with Mr. Bullington and Mr. Wingate, and it's important now for us to review where we are. Joe, talk about the background on Mr. Bennie Wright.'

Always smiling, Bullington squeezed his hands together and began, 'Yes, right, well, we ran the photo of this guy through our system. I won't bore you with the details, but we have some very sophisticated computers that store facial images of millions of people. When we feed in a suspect, the computers search and scan, and in general do their thing. With Mr. Wright, or whoever he is, we came up with nothing. No hit. No clue. We then sent it to the CIA, and they conducted a similar search, different computers, different software, same result. Nothing. We're surprised, frankly. We were pretty confident we could identify this guy.'

Kyle was not surprised, but he was disappointed. He'd read about the supercomputers used by the intelligence services, and after a lifetime of living with Bennie, he really wanted to know who he was.

Bullington brightened a bit and went on: 'Nigel might be a different story. We placed your composite of him into our system and came up empty. But the CIA got a probable hit.' Bullington opened a file, pulled out an eight-by-ten black and white, and handed it to Kyle, who immediately said, 'That's him.'

'Good. His real name is Derry Hobart, born in South Africa, raised in Liverpool, trained as a techie in the British intelligence services, got bounced ten years ago for hacking into the confidential files of some rich folks in Switzerland, generally regarded as one of the most brilliant hackers in the world. Brilliant, but a real rogue, a hired gun, warrants outstanding in at least three countries.'

'How much have you told these people?' Wingate asked. It was more of an accusation than a question. Kyle looked at his lawyer, who nodded and said, 'Go ahead, Kyle. You're not under any type of investigation. You've done nothing wrong.'

'I've given them the layout of the computer room, general stuff like that. Enough to keep them happy, but no data whatsoever.'

'Anyway,' Bullington said, 'the other two composites turned up nothing. If I understand things, these two boys are just part of the surveillance and not that important.'

'That's right,' Kyle said.

'Your composite of Mr. Hobart is remarkable, Kyle,' Bullington said.

'It's from a Web site. QuickFace.com. Anybody could do it.'

'What's your next step?' Wingate asked.

'We meet tomorrow night for an update. The plan is for me to somehow hack into the system, either download or divert the documents, and hand them over. I have no idea how this is supposed to be done. The computer system looks completely secure.'

'When is this supposed to happen?'

'They haven't told me, but I get the

impression it will be soon. I have a question for you.'

Neither Bullington nor Wingate offered to take the question, so Kyle plunged ahead. 'Who are these guys? Who are they working for?'

Bullington flashed all of his teeth and said with a boyish shrug, 'We honestly don't know, Kyle. Hobart is a whore who travels the world selling himself. We have no clue where Bennie comes from. You say he's not American.'

'He doesn't sound like it.'

'Without an idea as to who he is, we can't even begin to guess who he's working for.'

'There were at least five agents involved in the first encounter, back in February, the night I first met Bennie. All five were definitely Americans.'

Bullington was shaking his head. 'Probably hired guns, Kyle, thugs brought in for the job, paid, turned loose. There's a whole dark world out there of former cops and agents and former soldiers and intelligence types who got shoved out for a multitude of reasons. Most are misfits. They were trained in the shadows, and that's where they work. They'll hire on with anyone who'll pay them. Those five probably had no idea what Bennie was up to.'

'What are the chances of catching the ones who killed Baxter Tate?'

The smile went away for a moment. Both government faces looked sad and perplexed. Bullington finally said, 'First we have to catch Bennie, then we work our way up to the big boys who are paying him, then we'll work our way down to the street thugs who do his dirty work. If he's a pro, though, and it's quite obvious that he is, the chances of squeezing him for names are pretty slim.'

'How do you catch Bennie?'

'That's the easy part. You'll lead us to him.'

'And you arrest him?'

'Oh, yes. We'll have enough warrants to arrest him ten times – wiretapping, extortion, conspiracy, take your pick. We'll throw him under the jail, with Hobart as well, and no federal judge in the world will bond him out. We'll probably move him to a secured facility far away from New York so we can begin the interrogation.'

The image of Bennie chained to a chair as a couple of pit bulls screamed at him was rather pleasant.

Roy cleared his throat, glanced at his watch, and said, 'If you'll excuse us, I need to talk to Kyle. I'll call you later.' And with that Kyle stood, shook their hands again, and followed his lawyer back to his office. Roy closed the door and said, 'What do you think?'

'You trust those guys?' Kyle shot back.

'Yes. You don't?'

'Would you trust them with your life?'

'Yes.'

'Try this scenario. Currently there are at least eighteen intelligence outfits in this country, and those are just the ones on paper. There are probably a few more we know nothing about.

What if Bennie works for one of them? Suppose his project is just one of several to procure and protect all the secrets? What if the supercomputers couldn't find his face because they weren't supposed to?'

'That's a pretty ridiculous scenario, Kyle. A rogue operative working for the United States, spying on a U.S. law firm, killing U.S. citizens? I don't think so.'

'Sure it's ridiculous, but when your skull might be the next target, it does wonders for the imagination.'

'Take it easy. This is your only way out.'

'There's no way out.'

'Yes, there is. Let's take it one step at a time. Don't panic.'

'I haven't panicked in nine months, but I'm getting close.'

'No, you're not. Be cool. We have to trust those guys.'

'I'll call you tomorrow.' Kyle grabbed his brown trench coat and left the office.

Chapter 36

The Cessna 182 was owned by a retired doctor who flew it only in clear weather and never at night. He had known John McAvoy for over forty years and had flown him several times around the state for legal matters. Their little trips were as much pleasure as business, with John wearing a headset and taking the controls and thoroughly enjoying his time as the pilot. They always haggled over the rate. John wanted to pay more than just the fuel costs, and the doctor demanded less because flying was his hobby and he didn't need the money. Once they agreed on the cost of the trip, $250, they met at the York airport early on Tuesday morning and took off in perfect weather. Seventy-one minutes later they landed in Scranton. John rented a car, and the doctor left in the Cessna to drop in on his son in Williamsport.

The law office of Michelin Chiz was on the second floor of an old building on Spruce Street in downtown Scranton. John walked in promptly at 9:00 a.m. and was greeted coolly by a secretary. He had never met Ms. Chiz, never heard of her, but that was not unusual in a state with over sixty thousand lawyers. A Scranton lawyer he did know had told him that she ran an all-woman shop with a couple of associates, a couple of paralegals, and the usual assortment of secretaries and part-time help. No men need apply. Ms. Chiz specialized in divorce, custody, sexual harrassment, and employment discrimination, all from the female side, and had a busy practice. Her reputation was solid. She was a tough advocate for her clients, a good negotiator, and not afraid of the courtroom. Not bad looking either, the lawyer had informed John.

And he was right about that. Ms. Chiz was waiting in her office when John walked in and said good morning. She was wearing a black leather skirt, not too short, with a tight purple sweater and a pair of black and purple spiked-heeled platform sling backs that most hookers would shy away from. She was in her mid-forties, with, according to John's source, at least two divorces under her belt. She wore a lot of jewelry and makeup, far too much for John's taste, but he wasn't there to evaluate the talent.

For his part, he was wearing a boring gray wool suit and a plain red tie, nothing anyone would remember.

They settled around a small worktable in a

room adjacent to her office, and the secretary was sent for coffee. They played a few minutes of who-do-you-know, kicking around the names of lawyers from Philadelphia to Erie. After the coffee was served and the door was closed, Ms. Chiz said, 'Let's get down to business.'

'Great idea,' Mr. McAvoy said. 'Please call me John.'

'Sure, and I'm Mike. Don't know if that's the correct nickname for Michelin, but it stuck a long time ago.'

'Mike it is.' So far she had exuded nothing but charm and hospitality, but John could already tell that just behind the smile was a very tough lawyer. 'Would you like to go first?' John asked.

'No. You called me. You traveled here. There's something you want, so let's have it.'

'Very well. My client is my son, not the best arrangement in the world, but that's the way it is. As you know, he works for a law firm in New York. Law school at Yale, undergrad at Duquesne. I'm sure you know the details of the alleged rape.'

'Indeed I do. Elaine works here part-time, and we're very close. She wants to go to law school someday.'

'I hope she succeeds. As you know, the police in Pittsburgh closed the investigation not long after they opened it. Frankly, I knew nothing about it until very recently.'

Her surprise was obvious, and John continued. 'No, Kyle did not tell me when it happened. He was planning to, but the investigation was closed. This is upsetting because we are very close, but it's not important. I understand that you and Ms. Keenan met with Joey Bernardo here in Scranton a few weeks back, and the meeting did not go well, according to Joey's version. I also know that Baxter Tate contacted your client, and was evidently on his way here to talk to her when he was murdered.'

'That's correct.'

'They were planning to meet?'

'Yes.'

'So, it appears, Mike, that the episode five and a half years ago will not go away. My client would like to resolve things, to close this matter. It's a dark cloud hanging over these kids, and I'm here to explore ways to get rid of it. I'm representing only my son. The others know nothing of this meeting. The Tate family, of course, has no clue, and you can imagine what they're going through right now. Joey has a child on the way and is about to get married. Alan Strock, as far as we know, has forgotten the episode.'

Mike had yet to lift a pen. She listened intently as she softly tapped all ten fingertips together. Most fingers were adorned with rings, and both wrists were laden with inexpensive bangles. Her hard hazel eyes did not blink. 'I'm sure you have something in mind,' she said, content to listen.

'I'm not sure what your client wants. She might be thrilled if all three surviving roommates admitted there was a rape, got themselves convicted, and were sent off to prison. She might be satisfied with a quiet apology. Or she might entertain the idea of a financial settlement. Perhaps you could help me here.'

Mike licked her lipstick and rattled some bracelets. 'I've known Elaine for two years. She has a troubled past. She's frail, vulnerable, and at times subject to some very dark moods. It might be depression. She's been sober for almost a year, but she's fighting those demons. She has become almost like a daughter to me, and she has insisted from day one that she was raped. I believe her. She is convinced that the Tate family got involved, leaned on their friends, who leaned on the cops, who quickly backed off.'

John was shaking his head. 'That's not true. None of the four boys told their parents.'

'Maybe, but we don't know that for sure. Regardless, many of Elaine's problems stem from that episode. She was a healthy, fun-loving, vibrant coed who loved college and had big plans. Shortly after the rape, she dropped out and has been struggling ever since.'

'Have you seen her grades from Duquesne?'

'No.'

'Her first semester, she flunked one course, dropped out of another, and made horrible grades in the other three.'

'How did you gain access to her student records?'

'She improved slightly the second semester and made straight Cs. She took all four exams after the alleged rape, then went home and never returned to Duquesne.'

Mike's eyebrows arched and her spine stiffened. 'How did you gain access to her student records?' she snarled again. Ah, the woman had a temper after all.

'I didn't, and it's not important. How often do your clients tell you the entire truth?'

'Are you suggesting Elaine is lying?'

'The truth is a moving target here, Mike. But what's certain is that we'll never really know for sure what happened that night. These kids had been drinking and smoking pot for eight straight hours, and they were far more promiscuous than we'd like to believe. Your client was known to sleep around.'

'They were all sleeping around. That's no excuse for rape.'

'Of course not.'

Money was in the air. There were a few other obstacles to clear, but both lawyers knew they would eventually discuss the possibility of a 'financial settlement.'

'What does your client say about the episode?' Mike asked, her tone cool again. The flash of anger was gone, but there was a lot more where that came from.

'They had been by the pool all afternoon, then the party moved indoors, into the apartment. There were about fifteen kids, more boys than girls, but Elaine was not in the group. Evidently, she was next door at a different party. Around eleven thirty, the cops showed up and the party ended. Nobody was arrested, the cops gave them a break.'

Mike nodded patiently. This was all in the police report.

'After the cops left,' John continued, 'Elaine showed up. She and Baxter started making out on the sofa, and one thing led to another. My client was watching television in the same room, as was Alan Strock. My client was intoxicated, to say the least, and at some point he passed out. He is certain he did not have sex with Elaine that night, and at the time he was not certain if anyone else did either. He was too drunk to remember much the next morning, and, as you well know, no accusation was made by your client until four days later. The police investigated the matter. All four boys were on the verge of talking to their parents, but the investigators soon realized that they simply could not put together a case. In recent weeks, my client has talked to Baxter Tate and to Joey Bernardo, and both boys admitted to having sex with your client on the evening in question. Both are, were, adamant that it was consensual.'

'Then why was Baxter so anxious to apologize?'

'I can't answer that. I don't speak for Baxter.'

'Why did Joey apologize? He did so in my presence, you know?'

'Did Joey apologize for raping Elaine, or did he apologize for the misunderstanding?'

'He apologized. That's what's important.'

'There's still no case, and his apology adds nothing to the evidence. There's no way to prove rape occurred. There was sex, sure, but you can't prove anything else.'

She finally wrote something. Lavender legal pad, elegant strokes, noisy wrists. She took a deep breath and seemed to gaze out the window for a moment.

For Team McAvoy, it was time for the biggest gamble. They would never reveal every fact because successful negotiation does not hinge on full disclosure. But the one bomb that could wreck any deal had to be addressed.

'Have you talked to the detectives in Pittsburgh?' John asked.

'No, but I've read the entire file.'

'Anything mentioned about a video?'

'Yes, there were notes in the file. But the cops couldn't find one. Elaine even heard the rumor.'

'It's not a rumor. There is such a video.'

She took this without the slightest flinch. Nothing in her eyes, hands, or body registered surprise. What a great poker face, John admitted quickly. She simply waited.

'I haven't seen it,' he said. 'But my client saw it in February of this year. Don't know where it is now and don't know how many others have seen it, probably very few. There's a chance it might surface, perhaps on the Internet, perhaps in your mailbox.'

'And what would this video prove?'

'It would prove that your client was drunk and smoking pot when she sat down on the sofa with Baxter Tate and began kissing and groping. The angle of the camera does not allow a full picture of the two engaged in sex, but it's obvious from the knees down that they're having a fine time. Baxter is followed by Joey. At times Elaine is not active; at other times she's obviously engaged. My client thinks it proves that she was in and out of consciousness, but he's not certain. Nothing is certain, except that neither he nor Alan Strock had sex with her.'

'Where is the video?'

'I do not know.'

'Does your client?'

'No.'

'Who has the video?'

'I do not know.'

'Okay, who showed it to your client?'

'He does not know the person's real name. He had never met the person until the person showed him the video.'

'Gotcha. I take it there's a complicated story behind this.'

'Extremely complicated.'

'A stranger pops up, shows your son the video, then disappears?'

'Right, except for the disappearance part. The stranger is still in contact.'

'Extortion?'

'Something close.'

'Is that why you're here? Your client is scared

of the video? You wanna make peace with us so the extortion scheme goes away?'

'You're very astute.' She still had not blinked. She seemed to be reading his mind at this point.

'Must be a helluva video,' she said.

'My client found it troublesome, though he was not present during the sex portion of it. The video clearly shows your client happily getting involved in a good romp on a sofa. Whether she blacked out at some point is not clear, at least on the video.'

'She is seen walking and talking and moving around?'

'Clearly. These boys didn't drag her in off the street, Mike. She had been in their apartment many times, drunk and sober.'

'Poor thing,' Mike said, her first false move.

'Poor thing was having a wonderful time. She carried a purse full of drugs, along with her collection of fake IDs, and she was always looking for a party.'

Mike slowly stood and said, 'Excuse me for a moment.' She walked into her office, and John admired the black leather every step of the way. He heard her low voice, probably on the phone, and then she was back with a forced smile.

'We could debate this for hours,' she said. 'And not settle anything.'

'I agree. Baxter was in New York three weeks ago today to see my client. In the course of a long discussion about what happened, he told my client that he believed that he had forced himself on Elaine. The guilt was heavy. Maybe there was a sexual assault.'

'And the rapist is dead.'

'Exactly. However, my client was there when it happened. It was his apartment, his friends, his party, and his booze. He wants this thing off his back, Mike.'

'How much?'

John managed a nervous laugh. Such bluntness. She, however, did not crack a smile.

He made a note and asked, 'Is it possible to reach a financial settlement and have your client release all civil claims and agree not to prosecute?'

'Yes, assuming the settlement is sufficient.'

A pause as John made some more notes, then, 'My client does not have a lot of money.'

'I know how much your client earns. I've been practicing law for twenty years, and he earns more than me.'

'And me, after thirty-five years. But he has student loans, and it's not cheap living in New York City. I'll probably need to chip in a little, and I'm not a wealthy man. I don't owe anything, but a busy street practice in downtown York is not the road to riches.'

His honesty disarmed her for a moment, and she smiled and seemed to relax. They enjoyed a nice diversion swapping stories about the challenges of practicing law in small-town America. When the time was up, John said warmly, 'Tell me about Elaine. Job, salary, finances, family, and so on.'

'Well, as I said, she works part-time here for peanuts. She makes $24,000 a year as an assistant director of parks and rec for the city, not exactly a career job. She rents a modest apartment that she shares with her companion, Beverly, and drives a Nissan with a monthly note. Her family is from Erie, and I don't know how prosperous they once were, but things have taken a bad turn. She's on her own, twenty-three years old, surviving. She still has dreams of something beyond where she is now.'

John made a few notes, then said, 'Yesterday, I spoke with an attorney for the Tate family, big firm in Pittsburgh. Baxter had a trust that sent him six thousand a month, which was never enough. That sum would increase over time, but all the Tate trusts are now tightly controlled by an uncle who has a rather heavy hand. Baxter's trust folded when he died. There's very little in his estate, so any contribution from his family would fall under the category of charitable giving. These people are not known for their charity, and it's hard to imagine them entertaining notions of writing checks to Baxter's old girlfriends.'

Mike was nodding in agreement. 'What about Joey?' she asked.

'He's working hard, trying to provide for a growing family. He's probably strapped, and will be for the rest of his life. My client would like to keep both Joey and Alan Strock out of this.'

'That's admirable.'

'We propose two payments. One now, and one in seven years, when the statute of limitations expires on the rape charge. If your client puts this behind her, gives up the idea of pursuing these guys, then she gets a nice payment at the end. Twenty-five thousand now, and for the next seven years my client will add ten grand to an investment account that will render $100,000 when Elaine is thirty years old.'

Same poker face. 'Twenty-five up front is ridiculous,' she said.

'He doesn't have twenty-five thousand. It'll come from me.'

'We're not too concerned about where it comes from. We're much more interested in the amount.'

'Well, right now you have zero, and if we don't reach an agreement, then it's very likely you'll stay at zero. Your chances of recovery are slim at best.'

'Then why are you offering anything?'

'Peace of mind. Mike, come on, let's put this baby to sleep so these kids can get on with their lives. Kyle had almost forgotten the incident, hell, he's working a hundred hours a week, then Joey bumps into Elaine, then Baxter shows up all consumed with guilt because he remembers more now than he did before. This is crazy. They were just a bunch of drunk kids.'

Yes, they were, and Mike couldn't argue the point. She recrossed her legs, and John was compelled to glance at the high heels, just a quick down and up, but she noticed it.

'Let me talk to Elaine, and we'll make a counteroffer,' she said.

'Fine, but there's not much wiggle room here, Mike. The up-front money will be a loan from me to my client, and he is obviously nervous about taking on a seven-year obligation. He's twenty-five and can't see three years down the road.'

'I'll call Elaine, and she'll probably want to run over and discuss this face-to-face.'

'I'm not leaving town until we have a deal. I'll just walk down to the coffee shop and kill some time.'

An hour later he was back. They took their same positions, picked up their pens, and continued the negotiations.

'I assume you're not taking our offer,' John said.

'Yes and no. The seven-year scheme is okay, but Elaine needs more up front. She is two years away from her degree at the University of Scranton. Her dream is law school, and without some help it will be impossible.'

'How much help?'

'A hundred thousand now.'

Shock, disbelief, amazement, rejection. John grimaced and squirmed and allowed a lungful of air to whistle over his teeth. It was all an act, the long-practiced pretense of utter incredulity when the other side puts its first demand on the table. Exasperation, near defeat. 'Look, Mike, we're trying to reach an agreement here. You guys are trying to rob a bank.'

'In two years, Elaine will still be earning $24,000 a year. Your client, on the other hand, will be earning about $400,000, with guaranteed increases. This is not a stretch for him.'

John stood as if he were leaving, end of negotiations. 'I need to call him.'

'Sure. I'll wait.'

John walked outside the building, put a cell phone to his head, and called no one. The amount they would pay had less to do with what Elaine needed and much more to do with keeping her quiet. A hundred thousand dollars was a bargain, under the circumstances.

'We'll go seventy-five grand, and that's it,' John said, back at the table.

Her right hand rattled pleasantly as it came across. 'Deal,' she said. They shook on their agreement, then spent two hours haggling over the paperwork. When it was finished, he offered to buy lunch and she readily accepted.

Chapter 37

Nigel's latest workstation had been hastily assembled on a fine mahogany desk in the center of the sitting room in a spacious suite at the Waldorf-Astoria on Park Avenue. The computer was a sixteen-by-twenty-inch exact replica of the ten models on the eighteenth floor. The monitor, too, was a perfect match. Next to it was an ominous navy blue box the size of a larger laptop.

As Nigel proudly went through a detailed description of the various cords and cables, the spaghetti, as he called it, Bennie and Kyle watched without a word. There was a power cord, audio, monitor, and printing cables. 'Audio, Kyle? Do we have noise from these bad little boys?'

'No, no audio,' Kyle replied, and Nigel carefully rolled up the audio cable and put it away. He bent low behind the computer and pointed to the magic spot. 'Here we are, Kyle, the promised land, the USB port. Almost hidden, but I know it's there because I have a contact with Fargo. It has to be there, trust me.'

Kyle grunted but said nothing.

'Here's the plan, Kyle,' he said excitedly, thoroughly enthralled by his work. From his neat little hacker's high-tech tool kit he produced two small devices, identical in shape and length, three-quarters of an inch wide and about an inch and a half long. 'This is the wireless USB transmitter, hot off the press, state of the art, not yet available to the public, no sir,' he said, then quickly plugged it into the port that was under the power inlet. Once it was inserted, about a half an inch could be seen. 'You plug it in just so, and, presto, we're in business. It's virtually invisible.' He waved the other and explained, 'And this little bugger is the USB receiver that goes in the blue box there. With me, Kyle?'

'Got it.'

'The blue box goes inside your briefcase. You park the briefcase on the floor, directly under the computer, flip a switch, and the docs get themselves downloaded in a jiffy.'

'How fast?'

'Sixty megabytes per second, about a thousand documents, assuming you get the receiver within three meters of the transmitter, which should be easy. The closer, the better, Kyle. Are you with me?'

'Hell no,' Kyle said as he sat in the chair in front of the monitor. 'I'm supposed to somehow reach behind the computer, plug in the transmitter, leave it there, download, et cetera, while there are other people in the room and the video cameras are watching. How, exactly, do I pull that off?'

'Drop a pen,' Bennie said. 'Spill some coffee. Throw some papers around. Create a diversion. Go when the place is empty, and keep your back to the camera.'

Kyle was shaking his head. 'It's too risky. These people are not stupid, you know. There's a security tech on duty in a room next door. Name's Gant.'

'But does he work sixteen hours a day?'

'I don't know when he works. That's the point. You never know who's in there watching.'

'We know security, Kyle, and the grunts who are paid to watch closed-circuit screens all day are usually half-asleep. It's terribly boring work.'

'This is not a coffee room, Bennie. I'm supposed to be working in there. Stealing may be a priority for you boys, but the firm expects me to be plowing through the documents. I'll have a project due and a partner waiting on it.'

Nigel charged in. 'It could be over in two hours, Kyle, assuming you can find the documents quickly.'

Bennie shook off all concerns. 'Priority one is the air-breathing engines that Trylon and Bartin developed together. The technology is so sophisticated that the Pentagon is still orgasmic. Priority two is the fuel mix. Do a search for "cryogenic hydrogen fuel" and follow it up with one for "scramjet." There should be a ton of research in the files. Priority three is called "waveriders." Do a search. These are aerodynamic designs used to increase the B-10's lift-to-drag ratio. Here's a memo.' Bennie handed over a two-page summary.

'Any of this sound familiar, Kyle?' Nigel pleaded.

'No.'

'It's there,' Bennie insisted. 'It's the heart of the research, the crux of the lawsuit, and you can find it, Kyle.'

'Oh, thank you.'

For practice, Nigel withdrew the transmitter and handed it to Kyle. 'Let's see you do it.' Kyle slowly got to his feet, leaned over the computer, shoved away some cables, and with some effort finally managed to insert the transmitter into the USB port. He sat down and said, 'There's no way.'

'Of course there is,' Bennie scoffed. 'Use your brain.'

'It's dead.'

Nigel bounced around to the blue box. 'The software is some of my home brew. When you have inserted the transmitter, you reach down and flip this little switch, and the script automatically locates the computer and begins downloading the database. It will happen very quickly, Kyle, and if you like, you can take a break, leave the room, go for a pee, act like nothing at all is happening, and all the while my little gizmo is sucking up the documents.'

'Bloody brilliant,' Kyle said.

Bennie produced a black Bally briefcase identical to Kyle's, a stand-up model with a short leather flap that latched on one side. There were three compartments, with the middle one padded for a laptop. The substitute was complete with a few scuff marks and Kyle's Scully & Pershing business card firmly in the leather tag. 'You'll use this,' he said as Nigel carefully lifted the blue box and placed it in the center compartment of the briefcase. 'When you unzip this divide,' Nigel said, 'the receiver will already be in place. If for some reason you need to abort, just close the case and punch this button, and it locks automatically.'

'Abort?'

'Just in case, Kyle.'

'Let me get this straight. Something goes wrong, somebody notices me, maybe some alarm goes off in a supercomputer we know nothing about as soon as I start dickering with the database, and your plan is then for me to lock the flap on the briefcase, grab the transmitter that's almost hidden, and then do what? Sprint from the room like a shoplifter who's been caught? Where do I go, Nigel? Any help here, Bennie?'

'Relax, Kyle,' Bennie said with a fake smile. 'This is a piece of cake. You'll do fine.'

'No alarms, Kyle,' Nigel said. 'My software is too good for that. Trust me.'

'Would you please stop saying that?'

Kyle walked to a window and looked out at the Manhattan skyline. It was almost 9:30 on Tuesday night. He had not eaten since he and Tabor had enjoyed a fifteen-minute lunch in the firm cafeteria at 11:30. Hunger, though, was only a minor concern on a long, sad list.

'Are you ready, Kyle?' Bennie called from across the room. Not a question, but a challenge.

'As ready as I'll ever be,' he answered without turning around.

'When?'

'As soon as possible. I want to get it over with. I'll stop by the room a few times tomorrow, check the traffic. My best guess is that it'll be about eight tomorrow night, late in the day but with enough time to download, assuming I don't get shot.'

'Any questions about the equipment, Kyle?' Nigel asked.

Kyle walked stiffly back to the workstation and stared at the machines. He finally shrugged and said, 'No, it's pretty straightforward.'

'Super. One last thing, Kyle. The blue box has a wireless signal so that I know precisely when you're downloading.'

'Why is that necessary?'

'Monitoring. We'll be very close by.'

Another shrug. 'Whatever.'

The blue box was still in the center compartment, with Nigel handling it as if it were a bomb. Kyle then added the materials from his own briefcase, and when he grabbed the handle and lifted it off the table, he was surprised at the weight.

'A bit heavier, Kyle?' Nigel quizzed, watching every move.

'Yes, quite a bit.'

'Not to worry. We've reinforced the bottom of the Bally. It's not going to drop out as you're walking along Broad Street.'

'I like the other one better. When do I get it back?'

'Soon, Kyle, soon.'

Kyle pulled on his trench coat and made his way to the door. Bennie followed and said, 'Good luck, Kyle. It's all come down to this. We believe in you.'

'Go to hell,' Kyle said, and left the room.

Chapter 38

The briefcase grew heavier during the short, sleepless night, and when Kyle lugged it out of the rear of the taxi early Wednesday morning, he half-wished the bottom would indeed fall out, the blue box would crash onto Broad Street in a thousand pieces, and Nigel's precious home brew would be sent down the gutter. He wasn't sure what would happen after that, but any scenario was far better than what was planned.

Twenty minutes after he rode the elevator to the thirty-fourth floor, Roy Benedict entered the same elevator with two young men who were undoubtedly associates at Scully & Pershing. The signs were obvious. They were under thirty. It was 6:35 in the morning. They appeared to be fatigued and miserable, but they wore expensive clothes and carried handsome briefcases, black. He was prepared to see a familiar face, though felt it unlikely. It was not at all unusual to see attorneys from other firms in the building. Roy knew half a dozen partners at Scully, but with fifteen hundred lawyers arriving for work, he figured the odds were slim. And he was right. The two zombies riding up with him were just a couple of faceless souls who would be gone in a year or so.

The briefcase in Roy's hand was also a black Bally, identical to the one Kyle bought back in August, the third one required for this mission. He left the elevator alone on the thirty-fourth floor and walked past the vacant reception desk, down a hall to the right, four, five, six doors, and there was his client, sitting at his desk, sipping coffee, waiting. The exchange was brief. Roy swapped briefcases and was ready to go.

'Where are the feds?' Kyle asked, very softly, though no one was in the hall and the secretaries were just getting out of bed.

'Around the corner in a van. They'll do a quick scan to make sure there are no tracking devices. If they find one, I'll bring it back in a sprint and we'll concoct a story. If not, then they'll take it to their lab in Queens. This thing is heavy.'

'The blue box. Specially designed by some evil geniuses.'

'When do you need it?'

'Let's say 7:00 p.m. That's twelve hours. Should be enough, right?'

'That's what they say. According to Bullington, they have a small army of geeks just itching to unwrap it.'

'They can't screw it up.'

'They won't. You good?'

'Great. Do they have arrest warrants?'

'Oh, yes. Wiretapping, extortion, conspiracy, lots of good stuff. They're just waiting on you.'

'If Bennie is about to be arrested, then I'm a motivated young man.'

'Good luck.'

Roy was gone, leaving behind the Bally with the same scuff marks and name tag. Kyle quickly stuffed it with files and legal pads and pens and went to find more coffee.

Twelve long hours later, Roy was back with the second briefcase. He took a seat as Kyle closed the door. 'So?' he said.

'It is what it is. It's a customized computer built along the lines of those used by the military, everything is heavy-duty. Designed for nothing but downloading. Two hard drives, with 750 gigabytes each. Basically, enough memory to store everything in this building and the three next door. Highly sophisticated software that the FBI geeks have never seen before. These guys are good, Kyle.'

'Tell me about it.'

'And there is indeed a wireless signal so they can monitor you.'

'Dammit. So I have to download something?'

'I'm afraid so. The wireless signal cannot indicate what you are downloading, or how much. It just lets them know that you're inside and that you've started moving the database.'

'Shit!'

'You can do it, Kyle.'

'That seems to be the consensus.'

'Do you know where you'll meet these guys?'

'No. It'll be a last-second notice. Assuming I download without setting off alarms, I'll call Bennie with the happy news, and he'll tell me where to meet. I'm going to the room in an hour, and I plan to quit at nine, regardless of the download. So, by nine fifteen, if I'm lucky, I should be on the street.'

'I'll stay at my office. If you get a chance, please call. Pretty exciting stuff, Kyle.'

'Exciting? How about terrifying?'

'You're the man.' With that, Roy exchanged briefcases again and disappeared.

For sixty minutes, Kyle stared at the clock, did nothing but bill Trylon for an hour, and finally made a move. He loosened his tie, rolled up his sleeves, tried to look as casual as possible, and took the elevator to the eighteenth floor.

Sherry Abney was in the room, and he had to say hello. From the looks of her table, she'd been there for hours and the research had not gone well. Kyle chose a station as far away from her as possible. Her back was to him.

Despite his bitching and moaning, he foresaw little danger of being noticed by another member of Team Trylon. All ten chairs faced the outside walls, away from the center, so that while doing research, he could see nothing but the monitor, the computer, and the wall behind it. The danger was up above, lurking in the lenses of the video cameras. Still, he preferred to have the room to himself.

After fifteen minutes, he decided to visit the men's room. On the way out, he asked Sherry, 'Can I get you a coffee?'

'No, thanks. I'm leaving soon.'

Perfect. She left at 8:30, a nice breaking point that always made billing easier. Kyle placed a legal pad on top of the computer, then a couple of pens, things that could roll and slide and need retrieving. He scattered a couple of files beside the monitor and in general made a mess of things. At 8:40, he knocked on the locked metal door that led to the small printing room, and there was no answer. Then he tried a second metal door that led to places unknown, but he suspected it was the room where Gant hung out and secured things. He saw Gant occasionally and figured he worked close by. There was no answer. At 8:45, Kyle decided to plunge ahead before another associate arrived for one last hour of work. He walked to his table and bumped the legal pad on top of the computer, sending the pens flying against the wall. He threw up an arm, said 'Shit!' as loudly as possible, then leaned over as if to retrieve things. He found one pen, couldn't find the other, but kept searching. On the floor, behind the monitor, under the chair, then again behind the computer, where he deftly inserted the tiny transmitter into the USB port just as he found the missing pen and held it up so the cameras could see it. Settled down now, composed, not cursing, he took his seat and began clicking away at the keyboard. He slid the briefcase closer under the table, directly under the computer now, then he flipped the switch.

No alarms. No virus warnings screaming from the screen. No sudden entry by Gant with armed guards. Nothing. Kyle the hacker was downloading files, stealing at a dizzying rate of speed. In nine minutes, he transferred all Category A documents – letters, memos, a hundred different varieties of harmless information that had already been submitted to APE and Bartin. When he was finished with the Category A documents, he repeated the process and downloaded them again. And again, and again.

An hour after he entered the room, he again went through the charade of searching for lost pens, and while bumbling about, he plucked the transmitter from the USB port. Then he cleaned up his mess and left. He hurried to his office, got his jacket and trench coat, and made it to the elevators without seeing another person. As he rode down without a single stop, he realized that this was the moment he had always feared. He was leaving the office as a thief, with enough stolen files in his briefcase to get him convicted of numerous crimes and disbarred for life.

As he stepped into the raw December night,

he immediately called Bennie. 'Mission accomplished!' he said proudly.

'Great, Kyle. Oxford Hotel, corner of Lex and Thirty-fifth. Room 551, fifteen minutes away.'

'I'm on the way.' Kyle walked to a black sedan, one duly registered to a well-known car company in Brooklyn, and jumped into the backseat. The small Asian driver said, 'Where to?'

'And your name is?'

'Al Capone.'

'Where were you born, Al?'

'Tutwiler, Texas.'

'You're the man, Al. Oxford Hotel, room 551.'

Al the Agent immediately called someone and repeated the information. He listened for a few minutes, drove very slowly, then said, 'Here's the plan, Mr. McAvoy. We have a team on the move, and they should be at the hotel in ten minutes. We'll take our time here. When the supervisor is in the hotel, he will call me with more instructions. Would you like a vest?'

'A what?'

'A vest, bulletproof. There's one in the trunk if you'd like.'

Kyle had been too preoccupied with his thievery to contemplate the actual events surrounding the arrest of Bennie, and hopefully Nigel, too. He was sure he would lead the FBI to his handler, but he had not given much thought to the details of his betrayal. Why, exactly, might he need a bulletproof vest?

To stop bullets, of course. Baxter flashed through his overheated brain.

'I'll pass,' Kyle said, realizing how ill equipped he was to make such decisions.

'Yes, sir.'

Al looked for traffic, for detours, anything to burn some clock. His cell phone rang and he listened, then said, 'Okay, Mr. McAvoy. I'll stop in front of the hotel, and you'll walk into the lobby alone. Go to the elevators to the right, and punch the button for the fourth floor. Get off on the fourth, turn left, walk to the door leading to the stairs. In the stairwell, you will meet Mr. Bullington and several other agents. They will take over from there.'

'Sounds like fun.'

'Good luck, Mr. McAvoy.'

Five minutes later Kyle walked into the lobby of the Oxford Hotel and followed his instructions. In the stairwell between the fourth and the fifth floors, he met Joe Bullington and two other agents, all dressed exactly like the ones who'd snatched him some ten months earlier after a youth basketball game in New Haven. Except these were real, and he had no desire to inspect their credentials. Tensions were high, and Kyle's weary heart was pounding furiously.

'I'm Agent Booth, this is Agent Hardy,' one said, and Kyle was impressed with how large they were.

'Go to the door of 551,' Booth said. 'The second it starts to open, kick it very hard, then jump back out of the way. We'll be right behind you. We do not anticipate gunfire. We assume they're armed, but they're not expecting trouble. Once we're inside, you'll be removed from the scene.'

What! No gunfire! Kyle started to crack a funny, but his knees were suddenly weak.

'Got it?' Booth growled at him.

'Got it. Let's go.'

Kyle entered the hall and walked with as much confidence as possible to room 551. He pressed the button, took a deep breath, and glanced around. Booth and Hardy were fifteen feet away, ready to spring, shiny black pistols drawn. From the other end of the hall, two other agents were approaching, also with guns visible.

Maybe I should've opted for the vest, Kyle thought.

He pressed the button again. Nothing. Not a voice from within, not a sound.

His lungs had ceased working, and his stomach was a mess. The briefcase weighed a ton, much heavier now that it contained the stolen files.

He frowned at Booth, who looked perplexed as well. Kyle pressed the button for the third time, then tapped on the door and yelled, 'Hey, Bennie. It's Kyle.'

Nothing. He rang the doorbell for the fourth time, then fifth.

'It's a single room,' Booth whispered. Then he motioned for some type of well-rehearsed formation and said to Kyle, 'Please step aside. Go right down there and wait.' Hardy whipped out an electronic room key and inserted it. The green light came on, and the four FBI agents stormed in, high and low, right and left, barking, guns aimed in all directions. Joe Bullington was running toward them, and behind him were more agents.

The room was empty, of suspects anyway, and if anyone had been there recently, he'd left nothing behind. Bullington reappeared in the hall and commanded 'Lock the building!' into a phone or walkie-talkie. He shot Kyle a look of complete astonishment, and Kyle began to fade. Agents hustled about, frantic with indecision and confusion. Some ran to the stairs, others to the elevators.

An old woman in 562 stepped into the hall and shouted, 'Quiet!' but quickly lost her spunk when two frowning agents spun around with weapons. She retreated quickly, unharmed but awake for the night.

'Kyle, here please,' Bullington said, waving him into room 551. Kyle clutched the briefcase and entered the room. 'Stay here for a few minutes,' Bullington said. 'These two will remain with you.'

Kyle sat on the edge of the bed, briefcase between his feet, as his two guards closed the door and put away their guns. Minutes passed as he thought of a hundred scenes and scenarios, none particularly appealing. He thought of Roy, and called him. He was still at his office, waiting for the news.

'They got away,' Kyle said, his voice slow and weak.

'Whatta you mean?'

'We're in the hotel room, and it's empty. They're gone, Roy.'

'Where are you?'

'Room 551, Oxford Hotel, under guard, I guess. The FBI is searching the hotel, but they won't find anybody.'

'I'll be there in fifteen minutes.'

While the hotel was being searched, three FBI agents entered Kyle's apartment in Chelsea. Using his key, they entered quietly and began a sweep that would take four hours and produce three hidden cameras, a wiretap on his wall phone, and six other eavesdropping devices. Plenty of evidence to support indictments. A strong case for the feds, but what they really needed was some suspects.

Chapter 39

Roy arrived at 11:00 p.m. He was met by Joe Bullington at the front door and escorted through the lobby. The hotel was still locked down, a room-by-room search under way with lots of unhappy guests, and the front desk was chaos.

Roy's first question was 'How's Kyle?'

'Pretty rattled,' Bullington said. 'Let's take the stairs. The elevators have been stopped. Hell, we're all rattled.'

The second question was the most obvious one. 'What happened?'

'I do not know, Roy. It's confusing.'

Kyle was seated on the edge of the bed, briefcase still between his feet, trench coat still on, staring blankly at the floor and ignoring the two agents who were guarding him. Roy put a hand on his shoulder, then knelt down to face level and said, 'Kyle, you okay?'

'Sure.' It was somewhat helpful to see a trusted face.

Bullington was on the phone. He slapped it shut and said, 'Look, there's a suite on the second floor. It's easier to secure and much larger. Let's make a move.'

As they filed out, Kyle mumbled to his lawyer, 'Did you hear that, Roy? Easier to secure. I'm being protected now.'

'It's okay, Kyle.'

The suite had three rooms, one of which would work well as an office – desk, fax, wireless Internet, several comfortable chairs, and a small conference area at the far end. 'This'll do,' Bullington said as he ripped off his trench coat, then his jacket, as if they would be there for some time, and Kyle and Roy did the same. They took their seats and settled in. Two younger agents stayed by the door.

'Here's what we know so far,' Bullington began, very much the special agent in charge. 'The room was reserved this afternoon by a Mr. Randall Kerr, who used both a bogus name and a bogus credit card. Around 8:45, Mr. Kerr shows up to check in, alone, one small carry-on and a black briefcase, and in chatting up the desk clerk tells her that he just flew in from Mexico City. We've watched the video. It's Bennie, with no effort at disguise. He went to his room, and according to the electronic entry grid he opened the door to room 551 at 8:58. He opened it again eighteen minutes later, leaving evidently, because the door was never used again. No one remembers seeing him exit the building. There are some video cameras in the hallways and lobby, but so far nothing. He's vanished.'

'Of course he's vanished,' Kyle said. 'You won't find him.'

'We're trying.'

'What did you download, Kyle?' Roy asked.

'The Category A documents. Five or six times. I didn't touch anything else.'

'And this went smoothly?'

'As far as I know. There were no problems inside the room.'

'What time did you start downloading?' Bullington asked.

'About 8:45.'

'And what time did you call Bennie?'

'Just before 10:00.'

Bullington thought for a second, then stated the obvious. 'So Bennie waited until they got your signal, and once he knew you were downloading, he checked into the room. Eighteen minutes later he fled. That doesn't make sense.'

'It does if you know Bennie,' Kyle said.

'I don't follow,' Bullington said.

'Someone informed Bennie of our little plan, that much is obvious. It wasn't me. It wasn't my lawyer. And the only other parties involved would be you, Mr. Bullington, the FBI, and Mr. Wingate and his gang over at Justice. We have no idea at this point, and we probably never will. Regardless, Bennie got the tip and decided to have some fun. He knew I would lead you here to catch him, so this is all a setup. Bennie's probably down the street watching a hundred FBI agents swarm around the hotel and laughing his balls off.'

Bullington's cheeks turned a dark red. He suddenly had a call to make and left the room.

'Take it easy, Kyle,' Roy said softly. Kyle locked his fingers behind his head and bent over. The briefcase was still wedged between his feet. He closed his eyes and tried to control his thoughts, but that was impossible. Roy watched him but said nothing. He went to the minibar and pulled out two bottles of water.

'We should talk,' Roy said, handing a bottle to Kyle. 'We'll have to make some quick decisions.'

'Okay. What do we do with this damned thing?' Kyle asked, patting the briefcase. 'Scully doesn't need it, because the documents are not confidential. I just stole a copy. They haven't lost anything yet. Their files will appear to be untouched.'

'I'm sure the FBI will want it for evidence.'

'Evidence against who?'

'Bennie.'

'Bennie? Bennie's gone, Roy, listen to me. They'll never find Bennie, because he's a helluva lot smarter than they are. Bennie won't be arrested. Bennie won't go to trial. Bennie's on an airplane right now, probably a private one, looking at his fifteen passports and deciding which one to use next.'

'Don't be so sure.'

'And why not? Bennie outfoxed us tonight,

didn't he? Bennie has pals in high places, maybe not here in New York, maybe in Washington. Too many people got involved, Roy. The FBI, the Department of Justice, and the network of gossip spread. Plans here, authorizations there, meetings at high levels, more and more intelligence people in the loop. It was a mistake.'

'You had no choice.'

'My choices were limited. Looks like I made the wrong one.'

'What about the law firm?'

'I'm sure I'll screw that up, too. What's your advice? God knows I'm paying for it, if even at a discount.' Both managed smiles, but very brief ones.

Roy gulped his water, wiped his lips with a shirtsleeve, and leaned even closer. The two guards were still in the sitting room, within earshot. 'You could say nothing. Just report tomorrow for duty and act like none of this happened. The files are safe. Nothing has been compromised. Look, Kyle, you never planned to hand over anything to Bennie. You were forced to download some stuff to facilitate his arrest. The arrest didn't happen. The firm has no clue. Assuming there won't be a prosecution, the firm will never know.'

'But the plan was to bust Bennie, tell the firm everything, and beg for mercy. Sort of like the bank robber who brings back the cash and says he's sorry, can't we just forget about it. With a few more twists, of course.'

'Do you want to stay at the firm, Kyle?'

'My exit from Scully & Pershing was a foregone conclusion the day I walked into your office.'

'There might be a way to save the job.'

'I took the job because Bennie had a gun to my head. That gun has now been replaced by a different one, but at least the threat of blackmail is gone. There's a chance the video may still cause some embarrassment, but nothing more. I'd like to get out of here.'

A radio squawked in the sitting room, jolting the agents. It came and went with no further news.

Kyle finally abandoned the briefcase and stretched his legs. He looked at his lawyer and said, 'You're a big partner in a big firm. What would you do if an associate pulled this stunt?'

'Fire him immediately.'

'Exactly. On the spot, with little patience for a lot of talk. How can the firm ever trust me again? There are a thousand rookies out there ready to replace me. And there's something else here, Roy, something that Scully needs to know.' Kyle glanced at the sitting room, where his bodyguards were now watching TV.

'I'm not the only spy. Bennie knew too much. Someone else is planted there, passing along information to Bennie. I have to tell them.'

There was a commotion at the door, and the two guards quickly muted the television and hopped to attention. Kyle and Roy stood as

Bullington swept in with a small, important group, the center of which was a man of about sixty with short gray hair, a fine suit, and the air of someone in complete control of all things around him. Bullington introduced him as Mr. Mario Delano, director in charge of the New York office of the FBI.

He addressed both Kyle and Roy: 'Gentlemen, Mr. Bennie Wright has obviously left the building, and we have a serious problem. I have no idea where the leak was, but I assure you it was not my office. I doubt that's very comforting right now. We are searching frantically around the city – train stations, airports, subways, heliports, toll roads. Every agent under my authority is on the streets.'

If Kyle was supposed to be impressed, he was not. He simply shrugged as if to say, 'Big deal. The least you could do.'

Delano pressed on. 'It's urgent that you get out of town, Mr. McAvoy. I suggest that we take you into protective custody for a few days, let the dust settle, give us some time to track down Bennie Wright.'

'And if you don't find him?' Kyle asked.

'Let's talk about that later. We have a small jet waiting at Teterboro Airport. We'll have you there in thirty minutes. You'll have protection around the clock until something changes.' The crisp precision of Delano's plans left no doubt that the dangers were indeed substantial. Kyle could not argue. He was now the double agent, as well as the government's star witness in the event Bennie got caught. If they would murder Baxter to keep him away from Elaine, it was hard to imagine what they would do to Kyle.

'Let's go,' Delano said.

'I need a minute with my client,' Roy said.

'Certainly,' said Delano as he snapped his fingers and the room emptied. Roy closed the door, and when they were alone, he said, 'I'll call Scully and put them off.'

Kyle withdrew his FirmFone and said, 'No need. I'll check in with Doug Peckham and tell him I'm sick. Bennie never got his hands on my little phone here.'

'Fine. It's best if I keep the briefcase and the computer.'

'Just don't let the FBI have it.'

'I won't.'

They shook hands. Roy said, 'You did the right thing.'

'Right or wrong, it didn't work.'

'You didn't hand over anything, Kyle. You didn't breach a client's confidence.'

'Let's argue later.'

'Be safe.'

Chapter 40

John McAvoy was enjoying a peaceful Thursday morning at his desk when a secretary rang in with the news that two gentlemen from the FBI had dropped by for a surprise visit. They were quickly shown in. Introductions were made, badges flashed, coffee declined. 'Is he all right?' John asked.

'He's fine,' the agent named Halsey said. The one named Murdock agreed, nodding with smug assurance.

'What's happened?'

'Kyle has informed us that you are aware of the plans he had to help apprehend his handler,' Halsey said.

'Yes. I know the background and I know what he had in mind. What's happened?'

Both agents shifted weight. Murdock took over. 'Well, things didn't go as planned. Kyle secured the documents, and he was supposed to meet the handler around ten last night in a midtown hotel. The handler didn't show, fled at the last moment. As of now, we have not apprehended him.'

John closed his eyes, removed his reading glasses, and lit a cigarette. 'Where's Kyle?'

'He's with us, in protective custody. He's safe, and he's anxious to talk to you. That will not be possible at this moment.'

A blast of blue smoke escaped from John's side of the desk. 'Protective custody?' he repeated. The smoke drifted over and began settling on Halsey and Murdock.

'Afraid so. He could be in danger.'

'Who botched the operation?'

'Not sure it was botched, or how or why. Let's just say there is a lot of investigating going on right now.'

'When can I talk to him?'

'Soon,' Halsey said.

'We're out of Philly,' Murdock said. 'But we're here in York for the next few days. Our job is to relay messages to you.' Both agents withdrew business cards. 'Cell numbers on the back. Please don't hesitate to call.'

Kyle slept late into the morning, and awoke to the sounds of waves rolling onto a beach. He was adrift in the clouds – a thick white comforter, puffy white pillows, a thick white bedspread piled at his feet. The queen-sized bed was topped with a white canopy. He knew where he was, but it took a few minutes to convince himself he was really there.

The walls were adorned with cheap pastels of beach scenes. The floor was painted wood. He listened to the ocean and heard the distant calls of seagulls. There were no other sounds, quite a contrast to the early bustle of Chelsea. No alarm clock startling him at some obscene hour. No rush to shower and dress and hurry through the frantic rituals of getting to the office. None of that, at least not today.

This was not an unpleasant way to begin the rest of his life.

The bedroom was one of three in a modest two-story beach rental an hour east of Destin, Florida, on the Gulf, two hours and forty-eight minutes by Learjet from Teterboro Airport in New Jersey. They, he and his new friends, had landed at Destin just before 4:00 a.m. A van with armed drivers had scooped them up and raced along Highway 98, passing miles of empty condos and beach houses and small hotels. There were a few vacationers, judging by the parking lots, and many of the cars had Canadian license plates.

The two windows were half-open and the breeze blew the curtains. It was a full three minutes before Kyle thought about Bennie, but he fought the temptation and concentrated on the distant squawking of the seagulls. There was a slight knock at the door. 'Yes,' Kyle answered with a scratchy voice.

It opened slightly, and Todd, his new best friend, wedged through his chubby face and said, 'You wanted a ten o'clock wake-up call.'

'Thanks.'

'You okay?'

'Sure.'

Todd had joined the escape in Destin and was now assigned to guard their witness or snitch or whatever Kyle was considered to be. He was from the Pensacola office, went to Auburn, was only two years older than Kyle himself, and talked far more than any other FBI agent, real or fake, that he'd met so far in this ordeal.

Kyle, in boxers only, left the softness of the clouds and went next door to the large kitchen-den combo. Todd had been to the grocery store. The counter was covered with boxes of cereal, breakfast snacks, cookies, chips, all manner of boxed foods. 'Coffee?' Todd asked.

'Sure.'

There were a few items of folded clothing on the kitchen table. Kyle's other new best friend was Barry, an older, quieter type with premature gray hair and more wrinkles than any forty-year-old should have. Barry said, 'Good morning. We've been shopping. Bought you a couple of T-shirts, shorts, a pair of khakis, deck shoes. Really nice stuff from the local Kmart. Don't worry, Uncle Sam paid the bill.'

'I'm sure I'll look fabulous,' Kyle said, taking a cup of coffee from Todd. Todd and Barry, both in khakis and polos, were unarmed but not far from their weapons. There was also a Nick and a Matthew somewhere close by.

'I gotta call the office,' Kyle said. 'Check in, you know, tell them I'm sick and can't work today. By now they're already looking for me.'

Todd produced the FirmFone and said, 'Be our guest. We're told it's secure. Just don't give a hint as to where you are. Agreed?'

'Where am I?'

'Western Hemisphere.'

'Close enough.'

With his coffee and his phone, Kyle stepped outside onto a wide deck that looked over some dunes. The beach was long and beautiful, and deserted. The air was light, brisk, but far warmer than frigid New York. With great reluctance he looked at the phone. E-mails, texts, and voice mails from Doug Peckham, Dale, Sherry Abney, Tim Reynolds, Tabor, and a few others, but nothing to alarm him. He scanned them quickly, just the usual daily barrage of communications from very wired people with too much access to each other. Dale asked twice if he was okay.

He called Doug Peckham, got his voice mail, and reported that he was down with the flu, flat on his back, sick as a dog, and so on. Then he called Dale, who was in a meeting. He left the same message. One useless advantage of working with workaholics was that they had no time to worry about each other's minor ailments. Got the flu – take some pills and sleep it off, but do not spread your germs at the office.

Roy Benedict seemed to be waiting by the phone. 'Where are you, Kyle?' he asked, almost in a pant.

'Western Hemisphere. I'm doing well. How about you?'

'Fine. You're safe?'

'Safe. I'm hidden, stashed away, and I'm guarded by a posse of at least four, all anxious to shoot someone. Any news on our man Bennie?'

'No. They'll have indictments by noon, and they're adding one for murder. They'll splash these around the world and hope for a break. You were right. Your apartment had more bugs than a landfill. Good stuff, too, the latest in wiretapping technology.'

'I'm honored.'

'And they found a transmitter in the rear bumper of your Jeep.'

'I never thought of that.'

'Anyway, all this is being presented to the grand jury as we speak, so at least Bennie will have a thick indictment on record should he ever make a mistake.'

'Don't bet on that.'

'Have you talked to the law firm?'

'I left a message with Peckham, the flu routine. He'll buy it for a couple of days.'

'No alarms, nothing strange.'

'No. It's weird, Roy. I'm a thousand miles away now, and looking back, I can't believe how easy it was to walk in with the right gear and walk out with the files. I could've taken every single document in the database, four million plus, and handed them over to Bennie or another thug. And I could've gone back into my office this morning as if nothing happened. Scully has got to be warned.'

'So who tells them?'

'I do. I have a few things to get off my chest.'

'Let's talk about that tomorrow. I've been on the phone with Bullington all morning. Twice he's mentioned the witness protection program. The FBI is pushing it hard. They are pretty nervous about you, Kyle.'

'I'm nervous about me, too, but witness protection?'

'Sure. You're convinced they can't find Bennie. They're convinced they can. If they do, and they haul him back for a trial, with an incredible list of charges, then you're the star. If you're not around to testify, then the government's case falls flat.'

A pleasant morning at the beach was becoming complicated. And why not? Nothing had been simple for a long time now.

'That'll take some serious thought and consideration,' Kyle said.

'Then start thinking.'

'I'll call you later.'

Kyle dressed in the khakis and a T-shirt, not a bad fit, then ate two bowls of cereal. He read the *Pensacola News Journal* and the *New York Times*. The *Times* had nothing about last night's excitement at the Oxford Hotel. Of course not, Kyle said to himself. It happened far too late, and it was far too clandestine. Then why was he looking for it?

After breakfast and the papers, Todd joined him at the kitchen table. 'We have a few rules,' he said with a jovial face but a hard smile.

'What a surprise.'

'You can make calls, obviously, but only on that phone. Can't reveal your whereabouts. You can walk on the beach, but we have to follow, at a distance.'

'You're kidding? I'm walking down the beach, and there's a guy with a machine gun tagging along. How relaxing.'

Todd caught the humor and enjoyed a laugh. 'No machine gun, and we won't be conspicuous.'

'You're all conspicuous. I can spot an agent a mile away.'

'Anyway, stay close to the house.'

'How long will I be here?'

Todd shrugged and said, 'I have no idea.'

'Am I in protective custody or witness protection?'

'Custody, I think.'

'You don't know, Todd? Come on. Custody implies that I'm a suspect of some variety, doesn't it, Todd?'

Another shrug.

'But I'm not a suspect. I'm a witness, but I have not agreed to enter the witness protection program. So, according to my lawyer, the one I just talked to, I'm free to walk out that door anytime I want. Whatta you think about that, Todd?'

'That machine gun you just mentioned? We have at least six on the premises.'

'So I should stay here, right?'

'Right.'

'Okay, it's noon. What are we going to do?'

Barry had been hovering nearby, not missing a word. He walked to the table with a large basket of the usual board games the owners of all beach rentals leave behind. Barry said, 'We have Monopoly, Risk, Rook, Scrabble, Chinese checkers, your call, Kyle.'

Kyle studied the basket. 'Scrabble.'

Chapter 41

The flu raged unabated into Friday. Doug Peckham, while claiming to be sympathetic, was curious about any 'improvement.' They were getting hammered with motions in the Trylon case, and everyone was needed. His sympathy did not extend to a curiosity about where Kyle was staying, who, if anyone, was tending to him, what medications he was taking, and so on. Part of Kyle's ruse was the forbidding diagnosis that his particular strain of the flu was 'hotly contagious.' Since New York was going through its annual December flu warning, his story was easily digestible. Dale believed it, too, though she was much more sympathetic.

The temperature hit eighty degrees in the early afternoon, and Kyle was bored with the beach house. He said to Todd, 'I'd like to take a walk. Would you please prepare the beach?'

'My pleasure. Which way are you going?'

'East, toward Miami.'

'I'll round up the gang. They're getting bored with you.'

Kyle walked for an hour, and passed fewer than ten beachcombers going the opposite way. Thirty yards behind him were two of his guardians, a male and a female, a happy couple with receivers in their ears and handguns in their pockets.

He heard music, and saw a small crowd under a fake thatched roof. It was the Gator Hotel, a 1950s-style mom-and-pop motel with a small pool and low rates, a depressing little place, but it had the only action on the beach. Just for the hell of it, and to torment his followers, he sauntered away from the water, walked between two small dunes, and pulled up a chair at Pedro's Bar. Jimmy Buffett was singing softly about life in a banana republic. The bartender was mixing rum punch specials. The crowd numbered seven, all over the age of sixty, all overweight, all chatting in crisp northern accents. The early snowbirds.

Kyle sipped a rum punch and ordered a cigar. Between the dunes he saw his trailing couple stop and gawk and try to figure out what to do. Within minutes, another agent appeared from the front of the motel. He walked through the open bar, winked at Kyle, and kept going. We're here, buddy.

He drank and smoked for a while, and tried to convince himself that he was relaxed. No worries. Just another overworked professional enjoying a few days at the beach.

But there was too much unfinished business in New York.

After three days of thorough protection, Kyle was fed up. The Lear landed at Teterboro just after 6:00 p.m. on Saturday, December 6. At Kyle's insistence, he was booked into a suite at the Tribeca Grand Hotel, between Walker and White, near the Village. And at his request, all FBI agents remained below, in the lobby and atrium. He was tired of their overkill and silly rules – silly in his opinion.

Dale arrived promptly at eight. She was driven over by two agents and sneaked in through a service entrance. When they were alone, Kyle started with the fake flu and worked his way backward. It was a long journey, and she listened with the same disbelief that had been shared by Roy Benedict and John McAvoy. They ordered room service, lobster and a fine white burgundy, compliments of the government, and kept talking. He was leaving the firm, and not sure where he was headed. She was leaving the firm, a nice lateral transfer to a better life in downtown Providence. He wanted to talk about her future, but she was determined to finish up with his past. She found it fascinating, incredulous, frightening, and said over and over, 'Why didn't you tell me?' The best response he could offer was 'I didn't tell anyone.'

They talked until well past midnight. The back-and-forth was more a conversation between two good friends than between two casual lovers.

They said goodbye with a long kiss and a serious promise to meet in a few weeks, as soon as Kyle settled some issues.

At 1:00 a.m., he called downstairs and informed the boys that he was going to sleep.

Kyle McAvoy entered the opulent offices of Scully & Pershing for the last time at noon on Sunday. He was accompanied by Roy Benedict, Mr. Mario Delano of the FBI, and Mr. Drew Wingate with the Department of Justice. They were led to a conference room on the thirty-fifth floor, yet another room Kyle had never seen. They were met by half a dozen of the firm's partners, all with very somber faces. All offered stiff introductions. Only Doug Peckham showed the slightest trace of warmth to Kyle, and only for a second. They took seats on opposite sides of the table like enemies glaring across the battlefield: Howard Meezer, the managing partner; Peckham; Wilson Rush, who looked particularly upset; a retired legend named Abraham Kintz; and two slightly younger partners from the firm's management committee, men Kyle had never laid eyes on.

Late Saturday evening, Roy Benedict had sent them a twenty-five-page, detailed summary of Kyle's big adventure, and there was little doubt that every word had been read more than once by all six of the partners. Attached to the narrative was Kyle's letter of resignation.

Meezer kicked things off with a pleasant 'Mr.

McAvoy, your resignation is unanimously accepted.'

Not just accepted, but unanimously so. Kyle nodded but said nothing.

'We've read the summary prepared by your lawyer,' Meezer said slowly, methodically. 'It is fascinating, and troubling, and it raises a number of questions. I suggest we address them in order of priority.'

Fine, fine, yes, agreed all around the table.

'The first issue is what to do with you, Mr. McAvoy. We understand the reasons behind your theft, but it was a theft nonetheless. You took the confidential files of a valuable client for purposes that had not been authorized by this firm. A criminal prosecution is in order, do you agree?'

Kyle had been told to keep his mouth shut unless Roy approved a response.

'A criminal prosecution is possible,' Roy admitted. 'But there is nothing to be gained. The firm lost nothing.'

'Loss is not a requirement, Mr. Benedict.'

'Agreed, technically. But let's be practical. Kyle had no intention of turning over the documents once he'd taken them. He did so only to stop a conspiracy to seriously harm this firm and its client.'

'The FBI will not cooperate in a criminal prosecution, Mr. Meezer,' Delano said, the heavy hand of the federal government.

'Nor will the Department of Justice,' added Wingate.

'Thank you,' Meezer said. 'But we don't need your help. Theft can be a state charge, and we have some nice contacts with the authorities here in the city. However, we are not inclined to pursue this as a criminal matter.' Heavy emphasis on the word 'criminal.' 'There is little to be gained and much to be lost. We don't want our clients worried about confidentiality, and this little episode would make a wonderful story in the press.'

Wilson Rush was glaring at Kyle, but Doug occupied himself with a legal pad. He was there because Kyle fell under his immediate supervision, and because the firm needed bodies, a grim show of force at this unfortunate moment. Kyle watched Doug, ignored Rush, and wondered how many of the six partners over there were billing Trylon at a double rate since they'd been dragged in on a Sunday.

Billing. Billing. He hoped he never saw another time sheet, never again glanced at his watch and divided an hour into tenths, never again tallied things up at the end of the month to make sure he'd gone over two hundred hours, padding here and there if he came up a few hours short.

'As to the matter of ethics,' Meezer was saying, 'this is a serious breach of a client's confidence. The state disciplinary committee should be notified.'

He paused long enough for someone on the other side to respond. 'I thought you were trying to avoid publicity,' Roy said. 'These matters are supposed to be private, but we know that they're often leaked. And if Kyle gets reprimanded or disbarred, it becomes public record. A Scully & Pershing associate disbarred for taking confidential files. Is that the story you want splashed in the *New York Lawyer*?'

At least four of the six were slowly shaking their heads, and it dawned on Kyle that they were as nervous as he was. Their vaunted reputation was on the line. A major client might pull its business. Others could follow. Scully's competitors would use the breach of security as a piece of delicious gossip to spread all over Wall Street.

'Do you plan to stay in New York, Mr. McAvoy?' Meezer asked.

Roy nodded, and Kyle said, 'No, I can't.'

'Very well. If you agree to forgo the practice of law in the state of New York, we will agree to forget the ethical violations.'

'Agreed,' Kyle said, and maybe a bit too quickly because he couldn't wait to leave the city.

Meezer shuffled through some notes as if there were a dozen tough topics to cover, but the meeting was practically over. The meeting was important so that the firm could officially dismiss Kyle, perhaps flog him a bit, listen to his apology, and then both sides could say good riddance.

'Where is this blue box?' Wilson Rush asked.

'Locked in my office,' Roy said.

'And it has nothing but the Category A files?'

'That's correct,' Roy said.

'I'd like for our security people to see it.'

'Anytime.'

'But we would like to be present,' Delano added. 'If this Bennie character is caught, the box is exhibit No. 1.'

'Any progress on the search?' Meezer asked, veering off script.

Delano could never say there was no progress when searching for a suspect, so he gave the standard 'We are pursuing leads. We're still confident.'

In other words, no.

More shuffling of paper, more shifting of rear ends. 'In your summary, Mr. McAvoy, you allude to additional security issues within Scully & Pershing. Care to expand on this?'

A nod from Roy, and Kyle began, 'Yes, but first I want to apologize for my actions. I hope you understand the reasons behind what I did, but I was still wrong. And I apologize. As far as security, I met with these thugs ten times while I was in New York. The first meeting was in February, the tenth meeting was last Tuesday night. I took meticulous notes of each meeting – dates, places, duration, who was present, what was said, everything I could remember afterward. My attorney has these notes. The FBI has a copy. On three occasions, I was given information that could only be known by someone within this firm. I think there's another spy. For example, Bennie, and I hate to use that name because it's just an alias, but it's all we have, but Bennie knew about the warehouse full of documents, down south, as he said. During one meeting he and Nigel, another alias, hinted that they were making progress in breaching the security of the warehouse. They knew about the secret room on the eighteenth floor. Bennie knew every name of every partner and associate assigned to the lawsuit. Bennie knew that a young lawyer named McDougle was leaving, that he worked under a senior associate named Sherry Abney on the Trylon case, and Bennie told me to start playing squash because Sherry enjoyed the game. Bennie handed me copies of pleadings, motions, rulings – I have over six hundred pages of the court file that, as you know, is locked away and kept from the public.'

Three of the six jaws had dropped on the other side, not down to their chests, not the kick-me-in-the-gut shock of sudden, horrific news, but a stunning blow nonetheless. The nightmare of one lowly associate tapping into their impenetrable defenses was bad enough. Now there might be another?

And just to give them more heartburn, Kyle added something he truly believed, but couldn't prove. 'And I don't think it's an associate,' he said, then withdrew from the fray and settled back into his chair.

All six partners had the same thought. If it's not an associate, then it must be a partner.

Doug Peckham swallowed hard, cleared his throat, and attempted to speak. 'Are you saying—'

Next to him, Wilson Rush quickly raised his right hand, partially in Doug's space. Like a king calling for silence, a quick lifting of the hand, and all was quiet for the moment.

Roy finally said, 'Anything else?'

'I believe that's all,' Meezer said. After an awkward few seconds, Roy stood, followed by Kyle and Delano and Wingate. The six partners did not budge. They sat frozen, with matching scowls, as Kyle and his little entourage left the room.

Chapter 42

In the lobby of the building, they were met by the same three large young men who'd brought Kyle from the hotel. The group made it safely outside, onto Broad Street, then walked one block east to the building next door, where Roy worked, sixteen floors up. The three agents, bodyguards really, camped in a reception area and began waiting again. Inside Roy's office, Drew Wingate decided that his job was over. He excused himself and promised to help in any way possible. After he left, Kyle, Roy, and Delano gathered around Roy's small conference table. Some poor secretary, beckoned on a Sunday, served them coffee with a smile.

'What are your plans, Kyle?' Delano asked.

'Well, looks like I won't be practicing law in the state of New York, that's for sure. I'll go home for a few weeks, take some time off, enjoy the holidays.'

'I'm not sure that's a wise thing to do.'

'Thank you, Mr. Delano. I appreciate your concern, but I'm not about to go into hiding. Thanks for the offer to enter the dark little world of witness protection, but no thanks. I'm twenty-five years old, stumbling but not falling, and I'll do just fine on my own.'

Roy's coffee cup froze in midair, halfway to his mouth. 'Kyle, you can't be serious.'

'Dead serious, Roy. No pun intended. I've just survived three days of protection, guards all around me, hiding and watching for bad guys. No thanks. There's more to my future than fake names and nonstop Scrabble.'

'Scrabble?'

'Don't go there. Listen, I've been under surveillance for the last ten months. You know what that does to you? You get real paranoid. You suspect everyone. You seize upon every new face because it might belong to a bad guy. You notice every corner, alley, every bum on a park bench, every guy wearing a dark trench coat. You pick up a phone and you wonder who's listening. You send an e-mail and change the wording because the wrong eyes might see it. In your own apartment you change clothes in a hurry, back to the camera, trying to hide your crotch. You walk in a coffee shop and go straight to the front window to see who's on the sidewalk behind you. You learn all sorts of stupid little tricks because the more you know, the more you might need to know. And the walls close in. The world becomes a small place because somebody is always watching. I'm sick of it. I'm not going to live on the run.'

'These guys killed Baxter Tate without the slightest hesitation,' Roy said. 'What makes you think they won't do the same to you?'

'The operation was still hot when Baxter came barging in. The operation, at least that part that involves me, is now over. Bennie's gone. The operation failed. He might return with another plan—'

'I'm sure he will,' Delano said.

'But it won't involve me. What does Bennie gain by taking me out?'

'He takes out a material witness,' Roy said.

'Only if he's caught, which I seriously doubt. If Bennie gets hauled back for a trial, then we can talk about hiding.'

'Oh, it'll be too late then, Kyle,' Delano said. 'Believe me. The moment Bennie gets nabbed, there'll be a few guys headed your way.'

'Bring 'em on. We have at least five deer rifles at home. I'll carry a Luger in my briefcase. If they show up, we'll have a regular gunfight.'

'Get serious, Kyle,' Roy pleaded.

'The decision has been made. The FBI cannot force me into witness protection, and so I hereby officially, and respectfully, say no. Thank you, Mr. Delano, but the answer is no.'

'I hope you don't regret this,' Delano said.

'So do I,' Kyle said. 'And please don't follow me around. I might go berserk and shoot the next person I see lurking in the shadows.'

'Oh, don't worry. We have plenty of work elsewhere.' Delano stood and all hands were shaken. He said to Roy, 'I'll check in once a week with an update.'

Roy walked him to the door, and the FBI left Kyle's life. With the door closed, Roy took his seat and looked at Kyle as if he couldn't believe it. 'You're awfully brave,' he said.

'Brave or stupid. The line is often blurred.'

'Why not disappear for a few months, maybe a year? Let everything cool off.'

'A year means nothing. These guys have long memories. If Bennie wants revenge, he'll find me sooner or later, and it won't matter where I happen to be.'

'You don't trust the FBI?'

'No. I trust you, me, my father, a girl named Dale, and that's about it.'

'So it was an inside job?'

'We'll never know, will we? I have a hunch that Bennie works for the same government you and I send our taxes to. That's how he got away. That's why he'll never be found.'

'I still don't believe that.'

Kyle shrugged, and for a long time nothing was said.

Finally, Kyle glanced at his watch. 'Look, Roy, it's Sunday afternoon and you have a family. Go home.'

'What about you?'

'Me? I'm walking out the door, taking a long hike to my apartment, not once looking over my shoulder, and when I get there, I'll load up my clothes and as much junk as possible, cram all of it into my Jeep that has 200,000 miles on the odometer, and drive home. I should get there in time for a late dinner with my father. Tomorrow he and I will draw up a partnership agreement – McAvoy & McAvoy, Attorneys-at-Law – and I'll make partner faster than any graduate in the history of the Yale Law School.'

'I like it. The editor in chief of the *Yale Law Journal* practicing law on Main Street in York, Pennsylvania.'

'I like it, too. Real clients. Real people. Real cases. Deer hunting on Saturdays, Steelers on Sundays. A real life.'

'You're not kidding, are you?'

'I have never been more serious.'

'Come on. I'll walk you out.'

They rode the elevator to the lobby and walked out of the building. They shook hands and said goodbye, and Roy watched his client stride nonchalantly along Broad Street and disappear around a corner.

ALSO AVAILABLE IN ARROW

The Last Juror

John Grisham

In 1970, one of Mississippi's more colourful weekly newspapers, *Th Ford County Times*, went bankrupt. To the surprise and dismay of mar ownership was assumed by a 23-year-old college drop-out, named Wil Traynor. The future of the paper looked grim until a young mother w brutally raped and murdered by a member of the notorious Padg family. Willie Traynor reported all the gruesome details, and his new paper began to prosper.

The murderer, Danny Padgitt, was tried before a packed courtroom Clanton, Mississippi. The trial came to a startling and dramatic end wh the defendant threatened revenge against the jurors if they convict him. Nevertheless, they found him guilty, and he was sentenced to life prison.

But in Mississippi in 1970, 'life' didn't necessarily mean 'life', and ni years later Danny Padgitt managed to get himself paroled. He return to Ford County, and the retribution began.

'*The Last Juror* sees Grisham at the absolute peak of his form . . . page-turning urgency'
Mail on Sunday

'*The Last Juror* does not need to coast on its author's megapopularit It's a reminder of how the Grisham juggernaut began.'
New York Times

ALSO AVAILABLE IN ARROW

The Broker

John Grisham

In his final hours in the Oval Office the outgoing President grants a controversial last minute pardon to Joel Backman, a notorious Washington power broker who has spent the last six years hidden away in a federal prison. What no one knows is that the President issues the pardon only after receiving enormous pressure from the CIA. It seems that Backman, in his power broker heyday, may have obtained secrets that compromise the world's most sophisticated satellite surveillance system.

Backman is quietly smuggled out of the country in a military cargo plane, given a new name, a new identity, and a new home in Italy. Eventually, after he has settled into his new life, the CIA will leak his whereabouts to the Israelis, the Russians, the Chinese and the Saudis. Then the CIA will do what it does best: sit back and watch.

The question is not whether Backman will survive – there's no chance of that. The question the CIA needs answered is, who will kill him?

'A nail-biting story' *Sun*

'A killer combination of sheer story-telling nous and no-nonsense prose' *Independent*

'Grisham hasn't lost his touch' *Daily Mail*

arrow books

ALSO AVAILABLE IN ARROW

The Appeal

John Grisham

In a crowded courtroom in Mississippi, a jury returns a shocking verdict against a chemical company accused of dumping toxic waste into a small town's water supply, causing the worst "cancer cluster" in history. The company appeals to the Mississippi Supreme Court, whose nine justices will one day either approve the verdict or reverse it.

Who are the nine? How will they vote? Can one be replaced before the case is ultimately decided?

The chemical company is owned by a Wall Street predator named Carl Trudeau, and Mr. Trudeau is convinced the Court is not friendly enough. With judicial elections looming, he decides to try to purchase himself a seat on the Court. The cost is a few million dollars, a drop in the bucket for a billionaire like Mr. Trudeau. Through an intricate web of conspiracy and deceit, his political operatives recruit a young, unsuspecting candidate. They finance him, manipulate him, market him, and mould him into a potential Supreme Court justice. *Their* Supreme Court justice.

The Appeal is a powerful, timely, and shocking story of political and legal intrigue, a story that will leave readers unable to think about the electoral process or judicial system in quite the same way ever again.

'A brilliant career masterpiece . . . Grisham's flow of energy is seamless, collectively building a shockingly vivid scenario. Breathtaking.' *Sunday Express*

'An engrossing read' *Observer*

arrow books

The Archaeology of the M6 Toll 2000–2003

by Andrew B. Powell, Paul Booth, A.P. Fitzpatrick,

and

A.D. Crockett

The Archaeology of the M6 Toll 2000–2003

by Andrew B. Powell, Paul Booth, A.P. Fitzpatrick,

and

A.D. Crockett

with contributions by

Carol Allen, Michael J. Allen, Carl Champness, Catherine Chisham, Alan J. Clapham, Kate Cramp, H.E.M. Cool, Rebecca Devaney, Kirsten Egging, Rowena Gale, Jonathan Gill, Lisa Gray, Phil Harding, John Hunt, Fraser Hunter, Hugo Lamdin-Whymark, Ruth Leary, Jacqueline. I. McKinley, J. M. Mills, Cynthia Poole, Kelly Powell, Stephanie Rátkai, Kevin Ritchie, Robert G. Scaife, Ian Scott, Ruth Shaffrey, Wendy Smith, Chris J. Stevens, Andy Simmonds, Mike Trevarthen and Fay Worley

principal illustrator

Rob Goller

with

Sarah Lucas, Frances Chaloner, and Magda Wachnik, Simon Skittrell, Karen Nichols and Martyn Norris

Oxford Wessex Archaeology

Monograph No. 2

2008

This book is one of a series of monographs by Oxford Wessex Archaeology (OWA)
that can be ordered through all good bookshops and internet bookshops

ISBN 978–0–9545970–1–6

British Library Cataloguing in Publication Data
A catalogue record for this book is available from the British Library

The fieldwork and post-excavation assessment, analysis and publication were generously funded by CAMBBA Construction, a joint venture between Carillion plc, Alfred McAlpine plc, Balfour Beatty plc and AMEC Construction Ltd

Published by Oxford Wessex Archaeology,
a joint venture between Oxford Archaeology and Wessex Archaeology

Oxford Archaeology, Janus House, Osney Mead, Oxford OX2 0ES, Registered Charity No. 285627
Wessex Archaeology, Portway House, Old Sarum Park, Salisbury SP4 6EB, Registered Charity No. 287786

Designed and typeset by Wessex Archaeology
Printed and bound by Henry Ling (Dorset Press) Ltd, Dorchester

Contents

Chapter 15 Shenstone Linear Features (Site 13)

by Andrew B. Powell

Chapter 16 Shenstone Ring Ditch (Site 14)

by Andy Simmonds

Chapter 17 East of Birmingham Road Nurseries (Site 15)

by Andy Simmonds

Chapter 18 East of The Castle, Shenstone (Site 32)

by Andy Simmonds

Chapter 19 Round Wood, Shenstone (Site 33)

by Carl Champness

SITES AT THE SOUTH-WESTERN END OF THE ROUTE

Chapter 26 Curdworth Top Lock (Site 21)

by Andrew B. Powell

Chapter 27 Hawkeswell Farm, Coleshill (Site 24)

by Andrew B. Powell

SYNTHESES

Chapter 28 Environmental and material culture Studies

Chapter 29 Prehistoric discussion *by A. P. Fitzpatrick*

Chapter 30 Romano-British period discussion

by Paul Booth

List of Figures

List of Tables

Acknowledgements

The invaluable assistance received from Amy Baldry, Andy Bould, Keith Butterworth, Mike Edwards, Derek Graham, Richard Hill, Colin Jones, Tom Lawson, Paul Neal, and Richard Spicer from the CAMBBA construction joint venture is gratefully acknowledged. Particular credit is due to the Oxford Wessex Archaeology field team for their work in what were often difficult conditions.

The fieldwork was monitored on behalf of MEL by Pete Fasham and Kev Beachus of Jacobs, by Dr Mike Hodder for Birmingham City Council, by Chris Welch, Bill Klemperer and Stephen Dean for Staffordshire County Council, by Jonathan Parkhouse and Ed Wilson for Warwickshire County Council, and by Lisa Moffett of English Heritage and their collaborative role and also the contribution of Martin Leather of Jacobs is also acknowledged. Janet Miller and Andrea Bradley of Atkins acted as consultants to CAMBBA in the preliminary stages of the filedwork.

Materials conservation was undertaken by Vanessa Fell (Institute of Archaeology, Oxford) and the charred plant remains were assessed by Angela Monckton (University of Leicester). David Smith (University of Birmingham) and Matt Canti (English Heritage) commented on the insect remains and soils respectively at this stage, with Dan Miles (University of Oxford) and Cathy Groves (University of Sheffield) assessing the dendrochronological potential of the timber from Site 30.

Graham Eyre-Morgan (Sandwell Metropolitan Borough Council) and Chris Patrick (Coventry City Council) provided assistance in the analysis stage and Stuart Palmer (Warwickshire Museum Field Services), generously made available the drafts of a number of forthcoming excavation reports. Simon Esmonde Cleary (University of Birmingham) kindly provided very helpful comments on a draft of the Roman discussion chapter. Especial thanks are due to Mike Hodder (Birmingham City Council) for his unstinting help, advice and enthusiasm.

Sarah F. Wyles supervised the processing of the environmental samples and undertook the extraction of them. Michael J. Allen co-ordinated the environmental and radiocarbon dating programmes and Karen Nichols managed the graphics production with assistance from Paul Backhouse.

Alan Clapham wishes to thank the George Pitt-Rivers Laboratory for the provision of space and equipment. Phil Harding would like to thank Mick Aston and James Bond, and Viv Shears and Simon Scott of Sparsholt College, for their comments and advice. John Hunt is grateful to Stephanie Rátkai for discussing at length the nature and the implications of the pottery evidence, and for her generosity in sharing her wider contextual thinking relating to this material. Fraser Hunter is grateful to Lore Troalen for the XRF analysis of the beaded torc from Wishaw Hall Farm; and to Sally Worrell and J.D. Hill for information on unpublished torcs. Ruth Leary is grateful to Kay Hartley for advice on the mortarium types and to Hilary Cool and Mike Baxter for help with the pottery analysis. Jacqueline McKinley would like to thank Mrs. F.E. Fox of the South Staffordshire Archaeological and Historical Society and Diane Wilkes of the Walsall Local History Centre for their assistance and speedy dispatch of back-copies of articles and publications relating to Wall, and Andrew Fitzpatrick and Jörn Schuster for their advice and translations with regard to the cemetery at Wederath. Much of the work on the project up to 1994 was undertaken by George Lambrick and his role as well as that of the Oxford Wessex Joint Venture Board of Sue Davies, David Jennings, Clive Burrows and Simon Palmer, and the JV Management Team of John Dillon and Bob Williams, is also recognised.

Many, many, other people to numerous to mention have contributed to the project and to them we extend our thanks.

The project was led in the field by Andrew Crockett assisted by Paul Murray and Dave Score and was managed by Paul Booth and Andrew Fitzpatrick. The analysis programme was managed by Andrew Crockett, Andrew Powell and Karen E Walker assisted by Paul Booth, Lisa Brown, Bruno Barber, and Andrew Fitzpatrick.

Abstract

This volume presents the results of archaeological works carried out in advance of construction of the new M6 Toll motorway (formerly known as the Birmingham Northern Relief Road). The new road (44 km in length), leaves the M6 Motorway at Junction 3a, passing between Sutton Coldfield and Walsall to the south and Lichfield and Cannock to the north, and rejoins the M6 at Junction 11a. Forty-one sites were identified and investigated, spanning most archaeological periods from the Mesolithic to the post-medieval and modern industrial landscape of canals, railways and associated infrastructure.

Identification of over 1500 pieces of flint, provided evidence for a Late Mesolithic possible winter camp at Wishaw Hall Farm (Site 19) – a notable addition to the archaeological record for transient Mesolithic hunter-gatherers in the region. Isolated Neolithic finds and features were recorded including a later Neolithic burnt mound west of Crane Brook (Site 9); and a pair of Early Neolithic pits (containing pottery, charcoal and charred grain and hazelnut shells), fragments of a single Peterborough Ware vessel of Mortlake type and a collection of Early Neolithic pottery all at Shenstone (Sites 13, 15 and 32 respectively). Bronze Age remains were restricted to two burnt mound sites along Langley Brook (Site 39) and Collet's Brook (Site 40).

Middle Iron Age remains were discovered in various places. At Shenstone (Site 14) an oval enclosure and an adjacent roundhouse proved to be largely devoid of finds. At Langley Mill, a large enclosed settlement on the higher ground north of the mill (Site 29) contained at least five roundhouses, the largest having been rebuilt at least twice. This settlement overlooked a smaller enclosure and ring ditches (Site 30) at the foot of the slope on either side of Langley Brook.

A Middle Iron Age pit alignment was recorded at Wishaw (Site 19). The individual pits were quite variable, although set at a relatively regular intervals. Few finds were recovered with the exception of one placed deposit of stones, pottery and an inverted human skull. Pit alignments from this period are not uncommon in the region and they appear to characterise a period that focused on linear boundaries and land division. The pit alignment was just post-dated by a substantial. adjacent, segmented ditch – providing a boundary, which was recut in the Romano-British period. At nearby Site 20 were the probable remains of an isolated roundhouse. Burnt stone filled pits along the bank of the stream were certainly prehistoric, possibly Iron Age.

Romano-British archaeology is dominated by the small town of Wall (*Letocetum*) at the junction of two major roads; Watling Street running from London to Wroxeter, and Ryknield Street running from the Fosse Way, through Birmingham, towards Derby and on to Yorkshire. Outside Wall, cemeteries comprising 42 cremation and up to 21 inhumation burials were recorded either side of Ryknield Street (Site 12). Cremation burial dominated during the 1st–2nd centuries AD, with inhumation burials from the late 2nd century onwards, though some rare 4th century cremation burials were also recovered. At nearby Shenstone, four settlement enclosures with features including a well-preserved kiln lay within a linear zone defined by parallel ditches (Site 15). Other Romano-British discoveries included a field system alongside Watling Street at Washbrook Lane (Site 5), a substantial aisled building south of Watling Street beside Crane Brook (Site 34), a complex of at least five enclosures replacing the Middle Iron Age settlement north of Langley Mill (Site 29), and a smaller enclosure, at Wishaw (Site 19). The M6 Toll also crossed Watling Street twice; from south to north at Hammerwich and from north to south at Churchbridge (Site 4), though the latter produced no positive trace of the Roman road.

Medieval remains included ridge and furrow at Washbrook Lane (Site 5), a small 13th/14th century farmstead at Shenstone (Site 13), and an enclosure at Wishaw (Site 19). Of most significance were the Knights Templar fishpond complex east of Grove Lane (Site 20) and the settlement at Hawkeswell Farm (Site 24). The fishpond complex probably originated in the late 12th or early 13th century, on land probably granted as a gift from local major landholders. At Hawkeswell Farm, just north of the documented hamlet at Hawkeswell, poorly defined settlement from the 13th century onwards was indicated. Later medieval garden features and land-scaping suggest the area became part of the formal gardens for a precursor to the current Hawkeswell Hall.

South of Cannock free-standing structures of the 18th–19th century canal and rail network were recorded: the northern dam for Hatherton Reservoir (Site 2), the Churchbridge Railway and Accommodation bridges (Site 3), and long-since buried components such as Hawkins Canal Basin (Site 1). This was built in 1883 and was connected to the Hatherton Branch of the Staffordshire and Worcester Canal via an aqueduct crossing Wyrley Brook. Gilpin's Basin, built at Churchbridge in 1860 to allow direct transfer of materials between canal and rail, was also investigated, revealing the base of a quayside crane and footings of a large goods shed. A trench through the adjacent A5 Trunk Road (Site 4) revealed what may have been Telford's late 18th century improvements to what was then Watling Street turnpike (also seen at Site 41). The north side of the Hatherton Branch canal tunnel was revealed beneath the A5. Other post-medieval sites included a survey of Swan Farm at Norton Canes (Site 36), sections through the Cannock Extension (1858) and Wyrley and Essington Canals (1794) (Sites 6 and 8), the footings of a 19th century tramway between Lichfield Road and Barracks Lane (Site 34), and Curdworth top lock and lockkeeper's cottage at Dunton Wharf (Site 21). Infilled post-medieval ponds and other landscape features were recorded at Hawkeswell Farm (Site 24).

Foreign Language Summaries

Ce volume présente les résultats de travaux archéologiques effectués en avant de la construction de la nouvelle autoroute M6 à péage (connue antérieurement sous le nom de déviation de Birmingham nord. La nouvelle route (de 44 km de long) quitte l'autoroute M6 à la sortie 3a, passe entre Sutton Coldfield et Walsall, au sud, et Lichfield et Cannock, au nord, pour rejoindre la M6 à la sortie 11a. On a identifié et examiné 41 sites qui couvrent la plupart des périodes archéologiques, du mésolithique à la période post-médiévale et jusqu'à un paysage industriel moderne de canaux, chemins de fer et infrastructure associée.

L'identification de plus de 1500 éléments de silex a fourni des témoignages de ce qui pourrait être un campement hivernal à Wishaw Hall Farm (Site 19) – un remarquable ajout aux archives archéologiques concernant les chasseurs cueilleurs du mésolithique de passage dans la région. On a répertorié des trouvailles et des vestiges néolithiques isolés, y compris un monticule brûlé du néolithique final à l'ouest de Crane Brook (Site 9); et une paire de fosses du néolithique primitif (contenant de la céramique, du charbon de bois et des graminées et des coquilles de noisettes calcinées), des fragments d'un seul récipient en céramique de Peterborough de type Mortlake et une collection de céramique du néolithique primitif, le tout à Shenstone (Sites 13, 15 et 32 respectivement). Les restes de l'âge du bronze se réduisaient à deux sites à monticule brûlé le long de Langley Brook (Site 39) et Collet's Brook (Site 40),

On a découvert des vestiges de l'âge du fer moyen en différents endroits. A Shenstone (Site 14) une enceinte ovale et une maison ronde adjacente se sont avérées en grande partie dépourvues de trouvailles. A Langley Hill une importante occupation enclose sur des terres en hauteur au nord du moulin (Site 29) contenait au moins cinq maisons rondes, la plus grande ayant été reconstruite au moins deux fois. Cette occupation dominait une enceinte plus petite et des fossés circulaires (Site 30) au pied de la pente de chaque côté de Langley Brook.

Un alignement de fosses de l'âge du fer moyen a été enregistré à Wishaw (Site 19). Individuellement, les fosses étaient assez diverses, bien que disposées à des intervalles relativement réguliers. On n'a recouvré que peu de trouvailles à l'exception d'un dépôt de pierres placé, de céramique et d'un crâne humain renversé. Les alignements de fosses ne sont pas rares dans cette région et ils semblent caractéristiques d'une période qui se concentrait sur les limites linéaires et la division des terres. L'alignement de fosses précédait de peu un substantiel fossé segmenté adjacent – qui servait de limite, qui avait été recreusé à la période romano-britannique. Près de là, sur le Site 20, se trouvaient les vestiges probables d'une maison ronde isolée. Le long de la rive du cours d'eau, des fosses brûlées remplies de pierres étaient certainement préhistoriques, peut-être de l'âge du fer.

C'est la petite ville de Wall (*Letocetum*) qui prédomine en ce qui concerne l'archéologie romano-britannique, située au carrefour de deux routes majeures; Watling Street qui reliait Londres à Wroxeter, et Ryknield Street qui partait de Fosse Way, traversait Birmingham, prenait la direction de Derby pour finir dans le Yorkshire. A l'extérieur de Wall, on a répertorié, de chaque côté de Ryknield Street (Site 12) des cimetières comprenant 42 incinérations et jusqu'à 21 inhumations. Les sépultures à incinération étaient prédominantes au cours des premier et deuxième siècles av. J.-C., les sépultures à inhumation à partir de la fin du deuxième siècle, bien qu'on ait également retrouvé quelques rares sépultures à incinération du quatrième siècle. Dans la ville voisine de Shenstone quatre sites d'occupation à enceintes, dont les vestiges comprenaient un four à céramique bien préservé, se situaient à l'intérieur d'une zone linéaire délimitée par des fossés parallèles (Site 15). Les autres découvertes romano-britanniques comprenaient un système de champs le long de Watling Street à Washbrook Lane (Site 5), un important bâtiment avec bas-côté au sud de Watling Street à côté de Crane Brook (Site 34), un complexe d'au moins cinq enceintes qui a remplacé l'occupation de l'âge du fer moyen au nord de Langley Hill (Site 29) et une plus petite enceinte à Wishaw (Site19). La M6 à péage traverse aussi deux fois Watling Street; du sud au nord à Hammerwich et du nord au sud à Churchbridge (Site 4), bien que ce dernier n'ait fourni aucune preuve concrète de la voie romaine.

Les vestiges médiévaux comprenaient des billons et des sillons à Washbrook Lane (Site 5), un petit bâtiment de ferme du 13ème–14ème siècle à Shenstone (Site 13), et une enceinte à Wishaw (Site 19). Plus significatifs étaient le complexe d'étangs à poissons des chevaliers du Temple à l'est de Grove Lane (Site 20) et l'occupation d'Hawkeswell Farm (Site 24). Le complexe d'étangs à poissons avait probablement son origine à la fin du 12ème ou au début du 13ème siècle, sur des terres probablement offertes en cadeau par d'importants propriétaires terriens de la région. A Hawkeswell Farm, juste au nord du hameau documenté à Hawkeswell, existaient des traces d'une occupation mal définie qui s'était développée à partir de la fin du 13ème siècle. Des témoignages d'un jardin médiéval plus tardif et des aménagements du paysage donnent à penser que cette zone avait fait partie des jardins formels d'un précurseur de l'actuel Hawkeswell Hall.

Au sud de Cannock des structures isolées du réseau de canaux et de chemins de fer des 18 et 19ème siécles ont été répertoriées: la digue nord d'Hatherton Reservoir (Site 2), le chemin de fer de Chuchbridge et les ponts Accommodation (Site 3) ainsi que des éléments, maintenant depuis longtemps enterrés, tels que le Hawkins Canal Basin (Site 1). Celui-ci fut construit en 1883 et fut relié à l'Hatherton Branch du canal du Staffordshire et Worcester via un aqueduc qui traversait Wyrley Brook. On a également examiné Gilpin's Basin, construit à Churchbridge en 1860 pour permettre le transfer direct de matériaux entre le canal et le chemin de fer, il a révélé la base d'une grue de quai et les empiètements d'un gros entrepôt à marchandises. Une tranchée à travers la route nationale A5 adjacente (Site 4) a révélé ce qui pourrait avoir été les améliorations apportées par Telford à la fin du 18ème siècle à ce qui était alors la barrière à péage de Watling Street (également visible sur le Site 41). La partie nord du tunnel du canal de Hatherton Branch a été mise au jour sous l'A5. Les autres sites médiévaux comprenaient une prospection de Swan Farm à Norton Canes (Site 36), des coupes à travers Cannock Extension (1858) et Wryley et Essington Canals (1794) (Sites 6 et 8), les bases d'un tramway du 19ème siècle entre Lichfield Road et Barracks Lane (Site 34) et l'écluse supérieure de Curdworth et la maison de l'éclusier à Denton Wharf (Site 21). On a répertorié à Hawkeswell Farm (Site 24) des étangs post-médiévaux comblés et d'autres marques dans le paysage.

Traduction: Annie Pritchard

In diesem Band werden die Ergebnisse der archäologischen Untersuchungen vor dem Bau der „M6 Toll" (mautpflichtige Autobahn M6, ursprünglich Birmingham Nordumgehung genannt) vorgelegt. Die neue, 44 km lange Straße zweigt von der Autobahn M6 bei Anschlussstelle 3a ab, verläuft zwischen Sutton Coldfield und Walsall im Süden und Lichfield und Crannock im Norden, um sich bei Anschlussstelle 11a wieder mit der M6 zu vereinigen. Das Spektrum der 41 identifizierten und untersuchten Fundstellen entlang der Trasse lieferte Ergebnisse zu fast allen archäologischen Perioden zwischen der Mittelsteinzeit und der frühen Neuzeit sowie zur modernen Industrielandschaft mit ihren Kanälen, Eisenbahnlinien und zugehöriger Infrastruktur.

Die Identifizierung von mehr als 1500 Feuersteinstücken erbrachte den Nachweis eines möglichen spät-mittelsteinzeitlichen Wintercamps bei Wishaw Hall Farm (Fundplatz 19) – eine wichtige Ergänzung der archäologischen Quellen zu durchziehenden Jägern/Sammlern in der Region. Vereinzelt wurden neusteinzeitliche Funde und Befunde aufgenommen, darunter ein „burnt mound" (Ansammlung von verbranntem Flint) des späteren Neolithikums westlich von Crane Brook (Fundplatz 9), sowie ein Paar frühneolithischer Gruben (die Füllungen enthielten Keramik, Holzkohle, verkohltes Getreide und Haselnussschalen), Fragmente eines einzelnen Gefäßes aus Peterborough Ware und eine Ansammlung frühneolithischer Keramik bei Shenstone (Fundplätze 13, 15, und 32). Bronzezeitliche Befunde beschränken sich auf Fundplätze mit je einem „burnt mound" am Langley Brook (Fundplatz 39) und Collet's Brook (Fundplatz 40).

Mitteleisenzeitliche Befunde wurden an mehreren Stellen untersucht. Sowohl eine ovale Einfriedung als auch ein benachbartes Rundhaus in Shenstone (Fundplatz 14) waren größtenteils fundleer. In Langley Mill befand sich eine größere, eingefriedete Siedlung auf dem höher gelegenen Terrain nördlich der Mühle (Fundplatz 29). Von den wenigstens fünf dort aufgedeckten Rundhäusern wurde das größte mindestens zweimal erneuert. Diese Siedlung lag oberhalb einer kleineren Einfriedung und einiger Kreisgräben (Fundplatz 30) am Fuss der Hänge beiderseits des Langley Brook. Eine mitteleisenzeitliche Grubenreihe wurde in Winshaw dokumentiert (Fundplatz 19). Obgleich in relativ gleichmäßigen Abständen zueinander angeordnet, waren die einzelnen Gruben doch recht verschieden voneinander. Abgesehen von einem Depot aus Steinen, Keramik und einem umgekehrt deponierten menschlichen Schädel wurden nur wenige Funde geborgen. Grubenreihen dieser Zeitstellung sind in der Region nicht ungewöhnlich und scheinen eine Periode zu charakterisieren, in der vermehrt lineare Begrenzungen und Flureinteilungen aufkommen. Der Grubenreihe folgte als Abgrenzung in kurzem zeitlichen und räumlichen Abstand ein großer, in mehrere Abschnitte eingeteilter Graben, der in der römischen Kaiserzeit erneuert wurde. Auf dem nicht weit entfernten Fundplatz 20 fanden sich Hinweise auf ein einzeln stehendes Rundhaus. Einige mit verbrannten Steinen gefüllte Gruben entlang des Bachs sind sicherlich prähistorisch, möglicherweise eisenzeitlich.

Die meisten Befunde der römischen Kaiserzeit stammen von der kleinen Stadt Wall (*Letocetum*), die an der Kreuzung zweier wichtiger Straßen lag: der Watling Street von London nach Wroxeter und der Ryknield Street, die durch Birmingham und weiter nach Derby und Yorkshire führt. Vor den Toren Walls fanden sich beiderseits der Ryknield Street Gräberfelder mit insgesamt 42 Brand- und 21 Körperbestattungen (Fundplatz 12). Während des 1. und 2. Jhs. n. Chr. dominierte die Brandbestattung, Körperbestattung kommt ab dem späten 2. Jh. vor, es wurden jedoch auch einige seltene Brandbestattungen des 4. Jhs. gefunden. Im nahegelegenen Shenstone wurden vier eingefriedete Siedlungsstellen innerhalb eines von parallelen Gräben begrenzten langgezogenen Areals gefunden (Fundplatz 15); unter den Befunden befand sich u.a. ein gut erhaltener Töpferofen. Weitere kaiserzeitliche Befunde umfassen ein Flursystem entlang der Watling Street bei Washbrook Lane (Fundplatz 5), ein umfangreiches dreiflügliges Gebäude südlich der Watling Street bei Crane Brook (Fundplatz 34), ein Komplex von mindestens fünf Einfriedungen auf dem Areal der mitteleisenzeitlichen Siedlung nördlich von Langley Mill (Fundplatz 29) und eine kleinere Einfriedung bei Wishaw (Fundplatz 19). Die Trasse der M6 Toll kreuzte jene der Watling Street zweimal: von Süd nach Nord bei Hammerwich und von Nord nach Süd bei Churchbridge (Fundplatz 4), allerdings wurden an der zuletzt genannten Stelle keine Spuren der römischen Straße gefunden.

Mittelalterliche Befunde fanden sich in der Form von Wölbäckern bei Washbrook Lane (Fundplatz 5), eines kleinen Bauernhofs des 13./14. Jhs. bei Shenstone (Fundplatz 13) und einer Einfriedung bei Winshaw (Fundplatz 19). Am bedeutendsten war ein Komplex von Fischteichen des Templerordens östlich von Grove Lane (Fundplatz 20) und eine Siedlung bei Hawkeswell Farm (Fundplatz 24). Die Fischteiche wurden wahrscheinlich im späten 12. oder frühen 13. Jh. auf Land angelegt, das dem Orden von bedeutenden lokalen Landbesitzern vermacht worden war. Bei Hawkeswell Farm, unmittelbar nördlich des schriftlich überlieferten Weilers in Hawkeswell, fanden sich schwache Hinweise auf Besiedlung ab dem 13. Jh. Befunde spätmittelalterlicher Garten- und Landschaftsgestaltung legen nahe, dass das Areal Teil der Gartenanlage eines Vorgängers des derzeitigen Herrenhauses Hawkeswell Hall wurde.

Südlich von Cannock wurden noch aufrecht stehende Strukturen des Kanal- und Eisenbahnnetzwerks des 18. und 19. Jhs. dokumentiert: der nördliche Damm des „Hatherton Reservoir" (Fundplatz 2), die „Churchbridge Railway and Accommodation" Brücken (Fundplatz 3) sowie bereits seit längerer Zeit eingeebnete Komponenten wie das „Hawkins Canal Basin" (Fundplatz 1). Letzteres wurde 1883 gebaut und war über einen Aquädukt über den Wyrley Brook mit dem „Hatherton Branch" des Staffordshire und Worcester Kanals verbunden. Das 1860 in Churchbridge gebaute „Gilpin's Basin", das den direkten Materialtransfer zwischen Kanal und Eisenbahn ermöglichte, wurde ebenfalls untersucht. Dabei wurden die Fundamente eines Krans an der Kaianlage und eines großen Güterschuppens freigelegt. Ein Schnitt durch die benachbarte Fernstraße A5 (Fundplatz 4) erbrachte Befunde, bei denen es sich möglicherweise um von Telford im späten 18. Jh. ausgeführte Verbesserungsmaßnahmen an der damaligen Watling Street Mautstraße handelt (ähnliches fand sich auch an Fundplatz 41). Die Nordseite des Kanaltunnels des „Hatherton Branch" wurde unter den Schichten der Fernstraße A5 freigelegt. Weitere frühneuzeitliche Befunde stammen von der Vermessung von Swan Farm in Norton Canes (Fundplatz 36), Suchschnitten durch die Cannock Kanalverlängerung (1858) und die Kanäle von Wyrley und Essington (1794) (Fundplätze 6 und 8), den Fundamenten einer Straßenbahntrasse des 19. Jhs. zwischen der Lichfield Road und Barracks Lane (Fundplatz 34) sowie der Cudworth Oberschleuse samt Schleusenwärterhäuschen am Dunton Kai (Fundplatz 21). Verfüllte Teiche und weitere frühneuzeitliche Landschaftselemente wurden bei Hawkeswell Farm dokumentiert (Fundplatz 24).

Übersetzung: Jörn Schuster

Chapter 1
Introduction

by Paul Booth and Andrew B. Powell

Between December 2000 and August 2003, Oxford Wessex Archaeology (OWA), a joint venture between Oxford Archaeology (formerly Oxford Archaeological Unit – OAU) and Wessex Archaeology (formerly the Trust for Wessex Archaeology), carried out a programme of archaeological fieldwork in advance of the construction of the M6 Toll Motorway (M6 Toll). The work was commissioned by the construction consortium CAMBBA (Carillion, Alfred McAlpine, Balfour Beatty and Amec) on behalf of Midland Expressway Limited (MEL).

The M6 Toll, known prior to construction as the Birmingham Northern Relief Road (BNRR), was built to relieve pressure on the existing M6. It runs for 43 km from just west of Cannock, Staffordshire at the north-west to Maxstoke, Warwickshire at the south-east (Fig. 1). A total of 41 sites was investigated along its course, providing evidence of human activity from the Mesolithic to the modern period, including hunting and gathering, settlement, agriculture, fish farming, gardening, industry, communications and burial.

Archaeological and historical background

The archaeological and historical background to the scheme was considered at length in the 1994 *Archaeological Report for the Public Inquiry* (OAU 1994d). It was updated by supplementary work covering the period up to the end of 1999 and both sets of data were taken into account in the *Revised General Strategy and Methodology* (OAU and Babtie Group 2000). Much of the following summary is derived from the latter document. It is very condensed, since the period based overviews presented below give a more comprehensive view of the archaeology of the area in the light of the M6 Toll works and other recent archaeological projects. The present summary outlines the broad archaeological development of the scheme area as it was understood before the commencement of intrusive fieldwork in early 2001. 'The study corridor' refers to a 1 km wide transect across the area with the line of the new road at its centre.

Significant parts of the varied landscape through which the M6 Toll passes have traditionally been seen as forested and sparsely settled for much of their early history, though in recent years this has been brought into question. Nevertheless, the earlier periods are very poorly represented in the archaeological record of the region. Only one artefact of the Palaeolithic period (500,000–10,000 BC), a quartzite hand axe, was found within the study corridor. Mesolithic (8500–4000 BC) find scatters, indicative of a hunting and gathering population, within the study corridor (Thomas 1974) are evidenced principally by small scatters of flint tools at Wishaw (Hodder 1992) with a little further material from Langley Mill Farm (Site 29) in the same general area. No other traces of Mesolithic settlement are known. The material is generally too sparse to distinguish between hunting and base camps as has been attempted for some other parts of the country.

Again it is flint artefacts which constitute the evidence for the Neolithic period (4000–2400 BC). Within the study corridor a flint core, scraper, blade and flakes were located at Weeford Park, and two flints in the Wishaw area. Few Neolithic monuments have been definitely identified in the region, though they are known from aerial evidence outside the M6 Toll area, for example in the lower Tame valley. The Bronze Age (2400–700 BC) is equally characterised by a general lack of settlement evidence, but round barrows, burnt mounds and chance finds of metalwork, including bronze palstaves, are all known within the study area in this period. Offlow Tumulus, south of Lichfield, was perhaps the most prominent monument of the region but has been much diminished by ploughing, as has the ring ditch to its west. Further cropmarks of ring ditches, one with a central burial, occur in the adjacent cropmark complex to the south, crossed by the route. Two burnt mounds of probable late Bronze Age date occur within the study corridor, typically adjacent to streams, as with the possible example at Wishaw Hall Farm (Site 19) and the probable site located at Langley Mill (Site 30) (see Fitzpatrick, Chapter 29). A cropmark enclosure and linear feature immediately adjacent to the Langley Mill burnt mound material were undated but considered to be potentially contemporary with it. There are several Bronze Age find spots including flintwork and socketed axes. A late Bronze Age hoard was found at Shenstone, but bronzes are in general rare and their occurrence usually relates to chance finds, in some cases, at least, probably in a ceremonial context.

Some of the cropmarks identified at Shenstone are likely to have originated in the Iron Age (700 BC–AD 43) and include typologically characteristic features such as pit alignments (Whitehouse 1960–1), but none of the other cropmark features could be assigned to this period

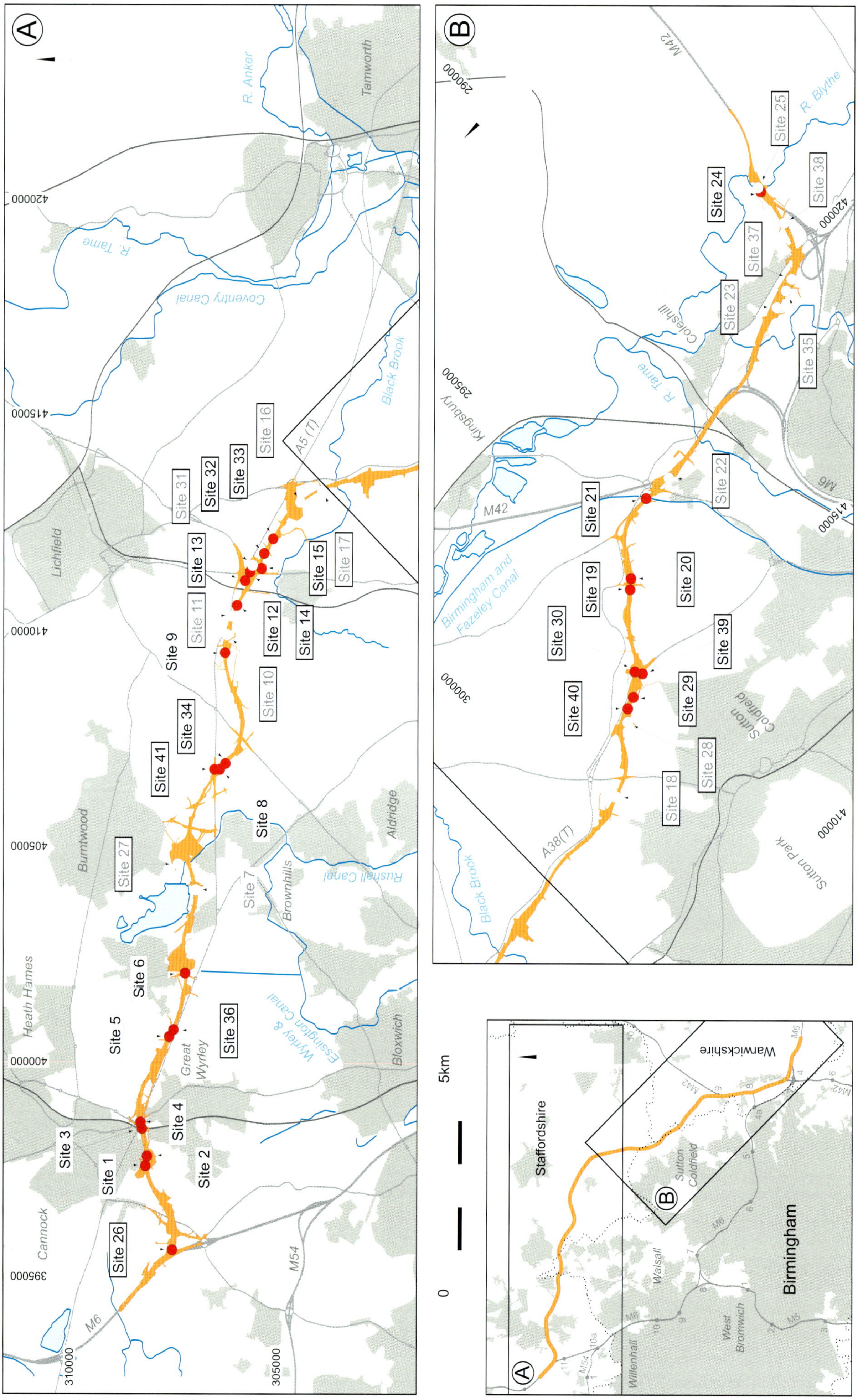

Fig. 1 The route of the M6 Toll, showing the locations of the sites

with certainty. It is likely that Iron Age settlements, especially around the Wall area, were predecessors of known Romano-British settlements. Occupation at the settlement excavated at Grimstock Hill, Coleshill in 1980, began in the middle Iron Age, extending into the Romano-British period. A Romano-British temple overlay a number of pre-Romano-British or early Romano-British circular buildings (Magilton 2006).

Two major routes were established in the Romano-British period (AD 43–410); Watling Street ran from London, north-west across the Midlands to Wroxeter, and thence to the military districts of the north-west; Ryknield Street ran north from the Fosse Way in Gloucestershire through Alcester, Birmingham, Wall and Derby to Templeborough in Yorkshire. These two roads crossed within the study area at Wall and were examined in Sites 41 and 12 respectively. At Wall, the scene of numerous, mostly small-scale excavations, a series of Roman forts dated from the mid-1st to the early 2nd century and a small town (*Letocetum*) developed on the line of Watling Street south of the forts, in line with a pattern of development widely observed in the West Midlands. Nevertheless, this area has been perceived as only a second rate growth area with a relatively thin spread of settlement sites, few of which exhibited the wealth of regions to the south (see Booth, Chapter 30). A Romano-British farming settlement with possible evidence of associated fields was known at Shenstone, west of East of Birmingham Road Nurseries (Site 15) (Hodgkinson and Chatwin 1944), and another late Romano-British settlement is indicated by finds at Wishaw Hall Farm (Site 19). Romano-British finds which have been discovered during fieldwalking may represent actual settlement sites, even where present only in small quantities. Romano-British finds are generally relatively numerous, and include a little material recovered in metal detector surveys.

Parts of the upland areas of the Birmingham Plateau and Cannock Chase were probably woodland which may have supported hunting and pannage and provided wood for charcoal burners, although none of these activities is directly attested at this time. The coalfields of the region were, however exploited during this period on a small scale. The most well known industrial site, however, is that of Mancetter-Hartshill in north Warwickshire, which was one of the largest pottery producing centres in the country. Production began in the later part of the 1st century and extended into the 4th, possibly as late as AD 350–370. It specialised in mortaria (mixing bowls) which have been identified across northern and central England. Romano-British pottery production on a smaller scale has been identified at Sherifoot Lane in Sutton Coldfield, dating to the 2nd century.

There are extensive prehistoric and Romano-British cropmarks in the Tame and mid Trent valleys as well as (to a lesser extent) in the valley of the River Blythe. The number of undated cropmarks interpreted as farmsteads and enclosures within the study corridor may point to a reasonable level of settlement and farming if they are of late prehistoric and Romano-British origin. There may have been little change in the character of Iron Age farmsteads after the Roman Conquest.

Relatively little is known of the end of the Romano-British period. Wall has been seen as a centre of particular potential interest, but there is little firm evidence to support this. The Roman administrative area centred on Wall may conceivably have been maintained into the 5th century in the form of a bishopric. Certainly the area is of considerable interest for the connection between Wall and nearby Lichfield, which became the major local ecclesiastical centre. There is even less evidence for the area in the Anglo-Saxon period (AD 410–1066), in complete contrast to areas such as the Trent valley and particularly the Avon valley where several cemeteries of this date are known (Ford 1996). There are no known Anglo-Saxon sites within the study corridor.

Most of the parishes crossed by the route are recorded as settlements in the *Domesday Book* of AD 1086, and the names given often have Saxon origins. The route passes through what was entirely a rural area during the medieval period, the only significant settlement in its immediate vicinity being Coleshill, although Lichfield was only *c* 3.5 km to the north and Tamworth 7–8 km distant to the east. A substantial length of the route crosses what were the chases of Cannock and Sutton. These were probably created because they were on relatively poor soils, well wooded and relatively thinly populated at the time of the Norman Conquest and before. In 1086 Cannock or Chenet was an estate directly held by the king, largely as a hunting forest, within which woodland was recorded as being six leagues long by four leagues wide. It became a free chase in 1290 when the metes and bounds covering Cannock and Rugeley were set out. The overlordship of Great Wyrley remained with the Crown apparently from before the Conquest until at least 1487. Prior to the Norman Conquest land in Great Wyrley appears to have been attached to the office of Keeper of the Royal Forest of Cannock.

The unevenly distributed hamlets and settlements and the characteristic moated sites of the 12th and 13th centuries and later reflect the practice of assarting as inroads were made back into the waste and woodlands after probable forest regeneration in the post-Romano-British period. The early Middle Ages saw substantial population expansion which led to many areas being taken into cultivation. Settlements were established on the edge of prosperous land gradually encroaching on the 'waste' land, taking it into use (see Hunt, Chapter 31). Moated sites were created primarily for prestige, often surrounding major dwellings, and occasionally had a limited defensive function. Medieval parks were formed as areas of land enclosed to keep in game, especially deer. These were often 'waste' land in so far as they were unenclosed tracts of rough grazing and heath. Parks of medieval origin of which traces survive within the landscape of the study area include Weeford and Coleshill. Weeford received its licence to empark in about 1288–9. Yates's map of Staffordshire (1769–75) shows it as woodland, and of similar extent to the present limits of Weeford Park.

The best known aspect of the more recent history of the region through which the route passes is that of its industrial development towards the end of the 18th century (see Gill, Chapter 32). The coal industry was expanding from the 16th century, and a further impetus to its development was the introduction of the smelting of iron ore using coke as opposed to charcoal. The North Warwickshire and South Staffordshire coalfields lie partly within the study corridor. The success of Brindley's canal of 1758 for the Duke of Bridgwater's colliery at Worsley meant that a canal network was rapidly established to aid in the transport of coal and other goods. In the 1830s and 1850s the canal network was extended by several branches to serve the collieries. A number of these late canals built in the railway age are crossed by the route. Other transport developments at this time included the improvement of turnpike roads and the appearance of early systems of primitive railways, some on wooden tramrails, that connected the mines. Main lines soon followed, such as the London and North Western. The route crosses a number of disused mid to late 19th century branch lines, which again reflect the industrial expansion of the Victorian era.

Population increased in areas where there was a concentration of industrial activity, as for example at Bridgtown. The pattern of smaller agricultural settlements remained similar to that of the later medieval period, however. The main enclosure of fields took place in the mid 19th century. Although not usually seen as a period of agricultural boom, some areas like North Warwickshire may have flourished in the late 19th century and the environs of both Canwell and Wishaw are notable for the numerous substantial estate cottages and farmhouses of this period. Most farms are likewise marked by good solid late 19th century farm buildings, though a few earlier buildings survive, of which Swan Farm, Norton Canes (Site 36), was an example.

Geology and topography

The underlying geology of the M6 Toll consists mainly of marls and shales of the Coal Measures in the north-west, a range of sandstones and pebble beds in the central section, and Mercian Mudstones in the south-east (Fig. 2). There are also extensive gravel terraces in the south-east, particularly in the Coleshill area (Cole valley) and in the Tame valley as far as Wishaw. These have been exploited for extraction, for example in the Curdworth and Water Orton area just north-west of Coleshill. Drift boulder clay covers some areas, more especially the region between Chasewater and Bridgtown, large parts of which were not considered suitable for field survey because of disturbance by mining and modern development. Elsewhere, boulder clay is patchy. There are small areas of floodplain alluvium in the valleys of the rivers Blythe and Tame, but these are not extensive and were generally covered by pastures.

The M6 Toll crosses three sheets of the British Geological Survey 1:50,000 Solid and Drift map series – sheet 153 (Wolverhampton, 2001), sheet 154 (Lichfield, 1922, 1 inch to one mile/1:63,360) and sheet 168 (Birmingham, 1996). As a result, the summary descriptions of site geology along the majority of the route (between Sites 1 and 29 on sheet 154) use different geological nomenclature to those at Site 26 at the north-west and Sites 30–25 at the south-east. Where possible the equivalent modern terminology has been added.

Despite this variety, the geology does not give rise to extreme variations in topography or soil conditions. The relief generally consists of undulating hills and broad valleys (Fig. 3). Altitude ranges from 76 m above Ordnance Datum (aOD) (the floodplain of the Tame) to 160 m aOD (near Weeford Park), with a general altitude around 100–130 m aOD.

The north-west end of the route crosses the South Staffordshire and South Cannock Plateaux (both divisions of the Birmingham Plateau), diverging from the original M6 line at Saredon at about 135 m aOD. On this gently undulating terrain, with the higher ground of the southern margins of Cannock Chase to the north, are situated (in geographical order) Sites 26, 1–5, 36 and 6, and finally Site 41, at *c* 120 m aOD in the valley of the Crane Brook at Hammerwich. This is the stretch quite significantly impacted in places by the results of mining and other industrial activities, and by the presence of settlements associated with these. The west to east flowing Crane Brook is the main stream to the south of Wall through the Wall and Shenstone wetlands (Leah *at al.* 1998, 113–7), drained in the late 18th and 19th century, lying in the Shenstone basin at *c* 95 m aOD. West of Wall Sites 8 and 34 lie close to the Crane Brook while a whole group of sites, 9–15, lay generally on slightly rising ground around the margins of the Shenstone basin both immediately south of Wall itself and a little further south-east, to the north of Shenstone. South-east of these sites on very level ground at *c* 100 m aOD are Sites 32 and 33. Both lie north of the Black Brook, fed from the west by the Crane Brook and itself an important tributary of the Tame, which it joins near Fazeley. The Black Brook cuts through the north-east tip of the Sutton Plateau at Weeford and Hints. No archaeological sites were encountered on the higher ground south of the Black Brook until the M6 Toll reached Collet's Brook and Langley Brook, just east of Sutton Coldfield. Here another cluster of sites (40, 29, 30 and 39) was encountered, all in streamside locations except Site 29, on higher ground between the two watercourses, of which the Langley Brook formed another west–east flowing tributary of the Tame, and therefore ultimately of the Trent river system. From Wishaw onwards (Sites 19 and 20, at about 90 and 85 m

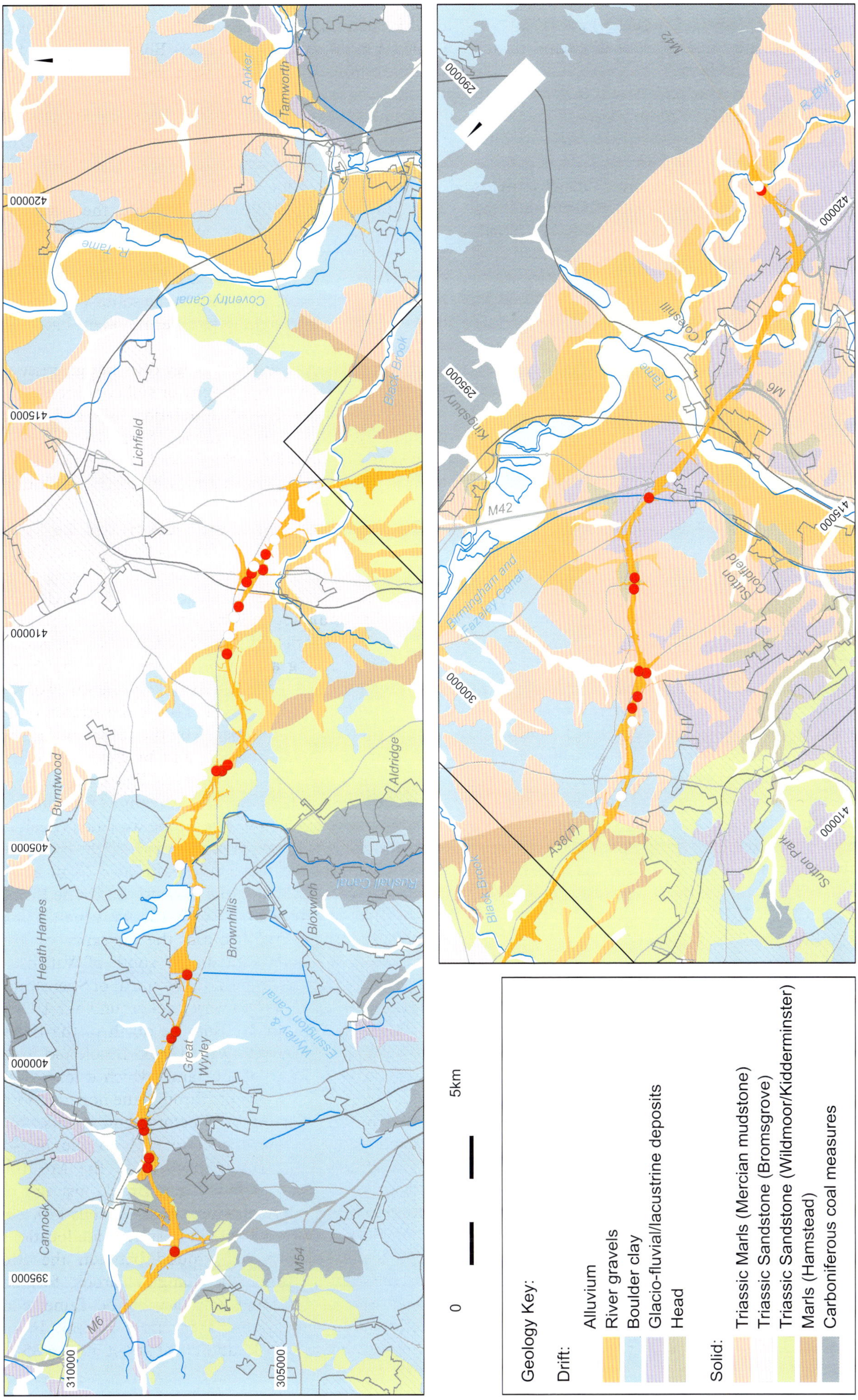

Fig. 2 The geology of the M6 Toll

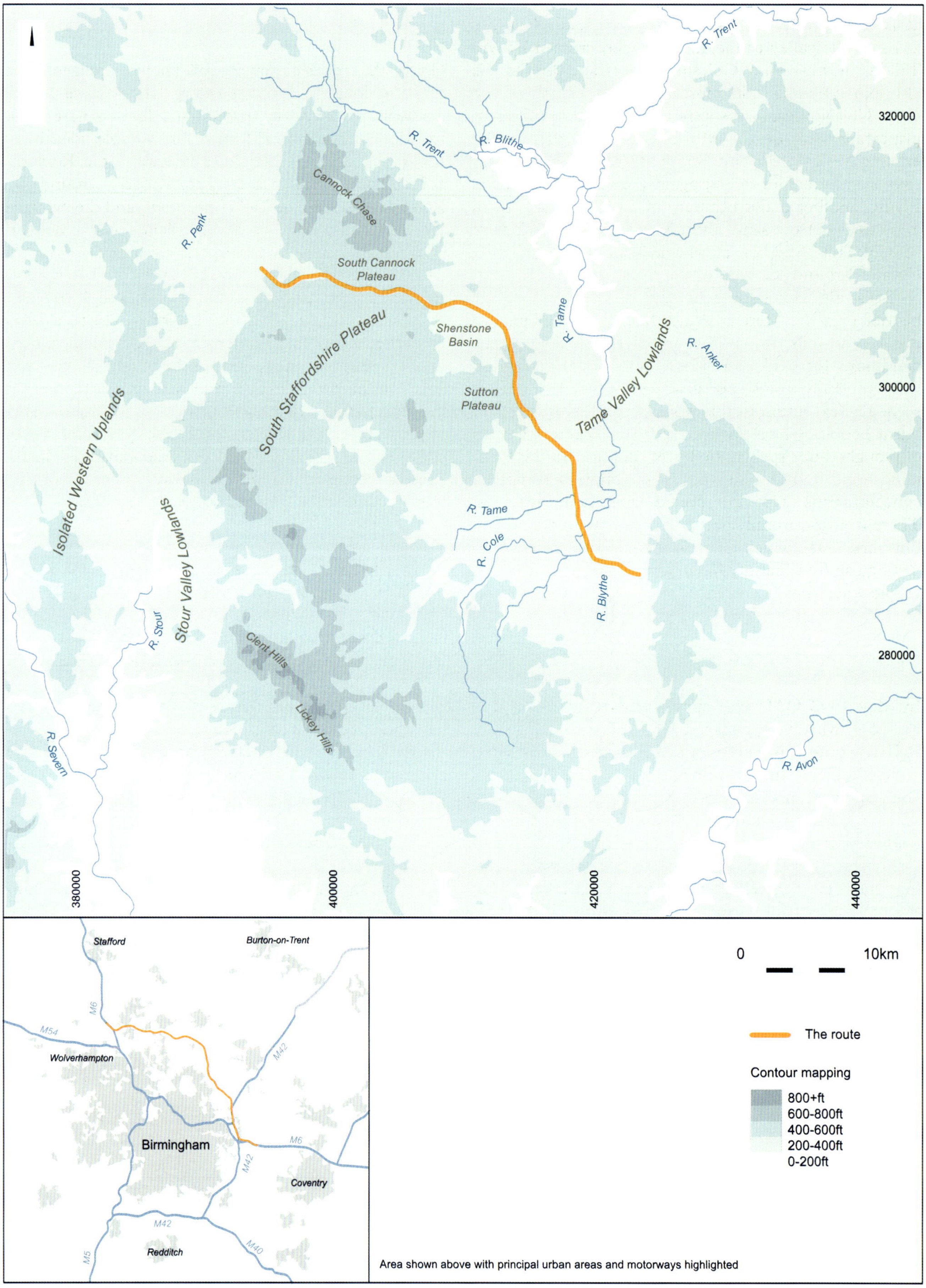

Fig. 3 Topography

aOD respectively) the ground drops gradually (via Site 21) into the valley of the Tame proper, crossed by M6 Toll just north-west of Coleshill, near where the Tame is also joined by one of its most important tributaries, the Cole. No significant sites were encountered in this area, principally because the M6 Toll followed that of the existing M42 at this point. South of Coleshill the ground rises slightly before falling again into the valley of the Blythe, another major tributary of the Tame. At *c* 76 m aOD this is at the same altitude as the Tame itself west of Coleshill. Site 24 at Hawkeswell lay on slightly elevated ground just west of the river.

Soils are generally light and sandy, but slightly heavier over the Mercian Mudstones. The tendency of the sandy soils to weather rapidly meant that the conditions for field observation and surface collection were generally good and all categories of finds easily seen. The exception to this would have been spreads of burnt pebbles which might have been expected on sites of ploughed-out prehistoric burnt mounds. In the event none were found and the only abnormally pebbly concentrations were interpreted as natural outcrops. There is little naturally occurring flint in the region and flint artefacts, which can sometimes be difficult to distinguish from natural flints, were consequently highly visible when they occurred.

Background to the project

In May 1992 OAU was appointed by Ove Arup and Partners, who were engaged by MEL to develop the BNRR route, to carry out an assessment of the archaeological implications of the BNRR. Field archaeological investigations in relation to the road scheme began in October 1992, with a programme of fieldwalking along approximately one-third (13.4 km, *c* 200 hectares) of the proposed route. The following year, four sites (Hawkeswell Farm, Coleshill; Shenstone Hall Farm; Wishaw Hall Farm; and Crane Brook, Wall) were evaluated by trial trenching (OAU 1993; 1994a–c). The results of this fieldwork, along with a desk-based assessment of the route, were incorporated in an *Archaeological Report* (prepared for Ove Arup & Partners on behalf of MEL) submitted to the 1994 BNRR Public Enquiry (OAU 1994d). Proposals for a programme of archaeological works to mitigate the effects of the road scheme, outlined in the conclusions to the Report and agreed by English Heritage and the Local Authority Archaeologists of Staffordshire and Warwickshire, were accepted by the Enquiry.

These proposals formed the basis of an Archaeological Project Design – the *Revised General Strategy and Methodology* (produced by OAU and subsequently revised by Babtie Group (now Jacobs) on behalf of MEL in June 2000) – which constituted a general *Written Scheme of Investigation* (WSI) defining the overall academic framework and methodological strategy of the programme of works.

Objectives

Given the relative paucity of known archaeological remains along much of the route, the objectives for the fieldwork were initially defined at a fairly general level, the 1994 *Archaeological Report*, for example, identifying two broad areas of particular interest – the Romano-British settlement pattern, particularly around the Roman small town at Wall (*Letocetum*), and the evidence for different phases of the Midlands canal network concentrated in the western part of the route.

Nonetheless, as the project represented a random transect across the West Midland landscape, it provided an opportunity to assess the extent to which existing records reflected the real density of archaeological sites, and so to examine the validity of the traditional view that much of the region had seen only limited settlement in the past, particularly in prehistory. As a result, the range of archaeological themes with the potential to be addressed by the M6 Toll work was expanded in the Project Design to encompass the following, although it was recognised that this list was not proscriptive:

1. the environmental development of the transect in relation to past human exploitation, contrasting the plateau country of the north-western part with the Shenstone Basin and Tame and Blythe valleys;
2. the nature of earlier prehistoric activity across the region;
3. later prehistoric predecessors to the Romano-British settlement pattern;
4. Romano-British settlement and landuse patterns in the vicinity of Wall;
5. variation in Romano-British settlement density and character in relation to proximity to the major road network (Watling Street and Ryknield Street);
6 the nature and settlement history of medieval rural sites;
7. the development of the region in the early post-medieval period (c 1500–1750), with particular reference to industrial development before the 'industrial revolution'; and
8. the physical characteristics, development and landscape impact of the 18th–19th century canal system.

On the basis of the initial assessment of the results of the excavations the research aims were revised to include both the period-based aims – A) earlier prehistoric, *cf* theme 2, B) later prehistoric, *cf* theme 3, C) Romano-British, *cf* themes 4–5, D) medieval, *cf* theme 6, and E) post-medieval industrial, *cf* theme 7 – as well as the following cross-period themes:

F) the environmental and economic development of the area through its changing settlement patterns from later prehistory to the medieval period, cf theme 1;

Table 1 The reported archaeological sites (from north-west to south-east)

Site name	No.	NGR	Fieldwork	Principal period(s)	Site code
Saredon	26	395300 307800	Trenching, targeted watching brief	Medieval, post-medieval	SARCM 01
Hawkins Canal Basin and Aqueduct	1	397570 308180	Watching brief	Industrial	CHHCQ 01
Hatherton Reservoir	2	397800 308120	Watching brief	Industrial	CHHAR 01
Gilpins Basin and Wharf	3	398430 308240	Watching brief	Industrial	BRGIL01
Churchbridge Complex	4	398550 308290	Watching brief	Post-medieval, industrial	BRCHB 01
Washbrook Lane, Norton Canes	5	400560 307590	Targeted watching brief	Romano-British	NCWBL 01
Swan Farm, Norton Canes	36	400700 307460	Building recording	Post-medieval/modern	NCSWF 01
Cannock Extension Canal	6	402030 307210	Watching brief	Industrial	NCCAN 01
Watling Street, Hammerwich	41	406414 306510	Watching brief	Romano-British, post-medieval	-
Wyrley & Essington Canal	8	406760 306380	Watching brief	Industrial	HAWYR 01
West of Crane Brook Cottage, Hammerwich	34	406900 306250	Targeted watching brief	Romano-British, modern	HACBC 01
West of Crane Brook, Wall	9	409400 306260	Excavation	Neolithic	WAWCB 01
Ryknield Street, Wall	12	410570 305970	Geophysical survey, trenching, excavation	Romano-British	WARYS 01
Shenstone Linear Features	13	411080 305780	Geophysical survey, trenching, targeted watching brief, watching brief	Neolithic, Romano-British, medieval	SHLIF 01
Shenstone Ring Ditch	14	411310 305620	Excavation	Iron Age	SHRID 01
East of Birmingham Road Nurseries, Shenstone	15	411430 305400	Targeted watching brief	Romano-British	SHEBN 01
East of The Castle, Shenstone	32	411760 305350	Geophysical survey, targeted watching brief	Neolithic, Romano-British, post-medieval	SHCAS 01
Round Wood, Shenstone	33	412130 305110	Geophysical survey, targeted watching brief	Romano-British, post-medieval/modern	SHRW 01
Collet's Brook Burnt Mound, Sutton Coldfield	40	415300 297440	Excavation	Bronze Age	SCCOB 01
North of Langley Mill, Sutton Coldfield	29	415410 297150	Geophysical survey, trenching, excavation	Iron Age, Romano-British	SCNLM 01
Langley Mill, Sutton Coldfield/ Middleton	30	415800 296750	Geophysical survey, trenching, excavation	Iron Age	SCLAM 01
Burnt Mound at Langley Brook, Middleton	39	415620 296620	Excavation	Bronze Age	MILAB 01
Wishaw Hall Farm, Wishaw	19	417190 295430	Excavation	Iron Age, Romano-British, medieval	WIPMS 01
Wishaw, Wishaw	20	417400 295280	Excavation	Iron Age, medieval	WISMD 01
Curdworth Top Lock, Curdworth	21	418450 293740	Building recording	Industrial	CUDUN 01
Hawkeswell Farm, Coleshill	24	421580 286720	Excavation	Medieval, post-medieval	COHAW 01

G) burnt stone technology (including burnt mounds)
H) artefact use (relating to the low incidence of finds from most sites); and
I) ritual and religion (in relation particularly to prehistoric placed deposits and Romano-British burial practices).

These themes are addressed in the relevant period discussions and in the chapter on Material Culture Studies which includes an overview of the environmental evidence, as well as, where appropriate, within individual site reports.

Methods

The Project Design outlined the generic methodologies to be used in the staged programme of archaeological works. Within this framework a separate site-specific WSI, defined for the purposes of the present project as a *Design Input Statement* (DIS), was prepared for each stage of work on each site. By referring to pre-agreed generic methodologies it was possible for each DIS to be focussed clearly upon the specific issues to be addressed, incorporating variations in the standard methodologies where these were appropriate to the particular circumstances of the site. Each DIS was reviewed by the relevant Local Authority Archaeologist, English Heritage, a representative of CAMBBA and by Babtie on behalf of MEL. The programme, involving fieldwalking, geophysical survey, evaluation trenching, excavation and watching brief, was structured so as to fulfil four strategic objectives:

- to minimise the risk of locating previously unrecognised sites during the construction process;
- to clarify the potential of known sites;
- to help establish the appropriate levels of recording of significant remains that could not be preserved; and
- to monitor the road construction so that any further remains could be investigated, and the success of the strategy assessed.

The Project Design, which incorporated the results of additional fieldwork by the Field Group of the Birmingham and Warwickshire Archaeological Society (BWAS) along the Birmingham sector of the route and an updated desk-based review of new archaeological information post-dating 1994, identified 30 numbered sites along the route as requiring archaeological investigation. Subsequently, a re-examination of the aerial photograph evidence for the route raised the number of sites to 37 (Babtie 2000) and as a consequence of further developments during the construction process the final total of numbered sites was 41. In addition, three potential borrow pit sites were evaluated in the summer of 2002.

The fieldwork stages

Stage 1
An initial stage of further field survey was undertaken to complete the scheme-wide phase of initial site location and thereby diminish the risk of locating unrecognised sites at a late stage in the project programme. This involved the systematic fieldwalking of all previously unexamined areas of suitable land (about 40% of the route), collecting artefacts from 20 m units along lines set 20 m apart. A significant number of fields were ploughed specifically to enable this work to be carried out.

Stage 2
This stage, in two parts, involved the phased investigation of specific sites. Stage 2(i), comprising geophysical (magnetometer) survey and machine trenching, was designed to evaluate known sites and areas of archaeological potential so that their research potential could be considered in detail, and their requirements for further investigation (or, if appropriate, preservation *in situ*) defined. The sampling rate of approximately 2% for machine trenching was designed to achieve a high statistical probability of locating sites of more than 30 m diameter (Hey and Lacey 2001). Twelve sites were subject to geophysical survey, and ten to machine trenching.

Stage 2(ii) involved excavation (either limited sample excavation, full excavation or total excavation, as defined in the Project Design) or targeted watching brief. These were carried out at those significant archaeological sites that required more detailed recording than that provided by geophysical survey or machine trenching, and which could not be preserved *in situ* (or whose long-term *in situ* burial was inappropriate in light of their critical research potential). Targeted watching brief, in which the topsoil was removed under archaeological supervision and to archaeological specifications, was employed at sites of local importance with a relatively low perceived archaeological potential, in advance of the principal earthmoving phase of the road construction. Fourteen sites were subject to excavation and 12 to targeted watching briefs. One earthwork survey and two standing building surveys were also undertaken.

Stage 3
The final stage was a programme of scheme-wide watching brief running intermittently during the construction programme, during which a further four sites were identified and investigated.

In reality, the compressed time scale of the project meant that it was not possible to carry out all the stages of this programme sequentially across the whole of M6 Toll. In some cases, therefore, different stages of work were under way at the same time and, in others, detailed mitigation strategies were implemented almost immediately upon receipt of data from the preceding phases of work.

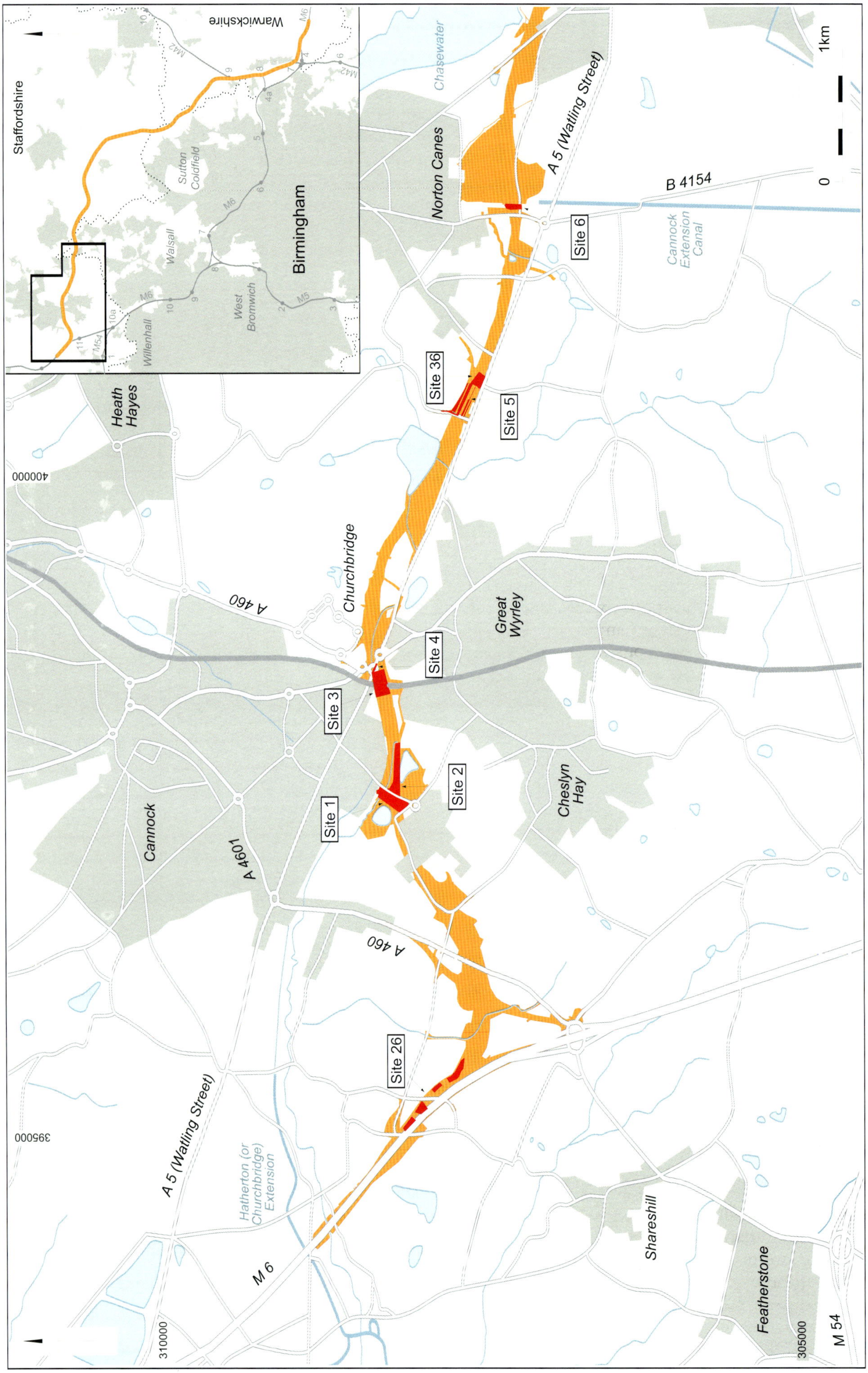

Fig. 4 Sites from Cannock to Norton Canes

Excavation and recording standards

The recording standards required for each level of fieldwork, as detailed in the Project Design, were applied to individual sites as set out in the site-specific DIS. Any methods specific to individual sites are detailed under the site descriptions.

Evaluation trenches and areas of excavation were machine stripped of topsoil or overburden down to the significant archaeological horizon or natural subsoil, whichever was encountered first, by mechanical excavator using a 1.8 m wide toothless bucket. The majority of trenches were 30 m long. A grid covering each site was laid out and related to survey points established for the scheme and to the Ordnance Survey grid, with temporary bench marks related to Ordnance Datum.

A sample of the archaeological deposits was excavated by hand. Structures and specific features of specialised activity (industrial, agricultural processing, ceremonial and funerary etc.) were fully excavated and all relationships recorded. A *c* 10% sample of all linear features was excavated, with significant relationships between them being investigated, and their terminals excavated. A sample of pits and postholes were half-sectioned or fully excavated as appropriate. Other archaeological features and deposits were sampled on the basis of their nature and significance.

Each site was assigned an alphanumeric site code (see Table 1), although for ease of reference in this report sites are referred to by their name and site number. A continuous unique numbering system was used. Written descriptions, comprising factual data and interpretative elements, were recorded on Oxford Wessex Archaeology's *pro forma* sheets. Features were normally planned at 1:20 and sections drawn at 1:10. A full black and white and colour (35 mm transparency) photographic record was kept, with additional digital photographs being taken. All features and sections, as well as evaluation trenches and site boundaries, were recorded using a Topcon Total Station Theodolite.

Metal detectors were employed as a means of finds recovery where appropriate. In general all identified finds and artefacts were retained, although for certain classes of building material or post-medieval pottery only a sample was kept.

Environmental methodology

Bulk samples were taken for the recovery of charred plant remains and charcoal, and in some cases for the recovery of waterlogged plant and insect remains to aid in the interpretation of function and activity on site. Samples for the analysis of soils, pollen, snails and animal bone were also taken where appropriate, although the acidic soils encountered along the route resulted in unburnt human and animal bone surviving only occasionally. Few contexts suitable for sampling for pollen, ie peats, buried soils or stratified and well dated

Table 2 Other sites (in archive)

Site name	*No.*	*NGR*	*Fieldwork*	*Principal period(s)*	*Site code*
Chasewater	7	404000 306800	Targeted watching brief	Post-medieval/modern	BHCAS 01
Brownhills Ring Ditch	27	404620 307390	Geophysical survey, trenching	-	HABRD 01
West of Ashcroft Lane, Wall	10	409730 306750	Geophysical survey, trenching, watching brief	-	WAWAL 01
East of Ashcroft Lane, Wall	11	410200 306100	Geophysical survey, trenching	-	WAEAL 01
Shenstone Compound	31	411500 305550	Excavation	Romano-British landscape	SHCOM 01
North of Brick Kiln Covert, Weeford	16	413300 304100	Targeted watching brief	Prehistoric	WEBKC 01
Thickbroom Deserted Medieval Village	17	413000 303800	Field inspection	-	
Fox Hill, Sutton Coldfield	18	414050 299080	Trenching	-	SCFOX 01
Collet's Brook Dam, Middleton	28	415100 297700	Site inspection	Medieval	MICBD 01
Curdworth, Curdworth	22	418500 292900	Geophysical survey, trenching	-	CURD 01
Coleshill Flint Scatter, Coleshill	23	419300 288400	Geophysical survey, trenching	-	COWC 01
Coleshill Hall Walk, Coleshill	35	419500 287900	Test pitting	Prehistoric	COHLK 01
West of Coleshill, Coleshill	37	419600 287700	Trenching	-	COWES 01
Packington Lane, Coleshill	38	420640 286850	Targeted watching brief	Medieval	COPAC 01
West of River Blythe, Coleshill	25	421700 286700	Targeted watching brief	-	COBLY 01

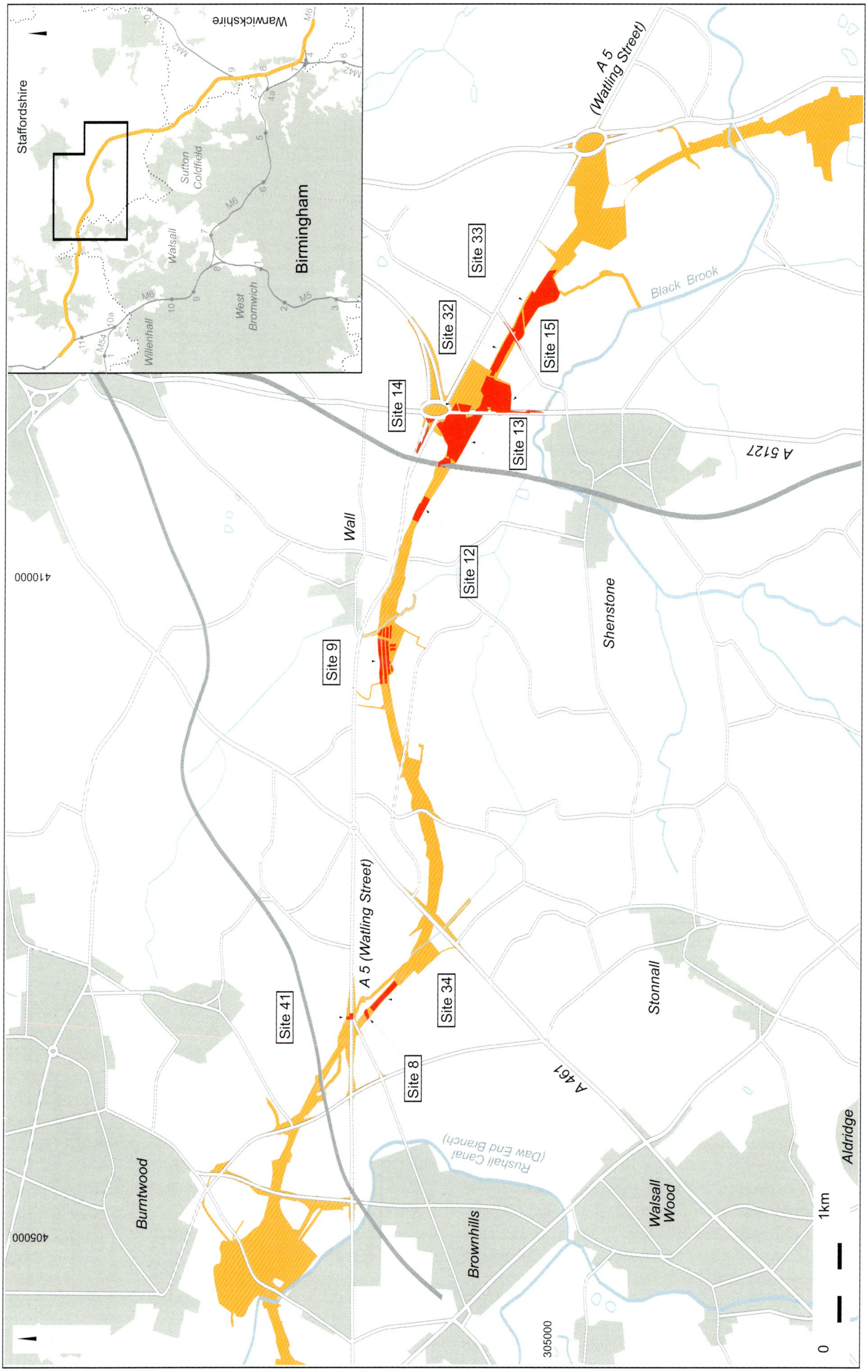

Fig. 5 Sites from Brownhills to Shenstone

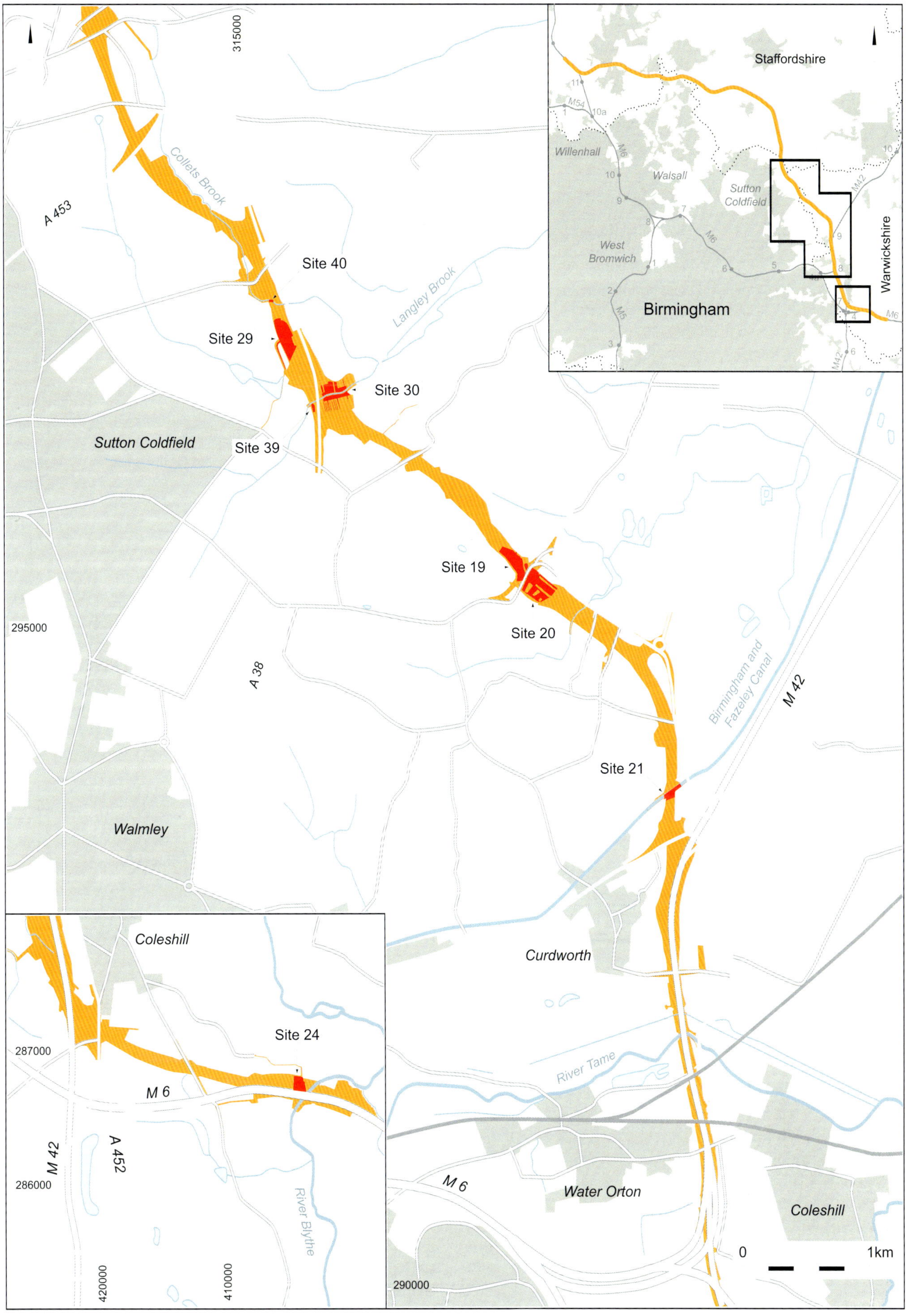

Fig. 6 Sites from Sutton Coldfield to Coleshill

Table 3 Sites providing the main evidence of activity in different periods (excluding individual finds and post-medieval/modern field boundaries)

Period	*Main evidence*	*Site Name*	
Mesolithic	Flint scatter	Shenstone Linear Features	13
	Flint assemblage	East of Birmingham Road Nurseries	15
	Flint scatter	Wishaw Hall Farm	19
Neolithic	Burnt mound	West of Crane Brook, Wall	9
	Pits	Shenstone Linear Features	13
	Pottery	East of Birmingham Road Nurseries	15
	Pottery	East of The Castle, Shenstone	32
Bronze Age	Early Bronze Age pottery	Ryknield Street	12
	Burnt mound	Langley Brook	39
	Burnt mound	Collett's Brook Burnt Mound, Sutton Coldfield	40
Iron Age	Old ground surface	Ryknield Street	12
	Settlement	Shenstone Ring Ditch	14
	Pottery	East of Birmingham Road Nurseries	15
	Pit alignment and ditch	Wishaw Hall Farm	19
	Round house and pottery	Wishaw	20
	Enclosed settlement	North of Langley Mill	29
	Open and enclosed settlement	Langley Mill	30
Romano-British	Field system	Washbrook Lane, Norton Canes	5
	Roman road	Watling Street, Hammerwich	41
	Aisled building and field ditches	West of Crane Brook Cottage, Hammerwich	34
	Roman road and cemetery	Ryknield Street	12
	Field ditches and pit	Shenstone Linear Features	13
	Settlement, enclosures and field system	East of Birmingham Road Nurseries	15
	Metalwork and pottery	East of The Castle, Shenstone	32
	Ditch and pit	Round Wood, Shenstone	33
	Enclosure and field ditches	Wishaw Hall Farm	19
	Settlement and enclosures	North of Langley Mill	29
Medieval	Ridge and furrow	Washbrook Lane, Norton Canes	5
	Settlement	Shenstone Linear Features	13
	Enclosure	Wishaw Hall Farm	19
	Fish ponds	Wishaw	20
	Possible settlement features	Hawkeswell Farm, Coleshill	24
Post-medieval/modern	Canal features	Hawkins Canal Basin and Aqueduct	1
	Reservoir	Hatherton Reservior	2
	Canal features	Gilpins Basin and Wharf	3
	Watling Street and bridges	Churchbridge Complex	4
	Building recording	Swan Farm, Norton Canes	36
	Canal features	Cannock Extension Canal	6
	Road	Watling Street, Hammerwich	41
	Canal features	Wyrley and Essington Canal	8
	Tramway	West of Crane Brook Cottage, Hammerwich	34
	Canal features and building recording	Curdworth Top Lock	21
	Garden features	Hawkeswell Farm, Coleshill	24
Undated	Enclosure	Cropmarks at Saredon	26

fine-grained deposits were encountered. Although many deposits were wet on excavation, few had been waterlogged in antiquity.

Some 1033 bulk samples for charred and charcoal remains were taken from the excavation and evaluation fieldwork. These were generally 20 litres, but their size varied according to the size of the features. All were processed by standard flotation methods; the flot was retained on a 0.5 mm mesh and the residues fractionated into 5.6 mm/4 mm, 2 mm and 1 mm fractions and dried. The coarse fractions (>5.6 mm/4 mm) were sorted, weighed and discarded. All flots (100%) were scanned under a low-power (x10–x40) stereo-binocular microscope, and all samples selected for analysis were fully extracted; selected residues were also scanned.

Charred plant remains were identified using the modern reference collections and reference manuals (such as Beijerinck 1947). Identifications were made (following Stace 1997) to species level where possible and genus and family where diagnostic features were less clear. For the identification of charred cereal grains and chaff, modern reference material was used with reference guides (such as Charles 1984 and Jacomet 1988).

With samples of waterlogged wood, a fine slice was taken from each wood fragment along three planes: transverse section (TS), radial longitudinal section (RL) and tangential longitudinal section (TL) using a razor blade. The resulting thin sections were mounted in water on a glass microscope slide, and examined under bi-focal transmitted light microscopy at magnifications of x50,

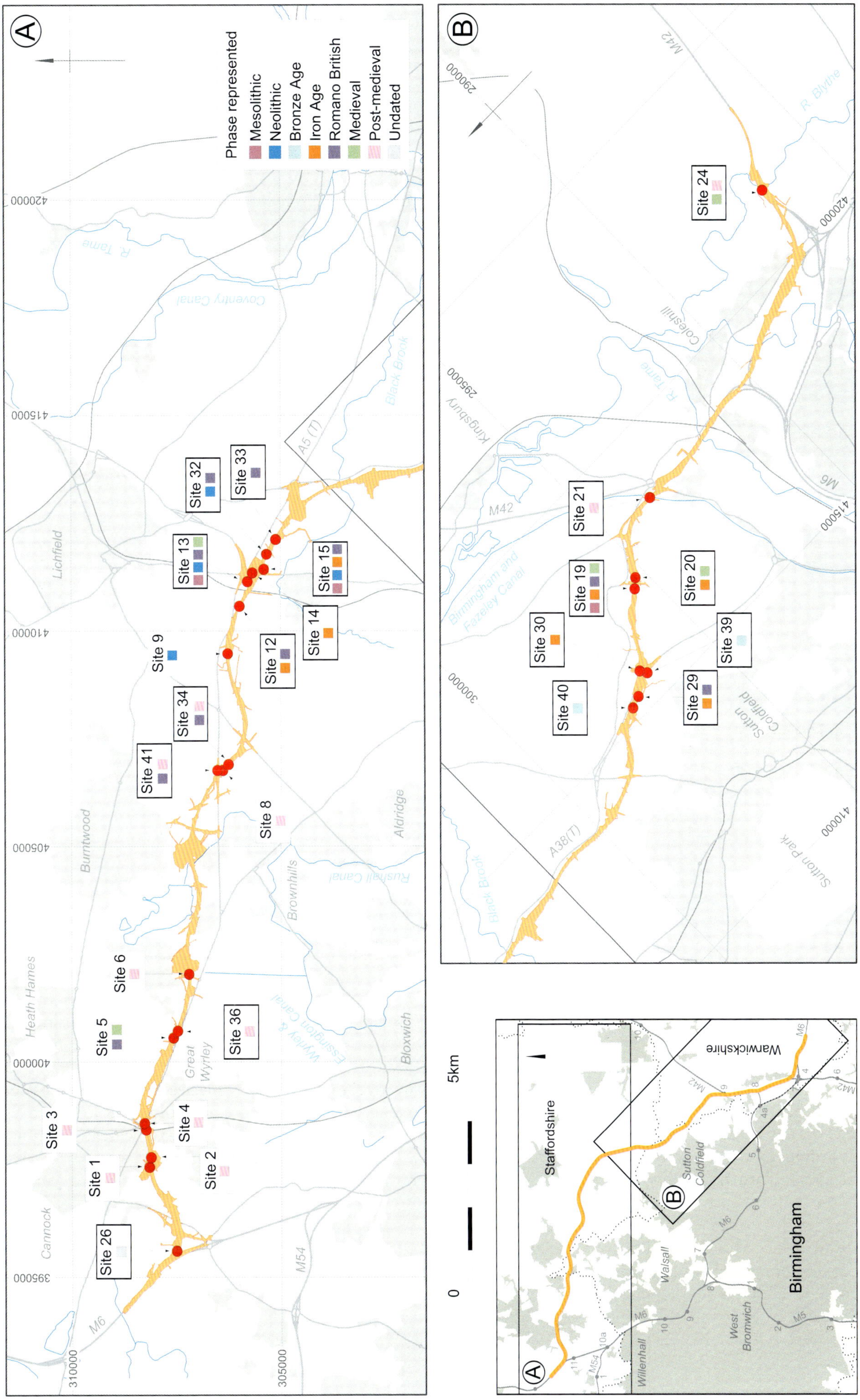

Fig. 7 Sites by period

x100 and x400 using a Kyowa ME-LUX2 microscope. Identification was undertaken according to the anatomical characteristics described by Schweingruber (1990) and Butterfield and Meylan (1980). Identification of waterlogged wood and other waterlogged plant material was to the lowest taxonomic level possible, usually that of genus, and nomenclature is according to Stace (1997).

Pollen samples were taken from two sites (Ryknield Street, Site 12, and Round Wood, Site 33). Standard techniques were used on samples of 2 ml volume from both sites (Moore and Webb 1978; Moore *at al.* 1991). Absolute pollen frequencies were calculated using added exotics to known volumes of sample (Stockmarr 1971). Pollen was identified and counted using an Olympus biological research microscope. All samples yielded copious numbers of pollen grains enabling identification, counting and the construction of pollen diagrams. Percentages for the latter are based on a total pollen sum comprising trees, shrubs and herbs. Percentages of fern spores are as percentage of the pollen sum plus spores. Taxonomy in general follows that of Moore and Webb (1978) modified according to Bennett *at al.* (1994) for pollen types and Stace (1997) for plant descriptions. These procedures were carried out in the Palaeoecology Laboratory of the Department of Geography, University of Southampton.

The radiocarbon dates are single entity AMS dates. Strict selection and scrutiny of material was made in an attempt to ensure that all items dated specific events (*cf* Allen and Bayliss 1995; Allen *at al.* 2004) and were not just datable items and it is considered that there is little prospect of residuality. All the radiocarbon results have been calibrated with the atmospheric data presented by Stuiver *at al.* (1993) and performed on OxCal v.3.9 (Bronk Ramsey 2003) and are expressed throughout this report at the 95% confidence level with the end points rounded outwards to 10 years following the form recommended by Mook (1986).

Post-excavation assessment

The full stratigraphic, artefactual and ecofactual record was subject to a post-excavation assessment, mostly undertaken in 2002. The report on this work (OWA 2003) presented a summary of all the findings to date, an assessment of the quality and significance of the evidence and proposals for further work based on this assessment.

In the light of the fieldwork results and the subsequent assessment programme the eight major research themes identified in the Project Design of 2000 were reconsidered and a further series of period-based and cross-period research aims defined, building on the earlier themes (OWA 2003, 73–7). These form the basis for the general discussions presented towards the end of this report.

An instruction to proceed with the programme of work defined in the post-excavation assessment report was received in August 2005.

Presentation of results

In total 41 sites were subject to archaeological investigation, of which 26 are reported here (Table 1, Figs 4–6). Reports on the remaining 15 sites (Table 2), which produced no significant archaeological remains, are retained in the archive (brief summaries of all sites can be found in the assessment report, see above). In most cases the unreported sites were ones identified on the basis of limited aerial photograph or surface (finds), evidence which proved on further investigation to be of minimal or no detectable significance.

The results are presented by individual named site along the road corridor from north-west to south-east. Because sites were identified during the various stages of preliminary work described above, and numbered from the north-west as they were identified, this numbering does not run consistently along the road corridor. Sites 1–25 are in geographical sequence from north-west to south-east with later numbers inserted into the sequence on an *ad hoc* basis. The site names are those assigned in the preliminary stages of the project. Table 1 provides a full concordance of site name, number and code. Table 3 lists sites by period, as shown in Figure 7.

Each site is described as a discrete entity, with a structural report followed by finds and environmental reports as appropriate, and discussion. The site reports are followed by a series of material culture studies, providing scheme-wide overviews of some of the artefact assemblages, then by broad period discussions – prehistoric, Romano-British, medieval and post-medieval.

SITES TO THE NORTH-WEST OF WALL

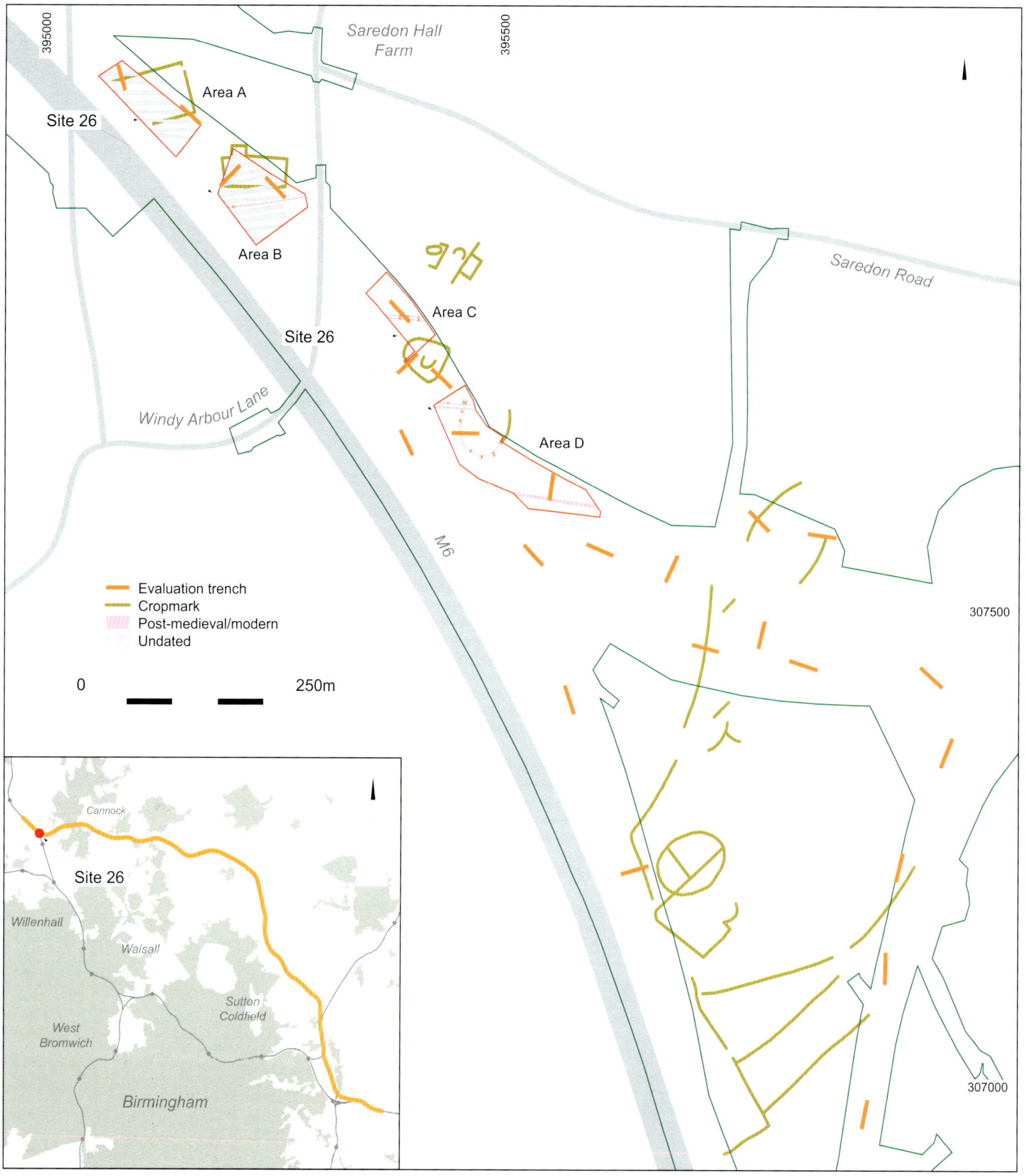

Fig. 8 Saredon (Site 26)

Chapter 2
Cropmarks at Saredon (Site 26)

By Andy Simmonds

Introduction

Trial trenching and a targeted watching brief were carried out within an area of indistinct cropmarks, south-west of Cannock, that appeared to represent a scatter of enclosures and linear boundaries, although fieldwalking in 1992 had failed to recover any significant finds associated with the cropmarks. The fieldwork revealed an area of medieval/post-medieval ridge-and-furrow bounded to the east by a lane, a rectilinear arrangement of field boundary ditches that is recorded on the 1899 OS 1st edition map and part of an undated sub-oval ditched enclosure (Fig. 8).

The site, centred on NGR 395750 307700, comprised an irregular area of arable land extending some 1.5 km along the M6 Toll, north of the junction of the M6 with the A460 Cannock–Wolverhampton road and south of Saredon Road. The geology is mapped as Late Devension till, with a small area of alluvium at the north-east (Geological Survey of Great Britain 2001, Sheet 153, Wolverhampton).

Twenty-five trenches were excavated (not all shown in Fig. 8), revealing a number of linear features in the north-western part of the cropmark complex, including the ditch of a U-shaped enclosure previously recorded as a cropmark, but no dating evidence. On the basis of these results, four areas (Areas A–D), extending over *c* 700 m in the northern part of the site, were targeted for excavation (Fig. 9). At the north-west, Areas A and B, with a combined area of *c* 1.3 hectares, were excavated in a large field between the M6 and Windy Arbour Lane extending south from Saredon Hall Farm. Area C (*c* 0.3 hectares) was on the eastern side of the Lane, and Area D (1.2 hectares) was situated to its south-east.

Results

Areas A and B

Areas A and B were positioned to investigate linear features recorded in the trial trenches (Fig. 9). These were shown to be the remains of an area of ridge-and-furrow, aligned east–west perpendicular to Windy Arbour Lane, only the furrows having survived truncation by modern ploughing. Nineteen furrows were recorded spaced at intervals of between 4.5 m and 6.7 m. They varied in width from 2.2 m to 5.8 m, and all had similar fills of mixed mid-brown sandy clay and gravel.

The only other feature was ditch 263070, which ran east–west across Area B. Its upper part had a gently sloping profile, with a vertical-sided slot, 0.25 m wide and at least 0.7 m deep, in its base. The profile suggests that a machine-excavated slot, most likely for a field drain, had been dug into an earlier ditch. The feature was filled with a loose mixture of brown, red and yellow sand.

Area C

No traces of the possible enclosure, as indicated by cropmarks extending into the southern part of Area C, were recorded either in the evaluation or the subsequent excavation. The only archaeological feature was an east–west trackway or field boundary defined by a pair of parallel ditches (269606 and 269607), 1.8–3.0 m apart, running for *c* 40 m across the area. The ditches had similar dimensions, averaging 1.0–1.2 m wide and 0.3 m deep, with shallow concave profiles and similar fills of light grey sandy silt.

The southern ditch (269607) was cut by a large feature (269532) *c* 5 m by 3 m, probably a tree hollow. It was irregular in shape and only 0.3 m deep with a fairly flat base, and filled with a brown sandy loam from which a sherd of 19th century pottery was recovered.

Area D

Area D was targeted on a U-shaped cropmark (Fig. 9), measuring *c* 50 m by 50 m, the north-eastern part of which lay outside the road corridor. The cropmark appeared to represent the west, south and east sides of an enclosure, but there was no trace of it north of a post-medieval field boundary.

The watching brief revealed a ditch (269589) up to 3.3 m wide and deepest on the southern side of the enclosure, where it was up to 1 m deep (Fig. 10). It became progressively shallower to the north-west and was only 1.6 m wide and 0.4 m deep where it was cut by post-medieval ditch 263051. It was generally V-shaped with asymmetrical sides, possibly resulting from the digging of a re-cut off-set slightly from its original line. The ditch was filled with a series of deposits of sand and gravel except for the deeper parts on the southern side, where the earliest fill was a gleyed clay indicating that the ditch had been subject to waterlogging. Charcoal appears to have been dumped in the base of the ditch around its entire perimeter. The final fill recorded in all the sections was a deposit of homogeneous greyish-brown silty sand with very few inclusions.

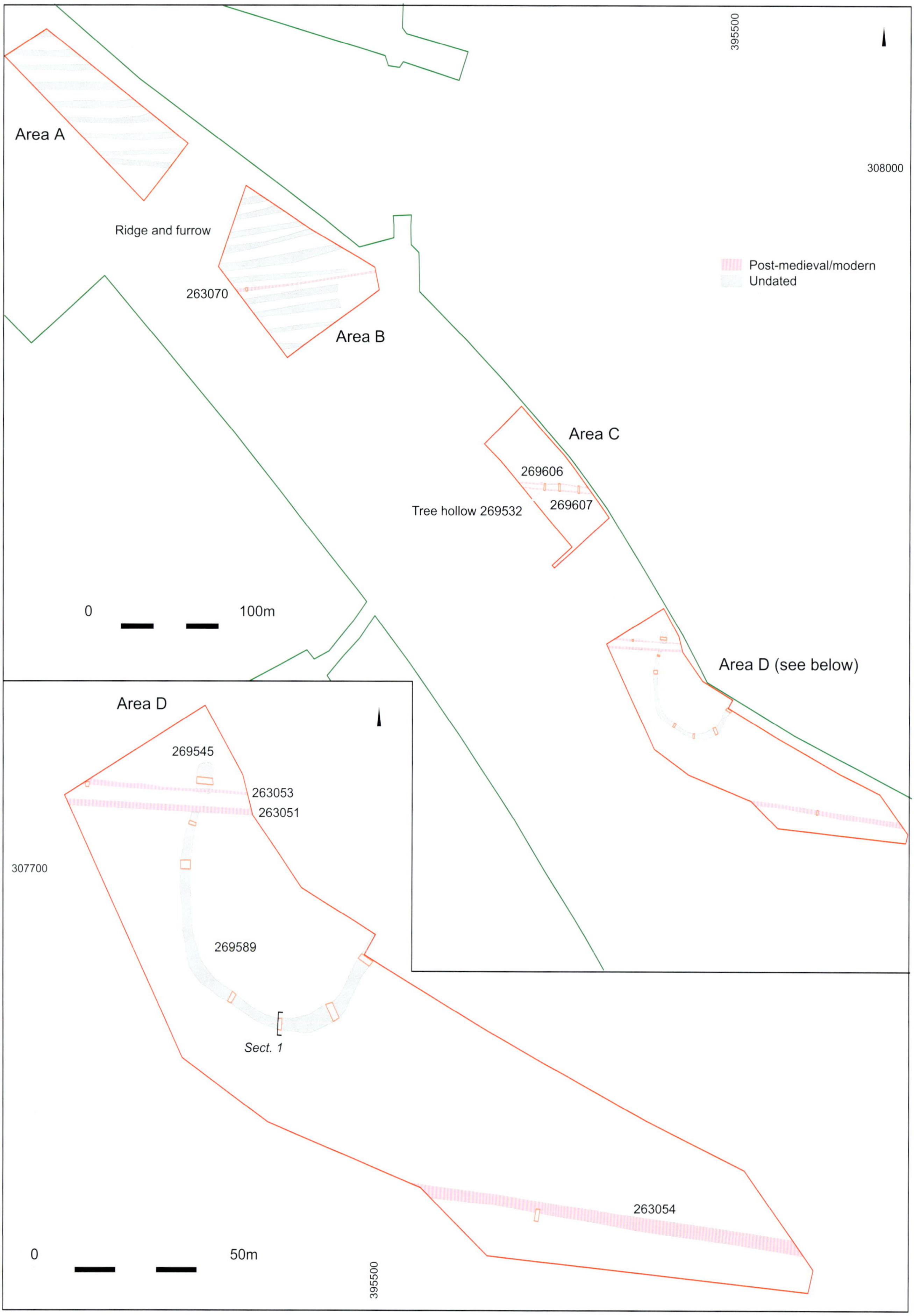

Fig. 9 Features in Areas A–D

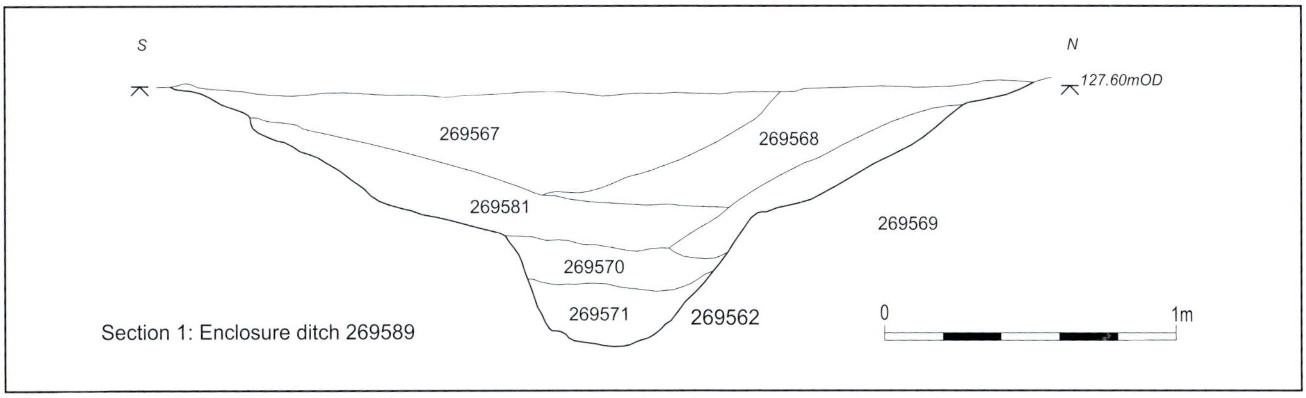

Fig. 10 Section across enclosure ditch 269589

A large oval feature (269545), measuring 7.5 m by 4 m, lay beyond the northern end of the ditch (cut by post-medieval ditch 263053). It was only 0.3 m deep with an uneven base and had a single fill of compact brown gravelly sand. Like feature 269532 in Area C, the feature may have been natural in origin.

Ditches 263051 and 263053 formed a double-ditched boundary running east–west across the northern part of Area D, parallel to the pair of ditches in Area C. The southern ditch (263051), which cut the northern end of ditch 269589, was not excavated. The northern ditch (263053), which cut feature 269545, was 1.2 m wide and 0.4 m deep, with an irregular, moderately steep northern side and a steeper southern side. It contained a gravelly primary fill overlain by a brown loamy sand.

Ditch 263054, also running approximately east–west, ran across the southern part of Area D. It was 2.3 m wide and 0.3 m deep with gently sloping sides. A ceramic drain had been inserted into its base, sealed by a single backfilled deposit of yellowish-brown sand from which a fragment of clay pipe stem was recovered. A subsequent re-cut (269598), measuring 0.7 m wide and 0.3 m deep with steep sides and a concave base, had a fill of brown sand (269599).

Environment

Charcoal, by Rowena Gale

Environmental samples were collected from five segments of the enclosure ditch (269589). Charcoal was present in all five samples but charred plant remains were all but absent. A single sample (264001) was recovered from the lowest level (context 269571) of ditch segment 269562 to record the character of the fuel debris and to assess possible origins of the fuel. The charcoal was poorly preserved and infiltrated with reddish deposits, making it difficult to examine the wood structure. It consisted mainly of blackthorn (*Prunus spinosa* – 18 fragments) but also included birch (*Betula* sp. – one fragment) and oak (*Quercus* sp. – two fragments) of undetermined maturity.

The function and date of the enclosure are unknown. It is possible that it was connected with the agricultural use of the land during the medieval period. Charcoal appears to have been dumped in the base of the ditch around its entire perimeter but there was little evidence to indicate the source of the debris. It is possible that it represents domestic fuel debris from activities conducted outside the site area but, probably more likely, given the dearth of food stuffs and other domestic waste materials (pottery and bone), it may have resulted from agricultural or craft use, for example, some type of bonfire. The high ratio of blackthorn could be indicative of the burning of scrub (perhaps from the clearance of invasive colonisation by this species) or hedgerow prunings. Had this resulted from industrial use, eg metal-working, a greater incidence of oak would be anticipated.

Soils in this region, situated on the South Staffordshire plateau, typically consist of marls and shales. Apart from noting the presence of blackthorn, oak, and birch, the sample offers little indication of the character of the local landscape or of woodland management. These species are commonly found on acid soils and could have grown in open woodland, hedgerows, scrub or as isolated specimens.

Discussion

Areas A–D were potentially thought to contain roughly rectilinear enclosures on the basis of aerial photographic evidence. However, the significance of this evidence was uncertain and no cropmarks were plotted in the rectified mapping survey carried out in July and August 2000. In the text section of that report it was observed of this site '... the AP evidence is very inconclusive, and was not considered to be of great importance ...' (Babtie 2000, 7). Features in Areas A–C proved to be linear in character, rather than forming parts of enclosures.

Only in Area D was an irregular enclosure identified, but this was quite undated and incomplete on its northern side. The interpretation of this is uncertain but rather than being open-sided it is perhaps more likely that the enclosure was completed by features which have left no archaeological trace, such as a substantial hedge or a piece of woodland. Alternatively, given that the enclosure ditch was increasingly shallow towards the north, it is possible that more intensive cultivation, in the post-medieval/modern period, in the field north of the parallel ditches (263051 and 263053) may have destroyed any traces north of the field boundary. The morphology of the U-shaped enclosure is not chronologically diagnostic and there was no evidence of activity in the interior that might have shed light on its date or function. A later prehistoric or Romano-British date can be tentatively suggested, but an even later date is possible.

Ridge-and-furrow cultivation like that recorded in Areas A and B is generally dated to the medieval and early post-medieval periods. The furrows recorded on this site are likely to relate to cultivation associated with the nearby village of Little Saredon. No evidence for ridge-and-furrow was seen in the areas east of Windy Arbour Lane which runs south from Saredon Hall Farm, suggesting that this lane is of some antiquity and formed the limit of the open field system.

The post-medieval ditches recorded in the excavation form a regular, rectilinear arrangement of field boundaries typical of the Inclosure period and are all depicted on the 1st Edition Ordnance Survey map of 1889 (Staffordshire sheet 56 NE).

Chapter 3
Hawkins Canal Basin and Aqueduct (Site 1)

By Andrew B. Powell

Introduction

A watching brief was carried out at the site of a 19th century canal basin, to the south of Cannock. The basin was linked to the Hatherton branch of the Staffordshire and Worcestershire Canal by an embanked aqueduct over the Wyrley Brook. The basin and aqueduct, which had been filled in with colliery spoil, were found to be well preserved, and those parts that were to be impacted by a new culvert over the Wyrley Brook were machine-excavated under close archaeological supervision and fully recorded.

The site covered *c* 0.5 hectares, centred on NGR 397570 308180, immediately south of the A5, and to the west of Walkmill Lane. It lay at *c* 112–119 m aOD on the south side of Wyrley Brook and adjacent to Hatherton Reservoir (Site 2) to the east (Fig. 11). The geology is mapped as Pleistocene Boulder Clay (Late Devension till), with alluvium along the Wyrley Brook (Geological Survey of Great Britain 1954, Sheet 154, Lichfield).

Historical background

The Staffordshire and Worcestershire Canal, opened in 1772, was a vital component of the 19th century industrial growth of Staffordshire, Warwickshire and the West Midlands, transporting coal and other goods over both short and long distances. The Hatherton branch (named after Lord Hatherton, chairman of the Staffordshire and Worcestershire Canal Company) was opened in 1841 running from the main canal east to Churchbridge, and so providing a direct link to the Cannock coalfields. The canal is unusual in having been constructed well into the railway era, and so was one of the last developments of the canal network in Britain. It would also have served other local industries, such as the Walk Mill, a large flourmill north-east of the site, in existence from at least 1775.

The Hawkins Canal Basin (also called the Walkmill Basin) was named after Joseph Hawkins & Sons, the owners of the Cannock Old Coppice Colliery south-west of the site. It was built in 1883 at the end of a short branch off the main canal just above Walkmill Lock. Hawkins' 35 year lease on the basin stipulated that underground coal workings beneath the basin were to be a maximum of 8 ft (2.4 m) wide and 8 ft (2.4 m) high. Twenty-three percent of sales from the colliery passed through the basin (Paget-Tomlinson 1993, 123).

The branch off the main canal passed under a draw bridge and across an aqueduct over the Wyrley Brook, entering the north-east corner of the basin. The 1st edition OS 25 inch map shows other elements of the complex, including another basin, the Walk Mill and mill leat. The canal was supplied, via the Hawkins Canal Basin, by a feeder running from a sluice (no longer visible) in the north-west corner of the Hatherton Reservoir, which covered *c* 5 hectares east of Walkmill Lane.

The 2nd edition OS map shows tram lines on either side of the basin converging at a wharf at its south-west end (Fig. 12), before continuing to the Cannock Old Coppice Colliery. The basin would have been used as a terminus for transferring onto the canal coal brought from this and other local mines (such as the Great Wyrley Colliery), as well the products of local brick and tile works.

In 1860, the South Staffordshire Railway (SSR) built a small interchange basin with a long siding at the Churchbridge (Site 4), allowing direct transfer from canal to railway, and in 1863 the Churchbridge locks linked the canal to the Birmingham Canal Navigation via the Cannock Extension Canal. By 1895, in the face of increased competition from other canal and railway companies, the Staffordshire and Worcestershire Canal Company joined with the Thames and Severn Trust, in order to secure the distribution of Staffordshire coal. Canal traffic ended at Hawkins Basin *c* 1949, and the Hatherton branch was abandoned in 1955. The basin was subsequently infilled with colliery spoil and a coppice planted on the infilled site.

Methodology

Although the fieldwork at the site began as a watching brief (with some limited preliminary recording prior to the start of site works), it was soon apparent that the level of preservation was considerably higher than expected. Because of the high level of impact of the road scheme, which involved the excavation of a large cutting resulting in destruction of part of the canal basin and much of the aqueduct, it was decided to carry out the equivalent to RCHM(E) Level 2 building recording of the impacted structures. This was undertaken intermittently over a period of three months.

Two main areas of the site were investigated. The larger (Area A), encompassing the north-east end of the

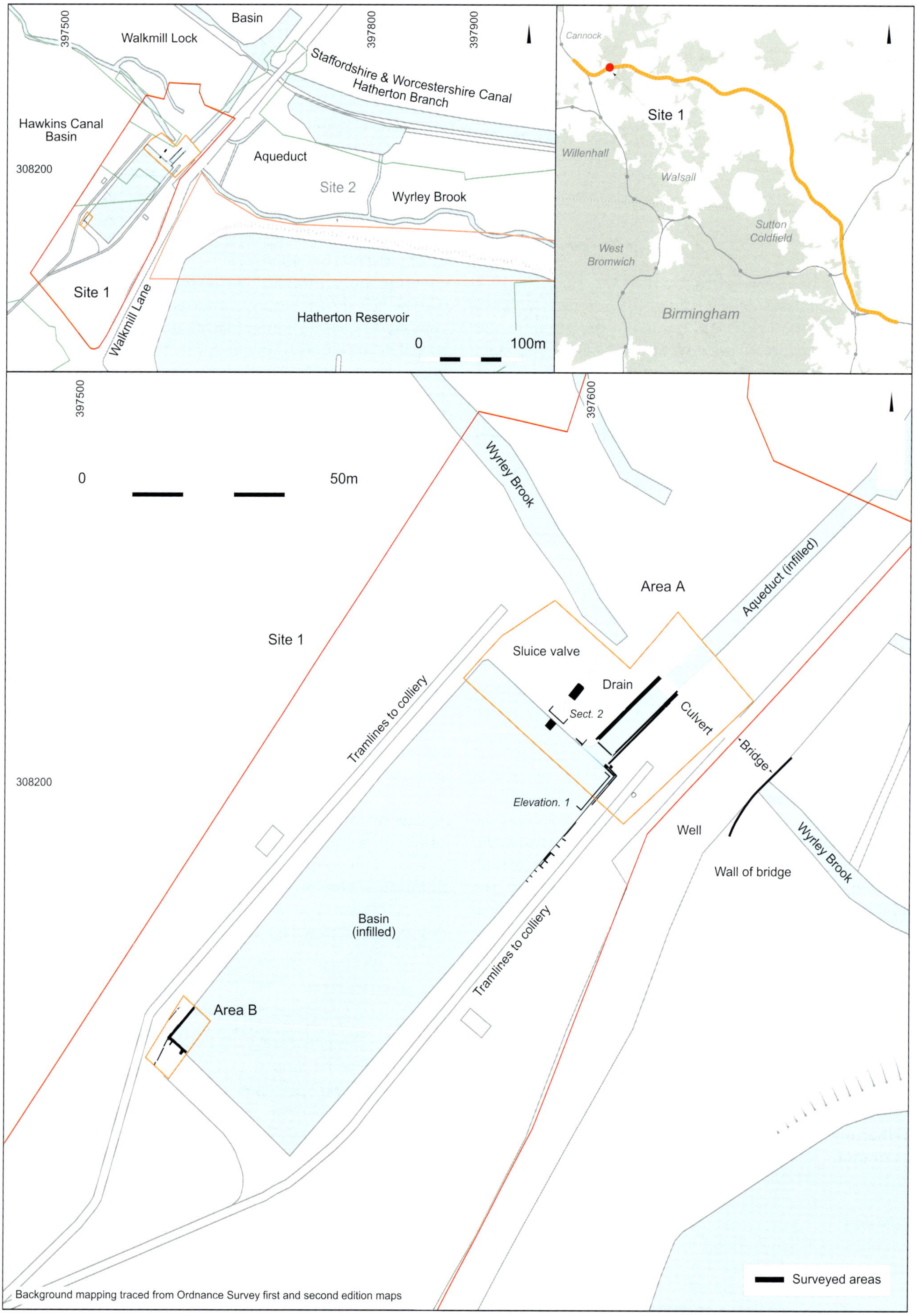

Fig. 11 Hawkins Canal Basin and Aqueduct (Site 1)

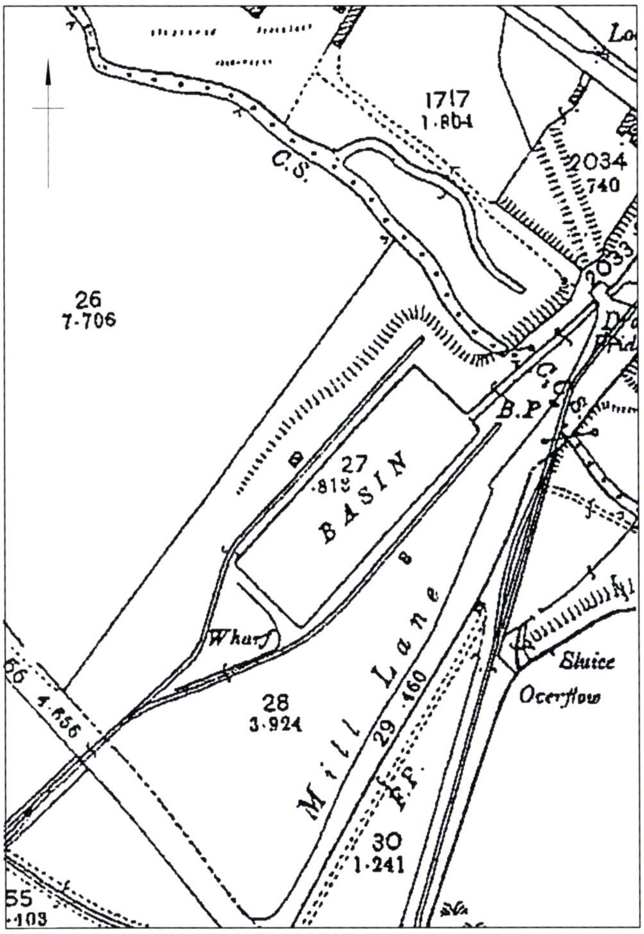

Fig. 12 2nd Edition 6 inch OS Map of the Hawkins Canal Basin

canal basin and the adjacent 30 m length of the aqueduct, measured *c* 43 m by 41 m. A smaller area (Area B), measuring 7 m by 4 m, was located at the south-western corner of the canal basin. These areas were excavated using a 360° excavator fitted with both toothed and toothless buckets as required. This involved the complete removal of colliery spoil from inside the impacted section of the aqueduct and canal basin walls, and the partial removal of spoil from the outside of the walls.

The structure was then surface cleaned by hand, recorded and digitally surveyed. A selection of building materials, including brick, cement and ceramics, was kept from each structure to allow comparison and analysis of building style and design. Subsequently, many of the surviving coping stones from the tops of the aqueduct walls were recovered by the Lichfield and Hatherton Canals Restoration Trust for use in canal restoration.

Results

Pre-canal basin features

Various forms of land drain – stone filled, brick-lined and ceramic pipe – were recorded underneath the canal basin and aqueduct, none of which appeared to be of any great age (the stone filled drain containing fragments of broken brick) (see Fig. 16). The presence of these drains suggests that the land had either been previously drained for agricultural purposes, and/or that it had been drained to aid in the construction of the canal features.

The original land surface, which was 3–4 m lower than the top of the canal basin, had been built up to the level of the top of the basin, so that the basin did not actually cut into the underlying ground. A section across the embanked aqueduct, adjacent to where it crossed the Wyrley Brook, showed that a thick concrete footing upon which it had been built rested on a 0.22 m thick layer made ground consisting of sandy clay and gravel and what appeared to be colliery waste. This overlay a layer of dark soil, 0.3 m thick, possibly the original land surface, below which was the natural clay within which the land drains had been laid.

The canal basin

The canal basin was *c* 95 m long and 33 m wide, aligned NE–SW. Its base was lined with *c* 0.5 m of pink clay. The basin walls were constructed of red brick in English bond, their three foundation courses stepped inwards on both faces from 1.1 m wide at the base. The bottom 12 courses of the wall (as recorded in a section on the north-west side of the basin) were 0.86 m (3½ brick lengths) wide. Its outer face then stepped inwards to 0.73 m (3 bricks) wide for the next 7 courses, and then to 0.6 m (2½ bricks) towards the top. The full height of the walls, as recorded at the south-west corner of the basin, was 3.1 m (Fig. 13). A number of brick buttresses were recorded against the outer faces of the walls, the outside of the basin being lagged with a packing of clay up to 1 m thick. The whole of the area around the canal basin and the aqueduct, had then been backfilled with clayey gravel up to the present ground level.

The tops of the walls had been severely damaged, although they were largely intact towards the north-east and south-west corners of the basin, where they had

Fig. 13 The south-west corner of the canal basin

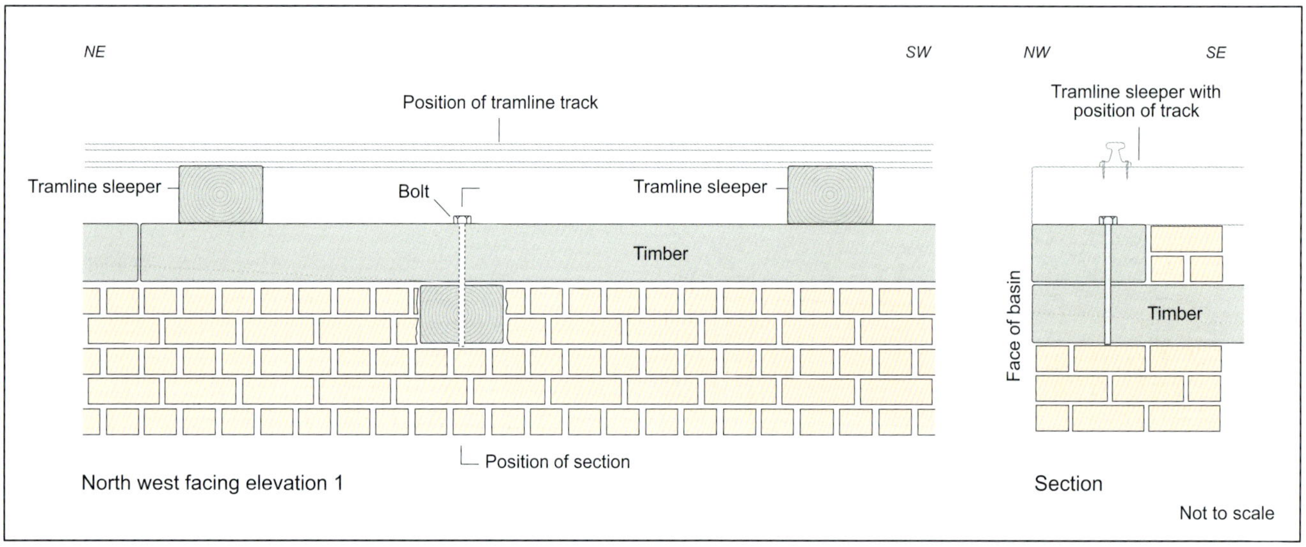

Fig. 14 North-west facing elevation and section of the canal basin wall

substantial longitudinal timbers laid along the top edge (Fig. 14). The timbers were secured by 33 mm diameter bolts to further timbers two courses below that ran back from the face of the wall (those at the corners set at an angle of 45°). These perpendicular timbers may have been tied to buttresses behind the walls, although these were not exposed. The longitudinal timbers were backed by two course of bricks set back *c* 0.3 m from the edge of the wall, across which lay a further series of lateral timber sleepers whose ends were flush with the edge of the basin. The sleepers, spaced between 1 m and 1.6 m apart, would have supported the tramway rails, running down both sides of the basin, that carried the trucks for loading coal onto the barges. Some of the nails securing the rails remained *in situ*, although the rails did not. As indicated on the 2nd edition OS map, these rails ended some 7 m beyond the end of the basin.

Drain, sluice valve and well

At the base of the north-east wall of the canal basin, some 10 m north-west of the mouth of the aqueduct, there was the arched opening to a brick drain (Fig. 15) that ran down to the Wyrley Brook, passing through a rectangular chamber, accessible from the top, containing a sluice valve. The opening to the drain was 0.5 m high and 0.68 m wide, the semicircular arch being constructed of two courses of brick headers. A shallow brick channel, ten bricks wide with the outer bricks at a slight angle, was laid in the clay floor of the canal basin in front of the opening.

A machine-cut section through the drain immediately behind the mouth indicated that the walls and floor of the drain were laid upon a single foundation course 1.43 m wide (Fig. 16). The walls, 0.35 m wide and five courses high, supported an arch comprising 17 bricks on the inner arc and 20 on the outer. The floor of the drain, sloping down towards the north-east,

Fig. 15 The arched opening of the drain in the canal basin

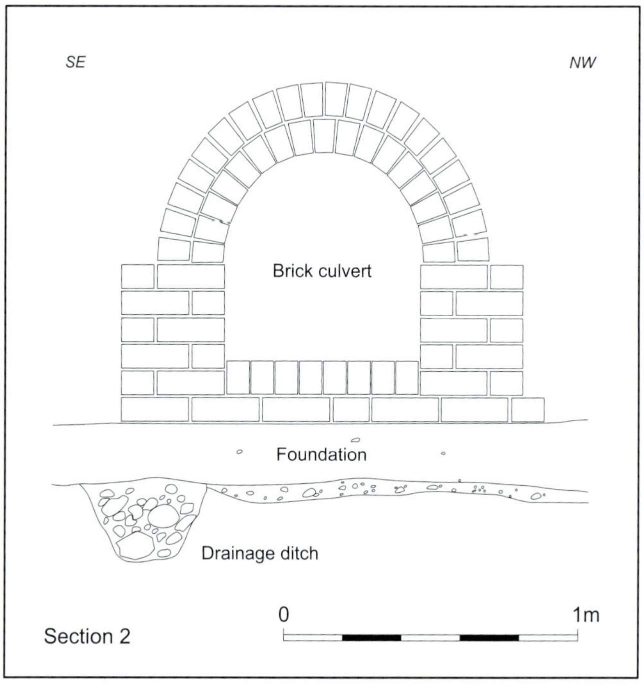

Fig. 16 Section through the brick drain between the canal basin and the sluice chamber

Fig. 17 The valve assembly in the sluice chamber

consisted of bricks laid on edge longitudinally, eight bricks wide – the same as the floor of the channel in the basin.

After some 8 m the drain opened, over a step of bullnose bricks, into a brick chamber, 2.1 m long and 0.7 m wide internally, and 3.2 m deep. The inner faces of the chamber walls, which were *c* 0.5 m thick, were partially covered with a screed of cement. There were opposed recessed slots on the side walls near the canal basin end, which would have held a raisable barrier or stop board, probably to isolate the chamber for maintenance purposes.

At the other end of the chamber, the water exited through a circular outlet pipe, 0.45 m in internal diameter, level with the floor of the chamber. The pipe was set within a step of brickwork extending out from the end wall. As the features had become covered with a hard concretion, it was not possible to determine what the pipe was made of. The pipe was blocked by an iron shut-off plate set back 0.22 m from its mouth, operated by a large cast iron valve assembly, set into the end of the chamber (Fig. 17). The top plate of the assembly, from which the square brass key (measuring 45 mm square) of the valve's screw mechanism protruded, was bolted down by eight square nuts.

Because of the shut-off plate, it was not possible to examine the drain beyond it. However, the other end of the drain was recorded, largely blocked by silt, in the south-western flanking wall of the culvert over the Wyrley Brook (below). The drain and valve would have acted as an overflow mechanism, as well as allowing the water in the basin to be drained, if necessary for cleaning.

On the other side of the aqueduct was a brick lined 'well', fed on its south-west side by a ceramic drain entering four courses below the top. It was 0.7 m in internal diameter, although not consistently circular. Each course comprised 11 rectangular handmade bricks, not bonded together but simply been laid in circle, each course turned half a brick from the one below. The well was at least 4 m deep, and it contained 0.5 m of water when recorded. This feature is unlikely to have been a well, and appears instead to have been a sump or soakaway draining water or waste from the area adjacent to the canal basin. A brown concretion lined the bricks on the lower courses.

The aqueduct

The canal basin was linked to the main canal, some 200 m to the north-east, by a short branch which narrowed as it crossed an embanked aqueduct over the Wyrley Brook. The Brook, some 23 m from the canal basin, passed under a brick culvert abutting the bridge that carried Walkmill Lane. Unlike the canal basin, the floor of the aqueduct was lined with a single course of bricks laid on edge in a thin bed of mortar resting on a 0.14 m thick layer of clay. The section recorded across the aqueduct just south-west of the culvert showed that at this point it had been built on a 1 m thick layer of concrete, comprising coarse gravel and lime-based mortar, resting on made ground. The concrete was sealed by a 0.15 m thick layer of clay, upon which the aqueduct walls and floor rested. The floor consisted of thick bricks set on edge in a layer of cement.

The aqueduct joined the canal basin some 2.4 m from the north-east corner, its mouth being 4.85 m wide at the basin, narrowing, after 2.2 m, to 3.65 m (Fig. 18). Just inside the point where the aqueduct narrowed, there were narrow recessed slots holding metal channels running down each wall, and a timber sill, from which two large square cut pins protruded, crossing the base of the aqueduct between them (marking the end of the brick floor). These would have allowed the lowering of some form of temporary barrier across the aqueduct.

The outside faces of the aqueduct walls were stepped inwards every seven courses, and lagged with a packing of clay up to 0.8 m wide behind them. The wall on the north-west side was thicker than that on the south-east side. Both walls were topped with large blue bullnose bricks (35 mm by 15 mm by 11 mm), behind which was a narrow strip of brick paving, then a compact gravel surface. There was a large sandstone block, 0.7 m by 0.9 m, on the eastern corner at the mouth of the aqueduct, and another, 0.9 m by 1.4 m, some 16 m further down the same side. The western corner of the mouth, on the

Fig. 18 The aqueduct

Fig. 19 The culvert carrying the embanked canal aquaduct over Wyrley Brook

other side of the aqueduct, had not survived, but a similar block was set in the north-west wall 9.3 m down the aqueduct, so that the blocks on either side were staggered. These 'nudging stones', which protruded slightly from the face of the wall, were designed to prevent damage to the brickwork.

The culvert and bridge

The Wyrley Brook flowed beneath two distinct structures abutting each other at a slight angle. To the west, the culvert beneath the embanked canal aqueduct had a low arch resting on low supporting walls (three courses showing above the water level) (Fig. 19), while, to the east, the bridge carrying Walkmill Lane had an elliptical arch with no visible wall below.

The arch of the Walkmill Lane bridge consisted of four courses of headers, although it appeared that the lowest course, set back slightly from the face, had been added at a later date presumably to strengthen the bridge; the second from bottom course employed bullnose bricks. The reddish-blue bricks in the face of the bridge were laid in English bond. At both ends there were shallow buttresses projecting out slightly from the face of the wall, topped with two courses of plinth bricks.

Immediately beyond the buttress on the south side there was a sidewall, topped with blue half round coping bricks, angled out slightly from the line of the bridge and appearing to be a later addition. The space behind it had been infilled with soil. The 1.5 m high bridge parapet was also a later addition, being constructed with a modern machine made brick, laid in stretcher bond with yellowy grey cement. It extended past the buttresses to square piers topped with concrete capstones, and curved slightly at the southern end to follow the line of the road.

To the west, the arch of the culvert carrying the aqueduct consisted of four courses of headers. The brickwork in the face above was plain English bond with no decorative features apart from a coping of blue/grey bullnose bricks (smaller than those used on the aqueduct). The face was bonded at either side to flanking walls of the same build, retaining the embankment and running at right angles along the side of the Brook. These walls sloped down steeply to the west, topped by an angled course of bricks and further bullnose bricks; the wall on north side levelled off as a low wall.

The outlet of the drain, running via the sluice chamber from the canal basin, exited above the water level in the southern flanking wall, partly covered by silt accumulated along the bank. An iron hinge on the left side probably held a metal grille/gate. A water out-fall pipe, probably for a road drain, had subsequently been cut into the opposite wall.

Discussion

The features recorded during the watching brief were found to be very well preserved, and revealed the main components of the canal basin's operation and use. The basin formed an integral part of a complex of canal features along this stretch of the Hatherton branch that highlight the importance of the canal for local industry. Development of the canal continued well into the age of the railways which, in many other parts of the country, saw the decline of the canal network.

Chapter 4
Hatherton Reservoir (Site 2)

By Andrew B Powell

Introduction

A watching brief was undertaken at the site of the former Hatherton Reservoir which supplied water for the Hatherton branch of the Staffordshire and Worcestershire Canal, to the south of Cannock. Examination of the reservoir dam demonstrated that the construction comprised merely an earth mound with no evidence of internal structures.

The site, at a height of between *c* 115.4–118.3 m aOD, covered *c* 2.1 hectares centred on NGR 397800 308120. It was located in an area of derelict land south of the Wyrley Brook to the east of Walkmill Lane, and adjacent to Hawkins Canal Basin (Fig. 20). The underlying geology is mapped as recent and Pleistocene Boulder Clay, with recent and Pleistocene Alluvium to the north along the Wyrley Brook (Geological Survey of Great Britain 1954).

Preliminary work consisted of a rapid photographic survey. More detailed recording was carried out in a later phase when intrusive site works impinged upon the dam enclosing the north end of the reservoir. This recording took the form of a machine dug section through part of the dam (which was battered to allow safe access into the trench for recording). The section was digitally surveyed to show the construction layers within the dam.

The reservoir was created by building a dam immediately to the south of the Wyrley Brook. The dam's original extent is shown on the first and second edition

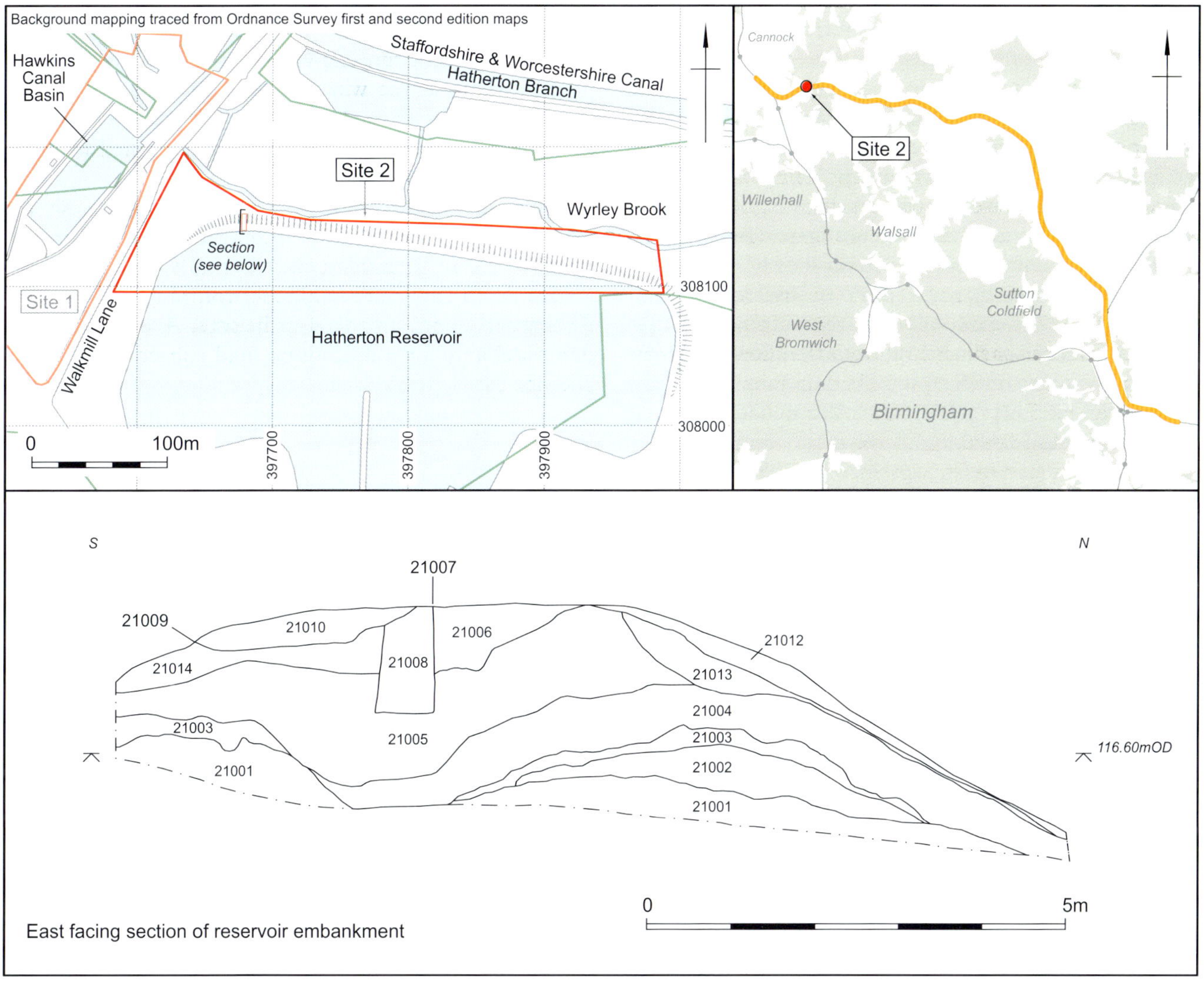

Fig. 20 Hatherton Reservoir (Site 2) and east-facing section through the reservoir embankment

Ordnance Survey 25 inch maps (1884, 1902) extending *c* 350 m in an east–west direction to the south of the brook and returning *c* 75 m to the south at its east end. The irregular southern edge of the reservoir was not dammed, being formed by the natural contours of the land, and is shown on the maps as marshland. The raised Walkmill Lane (then called Mill Lane) formed the western edge.

The Hatherton branch of the Staffordshire and Worcestershire Canal passed in an east–west direction *c* 100 m to the north of the reservoir and water appears to have been supplied to the canal via the adjacent Hawkins Canal Basin by means of a sluice, no longer visible, at the north-west corner of the reservoir.

Although the canal is no longer in use the reservoir is maintained as a nature reserve by the local authority and still holds water in its eastern half. A path extends along the northern edge of the reservoir, adjacent to the dam. The western section of the reservoir has been filled in so that its original extent is no longer visible and a section has been lowered for a concrete spillway.

Results

The location of the section had previously been quite severely impacted by the main contractors, so that the original height of the dam could not be ascertained. The section, which was over 11 m wide, did not reveal the full width of the dam, in particular the base of its inner slope.

The basal layer recorded in the section comprised two deposits (with a gap between them in the centre of the dam) of compact sandy clay up to 0.5 m thick (21001), the deposit on the outer (north) side being overlain by a 0.6 m thick layer of friable silty clay (21002) (Fig. 20). This was followed by separate inner and outer deposits of loose silty sand (21003) up to 0.3 m thick, the outer of which was overlain by a 0.7 m thick layer of compact silt clay (21004). Above these, spanning almost the full width of the dam, was a 1.5 m thick layer of friable silty clay (21005) that filled the central hollow between the inner and outer deposits, then the uppermost layer of silty clay (21006/21014). A hollow, possibly cause by erosion or slippage of this material near the top of the dam on its outer side, was filled with compact clay (21013), possibly as a repair. This was overlain by the subsoil and topsoil (21011 and 21012) which covered the outer slope of the dam's surface.

Two unidentified service pipes (most probably water) that had been cut into the top of the dam at some point after its construction. One lay in a backfilled trench (21007), 0.76 m wide and 1.7 m deep with vertical sides and a flat base, in the centre of the dam. The southern edge of this trench was cut by a concave cut (21009), 2 m wide and 0.6 m deep and running along inner edge of the dam's flat top, also holding a pipe.

Discussion

Although the location of the section across the reservoir bank was constrained by the presence of water in the reservoir and the ground works associated with the construction works, examination of the full length of the dam, and the areas that had been impacted by the ground works, indicated that the earth mound construction seen in the machine dug section was indicative of the dam as a whole. This comprised simple inner and outer earthen banks at the base, infilled by further deposits above. The local clay geology was used to provide the water proofing necessary to retain water within the reservoir.

The full dimensions of the dam could not be determined, but it is likely to have been at least 15 m wide and over 3 m high. As such it was considerably wider than the embankments of the Wyrley and Essington Canal investigated between Burntwood and Brownhills (Site 8), which were only 7 m wide. However, like the canal embankment, the dam section revealed no evidence for any structural component in the form of piling.

Chapter 5
Gilpin's Basin and Wharf (Site 3)

By Andrew B. Powell

Introduction

A watching brief was undertaken at the site of a 19th century canal basin on the Hatherton branch of the Staffordshire and Worcestershire Canal, at Churchbridge to the south of Cannock. Features were recorded during construction-related works, revealing phases of construction, use and abandonment. A double-arch brick railway bridge and an adjacent accommodation bridge over the former canal and the Wash Brook (a continuation of the Wyrley Brook) were also surveyed.

The site, covering *c* 2.1 hectares centred on NGR 398430 308240, consisted of part of the canal, and a railway interchange basin on its south side comprising a wharf and the site of a goods shed on a railway siding. The site included the embanked north–south aligned railway and railway bridge, immediately west of the basin (Fig. 21). The geology is mapped as Pleistocene Boulder Clay (Late Devension till), with alluvium along the course of the Wash Brook (Geological Survey of Great Britain 1954, Sheet 154, Lichfield). The excavation revealed a layer of possible alluvium up to 0.5 m thick overlying sandy gravel below modern ground levelling layers, with a sterile mid-brown/orange clay at greater depth (exceeding 4 m below ground level).

At the time of the excavation there was only limited visible evidence of the canal and basin on the site. The area on the south side of the canal, around the entrance to the basin, was stripped using a 360° excavator fitted with both toothed and toothless buckets as required, recorded and digitally surveyed. As ecological constraints at the former canal ruled out excavating a trench through it, a watching brief was also maintained during works to create two temporary diversions of the Wash Brook, the first diversion running to the south cutting across the basin, and the second running through the canal. This enabled sections across the basin and the north side of the canal to be recorded; a watching brief was also maintained during works at the southern end of the basin. The railway bridge and accommodation bridge (the latter allowing access between two parcels of land on either side of the canal) were also surveyed and recorded (Fig. 22) (in archive).

Historical background

In 1860, the South Staffordshire Railway (SSR) built a small interchange basin with a long siding on the south side of the Staffordshire and Worcestershire Canal (see Site 1, above), allowing direct transfer from canal to railway. It was known as Gilpin's Basin, after the Gilpin family who started coal mining in the area in 1817, and who owned the Edgetool Manufactory south-east of the site. The siding included two tracks entering a goods shed at the south end the basin, one continuing through it to the edge of the canal. Another track lay west of the shed, while others to the east had connections to the Gilpin's factory.

The 1st and 2nd edition OS 25 inch maps (1884 and 1902) show the layout of the canal at the site, and an adjacent mill stream fed by the Wash Brook on its south side (Fig. 23). The canal widened to *c* 17 m, between the bridge carrying the South Staffordshire Railway at the west, and the road bridge at the east, to facilitate access to the canal basin. North-east of the road bridge was a series of 13 docks along the side of the canal.

When the basin was constructed, the millstream, fed by the Wash Brook, was diverted sharply to the south, for some 75 m around the basin and goods shed, before turning again to the north-east to rejoin the Wash Brook.

Results

The canal and basin entrance

The north side of the canal was examined in section (Fig. 24). This revealed a 1.6 m wide foundation of roughly finished stones (up to 0.3 m by 0.2 m by 0.2 m), running ENE–WSW (31624) and laid without any uniform courses, bond or facing. The foundation was no more than 0.3 m deep and its upper surface was levelled with a layer of cement (31633). Sitting above the front edge of the foundation was a brick wall (31625) 0.7 m wide and surviving to a height of 0.65 m, both faces being of English bond construction. Behind the wall were layers first of sand and gravel (31634) and then rubble (31635). The construction cut for the canal was not exposed.

In front of the wall, a layer of decomposed organic material (31626) was overlain by two layers of silty gravel (31627 and 31268) abutting the wall and sloping into the canal at an angle of *c* 40°, possibly deposited during reconditioning of the canal. These, in turn, were overlain by a layer of brickearth (31629), possibly forming a lining for the canal, above which were layers of organic rich material (31631 and 31632) and a lens of redeposited brickearth (31630) which appear to have accumulated during the use of the canal.

On the south side of the canal, the canal wall was constructed of red, English bond brickwork. Its upper

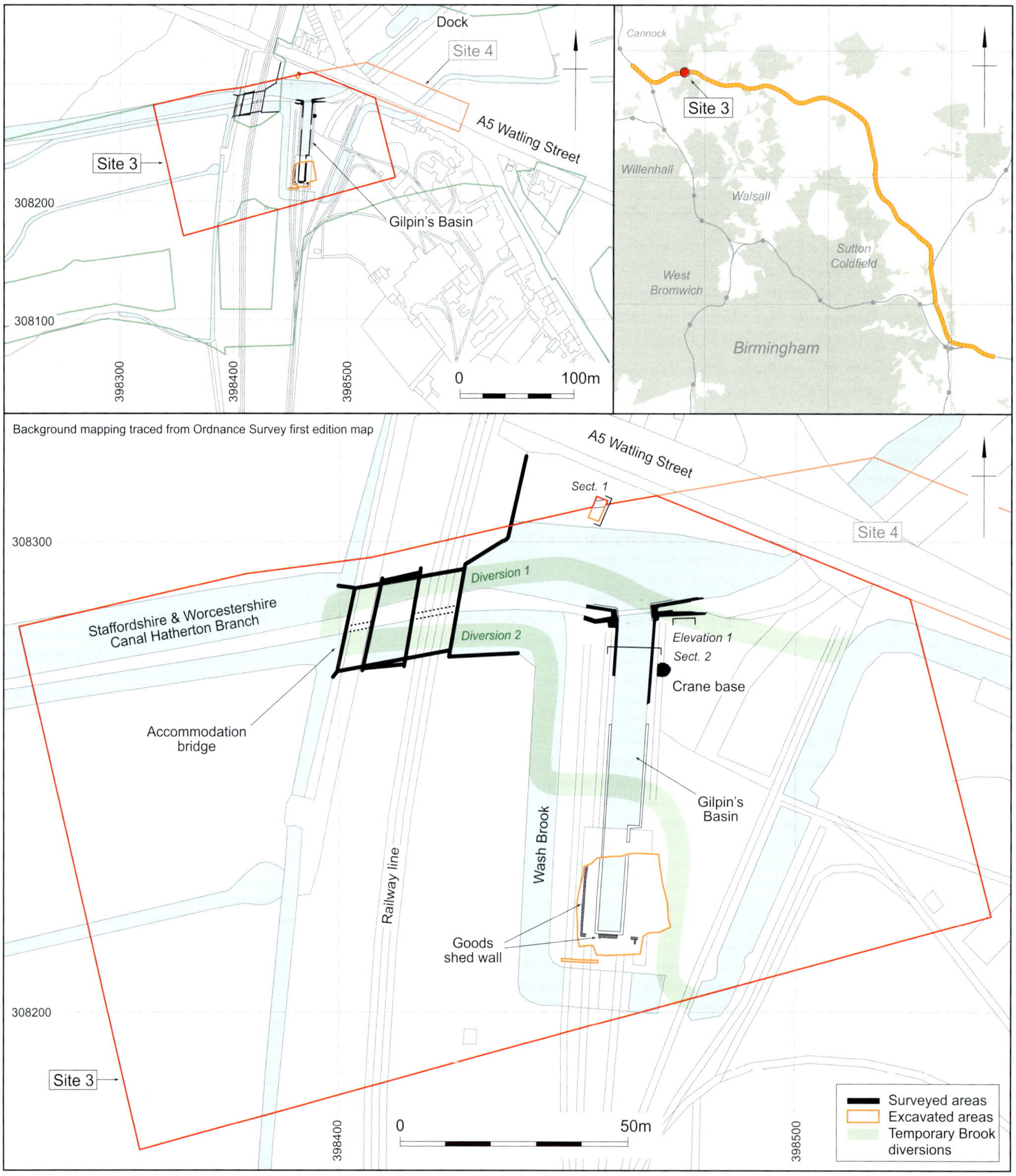

Fig. 21 Gilpin's Basin and Wharf (Site 3)

part had been demolished and only up to five courses survived. Both the front and back of the wall were pointed, although the back face was more roughly finished. Below the upper courses of the canal wall (and in the entrance to the basin) there was a course of bullnose bricks, with curved upper edges, protruding *c* 0.3 m out from the face of the wall, and forming a narrow (0.15 m) step just below water level (Fig. 25). West of the basin, this course was shown to rest on at least two further stepped courses of brickwork. In places, the corroded remains of a steel pipe or band ran along the front edge of the bullnose bricks.

On both sides of the canal basin the canal wall turned south to form a 7 m wide and 2.5 m long entrance to the canal basin. At the back of the basin entrance, on either side, two other walls ran parallel to the canal wall, the gaps between the front and back walls being filled with loose demolition rubble. There would probably have been a bridge across the mouth of the basin at this point, on the line of the towpath which ran along the south side

Fig. 22 The western side of the basin entrance looking west towards the railway and accommodation bridges

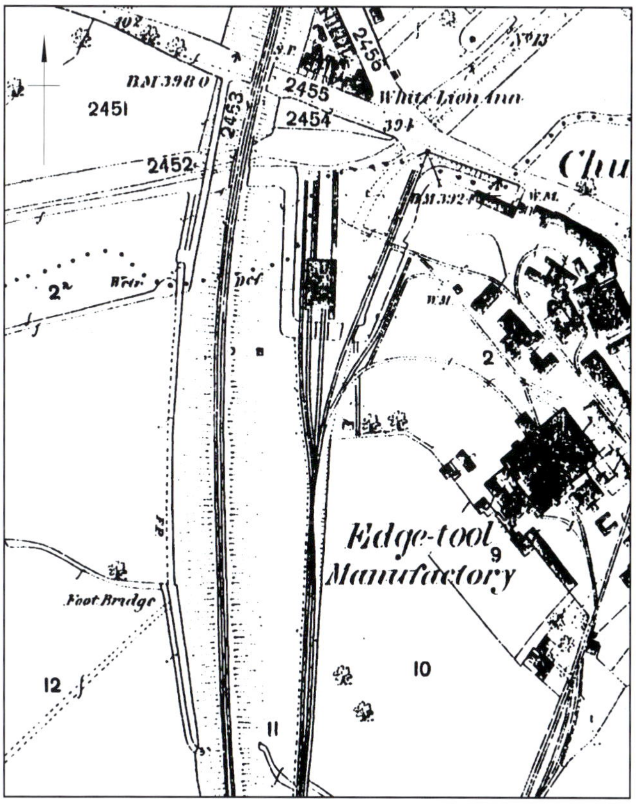

Fig. 23 1st edition 6 inch OS map of Gilpin's Basin

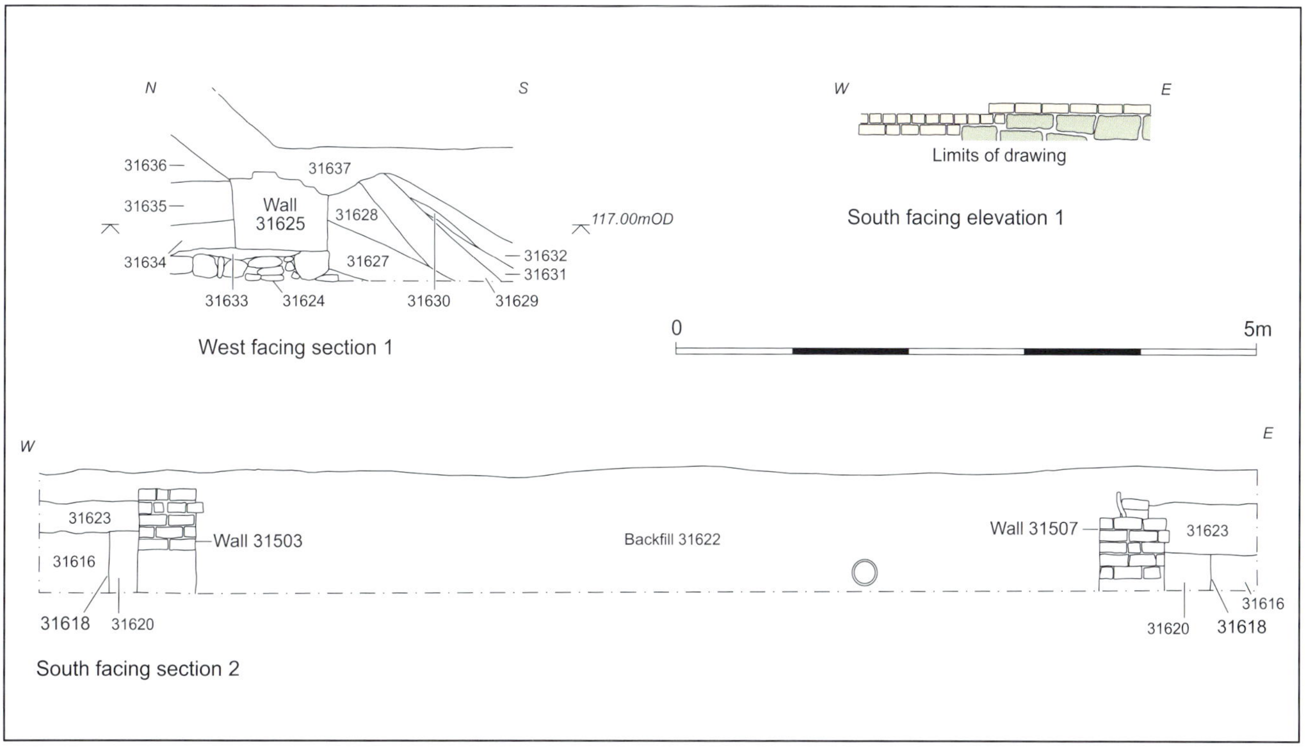

Fig. 24 West-facing section through the northern wall of the canal; elevation of the rear face of the inner canal wall, showing the change from stone to brick construction; south-facing section across the infilled basin

Fig. 25 The canal wall flanking the entrance to the basin

of the canal. Some 8.5 m east of the basin, the base of the back wall (at the rear of the towpath) changed from brickwork to stonework, with at least two courses of large stone blocks, mostly of sandstone (showing clear tooling marks) but including also a block of concretia/slag (Fig. 24, elevation 1). The lower of these stone courses was below the level of the water table but appeared to lie on a bed of concrete. The upper course was capped by a single surviving course of bricks. This stonework may represent the remains of an earlier phase of construction.

Abutting the south sides of the entrance walls were matching brick blocks or steps, bonded into the basin walls. That on the east measured 0.7 m by 1.3 m, but as it had been partly demolished it was not possible to determine the bond pattern, although the brickwork in the centre appeared to be random infill. That on the west, the top of which was two courses lower than the canal wall, measured 1.2 m by 1.5 m. It had an irregular bond and was partly covered by a screed of cement that also covered the adjacent face of the canal wall; behind it there was a roughly built, and possibly later, step made of broken half bricks.

The canal basin

The construction cut (31618) for the basin, revealed in section towards its north end, was 9.4 m wide with vertical sides cut into alluvium (31616). The gaps between the construction cut and the walls of the basin had been backfilled with a firm dark brown/black gravel (31620), overlain by a mixed rubble layer (31623) extending away from the basin above the alluvium, and possibly associated with a compacted tarmac surface (Fig. 24).

The basin was 70 m long, aligned at a slight angle to its entrance. At the north end it was 7.7 m wide *(c* 25 ft), but for 22 m at the south, within the site of the former goods shed, it narrowed on the east side to 4.9 m (16 ft) in order to accommodate the eastern of the two railway tracks that entered the shed from the south. The basin walls were 0.6 m wide, constructed of red brick with regular courses of English bond, and with cement mortar. The bricks measured 0.23 m by 0.11 m by 0.085 m (9 x 4¼ x 3¼ in). The wall was exposed to a maximum depth of 1.1 m in the south-west corner of the basin, revealing 12 courses of wall sitting on two foundation courses projecting 0.13 m out from the wall face.

Towards the south end of the basin a ceramic drainage pipe had been inserted through the upper course of the west wall. At intervals along the tops of the walls were a series of protruding 30 mm diameter metal rods with threaded ends, possibly for securing hand or guide rails or other fittings.

A machine excavated hole cut into the fill of the basin revealed that below a *c* 1 m thick layer of deliberate backfill (see below) there was a 0.6 m thick layer of organic dark grey/black clayey silt overlying a mid-brown/orange sterile clay at least 2.4 m deep.

The goods shed and crane

Remains of the goods shed covering the southern end of the basin (Fig. 21) were recorded. Its west wall, traced for *c* 15 m, was 0.3 m wide constructed of regular courses of brick; two wall courses and up to three foundation courses were exposed. The wall turned east at the south-west corner of the shed, being 0.6 m wide along the south end. After 1.1 m, a 2.8 m wide break marked the entrance for the western of the two railway tracks that entered the shed from the south. The wall then continued for a further 4 m, separated from the end wall of the basin by a gap of just 0.2 m, although its foundation courses abutted the basin wall. After a further 2.9 m wide break for the eastern railway track, the wall ran for a further 2.5 m to the south-eastern corner of the shed, with a short length of wall running south from near this corner. The east wall of the shed was not recorded.

On the east side of the basin was a brick base for a swivelling crane (Fig. 26). It measured 3 m by 3 m, being rounded on the east side. It was 0.4 m thick, the bricks

Fig. 26 The crane base

appearing to be poorly laid in no apparent order. The crane seems to have been set on a horseshoe-shaped bed of cement. On top of the bricks were the remains of a tiled surface, the red/bluish tiles, measuring 0.155 m *(c* 6 in) square and 0.032 m (1¼ in) thick, having been laid in a haphazard fashion. There were six, evenly spaced 30 mm diameter metal rods with threaded ends protruding through the centre of the tiled surface, presumably bolts by which the crane was secured.

Closure of the canal and basin

Following the closure of the canal, the basin was filled in (31622) and the ground levelled, predominantly with colliery waste. The backfill spread over the edge of the basin onto the adjacent tarmac surface, and was in turn overlain by further modern levelling layers. On the north side of the canal, the canal wall and all the associated layers exposed within the canal were covered by deposits of bank material (31636 and 31637) laid down during construction work on the A5 road to the north.

The bridges

The two bridges each had two arches, the southern arches spanning the Wash Brook, the northern arches spanning the former canal (Fig. 21). They were constructed of reddish-blue bricks, with regular English bond courses, bonded with a light grey cement, with flush pointing (in some areas re-pointed). As the bridges were set at an angle to the two watercourses, angled bricks were employed on the corners of the arches.

On the railway bridge, there were stepped brick mouldings at the top left and right corners of both the east- and west-facing abutments, and a single row of bricks overhanging each edge. Each face also had four large and five smaller bracing bosses above the level of the arches. Both arches displayed signs of re-building and re-pointing, with a number of cracks spanning the roofs of the arches. The south facing wall of the northern arch had a course of plinth-type bricks along its bottom edge, and at its right corner white brick quoins had been inserted at a later date; the other arch corners had been rebuilt using newer bricks.

The upper part of the south-east flanking wall had been rebuilt, with newer bricks used in places, and much of the wall had been re-pointed. The top course on the lower part of the wall consisted of bullnose bricks, but elsewhere these had been replaced by newer bricks. The upper part of the opposite flanking wall had also been rebuilt. In comparison to the bridge, this wall appears to have been poorly constructed, using bricks of varying size, and the wall displays a number of long cracks; it is possible that it was (re-)built at a later date. Approximately 11 m from the bridge this wall turned sharply to the north for a further 18 m, where one course in its face displayed a line of regularly spaced ¼-brick gaps, probably to aid drainage. The flanking walls on the western side of the railway bridge also showed signs of partial rebuilding.

The western flanking walls of the railway bridge joined to the smaller and lower accommodation bridge, on whose east and west faces the brickwork on the upper part of the parapet sloped to match the gradient of the footpath. The short flanking walls on the west side were topped, like those flanking the railway bridge, with a course of bullnose bricks.

A dividing wall ran between the canal and the brook, linking the central piers of both bridges, and continuing up to 10 m on either side.

Discussion

As at the Hawkins Basin (Site 1) to the west, the features recorded at this site – the canal and railway interchange basin, with its wharf crane base and the goods shed, and the railway and accommodation bridges – reveal the vital relationship between the local mining and manufacturing industries and the developing transport networks. It largely reflects the influence and interests of Thomas Gilpin, who in the first half of the 19th century was raising coal from his mines in Great Wyrley and Cheslyn Hay for, among other concerns, his edge tool factory at Churchbridge. It was largely on the basis of this network of interests that the Hatherton branch (also sometimes known as the Churchbridge Extension) of the Staffordshire and Worcestershire Canal was built in 1841. The surviving features at this site provide a clear illustration of the economic forces that shaped the surrounding area.

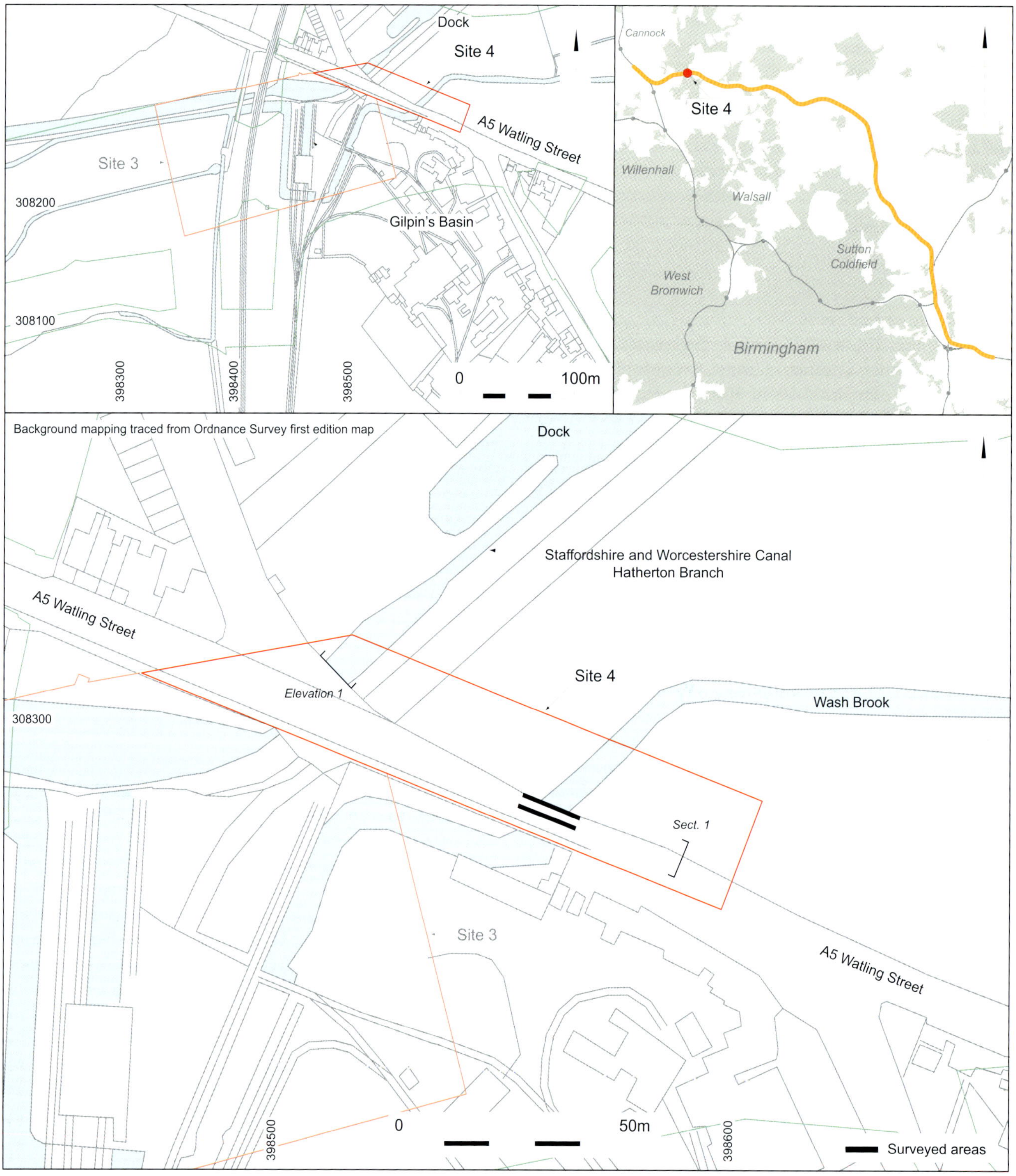

Fig. 27 Churchbridge Complex (Site 4)

Chapter 6
Churchbridge Complex (Site 4)

By Andrew B. Powell

Introduction

Two watching brief phases were undertaken on the A5 at Churchbridge, south of Cannock. The first comprised the excavation of a trench across the line of the A5 – which follows the line of the Roman road of Watling Street; the second involved the digital surveying of the bridge carrying the A5 over the Wash Brook.

The site, centred on NGR 398550 308290, was located on a decommissioned section of the A5, immediately east of Site 3, where the Wash Brook and the canal pass under the road (Fig. 27). The geology is mapped as Pleistocene Boulder Clay (Late Devension till), with alluvium along the course of the Wash Brook (Geological Survey of Great Britain 1954, Sheet 154, Lichfield).

The Roman road of Watling Street ran north-west from London across the Midlands to Wroxeter, and then on to the military districts of the north-west. It is likely to have continued in use in the Saxon period, its name, of Saxon origin, being interpreted as 'way of the sons of Waetla'. In the late 18th century, a new turnpike road was constructed along Watling Street by Thomas Telford. A bridge over the Wash Brook at this location is shown on a 17th century map of Staffordshire. Although it had been rebuilt several times, and the existing underside appeared to be largely of concrete, a 19th century sandstone parapet survived, and it was considered possible that elements of the 17th century bridge, or earlier bridges, may have survived within and beneath existing structure. A second bridge carried the road over the Hatherton branch of the Staffordshire and Worcestershire Canal.

A machine trench, measuring 13 m by 11 m, was excavated across the decommissioned A5 to the east of the Wash Brook bridge. The northern 4.5 m and the southern 2.5 m of the trench were abandoned after encountering live services. At the same time, a photographic record was made of the 19th century brick bridge carrying the A5 over the canal. Subsequently, the bridge over the Wash Brook was surveyed, accompanied by a digital photographic record to create a virtual model. Only those parts of the bridge that were exposed were recorded, and it was not possible to examine its foundations. No written record was made.

Results

A5 Watling Street

No remains that could be identified as belonging definitely to the Roman road were recorded in the section across the A5 (Fig. 28). At the base, overlying the natural gravel, were four dumped layers of mixed sand and gravel (contexts 26–23), representing levelling material on which had been laid a compacted road surface of sandy gravelly clay (22). The surface was indented by two wheel ruts (19 and 21), 0.6 m wide and up to 0.2 m deep, and 1.5 m apart centre to centre.

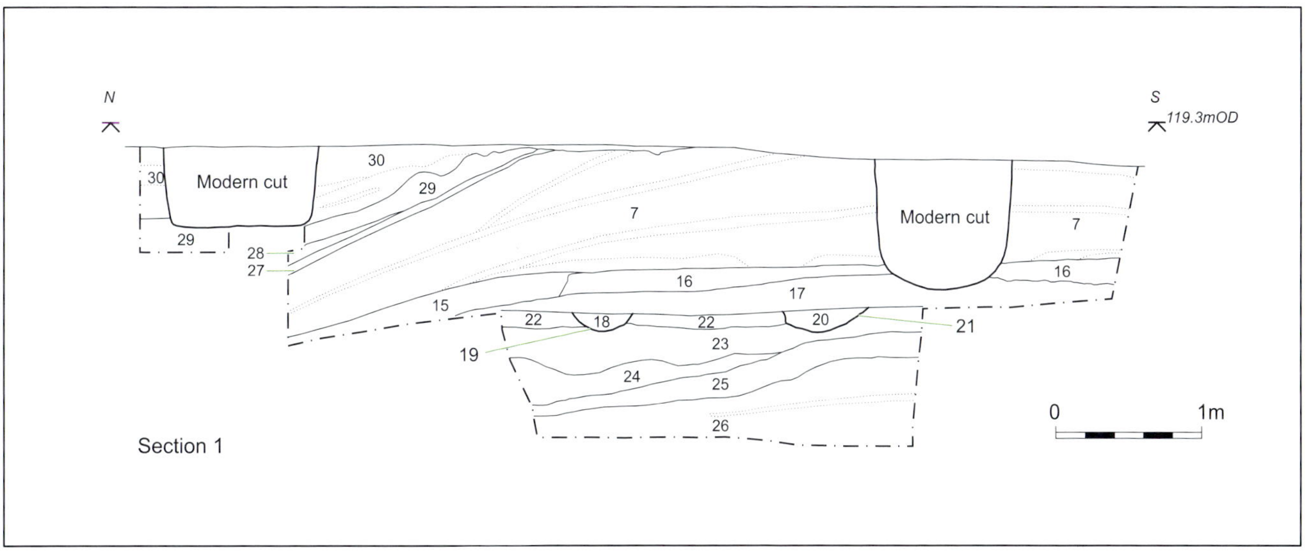

Fig. 28 West-facing section across the A5 Watling Street

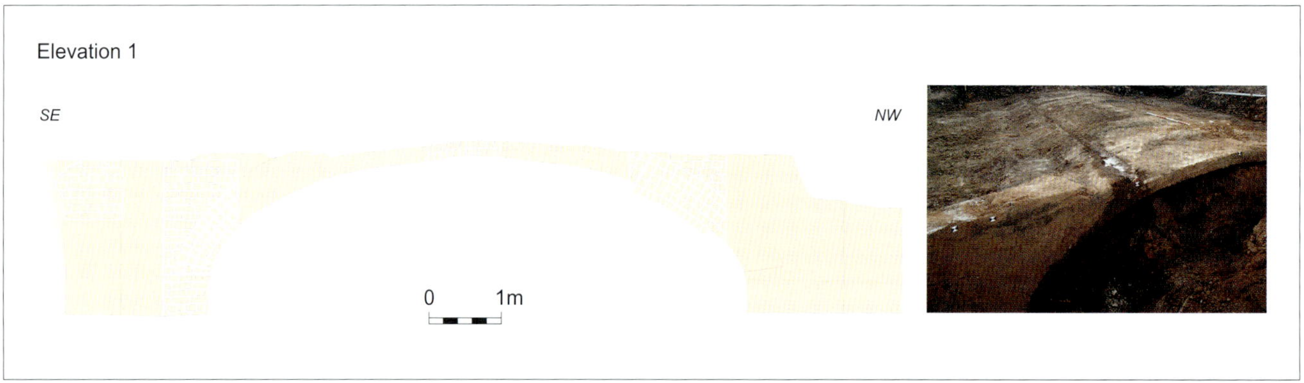

Fig. 29 Elevation and view from the north-east of the infilled bridge over the canal

No dating evidence was recovered from these layers. They are significantly different, however, from the cobbled road surface recorded on Watling Street at Hammerwich (Site 41) which was interpreted as probably representing the Roman road, or at Ryknield Street (Site 12).

This early road surface was sealed by further levelling deposits of clay and sandy gravel (17–15), on which a later surface of well compacted gravel (7) had been laid, sloping down towards the north edge of the road. These layers were also undated but may belong to Telford's late 18th century improvements along the Watling Street turnpike. A post-medieval road surface was also recognised at Hammerwich.

The uppermost 1 m of deposits relate to the construction of the present A5 and the backfills of modern service trenches (contexts 1–6, 8–14 and 27–30).

Fig. 30 The road bridge over the Wash Brook showing the relocated northern parapet

The canal bridge

A photographic and brief written record was made of the brick arch carrying the road over the canal (Fig. 29). It was 13 m long and 12 m wide, the canal at that point being 7.4 m wide. The upper part of the bridge had been demolished, but as it stood it was at least 2.2 m high; its full depth was not visible due to the water level and a gas main restricting access. The sides of the structure were constructed using English bond, with the arch made of four courses of headers. At some date after the closing of the canal a concrete culvert had been inserted beneath the arch.

The Wash Brook bridge

The bridge over the Wash Brook was digitally surveyed, although only its north-eastern side was fully recorded. The earliest visible elements of the structure appear to be of 19th century date, the bridge arch being constructed of sandstone blocks. The bridge had subsequently been widened on the north-east side, probably in response to heavier traffic in the 20th century (Fig. 30). The extension had a concrete arch with a bituminous waterproof covering on its exterior surface. At the same time, most of the original sandstone face and parapet on the north-east side was taken down and rebuilt over the extension. Because the level of the new road surface was high enough not to require the complete removal of the original stonework, the base of the wall was left in place, concealed within the bridge's structure.

The relocated parapet was 15 m long and curved outward at each end to octagonal piers topped by shallow pointed capstones. There was evidence of damage to the bridge, probably from traffic.

Chapter 7
Washbrook Lane, Norton Canes (Site 5)

By Carl Champness

Introduction

A targeted watching brief was undertaken on a site between Norton Canes and Great Wyrley, south-east of Cannock, in Staffordshire. The site, on the north side of the Roman road of Watling Street, was selected due to the presence, to its north, of cropmarks comprising a series of parallel linear features and a possible ovoid enclosure. The watching brief was changed to a full excavation following the discovery of ditches forming a Romano-British field system.

The site, covering *c* 1.64 hectares, centred on NGR 400560 307590, is situated on the north side of the A5, east of Washbrook Lane (Fig. 31). It lies just to the north of the road corridor, but was affected by the remodelling of the Washbrook Lane junction. The site lies on a flat plain at a height of 130.9–134.3 m aOD. The geology is mapped as Pleistocene Boulder Clay (Late Devension till) (Geological Survey of Great Britain 1954, Sheet 154, Lichfield). This consists of unstratified gravelly clays, with an expanse of periglacial patterning, comprising a series of interconnecting polygons filled with gravels and coarse material occupying the troughs. The soil was stripped from four wide strips running parallel to the A5, with an extension towards the north running adjacent to Westbrook Lane.

Results

The excavation revealed a series of ditches running parallel and perpendicular to the north side of the Roman road of Watling Street (the modern A5), forming a network of rectilinear field boundaries (Fig. 31). Superimposed upon and truncating them, across the site, were the remains of medieval ridge-and-furrow running perpendicular to the road. The areas where the ridge-and-furrow was preserved also contained the best preserved Romano-British features, suggesting that modern deeper ploughing was responsible for truncating archaeology in apparently blank areas of the site. A network of modern field boundaries and drains represented the present agricultural landscape in the area.

Romano-British

The Romano-British field system consisted of a series of shallow and ephemeral ditches and gullies that subdivided the landscape into rectangular fields aligned with reference to Watling Street. The majority of these field boundary ditches were shallow (50008, 50009, 50011, 50018, 50056, 50110, 50112, 50142, 50156 and 50164), between 0.12 m and 0.26 m deep and 0.35–0.90 m wide (Fig. 32). They generally had moderately sloping sides with a gentle transition into a concave/pointed base. They were typically filled with single deposits of mid-brown sandy silt that probably represented natural silting, and contained rare scatters of 2nd century Romano-British pottery and charcoal that are consistent with their interpretation as field boundaries. Ditch 50009 contained a slightly organic silty sand fill that produced pottery and charcoal, possibly providing evidence of manuring using rubbish deposits, as did an adjacent, slightly curved length of ditch (50011).

The most prominent ditch (50005), aligned NW–SE, was V-shaped, 1.25 m wide and 0.56 m deep, with steep sloping sides (Fig. 32). It had a sandy primary fill, and a secondary fill of loose dark brown sandy/silty clay representing the gradual silting up of the ditch with ploughsoil. It contained two sherds (118 g) of 2nd century Romano-British pottery and charcoal flecks. Ditch 50005 may have been one of the earliest ditches, possibly an ownership boundary, with the other, shallower ditches representing the later sub-division of individual fields, although where ditches intersected, excavation generally revealed that they were contemporary.

Associated with, but distinct from the field ditches was feature 50007, a shallow L-shaped gully possibly forming the north-east corner of a small rectangular enclosure. It was 0.35–0.4 m wide and 0.15 m deep, with well defined steep sides and a flat base, and its fill of greyish brown sandy silt containing frequent sub-rounded bunter cobbles and boulders (500242) may represent the erosion of a bank and/or dry-stone wall. Its southern end terminated near ditch 50008, whilst the north-western end had been truncated by medieval ridge-and-furrow. It contained three sherds (50 g) of 2nd century reduced coarse wares, and one (15 g) of black burnished ware.

A small oval pit (50048), measuring 0.6 m by 1.2 m, containing three Romano-British sherds, produced an assemblage of charred plant remains, including wheat, hulled barley, pea and beet, as well as mixed charcoal, probably the discard from a domestic hearth. A single posthole (50200), which produced two fragments (163 g) of locally produced Mancetter-Hartshill mortaria, had been significantly truncated by ploughing, indicating that subsequent cultivation may have removed other evidence of habitation.

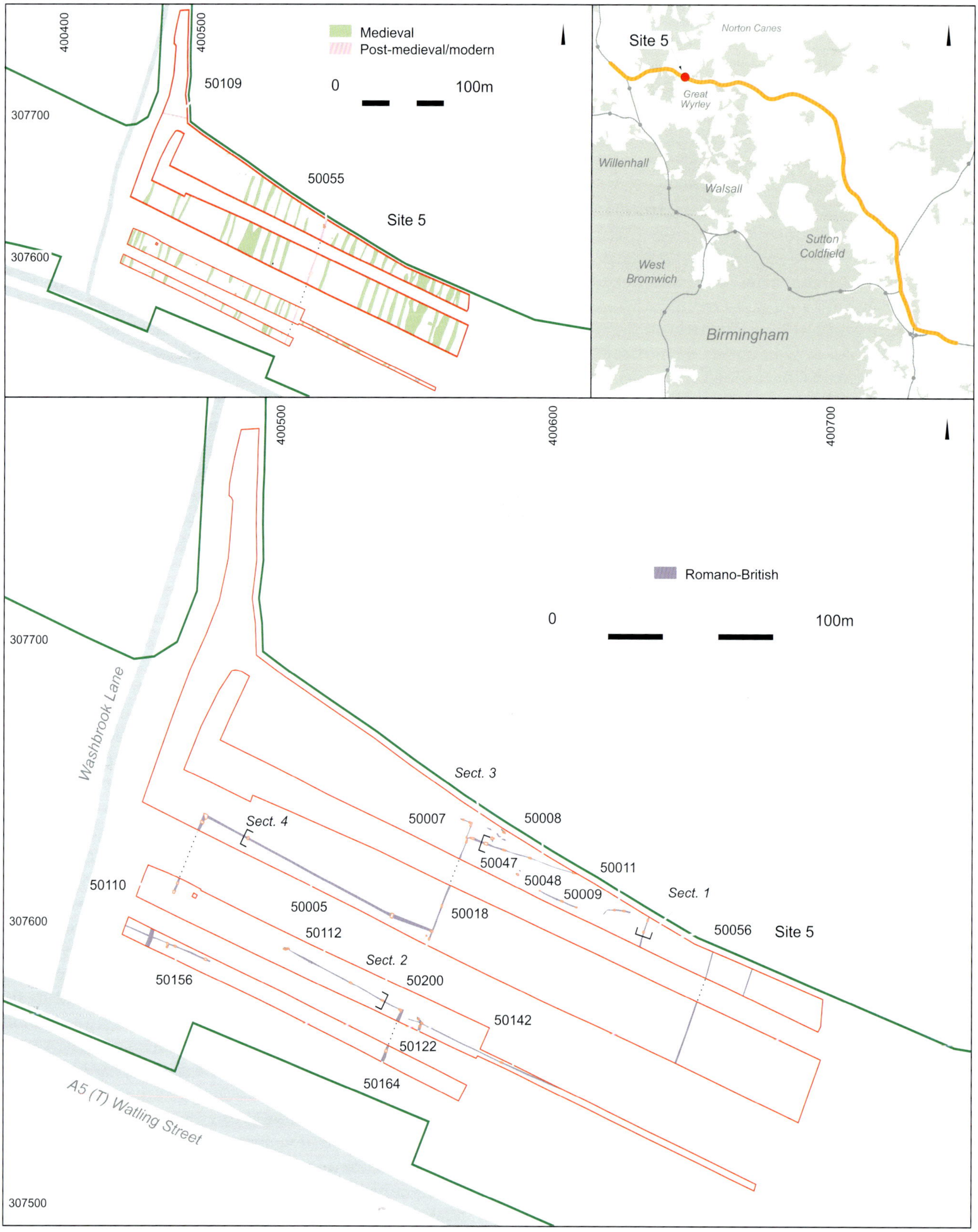

Fig. 31 Washbrook Lane (Site 5)

A short length of curved ditch (50122), which cut field ditch 50142, was one of the few features that had any stratigraphic relationship with the Romano-British field system. It was 1.2 m wide, 0.12 m deep and contained three sherds (30 g) of Romano-British pottery, and is of unknown function.

Medieval

The majority of Romano-British features were partly truncated by the remains of medieval ridge-and-furrow that ran NE–SW across the site and, like the earlier field system, was clearly oriented in relation to Watling Street.

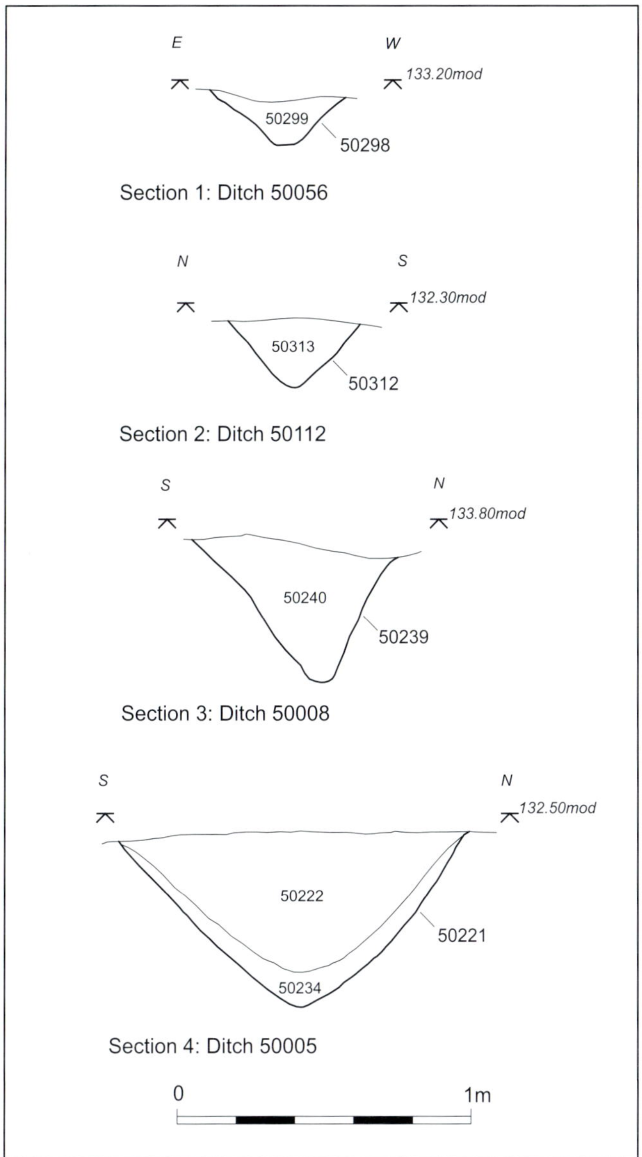

Fig. 32 Sections of Romano-British ditches 50056, 50112, 50008 and 50005

The furrows were 1.5–2.4 m wide and up to 0.2 m deep, and spaced on average 5–7 m apart, although many had been either disturbed or completely removed by modern ploughing.

Post-medieval and modern

Two modern field boundaries (50055 and 50109) and a network of ceramic field drains were recorded running NE–SW and E–W across the site. Both ditches had well defined edges and flat bases, and were probably dug by machine.

Undated

A cluster of irregular features near the northern edge of the site was investigated but proved to have poorly defined edges and undulating bases, measuring *c* 0.6 m wide, 1.8 m long and 0.2 m deep. They probably represent tree hollows.

Finds

Romano-British pottery, by Ruth Leary

A total of 70 sherds (1262 g) of Romano-British pottery was recovered from the site (Table 4).

Forms and fabrics

The most numerous wares were the reduced and oxidised groups (Table 5). The reduced wares did not include any of the Shenstone kiln fabrics (see Chapter 17), except R4, but comprised predominantly finer fabrics typical of the late 1st–mid-2nd century. Identifiable forms included three narrow-necked jars, an R15 carinated bowl and an R9 everted rim beaker. The beaker and narrow-necked jars are not closely datable and the carinated bowl is likely to be of mid-2nd century date. The oxidised wares included a storage jar, a wide-mouthed jar and a bowl in a form found in the Severn Valley ware range (Webster 1976, no. 50, dated late 2nd–late 3rd centuries). The Severn Valley ware wide-mouthed jar had the hooked rim found on types of the late 2nd–late 3rd centuries or later (Webster 1976, no. 26).

The imported wares comprised one Spanish Dressel 20 amphora sherd and a Central Gaulish form, Dr18/31 or 18/31R samian dish of Hadrianic–Antonine date. Traded wares included a Malvernian ware jar and a G2 jar, a type which seems to date to the late 1st–2nd centuries in north Warwickshire, a Mancetter-Hartshill mortarium, at least one BB1 jar of early–mid-2nd century type (Gillam 1976, no. 2) and probably two Severn Valley ware vessels.

Chronology and status

The sparse dating evidence suggests occupation probably from the early 2nd century, possibly extending into the 3rd century. The vessels and wares present indicate the proximity of a rural domestic settlement of fairly low status.

Environment

Charred plant remains, by A. J. Clapham

Six samples, each of ten litres were taken from Romano-British features during excavation. Only three samples were noted to contain charred plant remains, two from field ditches and one from a pit, and only these were analysed for charred plant remains. The number of remains in each sample was low and the material poorly preserved. The results are displayed in Table 6.

Ditches 50005 and 50009

The samples from the ditches were dominated by fragments of charcoal which had probably been discarded from domestic hearths. Charred plant remains were rare with only a glume base of emmer or spelt (*Triticum spelta/dicoccum*) and a single fragment of an

Table 4 Romano-British pottery: incidence of fabrics and forms by context

Ware	*Vessel form*	*Total*	*50008*	*50011*	*50056*	*50201*	*50207*	*50209*	*50231*	*50234*	*50240*	*50244*	*50252*	*50260*	*50266*	*50275*	*50280*	*50284*	*50308*	*50320*	*50327*
BB1		1	–	–	–	–	–	–	–	–	–	–	1	–	–	–	–	–	–	–	–
BB1	BB1 jar, fairly upright neck	1	–	–	–	–	–	–	–	–	–	–	–	–	–	–	1	–	–	–	–
BB1	closed vessel	1	–	–	–	–	–	–	–	–	–	1	–	–	–	–	–	–	–	–	–
DR20		1	1	–	–	–	–	–	–	–	–	–	–	–	–	–	–	–	–	–	–
G2		1	–	–	–	–	–	–	–	–	–	1	–	–	–	–	–	–	–	–	–
MALV	simple base	1	–	–	–	–	–	–	1	–	–	–	–	–	–	–	–	–	–	–	–
MH	simple base	2	–	–	–	2	–	–	–	–	–	–	–	–	–	–	–	–	–	–	–
O		2	–	–	–	–	–	–	–	–	–	–	–	–	–	–	–	–	–	2	–
O1		14	–	–	–	–	–	–	–	–	–	–	–	–	–	–	–	–	–	14	–
O1	Webster 50	3	–	–	–	–	–	–	–	3	–	–	–	–	–	–	–	–	–	–	–
O4		2	–	–	–	–	–	–	–	–	–	–	–	–	–	–	–	–	–	–	2
O5		2	–	–	–	–	–	–	1	–	–	–	–	–	–	–	–	–	1	–	–
O5	closed vessel	2	1	–	–	–	–	–	–	–	–	–	–	1	–	–	–	–	–	–	–
O9	storage jar, bead, undercut rim	1	1	–	–	–	–	–	–	–	–	–	–	–	–	–	–	–	–	–	–
R15	Carinated	6	–	–	–	–	–	–	6	–	–	–	–	–	–	–	–	–	–	–	–
R16	flange necked narrow-necked jar	2	–	–	–	–	–	–	–	–	–	–	–	–	–	–	2	–	–	–	–
R16	simple base	13	–	–	–	–	13	–	–	–	–	–	–	–	–	–	–	–	–	–	–
R4		1	–	–	1	–	–	–	–	–	–	–	–	–	–	–	–	–	–	–	–
R4	closed vessel	1	–	–	–	–	–	–	–	–	–	–	–	–	–	–	–	1	–	–	–
R4	everted rim narrow-necked jar	3	–	–	–	–	–	–	–	–	3	–	–	–	–	–	–	–	–	–	–
R9		3	–	–	–	–	–	–	–	–	–	–	–	–	1	2	–	–	–	–	–
R9	bead rim narrow-necked jar	1	–	–	–	–	–	–	–	–	–	–	1	–	–	–	–	–	–	–	–
R9	everted rim beaker	1	–	–	–	–	–	–	–	–	–	–	1	–	–	–	–	–	–	–	–
SV1	closed vessel	2	–	–	–	–	–	–	–	–	–	–	–	–	–	–	–	–	–	–	–
SV1	hooked rim	1	–	–	–	–	–	–	–	–	–	1	–	–	–	–	–	–	–	–	–
TS	DR18/31	2	–	2	–	–	–	–	–	–	–	–	–	–	–	–	–	–	–	–	–
Total		70	3	2	1	2	13	2	8	3	3	3	3	1	1	2	3	1	1	16	2
Date			2nd	early 2nd	Prob mid-2nd +	130/ 140+	Prob early–mid-2nd	2nd+	Mid–late 2nd	Late 2nd–late 3rd	2nd–4th	Late 2nd–late 3rd	120+	2nd+	2nd+	2nd+	Mid-2nd+	Prob mid-2nd+	2nd+	2nd+	2nd+

Table 5 Romano-British pottery: fabric quantification

Ware group	Ware	Vessel type	Form	Count	Weight (g)	Rim %	Rel % of count	Rel % of weight	Rel % of rim
A	DR20			1	165.4		1.4	13.1	
A total				*1*	*165.4*		*1.4*	*13.1*	
BB1	BB1			1	5		1.4	0.4	
	BB1	Jar		1	11.7		1.4	0.9	
	BB1	Jar	upright neck jar	1	14.5	9	1.4	1.2	6.9
BB1 total				*3*	*31.2*	*9*	*4.3*	*2.5*	*6.9*
G	G2			1	6.8		1.4	0.5	
	MAL V	Jar		1	81.6		1.4	6.5	
G total				*2*	*88.4*		*2.9*	*7.0*	
M	MH	Mortarium		2	162.2		2.89	12.9	
M total				*2*	*162.2*		*2.9*	*12.9*	
O	O			2	24.4		2.9	1.9	
	O1			14	23.3		20.0	1.9	
	O1	Bowl	Webster 1976, no. 50	3	71.4	16	4.3	5.7	12.2
	O4			2	19.7		2.9	1.6	
	O5			2	13.5		2.9	1.1	
	O5	Wide-mouthed jar		2	51.6			2.9	4.1
	O9	Storage jar	slightly hooked rim	1	203.8	12	1.4	16.2	9.2
O total				*26*	*407.7*	*28*	*37.1*	*32.3*	*21.4*
R	R15	Bowl	carinated	6	19.2		8.6	1.5	
	R16	Jar		13	47.8		18.6	3.8	
	R16	Narrow-necked jar	squared bead rim	2	43.4		2.9	3.4	
	R4			1	4.7		1.4	0.4	
	R4	Jar		1	37.1		1.4	2.9	
	R4	Narrow-necked jar	everted rim	3	61.3	22	4.3	4.9	16.8
	R9			3	63.2		4.3	5.0	
	R9	Beaker	everted rim	1	1.5	6	1.4	0.1	4.6
	R9	Narrow-necked jar	bead rim	1	43.7	25	1.4	3.5	19.1
R total				*31*	*321.9*	*53*	*44.3*	*25.5*	*40.5*
S	TS	Dish	Form 18/31	2	27.3	15	2.9	2.2	11.5
S total				*2*	*27.3*	*15*	*2.9*	*2.2*	*11.5*
SV	SV1			2	46.2		2.9	3.7	
	SV1	W-mouthed jar	hooked rim	1	12	26	1.4	1.0	19.9
SV total				*3*	*58.2*	*26*	*4.3*	*4.6*	*19.9*
Total				70	1262.3	131			

indeterminate cereal being found in ditch 50005 and a single seed of cleavers (*Galium aparine*) being identified from ditch 50009.

Pit 50048

The sample from pit 50048 contained more plant remains than the ditch samples; this is most likely a reflection of the larger size of the flot. A single grain of wheat was identified along with four of barley (*Hordeum vulgare*) of the hulled type. Other crops identified included pea (*Pisum sativum*) and beet (*Beta vulgaris*). Weed seeds included dock (*Rumex* sp.) and wild radish (*Raphanus raphanistrum*).

Conclusion

The paucity of charred plant remains means that it is not possible to provide a complete picture of the subsistence activities of this site, although the charred plant remains may represent dumping of the remains of domestic hearths into the ditches and pit, especially as they are associated with fragments of charcoal. It is possible to suggest that wheat – a hulled wheat, possibly spelt (*Triticum spelta*) – and hulled barley were cultivated, along with peas and beet. The presence of beet is of interest. The Romans are known to have cultivated beetroot and it is possible that it is this vegetable that is represented here. For a more complete picture of the agricultural activity in the area see Chapter 28, Environment and Agricultural Economy.

Table 6 Charred plant remains from Romano-British features

	Feature	Ditch 50005	Ditch 50009	Pit 50058
	Section	50221	50249	50251
	Context	50222	50250	50252
	Sample	53001	53005	53006
	Sample size (l)	10	10	10
	Flot size (ml)	40	80	750
Taxon	*Common name*			
Cereals				
Triticum sp. grain	Wheat	–	–	1
Triticum sp. glume base	Wheat	1	–	–
Hordeum vulgare hulled grain	Barley	–	–	4
Indet. cereal frags		1	–	–
Other crops				
Beta vulgaris	Beet	–	–	1
Pisum sativum	Pea	–	–	2
Other species				
Rumex sp.	Dock	–	–	1
Raphanus raphanistrum pod frag.	Wild radish	–	–	1
Galium aparine	Cleavers	–	1	–
Frag. Poaceae rhizome		–	–	1

Charcoal, by Rowena Gale

Localised burning activities were indicated by the presence of charcoal in all six of the samples that were taken during excavation, but it was unclear whether these were industrial or domestic in origin. The analysis of charcoal from pit 50048 and ditch 50008 was undertaken to indicate the character of the fuel and assess its origins. Preservation of the charcoal was poor and most fragments were permeated with reddish (?iron) deposits. The taxa identified are presented in Table 7.

Ditch 50008

The charcoal from the ditch fill (54240) was comminuted and degraded. It consisted mainly of oak (*Quercus* sp.) heartwood and roundwood, but also included birch (*Betula* sp.).

Pit 50048

A 25% sub-sample of the charcoal-rich deposit (50252) recovered from this small oval pit was difficult to examine due to extreme degradation. The charcoal identified was predominantly oak, mostly slow-grown heartwood but also sapwood and roundwood; the sample also included ash (*Fraxinus excelsior*), birch and the hawthorn/*Sorbus* group (Pomoideae). The pit also contained pottery and charred grains.

Table 7 Charcoal from features associated with the Romano-British field system (no. frags)

Feature	Context	Sample	Betula	Fraxinus	Pomoid.	Quercus
Ditch 50008	50240	53003	4	–	–	19h/u, 8r
Pit 50048	50252	53006	5	1	1	23h, 2r, 3s

Key: h = heartwood; r = roundwood (diam. <20 mm); s = sapwood (diam. unknown); u = maturity unknown (*Quercus* only)

Discussion

The samples from the ditch and pit produced fairly moderate deposits of charcoal. The charcoal was similar and thus may have had a common origin, which although unknown, clearly represents dumps of fuel debris. The frequency of oak heartwood suggests that this was the preferred fuel, although birch, ash and the hawthorn group were also employed. In the absence of supporting evidence from artefactual material, it is difficult to assign the charcoal to a specific use. The presence of charred cereal and other crop remains in pit 50048 may suggest that the deposit is related to domestic waste (see Clapham above), although other agricultural, such as the clearance of shrub or hedges, or industrial origins can not be ruled out.

A relatively narrow range of species was identified: oak, ash, birch and the hawthorn group, and given the open nature of the field system, woodland may have been fairly sparse in the immediate locality. It is feasible that the ditches were defined by hedges and, perhaps, hedgerow trees. The slow growth, such as that recorded in the oak charcoal, however, is more indicative of trees growing in competitive or stressed conditions. This implies either that there were stands of woodland relatively close to the site, or that firewood was brought in from further afield. There was no evidence to suggest that supplies were obtained from managed woodland.

Discussion

The differential preservation of archaeological features recorded across the site, affected both by medieval ridge-and-furrow and by modern deep ploughing, significantly hampered the interpretation of both individual features, and groups of features.

The Romano-British field system comprised an array of rectangular fields to the north of the Roman road, with evidence for the cultivation of wheat, hulled barley, peas and beet. Gaps between some ditches would have provided access between the fields, and other features may indicate the presence of small ditched enclosures, possibly also defined by banks and/or dry-stone walling, as well as nearby settlement activity. The recovery of a small assemblage of Romano-British pottery and scatters of charcoal from some of the ditches may reflect the practice of manuring with domestic waste, some of which was also dumped in the a pit and ditch. The pottery forms and fabrics indicate the presence within the vicinity of a rural settlement of fairly low status.

Although the extent of the field system could not be determined, many of the NW–SE aligned linear cropmarks to the north of the site are likely to be a continuation of it. Judging by the intensity of the cropmarks to the north, this area could contain a much greater concentration of surviving archaeological features with the potential to shed additional light on the activities in this site. Examples of large-scale planned Romano-British field systems are known from across the country (Dark and Dark 1997) and in places may represent a reorganisation of the landscape geared towards a market/military based economy. As there was no evidence for earlier field systems or activity on the site, it is possible that organised agricultural production along Watling Street was a response to the demand for foodstuffs generated by the establishment of forts and towns and the imposition of taxation.

The pottery dates the activity on the site to the early 2nd to 3rd centuries AD. The absence of late Romano-British material may reflect either the abandonment of the fields, a move away from the practice of manuring, or reversion to pasture during the later Romano-British period. Whatever the case, the demand for such a system of production would have been unnecessary in the post-Romano-British period with the decline in Roman villas and towns, and the landscape does not appear to have been reorganised again until the medieval period, as represented by the ridge-and-furrow.

Chapter 8

Swan Farm, Norton Canes (Site 36)

By Andrew B. Powell

Introduction

A rapid building survey was conducted of the brick farmhouse at Swan Farm, Norton Canes, south-west of Cannock, in order to provide a record of its observable fabric and structure prior to demolition. A number of episodes of building and alteration were noted, dating from the 18th century through the 20th century. The building had suffered from subsidence caused by coal mining.

The farmhouse, centred on NGR 400700 307460, stood on the immediate north side of the A5 Watling Street facing west-south-west (for ease of reference its front elevation is described below as south-facing) (Fig. 33). It had formed part of a larger complex of farm buildings extending to the north and east, most of which had been demolished before the survey was undertaken. A hand drawn plan of the ground floor was made at a scale of 1:50. The outside of the building was photographed using colour slide and black and white print film (35 mm format), and both the inside and outside were recorded using a digital camera. The photographic record was supplemented by written notes made at the time of survey.

Results

Two main phases of construction are evident in the layout and fabric of the building, although within both

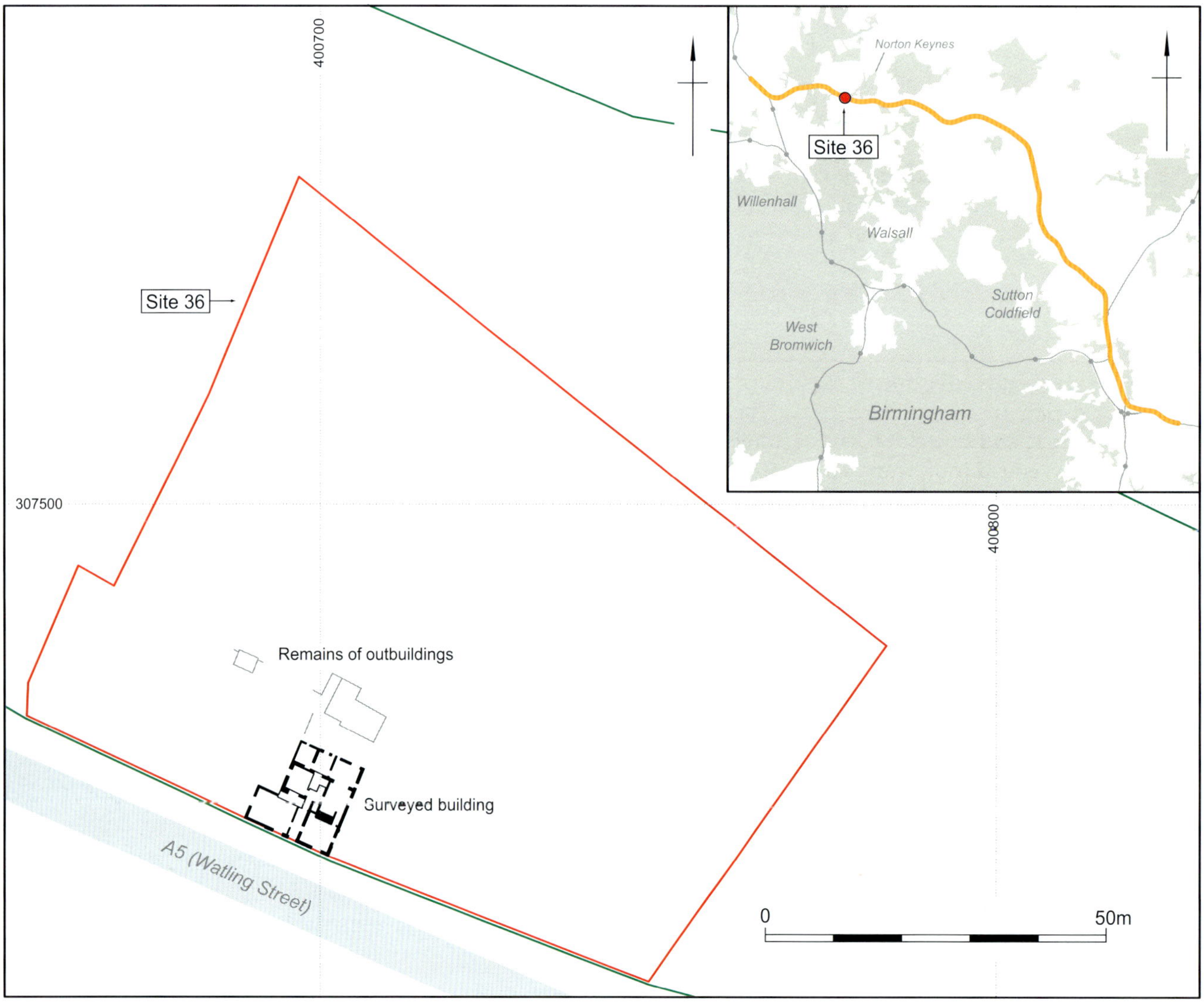

Fig. 33 Swan Farm (Site 36)

Fig. 34 Suggested phase plans of ground and first floors

phases there appear to have been a series of further additions and modifications (Fig. 34). Unfortunately, the rapid survey did not afford the opportunity for them to be examined in sufficient detail for more than the following tentative interpretation.

Phase 1

Phase 1 represents the main part of the building, probably dating to the 18th century. This comprised most of its front and side elevations, its three storeys and its tiled, gable-ended roof, with two main roof ridges and a low central ridge running between them. However, although this would appear on the surface to represent a single phase of construction, a number of anomalous features in its structure suggest, in fact, two distinct, although near-contemporary, construction phases (phases 1A and 1B), and a further phase of modification, particularly in relation to the windows (phase 1C), and subsequent remedial work in the face of subsidence in the western half of the building (phase 1D).

Phases 1A and 1B

The anomalous features include a small two-light window in the west wall of the ground floor stairwell, indicating that this wall must originally have been an external wall. The window had external hinges indicating that it opened outwards. The presence of this window suggests that the phase 1A building comprised (on the ground floor) only the two front rooms, the hallway between them leading to the rear staircase, and a rear room at the north-east. The presence of an open courtyard at the north-west corner is supported by the fact that brickwork, exposed in the attic, on the south side of that courtyard, was externally pointed (Fig. 35). The north-west quarter of the building, therefore, was added at a later date (phase 1B), as evident in the straight joint between its western wall and the externally pointed wall. The fact that it was constructed in exactly the same style as the phase 1A structure, however, may indicate that only a relatively short time had elapsed since the original construction.

The main elements of the front elevation also belong to Phase 1A, including the four 16-light sash windows, two on the ground floor and two above (Fig. 36). The

Fig. 35 External pointing in the south wall of the north-west attic room

Fig. 36 The front elevation

windows were of typical 18th century style, with rubbed brick, flat (skewback) arches above; the ground floor arches had been rendered over. While a faint joint scar in the brickwork in the centre of the first floor, above and to the right of the front door, might suggest the location of a blocked window, this seems unlikely given that it appears to be on the line of the internal wall between the two front rooms, and may simply indicate later repair or re-pointing.

It is notable that, although the arrangement of the four front windows was symmetrical, the door was placed left of centre. Moreover, chopped brickwork around the door suggests that the doorway which, unlike the front windows, had a curved arch above it, had been rebuilt.

The brickwork on the front elevation, which was mainly Flemish bond (alternate courses of headers and stretchers), showed many other signs of repair and re-pointing, and it had a random bond where it had been rebuilt with different bricks at the south-east corner. There was a rendered over plinth at the base, extending as far as the eastern window, beyond which the wall had been repaired. There was a treble string course above the ground floor (but not above the first floor as on the side elevations).

Fig. 37 The east elevation

Fig. 38 The west elevation

The eastern elevation had a mixture of brickwork bonds (most of the ground floor brickwork appearing to have been rebuilt at a later date). Three of the first floor windows and both of those in the attic floor had curved soldier arches, probably contemporary with the flat arched windows at the front, and it is likely that the fourth first floor window (later replaced) had originally been the same (Fig. 37). The original form and location of the ground floor windows, however, is uncertain due to the rebuilding of the ground floor wall. It is possible that the front range had a single window, or a pair of side windows, to match both those above and those in the rear range.

The western elevation provided no clues about the ground floor front range windows, since the wall of the front range had been cut through for the later extension (phase 2B), and only the top of an arched attic floor widow was visible above the extension roof. The rear range of the western elevation had, like the eastern elevation, pairs of windows on both floors (Fig. 38). This wall had an irregular bond comprising mostly stretchers, but with some headers, and there was a rendered over brick plinth along its base.

Phase 1C

Following the completion of the phase 1A–1B building, there were significant modifications to the external appearance of the resulting structure, in relation to the style and configuration of its windows. This involved the blocking of many of the earlier windows (possibly in response to the window tax that was levied between 1696 and 1851) and the replacement of others.

On the eastern elevation, four windows had been bricked in (three in the first floor and one on the attic floor). On the western elevation, the attic floor window of the front range had been bricked in (the rest of the range being concealed by the phase 2 extension), while on the rear range the forward of the pairs of windows on both the ground and first floors had been blocked.

It appears that the blocking of some windows provided the opportunity at this time to replace the remaining ground and first floor side windows, which showed evidence of relaid brickwork and different mortar in their surrounds. The neo-classical style of the new windows, with marginal panes of glass and decorated stone lintels, helps date this phase to the early 19th century (the remaining attic floor widows contain modern frames).

It seems the opportunity was also taken to rebuild the ground floor wall on the eastern side, the brickwork displaying a variable bond. During this process only two windows, in the same neoclassical style, were inserted – in the rear range in the place of the rearward of the two earlier windows, and in the front range in the centre of the wall.

Phase 1D

There is evidence that the western part of the house was subject to significant subsidence, causing damage to its structure and requiring considerable remedial work. This involved the massive thickening of the south wall of the northern range, significantly reducing the sizes of the north-west rooms of both the ground and first floors. The strengthened wall was now 1.7 m thick, extending part way across already blocked forward windows in these rooms. Some of the additional brickwork was visible in a straight joint in the hallway wall.

In addition, a series of external steel ties were put in place linking angled bracing plates attached to the brickwork at the corners of the building. The ties ran approximately level with the tops of both the ground floor and first floor windows on the east, south and north elevations. They ran behind the two phase 2 extensions on the west and north sides

The phase 1 interior

Behind the front door was the hallway from which the front and rear rooms on either side, and the staircase, were accessed. Although 1.5 m wide at the front, it seems likely that the hallway had originally been only *c* 1 m wide, which was the width some 4 m to the rear, between the front and rear ranges (Fig. 39). This widening involved the replacement of the wall between the hallway and the south-west room with a thin partition wall set back some 0.5 m from its original line (although reusing the original door frame). This may have been associated with the insertion of a new front door (above), which was placed centrally to the widened hallway.

Fig. 39 The hallway widened towards the front

The south-east ground floor room was entered from the hall through a six-panelled door with moulded door surrounds. The front sash window had shutters, and there was a chimney protruding from its back wall containing a modern fireplace. A door and short passage to the right of the fireplace, leading to the room behind, may not be an original feature, perhaps being inserted at the time of the phase 1C rebuilding of the ground floor east wall.

The rear room had a window in its east wall, but its rear wall had been broken through to link it to the phase 3 kitchen extension (below). The chimney on its south side contained a modern inglenook fireplace with a slightly arched bressumer, the eastern end of which was supported by a circular, cast-iron heck post. There was a corner cupboard in the north-west corner of the room, and a four-panelled, two-lighted doorway in the west wall.

This door, which had a simple latch, led back out into the hallway at the bottom of the staircase. On the south side of the stairwell was a door leading down to the cellar under the front room (this was filled with rubbish and not examined); this six-panelled, latched door to the cellar seemed to be contemporary with those leading from the hall to the front rooms. The south-west ground floor room was entered from the hall through a six-panelled door (similar to that on the east side), while the room behind had been significantly reduced in size by the phase 1D strengthening of the intervening wall.

The dog-leg staircase rose from the back of the hallway to the first floor and attic floor landings. It had a moulded handrail and turned balusters, and the central square-sectioned newel post survived right to the top of the stairs.

On the first floor, the south-east room had its original skirting and an ornate Georgian fire surround with floral garlands and fluted panels, and a moulded wooden mantel. The original door, in its moulded frame, had six plain panels and a pierced decorative hand-plate. The window had double panel shuttering. The south-west room had similar features.

The north-east room, which also had a similar door, had a blocked up fireplace with its surround removed, revealing a brick arch over the main opening. The inserted early 19th century sash window had no shutters. The north-west room had a Victorian fireplace, and like the room below, had been reduced in size by the strengthening of its south wall.

There were four garret rooms on the attic floor, accessed from an upper landing at the top of the staircase. The front rooms had Victorian fixtures and fittings, including fireplaces and surrounds. As the gable windows in the front rooms had been blocked this would have left them without light until the later insertion of dormer windows at the front (possibly in phase 2A when the rear extension also included a dormer window).

The presence of modern frames in the gable windows of the rear attic rooms may indicate these, too, had been blocked, but later re-opened. In the rear room on the east side a small fireplace and chimney had been added to the eastern side of the original chimney breast, bonded with a straight join. There was no equivalent fireplace in the western rear room, the brickwork of the chimney being externally pointed.

The roof was double-purlined, one of the purlins being a reused timber with an empty mortice and two peg holes. The rafters were wooden pegged to the top purlin, and joined to the ridge beam by mortice and tenon joints and wooden pegs.

Phase 2

There was no physical relationship between the two extensions that were added to the rear and the west side of the phase 1 building, and little in their respective and distinct characters to determine their relative dating. For this reason they are assigned to sub-phases 2A and 2B, although this does not imply that one was earlier than the other. Moreover, the irregular character of the rear extension suggests that its final form was the product of an extended process of rebuilding and modification, and this may well have spanned the point in time when the western extension was added.

The steel bracing ties added to the main building in phase 1D were not extended around the rear extension, although similar ties were installed around the western extension.

Fig. 40. The rear extension

Phase 2A

This phase saw the addition of a two-storey extension at the rear comprising three rooms on each floor (Fig. 40). It had a lean-to roof, blended into the original roof (Figs 37–8), across the full width of the building at the rear. The extension's first floor was accessed through an opening cut through the rear wall of the phase 1 building from halfway up the ground to first floor staircase (possibly at the location of an existing window lighting the lower part of the staircase). The extension, up a further three steps from this point, was, therefore, at a lower level than the first floor of the main building. A central dormer window was inserted in the extension roof to light the upper part of the staircase.

On the eastern elevation, the ground floor brickwork had been keyed into the phase 1 wall, but on the first floor and above there was a straight joint capped by a chimney stack. The rear elevation, the lower half of which was whitewashed, was quite irregular, and appears to have included at least two sub-phases, as well as other modifications. A step in the brickwork suggests that the eastern two-thirds was a separate build from the western one-third. The eastern part contained two unmatched windows and a back door on the ground floor (the western of the two windows had been later split into two parts by an internal wall). It appears that the door had been moved to the west, opening into a small central room, the original doorway having been bricked up.

The eastern ground floor room consisted of an extended kitchen created by breaking through the rear wall of the phase 1 building. It had a small, two-light window on its eastern wall. The room above, with a blocked fireplace in its south-east corner, had a modern window on its east side, possibly replacing what appeared to be a blocked window on its rear wall. The adjacent toilet, above the new doorway, had a four-light sash window.

It is possible that these various modifications were contemporary with the addition of the western end of the rear extension, which had an irregular bond and a straight joint to the existing brickwork. This part comprised a ground floor room with a small six-light casement window (not designed to open) to the rear and a low three-light window to the west, and a sealed room, possibly with a bricked in rear-facing window, above. The sealed room had originally been entered down two steps from the north-west room of the phase 1 building where an interruption to the skirting and a scar on the back wall indicated the position of the doorway.

The western corner of the rear extension appears to have been rebuilt, although the new brickwork matches that on its western face, raising the possibility that the entire western face of the extension had been rebuilt, possibly due to damage from subsidence. This brickwork, comprising sequences of three stretcher courses and one header course, was keyed into the phase 1 wall to its full height (in contrast to the eastern elevation).

Phase 2B

This phase saw the addition of a two-storey extension with a hipped roof onto the west of the front range, comprising the extension to the ground floor room, and the addition of a first floor room. The brickwork bond comprised sequences of three stretcher courses and one header course.

The phase 1 western wall of the ground floor room had been cut through to create a single large room, with large patio doors under a flat arch of gauged bricks in its western end. The fireplace had been moved to the western end of the original rear wall, so that it occupied a more central position within the extended room.

Access to the additional first floor room, which was at a slightly raised level, was through a door cut through the phase 1 wall at the likely point of its rearward window, and up two steps. This room had a large, west-facing six-light window with a wooden lintel.

Outbuildings

To the rear of the farmhouse were a number of surviving outbuildings. They included, at the east, a single storey brick building, recently used as a store. It had a large chimney with the remains of a boiler and under-grate, which suggests that this structure may have been used as a wash house. It is possible that the boiler is a later adaptation of an earlier forge, suggesting a possible earlier use as a smithy (Fig. 41). There was evidence of a rebuild in the brickwork on the front. The small extension to the west, probably used as a store or a toilet, was also a later build. Another small brick structure to the west may have been a store or shed.

Fig. 41 The outhouse

Discussion

As a substantial farmhouse fronting onto Watling Street, Swan Farm was clearly intended to make an impression, and although the essential structure of the building was established from the start, the various phases of construction suggested above indicate that a number of factors influenced its subsequent development. These include the desire to enlarge the farmhouse by extending it to the west and rear. Although there was accommodation in the attic, the temporary blocking of the attic windows, possibly in response to the window tax, suggests that this may not have been continuous. Changing fashions also appear to have played a part, particularly in the details of the architecture, such as in the windows and the front door. Perhaps the main factor, however, was the severe subsidence suffered by the farmhouse during the course of its life due to coalmining. Although this appears not to have deterred its occupants from both extending the building, and undertaking repeated remedial repairs, its effects are clearly visibly both internally and externally – in the off-square door frames (Fig. 39), the bracing ties and the areas of rebuilt brickwork – giving the building, in the end, a rather ramshackle appearance.

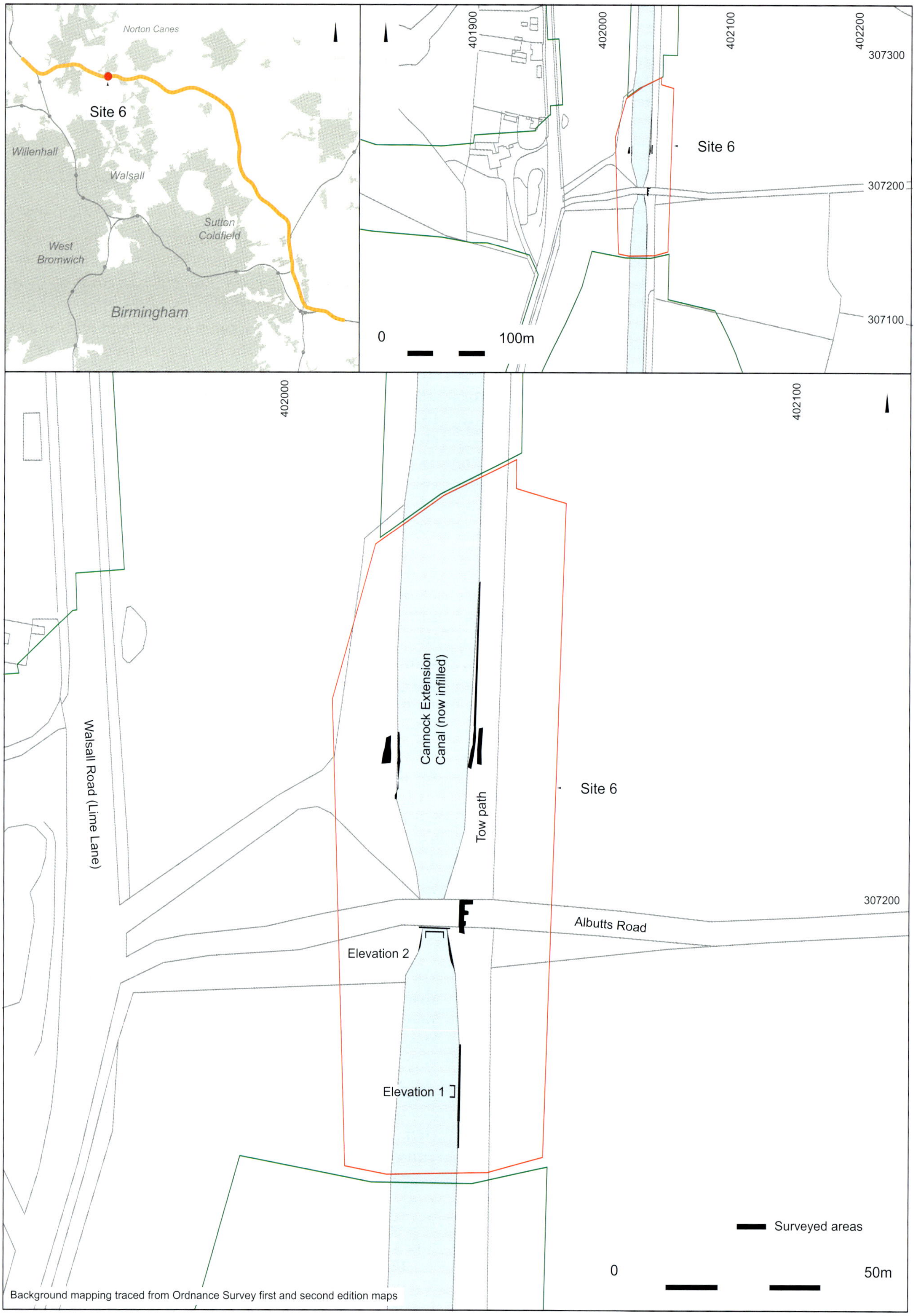

Fig. 42 Cannock Extension Canal (Site 6)

Chapter 9
Cannock Extension Canal (Site 6)

By Jonathan Gill

Introduction

An archaeological watching brief was undertaken where the M6 Toll cut at a right angle through the disused Cannock Extension Canal, in order to record the canal and any canal-related features exposed by the construction works prior to their removal. The profiles of the walls of the canal were revealed, as were a set of brick foundations which appeared to be the remains of a small bridge, and a series of overlying timber beams which may have tied the bridge foundations together.

The site covered *c* 0.5 hectares, centred on NGR 402030 307210, *c* 250 m to the north of the A5 on the south side of Norton Canes (Fig. 42). The geology is mapped as Pleistocene Boulder Clay (Geological Survey of Great Britain 1954, Sheet 154, Lichfield).

The main archaeological watching brief was undertaken over an area of *c* 135 m by 40 m where the construction for the new road cut through the former canal. The cut exposed the truncated ends of the canal walls, as well as other elements of the canal structure, and the investigation included the areas at either end of the cut where the embanked former canal remained *in situ*. The main recording works were undertaken on the surviving walls and bank of the canal, immediately south of the cut, where a plan and elevation of the walls were drawn by hand after the structure had been cleaned. A second area of recording concentrated on a timber structure which appears to have been the base of the former bridge and which was exposed by the construction works within the cut.

Historical background

The particular interest of the Cannock Extension Canal is that it represents one of the very last significant developments of the canal network in the country. It was constructed well into the railway era when investment into canals was very limited due to competition from railways and when the national rail network was expanding rapidly.

The act for the Cannock Extension Canal was first passed in 1854 and the canal was opened in stages between 1858, when the southern half was completed, and 1863 when it was extended to Hednesford Basin in the north. The stimulus for the construction of the Cannock Extension, as well as several other new canal branches in the same area, was the Cannock Chase coalfield, the importance of which developed rapidly in the mid-19th century with many new deep mines able to reach previously inaccessible mineral reserves.

The new canals extended the Birmingham Navigations northwards and linked the Cannock Chase collieries with the industrial works of the Black Country as well as with the wider canal system and with railway basins where coal could be transferred to the rail network. The 1 inch Ordnance Survey map of 1898 demonstrates the industrial nature of the canal and of the character of the mining landscape surrounding it. It shows a great many collieries punctuating the landscape to either side of the canal and with most of these connected to the canal by short branch tramways or railway lines which would have terminated at small wharves or basins. Among the collieries close to the Cannock Extension and connected to it were Conduit Colliery, Brownhills Colliery, Wyrley Grove Colliery and Cannock and Leacroft Colliery. Evidence of former collieries can still be seen along the navigable stretch of the canal including the trace of a former colliery basin south of the point where Lime Lane (B4154) passes over the canal.

The canal, which was *c* 8 km long, was a narrow gauge canal and contained no locks. The southern third, which largely survives today, extended in a dead straight, northward line from the Pelsall Junction of the Wyrley and Essington Canal as far as Norton Canes. From here it diverged north-westwards towards Rumer Hill, close to where it connected with the Hatherton branch of the Staffordshire and Worcestershire Canal via the Churchbridge Locks, and then on in a north-easterly direction to Hednesford Basin on the 473 foot level.

The second edition 25 inch:1 mile Ordnance Survey map (Fig. 43) shows in some detail the layout in 1902 of the site, where the M6 Toll has now cut the canal. The map shows that towards the centre of the site the canal narrowed and at this point a small bridge (Nortongreen Bridge) carried Albutts Road over the canal. A towpath is shown on the east side of the canal and a small wharf on the west side, immediately north of Nortongreen Bridge. To the north side of Albutts Road the maps show that the canal required much more substantial embankments to either side than to the south of the road suggesting that the surrounding ground level was lower to the north than to the south. This is also reflected in the fact that the maps show marshy land to the north and a field system to the south.

The Cannock Extension Canal remained in use into the 20th century but by the middle of the century it was suffering serious subsidence from previous mining in the

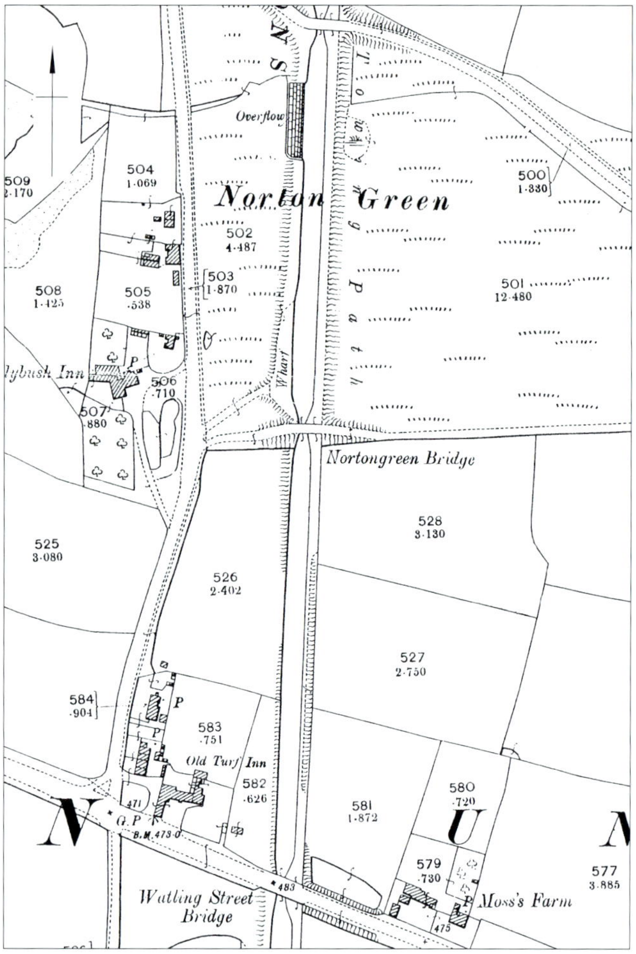

Fig. 43 2nd edition OS map of the site

area including a single week in 1960 when a section of the canal is reported to have dropped by 21 ft or 6.4 m (http://www.lhcrt.org.uk/history.htm). The line between the A5 and Hednesford Basin was abandoned by 1963.

Less than half of the original Cannock Extension Canal retains water and remains navigable. The surviving 2.5 km section extends from Pelsall Junction to a boatyard immediately south of the A5 (Watling Street) in Norton Canes. Immediately north of the A5 the line of the dry and partially infilled canal remains visible but after *c* 200 m it is cut by the new M6 Toll. Beyond this there is a *c* 500 m section where the canal has been fully infilled, although its line remains visible, but this is then truncated by an industrial estate which has been built over the canal and which completely hides the point where the canal formerly diverted to the north-west.

Much of the line of the northern two-thirds of the canal has been obliterated by various developments, including the Cannock eastern bypass which has been constructed directly over a section of the canal, but there are some small areas where its line is visible and there are a limited number of other features which provide evidence of its former existence. Among these is the west side of Norton Common Bridge (www.btinternet.com/~canals/canals/wyrleyessingtonroute.htm#cannock).

Results

Prior to the construction of the M6 Toll the canal held no water in the area of the site, but its line was apparent from a substantial embankment to either side which raised the level of the canal above the surrounding area. The outline of the wharf also remained visible on the ground as a widening to the embankment and the path up the embankment which allowed access to the wharf was also clear. The line of the former Albutts Road on the west side of the canal was also visible supported by a tapering embankment clearly shown on the OS map (Fig. 43). This road was historically carried over the canal by Nortongreen Bridge but this had been long demolished before any works had started on the M6 Toll.

At the base of the intersection between the embankments supporting the west side of the canal and the south side of Albutts Road was a brick wall, *c* 4 m long by 1.25 m tall which retained the base of the embankment and below which drained a significant water channel. This channel, which is presumably related to the former canal, extended westwards across the marshy field and continued beneath Lime Lane through a purpose-built culvert. The brick structure at the base of the embankment was heavily overgrown with vegetation at the time of the survey and its original form had been substantially hidden by this and by the partial collapse of the upper courses of brickwork. The lower half of the structure had been reinforced with a concrete beam and later brickwork but the upper half, which appeared to be primary, was constructed with old English bond Staffordshire Blue bricks, used widely on the Cannock Extension and other canals in this area.

The original purpose of the brick structure is not fully clear. It is possible that a small culvert was constructed beneath the canal to drain the surrounding fields but no such drain is shown on the 25 inch map and there was not a clear opening for a culverted drain within the brickwork. This may be because the lower half of the structure has been reconstructed in the 20th century. The wall may have been a section of retaining wall added at the point where the embankments meet.

The canal walls

The walls of the canal were brick built and were *c* 0.5 m in width. They were *c* 13 m apart in the surviving area immediately to the south of the excavation which provides the width of the canal in this area. The bricks on the east side were of a type stamped with the name 'Utopia' and these contrast with the bricks on the western side, which may indicate later repairs to the walls. Immediately to the south of the cut there is evidence of a substantial rebuild to the east wall where a large section of later brick (701059), *c* 2.5 m tall, has been constructed beneath what appears to be the surviving primary uppermost four courses (701005)

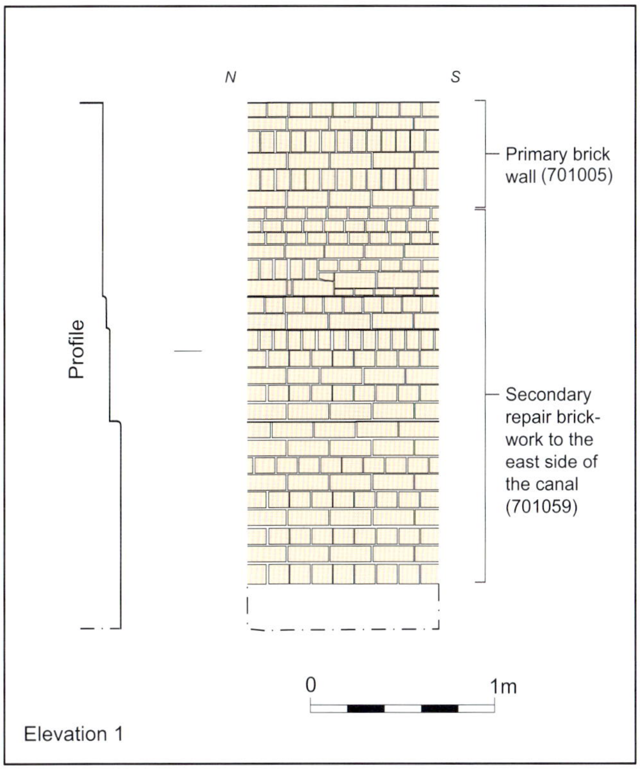

Fig. 44 Sample elevation of the rebuilt canal wall

(Fig. 44). These bricks were orange, in contrast to the original blue engineering bricks, and they were laid in an inconsistent English bond. At three points the coursing in these later bricks stepped out with bullnose special bricks. It is known that in the 20th century sections of the Cannock Extension Canal suffered from considerable mining subsidence and this may have necessitated the reconstruction of this wall.

Evidence indicates that, following the construction of the canal, a large amount of industrial waste and clay was deposited either side to provide support for the walls. The main bank of the canal which butts up against the clay deposits is a deposit of silty sand which also included industrial waste.

Excavations for the road construction did not reach the base of the canal and it was not therefore possible to see if it had been lined with bricks or clay. The whole of the canal appears to have been filled with industrial debris following its disuse.

The wharf

The site of the former wharf shown on historic maps was investigated for evidence of initial groundworks such as piling or foundations but neither evidence of this, nor of any structures used to transfer goods between the wharf and the barges, was recorded. The wharf was presumably a small simple platform where relatively small quantities of goods could have been manually loaded or unloaded.

Possible bridge foundations

Other than the canal walls the only feature revealed by the excavation was what appears to have been a set of foundations for the former Nortongreen Bridge which carried Albutts Road over the canal. The bridge is believed to have been removed long before the start of any works related to the M6 Toll but its location is clearly shown on historic maps. On the east side of the canal, within the general vicinity of the former bridge, the excavation revealed a section of brick wall which probably survived from the former foundations of the bridge.

At the southern end of this, at a 90° angle, were the remains of a wooden structure projecting towards the west, fixed in between two brick wall supports. The structure comprised four timber beams placed on top of each other (Fig. 45). Each beam was *c* 0.28 m tall by *c* 0.33 m wide and the brick walls between which the

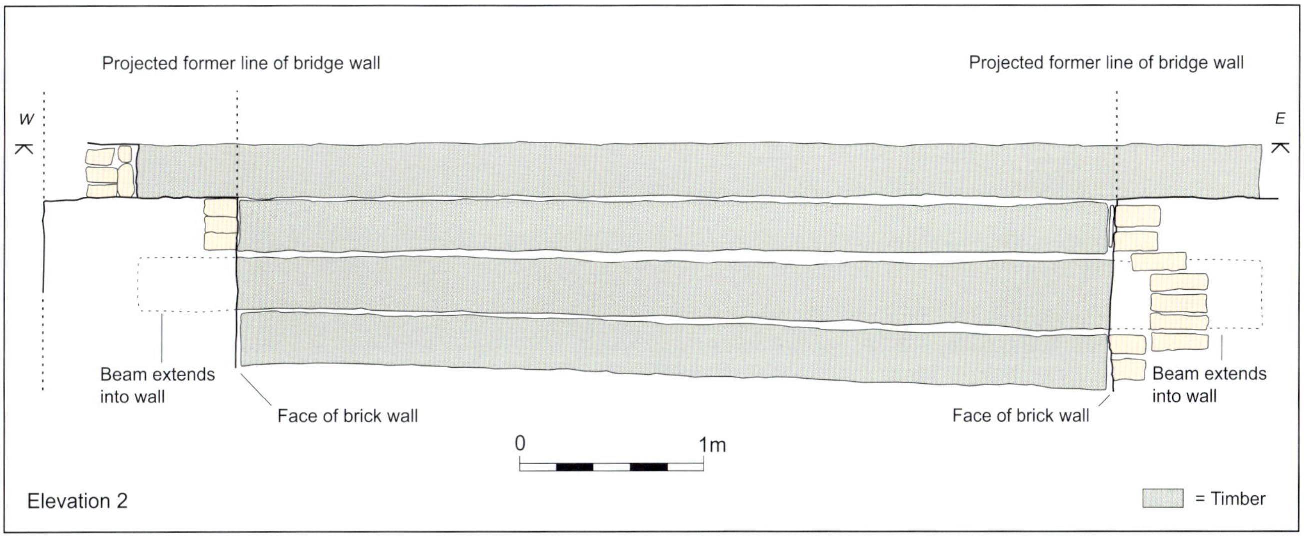

Fig. 45 Timber structure at the bases of the bridge piers

beams extended were *c* 4.75 m apart. This corresponds with the evidence of historic maps suggesting that at the point of the bridge the canal narrowed to *c* 4.5–5 m wide. The timber beams were keyed into the walls with every other one extending into the brickwork and it may be that they were designed to counteract the outward thrust of the bridge and to tie the two foundations together. It was only towards the bottom of the excavation for the road that the beams were exposed and they would clearly have been well below the water line to avoid interfering with the barges. Presumably the beams would have been immediately below the bottom of the canal, set within the likely deep layer of clay.

Discussion

The Cannock Extension Canal is representative of an interesting phase in the history of inland waterway navigation, long after the heyday of canal construction at the end of the 18th century, when competition from the railways had severely limited investment in new canals but before that investment had ceased altogether. It is sometimes assumed that with the initial establishment and dramatic growth of the national rail network in the 1830s and 1840s, canals were instantly rendered redundant and that no new canals were constructed from this time. The Cannock Extension Canal, which was not fully opened until the early 1860s, demonstrates that this is not entirely true and how in certain specific cases canals did, to a limited extent, remain competitive with the railways. The canals that could remain profitable tended to be short mineral-carrying routes and the Cannock Extension, whose trade was heavily based on carrying coal from the newly developed Cannock Chase Coalfield, was typical of these.

The archaeological work at this site on the Cannock Extension has recorded the construction of the canal as well as what appear to be the foundations for a former bridge. The site of a former wharf was also investigated but this appears to have been no more than a simple platform where limited quantities of goods could be loaded or unloaded.

Chapter 10
Watling Street, Hammerwich (Site 41)

By Carl Champness

Introduction

A watching brief was undertaken at a site along the A5, believed to be the route of the Roman road of Watling Street, just west of Wall, between Muckley Corner and Brownhills (Fig. 46). A 2 m wide and 15 m long machine excavated section revealed a sequence of four road surfaces (two of them cobbled), sandy foundations and a roadside ditch (Fig. 47). A length of the road to the west of the section was then machine stripped and its various surfaces exposed in plan in a series of 2.5 m wide steps (Fig. 48). The surfaces are undated but would appear to date from between the early Romano-British period and the present.

The site, centred on NGR 406414 306510, lies near the bottom of the gently sloping valley of the Crane Brook to the north, which the road passes over to the east of the site. The geology is mapped as Triassic Upper Mottled Sandstone with patches of surviving Pleistocene first terrace (Geological Survey of Great Britain 1954, Sheet 154, Lichfield). The excavated areas revealed the former natural deposits of mid-reddish sand containing sub-rounded bunter cobbles.

Results

The excavation revealed a roadside ditch, sandy road foundation layers and a sequence of four road surfaces (two cobbled surfaces and two modern asphalt surfaces) (Figs 46–7). Only sparse dating evidence was recovered and, apart from the partial section across a probably post-medieval road surface at Churchbridge Complex (Site 4), no other comparable sequences across Watling Street were revealed during the M6 Toll project for detailed comparison. Nonetheless, the completeness of the sequences did allow for reasonable interpretation of the early cobbled surface as being of early Romano-British date.

Romano-British

The earliest features within the sequence (411030, 411032 and 411034) were identified below the foundations of the earliest road surface, cutting into the natural sandstone (411036) that dipped down to the north. These were irregular in plan, *c* 0.4–0.8 m wide, with poorly defined edges and irregular or concave profiles, and may indicate tree clearance at some date prior to the construction of the road; a burnt tree stump was recorded in 411030.

The features were sealed by layers of colluvium (411029 and 411028), potentially a result of such clearance, although the moderately organic nature of the upper deposit (411028) suggests a brief period of stabilisation and soil formation, therefore indicating a time gap between clearance and construction.

The road was constructed of a series of sandy gravel foundation layers (411027, 411026, 411025 and 411019) with a combined thickness of *c* 0.4 m, laid down directly on top of the colluvial deposits and creating a slightly convex mound (*agger*). This profile would have aided drainage of the road surface, and elevated it above areas of land that would have been liable to flooding from the Crane Brook. The presence of irregular features (eg 411041) within a thick levelling layer (411025) suggests possible wheel rutting and surface disturbance during construction.

The earliest road surface (411018) consisted of a very compact layer of sub-rounded/rounded bunter cobbles, 0.06–0.08 m in diameter, contained within a fine/ medium sandy matrix. The surface was between 0.1 m and 0.18 m thick and *c* 5.5 m wide. A road edge deposit (411022), that formed the embankment to the north, had a very distinct boundary with the underlying colluvium, and consisted of loose, light yellowish coarse sand with little coarse component. It was 0.15 m thick, with signs of disturbance and distortion from the weight of the overlying material (411021). It appears to have been used to reduce the road bank gradient and so minimise the risk of erosion.

The road surface appeared to be stratigraphically related with a roadside ditch (411037) that ran parallel on its north side. The ditch was 1.1 m wide and 0.5 m deep, with moderately steep, concave sides and a concave base. The primary fills (411023 and 411024) in the base of the ditch suggest that its original profile may have been steeper. The main secondary fill (411017) consisted of a mid-greyish brown silt sand with 40% sub-rounded bunter cobbles that probably represents material eroded from the road bank and surface, combined with colluvium washed down from the surrounding hillside.

Post-medieval and modern

Overlying the earliest road surface was a layer of compact reddish-black sandy gravel (411100). Although it comprised 70% sub-rounded to sub-angular bunter cobbles, it did not appear to represent an actual road surface, but has been interpreted as a road accumulation deposit comprising a mixture of trample and colluvial

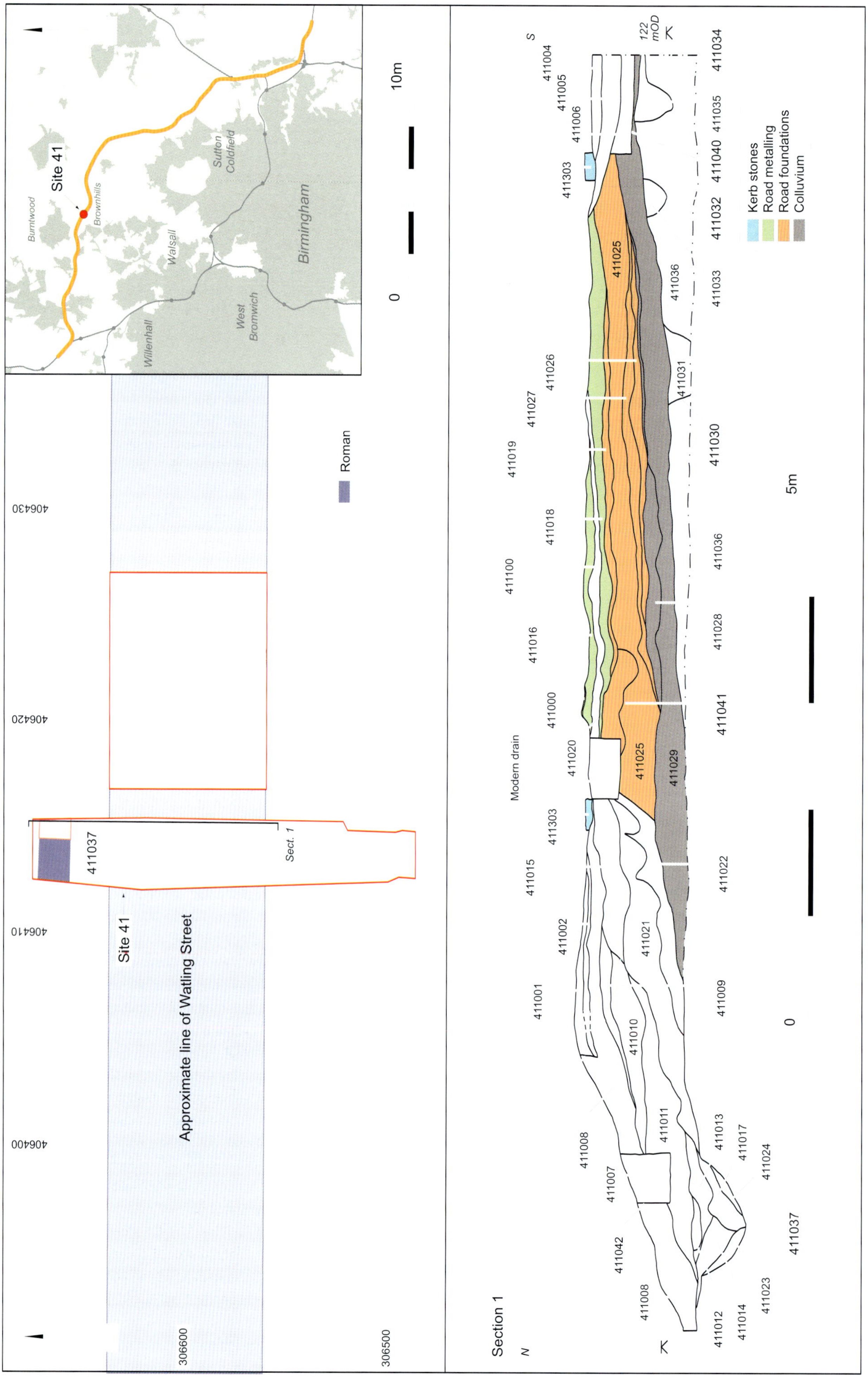

Fig. 46 Watling Street, Hammerwich (Site 41) and section across Watling Street

Fig. 47 Section across Watling Street

Fig. 48 Plough scars in the old road surface

ploughsoil. It was identified also within a series of well-defined parallel plough scars that cut NE–SW across the underlying cobbled surface, and contained a small quantity of post-medieval pottery (Fig. 48). The layer appears to indicate a period of abandonment of the road, subsequent soil formation above it and, eventually, probably a single episode of deep ploughing. The cobbled surface would have offered considerable resistance to the plough, and it is not surprising that this appears not to have been repeated, with the farmer most likely content with ploughing at a shallower depth, just above the road surface.

Signs of mineralisation within the layer 411100 probably resulted from its subsequent compaction by later traffic, and it appears likely that it was later truncated and levelled by the removal of the upper loose material in order to accommodate the second cobbled surface (411016). This consisted of very compacted sub-rounded bunter cobbles in a black sandy matrix, and was 0.05–0.1 m thick and *c* 6 m wide. This surface appeared less well constructed than the earlier surface, with a looser matrix and less consistent size of cobble.

Deposits 411015 and 411011, which accumulated against the northern edge of the road embankment, may represent material washed off the second road surface. They consisted of mid greyish brown silty sand with partially sorted sub-rounded and sub-angular cobbles. They were 0.25–0.40 m thick and extended down from the edge of the road to the top of the, by then silted up, ditch. Two further episodes of colluvial-derived road-edge accumulation (411010 and 411009) also occur during the period of use of the second road surface.

At some stage, stone curbs (411303) were laid down along the sides of the road, but due to the extent of modern truncation near the edges of the road it was not possible to establish with certainty to which phase they related. Stone curbs are known to have been used both in the construction of Roman and post-medieval roads.

The earliest asphalt surface (411000) was placed directly on top of the upper cobbled surface without the need for further foundations. Material was added to the northern road edge in order improve drainage (411001 and 411002), and to increase the size of the embankment (411008) to accommodate motor vehicles. This coincided with the addition of the modern curbs.

A further phase of major resurfacing and widening appears to have been carried out to help support increased traffic and to cope with larger vehicles on the A5, widening the road towards the south. This work involved cutting (411040) through the earlier layers into the underlying colluvium, and the laying down of several deposits of modern drainage gravel (411004, 411005 and 411006).

Discussion

The earliest cobbled surface (411018) is believed to represent the Roman road of Watling Street, and was probably of military construction. Its *agger*, possibly defined by a stone kerb, and ditch, are characteristic features of many other Roman roads in Britain (Mudd *et al.* 1999).

The accumulation of deposit 411017 in the ditch indicates that the road was in use for a considerable period of time, and potentially continued in use into the Saxon and medieval periods. The absence of evidence of resurfacing or major repairs probably reflects the well-constructed nature of the road.

The parallel plough scars that cut through the early road surface suggest there was a significant interval between the construction of the two surfaces. The few sherds of post-medieval pottery recovered from the intervening deposits suggest that the road probably went out of use during the medieval period, with colluvial deposits then accumulating to a sufficient depth to allow cultivation, probably during the post-medieval period.

In 1706, the section of Watling Street from Woburn to Hockliffe was converted into a turnpike by Act of Parliament in response for the need for improved road transport, and the second cobbled surface (411016) was probably constructed shortly afterwards; an interpretation supported by the recovery from it of a small amount of post-medieval finds. The re-instatement of the road indicates that either parts of the original surface were still identifiable in the area or that the 18th century road builders knew the former route of Watling Street from elsewhere.

Chapter 11
Wyrley and Essington Canal (Site 8)

By Andrew B. Powell

Introduction

A watching brief was undertaken during the excavation of a 27 m long machine cut trench across an embanked section of the Wyrley and Essington Canal between Burntwood and Brownhills. The section, along the line of the road corridor, revealed the construction of the embankment, and its subsequent reinforcement.

The site, covering *c* 0.46 hectares centred on NGR 406760 306380, was located to the north-east of Brownhills, immediately south of the junction of the A5 (Watling Street) and the B4156 Lichfield Road, and east of Meadow Farm (Fig. 49). It consisted of a section of the Wyrley and Essington Canal at a point where it was cut through by the road scheme. The canal, which was set on an embankment above the surrounding arable fields, was disused but retained a significant pool of water. Immediately to the west of the embankment are the remains of the 8-lock Ogley flight of locks. East of the site the canal crosses over Crane Brook.

The topography is generally flat (at *c* 118–120 m aOD) with a slight rise to the west through which the Ogley flight is cut. The geology is mapped as Triassic Bunter, Upper Mottled Sandstone (Geological Survey of Great Britain 1954, Sheet 154, Lichfield).

Historical background

The Wyrley and Essington Canal, nicknamed the 'Curly Wyrley' due to its contour hugging design, was opened in 1794, at the height of the canal-building boom, running from Horseley Fields to Sneyd. It was extended in 1797 past Brownhills and Lichfield to Huddlesford, and the embankment at the site dated to this phase of construction. Like many of the early canals it was narrow gauge making it cheap and easy to build. It was promoted to bring coal from the pits around Wyrley and Essington to Wolverhampton and Walsall (Crowe 1994, 20–1; Paget-Tomlinson 1993, 217).

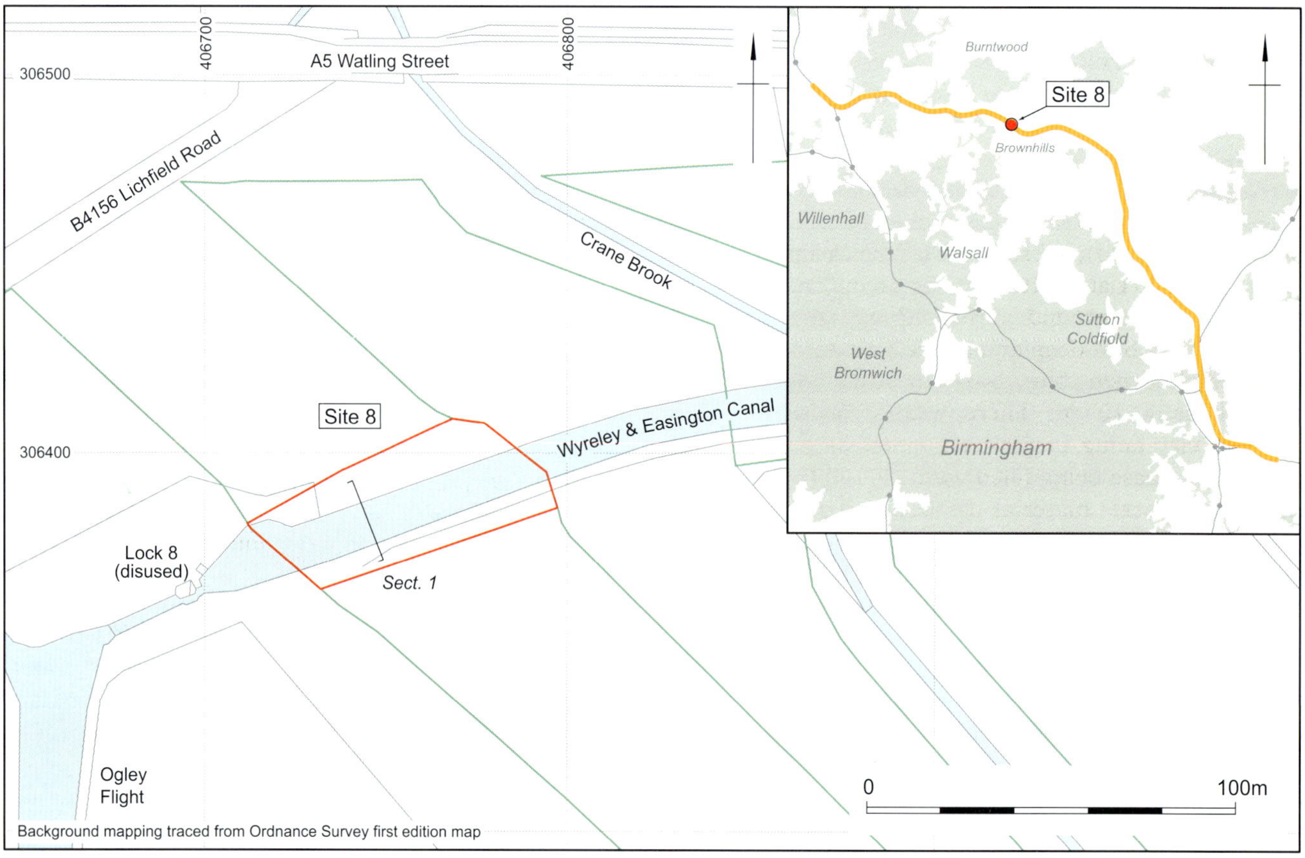

Fig. 49 Wyrley and Essington Canal (Site 8)

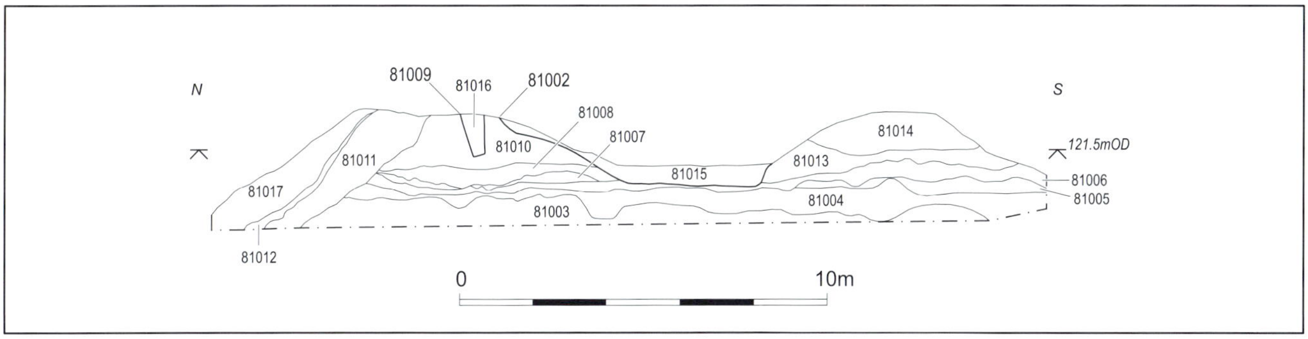

Fig. 50 West-facing section through the canal and embankment

Immediately west of the site are the substantially intact remains of Lock 8, built in 1858 as part of the rebuilding of the Ogley flight by the Birmingham Canal Navigations. The lock was built of red and blue local bricks with a coping of large, dressed stone blocks, one of which is inscribed 'No 8. 1858'. At the approach to its east end there are two curved brick wing walls narrowing into the lock chamber. The vertical timber bearers for the lock gates remain *in situ*, and the lock retains a low pool of water. Although late in the development of the canal network in Britain, the construction of the lock shows that a significant investment was still being made in the canal network well into the railway era, and several new sections of canal were built in the 1850s and 1860s.

The Ogley flight was closed in 1954 as traffic on the canal declined in the face of increased road and rail transport, and the contraction of coal mining in the region (Paget-Tomlinson 1993, 105). The importance of canals to the industrialisation of the West Midlands and south Staffordshire gives their surviving remains a relatively high significance.

Results

The entire canal at this location was built up over a buried soil (81006), subsoil (81005) and natural gravels and clay (81004 and 81003), with no excavation below the pre-existing ground surface (Fig. 50). The canal channel was 1.8 m deep and *c* 4 m wide at the base, the distance between the tops of the banks being approximately 10 m. There was no evidence of a puddled clay lining in the base or on the sides of the channel, the base being filled with a 0.5 m thick layer of industrial waste material (81015), including coal, clinker, gravels and clay, possibly dumped there after the canal's closure (as seen also at Hawkins Canal Basin, Site 1, and Gilpin's Basin, Site 3) (Fig. 51).

The banks on either side of the channel consisted of deposits of silty sand at the base (81008 to the north and 81013 to the south) some 7 m wide and up to 0.65 m thick, overlain by deposits of sandy clay (81010 and 81014) up to 1.2 m thick. This material may well have derived from excavations undertaken as part of the construction of the Ogley flight to the west. The banks were flat-topped with moderate slopes front and rear, but there was no evidence of a laid towpath on either side. Although the banks had no internal structures, there was a straight-sided trench (81009), 0.6 m wide and 1 m deep, filled with clay (81016), running along the top of the northern bank, possibly to plug a leak.

At some date after construction, the northern bank was widened and strengthened by the addition of a 0.75m thick layer of sand on its outer face (81011), covered by a 0.1 m thick layer of soil (81012). Subsequently, a second sand layer, 0.56 m thick, was laid down, containing brick rubble, coal and corroded metal (81017). It was not possible to ascertain whether there had been similar consolidation work on the southern bank as an unknown quantity of earth had already been removed from its outer face before the watching brief started.

Discussion

The section across the canal revealed the very basic nature of its initial construction, comprising simple earthen embankments with no internal structure, reinforcement or lining. This may reflect the relatively rapid rate of their construction, although it is evident that this had long term consequences, requiring repeated repairs. The reinforcement of the canal embankment may have been in response to slippage and leaks, which were likely to have been a continuous problem on the embanked sections of the canal. It is possible that one of these episodes was contemporary with the reconstruction of the adjacent lock in 1858.

Fig. 51 Section through the canal and embankment viewed from the north-west

Chapter 12

West of Crane Brook Cottage, Hammerwich (Site 34)

By Andy Simmonds

Introduction

A targeted watching brief was undertaken in an area of indistinct cropmarks, south of Hammerwich and east of Brownhills. It revealed a single Iron Age feature, following which the site was occupied by part of a Romano-British field/paddock system and then a Romano-British aisled timber building and well. The site also contained features of post-medieval and modern date (Fig. 52).

The site, covering *c* 1.6 hectares centred on NGR 406900 306250, was located just south of the Wyrley and Essington Canal (Site 8) at a point where an aqueduct carried it over a minor watercourse, Crane Brook, the canalised course of which lay just north-east of the site. The geology at the north-west end of the site is mapped as Triassic Bunter, Upper Mottled Sandstone, overlain to the south-east by Boulder Clay and Alluvium (Geological Survey of Great Britain 1954, Sheet 154, Lichfield). The site was on a gentle slope running down from the canal at the north-west end towards the bottom of the valley of the Crane Brook.

Watling Street passes *c* 300 m north of the site, and the Roman town of Wall (*Letocetum*) lay 3 km to the east. No other archaeological sites were known in the immediate vicinity of the site.

The site was identified as of potential archaeological significance on the basis of comments in the *Aerial Photographic Assessment* (Babtie 2000). The relevant part of the site was described as 'a definite area of archaeological potential ... very slight hints of possible ditches. Any further definition of the possible archaeological features is impossible from these photo sources alone'. The area covered by these features was indicated on the relevant figure in the report, but the individual features were not plotted. A fieldwalking survey of the site carried out in January 2001 recorded no significant surface finds.

Results

Iron Age

Prehistoric activity on the site was represented by a single irregular hollow (340145), measuring 2.7 m by 1.0 m and 0.13 m deep, located in the south-eastern part of the site. It single fill contained burnt and fire-cracked quartz pebbles up to 0.15 m across. The pebbles, generally rounded to sub-rounded with smooth surfaces diagnostic of river-rolling, lay in a soil matrix of greyish-brown silty sand which also contained flecks of charcoal. A sample of the charcoal produced a radiocarbon date of 800–520 cal BC (NZA-25164, 2515±30 BP) (Fig. 214). However, the date falls within a radiocarbon plateau and because the charcoal was oak heartwood, this date could be 250–300 years older than the date of the deposit which could, therefore, fall within the Middle rather than the Early Iron Age. The function of this feature is unclear.

Romano-British

Stratigraphically the earliest feature attributed to this period was pit 340478, situated in the north-western part of the site. It was cut on its north-western and north-eastern sides by later ditches, but prior to its truncation appears to have been oval or circular in shape. It was *c* 1 m across and 0.3 m deep, with a bowl-shaped profile. It was filled with two layers of silty sand (340479 and 340481) between which was a layer of soft orange clay (340480). The uppermost fill (340481) contained a small quantity of burnt small mammal bones.

Field/paddock boundaries

A group of ditches in the north-western half of the site formed part of a rectilinear arrangement of field or paddock boundaries. These features were clearly distinguishable from a group of undated ditches lying on similar alignments by the nature of their fills, which were orangy-brown to mid- brown in colour, in contrast to the darker, more humic fills of the undated features.

Ditches 348001 and 348009 extended across the excavation area on similar NE–SW alignments *c* 70 m apart. Ditch 348001 was exposed for 36 m, extending beyond the excavation area to the south-west and terminating at its north-eastern end 3 m from the edge of the site. It was 1.0–1.4 m wide and 0.4 m deep with quite steeply sloping sides and a base that varied from flat to concave. Ditch 348009 also terminated within the area of the excavation. It was exposed for a total length of 19 m and continued to the south-west beyond the edge of the site. It had a V-shaped profile and measured 0.7 m wide and 0.2–0.3 m deep. From its fill were recovered five sherds of black-burnished ware and the rim of a jar in an oxidised fabric broadly datable to the 2nd century.

The area between these ditches was sub-divided by ditch 348006, which lay roughly half way between them, on the same NE–SW alignment. It had been severely

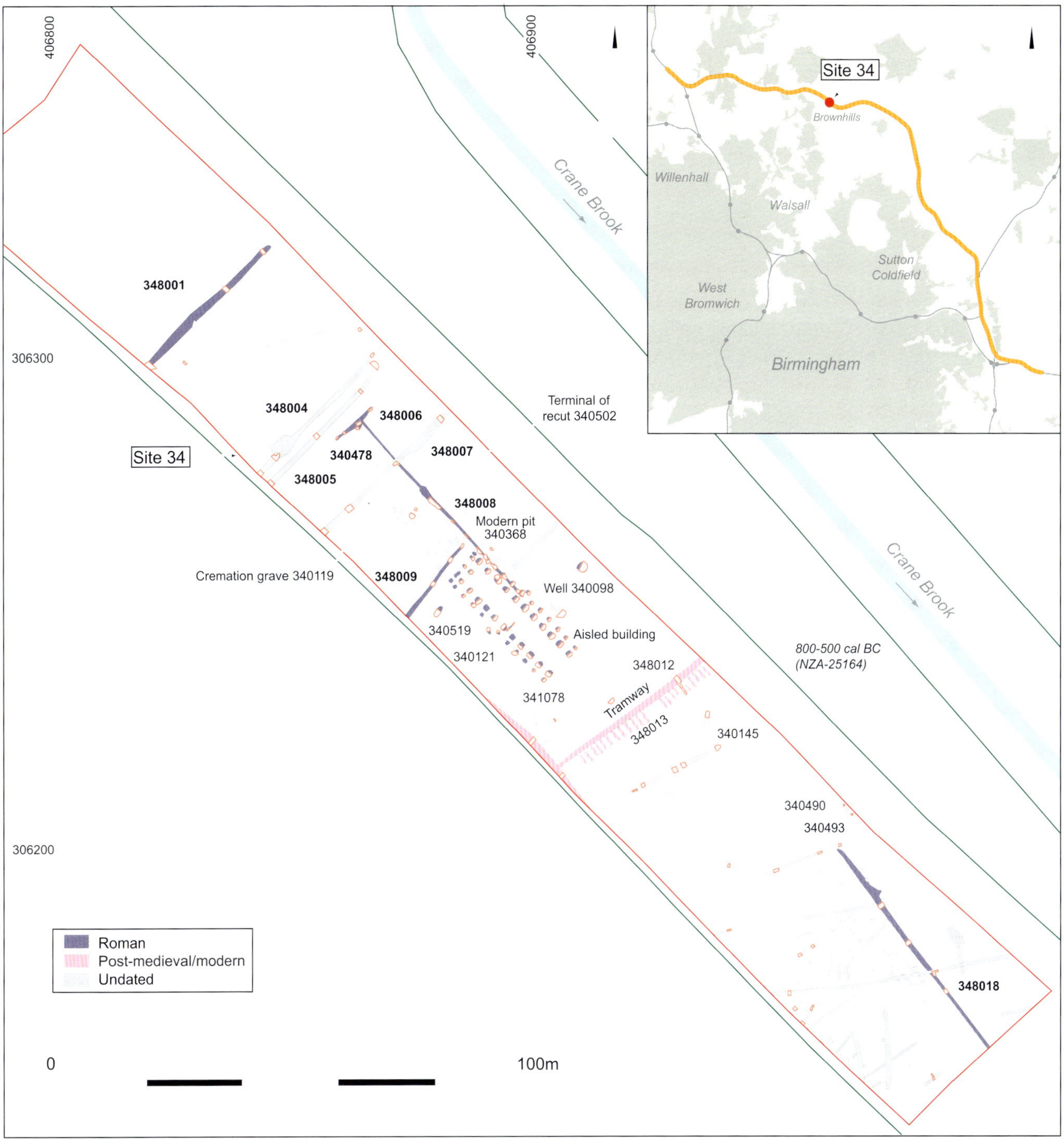

Fig. 52 West of Crane Brook Cottage (Site 34)

truncated by post-Romano-British ploughing and only a 10 m long stretch survived with a maximum depth of 0.2 m, petering out at either end.

Ditch 348008 branched off ditch 348006 at a right angle and extended for 49 m towards the south-east. At its north-western end, it too had been quite substantially affected by truncation and was only 0.13 m deep, but further south-east the depth increased up to a maximum of 0.37 m, decreasing again toward the south-eastern terminal. The ditch was 0.6–0.8 m wide with moderately steep sides and a flat base. Ditch 348008 formed the north-eastern boundary of a rectilinear field or paddock, the north-western and south-eastern sides of which were enclosed by ditches 348006 and 348009. The south-eastern end of 348008 extended beyond ditch 348009, suggesting that the system of enclosures continued further in this direction, but no further boundaries survived in this part of the site. An assemblage of pottery dating from the early to mid-2nd century was recovered from the south-eastern part of the ditch, and the dumping of this material into the ditch may have accompanied deliberate back-filling to accommodate the construction here of the aisled building (see below). What appeared to be the terminal of a re-cut (340502) of the north-western part of the ditch was recorded approximately half way along its length. The re-cut was 0.35 m deep, slightly deeper than the original ditch at this point, and contained three fills comprising a band of

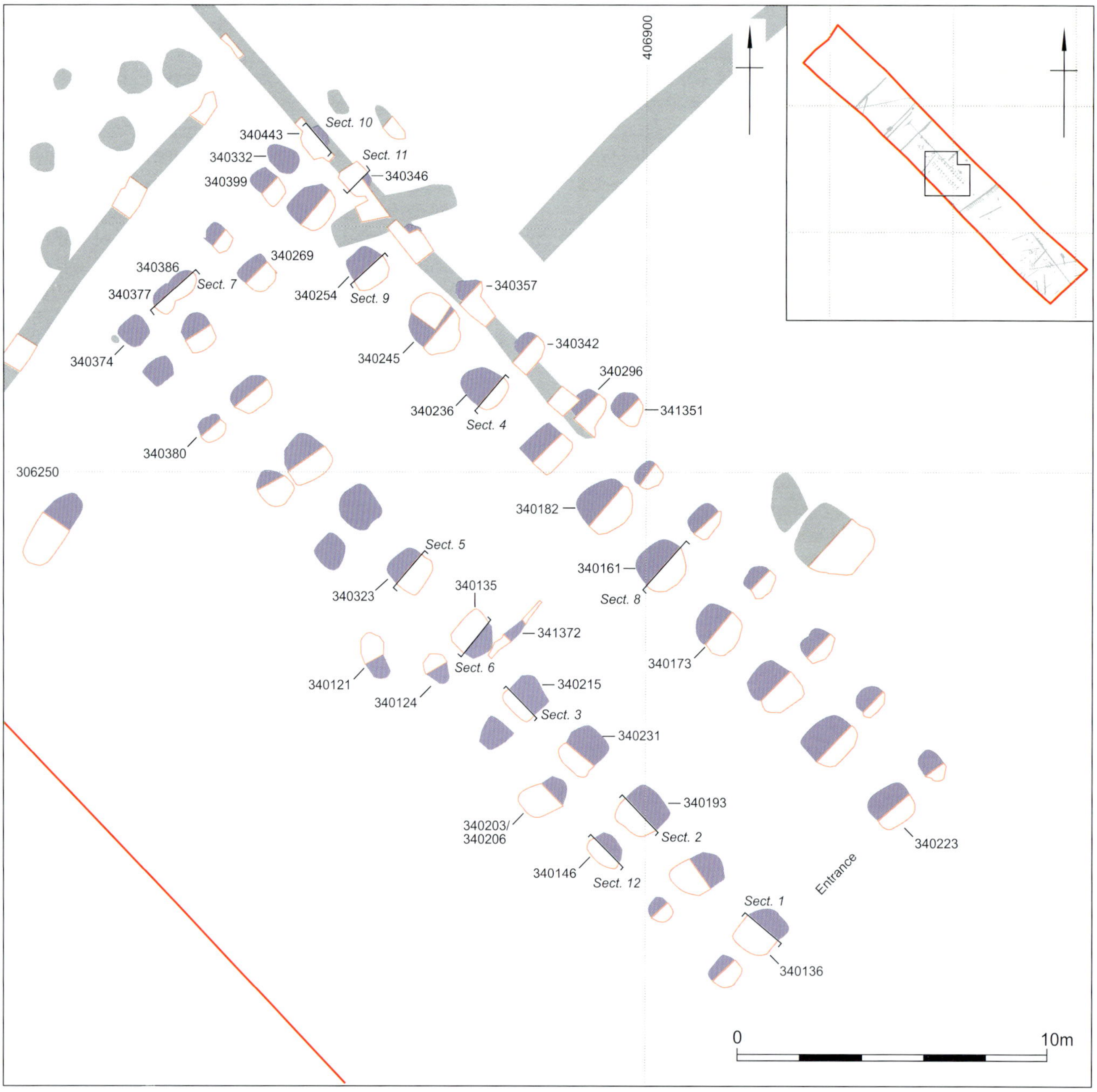

Fig. 53 The Romano-British aisled building

sandy gravel overlain by layers of reddish-brown and dark grey sand. No finds were recovered from the re-cut.

The excavation area was crossed by several largely undated boundary ditches, which were characterised by dark, humic fills different from those filling the above ditches. These included, towards the north-west of the site, ditch 348007, which cut across Romano-British ditch 348008, and a double-ditched boundary formed by ditches 348004 and 348005. None of these features appears on the 1st edition OS map of 1887–8 and, despite the character of their fills, they share the same alignment as ditch 348001, suggesting a possible relationship. A slot in the base of the latter containing two sherds of Romano-British pottery.

The system of ditched boundaries may have extended further to the south-east, where ditch 348018 was recorded at the south-eastern end of the excavation. The ditch was aligned NW–SE, on a slightly different orientation to ditch 348008, and was exposed for a total length of 52 m, although it continued further beyond the edge of the excavation. It was 0.4 m deep and generally V-shaped in profile, although the base became wider and flatter toward the terminal at the north-western end. Its fill contained sherds of pottery dating from the 2nd century.

Aisled building

In the central area of the excavation, a large aisled building was constructed over the back-filled south-eastern part of ditch 348008 (Figs 53–4). The building was post-built and survived as four rows of postholes with overall measurements of 29.5 m NW–SE by 10 m NE–SW, forming a structure of 10 bays. The two inner rows, *c* 6 m apart, comprised substantial postholes

Fig. 54 The Romano-British aisled building

which bore the greater part of the weight of the building's superstructure, while the smaller postholes of the two outer rows supported the outer wall. The south-east end of the building was open, but a central large posthole at the north-west end (and additional outer postholes) indicate that this end was closed.

There appeared to be a gap in the outer line of postholes near the midpoint of the south-west side – outside posthole 323. However, just outside the outer line of postholes in this area was the base of a shallow kidney-shaped pit (340121), measuring 1.2 m by 0.75 m, and 0.16 m deep with an irregular profile. It was filled with a single deposit of greyish-brown silty sand which contained 33 pottery sherds from the body and base of a jar and a single sherd from a second vessel dating from the second half of the 2nd century. There was a posthole (341351) in an equivalent position on the north-east side of the building.

The postholes were generally square in plan with rounded corners, although some were more nearly circular. Their size provides some indication of the scale of the building – those of the inner rows were up to 1.45 m wide with an average depth of 1.05 m, while those of the outer rows were up to 1.1 m wide with an average depth of 0.7 m. Postpipes preserved in the majority of the postholes indicated that they had held timbers that were round in section and measured 0.2–0.3 m in diameter, with occasional larger examples up to 0.4 m. The material forming each postpipe varied with depth, grading from brownish sand in the upper part of the feature where the greatest oxidation had occurred to darker, greyer material toward the base where waterlogging had resulted in the preservation of organic material in the deeper examples. In three postholes (340136, 340236 and 340323) (Fig. 55) waterlogging had preserved fragments of wood from the bases of the posts, identified as mature oak (see Chisham, below). The posts were secured in place by packing with dumps of sand and gravel excavated during the digging of the postholes.

Two postholes near the midpoint of the south-western side of the building each contained a pair of postpipes – 340141 and 340142 in posthole 340135, and 340249 and 340230 in posthole 340215 (only one visible in section) (Fig. 55). In both cases the twin posts had clearly been inserted at the same time as they were held in place by the same layers of packing material, and did not exhibit the disturbance to the original feature that would normally be associated with the replacement of an aged or damaged post. The reason for this arrangement was unclear, although it may be significant that these postholes were adjacent to each other. In a single posthole (340231), the post was supported on a post pad formed by several flattish stones laid centrally on the base.

The outer postholes along the north-western end wall were considerably shallower than those elsewhere in the structure, with only postholes 340322 and 340443 (Fig. 55) being more than 0.45 m deep. There was evidence for repairs in this part of the building, with posthole 340377 replacing posthole 340386, truncating the southern half of the earlier feature (Fig. 55). Postholes 340332 and 340399, on the opposite side of the building, may represent a similar replacement (although because they did not intersect their sequence is not known).

No floor surfaces or other features associated with the use of the building were identified, except for a single clay-lined gully (341372), aligned NE–SW laterally within the building adjacent to posthole 340135. It was 2.3 m long and 0.1 m deep with steep sides forming a U-shaped profile. The sides and base were lined with firm, light grey clay up to 0.02 m thick, possibly waterproofing for a drain. The gully was filled with a deposit of black charcoal-rich soil, the well-preserved charcoal component being dominated by oak roundwood, possibly derived from coppiced trees (see Gale below).

The building appears to have been deliberately demolished. Three postholes (340161, 340443 and 340254) (Fig. 55) showed evidence for the truncation of the top of the postpipe by a pit dug directly into the top of the posthole, presumably in order to dig out the base of the post. No postpipe was recorded in 11 postholes, suggesting that in these cases (eg 340346 and 340146) the posts had been completely removed and the resultant pit back-filled (Fig. 55). Since such efforts had been made to remove these posts, it is likely that in those

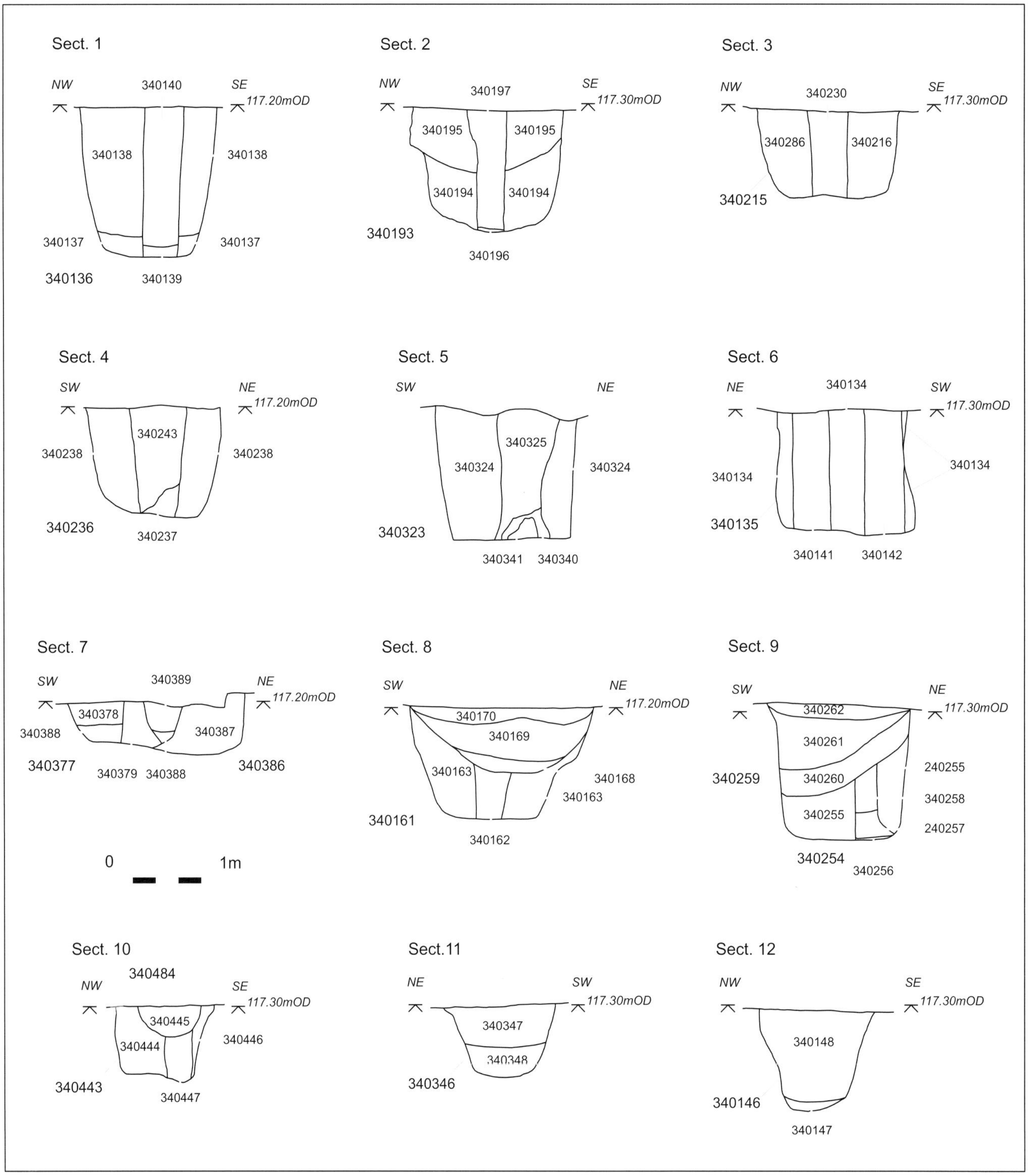

Fig. 55 Posthole sections

examples where a postpipe was recorded the post had been sawn off at ground level and the stump left to rot *in situ* (eg 340193, 340215) (Fig. 55).

Pottery recovered from the packing and postpipes of the postholes of the aisled building dated from the middle of the 2nd century. A small group of sherds was recovered from demolition-related contexts back-filling postholes after the posts had been removed, but these also dated to the mid-2nd century, suggesting either that the building stood for only a very short period or that this pottery is residual.

Well 340098

A stone-lined well (340098) lay *c* 10 m north-east of the aisled building (Fig. 56). The construction cut was roughly square and measured 2.7 m across. The lining, which had an internal diameter of 0.7 m, was well-constructed from blocks of pale brown sandstone measuring up to 0.6 m by 0.4 m by 0.2 m. The blocks had been roughly worked and their inner faces were shaped to fit the diameter of the shaft. The inner face of the stone-work had been stained to a reddish hue as a result of weathering. Hand excavation of the upper 1 m

Fig. 56 Stone-lined well 340098

of the well recorded three layers of greyish-brown sand from which a small quantity of undiagnostic Romano-British pottery was recovered. The lower part of the well was then half-sectioned by machine in order to retrieve any waterlogged organic remains. This revealed that the well was *c* 2.5 m deep, and filled with a homogeneous deposit of grey sand which, although wet, contained no waterlogged remains. Plans to install shoring to allow the collection of environmental samples were therefore abandoned.

Cremation burial

An urned cremation burial in a bowl-shaped grave (340119) was located *c* 20 m north-west of the aisled building. The grave was 0.4 m in diameter but had been substantially truncated by post-Romano-British ploughing and survived to a depth of only 0.07 m. It contained a deposit of cremated bone weighing 126.5 g, of a subadult/adult aged over 13 years, in a matrix of grey sand (340122) derived from the backfilled topsoil. Also in the grave were scattered 13 sherds of pottery representing the lower part of a grey ware vessel which clearly served as the urn for the cremated bone. The grave contained very little charcoal or charred plant remains, suggesting that the bone had been picked carefully out of the pyre debris for burial.

Other Romano-British features

A small number of other features of definite or presumed Romano-British date were recorded. South-west of the building, pit 340519 was interpreted as a deliberately cut feature due to its elongated oval shape, measuring 2.4 m by 1.16 m, and the regularity of its moderately steep sides with a flat base. The lower fill, a dark grey sand 0.2 m thick (340521), was overlain by a layer of lighter grey sand (340520) that may have been a deliberate back-fill.

There was also a pair of postholes (340490 and 340493) in the south-eastern part of the site, *c* 65 m from the aisled building. Posthole 340490 was 0.5 m in diameter and 0.4 m deep, with near-vertical sides and a flat base. The lower half was filled with a layer of mid-brown silty sand and gravel above which was a deposit of soft pink clay. Posthole 340493 was similar and measured 0.4 m in diameter and 0.5 m deep. It too had a lower fill of sand overlain by a deposit of clay. Fragments of undiagnostic fired clay were recovered from the lower fills of both postholes, but no datable artefacts. The postholes were 2 m apart and are likely to have formed part of a single structure, the rest of which may have lain beyond the adjacent edge of the excavation.

Post-medieval and modern

Along the south-western edge of the excavation, to the south of the aisled building, part of a post-medieval ditch (341078) was exposed which had been re-cut at least once. It was in turn cut by a SW–NE aligned ditch (348012), whose position appears to match that of a field boundary shown on the 1st edition OS map. This ditch, which was 1.5 m wide and 0.5 m deep, extended the entire 38 m width of the site, narrowing to *c* 0.8 m at the south-west.

Immediately adjacent and perpendicular to ditch 348012 on its south-east side was a series of railway sleeper-settings (348013), typically *c* 2.9 m by 0.8 m in

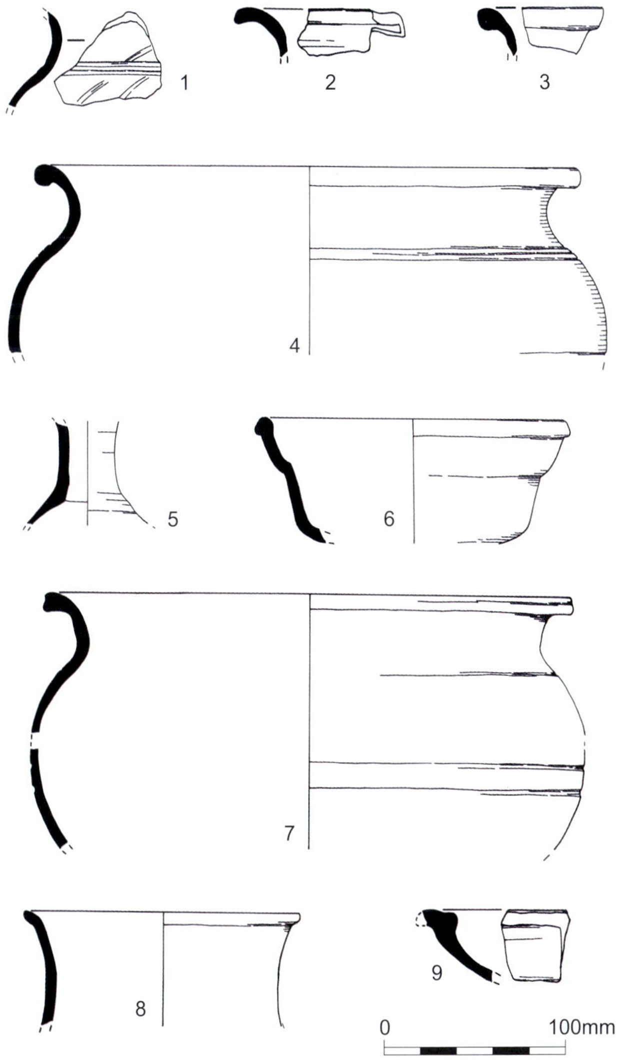

Fig. 57 Romano-British pottery

plan and with variable spacing, from *c* 0.5 m to 1 m. The single excavated example was only 0.1 m deep; from the slight irregularities of plan and profile it is clear that the sleepers were removed for re-use after the railway ceased to operate. The varying levels of disturbance resulting from this operation presumably explain why only 22 of the original 30 or so sleeper positions that would have spanned the site were located. There is no indication that the sleepers had been laid on a bed of ballast. The 1st edition map shows a trackway along the line of the sleepers, running between Lichfield Road and Barracks Lane, via a building located between Crane Brook and the Wyrley and Essington Canal to the north.

A number of modern field drains extended across the excavation, and the south-eastern end of the excavation was heavily disturbed by modern drainage features and rutting from farm vehicles. A modern pit measuring *c* 4 m by 1 m and 1.05 m deep was dug into the northern part of the aisled building but fortunately did not truncate any of its postholes.

Finds

Metal finds, by Kelly Powell

Only six iron finds were recovered, comprising five nails or nail fragments, one of which was unstratified, and a single unstratified hook (ON 345000). The hook had square corners, forming a truncated U-shape, 68 mm in length and 54 mm wide, and appeared to narrow to a point on its smaller arm, suggesting it may have been complete. Unfortunately it was very badly corroded and in poor condition and no further classification was possible. Although unstratified this find was located within the Romano-British aisled building, indicating a possible Romano-British date.

It is probable that all the nails were also Romano-British; ON 345001 was also unstratified but as with ON 345000 it was located within the Romano-British building. This particular nail was of a slightly less common form than the other three if Romano-British in date. It was of Manning type 7, which were probably used for upholstery on the basis of their potentially decorative flat discoidal heads. The remaining nails and nail fragments were all recovered from 2nd century AD features; ON 345003 from posthole 340380 within the aisled building, ON 345004 from ditch 348008 and notably ON 344005 (one of two from cremation grave 340119) which suggests it may have been part of funerary furniture. All these finds could be classified as Manning type 1 nails, ON 344005 almost certainly a type 1b (Table 8).

Table 8 Nail classification by context

	Type 1b	*Type 7*	*Total*
Unstratified	–	1	1
Posthole 340380	1	–	1
Ditch 348008	1	–	1
Cremation grave 340119	2	–	2
Total	4	1	5

Flint, by Kate Cramp

A single flake was recovered from context 340521 in pit 306250 (Table 150). The flake, which has been struck from a mid-brown flint with cherty grey inclusions, is technologically undiagnostic and can only be broadly dated to the prehistoric period. The presence of post-depositional damage on its edges indicates that it is probably residual.

Romano-British pottery, by Ruth Leary

Some 392 sherds of Romano-British pottery (2692 g) were recovered from the site. These came principally from the post-holes of the aisled building and the ditch pre-dating this structure (Table 9) with small amounts from other ditches, a well and a cremation burial on the site. Much of the pottery was fragmented and abraded. Cross-joins and sherds identified as the same vessel in both the postholes of the aisled building and ditch 348008 indicate that redeposition of sherds from the latter in the former was common. Indeed pottery sherds were further fragmented and redeposited in the backfill of postholes that had had the post removed. Very little pottery could, therefore, be related securely to the use of the aisled building although a *terminus post quem* could be obtained from the sherds derived from the earlier ditch fill. These give a date in the early–mid-2nd century. The BB1 sherds indicate that this was after AD 120.

Chronology

Overall the character of the site assemblage indicates a date range in the early–mid-2nd century. The absence of sherds in fabric group E (Table 10) may preclude a late 1st century date on the evidence from Tiddington (though such material is so scarce in this area, and the overall assemblage is so small, that arguments from absence are not conclusive), while the small amounts of BB1 and Severn Valley ware suggest the occupation

Table 9 Quantities of Romano-British pottery sherds from feature types

Feature	*Count*	*Weight (g)*
Ditch	215	739
Post-packing	10	122
Post-pipe	33	249
Pit dug into posthole	3	26
Posthole backfill	27	190
Undiff. postfill	22	202
Misc. feature	82	1164
Total	392	2692

ceased before the rise in these fabrics in the late 2nd and 3rd centuries at which time they reached 9.3% rising to 18.7% in the 3rd century and 8.6% rising to 8.8% in the 3rd century respectively at Tiddington. These figures contrast with 6% and 5% at this site. The presence of white and white slip wares is consistent with this dating and the absence of later mortarium types and fabrics also confirms a terminal date within the 2nd century. A jar sherd in a fabric similar to that made in the Shenstone kiln (Chapter 17) may indicate activity as late as the late 2nd century, but few of the other types need be dated this late.

Catalogue of illustrated sherds and discussion of stratified group (Fig. 57)

Ditch 348008

1. R16 narrow-necked jar with shoulder cordon. Distorted. A long-lived type, context 340356, cut 340355. Also in post-packing 340362, posthole 340357 cutting the ditch
2. SV1 four sherds from a wide-mouthed jar with everted rim. *Cf.* Evans *et al.* (2000), JWM5 M-L2. 340356, cut 340355
3. O4 41 sherds and scraps from a wide-mouthed jar with bifid, everted rim. This vessel compares well with the products of the Shenstone kiln in form but not fabric. The relatively upright neck and curving everted rim of this vessel suggests a 2nd century date and vessels with similar profiles but lacking the bifid rim appear in contexts dated as early as AD 120–150 at Coleshill (Booth 2006, nos 316–8). Such types are difficult to date closely but the similarity with the Shenstone kiln jars may make a mid-2nd century date preferable, context 340364, cut 340363
4. R15 wide-mouthed jar with cordoned shoulder and smoothly curving everted rim. This vessel was also found in backfill of the aisled building and posthole 340342 and appeared to have been broken in the recent past in all three contexts (340407 post backfill, and posthole 340342, perhaps plough damage). It would, therefore have been a near complete vessel when deposited in the ditch. The fine fabric and form compares with earlier types in the 2nd century. The flat shoulder cordon and fine burnish compares with the type of vessels which were made at Mancetter-Hartshill (unpublished) and occur in the early–mid-2nd century at related kilns on Derby Racecourse kiln 8 (Dool *et al.* 1985, fig. 78, nos 67–71) and kilns 1–6 (Brassington 1971, nos 21–36; 1980, nos 378–9 and 526), context 340411, cut 340410

Other sherds from the ditch included undiagnostic sherds of R2, R12, R15 and Dressel 20 amphora. Diagnostic sherds comprised fragments of a CC2 rough cast beaker, probably from the Argonne region, an R13 wide-mouthed jar with everted rim, an R15 wide-mouthed jar with everted rim thickened at the tip and a BB1 bowl or dish with burnished surfaces. A single South Gaulish samian sherd came from context 340363. The presence of a sherd from a BB1 bowl or dish implies the ditch infill must certainly date after AD 120 and a date in the mid-2nd century is a likely *terminus post quem* given the SV1 form and the O4 wide-mouthed jar. The lack of the early vesicular Severn Valley ware would support this dating. The fine grey ware R15 with brown core compares with a fabric also found at Rocester used for forms common in the late 1st–early 2nd centuries (Leary forthcoming GRA1B). CTA1 body sherds came from a combed storage jar in 340356, cut 340355 and also from 340364, cut 340363. A samian sherd from cut 340482 (context 340483) at the intersection with ditch 348006, was South Gaulish and of 1st century date, and a second, Central Gaulish, sherd from cut 340476 (context 340477) was dated *c* AD 120–160.

Aisled building

Post-packing

5. FLA3 fine, slender neck of flagon. This fabric corresponds to W21 in the Warwickshire series and this fabric is dated to the Antonine period at Tiddington (Booth 1996a), context 340134, posthole 340135
6. FLB2 carinated bowl with bead rim and double curved walls like a samian form 27. Similar vessels have been found at Mancetter-Hartshill (unpublished G12) and Derby Racecourse kilns (Brassington 1971, no. 23), the latter dating to the early 2nd century, context 340216, posthole 340215
7. R15 burnished wide-mouthed jar with expanded rim. The fabric of this vessel is closely comparable to No. 5 and a similar date range is likely, context 340362, posthole 340357

Other sherds from the post-packing included two fragments from a BB1 jar and one from a BB1 bowl or dish, both with acute lattice burnish, a scrap of samian and one of SV1. These sherds confirm the date range suggested for the pottery from ditch 348008 and may all derive from it.

Post-pipes

8. O6 bowl with flaring rim, probably from carinated bowl of late 1st–early 2nd century type. The fabric is unlike Severn Valley ware and is likely to be a local product, context 340174, posthole 340173
9. M1 incomplete rim sherd of bead and flange mortarium. The flange rises above the bead and the vessel is likely to date to the early–mid-2nd century, context 340297, posthole 340296

Body sherds of R3, R16, A10 and SV1 were present with a burnt FLA1 turned base, probably a flagon or beaker, and a short O4 everted rim, probably from a beaker. These vessel types and fabrics support the date range in the early–mid-2nd century suggested above.

Pit 340179, dug into posthole 340182

This feature contained sherds of FLB1, a BB1 bowl or dish with closely spaced acute lattice burnish, common in the early–mid-2nd century and an R15 bowl with moulded rim of a type found on carinated bowls in the late 1st–early 2nd century (*cf.* Brasssington 1971, no. 15).

Posthole back-fills

The backfill groups included six sherds from BB1 jars and bowls/dishes. The bowl/dish fragments bore closely spaced burnished lattice similar to the type found on vessels of the early–mid-2nd century (Gillam 1976, nos 35, 37, 53, 59 and 61). A further 18 sherds from vessel No. 5 were found and one R6 sherd.

Postholes undifferentiated
A further scrap of BB1 was found in posthole 340231 (340244), along with a scrap of R15, and a body sherd came from posthole 340161 (340163). These give a *termius post quem* of AD 120. A scrap of O4 was found in posthole 340215 (340230) and one of R16 in posthole 340161. A MWS1 mortarium sherd, from a bead and flange form broadly datable to the 2nd century, came from posthole 340182 (340183). A South Gaulish samian ware sherd probably of Flavian date came from posthole 340342

Two sherds from a BB1 jar and 12 body sherds from the R15 jar found in the ditch 348008 pre-dating the aisled building came from posthole 340342.

Miscellaneous features
The rest of the assemblage predominantly comprised undiagnostic body sherds. An R9 everted rim sherd, probably from a carinated bowl of late 1st–early 2nd century type was found in post-medieval/modern ditch 341078 (cut 340014, context 340012). Fill 340107 in well 340098 yielded a sherd of a BB1 jar and three R17 scraps. The slot on the base of undated ditch 348005 (cut 340112, context 340113) contained two oxidised sherds, probably SV4. Pit 340121 yielded sherds from two vessels: one from an R2 jar and 33 from the body and base of an R14 jar. These could not be closely dated but the R2 sherd compared with sherds from the Shenstone kiln suggesting a date in the second half of the 2nd century. Cremation grave 340119 contained 13 undiagnostic sherds of R16 from a vessel of uncertain form.

Fill 340207 in feature 340206 (cutting posthole 340203) contained one undiagnostic sherd of R17. Modern feature 340368 contained a rim sherd of a BB1 flat-rim bowl or dish. These were common in the 2nd century and the angle of the wall suggests a date in the mid-2nd century, although its rather small size precluded certainty. Ditch 348009 (cut 340435, context 340436) contained five scraps of BB1 and the rim of an O6 wide-mouthed jar with expanded, rounded rim broadly datable to the 2nd century. A samian scrap from ditch 348018 (cut 340453, context 340454) was of Hadrianic or Antonine date and a rim sherd from a samian dish form 18 came from the topsoil.

Fabrics
The assemblage was made up largely of reduced wares with only 6% of the group being BB1 and nearly 12% oxidised wares (Table 10). Both white and white-slip wares were represented in small quantities and the samian ware reached a level matched at sites such as Coleshill, Alcester and Tiddington (Booth 1991, fig. 2). In terms of national trends, this level of samian use is within the range found on rural sites but is relatively high (Willis 2004).

The sources of the coarse wares are, at times, difficult to determine. The wares are largely quartz tempered with little in the way of distinguishing characteristics where form typology is not present. The reduced fabrics are, however, quite different from those found at East of Birmingham Road Nurseries (Site 15) with only two groups of R2, the most common fabric at Shenstone, present here, in pit 340121 (33 sherds from a single vessel) and ditch 348008 (fill 340305). Fabric R16 was, by contrast, the most common and was represented by a narrow-necked jar of long lived type and sherds from a roughcast beaker. The fabric was broadly similar to fabrics from the Mancetter kilns but was not precisely matched. The distorted nature of the narrow-necked jar

Table 10 Romano-British pottery: fabric quantifications

Ware group	Fabric	Total	Wt (g)	Rel % wt	Rel % count
A	A10	2	14.9	0.5	0.6
	DR20	2	31.7	0.5	1.2
A total		*4*	*46.6*	*1.0*	*1.7*
BB1	BB1	24	153.7	6.1	5.7
C	C	22	151.8	5.6	5.6
F	CC2	4	1.4	1.0	0.1
M	M	2	131.3	0.5	4.9
O	O4	45	178.6	11.5	6.6
	O6	5	57.8	1.3	2.2
	O7	3	7	0.8	0.3
	SV	3	1.8	0.8	0.1
	SV1	14	26.1	3.6	1.0
	SV4	2	40.7	0.5	1.5
O total		*72*	*312*	*18.4*	*11.6*
R	R12	1	14.3	0.3	0.5
	R13	3	15.3	0.8	0.6
	R14	1	156.6	0.3	5.8
	R15	74	449	18.9	16.7
	R16	120	170.6	30.6	6.3
	R17	4	8.2	1.0	0.3
	R2	34	791.7	8.7	29.4
	R3	1	10.1	0.3	0.4
	R6	1	3.1	0.3	0.1
	R9	1	10.6	0.3	0.4
R total		*240*	*1629.5*	*61.2*	*60.5*
S	TS	9	125.3	2.3	4.7
W	FLA1	12	85.4	3.1	3.2
	FLA3	1	22.8	0.3	0.9
W total		*13*	*108.2*	*3.3*	*4.0*
WS	FLB1	1	6.4	0.3	0.2
	FLB2	1	25.4	0.3	0.9
WS total		*2*	*31.8*	*0.5*	*1.2*
Total		392	2691.6		

Table 11 Romano-British pottery: vessel types by estimated vessel equivalents

Vessel	Form	Ware group	Rim %	Rel %
Amphora	Amphora	Amph	*	
	Amphora	Amph	*	
Amphora total			0	
Bowl	Flat-rim	BB1	12	10.7
	carinated, double curve	WS	9	8.0
	Moulded-rim	R	5	4.5
	Flaring rim	O	15	13.4
	Flaring rim	R	7	6.3
Bowl total			48	42.9
Dish	DR18	S	6	5.4
Flagon	Neck	W	*	
	Turned base	W		**
Beaker	roughcast	F	*	
	roughcast	R	*	
	everted rim	O	5	4.5
Beaker total			5	
Jar	BB1	BB1	*	
Wide-mouthed jar	everted rim	R	7	6.3
	bifid everted rim	O	15	13.4
	curving, everted rim	O	2	1.8
	curving everted rim thickened at tip	O	9	8.0
	cordoned, curving everted rim thickened at tip	R	20	17.9
Wide-mouthed jar total			53	47.3
Narrow-necked jar	Narrow-necked jar	R	*	
Mortarium	bead & flange	M	*	
Total			112	

* = body sherds present; ** = <0.1%

from the site hints at the possibility of production in the vicinity.

Fabric R15 was fairly well represented by a large number of sherds from a cordoned, wide-mouthed jar of late 1st–early 2nd century type. The fabric with its brown core compared with Warwickshire fabric R41, given a date from the late 1st–4th centuries at Tiddington (Booth 1996a) and a fine grey ware found at Rocester used to make types of late 1st–early 2nd century type such as rusticated jars and Flavian Trajanic neckless, everted-rim jars (Leary forthcoming). A moulded rim from a bowl typical of the Flavian–Trajanic period supports this early date range, although such a small number of sherds invite caution.

The remaining reduced wares were present in very small numbers and were difficult to source or assess in terms of date. R13 was used to make a wide-mouthed jar so may be of mid-2nd century date or later, while a sherd of R9 came from a bowl with flaring rim which compares with carinated bowls of the late 1st–early 2nd centuries.

The oxidised wares include several examples which are closely comparable to the Severn Valley ware range of fabrics and included classic Severn Valley ware forms of the 2nd century. A wide-mouthed jar in fabric O4 may also be from this region or be a local version. Vessels in fabric O6 were a wide-mouthed jar with bifid, everted rim of a type found in the Shenstone kiln and a carinated bowl with flaring rim. These seem more likely to be local oxidised products than Severn Valley ware, although the source has not been located. O7 was scarcely represented but compared with Warwickshire O12, a local ware not precisely sourced as yet.

Two white ware fabrics were represented. FLA1 was fine and may have been a Mancetter-Hartshill product. FLA3 was an extremely fine ware identified as Warwickshire fabric W21 occurring in Antonine and 3rd century levels at Tiddington and Coleshill respectively, and thought to be a product of the Mancetter-Hartshill kilns.

The two white-slip ware vessels were in different fabrics. FLB1 was a fine ware with thin slip whereas FLB2 was coarser with a thicker more robust slip. The FLB1 sherd was undiagnostic, the fabric is not paralleled amongst the Warwickshire fabric series. The FLB2 sherd was very like fabric O6 and, on the basis of the consideration of that fabric, may also be local. The form belongs to the range made by the military potters in the early 2nd century and Mancetter-Hartshill is a possible source although the vessel is not matched there in this form and fabric combination.

A group of CTA sherds, perhaps all from a single combed storage jar, compared with Warwickshire fabric C41. This fabric was typically used for handmade jars in the 1st century but continued with lid-seated jars and storage jars into the 2nd century. This fabric was present in contexts dating to the first half of the 2nd century at Coleshill (eg Booth 2006, nos 473–6).

Amphora sherds were of southern Spanish type, principally Dressel 20. The samian assemblage, though small, includes South Gaulish, Central Gaulish and perhaps also East Gaulish material. Only four scraps of fine ware were recovered and these were from a roughcast beaker, probably from the Argonne region. The two mortaria were in an orange ware, possibly originally white-slipped, and a white-slipped fabric. Both were bead and flange forms of the 2nd century and neither compared closely with fabrics already identified, although fabric MWS1 was comparable to some fabrics from Wroxeter.

Vessel types

The quantity of bowls and dishes was relatively high with around the same amounts of jars and small amounts of flagons and beakers (Table 11). Very few cooking vessels were present and the number of food preparation vessels such as mortaria was also low. Very few BB1 jars were represented and other jars were overwhelmingly of the wide-mouthed type. In the writer's experience this latter type is rarely found with burnt matter adhering and may have had some specialist function related to the serving of food. The characteristics of the ceramic assemblage suggest a distinctive function, perhaps related to dining rather than cooking, with a relatively high status implied by the use of samian, beakers, flagons and amphora suggesting the adoption of Roman table manners. As the group is small and largely relates to occupation prior to the construction of the aisled building, these observations do not necessarily relate to the function of the latter.

The well yielded very little material, a BB1 jar sherd and scraps of reduced ware, unlike many wells which yield large groups of jars, often related to the activity of drawing water. Similarly the cremation yielded only abraded undiagnostic body and base sherds. The general impression of the site is, therefore, of one at which ceramic debris was not accumulating to any extent, at least within the excavated features and particularly during the use of the aisled building.

Pottery use

One BB1 jar sherd was sooted outside the body and a group of FLA1 flagon base and body sherds from posthole 340357 (340360) were burnt and abraded.

Worked stone, by Ruth Shaffrey

Three pieces of worked stone were retained, comprising two blocks of building stone with tool marks and one rotary quern fragment (ON 345002). The building blocks were recovered as samples from the lining (340099) of well 340098; both are of the same Keuper Triassic Sandstone found at all the M6 Toll sites (see Chapter 28). The rotary quern is made from a medium grained sandstone, probably Millstone Grit, and was used as packing (340273) in posthole 340245.

Catalogue of worked stone

1. Fragment of upper rotary quern. Probable medium-grained Millstone Grit. Deep uneven concentric grooves on grinding surface, otherwise pecked. Of flat-topped type. Posthole 340245. Second half 2nd century AD, context 340273. ON 345002
2. Roughly worked building stone. Triassic Keuper Sandstone – fine–medium grained well-sorted, well-rounded pale brown sandstone containing some mica and some plagioclase feldspar. Large block roughly worked and weathered. L 600 mm, W 400 mm; T 200 mm, context 340099, Well 340098
3. Building block. Triassic Keuper Sandstone – fine–medium grained well-sorted, well-rounded pale brown sandstone containing some mica and some plagioclase feldspar. Tool marks present on two sides. L 250 mm, W 200 mm; T 150 mm, context 340099, Well 340098

Building material, by Cynthia Poole

Only one fragment of Romano-British ceramic building material was found on this site. It was made in fabric S1, was heavily abraded and lacked any diagnostic features, but at 37 mm thick is probably a fragment of brick. It adds little to the interpretation of the site, but throws into stark relief the virtual absence of ceramic or stone building materials. This emphasises that the large aisled building excavated on the site must have utilised almost exclusively organic materials such as timber and thatch, though daub infill would also be unlikely to leave any trace.

Burnt animal bone, by Fay Worley

Animal bone was recovered from pit 340478 (contexts 340481 and 340479). All animal bone fragments were fully calcined and white in colour. Context 340481 contained two indeterminate mammal bone fragments and a medium mammal long bone fragment (1 g). Context 340479 contained a single fragment of indeterminate burnt bone weighing less than 1 g.

Environment

Charred plant remains, by A.J. Clapham

A total of 44 samples, of 3–30 litres, was taken during the excavations, mainly from Romano-British features. Seventeen samples were analysed for charred plant remains. The number of remains in each sample was low and they were poorly preserved. Ten samples were from postholes from the Romano-British aisled building; two were from well 340098, one from cremation grave 340119 and one from pit 340121. A single sample from Romano-British ditch 348008 (section 340299) was analysed as well as one from a Romano-British gully 341372. Plant remains were also identified from a sample from an Early Iron Age hollow (340145) containing burnt stone. The results are displayed in Tables 12–13.

Iron Age

Burnt stone hollow 340145

Few charred plant remains were recovered from the burnt stone spread in hollow 340145. These consisted of a single wheat grain, a barley grain and fragments of indeterminate cereal grains. Three fragments of hazel nutshell (*Corylus avellana*) were identified and probably represent a wild food resource. A tuber of onion couch grass (*Arrhenatherum elatius* var. *bulbosum*) was also found. It is most likely that these remains indicate a 'background' flora and cannot be used to interpret the function of this feature.

Table 12 Charred plant remains from postholes of the Romano-British aisled building

	Feature	340124	340135	340136	340161	340215	340231	340245	340269	340323	340346
	Context	340123	340134	340139	340163	340248	340244	340246	340271	340340	340348
	Sample	344007	344008	244009	344014	344031	344020	344038	344023	244036	344047
	Sample size (l)	16	20	8	20	4	8	10	3	8	10
	Flot size (ml)	10	20	125	75	5	40	40	100	50	20
Taxon	*Common name*										
Cereals											
Triticum dicoccum glume bases	Emmer	-	-	-	-	-	-	2	-	-	-
T. spelta glume bases	Spelt	-	-	-	10	-	9	-	8	1	-
T. spelta rachis fragments	Spelt	-	-	-	3	-	-	-	-	-	-
Triticum sp. Grain	Wheat	-	-	1	6+1f	1	2	-	1	2	-
Triticum sp. Spikelet forks	Wheat	-	-	-	1	-	-	-	3	-	-
Triticum sp. Glume bases	Wheat	-	-	-	25	1	1	4	6	3	-
Triticum sp. Basal rachis frags	Wheat	-	-	-	-	-	-	-	1	-	-
Hordeum vulgare hulled grain	Barley	-	-	2	2+1frag	-	-	-	2	-	-
H. vulgare rachis frags	Barley	-	-	-	2	-	-	-	-	-	-
Secale cereale rachis frags	Rye	-	-	-	-	-	2	-	2	-	-
Indeterminate cereal frags	-	-	5	1	18	1	11	2	2	3	-
Other species											
Spergula arvensis	Corn spurrey	-	-	-	-	-	-	-	1	-	-
Persicaria lapathifolia	Pale Persicaria	-	1	-	-	-	1f	-	-	-	-
Polygonum aviculare	Knotgrass	-	-	-	1	-	-	1	1	-	-
Fallopia convolvulus	Black Bindweed	-	1	-	1	-	-	-	-	-	-
Rumex acetosella	Sheep's sorrel	-	-	-	-	-	1	-	-	2	2
Rumex sp.	Dock	-	-	-	-	-	-	2	-	-	-
Raphanus raphanistrum pod frag.	Wild Radish	-	-	-	-	-	-	1	-	-	-
Vicia/Lathyrus sp.	Vetch/Tare	-	-	-	2	-	-	-	-	1	-
Trifolium sp.	Clover	1	-	-	-	-	-	1	-	-	-
Plantago lanceolata	Ribwort Plantain	-	-	-	-	-	-	-	1	-	-
Carex sp. (trigonous)	Sedges	-	-	-	-	-	-	-	1	-	-
Carex sp. (lenticular)	Sedges	-	-	-	-	-	-	-	1	-	-
Arrhenatherum elatius rootlets	False Oat Grass/ Onion couch grass	2	2	-	16	-	51	4	3	-	3
Avena sp.	Oats	-	-	-	-	-	-	1	-	-	-
Avena/Bromus sp.	Oats/Brome grass	-	-	-	-	1	-	-	3+1f	-	-
Bromus sp.	Brome grass	-	-	-	2frags	-	1f	1	-	-	-
Danthonia decumbens	Heath-grass	-	-	-	-	-	-	-	-	-	1
Small Poaceae	Small grass seeds	-	-	-	4	-	2	-	-	-	-
Culm bases (cereal)	-	-	-	-	34	-	-	-	11	-	-
Indeterminate flower head	-	-	-	-	-	-	-	1	-	-	-
Cenococcum geophilum	-	4	4	-	-	-	7	-	-	-	-
Unknown	-	1	-	-	-	-	-	-	-	-	-

Table 13 Charred plant remains from other features

Taxon	Common name							
	Period	Iron Age	Romano-British					
	Feature	Burnt stone spread in hollow 340145	Well 340098		Cremation grave 340119	Pit 340121	Ditch 348008	Gully 341372
	Section						340299	340263
	Context	340144	340101	340116	340122	340120	340300	340339
	Sample	344032	344003	344010	344006	344004	344026	344021
	Sample size (l)	20	20	20	3	13	17	7
	Flot size (ml)	500	175	20	10	40	125	2075
Cereals								
Triticum sp. Grain	Wheat	1	-	-	-	-	-	-
Triticum sp. Glume bases	Wheat	-	-	3	-	-	1	-
Triticum sp. Rachis frags	Wheat	-	-	1	-	-	-	-
Hordeum vulgare hulled grain	Barley	1	-	2	-	-	-	-
Secale cereale rachis frags	Rye	-	-	2	-	-	-	-
Indeterminate cereal frags	-	14	5	5	-	5	6	-
Other species								
Beta vulgaris	Beet	-	-	-	-	-	1	-
Corylus avellana nutshell frags	Hazel	3	-	-	-	-	-	-
Chenopodium album	Fathen	-	-	1	-	-	-	-
Stellaria media	Chickweed	-	1	-	-	-	-	-
Rumex acetosella	Sheep's sorrel	-	-	-	1	-	-	-
Rumex sp.	Dock	-	-	-	-	-	1	-
Crataegus monogyna fruit frag.	Hawthorn	-	-	1	-	-	-	-
Arrhenatherum elatius tubers	Onion Couch grass	1	-	-	-	-	-	-
Arrhenatherum elatius rootlets	False Oat Grass/Onion couch grass	-	-	-	1	5	-	-
Avena sp. Awn fragment	Oats	-	-	1	-	-	-	-
Small Poaceae	Small grass seeds	-	-	-	-	2	1	-
Culm node	-	-	-	-	-	-	1	-
Culm bases (cereal)	-	-	3	-	-	-	9	2
Cenococcum geophilum	-	-	-	15	9	6	-	-
Parenchyma fragments	-	-	1	-	-	-	-	-

Romano-British

Postholes of the aisled building

Overall there were quite a few charred plant remains identified from ten samples (Table 12). The remains represent cultivated cereals, such as glume bases of emmer wheat (*Triticum dicoccum*) and spelt wheat (*T. spelta*), the latter also represented by rachis fragments. Grains of wheat (*Triticum* sp.) were also recovered and it is also most likely that they are of spelt. Hulled barley (*Hordeum vulgare*) was also found along with barley chaff in the form of rachis fragments. Rye (*Secale cereale*) was represented by chaff remains (rachis fragments).

Weed seeds were represented by corn spurrey (*Spergula arvensis*), pale persicaria (*Persicaria lapathifolia*), knotgrass (*Polygonum aviculare*), black bindweed (*Fallopia convolvulus*), sheep's sorrel (*Rumex acetosella*), dock (*Rumex* sp.), wild radish (*Raphanus raphanistrum*), vetch/tare (*Vicia/Lathyrus* sp.), clover (*Trifolium* sp.), ribwort plantain (*Plantago lanceolata*), various species of grasses such as oats (*Avena* sp.), onion couch grass/false oat grass (*Arrhenatherum elatius*), brome grass (*Bromus* sp.) and heath-grass (*Danthonia decumbens*). It is most likely that all of these species were associated with the crops and were present as cornfield weeds. The identification of sedges (*Carex* sp.) suggests that there was damp ground to be found locally.

The presence of rye may be considered to be unusual as it is generally associated with later periods. Rye is usually grown on the lighter, sandy soils and the cultivation of this soil type can be confirmed by the presence of corn spurrey and heath-grass which can also indicate damper acidic conditions.

From the plant remains present from these postholes, it can be suggested that the timber aisled building was probably used to store locally grown cereals. It is even possible that some crop-processing may have been carried out inside the building prior to the cereals being taken to Wall via Watling Street. This might explain the presence of weed seeds.

Pit 340121

The sample from pit 340121, just outside the entrance to the Romano-British aisled building, contained very few charred plant remains. Five fragments of indeterminate cereal grains and five rootlets of false oat grass were recovered along with two small grass seeds. From these remains it is difficult to determine the function of the pit and it is possible that the assemblage represents a 'background flora'. However, given the presence of remains of false-oat grass within both this deposit and that from the cremation grave, it may suggest that some of this material was derived from a cremation pyre (see Gale below).

Well 340098

Two samples were analysed from well 340098 (contexts 340101 and 340116). Charred plant remains were rare with 340116 producing the greater number. In 340101 no cereal remains were identified apart from several fragments of indeterminate cereal grain. Other plant species identified include chickweed (*Stellaria media*) and a few cereal culm bases.

Context 340116 produced more in the way of cereal remains, including wheat chaff (glume bases and rachis fragments), barley grains and rye rachis fragments. Weed seeds identified include fathen (*Chenopodium album*), and oats. A fragment of a hawthorn fruit (*Crataegus monogyna*) was also identified. These remains most likely represent evidence of crop-processing although the hawthorn fruit may have originated from a shrub growing by the well or from scrub or hedgerows in the locality.

Cremation grave 340119

A single sample from a cremation grave was examined for charred plant remains (340122). Very few plant remains were recovered from this sample. These included a single nutlet of sheep's sorrel and rootlets of false oat grass. The rootlets may represent the remains of fuel used in the cremation but it is most likely that the remains represent a 'background' residual flora.

Ditch 348008 and gully 341372

Two samples, one from each feature were analysed for plant remains, both being dated to the Romano-British period. Little in the way of plant remains were recovered from these two samples. Only two cereal culm nodes were found in 341372 but 348008 contained more plant remains. Cereals were only represented by a single wheat glume base, other remains include a fruit of beet (*Beta vulgaris*) and a single nutlet of dock.

The presence of beet is of some interest and has already been identified from Washbrook Lane, Norton Canes (Site 5; Clapham, Chapter 7). It is most likely that the beet was deliberately cultivated as its natural habitat is the seashore, although it more probably represents the leaf beet variety.

Conclusions

In general, there were few plant remains recovered from the samples and therefore it is not possible to produce a full interpretation of the function of the features and the subsistence activities on the site. It is possible to suggest that wheat, barley and rye were grown locally with rye being cultivated on the poorer lighter sandy soils. Other crops that were grown include beetroot, and hazel nuts were probably harvested from the wild to supplement the diet.

It is possible to suggest that the aisled building was used for storing semi-cleaned crops as the postholes contained both cereal grains and chaff. There may have even been some crop-processing carried out in the building, as indicated by the presence of the chaff remains of barley and rye, especially when the weather was inclement. The significance of the results from this site, and on agricultural activities and their relation to the local environment in the Romano-British period are discussed in more detail in the report for East of Birmingham Road Nurseries (Site 15; Clapham, Chapter 17).

Table 14 Waterlogged wood identifications

Feature	Context	Sample	Identification	No.	Comments on sample
Posthole 340136	340139	344009	Mature *Quercus* sp.	2	14 frags >30 mm, plus several smaller, originally a single timber. Mature, very large growth rings
Posthole 340223	340225	344017	Mature *Quercus* sp.	2	1 large timber frag. (160 mm by 110 mm by 35 mm max.), plus 11 frags >30 mm and several smaller, originally a single timber. Mature, very large growth rings

Waterlogged wood, by Catherine Chisham

Waterlogged wood recovered by hand from postholes associated with the Romano-British aisled building was found in to be in excellent condition and was retained and prepared for identification. It was from large timbers of mature *Quercus* sp. (oak) and likely represents the posts preserved *in situ* (Table 14).

Charcoal,, by Rowena Gale

Twenty-six of the 44 bulk soil samples were collected from postholes associated with the timber structure, but proved to be very unproductive in terms of charcoal and charred plant remains. Eight samples of charcoal were selected for analysis from a range of features including two postholes, a pit, a cremation burial, ditches, a gully and the hollow containing burnt stone. The condition of the charcoal varied from very poor in the postholes to good (gully 341372). Identification was undertaken to obtain environmental data, to provide material for radiocarbon dating and to examine the type of fuel used on site. The taxa identified are shown on Table 15.

Iron Age

Burnt stone in hollow 340145

Charcoal associated with the burnt stones fill was abundant. The 50% sub-sample examined indicated the exclusive use of oak (*Quercus* sp.) heartwood. It produced a radiocarbon date of 800–520 cal BC.

Romano-British

Postholes 340136 and 340269

The timber aisled building measured some 30 by 10 m and the supporting posts were sunk into deep postholes. The remains of two posts, preserved through water-logging, were examined from postholes 340136 and 340223 and identified as oak (see above). Charcoal from the basal fills of postholes 340136 (sample 344009) and 340269 (sample 344023) was identified as oak heartwood and roundwood, and blackthorn (*Prunus spinosa*). The identification of multiple wood species and/or roundwood in these deposits indicates origins from hearths or bonfires (as opposed to structural timbers), which was either incorporated with packing material around the posts, dumped as backfill in the postholes after removal of the posts or accumulated naturally from scattered debris.

Pit 340121

The kidney-shaped pit 340121 lay close to the west flank of the building. The single fill (340120) contained large fragments from a pottery vessel and charcoal from oak, pine (*Pinus* sp.) and heather (Ericaceae). The oak included both narrow roundwood and heartwood. The function of the pit was not clear but may have been for waste disposal. However, the presence of tubers of false-oat grass in this deposit (see Clapham above) and the fact that the only other Romano-British find of pine wood is from the Ryknield Street cremation burials (Site 12; Gale, Chapter 14) might suggest that some of the material includes pyre waste.

Cremation grave 340119

A cremation burial was found a short distance from the northern end of the building. The body had been cremated off-site and the remains placed in a vessel. Associated charcoal (sample 344006) was very sparse but included moderate to fast-grown oak sapwood.

Ditch 348008

Charcoal was examined from segments 340299 and 340304 of the ditch 348008, which appeared to contain occupation debris. Although almost certainly hearth debris, it was not clear whether this resulted from domestic or agricultural activities. Oak was common to both samples; the large deposit in segment 340304 indicated the exclusive use of oak largewood, whereas the comparatively scrappy amount in segment 340299 also included birch (*Betula* sp.), hazel (*Corylus avellana*) and holly (*Ilex aquifolium*).

Gully 341372

This feature consisted of a shallow clay-lined gully with a charcoal-rich fill (context 340339). The charcoal was in unusually good condition and free from the contaminating sediments that had infiltrated deposits in other contexts. A 25% sub-sample was examined. The charcoal consisted entirely of narrow roundwood, predominantly oak, mostly <8 years of age, but also hazel, willow (*Salix* sp.)/poplar (*Populus* sp.), holly and heather. A single piece of uncarbonised oak roundwood was associated with slaggy material.

Discussion

A large amount of fuel debris was recovered from among the burnt stones in hollow 340145, radiocarbon dated to the Early–Middle Iron Age. Although there was no

Table 15 Charcoal (no. frags)

Feature	Section	Context	Sample	Betula	Corylus	Ericaceae	Ilex	Prunus	Quercus	Salicaceae	Pinus
Iron Age											
Burnt stone hollow 340145		340144	344032	–	–	–	–	–	43h	–	–
Romano-British											
Ditch 348008	340299	340300	344026	1	1	–	1	–	1h, 1r	–	–
	340304	340305	344033	–	–	–	–	–	42h/u, 2s	–	–
Posthole 340136		340139	344009	–	–	–	–	–	2r, 3s	–	–
Posthole 340269		340271	340023	–	–	–	–	2	5h/u, 10r	2s	–
Cremation grave 340119		340122	344006	–	–	–	–	–	3s	–	–
Pit 340121		340120	344004	–	–	2r	–	–	1h, 3r, 3s	–	2
Gully 341372		340339	344021	–	2r	2r	3r	–	91r	1r	–

Key: h = heartwood; r = roundwood (diam <20 mm); s = sapwood (diam. unknown); u = maturity unknown (*Quercus* only)

evidence for the hearth site being used to heat the stones, the charcoal indicated the selective use of oak heartwood.

The remainder of the discussion concentrates on the charcoal from features relating to the early to mid-Romano-British occupation of the site. Charcoal deposits from this period were mostly sparse and of uncertain origin. Samples collected from postholes in the timber structure, for example, were clearly not from the posts themselves but from hearth debris, possibly included as packing material around the posts or dumped as backfill. Alternatively, the material may have accrued from scattered agricultural or domestic waste.

The general character of refuse dumped in ditch 348008, however, was more indicative of domestic debris, probably from a farmstead sited close by. The large dump of fuel debris in this context, sample 344033, indicated the selective use of oak largewood and, given that domestic firewood usually consists of mixed species, often with a high ratio of roundwood (see, for example, domestic hearth debris from Site 15) the singular use of oak on this occasion may reflect its use for a particular purpose – or the recycling (as firewood) or disposal of discarded oak posts or off-cuts from wood-working waste. Oak largewood provides a long-lasting heat-source and requires less attention than roundwood.

A single cremation grave (340119) occurred just north of the timber structure. The cremated remains were contained in a vessel. Associated oak charcoal (sample 344006) probably represents pyre fuel but it would be necessary to examine a much larger sample of charcoal than was available to determine practical or ritual aspects of wood selection/use.

A charcoal-rich deposit in the gully 341372 was notable not only for its unusually good preservation but also because it consisted entirely of narrow roundwood, mainly oak, but also hazel, holly, willow/poplar and heather. Since the shallow clay-lined gully showed no signs of *in situ* burning, the charcoal was evidently dumped in this feature. The character of this deposit differed substantially from those examined from other contexts, and must relate either to the selective use of roundwood for a particular function or to the supply of fuel. It is feasible that the deposit derived from a casual bonfire used to dispose of, for example, hedge trimmings or discarded hurdles, but it seems less likely that bonfire debris would have been cleared and dumped in the gully.

The use of narrow roundwood would have produced an intensely hot, fast-burning but short-lived fire, such as that required for cooking or for some types of industrial activity, for example, firing pottery.

Environmental evidence

The site was based on sandy soils. Despite the (probably) intensively farmed land at this site, the charcoal indicated access to a range of arboreal species within the catchment area of the site. The frequency of oak in the deposits implies that oak formed the dominant woodland component in the area. Oak woodland may have been fairly open in character, perhaps mixed with birch, holly and hazel. Oak may also have grown as a hedgerow tree. The presence of heather suggests that patches of heathland were also present, perhaps in areas less suited to cultivation, and it may be that birch was also present in such areas. The presence of pine is again of some interest given its occurrence in cremation deposits from Ryknield Street (Site 12; Gale, Chapter 14), but also for its general absence from the pollen record for the preceding period (Scaife, Chapter 14). It may be that a few trees were able to colonise areas of heathland. Areas of damper soil (spring-lines or waterways) are indicated by the presence of willow or poplar.

The wood structure of some coppiced species, including oak, does not always demonstrate the initial spurt of growth typically seen, for example, in hazel coppice (Morgan 1982) and thus it is often difficult to establish the presence or use of managed woodland. But taking into account circumstantial evidence such as the (probable) open character of the agricultural landscape in the Romano-British period, it could be argued that small areas were probably maintained as managed woodland to fulfil the timber and fuel requirements of the working farm and associated farmstead. More secure evidence for the possible use of narrow roundwood was provided by large deposit of fuel debris (charcoal) from gully 341372 (sample 344021), which consisted entirely of narrow roundwood including mainly juvenile oak, less than 8 years of age but also hazel, holly, willow/poplar and heather. Pressure on agrarian use of the land suggests that coppicing and woodmanship would have been necessary. Some trees, however, clearly attained some degree of maturity, as indicated by deposits of oak largewood.

Discussion

Iron Age

A single feature, a hollow containing burnt stone (340145), was the only evidence for prehistoric activity identified on the site, radiocarbon dated to the Early–Middle Iron Age. In the absence of any artefactual material from this feature, or of other contemporary features either within or near the site, this single feature is hard to interpret. Deposits of fire-cracked stone might indicate a range of possible activities – domestic, industrial or ritual.

Romano-British

Use of the site in the Romano-British period began with the establishment of a system of rectilinear field or paddock enclosures. This is unlikely to have taken place before the 2nd century as no diagnostically earlier pottery was identified. A post-built aisled building was subsequently constructed partly over one of the back-filled ditches of the enclosure system. The re-cutting of the north-western part of ditch 348008 is, however, an indication that the enclosures probably continued in use in a slightly altered form after the construction of the building.

The aisled building presents certain problems in relation to its date and function. Pottery from ditch 348008, which preceded the building, and from the packing in the postholes of the building itself provided a *terminus post quem* for its construction some time around the middle of the 2nd century AD, but how long it was in use for is less certain. No floor surfaces associated with the building were preserved and the internal gully (341372) contained no dating evidence. The pottery derived from contexts associated with the demolition of the building is of a similar date to that dating the construction, so either the building was in use for only a very short period of time or, more likely, this material was residual. Cross-joins and sherds identified as originating from the same vessel in both the postholes of the aisled building and ditch 348008 indicate that residuality was a factor in the pottery assemblage recovered from the site. There was therefore no dating evidence associated with the use or demolition of the building, and its period of use is effectively open-ended. The only feature that may have been associated with the use of the building was clay-lined drainage gully 341372, but this is not particularly useful in interpreting the building's function. The pottery recovered from the postholes was not useful in establishing the function as the assemblage was small and not demonstrably related to the use of the building. The small size of the finds assemblage and the absence of obviously domestic artefacts suggest that the building was not domestic in function, an impression strengthened by the absence of its sub-division into rooms or of decorative embellishments such as flooring, wall plaster or tiles. The most likely function is as a barn, with the bays created by its aisled construction serving as separate storage areas.

The building is unlikely to have stood in isolation, but formed part of a larger site, as indicated by the cropmark evidence. However, the cropmarks lacked definition and so the details of the site are uncertain. The most likely interpretation is that the features recorded represent part of a villa complex, although none of the other major components of the complex can be identified on present evidence. This site is consistent with other villas known in Staffordshire both in terms of its location relatively close to a major road and of the date of its construction during the 2nd century (Wardle 2002a). Although a military interpretation is also an alternative, this seems unlikely as the establishment of a further military depot so close to the existing base at Wall seems unnecessary. In addition, the pottery assemblage was typical of a civilian rural settlement rather than a military one, and a military base would be likely to have been enclosed in a way that would create much clearer cropmarks than those recorded.

Despite the general non-domestic character of the aisled building, suggested also by the paucity of finds, the ceramic assemblage consisted largely of vessel types associated with dining, with relatively few types associated with cooking and food preparation present. The use of samian ware, beakers, flagons and amphora suggest the occupants had adopted Roman dining habits and had a status above that of people in other rural settlements in the area. The occurrence of some of this material in the fills of the ditch cut by the posts of the aisled building suggests that this status was already established by the time the building was erected. It also underlines the view that, while indicative of the character of the site, this material does not provide evidence relating to the use of the building itself.

Although the dating evidence is limited the pottery suggests that, in this part of the complex at least, activity probably did not extend beyond the late 2nd century at the latest.

Post-medieval

The post-medieval features require little comment. For the most part they seem to have been field boundaries. The most interesting feature was the minor railway, probably related to a nearby sand quarry, and in use in the period between the two World Wars. The fact that it does not appear on successive Ordnance Survey maps indicates the potentially transitory nature of relatively substantial structures.

SITES AROUND WALL AND SHENSTONE

Twelve sites, seven of them reported here, were investigated in an almost continuous transect, *c* 4.8 km long, across the landscape in the vicinity of Wall, Shenstone and Weeford (Fig. 58). Although not all of these sites produced evidence of Romano-British activity, their proximity to the Roman town at Wall and the Roman roads of Watling Street and Ryknield Street means that they share a common landscape and have, to a degree, a common archaeological background.

The principal sites in this group – West of Crane Brook (Site 9), Ryknield Street (Site 12), Shenstone Linear Features (Site 13), Shenstone Ring Ditch (Site 14) and East of Birmingham Road Nurseries (Site 15) – lay on the northern and eastern margins of the Shenstone Basin, a low-lying area with much wetland before 18th and 19th century drainage. These marginal areas are mostly quite level, raised only slightly above the basin floor, although the ground rises to the north behind Site 12 in the direction of Wall, and within Site 9 itself there was in local terms a notable rounded high point in the middle of the site, from which the ground sloped gently to east and west and more steeply down on the south side.

A series of Roman forts and marching camps was established at Wall, around which a small town, *Letocetum*, developed. *Letocetum* later became the site of an Imperial posting station, comprising a *mansio*, or hostel providing accommodation for officials travelling on the road, and a public bathhouse. The town, now a Scheduled Ancient Monument, was excavated in 1912–14 by the North Staffordshire Field Club, and on a number of occasions since (Gould 1998). Two major Roman roads intersected *c* 1.4 km east of the town – Watling Street, running from London across the Midlands to Wroxeter and on to the military districts of the north-west, and Ryknield Street, running north from the Fosse Way in Gloucestershire, through Alcester, Birmingham, Wall and Derby, to Templeborough in Yorkshire.

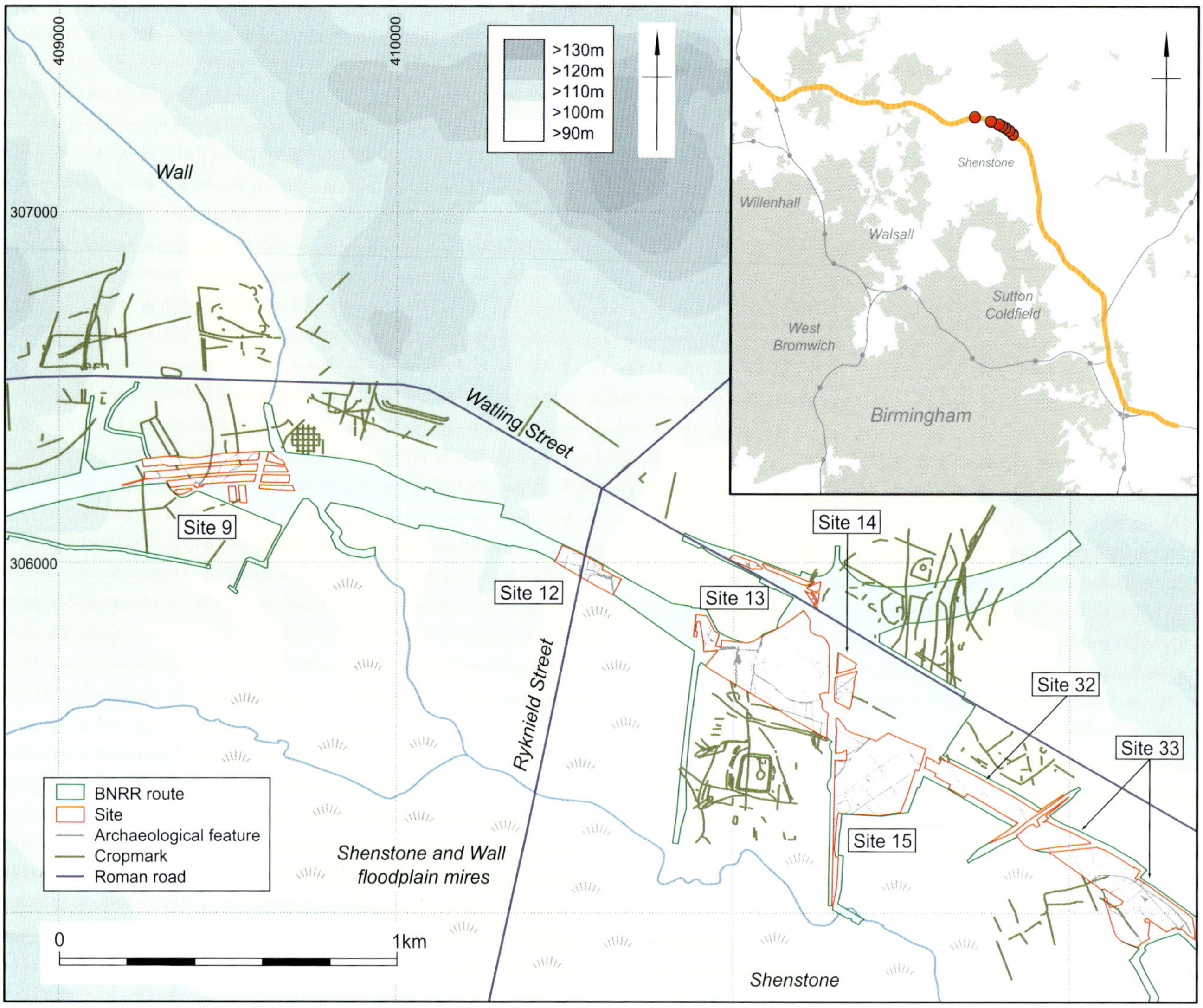

Fig. 58 Sites around Wall

Chapter 13

West of Crane Brook, Wall (Site 9)

By *Mike Trevarthen*

Introduction

An archaeological excavation was undertaken on land west of Crane Brook, immediately south-west of the Roman town of Wall (*Letocetum*). A small deposit of burnt stone was revealed on the southern flank of a small knoll. No artefacts were recovered, but charcoal from the deposit yielded a radiocarbon date within the later Neolithic. A number of other features, including a large curvilinear boundary ditch, drainage ditches and a borrow-pit or small quarry, were investigated but were all of post-medieval or recent date, and are not discussed in detail.

The site, covering 2.8 hectares centred on NGR 409400 306260, was located between the A5(T) and Bullmore Lane, *c* 0.3 km south-west of Wall (Fig. 59). The site's eastern boundary was defined by the Crane Brook, a small permanent stream that, before construction of the M6 Toll, may already have followed an artificial (or at least partially artificial) channel.

Underlying geology is mapped as Triassic Bunter Upper Mottled Sandstone, overlain by alluvium adjacent to Crane Brook (Geological Survey of Great Britain 1954, Sheet 154, Lichfield). A small outcrop of Pleistocene Boulder Clay, with a maximum elevation of 103.5 m aOD, corresponds with the site's central knoll. Low-lying areas of the site, at *c* 98.2–98.3 m aOD, were damp, and the lowest were seasonally saturated. Soils in these areas were dark and humic, sometimes overlying the remains of a slightly peaty subsoil. Anecdotal information from the former landowner indicates that groundwater abstraction has appreciably lowered the local water table since the early 1980s.

Fieldwalking was undertaken prior to an archaeological evaluation (OAU 1994c) targeted on cropmarks. The evaluation revealed a large curvilinear ditch likely to be Late Iron Age or Romano-British in date, possibly enclosing a small, much-truncated rural hilltop settlement. Little archaeological material had been recorded previously from the site's environs, although the Romano-British landscape is dominated by the settlement at Wall.

The original plan was for a watching brief of 3.72 hectares of land, to be followed by a review of the results to identify *c* 1 hectare within that area for full excavation. However, due to the wet ground conditions, critical constraints on access and the low level of archaeological remains this was revised. The requirement for a full excavation was withdrawn, and three principal *c* 20 m wide east–west strips were stripped of topsoil, with smaller trenches excavated to the south and south-east to ensure coverage of the site footprint. The site was *c* 0.43 km long aligned east–west, and 0.14 km wide. A machine-dug trial-trench extended the western edge of the site by a further 68 m, but no significant archaeological remains were discovered here and the trench was not expanded.

Results

Neolithic burnt stone deposit

A localised deposit of burnt stone in a charcoal-rich soil (90307) (Fig. 59) was discovered on the southern flank of the site's central knoll, immediately above ground which, until recent times, is likely to have been marshy or at least seasonally wet. The deposit was slightly machine-truncated on its northern edge (prior to its recognition), but survived as an irregular sub-oval layer measuring *c* 6 m by 7 m and up to 0.15 m thick. Concentrations of burnt stone were also noted filling the terminal of large post-medieval or recent curvilinear boundary ditch (90089) immediately to the north, suggesting the ditch may originally have cut through the burnt deposit, or lain close to its edge. Layer 90307 comprised abundant thermally shattered quartzite pebbles in a very dark, charcoal-rich sandy matrix.

No evidence for associated structures was found and no artefacts were recovered from the deposit. However, a sample of short-lived wood from the deposit (birch) provided a radiocarbon date of 2920–2660 cal BC (4230±35, NZA-25076) (Fig. 214). This places the deposit within the later Neolithic.

The burnt stone deposit sealed and preserved 0.2 m of mid–dark brown sandy loam (90308), probably a colluvial soil. Some charred material was noted within this layer, but most, if not all of this was probably intrusive from the overlying deposit. An undated irregular tree hollow (90309) was sealed below 90308.

Post-medieval/modern and undated

The majority of artificial features comprised land drains of 18th century or later date (often 'horseshoe' types), along with recent and modern drainage ditches, field-boundary ditches, and other intrusions. Irregular, and

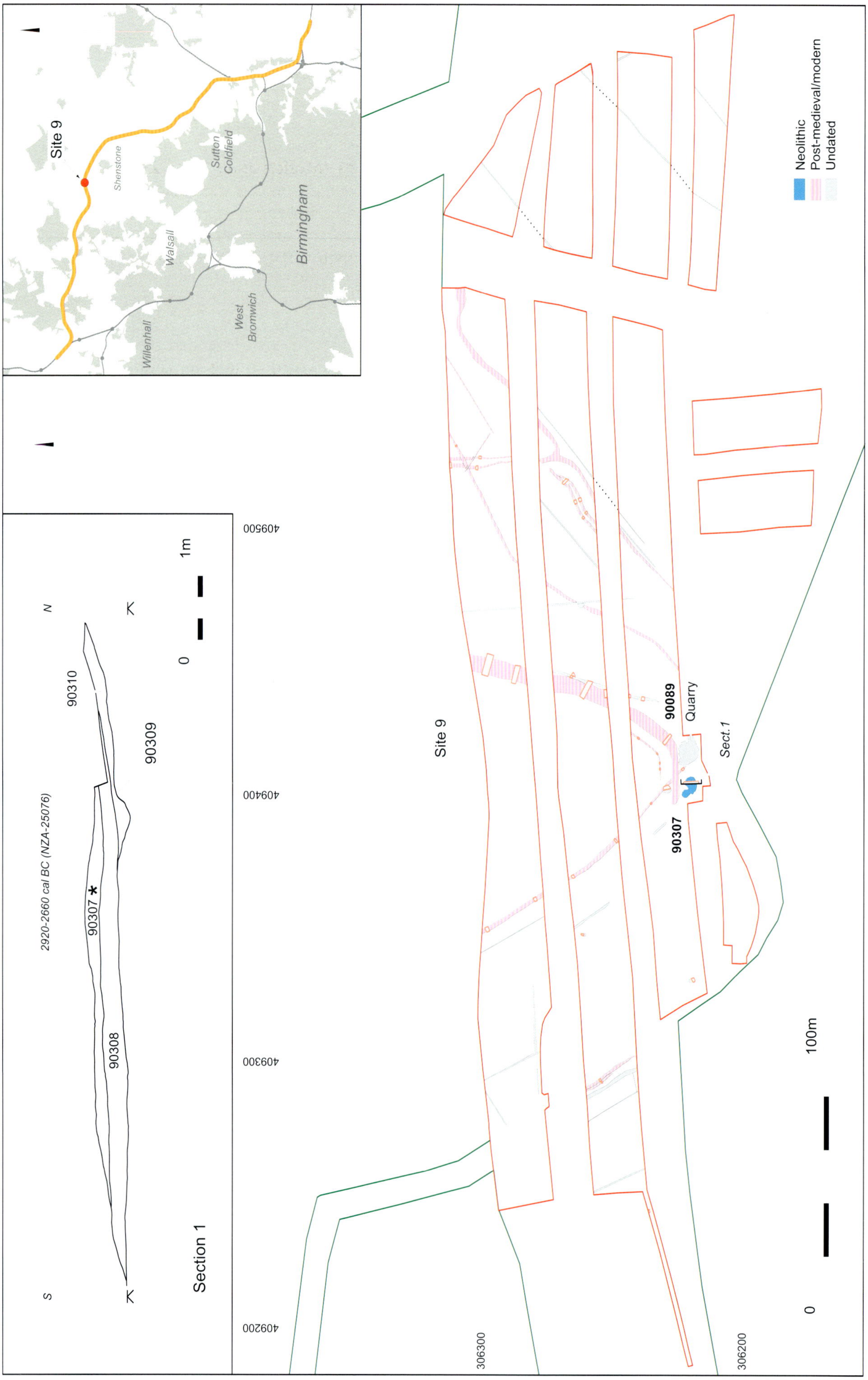

Fig. 59 West of Crane Brook (Site 9) and section of the burnt mound

often poorly defined, tree hollows were abundant, but none of those investigated yielded dating evidence. These features are not discussed further.

Finds

Flint, by Kate Cramp with Hugo Lamdin-Whymark

An end scraper was recovered from the ploughsoil *c* 120 m west of the main site. The scraper has been neatly retouched on a flake with platform edge abrasion and dorsal blade scars, technological traits that might support a Mesolithic or Neolithic date for the piece.

Romano-British pottery, by Ruth Leary

The site produced sherds from only two Romano-British vessels, all of them residual in later features. Six unabraded BB1 sherds (12 g) from a bowl or dish decorated with intersecting burnished arcs came from a tree hollow (90208) and a very abraded R2 jar bodysherd (30 g) with multiple horizontal grooves came from the ploughsoil. The BB1 vessel can be dated to the late 2nd century or later (Gillam 1976, 68). The grey ware sherd is not closely datable but as the fabric is similar to vessels from the Shenstone kiln (Chapter 17), it may be mid/late 2nd–3rd century.

Environment

Charred plant remains, by Lisa Gray

Two samples, each of 20 litres, were taken from within and below the burnt stone deposit, shown by radiocarbon dating to be of later Neolithic date, for the analysis of charred plant remains. Sample details and contents are given in full in Table 16.

Results

Very few charred plant remains were recovered from the samples. The burnt stone deposit (90307) produced no identifiable material, while a fragment of hazelnut (*Corylus avellana*) shell was recovered from the underlying soil (90308). Little can be gleaned from these remains, although hazelnut shells are commonly recovered from both Mesolithic and Neolithic sites and would seem to form an important part of the diet within these periods (Moffett *et al.* 1989; Zvelebil 1994). The scarcity of remains in this site is similar to those at the burnt mounds and burnt stone spreads from sites 19, 30, 39 and 40 and hazelnut shell fragments are the only non-wood plant they have in common.

Table 16 Charred plant remains

	Feature	Soil below burnt stone deposit	Burnt stone deposit
	Context	90308	90307
	Sample	90077	90075
	sample size (l)	20	20
	Flot size (ml)	1000	2600
Taxon	Common name		
Corylus avellana L.	hazel, shell frags	2	–
Brassica/Sinapsis sp.	Wild cabbage/ mustard, seed	*cf.* 1	*cf.* 1

Charcoal, by Rowena Gale

Both of the samples from within the burnt stone deposit and from the soil beneath were selected for wood charcoal analysis. Charcoal identification was undertaken to assess the character of the fuel used to heat the stones and to isolate short-lived species (from sample 90075) for radiocarbon dating. The taxa identified are presented in Table 17. Fragments of birch (*Betula* sp.) were selected for radiocarbon dating.

A 25% sub-sample of the large volume of charcoal available in the sample from the burnt deposit (90307) was examined, and identified as predominantly alder (*Alnus glutinosa*) and birch, but also oak (*Quercus* sp.), from slow-grown largewood, and the hawthorn/*Sorbus* group (Pomoideae). Charcoal was relatively sparse in the underlying soil (90308) but, apart from the absence of the hawthorn group and the addition of partially charred pine (*Pinus* sp.), the species content was roughly similar to that in the burnt deposit.

Discussion

The later Neolithic burnt stone deposit was located in a shallow depression, overlying natural accumulations of soil (the pebbles were almost certainly used to heat water). Charcoal was recovered from both contexts, and the evidence from the deposit indicates that firewood consisted predominantly of alder and birch. The divergent caloric values of these woods (birch provides a fast-burning, short-lived but intensely hot fuel whereas alder is slow to ignite and burns sluggishly; Edlin 1949; Lines 1984; Porter 1990) probably compensated for each other to some extent. Oak heartwood, on the other hand, produces a hot and longer-lasting heat-source. At first sight, the predominant use of alder would seem to be an unsuitable choice but, given the low-lying and often waterlogged soils in this area, it is probable that alder and birch dominated local woodland and offered the most readily available source of fuel.

The origin of the sample from beneath the burnt mound is not entirely clear. While most of the charcoal was probably intrusive from the overlying deposit, it could represent the earliest deposits of fuel debris associated with the burnt stone deposit or an unknown activity that pre-dated the build-up of the deposit. Interestingly, in addition to alder, birch and oak, this deposit included partially burnt pine. The resinous wood

Table 17 Charcoal from the Neolithic burnt mound (no. frags)

Feature	*Context*	*Sample*	*Alnus*	*Betula*	*Pomoideae*	*Quercus*	*Pinus*
Burnt stone deposit	90307	90075	43	28	2	3h	–
Soil below burnt stone deposit	90308	90077	2	8	–	5h	11

Key: h = heartwood

of pine burns quickly, although it has a tendency to spit (Edlin 1949). Why the pine fuel debris should be only partially burnt, in contrast to the fully carbonised residues from the remaining species, is perplexing but it may be because the fire was abandoned or doused before the firewood was fully consumed. In such an event, the resins inherent in the wood structure of pine would have enhanced its survival rate in aerobic soils, although possible waterlogging in the base of the hollow would also have improved its chances of long-term preservation.

Environmental evidence

The predominance of alder wood in the deposit suggests that alder carr dominated the lower lying riverine areas during the later Neolithic. It is probable that birch also grew within this fen woodland, and it is notable that birch also appears within the prehistoric peats of the Somerset levels and East Anglia (Rackham 2003). Oak and hawthorn would normally be found on drier soils, although the slow-growth noted in oak largewood from soil 90308 may record stressed growing conditions (perhaps due to excessive moisture in the soil) or a competitive environment.

The presence of pine is of some interest, although certainly pine today commonly invades alder-birch carr woodlands of this type (Rodwell 1991). However, it is largely absent from pollen diagrams by the Early to Middle Neolithic and is certainly not recorded at this date within a well dated sequence from Crose Mere, Shropshire (Beales 1980). It should be noted that the pine charcoal comes from under the later Neolithic dated deposit and as such may be much earlier, possibly even Mesolithic in date.

Discussion

The deposit of burnt stone, comprising a spread of burnt quartzite pebbles in a charcoal-rich soil, was initially interpreted as a burnt mound, but the later Neolithic date of 2920–2660 cal BC was early in relation to the expected Middle Bronze Age date for such features. It is notable, however, that nearly all the other evidence for Neolithic activity along the M6 Toll was found in the Wall/Shenstone area, including pits and a chisel arrowhead from Shenstone Linear Features (Site 13), and pottery from East of Birmingham Road Nurseries, Shenstone (Site 15) and East of The Castle, Shenstone (Site 32), as well as a possibly Neolithic flint scraper from this site.

The function of the deposit is unclear, although it is evident that local wood resources, predominately alder, were used in preference to better quality but less locally available fuels such as oak, to heat stones and therefore presumably water. Although sited in a damp, low-lying location, possibly subject to seasonal flooding, the deposit was not beside a stream course as was the case of the burnt mound deposits at Langley Brook (Site 39) and Colletts Brook Burnt Mound (Site 40), and the burnt stone spreads at Langley Mill (Site 30).

Although the majority of other features recorded at the site proved to be post-medieval or modern in date, the presence of Romano-British pottery is not unexpected given the site's proximity to Watling Street, the Roman town at Wall, and the extensive cropmarks in the area, some of which indicate Romano-British settlement and land-use, as well as the evidence of Romano-British activity recorded at the M6 Toll sites both to the east and west.

Chapter 14
Rykniald Street, Wall (Site 12)

By Jacqueline I. McKinley

Introduction

An archaeological excavation was undertaken along the course of the north–south Roman road, Ryknield Street. Archaeological evaluation had confirmed the position of the Roman road, which has long been known to pass to the east of Wall (Ordnance Survey 1956; Margary 1973; Oswald 1966–7a) through the location of a pair of parallel ditches following the road alignment, and revealed the presence of several cremation-related deposits to either side of the routeway suggesting the possible presence of a cemetery. The excavation revealed ditches marking the 'road-zone' of Ryknield Street, which ran north–south through the centre of the site, and elements indicative of the road's construction. A small, multi-rite cemetery lay to either side of the road, including four sub-rectangular mortuary enclosures to the east. A series of hearths/ovens, apparently contemporary with the early part of the cemetery, lay on its western boundary (Fig. 60).

The site comprised a rectangular area of *c* 1.1 ha (*c* 200 m by 60 m), formerly under agricultural cultivation, situated *c* 0.5 km to the south-east of Roman *Letocetum* (the village of Wall) and *c* 1.5 km north of the small town of Shenstone, centred on 410570 305970. The A5 (T) Wall by-pass, constructed in the 1960s – partly along the line of Roman Watling Street – lies *c* 135 m to the north of the site. The site lay towards the lower margins of a gentle, south-east facing slope, between *c* 100 m aOD in the north-west and *c* 97 m aOD in the south-east. The area occupied by the road and the cemetery appeared to lie on a natural terrace between 98.8 m and 100.1 m aOD. To the east the ground sloped down towards a small stream which joins the Crane Brook *c* 0.5 km to the south.

The underlying geology comprises Keuper Triassic Sandstones (Geological Survey of Great Britain 1954, Sheet 154, Lichfield), the natural subsoil forming a mottled brownish-yellow coarse sand with occasional flint gravel and pockets of gravel with sand. Consequently, most of the site was well drained. The eastern, downslope area of the site, however, was prone to water-logging due to the humic soils in that area, probably representing one of the humic sandy gley soil formations commonly seen close to the minor water-courses in this region ('The Wall and Shenstone wetlands'; Leah *et al.* 1998, 113; Godwin and Dickson 1964–5; Gould 1964–5, fig. 2; 1966–7 fig. 9).

Archaeological background

Two major Roman roads, Watling Street – the main routeway from London to Wroxeter, Chester and the north-west of the Province – and Ryknield Street – one of several major routes linking the south-west with the north-east – crossed *c* 0.5 km to the east of the Romano-British small town of *Letocetum* (Wall), at a point *c* 200 m north of the site (Fig. 61). The network of major Roman roads was established between AD 43 and 81 during the military advance (Margary 1973, 504). This part of Watling Street appears likely to have been constructed in the second phase of gradual advance to the north of the line formed by the Fosse Way in the second or third decade after the commencement of Roman occupation, and there is evidence to show that it was metalled by *c* 70 AD (*ibid.*, 496–504; Gould 1964–5; 1998, 24–6). There is no direct evidence to corroborate when this section of Ryknield Street was constructed; the timing is likely to have been similar to that of Watling Street although the layout suggests that the latter was constructed first (Margary 1973, 499; Gould 1998, 24–6; Wardle 2002a).

Sections across Ryknield Street have previously been recorded *c* 30 m and *c* 45–50 m south of its junction with Watling Street, the former by Hodgkinson in 1926 (Gould 1963–4, fig. 12) and the latter by Oswald during construction of the new A5 trunk road in 1965 (1966–7a, field 76). Hodgkinson observed a *c* 8.38 m width of metalling, *c* 0.15 m thick, with a V-shaped ditch to the east (Gould 1963–4, fig. 12). In the segment recorded by Oswald the cambered, gravel road surface (*agger*) was *c* 7.3 m wide, the gravel – laid on the ground surface – being a maximum of 0.38 m thick at its highest point. A single ditch, 0.6 m wide lay immediately adjacent to the road on its west side. Two further ditches, each *c* 1.4 m wide, lay parallel to either side of the road but at some distance from it – *c* 5.5 m on the west side and *c* 7.9 m on the east side; the distance between the two ditches being *c* 21 m. No graves were observed in the vicinity, but the remains of a timber structure were recorded on the east side of Ryknield Street (*ibid.*, field 77).

First and 2nd century buildings and evidence of later industrial activity were recorded by Gould on the east side of the junction of Ryknield Street with Watling Street during construction of the A5(T) in 1963–4 (1964–5). These remains probably related to a discrete

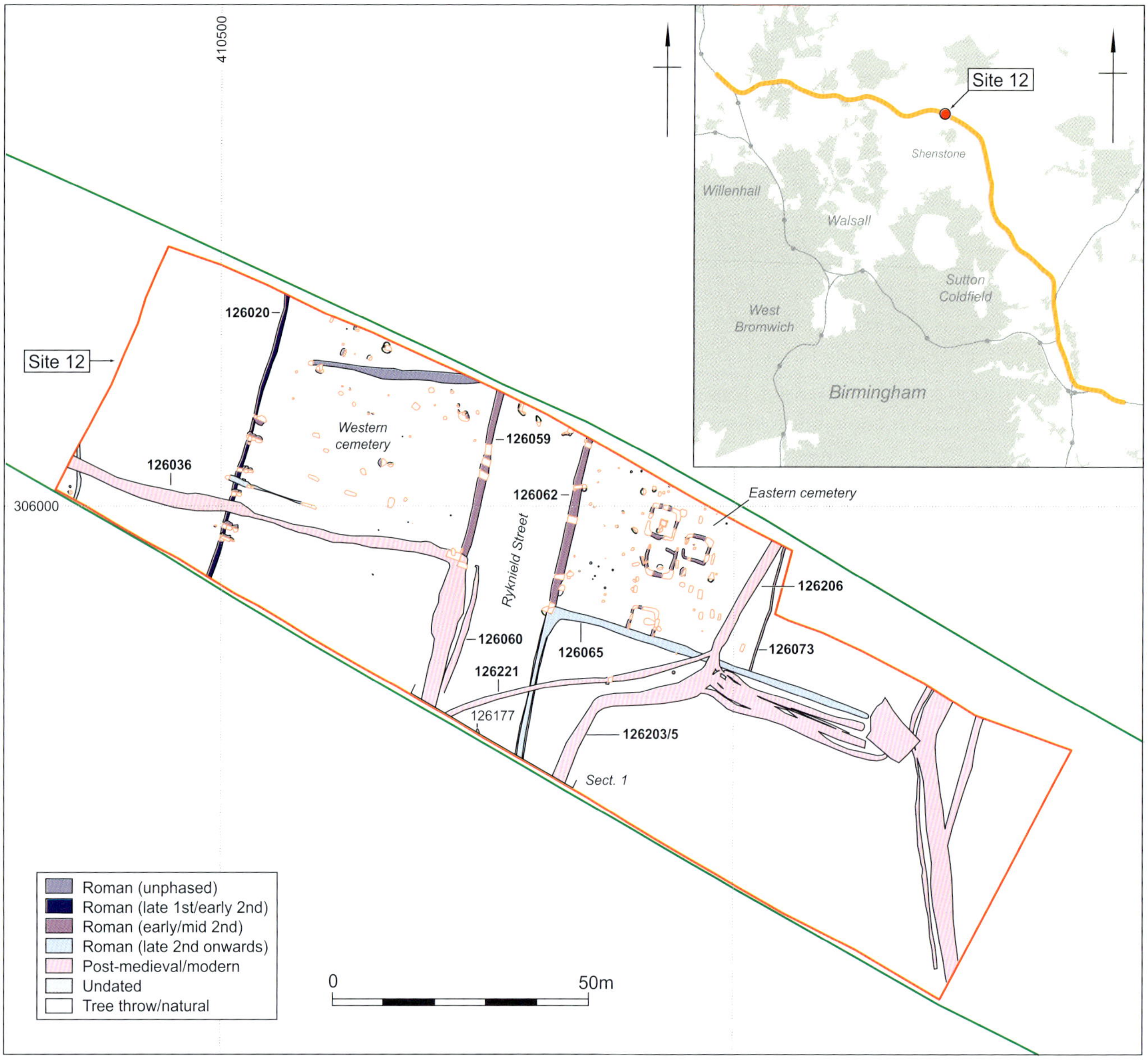

Fig. 60 Ryknield Street (Site 12)

settlement focused on the junction of these major routeways which lay *c* 0.5 km from *Letocetum* itself, although the buildings may feasibly have formed outliers to the town's suburbs (see below).

A considerable body of work has been undertaken on the Romano-British remains at Wall (Gould 1963–4; 1966–7; 1972; 1998; Round 1981–2; Ball and Ball 1983–4; Smith 1987, 227–9; Burnham and Wacher 1990, 274–8; Wardle 2002a; Fig. 61). A prolonged military presence, commencing in the first or second decade of the Roman occupation (post-AD 50) and including three or possibly four 1st–early 2nd century forts (Gould 1963–4; 1966–7; 1991–2; Round 1981–2; 1991–2; Fig. 61, 8), together with its position adjacent to the junction of two major routeways '... attracted a civil settlement which seems, in the second century, to have spread along both sides of Watling Street for a distance of about 3 km ...' (Burnham and Wacher 1990, 276–8; Gould 1963–4, 16, fig. 12) though this seems rather excessive based on the current evidence; 2 km would be more likely. The successive forts were constructed on the higher ground north of Watling Street (Fig. 61). Most of the excavated structures within the civil settlement appear to have been of timber construction but several stone buildings have been found. A bath house, possibly associated with what has been interpreted as a small *mansio*, lay close to the road on the west side of the settlement (Gould 1998, 14–21). *Letocetum* was one of five sites, possibly forming a chain of *burgi*, along Watling Street in the Midlands area, to possess a late Romano-British fortified enclosure through which the road passed (Webster 1974; Burnham and Wacher 1990, 276).

A minimum of 51 cremation graves have been recorded from a cemetery situated to either side – most finds being from the north – of Watling Street *c* 350 m to the west of Wall (Fig. 61, 1; Beckett 1925; Blay 1925; Hodgkinson 1927; Oswald 1966–7a, field 201). In 1921, E.D. Henderson and F. Jackson found *c* 30 cremation graves, all apparently containing the remains of urned

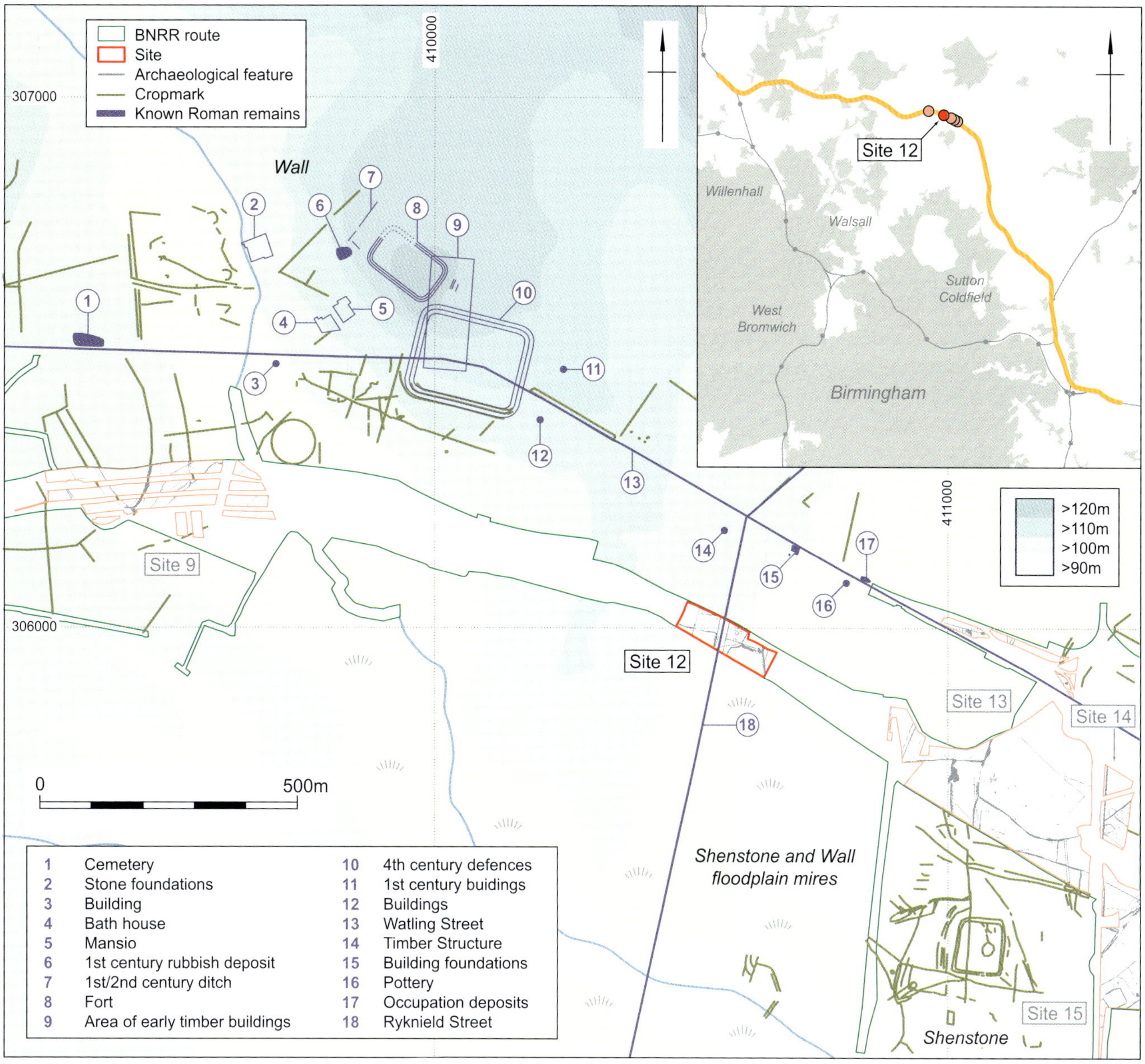

Fig. 61 The Romano-British town of *Letocetum* (Wall)

burials (although very little mention is made of the presence of any bone). At least one burial included '...charcoal, coffin and sandal nails [hobnails]' in addition to the bone but '... No article of adornment was found with the interments except a blue earthenware bead ...' (Beckett 1925). The cemetery reportedly extended '... for a considerable distance on both sides of the road ...' but there are no details as to how many of the *c* 30 graves lay to the north and how many lay to the south (*ibid.*). In 1924 '... many fragments of burial urns, charcoal, nails and pieces of subsidiary urns ...' were lifted by members of the Walsall Historical Association from a field to the north of the road (Blay 1925, 22). There is no mention of the number of cremation graves found, but at least three are described in some detail and Blay states that '... our rather irregular digging gave us the impression that the interments were two or three yards apart ...' suggesting they were relatively densely packed (*ibid.*, 23). At least four of the nine 'burials' excavated by Hodgkinson in 1927 appear to have been made urned; it is difficult to tell where the bone lay in the other deposits or even if they included any since little or no mention is made of the cremated bone itself (Hodgkinson 1927). Fragments of between one and seven vessels were recovered from each of these deposits including parts of a tettina from one; other objects were rare and included a few iron nails from two deposits and a glass vessel, bronze and glass items of personal ornamentation from one other. The recorded 'graves' were situated 3.0–19.5 m north of the Watling Street roadside ditch, with surviving depths of cuts of between 0.28 m and 0.66 m (*ibid.*). At least one of the nine graves excavated by Oswald contained the remains of an urned burial, two others being boxed; ceramic and glass grave goods were also recorded (1966–7a). The recorded graves all appear to be of later 1st or 2nd century date and a common theme throughout is the inclusion of pyre debris in the grave fills '... the urns were in black earth containing wood charcoal and, in some cases, calcined bones ... [which] ... appears to have been deposited over or round the urns after they had been placed in position ...' (Hodgkinson 1927). No inhumation graves were recorded in this western cemetery (Blay 1925, 24). The full size and extent of the cemetery are unknown but it appears likely to have been fairly extensive; unfortunately, changes to the form of the A5 trunk road during its construction made subsequent to Oswald's work on the site are believed to have resulted in the rest of the cemetery being destroyed without record (Gould 1998, 56–7).

Writing in the latter part of the 19th century, Bagnall recalls being told of a stone coffin containing human bone which was found in the 1820s when the road by *The Trooper* inn was lowered (1874, 40). The description and location render it likely that this is the same coffin as that reportedly deposited in the 19th century on the south side of Watling Street, adjacent to the west side of the 4th century enclosure, to serve as a water trough (Gould 1963–4, 6). Gould did not believe the coffin to necessarily be of Romano-British date, nor that it was conclusively from Wall, although the report of the find by Bagnall makes the latter likely. There is also mention of the recovery in 1924 of the remains of 12 coffined burials and one cremation burial 'close to the junction of the Chesterfield Road and Watling Street' (Collingwood and Taylor 1925, 226), presumably in the vicinity of the south-east corner of the 4th century enclosure, although Blay, in his publication on Wall (1925), makes no mention of any burials associated with the town other than those of cremated remains from the western cemetery. The stone coffin may have been dismissed for the same reasons as those postulated later by Gould but the supposed small cemetery on the eastern margins of the village was recorded at the same time as that to the west and should have been known to those working elsewhere in the village.

The remains of what has been referred to as a 'Romanised farm' lay *c* 600 m south-east of the site to the north of Shenstone (Fig. 61; Gould 1998, 53–6; Leah *et al.* 1998, 114). No *in situ* evidence for buildings has yet been recovered in the vicinity of the large double-ditched rectilinear enclosure (*c* 87 m by 80 m) and associated field-boundary and drainage ditches, but aerial photographs suggest the possible existence of a structure in the northern part of the enclosure (Gould 1998, 53–6). The location of a stone-lined well (found during ploughing) is uncertain but it was clearly in the vicinity of the earthworks. An unrecorded quantity of Romano-British building rubble – roof and flue tiles, ashlar sandstone blocks and ceramic *tesserae* – was recovered from the fill of the inner enclosure ditch together with pottery of predominantly 2nd century date. Gould suggested that the farm, which appears to have been occupied throughout most of the 2nd and into the early 4th century, may have been associated with the *mansio*/posting station in nearby *Letocetum* (1998, 55–6).

Evidence for agricultural activity and small scale settlement of Romano-British date has been found within much of the general vicinity, both as part of the M6 Toll project (Sites 13 and 15) and in observations made during the construction of the Wall by-pass in the 1960s (Oswald 1966–7a).

Methodology

All features believed to represent the remains of cremation or inhumation graves were fully excavated. No unburnt bone, human or animal, survived in the highly acidic burial environment of the site. Consequently, the targeted samples commonly collected from inhumation grave fills were not taken. All finds from the inhumation graves – generally representative of coffin furniture or the remains of grave goods – were 3D-recorded.

All cremation-related deposits were half-sectioned, plans and sections being drawn at 1:10 or 1:5. All deposits were subject to whole-earth recovery to ensure full collection of all cremated bone, pyre goods, pyre debris and grave goods. Recovery varied from that of a single 'sample' of the whole fill, to recovery of the fill by halves or quadrants, thereby providing information on the distribution of the archaeological components often indecernible by eye. Where possible the remains of the burial were recovered as a separate deposit from the remainder of the grave fill, but in some cases disturbance and heavy truncation due to ploughing and damage sustained during machine stripping made this distinction difficult. In several instances the grave cut for urned burials could not be discerned in excavation; consequently, the remains of the burial were excavated by cutting a box section. The remains of intact or largely intact urned burials were lifted whole on site for more detailed excavation, the vessel first being wrapped in crepe bandage to provide flexible support during subsequent excavation. The fills of the vessels were emptied in 20 mm spits.

All the remains were floated and wet-sieved to a minimum 1 mm sieve fraction. Bone in the large sieve fractions (10 mm and 5 mm) was separated from other extraneous material; the residues from the smaller sieve fractions (2 mm and 1 mm) were retained for scanning by the osteologist.

Results

Prehistoric

Evidence for pre-Romano-British activity in the area of the site was sparse and most of what was recovered was residual. No *in situ* features of conclusive prehistoric date were identified. One *in situ* deposit, in the form of an old ground surface (122596/7), was preserved below the metalled surface of the Roman road in the site's southern baulk.

Some, possibly all of the small assemblage of eight struck flints, date to the Mesolithic period (Cramp and Lamdin-Whymark below). Most were recovered from the subsoil or top of the natural and two were

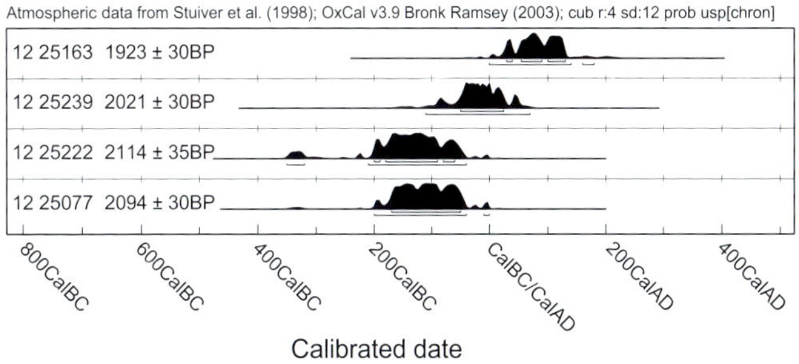

Fig. 62 Oxcal probability distributions of radiocarbon dates

redeposited in Romano-British features. All except one piece were recovered from a limited area (*c* 30 m by 5 m) in the central part of the site on the south-eastern edge of the natural terrace overlooking the lower, wetter ground to the south-east. The potential significance of this relatively concentrated spatial distribution, possibly reflective of a temporary station of limited hunting/ settlement activity, must be tempered by the unstratified location of the material, the possible effects of ploughing and the relatively high frequency of such finds in the general vicinity (Gould 1966–7, 10).

Small quantities of residual Early Bronze Age pottery (Allen, C., below) were recovered from the fills of four Romano-British inhumation graves in the eastern half of the cemetery (122609, 122376, 122675, 122405), and from a Romano-British pit of unknown function (122534) cut by one of the graves. The almost singular recovery of sherds from the fills of inhumation graves is somewhat strange given the range and extent of other, apparently earlier, excavated Romano-British features on the site, and although two sets of features were adjacent, the general distribution of sherds is fairly dispersed across the eastern half of the cemetery. The finds, which include parts of two Collared Urns, are suggestive of the presence of a Bronze Age mortuary-related feature in the general vicinity but probably not within the confines of the area of the site itself (*ibid.*). A single sherd of probably Iron Age pottery was recovered from a pit of uncertain function (122923) in the north-western area of the site. Although this comprised the only find, apart from occasional charcoal fleck, from this feature, it is most likely to be residual and the feature to be of Romano-British date.

One sample of short-lived charcoal (oak sapwood) from the old ground surface sealed by the surviving metalled surface of the Roman road was dated by radiocarbon analysis to 190–30 cal BC (2094±30 BP; NZA-20577), in the Middle–Late Iron Age (Fig. 62, Table 18). The old ground surface comprised a thin, immature soil with no developed horizon and had survived only in patches, probably having been truncated during construction of the Roman road (Figs 63–4; Allen, M. and Scaife, below); although there is a possibility that the road may have followed an earlier routeway (see below).

Analysis of pollen from the old ground surface showed a change – probably referable to the Iron Age – from alder, oak and hazel woodland to a more open environment dominated by hazel, with some indications of cereal cultivation most probably within the general vicinity rather than the area of the site itself (Scaife, below). The combined but limited evidence suggests the presence of at least one Late Iron Age settlement in the vicinity, the landuse within the area of the site itself being limited to woodland clearance, possibly for grazing and/or hazel coppicing.

An undated, small, sub-rectangular pit (129020) towards the western margins of the site was cut by the early Romano-British cemetery boundary ditch 126020 (Fig. 66), while a slightly larger pit (122299) was cut by the early Romano-British ditch 126062 flanking the east side of the Roman road-zone. Both features, of unknown function, may have been early Romano-British in date but could equally have been Iron Age or earlier.

Romano-British

The majority of the features and deposits from the site related to the Romano-British period. Ryknield Street is likely to have formed the primary focus of activity, the metalled surface apparently being laid directly over the Middle–Late Iron Age old ground surface. The road apparently underwent various stages of re-surfacing – possibly with some slight realignment – throughout the period, together with recutting of the associated road-zone boundary ditches. The establishment of the cemetery, predominantly containing the remains of early–middle Romano-British cremation burials with a smaller number of later inhumation graves and the rare continuation of cremation into the 4th century, is likely to have followed closely on the construction of the road. Various boundary ditches delineating the cemetery and running either parallel or perpendicular to the road were apparently abandoned and backfilled during the period of the cemetery's use, although the boundaries they formed were generally respected. A series of ovens/hearths ranged along the western boundary of the cemetery, most cutting through the early cemetery boundary ditch, appear contemporary with the earlier

Table 18 Radiocarbon dates from Ryknield Street

Feature	*Context*	*Material*	*Lab. No.*	*Result BP*	*Calibrated date (2σ)*
Pit 122922 with redeposited burial	122927	oak sapwood	NZA-25222	2114±35	200–30 cal BC
Old ground surface	122597	oak sapwood	NZA-25077	2094±30	190–30 cal BC
Cremation grave 122045	122139	oak sapwood	NZA-25239	2021±30	70 cal BC–cal AD 80
Oven 122517	122518	birch	NZA-26163	1923±30	cal AD 10–210

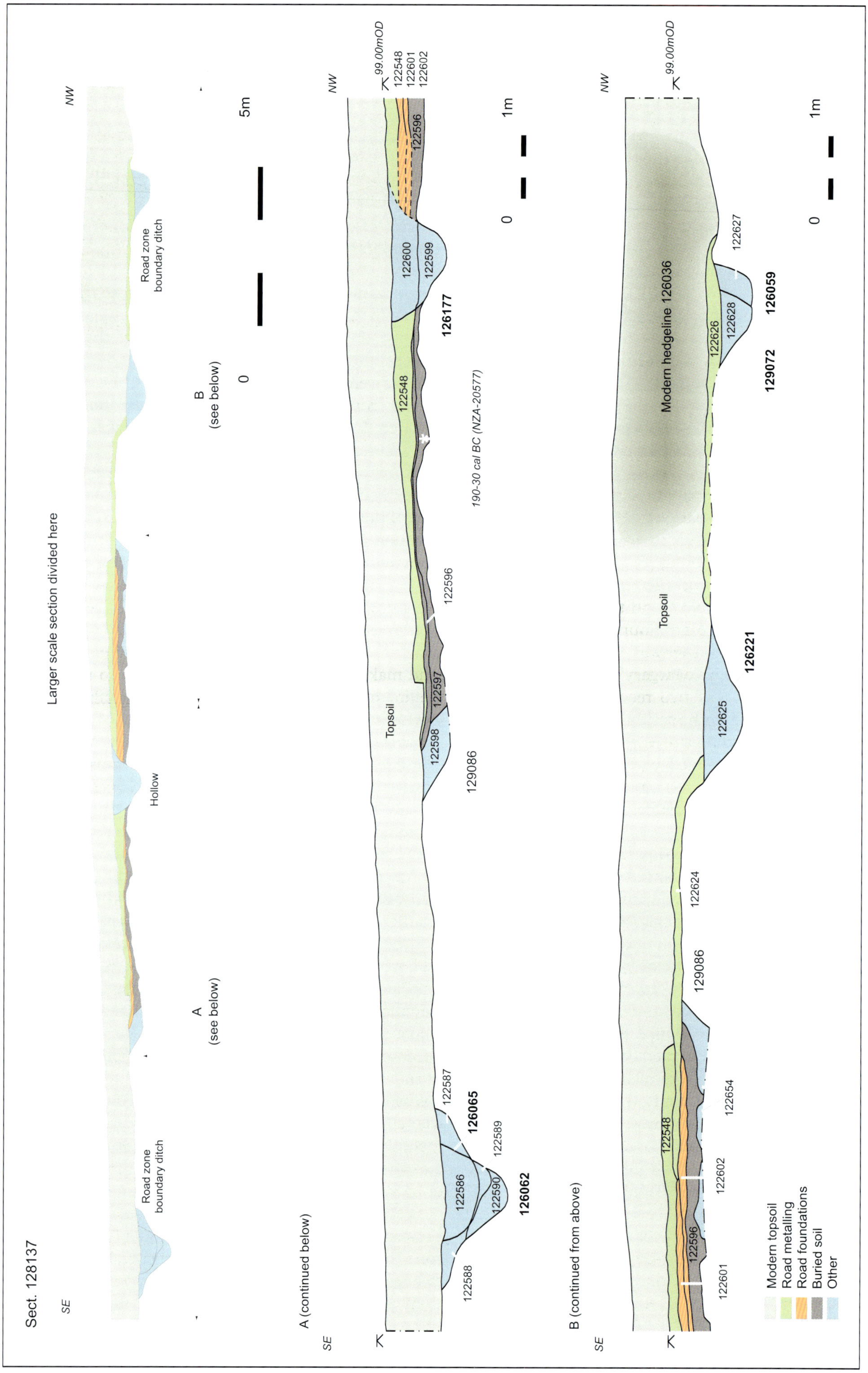

Fig. 63 Section across the Roman road

Fig. 64 Section across the Roman road

Fig. 65 Dump of building material in ditch 126059

phases of the cemetery, an *in situ* charcoal deposit from one being radiocarbon dated to cal AD 10–210 (1923±30 BP; NZA-26163) (Fig. 62, Table 18).

Road

The location of the Roman road, lying on the known plotted alignment of Ryknield Street, was clearly described by a series of parallel, north–south ditches crossing the central area of the site (Fig. 60). The distance between the inner edges of the two sets of ditches – 126062 and re-cut 126065 on the east side, and 126059 and re-cut 129072 on the west side – is *c* 17.5 m. These ditches represent boundaries marking out the 'road-zone' for the highway and the distance between them puts them in Margary's 'secondary class', describing the narrower of two recorded average zone widths of *c* 25.6 m and 18.9 m (Margary 1973, 22; NB latter distances from ditch centres).

Evidence for the road surface only survived in the site's southern baulk (Figs 63–4). There is clear evidence for a cambered *agger* comprising one, in places two layers of loose, coarse, rounded and sub-rounded gravel within a matrix of peagrit and silty sand. The maximum surviving depth of 0.23 m lay central to the area between the road-zone boundary ditches with a potential drop of 0.34 m from the crown to the sides (but see below). Over 4 m of the main 7.5 m of its width, as recorded in section, the metalled surface overlay make-up layers of reddish-brown sand (122601, 122602), overlying the Middle–Late Iron Age old ground surface which may have been truncated during construction of the road.

The position of the metalled surface corresponds largely with a 'hollow' in the natural, indicated by a steep boundary in the soil matrices (129086). Describing an area *c* 9.7 m wide (not fully excavated), and situated *c* 3 m from the eastern road-zone boundary ditch and *c* 6 m from that to the west, the hollow could have formed in response to the use of the road and compaction of the underlying deposits. Roads have been known to sink under their own weight where constructed over plastic soils (Margary 1973, 20). Post-depositional pedogenic effects, such as iron mobilisation and depletion, could have resulted in the observed edge-effects under and around the road surface (M Allen, pers comm); however, the road surface does in part extend over the natural where no such changes are apparent. Alternatively, the hollow may represent the remains of an old routeway which had been abandoned for a sufficient length of time to allow the formation of the old ground surface. This feature was only recorded in section, so the evidence for any of the alternatives is inconclusive.

Although this main area of road surface corresponds closely with the width, form and position of that recorded by Oswald (1966–7a) *c* 130 m to the north (see above), the arrangement is not quite as neat and straightforward. The *c* 4 m width of relatively shallow (0.1 m thick) 'primary' metalling (122624) lay on the west side of the main surface (122548), partly over a sand make-up layer (122602) but mostly to the west of the line of the possible early trackway directly on top of the natural. A third, shallow (maximum 0.12 m deep), 3.3 m width of metalling, 122626, apparently deposited directly onto the natural (Fig. 63), lay further to the west, extending over most of the width of the by then back-filled western road-zone boundary ditches, suggesting a middle–late Romano-British or possibly later date for this part of the surface.

All three metalled surfaces (122548, 122624 and 122626) lay physically immediately below the modern ploughsoil (0.34–0.9 m deep) and it is highly likely that at least some of the metalling will have been removed and/or partly redeposited. Some increase in the frequency of coarse gravel was observed between the flanking ditches but it showed no discrete distribution. There is a 1.21 m fall in the aOD level between the north and south parts of the site in the central area, and it may be that the higher ground was subject to more intensive scouring due to ploughing, and/or that there was a reduced depth of metalling along this slightly higher ground; Margary observed that the earthen embankments of the *agger* were sometimes left unmetalled (1948, 18; 1973, 20).

There was no evidence for the roadside ditches often associated with Roman roads (as distinct from the road-zone boundary ditches); these are generally positioned to one or both sides of the *agger* and may have served to ensure good draining and to provide up-cast for the surface (Margary 1948, 18). Oswald recorded a single ditch on the west side of the section of Ryknield Street

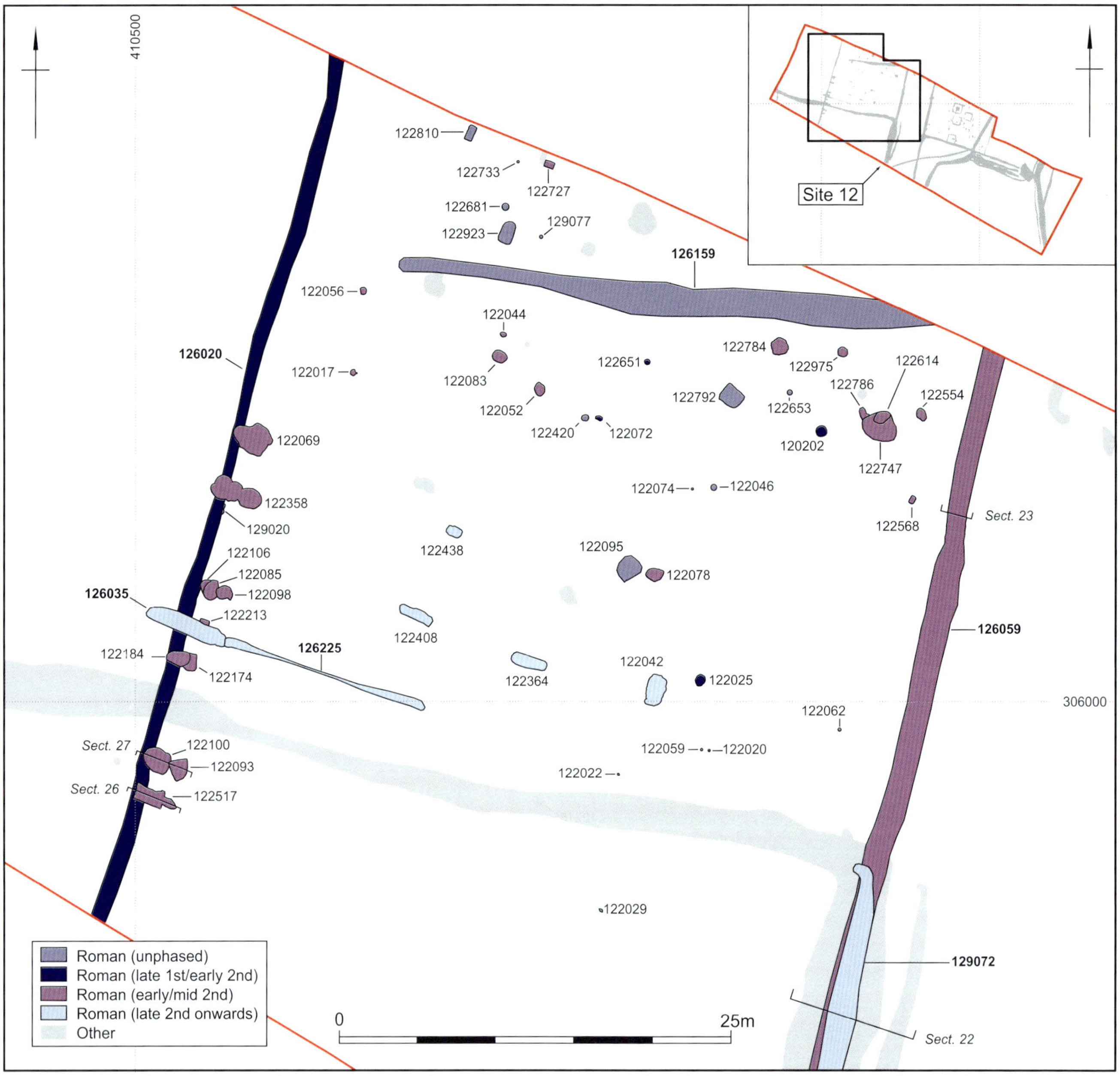

Fig. 66 Phase plan of the western cemetery

he investigated to the north of the site (1966–7a). He also observed a pair of parallel ditches flanking the road in a similar fashion to those recorded at this site (see above) and these clearly represented a continuation of the road-zone boundary ditches.

The primary cuts of the road-zone boundary ditches, 126062 to the east and 126059 to the west, ran the full width of the site, although there is evidence for some disruption or break in continuity in the central area of both ditches (see below). The excavated ditch segments varied in width from 1.2 m to 2.3 m and in depth, 0.65–0.85 m, with variations on both sides; the maximum widths were recorded in the northern halves. Although the standard form was that of a steep V-shaped ditch, often with a lower 'ankle-breaker', the road-side slope in both ditches varied, generally in the form of a shallow concave slope or upper lip (Fig. 82). Most segments contained two fills, an initial depth of silting within the 'ankle-breaker', followed by an indistinguishable accumulation of a similar sandy silt matrix with occasional flint gravel inclusions within the rest of the cut. There was generally no suggestion that silting predominantly occurred from one or other side of the ditch, although one segment in the northern half of the west ditch 126059 contained a substantial dump of building debris – worked building stone including part of a small moulded block and fragments of *tegulae* (Shaffrey and Poole, below) – clearly deposited from the west (cemetery) side (Fig. 65). A change in the form of both primary ditch cuts was recorded in the central area of the site, *c* 5 m north of the southern cemetery boundary ditch 126065, and extending south for a minimum 6 m length on the east side and 2.5 m on the west. Here the ditches had a shallow (0.17–0.45 m) U-shaped form, 0.65–1.3 m wide, with a single fill. This change corresponds with the southern margins of the cemetery and may relate to points of access from the road; although the width and form correspond more

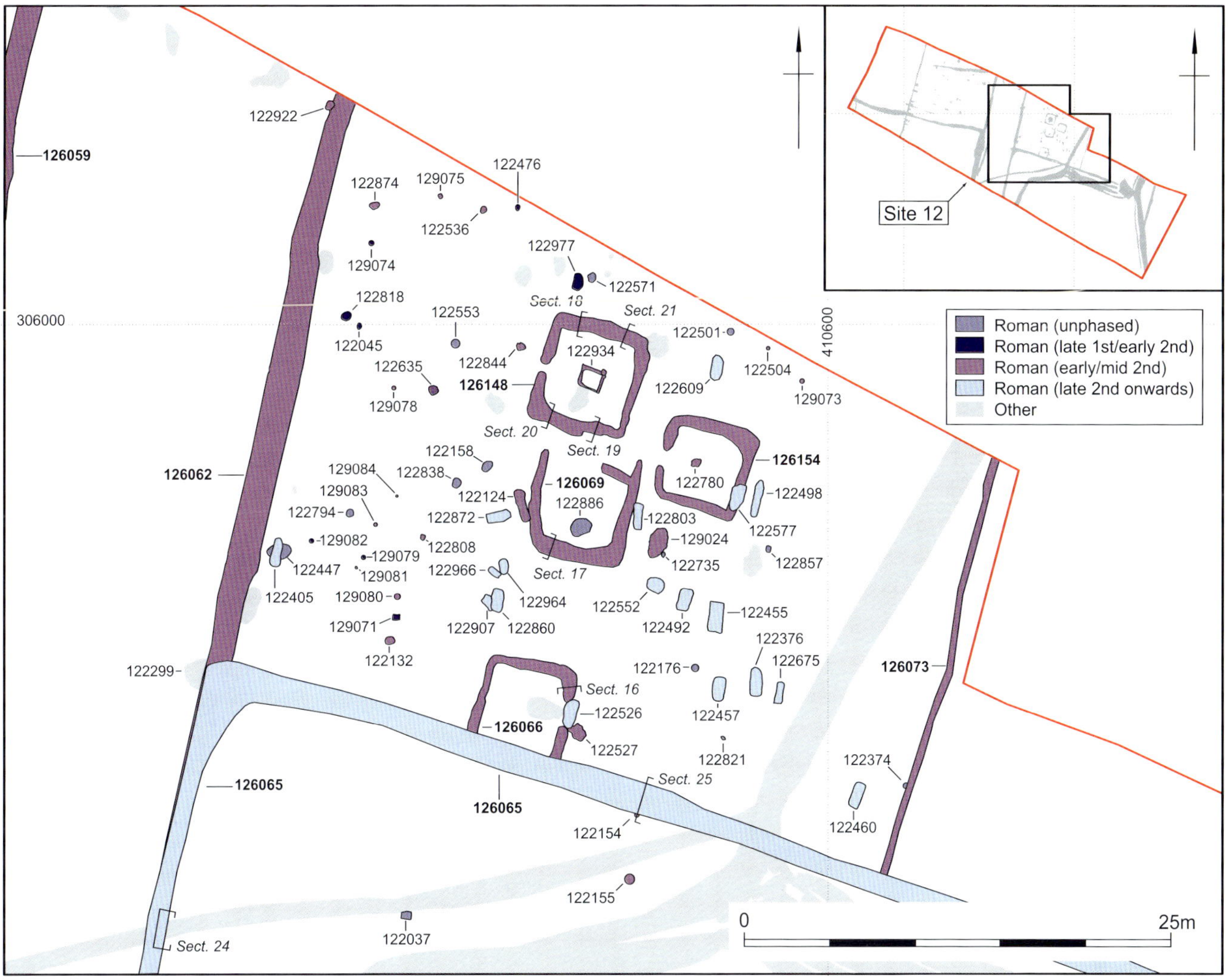

Fig. 67 Phase plan of the eastern cemetery

closely with those described by Margary for ditches of this type than does the wider, deeper form recorded elsewhere (1973, 22). Dating evidence from the fills suggests both ditches were probably largely backfilled by the late 2nd century AD, their cutting probably having coincided with the construction of the road and instigation of the cemetery in the second half of the 1st century AD.

With the exception of what appears to be a shallow V-shaped re-cut in the upper fill of one of the excavated segments in the northern half of 126059, close to the central area, there is no evidence for re-cuts to the primary ditches in the northern half of the site. Even this one re-cut must have been of limited extent since it was not seen in adjacent excavated segments. The ditch re-cuts in the southern half of the site differ slightly on either side. On the west side, 129072 had a U-shaped form, with a width of 0.7–1.1 m and depth of 0.3–0.45 m, and a single fill of light greyish-brown silty sand with occasional flint gravel inclusions, making it noticeably shallower and narrower than its predecessor. On the east side, the re-cut (126065) formed the north-south leg of an east–west southern boundary ditch to the eastern half of the cemetery. The shape of the cut was closer in form to the original, generally having a V-shaped form with a convex upper slope and an incipient 'ankle-breaker' in some segments (although not in the southern baulk). The width varied from 1.0–1.8 m, the surviving depth being 0.5–0.65 m. There were two or three fills, which were clearly angled-in from the east side in several segments – probably indicative of a slight bank formed of the upcast on this side – all comprising yellow/brownish-grey silty sands with occasional or rare flint gravel inclusions. The re-cuts are likely to have been made in the second half of the 2nd century AD, with silting continuing into at least the middle of the 3rd century.

The cemetery

The cemetery lay to either side of the road (Fig. 60), most mortuary-related features falling within the confines of a series of boundary ditches – including the road-zone boundary ditches – which may not all have been active contemporaneously (126020, 126059, 126062, 126065, 126073). Forty-two cremation graves and 15, possibly 21, inhumation graves were excavated, together with four mortuary enclosures and a series of features containing mortuary-related deposits. Most features lay in the eastern half of the cemetery: 61.9% (26) of the cremation graves, 86.7% (13) of the

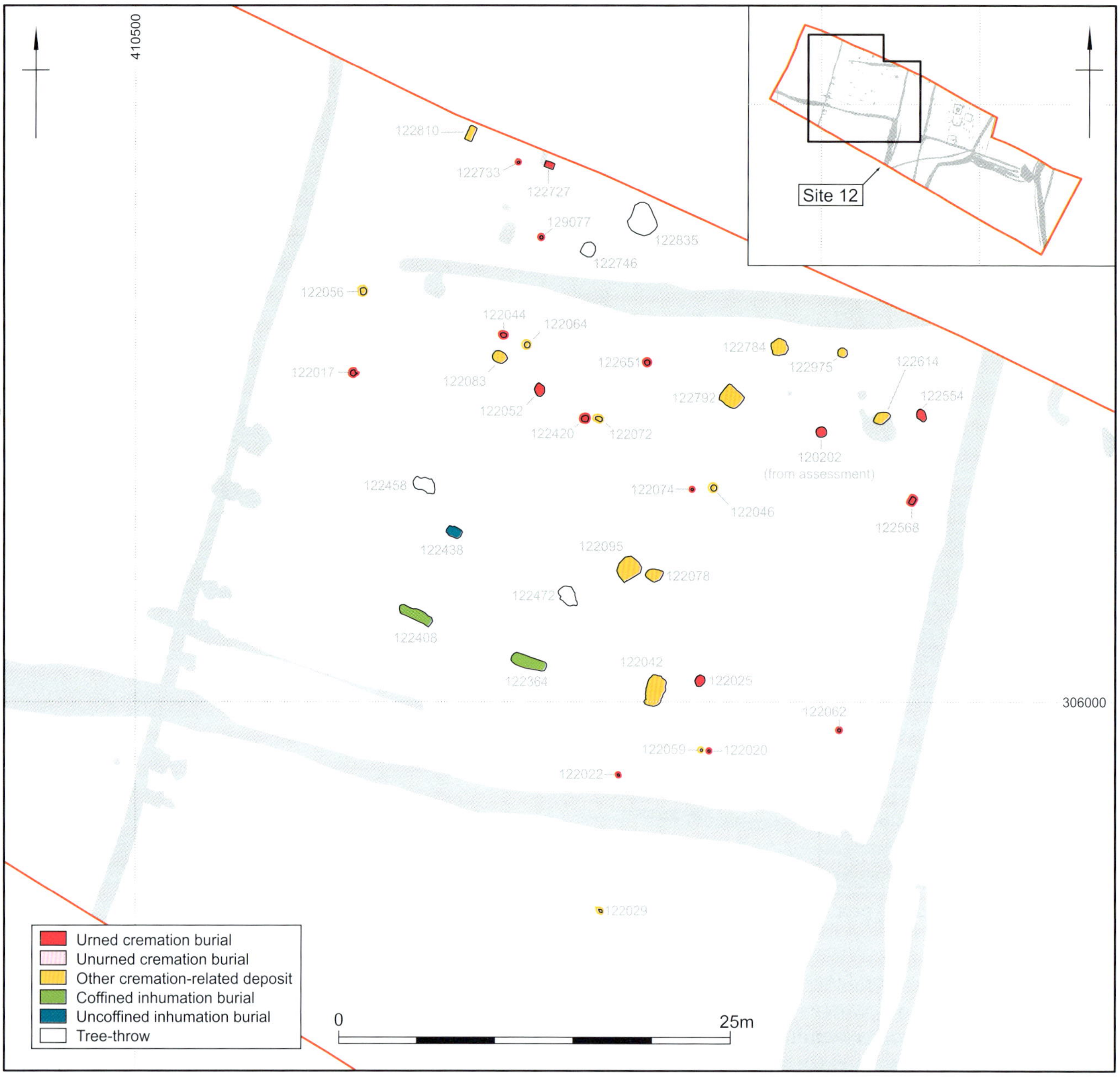

Fig. 68 Burial deposit types in the western cemetery

inhumation graves (80.9% including the possible graves) and all the mortuary enclosures. This imbalance may be slightly offset by the greater number of features containing redeposited burials and other cremation-related deposits (ie deposits of uncertain type) in the western half of the cemetery – six compared with three from the eastern half. The graves are generally fairly dispersed with no direct intercutting between either cremation or inhumation graves, although the presence of what appear to be redeposited cremation burials (mostly in the western half of the cemetery) indicates that some of the former had been completely removed from the excavated assemblage. The closest proximity between graves was seen in the eastern half of the cemetery where at the southern end two inhumation graves lay within 0.1 m of each other, and a cremation and inhumation grave were adjacent to within 0.3 m. There is no apparent ordered distribution of graves, other than a loose temporal distribution (see below), and the lack of intercutting suggests that the graves were marked in some way.

The full extent of the cemetery is unknown; the southern, western and eastern margins were established in excavation, but it must have continued northwards for an unknown distance towards the junction between Ryknield Street with Watling Street, *c* 200 m north of the site. Oswald (1966–7a) did not record any graves in his observations preceding the construction of the A5 trunk road, so the northern limits of the cemetery must lie within the intervening area, but could potentially extend up to the A5.

The major period of use of the cemetery occurred in the early–mid-2nd century (minimum 47.6% cremation burials), but burials appear to have been made throughout the Romano-British period, probably commencing in the late 1st century and potentially continuing into the early 4th century. The earliest graves (late 1st–early 2nd century; 28.6% cremation burials)

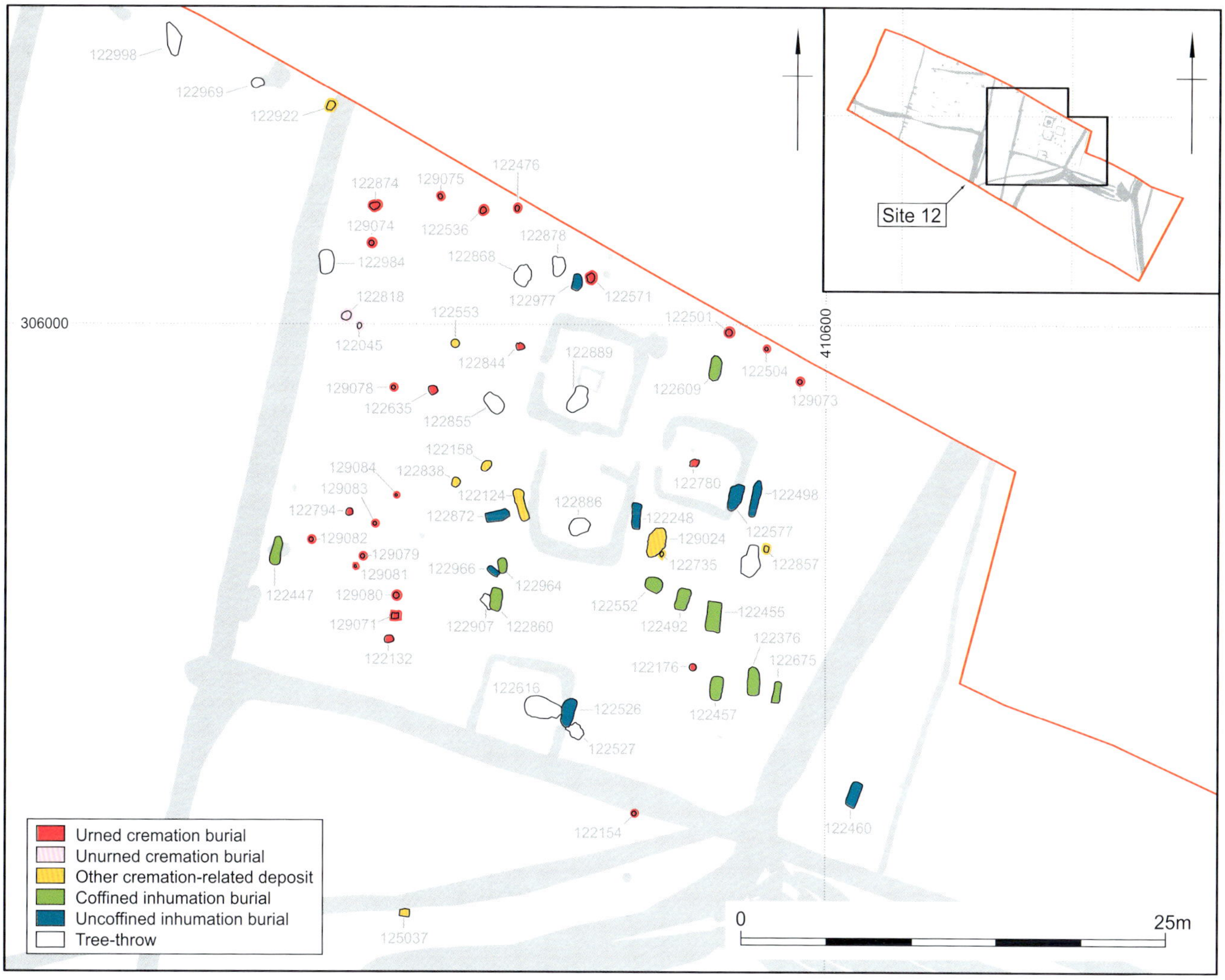

Fig. 69 Burial deposit types in the eastern cemetery

were concentrated within a 10–12 m wide strip to either side of the road-zone boundary ditches (Figs 66–7). The early–mid-2nd century graves were dispersed throughout the excavated area, extending to all the known margins of the cemetery. The few later cremation burials (4.8%) appear to have been made relatively close to the road; the latest identified cremation, of early 4th century date, was represented by a cremation-related deposit made in pit 122042 situated in the western half of the cemetery (Fig. 68). The inhumation graves, all likely to be of late 2nd–mid-4th century date, mostly lie towards the southern boundaries, predominantly on the east side of the road. Given this dispersed temporal distribution, it seems unlikely that cremation graves specific to any one phase would have been concentrated in the 'missing' northern part of the cemetery.

The top of most archaeological features/deposits lay immediately below the level of the modern worked soil/topsoil and many had been severely truncated by ploughing and further damaged during machine stripping of the site, the fills of some cremation burials having been spread within the adjacent subsoil. All the graves had cut into the natural sands and several were recorded as having cut through an undisturbed subsoil, through in most cases this had probably been subject to recent reworking.

Cremation graves and burials

The majority (83.3%) of the 42 cremation graves contained the remains of urned burials (that from grave 129077 missing in post-excavation) (Figs 68–9; age ranges given in Figs 71–2). Two graves appear to have held the remains of combined urned and unurned deposits (below); both were early–mid-2nd century burials made in the north-west area of the western cemetery. Three graves were so badly truncated as to render the form of the burial uncertain, although at least

Fig. 70 Grave 129071

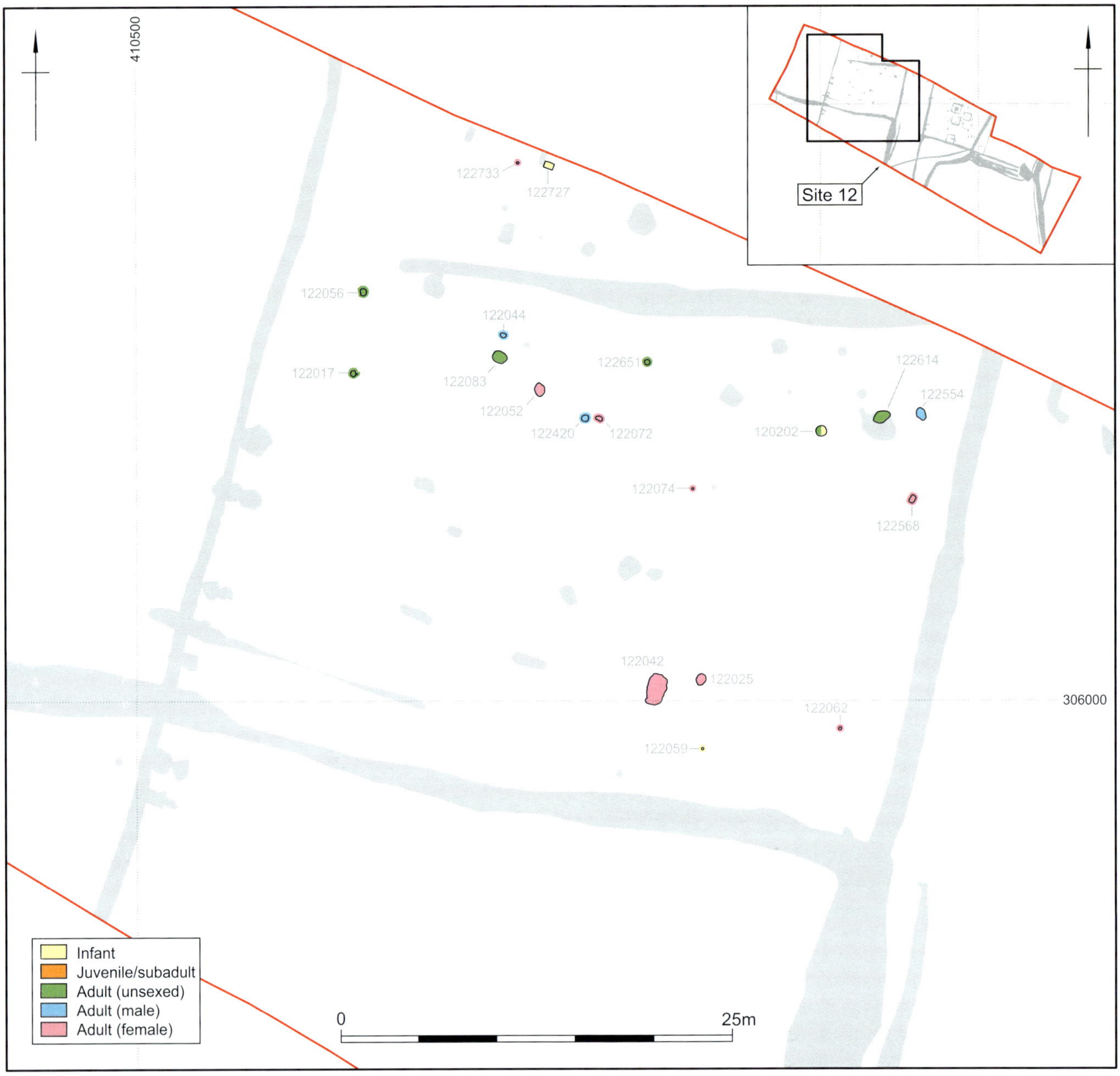

Fig. 71 Age ranges and sexing of burials in the western cemetery

one of these (grave 129084) is likely to have been made urned. What appear to be the two earliest burials were made unurned, the bone probably originally being held in some form of organic container. Four other contexts comprised the remains of redeposited burials and a further five features contained the remains of either redeposited burials with redeposited pyre debris or just redeposited pyre debris, including the remains of what appear to comprise the remains of the latest cremation undertaken (see Table 20, below).

All the graves, with the exception of 122780 (Fig. 73) situated centrally within mortuary enclosure 126154, had been truncated to some degree by post-medieval ploughing and during machine stripping of the site (for example, grave 129071, Fig. 70). Disturbance to the graves had not always had a great impact on the remains of the burial, the urns in at least four graves surviving complete and largely intact (graves 122132, 122554, 122635, and 122780), with little damage to those in five others (122536, 122571, 122794, 122874 and 129080; see below). All except one of these well preserved graves lay in the eastern half of the cemetery and all were within 13 m of the ditches flanking the road. Although most were of early–mid-2nd century date, at least one related to the earlier phase of cemetery use. The surviving depth of the graves had an overall range of 0.05–0.39 m, with the majority (58.5%) falling between 0.1 m and 0.2 m, although a substantial proportion (29.3%) survived to less than 0.1 m. All the better preserved burials were recovered from graves of more than 0.16 m in depth, most being over 0.2 m.

Most of the graves were circular (18; 42.8%) or sub-circular (14; 33.3%) in shape, generally with concave sides and bases, although seven (21.2%) had steep, straight sides and flat bases (see Grave catalogue). The circular cuts ranged in diameter from 0.13 m to 0.7 m. Many (14; 66.7%) were of small diameter, the vessels fitting snugly within them, and the looseness of the

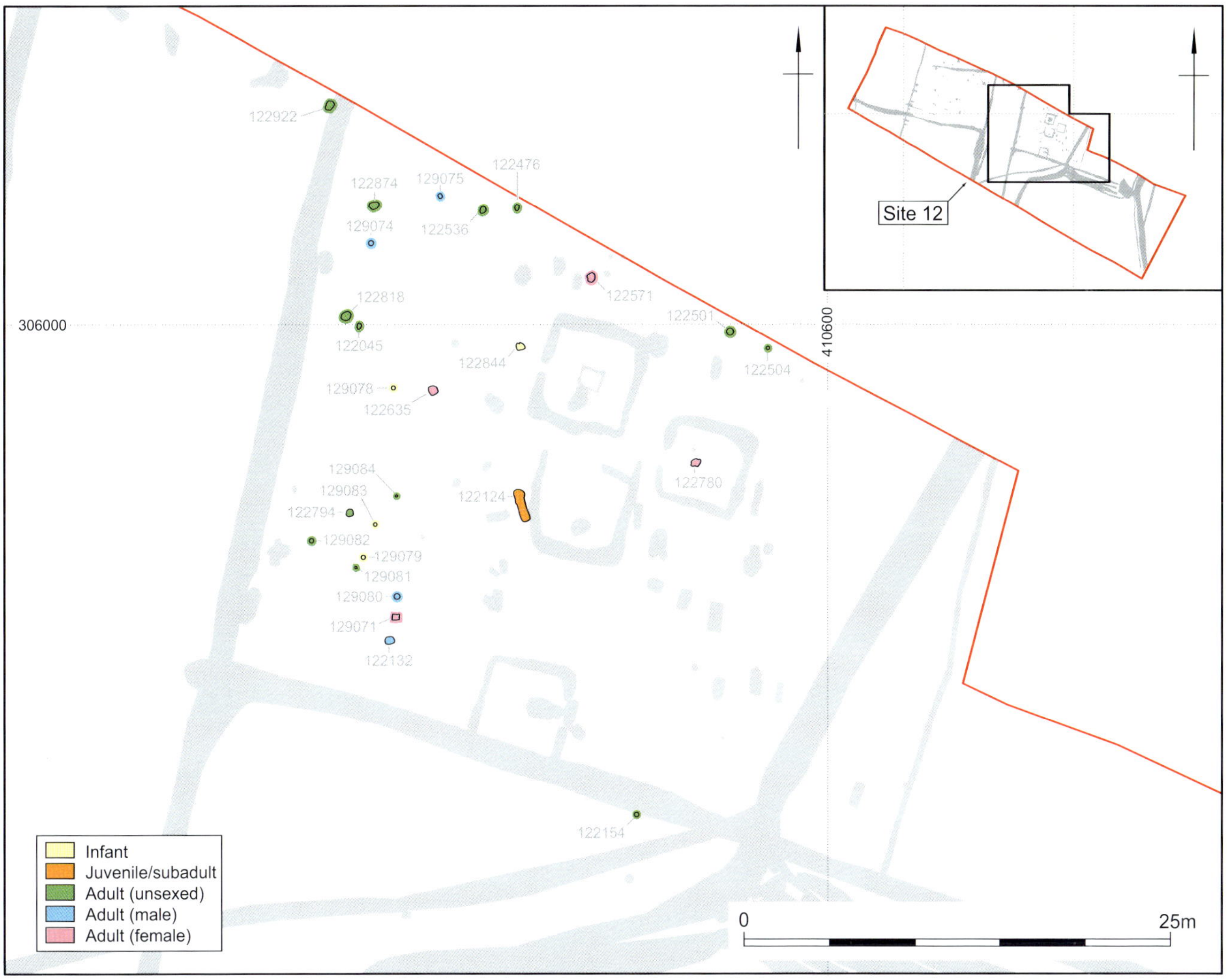

Fig. 72 Age and sexing ranges of burials in the eastern cemetery

sandy matrix had, over time, led to the material becoming compressed against the vessels, leaving little evidence for the cut other than the impression left by the vessels on their removal. The size of the sub-circular cuts also had a wide range of 0.2–0.83 m in length by 0.2–0.65 m in width; as with the circular cuts, the smaller figures tend to relate to the more heavily truncated deposits. Six graves (14.3%) were sub-rectangular and one (2.4%) rectangular, 0.36–0.86 m long by 0.3–0.6 m wide, all tending to have vertical or steeply sloping sides with flat bases. Grave 122780 lay central to the north-eastern mortuary enclosure 126154 and represented the most intact of the grave cuts (Fig. 73). The upper 0.18 m was sub-rectangular, *c* 0.85 m by 0.75 m, with an approximately central, 0.21 m deep, sub-circular cut *c* 0.25 m by 0.3 m; the rim of the urned burial sat slightly proud of the deeper central section of the grave. It is possible that this grave form, preserved here due to the depth to which it was cut, may have been used elsewhere within the cemetery but that only the lower, narrower and deeper sub-circular/circular sections have survived. Most of the graves lay a sufficient distant from their neighbours to have allowed for a wider cut than was apparently employed. Alternatively, this may represent a further distinction between this – the only grave directly associated with one of the mortuary enclosures – and the others within the cemetery. The shape of two other graves could not be confirmed, one having been removed by machine stripping in the evaluation stage of the project with only its position being recorded (grave 120202 in the western half of the cemetery), and the records pertaining to grave 122074 having been lost.

The backfills of most graves appear to have formed single deposits of mid-greyish-brown or reddish-brown silty sand, with occasional gravel inclusions. Many of the grave cuts were difficult to distinguish from the surrounding natural and it is likely that little or no worked-soil horizon existed across the cemetery area, the graves largely cutting through and being immediately backfilled with the natural sand. In the majority of cases the burial was made directly onto the base of the grave. In a few instances – graves 122176, 122635 and 122874 for example (Figs 73–4) – the burial was made several centimetres above the base of the grave on material generally indistinguishable from the rest of the fill. This suggests that graves were, at least occasionally, cut slightly in advance of their use – probably by no more than a day – and that either some weathering of the sides occurred and/or that the excavated material was left immediately adjacent to the cut allowing for some advanced silting.

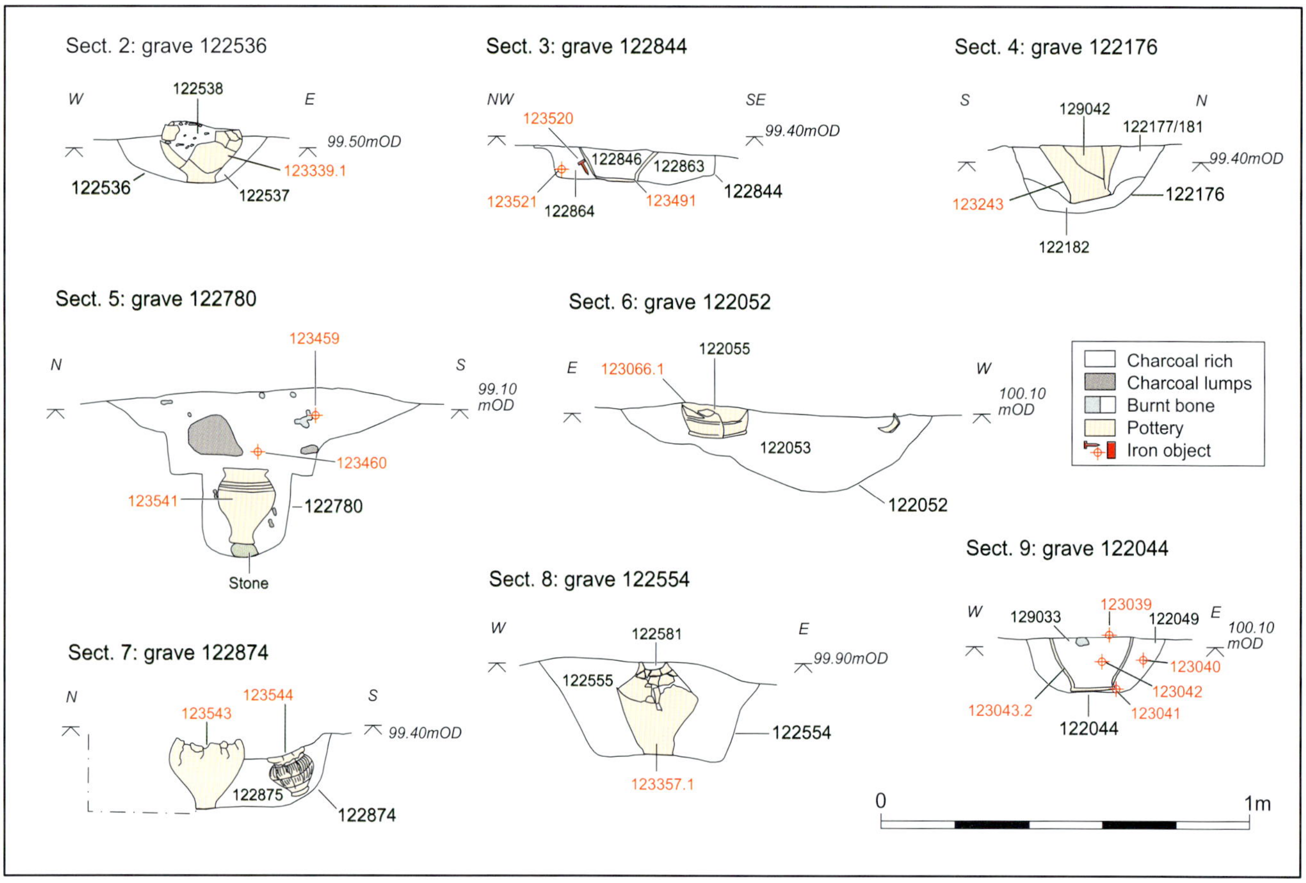

Fig. 73 Sections of cremation graves containing urned burials

In two graves, 122780 and 122132 (Figs 73–4), the urns were placed on three burnt stones arranged in the base of the cut (not all visible in section). In one other grave, 122044 (Fig. 73), there was some suggestion that rounded quartzite pebbles/gravel may have been used as packing, but it is more probable that this grave was simply cut through a pocket of natural gravel and, therefore, had more gravel inclusions in its backfill. One sub-rectangular grave, 122568 (Fig. 74), had a slight 'plinth' on which the urn sat (concealed by the urn in plan). The urned burial in grave 122052 appears to have been made in an inverted jar, positioned on a slight ledge on the east side of the grave (Fig. 73). All the other urned burials were made in upright vessels. Most burials were made central or close to central to the grave cut, only seven being made towards one side, including three to the east (graves 122052, 122874, 122420), two to the north (122635 and 122476) and one each to the south (122651) and west (122017). There is no discernible spatial or temporal distribution associated with the variable positioning of the burial within the grave, although both those placed towards the north are in the eastern cemetery and both fall within a late 1st–mid-2nd century date range; nor is there any obvious link with the age or sex of the buried individual.

The remains of artefactual pyre goods – that is items which were originally placed on the pyre with the deceased rather than being added to the grave at the time of burial – were recovered from a minimum of 26 (*c.* 61.9%) graves (see Cremated human bone, pyre goods, and Worley, below, for osseous pyre goods). The items predominantly take the form of ceramics (seven graves), iron (mostly nails including hobnails, seven graves), or both (eight graves), and glass vessels (two lone, two with iron objects and two with ceramics). Small fragments of copper-alloy items were also found in two graves with other materials (see Leary (ceramics) and Powell, K. (metalwork), below). In most of the graves from which pyre goods were recovered the fragments appear to have been deposited together with redeposited pyre debris in the grave fill (38.5%); in others, items were recovered either from the burial (23.1%) or from a combination of the burial and the general grave fill (23.1%); in 11.5% of cases fragments were recovered from a grave fill devoid of redeposited pyre debris; and in one case fragments of pyre goods came from both the burial and the redeposited pyre debris within the grave fill. No pyre goods were recovered from four graves containing redeposited pyre debris. In most cases, therefore, fragments of pyre goods were either being collected with the bone for burial, or lay within what probably amounted to a relatively small proportion of the debris from the pyre retained for inclusion in the grave fill. In all except one case, where fragments were recovered from a grave fill devoid of pyre debris, the remains of the burials were badly disturbed and the items will undoubtedly have been redeposited from within the urned burials. In grave 122874, a small jar that had originally served as a pyre good was recovered whole after cremation and included in the burial, being placed at the base of the grave to the south of the urn (Figs 73 and 75).

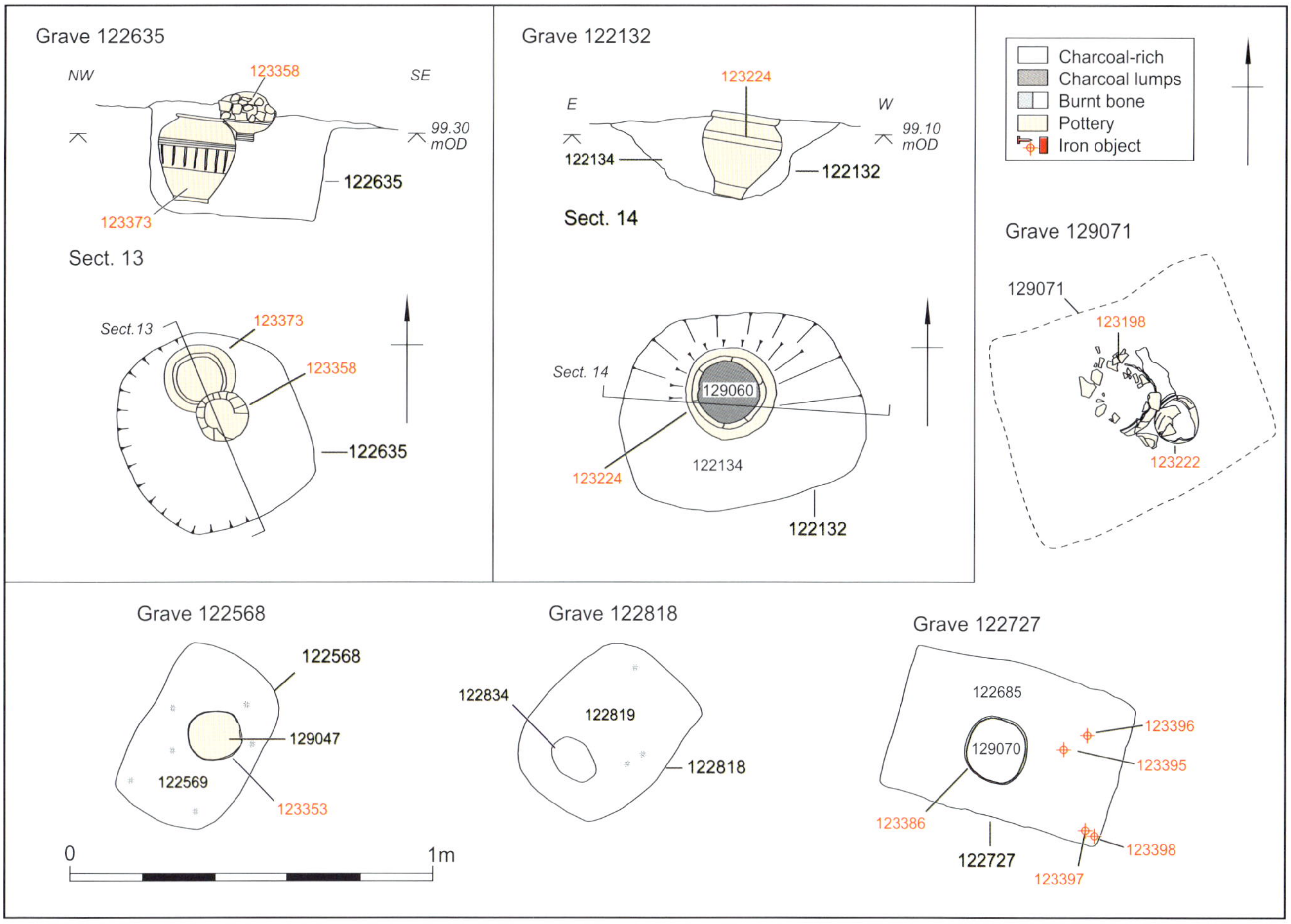

Fig. 74 Sections and plans of cremation graves containing urned and unurned burials

A higher proportion of the graves in the eastern half of the cemetery contained fragments of artefactual pyre goods than did those in the west (69.3% compared with 43.7%), although this may in part reflect the tendency for more of the better preserved graves to lie on the eastern side and the loss of material from the more truncated graves. Artefactual pyre goods also appear slightly more frequently in the early–mid-2nd century graves (78.9%) than in those of late 1st–early 2nd century date (55.5%). Most of the graves containing pyre goods were those of adults, although items were also recovered from three of the graves containing the remains of infants (42.8%) and from the one subadult grave. Although, given the relatively small proportion of the cemetery population for which it was possible to suggest a sex (38.7%, see below) so that the figures should be treated with caution, a substantially greater proportion of those individuals identified as probable males had artefactual pyre goods in their grave fills than did those identified as females (71.4% compared with 38.5%). There was no conclusive imbalance between the material types included with individuals of different sex, both ceramic and iron items occurring with both males and females – and infants – the exception being the two items of copper-alloy which were both from male graves. Iron hobnails were recovered from both male and female graves (14.3% male, 23.1% female) as were nails derived from funerary furniture of some form (biers, beds, boxes or caskets; see Powell K., below); nails from one of the infant burials are also suggestive of a casket.

Grave goods (items not included in the primary part of the mortuary rite but only in the secondary rite of burial) in the form of ceramic vessels, were recovered from six graves (14.3%), only two of which also included the remains of pyre goods. Unfortunately, it was not always possible to confidently deduce the position of these objects within the grave. In grave 122635, the urn was placed above a shallow depth of initial silting close to the northern edge of the cut. The accessory vessel was positioned 0.2 m above the base of the grave, to the

Fig. 75 Grave 122874

Fig. 76 Grave 122635

south of but probably touching the urn, and had either been added when the grave was partially backfilled or was a later addition (although no secondary cut was observed; Figs 74 and 76). It is possible that other graves could have contained similarly placed grave goods, the evidence for which has been destroyed by ploughing. In graves 129074 and 129075, both of narrow diameter, the accessory vessels each comprised a dish recovered from above the urns, and they may have functioned as lids.

The location of the accessory vessel – a jar – within grave 122733 is unknown, but since this grave too was of narrow diameter, the vessel is likely to have sat above the urn. The urn and accessory vessel from grave 122025 were both badly damaged and not recognised as separate items in excavation, consequently their positions within the grave is uncertain, but there is some indication that they may have been placed adjacent, in the centre of the cut.

The distribution of the six vessels recovered from grave 120202, excavated by machine in the evaluation stage, is unknown. Although some of them were interpreted as 'urns' it is by no means certain that this was an urned burial, or if the remains of the two individuals identified from the cremated bone, an adult and a young infant, were mixed or deposited as separate entities. Young immature individuals are commonly buried in smaller sized vessels than are older individuals and neither of the vessels tentatively identified as an 'urn' from this deposit is of a particularly small size.

A slightly higher proportion of the graves in the western half of the cemetery (18.7%) contained grave goods compared with those in the eastern half (11.5%), and although the numbers are low and should therefore be viewed with caution, a much higher proportion of the late 1st–early 2nd century graves contained grave goods than did the early–mid-2nd century ones (44.4% compared with 5.3%). Grave goods were recovered from both male and female graves (two each), the grave containing most items, 120202, being that of an unsexed adult buried with an infant.

Redeposited pyre debris, predominantly charcoal/fuel ash with variable inclusions of cremated human bone and fragments of pyre goods, was recovered from the backfills of 15 graves (35.7%) including 12 urned burials, one unurned and one combined burial, and one burial of uncertain form. Rare charcoal flecking was observed in several other grave fills. In all except one case, grave 129071, the pyre debris appears to have been deposited in the grave fill subsequent to the burial having been made. The high levels of disturbance and bioturbation make it difficult to define clearly whether this material was added as discrete deposits prior to the rest of the backfill or if the soil matrix was being added at the same time. As some deposits do appear fairly discrete, the former interpretation appears more likely, with subsequent mixing due to bioturbation. In grave 129071, the primary deposit comprised pyre debris above which the urned burial was made and sealed by two grave fills, one of which included a further small quantity of pyre debris.

There is no evidence to suggest that the pyre debris and the bone recovered from each grave did not derive from the same cremation (see Cremated human bone; Redeposited pyre debris). Most of the graves containing redeposited pyre debris lay in the eastern half of the cemetery (11 graves, 42.3%), material being recovered from a much smaller proportion of those in the western half (four graves, 25%). A higher proportion of the early–mid-2nd century graves contained redeposited pyre debris than did those of the late 1st–early 2nd century (42.1% compared with 25%), and no debris was recovered from either of the late 2nd–3rd century graves. One of the late 1st century graves containing unurned burials had a charcoal-rich fill, the other having only occasional charcoal flecks. Pyre debris was recovered from the graves of immature (infant and subadult) and adult individuals, and in association with the remains of both females and males.

The original nature of three of the four redeposited burials is unclear, but at least one – 12674, redeposited in the upper fill of pit 122614 in the western half of the cemetery – had been made urned. Two small pits 122059 and 122072 may each represent the remains of cremation graves, but if so the burials within them had been substantially disturbed and largely, if not completely redeposited, fragments of pottery (burnt and unburnt), cremated bone and pyre debris having been mixed and dispersed throughout the cuts, respectively 0.15 m and 0.2 m deep. All three of these redeposited burials lay in the western half of the cemetery. One other deposit, recovered from a small pit (122922) cut through the early–mid-2nd century upper fill of the eastern road-zone boundary ditch 126062, originally appeared to represent an *in situ* deposit. The charcoal-rich fill, containing a substantial quantity of cremated bone and a fragment of 2nd century mortarium, was dated by radiocarbon analysis to 200–30 cal BC (2114±35 BP, NZA-25222) (Fig. 62, Table 18). The material is clearly redeposited but what remains uncertain is whether the cremated bone pertains to a Middle–Late Iron Age cremation contaminated on redeposition by the fragment of burnt mortarium, or a 2nd century Romano-British cremation somehow contaminated by an earlier charcoal deposit.

A further five features (122042, 122056, 122083, 122124 and 122808) containing charcoal-rich fills, small quantities of cremated bone (<100 g), variable quantities of unburnt and burnt ceramics, and metal pyre goods (iron and copper-alloy), may represent the remains of disturbed, possibly redeposited burials with redeposited pyre debris, although this interpretation is not conclusive and they could represent lone deposits of pyre debris. One was recovered from a small, circular feature (122056) similar to many of the grave cuts; the others were all in larger sub-rectangular features, two of which were not commensurate with the other identified graves (122042 and 122124). The deposit in pit 122042 appears to represent the remains of the latest cremation undertaken at the site, dated to the early 4th century by a fragment of burnt, colour coated pentice moulded beaker probably from the Mancetter Hartshill kilns (*c.* AD 325+).

Redeposited pyre debris

Fifteen, possibly 16, pits contained fills that were interpreted as incidental or formal deposits of pyre debris (Figs 68–9). As with the cremation graves, most appear to be of early–mid-2nd century date (43.7%), with a few (12.6%) late 1st–early 2nd century deposits, although many could be dated no closer than Romano-British (43.7%). The charcoal-rich fills (including on occasions lumps of charred wood) mostly included very small quantities of bone (less than 10 g in 50% and less than 50 g in 88.9%), together with variable quantities of ceramic and/or metal pyre goods, the archaeological components forming a mixed deposit. The interpretation of one deposit (in cut 122046) as pyre debris is rendered dubious by the absence of any pyre goods and the recovery <1 g of possible cremated human bone; the fuel ash in this instance could have derived from some other form of fire.

The features varied in size and shape, including nine circular or sub-circular cuts of a similar appearance and size-range to many of the graves. Five larger, sub-rounded or sub-rectangular pits, 1.09–1.35 m in length by 0.66–1.2 m in width and all relatively shallow (0.2–0.4 m), may have included natural hollows or pits of unknown previous function as well as some possibly having been cut deliberately to hold the pyre debris. Two other features (122037 and 122810) have the appearance of deliberate cuts, both being rectangular with vertical or straight sides and concave bases (one disturbed by root action). Both were relatively shallow measuring 0.09–0.14 m, 122037 at 0.58 by 0.42 m and 122810 at 0.94 by 0.48 m; the latter held nine hobnails while the former included the largest single deposit of ironwork from the site (Fig. 77; Powell, K., below).

A minimum of eight (possibly nine) of the features lay to the west side of the road, one falling outside the area of the cemetery to the south, and six to the east, one again laying to the south of the southern boundary ditch (location of one other feature – 122030 – not recorded). The spatial distribution of these deposits, although scattered, appears slightly less random than that of the burials themselves (Figs 68, 69). Several of those located in the western half of the cemetery appear to form an arc around an open space adjacent to the road – possibly representing the location of at least some of the pyre sites. Those to the east of the road and some to the west are scattered amongst the graves, but their location does not suggest any links with specific burials.

Charcoal-rich deposits, apparently representative of redeposited pyre debris and inclusive of either small amounts of cremated bone and/or fragments of pyre goods, were found in several other features, including one of the ovens/hearths cutting the western cemetery boundary ditch (126020), a segment through the southern cemetery boundary ditch 126065, and one of the terminals of mortuary enclosure ditch 126148.

Inhumation graves

A possible 21 inhumation graves were recorded (Figs 68–9), mostly (18) in the eastern part of the cemetery. Fifteen graves were confidently identified by their shape assisted by the presence of coffin furniture and/or coffin stains. The remains of a minimum of ten coffined burials (recovered from both sides of the road) were identified; two others may have been coffined but the evidence was scanty and inconclusive. The only dating evidence, other than a general Romano-British date, was residual pottery in the grave fills, which included material of 1st–late 3rd century date. The position of one grave, 122526, across the eastern entrance to the most southerly of the mortuary enclosures (126066), suggests it post-dated the main period of use of the enclosures, the ditches of which had been backfilled by the later 2nd century. Taken together, what little evidence does survive – lack of grave goods, coffined burials and residual pottery from cremation burials/pyres – suggests that the cemetery followed the national trend of a shift to burial by inhumation of the unburnt corpse towards the latter part of the 2nd century.

The inhumation graves generally survived to a greater depth than the cremation graves, with a range of 0.15 m to 0.65 m, most (80%) being over 0.25 m deep. The majority survived above the depth of the coffin stain or furniture, although there was frequently evidence for bioturbation within the light sandy soils and some movement of coffin furniture had occurred as a result.

Most graves were sub-rectangular (seven) or sub-apsidal (five) in shape, with two rectangular cuts. One grave, 122552, appeared sub-circular at surface level, but the lower 0.11 m depth of the 0.28 m deep cut was rectangular (Fig. 78). The majority had steep or vertical sides and flat bases. The three rectangular graves, 122455, 122460 and 122492, were stepped on three or two sides respectively (Fig. 79); all lay in the eastern half of the cemetery, 122460 falling furthest to the east. The cuts varied in length from 1.27 m to 2.3 m (mean 1.46 m, SD 0.26 m), and in width from 0.49 m to 0.8 m (mean 0.65 m, SD 0.1 m), the two ends of the range for

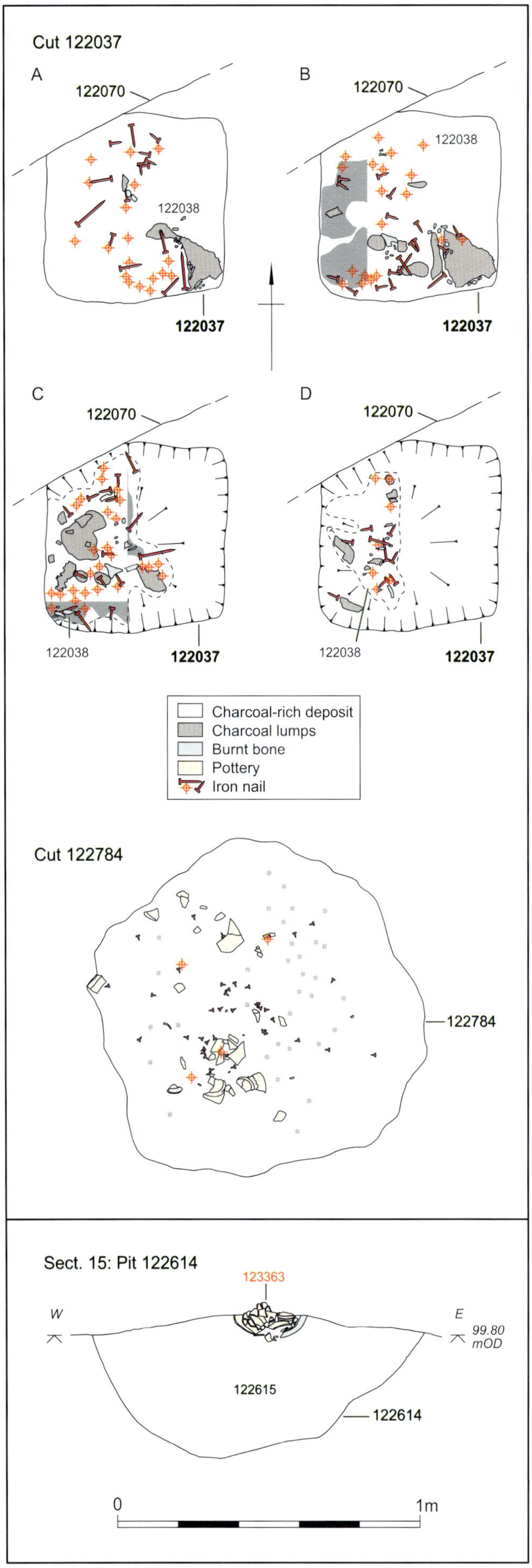

Fig. 77 Cremation-related features: cuts 122037, 122784 and 122614

both dimensions being from the same graves (122675, Figs 78, and 122364 respectively).

Most of the graves were orientated north–south (10, all in the eastern half of the cemetery), with three lying north-east to south-west (both halves), one east–west (east half) and one north-west to south-east (west half).

Coffin furniture was recovered from nine graves. This mostly comprised iron nails, but in one instance (grave 122552) fragments of lead sheet were also recovered; see Grave catalogue and Powell, K., below). Nine graves – not all the same as those with furniture – contained indications of a coffin stain (Figs 78–80). The latter tended to comprise a slightly darker version of the grave fill, which generally formed a mid-yellowish-brown silty sand with variable inclusions of flint gravel. In at least one instance (grave 122609) the shape of the coffin stain, narrower at the south end, suggests that the head was to the north (Fig. 78). Since no unburnt bone, human or animal, survived on the site due to the high soil acidity and no *in situ* grave goods were recovered from any of the features confidently identified as inhumation graves, the position of the bodies within most of the graves could not be deduced.

There is no evidence to suggest the age and sex of the individuals buried within the inhumation graves. Although the common burial position at this time, particularly for coffined burials, was supine and extended, it cannot be guaranteed that this would invariably have been the case. It may be pertinent to note, however, that only five of the graves were longer than 1.50 m and that the minimum estimated stature recorded for an adult from the Romano-British cemeteries within Roberts's and Cox's recent survey (2003, 163) was 1.59 m.

Six other features, one in the western half of the cemetery and five in the eastern portion, were identified as possible grave cuts, largely on the basis of their shape. All were either sub-apsidal (one) or sub-rectangular (five), with steep or vertical sides (except the northern end of 122977 which had a long concave slope; Fig. 78). The bases of three of the cuts were flat; two others were sloping, one with a central depression; and one other had an irregular base. A possible coffin stain was observed in three of the features, comprising slightly darker areas within the general grave fills of greyish-brown silty sand/sand with variable flint gravel inclusions. No coffin furniture was seen in any of these features. In general they tended to have a shallower surviving depth than the confidently identified grave cuts, with a range of 0.1–0.55 m, only half being over 0.25 m. The cuts varied in length from 1.0 m to 2.05 m and in width from 0.45–0.48 m, the maximum and minimum of both dimensions being from the same features. Most followed a north–south orientation (four), with one north-west to south-east and one south-east to north-west. One of the least convincing of these possible graves, 122977, contained two late 1st–early 2nd century vessels, laid on their sides in the centre of the southern half of the cut where the base was flat (Fig. 78). If these were to represent *in situ* grave goods it

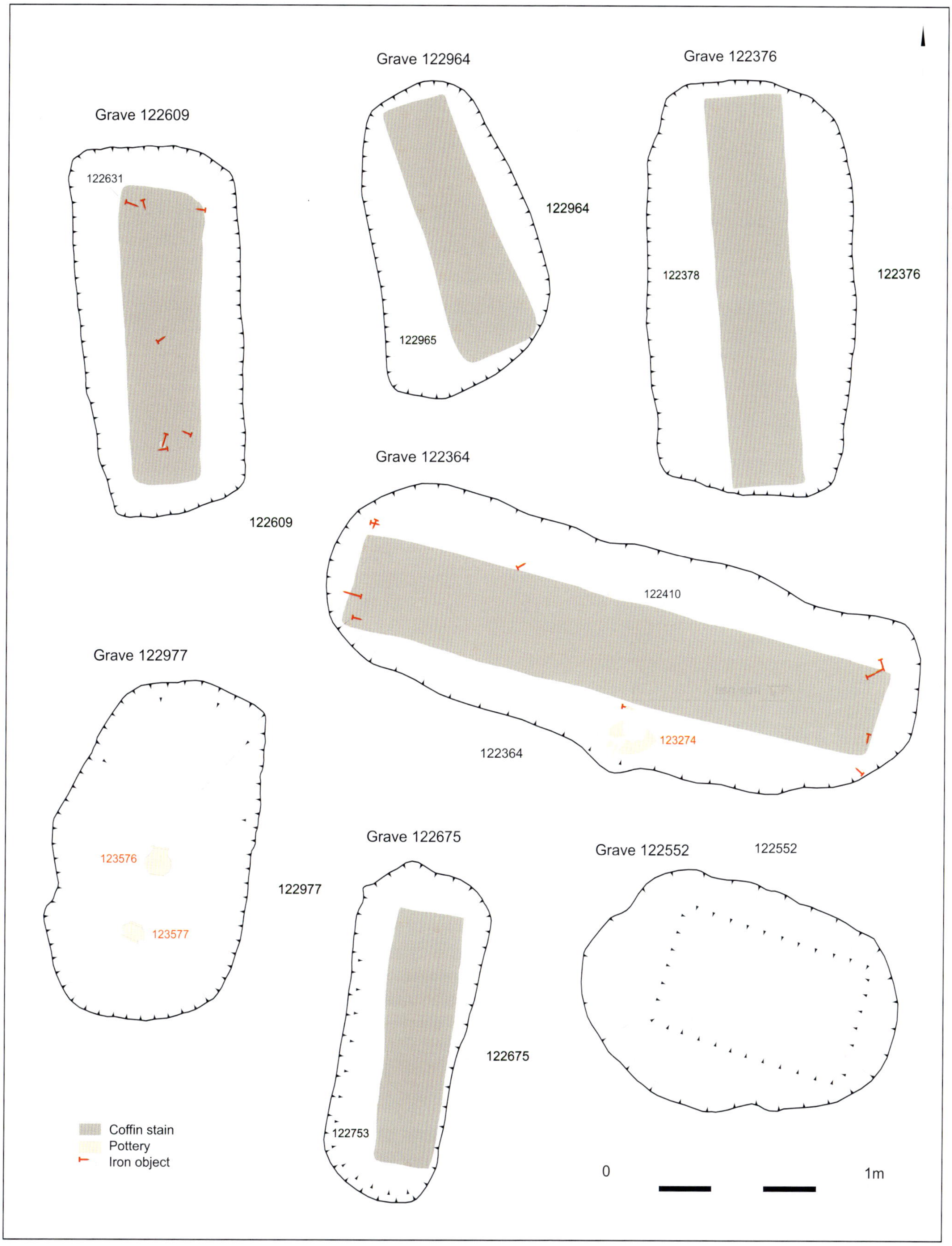

Fig. 78 Inhumation graves

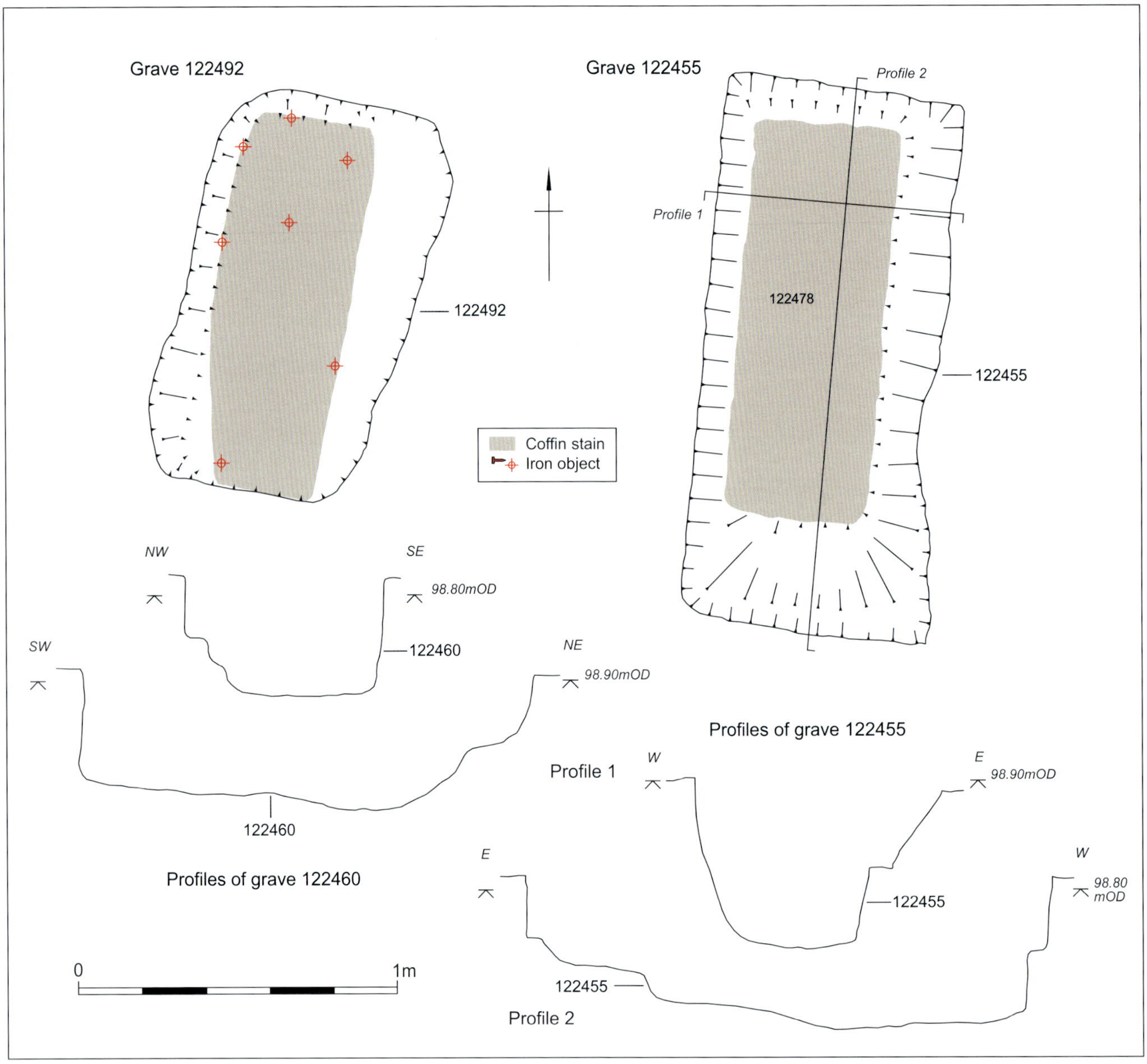

Fig. 79 Inhumation graves

would give an earlier date for the inhumation graves demonstrating the contemporaneous practice of both mortuary rites; the possible interpretation of this feature is far from conclusive, however, and the inhumation graves in general do not have the characteristics of such early Romano-British features. One of the possible graves (122577) was cut through the ditch of the eastern-most mortuary enclosure 126154, demonstrating the cutting of the feature post-dates the backfilling of the ditch, which seems to have occurred in the mid–later 2nd century AD.

The mortuary enclosures

The remains of four rectangular mortuary enclosures were excavated in the eastern half of the cemetery (Fig. 67). Three of the features (126148, 126069 and 126066) formed a dispersed north–south line parallel to the road, set back from the eastern road-zone boundary ditch 126062 by 13.7–14.7 m; the fourth enclosure (126154) lay on the same orientation but to the east of 126148 and 126069. Although technically rectangular as excavated, it is likely that the enclosures were intended to be square. All had similar dimensions but varied in the detail of their form, fills and associated features (Table 19). Datable material recovered from the ditch fills suggests they are likely to have been late 1st–mid-2nd century in date and to have been backfilled by the mid–late 2nd century; the southern-most enclosure, 126066, had been cut by the creation of the later 2nd century southern boundary ditch 126065.

Approximately 40–60% of each mortuary enclosure ditch was subject to excavation. The areas described by each enclosure were similar at between 5.33 m to 6.02 m east–west by 5.10 m to 6.74 m north–south, the northern-most (126148) representing the maximum size and the easternmost (126154) the minimum. The three westerly enclosure ditches all had steep sides, sometimes partially concave or convex, with flat or slightly concave bases (Fig. 81), whilst the easterly (126154) had a relatively gentle concave base and sides. The recorded

Fig. 80 Inhumation grave 122675 with coffin stain

widths of the ditches varied considerably both within one enclosure and between ditches. What is unclear is whether this reflects some functional variation occurring along the course of individual ditches or simply the product of different individuals cutting the ditch. There was no evidence for re-cuts but it is possible that in clearing out sections of the ditches during the course of their use, parts of them may have been accidentally widened; the soft nature of the natural sand is likely to have rendered such accidental remodelling in cleaning inevitable.

Two ditches, 126148 and 126154, had entrances in the centre of their west sides, facing the road. Although 126154 lay to the east of 126148 and 126069, the 1.41 m gap between the latter two left an unobscured line of vision from the road to the enclosure entrance and the cremation grave (122780) within it. The entrance to enclosure 126066 lay on the east side, away from the road, but had been blocked by the insertion of a (possibly 3rd century) inhumation grave, 122526. Enclosure ditch 126069 is somewhat unusual; the original intention appears to have been to leave the northern side open, but a short (*c* 1.8 m) length of east–west ditch was inserted commencing *c* 1 m south of the northern terminal to the eastern arm of the ditch; there was no apparent variation in the fill so presumably this had been cut shortly after the original.

Grave 122780 lay opposite the central entrance to enclosure 126154, but within the western half of the

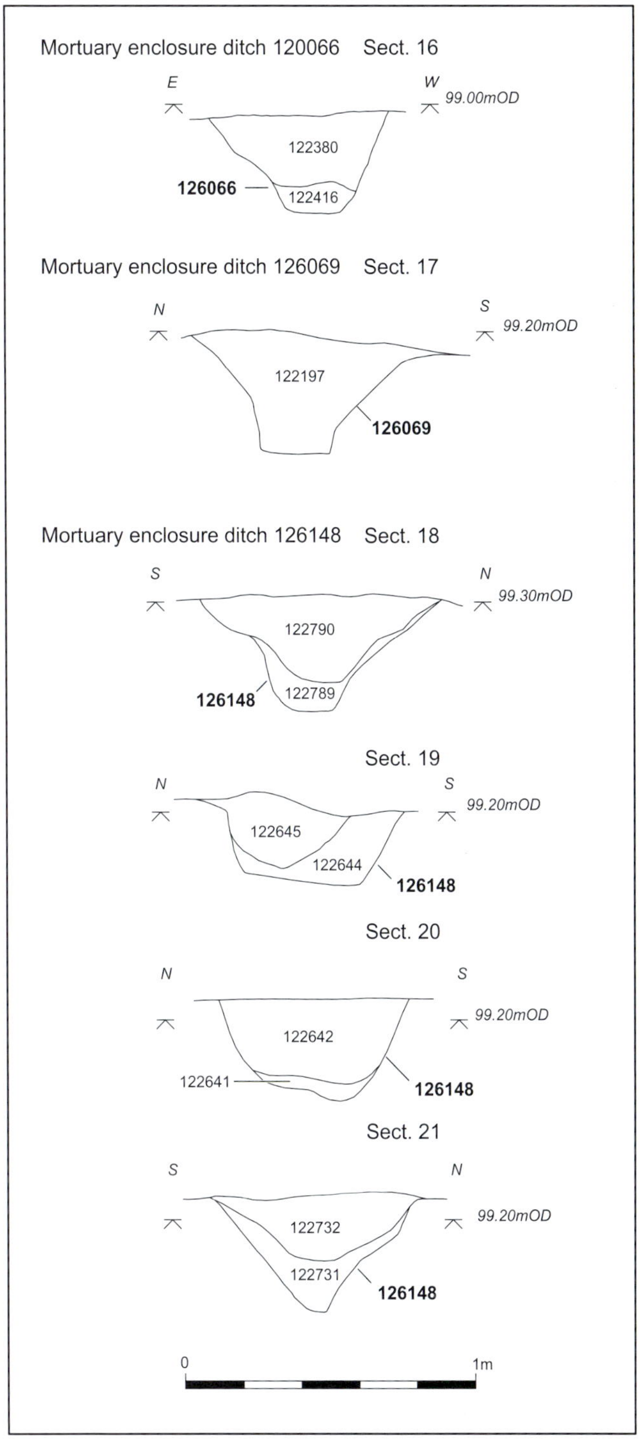

Fig. 81 Sections of mortuary enclosure ditches

enclosed area (Fig. 67). This grave represented the most intact feature of its type within the cemetery, having apparently been cut to a greater depth than those elsewhere (Fig. 73) (see above). The rectangular feature 122934, which lay central to enclosure ditch 126148, is likely to have supported a partly, if not wholly, wooden super-structure, possibly functioning as a mortuary house, cenotaph or shrine. Narrow (0.09–0.16 m wide), shallow (max. 0.4 m deep) slots described an area *c* 1.4 m by 1.2 m, with integral postholes at the north-east and south-east corners. The external slopes of the slot were vertical, the internal slopes steep and the base was flat; these appear to represent beam slots with posts at the

Table 19 Summary table of mortuary enclosure ditches

Ditch	Width (m)	Depth (m)	Dimensions (m)	Entrance (width (m)	No. fills	Associate features
126148	0.40–0.85	0.25–0.41	c 6.0 x 6.7	W side central (0.46)	2	'mortuary house' 122934
126068	0.45–1.10	0.28–0.40	c 6.0 x 6.2	N side to W (3.17)	1–2	?treethrow 122886
126066	0.33–0.90	0.22–0.33	c 5.7 x <5.2	E side towards N (1.39)	1–2	?treethrow 122616
126154	0.20–0.54	0.12–0.25	c 5.3 x 5.1	W side central (0.93)	1	urned burial, grave 122780

two corners away from the enclosure entrance. The only other negative feature within this enclosure was a tree hollow of unknown date which cut the beam slot. Tree hollows also represent the only internal features associated with the two remaining enclosure ditches, 126069 and 126066; that within the latter appears to have been cut by the insertion of the inhumation grave 122526 across the entrance, consequently, despite the absence of conclusive dating evidence, the trees may have been contemporaneous with the enclosures and their location may not have been wholly fortuitous.

The ditch fills were generally similar, comprising one or two fills of reddish- or yellowish-brown slightly silty sand/sand. A primary layer of silting, the recorded depths of which ranged from as little as 0.01 m to 0.22 m, was seen only in about half the excavated segments, possibly having been removed by cleaning in the rest. The main fills formed apparently homogenous deposits of material with variable inclusions of flint gravel. In most cases there was no evidence to suggest silting predominantly occurred from one side or the other; two of the eight excavated segments of ditch 126148 suggest that silting was predominantly from outside the ditch, the fills recorded in one other segment suggesting that it may have been mostly from the interior (Fig. 81). Small quantities of burnt and unburnt and often abraded pottery were recovered from one or occasionally two excavated segments in each enclosure ditch (between six and eight segments of each ditch excavated). Occasional charcoal flecking was observed in individual excavated segments from each ditch, and some metalwork was also collected from individual segments in all except ditch 126154. A very small quantity of redeposited cremated bone (<5 g) was recovered from one excavated segment of ditch 126066. One substantial deposit of metalwork, pot sherds and charcoal, including lumps of charred wood, was incorporated within the secondary deposit in the terminal to the north of the entrance to enclosure 126148. It is only in this latter case that a deliberate dump of material appears to have been made into one of the ditches.

Cemetery boundary ditches

The two road-zone boundary ditches, 126059 and 126062, clearly also functioned as boundary ditches to the cemetery. They were probably cut sometime before the establishment of the cemetery and appear to have maintained their function into the late 2nd and 3rd centuries despite having been backfilled by this stage (see above).

Ditch 126020, forming the north–south boundary on the west side of the cemetery, also appears to have been cut in the 1st century AD, probably at the time the cemetery was established. In most excavated segments the ditch showed a steep-sided V-shaped form with a slightly concave edge on the west side (Fig. 83); in one of the eight excavated segments the ditch sides were similarly steep but the base was flat. The width varied slightly from 0.6 m to 1.0 m, with a surviving depth of *c* 0.4–0.6 m; in one central segment (set only *c* 1.2 m from its nearest neighbour) the ditch narrowed to *c* 0.3 m with a reduction in depth to 0.15 m. It is possible, as was suggested with reference to the road-zone boundary ditches (see above), that the change in dimensions over a short stretch of the ditch was for ease of access to the cemetery. Most segments contained one or two fills – reddish-/greyish-brown silty sand with occasional gravel inclusions – with some indication of preferential silting from the steeper eastern side. No datable finds were recovered from the fills, but the ditch was cut by several ovens/hearths from one of which a radiocarbon date of cal AD 10–210 (NZA-26163, 1923±30 BP) (Fig. 62, Table 18) was obtained, and early–mid-2nd century pottery recovered from two; this suggests that the ditch was backfilled by the mid–late 2nd century AD.

The narrow (*c.* 0.5 m), shallow (surviving depth 0.1 m), north–south ditch 126073 appears to have formed the eastern boundary to the eastern half of the cemetery (Fig. 67). No mortuary-related features extended to the east of this ditch and the nearest graves (within 2.0–11.0 m) all appear to be of later 2nd century date. The shallow concave ditch held a single fill of dark brown sand from which no datable finds were recovered, but its southern end was cut by the later 2nd century southern boundary ditch 126065 (south of which no trace of it was recorded), indicating that it was largely, although not completely backfilled by this date and was probably cut in the early 2nd century.

The later Romano-British ditch 126065, which formed the re-cut to the road-zone boundary ditch 126062 in its north–south section (see Road above), appears to have formed a southern boundary to the eastern half of the cemetery, although extending *c* 27 m to the east of the eastern-most grave (Fig. 60). The ditch was dug in the latter part of the 2nd century, truncating the southern section of enclosure ditch 126066, the south end of the eastern boundary ditch 126073, and at least one urned cremation burial (grave 122154; Fig. 82). One, possibly two cremation-related features, 122037 (containing redeposited pyre debris) and

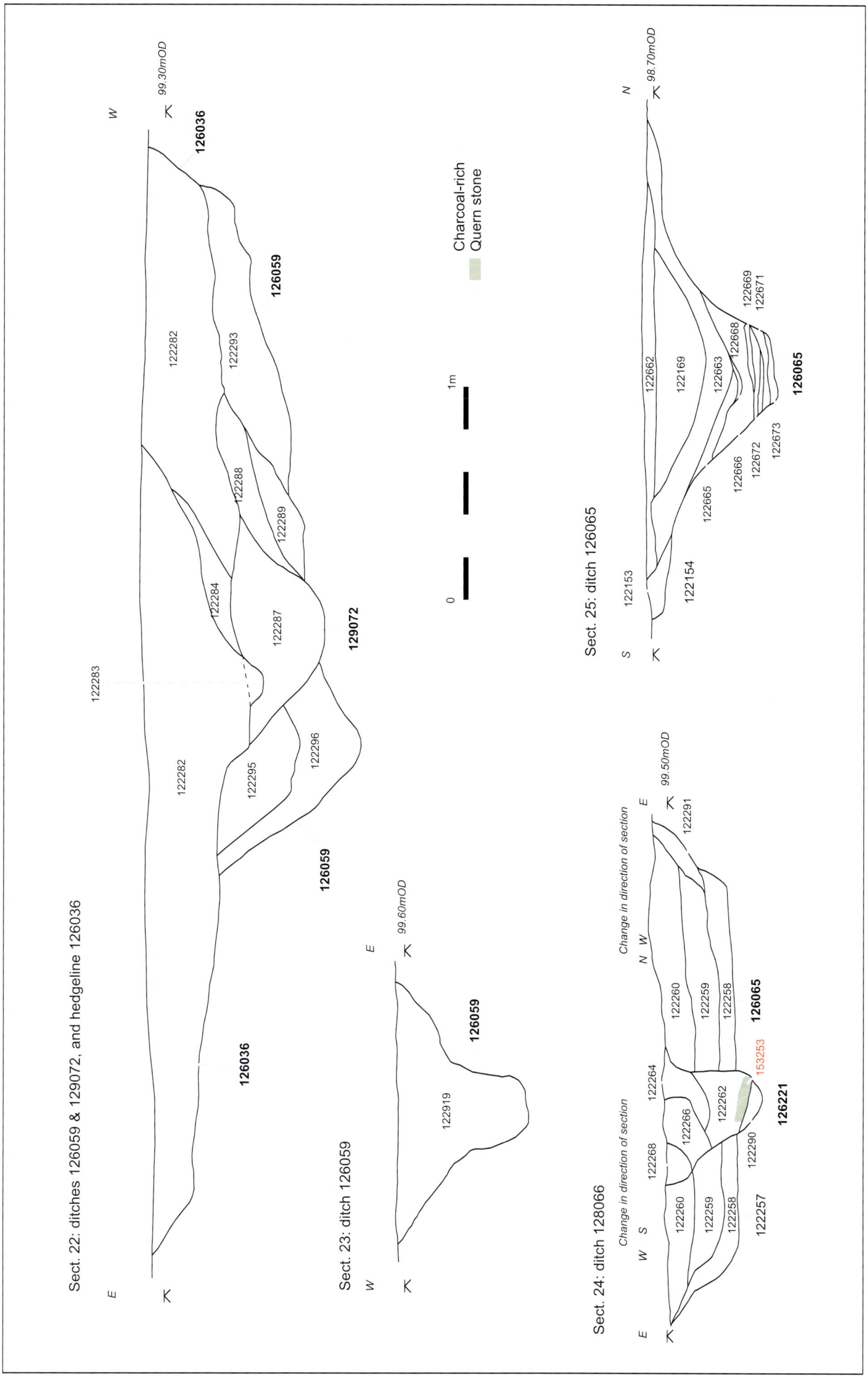

Fig. 82 Sections of cemetery road-zone ditches

122155 (pit with redeposited pot), lay to the south of the ditch, but in general its position corresponds with the southern extent of the graves and the location of the postulated access point to the cemetery across the road-zone boundary ditch 126062 (see above). The east–west section of the ditch was similar in shape and form to the north–south section; the sides were generally steep and convex with a narrow concave or, in two segments, flat base. The width varied from 1.06 m to 2.35 m, being widest in the central area of its east–west length and wider than at any point in the north–south section, although of similar depth (0.55–0.72 m). There were generally three fills of reddish- or yellowish-brown slightly silty sands with variable inclusions of gravel, although individual layers sometimes comprised several small lenses of material. The greatest variability was seen where the ditch cut through earlier features, their fills being incorporated in the silting (Fig. 82). There was some indication of preferential silting from the south side in some segments but generally silting appears to have occurred equally from either side.

There was no corresponding southern boundary ditch to the western half of the cemetery, although grave cuts and other mortuary-related features seem to cease at the same southerly point as those in the eastern half of the cemetery. Only one feature, containing redeposited pyre debris, lay to the south of the line formed by ditch 126065. The post-medieval hedgeline 129036 seems to fortuitously almost mirror ditch 126065; although it was found to cut the two ditches flanking the road in its north-south section, no underlying features were observed in the east–west section (Figs 60, 66).

Ovens/hearths

Six features (or associated groups of features), all with charcoal-rich fills, were distributed north–south along a *c* 25 m length of the western boundary ditch 126020, and cut into its upper fill (Fig. 66). They were similar in shape and form and probably related to similar activities.

Feature 122517, the clearest of the group, formed a sub-rectangular cut (1.9 by 0.95 m, max. 0.34 m deep) with three steep and one shelving side (latter to east), the flattish base having a shallow bowl at either end (Fig. 83). The natural across the base and at least part-way up the sides of the cut had been baked hard and red. The primary fill of greyish-red silty sand (125557) was overlain by a charcoal-rich deposit (122518) that spread out across the shallow, narrow 'tongue' (0.95 m by 0.55 m) forming the east end of the feature. The rectangular area appears to form the main body of an oven or hearth, for which there is no evidence of a super-structure, the eastern 'tongue' representing the flue and the point from which the spent fuel ash was raked-out.

None of the other features has quite such a distinctive shape as 122517, and only two others, 122100/122093 and 122085/122098, showed evidence for *in situ* burning. In the former, a sub-rectangular cut (122100; 2.2 m by 1.3 m, and 0.32 m deep) formed the main body of the feature incorporating a single shallow bowl in its east half. The shallow, sub-rounded cut (122093; 1.4 m by 1.2 m, and 0.1 m deep) which cut the east end of 122100 may have represented the flue area or at least the point for removal of ash from the hearth (Fig. 83). The primary fill of 122100 (122145) represents the remains of silting from the west; the main, charcoal-rich fill (122101) also contained moderate quantities of fired clay, suggesting a clay super-structure to the feature.

Cuts 122085 (1.1 m by 0.8 m, 0.18 m deep) and 122098 (1 m by 0.8 m, 0.1 m deep) were of a similar form and demonstrated a similar relationship to 122100/122093. No bowl was evident in the base of 122085 but the flat base was stepped-up towards the east end (Fig. 66). The fill again comprised several layers of charcoal-rich material, the upper two of which also contained fragments of fired clay. An extensive area (2.3 m by 2.2 m) of *in situ* burning spread to the north, east and south of these features suggesting either a more-extensive super-structure straddling the cuts or possibly collapse of the structure during firing. Feature 122106, to the west of and cut by 122085, may represent the remains of an earlier version of the hearth base although there is no direct supporting evidence for this in terms of *in situ* burning or the nature of the fill.

The remaining features, 122069, 122358 and 122174/122184, had similar sub-rectangular forms, 1.95–3.25 m long, 1.05–1.9 m wide and 0.35–0.4 m deep. Three sides generally had a steep straight or convex form, with a flat or single/double bowled base gently sloping up to the fourth side (west in two, east in the other). The two or three charcoal-rich fills contained rare fragments of burnt clay. The function of a small sub-rectangular feature (122213), cut by ditch 126035 (below) to the east of the boundary ditch is unclear, but the similarities between its fill and that of the ovens suggests it may have been associated with them.

Little direct dating evidence was recovered from this group of features, with a few fragments of early–mid-2nd century pottery recovered from two. A radiocarbon date of cal AD 10–210 (1923±30 BP, NZA-26163) (Fig. 62, Table 18), obtained from the charcoal deposits in 122517, indicates that the features were functioning at the same time as the cemetery was in use, probably in the 2nd century given that they cut through the backfilled early Romano-British boundary ditch 126020. The features appear to have had clay super-structures and to have been subject to several phases of use. However, there is little to indicate their function, which was clearly not linked to any industrial process or directly associated with cremation. The dense deposits of narrow, roundwood charcoal indicates hot, short-lived fires (Gale, below). Few charred plant remains were recovered and these largely comprised weeds and species commonly believed to have functioned as tinder. Rare cereal remains were recovered from two samples but as these were less than recovered from deposits elsewhere on the site they cannot be taken as indicative of use.

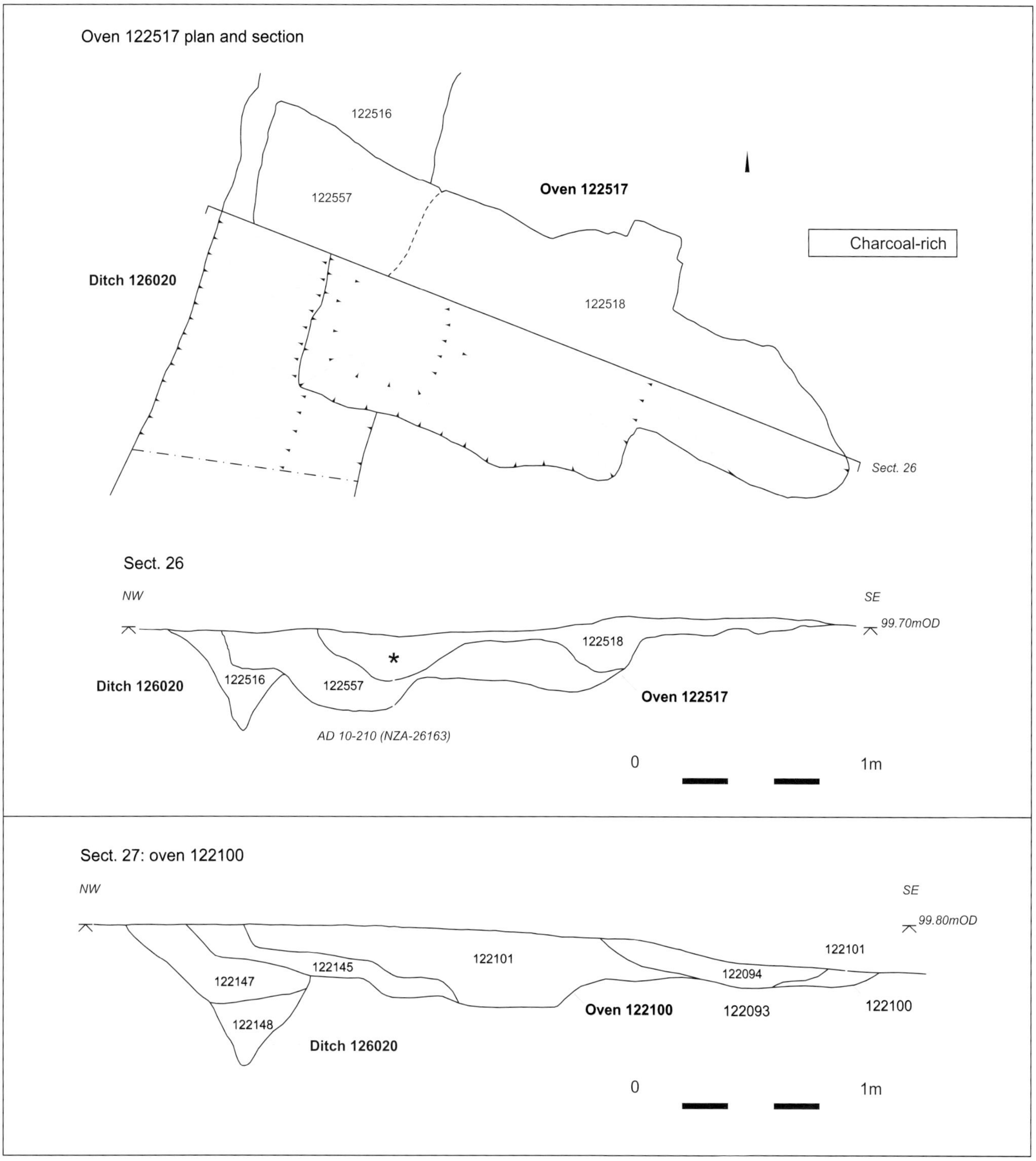

Fig. 83 Ovens 122517 and 122100

Miscellaneous features

Two adjoining, short lengths of ditch (126035 and 126225) running perpendicular to the road in the western half of the cemetery appear to have been cut in the 2nd century subsequent to the backfilling of the western boundary ditch (Fig. 66). The cuts had shallow concave sides and bases (0.5–0.82 m wide, 0.13–0.3 m deep), the single silty sand fills including fragments of burnt clay in places. The latter inclusions, and their apparent date and location, suggest that the ditches were associated with the ovens in some way, although ditch 126035 did cut the possible oven feature 122312.

No dating evidence was recovered from ditch 126159 (concave sides and base; 0.65–1.57 m wide, 0.2 m deep) in the western half of the cemetery, but its location and orientation (almost perpendicular to the cemetery's north–south boundary ditches), and the presence of charcoal flecking in the single fill, suggest a Romano-British date and some connection with the cemetery, possibly representing an internal boundary.

Several Romano-British or probable Romano-British pits of uncertain function were excavated in various parts of the cemetery (122614, 122681, 122747, 122786, 122858 and 122923). All were relatively small, of a commensurate size with others in the area, and the fills comprised similar soil matrices although with little or no artefactual or ecofactual material. Several Romano-British nails were recovered from a small feature (122820) in the eastern half of the cemetery, but the material is most likely redeposited, possibly within what comprised a natural scoop or depression. One possible posthole (122374) was cut by the early–mid-2nd century boundary ditch 126073, the post possibly functioning as an early boundary marker (Fig. 67).

Several features with the characteristics of tree hollows were cut by Romano-British features or contained residual Romano-British pottery, and the trees themselves may have been extant in the Romano-British period. Those possibly fortuitously situated within the mortuary enclosures have already been discussed above, but at least 14 possible tree hollows were recorded across the site.

Medieval, post-medieval and modern

There was very little evidence for post-Romano-British activity in the area of the site. Only two finds of later medieval date were recovered in excavation, a copper-alloy buckle from the topsoil in the eastern part of the site and an intrusive fragment of pottery from a Romano-British feature in the western half of the cemetery. There was a similar paucity of post-medieval artefactual material – a few items of unstratified metalwork from the topsoil (Powell, K., below) and odd fragments of pottery, mostly intrusive within the upper levels of Romano-British features (Leary, below).

Although no firm dating evidence was recovered from any of the series of *c* 17 intercutting ditch lengths on the eastern side of the cemetery (one fragment of post-medieval pottery from one), they are all likely to be post-medieval, although a later medieval origin cannot be discounted. The two longest lengths, 126203 and 126206, define the overall orientations, the former running roughly north–south with a central dog-leg to the east and the latter north–south with a 90° directional change to the east (Fig. 60). The ditches were of similar size and shape, those in the densest central area of intercutting demonstrating a shift southwards over time, with infilling apparently predominantly from the north. Their location was probably linked to the wet/boggy area in the low-lying eastern part of the site, the features functioning as relatively short-lived and frequently re-cut boundary and/or drainage ditches.

The north–south ditches at the eastern end of the site are modern. The hedge along the line of 126036 may have originated in the 18th century as part of the enclosures but it could have followed an existing boundary (see cemetery boundary ditches above); the hedge itself was extant at the commencement of excavation, being grubbed-out as part of the development preparations.

The date of the north-east to south-west ditch 126221 is difficult to define (Fig. 66). It cuts the later Romano-British ditch 126065 and is cut by two of the ditches early in the post-medieval series. The only artefactual material recovered from the fills is of Romano-British date (pottery and a quern fragment) but as the excavated segments were all at intersections with Romano-British features this is probably all residual (Fig. 82).

The apparent relationship of the ditch with the Roman road is confusing; one of the metalled road surfaces appears to overly the upper fill of the ditch – which otherwise lay in a gap between sections of metalling – by *c* 0.12 m (Fig. 63). Both the ditch fill and the road surface were physically below the modern topsoil/ ploughsoil and the part of the road surface overlying the ditch had clearly slumped; the ditch could have been cut from a higher level, traces of which were destroyed by subsequent ploughing, and over time the edge of the disturbed road surface could have slumped over the ditch fill. The most likely date for the ditch is later medieval or post-medieval, the line appearing to echo that of the later ditch series.

Undated and natural features

A few undated linear features and small pits of uncertain function lay chiefly in the western part of the site. One feature (126177) cut the metalled surface of the Roman road in the site's southern baulk (Fig. 63). A group of three possibly related postholes was excavated to the north of the mortuary enclosures and although they may be Romano-British there was no evidence to confirm this possibility. At least 14 probable tree hollows were identified across the site, some pre-dating and other post-dating the Romano-British features. A few other features indicative of root or animal activity were also investigated.

Grave catalogue, by Jacqueline I. McKinley and Kirsten Egging

(Including redeposited cremation burials and other cremation-related deposits)

KEY:
ON = object number; RE = rim equivalent; BC = base equivalent.

For Romano-British ceramic phases see Phasing (p. 158). See Chapter 28, Romano-British pottery fabrics for pottery codes.

Cremation graves

Grave 120202

No details of cut, removed by machine in evaluation stage. Uncertain if urned or unurned burial since all material recovered from spoil & distribution of archaeological comments unknown. Burial context (120203); cremated bone, several ceramic vessels, redeposited pyre debris.

Human bone : 431.8 g. 1) adult >30 yr 2) infant *c* 0.5–2 yr.

Animal bone: 7.7 g, 7 frags, medium mammal, mammal & u/id (20 frags).

Pyre/grave goods

ON 121201.1: 73 FLB2 sherds (freshly broken) from ring-necked flagon with evenly sized, slightly splayed rings. L1–E2 (*cf* Gillam 1970, no 2, dated AD 70–110). 275 g. RE 57%, BE 50%. (Fig. 87, 1)

ON 121201.2 54 sherds (freshly broken) from rim, body & base of R5 bifurcated everted-rim jar with shoulder groove & zone of double wavy line burnish around upper body. ?Conical, with slightly rebated rim (Lee and Lindquist 1994, R. 146). 476 g. RE 65%. BE 100%. (Fig. 87, 2)

ON 121201.3: 6 frags narrow mouthed R5 tettine with short everted rim & small spout (Brassington 1980, no. 555). 53 g; RE 70%. (Fig. 87, 3)

ON 121201.4: Frags Fe nail shank. L 24 mm.

ON 121202.1: 43 R5 sherds of base & lower body of jar with simple base. 706 g, BE 100%.

ON 121202.2: 42 rim & body sherds (freshly broken) from Malverniam were tubby pot with vertical burnish lines. Such vessels occur in 1st & 2nd C groups at Coleshill & Tiddington. Similar vessel found at Wall *mansio* (Round 1990–1, fig. 15.8) & fort (Gould 1963–4, fig. 14.84–5) 574 g. RE 61%. (Fig. 87, 4)

ON 121202.3: Abraded FLA4 body sherd. L1–E2. (*cf.* Ferguson 2001, table 124). 3 g.

ON 121202.4: 2 post-medieval sherds.

Bulk finds:

Copper-alloy box fittings. (Fig. 84, 18). See p. 144.

Phase: L1–E2 C.

Grave 122017

Sub-circular, moderately sloping, concave sides and base; 0.46 m by 0.4 m, 0.12 m deep. Urned burial (122065; ON 123098) in base, heavily truncated. Grave fill (122018): mid-yellowish-grey silty sand with redeposited pyre debris around & below bone of urned burial: plus unurned portion of burial + redeposited pyre debris.

Human bone: 276.6 g. Adult *c* 30–45 yr.

Pyre/grave-goods:

ON 123098: 98+ freshly broken (some abraded) sherds R16 narrow-necked jar; neck cordon & grooved body. 607 g; BE 80%. E–L 2 C. (Fig. 87, 5)

Bulk finds:

Bent Fe hobnail, Manning type 10. L 10 mm, D 9 mm. 7 frags min. 5 Fe nails, one with bent shank, min. 3 Manning type 1b (one small). L 19–53 mm, D 9–16 mm. 3 frags min. 2 Fe nail/studs one with faceted head; L 11–18 mm, D 11–13 mm. (Fig. 84, 17). See p. 144.

Phase: E–M2 C.

Grave 122020

Circular, moderately sloping, concave sides & base; 0.6 m diameter, 0.08 m deep. No clear cut observed in excavation. Urned burial (122028; ON 123012) in base, heavily disturbed. Grave fill (122021): soft reddish-brown sand with rare gravel, charcoal flecks.

Human bone: 2.7 g; >5 yr.

Pyre/grave-goods:

ON 123012: 84 frags CTA1 rebated-rim jar, horizontal combing/rilling outside upper body; some ?burning (grey) on outside rim & body sherd. Warwickshire series C41 1st–mid-2nd (Booth 2006, 116, table 2). 425 g; RE 10%; BE 80%. (Fig. 87, 6)

Phase: L1–E2 C.

Grave 122022

Sub-circular, moderately sloping, concave sides & base; 0.2 m diam., 0.08 m deep. Urned burial (122024; ON 123016), heavily truncated. Grave fill (122023): loose reddish-orange silty sand with occasional large pebbles & flecks charcoal.

Human bone: 17.5 g; Subadult/adult >13 yr.

Pyre/grave-goods:

ON 123016: 32 BB1 jar base & body sherds; burnt basal & lower body sherd. 202 g; BE 100%.

Phase: E–M2 C.

Grave 122025

Sub-circular, gradually sloping sides & concave base, but cut unclear; 0.77 m by 0.65 m, 0.15 m deep. Urned burial (122027; ON 123024.2) in base, heavily truncated. Grave fill (122026): soft light reddish-brown silty sand with rare gravel & charcoal frags.

Human bone: 374.8 g; adult *c* 18–30 yr, female.

Animal bone: 3.4 g; medium or large mammal rib.

Pyre/grave-goods:

ON 123024.1: 33 small frags mica dusted indented beaker with short everted rim. MG1. L1st–E2nd (Ferguson 2001, 177). 36 g; RE 65%. (Fig. 87, 7)

ON 123024:2 99 freshly broken FLA2 sherds. Flagon lower body & base, scorched on one side; 1192 g; BE 100%. (Fig. 87, 8)

Phase: L1–E2 C.

Grave 122044

Sub-circular, steep sides and flat base; 0.42 m by 0.3 m, 0.15 m deep. Combined urned (129033; ON 123043.2) & unurned (122049) burial, truncated. Grave fill (122049): soft mid-greyish-/reddish-brown sand silt with common quartzite stones. (Fig. 73)

Human bone: 810 g; adult *c* 30–45 yr; ?male.

Animal bone: 17.3 g; pig head & forelimb; fowl l & r wings.

Pyre/grave-goods:

ON 123039: Fe nail frag., Manning type 1b. L 39 mm, D 16 mm.

ON 123040: 2 frags Fe nail head & shank. Large flat head with turned over edges. Manning type 1. L 13 mm, D 19 mm.

ON 123041: frag. large flat Fe nail head with turned over edges, Manning type 1b. D 20 mm.

ON 123042; pebble with percussion wear at one end consistent with use as a pounder; unburnt. 100 mm by 60 mm by 40 mm.
ON 123043.1: 32 freshly broken sherds small bulbous flagon. Single handled vessel, cordon at base of neck. 342 g; BE 100%. (Fig. 87, 9)
ON 123043.2: 66 freshly broken R7 bowl, base & body sherds. Simple base. Scorched/burnt, internal crack in base. 594 g; BE 100%.
ON 123043.3: 4 frags. 2 near complete Fe nails, Manning type 1b. L 63 mm & L 56 mm, D 14 mm & 13 mm.
ON 123043.4: Fe hobnail. (Fig. 84, 2). See p. 144
ON 123589: Sherd R16 beaker; everted rim; 0.4 g.
Bulk finds:
87 R7 sherds, some from a carinated bowl with bifid rim (Booth 2006, fig. 45, nos 82 & 193, *cf.* Gillam 1970, no. 212 dated AD 160–200; Brassington 1971, no. 15) & some from unknown jar (same as 1 in 129033); M–L 2nd; 312 g; RE 7%.
Frag tile; 14 g.
3 small Fe nail heads & shanks (2 fused), Manning type 1b. L 21 mm, 20 mm and 22 mm; D 11 mm, 18 mm and 15 mm. 6 Fe hobnails (2 fused), Manning type 10. L 14–19 mm, D 8–10 mm.
Phase: E–M2 C.

Grave 122045
Sub-circular, concave sides & irregular base; 0.35 m by 0.25 m, 0.11 m deep. Unurned burial, disturbed by animal burrows. Grave fill (122139): soft, dark reddish-brown sand, sparse small pebbles, cremated bone in two disturbed concentrations with redeposited pyre debris.
Human bone: 389.5 g; adult *c* 30–40 yr.
Animal bone: 10.1 g; pig skull & r fore limb; >12 months; sheep/goat r fore limb; <30 months; bird wing.
Bulk finds:
Frag. molten blue/green glass. <1 g.
Fe nail frag., Manning type 1b. L 60 mm, D 14 mm.
0.8 g fuel ash slag.
Phase: ERB.

Grave 122052
Circular, steep sides, concave base; 0.7 m diam., 0.2 m deep. Urned burial (122055: ON 123066.1) ?inverted. Grave fill (122053): soft reddish-brown silty sand with moderate gravel inclusions. (Fig. 73)
Human bone: 210.3 g; adult *c* 35–55 yr, ?? female.
Animal bone: 0.6 g u/id.
Pyre/grave-goods:
ON 123065: Fe nail (missing tip), Manning type 1b. L 57 mm, D 15 mm.
ON 123066.1: 78 freshly broken, abraded R16 sherds. Neckless everted rim & double shoulder groove. Flavian–Trajanic type jar. 336 g; RE 86%. (Fig. 87, 10)
ON 123066.2: Rim sherd small BB1 jar/beaker. Short everted rim; burnt. L 2nd. 9 g; RE 10%. (Fig. 87, 11)
ON 123066.3: Frag. base small R18 jar. Burnt. 19 g; BE 55%. (Fig. 87, 12)
ON 123066.4: Frags base & lower body of small R18 jar. Burnt, 9 sherds very abraded. 57 g; BE 100%. (Fig. 87, 13)
ON 123066.5 16 frags molten blue/green glass. 32 g.
ON 123076: Fe nail shank frag. L 38 mm.
ON 123077: Fe nail, Manning type 1b. L 68, D 14 mm.
ON 123078: Fe nail (bent end), Manning type 1b. L 78 mm, D 17 mm.
ON 123090: Fe nail (?head damaged), Manning type 1b. L 57 mm, D 11 mm.
ON 123091: Fe nail head & shank frag., Manning type 1b. L 28 mm, D 12 mm.
ON 123092: Fe nail head & shank frags, Manning type 1b. L 40 mm & 21 mm, D 11/12 mm.
ON 123099: Fe nail, Manning type 1b. L 45, D 11 mm.
Bulk finds:
20 frags Fe nails including: 8 clear Manning type 1b heads & shank; 4 other shank frags, Manning type 1b; others small type 1b or 6. L 20–58 mm, D 10–14 mm. Frags min. 12 Fe hobnails, Manning type 10. L 12–18 mm, D8–10 mm. Fe nail/stud frag.; L 20 mm, D 15 mm.
Phase: E–M2 C.

Grave 122062
Circular, concave sides & base; 0.2 m diam., 0.06 m deep. Urned burial (122061; ON 123079). No grave fill observed, cut tight to vessel.
Human bone: 324.3 g; adult *c* 30–40 yr; female.
Animal bone: 5.5 g; pig leg; bird long bones.
Pyre/grave-goods:
ON 123079.1: 197 freshly broken sherds of necked BB1 jar. Acute lattice decoration. No wavy line burnish on neck, motif declined after mid-2nd century. Burnt one side (cracked) (*cf.* Gillam 1976, type 3). 992 g; RE 75%; BE 78%. M–L 2nd. (Fig. 87, 14)
ON 123079.2: 1 sherd Central Gaulish samian; 2nd; 0.1 g.
Phase: E–M2 C.

Grave 122074
Probably circular, close cut not seen in excavation; *c* 0.13 m diameter, depth unknown (<0.1 m). ?Urned burial (122075; ON 123118). Records incomplete.
Human bone: 114 g; adult *c* 20–45 yr, ??female.
Animal bone: <1 g; indeterminate medium mammal; bird long bone.
Pyre/grave-goods:
ON 123118.1: 52 freshly broken sherds. Simple base & lower body R2 jar. 542 g; BE 80%.
ON 123118.2: green glazed sherd; medieval.
Bulk finds:
52 R5 sherds; 39 g
15 frags 8–9 small Fe nails heads & shanks, Manning types 1b. L 47 mm, D 14 mm. 14 frags of min. 9 Fe hobnails/tacks, some flat heads, Manning type 1b/6 or 10. L 15–18 mm, D 9/10 mm.
Phase: RB.

Grave 122132
Sub-circular, steep NW & gradual NE side, concave base; 0.62 m diam., 0.22 m deep. Urned burial (129060; ON123224). Urn stood on 3 burnt stones at base prior to pyre debris being deposited around it. Grave fill (122142–4; 122134–5,

122137): brown sand, sparse pebbles, sparse redeposited pyre debris. (Fig. 74)
Human bone: 367.9 g; adult *c* 30–50 yr, ??male.
Animal bone: 103.5 g; pig head & l hind limb <27 months; fowl l leg.
Pyre/grave-goods:
ON 123224: 90 freshly broken sherds ovoid jar with rouletted decoration on body & short everted rim. Burnt 1 side, base to rim, rim sherds abraded; 2nd (*cf.* Dool 1985, fig. 76, nos 1–5, fig. 77, no. 38, fig. 80, nos 138–9, fig. 82, no. 200; Martin 2000, no. 77). 1389 g; 100%. (Fig. 87, 15)
Phase: E–M2 C

Grave 122154
Circular, moderately steep, irregular sides, flat base; 0.5 m diam., 0.15 m deep. Urned burial with redeposited pyre debris, heavily disturbed. Grave fill (122153): mixed pale grey & light brown sandy silt. Cut by ditch 126065.
Human bone: 87.9 g; adult >18 yr.
Animal bone: 1 g; indeterminate medium mammal.
Bulk finds:
22 FLA3 body sherds; 77 g.
Frags 3 Fe nails, min. 2 Manning type 1b. L 8–32 mm, D 10–16 mm. Frags *c* 15 Fe nail/hobnails, Manning type 10 and 8??. L 16–24 mm, D 9–10 mm.
Phase: E–M2 C

Grave 122176
Circular, steep sided, concave base; 0.41 m diam., 0.17 m deep. Urned burial (129042; ON 123243). Grave fills: (122170, 122177, 122179, 122181) black redeposited pyre debris in sandy silt; (122180; 122182) redeposited sand in base of grave. (Fig. 73)
Human bone: 26.2 g; subadult/adult >13 yr.
Animal bone: 3 g; pig head & r forelimb.
Pyre/grave-goods:
ON 123242: Fe hobnail/small Manning type 1b nail, point missing. L 11 mm, D 7 mm.
ON 123243.1: 64 freshly broken base & body sherds R9 jar. Moulded base & burnished lower body. 1098 g. BE 95%.
ON 123243.2: Fe nail head & shank (missing tip), Manning type 1b. L 31 mm, D 10 mm.
ON 123243.3: 2 Fe hobnails (bent), Manning type 10. L 14 mm, D 8 mm.
Bulk finds:
Fe hobnail frag., Manning type 10; L 8 mm, D 8 mm. Frag. small Fe nail, Manning type 1b/6. L 24 mm, D 8 mm.
Phase: RB

Grave 122420
Circular, steep sides, flat base; 0.45 m diam., 0.15 m deep. Urned burial (129044; ON 123297.1). Grave fill (122421–3; 122428–30): brown sand, rare gravel.
Human bone: 418.4 g; adult >50 yr, ?male.
Pyre/grave-goods:
ON 123297.1: 86 sherds recently broken R15 jar. Simple base & burnished lower body. 1040 g; BE 100%.
ON 123297.2: 5 frags min. 3 Fe nails; 1 almost complete (bent), 1 head & shank; 1 small shank. Manning type 1b. L 23–50 mm, D 14 mm.
Phase: RB

Grave 122476
Circular, steep sides, flat base; 0.35 m by 0.25 m, 0.15 m deep. Urned burial (122500; ON 123320). Grave fill (122477): friable, mid-brown sandy silt, rare gravel.
Human bone: 326.2 g; adult >18 yr.
Animal bone: 4.5 g; pig head & other parts; bird longbone.
Pyre/grave-goods:
ON 123320: 14 freshly broken R16 sherds. Base & lower body rusticated jar with applied vertical rustication around girth & groove at lower edge. Surface erosion; 585 g; BE 100%. (Fig. 87, 16)
Phase: L1–E2 C

Grave 122501
Circular, gradually sloping sides, irregular base; 0.4 m diam., 0.05 m deep. Urned burial (122502; ON 123321), badly plough damaged & bioturbated, none *in situ*. Grave fill (122502): soft dark brownish-black silty sand with rare charcoal & burnt bone spread out of vessel.
Human bone: 5.1 g; adult >18 yr.
Pyre/grave-goods:
ON 123321: 6 freshly broken sherds; base of small R16 jar. Burnt outside walls; 47 g; BE 100%.
Bulk finds:
Frag. small Fe nail shank. L 21 mm.
Phase: RB

Grave 122504
Sub-circular, concave sides, irregular base (extrapolated); 0.29 m by 0.4 m, 0.05 deep. Urned burial (122488; ON 124148), largely redeposited due to ploughing. Grave fill (122487): redeposited material from burial.
Human bone: 55.5 g; adult >18 yrs
Bulk finds:
31 FLA3 sherds, base & body, of small flagon. 4 sherds burnt & reduced to pale grey; 134 g. BE 50%.
Phase: E–M2 C

Grave 122536
Sub-circular, gradually sloping, concave sides & base; 0.53 m by 0.4 m, 0.16 m deep. Urned burial (122538; ON 123339.1). Grave fill (122537): friable mid-brown sandy silt, rare gravel. (Fig. 73)
Human bone: 569.4 g; adult *c* 35–50 yr.
Animal bone: 52.3 g; pig skull & limb; large; <17–22 months; bird longbone.
Pyre/grave-goods:
ON 123339.1: 65 freshly broken R5 base (plain) & body sherds of a jar. Shallow horizontal grooves. Possibly a waster. 896 g; BE 100%. (Fig. 87, 17)
ON 123339.2: R22 sherd with v-shaped 3-toothed combed motifs above a groove. 6 g. (Fig. 87, 18)
ON 123339.3: FLA3 body sherd; burnt. 6 g.
ON 123339.4: FLB body sherd; burnt. 7 g.
ON 123339.5: Fe nail (tip missing) small Manning type 1b with a flat head. L 23 mm, D 11 mm.

Bulk finds:
1.1 g fuel ash slag
Phase: E–M2 C

Grave 122554
Sub-circular, steep sides, flat base; 0.83 m by 0.58 m, 0.25 m deep. Urned burial (122581; ON 123357.1). Grave fills (122555; 122605): friable mid-brown sandy silt; moderate red sand flecks. (Fig. 73)
Human bone: 1203.3 g; adult *c* 35–50 yr; ?male.
Animal bone: 156.7 g; pig hind limbs, 24–42 months; poss. comp. pig post-cranial; poss. sheep/goat tibia; butchered medium mammal ribs; fowl carcass.
Pyre/grave-goods:
ON 123357.1: 221 freshly broken R2 sherds. Tall, chunky jar, everted-rim, simple base, neckless & shoulder/body junction marked with double grooves. Distorted waster/second. 1766 g; RE 5%; BE 100%. (Fig. 87, 19)
ON 123357.2: 7 sherds small BB1 jar with short everted rim & burnished lattice. Burnt. L2nd. Two further unburnt sherds poss. second BB1 jar (*cf.* Gillam 1976, no. 17); 29.9 g; RE 38%. (Fig. 87, 20)
ON 123357.3: 3 Fe nails; 1 near complete, 1 bent & in 2 pieces, 1 head & shank. Manning type 1b. L 50 mm, 52 mm & 16 mm; D 7 mm, 14 mm & 13 mm.
Phase: E–M2 C.

Grave 122568
Sub-rectangular, steep sides, irregular base; 0.5 m by 0.34 m, 0.18 m deep. Urned burial (129047; ON 123353) placed on a slight plinth S. central to grave, heavily truncated by ploughing. Grave fill (122569; 122608): friable, light reddish-brown sand, occasional gravel and charcoal flecks. (Fig. 74)
Human bone: 213.0 g; adult *c* 35–50 yr, ?female.
Animal bone: 1.6 g; indeterminate medium mammal.
Pyre/grave-goods:
ON 123353: 46 freshly broken sherds R4 jar; base & lower body complete with groove at girth. Blunt-ended everted rim (poss. 2nd vessel). L 2nd. 695 g; RE 5%; BE 100%. (Fig. 87, 21)
Phase: E–M2 C.

Grave 122571
Sub-rectangular/irregular (over-cut?); 0.86 m by 0.6 m, 0.2 m deep. Urned burial (122539; ON 123340). Grave fill (122572): soft mid-reddish-brown sand with rare gravel.
Human bone: 634.1 g; adult *c* 25–40 yr, female.
Animal bone: <1 g; bird long bone.
Pyre/grave-goods:
ON 123340: 161 R16 sherds, freshly broken body & base of shattered jar with low cordon or double groove. 945 g, BE 75%. (Fig. 88, 22)
Phase: RB.

Grave 122635
Sub-circular, straight sides, flat base; 0.53 m by 0.51 m, 0.28 m deep. Urned burial (129063; ON 123373). Grave fill (122632–8): firm reddish-brown sand, rare charcoal flecks. Undisturbed. (Figs 74, 76)
Human bone: 441.8 g; adult *c* 30–45 yr, ?female.
Animal bone: 22.7 g; pig l forelimb, 12–42 months; pig skull; fowl left wing.
Pyre/grave-goods:
ON 123373: R14 neckless, slightly globular jar with short everted rim, vertical rustication lines, girth groove & shoulder burnishing. Base holed (missing rectangle of base found in grave). 70–120; 1115 g; RE 97%; BE 100%. (Fig. 88, 23)
ON 123358: vessel missing in post-excavation.
Phase: L1–E2 C.

Grave 122651
Circular, steep sides, flat base; 0.35 m diam., 0.06 m deep. Urned burial (122677; ON 123382), heavily truncated by ploughing. Grave fill (122652, 122695): friable, dark brown sandy silt, rare gravel and charcoal.
Human bone: 104.3 g; adult >18 yr.
Animal bone: 43 g; pig r fore limb & l hind limb; <42 months.
Pyre/grave-goods:
ON 123382.1: 50 freshly broken R16 sherds from base & lower body of jar. Turned base, splayed. 265 g; BE 100%.
ON 123383.1: Small abraded body sherd; burnt; poss. same as ON 123382.
ONs 123382.2, 123383.2 and 123384: 39 FLA4 sherds; 2 adjoining sherds with complex graffito & 1 non-adjoining sherd with single incised line, possibly part of same graffito. Burnt, some completely reduced. 248 g. (Fig. 88, 24)
ON 123399: Glass vessel body frag.; light green appearing blue in section; 7 mm by 5 mm, 1 mm thick.
Phase: L1–E2 C.

Grave 122727
E–W, rectangular, vertical sides, flat base; 0.65 m by 0.42 m, 0.08 m deep. Urned burial (129070; ON 123386), heavily truncated. Grave fill (122685): firm reddish-brown sand; occasional gravel and charcoal. (Fig. 74)
Human bone: 3.1 g; neonate–infant *c* 0–2 yr.
Pyre/grave-goods:
ON 123386: 44 freshly broken sherds BB1 jar(s). Upright neck, wavy line burnish on neck. Slightly burnt. Most of body missing. *c* 120–150; 248 g; RE 15%; BE 80%. (Fig. 88, 25)
ONs 123395–7: Fe objects, missing in post-excavation.
Phase: E–M2 C.

Grave 122733
Circular cut, not fully observed in excavation (close to vessel); 0.15 m diam., 0.06 m deep. Urned burial (122742; ON 123387.?2), disturbed & truncated by ploughing. Grave fill (122686): hard reddish-brown sand.
Human bone: 535.8 g; adult *c* 18–50 yr, ??female.
Animal bone: 3.5 g; pig left fore limb; fowl right wing.
Pyre/grave-goods:
ON 123387.1: 64 sherds R15 base & lower body of a jar with moulded base. Burnt. 354 g; BE 100%.
ON 123387.2: 109 sherds base & lower body of a jar with moulded base. 967 g; BE 100%.
ON 123388: Frag. large Fe nail shank. L 42 mm.

ON 123410: Frag. Fe nail head and shank, Manning type 1b. L 42 mm, D 12 mm.

Bulk finds:

4 frags 3 Fe nails, 2 nearly complete, Manning type 1b. L 60–66 mm, D 13–16 mm.

Phase: RB.

Grave 122780

Sub-rectangular with deeper, central sub-circular section. Upper section: 0.85 m by 0.75 m, 0.18 m deep; steep sides, W/NW shallower & concave, flat base. Lower section: 0.25 x 0.3 m., 0.21 m deep; vertical sided, concave base. Cut made central within mortuary enclosure 126154. Urned burial (129050; ON 123541). Grave fill upper section (122781, 122783, 122799–800, 122805–6, 122848, 122850, 122852, 122854): loose dark greenish-black sandy silt, charcoal rich (redeposited pyre debris). Grave fill lower section (122903–4, 122906 & 122917): loose mid-greenish-black sandy silt, charcoal rich, rare burnt stone. Vessel placed on 3 burnt, flat angular stones. (Fig. 73)

Human bone: Upper grave fill: 24.3 g; lower grave fill: 22 g. Burial: 266.8 g; subadult *c* 13–18 yr; ??female.

Animal bone: 29.7 g; pig head, hind & fore limb <12 months; poss. sheep/goat mandible; bird longbone.

Pyre/grave-goods:

ONs 123420–3: 4 frags Fe nail including: 1 small tip, 1 probable head, 1 small shank, 1 shank projecting from large flat frag. L 19–28, D 18–30.

ON 123440: frag. small Fe nail shank. L 14 mm.

ON 123441: frag. Fe ?hobnail/ v. small nail shank. L 15 mm, D 10 mm.

ON 123442: 5 small frags. Fe ?hobnail head.

ON 123443: Fe hobnail, Manning type 10. L 18 mm, D 9 mm.

ON 123459: frag. Fe nail shank and poss. head; L 14 mm, D 15 mm.

ON 123460: 1 lump Fe ?hobnail/s; D 9 mm.

ON 123501–4: 7 frags Fe nail including; 1 head (corrosion product only?), 1 shank & head, & 2 ?nails. L 7 mm, D 8–10 mm.

ON 123505: Fe hobnail (bent), Manning type 10. L 15 mm, D 10 mm.

ONs 123512–3: 2 small Fe hobnails, Manning type 10. L 12–16 mm, D 8–11 mm.

ON 123515: frag. Fe nail/hobnail shank and poss. head. L 15 mm, D 19 mm.

ON 123516: frags 2 Fe nails, fused shafts. L 25 mm (combined), D 20 mm.

ON 123517: Bent Fe hobnail, Manning type 10. L 15 mm, D 10 mm.

ONs 123523–7: 5 frags. Fe nail including, 2 shanks, 1 head and 1 head with shank. L 8–22, D 8–9 mm.

ONs 123528–30: 3 Fe hobnails and frags. 2 others. Manning type 10. L 13–17 mm, D 8–9 mm.

ON 123539: frag. Fe nail ?head. D 10 mm.

ON 123541: complete R17 (9 fresh broken sherds) neckless jar with short everted rim (distorted) & double shoulder groove; eroded surfaces. 70–120; 617 g; 100%. (Fig. 88, 26)

ON 123542: frags Fe nail shank and poss. head. L 44 mm, D 8 mm.

ONs 123548–50: 4 Fe hobnails, Manning type 10; one bent & two fused together. L 6–20 mm, D 7–10 mm.

ON 123586: 32 burnt R18 sherds from a small BB1 jar/cooking pot, abraded; M 2nd (*cf.* Gillam 1976, nos 19–22, 20 mid-2nd century); 54 g; RE 24%; BE 40%. (Fig. 88, 27)

Bulk finds:

6 burnt sherds R18 everted-rim beaker; 7 g; RE 15%. 2 burnt base sherds from a closed vessel, FLA2?; 15 g; BE 1%. R17 sherd near base of jar with secondary burning; 56 g.

3 small Fe nails/hobnails with flat, circular heads; L 17 mm, D 8 mm. 8 frags Fe nails/small tacks, min. 2 with large flat heads & square section stems, others ?very small studs; L 10–21 mm, D 10–11 mm. 8 frags Fe hobnail, including 2 ?complete, 1 head & 5 shanks (3 with tips); Manning type 10. L 10–16 mm, D 9–10 mm.

Phase: E–M2 C.

Grave 122794

Sub-circular, moderately sloping sides, concave base; 0.45 m by 0.42 m, 0.3 m deep. Urned burial (129062; ON 123438), truncated. Grave fill (122811/12): loose reddish-brown silty sand, occasional pebbles.

Human bone: 126.8 g; adult >18 yr.

Animal bone: <1 g; indeterminate medium mammal; bird longbone.

Pyre/grave-goods:

ON 123438: 172 sherds R7 (fresh breaks), base & lower body of plain based jar. 2002 g. BE 100%.

Phase: RB.

Grave 122818

Sub-rectangular, shallow concave sides & base; 0.6 m by 0.46 m, 0.11 m deep. Unurned burial, upper grave fill (122834/122843): cremated bone formed concentration in S. half of cut. Mid-brownish-grey silty sand with small stones & charcoal flecks. Truncated. Grave fill in base of cut prior to burial (122819/122842): friable, light brownish-red silty sand with gravel inclusions. (Fig. 74)

Human bone: 179.0 g; adult *c* 18–40 yr.

Animal bone: 8.1 g; pig l fore limb; <42 months.

Pyre/grave-goods:

ON 124265: 3 frags molten blue/green glass. 2 g.

Phase: ERB.

Grave 122844

Sub-rectangular, steep sides, flat base; 0.47 m by 0.43 m, 0.09 m deep. Urned burial (122846; ON 123491), heavily truncated & bioturbated. Grave fill (122845; 122863–4): soft greyish-black, lenses orangy-brown sand, redeposited pyre debris below vessel. (Fig. 73)

Human bone: 53.4 g; infant *c* 2–5 yr.

Pyre/grave-goods:

ON 123491: 42 sherds R5 (fresh breaks), abraded lower body & base of jar with moulded base. Distorted – waster. 346 g; BE 100%.

ON 123490: frags Fe nail shank & poss. other pieces? L 30 mm.

ON 123520: frag. small Fe nail head & shank, Manning type 1b? L 29 mm, D 14 mm.
ON 123521: frag. small Fe nail shank. L 33 mm.
ONs 123534–5: 2 Fe nails head & shank (missing tips), Manning type 1b. L 21–29 mm, D 16 mm.
ON 123537: Fe nail head & shank (missing tip), Manning type 1b. L 32 mm, D 13 mm.
ON 123491: frag. Fe nail/hobnail fine shank & ?head, Manning type 1? L 14 mm, D 9 mm.
Bulk finds:
1 abraded sherd FLA2; 16 g. 4 burnt sherds FLA3; 38 g.
5 frag. Fe nail including; 1 with missing tip & 3 shanks (1 small). Manning type 1b?. L 15–56 mm, D 12 mm.
Phase: E–M2 C.

Grave 122874
Sub-circular, concave sides & flat base; 0.54 m by 0.4 m, 0.2 m deep. Urned burial (122891; ON 123543) in N. accessory vessel to S. Truncated. Grave fill (122875): soft light reddish-brown silty sand, rare gravel, very rare charcoal flecks. (Figs 73, 75)
Human bone: 774.8 g; adult *c* 35–60 yr.
Animal bone: 34.1 g; pig head & some vertebrae.
Pyre/grave-goods:
ON 123543: 212 sherds (fresh breaks) R7, base & body of plain-based jar. Heavily burnt. 1018 g; BE 100%.
ON 123544: 58 R16 sherds (fresh breaks) of small, globular rouletted beaker with short everted rim, slightly dished. Burnt one side; M2nd; 277 g; RE 95%; BE 100%. (Fig. 88, 28)
Phase: E–M2 C.

Grave 129071
Cut not identified in excavation; 0.36 m by 0.3 m, 0.2 m deep. Urned burial (122151; ON 123198). Redeposited pyre debris below & around burial (122149): firm, friable black & mid-greyish-orange silt & sandy silt, charcoal-rich, occasional rounded stones. Grave fill (122140): mid-greyish-orange silty sand with charcoal flecks. (Fig. 74)
Human bone: 122129/40 (grave fill): 54.9 g; 122149 (redeposited pyre debris): 82.6 g; 122151 (urned burial): 387.2 g. adult *c* 25–45 yr, ??female.
Animal bone: 3 g; pig head & poss. other parts; bird longbones.
Pyre/grave-goods:
ON 123198: 104 sherds (fresh breaks) R5 everted-rim jar with curving neck, turned base and grooves on body. ?L 1st/E 2nd. 615 g; RE 7%; BE 100%. (Fig. 88, 29)
ON 123222: R22 body sherd from a closed vessel; 13 g.
ONs 123226–32: 8 frags Fe nail including 4 shanks (2 with tips, 1 bent) & 2 heads with shank (1 small Manning type 1b). L 9–30 mm, D 8–12 mm.
ON 123233: Fe hobnail & 1 other, Manning type 10. L 19 mm, D 10 mm.
ON 123236: frag. Fe nail head & shank (small); Manning type 1b. L 13 mm, D 13 mm; heavy corrosion; human bone adhering.
ON 123237: frag. small Fe nail shank; L 23 mm; moderately heavy corrosion.
ON 123238: 2 frags (fit) flat round head, shank; Manning type 1b. L 30 mm; D 13 mm; heavy corrosion.
ON 123240: bent Fe nail with partial head & shank, Manning type 1b. L 39 mm, D 9 mm.
Bulk finds:
4 frags Fe nails, 3 with small shanks ?hobnails. Manning type 1b. L 12–18 mm, D 10–14 mm. Traces of red on one.
7.9 g fuel ash slag.
Phase: L1–E2 C.

Grave 129073
Circular cut, close to vessel & not identified in excavation; 0.25 m diameter, 0.16 m deep. Urned burial (122474; ON 122318), badly damaged. Grave fill not seen.
Human bone: 29.9 g; subadult/adult >13 yr.
Animal bone: 1.2 g; pig head.
Pyre/grave-goods:
ON 123313: 2 Fe nails (fused), Manning type 1b. L 38–48 mm, D 10–12 mm.
ON 123314: Fe strip/? blade with rectangular section. L 22 mm, W 15 mm, B 6/5 mm.
ON 123315: frag. upper portion Fe bow brooch with triangular arms, no fastening. L 18 mm, W 18 mm.
ON 123318 5 R4 base & body sherds from large, wide-mouthed jar with a moulded base & burnished exterior. Internally eroded; 160 g.
Phase: E–M2 C.

Grave 129074
Circular, close cut not identified in excavation; 0.3 m diam., 0.13 m deep. Urned burial (129045; ON 123330.2), truncated & disturbed.
Human bone: 865.8 g; adult >30 yr; ?male (poss. 2nd adult, ?? female).
Animal bone: 66.2 g; pig head & l hind limb; <12 months; fowl carcass.
Pyre/grave-goods:
ON 123330.1: 22 burnt base & lower body sherds from jar with moulded base, wide cordon; 106.9 g; BE 100%. (Fig. 88, 30)
ON 123330.2: 100 R5 sherds from everted-rim jar with upper flat cordon, raised zone of zigzag burnish. L1st–E2nd; 1241 g; RE 20%; BE 100%. (Fig. 88, 31)
ON 123330.3: burnt FLA3 body sherd; 2 g.
ON 123330.4: 14 (freshly broken) sherds from S. Gaulish36 dish with trailing foliage. Little abrasion. 219 g; RE 90%; BE 96%; L1st.
ON 123330.5: Copper-alloy stud. (Fig. 84, 16). See p. 144
ON 123330: frags 2 Fe nail shanks; L 13–26 mm.
ON 123337: Fe ?nails/ lump of Fe. L 38 mm.
Bulk finds:
Frag. Copper-alloy stud; x-ray shows groove & folded edge. L 10 mm.
0.9 g fuel ash slag.
Phase: L1–E2 C.

Grave 129075
Circular, close cut not seen in excavation; 0.25 m diameter, 0.06 m deep. Urned burial (122525; ON 123329.2/ 123338.2 – vessel mixed *in situ*), heavily disturbed. Grave fill not seen.
Human bone: 206.7 g; adult >18 yr; ??male.
Animal bone: 9.6 g; pig head & limb.
Pyre/grave-goods:
ON 123326: frag. copper-alloy coin. ?Sestertius; obverse: head r, bust possibly Trajan, legend illegible; reverse: ?standing figure.
ON 123327: cylindrical ?bottle body frag.; blue/green. Straight sides with slight curve at top & traces of vertical scratch marks. 40 mm by 19 mm.
ON 123328: frag. very small, folded copper-alloy sheet, irregular shape. ?wood adhering; L 15 mm.
ON 122329.1/122338.1: 16 R22 sherds (fresh breaks) from jar with moulded base, short everted rim & body with double grooves. 180 g. BE 100%, RE 12%. (Fig. 88, 32)
ON 122329.2/122338.2: 98 abraded & burnt sherds from BB1 jar with necked rim of E–M2 C type (*cf.* Gillam 1976, no. 2). 334 g. RE 5%, BE 98%, Re 10%. (Fig. 88, 33)
ON 123338.3: 6 sherds near complete (97%) S. Gaulish form 18 samian dish, severely abraded. Stamp almost illegible, poss. OFMOMO. AD 60–80. 225 g. RE 97%, BE 100%.
ON 122338.4: unburnt FLA3 sherd. 3 g.
ON 122338.5: abraded R7 sherd. 6 g.
ON 122338.6: very abraded R4 body sherd. 8 g.
Bulk finds:
0.4 g fuel ash slag.
Phase: E–M2 C.

Grave 129077
Circular, close cut not identified in excavation; 0.21 m diam., 0.12 m deep. Urned burial (122758; ON 123417), plough damaged.
Human bone: bone from burial missing in post-excavation. From cleaning: 1.4 g; subadult/adult >13 yr.
Pyre/grave-goods:
ON 123417: missing in post-excavation (section suggests jar).
ON 123439: 5 frags Fe nail, Manning type 1b. L 49 mm, D 10 mm.
Bulk finds:
3 R5 body sherds; 11 g.
Phase: ?L2–M3 C

Grave 129078
Circular, close cut not identified in excavation; 0.18 m diam., 0.08 m deep. Urned burial (122081–2; ON 123125), heavily truncated.
Human bone: 4.5 g; neonate/infant *c* 0–2 yr.
Animal bone: 1.4 g; bird r hind limb.
Pyre/grave-goods:
ON 123125: 85 sherds (fresh breaks) BB1 splayed, necked jar with beaded rim tip & acute lattice burnish. M2nd. 257 g. RE 8%, BE 45%. (Fig. 88, 34)
Phase: E–M2 C.

Grave 129079
Circular, close cut not identified in excavation; 0.22 m diam., 0.1 m deep. Urned burial (129041; ON 123170.1) heavily truncated.
Human bone: 32.9 g; infant *c* 0.5–3 yr.
Animal bone: 5 g; pig skull.
Pyre/grave-goods:
ON 123170.1: 66 R15 base & lower body sherds from moulded jar with splayed base & burnished lower body. 15 sherds abraded. 445 g. BE 100%. (Fig. 88, 35)
ON 123170.2: 3 R16 rim and body sherds from neckless beaker/small jar with everted rim; partially burnt rim & body; Flavian–Trajanic; 13 g; RE 40%. (Fig. 88, 36)
Bulk finds:
4 FLA3 sherds; 2 g.
Phase: L1–E2 C.

Grave 129080
Circular, close cut; 0.32 m diam., 0.2 m deep. Urned burial (122116l; ON 123159), truncated.
Human bone: 867.1 g adult >35 yr, ?male; ?second adult >18 yr, ??female.
Animal bone: 36 g. Pig head & r fore limb; approx. 12 months; bird longbone.
Pyre/grave-goods:
ON 123159: 57 R9 sherds (fresh breaks) R9 from jar with simple base & lower body; base cracked but probably in kiln. 1711 g. BE 100%.
ON 123590: 38 sherds of small BB1 beaker with short everted rim; all burnished. M2nd. 190 g. RE 50%, BE 75%. (Fig. 88, 37)
Bulk finds:
11.5 g fuel ash slag.
Phase: M2nd C.

Grave 129081
Circular, close cut not identified in excavation; 0.13 m diam., 0.1 m deep. Urned burial (122138; ON 123223) heavily plough damaged.
Human bone: 67.1 g adult *c* 18–40 yr.
Animal bone: 0.2 g u/id.
Pyre/grave-goods:
ON 123223: 14 R16 sherds from base & lower body of small jar/beaker with moulded base. 131 g. BE 100%.
ON 123229: 2 frags molten blue/green glass. 2 g.
Phase: RB.

Grave 129082
Circular, close cut not identified in excavation; 0.16 m diam., 0.06 m deep. Urned burial (122131; ON 123199): truncated.
Human bone: 82.8 g adult >18 yr.
Pyre/grave-goods:
ON 123199: 65 R15 sherds (fresh breaks) of body & base from nodular rusticated jar with sl. splayed base, ovoid profile & groove at neck & shoulder. L1/E2. 299 g; BE 95%. (Fig. 88, 38)
Bulk finds:
Abraded and burnt R4 body sherd; 24 g.
Phase: L1–E2 C.

Grave 129083
Circular, close cut not identified in excavation; 0.15 m diam., 0.06 m deep. Urned burial (122112; ON 123160), badly disturbed.
Human bone: 4.1 g infant *c* 0.5–3 yr.
Animal bone: <1 g; indet. medium mammal.
Pyre/grave-goods:
ON 123160: 11 R15 sherds from simple, narrow-necked jar with bifid rim & poss. applied handle/decoration. Much external cracking & internal flaking. L2/E3 (*cf.* Booth 2006, no. 113). 177 g. RE 14; BE 100%. (Fig. 88, 39)
Bulk finds:
FLA3 sherd; 3 g.
Phase: L2–M3 C.

Grave 129084
Sub-circular, close cut not evident in excavation; 0.15 m by 0.13 m, 0.13 m deep. Grave fill/?burial (122102: ON 123131) heavily plough damaged mix of cremated bone, fuel ash & pottery in sandy silt matrix.
Human bone: 72.4 g adult >18 yr.
Animal bone: <1 g; medium mammal limb.
Pyre/grave-goods:
ON 123131: 29 FLA5 sherds (fresh breaks) from base & lower body of flagon. ?burnt (slip grey). 228.7 g; BE 100%.
Phase: E–M2 C.

Pits containing cremation-related deposits
(inc. those incorporating redeposited burials and incidental/formal deposit pyre debris)

Cut 122029
Circular, concave base & sides; 0.4 m by 0.4 m, 0.13 m deep. Fill (122019): soft very dark grey/black sandy silt, 80% charcoal. Prob. redeposited pyre debris.
Human bone: 9.3 g; subadult/adult >13 yr.
Animal bone: 5 g; medium/large mammal.
Pyre goods:
ON 123006: Fe nail shank frag. L 16 mm.
ON 123007: Fe nail with large rectangular T-shaped head, ?Manning type 3. L 30 mm, D 14 mm.
ON 123008: small frag Fe ?nail head. D 8 mm.
ONs 123009–11: 3 frags Fe nail including; 1 complete, 1 head & shaft & 1 head. All Manning type 1b. L 12–17 mm, D 8–10 mm.
ON 123013: 2 frags near complete Fe nail, Manning type 1b. L 46 mm, D 12 mm.
ONs 123014–15: 2 frags Fe nail shank ; 1 bent, 1 with head. L 11–36 mm.
ONs 123017–19: 3 frags Fe nail including; head & shank, shaft & tip (bent) & ?head; min. 1 Manning type 1b. L 20–1 mm, D 14–17 mm.
ON 123022: frag. Fe nail head & shank, Manning type 1b. L 25 mm, D 12 mm
ONs 123027–32: 10 frags Fe nail including; 1 complete, 2 head & shank & 3 shanks; min. 3 Manning type 1b. L 9–40 mm, D 9–15 mm.
Bulk finds:
15 frags group small Fe nails; some complete, 6 heads Manning type 1b?, 6 other small. L 20–26 mm, D 7–9 mm.
Phase: ?RB.

Cut 122030
Sub-circular, concave base & sides; 0.3 m by 0.3 m, 0.05 m deep. Fill (122031–2): charcoal-rich deposit within loose reddish-brown silty sand, occasional small gravel. ?redeposited pyre debris.
Human bone: 38.4 g adult >18 yr.
Animal bone: 2.5 g medium mammal limb.
Pyre/grave-goods:
ON123033: 15 sherds BB1 jar/s. Upright neck with wavy line burnish & acute burnish on body. Slightly burnt & burnt material adhering. AD 120–150. 176 g; RE 7%. (Fig. 88, 40)
ON 123033: base sherd R16 small jar or beaker with splayed base. 113 g; BE 50%.
ONs 123034–6: frags 3 Fe nail heads & shanks, small Manning type 1b (1 ?6). L 22–39, D 8–13 mm.
Phase: E–M2 C.

Cut 122037
E–W rectangular cut, stright sides, shallow concave base; 0.58 m by 0.42 m, 0.09 m deep (max. SW). Fill (122038–41); homogen-eous compact charcoal-rich deposit, reddish-brown silty sand matrix, moderate gravel. Redeposited pyre debris. (Fig. 77)
Human bone: 117.4 g adult >18 yr.
Animal bone: 45.7 g cattle l. navicular cuboid, astragalus & calcaneum; pig skull? large/med. mammal.
Pyre goods:
ONs 123046–7, 123100, 123071, 123153–6, 123158, 123185–92, 123196–7, 123210–11: 39 frags *c* 33 hobnails, Manning type 10. L 12–24 mm, D 7–12 mm.
ONs 123045, 123048–9, 123050–1, 123053–59, 123063–4, 123068–9, 123073–4, 123080, 123082–97, 123089, 123093–4, 123101–2, 123107, 123135, 123137–8, 123140–42, 123143–51, 123153, 123157, 123162–69, 123172–3, 123175–80, 123182–3, 123194–5, 123203–6, 123209, 123212, 123214–17, 123219: 105 frags *c* 109 nails, mostly Manning type 1b. L 5–78 mm, D 4–21.
ONs 123060, 123105, 123139, 123144, 123152, 123181, 123184, 123193, 123207–8: 11 corroded Fe frags unknown form.
Bulk finds:
FLA3 bodysherd. 5 g.
12 frags min. 9 Manning type 10 Fe hobnails. L15 mm (ave), D 8 mm (ave). 6 Fe nails, Manning type 1b and 3 frags. L52 mm, D 11–12 mm. 7 frags min. 4 unclassifiable Fe nails. L 14–32 mm.
Phase: RB.

Cut 122042
NE–SW sub-rectangular cut; steep-concave sides, slightly un-dulating base; 1.85 m by 1.25 m, 0.62 m deep. Fills (122067, 122171–3): soft reddish-grey/brown sand, occasional gravel,

charcoal-rich upper & lower levels, pottery & cremated bone in upper level. Redeposited pyre debris or redep. burial + redeposited pyre debris.
Human bone: 27.5 g adult > 18 yr.
Pyre/grave-goods:
ON 123037: Copper-alloy bracelet. (Fig. 84). see p. 144.
ON 123038: 14 FLA body & base sherds from a flagon with turned base. 133 g. BE 18%.
ON 123113: frag Fe nail shank. L 20 mm.
ON 123587: 14 body & rim sherds from pentice moulded beaker with long neck & rouletted body. Vessel extensively burnt & grey throughout. Clear surface coating & appears to be burnt colour-coated beaker. Fabric somewhat different to Nene Valley series dated late 3rd–4th centuries & likely source is late kiln 6 at Hartshill whose output included pentice moulded beakers. Dated second quarter 4th century (Bird and Young 1981, fig. 17.5, no.5). Under x30 magnification surface can be seen to have hairline cracks all over indicating it has been burnt. 72 g. RE 17%. A further 9 sherds from this vessel recovered from context 122067. 9 g. (Fig. 88, 41)
ON 123588: 21 burnt sherds BB1 jar (*cf.* Gillam 1976, no. 2/3 mid–late 2nd century); 111 g; RE 5%; M–L2. 7 freshly broken, burnt sherds from rim & body of BB1 jar with everted rim (*cf.* Holbrook and Bidwell 1991, type 16; Buckland *et al.* 2001, no. 211); 59 g; RE 14%; M2. (Fig. 89, 42)
Bulk finds:
2 R5 body sherds, 1 burnt; 39 g. 3 sherds post-medieval pottery, 1 glazed.
Frags 97 Fe hobnails. Manning type 10. L 14–20 mm, D7–10 mm.
Phase: E 4th C.

Cut 122056
Circular, uneven base & sides; *c* 0.43 m diam., 0.26 m deep. Fill (122058): friable, mix charcoal-rich material in silty sand matrix. Redeposited pyre debris or redep. burial + redeposited pyre debris.
Human bone: 13.2 g adult >18 yr.
Pyre/grave-goods:
ON 123096: 22 FLA3 abraded base & lower body sherds from flagon with footring base. 265 g. BE 80%.
ON 123097: 4 R22 base & body sherds from jar with moulded base. 89 g. BE 35%.
Phase: ?RB.

Cut 122059
Oval with indistinct edges, concave sides & base with shallow W. edge & steep N. edge; 0.55 m by 0.2 m, 0.15 m deep. Fill (122060/122066): mixed charcoal-rich material within loose reddish-brown sand matrix. ?Redeposited urned burial + redeposited pyre debris.
Human bone: 2.8 g neonate/infant *c* 0–2 yrs.
Animal bone: 0.2 g animal bone.
Pyre/grave-goods:
ON 123095: 19 unabraded R22 base & lower body sherds (fresh breaks) from beaker with turned, splayed base. 157 g; BE 100%. (Fig. 89, 43)
ON 123095: 6 ?R22 base & body sherds from a jar; splintered & burnt. 35 g. BE 10%.
ON 123112: frag. Fe nail head & shank, Manning type 1b. L 34 mm, D 10 mm.
Bulk finds:
4 R5 sherds moulded base from a jar or beaker; 5 g.
Phase: RB.

Cut 122064
Irregular sub-rounded cut, irregular concave sides & base; 0.6 m diam., 0.17 m deep. Fill (122063): common charcoal dispersed within dark greyish-brown sandy silt, bioturbation. Redeposited pyre debris.
Human bone: 1.3 g no age/sex.
Pyre goods:
ONs 123108–10: 2 Fe nails; 1 Manning type 1b (L 69 mm, D 14 mm) & 1 Manning type 10 hobnail (L16 mm, D 9 mm). Fe nail frag.
ONs 123114 & 123119: 2 unidentified Fe frags.
ON 123120: Fe nail, Manning type 1b. L 80 mm, D 15 mm
Bulk finds:
7 sherds small beaker with splayed pedestal base; 4 burnt & oxidised; 32 g. BE 30%.
6 Manning type 10 hobnails. L 15–21 mm, D 8–11 mm.
Phase: RB.

Cut 122072
Oval cut, steep sides & undulating base; 0.75 m by 0.55 m, 0.2 m deep. Fill (122073, 122087): mixed charcoal-rich deposit within loose reddish brown sand, frequent gravel inclusions. Redeposited burial + redeposited pyre debris (most in upper fill).
Human bone: 10.2 g subadult/adult > 13 yr, ? female.
Pyre/grave-goods:
ON 123116: frag. small Fe nail shank. L 50 mm.
ON 123117.1: 27 R22 rim, base & body sherds from 2 small everted rim beakers: a) pedestal base & shoulder groove with hairpin motifs (off white paint) (Greene 1993, 45); L1/E2; 99 g; RE 35%; BE 100% (Fig. 89, 44): b) smaller. 4 g; RE 20%. (Fig. 89, 45)
ON 123117.2: sherd FLA2. 0.4 g.
ON 123121: frag. Fe nail shank & tip. L 30 mm.
ON 123122: frag. Fe nail head & shank, Manning type 1b. L 32 mm, D 10 mm.
ON 123127: frag. Fe ?nail. L 22 mm.
Bulk finds:
28 frags Fe nails/hobnails including 2 Manning type 1b, 12 small Manning type 1b/6 or hobnails & 13 hobnails (4 fused) min. 2 Manning type 10. L 12–38 mm, D 6–15 mm.
Phase: L1–E2 C.

Cut 122078
Sub-circular cut, concave sides & base; 1.09 m by 0.82 m, 0.25 m deep. Fill (122079); extensive bioturbation yellowish-grey sandy silt with frequent charcoal inclusions. Redeposited pyre debris.
Human bone: 1 g subadult/adult >13 yr.

Pyre goods:
ON 123123: head & shank frags. Fe nail, Manning type 1b. L 67 mm, D 14 mm.
ON 123124: Fe hobnail, Manning type 10. L 18 mm, D 9 mm.
ON 123129: Extremely burnt sherds BB1/R18 from a jar. 28 g.
Bulk Finds:
4 Manning type 1b Fe nails & frags 4 others; L 10–54 mm, D 9–16 mm. 13 Manning type 10 Fe hobnails, L18–20 mm, D 9–10 mm.
Phase: E–M2 C.

Cut 122083
Sub-rounded, variable sides & slightly concave base; 0.9 m by 0.72 m, 0.2 m. Fill (122084): soft mixed reddish-yellow-brown silty sand, sparse gravel, 80% charcoal (inc. charred timbers). Redeposited pyre debris or redeposited burial + re-deposited pyre debris.
Human bone: 93.7 g adult >18 yr.
Animal bone: 0.4 g u/id.
Pyre/grave-goods:
ON 123126: frag. Fe nail shank. L 38 mm.
ON 123128.1: 45 BB1 base, rim & body sherds from heavily burnt necked jar (*cf.* Gillam 1976, no. 2, dated mid-2nd century). 98 g. BE 100%. M2.
ON 123128.2: 146 R16 sherds (mostly fresh breaks; some v. abraded) from narrow-necked jar with out-curving rim, neck cordon, simple base & 2 grooves on body. One distorted sherd. 1517 g. RE 36%, BE 100%. (Fig. 89, 46)
ON 123132: fragmentary Fe nail ?Manning type 1b. L 53 mm.
Bulk finds:
5 frags Fe nail heads with shanks & shank frags, Manning type 1b. L 22 mm, D 15 mm. 9 frags Fe hobnails, 2 straight, other shank frags, Manning type 10. L 16–20 mm, D 7–10 mm.
Phase: E–M2 C.

Cut 122095
Sub-circular, irregular concave base & sides; 1.45 m by 0.66 m, 0.2 m deep. Fill (122096): compact mottled mid-yellowish-grey to dark grey/black, charcoal rich. Redeposited pyre debris.
Human bone: 12.3 g adult >18 yr.
Pyre goods:
ON 123133: Burnt sherd FLA3 flagon base. 15 g. BE 30%.
Bulk finds:
Frag. Fe hobnail with large head, Manning type 10; L16 mm, D 12 mm. Frags min. 4 Fe nails, including 3 Manning type 1b; L 19–55 mm, D 13–15 mm.
Phase: E–M2.

Cut 122124
Sub-rectangular/apsidal, steep side, irregular flattish base; 1.72 m by 0.6 m, 0.43 m deep. Fill (122125); mid-greyish-/reddish-brown with occasional gravel & charcoal-rich patches. ?Redeposited burial + redeposited pyre debris or redeposited pyre debris.
Human bone: 7.9 g juvenile/subadult *c* 6–18 yrs.
Animal bone: 0.4 g u/id.
Pyre goods:
ON 123202: 46 FLA3 sherds (fresh breaks) from body & base of flagon. 187 g. BE 15%.
ON 123221: frag. Fe nail head & shank, Manning type 1b. L 27 mm, D 15 mm.
Bulk finds:
Fe nail shank frag. L 28 mm.
Phase: E–M2.

Cut 122158
Circular, concave sides & base; 0.52 m diam., 0.3 m deep. Fill (122157, 122160): reddish-brown sand with occasional gravel, common charcoal in upper levels. Redeposited pyre debris.
Human bone: 3.2 g adult >18 yr.
Bulk finds:
7 frags min. 4 Fe hobnails, Manning type 10. L 14–15 mm, D 8–9 mm. Small Fe nail/tack (Fig. 84, 6). Frags 3 Fe nails, min. 1 with large head, Manning type 1b. L 14–32 mm, D 8–13 mm. (Fig. 84, 3). See p. 144.
Phase: RB.

Cut 122553
Circular, steep sides & flat base; 0.69 m diam., 0.1 m deep. Fill (122545): compact reddish-brown sand with common charcoal flecks. Redeposited pyre debris.
Human bone: 93 g adult >18 yr.
Animal bone: 4.2 g; 3 medium mammal long bone frags & 18 indeterminate frags.
Pyre goods:
ON 123347: Fe nail. (Fig. 84, 1). See p. 144
ON 123348: 3 abraded, burnt R23 sherds, 1 with double groove.
Bulk finds:
Frags 5 Fe nails/studs (heads), ?Manning type 1b. L 13–20 mm, D 13–20 mm.
Phase: L1–E2.

Cut 122614
Sub-circular pit with steep regular sides & concave base; 1.08 m by 0.77 m, 0.45 m deep. Urned burial (122674; ON 123363) redeposited in part of upper fill (*c* 0.35 m above base) towards N. edge of pit; cremated bone outside/under eastern side of broken vessel. Pit fill (122615/84): friable mid-brown sandy silt; gravel inclusions & few frags cremated bone spread throughout. (Fig. 77)
Human bone: 114.6 g adult >18 yr.
Animal bone: 0.8 g u/id.
Pyre/grave-goods:
ON 123363: 166 sherds v. fragmented FLB2 flagon with turned base & handle scar outside upper body. 498 g; BE 35%. 5 sherds unburnt.
Phase: E–M2 C.

Cut 122784
Sub-rounded, shallow concave sides, irregular base; 1.15 m by 1.1 m, 0.2 m deep. Fill (122785): firm light reddish-brown silty sand, moderate gravel & charcoal inclusions throughout. heavily bioturbated. Redeposited pyre debris. (Fig. 77)
Human bone: 23 g subadult/adult >13 yr.
Animal bone: 0.8 g medium mammal limb.

Pyre goods:

ON 123427.1: 6 very abraded, burnt sherds ?O4/grey ware from bifid rim lid.

ON 123427.2: 28 heavily burnt (grey) sherds S. Gaulish stamped (illegible) samian dish form18. Little wear on rim & footring edge. Flavian or Flavio-Trajanic. 183 g RE 46% BE 80%.

ONs 123432–3, 123437, 123449–50, 123452–55, 123469–71, 123480, 123487–8, 123496–8: 19 frags Fe representing remains 5 complete hobnails & 16 poss. hobnails (heads or heads with shaft). Min. 10 Manning type 10, 2 Manning type ?8/10. L 12–25 mm, D 9–15 mm.

ONs 123336 and 123486: frags 2 Fe nails/studs, 1 complete other head; ?Manning type 8. L20–27, D 9–12 mm. (Fig. 84, 20). See p. 144

ONs 123428–30, 123446, 123448, 123472–9, 123489, 123495, 123499–500: frags 19 Fe nails, 1 complete, others head & shaft, shaft or head. Includes min. 5 Manning type 1b & min. 3 type 8/10. L 10–41 mm, D 8–16 mm.

ON 123431: U/id Fe lump, ?collection of small objects.

ON 123583: Burnt mortarium sherd, probably Mancetter-Hartshill product, 6 g.

ON 123591: 75 abraded, burnt, R19 grey ware sherds from base, lower body & some rim of a narrow-necked jar with blunt ended everted rim, slightly grooved at the tip, and a neck cordon. 493 g RE 10 %. (Fig. 89, 47)

Bulk finds:

4 sherds from a barbotine dot beaker R20, 20 g.

Frags 5 Fe nail heads, one with shank. 1 Manning type ?8, 1 type 1b. L 17 D 12–15. Frags 2 Fe hobnails, 1 complete; Manning type 10. L 18 mm, D 11 mm.

Phase: E–M2.

Cut 122792

Rectangular, concave sides & irregular base; 1.35 m by 1.2 m, 0.16 m deep. Fill (122791, 122752): compact brown sand with common gravel. Charcoal-rich upper fill. Redeposited pyre debris.

Human bone: 3 g subadult/adult >13 yr.

Pyre goods:

ON 123424: 2 frags. Fe nail, head and shank, and shank. L 6–32 mm, D 9 mm.

Bulk finds:

Fe hobnail/decorative stud (head distorted; tip missing). L 12 mm, D 9 mm.

Phase: RB.

Cut 122808

Sub-rectangular, slightly concave sides & base; 0.4 m by 0.31 m, 0.05 m deep. Fill (122809): soft medium brown sand with occasional gravel. Redeposited pyre debris or redeposited burial + redeposited pyre debris.

Human bone: 4.1 g subadult/adult >13 yr.

Pyre/grave-goods:

ON 123461.1: burnt rim wide-mouthed FLA5 flagon/ jug with slightly rebated triangular rim. Late 1st–Hadrianic period (Birss 1985, 97 no. 49) RE 9%.

ON 123461.2: burnt basal sherd BB1 jar 10 g. BE 16%.

Phase: E–M2C.

Cut 122810

Sub-rectangular, steep sides, uneven flattish base; 0.94 m by 0.48 m, 0.14 m deep. Fill (122796): compact charcoal-rich deposit in black sand matrix. Finds from root/stakehole (122833) in base of cut. Redeposited pyre debris.

Human bone: 7.5 g subadult/adult >13 yr.

Animal bone: 0.2 g u/id.

Finds:

ON 123458: possible whetstone from naturally occurring pebble; unburnt.

Bulk finds:

8 Fe nails. L 13–62 mm, D 9–10 mm; very fine shanks, traces of red, some possibly tacks. Manning type 10 hobnail. L19 mm, D 9 mm.

Phase: RB.

Cut 122838

Sub-rounded, shallow concave sides & base; 0.55 m by 0.49 mm, 0.15 m deep. Fill (122837): charcoal-rich sand. Redeposited pyre debris.

Human bone: 18.3 g adult >18 yr.

Pyre goods:

ONs 123507–11: 5 Fe hobnails, 4 bent. Manning type 10. L 11–15 mm, D 5–10 mm.

Bulk finds:

Group of 10 Fe hobnails/nails with flat heads, Manning type 10. L 12–15 mm, D 8–9 mm.

Phase: RB.

Cut 122857

Sub-rectangular, steep sides & slightly sloping base (S–N); 0.38 m by 0.3 m, 0.21 m deep. Fill (122858): mid-reddish-brown silty sand with rare gravel inclusions. Occasional charcoal in upper levels with other archaeological components. Redeposited pyre debris.

Human bone: 10.2 g adult >18 yr.

Animal bone: 2.1 g; 4 frags. medium sized mammal longbone.

Pyre goods:

ON 123506.1: 6 burnt FLB2 sherds from flagon/beaker. 19 g.

ON 123506.2: 4 heavily burnt SV4 sherds. 40 g.

Phase: RB.

Cut 122922

Sub-circular, concave sides and base; 0.45 m diameter, 0.08 m deep. Fill (122928): soft mid-greyish-brown silty sand, charcoal-rich, rare gravel. ?Redeposited burial (122927). Cut ditch 126062.

Human bone: 355.9 g; adult >18 yr.

Animal bone: 4.8 g; indeterminate medium mammal limb.

Bulk finds:

2 sherds comprising bead rim & upper body of burnt mortarium with white quartz tempered fabric & quartz trituration grits; 2nd; 109 g.

0.1 g fuel ash slag.

Phase: 2nd C.

Cut 122975

Sub-circular, concave sides & flat base; 0.6 m by 0.56 m, 0.2 m deep. Fill (122976, 122981): compact mid-reddish-brown slightly silty sand, rare gravel. Occasional charcoal and other archaeological components throughout fill, possible central 'concentration'. ?Redeposited pyre debris.

Human bone: 21.4 g adult >18 yr.

Animal bone: 1 g; Pig lateral 3rd phalanx, 2 medium mammal phalanx frags & 8 medium mammal indeterminate frags.

Pyre goods:

ONs 123578, 123581, 123553 & 123558: 5 frags prob. 6 hobnails, Manning type 10; head or shank. L11–20 mm, D 8–11 mm.

ONs 123570–5, 123580, 123555–7, 123559–60: 13 frags prob. 14 Fe nails; 1 complete Manning type 7 (red on head) (Fig. 84, 4), see p. 144, & min. 2 type 1b head/shank. L 49 (type 7) & 11–35 mm, D 27 (type 7) and 8–15 mm.

ON 123554: frag. Fe nail/hobnail head & shank. L15 mm, D 12 mm.

Bulk finds:

1 sherd S. Gaulish form 27 samian cup; 4 g. 2 burnt sherds S. Gaulish form 18 samian dish; 8 g. Heavily burnt & cracked R12 rim sherd from small jar/beaker with stubby everted rim similar to BB1 jar of 2nd century date; 9 g, RE 10%.

12 frags Fe hobnails/nails, min. 3 heads & 2 shanks (1 with red colouring). L 13–20 mm, D 10–14 mm.

Phase: L1–E2C.

Cut 129024

Sub-rounded, steep concave slope with break/step on NE side & concave base; 1.8 m by 1 m, 0.4 m deep. Fill (129025–6): soft, light brown silty sand with moderate gravel inclusions & occasional charcoal flecks. Redeposited pyre debris.

Human bone: 24.2 g adult >18 yr.

Pyre goods:

ON 123584: 40 heavily burnt sherds from BB1 jar (*cf.* Gillam 1976, nos 2 or 3 dated early–mid-2nd century); 90 g. (Fig. 89, 48)

Bulk finds:

Burnt O4 sherd. Burnt R16 sherd; 16 g.

Burnt R12 sherd. 2 g.

Phase: E–M2C.

Inhumation graves

Grave 122364

NE–SW, sub-apsidal, steep sides, flat base; 2.3 m by 0.8 m, 0.4 m deep. Coffined burial. Grave fill (122365): friable light yellowish-brown sandy silt, moderate gravel. Coffin stain (122410 and 122426): friable mid-greyish-brown sandy silt, moderate gravel. (Fig. 78)

Human bone: no unburnt bone. Redeposited cremated bone: 0.2 g (122365 and 122410).

Grave goods:

ON 123274: fragmented (old breaks) splayed rim BB1 jar, obtuse lattice burnish, shoulder groove (*cf.* Holbrook and Bidwell 1991). Severely burnt – surface cracking & sooting on rim; *c* AD 270+; 1178 g; RE 88%; BE 85%. (Fig. 89, 49)

ON 123275: frag. small Fe nail shank (missing head). L 52 mm.

ON 123276: near complete Fe coffin nail shank, Manning type 1b. Wood adhering. L 48 mm, D 15 mm.

ON 123277: frags Fe coffin nail, Manning type 1b. Wood adhering. L 43 mm & 20 mm; D 16 mm.

ON 123278: frag. Fe nail shank. L 30 mm.

ON 123279: frag. Fe nail shank; mineralised wood adhering. L 34 mm.

ON 123281: Fe nail, Manning type 1b. Mineralised wood. L 42 mm, D 12 mm.

ON 123282: 2 frags Fe nail head & shank. L 20 mm, D 19 mm.

ON 123283: frag. Fe nail head & shank, Manning type 1b. L 30 mm, D 14 mm.

ON 123284: Fe nail, Manning type 1b. L 69 mm, D 19 mm.

ON 123285: 2 frags Fe nail, Manning type 1b. L 58 mm, D 14 mm.

ON 123286: frag. small Fe nail shank. L 36 mm.

ON 123287: frags Fe nail (missing tip), Manning type 1b. L 58 mm, D 14 mm. Mineralised wood.

ON 123288: frags ?2 Fe nails; shank & head, & shank. Manning type 1b. L 67 mm, D 14 mm.

ON 123289: 2 frags Fe nail head & shank; prob. Manning type 1b?; L 35 mm, D 20 mm.

ON 123290: 3 frags ?same Fe nail shank & head, ?Manning type 1b. L 25, 25 & 15 mm, D 13 mm.

ON 123291: Fe nail (missing tip), Manning type 1b. L 50 mm, D 17 mm.

ON 123294: frag. Fe nail head & shank, Manning type 1b. D 11 mm.

ON 123295: frag. Fe nail shank. L 37 mm.

ON 123300: frag. Fe nail head & shank, Manning type 1b. L 34 mm, D 11 mm. Mineralised wood.

ON 123301: frag. Fe nail head & shank, Manning type 1b. L 38 mm, D 15 mm. Mineralised wood.

ON 123302: 2 frags near complete Fe nail, Manning type 1b. L 64 mm, D 12 mm.

ON 123303: frags ?2 Fe nail shanks; L 43 & 10 mm. Mineralised wood.

ON 123306: 2 frags. Fe nail head & shank, Manning type1b. L21 and 9 mm, D 13 & 14 mm.

ON 123307: ?complete Fe nail, Manning type 1b. L 53 mm, D 15 mm.

ON 123308: 2 frags 2 fused Fe nails; heads separate, 1 shank partially missing. Manning type 1b. L 52 & 55 mm, D 15 & 23 mm. Mineralised wood.

ON 123309: frags Fe nail head & shank; Manning type 1b. L 43 mm, D 18 mm. Mineralised wood.

ON 123310: Frag. Fe nail head & shank, Manning type1b. L 34 mm, D 14 mm.

ON 123311: Fe nail missing tip, Manning type 1b. L 44 mm, D 13 mm.

ON 123312: Fe nail head & frag. shank, Manning type 1b. L 25 mm, D 15 mm.

ON 123585: 10 sherds small BB1 jar, short everted rim & obtuse lattice burnish (*cf.* Gillam 1976, no 18, dated late 3rd century). 6 freshly broken (Gillam 1976, no. 18, 3rd century) sherds burnt. 27 g. 3rd C (Fig. 89, 50)

Bulk finds:

Fe nail head & shank frag., 4 frags. shank. L 37 mm, 27 mm, 22 mm, 11 mm & 8 mm, D 12 mm. Mineralised wood.

Phase: L2–M4 C.

Grave 122376

N–S, sub-rectangular with apsidal N end, steep sides, flat base; 1.51 m by 0.8 m, 0.41 m deep. Coffined burial. Grave fill (122377): friable mid-reddish-brownish silty sand, sparse gravel, rare charcoal flecks. Coffin stain (122378/9): friable, very dark greyish-black silty sand & decayed wood. (Fig. 78)

Human bone: none.

Grave goods:

ON 123294: frag. Fe nail head & shank, Manning type 1b? L 13 mm, D 11 mm.

ON 123296: frag Fe nail head & shank, Manning type 1b? L 29 mm, D 10 mm.

Bulk finds:

1 FLA3 body sherd; 4 g.

Phase: RB.

Grave 122405

N–S, apsidal, steep sides, flat base; 1.65 m by 0.58 m, 0.65 m deep. Coffined burial. Grave fills (122406, 122462, 122521): friable mid-brown sandy silt/sand, occasional gravel, rare charcoal flecks. Coffin stain (122496): friable greyish-brown sand, occasional gravel. Cuts pit 122405.

Human bone: none

Bulk finds:

1 sherd Collared Urn, incised herringbone decoration. Small abraded R5 sherd; 1.3 g.

Phase: RB.

Grave 122408

NW–SE, sub-rectangular, vertical sides, flat base; 1.4 m by 0.6 m, 0.15 m deep. Coffined burial. Grave fill (122409): Compact, friable, mid-grey-orange silty sand, moderate gravel.

Human bone: none.

Grave goods:

ON 123298: frag. Fe nail head & shank, Manning type 1b. L 11 mm, D 11 mm. Mineralised wood.

ON 123299: frag. Fe nail head & shank, Manning type 1b. L 34 mm, D 10 mm. Mineralised wood.

ON 123304: frag. Fe nail, tip missing, Manning type 1b. L 59 mm, D 11 mm.

ON 123305: frag. Fe nail shank. L 29 mm.

Bulk finds:

4 post-medieval sherds.

Phase: RB.

Grave 122455

N–S, rectangular, slightly concave base. Stepped-in 0.05 m on N, S & E sides at upper level, second 0.3 m step at S end at lower level; 1.62 m by 1.75 m, 0.51 m deep. Coffined burial. Grave fill (122454) light brown sand, rare gravel. Coffin stain (122478–9) loose dark brown sandy silt, Fe flecks and gravel. (Fig. 79)

Human bone: none

Phase: RB.

Grave 122457

N–S, sub-rectangular, vertical sides, flat base; 1.33 m by 0.67 m, 0.35 m deep. ?Coffined burial. Grave fill (122456): loose mottled sand, patches of light grey compact sand, rare gravel & charcoal flecks.

Human bone: none.

Grave goods:

ON 123319: ?Fe/ ?soil stain. L 5 mm.

Bulk finds:

Very abraded oxidised sherd; O6; 1 g.

Phase: RB.

Grave 122460

NE–SW, rectangular, N & W sides stepped, flat base; 1.45 m by 0.65 m, 0.45 m deep. Grave fill (122461): soft mid-yellowish-brown silty sand, increasing brown-grey mottling with depth, rare flint gravel & charcoal flecks. (Fig. 79)

Human bone: none.

Phase: RB.

Grave 122492

N–S, sub-rectangular, steep sides, flat base; 1.3 m by 0.7 m, 0.15 m deep. Coffined burial. Grave fill (122491, 122535): brown sand, common gravel. Coffin stain (122513): dark brown sandy silt, moderate gravel. (Fig. 79)

Human bone: none.

Grave goods:

ON 123322: 2 fused Fe nails, tips missing, Manning type 1b. L 41 mm and 27 mm, D 12 & 11 mm.

ON 123323: frag. Fe nail head & shank, Manning type 1b. L 12 mm, D 12 mm.

ON 123324: frag. small Fe coffin nail head & shank (missing tip), Manning type 1b. L 36 mm, D 12 mm. Mineralised wood.

ON 123325: frag. Fe nail shank; L 21 mm.

ON 123333: ?complete Fe nail, Manning type 1b. L 35 mm, D 10 mm. Mineralised wood.

ON 123334: Fe nail head & part shank, Manning type 1b. L 10 mm, D 13 mm.

ON 123336: Fe nail in 2 frags, Manning type 1b. L 22 & 12 mm, D 12 mm. Mineralised wood.

Bulk finds:

Fe nail frag head & shank, Manning type 1b or small 7. L 25 mm, D 17 mm Mineralised wood. Distorted by heavy corrosion.

Phase: RB.

Grave 122526

N–S, sub-apsidal, vertical sides, flat base; 1.6 m by 0.6 m, 0.65 m deep. Grave fill (122528): soft greyish-brown sandy silt, gravel. Cuts mortuary enclosure ditch 122375, & tree hollows 122527 & 122616.

Human bone: none.

Grave goods:

ON 123345: frag. bent Fe nail; L 35 mm.

Bulk finds:

7 oxidised sherds; O6; 6 g.

1 rim sherd; MH1 mortarium; bead and flange; E2nd C; 14 g.

14 partially burnt, very abraded R16 sherds, everted rim jar. Probably Flavian–Trajanic. 23 g; RE 6%.

Phase: RB.

Grave 122552

NW–SE, sub-circular, irregular, steep sides with rectangular lower cut & flat base; 1.2 m by 0.8, 0.28 deep. Coffined burial. Grave fill (122541, 122582): reddish-brown sandy silt, patches

of compact sand and sparse gravel. Coffin stain (122649): loose reddish-brown silty sand, charcoal flecks. (Fig. 78)
Human bone: none.
Grave goods:
ON 123342: 2 frags Fe sheet plate, rounded corner with nail. L 54 mm, W 34 mm. Mineralised wood.
ON 123343: frag. Fe nail shank.
ON 123344: 5 frags. Fe sheet plate, 3 as 123342 & 2 larger, sub-rectangular with nails (1 with turned over edge), Manning type 1b. L 50 mm, 40 mm, 22 mm & 30 mm, W 35 mm, 40 mm and 13 mm.
ON 123349: frag. sheet lead binding from box or coffin; W 25 mm; nail not classifiable.
ON 123349: 5 frags square section Fe nail(s) originally attached to lead. L 30 mm (max), D 22 mm (head). Mineralised wood.
ON 123351: Fe nail (missing tip), Manning type 1b. L 46 mm, D 12 mm.
ON 123352: Fe joiners dog. (Fig. 84, 15). See p. 144.
ON 123354: frag. curved sheet lead & Fe studs with large heads; binding with fittings. L 38 mm (max), W 22 mm (max). Mineralised wood.
ON 123354: irregular flat lead sheet & 2 attached nail shafts. L 47 mm, W 33 mm. Mineralised wood.
ON 123354: Coffin binding (Fig. 84, 12). See p. 144.
ON 123354: Coffing binding (Fig. 84, 11). See p. 144.
ON 123355: Fe nail (missing tip), Manning type 1b. L 35 mm, D 18 mm.
ON 123356: 2 frags Fe nail head & shank, Manning type 1b. L 19 mm & 16 mm, D 13 m. mineralised wood.
ON 123359: Coffin binding (Fig. 84, 14). See p. 144.
ON 123359: 2 frags Fe nail shank; L 20 & 25 mm.
ON 123360: frags ?2 Fe nails (missing tip), Manning type 1b. L 23 mm, D 16 mm.
ON 123361: frag. lead/Fe binding; sub-rectangular plates with Fe corrosion & mineralised wood. Square hole at 1 end of one, other has 2 nails attached at ?corners. L 43 mm & 55 mm; W 40 mm & 43 mm.
ON 123362: 2 frags Fe nail head (unclear) & shank, Manning type 1b?. L 36 mm, D 20 mm.
ON 123364: frag. large Fe nail head & part shank (similar to 123362), Manning type 1b? or 7. L 13 mm, D 19 mm.
ON 123367: frag. Fe nail head & shank. L 12 mm, D 18 mm. Mineralised wood.
ON 123375: frag. small Fe nail shank. L 33 mm.
ON 123376: frag. distorted Fe nail shank. L 19 mm.
ON 123378: 7 frags corroded Fe studs with lead attached. Average D heads 21 mm, shaft L 10–20 mm. Mineralised wood.
ON 123378: Coffin binding (Fig. 84, 13). See p. 144.
ON 123379: frag. Fe nail shank with concretion; L 21 mm; heavy corrosion.
ON 123380: 2 frags ?1 Fe nail head & shank, Manning type 1b?. L 35 & 29 mm; D 9 mm. Mineralised wood.
ON 123381: frag. irregular-shaped lead sheet with Fe nail attached. L 57 mm, W 33 mm.
ON 123381: 2 frags lead sheet with Fe nails. L 35 & 28 mm, W 27 & 20 mm.
ON 123381: 5 frags lead sheet with square sectioned Fe nails & ?large round heads; studs type 7? L 35 mm (max), W 27 mm (max).
Bulk finds:
Fe shank & large domed head; Manning type 8?, ?possible stud. L 12 mm, D 16 mm. Mineralised wood.
Fe nail. (Fig. 84, 5). See p. 144.
7 frags Fe sheet; possible binding with folded piece. L 11–30 mm, W 9–20 mm. Mineralised wood.
8 frags Fe nail shanks. L 12–28 mm.
Irregular-shaped frag Fe sheet. L 31 mm.
Phase: RB.

Grave 122609

N–S, sub-apsidal, shallow straight sides, slightly concave base; 1.36 m by 0.6 m, 0.17 m deep. Coffined burial. Grave fill (122610): soft mid-greyish-brown silty sand, sparse flint gravel, charcoal flecks. Coffin stain (122631): soft mid-brownish-grey silty sand, rare gravel, charcoal flecking. (Fig. 78)
Human bone: no unburnt bone. Redeposited cremated bone: 12 g, subadult/adult>13 yr.
Grave goods:
ON 123360: 2 frags Fe nail. L 61 mm, D 19 mm.
ON 123369: 2 frags Fe nail head & shanks, Manning type 1b?. L 55 mm, D 14 mm. Mineralised wood.
ON 123370: frags Fe nail. L 48 mm.
ON 123371: 2 frags near complete Fe nail head & shank, ?Manning type 1b. L 48 mm, D 10 mm.
ON 123372: Fe nail (missing tip), Manning type 1b. L 65 mm, D 13 mm.
ON 123374: 2 frags Fe nail shank & head, Manning type 1b. L 66 mm, D 15 mm. Mineralised wood.
ON 123377: 2 frags ?complete Fe nail, Manning type1b. L 63 mm, D 15 mm.
Bulk finds:
Rim, samian (C Gaulish) cup form 27g, slightly burnt; Hadrianic–early Antonine. 3 g. RE 9%. 2 sherds, unburnt, R4 burnished jar. 7 g. 2 v. burnt sherds; flaked; prob. R16; 5 g. 1 small burnt frag. FLA, 0.6 g.
3 frags min. 2 Fe nail heads & shank, ?Manning type 1b. L 22 mm & 32 mm, D 16 mm & 11 mm.
Phase: L1–E2 C (ie date of redeposited pottery).

Grave 122675

N–S, sub-rectangular, vertical sides, flat base; 1.27 m by 0.49 m, 0.27 m deep. Coffined burial. Grave fills (122676, 122724) mid-reddish-brown silty sand, moderate gravel. Coffin stain (122723, 122753 and 122754): mottled mid- and light grey to reddish-grey silty sand, border of dark brown, occasional gravel. (Figs 78, 80)
Human bone: none.
Grave goods:
ON 123390: Fe nail in 3 frags, ?Manning type 1b. L 85 mm, D 19 mm. Mineralised wood.
ON 123391: frag. Fe nail head & shank, Manning type 1b. L 35 mm, D 13 mm.
ON 123408: Fe nail (missing tip), Manning type 1b. L 64 mm, D 14 mm.

ON 123409: Fe nail (missing tip), Manning type 1b. L 61 mm, D 15 mm.
ON 123410: Fe nail head & part shank, ?Manning type 1b. L 10 mm, D 17 mm.
ON 123414: 2 frags Fe nail shank & ?head(s). L 11 mm & 32 mm, D 24 mm & 14 mm.
ON 123415: frag. Fe nail head & 7 shank impression in corrosion product. L 22 mm, D 15 mm.
ON 123418: frag. Fe nail head & shank, & shank frag., Manning type 1b. L 35 mm & 30 mm, D 18 mm. Mineralised wood.
ON 123419: frags 2 Fe nail heads & shanks, Manning type 1b. L 57 mm and 32 mm; D 15 mm.
ON 123435: frag. Fe nail shank. L 26 mm.
ON 123444: frag. Fe nail shank. L 20 mm.
ON 123445: corrosion product from Fe nail (missing tip), Manning type 1b. L 50 mm, D 18 mm.
Bulk finds:
Cluster 2–3 Fe nail heads. L 33 mm. 2 frags Fe nail shank. L 33 and 20 mm. Mineralised wood.
Phase: RB.

Grave 122803
N–S, sub-rectangular, steep sides, flat base; 1.4 m by 0.49 m, 0.28 m deep. Grave fill (122804): loose brownish-red silty sand, common gravel. Cuts mortuary enclosure ditch 126069.
Human bone: none.
Phase: RB.

Grave 122872
E–W, sub-rectangular, steep sides, flat base; 1.35 m by 0.6 m, 0.35 m deep. Grave fill (122865): brown sand, moderate gravel, charcoal flecks.
Human bone: no unburnt bone. Redeposited cremated bone; 0.4 g; subadult/adult >13 yr.
Phase: RB.

Grave 122964
N–S, sub-apsidal, steep sides, flat base; 1.16 m by 0.7 m, 0.3 m deep. Coffined burial. Grave fill (122963): brown silt, rare gravel, charcoal flecks. Coffin stain (122965): mottled grey-green-black sandy silt, rare gravel. (Fig. 78)
Human bone: no unburnt bone. Redeposited cremated bone; 0.8 g u/id human.
Grave goods:
ON 123561: Fe nail head & shank (missing tip), Manning type 1b. L 44 mm, D 11 mm.
ON 123562: Fe nail head & shank (missing tip), Manning type 1b. L 50 mm, D 16 mm.
ON 123563: Fe nail, Manning type 1b. L 58 mm, D 13 mm. Mineralised wood.
ON 123564: near complete Fe nail, Manning type 1b. L 61 mm, D 13 mm.
ON 123565: frag Fe nail head & shank, Manning type 1b. L 41 mm, D 12 mm.
ON 123566: 2 frags Fe nail (missing tip), Manning type 1b. L 50 mm, D 13 mm.
ON 123567: 2 frags Fe nail (missing tip), Manning type 1b. L 60 mm, D 13 mm.
ON 123568: 2 frags Fe nail head & shank, Manning type 1b, & 1 other shank. L 14 mm and 33 mm, D 14 mm. Mineralised wood.
ON 123569: 2 frags Fe nail, Manning type 1b. L 84 mm, D 16 mm. Mineralised wood.
ON 123582: Fe nail head & shank (missing tip), Manning type 1b. L 40 mm, D 12 mm. Mineralised wood.
Phase: RB.

Possible inhumation graves

?Grave 122438
NW–SE, sub-rectangular, steep sides, sloping base; 1.35 m by 0.62 m, 0.17 m deep. Fill (122439): mid yellowish-brown silty sand, occasional gravel.
Human bone: none.
Phase: RB.

?Grave 122498
N–S, sub-apsidal, steep sides, undulating base with central depression; 2.05 m by 0.48 m, 0.21 m deep. Possible coffined burial. ?Grave fill (122499): friable, light to mid-brown silty sand, occasional gravel. ?Coffin stain (122540): friable, light brownish-red silty sand, charcoal flecks & gravel.
Human bone: none.
Phase: RB.

?Grave 122577
N–S, sub-rectangular, steep sides, flat base; 1.6 m by 0.75 m, 0.45 m deep. Fills (122593, 122648, 122578): loose mid-greenish-red/light greyish-red/reddish-brown sandy silt, rare charcoal flecks & gravel. Cut mortuary enclosure ditch 126154.
Human bone: no unburnt bone. Redeposited cremated bone: 0.1 g, subadult/adult >13 yr.
Bulk finds:
Base sherd R16 jar; 35 g; BE 22%. Body sherd BB1 jar; 3 g.
Phase: ?RB.

?Grave 122860
N–S, sub-rectangular, vertical sides & flat base; 1.35 m by 0.63 m, 0.55 m deep. Possible coffined burial. ?Grave fill (122859): soft, greyish-brown silt, rare charcoal & gravel. ?Coffin stain (122896): soft reddish-orange sand, patches of greyish-brown silt, rare charcoal & gravel. Cut pit 122900 & tree hollow 122907.
Human bone: none.
Phase: RB.

?Grave 122966
SE–NW, sub-rectangular, surviving sides steep concave, flat base; 1 m by 0.45 m, 0.1 m deep. Fill (122979): mid-greenish-brown silt, rare gravel.
Human bone: none.
Phase: RB.

?Grave 122977
N–S, sub-rectangular, vertical sides (N end obtuse & concave), flat base sloping at S end; 1.25 m by 0.75 m, 0.35 m deep. Fill (122913): compact brown sand, rare gravel. (Fig. 78)
Human bone: none.
?Grave goods:
ON 123576: 74 sherds small R14 jar/beaker with short everted rim, carinated shoulder, burnished rim & body. Heavily fragmented & much spalling. Cleat hole; some evidence of deliberate holing – missing piece in vessel; 70–120; 340 g; RE 100%; BE 100%. (Fig. 89, 51)
ON 123595: 10 sherds small Fabric R2 bulbous beaker, short everted rim, small splayed pedestal. Abraded patch (plough); 91 g; RE 100%; BE 100%. (Fig. 89, 52)
Phase: L 1–E 2 C.

Finds

Cremated human bone; pyre technology and ritual

Cremated bone from 168 contexts was received for analysis. All the deposits are probably Romano-British in date and included the remains of a minimum of 34 urned burials, two combined urned and unurned burials, three burials of uncertain form, four redeposited burials, and five contexts comprising either a redeposited burial with redeposited pyre debris or redeposited pyre debris (Table 20). Remains from other Romano-British contexts represent redeposited bone (from six inhumation grave fills, and five each from ditch and pit fills) which may originally have derived from burials, redeposited pyre debris or surface scatters of material. The remains – bone, urn and pyre/grave goods – from one other urned burial have been lost subsequent to excavation.

Charcoal from the remains of an unurned burial with redeposited pyre debris was radiocarbon dated giving a calibrated date of 70 cal BC–cal AD 80 (NZA-25239, 2021±30 BP) and metalwork recovered from the grave places it within the Romano-British phase of this range. The remains of a second unurned burial situated immediately adjacent to it is likely to be of a similar early Romano-British date. No unburnt bone, human or animal, survived in any of the excavated features including those interpreted as inhumation graves.

Methods
The remains from 12 urned burials were excavated (not by the writer) as a series of 4–15 x 20 mm spits to allow greater detail of the burial formation process to be ascertained. Seven grave fills were excavated in halves or quadrants for similar reasons. These divisions were maintained throughout analysis (the weights of bone from these contexts are shown together in Table 20 but separately within the archive).

Recording and analysis of the cremated bone followed the writer's standard procedure (McKinley 1994a, 5–21; 2000a; 2004a). The small fraction residues (1 mm and 2 mm) were scanned, and identifiable fragments recovered and included within the recorded bone weights. A subjective note of the quantity of bone remaining amongst the unsorted residue was made and is presented in the archive.

Age was assessed from the stage of skeletal and tooth development (Beek 1983; Scheuer and Black 2000), and the degree of age-related changes to the bone (Brothwell 1972; Buikstra and Ubelaker 1994). Sex was ascertained from the sexually dimorphic traits of the skeleton (Gejvall 1981; Wahl 1982; Bass 1987; Buikstra and Ubelaker 1994). The variable integrity of the attributed sex is denoted in Table 20 as '??'most likely, '?' probable, and unquestioned.

Results
A summary of the results from analysis is presented in Table 20 and in the Grave catalogue. Full details are in the archive.

Disturbance and condition
Most of the cremation graves had suffered some level of disturbance by plough damage and during machine stripping of the site. The levels of truncation varied widely and not all will have resulted in disturbance/removal of bone from the burial. The surviving depth of the graves ranged from 0.05 m to 0.39 m, with the majority (58.5%) at between 0.1 m and 0.2 m. Distribution of bone within the intact urned burials emptied in spits shows that most of the bone (*c* >95%) lay in the lower 0.1–0.12 m of the vessels. Consequently, it is likely that little or possibly no bone will have been lost as result of truncation from those graves which survived to a depth of 0.1 m or more. Many of the graves (29.3%), however, had depths of less than 0.1 m and it is probable that at least some, in a few cases much, bone will have been lost from these graves. Disturbance to burials, even where little or no bone loss occurs, may result in pressure damage to the bone and, particularly in the case of urned burials, expose the bone to greater soil infiltration, both potentially leading to a reduction in the size of the surviving bone fragments.

The majority of the bone is visually in good condition however, bone from 33 deposits (19.6%) is of a slightly (15.5%) or heavily (4.8%) worn and chalky appearance, implying deposition in or exposure to a more acidic burial environment. The worn bone all derived from either heavily truncated burials (five of the shallowest surviving graves), redeposited contexts – including bone redeposited in inhumation grave fills and at least two redeposited cremation burials – and occasionally from the backfills of cremation graves. This suggests that the original burial environment, particularly one in which the bone was protected from the natural acidic soil matrix (slightly silty sand) by being buried within a ceramic vessel, had a limited detrimental affect on the bone; once that microenvironment was disrupted or the bone was moved and redeposited, it became exposed to the detrimental effects of the soil matrix. The recovery of a single fragment of worn femur shaft from spit 6 of burial 122539 (grave 122571), where the rest of the

Table 20 Summary of results from human bone analysis

Context	*Cut*	*Deposit type*	*Phase*	*Bone wt (g)*	*Age/sex*	*Pathology*	*Pyre goods/ debris*
120203	120202	burial ?un./?u. + rpd	L1-E2 C	431.8	1) adult >30 yr. 2) infant *c* 0.5-2 yr.	osteophytes – C body surface margins; enthesophytes – femur shaft	7.7 g animal
122018, 122065 (inc. 122006)	122017	combined u. & un. burial + rpd	E-M2 C	276.6	adult *c* 30-45 yr	abscess – mandibular left M3 socket; periosteal new bone – mandible; enthesophytes – femur shaft	
122019	122029	rpd?	?RB	9.3	subadult/adult >13 yr.		5 g animal
122028 (inc. 122021)	122020	u. burial	L1-E2 C	2.7	>5 yr.		
122024 (inc. 122023)	122022	u. burial	E-M2 C	17.5	subadult/adult >13 yr.		
122027 (inc. 122026)	122025	u. burial	L1-E2 C	374.8	adult *c* 18-30 yr. female		3.4 g animal
122031/2	122030	?rpd	E-M2 C	38.4	adult >18 yr.		2.5 g animal
122038-41	122037	rpd	E-M2 C	117.4	adult >18 yr.		45.7 g animal
122061 (inc. 122048)	122062	u. burial	E-M2 C	324.3	adult *c* 30-40 yr. female		5.5 g animal
122049, 129033	122044	?combined u. & un. burial	E-M2 C	537.0	adult *c* 30-45 yr. ?male		17.3 g animal
122051	122050	redep.	?RB	0.1			
122055 (inc. 122053)	122052	u. burial	E-M2 C	210.3	adult *c* 35-55 yr. ??female	osteophytes – S1 body surface margins	0.6 g FAS
122058	122056	rpd/redep. burial + rpd	E-M2 C	13.2	adult >18 yr.		
122060/66	122059	redep. ?u. burial + rpd	RB	2.8	neonate/infant *c* 0-2 yr.		0.2 g animal
122063	122064	rpd	RB	1.3	?		
122067, 122171-3	122042	rpd/redep. burial + rpd	E 4 C	27.5	adult >18 yr. ?female		
122068	122069	rpd in pit fill	E-M2 C	<0.1	?		
122071	122070	redep. in ditch fill	?RB	0.2	?		
122073/87	122072	redep. ?burial + rpd	L1-E2 C	10.2	subadult/adult >13 yr. ?female		
122075 (inc. 122076)	122074	?u. burial	RB	114.0	adult *c* 20-45 yr. ??female		1 g animal
122079	122078	rpd	E-M2 C	1.0	subadult/adult >13 yr.		
122082 (inc. 122081)	129078	u. burial	E-M2 C	4.5	neonate/infant *c* 0-2yr.		1.4 g animal
122084	122083	rpd/?redep. burial + rpd	E-M2 C	93.7	adult >18 yr.		0.4 g animal; FAS
122096	122095	rpd	E-M2 C	12.3	adult >18 yr.		
122097	122098	redep. pit fill	?RB	<0.1	?		
122102 (inc. 122090)	129084	u. burial	E-M2 C	72.4	adult >18 yr.		2.2 g animal
122104	122103	redep. ditch fill	?RB	<0.1	?		
122112 (inc. 122111)	129083	u. burial	L2-M3 C	4.1	infant *c* 0.5-3 yr.		0.1 g animal
122116 (inc. 122114)	129080	u. burial*	E-M2 C	867.1	1) adult >35 yr. ?male ?2) adult >18 yr. ??female	osteoarthritis – 2T; solitary bone cyst/pseudo-erosion - capitate	31.1 g animal; FAS 11.5 g
122119	122120	redep. ditch fill	?RB	5.1	subadult/adult >13 yr.		0.4 g animal
122125	122124	?redep. burial + rpd/?rpd	E-M2 C	7.9	juvenile/subadult *c* 6-18 yr.		0.4 g animal
122129/40	129071	cremation grave fill	L1-E2 C	54.9	= 122151		0.4 g animal
122133 (inc. 122131)	129082	u. burial	L1-E2 C	82.8	adult >18 yr.		<0.1 g animal
122138 (inc. 122109)	129081	u. burial	RB	67.1	adult *c* 18-40 yr.		0.2 g animal
122139	122045	un. burial + rpd	L1 C	389.5	adult *c* 30-40 yr.		10.1 g animal; 0.8 g FAS
129041 (inc. 122108)	129079	u. burial	L1-E2 C	32.9	infant *c* 0.5-3 yr		5 g animal
122149	129071	rpd below burial	L1-E2 C	82.6	= 122151		1.8 g animal
122151	129071	u. burial	L1-E2 C	387.2	adult *c* 25-45 yr. ??female		5.6 g animal; 0.1 g FAS

Context	*Cut*	*Deposit type*	*Phase*	*Bone wt (g)*	*Age/sex*	*Pathology*	*Pyre goods/ debris*
122153	122154	u. burial + rpd	E-M2 C	87.9	adult >18 yr.		1 g animal
122157/60	122158	rpd	?RB	3.2	adult >18 yr.		
122365	122364	redep. inh. grave	L2-M4 C	0.1	?		
122370	122358	redep. pit fill	E-M2 C	0.3	?		
122380	122375	redep. ditch fill	?RB	0.3	?immature <18 yr.		
122407	122534	redep. pit fill	?RB	1.1	?		
122410	122364	redep. inh. grave	L2-M4 C	-	?		
122474	129073	u. burial	E-M2 C	29.9	subadult/adult >13 yr.		1.2 g animal
122500 (inc. 122477)	122476	u. burial	L1-E2 C	326.2	adult >18 yr.		4.5 g animal
122488	122504	u. burial	E-M2 C	55.5	adult >18 yr.		
122502	122501	u. burial	RB	5.1	adult >18 yr.		
122525 (inc. 122533)	129075	u. burial	E-M2 C	206.7	adult >18 yr. ??male		9.6 g animal; 0.4 g FAS
122538 (inc. 122537)	122536	u. burial*	E-M2 C	569.4	adult *c* 35-50 yr.	osteophytes – distal ulna, C1 anterior facet; enthesophytes – right navicular	52.3 g animal; 1.1 g FAS
122539	122571	u. burial*	RB	634.1	adult *c* 25-40 yr. female		0.1 g ?animal
122545	122553	rpd	L1-E2 C	93.0	adult >18 yr		4.2 g animal
122581	122554	u. burial**	E-M2 C	1203.3	adult *c* 35-50 yr. ?male	Schmorl's node – 2T; osteophytes – 1T, proximal radius	156.7 g animal (chop marks)
122610/31	122609	redep. inh. grave	L1-E2 C	12.0	subadult/adult >13 yr.		
122648	122592	redep. inh. grave	?RB	0.1	subadult/adult >13 yr.		
122663/5/8	122168	rpd in ditch fill	L2-M3 C	8.0	adult >18 yr		0.4 g animal
122674(inc. 122615/84)	122614	redep. u. burial	E-M2 C	114.6	adult >18 yr.	morphological variation – wormian	0.8 g animal
122677 (inc. 122652/95)	122651	u. burial	L1-E2 C	104.3	adult >18 yr.		43 g animal
122685	122727	?u./?un. burial	E-M2 C	3.1	neonate-infant *c* 0-2 yr.		
122736/41	122735	redep.	?RB	18.4	subadult/adult >13 yr.		
122742 (inc. 122738)	122733	u. burial	RB	535.8	adult *c* 18-50 yr. ??female		3.5 g animal
122752	122792	rpd	?RB	3.0	subadult/adult >13 yr.		
122755/7	129077	= *Missing Burial* 122758	?L2-M3 C	1.4	subadult/adult >13 yr.		
122799/81/83/ 122800/5/6/ 48-50/52-5	122780	upper grave fill	E-M2 C	24.3	= 129050		0.9 g animal
122785	122784	rpd	E-M2 C	23.0	subadult/adult >13 yr.		0.8 g animal
122796 (inc. 122832)	122810	rpd	?RB	7.5	subadult/adult >13 yr.		0.2 g animal
122809	122808	crd	E-M2 C	4.1	subadult/adult >13 yr.		
122834/43 (inc. 122819/42)	122818	un. burial	L1 C	179.0	adult *c* 18-40 yr.		8.1 g animal
122837	122838	rpd	?RB	16.3	adult >18 yr.		
122846 (inc. 122845/64)	122844	u. burial + rpd	E-M2 C	53.4	infant *c* 2-5 yr		
122858	122857	rpd	RB	10.2	adult >18 yr.		2.1 g animal
122865	122872	redep. inh. grave	?RB	0.4	subadult/adult >13 yr.		
122873	u/s	redep.	?	47.8	subadult/adult >13 yr.		1 g animal
122891 (inc. 122875)	122874	u. burial *	E-M2 C	774.8	adult *c* 35-60 yr.	*ante mortem* tooth loss – maxilla, mandibular right M2; abscess – mandibular right M1; enthesophytes – femur shaft	34.1 g animal

Context	*Cut*	*Deposit type*	*Phase*	*Bone wt (g)*	*Age/sex*	*Pathology*	*Pyre goods/ debris*
122903/4/6/ 122917	122780	lower grave fill	E-M2 C	22.0	=129050		1.5 g animal
122924	122923	redep. pit fill	RB	0.2	subadult/adult >13 yr.		
122927	122922	?redep. burial + rpd	E-M2 C	355.9	adult >18 yr.	fracture - rib	4.8 g ?animal; 0.1 g FAS
122965	122964	redep. inh. grave	RB	0.8	?		
122976/81	122975	?rpd	L1-E2 C	21.4	adult >18 yr.		1 g animal
129025	129024	rpd	E-M2 C	24.2	adult >18 yr.		
129042 (inc.122170/77/ 79/81)	122176	u. burial + rpd	RB	26.2	subadult/adult >13 yr.		3.9 g animal
129044 (inc. 122421-3/28-30)	122420	u. burial	RB	418.4	adult >50 yr. ?male	abscess – maxillary right C; periosteal new bone – right maxilla; osteoarthritis – 1L, distal humerus; osteophytes – C2 & T body surface margins, auricular surface, S1; degenerative disc disease – 1 T/L; enthesophytes – femur shaft	
129045 (inc. 122523/30)	129074	u. burial	L1-E2 C	865.8	adult >30 yr. ?male (??2nd individual, ??female)	osteophytes - finger phalanx; morphological variation – wormian bone	66.2 g animal; 0.9 g FAS
129047 (inc. 122608)	122568	u. burial	E-M2 C	213.0	adult *c* 35-50 yr. ?female		1.6 g animal
129050	122780	u. burial **	E-M2 C	266.8	subadult *c* 13-18 yr. ??female		29.7 g animal
129060 (inc. 122134)	122132	u. burial **	E-M2 C	367.9	adult *c* 30-50 yr. ??male	*ante mortem* tooth loss – mandibular left M1	103.5 g animal
129062	122794	u. burial *	RB	126.8	adult >18 yr.	osteophytes – T/L body surface margins	0.7 g animal
129063	122635	u. burial **	L1-E2 C	441.8	adult *c* 30-45 yr. ?female		22.7 g animal

KEY: u./un. - urned/unurned; rpd - redeposited pyre debris; crd - cremation-related deposit; inh. inhumation; ** undisturbed; * low level disturbance; Romano-British ceramic Phase equivalents: L 1st - E 2nd C = Phase 1; E-M 2nd C = Phases 2, 3, 6, 7, & 8; L 2nd - M 3rd/4th = Phases 4 & 5. C - cervical; T - thoracic; L - lumbar; S - sacral; FAS - fuel ash slag

bone was in good condition, suggests this bone derived from another cremation and was included in the burial either deliberately (eg as a 'token') or, more likely, accidentally (eg from re-use of an incompletely cleared pyre site).

Trabecular bone – articular surfaces, vertebral bodies, pelvic bones – is generally the first to be lost in acidic soil conditions, often crumbling away on being moved even if present at the time of discovery (McKinley 1997a, 245; Nielsen-Marsh *et al.* 2000). Even where bone is visually in good condition, a scarcity of trabecular fragments is likely to be as, if not more, reflective of poor survival rather than non-inclusion in the original deposit. Remains from a slightly higher proportion of deposits than those containing bone of worn appearance are devoid of trabecular bone (*c* 25–30%), but the distribution is very similar – the heavily truncated and redeposited burials, and various contexts containing redeposited bone. Obviously, where only a few fragments of redeposited bone were recovered the absence of trabecular bone may be fortuitous rather than reflective of poor bone preservation. More of the moderately–heavily disturbed burials, however, are lacking trabecular bone than contained worn bone; but not quite all those in which the bone appears worn are totally devoid of trabecular bone fragments (eg 122976, cut 122075). Remains from the well preserved/ largely intact burials all include a substantial proportion of trabecular bone. It is probable, therefore, that at least some trabecular bone was lost from some of the more heavily disturbed burials.

Demographic data

Minimum number of individuals (MNI)

The remains of a minimum of 48, potentially 52, individuals were identified (Table 21). With one, possibly three, exceptions, each of the burials contained the remains of one individual. Grave 120202 contained the remains of an adult and a young infant. A single duplicate skeletal element was recorded in burial 122116 (grave 129080) and some of the skull traits used for sexing were potentially slightly contradictory (Table 20). The evidence for the second individual here is not conclusive; the single duplicate fragment could have been included either as a 'token' or by accident following re-use of an incompletely cleared pyre site, and individual skull traits may show a variable range within both sexes. There was no duplication of skeletal elements amongst the bone from grave 129074, but contradictory sexing was suggested by different fragments of

Table 21 Summary of demographic data by phase

	L1C	L1–E2C	E–M2C	L2–M3C	Unphased RB	Total
Immature						
infant 0–5 yr	–	2	3	1	1	7
juvenile/ subadult 6–18 yr	–	–	1	–	–	1
subadult 13–18 yr	–	–	1 (?F)	–	–	A(F)
Adult	–	–	–	–	–	–
18–30 yr	–	1 (F)	–	–	–	1(F)
18–40 yr	–	–	–	–	2 (1F)	2 (1F)
18–50 yr	1	–	–	–	1 (??F)	2 (1F)
25–45 yr	–	2 (??F, ?F)	–	–	1 (F)	3 (F)
30–45 yr	1	–	3 (1F, 1?M)	–	–	4 (1F, 1M)
>30 yr	–	2 (1?M)	–	–	–	2 (1M)
>35 yr	–	–	7 (1?F, 1??F, 1M, 1?M, 1??M)	–	–	7 (2F, 3M)
>50 yr	–	–	–	–	1 (?M)	1 (M)
>18 yr	–	3/?4 (1?F)	6/?9 (1??F, 1?M)	1 (?F)	2	12/?16 (1M, 3F)
Indeterminate						
subadult/ adult >13 yr	–	1 (?F)	2	–	1	4 (1F)
?	–	1	–	–	–	1
Total	2	12/?13 (1/5F, 1M)	23/?26 (1/5F, 1/5M)	2 (1F)	9 (3F, 1M)	48/?52 (13/?14F, 7M)

the supra-orbital region of the skull; the evidence for more than one individual is, however, as with the previous case, not conclusive.

The two other potentially questionable individuals – both adults aged no closer than >18 yr (122058 and 122084) – derived from contexts interpreted as 'redeposited burial with redeposited pyre debris/redeposited pyre debris' (cuts 122056 and 122083). Context 122058 (cut 122056) contained very little bone (Table 20), and although context 122084 (cut 122083) contained slightly more there is no duplication of skeletal elements between this and several of the adult burials from the same phases. In the event that either of these deposits represented redeposited pyre debris rather than the remains of burials with redeposited pyre debris, then the bone could have derived from the same cremation as remains contained within a burial of the same phase, ie the individual(s) could already be represented within the assemblage. Five deposits of this type were identified. The bone from context 122125 (cut 122124) has been included in the number count since the remains are those of a juvenile/subadult and there is duplication of a skeletal element (petrous temporal) between this and the only other individual within this age range in the assemblage (129050); consequently, irrespective of the deposit type, this individual cannot be represented elsewhere. Although context 122067 (cut 122042) contained very little bone (Table 20) it has also been included in the minimum number count since it represents the remains of the latest cremation apparently undertaken on the site (early 4th century); although it could relate to one of the unphased Romano-British individuals. Cut 122808 contained very little bone (Table 20) and the bone from this deposit may have derived from an individual already represented within the assemblage.

As with the aforementioned deposits, most, if not all the bone from redeposited pyre debris not associated with a specific grave/burial could have originated from the same cremation as that of an individual already represented within the assemblage. The quantities of bone in these deposits, together with fragments redeposited in various pit, ditch and inhumation grave fills, is generally small, amounting to less than 50 g in 93.9% of cases and less than 10 g in 66.7%. The identifiable fragments recovered are too few and undistinguished to facilitate a realistic attempt to match them with each other or any other deposit.

Age

Of the total number of individuals identified the majority were adults 73.1%, with 17.3% immature individuals (<18 yr). Most of the latter were infants (0–5 yr; 77.8%), predominantly of less than 2 years old (55.5%) – a period of high susceptibility to disease in young individuals – but there is no conclusive evidence for individuals of less than 6 months old. There is little variation across the two main phases, with similar proportions of immature to adult individuals in both; the numbers in the earliest and latest phases are too few for comment (Table 21).

The proportion of immature individuals is not, in itself, particularly high, being less than may be expected in a 'normal population', but it is greater than that commonly encountered in archaeological cemetery populations. Figures of between 7.7% and 12.8% have been recorded from other early Romano-British cremation cemeteries at Puckeridge/Skeleton Green, Welwyn, Hertfordshire, and Cirencester, Gloucestershire (Wells 1981), East London (McKinley 2000b), Baldock, Hertfordshire (McKinley 1991) and Westhampnett, West Sussex (McKinley 1997a). Higher proportions have been observed in some contemporaneous cemeteries including 21% immature individuals at St Stephen's, St Albans, Hertfordshire (McKinley 1992) and a particularly high 29% from Brougham, Cumbria (McKinley 2004b). In addition to the well recognised cultural separation of neonates within cemetery groups, various other factors may affect the 'visibility' of immature individuals, particularly infants, within the population of a cremation cemetery (Philpott 1991, 98–9; McKinley 2000a), and all these figures are likely to represent an underestimate of the number of such individuals within the living population.

Only *c* 60.5% of adults could be placed within a more specific age range and there are substantial overlaps between most of these ranges (Table 21). The median range lies between 30–50 years, with only one individual (female) conclusively under 30 years of age and only one (male) conclusively over 50 years old. Although the data as presented in Table 21 may suggest that the adults in the early–mid-2nd century group tended to be older at the time of death than those in the earlier phase, the numbers in each group are small and the overlap between age ranges make this impression potentially misleading; there is no conclusive discernible temporal variation.

Sex

Sufficient evidence survived to indicate the sex of 38.7% of the total population, including 19 adults (50% of adults) and one subadult. This proportion of sexable individuals is within the average range for cremation cemeteries where the identification rate reflects the quality and quantity of sexually dimorphic criteria available for identification (McKinley 2000a). These overall figures include all confidence levels (Table 21) comprising unquestioned (five individuals), probable (10 individuals) and 'most likely' (five individuals) identifications.

A greater proportion of the overall population was sexed as female (23%) than as male (13.7%), that is 31.6% and 18.4% of the adult population respectively. The apparent discrepancy should be viewed with caution; half the adult population has not been sexed and it has been noted previously that there appears to be a bias towards the ease of the identification of females from cremated remains (McKinley 2000a). A slightly higher proportion of individuals were sexed in the earlier of the two main phases (late 1st – early 2nd century) in comparison with the later (early–mid-2nd century) – 46% and 38.5% respectively. The figures suggest a much higher proportion of females than males in the early phase (38.5% female compared with 7.7% male), with equal proportions in the later phase. Once again, however, these figures must be viewed with caution; they may be reflective of a temporal change but given the high proportion of unsexed individuals any such observation cannot be substantiated. There is no substantive difference between the ages of the sexed individuals, although there is no evidence for males of less than 30 years of age. Although the major period of use of the cemetery appears to have occurred in the early–middle part of the 2nd century (Table 21), there is evidence for a very early Romano-British origin. The latter part of the Romano-British period, in keeping with the national trend, saw the change to burial by inhumation of an unburnt corpse, although the two rites were obviously undertaken contemporaneously, the latest cremation apparently taking place in the early 4th century. No unburnt bone, human or animal, survived on the site, so it is not possible to deduce much information with respect to the late Romano-British population structure.

The cemetery population generally has a 'domestic' appearance, there being individuals of both sexes and a broad range of ages from young infant to older adult. The overall evidence cannot support the possible suggestions of temporal variations in the adult ranges, including those between the sexes, discussed above. The temporal stability in the proportions of immature to adult individuals probably reflects a similar stability in the form of the population, with no major fluctuations in fertility rates indicative of an aging population or influxes of young adults (also potentially suggestive of population migrations). There was no apparent spatial distribution within the cemetery in terms of age or sex (Figs 71–2).

The extent of the cemetery was established in three directions but the full extent to the north is unknown; consequently, only an unspecified proportion of the cemetery has been excavated. This absence of conclusive evidence as to the full size of the cemetery must temper any comment with regard to the probable size of the population being served by it. The current evidence for the number and density of graves, and the timescale over which burials were made, does not suggest the cemetery served a large population. The site lies *c* 0.5 km to the south-east of the Romano-British small town of Wall (*Letocetum*; Fig. 61), which is known to have had at least one other cremation cemetery situated to the west (See main text: Oswald 1966–7a; Smith 1987, 229; Burnham and Wacher 1990, 278; Gould 1998, 56–7). It is not unusual for Romano-British towns to be served by more than one cemetery and it is probable that at least part of the population of Wall was being buried in the Ryknield Street cemetery. It is also likely that the cemetery served the eastern suburbs of the town and farmsteads close to the route of the road.

Pathology

Pathological lesions were observed in the remains of 11 adults (21.1%, 32.3% adults; Table 20). The data presented here represent only a sample of the pathological conditions which would have affected the population. The recording of pathological lesions within cremated remains is the product as much of the quantity and range of skeletal elements included in the burial (see below), and their survival, as of the pathological conditions the population experienced. The nature of the material generally renders it impractical to create the type of skeletal inventory required for the calculation of prevalence rates; consequently, only a summary of the nature and occurrence of lesions is presented, and the crude prevalence rates (number of affected individuals) should be treated with caution for the reasons outlined.

Dental lesions were observed in four dentitions, all those of adults greater than 30 years of age. Two individuals showed *ante mortem* loss of one or more tooth; both individuals had lost one mandibular molar and one (122891, grave 122874) had also suffered the loss of several maxillary teeth resulting in a severe reduction in alveolar height. Dental caries, dental abscesses (infection often being related to caries) or occasionally excessive tooth wear may all lead to *ante mortem* tooth loss. The common loss and non-recovery of the exposed part of the tooth during the cremation process means that evidence for at least two of these possible causes very rarely survives. One individual with ante mortem tooth loss, 122891, did have evidence for a dental abscess in the same area as some of the tooth loss and both are likely to be linked to dental caries. Dental abscesses (infection) were observed in two mandibles and a maxilla, the former both involving molar teeth and the later a canine. The maxillary lesion had drained labially, resulting in a limited infection of the overlying facial soft tissues and the formation of periosteal new bone on the underlying bone surface. Slight periosteal new bone was also observed on the buccal margins of one of the mandibular lesions. None of the lesions were large or particularly severe, but they would still have caused a considerable amount of pain and, as with all infections, have resulted in a general debility in the individual's health.

A well-healed rib fracture was observed in the remains of one individual. Although fractures to the ribs, which may result from a fall against a hard object or a direct blow to the chest (Adams 1987), represent one of the most common fracture types recorded in archaeological material (Roberts and Manchester 1997, 77), fracture lesions of any type are very rarely recorded in cremated remains, this being the first such lesion the writer has observed in the analysis of >5000 cremation burials. The scarcity of such lesions is unlikely to reflect a less traumatic lifestyle for those choosing to cremate their dead, rather reflecting the lack of complete skeletal recovery for burial after cremation (see below) and, probably, the preferential fracturing during cremation along lines of weakness/change in bone density.

The majority of observed lesions were indicative of some form of joint disease. Eight individuals (*c* 15.4% total population, 23.5% of adults) had lesions in one or more joint, including four males (57.1% males) and one female (7.8% females). Two males, both >35 years, each had lesions indicative of osteoarthritis (Rogers and Waldron 1995, 32–46) in two joints, the lower spine (thoracic and lumbar) being most affected and one distal humerus. Degenerative disc disease (*ibid.*, 27), resulting from a breakdown in the intervertebral disc, was recorded in one lower thoracic/lumbar vertebra in the older adult male 129044 (grave 122420); the condition generally reflects wear-and-tear and is age-related. Schmorl's nodes, resulting from a rupture in the intervertebral disc (*ibid.*), were observed in one male spine, affecting a minimum of two mid-lower thoracic vertebrae. Osteophytes (new bone on joint surface margins) may occur alone, where they are largely seen as age-related, or in association with other lesions where they may be indicative of diseases such as osteoarthritis or degenerative disc disease (*ibid.*, 20–1). Lone lesions were seen at between one and four sites in seven individuals, including three males and one female. Vertebral body surface margins were most commonly affected (three cervical, three thoracic, two sacral); other sites included the forearm and hand, and the auricular surface of the pelvis (all single instances).

Enthesophytes (new bone at tendon insertions) may develop in response to a number of conditions and it is not always possible to ascertain the specific cause of individual lesions (*ibid.*, 24–5). Lesions were observed in four individuals, mostly along the major dorsal muscle attachments of the femora (three cases) and are most likely to be indicative of repetitive minor muscle stress.

Pyre technology and cremation rituals

Efficiency of cremation

The majority of the bone is white in colour, indicating a high level of oxidation of the bone (Holden *et al.* 1995a; 1995b). Some very slight blue/grey colour variations, indicative of incomplete oxidation (*ibid.*), were observed in 35% of deposits, including 44% of the urned burials. Variations were generally seen in one or more fragments of a single skeletal element, occasionally two or three elements. In 69% of cases only one skeletal area was involved, with two or three areas affected in 12% of cases and all four skeletal areas (skull, axial skeleton, upper and lower limb) in 6%. As is commonly observed (McKinley in press, table 2), elements of the skull and lower limb were most frequently affected (50% and 44% respectively); elements of the upper limb and axial skeleton being involved in 31% of cases. No variations were observed in the remains of the young immature individuals. Amongst the adult remains 40% showed some variation, including 50% of those sexed as female and 67% of those sexed as male. All the variations were minor and suggestive of some general, overall shortfall.

Factors affecting the efficiency of oxidation have been discussed elsewhere by the writer (McKinley 1994a, 76–8; 2004b, 404–6). In a recent review of levels of oxidation in Romano-British cemeteries, the writer concluded that the main overall contributory factor related to body mass (greater variability within the adult male remains) and the apparent lack of adjustment in the size of the pyre/quantity of fuel used to construct it. The greatest variability was seen in town cemeteries – as compared with rural sites or those within the northern frontier fort zone – and it is believed that this was linked to the undertaking of the cremation by professional *ustores* rather than the 'family' or military personnel/comrades (McKinley in press).

Bone weight

A variety of cultural and non-cultural influences may affect the weight of bone recovered from a burial including levels of disturbance, the burial environment (preservation), type of deposit, number of individuals, the age (immature versus adult) and, potentially, the sex of the individual and presence of pyre goods (eg cremated animal bone; McKinley 1993; 2000a). Cremation burials of any period very rarely, if ever, contained all the bone which would have remained at the end of cremation (McKinley 1997b) and a wide range in bone weights are common. It is not clear why such great variations existed and no consistent pattern has yet been demonstrated for the Romano-British period.

The weight of bone recovered from the *in situ* burials at Ryknield Street varied greatly from a minimum of 2.7 g from the truncated urned burial in grave 122020 (depth 0.08 m) to a maximum of 1203.3 g (13.0% animal bone pyre goods) from the undisturbed urned burial in grave 122554 (depth 0.25 m). Many of the burials had been subject to some level of truncation which is likely to have removed at least some bone from the deposit or have led to its poor preservation (see above). The most reliable view of the quantity of bone originally included is provided by the undisturbed burials (Table 20, ** intact, * slight damage to urn but loss of bone unlikely). Even within this group there is still a wide weight range; 126.8 g–1203.3 g, with a mean of 583.5 g.

Most of the burials were made urned, with only two conclusive unurned burials and two combined urned/unurned burials, and it is difficult to draw any conclusions as to the potential significance of the burial type in relation to the weight of bone included. The unurned burials contained an average of 284.2 g of bone, but both were from relatively shallow graves (0.11 m) and some of their contents could have been lost; consequently, it cannot be stated with confidence that the unurned burials consistantly held less bone than the urned ones. The same considerations may be pertinent with respect to the combined burials (average 406.8 g, grave depths 0.12–0.14 m).

The number of individuals within the burial is likely to have been of limited, if any, significance to the weight of bone it contained. The one conclusive dual burial, 120203 (grave 120202), held less than the average weight of bone, although the two other possible duals (122116 and 129045, graves 129080 and 129074) contained higher than average weights. The four *in situ* infant burials obviously contained much less bone than their adult counterparts, although here too there is a wide range of 4.1–53.4 g, the latter being more than remained in some of the disturbed adult deposits. The undisturbed burial of the subadult female 129050 (grave 122780) held a relatively low weight of bone, but even this was greater than that within one of the undisturbed adult burials. The average bone weight from undisturbed burials where the remains were sexed as male is higher than that for the female burials (637.9 g and 447.5 g respectively) but the weight from some individual female burials was higher than those of some males. Although greater weights of animal bone were recovered from some of these burials in comparison with those of the females, the weight of human bone remained proportionally higher.

The average weight of bone recovered from the undisturbed urned adult burials (583.5 g) represents a maximum of only *c* 58% of the expected weight of bone from an adult cremation (McKinley 1993), probably more in the region of 36.5%. The maximum weight of bone (1203.3 g, which includes a minimum of 156.7 g animal bone), although within the upper range of weights from cremation burials of any period (McKinley 1997b), represent *c* 75.2% of the entire cremated remains which would have existed. The minimum weight of 126.8 g from the undisturbed urned adult burials represents a maximum of only *c* 13%, probably more in the region of *c* 8%.

Table 22 Human bone fragmentation within different deposit types and conditions

Deposit type/condition	*10 mm fraction (%)*	*Max. fragment (mm)*
**undisturbed urned burial	range: 58.6–75.5 average: 67.9	59–71 average: 67
* undisturbed urned burial	range: 41–64 average: 52.1	36–68 average: 48.8
disturbed *in situ* urned burial	range: 2.8–80.5 average: 39.8	7–72 average: 33.4
unurned burial	range: 58–68.9 average: 63.4	37–58 average 47.5

The average weight of bone from the undisturbed burials is within the median range of those recorded in contemporaneous cemeteries, being higher than that from the northern/western frontier forts, and less than that from some of the large town cemeteries, falling closest to those from Welwyn (Wells 1981), and Westhampnett, (McKinley 1997a; 2004b, table 6.6).

Fragmentation

Dehydration of the bone during cremation leads to shrinkage and the formation of cracks and fissures rendering the material brittle and fragmentary. Burial, excavation and post-excavation processing of the bone leads to further fragmentation along the dehydration fissures, particularly if the deposit is disturbed in the ground (McKinley 1994b; 2004b).

Table 22 presents the maximum recorded fragment sizes together with the percentage of bone recovered from the 10 mm sieve fraction (the very wide range of percentage recovery from the 10 mm fraction for the disturbed burials is due to the skewing effects of the very low weights of bone recovered from some deposits). These figures demonstrate increased bone fragmentation as a result of disturbance to a deposit and the additional protection which may be afforded by burial within an urn, generally by exclusion of the soil matrix which, once in direct contact with the bone, will infiltrate the dehydration fissures and lead to increased fragmentation. There is no evidence to suggest that deliberate fragmentation of the bone occurred prior to burial.

Skeletal elements

Cremation burials generally comprise a range of bone fragments from all skeletal areas. Cases where this may not occur include deposits containing small quantities of bone (particularly <50 g), which may include heavily disturbed deposits or immature individuals. Most burials will contain a substantial proportion of 'unidentifiable' fragments comprising long bone shaft or undistinguished fragments of trabecular bone, the proportion tending to be greater where deposits are disturbed and the bone more fragmentary (McKinley 2004b,

298–9). Skull elements are often disproportionally represented due to the ease of identification of even very small fragments of skull. Conversely, elements of the axial skeleton are commonly under-represented due to the frequent preferential destruction of trabecular bone (see above).

As with bone weights, the most representative view of what was originally included in the burials from Ryknield Street is likely to be obtained from the least disturbed deposits. The most intact burials show a close to 'normal' distribution by weight of elements within the four skeletal areas (McKinley 1994a, 6); eg burial 129063 (grave 122635) with 19.6% skull elements, 24.1% axial skeletal, 26.2% upper limb and 30.1% lower limb. One burial (122581, grave 122554) contained a disproportionally high percentage of axial skeleton (30.9%), largely at the expense of upper limb (15%), while two others (129050 and 129060, graves 122780 and 122132) have the more common lower percentage of axial skeletal elements (9.5% and 7.3% respectively); the latter may reflect a problem with preservation rather than the inclusion of elements within the burial. Three of other better preserved burials (122538, 122116 and 129062 in graves 122536, 129080 and 122794) all have a disproportionally high percentage of lower limb elements (>50%) but none is at the expense of skull elements.

The levels of disturbance and small quantities of bone remaining in many of the other burials render detailed appraisal of their contents open to debate since the results are likely to have been skewed by the effects of poor bone preservation and higher fragmentation. In 12 of these burials there appears to be a disproportionally high percentage (>45%) of lower limb elements and, although this cannot be taken as indicative of preferential selection, since in many cases only the lower portions of the burials survived *in situ*, it may be indicative of more of the lower limb elements being positioned towards the base of the urn (see burial formation processes).

There is no noticeable difference between the few unurned burials and the majority of urned depositions. Although there are some indications of 'preferential' inclusion of skeletal elements from some areas in a few cases (no discernible pattern linked to age/sex), with one exception it is difficult to state with any confidence that this was the result of a deliberate act of selection. The depth (0.2 m) of grave 122052 renders it highly unlikely that any bone was lost from burial 122055, yet it contained a very disproportionally low percentage of the easily identifiable skull elements (1.2%), suggestive of deliberate exclusion. An absence or paucity of skull elements has occasionally been observed in other contemporaneous cremation cemeteries including Puckeridge (Wells 1981, 291), East London (McKinley 2000b, 271) and Brougham (McKinley 2004b, 301), and it has been postulated that rather than exclusion from the burial as such, the symbolic significance of the skull may have rendered it suitable for some other ritual purpose in these instances (*ibid.*), fragments perhaps being used as tokens of remembrance.

Tooth roots and the small bones of the hands and feet are commonly recovered in cremation burials of all periods, and it is believed their frequency of occurrence may provide some indication of the mode of recovery of bone from the pyre site for burial. Tooth roots – the enamel and crown of erupted teeth commonly shattering into small fragments during cremation and subsequently being lost – were recovered from 23 deposits in the Ryknield Street assemblage, including 19 burials (44%) and one non-cremation grave deposit of pyre debris (7.7%). All burial types contained tooth roots, including both unurned burials, both combined urned/unurned burials and 43% of the urned burials. The majority (78.9%) contained the remains of only one or two roots, the maximum of five being recovered from an urned adult female burial; amongst the sexed individuals, a similar proportion of male and female remains included fragments of tooth root (42.8% compared with 38.5%). Fragments of hand/foot bones were identified in 62.3% of the burials and one non-cremation grave deposit of pyre debris; the burials again included both unurned and both combined burials, and 66% of the urned burials. Most (51.8%) contained fragments of one or two elements, with a maximum of 13 elements being identified from the adult male burial 122116 (grave 129080). Of the sexed individuals, similarly high proportions contained some of these elements (76.9% females, 85.7% males), with no clear difference in frequency. The various potential modes of recovery of bone for burial have been discussed elsewhere by the writer (2000a; 2004b, 303). Although the numbers of small elements are not particularly high at Ryknield Street, it seems probable that there was at least some element of collection of bone for burial by raking-off and winnowing of the cremated remains rather than individual hand-recovery of fragments, thereby easing the recovery of the smaller skeletal elements as well as the larger ones. The relative scarcity of such fragments amongst the deposits interpreted as redeposited pyre debris lends some support to this interpretation, although it is clear that a mass of material is missing from all of the surviving deposit type at Ryknield Street.

Pyre goods

Artefactual pyre goods had been removed from amongst the cremated bone during excavation and in post-excavation processing of the remains, and this material had been catalogued and assessed/analysed before osteological analysis commenced. Fragments of cremated animal bone were distinguished in 52 deposits (30.9%) during osteological analysis, including 80% of the urned burials, both unurned burials and one of the combined burials. Animal bone was found with both immature and adult individuals including 71.4% of the infants, the one juvenile/subadult and one subadult, and adults of both sexes including 69.2% of the females and 85.7% of the males.

Five of the six individuals sexed as male were accompanied by two taxa, as were five of the nine females; the younger immature individuals were accompanied by single taxa (see Grave catalogue and Worley below). All of the males were accompanied by pig remains, 83.3% of those with animal bone also having some bird species – fowl where this was distinguishable (*ibid.*). Of the females with animal pyre goods, 55.5% included some pig, 77% some bird and 33.3% fragments of indeterminate medium-sized mammal. One infant was accompanied by pig remains, one by bird remains and the others by indeterminate medium-sized mammal.

The inclusion of cremated animal remains in Romano-British burials is relatively common, although there is a wide range in the number of burials with animal bone from different cemeteries, for example, 3.5% from Westhampnett (McKinley and Smith 1997), 13% from Baldock Area 15 (McKinley 1991), 36% from Puckeridge (Wells 1981) and 47% from St Stephens (McKinley 1992) (see Worley, below, for further discussion). The very high percentage of burials inclusive of animal pyre goods from Ryknield Street appears slightly unusual and certainly calls into question Philpott's observation (made prior to the examination of many of the examples cited here and by Worley) that animal remains were most common in the 'richer' cremation cemeteries of the south-east (1991, 199). The Ryknield Street burials generally appear poor in both pyre goods and grave goods and it may be that the increased inclusion of animal offerings on the pyre comprised a local variation in suitable accompaniments for the deceased.

There are several examples of complete or, more commonly, fragmentary iron objects adhering to bone fragments; this is most likely to represent post-depositional 'rusting' of iron pyre/grave goods to the bone. Blue/green spot staining, probably indicative of the proximity of copper-alloy items during cremation, was observed to fragments of skull vault (two cases), anterior mandible and a cervical vertebra (one case) from three burials; two adults, one female, and the subadult female 129050 (grave 122780). No remains of copper-alloy pyre goods were recovered with any of these burials, but the staining suggests any such items may have melted in the heat of the pyre and, since not all the human remains were collected for burial, it is probable that the remains of pyre goods were also overlooked (accidentally or deliberately) in this secondary part of the mortuary rite. The areas affected suggest that items may have represented personal ornamentation such as earrings, brooches or necklaces.

Dual deposits

The potential number and nature of the dual deposits from Ryknield Street have been discussed above. Only one grave conclusively contained remains representing the formal burial of two individuals (2.2% burials); the nature of a further two burials is questionable. The percentage, while rather low, is within the range commonly identified from all periods in which the rite was practiced, the combination of adult and young immature individual being that most frequently encountered (McKinley 1994a, 100–2; 1997b; 2000b, 272). In other Romano-British cemeteries the range varies from 2% at Welwyn to 8% at Owslebury, Hampshire (Wells 1981) and Plot 2 at East London (McKinley 2000b, 272). No multiple burials, however, were recorded from Derby Racecourse (Harman 1985b, 279), Lankhills, Hampshire (Clarke 1979), Walls Field and Walls Common, Baldock (Stead and Rigby 1986), Puckeridge (Wells 1981) or many of the Northern frontier fort cemeteries, although in the latter at least there may have been circumstances mitigating against the recognition of such deposits (McKinley 2004b, 303–4).

Redeposited pyre debris

A minimum of 12 urned, one unurned and one combined burial, one burial of uncertain form, and four of the redeposited/burials of uncertain type (66.7%) included redeposited pyre debris somewhere within the grave fill. The bone, if any, from the pyre debris had not/could not always be distinguished in excavation due to the levels of disturbance. In all except one case, grave 129071, the pyre debris appears to have been deposited in the grave fill subsequent to the burial. In grave 129071, the primary deposit comprised pyre debris including 82.6 g of bone (context 122149); the urned burial 122151 was made above this and sealed by two grave fills, one of which included a small quantity of pyre debris (including 54.9 g of bone), a fragment of middle finger phalanx from which joined a fragment from the debris deposited below the burial. Although there were no joins between bone fragments from the pyre debris in grave 129071 and those from the burial, there was no duplication of skeletal elements and the remains from all three deposits, both human and animal pyre goods, were commensurate with each other and can be taken to have derived from the same cremation. Although the quantities of bone from the pyre debris in other cremation grave fills tended to be smaller and, again, no direct joins could be seen, as with grave 129071, there was no evidence in any of these cases to suggest the pyre debris derived from other than the same cremation as that within the burials.

The recovery of redeposited pyre debris from Romano-British grave fills is relatively common (McKinley 2000c; 2004b, 304–6). Reference to 'remnants of the pyre' frequently being recovered from cremation graves in Raetia (Struck 1995) indicates that the trait may also be seen elsewhere in the Roman Empire.

Fifteen, possibly 16 deposits (latter not included in Table 20) were interpreted as incidental or formal deposits of pyre debris. Most contained very small quantities of bone; less than 10 g in 50% and less than 50 g in 88.9% of cases. None of the deposits appeared to contain debris from the remains of more than one cremation. As observed above, although the material from some, if not all, of these deposits is likely to have derived from the same cremations as that within at least some of the excavated burials, the identifiable fragments recovered are too few and undistinguished to enable a realistic attempt to match deposits. The spatial distribution of these deposits, although scattered, appears slightly less random than the burials themselves, several of those in the western half of the cemetery possibly forming an arc around an open space adjacent to the road – possibly the location of the pyre sites? Those to the east of the road and some to the west are scattered amongst the graves, but their location does not suggest any links with specific burials.

Deposits of this type have been recognised within other Romano-British cemeteries and their occurrence is likely to have been more widespread, but a reluctance to see deposits containing cremated bone as anything other than 'burials' has probably limited the numbers identified (McKinley 2000c; 2004b, 304–6). The walled cemetery at Derby Racecourse:

> '... contained large quantities of charcoal, and scattered fragments of calcined bone, both on its surface and in the features within it. The bottoms of small pits filled with charcoal and ash were found in all parts of the walled enclosure...' (Wheeler 1985, 231)

Although 20 of these features were, as with the Ryknield Street graves, less than 0.2 m deep, the quantities of bone were very small (commonly <25 g). Whilst the description of the 'charcoal laden' fills may suggest that some represented pyre debris deposited in the base of a grave prior to insertion of the burial (rather than the more common deposition over the burial), others are likely to be formal or possibly incidental deposits of pyre debris. In unurned burials with redeposited pyre debris, the bone for 'burial' forms a concentrated mass, originally held within some form of organic container,. commonly (although not exclusively) at or towards the base of the grave.

A small quantity of fuel ash slag (FAS) was recovered from nine burial contexts including five urned burials and one unurned burial. This general hearth slag largely comprises silica and is commonly formed where fires are constructed over a sandy soil matrix as exits at Ryknield Street. It is commonly found in cremation-related contexts in the Western and Northern Isles of Scotland and parts of East Anglia.

Burial formation processes

The primary deposit in grave 122017 comprised an unurned collection of 215.9 g of bone with redeposited pyre debris, above which was placed a vessel containing (at time of excavation) 58.1 g of bone from the same cremation. The vessel was truncated, leaving only the lower 0.04–0.08 m *in situ* and it may originally have held substantially more bone. A second, possibly similar deposit was recovered from grave 122044. Here, an urned burial, surviving to 0.12–0.14 m depth, contained 415.8 g of bone, most of which (78.3%) lay in the central 0.08 m of the vessel. A further 121.2 g of bone was recovered from the upper grave fill, apparently forming an additional unurned deposit made within the partially backfilled grave. Although rare, similar deposits have been observed at a few other contemporaneous cemeteries (McKinley 2004b, 304).

Most of the small amount of bone in the upper 0.06 m depth of the urned burial 122116 in grave 129080 (0.22 m total surviving depth) is likely to have been there as a result of bioturbation, lying within a mixed soil matrix also containing fragments of sherds from the broken upper part of the vessel. Most of the bone (95.8%) lay in the lower 0.16 m depth of the vessel within which a mix of skeletal areas, left and right side, lay with fragments of pyre goods (animal bone and iron objects); there was no apparent ordered deposition. The upper 0.04 m of the intact urned burial 122891 (grave 122874) again contained little bone (8% of total). Most of the mandible and other facial bones were confined to the central 0.06 m depth of the vessel, but otherwise a range of elements from all skeletal elements were distributed throughout the depth together with fragments of animal bone pyre goods. There are joins between bone fragments from spits 2 and 6 (base) in burial 129044 (grave 122420), where, once again, most of the facial bones lay in the central surviving 0.06 m of the vessel. The upper 0.04 m of the undisturbed burial 129050 from grave 122780 held only 2.2 g of bone (0.8% of total). The urned burial of greatest surviving depth, 129062 from grave 122794, at 0.25–0.6 m, contained relatively little bone, 126.8 g, most of which (93%) lay in the lower 0.12 m depth of the vessel.

What these figures demonstrate is that the vessels functioning as burial urns were not used to full capacity, despite there easily being more than enough bone to fill them – this secondary part of the mortuary rite did not demand deposition of all, or even nearly all the cremated remains. There appears, in general, to have been no ordered deposition of remains within the vessels; other than the apparent concentration of some skeletal elements in the central section, the evidence from the more complete vessels does not lend support to the suggestion from the disturbed burials that more of the lower limb elements may have been concentrated towards the lower part of the urn fills (see skeletal elements). This apparently random distribution – common across the temporal range of the rite – could reflect one or more factors including mixing of skeletal elements on collection via raking of material from the pyre, and original collection in a different receptacle to that eventually used for burial with mixing/more mixing occurring during transfer.

Metal finds, by Kelly Powell

This site produced a large amount of metalwork (978 objects) by comparison with others on the M6 Toll, mainly because of its function as a cemetery during the Romano-British period. Overall, 18 copper-alloy objects including coins, 26 lead or mixed lead and iron items and 934 iron finds were recovered, the majority of which were Romano-British in date and associated with primarily funerary features. The notable exception to this trend were the copper-alloy objects, nine of which (50%) were post-Romano-British, recovered from the topsoil layer. A number of objects were recorded as small finds but on examination were found to be cremated bone and charcoal with iron staining suggesting the original presence of further iron. Of the iron objects recorded, a minimum of 913 proved to be nails or probable nails. For this reason much of the following discussion is concentrated on these common artefacts, which were classified using W H Manning's typology (1985). The remaining objects from the cemetery features are listed in the Grave catalogue.

Nails

The most common type of metalwork found on Romano-British sites are Manning type 1 nails (Fig. 84,1; Manning 1985, 134) and this site is no exception. Of the 913 nails or probable nail fragments recovered, 598 could be positively classified by Manning type (Table 23), 298 (50%) of which were type 1b. Although a similar number of hobnails (Manning type 10) (Fig. 84,2) was identified this is likely to be a result of the distinctiveness of this nail type. The majority of the uncategorised nails were deemed unclassifiable due to their fragmentary nature but based on the rest of the assemblage, the size and form of most would indicate that these are also likely to be type 1.

With the exception of the type 10 nails, which are fundamentally different in character, the average length for complete nails across the site was 43 mm, with a range of 13–85 mm. This indicates that most, if not all of the type 1 nails were type 1b (less than 150 mm in length), and illustrates the generally small size of the nails on the site as a whole. It is likely, therefore, that the structures or artefacts from which the nails were

Table 23 Nail classification by context type

	Type										
	1b	10	8/stud	1b/10	Facetted stud	Tack	7	10/stud	10/8	Unclass.	Total
Cremation grave	99	73	–	1	3	9	–	–	12	59	246
RPD	107	110	–	5	1	22	1	23	–	105	364
CRD	8	104	–	–	–	–	–	–	–	2	115
Inhumation grave	63	–	2	–	–	–	–	–	–	47	112
Ditch	13	20	–	–	–	–	–	–	–	6	39
Discrete feature	4	2	–	–	–	–	–	–	–	8	14
Unstrat.	4	–	–	–	–	–	–	–	–	9	13
Total	298	299	2	6	4	31	1	23	12	237	913

RPD = redeposited pyre debris; CRD = cremation-related deposit

originally derived were not particularly substantial and in a funerary context may represent small coffins and boxes or biers.

The frequency of complete nail lengths indicates a generally even spread between 25 mm and 70 mm, although clusters are clearly visible (Table 24). For instance 14% of the complete nails fell within the range of 20–25 mm indicating that a particular type of small type 1b nail was being manufactured (Fig. 84, 3). Additionally, 29% of the complete nails were 40–55 mm and 31% 55–70 mm. Overall trends indicate that the longer nails tended to be found in inhumation graves, presumably because they were used in coffins, whilst the smaller nails were found in cremation graves (Table 25). However, the nature of the objects from which these originated are unknown.

Unsurprisingly the Manning type 10 nails (hobnails) from this site were of relatively standardised lengths within the range of 10–24 mm; they were on average 16 mm long. Where hobnails were fragmentary and lengths unclear, head diameter is given as an indication of the overall length, as the two measurements are often related proportionally.

Few other Manning nail types were represented in the assemblage, although one definite type 7 nail (Fig. 84, 4) was identified and a number were classified as definitely or possibly type 8 (Fig. 84, 5). The difficulty with the latter class of nail is that it is not easy to distinguish from incomplete studs of different kinds; consequently identification is tentative. In addition to these standard Manning nail types a class of small 'tacks' (Fig. 84, 6) was identified. The predominance of the small (20–25 mm) type 1b nails and hobnails, in addition to the presence of such 'tacks' made identification complex at times, particularly when the nails were exceptionally badly corroded, and the tables consequently take account of these blurred distinctions.

Overall preservation of the metal finds from Ryknield Street was poor, particularly with respect to the iron nails. It is notable, therefore, that there are a few examples of exceptional or localised variable preservation. This is particularly evident in the more unusual nail types and is often accompanied by red staining on the metal surface (Figs 84, 4 and 84, 6). This phenomenon may indicate some form of surface treatment, not unexpected for objects such as decorative studs, but there are also a number of type 1 and type 10 nails which exhibit this trait. An alternative possibility is that the staining is the result of intense burning through cremation in association with a material which has reacted with the metal.

Due to the size and nature of the site and the number of finds, discussion will be organised by the type of feature from which metal finds were recovered. Table 23 illustrates the number of nail types present in each feature type and immediately reveals patterns in distribution. Type 1 nails were found ubiquitously in more feature types than any other class of nails, suggesting they had a more diverse use. Hobnails (type 10) do not appear to have survived in inhumation graves and are only present in any quantity in features containing deposits related to the cremation rite. Additionally, the more unusual nail types were also generally found within cremation-related deposits.

Cremation graves

Cremation graves mainly produced iron nails, although graves 129073 and 129074 are the exception. In total 219 metal finds (215 iron and 4 copper-alloy) were recovered from the grave fills. Overall a smaller number of nails were recovered per feature than from the inhumation graves. The nail assemblage is also more mixed (Table 23), containing the common type 1 nails (and the smaller variety of these type of nails, see above), as well as hobnails and, potentially, a type of 'tack'. Here the cremation graves are subdivided into those containing the remains of urned, unurned and combined burials and those of uncertain burial form.

Table 24 Frequency of complete nail lengths

Length (mm)	10–15	15–20	20–25	25–30	30–35	35–40	40–45	45–50	50–55	55–60	60–65	65–70	70–75	75–80	80–85
No.	4	3	11	4	4	6	7	10	5	12	7	5	0	1	2

Table 25 Average nail length (complete) including hobnails, by context type

Context type	*Average length (mm)*
Cremation grave	29.0
Redeposited pyre debris	27.0
Cremation-related deposit	17.0
Inhumation grave	54.0
Discrete feature	14.0
Ditch	40.5
Unstratified	60.0

Urned burials

The majority of cremation graves from which metal finds were recovered contained the remains of urned burials (15 of a minimum of 35). The metalwork assemblages from these urned burials are characterised by their small size and fragmentary nature. In most cases the nails were recovered from the grave fill (see above). Details of the individual items recovered from each grave are presented in the Grave catalogue.

One of the most interesting finds was a type of nail or stud with a facetted head and short shank (eg graves 122052 and 122017 (Fig. 84, 17), and in the redeposited pyre debris from 122784). The head of this nail or stud was flattened in sections from the central point, dividing it into separate parts. The function of these nails/studs is unknown. Parallels include an example from the Uley shrine (Woodward and Leach 1993, 183, no. 12), although this has a steeper head than the examples seen here. Woodward and Leach class this as a type 8 or 10 nail, although whether these objects can be classified as such is open to debate. A similar style of copper nail can be seen from Colchester (Crummy 1983, 116, no. 3093) and *Verulamium* (Frere 1972, fig. 37, no. 98). It is likely that their function was decorative.

Finds other than nails were occasionally recovered including a possible iron bow brooch fragment (ON 123315) and a fragment of iron strip or bar (ON 123314) both from grave 129073. The possible brooch was very heavily corroded and clearly burnt, barely retaining its shape. Only part of the top of the bow and arms remained, forming a triangular shape, with no indication of fastening. A fragment of copper-alloy sheet and a Roman coin were found in grave 129075. The fragment of sheet is very small and folded over; it appears to have wood adhering to the reverse and may have been fixed to some form of wooden funeral furniture, but its exact nature is unknown.

Fragments of similar copper-alloy studs were collected from grave 129074; the most complete was folded over at the edge with a single groove running around the head (Fig. 84.16). A similar object is recorded from *Verulamium* (Frere 1984, 152, no. 45) from a context dated AD 150– 250. The studs presumably had a decorative function.

The largest assemblage of nails from a cremation grave was from 122780, the central grave within mortuary enclosure 126154, which survived to a much greater depth than the others (see above). This included a minimum of 19 large nails and 21 hobnails, and what are best described as small tacks (minimum of nine) which do not seem to have a parallel in Manning's classification system; another well preserved example was found amongst the redeposited pyre debris from pit 122158 (Fig. 84.6). These are small (10–15 mm) nails with proportionally large (10–11 mm) flat heads, possibly for use in upholstery or similar. The nails are heavily corroded. Several examples within this particular assemblage exhibit variable preservation often seen on nails of a decorative or unusual kind from the site, suggesting some sort of surface treatment, although this may be a result of the burning process.

Unurned burials

A type 1b nail was recovered from one of the two unurned burials from the site (grave 122045).

Combined burials

Metalwork was recovered from both graves (122044 and 122017) which contained the remains of combined urned and unurned burials; predominantly nails and hobnails (Fig. 84.2). Grave 122017 also contained two of the studs with facetted heads discussed above, one of which was extremely well preserved; the head was flattened in sections from the central point, dividing it into five parts (Fig. 84.17).

Burials of uncertain form

The burial recorded during the evaluation (grave 120202) contained a single fragment of standard-sized nail in addition to a probable copper-alloy box fitting, consisting of a catch with a split pin attachment still *in situ* (Fig. 84.18). A badly corroded copper-alloy ring with a D-shaped section was also found associated with the catch. It is probable that this object originally formed part of the catch on a box or casket in a cremation or funerary context (*cf.* eg Partridge 1981, 319, fig. 122).

Redeposited pyre debris

A total of 364 nails (40% of the overall nail assemblage) came from 14 pits containing formal or incidental deposits of pyre debris (Table 23). The only other metal finds from this deposit type were unidentified iron objects. The number of nails per feature varied from one to 106 (see Grave catalogue).

Most notable amongst the various iron nails/hobnails (33) recovered from the pyre debris within pit 122975 is a possibly complete and very well preserved Manning type 7 nail (Fig. 84.4), which Manning suggests is most likely to have been used in upholstery work. The nail exhibited the traces of red seen on other well preserved nails, particularly on the head. This item certainly seems to indicate that some form of funerary furniture was included in the cremation.

Cremation-related deposits

This context type – which mostly comprised deposits which could be interpreted as either unurned burials with redeposited pyre debris or redeposited pyre debris (see above) – is difficult to assess in terms of metal finds due to the burnt and corroded nature of the remaining artefacts, which makes classification tentative at best. Overall a much larger proportion of hobnails is evident within these deposits in comparison with the grave fills/burials. It is difficult to say with any certainty whether items classified as nails or studs with domed heads and potential 'tacks' are in fact further distorted and corroded hobnails.

Deposits from five features contained iron finds the majority of which are nails (Table 23).

The largest assemblage from the site was recovered from pit 122042 and included at least 97 hobnails, many complete with an average length of 17 mm and head diameter of 8 mm. A fragment of copper-alloy bracelet was also recovered (Fig. 84.19). The fragment was heavily encrusted and appears to be plain, although it is doubtful that any decoration would be visible. It is unlikely to be closely datable but potential parallels exist at South Shields (Allason-Jones and Miket 1984, 127 3.224) and in a grave from the Eastern Cemetery of Roman London (Barber and Bowsher 2000, 185 B381).

Inhumation graves

A minimum of 142 metal objects (118 iron and 24 lead) was recovered from eight inhumation graves, 112 of which were nails or nail fragments (Table 23). The remaining collection of fragments of iron and lead sheet (Fig. 84.11–14) and a joiner's dog (Fig. 84.15) were retrieved from a single grave (122552). The majority of the nails recovered from this context type are probably coffin nails and are all of a similar nature. Many conform to Manning type 1b and fall within discrete size ranges. In addition, many were associated with mineralised wood (details of individual finds from each grave may be found in the Grave catalogue).

Grave 122492 contained nine nails, seven of which were certainly and another probably of Manning type 1b. It is notable that the three possibly complete examples vary in size from 25 mm to 44 mm, and all the remaining nails fall within this size range. They are particularly small for coffin nails, although the context type and presence of mineralised wood on at least four suggest that this was their purpose.

The metal finds from grave 122552 are of a slightly different nature to those from the other graves (including nails, fragments of lead and iron sheet and a joiner's dog), although it is unclear whether this is partly a result of preservation conditions. It is, however, immediately apparent that more significant coffin furniture was present. There was a minimum of 24 fragments of lead sheet 28–85 mm long, many with iron nails or studs still attached through perforations in the lead (Fig. 84, 11–13). Some of the fragments were clearly shaped. In particular the fragments ON 123361 appear to be sub-rectangular in form with nails still attached at what would constitute corners and have mineralised wood on the reverse (Fig. 84, 14). Some of the fragments are curved in the centre (ON 123378 and ON 123354) (Fig. 84, 12), probably originally functioning as binding for the edges of a coffin, an interpretation reinforced by the presence of mineralised wood. The most interesting of these is a definite three-dimensional corner piece with an iron nail still attached (Fig. 84 11). The nails attached to these fragments are for the most part quite heavily corroded and not easily identified. However, they do appear to have quite short shanks (10–20 mm) with heads of similar or larger dimensions and may possibly be decorative studs. ONs 123342, 123344 and 123361 (Fig. 84, 14) may also have been fittings from the same coffin. Like the lead sheet, some of these fragments are sub-rectangular and some are clearly designed to fit around edges, with nails still attached and mineralised wood adhering.

Ditches

The metal finds from ditches (43 iron and one copper-alloy) were once again mainly nails (Table 23), with a few notable exceptions. Four complete hobnails ranging from 15 mm to 18 mm in length were collected from one of the excavated segments in the northern half of the western road-boundary ditch 126059. These were heavily corroded and recovered together with a deposit of fuel ash suggesting they may have formed part of a cremation-related deposit (no bone). A collection of nails was recovered from one of the excavated segments of the post-medieval ditch 126221, probably derived from the redeposited pyre debris in pit 122037 through which it cut at this point (Fig. 67). This included a minimum of four type 1b nail fragments, ranging in size from 35 mm to 40 mm with head diameters 10–15 mm, in addition to a minimum of 14 hobnails, many of which were complete and within the range 16–20 mm.

Several fragments of nail and five tiny pieces of irregular shaped iron sheet were recovered from an excavated segment of the cemetery southern boundary ditch 126065 where it cut through cremation grave 122154. The nail was probably of type 1b, within the standard sizes for the site overall (head diameter 14 mm); the fragments of sheet were unidentifiable.

Iron finds were recovered from several of the mortuary enclosure ditches. For example, four nails or nail fragments were recovered from three of the five excavated segments of ditch 126069 (from all sides); three of the four were identified as Manning type 1b, on average 50 mm long. Nails were recovered from two of the three fills within the north-west segment excavated through ditch 126066, mostly from amongst a deposit of fuel ash (possibly pyre debris). A shank fragment of a large nail (73 mm long) is notably bigger than the standard size of nail from the site, with the breadth of the shank itself 15 mm, but as a single find the function of this nail is unknown. A more standard assemblage of six nails or nail fragments was also found, including two hobnails, on average 18 mm long and two or possibly three type 1b nails. Two of these were considered to be complete or near complete, measuring a more standard 44 mm and 58 mm respectively, with head diameters of 13 mm and 14 mm.

Lastly, metal finds were recovered from three of the segments excavated in the northern half of ditch 126148. A fragment of probable type 1b nail within standard size ranges was retrieved from the north-east segment. A single copper-alloy nail, the form of which is of Manning type 1b, was recovered from one segment in the northern side (Fig. 84, 8) and was the only example of this type from the site and the project as a whole. Similar copper-alloy nails have been recovered from South Shields (Allason-Jones and Miket, 183, no. 3.577) and Colchester (Crummy 1983, 115, no. 3057) and although no indication of purpose is given in these contexts, copper-alloy nails are likely to have been used for more decorative purposes than the iron variety. Three or possibly four nails, two fragments of strip or bar, a potentially complete joiner's dog (Fig. 84, 9) and a double-spiked loop (Fig. 84, 10) were found in the north-west segment of the ditch, within a probable deposit of pyre debris (see The mortuary enclosures above). One of the nails was complete enough to be identified as a Manning type 1b, with an incomplete length of 48 mm. All were heavily corroded and at least two had quite a large quantity of mineralised wood adhering. The strips measured 17 mm and 34 mm long but were clearly incomplete.

The double spiked loop (ON 123467) and the joiner's dog (ON 123465) may have been complete. This small assemblage appears to represent the remains of a wooden artefact such as a box, with mineralised wood remaining on the nail fragments and double spiked loops and joiner's dogs known for use in wood working (see Manning 1985, pl. 61, R39–47). Given its position together with other material suggestive of pyre debris this probably had a funerary function.

Discrete non-funerary features

A total of 14 scattered finds of nails was recorded from isolated non-funerary features. In most cases these consisted of fragments of heavily corroded nails (Table 23). One such fragment was recovered from hearth/oven 122517, one from tree hollow 122878 and one from tree hollow 122616, which had been cut by inhumation grave 122526. A number of pits with no apparent funerary function produced nail fragments. For example, two possible nail fragments were recovered from pit 122820, one possibly complete hobnail measuring 14 mm from pit 122924 and one probable hobnail from pit 122792, although in its distorted and corroded state this does resemble a decorative stud. A total of six nails and a further possible nail were recovered from pit 122156, four of which could be identified as Manning type 1b. One example, which may have been complete, measured 42 mm in length with a head diameter of 12 mm and all fragments were within this size range. Many of the nails were associated with charcoal and were heavily corroded indicating that they derived from some form of burnt deposit.

Unstratified

A total of 26 objects (14 iron, 10 copper-alloy and 2 lead), were recovered from unstratified locations, including topsoil and subsoil. This group included 10 of the 18 copper-alloy finds, which were retrieved from the topsoil. Of particular note is an oval-sectioned copper-alloy handle (Fig. 84, 7). An almost identical parallel is recorded from the excavations at South Shields (Allason-Jones and Miket 1984, 167, no 3.427) and identified as a helmet handle. Bearing in mind the funerary, rather than military, nature of this site it is possible that the handle may have originally functioned as a coffin or box fitting. Although not identical, handles were recovered from grave 6 at Baldock cemetery (Stead and Rigby 1986, 68, no. 16) and grave 198 at Pepper Hill (Biddulph 2006). All of these finds indicate a Romano-British date for the handle. Unfortunately because the handle was recovered unstratified alongside four post-medieval or modern objects (a button, a miscellaneous housing and two sheet fittings), no further interpretation is possible.

The remaining unstratified copper-alloy objects were all of medieval or post-medieval date and included a very worn 'Cartwheel' coin (ON 123003) of George III (1797), a fragment of curved strip, flat on the interior and grooved on the exterior and a potentially modern ring, perhaps a water-pipe junction. Buckle ON 123002 was post-medieval, square in form, measuring 17 mm across with a central bar but missing its pin. ON 123003 is a medieval cast buckle loop and integral plate, 47 mm long, probably dating to the 13th or 14th century (Scott, pers. comm.). It has an oval frame, 20 mm wide with a decorative knop on the outer edge, a large hole at the base of which would have held the tongue, now missing. The plate has a central baluster-like expansion with a flat, decorative terminal pierced by three possible rivet holes (*ibid*).

Additionally, two lead objects of probable post-medieval date were recovered from the topsoil. These were a token, ON 123001, and ON 123005, a domed weight, clearly missing a hook or loop of iron from the top.

A number of iron nails and an unidentified lump of iron were also recovered from topsoil, subsoil and redeposited natural and therefore have limited archaeological value. Overall, 13 nails or nail fragments were recorded from such contexts; these were mostly fragmentary and heavily corroded, although four can be identified as Manning type 1b, none larger than 49 mm long where approaching completeness.

Discussion

Pyre/grave goods

If we conclude that this large collection of nails mainly represents funerary furniture (see below), the assemblage from Ryknield Street is most notable for the apparent scarcity of pyre or grave goods. Comparatively, sites such as the contemporary Romano-British cemeteries of Derby Racecourse (Wheeler 1985), Brougham in Cumbria (Cool 2004) and Pepper Hill, Kent (Biddulph 2006) produced a range of pyre and grave goods. These assemblages were dominated by jewellery such as brooches and bracelets, including a number of gold items from Brougham, but also extended to personal effects such as tweezers and iron needles. The prominent exceptions from Ryknield Street include the probable badly burnt iron bow brooch from urned burial 122474 (grave 129073) and the fragment of encrusted copper-alloy bracelet from cremation-related deposit 122067 (cut 122042). However, in this context these finds are not only the sole remaining items of jewellery but, alongside the Roman coin from the urned burial in grave 129075, the only individual metal pyre goods of real significance to have survived. Notably, no obvious metal grave goods were recovered at all.

This said, Ryknield Street is similar to the aforementioned sites with relation to the retrieval of hobnails from a number of funerary deposits. Overall a large quantity of hobnails was recovered from cremation-related deposits and redeposited pyre debris suggesting these items would have been pyre goods. It is notable that no hobnails survived from inhumation graves; in view of the fact that coffin nails survived in these features it is likely that any hobnails present within them would also have survived. Their absence indicates the existence of two separate funerary traditions.

Hobnails appear commonly as funerary goods in the 2nd century AD, although the minor amounts involved in many cases do not constitute whole pairs of shoes. This is true of Ryknield Street, with the exception of cremation-related deposit 122067 in cut 122042. This feature produced 97 hobnails that may have been the remains of a single pair of shoes worn by the deceased or placed on the pyre. The bracelet fragment was also recovered from this deposit which may have derived from a relatively rich cremation. It has been suggested that a handful of hobnails were thrown into graves at this time as a symbolic gesture (Salway 1981), although it is more likely that the survival of small numbers of hobnails is a result of collection of an arbitrary amount of cremated remains, human and artefactual, for deposition (McKinley 2000c, 41; Cool 2004, 391). It is rare for the entire cremated remains of an individual to have been collected for burial and evidence indicates goods were sometimes selected from the pyre for inclusion in the grave, the remainder were discarded with pyre debris (McKinley 2000c, 41).

On a regional level, Ryknield Street differed considerably from the Derby Racecourse cemetery which produced a variety of copper-alloy and iron grave goods. In particular, three possible military graves at the latter contained copper-alloy plates and buckles, a brooch and an iron blade, and two infant burials produced copper-alloy bracelets and a finger ring (Wheeler 1985). Significantly, unlike Ryknield Street, at least 143 hobnails and 15 'bootplates', possibly more, were recovered from inhumation graves (*ibid.*). Only scattered hobnails and no pyre goods were recorded from cremation graves. Therefore the traditions seen at Ryknield Street do not seem to have been regional.

Funerary furniture

The large number of nails recovered indicates that funerary furniture was quite common. It is no surprise that the inhumation graves produced the larger nails, the discrete size ranges of which and presence of mineralised wood indicate their use as coffin nails. The occasional much larger nails, such as those from graves 122964 and 122676 are more difficult to interpret but may equally have been part of coffin manufacture. Of a possible 21 inhumation graves only eight produced metalwork which may be a result of preservation or may signify the use of wooden pegs as fastenings, or the use of unfastened boards. Other coffin fittings were limited to a single grave (122552) and seem to indicate that the coffin was bound mainly with lead in addition to some iron fittings, with no sign of decoration on either. Whilst rare coffin fittings were found at Derby Racecourse, Brougham and Pepper Hill the presence of lead is unknown with the exception of a large lead sheet from an *ossarium* at Brougham (Mould 2004). The use of lead in this way at Ryknield Street also contrasts with well-known practices such as the provision of lead lining in wooden coffins (Toller 1977) or the use of iron fittings in later Romano-British contexts as for example at Poundbury (Farwell and Molleson 1993, 117–27, 129). Grave 122552 may therefore have contained the remains of a burial of some significance.

The nails recovered from cremation graves and related contexts hint at the presence of specialised cremation furniture. Notably the presence of nails seems to suggest that objects, perhaps biers or boxes, were included on the pyre, as noted at Pepper Hill and Brougham. In addition, boxes or caskets may have served as pyre goods.

A large number of the nails from these contexts fell within the range of 20–25 mm. These small nails, also found at sites discussed above, are generally interpreted as fastenings from biers (Cool 2004, 393; Biddulph 2006) and are likely to have performed the same function here. At Brougham these items of furniture appear to have been highly decorated with fittings of bone and antler (Greep 2004), although no such objects survive from either this site or Pepper Hill. Unfortunately the distribution and function of nails from Derby Racecourse were not discussed in the publication.

The presence of boxes or caskets may be hinted at by the occasional larger nails in cremation-related contexts in addition to more obvious box fittings, most notably the probable hinge with split pin attachment and ring from deposit 120203 (Fig. 84.18). The ring may have functioned as a handle, similar to one recovered from a box at Pepper Hill (Biddulph 2006). Other possible box fittings include the collection of iron objects and a copper-alloy nail from the mortuary enclosure ditch

126148 and the fragment of copper-alloy sheet from the urned burial in grave 129075 which clearly had wood adhering to the reverse. Whilst caskets from contemporary sites appear to have been decorated with metal fittings there is no evidence of this from the current site. However, the 'tacks' and type 7 nail, probably for use in upholstery, domed and facetted iron studs, and copper-alloy studs may have functioned as decoration on either type of cremation furniture.

Overall the dearth of metal finds as pyre or grave goods is typical of the M6 Toll sites, possibly representing a Romano-British community of less conspicuous wealth or status. However, the metal finds from the cemetery indicate that specialised funerary furniture, although not necessarily highly decorated, was probably an integral part of the funerary tradition in the area at this time. Comparisons with the cemetery at Derby Racecourse indicate that some burial traditions noted at Ryknield Street, in particular the lack of pyre goods and/or grave goods, were not representative of the area as a whole.

Illustrated metal finds (Fig. 84)

1. Nail. Iron. Complete or near complete. Manning type 1b. Flat circular head and square sectioned shank. L 59 mm, head D 13 mm. ON 123347, cut 122553, context 122545
2. Hobnail (Manning type 10). Iron. Complete. Hollow pyramidal head and square sectioned shank, bent at the tip. Adhering corrosion contains a further 2 hobnails and fragments of human bone. L 15 mm, head D 9 mm; grave 122044
3. Nail. Iron. Possibly complete. Small Manning type 1b. Flat circular head and square sectioned shank. L 23 mm, head D 8 mm; cut 122158
4. Nail. Iron. Complete or near complete. Manning type 7. Large flat circular head with square sectioned shank. Traces of red visible on head. L 49 mm, head D 27 mm. ON 123560, grave 122975, context 122976
5. Nail. Iron. Incomplete, part of head and possibly tip missing. Probable type 8 nail, hollow domed head and short square sectioned shank. Possibly iron sheet below head of nail and mineralised wood adhering. L 40 mm, head D 16 mm; grave 122552
6. Nail/tack. Iron. Possibly complete. Very small nail with irregular shaped flattened head, damaged and short square sectioned shank, tip damaged. Traces of red visible on head. L 14 mm, head D 10 mm; grave 122158, context 122157
7. Handle. Copper-alloy. Incomplete. Possible coffin/furniture/helmet handle. Oval section thickens towards centre and remaining 'rivet' terminal. L 67 mm, max. W 8 mm, max T 6 mm; topsoil 122007
8. Nail. Copper-alloy. Complete or near complete. Flat sub-circular head and square sectioned shank. As Manning type 1b. L 36 mm, head D 7 mm. ON 123366, ditch 126148, context 122620
9. Joiner's dog. Iron. Possibly complete. Mineralised wood adhering. L 40 mm, W 7 mm. ON 123465, ditch 126148, context 122815
10. Double-spiked loop. Iron. Possibly complete, spike may be broken. Heavily corroded. L 39 mm, loop D 17 mm. ON 123467, ditch 126148, context 122815
11. Coffin binding. Lead with iron nails. Incomplete. Fragment of sheet with three sides from the corner of a box/coffin, iron nail attached through the sheet. L 60 mm, W 50 mm. ON 123354, grave 122552, context 122582
12. Coffin binding. Lead with iron nails. Incomplete. Fragment of curved/bent sheet from the edge of a coffin. Two iron nails still attached through the sheet with mineralised wood. L 84 mm, W 35 mm. ON 123354, grave 122552, context 122582
13. Coffin binding. Lead with iron nails. Incomplete. Fragment of sheet, bent up at a right angle at one end. Pierced by two iron nails with mineralised wood on the reverse. L 84 mm, W 56 mm. ON 123378, grave 122552, context 122582
14. Coffin binding. Iron. Incomplete. Length of strip bent at a right angle. Two square sectioned nails attached through the strip and mineralised wood on the reverse. Heavy corrosion. L 109 mm, W 24 mm, T 4 mm ON 123361, grave 122552, context 122541
15. Joiner's dog. Iron. Complete. Mineralised wood adhering. L 38 mm, W 8 mm. ON 123352, grave 122552, context 122541
16. Stud. Copper-alloy. Circular head with some edge damage. Square sectioned pin, missing tip. The head is constructed from very thin metal, folded over at the edge. A groove runs around the head, 2 mm away from the folded edge. D 18 mm, T <1 mm. ON 123330.5, grave 129074
17. Nail/stud. Iron. Incomplete, tip missing. Head flattened into at least five sections with a central point in a floral-type design. Square sectioned shank, bent, becomes very circular towards the point. L 17 mm, head D 11 mm; grave 122017
18. Box fittings. Copper-alloy. Strip of varying thickness with a raised lip (exterior) and perpendicular sub-square lug with circular central perforation (interior), at the smaller end. The thinner part of the strip is also bevelled at the edges. Becomes thicker at a distance of 35 mm from this end and bends towards the interior to form an approximate right angle. At the thicker end is a rectangular hole with a fragment of split pin attachment still *in situ*. Associated with this probable catch is a D-sectioned ring. Strip L 60 mm, min. W 11 mm, max. W 24 mm, T 2 mm, lip T 4 mm, lug L 11 mm, lug hole D 5 mm, rectangular hole L 8 mm, split pin W 5 mm, ring D 29 mm, T 2 mm; grave 120202
19. Bracelet. Copper-alloy. Incomplete. D-shaped section, undecorated. L 55 mm, W 5 mm, T 4 mm ON 123037, cut 122042
20. Nail/stud. Iron. Complete. Head flattened into five sections with central point in a floral-type design. Short square sectioned shank, bent towards the point. Traces of red on head and shank. L 27 m, head D 9 m. ON 123486, cut 122784

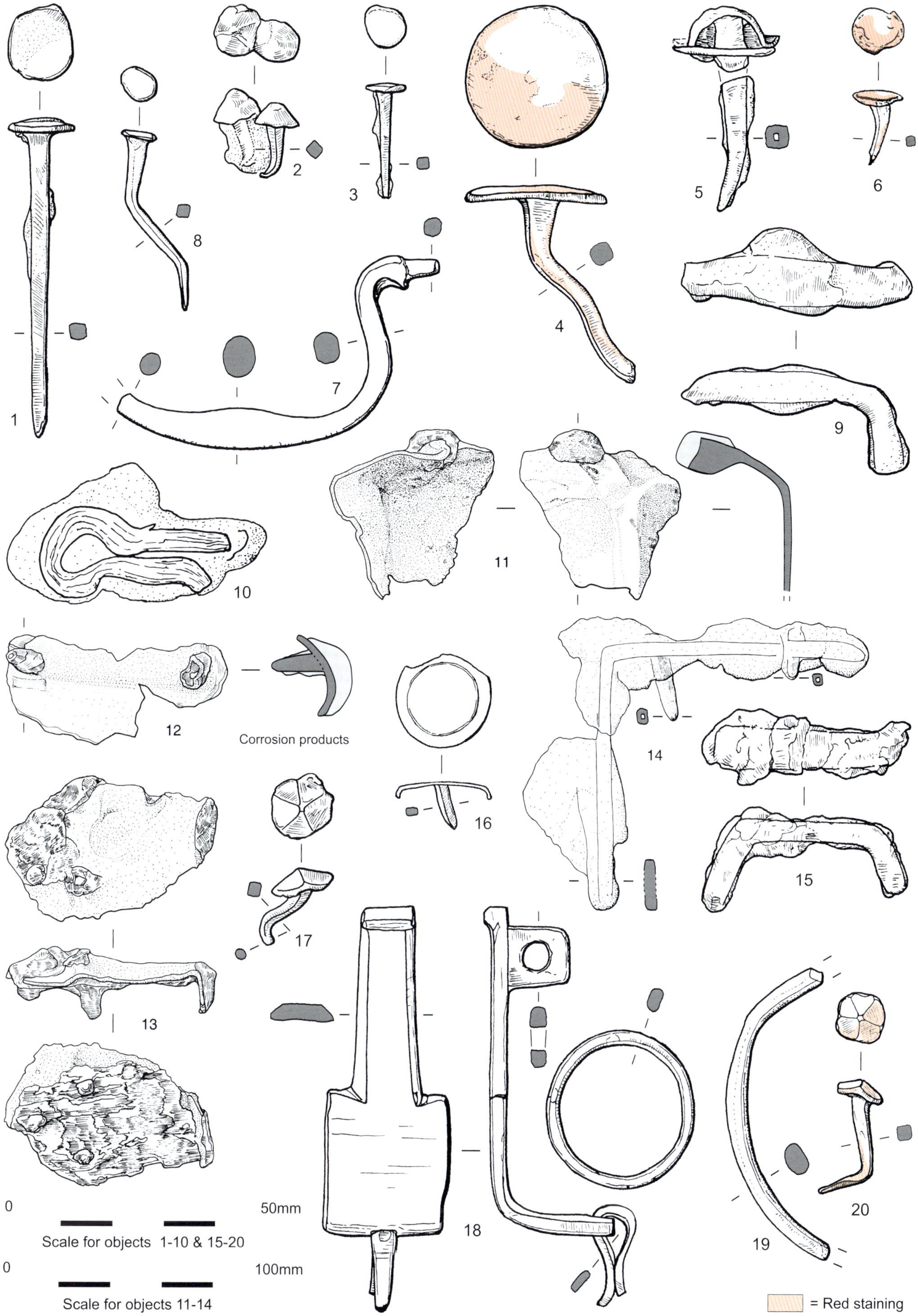

Fig. 84 Metal finds

Flint, by Kate Cramp with Hugo Lamdin-Whymark

A total of eight struck flints and a single piece (1 g) of burnt unworked flint were recovered from the excavation (Table 150). Datable types suggest that some or perhaps all of the flintwork dates to the Mesolithic period. All of the flints have been manufactured from pebble flint, which would have been available relatively locally (see Chapter 24 below for a more detailed description of raw material use).

The assemblage contains two flakes, one blade and one partially-worked nodule, the majority of which are chronologically undiagnostic. Retouched tools are relatively numerous and include one microlith, one burin, one retouched blade and one flake with slight abrupt edge retouch.

The microlith (Fig. 85, 1; context 123021), compares most closely to Jacobi's class 1bc (Jacobi 1978, 16, fig. 6), a shape that is usually associated with assemblages of early Mesolithic date. The particularly narrow proportions of this example, however, align it more closely in metrical terms with microliths of late Mesolithic date (Pitts and Jacobi 1979, 170). As an isolated find and in the absence of independent dating means, a broad Mesolithic date is therefore proposed for the piece.

The utilised burin (Fig. 85, 2; context 123023, has been made on a flake by means of a plunging spall struck from the distal edge (see Tixier *et al.* 1980, fig. 30, no. 4). This piece is a distinctively Mesolithic artefact and may be contemporary with the microlith from the same site. An unstratified minimally-retouched blade was also recovered from the site.

The flint was found scattered across several contexts and the frequent incidence of post-depositional edge damage implies that much of it is residual. Technologically, however, the flintwork is similar in character and forms a fairly coherent group. In view of the presence of a microlith and a burin, a broad Mesolithic date would not be unreasonable for all the pieces.

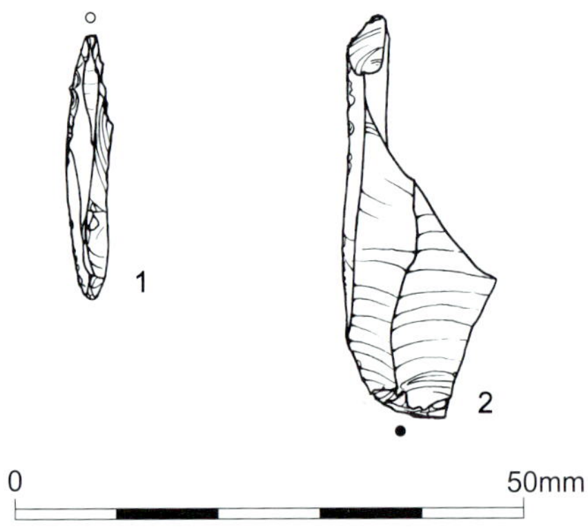

Fig. 85 Flint microlith and burin

Roman glass, by H.E.M. Cool

Molten blue/green glass was found in six cremation graves. Given the colour, it is virtually certain that this was derived from vessels that had been placed on the pyre, rather than items of jewellery bedecking the corpse. In all cases the temperature the pyre had achieved had been so high that the vessels had deformed and, in some cases, completely melted; so it is not possible to identify what types of vessels are represented.

The amount of glass recovered from grave 122052 though (ON 123066), suggests that at least in this case it may have been a vessel such as a bottle rather than a small unguent bottle of the type that was frequently used as a pyre good. That bottles were present on the pyres is hinted at by ON 123292, recovered from a layer in the eastern half of the cemetery, adjacent to the western boundary ditch. This is a blue/green base fragment (23 mm by 17 mm) most probably coming from a square bottle. It has not been melted or deformed by heat, but the strain cracking and jigsaw-like fractures on the edge are typical of glass that has been subject to high temperatures.

Another bottle is probably represented by ON 123327 from the urned cremation burial made in grave 129075. The slight flexing seen at one edge might be from the lower part of the bulge often seen at the shoulder, and the vertical scratches are typical features on such bottles. The fragment shows no evidence of having been burnt and given that the burial was disturbed it might be a chance inclusion. If the identification is correct, it indicates activity on the site in the late 1st to early 2nd centuries, as cylindrical bottles have a relatively short floruit in comparison to the square bottles which continued in use into the 3rd century (Price and Cottam 1998, 191–8).

In addition to the glass vessels, part of an opaque white glass gaming counter (plano-convex, half extant; D16 mm, 7 mm thick) was found in the cemetery boundary ditch 126065 (segment excavated at north-west angle). Although such counters are found later, the majority were in use during the mid 1st to mid-2nd centuries (Cool *et al.* 1995, 1555).

Earlier prehistoric pottery, by Carol Allen

All the 21 prehistoric sherds found on this site originated from the fills of Romano-British features, mostly inhumation graves but also two pits of unknown function (Table 15). Some sherds are very abraded but most are unabraded or only slightly abraded and the average sherd size of 6 g indicates the assemblage is fragmentary. Some of the quartz-tempered sherds may be Neolithic but there is no form or decoration to confirm this.

Early Bronze Age Collared Urns

Inhumation grave 122405 and pit 122534 contained grog-tempered sherds of Early Bronze Age date. Grog tempering may have been an important recycling ritual

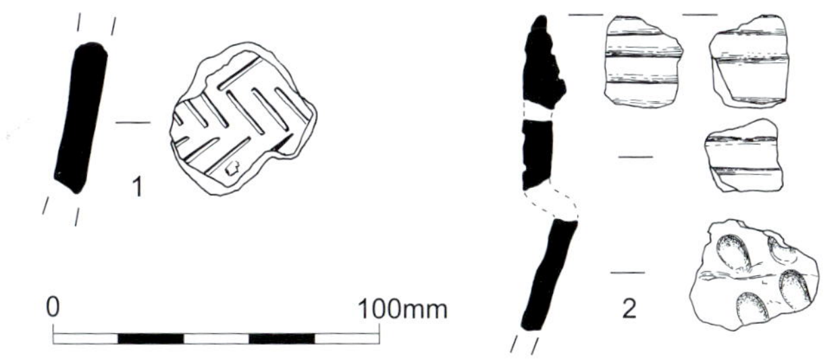

Fig. 86 Prehistoric pottery

employed in the manufacture of vessels used for burials (Allen and Hopkins 2000, 310). These sherds are parts of two Collared Urns suggesting that a ring ditch, barrow or cemetery of this period lay nearby. The fragmentary and partial nature of the pots indicates that this pottery has been disturbed by subsequent activity in the area and transported to these contexts. However, the condition suggests that the pottery has not moved a great distance.

One of two sherds (Fig. 86, 1) found in inhumation grave 122405, was decorated with incised herringbone decoration. Similar decoration is found on Food Vessels but the grog tempering and the orange finish of the sherds indicates that this is part of the collar of a Collared Urn. The second smaller sherd is undecorated. Identical pottery is known in the region for example from Coneygre Farm, Nottinghamshire (Allen *et al.* 1987, fig. 10.54) and Harston, Leicestershire (Longworth 1984, pl. 8c).

Sherds from pit 122534 (Fig. 86, 2) are also from a Collared Urn. One sherd is from the upper part of the collar with an internally moulded rim, and there are deeply incised horizontal grooves both inside the moulding and on the exterior of the collar. A second sherd is from the collar, showing the incised horizontal decoration and the third sherd from the shoulder has small jabbed circular impressions. A Collared Urn with the same decoration on the collar and rim was found at Kirkby Green in Lincolnshire (Longworth 1984, pl. 130c). A Collared Urn with jabbed circular impressions on the neck and shoulder is known from Wetton, Staffordshire (*ibid.*, pl. 80a).

Both these vessels are therefore fairly typical of Collared Urns found in the region but no firm dates have been established in this area. It is generally considered that this type of pottery came into use about 2000 cal BC and was widely used by 1750 cal BC (Allen and Hopkins 2000, 307; Needham 1996, 131). As the precise form of the vessels is not apparent no closer date can be given.

Romano-British pottery, by Ruth Leary

A total of 5462 sherds (42868 g) from a minimum of 248 vessels was recovered during the course of excavation. The site had suffered from extensive plough damage resulting in only 10 vessels out of those recovered from the minimum of 37 urned cremation burials (including the combined urned and unurned burials) retaining rim sherds to any extent. Most of the pottery came from the cremation graves containing the remains of urned burials, the deposits of pyre debris and the mortuary enclosure ditches (Table 26, Figs 87–9).

Table 26 Quantification of Romano-British pottery in features

Feature type	*ESC*	*ASC*	*Wt (g)*	*Rel % ESC*	*Rel % ASC*	*Rel % wt*
urned cremation burial	389	3908	31,539.7	42.28	71.64	73.62
unurned cremation burial	2	2	106.9	0.22	0.04	0.25
RPD from pits	116	356	1319.0	12.61	6.53	3.08
CRD	38	388	3938.0	3.15	6.07	6.16
inhumation grave	7	110	483.0	0.76	2.02	1.13
ditch	30	52	366.8	3.26	0.95	0.86
RPD from ditch	17	17	176.5	1.85	0.31	0.41
redeposited in inhumation grave	13	105	1220.4	1.41	1.92	2.85
mortuary enc. ditch 126069	23	23	356.6	2.50	0.42	0.83
mortuary enc. ditch 126066	51	59	761.3	5.54	1.08	1.78
mortuary enc. ditch 126154	3	2	35.7	0.33	0.04	0.08
mortuary enc. ditch 126148	81	108	480.3	8.80	1.98	1.12
pit	39	64	333.7	3.48	1.04	0.71
Romano-British pit	2	2	14.2	0.22	0.04	0.03
road-zone ditch	48	78	1385.8	5.22	1.43	3.23
subsoil	16	20	338.2	1.74	0.37	0.79
tree-throw hole	15	15	109.7	1.63	0.27	0.26
unstratified	30	153	902.2	3.26	2.68	2.04
Total	920	5462	42,868	100	100	100

Key: ESC = equivalent sherd count; ASC = actual sherd count; RPD = redeposited pyre debris; CRD = cremation-related deposit

Study of the ceramics allowed the features to be assigned to ceramic groups according to date range and this indicated that use of the cemetery was concentrated in the late 1st–mid-2nd centuries. There was evidence that cremations were still carried out in the mid-3rd century. The material provided valuable evidence for aspects of cremation ritual, including burial procedures. Although the deposition of ceramic grave goods was commonly limited to a single urn containing the remains of the dead, fragments of ceramic pyre goods demonstrated both the range of vessels being placed or thrown on the pyre during the cremation and the careful collection of this material for in clusion in the burial. The dated material showed that different types of vessels were selected for use during the cremation rituals in the late 1st–early 2nd centuries compared to after *c* AD 120. It appears that there was a greater tendency to select burnt coarse ware beakers for inclusion in the grave in the later period. Material from other features, such as the mortuary enclosures and ditches, suggested that these were foci of different types of rituals both from each other and to those carried out at the pyres and graves.

Methodology

A number of problems arose regarding the quantification of the ceramic assemblage. The plough damage and recovery methods had resulted in severe fragmentation of the majority of the burial urns and this resulted in an unacceptable inflation of the sherd count values. In addition many of the urns had lost their upper halves which compounded the quantification dilemma by precluding the possibility of recording estimated vessel equivalents (EVES) using rim percentage values. Assessing the significance of sherd weight difference was problematic when comparing assemblages from graves with those from other earth-dug features because the former originally contained complete, and heavy vessels whereas the latter contained token deposits or random debris, both with smaller lighter sherds representing complete vessels, from already broken vessels.

To try and counter these distortions, two further methods were added. The first was a modification of the count where a vessel which was thought to have been deposited as a single entity, such as a cremation urn, was counted as one sherd rather than 160 or more. This was not altogether satisfactory since it was difficult to assess some of the fragmentary auxiliary vessels such as the small BB1 jars/beakers. Often these were burnt, incompletely represented and in fragments. As some cremation urns were also burnt, in fragments and incomplete, it was not possible to be sure if these auxiliary vessel fragments were pyre debris deposits or smashed vessels, deposited complete. Thus this method did not altogether eradicate the problem but is included to counterbalance the extreme distortion caused by post-burial fragmentation.

In addition, minimum vessel count was added. This was assessed for each discrete feature in terms of how many vessels were represented. One difficulty here was encountered with the road-zone ditches where sherds in the same fabric which were scattered along the ditch were not always easy to assess in terms of minimum number of vessels. In addition, sherds in the same fabric from different features could, in theory, come from the same vessel. This was discounted unless joins could be found and as the principal interest of investigation lay in the nature of individual features on the site and their similarity to other features, this seemed an acceptable procedure. All five means of quantification are included in the tables to facilitate comparison with as wide a range of sites as possible, but the limitations of the data should be borne in mind when they are used. For these reasons analyses of fragmentation and average sherd weights would not be meaningful for this site.

Fabrics and forms

The pottery was divided into detailed fabrics grouped into wares based on the Warwickshire fabric series. Individual fabrics were correlated with the Warwickshire fabric series and this is detailed in Chapter 28, Romano-British pottery fabrics. For the purposes of the study of the cemetery assemblage, the broad ware groups are the most useful for most purposes (Table 27). The most varied ware groups were the reduced and oxidised wares, the latter being uncommon in any case. The reduced wares, apart from BB1 sherds, were all likely to be local wares from nearby kilns, the kilns at Sherifoot Lane and the Mancetter-Hartshill kilns. Distorted and warped sherds from the site suggest that some kilns were operating in the vicinity of Wall which preceded those excavated at Shenstone (Chapter 17). These are easily distinguished from the Shenstone kiln products on grounds of fineness alone. However, although comparison was made with fabric samples from, or identified as from Mancetter-Hartshill and Sherifoot Lane it was difficult to source the reduced wares to individual kilns with much certainty. Detailed comparisons are given below.

Amphora

A single sherd of amphora, the most common type, Dressel 20 from southern Spain, was found on the site and this came from upper fill of the road-boundary ditch 126059 (context 122338, northern-half). Amphorae were scarce on other cemetery sites such as at Brougham and are rare or completely absent on northern cemetery sites (Evans 2004, 337). However at Derby Racecourse, although amphorae were not used as cremation urns or grave goods as at the East London cemetery (Barber and Bowsher 2000, 121), sherds were by no means uncommon in both cremation and inhumations graves (Birss 1985 table 20). The amphora sherds at Derby were not burnt, unlike other non-grave good ceramics from the site, and presumably served some other role in the ritual feasting carried out on the site. In London, amphora sherds were present in the pyre debris (Barber and Bowsher, 2000 table 104) in significant quantities while at Brougham, Cool notes the possibility of the use of olive oil as a base for perfumes used in the preparation of the dead for burial (2004, 439). This aspect of ritual activity was either not carried out at Ryknield Street or was fulfilled by some other, perhaps perishable container.

Black burnished ware 1

This was the second largest single ware group and accounted for some 11–25% of the assemblage with a total centring on 20% suggested by the EVES and minimum vessel count values although, by minimum vessel count, group W was more numerous. Most of this group was identified as normal BB1 but a small group of sherds from small jar/beakers were grey in colour and were classified as fabric R18. These were probably burnt BB1 vessels but the thorough burning made identification rather difficult so a sub-group was used for them. If not true BB1 their forms suggest they were contemporary copies.

Most of the BB1 vessels were jar forms with nearly 60% being full sized jars and *c* 30% small jar/beakers. A

Table 27. Actual and relative quantities of Romano-British fabrics and ware groups

Ware group	Fabric	Totals: Equivalent sherd count	Totals: Actual sherd count	Totals: Weight	Totals: Rim %	Totals: Vessel count	Relative % of whole: Equivalent sherd count	Relative % of whole: Actual sherd count	Relative % of whole: Wt (g)	Relative % of whole: Rim %	Relative % of whole: Vessel count
A	DR20	1	1	119.1		1	0.1	*	0.3	*	0.4
BB1	BB1	216	774	4641.2	424	34	23.5	14.2	10.8	17.7	13.7
	R18	43	48	171.1	39	6	4.7	0.9	0.4	1.6	2.4
BB1 Total		*259*	*822*	*4812.3*	*463*	*40*	*28.2*	*15.0*	*11.2*	*19.3*	*16.1*
C	CT	1	1	0.7		1	0.1	*	*	*	0.4
	CTA1	2	104	424.8	10	1	0.2	1.9	1.0	0.4	0.4
C Total		*3*	*105*	*425.5*	*10*	*2*	*0.3*	*1.9*	*1.0*	*0.4*	*0.8*
F	CC	4	24	80.7	17	2	0.31	0.4	0.2	0.7	0.5
	MG1	1	53	36.2	66	1	0.1	1.0	0.1	2.8	0.4
F Total		*5*	*77*	*116.9*	*83*	*3*	*0.4*	*1.4*	*0.3*	*3.5*	*0.9*
M	M1	2	3	131.8	5	2	0.2	0.1	0.3	0.2	0.8
	MH	19	20	743.1	37	8	2.1	0.4	1.7	1.5	3.2
M Total		*21*	*23*	*874.9*	*42*	*10*	*2.3*	*0.4*	*2.0*	*1.8*	*4.0*
MALV	MALV	1	42	573.5	61	1	0.1	0.8	1.3	2.6	0.4
O	O1	29	29	173.4		4	3.2	0.5	0.4	*	1.6
	O4	12	21	39.5	24	3	1.3	0.4	0.1	1.0	1.2
	O6	3	17	13.3		3	0.3	0.3	*	*	1.6
O Total		*44*	*67*	*226.2*	*24*	*11*	*4.8*	*1.2*	*0.5*	*1.0*	*4.4*
P	P	1	1	3		1	0.1	*	*		0.4
	P3	11	11	21.4		2	1.1	0.2	*		0.8
P Total		*12*	*12*	*24.4*		*3*	*1.2*	*0.2*	*		*1.2*
R	R10	3	3	7.2		1	0.3	0.1	*	*	0.4
	R12	2	2	10.5	10	2	0.2	*	*	0.4	0.8
	R13	1	1	19.7		1	0.1	*	*	*	0.4
	R14	8	111	1502.9	197	4	0.9	2.0	3.5	8.2	1.6
	R15	27	327	2567.7	41	9	2.9	6.0	6.0	1.7	3.6
	R16	105	984	6486.8	349	31	11.4	18.0	15.1	14.6	12.9
	R17	2	10	672.6	100	2	0.2	0.2	1.6	4.2	0.8
	R19	6	79	599.9	10	3	0.7	1.4	1.4	0.4	1.2
	R2	17	297	2605.7	108	9	1.8	5.4	6.1	4.5	3.6
	R2/5	6	6	10.4	12	1	0.7	0.1	*	0.5	0.4
	R20	4	4	19.7		1	0.4	0.1	*	*	0.4
	R21	1	2	24.2	20	1	0.1	*	0.1	0.8	0.4
	R22	30	160	2325.5	167	9	3.3	2.9	5.4	7.0	3.6
	R23	3	3	10		1	0.3	0.1	*	*	0.4
	R24		8	6.5		0	*	0.1	*	*	*
	R4	8	55	894.6	5	6	0.9	1.0	2.1	0.2	2.4
	R5	27	601	4951.3	163	20	2.9	11.0	11.6	6.8	8.1
	R7	39	541	3951.7	7	4	4.2	9.9	9.2	0.3	1.6
	R8	1	1	11.6		1	0.1	*	*	*	0.4
	R9	3	122	2830.8		3	0.3	2.2	6.6	*	1.2
R Total		*293*	*3317*	*29509.3*	*1189*	*110*	*31.8*	*60.7*	*68.8*	*49.7*	*44.4*
S	TS	43	216	786.8	247	12	4.4	4.0	1.8	10.6	4.9
SV	SV1	11	11	82.1		2	1.2	0.2	0.2	*	0.8
	SV4	3	4	40.3		1	0.3	0.1	0.1	*	0.4
SV Total		*14*	*15*	*122.4*	*0*	*3*	*1.5*	*0.3*	*0.3*	*	*1.2*
W	FLA	2	1	14.4	21	2	0.2	*	*	0.9	0.8
	FLA2	42	139	1760.2	63	12	4.3	2.6	4.1	2.7	4.9
	FLA3	127	282	2081.2	125	28	13.1	5.2	4.9	5.4	11.4
	FLA4	40	40	230.5		3	4.1	0.7	0.5		1.2
	FLA5	3	57	442.4	9	3	0.31	1.1	1.0	0.4	1.2
W Total		*214*	*519*	*4528.7*	*218*	*48*	*22.1*	*9.5*	*10.6*	*9.4*	*19.5*
WS	FLB	1	1	7.4		1	0.1	*	0.02		0.4
	FLB2	9	245	740.6	57	3	0.9	4.5	1.7	2.5	1.2
WS Total		*10*	*246*	*748*	*57*	*4*	*1.0*	*4.5*	*1.7*	*2.5*	*1.6*
Total		920	5462	42868	2394	246	100%	100%	100%	100%	100%

* = <0.1%

very small number of sherds from open vessels were identified and these came from ditches 126059 and 126065. All but one of the jars with rims surviving had slightly splayed necks with everted or beaded rim tips. These would be consistent with a date in the Hadrianic or early Antonine period. Only two of the jars had wavy line neck burnish. One of these, from cremation grave 122727, had a fairly upright neck and may be as early as the Hadrianic period (Fig. 87, 5). The other, from redeposited pyre debris in pit 122030, had a more splayed neck, perhaps of the mid-2nd century (Fig. 88, 40). Jars with taller splayed rims such as Gillam's (1976) nos 3 and 4 were absent suggesting activity declined after the early Antonine period. The jar from inhumation grave 122364 was of much later date with its splayed rim, obtuse lattice burnish and grooved shoulder (Fig. 89, 49). This must date from the late 3rd century, *c* AD 270+ (*cf.* Holbrook and Bidwell 1991) at the earliest and it was from this grave that another BB1 jar, a small beaker form, with obtuse lattice was recovered. A third jar with this late form of decoration was found in tree hollow 122907 while one with right-angled lattice came from ditch 126065 (upper fill 122483).

The small jars/beakers are a group given an inception date in the early Antonine period by Holbrook and Bidwell but continuing through the 3rd century and into the first half of the 4th century (1991, 94). Gillam does propose some dating guidelines within his scheme (1976) in which those which copy the typology of larger jars are dated accordingly and those with simpler forms, particularly the rim, are all dated within the 2nd century. Gillam noted that the Nene Valley beakers may have ousted this form in the North in the late 2nd century. The dating of these vessels is not very satisfactory unless diagnostic decoration is present such as the obtuse lattice on the beaker from inhumation grave 122364. Although some vessels are dated mid–late 2nd century in the catalogue by reference to Gillam 1976, an extension of the dating into the late 2nd century cannot be suggested on the basis of these beaker types alone without a better dated sequence.

In the Midlands the type is rare at sites like Derby Little Chester, where it only occurred in Antonine phases (Birss 1985, table 4) with only one unburnt example from the Racecourse cemetery, a sherd from inhumation grave 160 (Birss 1985, table 20 and archive catalogue). At Alcester very few of these small jars are recorded (Lee and Lindquist 1994, 43 B2 and 3, both dated early–mid-2nd century; Ferguson 2001, 50–1 and 182–3) while at Tiddington only one handled beaker was noted (Booth 1996a) and at Coleshill only two vessels of this type, both in Antonine groups (Booth 2006, nos 132 and 268). Other sites in the Midlands tell a similar story.

At the New Cemetery site, Rocester, nine examples were recorded (of at least 660 vessels; Leary 1996, fig. 19, no. 9 and archive catalogue) and at Rocester Old Shops some ten small jars of this type were represented (of at least 400 vessels; Leary forthcoming a). At Ryknield Street the 12 small BB1 jars represent a larger than normal proportion of the total of 242 vessels by minimum vessel count. It would appear that in the absence of fine ware beakers, small jars in BB1 and reduced wares were being selected for use in the funerary rites and in subsequent deposition in the graves whether whole or in pieces. Certainly only two examples were apparently unburnt.

Fabric group C

This very small group comprised shell-tempered wares. Only one vessel form was found, a rebated-rim jar with horizontal combing/rilling outside upper body. This compared with Warwickshire series C41 which occurred in late 1st–early 2nd century phases but seemed particularly common in the early 2nd century (Coleshill; Booth forthcoming, table 2). The fabric was associated with forms such as rebated-rim jars and storage jars of 1st–2nd century type at Coleshill.

Fabric group F fine wares

Fine wares were very poorly represented. Only three vessels were identified in this category: a tiny burnt scrap of roughcast ware, probably from a beaker, a colour-coated pentice-moulded beaker and a mica-dusted ware beaker. The MG1 beaker was from cremation grave 122025 (Fig. 87) while the roughcast ware scrap was from the mortuary enclosure ditch 126148. The roughcast ware sherd was too small and burnt to either source the ware or reconstruct the form. The MG1 beaker was indented and belonged to a group common in the early 2nd century (Marsh 1978, type 21) and the fabric is found in late 1st–early 2nd century deposits at Alcester (Ferguson 2001, 177). The pentice-moulded beaker was extremely burnt and fragmented. It bore fine surface cracks all over making fabric identification difficult. It had clearly been slipped/colour-coated and its fairly fine quartz-tempered fabric was not a close match to the range of Nene Valley pentice moulded beakers of the late 3rd–4th centuries. A likely source would be the late kiln at Hartshill producing very similar vessels in the early 4th century (Bird and Young 1981, fig. 17.5, no.5).

Mortaria

Only ten mortaria were identified from the site and these were predominantly of Mancetter-Hartshill type. Undiagnostic sherds from one white ware mortarium were badly burnt but were probably from Mancetter-Hartshill while a further vessel may have been of local manufacture, perhaps at Shenstone. All but one vessel were bead and flange mortaria of the early 2nd century with one painted smooth hammerhead mortarium of the mid-3rd–mid-4th century (Fig. 89, 53). Two of the mortaria were associated with a redeposited cremation burial (from pit 122922), and this vessel had been burnt. A small and very abraded sherd of mortarium came from inhumation grave 122526 and this was probably residual.

Another small, burnt sherd came from redeposited pyre debris in pit 122784 and three larger sherds came from mortuary enclosure ditch 126066 (Fig. 89, 54). The latter appeared to be misfired and were distorted suggesting the vessel may have been a waster from a local kiln.

Several sherds from a bead and flange mortarium came from the secondary fill of the road-flanking ditch 126062 (context 122926, north end) (Fig. 89, 55) and these were singed in places in a way that suggested burning through usage rather than burning on a pyre. A further sherd from the waster from mortuary enclosure ditch 126066 was found in tree hollow 122527. The remaining mortaria came from the subsoil or were unstratified.

Oxidised ware

These wares were uncommon and often comprised small, abraded undiagnostic sherds. The majority were likely to be local oxidised wares but some 16%

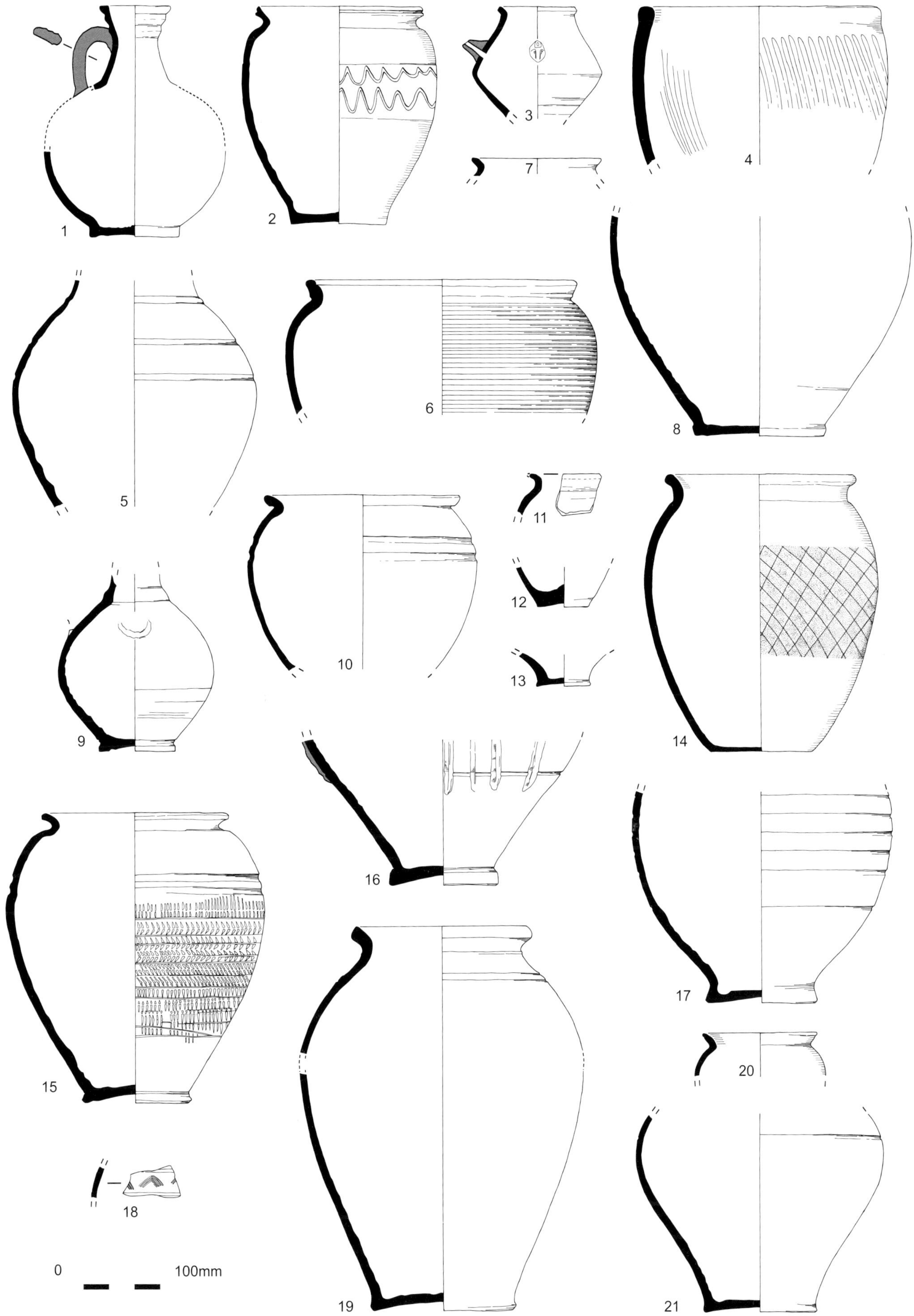

Fig. 87 Romano-British pottery

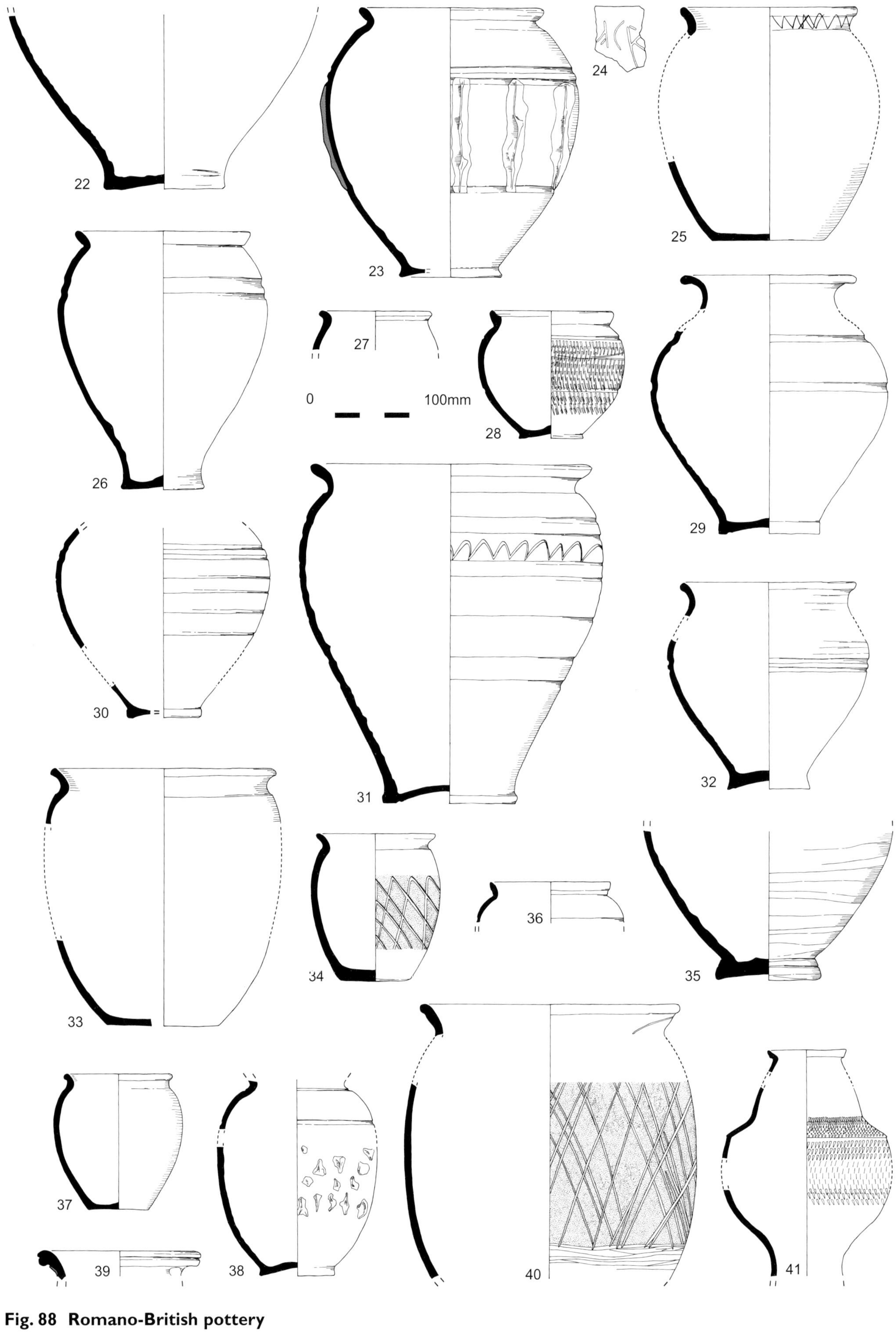

Fig. 88 Romano-British pottery

compared well with Severn Valley ware. Only two forms were identified – a rebated rim jar and a bifid rim lid. At Mancetter-Hartshill and Derby Little Chester kilns the former type is present in oxidised wares and is current from the late 1st to the mid-2nd century at Derby, being replaced by the cupped-rim Derbyshire ware jars from AD 140 onwards.

The lack of oxidised wares dating to the late 1st–mid 2nd century on the site is noticeable. At Tiddington, oxidised coarse wares only account for 12–8% of the assemblages (using sherd count) and the majority of these were Severn Valley wares. In spite of one of the oxidised wares at Tiddington being a product of its kiln, only 3.8% was recovered from the contemporary early 2nd century phase of the nearby settlement. At Coleshill just over 12% of the assemblage comprised oxidised coarse wares and most of these were identified as Mancetter-Hartshill products. This level was more or less constant throughout the occupation. Similarly at Rocester oxidised wares contributed some 7% of the total assemblage with a greater proportion in the late 1st–early 2nd centuries when military potters are likely to have been producing fine oxidised table wares for the fort (Leary 1996, fig. 28). To the north, at Derby, oxidised wares were also low in number (Martin 2000, table 5). Sites to the south such as Metchley (Hancocks 2004, 66 and table 10) do have more oxidised coarse wares but these are predominantly Severn Valley ware. Similarly at Greensforge, Severn Valley wares were not only the largest fabric group but were the only oxidised ware represented (Evans 1996–7, table 4). At Alcester a similar situation arises with Severn Valley dominating the oxidised ware group which made up 33% of the total assemblage (Evans 1994, 149). It would appear that Wall was situated on the periphery of the distribution zone for this ware, and indeed on the edge of a zone where oxidised wares were favoured, in the same way as Tiddington and Coleshill seem to be (Evans 1994, 149; Booth 1986, 35).

Reduced wares

This group was the largest from the site and this was undoubtedly partially a result of the use of reduced ware jars as cremation urns in the early 2nd century. The most numerous fabrics were R16 then R5 and R2. R5 tended to have larger quartz inclusions but other attributes were very similar to R16. R5 and R16 were very similar and merged into one another suggesting they may be part of a larger related group of fabrics. Rusticated jars and neckless, everted-rim jars with a shoulder groove(s) of the late 1st–mid-2nd century, small jar/beakers, a narrow-necked jar with everted rim (Fig. 88, 46), and carinated bowls with plain and bifid rim were identified in fabric R16 (Fig. 89, 56) and rusticated jars, neckless, everted-rim jars and small jar/beakers in fabric R5 with the addition of a wide-mouthed jar with everted rim, a bifid-rim narrow-necked jar, possibly a facepot or flagon (Fig. 88, 39), and a tettine (Fig. 87, 3). One of the R5 neckless jars was decorated with a burnished zigzag line motif (Fig. 87, 31) rather than the more common shoulder groove or rustication while a second jar with a bifurcated rim had a double wavy line burnish. One of the R16 beakers had rouletted decoration (Fig. 88, 28).

The carinated bowls have been given various date ranges. At Coleshill quite a number of well preserved examples were found in a group dated to the mid–late 2nd century and at Tiddington a similar date range was suggested. Gillam (1970) dated this form AD 160–200 in the north. At Leicester a general 2nd century date is given (Clarke 1999, no. 316). At York the form was dated by Perrin to the mid–late 2nd century (1990, no. 1217) but by Monaghan to the early–mid-2nd century (1997, form BB). This type is also known in phases given a date range in the late 1st–mid-2nd century type, as at Wall, where Ball and Ball (1983–4, fig. 13, no. 2), in phase 2, dated it to the late 1st–early 2nd centuries by the associated mortaria, and at Derby (Brassington 1971, no. 524; Dool *et al.* 1985, fig. 78, no. 59). A date range centring on the mid-2nd century but extending into the late 2nd century would accommodate the existing evidence. The earlier date range of the jar and beaker forms in these fabrics would support a date earlier rather than later in the period. R16 compares with fabrics made at Mancetter-Hartshill and is also similar to wares from the kiln at Sherifoot Lane. However, kilns closer to Wall may have existed at this period, as suggested by the evidence of wasters and distorted vessels, perhaps 'seconds', both at the cemetery (see below, cremation grave 122780 and cremation-related deposit in cut 122083) and from Wall itself (fine grey ware jars and a white ware beaker; Leary 1995–6, nos 18, 19 and one as no. 25). Such kilns may be the precursors of the Shenstone kiln.

R7 and R15 (Fig. 89, 57) were a similar pair with R7 being rather coarser than R15. These fabrics had a distinctive brown core like the coarser R4 fabric from the Shenstone kiln. Carinated bowls from Coleshill, thought to be from the Sherifoot Lane kiln or Mancetter-Hartshill, were in a similar fabric (Warwickshire R18). Similar carinated bowls with bifid or bead rims were present at Ryknield Street in R7.

Other fabric groups with smaller numbers of sherds may have been variations in the clay sources or from other small kilns. Only undiagnostic bodysherds were found in fabrics R8, R9 and R10. Fabrics R12, R14, R20, R22 and R24 were used to make small jars/beakers with short everted rims while examples of the neckless everted-rim jars of late 1st–early 2nd century type were found in R17, R22 and R23. One of the small jar/beakers in R20 was particularly notable in having hairpin decoration *en barbotine* which had fired a greyish white. This may have been white paint intended to appear more prominently than it does now. This decorative motif is found on Central Gaulish beakers of the Flavian–Hadrianic period and may be copying such imports. Examples of ring-and-dot type beakers from Mancetter-Hartshill are known with hairpin decoration replacing the rings.

An R22 jar/beaker had a central rouletted zone around the body (Fig. 87, 15). Another R22 sherd from an unknown vessel type was decorated with combed inverted V motifs. A narrow-necked everted rim jar was identified in R19 and another bead rim bowl, possibly one of the carinated types, was identified in R21. A ribbed flagon handle was also present in R22 (Fig. 89, 58). From the vessel typology these fabrics are likely to be of similar date in the early–mid-2nd century, perhaps extending into the late 2nd century after they may have been superseded by the coarser fabrics from the Shenstone kilns.

The small amounts of R2 and R4 fabrics found in the Shenstone kiln (Chapter 17) are not surprising given the suggested date range of the cemetery. The only identifiable form in R4 was a wide-mouthed jar similar to those made at Shenstone. Two definite examples were present. Wide-mouthed jars were uncommon finds on the site but the definite examples, from cremation graves, suggest activity at the cemetery overlapped with the industry represented by the Shenstone kiln to a limited extent.

The selection of reduced ware forms was clearly heavily influenced by the need for cremation urns and the desire to accompany these with small jars, interpreted here as beakers. This latter group has been noted elsewhere as a type often found in ritual or burial contexts (Monaghan 1997, type JZ). The use of this vessel type in a possible foundation deposit at the *mansio* site, Wall, is instructive here (Round 1990–1, 62 no. 165).

No platters, dishes or cups were present. Narrow-necked and wide-mouthed jars are rare, although this may be due to chronological considerations since white ware flagons served as liquid holders during the main period of activity on the site and wide-mouthed jars did not become generally abundant until the late 2nd century onwards. The latter do not seem to be a type favoured for use on cemetery sites, *cf.* the low number at Brougham in a region and period where wide-mouthed jars might be expected to be found in reasonable quantities in the ceramic population (Evans 2004, tables 8.11 and 8.19).

Lids are also rare and specialist items such as strainers, colanders or cheesepresses are absent apart from the tettine and the possible face pot. This last form is commonly associated with graves in the Rhineland and also with temples or bath buildings (Braithwaite 1984, 124). At Brougham a facepot and two headpots came from the cemetery (Evans 2004, 49, burial 7 and p. 261, P6 and P8). The function of the tettine is not clear but Webster traced its ancestry at least to Mycenaean times and noted that samian examples were restricted to the 2nd century (1981). Suggested functions include feeding cup, lamp filler, invalid cup and vessel for applying liquid clay *en barbotine*. At Usk, Greene favoured the lamp filler function and noted an example of one found with a lamp (1993, 34 type 16). It was present at the Derby Racecourse kilns (Brassington 1980, no. 555 from kiln 7) and also at Alcester (Lee and Lindquist 1994, nos O439). Its association here with an infant burial makes the feeding cup interpretation particularly appealing. However, at Brougham and London's Eastern cemetery these vessels occurred with adult burials (Evans 2004, 157, 166.2; Barber and Bowsher 2000, 228, B713).

White ware

This category of fabrics was used almost exclusively for flagons or jugs with one possible beaker represented by a small everted rim, although a jug is possible. Three fabric groups are represented, two of which are likely to come from the Mancetter-Hartshill kilns and the third is in the *Verulamium* region tradition. The *Verulamium* region examples are uncommon. This could reflect the site chronology, since the widespread distribution of *Verulamium* products in the late 1st–early 2nd centuries may have preceded the most intensive use of the cemetery. The other two fabrics were used to make ring-necked flagons with upright necks and even-sized rings and splayed necks with prominent upper rings. The ring-necked form is well-known with a chronological progression from upright even spaced rings to widely splayed rings with a prominent upper ring. The examples present compare with examples from the late 1st–early 2nd and early–mid-2nd centuries. Two other forms were present – a small flagon with upright bead rim above a groove, perhaps as Gillam (1970, no. 17) dated AD 150–250 (Fig. 89, 59), and a large jug or flagon with an out-curving rim. In both cases little of the vessel was present and firm form identification was difficult. It was, however, clear from the bodysherds that fine, thin-walled small flagons and large, thick walled flagons or jugs were both present. The contrasting size of these types suggests that they may have had different functions.

White slipped ware

Only one white-slipped vessel was identified, a flagon with splayed ring-necked rim of late 1st–early 2nd century type.

Handmade fabrics

Four contexts contained handmade sherds of pre-Roman Iron Age type – inhumation grave 122405 and two pits of unknown function (122653 and 122923) contained single sherds or small scraps from vessels of the type and these seem best explained as residual material. However, cremation grave 120202 contained a substantial amount of a MALV tubby jar with rounded rim oblique burnished streaks (Fig. 87, 4). Such vessels occur in 1st and 2nd century groups at Coleshill and Tiddington. Similar vessels have been found at the *mansio* site at Wall (Round 1990–1, fig. 15, no. 8) and in an Antonine pit at site K at the fort (Gould 1963–4, fig. 14, nos 84–5). At Metchley this ware accounts for nearly 10% of the assemblage by weight (Green 2001, table 17) and at Alcester similar tubby jars with oblique burnish lines were given an Antonine date.

Chronology

The date of activity on the site overall can be assessed in terms of the date range of the fabrics and forms present

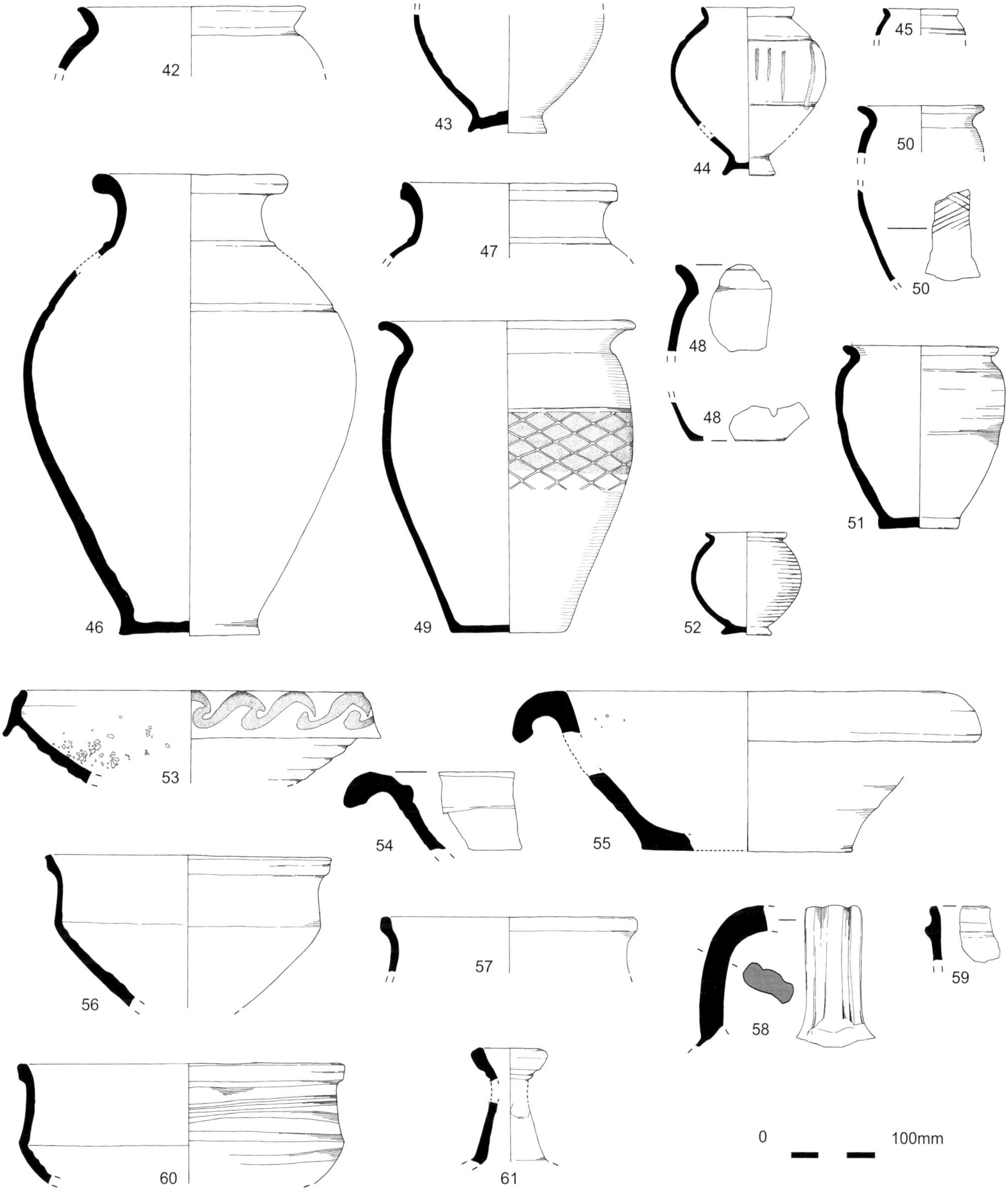

Fig. 89 Romano-British pottery

from all features and the date of individual features. The former evidence is discussed here whereas the latter is discussed below by feature type.

The absence of fabric group E and 1st century types present at Wall such as platters, early flagons, butt beaker types, early fine wares and the small amount of early wares such as the *Verulamium* region fabrics suggests activity commenced in the late 1st or, perhaps, the early 2nd century AD (Table 28).

The largest fabric group by weight was R16, a fine local reduced ware, used in the manufacture of rusticated jars, neckless beakers and jars with short everted rims of late 1st–early 2nd century date and bowls with everted or bifid rims of a type common in the mid–late 2nd centuries at Coleshill and Tiddington and in the early–mid-2nd century at Derby. The second largest group by weight was fabric R5, a slightly coarser fabric than R16 but probably part of a fabric continuum.

Table 28 Quantities of Romano-British wares, fabrics and vessel types by minimum vessel count

Ware group	*Fabric*	*Bowl*	*Dish*	*B/D*	*Cup*	*BKR*	*JMINI*	*F*	*Tettine*	*J*	*N-N jar*	*W-M jar*	*Lid*	*Mortarium*	*Unid.*	*Total*
A	DR20	–	–	–	–	–	–	–	–	–	–	–	–	–	1	1
BB1	BB1	–	–	3	–	–	7	–	–	23	–	–	–	–	1	34
	R18	–	–	–	–	–	4	–	–	–	–	–	–	–	2	6
C	C	–	–	–	–	–	–	–	–	1	–	–	–	–	1	2
F	CC	–	–	–	–	2	–	–	–	–	–	–	–	–	–	2
	MG1	–	–	–	–	1	–	–	–	–	–	–	–	–	–	1
M	M	–	–	–	–	–	–	–	–	–	–	–	–	2	–	2
	M1	–	–	–	–	–	–	–	–	–	–	–	–	1	–	1
	MH	–	–	–	–	–	–	–	–	–	–	–	–	6	–	6
	MW	–	–	–	–	–	–	–	–	–	–	–	–	1	–	1
MALV	MALV	–	–	–	–	–	–	–	–	1	–	–	–	–	–	1
O	O1	–	–	–	–	–	–	–	–	1	–	–	–	–	3	4
	O4	–	–	–	–	–	–	–	–	1	–	–	1	–	1	3
	O6	–	–	–	–	–	–	–	–	–	–	–	–	–	3	3
	SV1	–	–	–	–	–	–	–	–	1	–	–	–	–	1	2
	SV4	–	–	–	–	–	–	–	–	–	–	–	–	–	1	1
P	P	–	–	–	–	–	–	–	–	–	–	–	–	–	1	1
	P3	–	–	–	–	–	–	–	–	–	–	–	–	–	2	2
R	R10	–	–	–	–	–	–	–	–	–	–	–	–	–	1	1
	R12	–	–	–	–	–	1	–	–	1	–	–	–	–	–	2
	R13	–	–	–	–	–	–	–	–	1	–	–	–	–	–	1
	R14	–	–	–	–	–	1	–	–	1	–	–	–	–	2	4
	R15	2	–	–	–	–	–	–	–	6	–	–	–	–	1	9
	R16	3	–	–	–	–	10	–	–	11	2	–	–	–	5	31
	R17	–	–	–	–	–	–	–	–	2	–	–	–	–	–	2
	R19	–	–	–	–	–	–	–	–	2	1	–	–	–	–	3
	R2	–	–	–	–	–	1	–	–	4	1	1	1	–	1	9
	R2/5	–	–	–	–	–	1	–	–	–	–	–	–	–	–	1
	R20	–	–	–	–	–	1	–	–	–	–	–	–	–	–	1
	R21	1	–	–	–	–	–	–	–	–	–	–	–	–	–	1
	R22	–	–	–	–	–	4	1	–	4	–	–	–	–	–	9
	R23	–	–	–	–	–	–	–	–	1	–	–	–	–	–	1
	R24	–	–	–	–	–	–	–	–	–	–	–	–	–	–	0
	R4	–	–	–	–	–	–	–	–	2	–	3	–	–	1	6
	R5	–	–	–	–	–	1	–	1	12	–	1	–	–	5	20
	R7	1	–	–	–	–	–	–	–	3	–	–	–	–	–	4
	R8	–	–	–	–	–	–	–	–	1	–	–	–	–	–	1
	R9	–	–	–	–	–	–	–	–	2	–	–	–	–	1	3

Ware group	*Fabric*	*Bowl*	*Dish*	*B/D*	*Cup*	*BKR*	*JMINI*	*F*	*Tettine*	*J*	*N-N jar*	*W-M jar*	*Lid*	*Mortarium*	*Unid.*	*Total*
S	TS	5	5	–	2	–	–	–	–	–	–	–	–	–	1	12
W	FLA	–	–	–	–	–	–	1	–	–	–	–	–	–	1	2
	FLA2	–	–	–	–	1	–	10	–	–	–	–	–	–	1	12
	FLA3	–	–	–	–	–	–	26	–	–	–	–	–	–	2	28
	FLA4	–	–	–	–	–	–	2	–	–	–	–	–	–	1	3
	FLA5	–	–	–	–	–	–	3	–	–	–	–	–	–	–	3
WS	FLB	–	–	–	–	–	–	1	–	–	–	–	–	–	–	1
	FLB2	–	–	–	–	–	–	3	–	–	–	–	–	–	–	3
Total		12	5	3	2	4	31	47	1	81	4	5	2	10	40	246

This fabric was used principally in the manufacture of neckless, everted rim jars of the late 1st–early 2nd century but included a tettine and one wide-mouthed jar similar to those made at site 15. The predominance of these two fabrics with their early forms strongly indicates activity in the late 1st–early 2nd centuries.

A group of carinated bowls with bead or bifid rims (see discussion under fabric R) were paralleled locally in contexts dated to the mid–late 2nd century but, given the absence of late 2nd century pottery generally, these may all belong to the earlier part of that date range.

The third largest fabric group was BB1. The forms present included jars and beakers with only three bowls or dishes represented. These last came from ditch deposits and had acute lattice decoration suggesting a Hadrianic–early Antonine date. The jars were predominantly of the type with slightly splayed necks belonging to the Hadrianic–early Antonine period. Two had wavy line neck burnish, a feature which declined after the mid-2nd century, and where detectable, four jars had acute lattice burnish. There were four vessels with obtuse or right-angled lattice, three jars and a beaker. Two of these, a jar and a beaker (Fig. 89, 49–50), came from inhumation grave 122364, but were both burnt suggesting they may have derived from a disturbed late cremation burial. The rim of the jar is just greater than the girth suggesting a late 3rd century date, *c* AD 270+ (*cf.* Holbrook and Bidwell 1991). The other two vessels came from ditch 126065 and tree hollow 122907. The small BB1 beakers were difficult to date precisely and all but one seemed to lack lattice burnish. Holbrook and Bidwell (*ibid.*, 94) indicated these should be dated from the early Antonine period onwards and comparison with Gillam suggests that most may belong to the mid–late 2nd century (1976, nos 17, 20 and 21). The BB1 vessels therefore extend the date range as late as the late 3rd century and indicate that this may have included the rite of cremation.

Overall white wares accounted for some 11% of the assemblage by weight but only four forms were represented: an upright ring necked flagon of the early 2nd century, two splayed neck, ring neck flagons with prominent upper rings of the early–mid-2nd century, a large flagon with outcurving heavy rim, perhaps of the early 2nd century and a very abraded rim sherd which seems to have an upright beaded rim with grooved neck, which compares with examples dated from the mid-2nd to mid-3rd centuries. Unfortunately the other vessels were represented by body and base sherds only. A white slipped ring necked flagon with splayed neck also belongs to the late 1st–early 2nd century.

Other types which extend this date range included a colour coated pentice moulded beaker dated to the early 4th century from the cremation-related deposit in pit 122042 and a smooth MH2 hammerhead mortarium with painted 'S' motifs from subsoil layer 122006, dated to the mid-3rd–mid-4th centuries.

There were very few fine wares, a mica-gilt beaker and a colour coated roughcast ware beaker, and no Nene Valley colour coated ware. The lack of Nene Valley colour coated wares might suggest a decline in activity which left traces in the ceramic record around the mid–late 2nd century. However, at Tiddington, Nene Valley wares were also uncommon before the 3rd–4th centuries while at Coleshill only small quantities are found in the Antonine period. Nonetheless its complete absence agrees with the date range suggested by the other types which centres on the early–mid-2nd century with some activity which may extend into the late 2nd century and only a small amount of material dating to the late 2nd–early 4th centuries.

Phasing

The contexts were put into groups to facilitate examination of the chronological phasing of the site. The groups were: 1. late 1st–early 2nd, 2. early–mid-2nd, 3. mid-2nd, possibly extending into the late 2nd century, 4. late 2nd–early/mid-3rd, 5. mid-3rd–mid-4th, 6. mid-1st–2nd, 7. AD 120–200, 8. AD 120+ and 9 undated. The groups overlap and undiagnostic sherds such as white ware bodysherds were given wide date ranges such as mid 1st–2nd century. These were not very satisfactory but did allow some quantification of the number of features datable to each period (NB. for stratigraphic purposes and other finds analysis these groups were simplified to L1st – E 2nd C = Phase 1; E–M 2nd C = Phases 2, 3, 6, 7 and 8; L 2nd – M 3rd /4th C = Phases 4 and 5; see Grave catalogue). The number of undated groups, however, highlights the unreliability of the sample. The pottery was grouped for this purpose either by features such as cremation grave, inhumation grave and pit or by context, such as primary ditch fill, secondary ditch fill unless the date of each was identical. Pottery from each mortuary enclosure ditch made up one group as they seemed to be chronologically homogeneous. The pottery shows a strong presence in the 2nd century with very little thereafter. Although the date range extends into the 1st century, the lack of any sherds of ware group E on the site suggests that this would be late in that century. There is only one sherd from a ring and dot beaker and a Trajanic or Hadrianic date would be acceptable for most of the vessels dating to the broad period covered by the late 1st–early 2nd centuries. The neckless everted rim jars and rusticated jars were mostly of the conical or pear shape rather than the globular form common in the pre-Flavian and Flavian period.

The later groups dating to the late 2nd to mid-3rd–mid 4th centuries were restricted to sherds from subsoil deposits, a BB1 jar sherd with obtuse lattice burnish from tree hollow 122907, a second similar sherd with right-angled lattice burnish from ditch 126065, the colour coated pentice moulded beaker from the cremation-related deposit in pit 122042, the late burnt BB1 vessels from inhumation grave 122364 and possibly the bifid rim vessel from cremation grave 129083.

The road-zone ditches

A minimum of 18 vessels was found in the road-zone ditches 126059 and 126062. Only an abraded mortarium rim from ditch 126062 could be dated; the profile of this vessel suggested a date in the early 2nd century, *c* AD 100–130. Ditch 126059 contained rather more material but this came from the upper fills including a dump of stone rubble from the central excavated segment in the northern half of the ditch. This group included a carinated bowl of the type associated with pottery of the mid–late 2nd century at Tiddington and Coleshill (Fig. 89, 60). In other secondary and upper fills undiagnostic BB1 sherds were found giving a date after AD 120.

There was a possible deposit of pyre debris (no bone) in the adjacent excavated segment of ditch 126059 (context 122077). This included a scrap of undated samian, sherds of R1 and a FLA3 flagon rim with a pronounced upper ring and splayed profile, of the early–mid-2nd century (Fig. 89, 61).

Cremation graves

The small numbers of types datable to the 1st century suggest there was little activity until the turn of the century. There are few globular jars of early date and ring-and-dot beakers were scarcely represented. Early flagon types are also missing as are platters, reeded-rim bowls, early beaker types and early jar forms, all present at the military sites at Wall (Gould 1963–4, pottery nos 120, 125, 143–4, 151, 155–6; Leary 1995–6, nos 9, 10, 39, 52 and 46). None of the early 'Belgic type' fabrics typical of the mid–late 1st century were present on the site. At Tiddington fabrics of this group went out of use by the end of the 1st century AD (Booth 1996a). Early wares such as the products of the *Verulamium* region kilns are scarce, also while handmade vessels are absent apart from some residual Iron Age material and the Malvernian tubby jar from grave 120202. Sherds from *Verulamium* region flagons occurred in grave 122651 including a sherd with graffiti (Fig. 88, 24) but this group did not include any other datable ceramics so the generally broad range of late 1st–early 2nd century for this ware could not be narrowed down with confidence. An inception date towards the end of the 1st century AD or at the start of the 2nd century would fit the known ceramic sequence.

The vessels in the mid–late 2nd century group could all date to the mid-2nd century and thus shorten the overall date range for the majority of the cremations. The dated types were BB1 jars and small jars/beakers the dating of which may extend into the second half of the 2nd century, the carinated bowls which seem to be of mid–late 2nd century date (see above) and the wide-mouthed jars which are similar to those from the Shenstone kiln (Chapter 17).

All of these types are likely to overlap chronologically with the group 2 ceramics and the lack of BB1 jars best placed in the late 2nd century suggests a decline in activity after the mid-2nd century. None of the sherds from the cremation graves dates to the 3rd–4th centuries but the substantially complete burnt vessels from inhumation grave 122364 may have derived from a disturbed cremation burial which, if so, would make this the latest cremation undertaken on the site. The cremation grave with the latest date range is 129083 dated thus on account of the bifid rim on a narrow necked jar. Clearly bifid rims were used earlier and are present on a neckless jar of late 1st–early 2nd century type in cremation grave 120202. If the vessel is a facepot then the dating would not be less secure since the sherd is too small to reconstruct the form and such vessels do not have a well established typology.

Redeposited pyre debris

Most of the deposits had only one or two vessels represented although one, from pit 122784 had six vessels. The quantity of burnt sherds in the redeposited pyre debris from the grave fills suggests that a significant proportion of the pyre goods were collected after cremation and deposited with the urn in the grave. The small size of this part of the assemblage coupled with the burnt and abraded condition of the sherds resulted in poor dating for these deposits. The sherds from deposits of pyre debris in pits 122064 and 122857 could only be given a Romano-British date. Pit 122078 was given a *terminus post quem* of AD 120 by the BB1 sherd, while pits 122037 and 122095 could only be broadly assigned to the late 1st–2nd centuries by the white ware sherds present. A grey ware sherd from pit 122553 was from a jar with the typical shoulder grooves of jars of the later 1st–early 2nd centuries, while the samian cup and dish from pit 122975 are also of late 1st century date and the coarse ware is likely to date after AD 120.

Pit 122030 contained sherds from a BB1 jar of early–mid 2nd century date. Pit 122784 was likely to date to the early–mid-2nd century or later on account of the samian. A white ware sherd assigned to ceramic group 4 in the early–mid-3rd century was recovered from an excavated segment of the cemetery boundary ditch 126065 where it cut through the cremation burial made in grave 122154; the redeposited pyre debris from the ditch may have derived from the grave.

Cremation-related deposits

In addition to redeposited burials, these deposits commonly comprised those which could be interpreted as either burials with redeposited pyre debris or redeposited pyre debris, ie the nature of the deposit is uncertain. Pit 122808 was given a date after AD 120 by the BB1 sherd and FLA5 jug. The beaker from pit 122072 is likely to belong to group 1. Pit 122083 contained a BB1 jar of mid-2nd century type. The deposit in pit 122042 contained the remains of six vessels including a burnt, colour-coated pentice moulded beaker dating to the late 3rd–early 4th centuries on present evidence. The redeposited burial in pit 122922 had sherds from a bead and flange mortarium dating to the 2nd century in its fill. The redeposited burial from pit 122059 had sherds of R22, R5 and R24, the first two probably from small jars/beaker. These cannot be precisely dated.

Inhumation graves

Five of the inhumation graves, 122405, 122376, 122408, 122457 and 122964, lacked diagnostic sherds. The burnt condition of the sherds in grave 122964 suggests that these were redeposited from an earlier cremation-related deposit. Grave 122609 contained a burnt sherd from a samian cup form 27g of Hadriantic–early Antonine date, an FLA scrap, two R4 bodysherds and some burnt R16 sherds. It is likely that these sherds were also all redeposited. The two beakers from the possible grave 122977 belong to the late 1st–early 2nd centuries and may be grave goods (Fig. 89, 51–2). Burnt and much abraded sherds from a R16 rusticated jar from grave 122526 dated to the late 1st–early 2nd centuries. These and the incomplete mortarium rim of similar date were residual. Grave 122364 contained large amounts of a burnt BB1 jar and small jar/beaker. Both were extensively burnt and bore all the characteristics of being from a disturbed cremation burial of late 3rd century date.

Thus only one possible inhumation grave, 122977, may have contained grave goods and the rest can only be given a *terminus post quem* from the residual pottery from their fills. Since the grave goods are of late 1st–early 2nd century date and some of the 'residual' pottery is as late as the late 3rd century, the date of the unaccompanied graves cannot be implied.

Mortuary enclosure ditches

The ceramics from the ditches of mortuary enclosures 126069, 126066 and 126154 belonged to group 2. The BB1 sherds and flagon type suggested infilling of these ditches took place around the mid-2nd century. The material from enclosure ditch 126148 may be later as the three carinated bowls from this feature have a date range from the mid–late 2nd century. Ditch 126066, which contained sherds from a ring-necked flagon in fabric FLA3, was cut by the southern cemetery boundary ditch 126065, and some of the small group of pottery from the latter in the vicinity of the mortuary enclosure may have derived from the fill of the former.

Other ditches

The largest fabric group recovered from ditch 126065 was white ware FLA3 and also some FLA2. The diagnostic sherds indicated these were flagon or jugs. They were recovered from an excavated segment where the ditch cut through the cremation burial made in grave 122154 and may have derived from that grave. Other diagnostic sherds from the ditch included a sherd of BB1 with right-angled lattice burnish dating to the first half of the 3rd century from a segment excavated adjacent to the mortuary enclosure ditch 126066.

The post-medieval/modern ditch 126221 contained a residual sherd from a FLA3 flagon body and neck and an R5 sherd from a wide-mouthed jar similar to those from the Shenstone kiln. The later vessel is in a finer fabric than that from the Shenstone kiln and probably dates from the mid-2nd century or later.

Miscellaneous pits, ovens and other features

The pits contained small groups of pottery and were not well dated. A small handmade sherd, smoothed or burnished, which is probably of Iron Age date, was recovered from pit 122923. Pit 122681 could be dated to the Hadrianic–Antonine period by the presence of BB1 sherds in its fill, while white ware sherds from pits 122155 and 122162 made a date range in the early Romano-British period likely. Oven 122358 contained sherds of BB1 giving a date after AD 120. The samian from oven 122069 gave a date in the early–mid-Antonine period.

Vessel form selection

Medium necked jars are the most common single group (Fig. 90). These were selected as cremation urns in nearly every case. There are three examples of small coarse ware jar/beakers, five flagons, possibly two wide-mouthed jars and one example of a narrow-necked jar being used to contain cremated remains but the remainder seem to have been using medium necked jars. Of these types the BB1 jars are commonly associated with cooking activities on domestic sites on the basis on the common occurrences of burnt matter on the rim and shoulder. The neckless, short everted rim jars of the late 1st–early 2nd centuries seem to have been the equivalent of these BB1 jars during the earlier period in that their numbers declined as BB1 jars increased. Sooting is not as common on those types (*cf.* the same situation at Alcester; Lee and Lindquist 1994, 9), however, suggesting perhaps differences in cooking methods. Their overall size also contrasted with the BB1 jars being slightly smaller in rim diameter. The basis of selection was probably the convenient size and shape, ideal for the deposition of the ashes. Most of the vessels of uncertain form were almost certainly jars. If all the jars and unknown vessels are combined a total of 52% is reached, a proportion which would compare with that found at Alcester (*ibid.*, fig. 44), rather less than that found at the rural site of Tiddington (*c* 75%) but a similar quantity to that found at Coleshill (53%).

Flagons were the next most common vessel type at nearly 20% of the assemblage. This number of flagons would be outstanding on a domestic site in Warwickshire. At Coleshill a proportion of 2% of flagons was considered unusually high and a consequence of the proximity of kilns at Mancetter-Hartshill producing flagons. On cemetery sites, however, flagons or equivalent liquid containers (Evans 2004, 353) are disproportionately common. At Derby Racecourse cemetery flagons were used both as urns and as auxiliary vessels, one accompanying a pig burial. The disproportionate amount of flagon and fine ware beaker sherds from the fills of both cremation and inhumation graves in the walled cemetery along with the frequency of burning on them, at Derby, suggested that these vessel groups were an important part of the cremation rituals carried out on the site (Birss 1985, 166–7 and table 20).

Three flagons were used as cremation urns, a further two were probably deposited as auxiliary vessels in the graves and two more were either damaged auxiliary vessels or pyre goods. Two of the flagons used as urns were burnt. Further burnt sherds from flagons in the cremation graves seem to be fragments of pyre goods. Six examples of this were identified with a further two that may be pyre goods or damaged auxiliary vessels. The status of unburnt sherds in the cremation graves was difficult to determine. These could be pyre related goods which had escaped fire damage, or fragments from flagons used in the primary stage of mortuary rite but not deposited on the pyre.

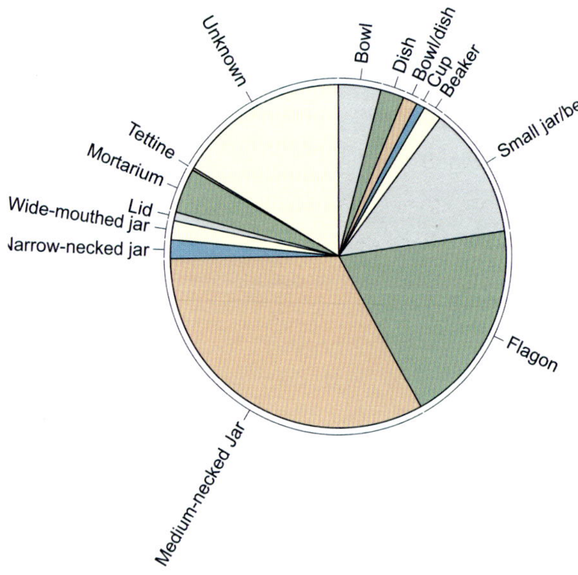

Fig. 90 Romano-British pottery: proportion of vessel types using vessel count

The small jars or beakers were the next most numerous category (Table 29). These came predominantly from urned burials and were made either in BB1 or reduced ware, being smaller versions of the larger jars. The majority of the small jars/beakers from cremation graves were burnt. Relatively similar numbers of this type were found in the redeposited pyre debris and cremation-related deposits with all the identifiable vessels from the latter being of this type. Unlike in the case of the medium-necked jars, the burnt examples were divided fairly evenly between the two ware groups with one more BB1 vessel being burnt. The burning was often thorough and severe, and the vessels were more often fragmentary with only one complete example (unstratified). The burnt examples of this type were found principally in the cremation graves, cremation-related deposits, amongst the redeposited pyre debris and in the inhumation graves. This last comprised a vessel which was probably from a redeposited cremation burial in inhumation grave 122364. Unburnt examples were found in a greater range of features.

These small jars were undoubtedly related to the drinking activity evidenced by the flagons. Their burnt condition may indicate that they were thrown, with their contents, onto the pyre at some point, perhaps as a libation. The sherds or complete vessels of this type made up a greater proportion of the assemblage from the graves than the redeposited pyre debris and,

Table 29 Incidence of small jars/beakers

Deposit	*BB1*	*Reduced ware*
Cremation grave	7	6
Redeposited burial	–	1
Redeposited pyre debris	–	5
Cremation-related deposit	–	3
Inhumation grave	3	2
Mortuary enclosure ditch	–	1
Road-zone ditch	–	2
Uncertain	1	–
Total	11	20

significantly, a higher proportion of burnt examples were found in the cremation graves than amongst the redeposited pyre debris. Presumably this was because they had been collected from the pyre site for inclusion in the grave.

Cups and fine ware beakers were uncommon but included a burnt beaker from the cremation-related deposit in pit 122042. Table wares such as bowls and dishes were also uncommon. Only two of these were burnt, both samian dishes from redeposited pyre debris in pits 122975 and 122784. Three came from cremation graves – a carinated bowl from 122044, a form 36 dish from 129074 and a near complete form 18 dish from 129075. The majority of these bowls and dishes came from the mortuary enclosures with moderate amounts from the ditches and redeposited pyre debris, and the least from the cremation graves. This compares well with evidence from elsewhere in the Roman world for vessels associated with feasting being concentrated around the *ustrina* (the cremation areas; Polfer 2000, fig. 3.5).

Lids and mortaria were rare and represented only in the inhumation graves, mortuary enclosure ditch 126066, road-zone boundary ditches, a tree hollow, a cremation-related deposit and one unurned cremation burial. The numbers are rather small for analysis but several were burnt. They may have been used for the production of foodstuff for the ritual ceremonies but not selected for inclusion in the burial. The burnt condition of some examples is misleading. Except for the example from pit 122922, the burning on the others seems to be singeing through usage, not an uncommon condition in mortaria. One example, from mortuary enclosure ditch 126066 and the adjacent tree hollow, was distorted and is likely to be a waster.

Evidence for rituals

The redeposited pyre debris and an inhumation grave with what appeared to be a redeposited cremation burial within its fill had the greatest proportion of burnt vessels with significant amounts also found in the cremation graves, mortuary enclosure 126124 (but only three vessels *in toto* in the latter) and amongst the unstratified material. The relative quantities of burnt vessels in each vessel type can be seen in Table 30 and are compared with overall proportions of vessel types in the site assemblage in Table 31. This shows clearly that a disproportionate number of flagons and small jar/beakers were burnt. The concentration of burnt vessel fragments in pyre debris deposits is likely to be due to the location of some of the urns beside or on the pyre during cremation, and deposition or casting of drinking vessels onto the pyre at some point. The pits containing redeposited pyre debris seem to have contained a greater proportion of burnt flagons than any other feature suggesting these may have been the favoured place for deposition of burnt flagon sherds. By contrast small jars/beakers were rare whether burnt or unburnt. On the basis of the singed character of the burning, it was considered that the disproportionate amount of burnt mortaria is likely to relate to domestic usage rather than rituals.

The proportion of medium-necked jars from cremation graves was rather more than that from the mortuary enclosure ditches, the cremation-related deposits and the redeposited pyre debris. Mortuary enclosure ditch 126154 had a greater proportion of jars but the size of this group, only three vessels, made this insignificant. Mortuary enclosure ditch 126066 with nine vessels, by contrast, had only one certain jar but the unidentified vessels were probably jars. The road-zone ditches had relatively few jars but again most of the unidentified vessels were likely to be jars.

Less than a quarter of the medium-necked jars from cremation graves were burnt (Table 30). Although burnt matter was noted on three BB1 jars from the site, two large jars and one small jar/beaker, it is difficult to decide whether these accretions were deposited during domestic cooking activity or during cremation. Burnt matter was noted adhering to only two other sherds. One of the urns, a BB1 jar, was burnt down only one side. At Brougham the burning pattern on the jars suggested they were being placed next to the pyre and the near side was being burnt (Evans 2004, 358). At Ryknield Street, some of the vessels seemed to have been burnt on one side (cremation grave 122062 and a redeposited urn in inhumation grave 122364) while in other cases all the sherds present were heavily burnt all over (redeposited pyre debris from pit 129024). The jar from inhumation grave 122364 was severely burnt resulting in surface cracking and deterioration. Relatively more burnt jars were represented in the assemblages from redeposited pyre debris and mortuary enclosure ditches 126069 and 126154, the last two being small groups, than other feature types. It must be concluded that much of this damage to the large jars was caused by their inclusion on or within the pyre and subsequent reuse as urns.

Twelve out of 18 of the burnt jars from the site were BB1 jars. This may indicate a chronological change in cremation rites and/or cooking methodology. If in the late 1st–early 2nd centuries food was prepared in such a way that these medium-necked jars did not get burnt or become covered with burnt deposits then they may also have been considered inappropriate vessels to place on or near the cremation pyres. Alternatively or in addition,

Table 30 Relative proportions (%) of burnt and unburnt sherds by vessel type in each feature group

Vessel type	*Condition*	*Urned cremation burial*	*Unurned cremation burial*	*Redeposited burial*	*Redeposited pyre debris*	*Other cremation-related deposit*	*Inhumation grave*	*Mortuary enclosure ditch 126069*	*Mortuary enclosure ditch 126066*	*Mortuary enclosure ditch 126154*	*Mortuary enclosure ditch 126148*	*Pit*	*Ditch*	*Road-zone ditches*	*Subsoil*	*Tree throw hole*	*Unstratified*
B		–	–	–	2.6	–	–	20.0	11.1	–	36.4	–	–	9.1	–	–	–
B	BR	1.2	–	–	–	–	–	–	–	–	–	–	–	–	–	–	–
D		3.5	–	–	–	–	–	–	–	–	–	–	–	–	–	–	6.3
D	BR	–	–	–	5.3	–	–	–	–	–	–	–	–	–	–	–	–
B/D		–	–	–	–	–	–	–	–	–	–	–	10.0	9.1	–	–	–
BKR		1.2	–	–	–	–	–	–	–	–	–	–	–	–	–	–	6.3
BKR	BM	–	–	–	–	–	–	–	–	–	9.1	–	–	–	–	–	–
BKR	BR	–	–	–	2.6	–	–	–	–	–	–	–	–	–	–	–	–
C		–	–	–	2.6	–	–	–	–	–	–	–	–	–	–	–	–
C	BR	–	–	–	–	–	5.9	–	–	–	–	–	–	–	–	–	–
F		11.6	–	–	10.5	–	5.9	20.0	11.1	33.3	27.3	–	30.0	9.1	33.3	11.1	25.0
F	BR	8.1	–	–	7.9	–	–	–	–	–	–	25.0	–	4.5	–	11.1	–
F	BR GRF	1.2	–	–	–	–	–	–	–	–	–	–	–	–	–	–	–
Tettine		1.2	–	–	–	–	–	–	–	–	–	–	–	–	–	–	–
J		34.9	–	–	18.4	–	11.8	–	11.1	–	–	37.5	20.0	13.6	33.3	33.3	25.0
J	BR BM	–	–	–	2.6	–	5.9	–	–	–	–	–	–	–	–	–	–
J	BR	7	–	–	15.8	–	–	20.0	–	33.3	–	–	10.0	–	–	–	12.5
J	BR CRCK	1.2	–	–	–	–	–	–	–	–	–	–	–	–	–	–	–
J	DIS	2.3	–	–	–	–	–	–	–	33.3	–	–	–	–	–	–	–
J	PTBAS	1.2	–	–	–	–	–	–	–	–	–	–	–	–	–	–	–
JMINI		3.5	–	25.0	7.9	66.7	11.8	20.0	–	–	–	–	–	9.1	–	–	–
JMINI	BR	11.6	–	–	5.3	33.3	11.8	–	–	–	–	–	–	–	–	–	–
JMINI	BR BM	–	–	–	–	–	–	–	–	–	–	–	–	–	–	–	6.3
JMINI	PTBY PTBAS	–	–	–	–	–	5.9	–	–	–	–	–	–	–	–	–	–
NNJ		–	–	–	2.6	–	–	–	–	–	–	–	–	4.5	–	–	–
NNJ	DIS	1.2	–	–	2.6	–	–	–	–	–	–	–	–	–	–	–	–
WMJ		3.5	–	–	–	–	–	–	–	–	–	–	10.0	–	16.7	–	–
M		–	–	–	–	–	5.9	–	11.1	–	–	–	–	–	16.7	–	6.3
M	BR	–	100.0	–	2.6	–	–	–	–	–	–	–	–	4.5	–	–	6.3
M	BR DIS	–	–	–	–	–	–	–	11.1	–	–	–	–	–	–	11.1	–
L		–	–	–	2.6	–	–	–	–	–	–	–	–	4.5	–	–	–
UNK		2.3	–	50.0	5.3	–	23.5	20.0	44.4	–	27.3	37.5	20.0	27.3	–	33.3	6.3
UNK	BR	3.5	–	25.0	2.6	–	11.8	–	–	–	–	–	–	4.5	–	–	–
Total no.		86	1	4	38	3	17	5	9	3	11	8	10	22	6	9	16

B = bowl; D = dish; B/D = bowl/dish; BKR = beaker; C = cup; F = flagon; J = medium-necked jar; JMINI = small jar/beaker; NNJ = narrow-necked jar; WMJ = wide-mouthed jar; M = mortarium; L = lid; UNK = uncertain; BR = burnt; BM = burnt material; GRF = fraffiti; CRCK = cracked; DIS = distorted; PTBAS = perforated base

the jars may only have been placed on, or near enough to, the pyre to get burnt after BB1 jars were in circulation.

The tendency to collect pyre goods for inclusion in the cremation grave can be seen even more clearly in the case of the small jar/beakers. This type made up a similar proportion of the assemblages from the graves and the redeposited pyre debris but a greater number of those from the former were burnt, giving strong evidence for their careful collection for inclusion in the grave. In contrast, few of the fine ware beakers were selected for burial and no burnt examples were taken. The small jar/beakers tended to be severely burnt resulting in extensive surface cracking and disintegration into many small sherds. An example from Beckfoot cemetery handled by the writer elucidates the procedure. This small BB1 jar/beaker was delivered unwashed, thanks to the foresight of the excavator, and presented a complete vessel, burnt all over with fine cracking, particularly concentrating on one side. Although fairly robust as delivered, customary finds washing, even done with particular care, will result in the vessel fragmenting into small sherds (at the severely burnt side) and larger sherds (on the less severely affected side). Compared with some of the small BB1 jar/beakers from Ryknield Street, it is easy to envisage a situation where complete or near complete vessels (the Beckfoot jar had a chipped rim) could fragment for several more reasons, in addition to mere finds washing. Burial conditions, particularly seasonal temperature changes, would exacerbate the existing cracking and cause fragmentation. Machine stripping has clearly damaged many pots at Ryknield Street and caused shattering. Vessels with more intense cracking would easily fragment however careful excavators were. In grave 122874, a small beaker recorded as complete prior to excavation numbered 58 burnt sherds on arrival with the writer (it is not clear from the records if it was found intact). It is additionally clear that the vagaries of the cremation process resulted in partial burning of pyre goods and unburnt fragments within the graves may also be parts of pyre goods collected for inclusion in the burial.

As with the jars, most of the burnt small jars and beakers were BB1 vessels. Of the eight non-BB1 burnt small jars, one was a BB1 copy, two were everted rim

Table 31 Relative amount of burnt vessels by vessel type, and proportion of each vessel in total assemblage

Vessel type	*No. burnt*	*% of total burnt vessels in group*	*% of total vessel count*
Beaker	–	–	4.0
Cup	2	2.9	2.4
Bowl	–	–	1.2
Bowl/dish	1	1.5	1.6
Dish	1	1.5	0.8
Flagon	15	22.1	19.4
Tettine	–	–	0.4
Medium-necked jar	19	27.9	32.7
Small jar/beaker	16	23.5	12.5
Narrow-mouthed jar	–	–	1.6
Wide-mouthed jar	–	–	2.0
Lid	–	–	0.8
Mortarium	6	8.8	4.0
Uncertain	8	11.8	16.5
Total	68	27.4	248

rouletted jars and one was a neckless everted jar similar to the medium-necked jar type of the late 1st–early 2nd centuries. The rouletted beakers were most likely to date to the mid-2nd century. This dating evidence again suggests that the pattern of putting pottery jars on the pyre and collecting them for burial may belong to the Hadrianic–Antonine period (early–mid-2nd century).

Flagons were relatively well represented in the subsoil and ditch assemblages and the sherds from these groups were unburnt suggesting some other activity on the site, which did not result in burning, involved flagons. Significantly the pyre debris deposits had a similar quantity of flagons to the cremation graves. The urned burials and pits containing redeposited pyre debris had the most burnt flagons with no burnt examples from the mortuary enclosure ditches. This contrasts with Polfer's findings in Luxemburg where vessels related to drinking were found in decreasing quantities as grave goods (unburnt), pyre goods in graves and in the *ustrinum* (2000, fig. 3.5) with similar levels of burning and flagons recorded in the pyre debris and urned cremation burials. Three of the burnt flagons came from groups dated to the late 1st–early 2nd centuries (Flavian–Trajanic), although as seven were not typologically diagnostic, these could increase this figure. The remaining eight could be dated to the Hadrianic–Antonine period. This rather strengthens the impression for an increased tendency to place pottery flagons, jars and small jar/beakers on the pyre at this time.

Table wares such as fine ware beakers, bowls and dishes were uncommon. The low numbers of bowls and dishes generally from the site suggests either that eating was not a major feature of the rituals or that some organic vessels were being used due to relative poverty or cultural choice, or, perhaps, that the foci of eating activity did not lie within the excavated area. Certainly at the Derby Racecourse cemetery rather more samian ware was excavated and fine ware beakers were found in reasonable quantities (Birss 1985, table 20). Most of these tablewares were unburnt as were storage-related items such as lids. This may be due to their use in the ritual feasting but not in rites involving burning. Similar observations were drawn by Polfer in a larger group from Luxemburg, but in this case altogether more vessel types had associations with eating (2000, fig. 3.5).

The redeposited pyre debris from pit 122784 included a large proportion of a burnt stamped samian dish, and burnt R20 sherds from a beaker with barbotine dots, a type common in the late 1st century, rim and neck sherds from a narrow-necked R19 jar, a burnt mortarium scrap, An O4 sherd from a lid and around half a R19 jar base. These vessels bring out an interesting aspect of the pyre debris deposits, namely the presence of tablewares and fine ware fabrics, such as samian, and the inclusion of types associated with food preparation or storage such as a mortarium and a lid. The narrow-necked jar, a form often associated with liquids and present in well groups, may have played a role in procedures associated with ritual cleansing. Another burnt fine ware beaker was also present in the pyre debris deposit found in pit 122042. It is a thin walled vessel, with an elaborate shape and decoration. This group also contained unburnt flagon sherds and burnt BB1 sherds from a jar. Sherds from another burnt beaker were present amongst the redeposited pyre debris from pit 122064.

The incidental/discrete deposits of pyre debris from pits differed from the pyre debris included in the grave fills in having more burnt dishes and fine beakers, cups, slightly fewer flagons and rather less burnt flagon sherds, more burnt jars sherds but fewer jars altogether, similar numbers of small jars/beakers but with less evidence of burning and more burnt mortarium sherds. This indicates a degree of selection for inclusion within the grave, with beakers being particularly singled out and large burnt jars less popular compared with the parent population indicated by the redeposited pyre debris from pits. The burnt dishes were not favoured at all although one burnt bowl was chosen and the only mortarium sherd was from an unurned cremation burial. The proportions of flagons were almost identical.

The pottery vessels from the mortuary enclosure ditches were quite different from each other. The group from enclosure ditch 126148 was the largest group and was dominated by bowls and flagons; this was the only mortuary enclosure ditch to have a fine ware beaker represented. The sherds from ditch 126069 represented five vessels only, single examples of a bowl, a flagon, a jar, a small jar/beaker and an unknown type. The jar was burnt. This group was nearest in composition to the redeposited pyre debris assemblage. Ditch 126154 had very little pottery – a flagon and two jars, one of which was burnt and the other distorted while enclosure ditch 126066 had nine vessels. These included two mortaria, one of which was burnt and distorted, a bowl, a burnt flagon, a burnt jar and four undiagnostic sherds from other vessels. The preponderance of tablewares and food preparation ceramics suggest a place for feasting as well as drinking but the diversity of the four groups hints at more complex and varied rituals in these spaces.

Other pottery conditions

A flagon from cremation grave 122651 had traces of graffiti. The bases of two vessels may have been deliberately holed. A small R14 jar or beaker from inhumation grave 122977 had much surface spalling and was very fragmentary. One of its sherds had part of what appeared to be a cleat hole and the base seemed to have been holed deliberately; the missing rectangle of base was found in the grave. The near complete rusticated jar from cremation grave 122635 also seems to have been deliberately holed. No signs of mending other than cleat hole on the pot from grave 122977 were identified.

Several vessels showed signs of distortion and were considered seconds or wasters – an R13 jar from mortuary enclosure ditch 126066, a mortarium from mortuary enclosure ditch 126154, an R5 jar base from cremation grave 122844, an R2 narrow-necked jar from cremation grave 122554, an R16 narrow-necked jar from the cremation-related deposit in pit 122083 and a complete everted rim jar from cremation grave 122780 whose rim seemed distorted.

Numbers and types of vessels in burials

The analysis of the number of vessels accompanying the cremation burials is complicated by the fragmentation of vessels after burial and the loss of parts of vessels through plough and/or machinery damage. It was not always clear if complete vessels or only parts of vessels had been deposited. This was especially acute if the vessels were burnt but even unburnt sherds may have been pyre goods originally.

A single vessel was present in just under half of the cremation graves (Table 32). In most cases these were jars but instances of a wide-mouthed jar, two instances of a flagon and three of a small jar/beaker being the only vessel recovered were identified. In five cases the urn was burnt. In two cases there was another jar present – two bases in grave 122733 and probably two vessels in grave 129083. In one example the urn, a burnt flagon, was accompanied by sherds from an MG1 beaker recorded on site as being broken. This latter vessel may have been a collected pyre good but was not obviously burnt. In two cases, the second vessel was a samian dish (graves 129074 and 129075), which had in the case of 129074 been placed over the urn. In the grave 120202, substantial parts of six unburnt vessels were recorded, two flagons, a tettine and three jars. Additionally grave 122635 had a second vessel now mislaid.

The remaining vessels appear to have been pyre goods collected for inclusion in the grave fill or, in the case from grave 129080, inside the urn. A small number of sherds were unburnt and where these are single sherds or abraded, they have been categorised as probably redeposited. However, given the numbers of sherds clearly representing pyre good deposition, it is equally, if not more likely that these are pyre goods which have survived unburnt. Small jars/beakers as pyre goods were very commonly included in the grave, with only slightly fewer flagons. Only one bowl was present and two mortarium sherds.

Grave goods, apart from those from grave 120202, are very limited with only five graves accompanied by a second vessel. However, the buried pyre goods considerably increase the number of vessels used within the funerary rite and indicate that a rather different level of expenditure was undertaken than might at first be suggested. The animal remains similarly disclosed a large proportion of individuals accompanied by food offerings (Worley, below).

The inhumation graves

Only one of the possible inhumation graves, 122977, had what may have comprised ceramic grave goods, two small grey ware beakers. One was badly fragmented and had been repaired while the other was a very small complete vessel. Graves 122609, 122526 and 122364 all contained burnt pottery, probably derived from disturbed cremation-related deposits. The vessels in grave 122364 were near complete and contemporary suggesting their intentional inclusion within the grave. Graves 122408 and 122964 had no Romano-British pottery while the remainder only contained small sherds.

Changes through time

The damage sustained by the assemblage made analysis by quantification fraught with difficulties and the loss of chronologically diagnostic parts of the vessels resulted in a less robust sample for analysis. Nevertheless, some significant trends emerged from a study of the wares and vessel types being selected for inclusion in the various forms of deposit in each chronological group (Tables 33 and 34). The analysis of the vessel types showed a decrease in the relative quantities of jars in the cremation burials during the 1st and 2nd centuries, and a detailed study of the vessels used as urns in group 3 burials bore this out. By the mid-2nd century there seems to have been a greater flexibility in the vessels chosen, so much so that only two of the urns were medium-necked jars, the other being narrow-necked and wide-mouthed jars or, in one case, a bowl.

It was also clear that flagons were considerably more common in group 1 with a marked decline by group 3. Fine ware beakers are only present in group 1 and dishes in groups 1 and 2. The only tettine came from group 1 also. However, the disappearance of dishes may have been offset by the appearance of bowls. This may reflect a difference in the type of food being consumed at the funeral feasts, perhaps, stews which need to be contained in deeper bowls rather than roasts which can be set on a flat, open dish. Although numbers are too small for certainty, the same pattern was detected in the material from the redeposited pyre debris (Table 35).

Table 32 Number and type of pots represented in cremation graves

Grave	*Bowl*	*Dish*	*Beaker*	*Flagon*	*Tettine*	*Jar*	*Small jar/ beaker*	*N-necked jar*	*W-mouthed jar*	*Mortarium*	*Uncertain*	*Total*
122017	–	–	–	–	–	1**	–	–	–	–	–	1
122020	–	–	–	–	–	1**	–	–	–	–	–	1
122022	–	–	–	–	–	1**	–	–	–	–	–	1
122132	–	–	–	–	–	–	1**	–	–	–	–	1
122154	–	–	–	1**	–	–	–	–	–	–	–	1
122176	–	–	–	–	–	1**	–	–	–	–	–	1
122420	–	–	–	–	–	1**	–	–	–	–	–	1
122476	–	–	–	–	–	1**	–	–	–	–	–	1
122501	–	–	–	–	–	–	1**	–	–	–	–	1
122504	–	–	–	1**	–	–	–	–	–	–	–	1
122571	–	–	–	–	–	1**	–	–	–	–	–	1
122797	–	–	–	1**	–	–	–	–	–	–	–	1
122635	–	–	–	–	–	1**	–	–	–	–	* lost	2
122727	–	–	–	–	–	1**	–	–	–	–	–	1
122794	–	–	–	–	–	1**	–	–	–	–	–	1
122922	–	–	–	–	–	–	–	–	–	1 p?	–	1
129073	–	–	–	–	–	–	–	–	1 **?	–	–	1
129078	–	–	–	–	–	1**	–	–	–	–	–	1
129081	–	–	–	–	–	–	1**	–	–	–	–	1
129084	–	–	–	1**?	–	–	–	–	–	–	–	1
122025	–	–	1*	1**	–	–	–	–	–	–	–	2
122062	–	–	–	–	–	1**	–	–	–	–	1 r (samian)	2
122568	–	–	–	–	–	–	–	–	2**	–	–	2
122733	–	–	–	–	–	2 ** + *	–	–	–	–	–	2
122874	–	–	–	–	–	1**	1p	–	–	–	–	2
129071	–	–	–	–	–	2** + r	–	–	–	–	–	2
129080	–	–	–	–	–	1**	1p inside urn	–	–	–	–	2
129082	–	–	–	–	–	1**	–	–	–	–	1 p	2
122074	–	–	–	–	–	1 **	–	–	–	–	1 r	2
122044	1p	–	–	1**	–	–	1r?	–	–	–	–	3
122554	–	–	–	–	–	1 r	1p	1 **	–	–	–	3
122844	–	–	–	2 p+p/r	–	1**	–	–	–	–	–	3
129079	–	–	–	1 r	–	1 **	1 p	–	–	–	–	3
129083	–	–	–	1 r	–	?2 ** + ?	–	–	–	–	–	3
122052	–	–	–	–	–	1**	3 p	–	–	–	–	4
122536	–	–	–	2 p	–	2 **+ r	–	–	–	–	–	4
122651	–	–	–	1 p	–	1 **	–	–	–	–	2 p	4
129074	–	1*	–	1 p	–	2** + p	–	–	–	–	–	4
122780	–	–	–	1 p	–	2 ** + r	2 p	–	–	–	–	5
120202	–	–	–	2*+ r	1*	3** +*	–	–	–	–	–	6
129075	–	1*	–	1 r	–	1** +1* + 2r	–	–	–	–	–	6
Total	1	2	1	18	1	41	13	1	3	1	5	87

**=urns, *=grave goods, p=pyre goods, r= unburnt sherds possibly redeposited

Table 33 Vessel types in ceramic groups (min. vessel count/relative %)

Ceramic group	*B*	*D*	*BKR*	*F*	*Tettine*	*J*	*JMINI*	*NNJ*	*WMJ*	*Mor*	*Unk*
1	–	1/3.85	1/3	6/23.08	1/3.85	13/50.00	1/3.85	–	–	–	3/11.54
2	–	1/4.76	–	3/14.29	–	10/47.62	7/33.33	–	–	–	–
3	1/7.69	–	–	1/7.69	–	3/23.08	3/23.08	1/7.69	3/23.08	–	1/7.69
4	–	–	–	1/33.33	–	2/66.67	–	–	–	–	–
6	–	–	–	6/66.67	–	3/33.33	–	–	–	–	–
7	–	–	–	–	–	1/50.00	–	–	–	1/50.00	–
8	–	–	–	–	–	1/100.00	–	–	–	–	–
9	–	–	–	–	–	7/77.78	2/22.22	–	–	–	–
Total	1	2	1	17	1	40	13	1	3	1	4

Key: B = bowl; D = dish; BKR = beaker; F = flagon; J = medium-necked jar; JMINI = small jar/beaker; NNJ = narrow-necked jar; L = lid; M = mortarium; Unk = uncertain

This would accord with the rise in burnt BB1 jars in groups 2 and 3. The lack of burning on the earlier jar forms in reduced wares suggests a difference in cooking practices. A credible explanation might be that the earlier jars were used to boil food in water, which would 'burn on' to a lesser degree, while the BB1 jars were used to make stews which would 'burn on' more readily. The tendency of the BB1 jars to have a slightly wider mouth compared with the reduced ware jars may also be related to this difference in function, as today stews are served from larger casseroles with open, wide mouths and pans for boiling are often narrower. Boiled foodstuffs could be served on dishes with the different foods arranged individually (Cool 2006) whereas the stews could be served in higher sided bowls with no need for such distinctions. The change of vessel types in both the table wares and the cooking vessel types may therefore reflect these changes in cooking practices. The numbers of bowls and dishes from the site are very small but the same pattern can be seen in the cremation-related deposits and redeposited pyre debris where dishes are restricted to group 1 as is the only identified cup. Indeed the majority of the samian dishes were of early date.

Although fine ware beakers are restricted to group 1, small jars/beakers are uncommon generally in group 1 and peak in group 2. Since half the small jars/beakers from the cremation graves were in reduced wares, this change does not seem to be simply due to the availability of these vessels in BB1 ware in groups 2–3. The number of these vessels from the group 2 graves, however, leads to the conclusion that they were deliberately selected both as accompanying vessels and as pyre goods collected for burial. It may be that the flagons favoured in group 1 graves served a similar purpose, perhaps either providing the dead with drink or the gods with libations, but were less commonly placed on the pyre in the late 1st–early 2nd century. Another possible explanation is that the drink being consumed differed, so group 1 cremation burials were accompanied by wine while group 2 and 3 cremation burials were accompanied by beer. Certainly Cool's study of eating and drinking in Roman Britain (2006) demonstrated the association of flagons with wine preparation and suggested large capacity beakers may be associated with beer drinking, although some, such as imported motto beakers, may have been used to mix wine or for large amounts of wine. Quantified ceramic data is not available for Wall but at Derby Little Chester fort the relative quantity of flagons did not decrease from the later 1st–early 2nd to mid-2nd centuries (Birss 1985,

Table 34 Wares in cremation graves by ceramic group (min. vessel count/relative %)

Ceramic group	*BB1*	*C*	*F*	*M*	*MALV*	*R*	*S*	*W*	*WS*
1	–	1/3.85	1/3.85	–	1/3.85	14/53.85	2/7.69	6/23.08	–
2	8/38.10	–	–	–	–	9/42.86	1/4.76	3/14.29	–
3	4/30.77	–	–	–	–	7/53.85	1/7.69	1/7.69	–
4	–	–	–	–	–	2/66.67	–	1/33.33	–
6	–	–	–	–	–	3/33.33	–	5/55.56	1/11.11
7	–	–	–	1/50.00	–	1/50.00	–	–	–
8	1/100.00	–	–	–	–	–	–	–	–
9	–	–	–	–	–	1/100.00	–	–	–

Table 35 Numbers of vessel types in redeposited pyre deposits

Ceramic group	B	D	BKR	C	F	J	JMINI	NNJ	L	M	Unk.	Total
1	–	1	–	1	–	1	1	–	–	–	–	4
2	–	1	–	–	1	3	2	1	1	1	–	10
3	1	–	–	–	–	4	1	1	–	–	1	8
4	–	–	1	–	2	4	–	–	–	–	–	7
6	–	–	–	–	3	1	–	–	–	–	1	5
8	–	–	–	–	–	1	–	–	–	–	–	1
9	–	–	–	–	1	–	1	–	–	–	1	3

Key: B = bowl; D = dish; BKR = beaker; C= cup; F = flagon; J = medium-necked jar; JMINI = small jar/beaker; NNJ = narrow-necked jar; L = lid; M = mortarium; Unk = uncertain

table 8). However the small BB1 jars/beakers were restricted to the mid–late 2nd century groups and the reduced ware small jars/beakers were absent in the late 1st–early 2nd centuries and present in the Hadrianic–Antonine period equivalent to groups 2 and 3 (Birss 1985, tables 4 and 9), suggesting the introduction of this vessel type may have been a regional trend. At Rocester Old Shops, although beakers were relatively more common, 24%, in phase 1 (Flavian–Trajanic) they were predominantly fine wares. In the later phases the beaker component dropped to around 10% but in phase 2 (Hadrianic– Antonine) the coarse ware small jar/beaker form outnumbered the fine ware types and by phase 3 (late 2nd–early 3rd centuries) all the beakers were in coarse wares (Leary forthcoming and archive data). The alteration in drinking vessels deposited may partially reflect a change in drinking habits.

Changes in the fabrics were partially affected by the changes evidenced by the incidence of vessel type study. The decline in group W (see Chapter 28, Romano-British pottery fabrics) clearly reflects the changes in flagons being deposited. The restriction of groups WS and the fine wares, F, to group 1 also reflect the concentration of flagons and tables wares respectively in group 1. The fluctuations in groups BB1 and R mirror the arrival of BB1 in the region in the Hadrianic period and the related decline in local coarse wares. Groups C and MALV were limited to group 1 burials and this is likely to indicate their main period of circulation in the region. The larger quantity of samian in group 1 again results from the deposition of dishes during that period. The rise in group 3 is illusory and comprised a tiny residual scrap.

Distribution patterns

The chronological groups indicated by the pottery did not reveal a strong spatial patterning of cremation graves within the cemetery. There was a cluster of three group 1 (late 1st–early 2nd century) burials in the south-west corner of the eastern half of the cemetery and the group 2 (early–mid-2nd century) grave in this area, 122132, could be a near contemporary deposition. The latest burial lay in the south-west corner of the eastern half of the cemetery but the material from inhumation grave 122364, probably from a redeposited cremation-related deposit, came from the southern part of the western half of the cemetery, as discussed above.

The inhumation graves were harder to date as most lacked certain accompanying vessels. Two graves, 122609 and 122977, with pottery of the late 1st–early 2nd centuries were situated near mortuary enclosures 126148 and 126154. In the case of the possible grave 122977, two small beakers were found in the grave in near complete unburnt condition. The material from grave 122609 comprised sherds of a samian cup and bodysherds from unidentified vessels in fabrics R4, R16 and FLA. All the vessels were burnt except the R4 sherds and could easily be redeposited material from earlier cremation rites in this area of the site. The possible grave 122977 may be of more significance given its two small beakers of early type and its position near the mortuary enclosure; however, the interpretation of this feature as a grave is far from secure (see above).

In terms of the number of vessels found in each cremation grave, a cluster of burials with multiple pots, ranging from two to six vessels, lay in the north-west corner of the eastern half of the site and the early group in the south-west corner had two to three pots each. Another cluster of three graves in the north-east of the western half of the cemetery also contained three to four pots. Grave 122780, inside mortuary enclosure 126154, had six vessels associated with it. Its central position suggests contemporaneity with the enclosure and the pottery from it would be consistent with this.

Pyre and grave goods: selection by age and sex of the individual

There were rather too few burials with both aged and sexed remains and diagnostic pottery to provide good evidence for trends in the association of ceramic types with categories of the dead. The evidence is tabulated, however, and some associations are worth noting (Tables 36 and 37).

Adults have the greatest variety and number of pottery vessels associated with them as urns, with little difference relating to gender. Immature individuals do

Table 36 Cremation urns by age and sex of individual

	F	J	JMINI	NNJ	WMJ
neonate/infant	–	2	–	–	–
infant	–	4	–	–	–
juvenile/subadult	–	1	–	–	–
subadult	–	2	–	–	1
subadult female	–	1	–	–	–
adult + infant	–	1	–	–	–
adult	4	7	2	–	–
adult female	1	6	–	–	1
adult ?female	–	1	–	–	–
adult male	1	2	1	1	–
adult male + adult female	–	1	–	–	–
adult male ?+ adult female	–	1	–	–	–

Key: F = flagon; J = medium-necked jar; JMINI = small jar/beaker; NNJ = narrow-mouthed jar; WMJ = wide-mouthed jar (see Cremated human bone for age categories)

not seem to have been given smaller vessels as urns. Amongst the urned burials, all but one female were buried in medium-necked jars, whereas the males were also deposited in a flagon, a narrow-necked jar and a small jar/beaker. The infant from grave 129083 may have been deposited in a facepot but not enough of the upper part of the vessel survived to be certain. Flagons and small jars/beakers were only used as urns for adults although both were found amongst the pyre goods of infants.

Multiple pots of all functions seem to be associated primarily with adults, although the adult and infant burial made in grave 120202 may have included five near complete vessels including a tettine. The female subadult from grave 122780 and the adult male from grave 129075 were accompanied by a significant number of ceramic pyre goods, as was the possible double burial of an adult male and ?adult female in grave 129074. Second vessels as grave goods were all associated with adults with the possible exception of the double burial in grave 120202 (from evaluation; see The cemetery; Table 38).

Table 37 Number of vessels of any type associated with graves by age and sex of individual

No. of pots / *Age and sex*	1	2	3	4	5	6
neonate/infant	2	–	–	–	–	–
infant	–	–	3	–	–	–
juvenile/subadult	1	–	–	–	–	–
subadult	3	–	–	–	–	–
subadult female	–	–	–	–	1	–
adult + infant	–	–	–	–	–	1
adult	9	2	–	2	–	–
adult female	2	5	–	1	–	–
adult ?female	–	1	–	–	–	–
adult male	2	–	2	–	–	1
adult male + adult female	–	1	–	1	–	–

Table 38 Second pots as grave goods

Grave good	JMINI	BKR	D	F	T	J
adult+infant	4	–	–	1	1	2
adult female	2	1	–	–	–	1
adult male	1	–	1	–	–	–
adult male + adult female	1	–	1	–	–	–

See previous tables for key. T = tettine

The pyre goods showed little patterning by sex, although only young females or females buried with men had more than one small jar/beaker and the flagons were not found with adult females (Table 39). Most of the pyre goods were associated with adults or subadults. Two flagons and a small jar were associated with infants. The flagons both came from the same burial (in grave 122844) but the infant burial (from grave 129079) with the small jar pyre good may well have also had a flagon on the pyre represented in the grave by four unburnt flagon sherds.

Worked stone, by Ruth Shaffrey

The most significant worked stone was a moulded block in two fragments (Fig. 91; ON 123552). The moulding continues around all four faces and the shape of the detail on top of the block suggests this was a corner focus on top of a low wall. The most likely interpretation, given its context, is that it was part of a funerary monument. It was recovered from the northernmost excavated segment through the western road-zone ditch 126059 together with 14 other large

Table 39 Pyre goods from burials

Pyre goods	BKR	F	J	JMINI	Unk.
infant	–	2	–	1	–
subadult female	–	1	1	2	–
adult	–	3	–	1	3
adult female	–	–	–	3	–
adult male	1	–	1	1	–
adult male + adult female	–	1	1	1	–

See previous tables for key

building blocks; a single block was also recovered from the terminal of mortuary enclosure ditch 126066 (Table 40).

Most of the blocks are heavily weathered and have lost tool marks but those classed as building blocks carry some tooling marks on one or more faces. All the building stones, including the moulded block, are made from the same locally available, light reddish brown, slightly micaceous and feldspathic sandstone (Keuper Sandstone, see Chapter 28).

In addition to the structural fragments, several items suggestive of nearby occupation or subsistence activities were recovered, but some were residual within post-medieval features. Rotary quern fragments were retrieved from two contexts – the fill of the Romano-British boundary ditch 126159 in the western half of the cemetery and the post-medieval ditch 126221, possibly redeposited from one of the Romano-British ditches cut by it at this point – but both were only very weathered fragments from lava querns.

There are also two possible polishing stones from a post-medieval pit 122932 at the north end of the road-zone. A possible whetstone that also made use of a naturally occurring pebble (ON 123458) was recovered from amongst the redeposited pyre debris in pit 122810 and a single pebble (ON 123042) with wear at one end consistent with use as a pounder was found in cremation grave 122044, but neither showed signs of burning and both could be residual rather than representing pyre/grave goods.

Catalogue of worked stone from non-grave/cremation-related contexts

ON 123552 Square moulded block (Fig. 91): Keuper Sandstone: slightly irregular square block with complete zone of moulded decoration *c* 210–220 mm deep running horizontally around all sides. Detail on top of block heavily damaged but appears to have consisted of small, carved, asymmetrical pyramid suggesting corner piece. Underside of block has outline of slightly smaller square where it connected with lower stone. Designed to be visible from all sides & from above. L 300, W 300, T 250, ditch 126059, context 122919

ON 123253 Frag. upper rotary quern: lava; very weathered, broken into *c* 10 frags with flat surfaces & straight edges. T 42 mm, ditch 126221, context 122262

Bulk finds:

Probable rotary quern frag.: lava; tiny weathered, cditch 126159, ontext 122692

Possible polishing stones: frags 2 pebbles, 1 showing signs of polish on one side; L 60, W 50, T18; L 100, W 62, T 40, pit 122932, context 122933

Building material, by Cynthia Poole

Six fragments of ceramic building material, weighing 600 g, were recovered from six contexts together with two fragments of stone, weighing 30 g. All of the identifiable ceramic fragments were *tegulae*, made in fabrics S2 and S7 (see Chapter 28). Two had quite wide type E flanges with C1 and D1 cutaways. A narrower very worn flange was possibly type B or D. The other fragments were flat tile or unidentified. A single limestone *tessera* 15 mm by 14 mm was the only stone building material.

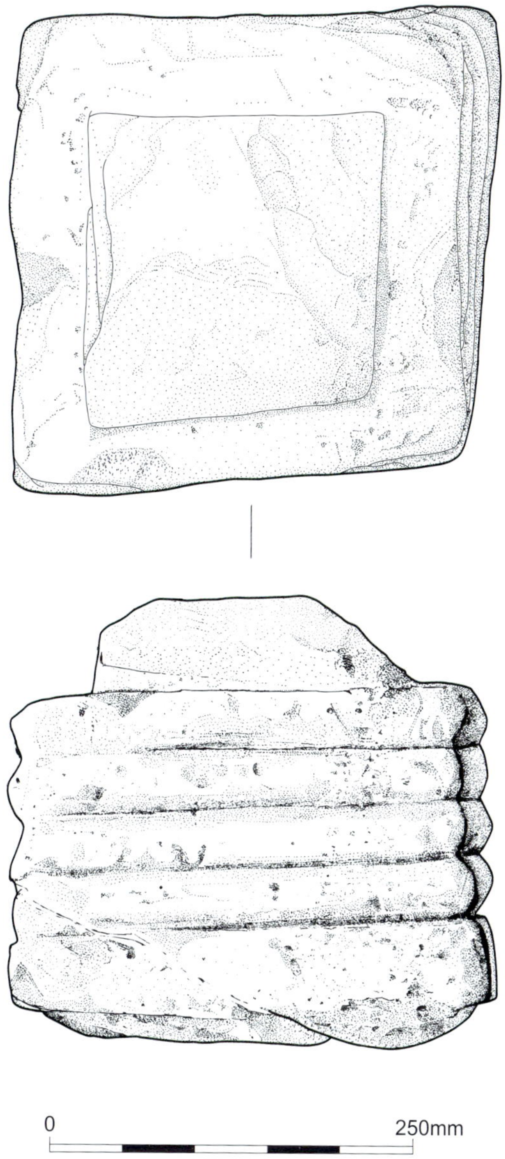

Fig. 91 Stone block

The building material was recovered from the fills of various ditches including the western road-zone ditch 126059 (together with the dump of worked stone), mortuary enclosure ditch 126066, and two of the post-medieval ditches (126060 and 126205). The material may have been associated with some form of mortuary structure within the cemetery, and *tegulae* and *imbrices* have been found used as covers for cremation burials in other contemporaneous cemeteries.

Cremated animal bone, by Fay Worley

The cremated animal bone assemblage was recovered from a variety of deposit types including urned and

Table 40 Other building blocks

ON	Context	Feature	Notes	Size (mm)
	122325	126059	Square block with 4 tooled faces remaining	160 x 180 x 130
123262	122325	126059	1 flat face & 1 flat edge square to each other	210 x 240 x 110
123257	122325	126059	No tool marks	140 x 100 x 70
123264	122325	126059	Weathered block	150 x 110 x 90
1233260	122325	126059	Square edges but no tool marks	110 x 80 x 60
123258	122325	126059	Square edges but no tool marks	150 x 130 x *c*80
123259	122325	126059	Small square block without tool marks as weathered	110 x 80 x 70
123255	122325	126059	Rectangular block tooled all over although broken at 1 end	310 x 130 x 110
123256	122325	126059	Large rectangular block tooled all over & 5 chunks probably weathered from this block	170 x 160 x 90
123254	122325	126059	Small rectangular block with squared edges & tooled all over	140 x 100 x 70
123267	122339	126059	Rectangular block tooled all over	210 x 160 x 100
123270	122339	126059	Tooled on 3 sides	80 x 130 x 120
123272	122339	126059	Roughly square, tooled on 4 sides & more finely on 1 side	160 x 150 x 70
123551	122425	126066	Probably building stone although no tool marks present	130 x 110 x 80
	122919	126059	Rectangular block with tooling & more finely tooled on 1 face	550 x 350 x 200

unurned cremation burials, redeposited cremation burials, redeposited pyre debris, cremation-related deposits and other archaeological features. The animal bone assemblage indicates that portions of pigs, sheep or goats, cattle and domestic fowl were burnt at cremation ceremonies and that, often, their remains were incorporated into the cremation burials. Although other taxa have been identified in Romano-British cremation burials in Britain, those at Ryknield Street primarily included pigs and domestic fowl with very few contexts containing other taxa. This is similar to the range of faunal pyre goods identified from the Romano-British cemetery at Derby Racecourse (Wheeler 1985), the only other large Romano-British cemetery with cremated animal bone identified in the Midlands.

Methods

The cremated animal bone was separated from the cremated human bone by McKinley prior to analysis. It was identified by comparison with faunal reference material at Oxford Archaeology. Each fragment was examined for indications of butchery marks, pathological lesions and sexually distinctive characteristics. Epiphyseal fusion was noted and interpreted (following Silver 1969) to indicate age-at-death of mammal bones. Teeth rarely survive cremation intact. However, unerupted tooth crowns may be recognisable in cremated material. These were recorded and used to indicate age-at-death from tooth eruption (following Silver 1969).

Cremation can shrink and warp bone fragments negating the interpretation of metric data. As all recovered bone fragments had been burnt, no measurements were recorded. The bone fragments were recorded using a zone method (Serjeantson 1996). Zones were recorded as present when any part of that zone could be identified.

The condition of bone fragments was recorded. As all fragments were calcined and white in colour, this information was only recorded in the total assemblage entry for each field in the database. Erosion of the burnt bone's surface was noted, as was evidence for iron and copper-alloy staining or pieces of metal or glass fused to the bone fragments. Tissue regression fractures have been shown to indicate that bones were fleshed when burnt (Buikstra and Swegle 1989; Pope *et al.* 2004), these were noted when present.

The animal bone fragments were recorded in a *Microsoft Access* database. The total fragment count and weight of animal bone in each context was recorded, followed by individual weights and refitted fragment counts for each element. A hard copy of the database can be found with the site archive.

Results

A total of 1519 fragments (668 g) of cremated animal bone was recovered from 78 contexts. This fragment count includes a large number of recently broken pieces. This can be attributed to the brittle nature of calcined bones. All the animal bone was fully calcined and predominantly white in colour.

Only a very restricted range of taxa was identified comprising pig (*Sus scrofa*), sheep or goat (*Ovis aries* or *Capra hircus*), cattle (*Bos taurus*) and domestic fowl (*Gallus gallus*). Further fragments were recorded as large or medium mammal size, bird or indeterminate. No medullary bone or tarso-metatarsal spurs were present in the bird bone assemblage preventing the identification of male and female individuals. Similarly, no pig remains could be sexed as tooth enamel is usually destroyed during cremation.

Animal bone was recovered from 30 cremation graves, 28 of which contained the remains of urned burials. Burnt bone from the remaining two burials was probably originally held in an organic container. Burnt animal bone was also recovered from 11 contexts comprising redeposited pyre debris, two cremation-related deposits, three redeposited burials, five ditch fills, two pit fills, six subsoil contexts and redeposited material.

Tissue regression fractures were identified on a pig tibia from grave 122132, a pig ulna from grave 122635 and a medium mammal long bone fragment from grave 122554. These fractures suggest that the pig remains were burnt while in a fleshed state. Element representation indicates that the mammal remains were probably burnt as carcass portions. Often only a restricted range of skeletally adjacent elements were present in each deposit. Butchery marks were identified on medium mammal ribs from grave 122554 (see below). These butchery marks suggest that the rib cage had been portioned or disarticulated and possibly that some of the meat had been filleted.

Evidence for pathology

A fowl left tarso-metatarsal from grave 129074 had a small area of pathological bone growth on its metatarsal facet. A second possible pathology was noted on a pig phalanx fragment from the same grave; the unfused proximal epiphysis appeared to have a pathological bone extension.

Burnt animal bone from urned cremation burials

Burnt animal bone was recovered from 28 urned cremation burials (Table 41). The number of animal bone fragments (total fragment count) in each case varied from one to 200 (<1–148 g). The burials included pig, sheep or goat and domestic fowl remains with further fragments identified as medium mammal sized or bird. All bird bones were domestic fowl sized and no other bird species were identified. Only one fragment was identified as possible sheep or goat; a piece of distal tibia from grave 122554. All other identified mammal bones were from pigs.

Medium mammal pyre goods were found in 25 burials. Of these, 18 contained the remains of pigs and 14 contained the remains of medium mammals (including pigs) and birds; in six of these the birds could be identified as domestic fowl. Two burials contained only bird bones.

Pig pyre goods and evidence for butchery

Pig skull fragments were recovered from 14 urned burials, being the only skeletal element present in three. In the remainder, the pig's head was accompanied by at least one limb. Head and forelimb portions were recovered from three burials (two included the right fore limb). Head and hind limb portions were recovered from two burials (both included the

Table 41 Cremated animal bone from cremation graves

Grave	Mammal pyre goods	Bird pyre goods	No. frags	Wt (g)
122025	poss. medium or large mammal rib		11	3
122044	pig head & fore limb	fowl l. & r. wings	94	15
122045 *	pig skull & r. fore limb >12 months. Sheep/goat, 30 months	wing	30	10
122052	indeterminate		1	<1
122062	pig leg	long bones	36	5
122074	indet. medium mammal	long bone	3	<1
122132	Pig head & r. hind limb <27 months	fowl l. leg	200	101
122154	Indet. medium mammal		3	1
122176	pig head & R. fore limb		9	3
122476	Pig head & possible further regions	long bone	23	3
122536	Pig head & limb, large individual <17–22 months	long bone	102	50
122554	Pig l. & r. hind limbs, 24–42 months. Poss. complete pig post-cranial skeleton & poss. sheep/ goat distal tibia. Butchered medium mammal ribs	fowl carcass	184	148
122568	indet. medium mammal		3	1
122571		long bone	1	<1
122635	pig l. fore limb, 12–42 months & prob. pig skull	fowl l. wing	31	20
122651	pig r. fore limb & l. hind limb, <42 months		58	43
122733	pig l. forelimb	fowl r. wing	9	2
122780	pig head, fore & hind limb, <12 months. Poss. sheep/goat mandible	long bone	101	30
122794	indet. medium mammal	long bone	7	<1
122818 *	pig l. fore limb, <42 months		12	7
122874	pig head inc. some vertebrae		53	33
129071	pig head & poss. other regions	long bones	31	3
129073	pig head		5	1
129074	pig head & l. hind limb, <12 months	fowl carcass	183	61
129075	pig head & limb		24	9
129078		bird r. limb	19	1
129079	pig head		11	5
129080	pig head & r. forelimb *c.* 12 months	long bone	83	36
129083	indet. medium mammal		1	<1
129084	medium mammal limb		4	<1

* = unurned burial

left hind limb). Head and both fore and hind limb portions were recovered from two burials (in one both limbs were from the left hand side). Head and indeterminate limb was recovered from three burials, and head and further indeterminate regions was recovered from one burial.

Pig legs without accompanying heads were recovered from three urned burials; grave 122651 contained a right fore limb and a left hind limb, grave 122733 a left fore limb, and grave 122554 both left and right limbs but may have included a complete post-cranial skeleton with further fore limb and thoracic fragments from a medium sized mammal. A single fragment of possible sheep or goat was recovered from this context raising the possibility that the medium mammal fragments may be sheep or goat rather than pig. Grave 122554 also contained the only evidence for butchery in the animal bone assemblage; transverse cuts were identified on the medial and lateral faces of three medium mammal rib fragments.

Bone fusion and the presence of unerupted tooth crowns indicated an age at death for the pigs from eight burials. There was no evidence of animals aged over 42 months at death. Pigs from two graves (122780 and 129074) were less than 12 months old and in grave 129080 the pig was *c* 12 months old. Grave 122536 contained a pig less than 22 months old, grave 122131 one less than 27 months old and grave 122651 a pig less than 42 months old. Graves 122635 and 122554 contained the remains of animals 12–42 months old and 24–42 months old at death respectively. No animals were neonatal.

Bird pyre goods

No bird cranial fragments were identified. However bones from both legs and wings were recovered from graves 122554 and 129074, indicating that a complete carcass might have been present on the pyre. Wing bones were identified in graves 122044, 122635 and 122733, and leg bones in 122132 and 129078. The remaining bird pyre goods comprised long bone fragments which could not be further identified.

Burnt animal bone from unurned cremation burials

Burnt animal bone was recovered from two urned burials (Table 41). The unurned burials contained 2–30 fragments of animal bone (4–10 g). Grave 122045 contained pig, sheep or goat and bird (probably domestic fowl) bones, and grave 122818 only pig. With the exception of the definite presence of sheep or goat, the form of animal pyre goods from unurned burials was consistent with those found in urned burials at the site.

Pig pyre goods

A pig skull and right fore limb from an individual aged over 12 months old at death were recovered from grave 122045. A pig left fore limb from an individual of less than 42 months old was recovered from grave 122818.

Sheep or goat pyre goods

Grave 122045 contained a sheep or goat right fore limb from an animal aged less than 30 months old at death.

Bird pyre goods

Grave 122045 contained a bird wing, probably from a domestic fowl.

Table 42 Cremated mammal bone from redeposited pyre debris

Fill of	*Mammal*	*No.*	*Wt (g)*
122029	medium or large indet.	15	5
122030	medium mammal limb	6	2
122035	large or medium indet. frag. (with Fe stain)	1	1
122036	cattle l. astragalus & calcaneum	6	31
122037	prob. pig skull	1	<1
122037	cattle l. navicular cuboid	3	12
122553	medium limb	21	4
122784	medium limb	4	<1
122833	medium indet. frag.	1	<1
122857	medium limb	4	1
122975	pig limb	13	1

Burnt animal bone from redeposited pyre debris

Burnt animal bone was recovered from ten pits containing redeposited pyre debris (Table 42). Each contained between one and 21 fragments of burnt animal bone (<1–31 g). All the animal bone was identified as mammal with pig bones recovered from pits 122037 and 122975 and cattle bones from 122037. The remaining deposits contained only medium mammal sized fragments.

Burnt animal bone from cremation-related deposits

Cut 122083 (context 122084) contained a bird long bone and a medium mammal indeterminate fragment (total weight of less than 1 g). Cut 122124 (context 122125) contained two indeterminate burnt bone fragments (total weight of less than 1 g).

Burnt animal bone from redeposited burials

Pits 122059 and 122614 contained the remains of redeposited cremation burials, both of which included cremated animal bone. Context 122060 from pit 122059 contained a single bird long bone fragment (weighing less than 1 g). Contexts 122615 and 122674 from pit 122614 contained three medium mammal unidentified fragments and two adjoining fragments of indeterminate long bone (total weight of 1 g).

Burnt animal bone from other archaeological contexts

The range of taxa identified in these deposits was limited to pig, sheep or goat, domestic fowl, medium mammal and indeterminate mammal (summarised in archive).

Discussion

The cremation rite practiced at the site included burning fleshed pig portions and domestic fowl carcasses or carcass portions. Occasionally sheep or goat and cattle portions were also burnt. Some of the burnt animal remains were incorporated into cremation burials with the human remains, but some were redeposited with the pyre debris. Animal pyre goods were recovered from 30 burials, each containing 1–3 taxa. Burials with three taxa were uncommon (two occurrences), 16 contained one taxon and 13 contained two. Where pig remains could be aged, the animals were less than 42 months old at death; most were over 12 months.

A recent survey of faunal pyre goods in Romano-British cremation burials (Worley forthcoming) identified 32 sites in the UK with animal pyre goods. Of these, only two sites (Derby Racecourse and Alcester Birch Abbey burials) are in the Midlands. Derby Racecourse included 70 analysed cremation burials, 30% of which contained burnt animal bones. The burials were dated between the mid-1st and 4th centuries AD. A single 4th century cremation burial was excavated in the inhumation cemetery of Alcester Birch Abbey, Warwickshire (Denston 1994). The grave contained the cremated remains of an adult female and the bones of a sheep or goat and a bird.

The majority of mammalian pig pyre goods at Derby Racecourse were also immature pig (Harman 1985a). Fewer identified fragments were recovered from each burial, but, the skeletal distribution of pig pyre goods from Derby Racecourse Cemetery does not appear to be as consistent as that from Ryknield Street.

A similar pattern of pig pyre goods can be found in the assemblage from the Romano-British cemetery of East London (Barber and Bowsher 2000) where 20% of the 377 various forms of cremation-related deposits analysed contained burnt animal bone. At the East London cemetery the majority of animal pyre goods were identified as pig or domestic fowl, although a wide range of other taxa was also present. The pig pyre goods often comprised skeletons or forelimbs with cranial parts also well represented (Reilly 2000). Pig skulls and limbs, and domestic fowl remains were also the most common pyre goods at the Late Iron Age cremation cemetery of King Harry Lane at *Verulamium* (Stead and Rigby 1989). Davis reports that at King Harry Lane, pig pyre goods consisted of portions of head and/or single limbs (Davis 1989), a remarkably similar pattern to that at Ryknield Street. Davis goes on to suggest that the pigs' feet were not included in the pyre good (*ibid.*); however this is not consistent with the assemblage being reported here. Finally, a predominance of pig and domestic fowl pyre goods was also a feature of the Late Iron Age and Romano-British cemetery of St Stephens' at *Verulamium* analysed by the writer.

Although this report has identified several Late Iron Age and Romano-British cremation cemeteries with a high occurrence of pig and domestic fowl pyre goods, this pattern is not found at all contemporaneous cemeteries in Britain. Several cemeteries have higher proportions of sheep or goat and cattle remains with other identified taxa including fish, dogs and, very rarely, horses. The high proportion of pig and fowl remains amongst pyre goods appears to be a pattern restricted to south-eastern England in the Late Iron Age and Romano-British periods. The remains from Ryknield Street extend that range into the Midlands.

The motivation behind the inclusion of animal pyre goods remains unclear. The pigs and domestic fowl burnt at Ryknield Street may have been food offerings or sacrifices. Pork and poultry were both popular meats in the military and urban Roman diet and are found frequently in settlement assemblages (Grant 1989; King 1991; 1999). However, both pigs and domestic fowl are also recorded as suitable sacrificial species in Roman writings and both had chthonic or funerary significance (for example see Simoons 1994). Perhaps the two associations should be seen as acting together increasing the suitability of pigs and fowl as pyre goods.

Environmental

Charred plant remains, by Lisa Gray

Of the 289 samples taken, 60 were selected for analysis from a variety of features predominantly associated with the cemetery. Charred plant remains were recovered from 32 of the samples, the contents of which are given in full in Tables 43–9 (for key to tables see Table 43).

One of the 32 samples containing charred plant remains, taken from the old ground surface below the Roman road, has been allocated a Late Iron Age date by radiocarbon analysis. A variety of Romano-British features were sampled including cremation graves and other deposits associated with the cremation rite, a possible inhumation grave, ditches, ovens and pits (several of the latter are undated). Charred remains included legume and weed seeds, cereal grains, tuber fragments and wood fragments. All scientific names for the plants are taken from Stace (Stace 1997) and will be given once, in brackets, with the common name and the common name, alone being used thereafter. For ease of reading the term 'seed' includes the more botanically correct terms such as achene and nutlet.

Results

The most frequent macro-remains were fragments of wood and tuber. The tubers were those of false oat/onion couch grass (*Arrhenatherum elatius var. bulbosum*) and were present in 18 of the samples. The remaining plant remains were seeds of legumes, weed seeds, grains and nutshells. Fragments of grass (Poaceae) stem were recovered but these are likely to belong to the false oat/onion couch grass tubers. No chaff was observed.

The legumes and grains were generally much abraded and in fragments. The most frequent grain was barley (*Hordeum* sp.) and the most frequent legume was lentil (*Lens culinaris*). These were recovered in small quantities in six samples with most being found in two samples from the mortuary enclosure ditch 126066 (samples 124123 and 124216). Samples from the fills of two cremation graves also contained lentils (Table 48). A fragment of sloe (*Prunus spinosa*) was also found in the redeposited pyre debris from pit 122975.

The weed seeds were dominated by ruderals such as black bindweed (*cf. Fallopia convolvulus*) and knotgrass (*Polygonum aviculare*). Most of the cereal grains were

Table 43 Charred plant remains from old ground surface 122597

Taxon	Common name	Sample 124248
	Sample size (l)	18
	Flot size (ml)	100
Rubus fruticosus agg. seed	blackberry	1
Polygonum aviculare seed	knotgrass	1
Arrhenatherum elatius tubers	false oat/onion couch grass	6
indet. frags (>4 mm^3)	wood	++
indet. frag.	nutshell	1

Key to estimated levels of abundance codes: + = 1–10; ++ = 11–50; +++ = 51–150; ++++ = 151–250; +++++ = > 250

Table 44 Charred plant remains from the ovens

Taxon	Common name				
	Cut	122085	122358	122100	122098
	Context	122088	122370	122101	122097
	Sample	124032	124121	124050	124036
	Sample size (l)	10	6	10	10
	Flot size (ml)	500	500	700	175
Cereal remains					
Triticum sp. grain	wheat	–	–	1	–
Hordeum/*Triticum* sp. grain	barley/wheat	2	–	–	–
Other remains				–	–
Lens culinaris seed	lentil	–	–	–	–
Arrhenatherum elatius tubers	false oat/ onion couch grass	–	3	–	–
Poaceae stem frag.	grass	–	–	7	–
indet. frag. (>4 mm^3)	wood	+++++	++++	+++++	+
indet. frag. (<4 mm^3)	wood	+++++	–	+++++	+++++

Table 45 Charred plant remains in pit samples

Taxon	Common name			
	Cut	122876	122923	122797
	Context	122877	122978	122798
	Sample	124288	124301	124244
	Sample size (l)	10	10	10
	Flot size (ml)	90	30	40
Cereal remains				
Triticum cf. *dicoccum* 1-seeded/ terminal grain	emmer wheat	1	–	–
T. spelta grain	spelt wheat	4	–	–
T. dicoccum/*spelta* grain	emmer/spelt	3	–	–
T. spelta/*aestivum* grain	spelt/bread wheat	2	–	–
Triticum sp. grain	wheat	17	–	–
cf. *Hordeum* sp (abraded) grain	barley	16	–	–
cf. *Avena* sp. (abraded grain)	?oat	1	–	–
Other remains				–
Vicia cf. *tetra-sperma* seed	smooth tare	1	–	–
Vicia cf *cracca* seed	tufted vetch	1	–	–
Vicia/*Lathyrus*/*Pisum* sp. seed	vetch/tare/vetchling/pea	6	–	–
Polygonum sp. seed frag.	knotgrass	–	1	–
Persicaria seed	persicaria/redshank	1	–	–
Fallopia convolvulus seed	black bindweed	4	–	–
Arrhenatherum elatius tuber	false oat/onion couch grass	–	1	1
Lamiaceae/Urticaceae stem frag.	dead-nettle/ nettle family	1	–	–
Poaceae stem frag.	grass family	–	1	–
indet. frag. (>4 mm^3)	wood	+++	–	++
indet. flecks (<4 mm^3)	wood	–	++++	++++

Table 46 Charred plant remains from redeposited pyre debris

	Cut	122784	122975	122029	129024	122037	
	Context	122785	122976	122019	129025	122038	122039
	Sample	124245	124306	124007	124310	124025	124027
	Sample size (l)	10	10	8	10	8	6
	Flot size (ml)	50	40	90	10	450	450
Taxon	Common name						
Cereal remains							
cf. *Triticum* sp. (abraded) grain	possible wheat	–	–	–	1	–	–
cf. *Hordeum* sp. (abraded) grain	possible barley	–	–	–	–	–	1
Other remains							
Lens culinaris seed	possible lentil	–	–	–	–	1+cf. 1	–
Brassica/Sinapsis seed	cabbage	cf. 1	–	–	–	–	–
Polygonum aviculare seed	knotgrass	–	–	–	1	–	–
Arrenatherum elatius tuber	false oat/onion couch grass	4	12	6	–	12	1
Poaceae stem frag.	grass family	1	4	7	–	–	–
indet. frag. (>4 mm^3)	wood	+	+++	+++	–	+++++	++
indet. fleck (<4 mm^3)	wood	+++	++++	++++	++++	+++++	–
indet. frag.	nutshell	–	–	–	–	–	–

Table 47 Charred plant remains from cremation-related features

		Cut	122124	122922	122083	122072
		Context	122125	122927	122084	122087
		Sample	124053	124297	124030	124031
		Sample size (l)	10	9	10	2
		Flot size (ml)	40	90	60	40
Taxon	Common name	Habitat/use				
cf. *Hordeum* sp. (v. abraded) grain	barley	FI	–	–	1	–
Lens culinaris seed	possible lentil	FI	–	–	1	–
Rubus fruticosus agg. seed	blackberry	CFGH	–	2	–	–
Polygonum aviculare seed	knotgrass	ABG	–	4	–	–
Prunus spinosa frag.	sloe	FHI	–	1	–	–
Arrhenatherum elatius tuber	false oat/onion couch grass	BCD	–	–	4	5
Poaceae stem frag.	grass family	–	–	5	–	–
indet. frag. (>4 mm^3)	wood	–	–	+++	++	–
indet. fleck. (<4 mm^3)	wood	–	++++	++++	++++	+++++

Table 48 Charred plant remains from cremation graves containing urned burials

	Cut	122025	122132	129079	122154	122017	122501	129074	122568	122651
	Context	122026	122142	122108	122153	122018	122502	122523	122608	122652
	Sample	124003	124064	124047	124226	124001	124152	124162	124282	124210
	Sample size (l)	10	10	10	9	10	3.5	10	3	5
	Flot Size (ml)	20	10	40	40	300	50	5	5	30
Taxon	Common name									
Cereal remains										
cf. *Triticum* sp. (abraded) grain	possible wheat	–	–	–	1	–	–	–	–	–
Other remains										
Lens culinaris seed	lentil	–	–	–	1	–	–	–	–	–
cf. *Lens culinaris* seed	possible lentil	–	–	–	–	1	–	–	–	–
Prunus spinosa seed	sloe	–	–	–	–	–	–	–	–	1
Arrhenatherum elatius tuber	false oat/onion couch grass	–	–	9	74	2	5	–	–	–
Poaceae stem frag.	grass family	–	–	1	–	8	–	–	–	2
indet. frag. (>4 mm^3)	wood	–	–	–	–	++++	–	–	–	++
indet. fleck (<4 mm^3)	wood	++	+++	+++	+++	+++++	+++++	++++	+++	+++++

Table 49 Charred plant remains from cremation graves containing urned and unurned burials plus possible inhumation grave

	Cut	122780		122045	122977
	Context	122781	122903	122139	122913
	Burial type	urned	urned	unurned	?inhumation grave
	Sample	124231	124292	124066	123298
	Sample size (l)	6	5	10	9
	Flot size (ml)	60	50	30	40
Taxon	*Common name*				
cf. *Lens culinaris* seed	possible lentil	1	–	–	–
Lens culinaris seed	lentil	–	1	–	–
Rumex cf. *acetosella* seed	sheep's sorrel	2	–	–	–
Rumex sp. seed	dock	1	–	–	–
Arrhenatherum elatius tuber	false oat/onion couch grass	2	8	9	1
cf. *Arrhenatherum elatius* tuber	possible false oat/onion couch grass	–	1	–	–
Poaceae stem. frag.	grass family	9	1	3	1
indet. frag. (>4 mm^3)	wood	+++++	++	–	–
indet. frag. (>4 mm^3)	wood	–	+++++	++++	++++

recovered from an undated pit (122876) in the south-west corner of the site. These included barley grains and a small number of grains of emmer (*Triticum dicoccum*), spelt (*T. spelta*), emmer/spelt (*T. dicoccum/spelta*) and spelt/breadwheat (*T. spelta/ aestivum*). One poorly preserved possible oat (*cf. Avena* sp.) grain was also recovered from this pit.

A number of weed seeds of similar species to those seen within the other samples were recovered from this sample, along with several seeds of vetch/tare/wild pea (*Vicia/Lathyrus* sp.)

Discussion

Resources associated with cremation

Tubers of false-oat grass are commonly recovered from Bronze Age cremation deposits (Robinson 1988; Greig 1991; Moffett 1999), where they have been interpreted as possible deliberate deposits or kindling (Murphy 1983b, 127). Robinson suggested that a possible way these tubers entered the archaeological record was because the whole plant was gathered by being pulled out of the ground with the intention of the dried stems being used as kindling for pyres and the tubers surviving by charring because the stem bases would have been uprooted too (1988, 102). False oat/onion couch grass tubers were not observed in the analysis of samples from the Eastern or Western cemeteries of Roman London (Davis with de Moulins 2000; Gray 2003), but are present from Site 12. This would tend to support the hypothesis that they represent the use of locally available resources rather than the deliberate gathering of these tubers as ritual offerings.

It is also possible that many of the seeds of wild species entered the samples with plants uprooted with the false oat/onion couch grass as it was gathered for kindling; all gathered dry and *en masse* to provide fuel for the pyres. However, evidence was also recovered for other plants more commonly associated with the collection of wild food resources. A sloe/blackthorn stone was found in the sample from cremation grave 122651, and three blackberry seeds were found in the cremation-related deposit from cut 122922 (Table 47).

Funerary practices

Although not all of the following plant remains were found in pyre debris, they may have ritual significance as funerary offerings. Lentil has been found in samples from cremations in Roman London (Davis 2000, 369; Giorgi 2000). It is possible that a Roman cultural practice could have travelled this far and that these lentil fragments were the remains of a ritual offering. It may be significant that one lentil was found in one of the ovens (122100) on the western margins of the cemetery. The remaining small-seeded legumes could have arrived as crop weeds with grain, tinder or kindling.

None of the other edible legumes or fruits observed at some other Romano-British cremation cemeteries, such as pea (*Pisum sativum*) and bean (*Vicia faba*), was observed here (Davis 2000, 369).

Environment

The general environment indicated by the finds of false-oat/onion couch grass is one of dry long grassland, possibly previously abandoned agricultural land. Robinson described the natural habitat of false oat/onion couch grass as well-drained soil where grazing had been withdrawn, and suggested that the material in the pyres came from land that had been cleared and was no longer being used agriculturally (Davis 1988).

Charcoal, by Rowena Gale

Soil conditions at the cemetery were not conducive to the long-term preservation of organic material and despite the frequency of charcoal in some contexts much of this material was degraded and difficult to examine. Sixty-seven samples were selected for full analysis: one prehistoric; three prehistoric/Romano-British; 57 Romano-British; one post-medieval; five undated. The samples mainly derived from cremation graves (containing the remains of urned and unurned burials), pits containing redeposited pyre debris and other forms of cremation-related deposit, although charcoal was also examined from ovens, ditches and pits of unknown function. Sample selection was initially based on context type and sample size but also prioritised contexts in which charred plant remains were present. Charcoal analysis was undertaken to examine species selection for pyre construction and to identify the ritual use of woods for funerary practices during the Roman-British period; and also to obtain environmental evidence.

Results

The taxa identified are presented in Table 50.

Prehistoric/Romano-British

The tree hollow (122907), situated between mortuary enclosures 126066 and 126069, had been cut by inhumation grave 122860 providing a Romano-British *terminus ante quem*. The charcoal-rich samples from its fill (124296, 50% sub-sampled, and 124361) consisted of degraded oak (*Quercus* sp.) largewood. The origin of these single species deposits may have been from the tree itself.

Romano-British

Cremation graves with urned burials

Charcoal from 14 grave fills was examined. Most contexts included multiple species with oak common to almost every sample. Other taxa identified included birch (*Betula* sp.), ash (*Fraxinus excelsior*), the hawthorn/*Sorbus* group (Pomoideae), willow (*Salix* sp.) or poplar (*Populus* sp.), pine (*Pinus* sp.) and an unidentified conifer (the latter too degraded to name). Single species deposits of oak were recorded in five graves but in quantities too small to be of significance.

Cremation-related deposits

Charcoal was examined from four pits containing the remains of deposits which could be interpreted either as redeposited pyre debris or as unurned burials with redeposited pyre debris. These deposits tended to be larger than those from graves containing urned burials but were similarly dominated by oak, with the sporadic occurrence of other species. The range of non-oak species differed slightly to that from the urned burials but probably not in any significant way.

The sample from pit 122083 (sample 124362) included short lengths of oak and elm (*Ulmus* sp.) roundwood measuring about 50–70 mm in diameter; these pieces retained their original morphology and measured up to 150 mm in length.

Redeposited pyre debris

Samples recovered from nine pits containing redeposited pyre debris were examined. The charcoal from pit 122095, while not particularly abundant, included an unusually wide range of taxa.

A fairly large quantity of oak was identified in the sample from pit 122784, which also contained about 40 nails, some of which were embedded in large pieces of wood. This could suggest debris either from the recycling of structural waste as pyre fuel or the inclusion of a nailed structure/artefact in the pyre, such as a wooden stretcher to support the body.

Similar observations were made with regard to the material from pit 122037, located outside the south-east boundary of the cemetery, which was recovered by quadrant (samples 124025: 25% sub-sampled, 124027 and 124357). The charcoal was degraded with some pieces vitrified and/or slaggy. All three samples were composed almost entirely of oak largewood, although oak and birch were also present as roundwood. On excavation, nails were recorded as *in situ* in some of the wood.

The huge amount of charcoal collected from pit 122078 (25% sub-sampled) consisted mostly of moderate- to fast-grown oak roundwood, mainly about 60–70 mm in diameter, but also birch wood, probably of similar dimensions.

Inhumation burials

Small fragments of oak roundwood (sample 124356) were collected from grave 122609, in which a coffin stain and loose nails were recorded. The possible grave 122977 included both oak and pine. It is most likely that this material was redeposited within the inhumation graves from disturbed cremation graves or some other form of cremation-related deposit; cremated bone was recovered from the fill of grave 122609.

Mortuary enclosure ditches

Charcoal was examined from ditches defining the four mortuary enclosures. This material almost certainly originated from pyre fuel, probably from discarded/dumped material from pyre sites although ritual deposits may also be relevant. None of the samples was particularly large and all were in poor condition. The charcoal was similar in character to that from the cremation graves, with oak as the most frequent taxon, and, more sporadically, birch, hazel (*Corylus avellana*), ash, willow and/or poplar, the hawthorn/*Sorbus* group and pine. Many of these deposits also included pottery fragments and nails (see above).

Ovens

Three features interpreted as ovens or hearths were located along the western boundary of the cemetery. The charcoal-rich sample 124121 (50% sub-sampled) from oven 122358 was composed mainly of oak roundwood ranging in diameter from <20–50 mm in diameter, some of which included very slow-grown wood. Additional narrow roundwood was named as hazel (fast-grown), ash and willow and/or poplar. The remains of charred grain and bone suggest a possible use for cooking food. Ovens 122085 (10% sub-sampled) and 122100 (10% sub-sampled) also contained large amounts of burnt fuel debris, which included various other species in addition to those named above. Overall, these ovens demonstrated the use of roundwood gathered from a broad mix of species.

Pit

Samples from two pits of unknown function were analysed. Pit 122681 included mainly oak but also holly (*Ilex aquifolium*). The origin of the charcoal from these pits is unknown.

Table 50 Charcoal (no. frags)

Cut	Context	Sample	Acer	Alnus	Betula	Corylus	Fraxinus	Ilex	Pomoidaea	Prunus	Quercus	Salix/ Populus	Sambucus	Ulex/ Cytisus	Ulmus	Pinus	Conifer
Prehistoric																	
Old ground surface																	
-	122597	124248	-	-	2	-	-	-	-	-	12h/u,2s	-	-	-	-	-	-
Prehistoric/Romano-British																	
Pit																	
122900	122901	124291	-	-	-	-	-	-	-	-	5h, 1s	-	-	-	-	-	-
Tree-throw																	
122907	122905	124296	-	-	-	-	-	-	-	-	81h/u	-	-	-	-	-	-
		124361	-	-	-	-	-	-	-	-	38h/u	-	-	-	-	-	-
Romano-British																	
Cremation graves containing urned burials																	
122017	122018	124001	-	-	-	-	6h, 18s	-	-	-	28h	-	-	-	-	-	-
122025	122026	124003	-	-	1	-	-	-	-	-	8u	-	-	-	-	-	-
122052	122053	124010	-	-	1	-	-	-	3	-	2h,15r,4s	3	-	-	-	-	1
129082	122131	124055	-	-	1	-	-	-	-	-	31h/u	1	-	-	-	-	-
122132	122142	124064	Insufficient charcoal														
122154	122153	124226	-	-	1	-	-	-	-	-	15r	5	-	-	-	-	-
122176	129042	124333	-	-	-	-	-	-	-	-	8h,1r,17s	-	-	-	-	-	-
122501	122502	124152	-	-	7	-	-	-	-	-	2h,11r,2s	-	-	-	-	-	-
129074	122523	124162	-	-	-	-	-	-	-	-	2u	-	-	-	-	-	-
122568	122608	124182	-	-	-	-	-	-	-	-	4u	-	-	-	-	-	-
122651	122652	124210	-	-	-	-	-	-	-	-	9u	-	-	-	-	-	-
122780	122781	124231	-	-	-	-	8	-	-	-	22h/u	1	-	-	-	1	-
	122903	124292	-	-	-	-	12	-	3	-	30h/u,2r,1s	-	-	-	-	-	-
129078	122081	124038	-	-	1	-	-	-	1	-	5u	-	-	-	-	-	-
		124354	-	-	-	-	1r	-	-	-	-	-	-	-	-	-	-
129079	122108	124047	-	-	-	-	-	-	-	-	6h, 5s	-	-	-	-	-	1
Cremation graves containing unurned burials																	
122045	122139	124066	-	-	1	-	-	-	-	-	6h/u, 3s	-	-	-	-	-	-
Redeposited burials																	
122922	122927	124297	-	-	-	-	-	-	*cf.*1	-	14h,1s	-	-	-	-	-	-
Cremation-related deposits																	
122059	122066	124017	-	-	-	-	-	-	-	-	3u	-	-	-	-	-	-
122072	122087	124031	-	-	-	-	-	-	9	-	11h, 1s	-	-	-	-	-	-
	122073	124355	-	-	-	-	-	-	1	-	-	-	-	-	-	-	-
	122097	124036	-	-	-	2r	-	-	1	-	27u	6	-	-	-	-	-
122083	122084	124030	-	-	-	-	-	34	-	-	35h/u,6r,10s	-	-	-	3	-	-
		124358	-	-	-	-	-	-	-	-	3h	-	-	-	-	-	-
		124362	-	-	-	-	-	15	-	-	41h, 8r	1	-	-	14	-	-

Cut	Context	Sample	*Acer*	*Alnus*	*Betula*	*Corylus*	*Fraxinus*	*Ilex*	*Pomoideae*	*Prunus*	*Quercus*	*Salix/ Populus*	*Sambucus*	*Ulex/ Cytisus*	*Ulmus*	*Pinus*	Conifer
122124	122125	124053	-	1	-	-	-	-	-	4	31h/u, 18s	-	3	-	-	-	-
Redeposited pyre debris																	
122029	122019	124007	-	-	-	-	2r	-	-	-	21h, 3s	-	-	-	-	-	-
122046	122047	124011	-	-	1	-	-	-	1	-	1h, 18r, 6s	-	-	-	-	-	-
122078	122079	124034	-	-	12	-	-	-	-	-	74s	-	-	-	-	-	-
122095	122096	124042*	1	-	21	-	1	4	5	-	2h, 1r, 13s	1	-	-	-	-	-
122037	122038	124025	-	-	2r	-	-	-	-	-	26h/u	-	-	-	-	-	-
	122039	124027	-	-	-	-	-	-	-	-	51h	-	-	-	-	-	-
	122041	124357	-	-	-	-	-	-	-	-	1h	-	-	-	-	-	-
122784	122785	124245	-	-	-	-	-	-	-	-	39h/u, 2s	-	-	-	-	-	-
122810	122796	124260	-	-	-	1	-	-	13	-	6h, 8r, 5s	-	-	-	-	-	-
122975	122976	124306	-	-	-	-	-	-	-	-	8h, 3s	-	-	-	-	-	-
129024	122025	124310	-	-	-	-	-	-	-	-	3h, 1s	-	-	-	-	1	-
Inhumation grave																	
122977	122913	124298	-	-	-	-	-	-	-	-	6h, 2s	-	-	-	-	4	-
122609	122610	124356	-	-	-	-	-	-	-	-	8r	-	-	-	-	-	-
Mortuary enclosure ditches																	
126066	122380	124123	-	-	-	-	-	-	-	-	18u	-	-	-	-	6	-
	122722	124216	-	-	-	-	-	-	-	-	22h/u	1r	-	-	-	-	-
126069	122166	124089	-	-	2	-	-	-	-	-	7h, 4s	-	-	-	-	1	-
	122218	124104	-	-	-	-	-	-	-	-	15h/u	-	-	-	-	-	-
126154	122520	124156	-	-	-	1	-	-	1	-	2u	-	-	-	-	-	-
	122576	124191	-	-	-	1	-	-	-	-	7h, 1s	-	-	-	-	-	-
126148	122815	124252	-	-	-	-	-	-	-	-	8h, 8s	-	-	-	-	-	-
Ovens																	
122085	122088	124032	-	-	-	36	-	35	1	-	31h/u,2r, 5s	-	-	-	-	-	-
122100	122101	124050	-	1	8	-	2	-	-	1r	66h/u,2r, 13s	2	-	-	-	-	-
122358	122370	124121	-	-	-	1r	2r	-	-	-	29s/r, 4r	2	-	-	-	-	-
Pits																	
122681	122682	124214	-	-	-	-	-	3	-	-	25h/u,1s	-	-	-	-	-	-
122923	122978	124301	-	-	3	-	-	-	-	-	7s	-	-	-	-	-	-
Road-zone ditches																	
126059	122077	124353	-	-	1	-	-	-	-	-	1r	-	-	-	-	-	-
126065	122169	124119	-	-	-	-	-	-	-	-	1h, 2s	-	-	-	-	-	-
		124225	-	-	2	-	1	-	-	-	11h, 4r, 2s	-	-	-	-	-	-
	122663	124233	-	-	3	-	-	-	-	-	33u	1	-	-	-	-	-
	122668	124234	-	-	-	-	-	-	-	-	20h/u, 3s	1	-	-	-	-	-
	122665	124235	-	-	5	-	-	-	-	-	23h/u, 1s	3	-	-	-	-	-

Cut	Context	Sample	Acer	Alnus	Betula	Corylus	Fraxinus	Ilex	Pomoideae	Prunus	Quercus	Salix/ Populus	Sambucus	Ulex/ Cytisus	Ulmus	Pinus	Conifer
Post-medieval																	
Ditch																	
126221	122071	124070	-	-	2r	-	-	-	-	-	27h, 1s	3r	-	-	-	-	-
Undated																	
Pits																	
122739	122740	124243	-	47	10	-	-	1	11	2	2r	-	-	1r	-	-	-
122797	122798	124244	-	5	1	-	8	1	3	-	-	-	-	-	-	-	-
122816	122817	124267	-	4	10	-	-	-	3	-	35h	-	-	-	-	-	-
122876	122877	124288	-	-	-	4	-	-	-	-	16h/u	-	-	-	-	-	-
Tree-throw/hollow																	
122870	122884	124289	-	-	-	-	-	-	-	-	61h	-	-	-	-	-	-

Key: h = heartwood; r = roundwood; (diam. <20 mm); s = sapwood (diam. unknown); u = maturity unknown (*Quercus* only)

Discussion

The Romano-British cemetery extended on both sides of Ryknield Street, with its outer boundaries defined by ditches. The eastern half included four rectilinear ditched mortuary enclosures. Cremation graves were distributed across both halves of the cemetery but were more frequent in the eastern half. The series of ovens or hearths was located on the western fringe of the site, the function of these is uncertain although food preparation for ceremonial or celebratory feasting is a possibility.

The charcoal recovered from this range of features, although sometimes abundant (particularly in the ovens and in some pits and ditches) was mostly degraded, friable and infiltrated with reddish deposits. In some instances only a small percentage of the sample was suitable for identification.

Pyres and cremations

No evidence for pyre sites was recovered in excavation. The charcoal (pyre debris) associated within the cremation graves and other forms of deposit associated with the rite provides evidence of the type and character of the fuel used in pyre construction. Table 50 shows that in the 15 cremation graves, nine pits containing redeposited pyre debris and the four cremation-related deposits, oak occurred more frequently and (usually) in greater quantity than other taxa, suggesting that this was the preferred and, indeed, probably most practical wood for pyre construction.

The remains of substantial roundwood in the cremation-related deposit from pit 122083 included large chunks of charred oak and elm roundwood. These measured 50–70 mm in diameter and up to 150 mm in length. Since charcoal fragments of these dimensions could easily have been separated out during the collection of cremated bone from the pyre site if this was undertaken as hand recovery of individual bone fragments, the inclusion of such fragments supports the collection procedure discussed here and elsewhere by McKinley recovery by raking and winnowing (see above). Assuming these to have been collected from a pyre site, the dimensions of the charcoal demonstrates the use of poles up to 100+ mm in diameter in the pyre structure. This particular deposit was the only one in the current study to include elm. The pyre debris from pit 122078 included the remains of fast-grown oak poles measuring about 60 mm or 70 mm in diameter, probably obtained from managed woodland (see below); the birch was of similar dimensions.

In most instances, sparse additional taxa occurred rather randomly in the various deposits incorporating pyre debris. It is possible that some represent the remains of funerary furniture (eg the funeral bier/ wattle stretcher) and/or pyre goods such as wooden boxes or caskets (see above), and were not integral to the fabric of the pyre structure.

Maple wood, for example, was particularly prized for making boxes and caskets in the Romano-British period (Gale and Cutler 2000) and the rare inclusion of maple wood in the redeposited pyre debris from pit 122095 (not recorded from elsewhere on site) may be attributable to such origins. The presence of numerous nails in some contexts, for example cremation grave 122784 and the redeposited pyre debris from pit 122037 where nails remained *in situ* in large pieces of wood, may suggest the recycling of structural waste or they could relate to funerary furniture (see above).

Experimental work has indicated that *c* 146 kg of wood is required to cremate an adult human body. A rectangular platform has traditionally served as the most usual type of pyre structure, built from stout poles and in-filled with brushwood/smallwood (*ibid.*).

Charcoal from four cremation graves, one cremation-related deposit and two pits containing redeposited pyre debris, consisted solely of oak but in view of the small amount of charcoal available from most of these samples, it would be unsafe to base conclusions on these results. The unusual and interesting inclusion of pine/conifer was recorded in cremation graves 122052, 122780 and 129079, and in the redeposited pyre debris from pit 129024 and is discussed in more detail below (see Funerary custom/ritual). There was no evidence to indicate spatial differences in the type of pyre fuel recovered from the different mortuary enclosures or between the eastern and western sides of the cemetery.

Charcoal samples from the mortuary enclosure ditches were small and degraded. Funerary activities (sweepings from pyre sites) would have provided the most likely source for this material, and, indeed, the range of species in the ditches (including pine in ditches 126066 and 126069) reflects those identified from the cremation deposits and pyre debris.

Ovens

The charcoal from the ovens/hearths on the western margins of the cemetery was extremely abundant and in some contexts may represent multiple rake-outs from the ovens rather than debris from the final firing. In all instances, the charcoal indicated the extensive use of (usually) narrow roundwood from a wide range of species and thus differed substantially from the wider roundwood recorded in some pyre debris. Non-oak species often included fast-grown wood, perhaps from managed woodland, whereas oak roundwood was sometimes extremely slow-grown. Narrow roundwood makes particularly efficient fuel for ovens, as the high ratio of wood surface to atmospheric oxygen rapidly produces a very hot, although short-lived, fire. The addition of wider roundwood/logs would have extended the life of the heat source.

Tree throws/hollows

Large quantities of charcoal from the fills of the prehistoric/Romano-British (122907) and undated (122870) tree hollows consisted entirely of oak heartwood. The origin of this material is unknown. Although it could relate to the burnt remains of the trees, the location of sample 124289 from an upper layer of the fill of tree hollow 122870, in which burnt or scorched soil was recorded, suggests possible origins from activities or events some time after the tree had fallen.

Funerary customs/ritual

Tacitus (*Germania*, 27) wrote in the 1st century AD, while travelling through Germany, that the Gauls used specially selected wood for high-ranking cremations (perhaps inferring disparity between Gaulish and Roman cremations).

Charcoal deposits from the cemetery at Ryknield Street produced inconclusive evidence of the selection of single wood species for pyre construction, although oak was clearly the preferred fuel. Such evidence, however, may have been masked by the inclusion of pyre goods or funerary furniture (as discussed above). Although large deposits of oak occurred in the redeposited pyre debris from pit 122784, this appears to have included recycled oak planks, which, in this instance, may suggest that practical aspects of wood supply were more important than the ritual selection of wood species.

Although there is a growing body of evidence from Bronze Age cremation graves linking the exclusive use of certain woods with status, gender and age (Smith 2002), there are less data available to provide convincing proof of similar customs in later periods. For example, at the Late Iron Age/Romano-British cemetery at Westhampnett in West Sussex, which also included the sites of numerous Late Iron Age pyres, oak and ash provided the bulk of the pyre fuel, supplemented with a range of other species; the Late Iron Age pyre structures here also included (?discarded) planks and structural timbers (as indicated by iron nails; Gale 1997). One grave, however, differed in character from the others, which may allude to special status: deposits of cremated bone had been placed in each corner of the square grave and a layer of charcoal spread over the entire feature (the abundant single-species pyre fuel consisted of large fragments of ash). Pyres constructed from single wood species were also recorded at the Romano-British cemetery at Baldock Bypass, in this instance from oak poles (Gale 2005). Campbell (2004) has suggested that at Brougham there may have been some link between age/gender of the individual and wood species.

Almost certainly of ritual significance, however, was the occasional inclusion of coniferous evergreen species in the pyre deposits at Westhampnett, Baldock Bypass and in the cemetery here, at Ryknield Street. Pine and unidentified conifers (too degraded to identify to species) were recovered from cremation graves 122052 (western half), 129079 (eastern half) and 122780 (within mortuary enclosure), the redeposited pyre debris from pit 129024, the possible inhumation grave 122977 (probably redeposited pyre debris) and the mortuary enclosure ditches 126066 and 126069. At Westhampnett and Baldock Bypass, yew (*Taxus* sp.) fronds were included in pyre debris and a cremation burial respectively (Gale 1997; 2005).

In the writer's experience, yew and pine rarely occur in archaeological contexts and thus their specific association with burials at these sites must be of symbolic and/or ritual importance. Placing coniferous boughs or fronds on the burning pyre may have ensured renewal or perpetuity in the afterlife. Such action would accord with ancient beliefs held by many cultures throughout Europe, where evergreen trees, including pine and yew, were associated with death and immortality; yew wood, for example, was burnt on funeral pyres in Roman Italy (Dallimore 1908; Cornish 1946; Cooper 1978). The type of evergreen involved was probably determined by the local environment (pine grows on acid soils whereas yew favours chalk). The Roman practice of lining coffins with box (*Buxus*) leaves probably had similar connotations (Godwin 1956).

Environmental evidence and the provisioning of pyre fuel

The charcoal deposits indicate that pyre wood consisted predominantly of both fast-grown and slow-grown oak poles, suggesting that some supplies were obtained either from managed woodland or from trees in open habitats. The greater use of narrow roundwood to fuel the ovens, particularly fast-grown hazel (oven 122085), could also be indicative of woodland management, and it is notable that the species appears to increase in the period prior to the construction of the road (see below). The slow-grown oak, on the other hand, suggests trees growing in competitive or stressed conditions. Timber and wood for pyre construction would have been obtained from the closest sources available, especially given the large volume of wood required. Access to more distant woodlands would have been relatively easy via Ryknield Street, should this have been necessary.

Other woodland trees represented in the fuel debris and probably growing locally in oak woodland included birch, holly, hazel and ash. Elm, alder and willow/poplar prefer damper soils; and in waterlogged situations, alder and willow form alder carr. Blackthorn, the hawthorn group and elder typically grow in marginal woodland, whereas heathers, gorse/broom, birch and pine characterize impoverished soils or open heathland. It might be noted that while traces of pine pollen were present there is little evidence to suggest that the species had any real presence in the local environment (see below).

Despite the possible frequency of alder in the environment (see below), there was little evidence to indicate its use either as pyre fuel or to fuel the ovens. Although generally considered to make poor fuel (Edlin 1949; Porter 1990), it was, nonetheless, used on some occasions, as indicated by deposits in the undated pits 122797, 122816 and, particularly, in 122739.

Conclusion

The data indicate the consistent and predominant use of oak (poles) for pyre construction and, sometimes, recycled structural elements (planks). In almost all contexts small quantities from other species were also present, some of which may have been artefactual in origin. There were no apparent differences in the character of the pyre/fuel deposits in the two halves of the cemetery or between that included in the cremation graves, redeposited pyre debris or cremation-related deposits. A particularly interesting aspect, however, related to evidence of the ritual burning of coniferous branches, a practice rarely recorded from other Roman cremation burials in Britain, although described by Roman sources as common place in Italy.

Although the function of the ovens is uncertain, possible uses include food preparation for funerary feasts. The ovens were fired with narrow roundwood from a wide range of species.

Comparative analyses of the charcoal and pollen records indicate that, despite the possible dominance of alder woodland close to the cemetery immediately prior to the construction of Ryknield Street, alder wood was only sparsely represented in the fuel deposits (see also Scaife, below). The diversity of trees and shrubs named from the charcoal indicates the exploitation of woodland in differing habitats.

Pollen, by Robert G. Scaife

Pollen and spores were recovered from a sequence of five samples taken through the palaeosol (122597) underlying the Roman road, which has been dated by radiocarbon analysis to 190–30 cal BC (2094±30 BP; NZA-20577). The principal aim of this study was to reconstruct the past vegetation and environment, especially in relation to human impact and activities which might be related to the local archaeology.

The upper sample comes from sand which appears to form the lower part of the road make-up. The source and hence date of the pollen in this upper layer is of some question. It is probable that the sand was locally quarried from open exposures and hence contains pollen of more recent date. As such this uppermost sample is treated as the most recent in date.

Absolute pollen frequencies (APF) are notably high being greater than 1 million grains/ml. This abundance is attributed to the sandy, acidic character of the soil. Substantial pollen counts were thus made ranging from 750 grains to 1200. These data are presented in Figure 92.

Overall, tree and shrub pollen are dominant throughout the profile although the values of the former are greater in the lower levels whilst shrub values are higher in the upper assemblages. Heath taxa (*Calluna* and *Erica*) are also present and along with herbs become progressively more important towards the top of the profile.

Trees comprise largely *Alnus* (alder, 46% of total pollen) which is more important at the base of the profile declining to 12% in the upper sample within the sand of the road make-up. Also present are *Quercus* (oak, to 22%), *Tilia* (lime, to 10%) and *Betula* (birch, 10% at the top of the profile). *Ilex* (holly, to 1%) is considered important, being a very small pollen producer.

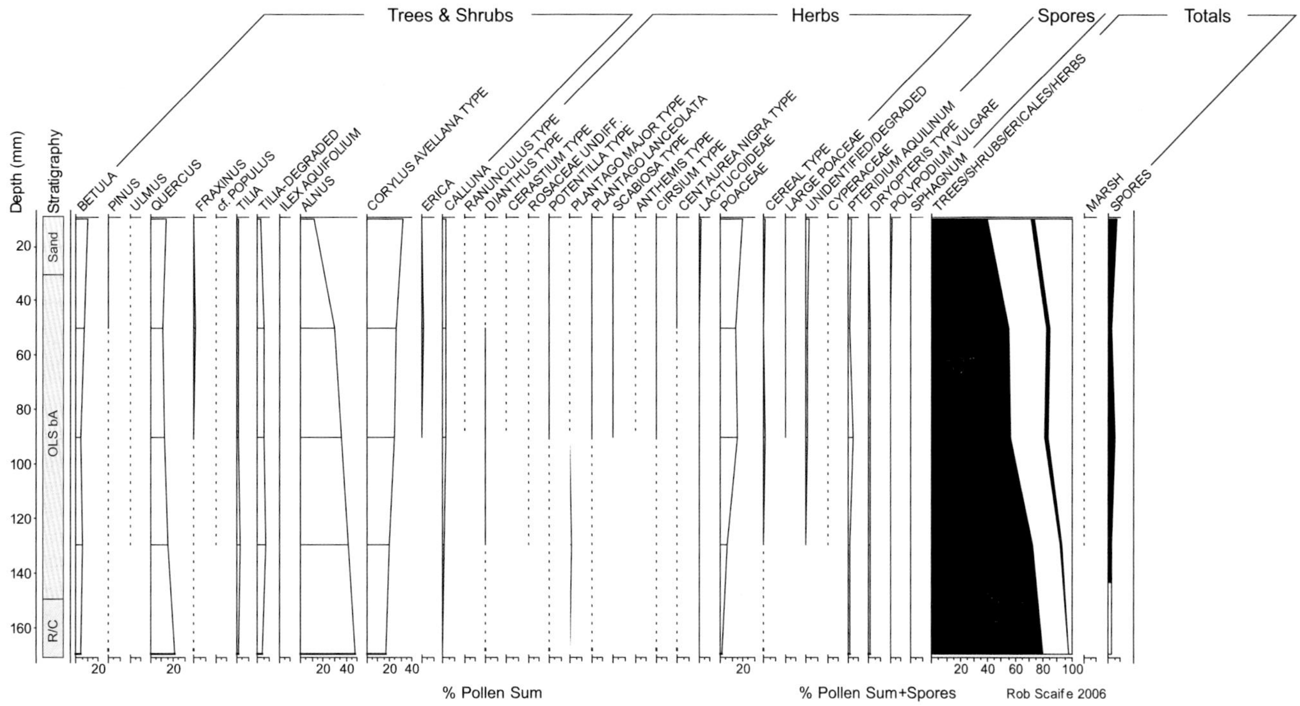

OLS = old ground surface; R/C = top of natural sand

Fig. 92 Pollen diagram

Shrubs are dominated by *Corylus avellana* type (31%; likely to be hazel but may include sweet gale). This taxon becomes more important in the upper levels. Dwarf shrubs comprise *Calluna* (ling) and *Erica* (heather) with values to 3%.

Herbs become progressively more important upwards in the profile. Poaceae (grasses) are most important increasing to 21%. There are occasional occurrences of cereal pollen along with other herbs including *Plantago lanceolata* (ribwort plantain), *Plantago media/major* type, Asteraceae types (daisy/dandelion types), *Potentilla* (cinquefoil), *Ranunculus* (buttercup) and Caryophyllaceae (pink family).

Ferns are represented by small numbers of spores of *Pteridium aquilinum* (bracken), *Dryopteris* type (monolete spores of typical ferns) and *Polypodium vulgare* (common polypody fern).

The inferred vegetation

The pollen data show clearly that trees and shrubs were important and probably dominant on and adjacent to the site. There is, however, evidence that there was progressive opening of this woodland as evidenced by the expansion of herbs. Alder is extremely important and although it is a high pollen producer, the values here suggest that it was locally important perhaps growing in nearby wetter valley habitats fringing rivers or as part of a more extensive floodplain carr woodland. Drier, better drained soils supported oak and hazel woodland with holly. Lime is present but has rather degraded pollen grains. This may indicate that its pollen may have remained in the soil from a period of its earlier importance on the site. This is a frequent occurrence, since although its pollen is generally under-represented in pollen spectra, it has robust pollen grains which may remain in soils for much greater periods than thin walled pollen taxa. The importance of lime woodland (small leaved lime) over much of southern and eastern England is now well documented and data here provide useful information for central England.

The expansion of herbs in the upper levels of this sequence implies that there was increasing pressure on the woodland. The expansion of hazel and the peaks of holly and bracken from 8 cm to 10 cm may reflect removal of oak, and opening of the woodland allowing the more heliophilous shrubs to flower more freely. This is also accompanied by occurrences of cereal type and other herbs which may come from near the site or from further distances by virtue of long distance/regional transport, since any opening of the woodland canopy would allow easier ingress to the site as the pollen catchment was enlarged. It should be noted that proximity of human habitation may also have resulted in cereal pollen and associated herbs coming from crop processing activities.

This palaeosoil underlies a Roman road and the absence of an upper humic soil layer (Ah) suggests that it was truncated during the road's construction. Information pertaining to the environment of the Romano-British period has been lost and the environment described relates to the preceding Iron Age.

Summary

The palaeosol underlying the Roman road was found to be exceptionally rich in sub-fossil pollen. Analysis of these pollen assemblages has shown that there was a change from a dominant alder, oak, hazel woodland to a more open environment. This comprised open woodland in which hazel was important with some evidence of cultivation or use of cereals. The environment described may be referable to the Iron Age. There is residual evidence of lime (*Tilia*) in the soils which is attributed to an earlier period (middle Holocene and Neolithic/Bronze Age).

Mollusca from cremation graves, by Michael J. Allen

During the routine processing of the 289 bulk samples, three were noted to contain rare snail shells. One was noted to contain freshwater snails in the flot. Sorting of the residue did not recover any further fragments. The snails from grave 122022, pit 122072 and a pit containing possible redeposited pyre debris (122046), survived where rare preservation was probably due to increased calcium carbonate levels created by the presence of ash waste (calcium phosphate) in the sampled context (Table 51).

Only four specimens were present, three of which were freshwater/amphibious and the fourth was probably typical of marsh and mesic habitats. All species are common in their preferred typical habitat and these habitats range from small bodies of water (*Hippeutis complanta*), running freshwater (*Gyraulus albus*), freshwater and floodplains subject to drying out (*Anisus leucostoma*), to marshes and dry damp terrestrial ground (*Carychium cf. minimum*).

Of particular interest is the presence of aquatic species, and even the single terrestrial species, *Carychium cf. minimum* is essentially a marsh dweller (Evans 1972), thus all of the species present are ones typical of small bodies of water, rivers or riversides. This, therefore, indicates the exploitation of riverine and floodplain resources for the cremation and burial practice. The site is located on the Shenstone and Wall floodplain mires and a small stream lies within 100 m of the cemetery and may have been the source, but even this runs into the Crane Brook within less than 0.5 km.

This evidence may suggest that, for instance, rushes may have been used to fuel or set the pyres, or water retained to quench them, but the precise activity cannot be discerned, just that local watery resources were exploited. The lack of terrestrial species in the same samples is, however, puzzling.

Table 51 Mollusca from cremation graves and cremation-related features

Cut	*Context*	*Sample*	*Mollusc*
122022	122024	124005	*Hippeutis complanta*
122072	122073	124024	*Carychium* cf. *minimum*
122046	122047	122011	*Anisus leucostoma* and *Gyraulus albus*

Buried soil beneath the Roman road, by Michael J. Allen

The buried soil (122597) sealed beneath the metalled road surface of the Roman road was examined and described in the field (M. Canti and M.J. Allen). A 180 mm high kubiena tin (sample 124317) was taken across the soil and sub-sampled for both pollen (see Scaife, above) and soil magnetic susceptibility. The soil and associated sediments were described following the terminology outlined by Hodgson (1976), and sub-samples removed for the measurement of magnetic susceptibility help define the local pedological and palaeo-environment (Allen and Macphail 1987; Allen 1986). This was recorded on 10 g air dried samples <2 mm using a Bartington MS2 meter coupled to a MS2B sensor calibrated for 10 g of soil.

At the sampling point, well within the road *agger*, the gravel metalling of the road rested on a thin sand layer which overlay the buried soil (Fig. 63). Elsewhere, on the edges of the road, this thin sand layer and the gravel metalling lay directly on subsoil, without the buried topsoil layer being present at all.

The geology locally comprises Triassic sandstones or pebble beds and is free of significantly different drift. The buried soil is developed in these loamy to medium sands. The profile at the sampling spot was described as follows and augmented with additional descriptive comments by Canti:

0–340 mm Modern deep ploughed topsoil

340–530 mm Gravel metalling. Brown (7.5YR 5/4) dry and dark reddish-brown (5YR 3/4) (ferruginous) moist loamy sand matrix surrounding 40–60% rounded stones of 10–70 mm. Patches of reddish-brown (5YR 4/4) in some parts of matrix. Abrupt wavy boundary.

530–640 mm Sand layer. Brown (10YR 4/3) dry and brown (7.5YR 5/4) and reddish-brown (5YR 5/4), loose sandy loam. Stoneless, with clear irregular boundary.

640–760 mm Buried soil (A horizon). Dark brown (7.5YR 4/2) dry and dark brown (7.5YR 3/4) moist sandy loam, with an incipient iron/manganese pan at about 670–700 mm where sand is darker – very dark grey (5YR 3/1) – and loosely cemented and partially cemented. Infilled worm burrows of 10YR 4/3 from horizon above. Also streaks of dark brown (7.5YR 3/2) and patches of brown (7.5YR 4/2). <5% stones of 1–10 mm. Abrupt wavy boundary.

760–*c* 800 mm+ Sand layer (R/C horizon). Brown (7.5YR 5/4) dry and pinkish-grey (7.5YR 6/2) moist, loamy sand. Excavated to a few centimetres only <5% stones 1–10 mm

The buried soil is an acid ranker developed on sandy loam and no horizonation was noted, but some local gleying or panning (incipient pan) was noticed only beneath the central portion of the road. Magnetic susceptibility (Table 52) shows very low background susceptibility levels (1.0), and very low enhancement in the soil (2.0–2.8), and magnetic susceptibility

Table 52 Magnetic susceptibility results (mag. sus. in SI x 10^{-8} SI/kg)

Depth (mm)	Depth* (mm)	Sample	Description	Magnetic susceptibility		
				Low frequency (0.1)	Low Frequency (1.0)	High frequency (1.0)
620–640	0–20	@ 10 mm	sand, beneath road	3.2	3	3
640–760	20–160	@ 30 mm	buried soil	2.8	2	2
		@ 60 mm		0.8	1	1
		@ 80 mm		2.1	3	2
		@ 100 mm		2.0	3	3
		@ 140 mm		1.0	1	1
760–800	160–180	@ 160 mm	top of natural sand	1.0	1	1

* = in Kubiena tin

suppression or reduction in the pan (presumably non ferromagnetic, or manganese dominated). Higher magnetic susceptibility levels in the sand above, probably derived from the ferruginous elements within the gravel of the road surface itself.

Interpretation

The buried soil is the slightly disturbed remains of a ranker soil and was part of the soil cover that would be expected on this substrate. Patches of discrete colour change within it (including occasional quite dark organic stains) suggest disruption (eg trampling?) over and above that simply caused by post-burial earthworm burrowing. This trampling may be related to the construction of the road itself, or Late Iron Age activity (dated from a sample of charred oak sapwood to 190–30 cal BC, 2094±30 BP; NZA-20577) evidenced from charcoal and burning activity in the buried soil.

The sand layer which seals the buried soil protected it prior to the emplacement of the gravel metalling. This sand may have been laid as a make-up layer for the gravel surface. Where this sandy layer is absent, the buried soil is also absent – even where the gravel layer is in place.

Discussion

Pre-Romano-British activity in the area of the site appears to have been of a marginal and mostly of a transient nature, probably influenced by the presence of the marshy/peaty ground to the south and east. Although flintwork of Mesolithic to Bronze Age date has been recovered from the area, predominantly from the higher ground around Wall and to the south around Shenstone, as at Ryknield Street it has all been unstratified (Gould 1966–7). The recovery of redeposited, largely unabraded fragments of Collared Urn from several later Romano-British features in the eastern half of the site, strongly suggest the one-time presence of Early Bronze Age burials in the immediate vicinity, possibly in association with a ring ditch or barrow (Allen, C., above). Given the location of the redeposited material this is most likely to have lain somewhere to the north-east of the site and to the south of the A5.

There is similarly limited evidence for Iron Age activity within the vicinity, with very few artefactual remains of this date having been recovered, although crop marks to the north, and possibly to the south of Watling Street on the east side of Wall do indicate a native British presence in the area prior to the Roman settlement (Gould 1972; 1998, 7–12). Gould believes this is likely to have taken a 'ranching' rather than agricultural (?arable) form, a belief supported by the limited evidence recovered from this site suggestive of woodland clearance – possibly for grazing and/or hazel coppicing – and the possible presence of a north–south drove-way along the margins of the peaty ground to the east. The pollen spectrum from beneath Ryknield Street included some evidence for cereal crops which may have derived from a location near the site or from further afield (see Scaife above).

Commencement of occupation at *Letocetum* and construction of the roads in this area will have been intimately connected, the latter being undertaken in response to military requirements (Margary 1973, 18). The earliest occupation of *Letocetum* is believed to have been between AD 50–60, although whether the original establishment was Claudian (AD 41–54) or Neronian (AD 54–68) remains a point of some discussion (Gould 1966–7; 1991–2; Round 1981–2; 1990–1). The date of the roads must be closely similar as they would have been required to serve the military needs of the fort at *Letocetum* and beyond to the north and west: Watling Street, which apparently preceded Ryknield Street in its construction at this point, was certainly metalled by AD 70 (Gould 1964–5; 1998, 24–6; Wardle 2002a). The earliest burials in the Ryknield Street cemetery and that to the west of the town (see Archaeological background above) were made in the latter part of the 1st century AD, and both are likely to have been established in the early years of occupation.

The position of Ryknield Street within the area of the site was largely defined by the boundary ditches marking the 'road-zone'. Such ditches do not appear to have been a universal feature associated with road construction, although they may have been more common than their known survival suggests – most recorded examples being in remote areas (Margary 1973, 22). Probable boundary ditches were identified to either side of a section of Ryknield Street in Alcester, Warwickshire (Booth 1982, 143). At 1.2–2.3 m, the width of the ditches recorded at this site is greater than those observed elsewhere, which tend to be small (0.6–1.2 m wide) and shallow. The central sections of each ditch, notably diminished in size and form (possible points of entry to the cemetery from the road), bear the closest similarities to those observed at other sites. It may be that the apparently secondary function of these ditches as boundaries to the cemetery was the reason for their being more substantial than is normally seen. The segments excavated to the south of the cemetery tended to be narrower and shallower than those bounding it, particularly on the west side. The ditches observed by Oswald to the north were *c* 1.4 m wide, but as they were not excavated their form and depth is unknown (1966–7a).

Wide variation in the size and form of the *agger* is a well recognised feature of Roman roads, including across the same route, differences reflecting the type of land being traversed, the variability of local materials and the importance and frequency of use of the routeway (Margary 1973, 19–20, 504–5). The presence of roadside ditches – generally providing material for construction of the *agger* – is, whilst common, not a universal feature (Margary 1948, 18; 1973, 19). Roadside ditches were observed on only the west side of the segment of Ryknield Street observed by Oswald towards its junction with Watling Street (1966–7a, 39) and on only the south side of Watling Street in a section investigated to the east of the junction (Gould 1964–5, 3); where Watling Street was encountered at Hammerwich (Site 41, Chapter 10) to the west of Wall, the roadside ditch was apparent only on the north side. The width of the road-zone suggests that, at least in this section, Ryknield Street represented a second class road (Margary 1973, 22), and at *c* 7.3–7.5 m wide (the Ryknield Street cemetery and Oswald 1966–7a) it is narrower than the *c* 8.2 m width recorded for Watling Street (Gould 1964–5, 3). None of the excavated segments approaches the maximum width of *c* 9.1 m seen in the most important roads, but all are close to the *c* 7.3 m most commonly observed (Margary 1973, 21).

The general construction of both roads appears similar in all the segments investigated on this east side of Wall. A layer of sand overlay the natural; 0.06–0.11 m thick at Ryknield Street and 0.01 m thick in the Watling Street segment. The metalling was formed of varying depths of gravel with a sandy matrix (max. 0.34 m at the Ryknield Street cemetery site, 0.38 m Ryknield Street towards the junction, and 0.15–0.23 m (ploughed-out) on Watling Street). The metalling material appears to have derived from roadside ditches in the earlier investigated segments but such was not the case at the Ryknield Street cemetery. Pockets of gravel were observed within the natural sand (see above) and it is possible that some of the larger pits of unknown/uncertain function within the cemetery area, including those incorporating small amounts of redeposited pyre debris, were originally excavated as gravel quarries for road metalling material (Margary notes that roadside pits of this type have been observed elsewhere; 1973, 19). It is also possible that the road was not metalled across its entire route since *aggere* were sometimes left unmetalled (Margary 1948, 18; 1973, 20; see above).

Of the two routes, Watling Street was undoubtedly the more important and of slightly earlier construction. Ryknield Street was, however, a major routeway and the positioning of a cemetery close to the junction of the two roads, and doubtless visible from it, will have represented a prime location. In the early part of the 20th century, it was on this side of Wall that '... authorities had stated [the cemetery serving *Letocetum*] "undoubtedly exists" ...' (Beckett 1925, quoting E.D. Henderson speaking in 1924). The discovery of the western cemetery, *c* 375 m from the apparent western limits of the settlement seems to have dispelled this notion: there is no evidence to suggest that the 20th century archaeologists working in Wall were aware of the 13 burials reported as being recovered close to the Chesterfield Road near to where the line of Watling Street angles to the south-east (Collingwood and Taylor 1924, 226; see Archaeological background). One may expect that the Watling Street cemetery will have represented an equally if not more prestigious location situated on the more important routeway, and may have slightly pre-dated that on Ryknield Street *c* 500 m to the west of the late Romano-British fortifications.

The known numbers from the Watling Street cemetery (minimum of 51 cremation burials) and Ryknield Street (minimum 42 cremation and 15 inhumation graves) are similar, but both represent an unknown proportion of the overall number of burials. The Watling Street cemetery was not subject to organised area excavation; most cremation graves were recognised by the presence of pyre debris in or over the grave fill and since a similar number of graves, as at Ryknield Street, may not have contained much pyre debris (*c* 64%), some cremation graves may have been overlooked; no inhumation graves were recorded and whilst this absence may be genuine, the inhumation grave cuts were very difficult to distinguish in the recent excavations and again, may have been missed in the earlier investigations.

If the lack of inhumation graves in the Watling Street cemetery was genuine, it would probably indicate that the cemetery went out of use in the later Romano-British period at which stage burials may have been concentrated in the Ryknield Street cemetery. The Ryknield Street cemetery, whilst defined and fully excavated in three directions, clearly continued for some unknown distance to the north towards the road junction. There can be little doubt that the Watling Street cemetery served the population of *Letocetum*, but what of the Ryknield Street cemetery? It lay further from the early forts and the core of the town than its western counterpart, and along a road to the south of that passing through the town itself. Several 1st and 2nd century buildings, possibly representing a discrete settlement or part of the town's western suburbs lay at the road junction (Gould 1963–4, 16; 1964–5; Oswald 1966–7a) and at least one farmstead, the occupants of which may have used the cemetery, lay close to the road (Gould 1998, 53–4; Fig. 61).

There are no demographic data for the Watling Street cemetery since none of the bone was subject to osteological examination, but the Ryknield Street cemetery population generally has a 'domestic' appearance, there being individuals of both sexes and a broad range of ages from young infant to older adult, with no convincing evidence for temporal variations (see Human bone). It is probable that the latter cemetery served at least parts of the town, its eastern suburbs and the immediate rural hinterland.

There are no details of the grave group reported to have been situated close to the Chesterfield Road (Collingwood and Taylor 1924, 226). It may have formed part of a larger cemetery or represented a small, discrete group of burials associated with a specific household. The presence of coffined inhumation burials and the apparent lack of finds suggest a late Romano-British date.

In common with many Romano-British cemeteries, most of the cremation burials from the Ryknield Street cemetery were made urned, although there were some unurned and combined deposits (Philpott 1991, 8); in a survey undertaken by the writer of 1720 burials from 60 sites the average was *c* 48.2% urned, 24.4% unurned and 0.6% combined (in press). Also in common with contemporary features, most of the graves were circular or sub-circular with a small number of rectangular cuts (Philpott 1991, 8).

The inclusion of pyre goods – items which were originally placed on the pyre with the deceased, as distinct from those added to the grave at the time of burial – within the grave was common; artefactual pyre goods were recovered from *c* 62% of the cremation graves and animal remains from an unusually high 80% of the urned burials, both unurned burials and one of the combined burials. Much of the artefactual material derived from the pyre debris within the grave fills and probably represents only a proportion of the materials originally placed on the pyre, although finds from non-grave deposits of pyre debris do not suggest a wider range of materials or types of goods (but see Leary, above, for apparent selection of ceramic vessel forms for inclusion in the burial). Material types were limited to ceramic and glass vessels and iron nails (hobnails and funerary furniture). No items of personal ornamentation or equipment were recovered from graves, but parts of a bracelet, a coin and a possible brooch were found in other deposits of pyre debris (Powell, K, above). The possible presence of copper-alloy jewellery as pyre goods is, however, suggested by the presence of blue/green spot staining to bone from three burials (see Human bone). The ceramic vessels were predominantly those associated with drinking (eg flagons), three items being the most recovered from any one grave. There is some indication that the vessels functioning as urns were also placed on or beside the pyre during cremation (Leary, above). The animal remains included the usual Romano-British taxa of pig and bird (fowl where distinguishable), with some other indeterminate medium-sized mammal (Worley, above).

Grave goods – items only included in the secondary rite of burial – were recovered from only 14.3% of the cremation graves, all comprised ceramic vessels of some form; the most items additional to the urn recovered from any one grave was five.

Although the details are incomplete and sometimes imprecise, the cremation graves from the Watling Street cemetery appear to have been very similar in terms of the associated artefacts. There was an absence of items of personal adornment. Finds included iron nails (hobnails and furnishings) and fragments of ceramic vessels which, although not described as burnt, from the description of their condition and the depth of the features they derived from, are likely to have been (Beckett 1925; Blay 1925; Hodgkinson 1927). The frequent lack of distinction made between pyre and grave goods, especially in older site reports and particularly with reference to the ceramic remains – that may be difficult to distinguish anyway (Cool 2004, 441–2) – renders extracting clear comparable data difficult. Both cremation and inhumation graves at Derby Racecourse contained burnt pottery, that in the latter probably being redeposited from cremation-related deposits (Wheeler, 1985, 266). Although it is unclear how many of the cremation graves contained pottery, it appears that few contained '... more than a handful of sherds ...' (*ibid.*, 235) and very few – eight of the possible 39 graves – contained (?unburnt) vessels including an urn (*ibid.*, 231, table 18); as at the Ryknield Street cemetery, flagons appears to have been most common.

A similarly limited range of other pyre goods – iron hobnails, possibly glass vessels and a worked bone pin – appears to have been included in either the burials or other cremation-related deposits. A wider range of pyre goods was recovered from the East London cemeteries, where 53% of the burials contained non-ceramic goods, including glass, copper-alloy and worked bone, with iron nails being the most frequent find (Barber and Bowsher 2000, 67–9). Although ceramic items were recovered from non-grave deposits of pyre debris, no ceramic pyre goods were found in the graves; as has been noted elsewhere, drinking vessels were more common that those associated with food preparation or serving (*ibid.*). A higher proportion of burials (21%) included grave goods, predominantly ceramic items. An even wider range of artefactual pyre goods was recovered from a minimum of 58% of the urned burials at the late

Romano-British northern frontier fort cemetery at Brougham, Cumbria, including worked bone from 35% (Cool 2004, 441–3; McKinley 2004b, 301). Although burnt and scorched pottery was recovered it was difficult to deduce the role of much of this material and it was postulated that relatively little pottery may have functioned as pyre goods. Ceramic vessels represented the most common form of grave good, just under half the graves containing one or two accessory vessels. The common arrangement of such burial groups is admirably demonstrated by figures 99–102 in Partridge (1981), showing the graves from Skeleton Green, Hertfordshire. The inclusion of cremated animal remains in Romano-British burials is relatively common, although there is a wide range in frequency within different cemeteries, for example 3.5% of burials from Westhampnett, West Sussex (McKinley and Smith 1997), 13% from Baldock (Area 15), Hertfordshire (McKinley 1991), 29% of deposits from Derby Racecourse (Harman 1985b; although these may not all have been burials), 36% from Puckeridge, Hertfordshire (Wells 1981) and 47% from St Stephen's, St Albans (McKinley 1992).

In general the Ryknield Street cemetery appears to include a higher proportion of pyre goods, although with a reduced range of material/object types compared with most of its contemporaries. This decreased range of materials (but not the frequency of occurrence) seems to be shared with one of its near neighbours – the Derby Racecourse cemetery; both also have a substantially lower proportion of burials with grave goods. Philpott observed the absence of large or even modest ceramic (presumably grave good) assemblages outside the south-east and attributed it to the difference between areas where the native Iron Age tradition was for cremation and those where the rite had been introduced by the Romans, as is the case at Wall, the Romans placing less emphasis on items placed in the grave than on the pyre (1991, 42). He also suggested, however, that the inclusion of animal remains on the pyre was more prevalent in the northern areas, but whilst the Ryknield Street cemetery contained the highest frequency of burials with animal bone recorded to date, and 54% of the unurned burials from Brougham contained animal remains (McKinley 2004c, 331), such material is also common in burials from the south-east.

The persistence of the mortuary rite of cremation into the late Romano-British period has most commonly been observed in cemeteries within the northern frontier zone (Philpott 1991, 50–2; Cool 2004). Smaller numbers of late burials have been recorded in some of the large urban cemeteries and, to a lesser extent, in smaller towns and rural locations (McWhirr *et al.* 1982; Philpott 1991, 50–2). The numbers, although remaining low, and distribution have increased in recent years, particularly with radiocarbon dating being undertaken on unaccompanied cremated remains (eg Barber and Bowsher 2000; Birbeck and Moore 2004; Lovell 2005). Isolated 4th century examples from the Midlands include those from Alcester (Warwickshire), Barton (Gloucestershire) and Barrow Hills, Radley (Oxfordshire; Philpott 1991, 50–1). The late continuance of the rite has been taken as indicative of conservatism within possibly isolated communities, though its persistence in cities and towns such as London and Winchester renders the latter questionable, and it is seems more likely to have been a reflection of individual/family inclination (*ibid.*). Cremation had remained predominant amongst the northern Germanic peoples, particularly in the Saxon coastlands (Todd 1980, 147–51) and north of the Alps (Topal 1981, 75); since the military in Britain are known to have included non-native personnel (Jarrett 1994) the persistence of the rite in the northern frontier zones may be linked to this fact (McKinley 2004b; Cool 2004).

The use of square or rectangular mortuary enclosures to contain one or more inhumation (associated with barrows, predominantly in Yorkshire) or, less frequently, cremation grave (south-east England), was a common tradition in the later Iron Age, although neither occurrence was prevalent in the West Midlands (Whimster 1981, 34, 75–129; Black 1986; Niblett 1999, 400; Stead and Rigby 1986, fig. 25; Stead and Rigby 1989, fig. 182; Hill *et al.* 1999). The practice of placing individual or small groups of cremation graves within small square enclosures was common across northern France and the Rhineland from the 2nd century BC through into the 2nd century AD, the features in the latter area being termed *grabgärten* (Decker and Scollar 1962; Whimster 1981, 128; Black 1986; Cordie-Hackenberg and Haffner 1997; Haffner 1989; Cordie in press). The occurrence of such or similar features in Roman Britain is less common than in parts of continental Europe; Struck (2000) has noted their presence in small numbers at a minimum of 16 sites, with a concentration in south and south-west England, but none havs previously been recorded in the Midlands, although occasional examples are known from the Upper Thames valley (Booth 2001a, 20). Their area of occurrence appears to largely correspond with those in which the tradition existed in the Late Iron Age, the use of an enclosure ditch, with or without a wooden barrier, being succeeded by walled enclosures in some places (Black 1986; Struck 2000).

There is considerable variability in the few British examples in terms of their size and form (range 2.7–8.0 m, complete/incomplete square or rectangle), the presence/absence and position of an entrance, their date, and the associated burial type. The 1st–2nd century features at St Stephen's, for example, were of a commensurate size to those from the Ryknield Street cemetery (describing areas with sides of 4.5–6.3 m), either associated with cremation graves or 'empty' and interpreted as possible 'mortuary houses' (Niblett 1999, 401). At Poundbury, Dorset, features were of commensurate size to those at the Ryknield Street cemetery but were associated with late Romano-British inhumation burials (Farwell and Molleson 1993, fig. 10,

235). The closest direct parallels in terms of date, size, form and associated – or lack of – deposits, appear to lie in continental sites such at Wederath. There, although commencing in the Iron Age, many of the features were of 1st–mid-2nd century AD date, describing areas of between 4 m by 6.5 m, and 7.5 m by 9 m, with no indications of an internal/external bank; many ditches formed unbroken squares/rectangles but others included entrances and partial ditches were common, and most, if not all, appeared to have been backfilled relatively quickly after being dug (Cordie-Hackenberg and Haffner 1997; Haffner 1989; Cordie in press). The features generally enclosed between one and three graves, although many had no associated internal features (*ibid.*).

In France such 'empty' enclosures have been interpreted as possible 'banqueting enclosures', with potential links to the Roman custom of holding funerary banquets and/or commemorative feasts at cemeteries in memory of the dead (Alcock 1980; Toynbee 1996, 95). A pertinent point with respect to this possible interpretation is the recovery of pottery forms used as tablewares and in food preparation – indicative of feasting as well as drinking, only the latter being visible amongst the pyre goods recovered – from each of the enclosure ditches at Ryknield Street, albeit in small quantities (see Leary, above). This interpretation may also explain and be supported by the presence of the 1st–early 2nd century ovens on the cemetery's western boundary. Although there is little to indicate their specific function (they were clearly not directly associated with cremation), the narrow, roundwood charcoal indicates hot, short-lived fires (Gale, above), and if feasting was taking place within the cemetery precincts they may have been used for cooking food.

The possible presence of trees within some of the otherwise 'empty' enclosures could reflect their function as miniature versions of funerary gardens, some of which have also been linked with banqueting (Toynbee 1996, 94–100). It is possible that at least the three enclosures nearest to the road could have held wooden superstructures; although no postholes were observed within the ditches, the cuts tended to have flat bases with relatively steep sides and could have acted as beam slots, although there was no conclusive evidence to support this. The presence of such enclosures at Ryknield Street, in an area where no native tradition for such features existed, suggests they were associated with an incoming rather than the indigenous population.

The small rectangular feature 122934, central to enclosure ditch 126148, has probable parallels with a number of wooden 'shrines', often with four-post structures, recorded from mostly urban and occasionally military sites predominantly in southern England and south Wales (Black 1986; Struck 2000). The recorded structures were of a similar size and form to feature 122934, describing areas of 0.76–2 m square, for example that from St Stephen's, Winchester Hampshire (Black 1986). Struck (2000) has suggested that these features represent cheaper versions of stone mausolea or possibly a native alternative to them. There are also possible parallels with Anglo-Saxon features, where similarly proportioned four-post structures were sometimes associated with a central cremation grave; where no central grave was recovered it has been postulated that the mortuary structure itself contained the remains (Black 1986; Down and Welch 1990, fig. 2.13; Lucy 2000, 118–9). An above ground repository for cremated remains is also the interpretation given for the plinth within the Harpenden mausoleum in Hertfordshire (Black 1986). The structure represented by feature 122934, which would have been visible through the entrance to the enclosure to those travelling on the road, could, therefore, have represented a mortuary house/repository for cremated remains or a shrine. The presence of a masonry funerary structure within the area of the site was suggested by the recovery of a dump of 14 building blocks, and fragments of a small decorated block, from the fill of the western road-zone boundary ditch (Shaffrey, above) (Fig. 91). The location of this material, clearly deposited from the west side of the ditch, renders it unlikely that it related to any features in the eastern half of the cemetery where the mortuary enclosures lay.

Cremation cemeteries were not only places of burial but also functioned as crematoria, containing one or more *ustrina*, ie areas in which the cremations were conducted (Wheeler 1985, 234; Black 1986; McKinley 2000c). Although some evidence for pyre sites has been found in Romano-British cemeteries, pyres constructed on a flat ground surface may leave little or no evidence of their presence, particularly at a site such as Ryknield Street where it is known that truncation of the old ground surface has occurred (Black 1986; McKinley 2000c). There was no direct evidence to indicate the location of the *ustrina* or individual pyre sites at Ryknield Street, but the recovery of pyre debris from grave fills and other features within the confines of both halves of the cemetery, indicates the relatively close proximity of the pyre sites to the graves. In the western half of the cemetery, formal and incidental deposits of pyre debris were concentrated in features forming an arc around an open space beside the road, where an *ustrinum* may have been located; one may have expected deposits of pyre debris in the road-zone boundary ditch if this was the case, but only a few of segments were excavated in this area.

The rare presence of redeposited bone fragments within the fill of the western boundary ditch may indicate the location of some pyre sites towards the western margins of the cemetery. The distribution of redeposited pyre debris in the eastern half of the cemetery was more scattered and could be indicative of the use of individual pyre sites. There were no large deposits of pyre debris, however, such as those recorded at Derby Racecourse, Baldock, or in the East London cemeteries (Wheeler 1985; Barber and Bowsher 2000; McKinley 2000b). This could, in part, reflect the scale of operations but may also indicate that an *ustrinum* lay to the north outside the confines of the excavation.

The very limited recovery of medieval or post-medieval material from the topsoil, subsoil and excavated features of the same date suggests agricultural activity may have been of a pastoral nature, much of the land within the vicinity of the site being too wet for ploughing with consequent limited manuring /middening.

Chapter 15
Shenstone Linear Features (Site 13)

By Andrew B Powell

Introduction

Following a programme of fieldwalking, geophysical survey and trenched evaluation, targeted and general watching briefs were undertaken on land south-east of Wall, south-west of the Roman road of Watling Street. Cropmarks visible in aerial photographs (Fig. 58) showed a series of linear features in the southern part of the site, possibly associated with a large square enclosure, of probable Iron Age or Romano-British date, to the south, as well as with settlement features to the south-east in East of Birmingham Road Nurseries (Site 15; Chapter 17). In addition, the site was close to the Romano-British cemetery uncovered at Ryknield Street (Site 12). The watching briefs revealed a scatter of Mesolithic flints, a small number of Iron Age (or possibly Anglo-Saxon) and Romano-British features, a rectangular medieval enclosure and post-medieval ditches.

The site was an irregular parcel of land, covering *c* 7.5 hectares, centred on NGR 411080 305780, and bounded by the A5 Watling Street to the north-east, the A5127 to the east and the Sutton Coldfield to Lichfield railway to the west (Fig. 93). It sat on a small promontory of higher, sandier ground, at *c* 92–98 m aOD, protruding into the surrounding Shenstone wetlands. The geology is mapped as Triassic Keuper Sandstone (Geological Survey of Great Britain 1954, Sheet 154, Lichfield).

The site was located south of the Roman road of Watling Street, *c* 1.5 km south-east of Wall (see above). Extensive cropmarks have been identified from aerial photographs around, and extending into, the site. These include, to the north-east, an enclosure of possible Iron Age date (Gould 1972), boundary ditches, trackways and a pit alignment, and to the south, a large (*c* 0.7 hectares), double-ditched square enclosure, possibly a Romanised farmstead (Hodgkinson and Chatwin 1944), from the inner ditch of which were recovered dressed sandstone blocks, window glass, *tesserae*, and roofing and flue tiles. Together these features suggest intensive occupation and exploitation of the landscape spanning the Iron Age and Romano-British period.

The excavation at Shenstone Ring Ditch (Site 14), immediately to the east across the A5127, produced Iron Age settlement evidence and extensive Romano-British features, including major linear boundaries, an enclosure and a 2nd century pottery kiln. To the west, Ryknield Street (Site 12) produced evidence of the Romano-British cemetery complex described in the previous chapter (Fig. 58).

Results

Mesolithic

A total of 98 worked flints, including flakes, blades, cores and debitage, was recovered from the site. Of these, 69 were recovered from an extensive cleaning layer (133811), concentrated in an area some 100 m across in the centre of the site. The significant proportions (39%) of blades and blade-like flakes and the presence of two microburins suggest a Mesolithic, probably later Mesolithic, date. Most of the flints were in relatively fresh condition although a few displayed post-depositional damage. The remaining flints (29 pieces) were residual in later contexts and again appear, technologically, to be largely of Mesolithic date.

Neolithic

Two adjacent oval pits produced pottery, charcoal and charred hazelnut shells (Fig. 94). Pit 133089 measured 0.5 m by 0.7 m, and was 0.13 m deep with a concave profile. Its single fill of sandy silt, which appeared to have been a deliberate deposit, contained 35 sherds (214 g) of fragmented but unabraded coarse pottery, large amounts of charred hazelnut shells and cereal grains (barley and probable emmer/spelt). Just over 1 m to the north-north-west was a similar feature (133090), measuring 0.8 m by 1 m, and 0.18 m deep with concave sides and a flat base. Its sandy silt primary fill, contained 24 sherds of similar pottery (153 g) and further charred hazelnut shells and cereal grains, which may also have deliberately deposited. The upper sandy fill contained a further seven sherds and medium to large fire-cracked pebbles, and appeared to have accumulated naturally.

The pottery from both pits was provisionally identified as Iron Age, so perhaps associating these features with the Iron Age settlement *c* 100 m to the east at Shenstone Ring Ditch (Site 14, Chapter 16), or possibly Saxon. Consequently, a sample of charred oak sapwood from pit 133089 was submitted for radiocarbon dating to determine the date of this phase of activity on the site. However, the date of 3940–3700 cal BC (5004±30, NZA-25056) places this pit within the Early Neolithic. The added significance that this date gave to the presence of cereal grain within the pit led to the additional submission of a carbonised grain of barley for radiocarbon dating. This provided a result of 3710–3530 cal BC (4846±30 BP, NZA-25898), providing confirmation of cereal cultivation in the Midlands

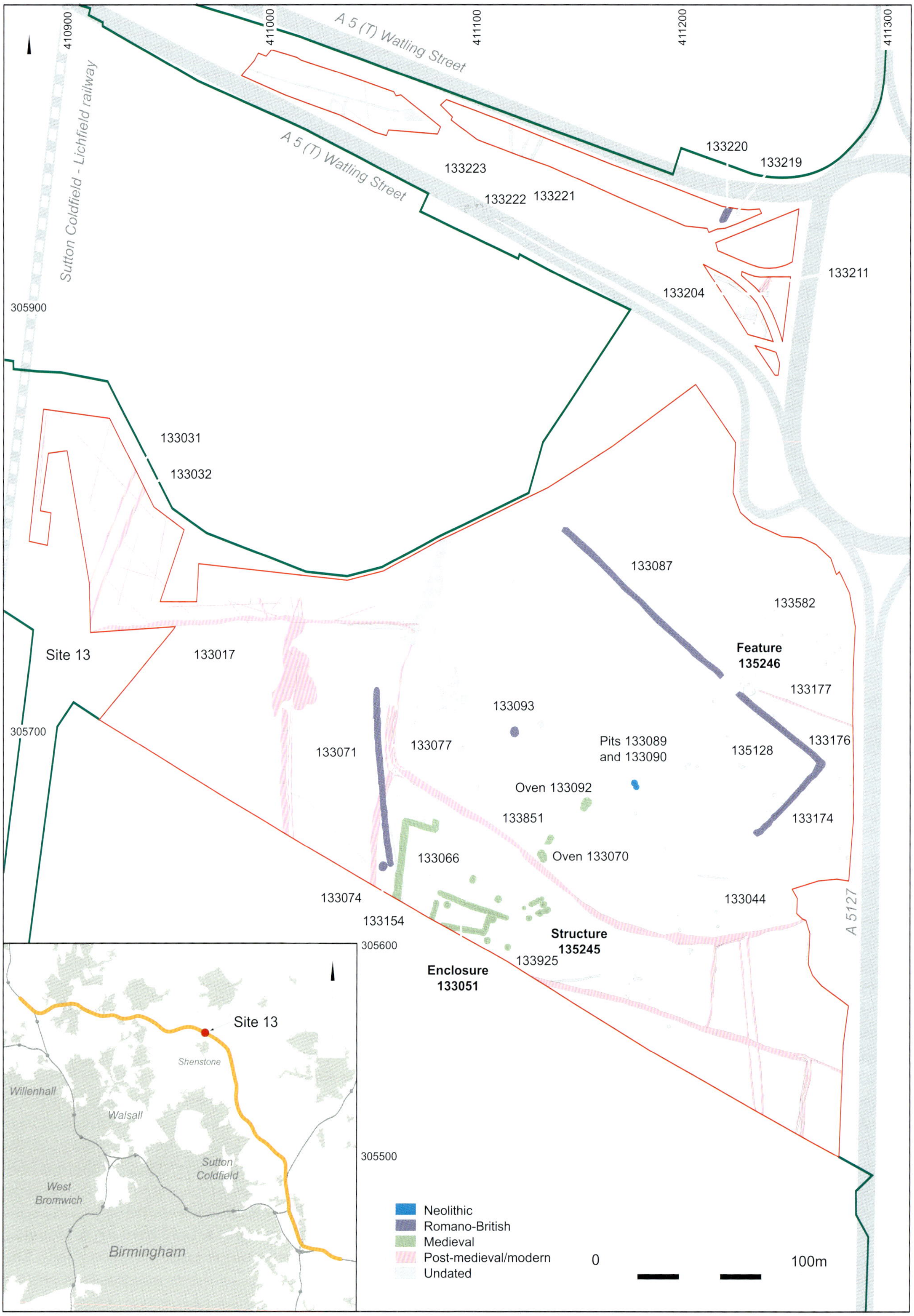

Fig. 93 Shenstone Linear Features (Site 13)

Table 53 Radiocarbon dates for Shenstone Linear Features

Feature	*Context*	*Material*	*Lab. No.*	*Result BP*	*Date cal BC (2σ)*
Pit 133089	133659	Oak sapwood	NZA-25056	5004±30	3940–3700
		Barley grain	NZA-25898	4846±30	3710–3530

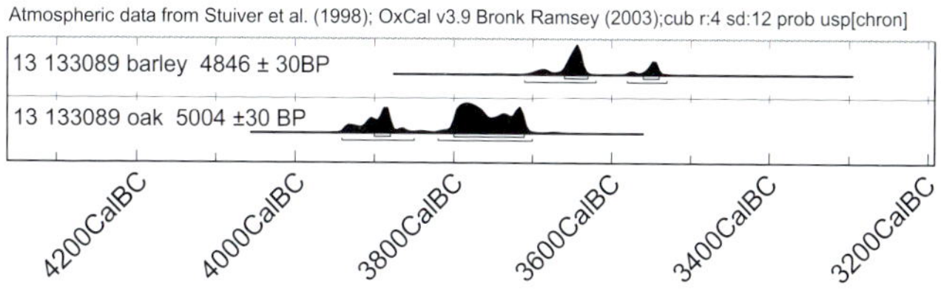

Fig. 95 Oxcal probability distributions of radiocarbon dates

during the earlier Neolithic (Fig. 95, Table 53). However, the fact that the two dates are not contemporaneous (there is no statistical overlap in their probability distributions; Fig. 95) suggests that the event which pit 133089 represents (and by comparison also pit 133090) was not chronologically isolated, but rather was a component of the longer-term occupation and sustained exploitation of a particular location within the landscape. The single deposit in pit 133089 appears to have either incorporated earlier material, including hazelnut fragments, redeposited from some other context, or have been contaminated by later activity at the same location, with grain being reworked, possibly through bioturbation, into its fill.

A rather perplexing clue to the use of the pits is provided by the presumably accidental incorporation of a single freshwater snail, *Anisus leucostoma*, in the fill of pit 133089, perhaps along with water, vegetation (reeds, rushes) and/or mud from Crane Brook some 0.5 km to the south. Its survival suggests the discard of calcium-rich material in the pit, but the lack of any local terrestrial species is puzzling.

Eight sherds (68 g) of similar pottery had been found with occasional charcoal pieces in a large shallow feature (132104), possibly a tree hollow, *c* 40 m north-east in evaluation trench 13021 (along with a single Romano-British sherd), and a further 10 sherds were recovered unstratified during the watching brief.

Among the residual flints found in later features across the site was a Middle–Late Neolithic chisel arrowhead.

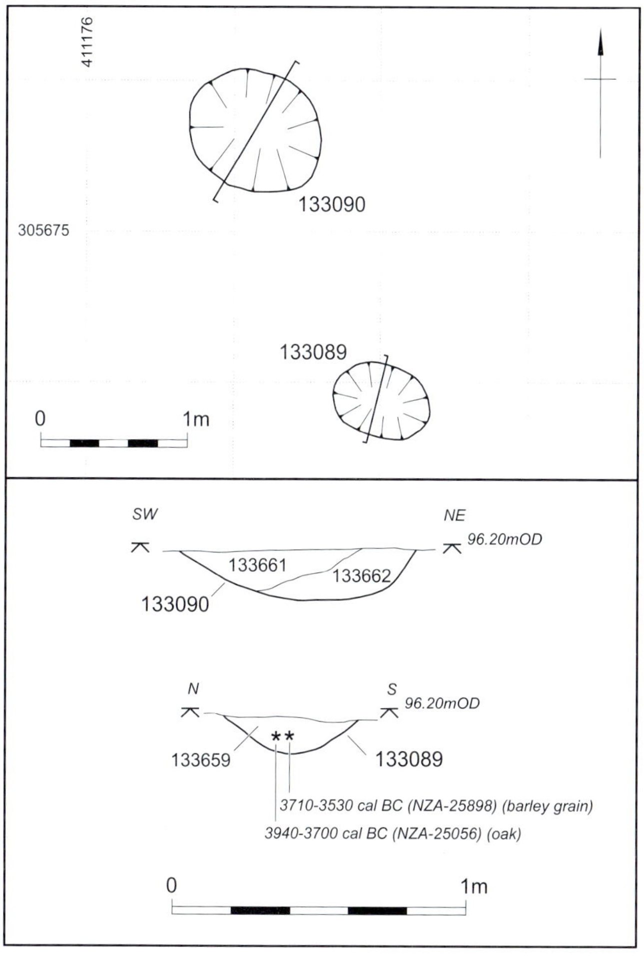

Fig. 94 Neolithic pits 133089 and 133090

Romano-British

A series of lengths of straight ditch producing Romano-British pottery formed what appeared to be part of a field boundary (Fig. 93). Towards the east of the site, ditch 133174 was recorded running north-east for 45 m before turning at a right-angle and running north-west for 52 m (as 133176). At that point machining had truncated the ditch for some 13 m, but it continued on the same line for over 100 m (as 133087) to a possible terminal.

Ditch 133174 varied in dimensions and profile along its length, measuring 0.3–0.9 m wide and 0.1–0.3 m deep, and had only a single fill, suggesting that in places it had been severely truncated. A number of apparent gaps recorded towards its south-west end may also be due to truncation, rather than being original features. Two excavated sections (135092 and 135102) each produced single sherds of Romano-British mortaria. Ditches 133176 and 133087 had been less severely truncated, averaging 0.7 m wide and up to 0.5 m deep, one section (133580) of ditch 133087 producing a single sherd of 2nd century AD samian.

To the south-west, a slightly curved ditch (133071) ran north for over 80 m from near the southern edge of the site. It was up to 0.85 m wide and 0.35 m deep with a U-shaped profile and had, in most excavated sections, two fills. At its southern end it was only 0.25 m wide and 0.1 m deep, suggesting that it may have been ploughed away beyond that point rather ending at a terminal. This most southerly section (133744) produced two sherds of Romano-British pottery from the single fill, as well as a small amount of charcoal. A number of the undated ditches on the site were of similar form and dimensions as those shown to be Romano-British in date, and potentially belong to the same phase.

A sub-circular pit (133154), some 3 m west of the southern end of ditch 133071, produced a large assemblage of Romano-British pottery. It measured 1.8 m by 2.2 m, and was up to 0.3 m deep with shallow concave profile. Its primary silty sand fill, which appeared to derive from the erosion of its eastern side, contained no finds, but the upper fill produced 47 sherds of late 3rd–4th century pottery, of varied forms and fabrics. The upper fill also contained burnt stone, ceramic building material and charcoal. The pottery was in variable condition, suggesting that the material had not been subject to repeated movement before deposition. A number of residual sherds of Romano-British pottery were recovered from the nearby ditch of the medieval enclosure (below), and a single sherd was recovered from a shallow ovoid scoop (133093), possibly a natural hollow, measuring 2 m by 2.7 m and up to 0.1 m deep in the centre of the site.

A pair of approximately parallel ditches (133219 and 133220) were recorded running SSW–NNE in the watching brief area to the north of the main site, corresponding to the southern ends of two short linear features visible as cropmarks in aerial photographs. Ditch 133219, running approximately north–south, was 1.7 m wide and 0.55 m deep, with a U-shaped profile and two fills, while ditch 133220 was 1.3 m wide and 0.4 m deep with moderately steep V-shaped profile and with a narrow steep-sided slot in the base. The uppermost fill of ditch 133220 was recorded as containing Romano-British pottery.

Medieval

As mentioned above, sherds of coarse handmade pottery recovered during the evaluation of the site were tentatively identified as either Iron Age or Anglo-Saxon. Further sherds, recovered during the excavation and similarly identified during the assessment stage (OWA 2003), have since been identified as Neolithic on the basis of radiocarbon dates. Nonetheless, two sherds of ?grano-diorite tempered pottery from a post-medieval feature (133916) may still be of Anglo-Saxon date (medieval pottery, below). Otherwise, medieval activity was represented by a small complex of 13th–14th century features concentrated towards the southern edge of the site, including a small sub-rectangular enclosure (133051) and adjacent ditch (133078), a rectangular timber building (135245), two ovens and a number of pits (Fig. 96).

Enclosure and ditches

The enclosure (133051) abutted the south side of an earlier east–west ditch (133196) running for 35 m from a terminal at the west but truncated at the east, some 8 m beyond the eastern end of the enclosure. The ditch was on average 0.5 m wide and up to 0.23 m deep with a variable profile and a single fill. That fill was cut by the ditch forming the eastern and southern sides of the enclosure (133303).

The enclosure was 26 m long internally aligned approximately east–west, by 10 m wide at the east and an estimated 14 m at the west (its south-west corner lying just outside the site). The ditch forming the west end (133052) ended at a terminal 4.5 m short of the eastern terminal of ditch 133196, the resulting gap forming the enclosure's entrance. The enclosure ditch, which produced seven sherds of pottery with a date range of 12th–14th century, was similar in form and dimensions to ditch 133196 on the north side, which produced two 13th–14th century sherds.

Sharing similar alignments to, and probably associated with the enclosure was a zigzagging length of ditch (133078), some 20 m to the north-west. This ran approximately north for over 30 m from near the southern edge of the site, before turning at a sharp angle to the east-south-east for 15 m, then again to the north for a further 3 m, beyond which it was not traced. It was up to 1 m wide and 0.4 m deep with a shallow U-shaped profile, and its single fill produced four sherds (31 g) of mid-13th–early 14th century pottery.

The absence of any archaeological features within the enclosure, and the low level of finds suggest that it was probably an animal enclosure, rather than having a domestic function, ditch 133078 possibly being part of a more extensive arrangement for controlling the movement of stock, extending to the south.

Post-built structure

Some 16 m east of the enclosure, and north of the projected line of ditch 133196, there was a rectangular post-built structure (135245), aligned NE–SW, comprising 15 postholes (Fig. 96). Externally, it was 10.5 m long by 6.5 m wide at the north-east, narrowing slightly to 6 m wide at the south-west. The north-west side consisted of a straight line of six postholes, all but one being regularly spaced *c* 2 m apart, centre to centre. The south-east side was less regular, having a slightly wavy line of seven irregularly spaced posts, one of them well out of line. The 4 m wide gap between the two south-westerly postholes on this side, may correspond to the smaller, but still noticeably wider gap at the same point on the opposite side.

The south-west end of the structure appeared to be open, but at the other end a large posthole (133930) and an internally adjacent shallow circular cut, 0.1 m deep (133556), were placed centrally along the building's long axis.

As with the post spacing, the postholes on the north-west side were of similar dimensions, being 0.4–0.5 m in diameter and 0.2–0.27 m deep, all with single fills. Those on the opposite side however, were more variable both in shape and size, having up to three fills, with some displaying post-pipes and evidence of the posts having been removed. Two of the postholes on this side (133554 and 135000), although over 0.5 m in diameter, were

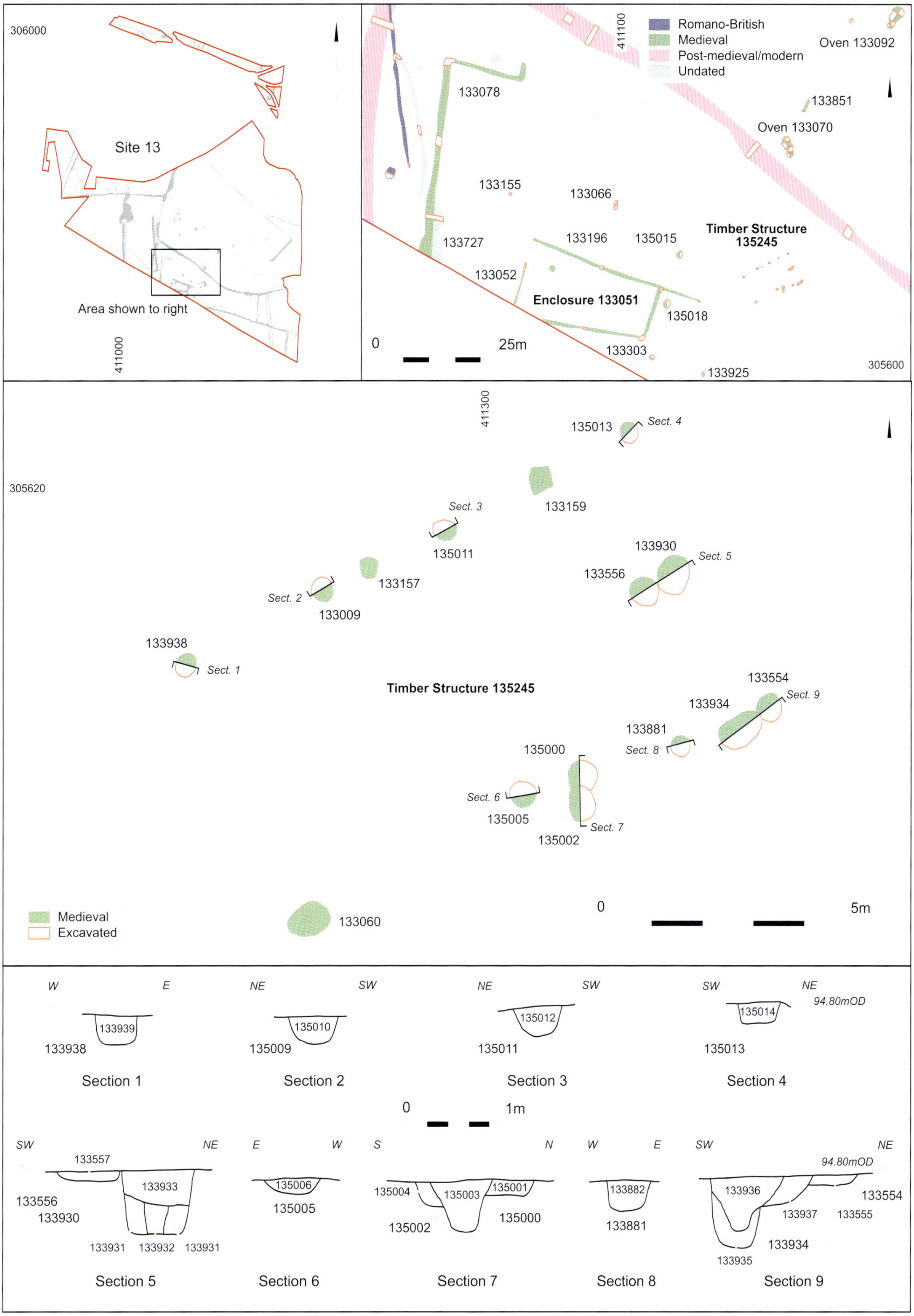

Fig. 96 Medieval features including timber structure 135245

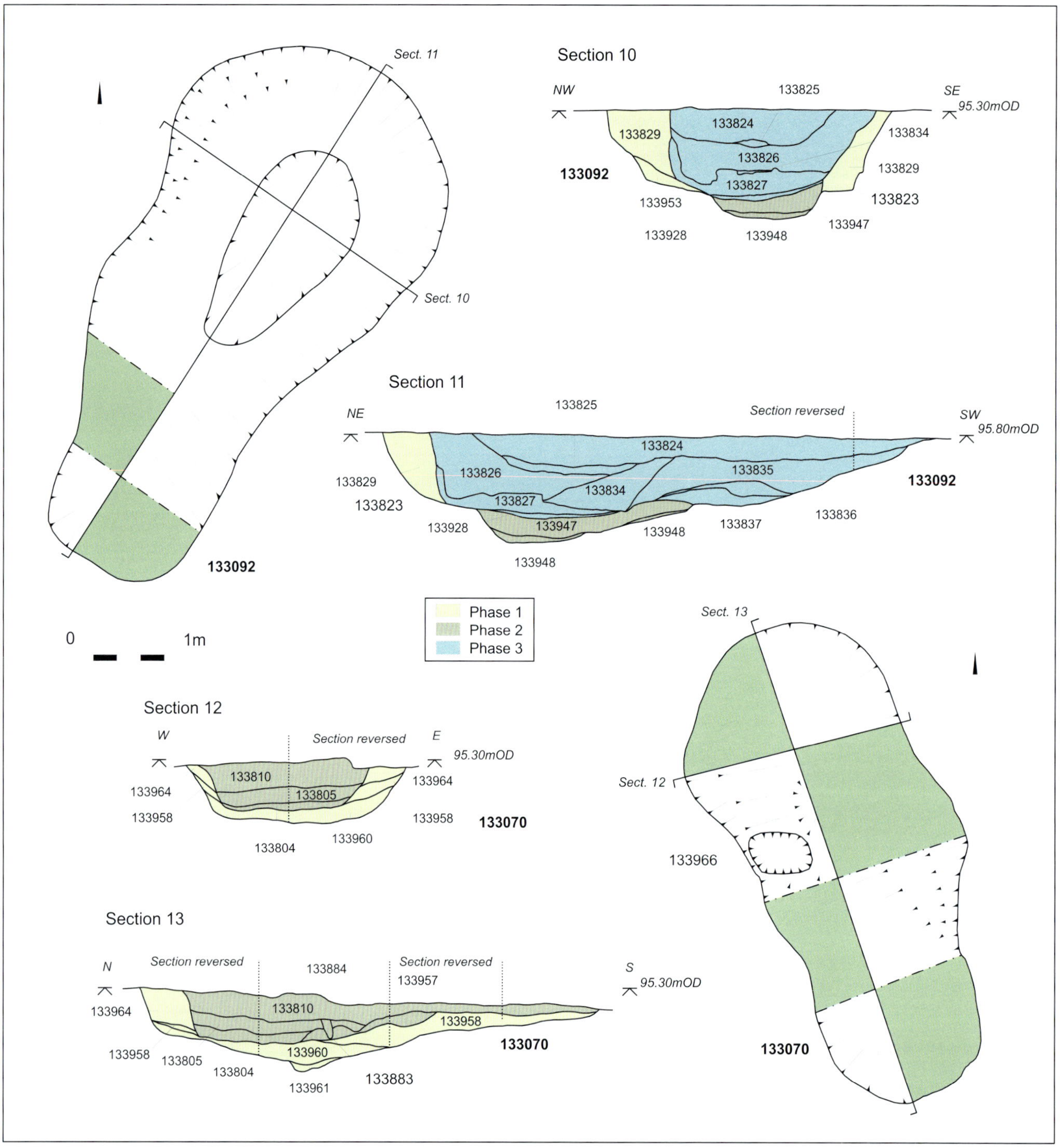

Fig. 97 Medieval ovens 133070, 133092

only *c* 0.1 m deep, and both had deep postholes immediately adjacent to them (similar in arrangement to features 133556 and 133930 at the north-east end of the structure). It is possible that these shallow features represent the remnants of truncated postholes; alternatively they may reflect the impressions left in the sandy subsoil by either substantial posts resting directly on the ground, rather than set in it, or more likely by post-pads.

The low level of finds from this structure – three sherds of mid-13th–early 14th century pottery from posthole 133881 on the south-east side – suggest that, like the enclosure, it was not a domestic structure, and may instead have been a barn or byre.

Ovens

Two clay-lined ovens were recorded, one (133070) 18 m north of structure 135245, the other (133092) a further 28 m to the north-east (Fig. 97). In addition, a smaller clay-lined feature (133066) was recorded 11 m north of the enclosure.

Oven 133070 was an irregular pear-shaped cut, 4 m long and 1.85 m wide at the north-west but narrowing to 1.3 m at the south-east. Four segments (constituting half the feature) were excavated, indicating two phases of construction and use. In both phases the wide end and sides of the cut were moderately steep, the base sloping gradually up to the narrower end.

The original cut was up to 0.6 m deep. A small depression in the centre of its base, containing a lens of sand and charcoal (133961), was overlain by a layer of clay (133960) up to 0.2 m thick, lining the base of the cut from the midpoint to the wider end. This showed evidence of having been burnt, but not at very high temperatures. Near the oven's midpoint, on the south-west side, the clay layer was cut by a subrectangular feature (133966) with the appearance of a posthole, *c* 0.5 m by 0.3 m, filled with silty sand containing flecks of charcoal (as the opposite segment was not excavated it was not possible to ascertain whether there was a corresponding feature on the other side). There was a charcoal-rich layer of dark sand (133958), up to 0.25 m thick, above the clay lining, containing two sherds of 13th–14th century pottery, the layer having the appearance of mixed dump of material. This, in turn, was overlain by a mixed clay deposit (133964) possibly resulting from the collapse and erosion of the original clay oven structure.

These fills were truncated by a smaller recut of the feature, 1.45 m wide and 0.4 m deep. On its base was further deposit mixed clay (133957), 0.1 m thick, containing lenses of dark sandy soil, above which was a 0.1 m thick layer of silty sand (133804) containing *c* 10% charcoal. This was sealed by a 0.12 m thick layer (133805) comprising *c* 60% clay, mixed with sand, probably material deriving from the second phase oven structure. This layer was cut by two possible stakeholes, one of which (133883) was 0.06–0.1 m wide and 0.15 m deep; they were 0.2 m apart on the long axis of the oven, and clearly post-dated the period of the oven's used. They were sealed by the uppermost fill (133810), a further mixed deposit of clay, silty sand and charcoal, producing 50 sherds (653 g) of mid-13th–14th century pottery.

Oven 133092, which was almost fully excavated, was similar in overall form to 133070, being 4.7 m long, 2.5 m wide at its rounded wider end (at the north-north-east) and 1.3 m wide at the other end, which was slightly squared. Overall, it was 0.9 m deep, there being a distinct depression in its base. This depression, which was 0.3 m deep had steep sides around three sides, its base sloping up gradually toward the south-south-west.

The drawn sections indicate more than one phase of construction and use. The earliest phase consisted of a steep-sided, flat-based cut (133823), 0.6 m deep. Its silty sand fills (133953 and 133829) had been cut through by a deeper but narrower cut creating the depression in the base of the feature. This had on its base a thin layer of mixed sand and charcoal (133948), containing medium sized cobbles, overlain by a clay lining (133947) filling the rest of the depression.

The clay lining was truncated by a second re-cut, again largely within the extent of the original feature. Like the first recut, this had a spread of sand and charcoal (133928) on its base overlain by a clay lining (133827), up to 0.2 m thick, that extended up the sides of the cut. In the shallow end there was a series of apparently dumped layers of silty sand, rich in charcoal. Layer 133837 (sealed by a patch of redeposited natural (133836) collapsed from the side of the cut), was 0.15 m thick and produced 16 sherds (290 g) of mid-13th–14th century pottery. It was overlain first by layer 133835, up to 0.3 m thick and containing a further 82 sherds (954 g), a nail, animal bone and large burnt cobbles, and then by dump layer 133834, only the latter extending over clay lining 133827.

The remaining hollow of the cut, up to 0.5 m deep in the centre, was filled with two layers (133826 and 133824) of mixed sand, clay and charcoal, the clay probably deriving from the collapse and erosion of the final oven structure, with an intervening layer containing numerous large burnt stones (133825). These layers produced significant amounts of mid 13th–14th century pottery (156 sherds/913 g) as well as five sherds (54 g) possibly as early as the 12th century, and one 15th–16th century sherd.

A series of 36 environmental samples was taken from the two ovens to determine the nature of the charcoal and other charred remains, and so, *inter alia*, to help identify the function of the ovens. They produced large quantities of charred grain, some charred chaff fragments, and a high number of charred weed seeds, as well as pea/bean fragments, hazelnut fragments and fruit stones.

The evidence suggests that these features were drying ovens. There is clear evidence of fire, but not apparently within the base of the features, nor at the temperatures that would have been needed in a pottery kiln. If the feature in the base of oven 133070 was a posthole, this would suggest that the purpose of the fire would have been to provide low temperature heat for drying rather than combustion. It is likely, therefore, that these features represent the chambers underneath above-ground driers, that could be used for drying grain, smoking foods and other similar activities. Hot air from a fire at its entrance would by drawn into the chamber and up through the structure, the clay lining (and the cobbles in oven 133070) aiding heat retention, and facilitating the recovery of the foodstuffs after drying.

A related activity appears to be represented by feature 133066 (Fig. 98). This was an irregular oval in plan, measuring 1.7 m by 0.9 m long, aligned NNE–SSW, and 0.25 m deep with moderately steep sides and a slightly concave base. On the base there was a black discoloration to the natural, possibly caused by the incorporation within it of fine charcoal. Above the natural was a layer of burnt clay (133949) up to 0.1 m thick, punctured by a series of stakeholes both around the edge and in the centre of the feature. This was overlain by a dark brown/black soil (133790) containing numerous pieces of sandstone, and producing charcoal, charred cereal grains, seeds and nutshell, as well as nine sherds (205 g) of 13th–14th century pottery, including the base of a bowl containing a brown deposit. There was also a small piece of square stone, possibly a gaming piece (ON 134580). Again, some form of drying,

Fig. 98 Medieval clay lined feature 133066

smoking or curing function can be suggested for this feature.

Other features

There was a loose cluster of other features in the same area of the site, five of which produced medieval pottery. Pit 133015 was *c* 1.3 m in diameter and 0.5 m deep with moderately steep concave sides and concave base. The upper of its two silty sand fills produced five sherds (55 g) of mid-13th–early 14th century pottery.

Subcircular pit 135018, located immediately east of the enclosure, measured 1.5 m by 1.8 m, and was 0.1 m deep with moderately steep sides and a flat base. Its single fill of silty sand containing patches of clay produced ten sherds (173 g) of mid-13th–14th century pottery and a rotary quern fragment.

Pit 133155 was 0.7 m in diameter and 0.1 m deep with a shallow concave profile. Its single silty sand fill, containing *c* 10 % charcoal, produced three sherds (52 g) of mid–late 13th century pottery.

A shallow, irregular feature (133851), 2.2 m long, 1.3 m wide and up to 0.17 m deep, had three fills, a sandy primary fill similar to the natural, a loose brown soil containing 11 sherds (77 g) of mid-13th–14th century pottery concentrated just below its surface, and a compact silty clay upper fill containing a further 11 sherds (354 g).

Pit 133925 had an irregular shape, 1.4 m by 1 m, and was 0.12 m deep with mostly steep sides and a flat base. The sides showed evidence of burning and on the base, near the centre, was a spread of burned material, including rye grains, weed seeds, pea/bean fragments and straw, containing 31 sherds (680 g) from a single mid-13th–14th century storage jar. The upper silty sand fill also contained substantial amounts of charcoal.

A fragment of a very worn, glazed and decorated medieval floor tile was recovered from post-medieval or later ditch 133039.

Post-medieval and modern

Activity in the post-medieval period is represented primarily by a series of substantial linear features representing field boundaries, tracks and drainage ditches, all of which appear to have silted up naturally, in some cases requiring the digging of repeated recuts (Fig. 93). A number of stratigraphical relationships allow some limited phasing, particularly between the ditches in the south-eastern part of the site (all of which had been visible as cropmarks in aerial photographs). Some of the ditches – 133017, 133031, 133032, 133044, 133074, 133077 and 133177 – correspond to boundaries shown on the 1st edition OS map of 1887–8.

Undated

Three undated features in the eastern part of the site contained large quantities of burnt stone, and could possible have related functions. Feature 135246 (Fig. 99), immediately north of Romano-British ditch 133176 and on a line of 19th century field boundary (133177), consisted of two arcs of gully in an approximately circular arrangement, with a projected external diameter of *c* 6 m, separated by gaps of 5 m at the north and 3 m at the south. The arc to the west (135194) was *c* 3.6 m long, that to the east (133185) *c* 5.6 m. The gullies, which were up to 0.6 m wide and 0.2 m deep with generally U-shaped profiles, contained single sandy silt fills containing significant quantities of burnt stone. The nature of these gullies is unclear, although they would appear to define some form of structure. This was probably too small to have been a domestic roundhouse, having an internal diameter of only 5 m, and it is possible that the gullies, open at two ends, formed screens for some form of craft or industrial activity as represented by the burnt stone. At the north end of the western gully was a small pit or posthole (135149) *c* 0.7

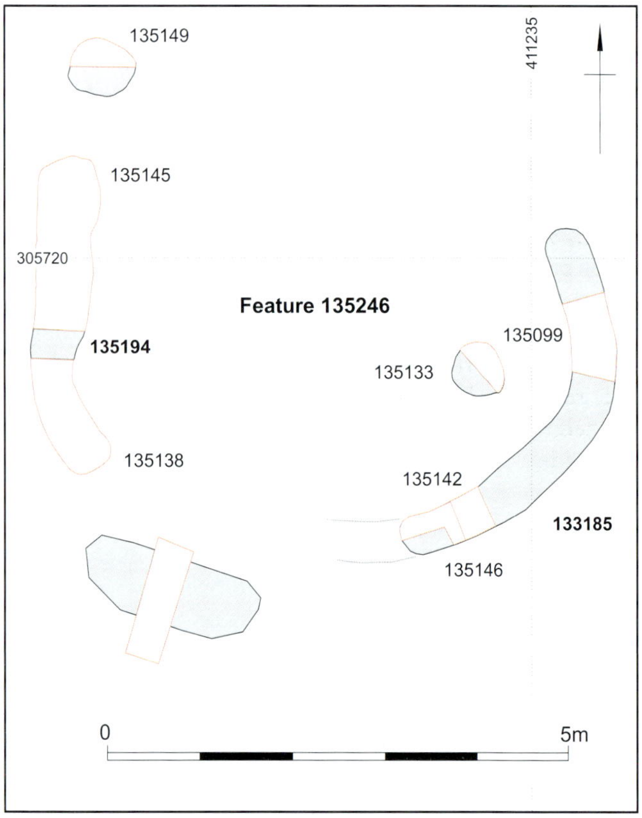

Fig. 99 Undated penannular gully feature 135246

m in diameter and 0.2 m deep; a similar feature (135133), 0.6 m by 0.15 m deep, lay just inside the eastern arc. The proximity of these features to the gullies suggests they were associated with the structure.

Some 30 m to the north-north-east, an isolated pit (133582), measuring 0.8 m in diameter and 0.3 m deep with a U-shaped profile, also contained burnt stone. On the base of the cut was a *c* 0.1 m thick layer of silty sand containing some charcoal, overlain by a layer of burnt stones and charcoal, then further sand. A large quantity of burnt, cracked stone was also recorded in pit 135128, *c* 20 m to the south-south-west of the gully structure. This measured 0.7 m by 1.2 m, and was 0.4 m deep with steep sides and an irregular base; its loose dark silty sand fill contained a piece of unidentified burnt bone.

There was a spread of burnt stone (133728), with occasional charcoal, in a shallow hollow (133727) on the east side of medieval ditch 133078, although no relationship with the ditch was recorded (Fig. 96).

As well as the features described, there were other lengths of undated ditch within the main site, as well as isolated pits of varying form and size, and a number of possible postholes, none forming part of any recognisable structure. The pits contained no evidence to indicate their date or function, and some of which may in fact have been tree hollows.

In addition, the watching brief maintained in the smaller areas along the line of the A5, to the north of the main site, recorded a series of ditches, most of which were undated. They included ditch 133204 which was recorded running WNW–ESE, and therefore approximately parallel to Watling Street, for *c* 27 m. It was 1.4–2.3 m wide and up to 0.5 m deep with variable irregular sides and a irregular flat base, containing up to four fills. It was cut by post-medieval ditch 133211 (above).

Approximately 100 m west of the possible Romano-British ditch in this area (133220), was a group of three ditches, the eastern two (133221 and 133222) running parallel aligned SSW–NNE, *c* 4 m apart, and ditch 133223, to their immediate west, aligned north–south. The parallel ditches were similar in form, measuring 1.6–1.8 m wide and 0.45–0.6 m deep, with moderately steep sides and concave bases, ditch 133222 having a shallow lip on the east side. They contained four and five fills respectively. Ditch 133233 was 1.5 m wide and 0.3 m deep with a concave profile and a shallow ledge on east side.

Finds

Post-Romano-British metalwork, by Ian Scott

This site produced six iron objects, including two possible bucket handles (undated context 133053 and post-medieval spread 133086), two nails (undated context 133646 and layer 133835 in oven 133092), a large post-medieval horseshoe (context 133043) and a post-medieval horseshoe nail (a so-called 'fiddle-key' nail) (context 133784). The bucket handles could be of relatively recent date. Overall the assemblage was very limited and of minor significance.

Flint, by Kate Cramp

An assemblage of 98 struck flints, the second largest from the M6 Toll, was recovered from the site (Table 150). The majority (69 pieces) came from a cleaning layer 133811 (Table 54); the remainder formed a fairly disparate spread across numerous contexts. The presence of several diagnostic tools (including two microburins), along with the general technological appearance of the flintwork, suggest a broadly Mesolithic date for the assemblage. The flintwork was in variable condition but generally fresh. A small number of flints, including some from layer 133811, were in a worn condition and probably redeposited. The raw material represented by the flintwork was entirely pebble flint, similar to that used at Wishaw Hall Farm (Site 19, Chapter 24).

The assemblage was dominated by flakes (43 pieces), although blades, bladelets and bladelike flakes were relatively numerous (23 pieces); these provided around 35 % of all unretouched removal types, a percentage that falls within the range given for assemblages of Mesolithic date (Ford 1987, 79). The flakes and blades showed careful preparation and removal. Platform edge abrasion was present on most pieces and soft-hammer percussion seems to have been the preferred hammer mode; dorsal blade scars were not uncommon and reflect the blade orientation of the reduction strategy. Some of the blades (eg Fig. 100, 1) had been struck from opposed platform blade cores.

The assemblage from layer 133811 contained a mixture of flake and blade material, and it was noticeable that some of the flakes were of unusually squat proportions. All three of the cores from layer 133811 were directed at the production of corres-

Table 54 Quantification of struck flint from layer 133811

Category	*Total*
Flake	28
Blade	12
Bladelet	3
Bladelike flake	3
Unclassifiable waste	5
Microburin	2
Chip	11
Core on flake	2
Multi-platform flake core	1
Retouched flake	1
End scraper	1
Total	69
No. (%) burnt struck flints	1 (1.5)
No. (%) broken struck flints	15 (21.8)
No. (%*) retouched pieces	2 (3.4)

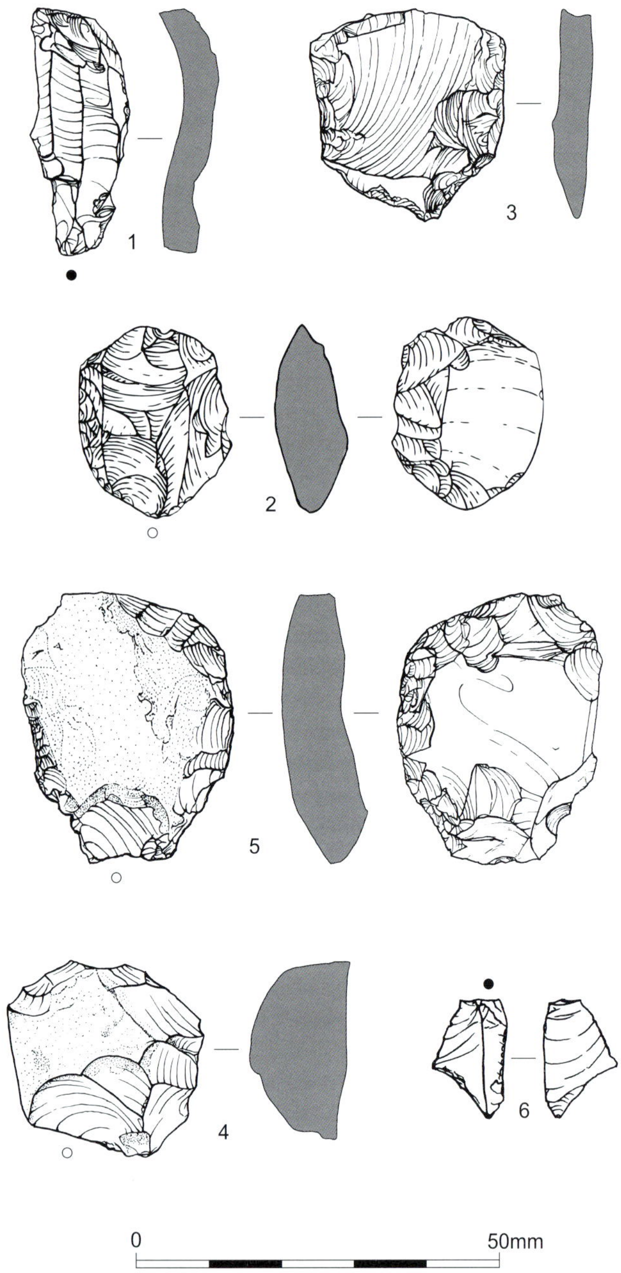

Fig. 100 Flints

pondingly squat removals; two examples were manufactured on flakes, a core type not observed elsewhere along the M6 Toll. In one case, the flake had undergone an intermediate stage as a finely-retouched side scraper (Fig. 100, 2). A further three cores were recovered from elsewhere on the site, two of which were aimed at bladelet production; one of these originally had opposed platforms but was worked from multiple directions as it neared exhaustion.

Retouched tools included two flakes with slight edge retouch, one end scraper, one chisel arrowhead and an unclassifiable retouched piece. The chisel arrowhead (Fig. 100, 3) had been manufactured transversely on the proximal fragment of flake. The unretouched blade edge was rather irregular, and was subsequently created (or perhaps rejuvenated) by a transverse flake removal. The end scraper (Fig. 100, 4) had been perfunctorily retouched on a preparatory flake, and displayed some macroscopically visible use-wear. The unclassifiable retouched tool (Fig. 100, 5) exhibited fine, curving, slightly invasive bifacial retouch along the right-hand edge; the bulb had been removed by two flake removals and a corresponding removal made at the distal end. This proximal and distal retouch may have been intended to assist in hafting the implement, which would presumably have been used as a knife or scraper.

Dating the assemblage is somewhat problematic. In the assemblage from layer 133811, significant numbers of blades, bladelets and bladelike flakes (*c* 39% of the flake material) were combined with two microburins (eg Fig. 100, 6), a composition strongly suggestive of a Mesolithic date. The presence of three flake cores and several squat flakes was unexpected and would normally herald the intrusive presence of later flintwork; given the generally low numbers of flints present on site, however, it is unlikely that the assemblage is mixed. The dominant traits of blade production are therefore considered to date the assemblage to the Mesolithic, and perhaps to the later Mesolithic.

The flintwork from elsewhere on the site seems to be more mixed. The chisel arrowhead indicates the presence of some Middle–Late Neolithic activity, but no other material contemporary with this piece was conclusively identified. Also recovered were a number of residual blades and bladelet cores which, technologically, would belong in a Mesolithic assemblage.

List of illustrated flints (Fig. 100)

1. Blade, plunging blade from opposed-platform blade core. Heavily utilised, context 133811. ON 134541
2. Core on a flake, finely-retouched side scraper, reworked to produce series of small flakes from ventral surface. 8 g, context 133811, ON 134518
3. Chisel arrowhead, crude and irregular example, with transverse removals to create blade edge. ON 134536
4. End scraper, crude, abrupt retouch on preparatory flake. Utilised, context 133811. ON 134567
5. Unclassifiable retouched tool, cortical flake with invasive bifacial retouch along one edge. Bulb removed, perhaps for hafting purposes. Knife or scraper? Possibly Neolithic
6. Microburin, proximal, right-hand notch, context 133811. ON 134568

Worked stone, by Ruth Shaffrey

Two pieces of worked stone were recovered from medieval contexts. A single fragment of a large millstone measuring at least 850 mm diameter and 53 mm in thickness was recovered from the only fill of pit 135018 (135019) dated to the 13th–14th century (ON 134580). Its presence is a good indication of the existence of a watermill on or near the site. A single, square, probable gaming piece (ON 134580), in red siltstone, was recovered from the only fill of a clay-lined medieval feature 133066 (133792); it is well polished all over.

Table 55 Romano-British pottery: fabrics and forms

Ware group	Ware	Vessel type	Form	Count	Wt (g)	Rim %	Rel % of count	Rel % of weight	Rel % of rim
BB1	BB1	Jar	jar with short everted rim	1	11.1	3	1.6	0.8	2.1
M	M			1	8.2	–	1.6	0.6	
	M	mortarium	bead and flange	4	293.9	30	6.3	19.9	20.6
	M	mortarium	multi-reeded	3	278	27	4.7	18.8	18.5
	MH			1	6.4	–	1.6	0.4	
	MH	mortarium		1	16.6	–	1.6	1.1	
	MH	mortarium	reeded	1	53	10	1.6	3.6	6.9
	MH	mortarium	multi-reeded	1	14.6	4	1.6	1.0	2.7
	MH	mortarium	multi-reeded	1	17.1	5	1.6	1.2	3.4
M total				*13*	*687.8*	*76*	*20.3*	*46.6*	*52.1*
O	O			1	17.1	–	1.6	1.2	
	O4			2	21.7	–	3.1	1.5	
	O7	jar		2	98.9	–	3.1	6.7	
O total				*5*	*137.7*	*0*	*7.8*	*9.3*	
R	R15	tankard?		1	15.7	–	1.6	1.1	
	R2			2	38.5	–	3.1	2.6	
	R2	bowl	bead and flange as kiln	2	17.8	3	3.1	1.2	2.1
	R21	bowl	bead and flange	4	99.6	12	6.3	6.8	8.2
	R5			1	11	–	1.6	0.8	
	R5	W-mouthed jar		4	49.1	–	6.3	3.3	
	R9			1	23.6	–	1.6	1.6	
	R9	bowl	grooved flange rim	19	160.7	7	29.7	10.9	4.8
R total				*34*	*416*	*22*	*53.1*	*28.2*	*15.1*
S	TS			1	2.6	–	1.6	0.2	
SV	SV1			1	1.5	–	1.6	0.1	
	SV3			1	2.8	–	1.6	0.2	
SV total				*2*	*4.3*	*0*	*3.1*	*0.3*	
W	FLA2	flagon	ring-necked	1	8.5	45	1.6	0.6	30.8
	FLA2	flagon		2	160	–	3.1	10.9	
	FLA3			4	30	–	6.3	2.0	
W total				*7*	*198.5*	*45*	*10.9*	*13.5*	*30.8*
Total				63	1458	146			

Early prehistoric pottery by Carol Allen

The 78 sherds came from two adjacent pits. Most sherds came from pit 133090 which also contained fire-cracked pebbles, and a further 37 sherds were found in pit 133089. This small shallow U-shaped pit also contained hazelnut shells and cereal grains dated to 3940–3700 cal BC (5004±30, NZA-25056) and 3710–3530 cal BC (4846±30 BP, NZA-25898), respectively. Special deposition of material in such Neolithic pits has been noted elsewhere (Thomas 1999, 64).

All the sherds were tempered with angular coarse to very coarse quartz. The sherds had a smoothed exterior finish but there were no sherds which had a form or decoration which could assist with identification of the type or date. However, the context, tempering and appearance of the sherds tends to confirm the earlier Neolithic date obtained.

Iron Age pottery, by Paul Booth

Six sherds of Iron Age pottery (85 g) were recovered from a single evaluation context, 132103, of Romano-British date. Five sherds (83 g), in fabric AQ3/4, may have been from the same irregularly-fired vessel and the sixth fragment (2 g), in fabric QA4, had an oxidised exterior surface. There were no diagnostic features or indications of decoration. A broadly Middle Iron Age date is likely on the basis of the general characteristics of the sherds.

Romano-British pottery, by Ruth Leary

The site produced 63 sherds (1458 g) of Romano-British pottery. The site was unusual in having a large number of mortaria and was the only site, other than Site 15 itself (Chapter 17), to have an example of the flanged bowl made at the Shenstone kiln. The majority

Table 56 Romano-British pottery by context and sherd count

Ware	*Vessel Form*	*Total*	*132103*	*133580*	*133675*	*133745*	*133778*	*133796*	*135092*	*135103*
BB1	Jar with short everted rim (Gillam 1970, no. 20)	1	–	–	–	–	1	–	–	–
FLA2	splayed ring-necked, larger rebated top ring	1	–	–	–	–	1	–	–	–
FLA2	turned base	2	–	–	–	–	2	–	–	–
FLA3	closed vessel	4	–	–	–	4	–	–	–	–
M1	bead & flange	4	–	–	–	–	4	–	–	–
M2	multi-reeded hammerhead (6 reeds)	3	–	–	–	–	3	–	–	–
MH		3	–	–	–	–	2	–	–	1
MH	collared (3 reeds)	1	–	–	–	–	1	–	–	–
MH	multi-reeded hammerhead (5 reeds)	1	–	–	–	–	1	–	–	–
MH	multi-reeded hammerhead (7 reeds)	1	–	–	–	–	–	–	1	–
NP		2	–	–	–	–	2	–	–	–
O		1	–	–	–	–	1	–	–	–
O4		2	–	–	–	–	2	–	–	–
O7	simple base	2	–	–	–	–	2	–	–	–
P		6	6	–	–	–	–	–	–	–
R15	double-ribbed handle	1	–	–	–	–	1	–	–	–
R2		2	–	–	–	–	2	–	–	–
R2	grooved flanged bowl as Shenstone kiln	2	–	–	–	–	2	–	–	–
R21		4	4	–	–	–	–	–	–	–
R5		1	–	–	–	–	1	–	–	–
R5	closed vessel	4	–	–	4	–	–	–	–	–
R9		1	–	–	–	–	1	–	–	–
R9	grooved flanged bowl	19	–	–	–	–	19	–	–	–
SV1		1	–	–	–	–	–	1	–	–
SV3		1	–	–	–	–	1	–	–	–
TS		1	–	1	–	–	–	–	–	–
Total		71	10	1	4	4	49	1	1	1
Date			late 2nd–mid-3rd	1st–2nd	2nd+	1st–prob. early–mid-2nd	late 2nd–early 3rd–mid-3rd–mid-4th	2nd+	mid-3rd–mid-4th	130/40+

of the diagnostic sherds dated to the late 2nd to 3rd/mid-4th centuries with the exception of a 2nd century BB1 jar (Gillam 1976, no. 30) and an FLA2 ring-necked flagon, both from context 133778, pit 153154.

Fabrics and forms

Taking the high incidence of mortaria into account the remainder of the assemblage was dominated by local reduced wares with rather smaller numbers of oxidised wares, including Severn Valley wares. The wide-mouthed jar and bead and flange bowl with upturned flange provided direct comparison with the products of the Shenstone kiln while the other bead and flange bowls could also come from that pottery. The handled vessel, perhaps a tankard, did not necessarily come from the kiln since its fabric was unlike the wares identified from there. The source of the oxidised wares is uncertain but a small percentage (Table 55) are likely to come from the potteries working in the Severn Valley tradition. The white ware is comparable to that identified at the Mancetter-Hartshill potteries and only one sherd of BB1 was present.

The assemblage is too small for in-depth analysis but the proportion of different forms and fabrics is unusual, suggesting that the site had a special function. The waster and the presence of kiln forms suggest that this was related to pottery production rather than domestic occupation.

Chronology

Most of the pottery came from the upper fill in pit 133154 (context 133778), and this was the only group meriting detailed treatment (Table 56). It included sherds dating from the late 2nd/early 3rd to the mid-

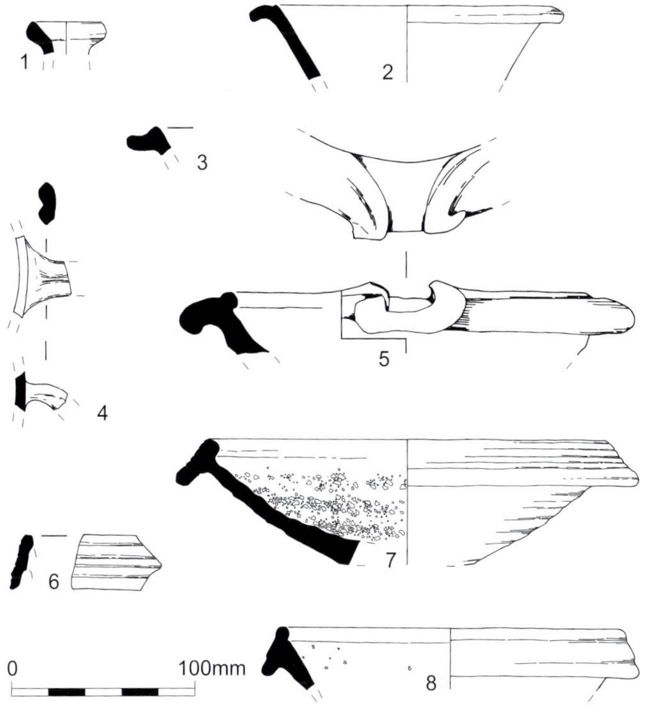

Fig. 101 Romano-British pottery

3rd/mid-4th centuries. The group is important on account of the presence of a relatively high proportion of mortaria, including two wasters, dating to the late 2nd–early 3rd and the mid-3rd–mid-4th centuries. These were in different fabrics, M1 and M2. A reeded-rim mortarium with three reeds in M2 was also present on Site 15. Fabric M1 was present on Sites 12, 15, 19, 29 and 34 and M1 was used to make bead and flange mortaria in types dating to the second half of the 2nd century and perhaps the early 3rd century. The fabric is very similar to some of the smooth yellowish-cream Mancetter-Hartshill mortaria and apart from their greyish burnt surfaces and distorted condition, they would have been classified as a Mancetter fabric. The M2 mortaria were both reeded rim mortaria of the 3rd–mid-4th centuries. The M2 fabric is quite distinct and like a fine Derbyshire ware. Similar mortaria have been noted at Derby (Hartley 1985, 126, fabric 8) and at Rocester (Ferguson 1996, 62). There is no reason to suppose that these two fabrics were not being produced in the vicinity of Wall.

Other chronologically diagnostic sherds from the features included a bead and flange bowl in fabric R21 from context 132103 (during the evaluation stage) dating from the mid-3rd century; the same context contained several sherds of Iron Age pottery (see above). A very abraded sherd of samian ware of 2nd century date came from ditch 133087 (context 133580) and a multi-reeded MH2 mortarium dated mid-3rd–mid-4th century came from ditch 133174 (context 135092). A further MH2 body sherd, in a fabric dating after AD 130/40, came from context 135103 of the same ditch and a FLA3 flagon base came from ditch 133071 (context 133745) and is likely to date to the 2nd century. Feature 133093 (context 133675) contained an R5 wide-mouthed jar sherd of mid–late 2nd century or later. A small abraded scrap of Severn Valley ware was found in the ditch of medieval enclosure 133051 (context 133796).

Catalogue of illustrated Romano-British pottery from context 133778, pit 133154 (Fig. 101)

1. FLA2 ring-necked flagon with pronounced upper ring. Early–mid-2nd century. 9 g. RE 45%
2. R9 grooved flat rim bowl. 71 g. RE 7%
3. R2 bead & flange bowl with upturned flange as those from the Shenstone kiln, Site 15. 18 g. RE 3%
4. R15 handle from small vessel, probably a tankard. 16 g
5. M1 bead & flange mortarium with hooked flange & bead rising above the flange. Mid–late 2nd century. Clearly a waster, both distorted & cracked & fired slightly greyish along flange edge. Evans 2002b, M74–5, dated AD 150–200 & 160–210 respectively. 294 g. RE 30%
6. MH2 multi-reeded hammerhead mortarium with 5 reeds, Evans 2002b, M104–6 dated mid-3rd–mid-4th. 15 g. RE 4%
7. M2 multi-reeded hammerhead mortarium with 6 reeds, Evans 2002b, M104–6 dated mid-3rd–mid-4th. 278 g. RE 27%
8. MH2 abraded collared mortarium with upright bead and grooved distal, Evans 2002b, M85 AD 170–220. 53 g. RE 10%

Medieval pottery, by Stephanie Rátkai

Ten unstratified sherds (weighing 68 g) may be the oldest post-Romano-British sherds from the site, being possibly Early-Middle Anglo-Saxon in date. One of the sherds contained granitic inclusions, possibly grano-diorite, the remainder being tempered with quartz, sandstone with some feldspar and burnt out organics. The range of inclusions was much the same as those found in Anglo-Saxon pottery at Catholme, Staffordshire (Kinsley 2002; Vince 2002). However, Kinsley notes the difficulty of distinguishing between the Iron Age and Anglo-Saxon pottery from the site. Although the Shenstone sherds could just be scratched with the finger nail, they did seem a little too hard and the inclusion size a little too small to be prehistoric. That said, there was no trace of burnishing on the sherds, although this need not be the *sine qua non* of Anglo-Saxon pottery. Sherds from a sunken-featured building at Grange Park, Northamptonshire (Rátkai forthcoming a) were mainly unburnished. Secondly, it is not clear how much abrasion had affected the Shenstone sherds. The interior surfaces of all but one sherd were quite rough with some indication of light sooting, whereas the external surfaces were rather smoother. There was no indication as to vessel form.

A small assemblage of medieval pottery was recovered, numbering some 457 sherds weighing 4708 g. Over half of the pottery came from oven 133092. The amount of pottery found in the other features was small,

Table 57 Medieval pottery: quantification by percentage sherd count

Fabric	Oven 133092						Oven 133070		Feature 133066	Other	Total
	133824	133826	133835	133837	133827	133834	133810	133958			
COVT03(WCTS Sq20.4)	–	–	–	–	–	–	–	–	–	0.66	0.22
CPJ10	18.31	95.00	13.25	64.71	–	62.50	38.46	60.00	–	18.54	24.07
CPJ10?	–	–	–	–	–	–	–	–	–	1.32	0.44
CPJ11	–	–	8.43	17.65	–	–	–	40.00	–	6.62	4.38
CPJ12	3.52	–	1.20	–	–	–	3.85	–	–	–	1.53
CPJ13	1.41	–	–	–	–	–	7.69	–	–	–	0.88
CPJ14	–	–	–	–	16.67	–	–	–	25.00	7.28	2.84
CPJ14?	–	–	–	–	–	–	–	–	25.00	–	0.22
Deritend ware? (WCTS Sg12?)	–	–	–	–	–	–	–	–	–	0.66	0.22
Reduced deritend ware	–	–	3.61	–	–	–	–	–	–	0.66	0.88
IP02	–	5.00	–	–	–	–	–	–	–	–	0.22
IRG02 (WCTS Sg12?)	–	–	–	–	–	–	–	–	–	0.66	0.22
WW01/WW05 (WCTS WW01.4)	–	–	24.10	–	–	–	–	–	–	11.26	8.10
WW04 (WCTS WW01.5)	–	–	–	–	–	–	–	–	–	0.66	0.22
WW07	76.76	–	49.40	17.65	83.33	37.50	50.00	–	50.00	51.66	55.58
Sherd count	142	20	83	17	6	8	26	5	4	151	457

often fewer than ten sherds, precluding any detailed analysis of the pottery (Tables 57–8).

Over half the pottery was made up of whitewares, which were divided into four fabric groups. The dominant whiteware was WW07 which was not recorded on the M6 Toll sites to the south-east at Wishaw and Coleshill (Sites 19, 20 and 24) but follows in the same tradition as the whitewares previously found there. The preponderance of WW07 strongly indicates a local source of manufacture. The other whiteware fabrics (WW01, WW04 and WW05) could be paralleled at the Warwickshire sites (for codes see Chapter 28).

Roughly a third of the pottery was made up of cooking pot fabrics CPJ10–CPJ12. Again their high proportion relative to other cooking pot fabrics found at Shenstone suggests local manufacture. With the exception of one Coventry-type ware sherd, four possible reduced Deritend ware-type sherds and two glazed Deritend ware sherds none of the cooking pot fabrics could be paralleled on the other M6 Toll sites.

Enclosure and ditches

Only seven sherds were found associated with the medieval enclosure (133051). Six of these were small fabric CPJ10 cooking pot sherds (weight 42 g) including one rim sherd, too small for illustration. The remaining sherd (weight 2 g) was from a CPJ14 cooking pot. Ditch (133078) which may have been associated with the enclosure, contained a possible white-slip decorated Deritend ware jug sherd and three unglazed whiteware sherds of indeterminate form, although one flat base sherd was present. The pottery from both the enclosure and the ditch was very fragmentary but some of the CPJ10 form sherds from elsewhere on the site suggest a 13th century or possibly early 14th century date for this fabric. This would be roughly the same date range as the Deritend ware jug from the enclosure. The whitewares in 133078 give a terminus post quem of about 1250 but could be as late as the mid- or late 14th century. So the ceramic evidence need not disprove that the enclosure and ditch were coeval although it cannot confirm it definitively.

Post-built structure

The post-built structure (135245) produced even less ceramic evidence than the enclosure and ditches. The pottery which came from post-hole 133881 (fill 133882) consisted of a reduced Deritend ware sherd, a CPJ10 sherd and a whiteware (WW07) cooking pot sherd. These sherds weighed 2 g, 2 g and 11 g respectively and presumably represent general pottery scatter incorporated into the backfill of the post-hole and are consistent with the interpretation of the structure as a barn or byre. The evidence is somewhat ephemeral but probably indicates that the structure, and enclosure and ditch, discussed above, are more or less contemporary or fell out of use at about the same time.

Ovens

The uppermost fill (133810/133815/133873) of oven 133070 contained an equal number of whiteware sherds and iron-rich cooking pot sherds, suggesting a deposition no earlier than the later 13th century. Cooking pot fabrics CPJ10, CPJ12 and CPJ13 were present. Most of the whiteware sherds were also from cooking pots with the exception of two sherds from jugs. Most of the cooking pot sherds were sooted or burnt and the two jug sherds were sooted. The environmental sample contained rather more substantial sherds than from the other fills and included a whiteware (WW07) CPJ rim sherd (Fig. 102, 2) and rilled CPJ10 rim-body sherds (Fig. 102, 1). Two further rilled fabric CPJ10

Table 58 Medieval pottery: quantification by percentage sherd weight

Fabric	*Oven 133092*						*Oven 133070*		*Feature*	*Other*	*Total*
	133824	*133826*	*133835*	*133837*	*133827*	*133834*	*133810*	*133958*	*133066*		
COVT03(WCTS Sq20.4)	–	–	–	–	–	–	–	–	–	0.89	0.36
CPJ10	35.89	73.08	19.34	76.24	–	81.48	47.52	43.75	–	6.86	24.30
CPJ10?	–	–	–	–	–	–	–	–	–	0.84	0.34
CPJ11	–	–	13.71	19.50	–	–	–	56.25	–	4.08	5.56
CPJ12	6.89	–	3.19	–	–	–	9.69	–	–	–	2.63
CPJ13	0.26	–	–	–	–	–	2.13	–	–	–	0.23
CPJ14	–	–	–	–	26.00	–	–	–	7.38	9.63	4.42
CPJ14?	–	–	–	–	–	–	–	–	6.04	–	0.19
Deritend ware? (WCTS Sg12?)	–	–	–	–	–	–	–	–	–	0.47	0.19
Reduced deritend ware	–	–	0.64	–	–	–	–	–	–	0.10	0.17
IP02	–	26.92	–	–	–	–	–	–	–	–	0.74
IRG02 (WCTS Sg12?)	–	–	–	–	–	–	–	–	–	0.05	0.02
WW01/WW05 (WCTS WW01.4)	–	–	17.53	–	–	–	–	–	–	20.21	11.70
WW04 (WCTS WW01.5)	–	–	–	–	–	–	–	–	–	0.10	0.04
WW07	56.96	–	45.59	4.26	74.00	18.52	40.66	–	86.58	56.75	49.09
Sherd weight (g)	769	130	941	282	50	54	423	32	149	1910	4708

cooking pot sherds were found in this layer. A CPJ12 base sherd had heavy external soot and heavy abrasion on the exterior base and base angle.

The remaining fill (133958) contained no whitewares and only three CPJ10 cooking pot sherds. Two of these were horizontally rilled or lightly combed and were similar to those found in pit (135015), which lay between enclosure 133051 and post-built structure 135245.

Oven 133092, more fully excavated than the above, produced a good sized pottery group of 276 sherds, the largest from the site. However the sherds were very small, with an average weight of 8 g. Only seven rim sherds were present, two too small for accurate identification, and 17 base sherds.

Five fills contained pottery (133824, 133826, 133835, 133837 and 133827). There were cross-joining sherds (ie sherds from the same vessel but found in different contexts) from 133835 and 133837 in CPJ11, from a possible jug or pipkin which had been knife trimmed above the base-angle, and from a cooking pot with patches of heavy sooting on the interior base. The jug/pipkin had reddish patches on the interior surface possibly indicating areas where glaze had burnt away. Fills 133824 and 133835 also appeared to contain fragments of the same whiteware vessels. It would therefore appear that the fill sequence represents a series of contemporary dumps or backfilling and there is no reason to assume that the earliest fill with pottery (133827) is not also part of the same event.

Crushed fragments of a Red-Painted whiteware jug (fabric WW07) were found in fill 133824 and several sherds from another Red-Painted whiteware jug (fabric WW01), still badly broken but not so badly as the previous, were found in fill 133835. Other Red-Painted whiteware sherds were found in these layers.

Overall, cooking pots were the best represented by all measures of quantification in the oven fills. Given the degree of brokenness noted in many of the jug sherds, quantification by weight perhaps reflects most accurately the relative frequencies of cooking pots, jugs and bowls (Table 59). Despite the predominance of cooking pots the greater number of these sherds were unsooted, which may indicate a greater use of metal cooking vessels. Eleven sherds (representing six vessels) had patches of soot on the interior base but otherwise what sooting there was, was rather undiagnostic and could have derived from culinary or any other use. In contrast the greater number of bowl sherds were sooted externally, usually heavily. This presumably shows a preference for using bowls for cooking – the very heavy sooting would suggest too intense a heat for use in dairying, for example.

Seventeen whiteware cooking pot sherds and three sherds from a finger-impressed whiteware jug base, three from fill 133824 and the remainder from fill 133835, appeared to have been burnt, which presumably occurred when the oven was in use, although the sherds must have been redeposited and not burnt *in situ* since the remainder of the pottery from the two contexts was unburnt. Fifty whiteware and CPJ10 sherds were abraded, 16 heavily, and were found scattered throughout the oven fills. A CPJ12 cooking pot was heavily abraded on the external base and base angle and heavily sooted on the exterior. The wear pattern may have occurred whilst the pot was in use. Eleven sherds, mainly CPJ10 cooking pots but also including the finger-impressed whiteware base (above), had brown surface discoloration or perhaps the remnant of some deposit. Similar brown staining was found on sherds from oven 133070 and ditch 133078.

Table 59 Medieval pottery: functional analysis

Vessel type/function	Sherd no.	Sherd wt (g)	% sherd no.	% sherd wt
Food preparation/cooking				
bowl	18	217	3.94	4.61
Cooking/storage				
cooking pot/jar	234	2805	51.20	59.58
cooking pot/jar?	18	180	3.94	3.82
Liquid consumption				
jug	118	1073	25.82	22.79
Indet. jug/pipkin	7	133	1.53	2.82
Unknown	62	300	13.57	6.37
Total	457	4708	100.00	100.00

The ceramic composition of the fills of oven 133092 seems broadly similar, consisting for the main part of whitewares including some Red-Painted whitewares and CPJ10, CPJ11 and CPJ12 cooking pot sherds. Red-Painted whitewares seem to be current from the mid 13th century and throughout much of the 14th century. The CPJ10 cooking pot form (Fig. 102, 5) is the same as one from the second oven 133070 (Fig. 102, 1), indicating a broadly similar date for the disuse of the ovens. Rilled CPJ10 sherds came from ovens 133092, 133070, pit 135015 and post-medieval/modern ditch 133044 which again suggests a rather limited time-frame for activity in this part of the Shenstone settlement. Likewise brown stained sherds were found in both ovens and ditch 133078.

Feature 133066 which appears to have been related to the use of the ovens contained four sherds comprising an 88 g bowl base sherd (fabric WW07) a 41 g cooking pot rim sherd (fabric WW07) and two smaller CPJ14 cooking pot sherds.

The presence of charred cereal and other plant remains associated with the ovens does make it unlikely that they used for anything other than crop processing. However, intriguingly an overfired sherd (fabric ?CPJ11) with fine cracking over the surface, which could conceivably have been a waster, was found in the fill 133784 of pit 133155. In addition a small daub or burnt clay fragment from the fill of pit/oven 133066 had a vitreous or slaggy coating on one surface, suggesting that it had once been part of a kiln or furnace lining. The clay body was very similar to the fabric of CPJ10 and had become partly vesicular beneath the vitreous surface. Although there was no evidence of high temperatures associated with ovens 133070 and 133092, nor with feature 133066, clearly some hot industrial process had been carried out at some point on the site. Three small daub fragments, each weighing *c* 4 g were also found within the fill of oven 133092.

Other features

A series of pits (133155, 133851, 133925, 135015 and 135018) produced pottery. The pottery was much the same as that recovered from the features discussed above. Cooking pot sherds formed the majority of the pottery. Jugs and bowls were very poorly represented, with jugs outnumbering the bowls by both sherd count and weight. Pit 133851 was unusual in having only whiteware sherds and pit 133155 in having no whiteware sherds. A number of form sherds have been illustrated from these features; a whiteware (WW07) cooking pot rim from 1335015 (Fig. 102, 13), a burnt and sooted whiteware (WW07) cooking pot (Fig. 102, 12) from 133925 (a group of whiteware body sherds from the same pit also appeared to have been burnt) and a CPJ14 rim sherd from 133155 (Fig. 102, 9). Pit 133851 was the only pit to contain jug sherds including the base of a Red-Painted whiteware (WW05) baluster jug (Fig. 102, 11) which was found with two further glazed whiteware sherds (WW07) representing a second jug. A fabric CPJ10 squared cooking pot rim sherd (Fig. 102, 10) was also found in the pit.

Discussion

The presence of possible Early–Middle Saxon sherds is of interest, particularly as there is something of a shortage of pottery of this date in the West Midlands, making it extremely difficult to map and understand the extent and nature of Early–Middle Saxon occupation in the area. However, Shenstone is not that far from the Early–Middle Saxon sites at Catholme and Wychnor (Losco-Bradley and Kinsley 2002), both of which, like Shenstone, lie close to Ryknield Street.

There was a very limited range of medieval fabrics present. Just under 80% by sherd count and 73% by weight of the medieval assemblage was made up of two fabrics, WW07 and CPJ10, and all five whiteware fabrics made up 61–4% of the assemblage. The high proportion of whitewares may simply reflect chronological factors, ie most of the activity associated with the site would seem to have taken place in the 1250–1350 date range. The predominance of just two fabrics is perhaps stranger and may reflect a narrow range of socio-economic contacts for the settlement. Pottery which could be said to have been manufactured outside the immediate Shenstone area with any degree of certainty was limited to a single Coventry-type ware sherd and four sherds probably from the Deritend kilns in Birmingham. Some further contact with Birmingham is perhaps indicated by the fact that the rounded reduced cooking pots with angular rim and external rilling (like Fig. 102, 1 from 133810) and the rim form of the cooking pot from 133824 (Fig. 102, 3) are paralleled in reduced Deritend ware (Rátkai forthcoming b) and could just conceivably represent a migrant potter.

Vessel forms were also very limited. The predominance of cooking pots may suggest a lower status settlement but may equally simply reflect a functional bias in the areas from which the pottery was derived. Cooking pots were found in all fabrics but jugs and bowls were only found in the whitewares with the possible exception of the putative jug/pipkin in fabric CPJ11 from the fill of oven 133092.

The earliest medieval pottery from the site is probably the Coventry-type ware sherd which should

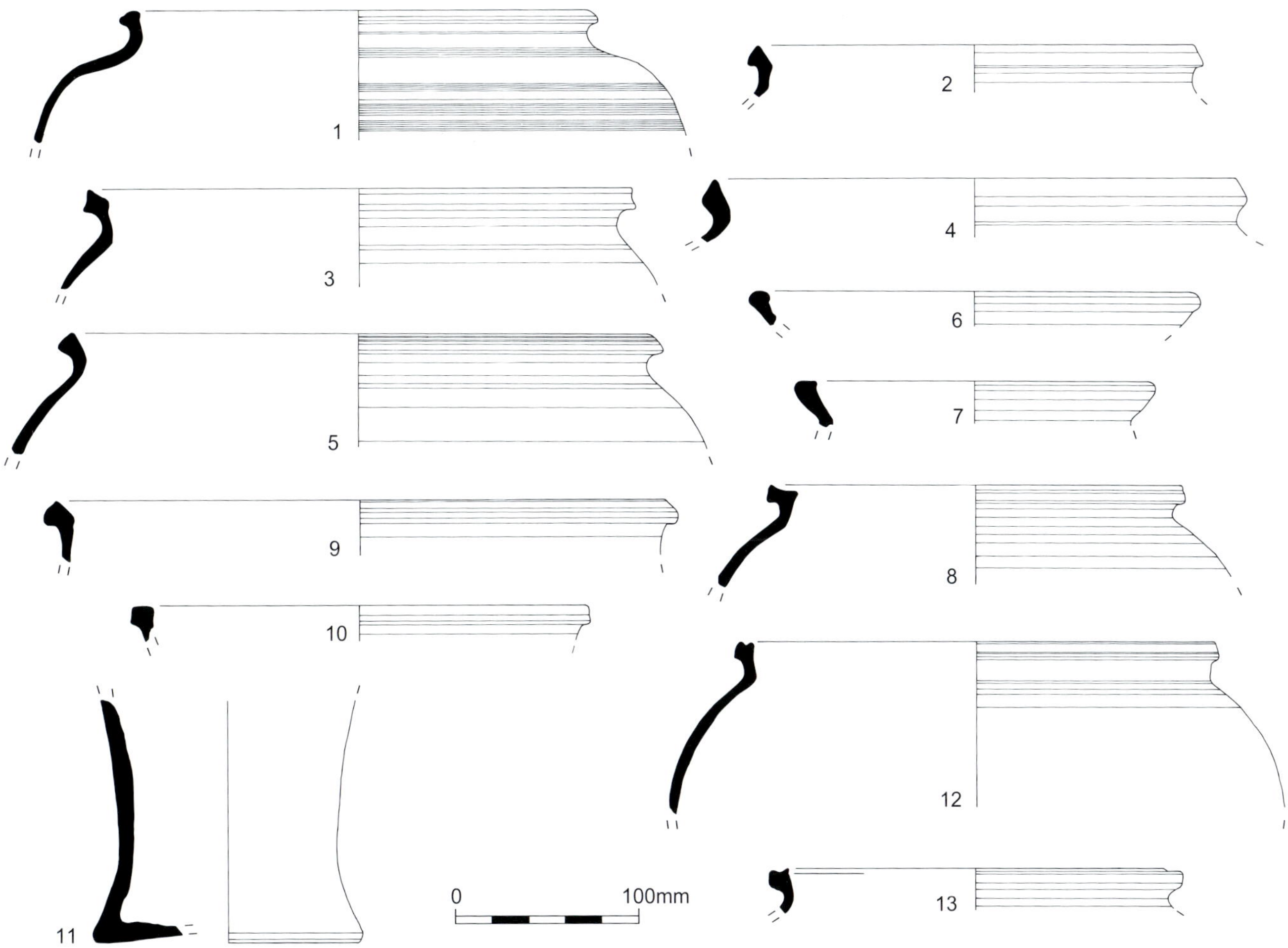

Fig. 102 Medieval pottery

pre-date the mid-13th century and it is just possible that fabrics CPJ12, CPJ13 and CPJ14 belong to the first half of the 13th century. The absence of anything which could be said with any certainty to date to the 12th century implies that this area of the site was not fully utilised until the mid-13th century.

It is obviously tempting to see the abandonment of the various features, particularly the ovens as being associated with the Black Death in the mid-14th century, especially in the absence of any very closely datable ceramics. However the Black Death was merely the culmination of a series of catastrophic events beginning much earlier in the century with worsening climatic conditions and crop failures. The absence of any clearly 15th century pottery does suggest that there must have been contraction or even abandonment of the settlement in the 14th century which could have occurred at any time after the first decade of the century.

llustrated vessels (Fig. 102)

Ovens

1. CPJ10. Cooking pot, wheel-thrown/-finished, light ext. rilling, context 133810 oven 133070
2. WW07. Cooking pot, context 133810 oven 133070
3. CPJ10. Cooking pot, context 133824 oven 133092
4. CPJ10. Cooking pot, heavy abrasion, some brown staining, context 133835 oven 133092
5. CPJ10. Cooking pot, very heavy abrasion, context 133835 oven 133092
6. CPJ14. Cooking pot, some ext. soot, context 133790 oven/pit 133066
7. CPJ14. Cooking pot, some int. blackening/soot, context 133790 oven/pit 133066
8. WW07. Cooking pot, context 133790 oven/pit 133066

Pits

9. CPJ14. Cooking pot, some ext. soot, context 133784 pit 133155
10. CPJ10. Cooking pot, context 133853 pit 133851
11. WW05. Baluster jug base splashes of olive glaze & vertical red slip bands, some burning around base/base-angle, context 133854 pit 133851
12. WW07. Cooking pot ?burnt, context 133929 pit 133925
13. WW07. Cooking pot, context 135016 pit 135015

Environment

Charred plant remains, by Wendy Smith

Of the 67 bulk samples taken from a number of pits and kilns/ovens, 28 were selected for full analysis of charred archaeobotanical remains, on the basis of their richness or their archaeological significance. Three samples came

Table 60 Charred plant remains from Neolithic and Medieval pits

		Neolithic pits		Medieval features				
	Type							
	Feature	*133089*	*133090*	*133925*		*133066*		*133155*
	Context	*133659*	*133661/ 133672*	*133926*	*133929*	*133790*	*133787*	*133784*
	Samples	*134005*	*134004/ 134006*	*134040*	*134045*	*134012*	*134063*	*134011*
	Sample size (l)	*9*	*38*	*20*	*10*	*20*	*8*	*8*
	Flot size (ml)	*25*	*355*	*625*	*450*	*250*	*140*	*60*
Taxon	*Common name*							
Cereal grain								
Hordeum sp.	Indeterminate barley	1[1]	-	-	-	-	-	-
cf. *Hordeum* sp. hulled	Possible hulled barley	1	-	2	-	-	-	-
Secale cereale grain	Rye	-	-	2	-	-	-	8
cf. *Secale cereale*	Possible rye	-	-	3	3	-	-	-
Secale cereale /*Triticum* sp. – indeterminate	Rye/wheat	-	-	74*	26*	9*	-	42
Triticum dicoccum/*Triticum spelta*	Emmer/spelt	1	-	-	-	-	-	-
Cereal/Poaceae - Indet.	-	1	3	155*[E]	140	42[E]	25[E]	42
Cereal/Poaceae - detached embryo	-	-	-	1	1	-	-	1
Cereal chaff								
cf. *Hordeum* sp. rachis node	Possible barley	-	-	1	-	-	-	-
Secale cereale rachis node	Rye	-	-	88	110	4	-	-
cf. *Secale cereale* rachis node	Possible rye	-	-	15	28	-	-	1
Triticum spelta glume base	Spelt	-	-	-	1	-	-	-
Cereal - indet. cereal rachis internode	-	-	-	9	17	1	1	-
Cereal/Poaceae - culm node	-	-	-	44	25	5	1	1
Cereal/Poaceae - culm base	-	-	-	2	-	-	-	1
Cereal/Poaceae - glume	-	-	-	-	1[E]	-	-	-
cf. Cereal/Poaceae - culm base	-	-	-	-	4	1	-	-
Pulses								
cf. *Vicia* sp./ *Pisum sativum*	Vetch/garden pea	-	-	1	-	-	-	-
Tree/shrub								
Corylus avellana – nutshell frag.	Hazel	162[2]	869	1*	-	2	1*	3
cf. *Prunus spinosa* – frag.	Possible blackthorn/sloe	-	-	1	-	-	-	-
Weed/wild								
Ranunculus acris /*repens*/*bulbosus*	Meadow/creeping/bulbous buttercup	-	-	-	-	-	1	-
Spergula arvensis	Corn spurrey	-	-	7	7	29[E]	14[E]	2
Persicaria sp.	Knotweed	-	-	-	2[E]	-	-	1
Polygonum aviculare	Knotgrass	-	-	-	1	1	-	-
Polygonum sp.	Knotgrass	-	-	-	-	1	-	-
Polygonum sp./*Rumex* sp./*Carex* sp. – internal structure	Knotgrass/dock/sedge	-	-	-	3	-	-	-
Fallopia convolvulus	Black-bindweed	-	-	-	-	1	-	-
Rumex acetosella	Sheep's sorrel	-	-	8	4	1	2	4
Rumex cf. *acetosella*	Possible sheep's sorrel	-	-	5	-	-	-	-
Rumex sp.	Dock	-	-	-	1	2	-	-
Raphanus raphanistrum – capsule segment	Wild radish	-	-	7*	8	1	-	-

	Type	*Neolithic pits*		*Medieval features*				
	Feature	*133089*	*133090*	*133925*		*133066*		*133155*
	Context	*133659*	*133661/ 133672*	*133926*	*133929*	*133790*	*133787*	*133784*
	Samples	*134005*	*134004/ 134006*	*134040*	*134045*	*134012*	*134063*	*134011*
	Sample size (l)	*9*	*38*	*20*	*10*	*20*	*8*	*8*
	Flot size (ml)	*25*	*355*	*625*	*450*	*250*	*140*	*60*
Rubus section Rubus	Bramble/ Blackberry	-	-	-	-	1	-	-
Vicia sp./*Lathyrus* sp.	Vetch/vetchling	2	-	-	4	5	1	2
Galeopsis sp.	Hemp-nettle	-	-	-	1	-	-	-
cf. *Galeopsis* sp.	Possible hemp-nettle	-	-	-	2*	-	-	-
cf. *Plantago major*	Possible greater plantain	-	-	-	-	1	-	-
Anthemis cotula	Stinking chamomile	-	-	-	1	7	-	-
Chrysanthemum segetum	Corn marigold	-	-	134	165^{E}	130^{E}	78	2
Tripleurospermum inodorum	Scentless mayweed	-	-	-	-	2	1	-
Eleocharis palustris uniglumis	Common/slender spike-rush	-	-	10	-	-	-	-
Schoenoplectus lacustris /tabernaemontani	Common club-rush/grey club-rush	-	-	-	-	3	-	-
Carex sp. – 2-sided	Sedge	-	-	3	1	-	-	-
Carex sp. – 3-sided	Sedge	-	-	-	1	1	-	-
Cyperaceae – unidentified	Sedge family	-	-	1	1	-	-	-
Avena sp. – caryopses	Oat	-	-	1	-	1*	-	2
Avena sp. – floret base	Oat	-	-	2	-	2*	-	-
Avena sp. – awn	Oat	-	-	1^{E}	1^{E}	2^{E}	1^{E}	1
Avena sp./ *Bromus* sp.	Oat/brome grass	-	-	42	46*^{E}	34*^{E}	15*^{E}	6
Poaceae – small caryopsis	Small-seeded wild grass	-	-	-	-	2	-	-
Poaceae – medium caryopsis	Medium-seeded wild grass	-	-	-	-	1	-	-
Fungal body	-	-	(1)	-	-	-	-	-
Unidentified – bud scar	-	-	-	-	2	-	-	-
Unidentified – calyx	-	-	-	-	1	-	-	-
Unidentified – leaf fragment	-	-	-	-	3	-	-	-
Unidentified – stalk	-	-	-	-	-	1	-	-
Unidentified – root/ tuber/ culm	-	-	-	12	-	-	-	-
Unidentified	-	-	2	6	-	6	-	1
Indeterminate	-	-	2	39*	50	72*	13*	52

Key: Numbers in parentheses [eg (9)] are not included in total; N^{E} = estimate count. Scores from the heavy residue which have been adjusted to match the proportion of the flot sorted have been indicated with an asterisk (eg N*) [1] The cereal grains recovered from sample 134005 were initially all identified as indeterminate cereal grain. I am grateful to Chris Stevens, who has returned to this material and made the barley and emmer/ spelt grain identifications presented here. [2] Volume of hazel nutshell fragments for the flot of sample <134005> Feature 133089, context 133659 = c. 15 ml and estimated volume for the heavy residue = < 2 ml.

Table 61 Charred plant remains from medieval kiln/oven 133070

	Feature		*Medieval kiln/oven 133070*		
	Context	*133804*	*133810*	*133958*	*133960*
	Sample	*134032*	*134017/ 134036*	*134033/ 134047*	*134061*
	Sample size (l)	*5*	*30*	*17*	*6*
	Flot size (ml)	*80*	*400*	*430*	*40*
Taxon	*Common name*				
Cereals grain					
Secale cereale	Rye	-	1	3	-
cf. *Secale cereale*	Possible rye	-	3	9	5
Secale cereale/Triticum sp. – indet	Rye/wheat	4	26	50	20
Cereal/Poaceae - indet	-	12^{E}	133^{E}	129^{E}	102^{E}
Cereal/Poaceae - detached embryo	-	-	-	4	2
Cereals chaff					
Hordeum sp. rachis node	Barley	1	-	-	1
Hordeum sp./*Secale cereale* indet rachis node	Indeterminate barley/rye	-	3	1	6
Secale cereale rachis node	Rye	1	6	41	367
cf. *Secale cereale* rachis node	Possible rye	-	1	2	-
Triticum spelta glume base	Spelt	3	-	-	1
Triticum cf. *spelta* glume base	Possible spelt	-	1	-	-
Triticum sp. glume base	Wheat	-	3	2	-
Cereal/Poaceae - indet rachis internode	-	2	4^{E}	10^{E}	326
Cereal/Poaceae - culm node	-	-	7	9	14
Cereal/Poaceae - glume	-	-	1	1	1^{E}
cf. Cereal/Poaceae - awn	-	-	1	-	-
Tree/shrub					
Corylus avellana – nutshell frags	Hazel	1	2	-	1
Wild/weed					
Fumaria sp.	Fumitory	-	1	-	-
Chenopodium sp. - ? modern	Goosefoot (poss. modern)	1	-	1	-
Atriplex sp.	Orache	-	1	-	-
cf. *Scleranthus sp.*	Knawel	-	1	-	-
Spergula arvensis	Corn spurrey	16	34	126^{E}	20
Persicaria sp.	Knotweed	-	2	1	1
cf. *Persicaria* sp.	Possible knotweed	-	-	1	1
Polygonum aviculare	Knotgrass	1	-	-	-
Polygonum cf. *aviculare*	Possible knotgrass	-	1	1	-
cf. *Polygonum* sp.	Possible Knotgrass	-	-	1*	-
Polygonum sp./*Rumex* sp./*Carex* sp. – internal structure	Knotgrass/Dock/Sedge	-	2	-	-
Rumex acetosella	Sheep's sorrel	9	3	29^{E}	8
Rumex cf. *acetosella*	Possible sheep's sorrel	-	6	33^{E}	-
Rumex sp.	Dock	-	-	1	2
Raphanus raphanistrum – capsule segment	Wild radish	-	-	1	-
Rubus section Rubus	Bramble/Blackberry	-	-	1	-
Vicia cf. *hirsuta* (L.) Gray	Possible hairy tare	-	-	1	-
Vicia sp./*Lathyrus* sp.	Vetch/Vetchling	2	4	8*	2
Galeopsis sp.	Hemp-nettle	-	1	-	-
cf. *Galeopsis* sp.	Possible hemp-nettle	1	-	1	-
Prunella vulgaris	Selfheal	-	-	1	-
Centaurea cf. *cyanus*	Possible cornflower	-	-	-	1
Lapsana communis	Nipplewort	-	2	-	-
Anthemis cotula/Chrysanthemum segetum – indet.	Stinking chamomile/corn marigold	-	-	-	1
Chrysanthemum segetum	Corn marigold	15	69	146	70
Tripleurospermum inodorum (L.) Sch. Bip.	Scentless mayweed	1	1	5	-
Asteraceae – unidentified	Daisy Family	1	-	3	-
Carex sp. – 2-sided	Sedge	-	-	1	-
Cyperaceae – unidentified	Sedge Family	-	1	1	-

Table 61 continued

	Feature		Medieval kiln/oven 133070		
	Context	133804	133810	133958	133960
	Sample	134032	134017/ 134036	134033/ 134047	134061
	Sample size (l)	5	30	17	6
	Flot size (ml)	80	400	430	40
Taxon	*Common name*				
Avena sp. – caryopses	Oat – caryopsis	-	-	-	1
Avena sp. – floret base	Oat – floret base	-	-	-	1
Avena sp. – awn	Oat - awn	-	2	2	1^{E}
Avena sp./*Bromus* sp.	Oat/Brome grass	3	44	30	13
Poaceae – small caryopsis	Small-seeded wild grass	-	2	7	1
Poaceae – medium caryopsis	Medium-seeded wild grass	-	-	5	-
Poaceae – basal rachis node	Wild grass basal rachis node	-	-	-	2
Unidentified – bud scar	-	-	-	1	-
Unidentified – seed coat – frags	-	-	-	12	-
Unidentified	-	-	9	18	50
Indeterminate	-	14	43	46	-

Key: Numbers in parentheses [eg (9)] are not included in total; N^{E} = estimate count; Scores from the heavy residue which have been adjusted to match the proportion of the flot sorted have been indicated with an asterisk (eg N*)

from earlier Neolithic pits 133089 and 133090, while 23 were from medieval pits or oven/kiln features (13th/14th century). A further two samples were clearly unusually well-preserved and, upon full analysis, it was clear that these were modern, possibly from the burning of a modern telegraph pole; these are not considered below (but are briefly discussed in archive).

Results

Tables 60–2 list the taxa identified in all 26 securely ancient samples. Table 63 presents the relative proportions of plant remain categories for each sample by period and feature group. Botanical nomenclature follows that of Stace (1997).

All of the Neolithic samples primarily contained charred hazel (*Corylus avellana*) nutshell fragments. The medieval samples all contained mixtures of cereal grain, cereal chaff and weed/wild plant seeds. The main cereal crop recovered in the medieval assemblage was rye (*Secale cereale*). Both rye grain and chaff were recovered, but rye chaff was the most frequently identified. However, this may be due to the generally poor preservation of cereal grain. Small quantities of barley (*Hordeum* sp.) grain and rachis nodes and spelt (*Triticum spelta*) glume bases were also recovered.

The weed/wild plants recovered from the medieval samples most likely arrived in these deposits as weeds of the cereal crops, although it is possible that they could represent gardening waste or some other weeding debris (perhaps in field preparation). Modern agricultural practice, especially the use of herbicides, means that many of these taxa are rarely seen as weeds of cereal crops today; however, the weed/wild flora recovered from Shenstone clearly contained species which are found frequently in association with ancient crop-processing waste at other sites in Britain (eg Greig 1990; Jones 1988a, 90; 1988b, 46).

The Neolithic assemblage

Neolithic farming

Pit 133089 contained four grains (estimated) of cereals including barley (*Hordeum vulgare*), possible barley (*cf. Hordeum* sp.), indeterminate glume wheat (emmer/spelt – *Triticum dicoccum/spelta*) and indeterminate cereal/large grass (Poaceae) caryopsis. Adjacent pit 133090 contained indeterminate cereal grains.

A sample of charred oak sapwood from pit 133089 produced a radiocarbon date of 3940–3700 cal BC (5004±30, NZA-25056) and, as it was deemed important to confirm earlier Neolithic farming in the Midlands, one barley grain from the same pit was re-examined, its identification confirmed (C. Stevens) and submitted for dating. The result of 4846±30 BP (NZA-25898) calibrates to 3710–3530 cal BC, confirming that the grain was in use, and possibly even locally cultivated, in the earlier Neolithic. Although the two items submitted for radiocarbon determination date to the earlier Neolithic, they are not contemporaneous and fail $\chi 2$ (T' = 13.86; T'(5%) = 3.8; υ = 1; Ward and Wilson 1978). This indicates at least that two separate Neolithic events are represented in the debris in pit 133089, and they might be as much as five centuries apart, but possibly as little as one and half centuries. This suggests that the charred plant remains (including charcoal) associated with this feature were deposited over a long period of time or later deposits were re-worked into earlier deposits, possibly through bioturbation. With respect to the latter, it might be noted that the other analysed pit (133090) was attributed to the Neolithic.

Limited evidence for scrub/woodland in the area during the Neolithic

The recovery of hundreds of charred hazelnut shell fragments from Neolithic deposits is typical for the British Isles (eg Robinson 2000; Moffett *et al.* 1989). The nutshells could have entered the deposits either as waste from collected wild foodstuffs or as accidentals with wood fuel. However, although hazel charcoal was present it was much less common than oak (Gale, below) and it is more likely than the hazelnuts were collected for food, with the charred nutshells simply representing burnt refuse. Their recovery may provide limited evidence for the presence of scrub/woodland in the vicinity during the period. However, with their robust outer shells, hazelnuts are particularly well suited to transport and storage, so although hazelnuts may have been available locally, they may have been brought into the area.

Comparison with other Neolithic sites

According to the English Heritage Environmental Archaeology database (English Heritage 2004), no other Neolithic archaeobotanical material has been published for the county of Staffordshire.

In surrounding counties, only a handful of sites are published or exist as unpublished reports. Two sites are published from this period in Derbyshire – a preliminary summary of results from Early Neolithic settlement at Lismore Fields, Buxton (Jones 2000; forthcoming) and the Bronze Age (including Neolithic features) Barrow at Big Lane, Hognaston (Hunt 1996). Comparison with Lismore Fields is problematic, because this is a settlement site and with an assemblage (although not yet published) that is clearly remarkably rich in charred cereal remains and, therefore, quite different from the assemblage encountered at Shenstone. The Hognaston results are also difficult to compare.

A total of eight samples were reported, three of which produced a total of seven charred seeds (Hunt 1996, 158). Such a limited assemblage is difficult to interpret, but in her discussion of the results, Hunt (*ibid.*, 159) discusses the recovery of 'well-preserved grass rhizomes' (which are not listed in her table of results), together with 'some leaves, stems and seeds, strongly suggest[ing] that these samples represent the remains of turves'. The Neolithic site of Bromfield in Shropshire (Colledge 1982) has also only produced a very small assemblage (including a few cereal grains, weed seeds, apple and hazel nutshell fragments), but this may be an artefact of sample size, which was extremely small. To date, the nearby counties of Cheshire and Leicestershire and the West Midlands have no published Neolithic archaeobotanical assemblages.

However, results from Neolithic pits in the Arrow Valley, Warwickshire (Moffett and Ciaraldi 1999) and Mill Farm, Kemerton, Worcestershire (de Rouffignac 1990) are very similar to those from Shenstone. In all cases the pits have produced a large quantity of hazel nutshell fragments. However, unlike Shenstone, these sites have produced crab apple (*Malus sylvestris*) pips, as well as partial and whole fruits. Further unpublished cereal remains dating to the early part of the 4th millennium have also been discovered in Hereford (Ray 2002), while emmer wheat is recorded from Early Neolithic pits at Wellington Quarry, Herefordshire (Jackson 2002).

The medieval assemblage

The charred plant remains from medieval features provided evidence for which cereal crops were in use in the medieval period, as well as crop-processing activities. Because of the consistency of cereal remains recovered in all the medieval samples, it is highly likely that the weed/wild plants recovered represented weeds of crop and, therefore, provide some information on cultivation conditions, timing and harvesting methods. It is likely that the spelt glume bases (as well as the indeterminate wheat (*Triticum* sp.) glume bases) recovered were residual from Romano-British activity at the site.

Cultivation of rye

The dominance of rye (*Secale cereale*) grain and chaff in the medieval pit and kiln/oven samples was notable. The 23 samples, however, only represented seven pits or kiln/oven features and, therefore, may not have been representative of the full range of cereal crops cultivated in the area. Nevertheless, the consistency of results suggested that charring events involving rye were repeatedly occurring at Shenstone in the period.

The cultivation of rye became widespread during the Saxon period in the British Isles and it became a significant crop in certain areas of England by the Late Saxon period (eg Romsey, Hampshire or Gloucester (Green 1994, 85)) and is also known from Stafford (Moffett 1994).

Like any crop, rye presented certain advantages and disadvantages to the ancient farmer. Rye tillers easily, so can better tolerate trampling/grazing by livestock (Langer and Hill 1991, 75–6). It is favoured in colder climes of northern Europe because it is more tolerant of frosts/cold temperatures, is also drought tolerant and can be cultivated on acid or sandy soils (*ibid.*, 75–7; Zohary and Hopf 2000, 69); all of which are situations where wheat crops might easily fail. The lack of gluten in rye grains means that, today, it is considered inferior to wheat for baking; however, it is much prized in northern Europe for slow-baked (ie 18–36 hours) dark breads (eg pumpernickel in Germany) (Langer and Hill 1991, 77). Rye straw was greatly valued in the past for thatching (*ibid.*; Letts 1999). Today, rye is considered a useful high energy feed for livestock (Zohary and Hopf 2000); however, if livestock are fed the grain alone it will turn into 'a sticky mass in the mouth of livestock' and so must be put into an admixture with other cereal grain (Langer and Hill 1991, 77).

Evidence for crop processing

Charred rye grain and rachis fragments were abundant in the medieval pit and kiln/oven deposits. Rye is free-threshing and, when fully mature, the grains easily fall free from their surrounding chaff. Although classed as free-threshing, rye cereal ears are non-shattering (Zohary and Hopf 2000, 70) and, therefore, can be intentionally harvested slightly damp (a method of harvest use to ensure the retention of as much grain as possible; Oelke *et al.* 1990)) and the ears are then dried whole before threshing. Some have argued that parching rye to ease crop processing is not necessary (eg Hillman 1978); however, the dry roasting of grain is highly likely, as this would improve flavour and make milling more efficient, since wet grain will turn to a paste when milled (eg Moffett 1994, 61).

Table 62 Charred plant remains from medieval kiln/oven 133092

Taxon	Common name	133824	133826	133827	133928	133834	133835	133837	133947	133948
	Feature	*Medieval kiln/oven 133092*								
	Context(s)	*133824*	*133826*	*133827*	*133928*	*133834*	*133835*	*133837*	*133947*	*133948*
	Sample	*134024/ 134022*	*134020*	*134051*	*134047*	*134026/ 134041*	*134025*	*134027*	*134054*	*134049*
	Sample size (l)	*14*	*9*	*8*	*9*	*17*	*110*	*10*	*9*	*20*
	Flot size (ml)	*175*	*60*	*20*	*40*	*390*	*100*	*60*	*40*	*250*
Cereal grain										
cf. *Hordeum* sp. hulled	Possible hulled barley	-	-	1	-	-	-	-	-	-
Secale cereale	Rye	-	-	-	-	1	-	3	7	4
cf. *Secale cereale*	Possible rye	-	1	2	4	1	-	1	5	1
Secale cereale/*Triticum* sp. indet	Rye/wheat	76*	16	30	21	57	17*	15	55	33*
Cereal/Poaceae - indet cereal	-	146*^{E}	36*^{E}	48^{E}	80^{E}	137^{E}	51*^{E}	31*^{E}	87^{E}	102*^{E}
Cereal/Poaceae - detached embryo	-	-	1	4	11	7	1	2	15	10
Cereal chaff										
Hordeum sp. rachis node	Barley	-	-	-	1	-	-	-	1	-
Hordeum sp./*Secale cereale* indet. rachis node	Indeterminate barley/rye	4	3	-	4	3	-	1	6	-
Secale cereale rachis node	Rye	5	50	36	245	74	21	14	76	564
Secale cereale basal rachis node	Rye	51	1	-	-	-	-	-	-	-
cf. *Secale cereale* rachis node	Possible rye	19	2	2	1	5	3	4	12	100^{E}
Secale cereale/*Triticum* sp. awn	Rye/wheat	-	-	-	-	1	-	-	-	248
Triticum sp. glume base	Wheat	-	-	-	-	-	-	-	1	-
Cereal - indet rachis internode	-	37	13	19	120^{E}	23	8	12	29	-
Cereal/Poaceae - culm node	-	3	3*	3	10^{E}	6	2	3	8	30^{E}
Cereal/Poaceae - culm base	-	-	-	1	-	-	-	1	-	-
Cereal/Poaceae - glume	-	1*	-	1	-	-	-	-	3^{E}	1
cf. Cereal/Poaceae - culm base	-	-	-	-	1	-	-	-	1	-
cf. Cereal/Poaceae - rachis internode	-	-	-	-	-	3	-	-	-	-
Pulses										
cf. *Vicia* sp./*Pisum sativum*	Vetch/garden pea	-	-	-	-	1	-	-	-	2
Tree/shrub										
Corylus avellana – nutshell frag.	Hazel	5*	-	-	-	-	1*	-	-	-
cf. *Prunus domestica* ssp. *institia* frag.	Possible bullace/damson	1	-	-	-	1	1	-	-	-
Wild/weed										
Ranunculus acris/*repens*/*bulbosus*	Meadow/creeping/bulbous buttercup	-	-	-	-	-	1	-	-	-
cf. *Urtica dioica*	Possible common nettle	-	1	-	-	-	-	-	-	-
Chenopodium sp. - ? modern	Goosefoot (possibly modern)	-	-	-	-	3	-	-	-	-
Chenopodium sp./*Atriplex* sp. - indet	Goosefoot/orache	-	-	-	-	-	-	-	-	1
Atriplex sp.	Orache	-	-	-	-	3	-	-	-	-
Spergula arvensis	Corn spurrey	49	18	13	45	168	51^{E}	46	24	33
cf. *Agrostemma githago*	Possible corncockle	-	-	-	1	-	-	-	-	-
Persicaria sp.	Knotweed	-	-	-	2	1	-	-	-	1
Polygonum cf. *aviculare*	Possible knotgrass	1	-	-	-	2	-	-	-	-
Polygonum sp.	Knotgrass	1	-	-	-	2	-	-	-	-
cf. *Polygonum* sp.	Possible knotgrass	2	1	-	-	-	-	-	1	-
Polygonum sp./*Rumex* sp./*Carex* sp. – internal structure	Knotgrass/dock/sedge	7	-	-	-	3	-	-	2	-

Taxon	Common name	Feature / Context(s) / Sample / Sample size (l) / Flot size (ml)	Medieval kiln/oven 133092							
		Context(s)	133824	133826	133827	133928	133834	133835	133837	133947	133948
		Sample	134024/ 134022	134020	134051	134047	134026/ 134041	134025	134027	134054	134049
		Sample size (l)	14	9	8	9	17	110	10	9	20
		Flot size (ml)	175	60	20	40	390	100	60	40	250
Fallopia convolvulus	Black-bindweed		-	-	-	-	2	-	-	-	-
Rumex acetosella	Sheep's sorrel		42	-	6	37^{E}	57	24	5	7	35
Rumex cf. *acetosella*	Possible sheep's sorrel		-	8	4	-	27	-	18	11	-
Rumex sp.	Dock		7*	-	-	1	4	1	2	-	-
Raphanus raphanistrum – capsule segment	Wild radish		5	1	2	3	2	2	-	1	4^{E}
Vicia cf. *hirsuta*	Possible hairy tare		-	-	-	-	1	1	-	-	-
Vicia sp./*Lathyrus* sp.	Vetch/vetchling		14	4*	3	6^{E}	17^{E}	3^{E}	2	5	2*
Melilotus sp./*Medicago* sp./*Trifolium* sp.	Melilot/medick/clover		1	-	-	-	-	1	-	1	1
Galeopsis sp.	Hemp-nettle		-	-	-	1	1	-	1	-	-
cf. *Galeopsis* sp.	Possible hemp-nettle		-	-	-	-	-	-	1	-	-
Prunella vulgaris	Selfheal		-	-	-	-	-	1	-	-	-
Plantago major	Greater plantain		-	-	-	-	-	-	-	1	-
Plantago media/lanceolata	Hoary plantain/ribwort plantain		3	1	-	-	4	-	2	-	-
Galium cf. *mollugo*	Possible hedge bedstraw		-	-	-	-	-	1	1	-	-
Centaurea cf. *cyanus*	Possible cornflower		1	-	-	2	2	-	-	-	1
cf. *Centaurea* sp. – internal structure	Possible knapweed		1	-	-	-	-	-	-	-	-
Lapsana communis	Nipplewort		1	1	-	-	-	-	1	-	1
Anthemis cotula	Stinking chamomile		11	4	1	6	68	12	17*^{E}	-	-
Anthemis cotula/Chrysanthemum segetum – indet.	Stinking chamomile/corn marigold		-	-	-	-	72	-	-	-	-
Chrysanthemum segetum	Corn marigold		610*	57^{E}	50^{E}	246	635	340^{E}	301*^{E}	96	228^{E}
Tripleurospermum inodorum	Scentless mayweed		7	-	-	3	6	3	6	1	7^{E}
Asteraceae – unidentified	Daisy family		-	-	-	-	1	12^{E}	-	-	1
Schoenoplectus lacustris/tabernaemontani	Common club-rush/grey club-rush		1	1	-	-	-	-	3	-	-
Carex sp. – 2-sided	Sedge		-	-	-	-	-	-	1	-	-
Carex sp. – 3-sided	Sedge		1	1	-	-	2	1	-	2	-
Cyperaceae – unidentified	Sedge family		1	-	-	-	6	-	-	-	-
Avena sp. – caryopsis	Oat		-	-	-	-	1	-	-	-	-
Avena sp. – floret base	Oat		-	-	1	6	3	-	1	9	11^{E}
Avena sp. – awn	Oat		2^{E}	-	1^{E}	1^{E}	2^{E}	1^{E}	-	1^{E}	1^{E}
Avena sp./*Bromus* sp.	Oat/brome grass		90*	19*^{E}	11	55	54	17*	41*^{E}	40	46*
Poaceae – small caryopsis	Small-seeded wild grass		-	1	-	1	8	3	2	5	8
Poaceae – medium caryopsis	Medium-seeded wild grass		4	-	-	-	1	-	-	-	3
Poaceae – basal rachis node	Wild grass		-	-	-	-	-	-	1	-	-
Poaceae – rachis node	Wild grass		-	-	-	-	-	-	-	-	2
cf. Poaceae – culm node	Possible wild grass		-	-	-	-	1	-	-	-	-
cf. Poaceae – basal rachis node	Possible wild grass		-	-	-	-	1	-	-	-	-

Taxon	Common name	Medieval kiln/oven 133092								
	Context(s)	133824	133826	133827	133928	133834	133835	133837	133947	133948
	Sample	134024/ 134022	134020	134051	134047	134026/ 134041	134025	134027	134054	134049
	Sample size (l)	14	9	8	9	17	110	10	9	20
	Flot size (ml)	175	60	20	40	390	100	60	40	250
Unidentified – bud scar		-	-	1	-	-	-	1	1	-
Unidentified – calyx		-	-	1	-	-	-	-	1	-
Unidentified – flower structure – frag.		-	-	-	-	-	-	-	11	-
Unidentified – leaf fragments		-	-	-	-	5	-	-	-	-
Unidentified – seed coat – frag.		-	-	-	-	-	-	-	-	-
Unidentified – stalk		-	-	-	-	-	-	-	-	-
Unidentified – root/ tuber/ culm		-	-	-	-	4	-	-	-	-
Unidentified		-	-	11	1	4	88	8	-	-
Indeterminate		18	83	13	50^E	52	44	39	43	1*

Key: Numbers in parentheses eare not included in total; N^E = estimate count; Scores from the heavy residue which have been adjusted to match the proportion of the flot sorted have been indicated with an asterisk (eg N*)

The assemblages recovered from all but one medieval sample could be described as cereal crop-processing by-products, primarily comprised of cereal chaff elements (ie primarily rachis nodes of rye and indeterminate cereal rachis internodes), with small quantities of cereal grain and similarly sized weed/wild seeds. Although cereal chaff is less likely to survive charring than cereal grain (Boardman and Jones 1990), it was clearly abundant in these samples. With the exception of the sample from pit 133155 (context 133784) where cereal grain was dominant, all the other medieval deposits were dominated by weeds of crop (12 samples), cereal chaff (2 samples) or contained a fairly even mixture of cereal grain: cereal chaff: weeds of crop (8 samples) (see Table 63). As a result, the charred plant remains recovered from both the pit and the kiln/oven deposits are likely to have contained cereal crop-processing by-products.

What is notable about the medieval Shenstone samples is that, although the proportion of cereal grain:cereal chaff: weeds of crop can vary, all of the samples produced similar assemblages. This suggests that this by-product of cereal-processing was repeatedly charred (most likely as a result of use of cereal chaff as fuel in the kiln/oven structures) and, in some cases, disposed of in pits on site.

At least two obvious routes of arrival for this material into deposits at Shenstone are possible. It may be that a sieving by-product was intentionally destroyed or used as fuel. The combination of cereal chaff, with small quantities of cereal grain and weed seeds may represent 'chob' or 'cavings' (extraction by hand of weed seeds, cereal chaff, and tail grain during sieving; see Hillman 1984, 2–3; Jones 1984, 46). Or it may be waste generated during small-scale crop processing (ie cleaning small amounts of grain prior to hand-milling), which was intentionally burned as fuel. Alternatively, it could be that this material represented crop-processing waste that had been collected and stored, perhaps destined for use as livestock feed, that had become accidentally burned. However, the fairly limited dominance of cereal grain, which is more likely to survive charring than cereal chaff (Boardman and Jones 1990), makes this second interpretation unlikely.

All of the pit samples were clearly secondary and, therefore, it is possible that much of the charred material had been re-worked and/or represented a mixture of a series of dumping events. The deposits excavated from the kiln/oven structures were more likely to be primary, but, some mixing and re-deposition cannot be ruled out. As a result, any precise identification of the route(s) of arrival of the mixture of cereal chaff, cereal grain and weed seeds recovered from these deposits is not possible. Use of cereal processing waste as fuel is well attested (Hillman 1981; 1984) and spent fuel from the final firing(s) of a kiln/oven and/or the disposal of spent fuel on site into pits seems a likely explanation for the assemblages encountered.

However, one further explanation for the abundance of rye chaff in these deposits is possible. Campbell (1994, 69) citing Markham's 1681 treatise on agriculture (*An English Husbandman: A Way to Get Wealth*) states that he recommended the use of rye straw as bedding for malting grain, in order to protect the grain from charring during the malting process (where cereal grain is heated to arrest the growth of the sprouting of the grain). In this way, the rye chaff could become

Table 63 The proportion of charred plant remains recovered (%)

Feature	Context	Sample	Cereal grain	Cereal chaff	Pulse	Tree/shrub	Weed/wild	Unident./indet	Total
Neolithic pits									
133089	133659	134005	3.0	–	–	95.9	1.2	–	169
133090	133661	134004	0.4	–	–	98.8	–	0.8	498
	133672	134006	0.3	–	–	98.7	–	1.0	382
Medieval kilns/oven									
133070	133810	134017	38.0	5.6	–	0.4	48.7	7.3	234
	133804	134032	18.2	8.0	–	1.1	56.8	15.9	88
	133958	134033	26.9	8.0	–	–	52.2	12.8	312
	133810	134036	39.6	7.5	–	0.5	33.7	18.7	187
	133958	134057	25.4	9.4	–	–	59.7	5.5	437
	133960	134061	12.6	70.1	–	0.1	12.2	4.9	1021
133092	133824	134022	16.2	18.0	–	0.3	57.8	7.6	604
	133824	134024	17.7	1.6	–	0.3	73.6	6.9	700
	133826	134020	17.5	28.6	–	–	46.8	7.1	252
	133827	134051	33.6	24.5	–	–	36.4	5.5	253
	133834	134026	17.8	10.6	–	–	63.0	8.6	500
	133834	134041	11.1	5.5	0.1	0.1	74.6	8.6	1132
	133835	134025	10.9	5.4	–	0.3	75.2	8.2	633
	133837	134027	8.8	5.9	–	–	78.7	6.6	591
	133928	134047	11.9	39.1	–	–	43.5	5.5	977
	133947	134054	30.3	24.6	–	–	37.3	7.7	557
	133948	134049	9.9	62.3	0.1	–	27.6	0.1	1514
Medieval pits									
133925	133926	134040	35.0	23.5	0.1	0.3	34.4	6.6	677
	133929	134045	25.7	28.1	–	–	38.6	7.6	661
133066	133790	134012	13.3	4.2	–	–	66.7	15.8	165
	133786	134013	14.1	1.9	–	1.0	57.8	25.2	206
	133787	134063	16.2	1.3	–	0.6	73.4	8.4	154
133155	133784	134011	54.1	1.7	–	1.7	11.6	30.8	172

Key: Shading indicates clearly dominant (ie >50% of all identifications) plant remain category; assemblages with more of a mixture of plant categories are unshaded

charred, and potentially preferentially survive in archaeological deposits. Notably, he suggests that the rye should be cut off at the ear and the straw spread out to protect the malt grain (Markham 1681 cited in Campbell 1994, 69). This would potentially leave a by-product rich in rye rachis nodes and possibly weeds of crop, as well as small quantities of cereal grain; which would be useful as kindling or fuel for a kiln/oven. This may also explain the deposits encountered at Shenstone.

Evidence for cultivation conditions

The majority of taxa identified in the weed/wild component are all typically recovered with cereal remains in the British Isles (eg Jones 1988a; 1988b). Those taxa identified to species or genera level with specific habitat information have been summarised in Table 64. The vast majority of taxa are strongly associated with arable/cultivated ground or waste ground. These taxa include corn spurrey (*Spergula arvensis*), possible corncockle (*cf. Agrostemma githago*), black-bindweed (*Fallopia convolvulus*), sheep's sorrel (*Rumex acetosella*), wild radish (*Raphanus raphanistrum*), greater plantain (*Plantago major*), possible cornflower (*Centaurea cf. cyanus*), nipplewort (*Lapsana communis*), stinking chamomile (*Anthemis cotula*), corn marigold (*Chrysanthemum segetum*), scentless mayweed (*Tripleurospermum inodorum*), and oat (most likely wild).

Several of the taxa recovered suggest that the cereal (most likely rye) was cultivated on or near damp to wet (possibly seasonally flooded) ground. For example, the recovery of common/slender spike-rush (*Eleocharis palustris/uniglumis*), common/grey club-rush (*Schoenoplectus lacustris/tabernae-montani*) and sedge (*Carex* sp. – 2-sided and 3-sided urticles) all suggest damp to wet conditions. Some of the taxa can be indicative of acid (eg *Rumex acetosella*) or basic (eg *Plantago media/lanceolata* or *Galium cf. mollugo*) soil conditions; however, they are not exclusively found on such soil types. The recovery of stinking chamomile suggests that heavier soils were cultivated, while corn marigold and corn spurrey are characteristic of the cultivation of sandier soils. Combined they suggest either the cultivation of a range of different soil types, or perhaps that fields traversed differing soil types.

Timing of cultivation

As a crop, one of the advantages of rye is that it can be grown as a winter cereal in Britain (eg Langer and Hill 1991, 77). It might be noted though that both corn marigold and corn spurrey are often associated with spring sown or summer crops, (Hanf 1983; Ellenburg 1988). Rodwell (2000) classifies them as part of the *Chrysanthemum segetum–Spergula arvensis* community growing alongside field edges on acidic, light sandy

Table 64 Habitats of weed/wild taxa identified to species from medieval deposits

	Habitat	*Acid soils (low pH)*	*Basic soils (high pH)*	*Arable/cultivated ground*	*Grassland*	*Heavier soils*	*Hedgerows*	*Nitrogen –rich soils*	*Open ground*	*Rough ground*	*Sandy soils*	*Waste ground*	*Water*	*Waterside/ wet places*	*Woodland*
Ranunculus acris/repens/ bulbosus	Buttercups				✓									?	
cf. *Urtica dioica*	Possible common nettle							✓							✓
Spergula arvensis	Corn spurrey		✓	✓							✓				
cf. *Agrostemma githago*	Possible corncockle			✓								✓			
Polygonum aviculare	Knotgrass								✓						
Fallopia convolvulus	Black-bindweed			✓					✓			✓			
Rumex acetosella	Sheep's sorrel	?		✓	✓										
Raphanus raphanistrum – capsule segment	Wild radish			✓						✓		✓			
Rubus section Rubus	Bramble/ Blackberry											✓			✓
Vicia cf. *hirsuta*	Possible hairy tare				✓					✓					
Prunella vulgaris	Selfheal				✓					✓					
Plantago major	Greater plantain			✓	✓				✓	✓					
Plantago media/ lanceolata	Hoary plantain/ Ribwort plantain		?		✓										
Galium cf. *mollugo*	Possible hedge bedstraw		?		✓		✓								
Centaurea cf. *cyanus*	Possible cornflower			✓								✓			
Lapsana communis	Nipplewort						✓			✓		✓			
Anthemis cotula	Stinking chamomile			✓		✓				✓		✓			
Chrysanthemum segetum	Corn marigold			✓								✓			
Tripleurospermum inodorum	Scentless mayweed			✓								✓			
Eleocharis palustris /uniglumis	Common/ Slender spike-rush												✓	✓	
Schoenoplectus lacustris/ tabernaemontani	Common club-rush/ grey club-rush												✓	✓	
Carex sp.	Sedge													✓	
Avena sp.	Oat			✓								✓			

soils, following the *Spergulo-Chrysanthemum segetum* of the continent. It is also interesting to note that while rye was recovered from the Romano-British site, East of Birmingham Nurseries (Site 15; Clapham Chapter 17), these two species were absent from the weed flora. However, it is noted that this association is replaced by others in summer sown crops, implying that the association with spring sowing may be less strong than suggested by the other authors.

Evidence for harvesting height

The frequent presence of taxa such as sheep's sorrel, stinking chamomile and corn spurrey in the Shenstone samples strongly suggests a low harvesting height. For example, sheep's sorrel can actually be procumbent (growing flat across the ground), but is typically quite low-growing (Stace 1997, 190) and, therefore, would most likely require a harvesting height quite low, perhaps <150 mm). As a result of the frequent recovery of fairly low-growing taxa in these samples, it suggests a general trend for harvesting the cereal to recover the greatest length of straw possible. Again, the importance of rye straw for such activities as thatching (eg Letts 1999, 21–2) may somewhat explain the low harvesting height.

Potential residual Romano-British charred plant remains

By the Saxon period hulled wheats, emmer and spelt, appear to be rarely cultivated in England, although some exceptions exist (*cf.* Pelling and Robinson 2000), and are replaced by the more easily processed free-threshing wheats (eg *Triticum aestivum/T. durum*). The recovery of small quantities of spelt and indeterminate wheat glume bases in some of the medieval samples does suggest that a certain amount of residual material is re-deposited on site.

Although no samples from Romano-British phases at Shenstone were sufficiently rich to merit full analysis, there clearly was Romano-British activity on site and this may explain the presence of small quantities of charred remains more typical of Romano-British assemblages within some of the medieval samples.

Comparison with other medieval sites in Staffordshire

The medieval results from Shenstone suggest that rye may have been a significant cereal crop in this area of the Midlands during the medieval period. Moffett (1994) has already reported rye remains from Late Saxon deposits at Stafford. The examination of later (15th century) deposits from Stone (Moffett and Smith 1996) has also resulted in the recovery of rye. Unpublished evidence from Stafford College, Broadeye, Stafford (Smith 2004) for charred plant remains from two pits which contained a mixture of cereal grain, cereal chaff and weed seeds is quite similar to that produced at Shenstone. Rye was not dominant at Stafford College, it was also recovered with barley and free-threshing wheat. Most strikingly the range of weed taxa were very similar to that recovered from Shenstone, with corn marigold and corn spurrey abundant. The limited number of sites from the 13th/14th century makes wider comparison in Staffordshire, or the Midlands, quite difficult, but clearly these results from Staffordshire now strongly suggest that there is a definite trend for the cultivation of rye from the Saxon and medieval periods in the county.

Conclusions

Excavations at this site resulted in the recovery of three earlier Neolithic and 23 medieval (13th–14th centuries) archaeobotanical assemblages. The earlier Neolithic samples were from pits, all of which primarily contained charred fragments of hazelnut shell, probably collected as a food resource.

The medieval samples included five pit samples and 18 kiln/oven samples. All contained a mixture of cereal grain, cereal chaff and accompanying weeds of crop. Although the precise proportions varied, they were remarkably uniform with rye chaff the most dominant and frequently recovered cereal remain in all samples. The frequent presence of weed taxa such as sheep's sorrel, stinking chamomile and corn spurrey strongly suggests a low harvesting height, most likely for the intentional recovery of rye straw, which was highly prized for thatching in the period. With the exception of one deposit (pit 133155, context 133784 (54.1% cereal grain, either indeterminate rye/wheat or indeterminate cereal/large grass)), the limited recovery of cereal grain in these deposits strongly suggests that these samples contain a crop-processing by-product most likely used as fuel for the kiln/oven structures found on site.

The medieval deposits from Shenstone have added important information on cereal cultivation for the period, which is not particularly well studied in the region. The possibility that rye was a significant crop in the vicinity of Stafford is suggested by these and unpublished results from Stafford College, Broadeye, Stafford (Smith 2004). However, further archaeobotanical sampling of deposits dating to the Late Saxon and medieval periods is essential to test this hypothesis.

Charcoal, by Rowena Gale

Sixty-seven bulk samples were collected. Despite the abundance of charcoal in many contexts, the condition of the charcoal was generally very poor. Fifteen samples were selected for charcoal analysis from earlier Neolithic and medieval pits, two medieval kilns/ovens and a shallow feature containing burnt stone. Charcoal analysis was undertaken to evaluate the character of local woodland and to indicate the selection and use of wood resources. The taxa identified are presented in Table 65.

Earlier Neolithic pits

The two adjacent pits (133089 and 133090) were roughly in the centre of the site. Charcoal from context 133659, the single fill of pit 133089, was identified as oak (*Quercus* sp.) and alder (*Alnus glutinosa)*. A piece of oak sapwood was submitted for radiocarbon dating and provided an Early Neolithic date (see Smith above). Samples from context 133661 were obtained from the top fill of pit 133090; the charcoal included oak heartwood and sapwood (some slow-grown), hazel (*Corylus avellana*), ash (*Fraxinus excelsior*) and pine (*Pinus* sp.). In view of the large quantities of pottery and charred hazel nutshells associated with the charcoal, these deposits are ascribed as domestic refuse. In contrast, charred grain was infrequent. A number of pebbles in pit 133090 appeared to have been fire-cracked.

Medieval

Pits and feature 133066

Charcoal was examined from pits 133925 and 133155 , and feature 133066, on the south-west boundary of the site. The frequency of charred food remains (grain, pulses and hazelnuts) and pottery in these features suggested that associated charcoal deposits represent domestic hearth debris.

Slight scorching on the sides of pit 133925 could suggest *in situ* burning – the pit, perhaps, having been used for burning refuse. The charcoal-rich sample 143040 (50% sub-sampled), from the secondary fill of this pit indicated the predominant use of narrow roundwood measuring <15 mm in diameter, mainly from birch (*Betula* sp.) and hawthorn/*Sorbus* type (Pomoideae), but also oak and alder.

Pit 133066 may also have been a fire-pit, as suggested by the baked clay lining. Although very fragmented, the charcoal-rich deposit from context 133790 appeared to consist almost entirely of narrow roundwood measuring <10 mm in diameter from birch, holly (*Ilex aquifolium*), hazel, the hawthorn/*Sorbus* group, blackthorn (*Prunus spinosa*), gorse (*Ulex* sp.)/broom (*Cytisus scoparius*) and oak. A similar range of taxa was identified from context 133949, which also consisted of narrow roundwood. The similarity of the charcoal in these contexts suggests that these deposits either accrued from the same burning event or, if from different events/activities, from the use of the same type of firewood.

The shallow and heavily truncated pit 133155 appears to have been used as a dump. Sample 134011, from context 133784, the single fill of the pit, consisted almost entirely of oak heartwood and thus differed in character to that from the other two pits. A small amount of hazel was also present.

Kilns/ovens

The two kilns/ovens 133070 and 133092 were located roughly in the middle of the site. Large quantities of charred grain associated with these features suggested their use as grain-driers. The initial assessment of the charred plant remains suggested that some contexts within these features contained different types of grain assemblages, perhaps representing different events/activities (OAU 2003).

Table 65 Charcoal from Neolithic and medieval contexts (no. frags)

Feature	*Context*	*Sample*	*Alnus*	*Betula*	*Corylus*	*Fraxinus*	*Ilex*	*Pomoideae*	*Prunus*	*Quercus*	*Salicaceae*	*Ulex/Cytisus*	*Pinus*
Early Neolithic													
Pits													
133089	133659	134005	2	–	–	–	–	–	–	6h, 5s	–	–	–
133090	133661	134004/6	–	–	14	5	–	–	–	3h, 6r	–	–	4
Medieval													
Pits													
133925	133926	134040	1	27r	–	–	–	5r	–	2h	–	–	–
Feature													
133155	133784	134011	–	–	2	–	–	–	–	33h	–	–	–
133066	133790	134013	–	1r	3r	–	3r	4r	11r	2h	–	8r	–
	133949	134063	–	3	–	–	1r	1r	3r	1r	–	2r	–
Kilns/ovens													
133070	133958	134057	–	6	3	–	–	–	1	24h	–	–	–
	133958	134033	–	13	1	–	–	–	–	35h,1r, 2s	1	–	–
	133810	134017	–	18	1	–	4r	4r	–	24h, 3r, 2s	–	–	–
133092	133835	134025	–	15r	–	–	–	–	–	1h, 2r	–	–	–
	133834	134041	–	7	2	–	–	4	2	66h, 2r, 1s	1	–	–
	133928	134047	–	3	2	–	–	–	–	4h	–	–	–
	133948	134049	4	9	–	–	–	1	–	18h, 2r, 1s	–	1	–
Shallow feature containing burnt stone													
133727	133728	134008	–	–	–	–	–	–	–	8u	–	–	–

Key: h = heartwood; r = roundwood (diam. < 20 mm); s = sapwood (diam. unknown); u = maturity unknown (*Quercus* only)

Charcoal from contexts 133958 (lower) and 133810 (upper) in the kiln/oven 133070 included a relatively wide range of taxa: oak, birch, hazel, holly, the hawthorn/*Sorbus* group, blackthorn and willow (*Salix* sp.)/poplar (*Populus* sp.).

Charcoal was examined from four contexts from kiln/oven 133092. Context 133948 underlay the clay-lining of the pit and thus appears to represent an earlier dump of charcoal (?prior to its use a grain-dryer); the taxa named included oak heartwood and roundwood, birch, alder, the hawthorn/*Sorbus* group and gorse/broom. Charcoal was less abundant in context 133928, a burnt sandy charcoal lens between two clay layers near the base of the re-cut feature, and identified the use of oak, birch and hazel. Context 133835 was described during excavation as possibly backfill using rubbish; this context contained burnt cobbles, bone, pottery, charred grain and charcoal, the latter named as oak and birch. It was not clear whether charcoal in context 133902 had been burnt *in situ* or dumped; this charcoal-rich context contained fragments of burnt wood up to 15 mm in length. A 50% sub-sample was examined and identified as mostly oak heartwood from slow-grown wood; additional but infrequent taxa included blackthorn, the hawthorn/*Sorbus* group, birch, hazel, willow/poplar and a quantity of unidentified bark about 10 mm thick.

Ditch

Context 133728 was the single fill of a shallow hollow on the edge of ditch 133078, close to the south-west edge of the site. Due to heavy truncation, it was difficult to determine the true character of the feature. Apart from burnt stone, charcoal and charred cereal grain, no artefactual material was recorded. The charcoal was abundant but in such poor condition that only a few fragments retained sufficient diagnostic information to enable identification; these were named as oak.

Discussion

Early Neolithic

The remains of refuse, including fuel debris were recovered from two isolated pits 133089 and 133090. The origin of this material is uncertain. The charcoal indicated that firewood was gathered from a range of species including oak, alder, ash, hazel and pine. Pine wood occurs infrequently in archaeological contexts, perhaps due to its (assumed) low distribution in the environment in the later prehistoric period, but possibly also because the resinous wood has a tendency to spit when burning (Porter 1990), thus posing a serious fire-risk to flammable structures. It might be noted that pine wood of probable Neolithic date was also recorded from West of Crane Brook (Site 9, Chapter 14). None of the charcoal examined suggested the use of coppiced wood, in fact, some fragments of oak heartwood were indicative of slow-growth, consistent with competitive or stressed habitats, such as dense woodland.

Medieval

Medieval occupation was agrarian. In addition to numerous linear features and a small enclosure, some type of activity (possibly grain-drying) centred around the two large clay-lined kiln/oven features 133070 and 133092. Some other features in this locality may also have been used for burning, for example feature 133066, which contained a baked clay lining, and pit 133925, which showed slight scorching of the walls, perhaps the result of burning waste materials.

Since charcoal deposits were frequently associated with dumps of household refuse (pottery, bone, charred foodstuffs and grain), similar origins seem likely for the charcoal, as, for example, in pits 133925 and 133155, feature 133066 and perhaps also contexts 133835 and in the kiln/oven feature 133092, which probably included material dumped as backfill. With the exception of pit 133155, the character of the fuel debris recovered from these features was remarkably similar and indicated the frequent use of narrow roundwood mainly from shrubby species such as hazel, the hawthorn/*Sorbus* group, alder, holly, birch and gorse/broom but also oak heartwood. Deposits in pit 133155, however, appear to have originated from an activity (either domestic or otherwise) for which the fuel consisted predominantly of oak heartwood. Charcoal from context 133834 (kiln/oven 133092), included a fairly wide range of species but demonstrated the selective use of oak heartwood, perhaps for a specific activity. Charcoal from context 133835, in the same feature but interpreted as possible backfill material, was less frequent and consisted of birch roundwood and oak.

A common theme recorded from deposits/residues from the two kiln/oven features 133070 and 133092 is the predominant use of oak and birch, with more sporadic use of (mostly) roundwood from hazel, alder, holly, blackthorn, the hawthorn/*Sorbus* group and willow/poplar. It is difficult, however, to attribute any of the deposits examined specifically to residues arising from burning events within the kiln features with any certainty. Even deposits obtained from the basal layers, which might be assumed as *in situ* deposits can mislead, for example context 133948 (kiln/oven 133092) was actually recovered from beneath the clay-lining – which suggests that the material was dumped in the pit prior to its use as a grain-drier. Context 133928, also from kiln/oven 133092, however, occurred as a lens of charcoal between layers of clay, which suggests the re-use of the feature and, thus, more securely implicates the charcoal (oak, birch and hazel) as the remains of fuel dedicated to the use of the feature.

Charcoal was also obtained in large quantity from the fill of a shallow hollow 133727 containing burnt stone (133078) but its condition had deteriorated to the extent that very little could be identified; a few fragments of oak were named. The origin of this material is unknown.

Evidence from both pits and the kiln/oven features illustrates the common use of narrow roundwood (probably from coppiced sources – see below), particularly birch, combined with oak heartwood, the latter probably from wider roundwood or largewood. The lack of distinction between fuel deposits from (probably) exclusively domestic contexts and those from agricultural use of the grain-driers suggests either the common use of available wood resources for any fire-based event or that the act of discarding refuse (including fuel debris) was practised on an *ad hoc* basis, which resulted in considerable mixing of deposits.

Environmental evidence

Underlying soils at the site were sandy and well drained. The range of woodland taxa identified were typically acid-tolerant and included pine from the Neoltihic, oak and hazel from both periods, and birch, holly, gorse/broom, blackthorn, the hawthorn/*Sorbus* group and ash recovered only from medieval contexts. This combination of species suggests that the medieval woodland consisted mainly of oak/birch/holly communities, with shrubby species such as gorse and hazel growing in more open areas or scrub. The proliferation of nutshells suggests that hazel was common in the environment. Wetland species included alder and willow and/or poplar. Given the extensive agricultural land-use, hedgerows were probably a common feature in the medieval landscape and would have provided a useful source of smallwood.

Woodland management and fuel resources

Charcoal deposits from the earlier Neolithic pits were generally too fragmented to assess origins from roundwood/managed woodland, although oak heartwood from pit 133090 included narrow growth rings more characteristic of trees growing in competitive woodland or stressed environments. Large quantities of narrow roundwood were present in nearly all the medieval samples but owing to the poor structural condition of this material it was usually very difficult and often impossible to examine growth patterns and therefore no conclusive evidence for the use of coppiced wood was forthcoming. The following points are offered as alternative evidence for the use of coppiced stems during the medieval period:

- The high ratio of narrow roundwood (often <15mm in diameter but <10mm in feature 133066) from a wide range of species, present in most samples, is consistent with the use of coppice stems grown on short-rotation. The combination of narrow roundwood with oak heartwood from wider roundwood or largewood could imply a system of growing coppice with standard oaks.
- By the 13th/14th centuries, the conversion of woodland to agricultural land in most parts of the country had reduced available woodland to such an extent that woodmanship/management was the only means of sustaining adequate supplies for fuel and timber (Rackham 1986).

Mollusca, by Michael J. Allen

During the routine processing of the bulk samples, one was noted to contain a freshwater snail in the flot. Sorting of the residue did not recover any further fragments but the presence of a single specimen of the amphibious species *Anisus leucostoma* from Neolithic pit 133089 (context 133659) is not expected on this site and indicates the exploitation of riverine resources. The site is located on the Shenstone and Wall floodplain mires and the Crane Brook lies about 0.5 km to the south and within easy access.

We can assume that this was an accidental incorporation into the pit along with something like water, vegetation (reeds, rushes) or mud from the river and river's edge for use on site. This use of riverine resources and their removal to a dry occupation location is a feature commonly seen in southern England where freshwater snails have been found in pits from a numbers of sites: including Balksbury in the Anton and Pilbrook valley, Hampshire (Allen 1995; 2001), Winklebury, Hampshire (Thomas 1977), The Bowsings, Gloucestershire (Allen 1998), and also Battlesbury (Allen forthcoming) and Codford Circle in the Wylye Valley, Wiltshire (unpublished).

The survival of a shell here suggests the discard of calcium-rich refuse or material in this pit, and the presence of numerous different types of material (*cf.* Thomas 1977; Shackley 1976). The presence of the single freshwater species and lack of local terrestrial species is, however, puzzling.

Discussion

This site was notable for the number of periods represented, with evidence of Mesolithic, Neolithic, Iron Age, Romano-British, possible Anglo-Saxon, medieval and post-medieval/modern activity. This may be due in part to its position on a small promontory of higher, sandier ground, protruding into the surrounding Shenstone wetlands, which would have made it a suitable location for temporary occupation by hunter-gatherer groups exploiting an ecologically rich wetland environment, and for more permanent settlement in later periods.

The significant evidence for Neolithic activity in the area, comprising hunting (as represented by the chisel arrowhead), food gathering (hazelnuts) and the likelihood of cereal cultivation as represented by the contents of the two small pits, adds to the other evidence for Neolithic activity along the M6 Toll, all of which was found in the Wall/Shenstone area. An assemblage of Early Neolithic pottery was found at East of The Castle (Site 32, Chapter 18), while Peterborough Ware pottery of Mortlake type was found at East of Birmingham Road Nurseries (Site 15), both sites to the immediate south-east, while West of Crane Brook (Site 9), under 2 km to the north-west, produced a later Neolithic radiocarbon date of 2920–2660 cal BC (4230±35, NZA-25076) from the burnt stone deposit, along with a possible Neolithic flint scraper.

The few Romano-British features, dated mainly to the late 2nd–3rd/mid-4th centuries and lying within the landscape around the Roman town at Wall, are suggestive of both domestic and agricultural contexts. However, they represent a relatively low level of activity in comparison with that suggested by the possible Romanised farmstead indicated by cropmarks to the south, and that found on the adjacent sites, particularly by the Romano-British enclosures and field system uncovered at East of Birmingham Road Nurseries (Site 15) to the south-east, the ditches on the two sites having a similar orientation and probably being associated.

The distribution of medieval features on the southern edge of the site suggests that further features, including possibly those relating directly to domestic occupation, may have lain to the south. If the enclosure, ditches and timber structure were, as suggested, related to animal farming, it is likely that these would have been located close to the edge of the settlement. The ovens, in contrast, were sited at a greater distance, both to avoid the risk of fire spreading to the settlement, and because of the smoke they would have produced. Although their function remains uncertain, ie whether for parching or malting grain, it is possible that they were used to dry-roast grain to improve its flavour and facilitate its milling. Other forms of evidence suggest milling in the vicinity of the site, including the recovery of part of a large millstone; and according to documentary reference (see Chapter 31 below), the appurtenances of the manor of Shenstone held by William de Bray, included at least two mills in the late 12th century.

In combination, however, the medieval features suggest the presence of a substantial settlement, dated mainly to the 13th–14th centuries but perhaps with its origins in the 12th century. The finds and features indicate a range of domestic and subsistence activities, including food production and processing. There is indirect evidence of animal husbandry, with more direct evidence for the cultivation of cereals (wheat and rye) and legumes (peas and beans) and the exploitation of wild food resources (hazelnuts).

The series of post-medieval ditches is likely to represent the evolution of the field system over a considerable period. The limited dating evidence points to a post-medieval to modern date, but it is possible that elements of the ditch system had their origins in the medieval period, and it is clear that it continued to be modified into the 19th century, particularly with those straight boundaries characteristic of parliamentary inclosure.

Chapter 16
Shenstone Ring Ditch (Site 14)

By Andy Simmonds

Introduction

Following a programme of fieldwalking, geophysical survey and trenched evaluation, an archaeological excavation was undertaken on land south-east of the village of Wall and north of Shenstone. This revealed a Middle Iron Age oval enclosure and an adjacent smaller ring gully enclosing a roundhouse, as well as post-medieval boundary ditches and modern features (Fig. 103).

The site, covering *c* 1 hectare centred on NGR 411310 305620, lay in the south-eastern angle of the junction of the A5 and the A5127 Birmingham to Lichfield road. The geology is mapped as Triassic Keuper Sandstone (Geological Survey of Great Britain 1954, Sheet 154, Lichfield). This comprised a compact, slightly clayey sand.

The site was initially identified on the basis of cropmark evidence, which appeared to represent a ring ditch. An evaluation carried out by Oxford Archaeological Unit in October 1993 concluded that the feature was oval in shape rather than completely circular, but was unable to further clarify its date or character due to an absence of finds (OAU 1994a). The evaluation also identified a number of possible discrete features within the area enclosed by the ditch, including a scatter of six postholes.

Results

Mesolithic

Mesolithic activity was represented by a single unstratified flint blade (ON 143002). A wide spread of similar flints was recorded to the immediate north-west at Shenstone Linear Features (Site 13), and a small assemblage was recorded at East of Birmingham Road Nurseries (Site 15) to the south.

Iron Age

The oval enclosure previously identified from cropmark evidence and sampled in the evaluation was exposed in the southern part of the site, with a smaller ring gully containing a roundhouse adjacent to it on its north side.

Oval enclosure

The enclosure was oval in plan with a slightly asymmetrical entrance, *c* 5.5 m wide, facing east-south-east. Internally the enclosure measured *c* 21 m north–south and 23 m east–west, although its western extent had been removed by the digging of a modern drain (141001), excavated since the 1993 evaluation. The enclosure ditch was up to 2 m wide on the north side (141003) but was less substantial on the south side (141004), where its width varied from 1.1 m to 1.5 m. It was 0.5–0.7 m deep, with sides that sloped moderately to a narrow, flat base (Fig. 104). It is likely that this profile is the result of erosion of the surrounding sand, and that the original profile was steeper.

The basal fill in the southern ditch terminal was a layer of grey or dark brown clay with occasional darker mottling (140029), which is likely to represent material accumulating in standing water, indicating that the base of the ditch was waterlogged. Forty-one sherds (218 g) of Iron Age pottery, probably from a single vessel, were recovered from this layer, and a carbonised residue from one sherd produced a radiocarbon date in the Early Iron Age of 770–410 cal BC (NZA-25166, 2463±30) (Fig. 105, Table 66). Throughout the length of the ditch, this earliest fill was overlain by two layers of sandy material resulting from natural in-filling and the stabilisation of the ditch profile. At the southern terminal the upper of these sandy layers was cut by an oval pit (140011), measuring 1.3 m by 0.85 m, its sides sloping gently to a rounded base at a depth of *c* 0.4 m (Fig. 104). A primary fill, consisting of light brown sand (140031) eroded from the pit edges, was overlain by a layer of grey sandy silt (140030), then a layer of compact grey sand with orange mottling (140012) containing the lower part of a saddle quern (ON 143001). The pit was sealed by the final fill of the enclosure ditch, a layer of dark greyish-brown sandy silt (140009). The northern terminal of the enclosure ditch had been truncated by a modern field drain.

A scatter of six possible postholes (140054, 140056, 140058, 140060, 140062 and 140068) was identified in the central part of the enclosure, in addition to two recorded during the evaluation (12 and 14), but formed no coherent pattern. A further four possible postholes recorded during the evaluation could not be identified during the excavation. All the postholes were circular or oval in plan and had concave bases, the smallest (140060, 140068) measuring no more than 0.11 m in diameter and 0.04 m deep, while the largest (140054) measured *c* 0.45 m wide and 0.1 m deep. They all contained similar fills of brown silty sand with no evidence for post-pipes, and none yielded any finds. It is possible that some, particularly the smaller examples, were produced by root action rather than being archaeological features.

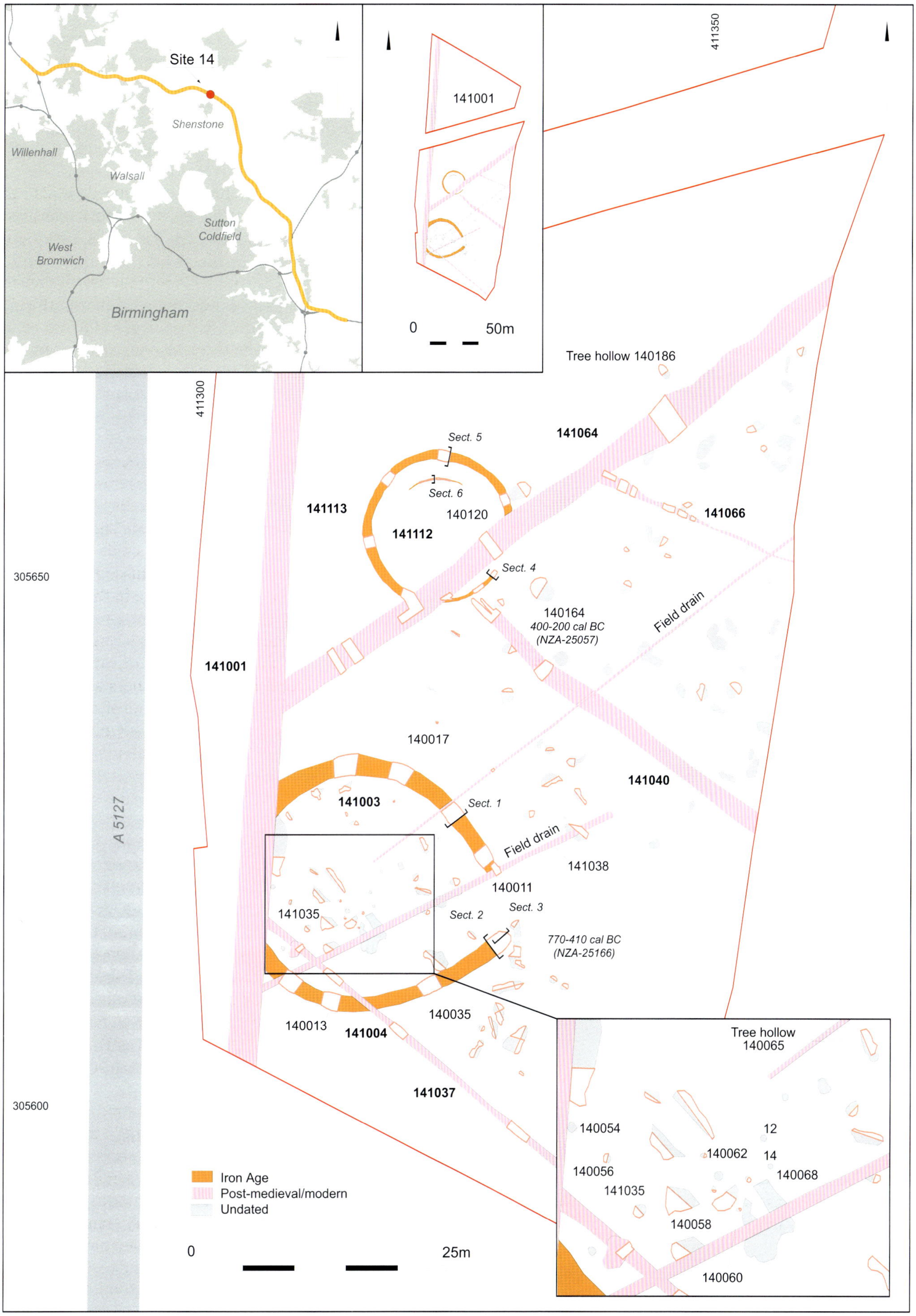

Fig. 103 Shenstone Ring Ditch (Site 14)

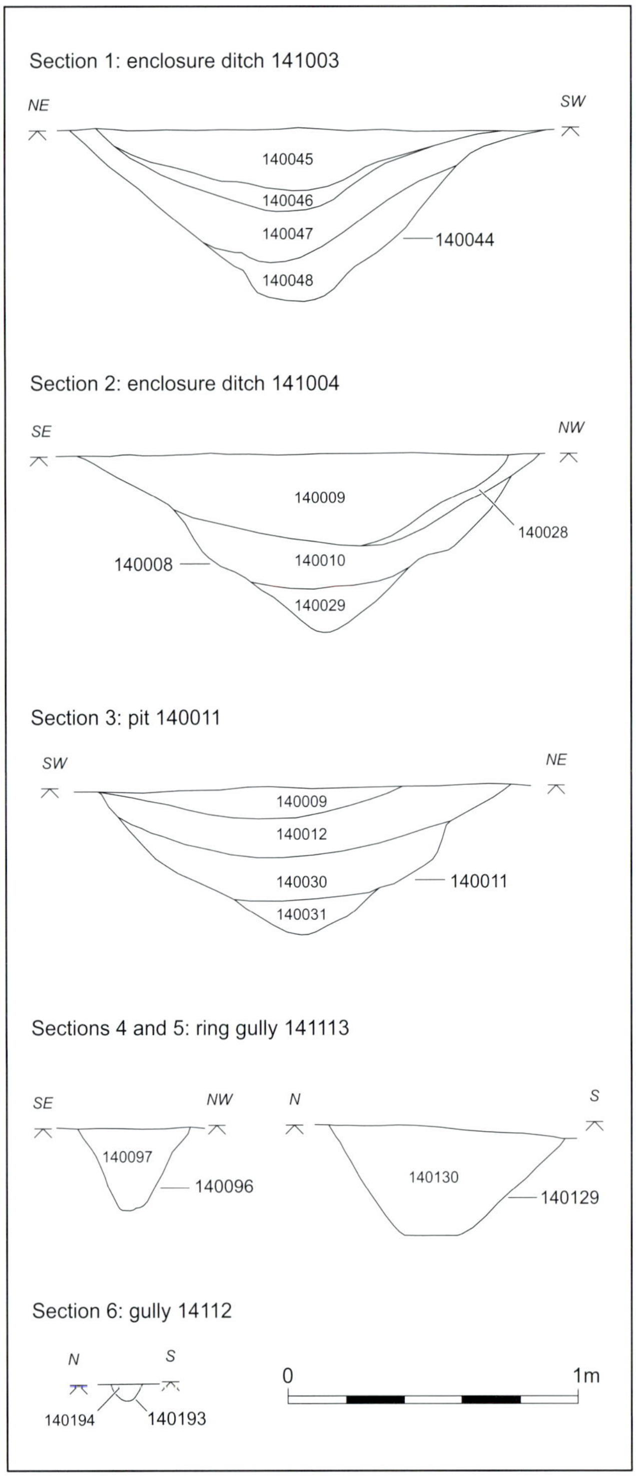

Fig. 104 Ditch and gully sections

Table 66 Radiocarbon dates

Feature	*Context*	*Material*	*Lab. No.*	*Result BP*	*Date cal BC at 2 σ*
Oval enc. ditch 141004	140029	residue on pot	NZA-25166	2463±30	770–410
Roundhouse gully 141113	140165	oak round-wood	NZA-25057	2260±35	400–200

Roundhouse ring gully

A penannular ring gully (141113) lay 15 m north of the enclosure, probably representing a roundhouse. In contrast to the larger oval enclosure, the ring gully was almost exactly circular, and measured 13 m in diameter with an entrance facing east-south-east. It was 0.75–1.06 m wide and up to 0.6 m deep with a U-shaped profile (Fig. 104). On the southern side it appeared to have been subject to greater truncation and was only 0.4 m wide and 0.5 m deep. Only the southern terminal of the entrance survived, the northern having been truncated by post-medieval boundary ditch 141064. The entrance would have been between 2 m and 5 m wide. The gully contained a single fill of grey silty sand from which the only finds were four pieces of burnt stone weighing 650 g. Varying quantities of charred plant remains recorded in the excavated sections suggest that it was the site of localised episodes of dumping of burnt waste from crop processing.

A sample of oak charcoal from the fill of the gully provided a radiocarbon date in the Middle Iron Age of 400–200 cal BC (NZA-25057, 2260±35 BP), considerably later than, and not overlapping with, that obtained from the oval enclosure ditch (Fig. 105, Table 66).

Within the northern part of the ring gully, and concentric with it, was a *c* 5.8 m long arc of a very slight gully (141112), 0.11 m wide and no more than 0.06 m deep (Fig. 104). It is possible that this represents the surviving part of the wall-line of the roundhouse, and its shallowness would be consistent with the rest of the feature having been truncated by recent ploughing. The curvature of the surviving arc suggests a diameter of *c* 10 m for the roundhouse, which is consistent with the dimensions for such structures recorded elsewhere (eg Allen *et al.* 1984).

Post-medieval and modern

The southern part of the excavation area was crossed by boundary ditches aligned NW–SE and NE–SW and forming the north-western edge of a post-medieval field system. The most substantial of these features, ditch 141064, was up to 2 m wide and 0.7 m deep, and extended across the site aligned NE–SW. Ditches 141037, 141040 and 141066 were all aligned NW–SE and sub-divided the area south of ditch 141064 into

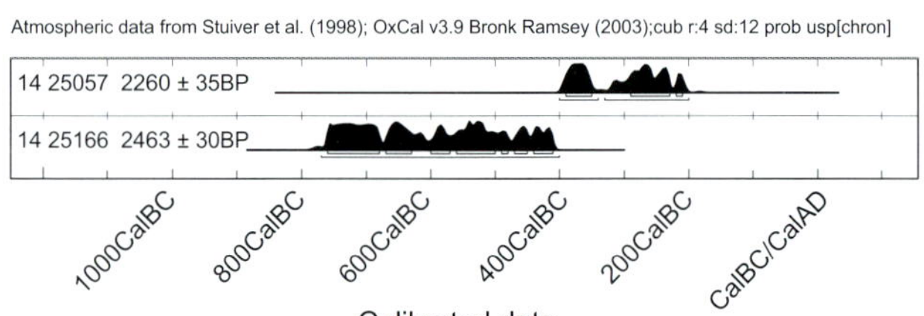

Fig. 105 Oxcal probability distributions of radiocarbon dates

approximately rectilinear fields. Pit 141035, which cut ditch 141037 and produced a single piece of post-medieval tile, was sub-rectangular in plan and measured 1.6 m by 1.2 m, with vertical sides and was excavated to a depth of 0.45 m without reaching the base. Field drain 141038, which was oriented ENE–WSW, may be associated with this field system.

In addition to the possible postholes identified within the oval enclosure, a total of 96 discrete features was recorded; all but two lay south-east of boundary ditch 141064. Sixty-five were investigated and found to be oval or irregular in plan, measuring up to 2.75 m by 1.45 m, and had poorly defined edges and irregular or concave profiles. Their shape and character suggest that they were tree hollows. Pottery recovered from tree hollow 140186 and a brick from tree hollow 140065 suggest that some were of post-medieval date.

A modern service trench (141001) extended north–south along the western edge of the site and truncated the western side of the oval enclosure. This feature was not recorded in the evaluation and had presumably been laid subsequent to that investigation.

Finds

Flint, by Kate Cramp

A single flint blade was recovered (Table 150). It has an abraded, faceted platform and is probably Mesolithic; the slightly damaged condition of the piece suggests that it is probably residual.

Worked stone, by Ruth Shaffrey

A saddle quern (ON 143001) was the only worked stone from the site; this was retrieved from the upper fill (140012) of pit 140011, which was cut into the terminal of enclosure ditch 141003. It was well used as a saddle quern but was manufactured from a boulder and was unshaped on the underside. It was made of blue–green gneiss and, most likely to be an erratic from the glacial deposits overlying the South Staffordshire Coalfield, as these contain boulders from suitable source areas such as southern Scotland (Barrow *et al.* 1919, 179). It measures 390 mm by 220 mm by 70 mm. The quern is of special importance because it was one of very few finds from the site and was almost certainly part of a deliberate or structured deposit. The unusual fabric of the quern may also have marked it out as being of extra significance. It was clearly still functional when it was deposited and although there was heavy burning on the base that could suggest re-use, it is equally plausible that it had undergone a 'ritual' death to mark the end of its functional existence. Querns are often found at the ends of enclosure ditches (Brück 1999a, 152) and the suggestion is that they emphasise the significance of that boundary (*ibid.*, 153). A general overview of the deposition of querns in contexts of special significance is

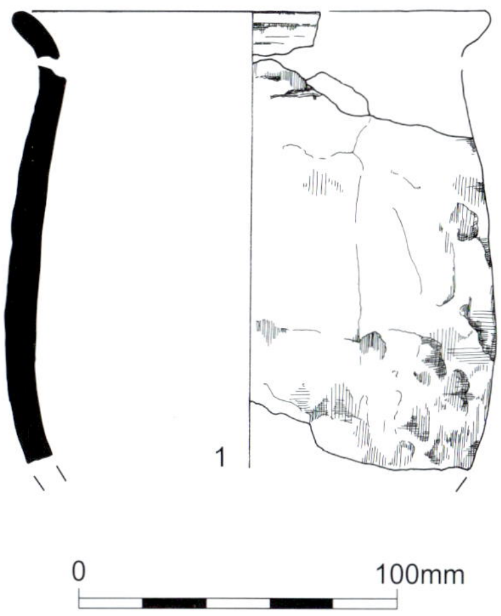

Fig. 106 Iron Age pottery

yet to be carried out but its occurrence during all periods is becoming increasingly well known. Examples of Middle Iron Age date include not only those placed in boundary ditches, such as here, but also those placed in pits in the entranceway to roundhouses (Shaffrey in prep.).

Iron Age pottery, by Paul Booth

Some 41 sherds and fragments of Iron Age pottery (218 g) were recovered from a single vessel – a simple jar with a slightly everted rim – in context 140029, in the southern terminal of the oval enclosure. The vessel, in fabric QAM4, was a simple fairly straight-sided jar with a slightly everted rim (Fig. 106). The vessel was undecorated, but had some internal and external sooting and carbonised material on the surface provided a radiocarbon date of 770–410 cal BC (NZA-25166, 2463±30), indicating an Early Iron Age date.

In addition, a single fragment of poorly-fired, very coarsely tempered oxidised ceramic came from a sample (142023) in ring gully fill 140165. This is of Cheshire Stony VCP (briquetage), which has a wide period of use in the Iron Age (Morris 1985).

Environment

Charred plant remains, by Lisa Gray

Twenty-four samples were taken from Iron Age features, averaging 20–30 litres. The majority of the samples, however, produced very few remains and only 18 were chosen for analysis.

Results

Charred remains consisted of wood and occasional cereal grains, chaff, seeds and nutshell fragments. Very little was recovered from these samples. The results of the analysis are presented in Tables 67–8; six samples are omitted as no identifiable plant remains were recovered

Table 67 Charred plant remains from Iron Age ring gully and gully 141112

Taxon	Common name									
	Feature	Roundhouse ring gully 141113								Gully 141112
	Section	140120		140127	140129	140142	140145		140164	142024
	Context	140121	140122	140128	140130	140143	140146	140147-50	140165	140194
	Sample	142015	142016	142018	142017	142019	142020	142021	142023	142024
	Sample size (l)	20	18	20	18	18	19	20	40	10
	Flot size (ml)	60	40	90	40	20	15	60	2000	15
Triticum cf. dicoccum/spelta glume bases	Emmer/spelt wheat	–	–	–	–	–	–	–	1	–
Triticum cf. spelta glume base	?Spelt	–	–	–	–	–	–	–	1	–
Triticum cf. dicoccum glume base	Emmer	–	1	–	–	–	–	–	–	–
Triticum. sp. grain	Wheat	–	1	–	–	–	–	–	1	–
Avena/Hordeum/Secale/Triticum grain	indet. cereal	–	1	–	–	–	–	–	–	–
Avena/Hordeum/Secale/Triticum stem frag.	indet. cereal	–	–	–	–	–	–	–	1	–
Chenopodium album seed	Fat-hen	–	–	–	–	–	1	–	–	–
Brassica/Sinapsis sp. seed	Wild cabbage/ mustard	–	2	–	–	–	2	–	1	–
Corylus avellana shell frag.	Hazel	1	–	–	–	3	–	–	1	–
Indet. wood frag (>4 mm^3)		++++	–	++++	–	–	–	++++	–	+++
Indet. wood fleck (<4 mm^3)		–	+++++	+++++	++++	++++	–	–	+++++	–
Indet. plant tissue? grain frag.		–	–	–	–	–	+	–	–	–

Key to estimated levels of abundance codes: + = 1–10; ++ = 11–50; +++ = 51–150; ++++ = 150–250; +++++ = >250

from them. Two features, ring gully 141113 and enclosure ditch 141003/4, produced some plant remains. The remaining features produced very low quantities of identifiable plant remains, for example occasional, sometimes fragmentary seeds of chickweed (*Stellaria media*). In several samples, for example those from contexts 140038, 140076 and 140194, charred wood was the only charred plant remain.

Roundhouse ring gully 141113

Two poorly-preserved wheat (*Triticum* spp.) grains were observed in the sample from context 140122 (section 140120). This sample also produced a fragment of emmer (*Triticum cf. dicoccum*) chaff, a glume base. Glume bases were also observed in context 140165 and had characteristics of emmer and spelt (*Triticum cf. spelta*). Unfortunately, in the absence of better preserved

Table 68 Charred plant remains from the Iron Age oval enclosure ditch

Taxon	Common name									
	Feature	Enclosure ditch 141003				Enclosure ditch 141004				
	Section	140017	140022		140069	140008	140013	140035		140040
	Context	140020	140023	140033	140076	140029	140015	140038	140039	140041
	Sample	142001	142011	142013	142010	142002	142009	142004	142003	142008
	Sample size (l)	19	40	34	20	13	33	10	24	31
	Flot size (ml)	15	60	50	25	130	60	15	125	250
Brassica/Sinapsis seed	Wild cabbage/ mustard	–	–	1	–	–	1	–	–	–
Stellaria media seed frag.	Chickweed	–	–	–	–	–	–	–	+	–
Corylus avellana shell frag.	Hazel	2	–	–	–	–	–	–	–	–
Cyperaceae stem frag.	Sedges	–	–	1	–	–	–	–	–	–
Avena/Hordeum/Secale/ Triticum stem frag.	Indet. cereal	–	–	–	–	–	–	–	+	+
Indet. wood frag. (<4 mm^3)		–	–	+	–	++++	–	–	–	+++
Indet. wood fleck (<4 mm^3)		++++	+++++	+++	++++	++++	++++	++++	+++	+++++
Indet. plant tissue ?grain frag.		–	–	1	1	–	++	–	–	–

grains and more chaff, it was not possible to make clear identifications. Three of these samples produced low quantities of seeds of ruderals such as fat-hen (*Chenopodium album*).

Enclosure ditch 141003/4
The ditch produced only small quantities of cereal chaff, two hazelnut shell fragments and a few weed seeds.

Interpretation and discussion
The charred remains are scarce and with such a sparse assemblage it is not wise to infer much about the farming or crop-processing activities at this site but the grains, chaff and seeds found are typical of Iron Age assemblages. In the Late Iron Age emmer and spelt are often found together with spelt being more numerous (Green 1981, 132).

The mixture of small seeds, glume base chaff, stem fragments and grain fragments observed, thinly scattered through these samples, could be the remains of sieving waste used as tinder or kindling (Hillman 1984, 4–5).

The charred hazelnut shell fragments, present in low quantities in several samples, are the only clear evidence of the use of an additional food plant. The charred shell fragments could be the result of the nuts being roasted prior to consumption. The only other possible food plants come from the seeds of fat-hen (*Chenopodium album*) that can be eaten in their own right as can the leaves of these plants, although they are perhaps more likely to come in as weeds of the crop.

Charcoal, by Rowena Gale

Twenty-four bulk soil samples were collected from sections of the enclosure ditch and ring gully and processed. Charred plant remains and charcoal were generally sparse. Charcoal was degraded and many fragments were infiltrated with red deposits which obstructed diagnostic features on the cell walls. Intact sections of roundwood were not recorded. Seven samples were selected for detailed analysis from ditch sections from the enclosure and ring gully and from a pit located in the southern terminal of the enclosure. Charcoal identification was undertaken to indicate the character of local woodland and to assess species selection for use as domestic firewood. The taxa identified are presented in Table 69. None of the wood structure examined used was indicative of fast-growth.

The oval enclosure
The character of ditch infill material in context 140020, ditch section 140017 on the northern side of the enclosure, was recorded as differing from other deposits on this side. Associated charcoal was sparse but included birch (*Betula* sp.), oak (*Quercus* sp.) and yew (*Taxus* sp.). Charcoal was also examined from two ditch sections on the southern side of the enclosure, both of which may represent either the natural accumulation of debris through silting or dumps of fuel debris from an unspecified activity. These included the secondary fill, context 140015, of section 140013, which contained small fragments of oak largewood, birch, hazel (*Corylus avellana*), ash (*Fraxinus excelsior*), blackthorn (*Prunus spinosa*) and the hawthorn/*Sorbus* group (Pomoideae); and context 140039, the top fill of section 140035, from which oak, hazel and *cf.* birch were named. Charcoal in the latter section was particularly poorly preserved and some appeared to be partially mineralised.

Pit 140011 was located in the southern terminal of the enclosure ditch. A placed deposit of a saddle quern was recorded in fill 140012. Charcoal from the underlying fill (140030) was extremely sparse but named as oak heartwood.

The ring gully
Charcoal deposits recovered from the ring gully (141113) are likely to have originated from hearth debris discarded from the roundhouse. Charcoal was examined from the upper and lower fills (contexts 141121 and 141122) of the eastern ditch section 140120. A more or less similar range of taxa was present in each sample: oak heartwood and sapwood, blackthorn, birch and hazel. In contrast, a large amount of charcoal was recovered from context 140165 from the southern ditch section 140164, and a correspondingly wider range of taxa was identified: predominantly alder (*Alnus glutinosa*) and hazel but also oak, birch, holly (*Ilex aquifolium*), ash and gorse (*Ulex* sp.)/broom (*Cytisus scoparius*). This section also produced charred plant remains including grain, chaff and hazelnut shell. Both gully sections were located near the entrance of the gully.

Discussion
It is probable that charcoal in both the features examined represents dumped deposits of domestic hearth debris, although agricultural origins, for example, bonfires from scrub clearance, may account for deposits in the oval enclosure ditch. There was no evidence to suggest industrial activity. The samples examined suggest that while domestic fuel was gathered from a range of species, oak, birch and hazel were used more frequently than the other taxa named: alder, ash, holly, the hawthorn group, blackthorn, gorse and yew. Yew was only present in a sample from the northern side of oval enclosure (141003) and, interestingly, on excavation, the fill of this context was described as differing from others in that particular section of the ditch. This could suggest different origins for the fill of this context, which may explain the unusual inclusion of yew.

The use of coppiced wood seems unlikely since none of the fragments examined demonstrated the fast growth usually associated with woodland management but the absence of sufficiently intact pieces of roundwood prevented a more accurate assessment. A placement of a quern stone was recorded in pit 140011 in the southern terminal of the oval enclosure. Oak charcoal was identified in the underlying fill 140030 and, although

Table 69 Charcoal from the Iron Age enclosure and ring gully (no. frags)

Section	*Context*	*Sample*	*Alnus*	*Betula*	*Corylus*	*Fraxinus*	*Ilex*	*Pomoideae*	*Prunus*	*Quercus*	*Ulex/ Cytisus*	*Taxus*
Oval enclosure (N ditch 141003)												
140017	140020	142001	–	4	–	–	–	–	–	3h, 1s	–	7
Oval enclosure (S ditch 141004)												
140013	140015	142009	–	3	–	1	–	1	1	14h, 1s	–	–
140035	140039	142003	–	–	1	–	–	–	*cf.* 3	8u	–	–
Pit in terminal of oval enclosure ditch												
140011	140030	142006	–	–	–	–	–	–	–	5h	–	–
Ring gully (141113)												
140120	141121	142015	–	8	1	–	–	–	1	18h, r, 1s	–	–
	140122	142016	–	2	2	–	–	–	–	4h, 1r, 1s	–	–
140164	140165	142023	16	3	18	1	3	–	–	8h, 1r	1	–

Key: h = heartwood; r = roundwood (diam. <20 mm); s = sapwood (diam. unknown); u = maturity undetermined (*Quercus* only)

this may be related to the (?ritual) placement activity, it is more likely to represent an earlier and independent fill.

Environmental evidence

The site was based on sandy, acidic soils. In the present day, low-lying wetlands occur in the Shenstone area. The range of taxa identified from the settlement area suggests that during the Iron Age period woodland was composed predominantly of oak/birch/holly communities. Hazel and ash may also have been constituents of this type of woodland environment. It is notable that these species are largely reflected also in the pollen analysis of later Iron Age soils from Ryknield Street, Site 12; Scaife, Chapter 14), although some species, such as holly and ash are under-represented in the pollen spectra, the former being entomophilous (insect pollinated), the latter a poor pollen producer. Due to difficulties in identification yew is often absent from the pollen spectra, but its charcoal was recovered from a single feature. The species may also have formed part of this local woodland on sandy, acidic soils although it is generally more characteristic of alkaline soils. If yew did, in fact, grow in the vicinity of the site, its infrequency in the charcoal is probably due in part to the difficulty of cutting the dense hard wood and also to its poor quality as firewood (Porter 1990). A number of shrubby/scrubby species were also named, blackthorn, gorse/broom and the hawthorn group; the presence of hazel nutshells suggests that this taxon also grew in a more shrubby form in open well-lit areas. Alder indicates the presence of wetter soils, perhaps near spring lines or on the low-lying ground in the Shenstone Basin, and was seen in the pollen record to form a substantial part of the local woodland during the Iron Age. Land division and enclosures were probably defined by hedges.

There was no evidence from this site to suggest that woodland was managed during the Middle Iron Age period and, if population levels were still fairly low, it is possible that 'natural' woodland was able to sustain local demand.

Discussion

The site appears to represent a small rural settlement spanning the Early and Middle Iron Age, comprising a ring gully surrounding a roundhouse, and a larger oval enclosure that may have been used for penning stock or, alternatively, could also have enclosed a domestic structure. Settlements comprising roundhouses in association with circular or near-circular stock enclosures have been recorded in the south Midlands at Finmere, Oxfordshire (Kenyon 2001) and Oxley Park, Milton Keynes (Archaeological Investigations 2005). The only indication as to the structure of the roundhouse in the ring gully is the short arc of gully, possibly the truncated remains of a wall trench. This is a form of structure well-known from other sites of this period and interpreted as representing a domestic dwelling (Cunliffe 1984).

Artefactual material was extremely scarce, and this is consistent with the general pattern for Iron Age sites in the West Midlands. This paucity of material remains has been observed throughout the Iron Age and continued into the Romano-British period, and is likely to be explained to be explained by cultural factors. The site lies near the interface between Cunliffe's 'bowl continuum' of south-central England and the more aceramic areas to the west (Cunliffe 1991, fig. 4.10).

Little evidence was recovered for the economy of the settlement, as bone did not survive in the acidic soil and only small quantities of charred plant remains were present. Both these deficiencies are commonly encountered throughout the West Midlands (Pearson 2002). The charred plant remains derived from dumps of burnt crop-processing waste deposited in the ring gully and the enclosure ditch, indicating that crop-processing was being carried out nearby, but no crop storage features were identified. Indeed, the site displayed a notable absence of storage pits or other cut features associated with the Iron Age occupation. This may be in part due to the sandy nature of the natural geology, which would cause the sides of such features to be liable to collapse, rendering them impractical, and also perhaps to the possibility of such features becoming waterlogged, as the drainage was observed to be poor during the excavation. If the enclosure was used for penning stock this would indicate pastoral farming and so provide evidence for the structure of the economy. Pearson has suggested that the low level of charred plant remains recorded on Iron Age sites in the region may reflect the relative unimportance of arable farming compared to pastoral farming. If this were the case, it would also explain the absence of storage pits.

The roundhouse and enclosure shared the same east-south-east orientation, a common alignment for such structures which has been attributed to symbolic concerns (Oswald 1997). The placing of objects at key locations within settlements has also been linked to structuring principles associated with propitiation and the symbolic importance of boundaries. Palmer (2002a) has remarked on the prevalence of threshold locations, such as the terminals of enclosure ditches, as loci for concentrations of artefacts on sites elsewhere in the West Midlands. It is therefore likely to be significant that the only artefacts recovered during the excavation were found at the ditch terminal defining the southern side of the entrance to the oval enclosure. If the presence of artefacts at this location singles it out as having some symbolic significance, the digging of pit 140011 into the fills of the partly-silted ditch terminal and the placement within it of a quernstone is also likely to represent a significant act, possibly forming some form of rite of closure at the end of the use of the enclosure. The uppermost fill of the enclosure ditch, which seals the pit, would then represent the final silting of the ditch after it had passed out of use.

Chapter 17
East of Birmingham Road Nurseries, Shenstone (Site 15)

By Andy Simmonds

Introduction

A targeted watching brief was undertaken on a site south-east of Wall, identified on the basis of cropmarks interpreted as representing three sides of a rectilinear enclosure within a complex of linear features, with some additional, more indeterminate features. This led to an excavation which revealed a Romano-British settlement comprising a series of enclosures bounded by a pair of parallel ditches, as well as a small Mesolithic flint assemblage, a small amount of residual Neolithic and Iron Age pottery and post-medieval boundary ditches (Fig. 107).

The site, covering 4.4 hectares centred on NGR 411430 305400, was located north-east of the village of Shenstone, opposite Birmingham Road Nurseries on the eastern side of the A5127 Birmingham to Lichfield road. It was bounded to the east by Mill Lane, to the north by Site 14 (Shenstone Ring Ditch) and on the south side by fields. The area of the excavation was *c* 270 m square, with a strip 265 m long and *c* 12 m wide extending southward from its south-western corner alongside the A5127.

The geology over most of the site is mapped as Triassic Keuper Sandstone, its southward extension into the Crane Brook floodplain overlying First Terrace deposits and alluvium (Geological Survey of Great Britain 1954, Sheet 154, Lichfield). This geology comprised silty sand with areas of clay, and varied in colour from yellow in the western part of the site to orange-brown in the east. Two layers of colluvium with a combined thickness of *c* 0.25 m extended *c* 50 m into the western edge of the site.

Stripping of the overburden was carried out by the contractor's plant as and when machinery was available, with the result that the work was carried out intermittently over a number of months, with small areas of the site being open at various times. The northern part of the site in particular was subject to tracking by plant moving across it and was used for some time as an area for storing spoil.

A field evaluation carried out in 1993 (OAU 1994a) interpreted the two main linear features as being Romano-British field boundaries, but was unable to locate the enclosure identified from cropmarks, which was assumed to have been destroyed by modern ploughing. A possible hollow-way identified in the western part of the site could not be dated.

Watling Street passes within *c* 250 m of the northern boundary of the site and the Roman town of Wall (*Letocetum*) lies *c* 2 km to the west along the line of the road. Gould (1972) has suggested that the site may be associated with a double-ditched enclosure situated c 200 m to the west which has been interpreted as a possible villa site.

Results

Mesolithic

Tree throw 150474

Evidence for Mesolithic activity consisted of a small assemblage of 11 pieces of knapped flint. Most were residual in later features, but three pieces, comprising an opposed platform blade core and two blades, were recovered from a tree hollow located toward the south-eastern corner of the site (150474) (Fig. 107). In contrast to the residual pieces, these were in fresh condition and were probably contemporary with the formation of the tree hollow. The feature was irregular in plan with steeply sloping sides, and measured *c* 2 m in diameter and 0.36 m deep (Fig. 108). The flints were recovered from fill 150476, one of three layers of redeposited natural sand and gravel, created by the toppling of the tree, and sealed by an uppermost fill of greyish-brown silty sand (150484) resulting from the silting up of the resultant hollow. Charcoal flecks within fills 150476 and 150484 indicated that the Mesolithic activity on the site was associated with burning of some sort, although there was no evidence that this was directly associated with the creation and use of the tree hollow, and the flints themselves were unburnt.

Other possible Mesolithic tree hollows

It is possible that others among the 21 tree hollows identified in the excavation may also date from the Mesolithic period, although no others contained artefactual evidence of this date. Tree hollow 150489 was of a similar size to tree hollow 150474, measuring *c* 2.15 m in diameter and 0.24 m deep. It also contained a similar sequence of fills, comprising an initial layer of orange-brown sand and gravel disturbed by the up-rooting of the tree (150490), overlain by a deposit of brownish-grey silty sand (150491) formed by the gradual in-filling of the remaining hollow. Both fills contained flecks of charcoal but no finds.

Tree throws 150162, 150723 and 150909 are also possible candidates as they were cut by Romano-British features and are thus likely to be prehistoric in date. Tree hollow 150723 was irregular in shape with a diameter of *c* 1.6 m and survived to a depth of 0.5 m. It contained a

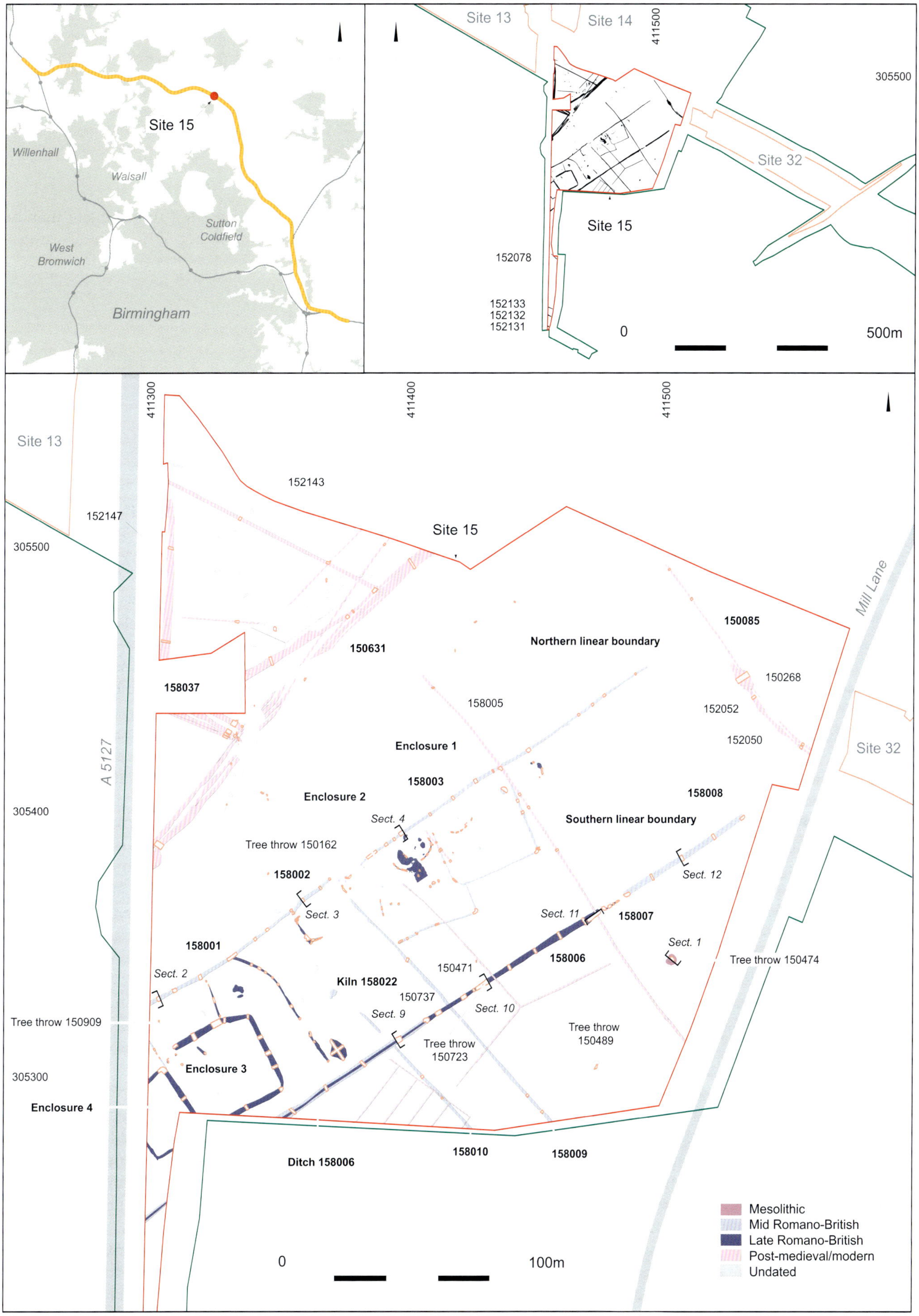

Fig. 107 East of Birmingham Road Nurseries (Site 15)

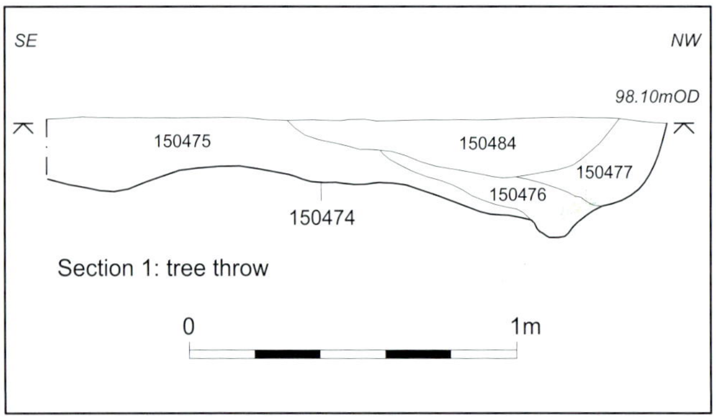

Fig. 108 Section of tree-throw 150474

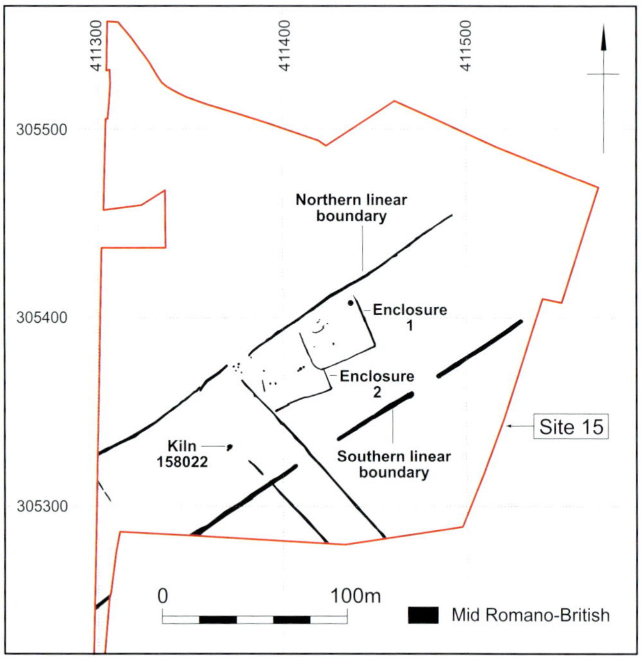

Fig. 109 Mid-Romano-British features

single fill of reddish-brown sandy clay (150724) which contained no artefacts but was flecked with charcoal. Tree hollow 150162 was approximately oval in plan, although its south-western edge had been removed by Romano-British ditch 158002. It measured *c* 0.95 m by 0.8 m with a depth of only 0.13 m, and contained a single sterile fill of reddish-brown sandy silt with small flint gravel (150163). Tree hollow 150909, near the western edge of the excavation, measured 0.45 m by 0.3 m and was 0.25 m deep with steep sides and an irregular base. Its single fill of reddish-brown sandy silt was cut by posthole 150907.

Neolithic

A group of 42 sherds of a single Peterborough Ware vessel of Mortlake type in a quartzite-tempered fabric was recovered from a subsoil context (150031) in the northern part of the site. The context of the sherds is curious, but it is most likely that the pottery derived from a pit and had been disturbed by recent ploughing. Extended exposure to such activity would have resulted in greater fragmentation and dispersal of the sherds.

Middle Iron Age

Activity dating from the Middle Iron Age was represented by pottery found as residual material in features of later periods. An assemblage of 95 sherds of pottery weighing 1335 g was recovered, most of which derived from two contexts. The largest assemblage consisted of 40 sherds (856 g) recovered from the uppermost fill (150168) of Romano-British southern boundary ditch 158006, toward the southern edge of the excavation. This material represents the majority of a single vessel. Some 15 m south-west of this group, two further sherds in the same rock-tempered fabric were found, in the uppermost fill (150193) of the same ditch. The remainder of the Middle Iron Age assemblage consisted of 53 sherds weighing 437 g recovered from the only fill (155000) of Romano-British ditch 158009 in the central part of the excavation. This group is in a different fabric to the material from ditch 158006, but may similarly represent the remains of part of a single vessel.

Romano-British

Evidence for Romano-British activity consisted of four ditched enclosures (Enclosures 1–4), boundary ditches and part of a possible field system, and a variety of discrete features including a well-preserved pottery kiln (Fig. 107). The ceramic evidence indicates that occupation lasted from the mid–late 2nd century until the late 3rd century, with the possibility of some activity continuing into the 4th century. Few stratigraphic relationships were present, as there was very little intercutting of features, but a combination of ceramic and spatial analysis was able to divide the occupation into two broad phases with a break around the middle of the 3rd century (Fig. 109). This break coincides both with a change in the ceramic assemblage and a re-organisation of the site.

Throughout the occupation of the settlement, structural activity was confined to the area between a pair of parallel linear boundaries. These boundaries were defined by a series of ditches aligned NE–SW and *c* 65 m apart. The more northern boundary was formed by ditches 158001, 158002 and 158003, while ditches 158006 and 158008 defined the southern boundary. It is probable that the up-cast of the excavation of these ditches was used to form banks beside them, adding to the effectiveness and monumentality of the boundaries, although no evidence for such earthworks survived. As these boundaries appear to have had a determining role in the positioning and arrangement of the rest of the features, it is assumed that they were established at the very outset of the settlement. They were in use for the

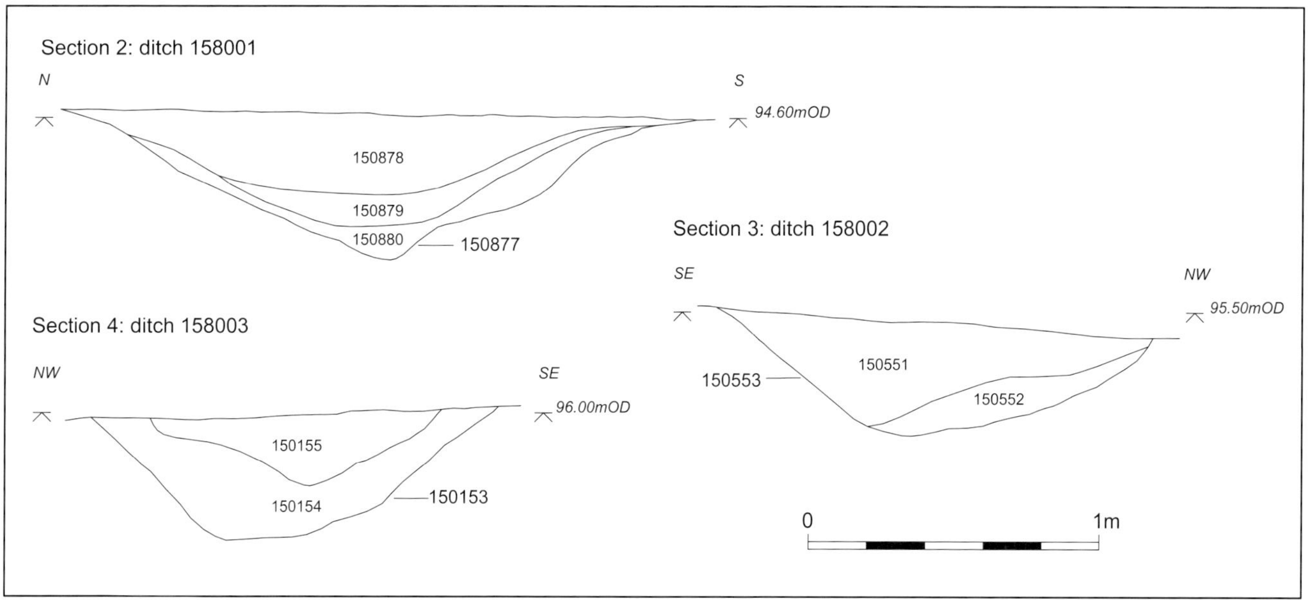

Fig. 110 Sections through the northern linear boundary ditches 158001, 158002 and 158003

entire occupation of the site and continued to be respected by the features of the later phase.

Mid-Romano-British (mid-2nd–mid-3rd centuries)

The northern linear boundary: ditches 158001, 158002 and 158003

The north-western extent of the Romano-British features was delineated by three ditches (158001, 158002 and 158003) lying on the same NE–SW, although slightly meandering, alignment. These ditches were exposed for a total length of 237 m, and continued to the south-west beyond the edge of the excavation. Toward the north-east, the ditches became progressively shallower until the boundary petered out. The northern part of the site had been subject to truncation due to plant tracking across it and had been used for spoil storage, in addition to the truncation resulting from ploughing during its previous use as arable land, and it is likely that the petering out of this ditch is the result of this truncation rather than representing the original end of the boundary.

The south-western part of the boundary was represented by ditch 158001, which extended for 72 m from the baulk at the western edge of the site before ending in a rounded terminal. The south-western part of the ditch was overlain by colluvial layers 150027 and 150028, which formed a buffer protecting the ditch from the truncating effect of post-Romano-British ploughing. Where the ditch was thus protected it was up to 2.1 m wide and survived to a depth of between 0.42 m and 0.66 m (Fig. 110). The sides of the ditch were slightly irregular and sloped quite gently to a concave base. Three sections were excavated across this part of the feature, recording from three to five fills. The primary fill was a deposit of orange gravelly sand resulting from the initial phase of erosion of the sides of the ditch. This was overlain by secondary in-filling composed of reddish-brown silty sand with small amounts of gravel and occasional charcoal flecks and representing the stabilisation of the profile of the feature. Both these phases of silting contained small quantities of pottery dating from the 2nd or early 3rd century. The final silting of the ditch resulted in an uppermost fill composed of greyish loamy sand. The majority of the pottery assemblage from the ditch was recovered from this latest layer. This material was also later in date, dating from the mid-3rd to mid-4th centuries. Four sections excavated across the northern part of the ditch, beyond the area protected by the layers of colluvium, revealed that it had been significantly reduced by ploughing and survived to a maximum depth of 0.32 m. This truncation had resulted in the loss of the upper fills in this part of the ditch.

North-east of ditch 158001 the boundary was continued by ditch 158002. This ditch was 20 m in length and was somewhat sinuous in plan, its south-western end in particular curving to the south so the terminal lay beside the corresponding terminal of ditch 158001, separated by a gap of 0.45 m. The terminal at the north-eastern end of the ditch was dug partly into the fill of an earlier tree hollow (150162). The ditch measured between 1.2 m and 1.5 m in width and was up to 0.4 m deep (Fig. 110). The profile formed a shallow V-shape, with the sides sloping gently to a concave base. The primary fill, formed by erosion of the sides of the feature, was composed of orangy-brown silty sand with some small flint gravel and was overlain by a secondary fill of greyish-brown silty sand containing less gravel, with occasional flecks of charcoal.

At the terminals, where the ditch became slightly shallower, only the primary fill was present. As was observed in the case of ditch 158001, a small assemblage of pottery was recovered which dated predominantly from the second half of the 2nd century to the mid-3rd century.

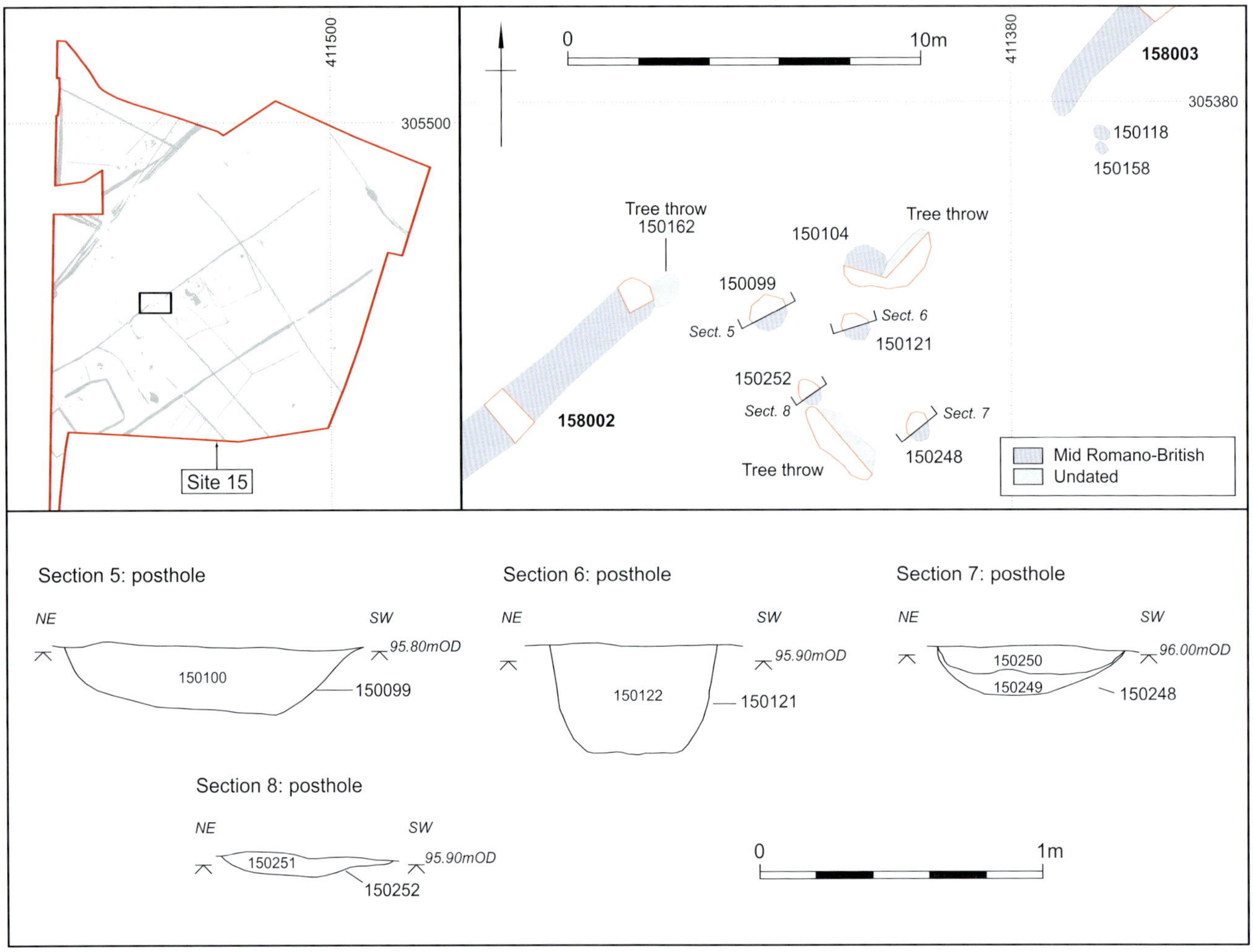

Fig. 111 Postholes associated with the entrance through the northern linear boundary

Ditch 158003 started 12.5 m beyond the end of ditch 158002 and extended on the same alignment for a further 134 m. It had similar dimensions to ditch 158002, measuring 1–1.5 m wide and surviving to a maximum depth of 0.42 m (Fig. 110). Its profile, however, was more variable, with an open V-shape being recorded in some sections while others revealed a wider, somewhat flatter, or occasionally more rounded base. In a number of sections a very thin primary fill of orangy-brown sand was recorded, which was only a few centimetres thick. The thinness of this deposit compared to the equivalent fills in ditches 158001 and 158002 may indicate that the ditch had been cleaned out during its use, resulting in the partial removal of these lower silts. This primary fill was completely absent from some sections, where it may have been completely removed by such cleaning. All 15 sections excavated across this ditch revealed a main fill of brown silty sand containing small quantities of gravel and occasional flecks of charcoal.

The pottery recovered from the early fills of the ditches forming the northern linear boundary appears to have begun to accumulate around the middle of the 2nd century. The ceramic evidence indicates that the ditches continued to silt up through the following century, with the final in-filling of ditch 158001 not occurring until the early part of the 4th century. This final phase was not recorded in ditches 158002 and 158003, but this is likely to be due to the removal of the later fills by post-Romano-British ploughing rather than because these features were in-filled at an earlier date. Pottery dating from the 2nd to mid-3rd centuries was recovered largely from sections of ditch 158003 adjacent to Enclosure 2. A ceramic lamp, complete except for a broken handle, and a fine ceramic figurine base were also recovered from this part of the ditch. Later pottery was concentrated both in this area and at the south-western end of the site near Enclosure 3. The north-eastern part of the boundary, beyond Enclosure 1, produced only two sherds despite the excavation of a total of five sections in this area.

Features associated with the northern linear boundary

Two straight ditches (158009 and 158010), running perpendicular to the northern linear boundary in the central part of the site, appear to be associated with it (Fig. 107).

Ditch 158009, ran for *c* 115 m from the southern edge of the excavation to within 10 m of the eastern terminal of ditch 158002, on which it appeared to have been aligned. It passed through the 24 m wide gap in ditch 158006 of the southern linear boundary, a gap that was subsequently blocked when part of the boundary ditch was re-cut. The stratigraphical relationship between ditch 158009 and the re-cut was not recorded. Ditch 158009 was 1.2 m wide and up to 0.26 m deep and had an open V-shaped profile with gently sloping sides. It contained a fill of orangy-brown silty sand. An assemblage of 53 sherds of Middle Iron Age pottery likely to derive from a single vessel was recovered from a section excavated across this ditch *c* 6 m south of Enclosure 4. A single fragment of post-medieval ceramic building material is likely to have been intrusive.

There was a group of five postholes (150099, 150104, 150121, 150252 and 150248) near the northern end of ditch 158009, which may have formed part of a gate or other structure associated both with the entrance through the linear boundary, and that between ditches 158009 and 158002 (Fig. 111).

Postholes 150099 and 150104 lay 1.9 m apart on the same alignment as the boundary ditches. Both measured *c* 1 m in diameter and had similar fills of greyish-brown silty sand. Posthole 150099 was the shallower of the two at 0.24 m, and had a bowl-shaped profile with a flat base, while posthole 150104 had steeper sides and a depth of 0.35 m. Posthole 150121 was located a short distance south-east of postholes 150099 and 150104 and was oval in plan, measuring 0.84 m by 0.6 m and 0.38 m deep. The two remaining postholes, 150248 and 150252, were both substantially truncated, surviving to depths of only 0.1 m and 0.08 m respectively.

Posthole 150099 contained a small quantity of undiagnostic pottery and two pieces of rotary quern (ONs 154003 and 154010). One fragment was from an upper stone (ON 154003) and one from a lower (ON 154010), but they were of two different types of sandstone and therefore presumably represented parts of two different querns. Posthole 150104 yielded a pottery assemblage indicative of a date in the second half of the 2nd century. The handle of a bronze *patera* (ON 154004) was recovered from the surface of posthole 150121 during topsoil stripping (Fig. 120).

Two small postholes or stakeholes (150118 and 150158) located near the south-western terminal of ditch 158003 may also have been associated with this group of features.

Ditch 158010 ran parallel to, and *c* 24 m west of, ditch 158009, and may have been aligned approximately on the north-east terminal of ditch 158001. It was 1.28 m wide and 0.2 m deep with an open, V-shaped profile, and was filled with a single deposit of orangy-brown silty sand. It extended *c* 46 m from the southern edge of the excavation, also crossing (unrecorded) the line of the southern linear boundary, and continued after a 4.7 m gap, for a further 11 m.

Together these features suggest part of an organised landscape, with a series of fields bounded to the north-west by the northern linear boundary, beyond which was open, unenclosed land. The group of postholes suggests some form of structure designed to control movement both between the two fields to the south, and between the fields and the open land to the north.

The southern linear boundary: ditches 158006 and 158008

Ditches 158006 and 158008 defined a linear boundary at least 280 m long, running parallel to and *c* 65 m south-east of the northern linear boundary. Ditch 158006 was exposed for a total length of 213 m, and continued to the south-west beyond the edge of the excavation. It originally consisted of two parts, separated by a 24 m wide gap defined by a pair of terminals (150471 and 150737), *c* 53 m from its north-eastern end (Fig. 107). The position of the gap (through which passed ditch 158009 but which was subsequently blocked when part of ditch 158006 was re-cut) corresponded approximately with the gap between ditches 158002 and 158003 in the northern boundary.

To the north-east, a second, 11 m wide, entranceway separated ditch 158006 from ditch 158008, which extended on the same alignment for a further 56 m. During the later part of the site's occupation, this gap was blocked by a short length of ditch (158007). Although running on a parallel course to the northern boundary, the southern linear boundary is noticeably straighter, suggesting either that the two features may not have been laid out at exactly the same time, or that they had slightly different functions.

Ditch 158006 was also significantly more substantial than the northern boundary, varying in width from 2.0 m to 3.0 m and being up to 0.8 m deep (Fig. 112). In profile, its sides sloped gently to a generally flat or occasionally more concave base. In a number of sections the profile was steeper in the lower part of the ditch, and it is likely that this steeper profile preserved the original shape of the ditch, with the more gentle slope of the upper part of the sides being the result of modification by subsequent erosion. The primary ditch fill varied in character from an orange gravelly sand to a red silty clay, according to localised variations in the natural. This was overlain by a secondary fill which was generally mid-brown or brownish-grey in colour and varied from silty sand to clay silt, again according to variations in the geology. The ceramic assemblage from the original phase of ditch 158006 was small, but indicated that the ditch was silting up during the 2nd and early 3rd centuries.

The upper part of the ditch had been removed by the digging of a re-cut which was consistently shallower than the original cut, generally ranging from 0.6 m to 0.76 m in depth. Toward the south-west end it had a more V-shaped profile than the earlier phase, but to the north-east the base became wider and more concave. The re-cut was continued across the entrance gap in the ditch 158006, but was found to be very shallow at this point, its depth diminishing to between 0.1 m and 0.33 m. At the north-eastern end of the ditch, the re-cut extended for 4 m beyond the original terminal. The re-cut had two to six fills indicative of natural in-filling, comprising a series of layers of brown or orangy-brown sandy silt sealed by a final deposit of darker, greyish material representing the final silting of the ditch. The few sherds of pottery recovered from the re-cut date from the same period as the material from the earlier cut and are thus probably residual.

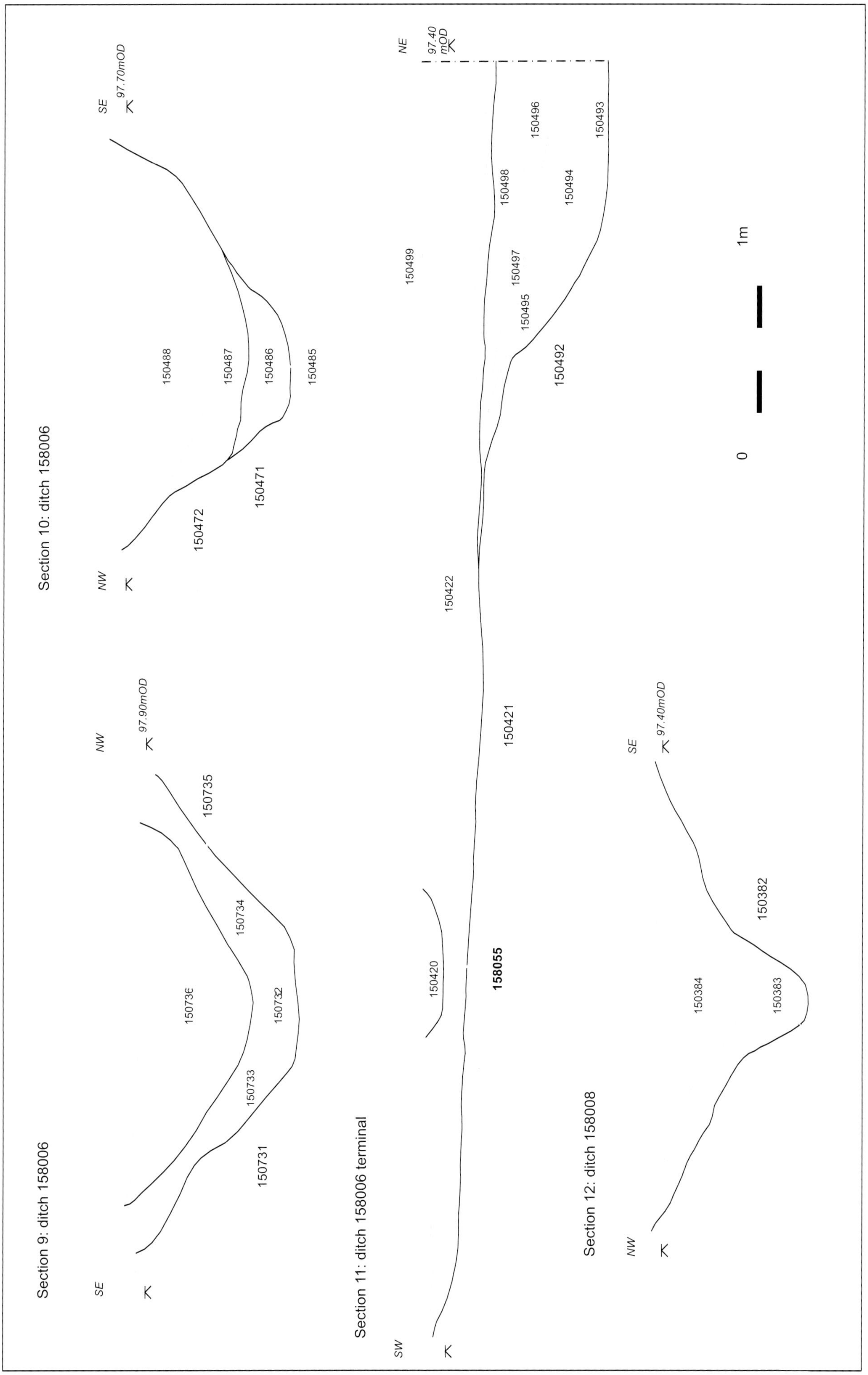

Fig. 112 Sections through the southern linear boundary ditches 158006 and 158008

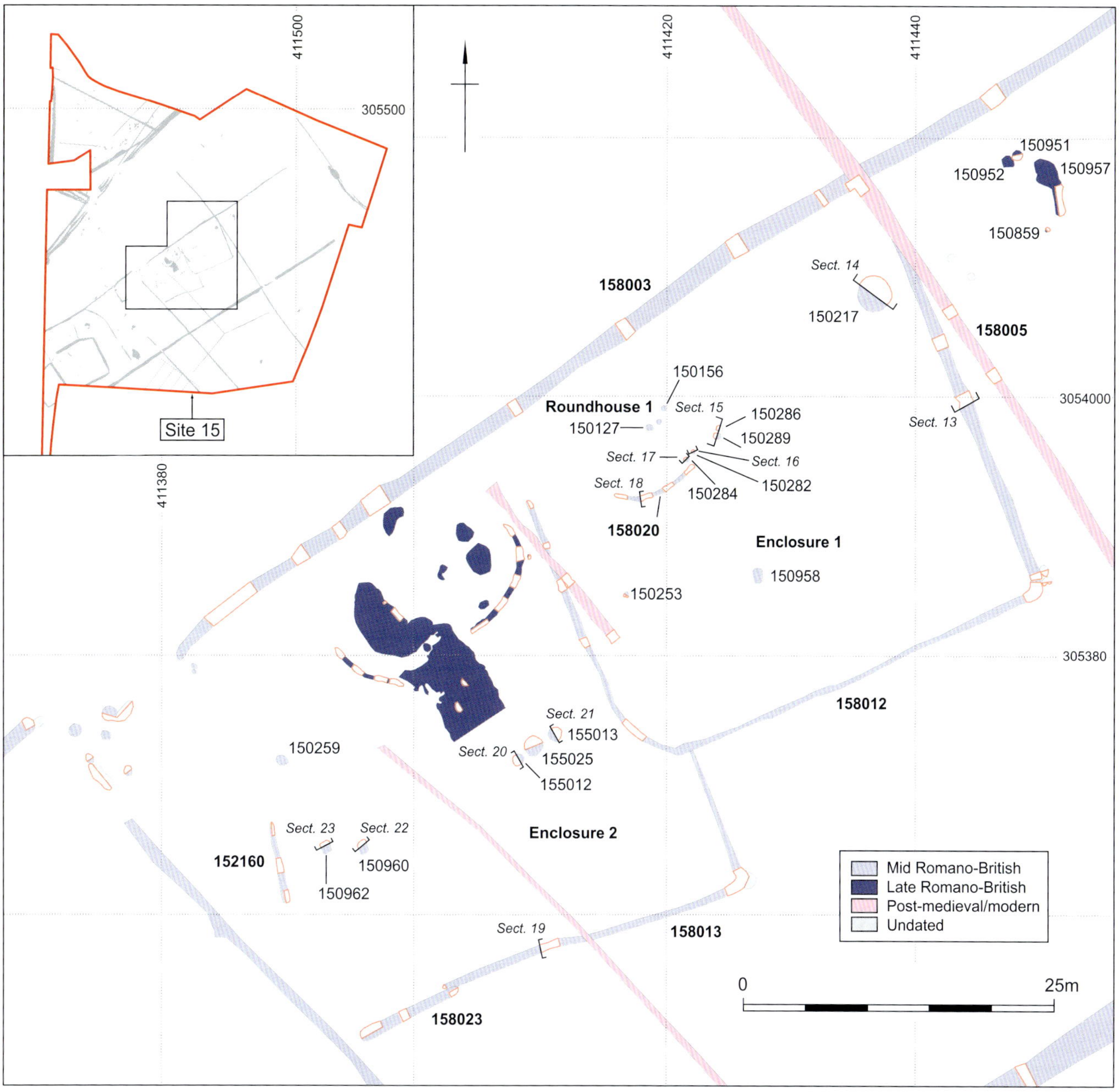

Fig. 113 Mid-Romano-British enclosures 1 and 2 and ditch 158026

Ditch 158008 was 2.0–2.4 m wide and up to 0.9 m deep, the depth decreasing to *c* 0.4 m toward each terminal. It was much more steeply V-shaped in profile than the other boundary ditches (Fig. 112). The primary fill was an orangy-brown silty sand containing much gravel, which was particularly extensive on the southern side of the ditch and may have been partly the result of the slumping of this side of the feature. This was overlain by a main fill of brownish-grey silty sand resulting from secondary silting. Unlike ditch 158006, ditch 158008 showed no evidence for having been re-cut.

Ditch 158007 appears to have been dug to block the entrance gap between ditches 158006 and 158008. The ditch was 6.7 m long and 0.7 m wide with a depth of 0.19 m. It had regular, gently sloping sides and a concave base and contained a single fill of mid-brownish-grey sandy silt with 5% gravel. A sherd of Mancetter-Hartshill mortarium from this ditch dated it to the mid-3rd–mid-4th centuries. The blocking of the entrance through the linear boundary would thus appear to be part of the more widespread re-organisation of the settlement that occurred at this time.

Enclosure 1

Enclosure 1 was a three-sided rectilinear enclosure measuring *c* 34 m square. It abutted the northern linear boundary ditch 158003, which may have served as its north-western side (Fig. 113). It was defined on its other three sides by a shallow V-shaped ditch (158012), its eastern corner forming a sharp right angle, but the southern corner being more rounded. The ditch was 0.5–1.0 m wide and up to 0.23 m deep and was filled with a single deposit of greyish-brown silty sand with gravel inclusions, from which a single sherd of pottery dating from the mid-2nd to late 3rd century was recovered (Fig. 114). At the enclosure's western corner the ditch terminated short of ditch 158003, leaving an entrance 6.5 m wide. It was not possible to determine whether there had been a second entrance at the northern corner, as this part of the enclosure ditch had been truncated by post-medieval field boundary ditch 158005, although it did not appear to continue up to ditch 158003.

A possible roundhouse (Roundhouse 1) was located in the western part of the enclosure. The only surviving elements of the structure were the postholes of a south-east-facing entrance, a length of curved gully (158020) and two possible internal postholes (150127 and 150156). Most of the gully had been truncated, and only a 6.7 m length on the southern side survived (158020) with a maximum depth of 0.12 m and up to 0.4 m wide, with a single fill of brownish-grey silty sand. At its north-eastern end it terminated adjacent to posthole 150284, but petered out to the west. Although only a short length of gully was recorded, the circle it would appear to describe has a projected diameter of *c* 14 m. For the roundhouse not to extend over the line of the northern linear boundary, therefore, it would need have to have been slightly oval in shape. Alternatively it need not have been contemporary with the boundary, possibly pre-dating it given the date range of the silting of the ditch.

The roundhouse entrance was flanked by two pairs of postholes that held the jambs of a doorway or porch between 1.8 m and 2.5 m wide. It is uncertain whether the four postholes were part of a single-phased entrance structure or represent two phases of an entrance formed in each phase by two posts. The south side of the entrance was defined by postholes 150282 and 150284 (Fig. 114). Both features were circular in plan with very steep or vertical sides and a concave base. Posthole 150284 was the larger of the two, with a diameter of 0.4 m and a depth of 0.32 m, while posthole 150282 was 0.32 m in diameter and 0.16 m deep. Each was filled with a single deposit of grey silty sand with small quantities of fine gravel. Neither posthole contained any artefactual material.

Postholes 150286 and 150289, which formed the northern side of the entrance were more substantial than those to the south (Fig. 114). The largest of the four was posthole 150286, which measured 0.54 m in diameter and was 0.42 m deep. The sides of this posthole dropped vertically to a concave base which was filled with a layer of re-deposited natural, composed of orange, slightly gravelly sand 0.08 m thick (150287). This layer was overlain by a main fill of grey silty sand (150288) which contained two undiagnostic scraps of pottery and a fragment of tile. Posthole 150289 measured 0.46 m in diameter. It had a more tapering profile than the other postholes, with a concave base at a depth of 0.34 m. Like the adjacent posthole 150286 it had a thin initial fill of redeposited natural sand (150290) overlain by a main fill of grey silty sand (150291).

It is uncertain whether the redeposited natural sand in the bases of these postholes results from the initial digging of the features and erection of the posts, or represents disturbance caused by the later removal of the posts. That the posts were removed rather than left to rot *in situ* was indicated by the absence of post-pipes in any of these features.

Two postholes (150127 and 150156) were located near the centre of the roundhouse. Posthole 150127 was slightly irregular in plan, most likely due to root disturbance. The steep-sided cut was 0.6 m in diameter and 0.3 m deep. It was filled with a charcoal-rich soil (150128), containing a handful of pottery sherds dating from the 1st or early 2nd century. Posthole 150156 had been substantially truncated with the result that only 0.05 m of the feature survived. It measured 0.4 m in diameter and was similarly filled with a deposit of black, charcoal-rich silt (150157).

A waterhole (150217) was located within the northern corner of the enclosure. It was circular in plan, with a diameter of 2.65 m and 1.45 m deep (Fig. 114). The sides dropped sharply to a concave base with a distinct step on the northern side. Following some initial slumping of the sides (150218) the earliest silting deposits were two layers of grey sandy silt (150407, 150408) with a total thickness of 0.5 m. Pottery from these layers indicates that the feature began silting during the second half of the 2nd century, and it had presumably been created not long before this. The bulk of the feature was filled with a substantial deposit of orangey pink silty sand (150219/150406) that may be deliberate back-filling, above which was a final silting represented by two deposits of grey silty sand (150220, 150221). The presence within the upper fills of fragments from mortaria current during the late 3rd–mid-4th centuries suggests that the waterhole was not finally filled in until the later stages of the occupation of the site. Plant remains from the waterhole appear to consist of crop-processing waste which was used as a fuel and then dumped with charcoal into the feature.

Two features were recorded in the southern part of the enclosure: a shallow pit (150958), and a posthole (150253). Both features were filled with dumps of burnt material composed of mixed grey and brown sand and charcoal and are likely to be associated with the occupation of the enclosure. Pit 150958 contained two fragments of box flue tile, possibly indicating its use as an oven structure.

Enclosure 2

Enclosure 2 abutted the south-western side of Enclosure 1, and although the stratigraphical relationship between their ditches was not established, it seems likely that they were either contemporary, or that Enclosure 2 was added while Enclosure 1 was still extant (Fig. 113). The northern linear boundary ditch 158003 formed its north-western side. Its south-eastern side was formed by an L-shaped ditch (158013), 0.6 m wide and 0.15 m deep with a moderately sloping profile and a concave base (Fig. 114), which branched off the southern corner of Enclosure 1. This ditch extended south-eastward for *c* 11.5 m before turning a right angle toward the south-west for a further 25 m. Its only fill was a reddish-brown sandy silt (150978) from which was recovered a single

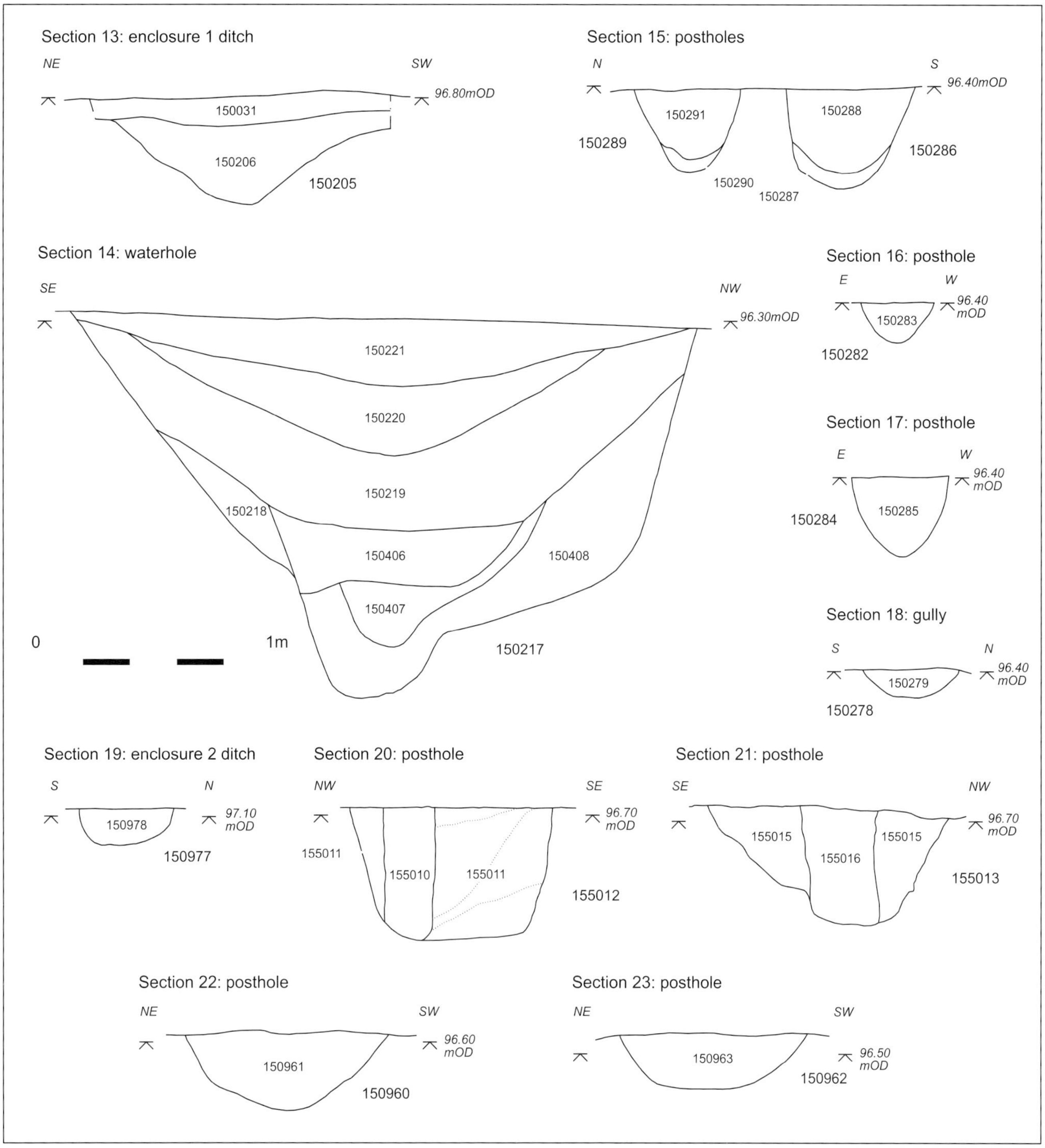

Fig. 114 Sections of mid-Romano-British features in Enclosures 1 and 2 and ditch 158026

small sherd of black burnished ware dating from AD 120 or later.

Early in the 3rd century ditch 158013 was extended to the south-west by the digging of an additional 8.5 m length of ditch (158023). This was a similarly shallow feature, with a U-shaped profile and 0.19 m deep, and filled with a single deposit of reddish-brown silty clay, containing a small group of pottery. This extension stopped just short of ditch 158009, which appears to have formed the enclosure's south-western side.

Three pairs of postholes were recorded within Enclosure 2, two of which may date from the mid-Romano-British phase (155012 and 155013; 150960 and 150962) (Fig. 113). The occurrence of three similar sets of features within a single enclosure suggests that they represent a specific form of structure related to the activities taking place here. It has been suggested that pairs of postholes may be the doorposts of stake or surface-built roundhouses which have otherwise been truncated away, although two-posted structures could also have other uses, such as drying racks or food troughs. The only dating evidence for these features was a group of pottery from post-pipe 155010 within posthole 155012 datable to the late 2nd–3rd centuries. Postholes 150960 and 150962 were undated but may also belong to this phase.

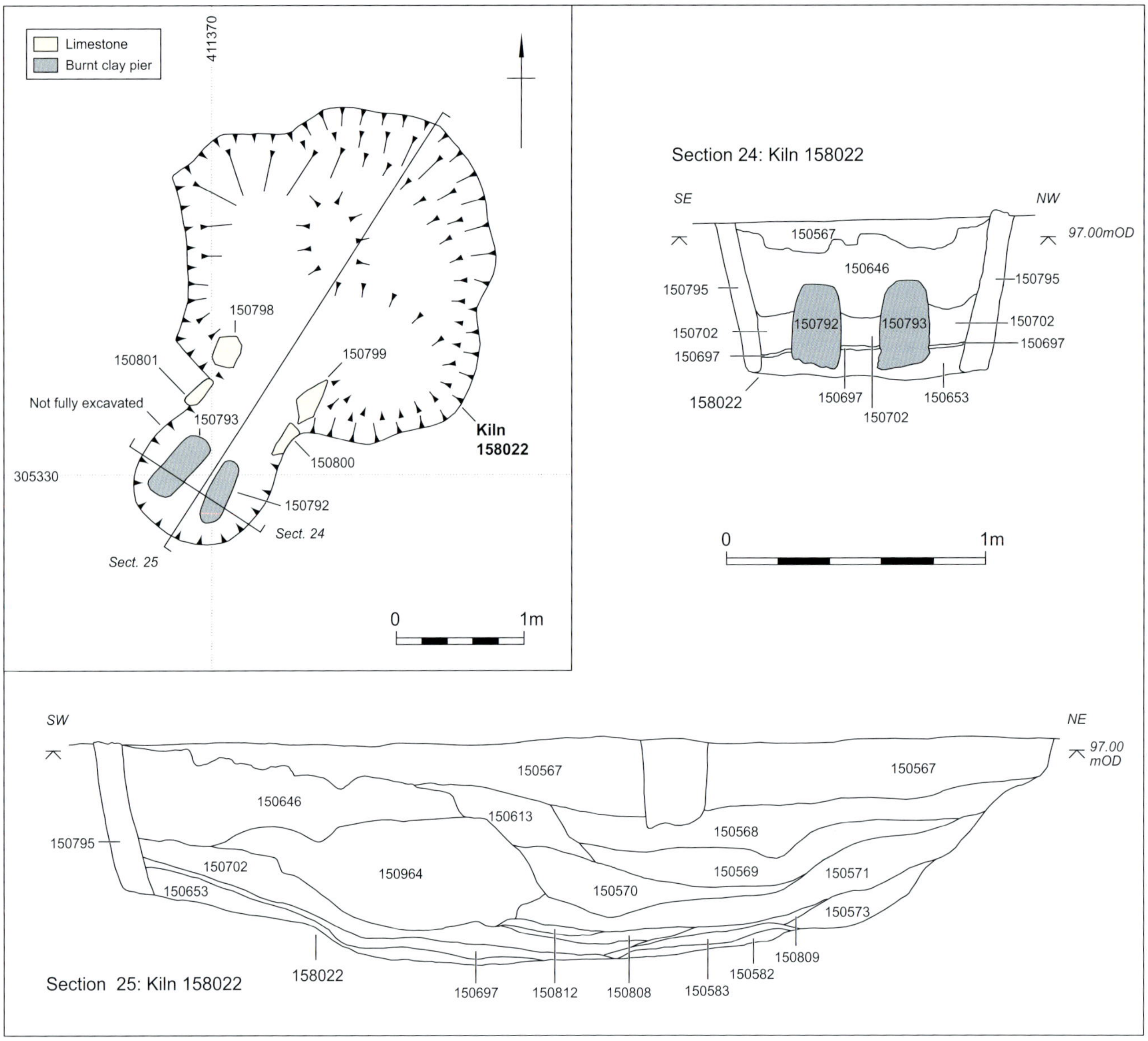

Fig. 115 Pottery kiln 158022

The postholes had similar dimensions, ranging from 0.7 m to 1.1 m in diameter, and each pair had closely similar depths, postholes 150960 and 150962 being the shallowest at 0.32 m and 0.23 m respectively and postholes 155012 and 155013 the deepest at 0.57 m and 0.6 m (Fig. 114). The profiles were generally steep-sided except for posthole 155013, which had a more gentle slope on its southern side that may have acted as a ramp to facilitate the insertion of its post. All of the postholes were filled with deposits of brownish-grey silty sand. Post-pipes composed of darker, charcoal-flecked material were identified in postholes 155012 and 155013.

Post-pipe 155010, in posthole 155012, was located toward the northern side of the posthole and was square in plan with a width of 0.27 m. Post-pipe 155016 was more centrally placed within posthole 155013, and was sub-circular in plan with a diameter of 0.3 m. The post-pipe became less well defined with depth as the deposit became more similar to the surrounding packing material.

The only other probable mid-Romano-British features recorded within the enclosure were two pits and a short length of ditch. Pit 155025 was located between paired postholes 155012 and 155013, although whether it was associated with them is unclear. The pit was circular in plan with a diameter of 1.45 m. The sides sloped steeply to a flat base at a depth of 0.35 m. The only fill of the pit, a reddish-brown silty clay, contained no finds and its function is uncertain.

Pit 150259 was a rather isolated feature located in the western part of the enclosure. It measured 0.85 m in diameter and was 0.34 m deep with steep sides and a flat base. It contained a lower fill of reddish-brown silty sand (150260) overlain by a dump of charcoal-rich soil (150261). Both fills contained pottery, the majority of which came from the upper fill. The pottery was dated to the late 2nd–early 3rd centuries, although a single medieval sherd was also present, indicating that the feature had experienced some later disturbance.

In the western part of the enclosure was a 6.3 m length of ditch (152160), running north–south, which

Fig. 116 Pottery kiln 158022 showing the sandstone slab used to roof the flue collapsed *in situ*

was 0.5 m wide and up to 0.18 m deep with a shallow, V-shaped profile. It contained a single fill of brown silty sand similar to the fills of the enclosure ditches.

The largest groups of pottery dating from the mid-2nd to mid-3rd centuries found on the site were recovered from that part of the northern linear boundary ditch adjacent to this enclosure, suggesting that this area was a main focus of occupation at this time. However, the datable material from those features in this part of the enclosure dated from the mid-3rd and 4th centuries, meaning that whatever activity took place in this part of the enclosure during the earlier phase has left no structural evidence.

Ditch 158026

Ditch 158026 was located near the western edge of the excavation and lay on a NW–SE alignment (Fig. 118). A total length of 13.6 m was exposed, the south-eastern end of which was cut by the ditch of the conjoined late Romano-British Enclosures 3 and 4. To the north-west it continued beyond the edge of the excavation. The ditch was 0.5 m wide and up to 0.24 m deep, with steep sides and a base that varied from flat to concave (Fig. 119). Approximately 5 m from the point at which it was cut by the later enclosure ditch it was interrupted by an entrance 0.8 m wide, wide enough to allow pedestrian access. The ditch was filled with a single deposit of pinkish brown clayey sand that contained sherds of pottery giving a date after AD 130/140. This ditch appears to have been a lateral division between the linear boundary ditches, the line of which was adopted as the boundary between Enclosures 3 and 4 during the later phase of the occupation of the site.

Kiln 158022

Pottery kiln 158022 was located in a rather isolated position *c* 11 m north-west of the end of ditch 158010 (Fig. 107). There were no associated features in the vicinity. It comprised a firing chamber set within a circular pit, with a large stokehole on its north-eastern side (Figs 115– 16).

The firing chamber measured 1.2 m in diameter and was sunk to a depth of 0.65 m. The sides of the chamber and flue had been lined to a thickness of 70–120 mm with a layer of clay (150795), the inner face of which had been fired to a dark blue colour by the heat generated within the kiln. There was some evidence for repairs to this lining in the form of patches which were less intensively fired, and which may have been replaced during the use-life of the kiln. The presence of areas of similar clay *c* 20 mm thick found intermittently across the base of the chamber (150794) suggests that the lining may originally have been continuous across the chamber floor. In the centre of the chamber stood the two clay piers (150792, 150793) which had supported the raised firing surface. These were made from the same clay as the lining and each measured 0.45 m by 0.2 m and were 0.3 m high. They were fired to the same dark blue hue as the lining. Archaeomagnetic dating of one of the piers gave a date of AD 125–175 for the kiln's final firing.

The firing chamber was fed through a short flue 0.8 m wide, which had been covered by a rectangular sandstone slab (measuring 815 mm by 670 mm wide and 190 mm thick), found in a fragmentary state in layer 150964. The slab had been deliberately shaped and bore clear tool marks, and may have been a re-used building stone. It was supported on four unworked limestone uprights (150798, 150799, 150800, 150801) placed against the sides of the flue. Each of these uprights measured *c* 0.25 m by 0.1 m and was 0.75 m high, except the eastern stone (150799), which had broken and was only 0.6 m high when found. The stokehole consisted of an irregular pit *c* 2.6 m in diameter and 0.8 m deep dug into the natural sand.

The base of the structure was covered throughout by deposits of loose sand disturbed during work on the kiln (150653, 150582). These were overlain within the firing chamber by a layer of black, ashy silt 0.05 m thick, interpreted as spent fuel from the firing of the kiln (150697 and 150704). The ashy layer extended throughout the chamber and the flue, and spilled out partly into the stokehole. The absence of greater accumulations of material derived from the firing of the kiln indicates that the base of the firing chamber was cleaned out regularly and the resulting debris shovelled out of the stokehole.

The ashy layer was partly overlain by deposits of brown silty sand (150583, 150573, 150809) up to 0.13 m thick that extended along the base of the stokehole, thickening toward the edge of the feature. This is likely to be a natural accumulation of material eroded from the sides of the stokehole pit, and may indicate that the feature was left open for a period after the final firing.

The in-filling of the disused kiln began with the partial back-filling of the firing chamber with a layer of dark reddish-brown sandy silt 0.15 m thick which contained a high density of pottery (eg, 150702). This included distorted and misfired sherds which are likely to be discarded wasters produced in earlier firings of the kiln. At about the same time a series of discrete dumps of ashy silt (150808, 150812, 150586) and dark reddish-brown charcoal-rich soil (eg, 150571, 150603) were deposited in the stokehole to a depth of 0.3 m. This was followed by the collapse of the stonework in the flue. The back of the stone slab covering the flue was broken, possibly deliberately, and the stone slumped into the flue, some fragments tumbling into the firing chamber (150964). One of these fragments came to rest on the clay piers. The firing chamber was then back-filled with a single deposit of red sandy silt (150646 etc) that again contained a large quantity of waster sherds, as well as a large amount of fired clay. This layer also spilled out through the flue and into the stokehole.

The remainder of the structure was filled with a series of dumps of greyish-brown silty sand (the rest of the fills from 150570 onwards), during the course of which there was some collapse of the southern side of the stokehole, represented by deposits 150610 and 150745. The uppermost fill (150567) was the only layer to contain sherds unequivocally not produced in the kiln, suggesting that by this time the kiln was being used as a convenient dump for settlement refuse. The structure appears to have been derelict for some considerable time before its final in-filling, as the imported pottery in this layer can be dated to the third decade of the 3rd century.

Late Romano-British (mid-3rd–4th centuries)

The 3rd century witnessed a major re-organisation of the site, including possibly the recutting of the southern linear boundary, so blocking the entrance in ditch 158006, and the cutting of ditch 158007, partly blocking the entrance between ditches 158006 and 158008 (Fig. 107). Enclosures 1 and 2 appear to have passed out of use at this time, as no pottery dating from the mid-3rd–4th century occupation of the site was recovered from their ditches. Enclosures 3 and 4, which were constructed at this time near the south-western limit of the excavation, may have been intended as direct replacements for the earlier enclosures.

Features in Enclosure 2

Use of the area of the earlier enclosures did not end completely, however, as activity continued in the northern part of Enclosure 2 (Fig. 117). Two curved gullies (158017 and 158019) were dug to enclose an area in the northern part of the enclosure. This area measured *c* 16 m NE–SW by 11.5 m NW–SE and abutted the south-eastern side of linear boundary ditch 158003. The gullies varied in width from 0.4 m to 0.6 m and had been substantially truncated, surviving to a depth of no more than 0.12 m. Both were filled with deposits of light brownish-grey silty sand with some flint gravel, and were dated by a group of pottery sherds dating from the late 3rd or early 4th century recovered from the fill of 158019. Between the terminals of the two gullies was a south-east facing entrance 6.75 m wide.

Cobbled surface 150411 extended through this entrance and may have been intended to mitigate the effects of trampling on the soft, poorly drained underlying geology. The surface measured at least 8.5 m NW–SE by 5.5 m NE–SW and was composed of rounded pebbles up to 0.1 m across. It had an irregular shape that probably results from truncation rather than preserving its original form. It was overlain by a layer of trample (150412) consisting of light brown sandy silt with patches of orange clay, from which was recovered a handful of pottery and tile.

At its northern end the cobbled surface was cut by a large, irregular hollow (158018). The hollow measured 7 m by 3.5 m but was quite shallow, with an irregular base that varied up to 0.3 m deep. Slots excavated across it revealed from one to four fills of brown silty sand. Part of the hollow's eastern side respected the line of gully 150391. The gully was straight, aligned NW–SE and 3.6 m long. It had a maximum width of 0.35 m and was only 0.05–0.1 m deep. It had a single fill of greyish-brown sandy silt from which no finds were recovered.

On the north-eastern side of gully 150391, the central part of the area enclosed by gullies 158017 and 158019 was largely devoid of features, with a small group of smaller hollows (150110, 150300, 150320, 150322) around the north-eastern end. These hollows varied in size up to 2.5 m by 2.0 m and were all only a few centimetres deep, with similar brown sandy fills. The reason for the apparently blank area gully 150391 and the hollows to the north-east may be that this was the location of a structure for which no direct evidence survives.

A pair of postholes (150296 and 150329) similar to the sets recorded elsewhere within Enclosure 2 were cut into cobbled surface 150411. The postholes were 1.2 m apart and both measured 0.7 m in diameter. Posthole 150329 was slightly the deeper at 0.42 m, compared with a depth of 0.36 m for posthole 150296. Posthole 150329 contained a sequence of three fills including a deposit that contained a high concentration of flint pebbles and may have been collapsed post packing.

Three other postholes were recorded in this part of Enclosure 2, two (150306 and 150333) within the area enclosed by the gullies and one (150302) just outside, none of which formed part of any coherent structure.

Feature in Enclosure 1

The sequence of pottery recovered from the fills of waterhole 150217 in Enclosure 1 indicates that it also

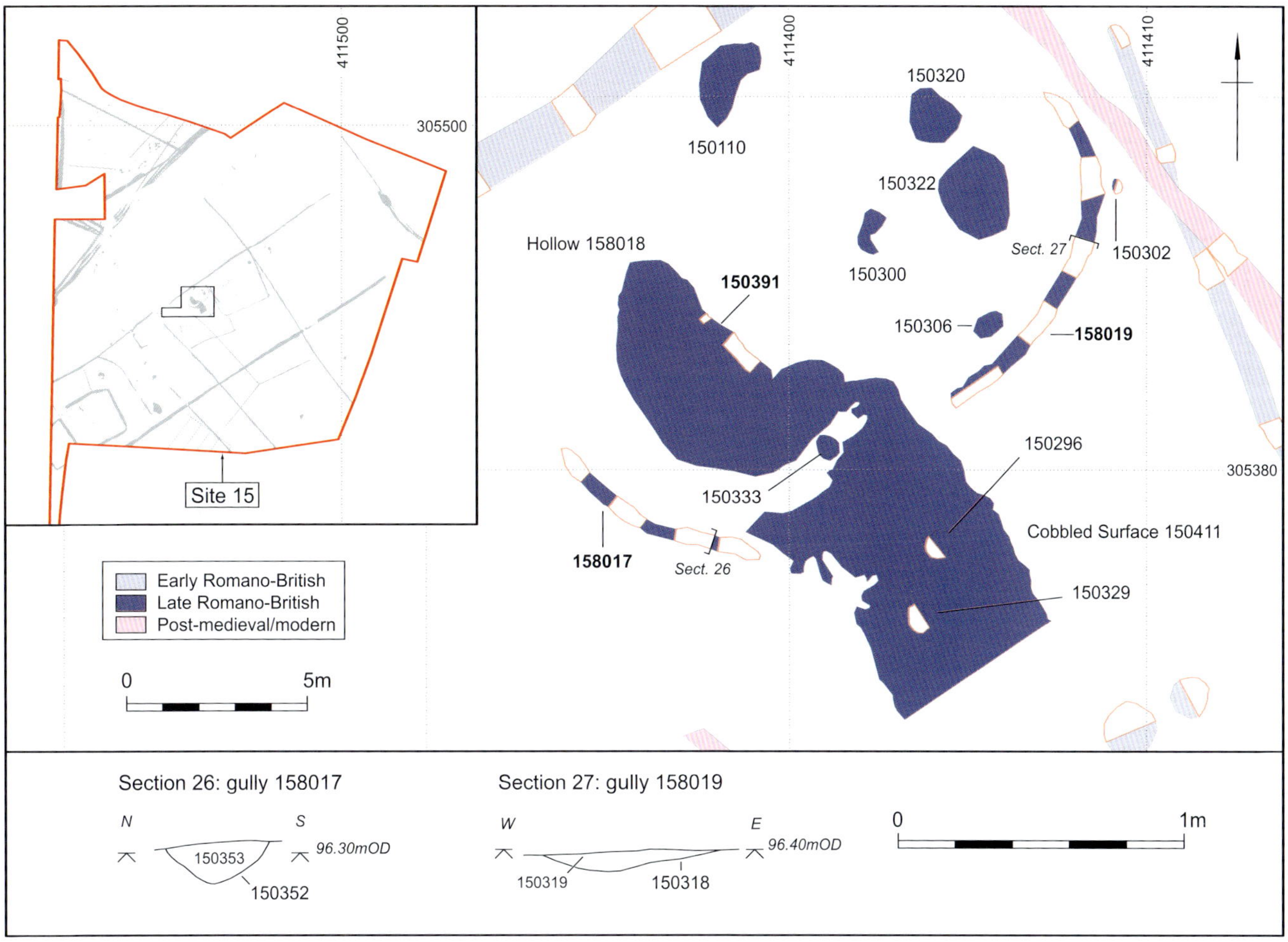

Fig. 117 Late Romano-British features in Enclosure 2

continued in use in this period, possibly not being finally in-filled until as late as the mid-4th century.

Features north-east of Enclosure 1

A small group of features comprising an irregular hollow (150957) and three postholes (150859, 150951 and 150952) were recorded *c* 11 m north-east of Enclosure 1 (Fig. 113).

Hollow 150957 was irregular in shape and measured 4.75 m by 1.75 m. It had an irregular base and was 0.14 m deep, and was filled with a deposit of brown sand (150956) with occasional rounded pieces of gravel that contained pottery dating from the 3rd and 4th centuries and a small quantity of ceramic tile. It also contained a flat, squared piece of sandstone that probably originated as a building stone (ON 154019).

A posthole and a pit or posthole were located on the north-western side of the hollow. Posthole 150951 was 0.85 m in diameter and 0.32 m deep with steep sides and a flat base. It contained a post-pipe (150953) composed of dark brown humic sand, which was 0.46 m in diameter. The post-packing was a deposit of light brown, slightly gravelly sand (150954). Next to the posthole was a circular, bowl-shaped feature 0.9 m in diameter and 0.23 m deep (150952), which could have been either a second posthole or the base of a small pit.

Posthole 150859 was situated 1 m south-west of hollow 150957. It was 0.35 m in diameter and 0.4 m deep with vertical sides and a flat base and contained a single fill of brown sand (150858).

The function of these features is unclear, but they represent the north-eastern extent of structural features recorded in the excavation.

Enclosures 3 and 4

Enclosures 3 and 4 were conjoined, sharing boundary ditch 158015 (Fig. 118). Enclosure 3 was almost square in plan, measuring 34 m NE–SW by 31 m NW–SE internally, bounded to the south-west by ditch 158015, and on the other three sides by ditch 158014, and with a 4.5 m wide entrance at its western corner. The two ditches were generally between 2.0 m and 2.78 m wide and up to 0.85 m deep (Fig. 119). These dimensions decreased considerably at the northern and eastern corners of the enclosure, measuring as little as 1.05 m by 0.41 m at the latter. The profile of the ditch was recorded as a V-shape with moderately sloping, occasionally irregular sides, which probably derived from the erosion of an original steeper profile due to the friable nature of the geology into which it was dug.

Ditch 158014 containied 1–5 fills, the former occurring only at the eastern corner where it was most shallow. The primary fill was a reddish-brown gravelly sand, except at the western corner of the enclosure where the natural geology was clay and the fill was a brown sandy clay. This was overlain by up to three layers

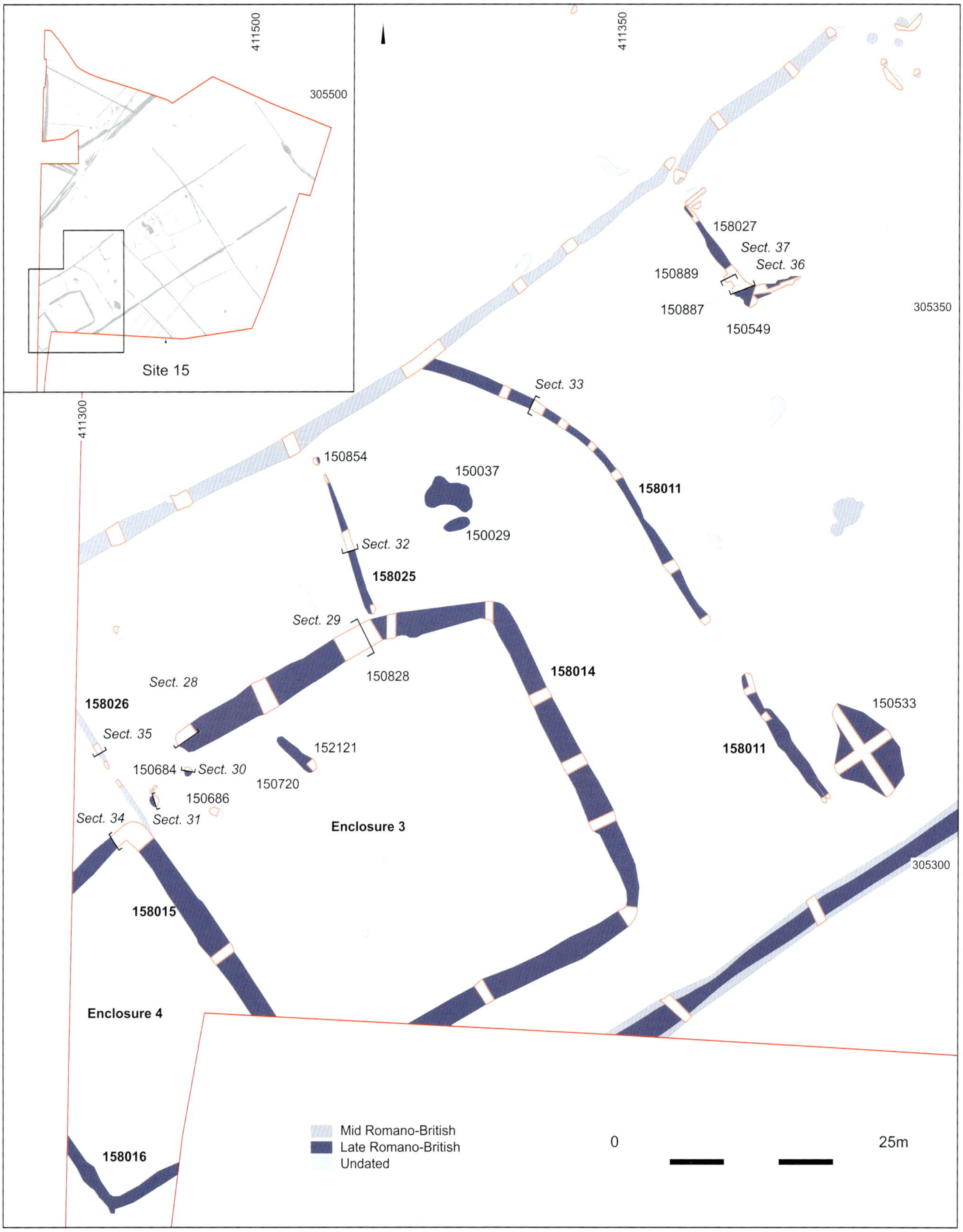

Fig. 118 Late Romano-British Enclosures 3 and 4 and adjacent features

of secondary in-filling that consisted of brown or greyish silty sand containing varying amounts of gravel.

Occupation debris had accumulated or been dumped into the ditch, particularly on the northern side of the enclosure. In segment 150828, the secondary fill (150826) was almost black due to a very high charcoal content and contained the largest assemblages of both pottery and roof tile from any single context in the excavation, as well as two fragments of rotary quern. Smaller groups of finds, which were nonetheless large in

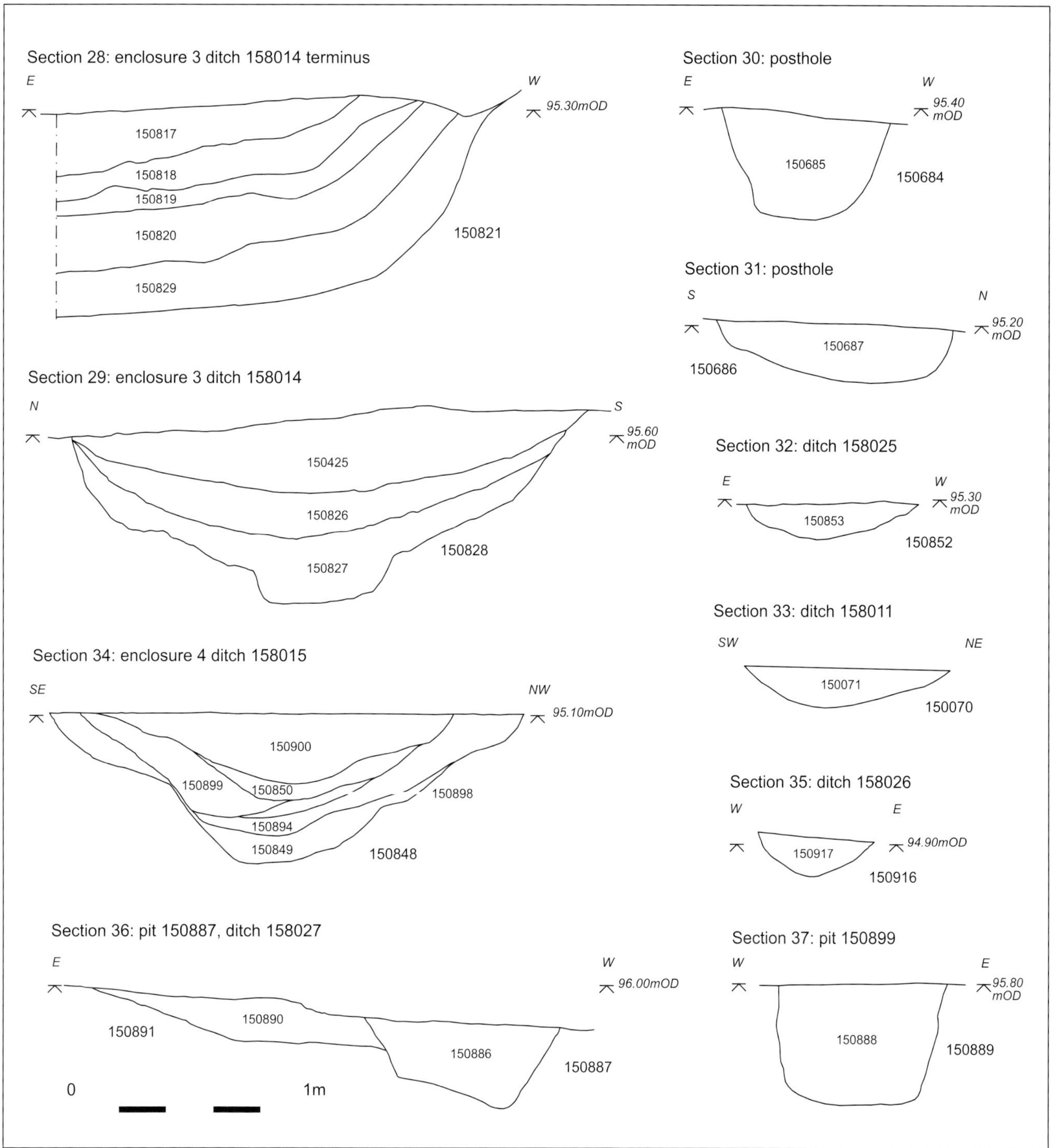

Fig. 119 Sections of late Romano-British features in Enclosures 3 and 4 and adjacent features

the context of this site, were recovered from the secondary fills in other segments of the northern part of the enclosure ditch. A dump of charcoal-rich soil (150818) overlying the later of two layers of secondary silting (150820, 150819) in the terminus (150821) on the north-eastern side of the entrance into the enclosure is also likely to represent occupation debris.

In the deeper sections of the Enclosure 3 ditches a tertiary fill of brown silty sand was recorded. This generally contained smaller quantities of finds than the secondary fills and may have formed when the level of activity in the enclosure had declined or ceased altogether. In this latest fill the greatest concentration of pottery and tile was again located in ditch segment 150828. The pottery recovered from the ditch presumably derived from activities taking place within the enclosure, and dated from the late 3rd to early 4th centuries.

The entrance into Enclosure 3 at its western corner had a gateway formed by postholes 150684 and 150686, which lay 3.2 m apart (Fig. 118). The postholes were set back *c* 1 m from the line of the inner edge of the enclosure ditch, and may have been positioned in line with a bank constructed from the upcast of the ditch, although no remains of such a bank survived. Posthole 150684, at the north-east, was 0.8 m in diameter and

0.36 m deep, with almost vertical sides and a flat base (Fig. 119). Posthole 150686, at the south-west, was oval in plan, measuring 1.0 m by 0.8 m. It was more shallow than its companion, with a depth of 0.23 m, and had more concave sides that curved to join the base with no clear break. The two postholes were filled with similar deposits of brown silty sand (150685 and 150687), neither of which contained any artefactual material.

The only other archaeological features within Enclosure 3 were a shallow gully 4.5 m long (152121) and a posthole (150720) cut into the gully's south-eastern end.

Enclosure 4 was slightly smaller and more rectangular than Enclosure 3, measuring 25 m NW–SE by 20 m NE–SW. At its northern corner, ditch 158015 turned a right-angle to the south-west to enclose the northern part of the enclosure, while ditch 158016, which formed its southern corner, was exposed only within the narrow strip extending south from the south-western corner of the main excavation area. As the eastern and western corners of Enclosure 4 lay beyond the excavated area it was not possible to establish whether its ditches were a single feature, nor to establish its relationship with Enclosure 3. At the western corner of the enclosure, beside the entrance to Enclosure 3, the secondary fills of reddish-brown sand resulting from the gradual silting of the ditch (150894, 150899) were interleaved with darker, greyer deposits containing frequent fragments of charcoal (150898, 150850), of which context 150850 contained a substantial amount of pottery and tile (Fig. 119). These layers are also likely to have resulted from periodic episodes of dumping.

Ditch 158016, at the southern corner of Enclosure 4, was markedly less substantial than ditch 150815 to the north (Fig. 119), being between 0.8 m and 1.42 m wide and up to 0.46 m deep. It had the same V-shaped profile, but was partly truncated by a modern drain, and contained a sterile sandy fill with no dumps of occupation debris, and only a single, undiagnostic sherd of pottery. Enclosure 4 contained no features.

Ditch 158025

Ditch 158025 ran approximately north–south for 13.4 m between the north-western side of Enclosure 3 and northern linear boundary ditch 158001 and appears to have been intended to block access round this side of the enclosure. It was up to 0.76 m wide, narrowing to 0.3 m toward the north-western end, and had been substantially truncated, surviving to a depth of no more than 0.2 m (Fig. 119). It was filled with a deposit of light yellowish-grey silty sand from which no finds were recovered.

At its north-western end the ditch terminated 3 m from 158001. Posthole 150854 was in the middle of this entrance gap and may have been associated with a gate or similar structure that enabled the entrance to be closed. The posthole measured 0.8 m in diameter and had a shallow bowl-shaped profile with a depth of 0.08 m. It was filled with a similar material to the ditch.

Ditch 158011

A further part of the changes to the organisation of the settlement at this time was the separation of the south-western area, including Enclosures 3 and 4, from that to the north-east by the digging of ditch 158011 running between the northern and southern linear boundaries. The ditch, curving at the north-west, ran south-east for 54 m from ditch 158001, terminating 6.8 m from ditch 158006, with a 5.5 m wide entrance gap *c* 13 m north of its southern terminal. South of this gap it was possible to identify two distinct phases of the ditch, with two cuts lying parallel to each other but not overlapping sufficiently for any stratigraphic relationship between them to be established. Both cuts were 0.7–1.0 m wide and were heavily truncated, with only the lower 0.1–0.2 m of their bases surviving. They were filled with similar deposits of greyish-brown sandy silt. A small quantity of pottery was recovered from the fill of the western cut giving a date range in the late 3rd to mid-4th centuries. North of the entrance gap only one phase of the ditch was identified, the dimensions of which were similar to those recorded to the south.

Hollows 150533, 150037 and 150029

North-east of ditch 158011's southern terminal was an irregular hollow (150533) which may have been formed by trampling by animals passing through the second gap – between the terminal and ditch 158006. The hollow, which measured 9.55 m by 6.15 m and was 0.1 m deep, was filled with a deposit of greyish-brown sandy silt (150534) which contained a small assemblage of pottery including a mortarium base and late shell-tempered wares suggesting a date in the late 3rd–4th century.

A second (150037) hollow was recorded between ditches 158025 and 158011. This measured 4.25 m by 2.6 m and 0.24 m deep and was irregular in shape with an equally irregular base. It was filled with a deposit of greyish-brown silty sand (150038) from which a small assemblage of pottery and tile dating from the mid-3rd century or later was recovered. To its immediate south, hollow 150029 was smaller and oval measuring 2.5 m by 1.1 m and 0.1 m deep. It was filled with a greyish-brown silty sand (150030) similar to the fill of hollow 150037, and it is likely that these were originally part of a single hollow, truncated by later ploughing.

Ditch 158027

An L-shaped ditch (158027), possibly the south-western end of a small rectilinear enclosure, was located next to the south-western end of linear boundary ditch 158002. It ran south-east for 11 m, turning a right-angle toward the north-east for a further 6 m, beyond which it had been truncated by post-Romano-British ploughing. The ditch was 0.8 m wide and up to 0.35 m deep with a V-shaped profile and gently sloping sides. It was filled with a single deposit of dark brown gravelly sand from which were recovered a small assemblage of pottery and part of a rotary quern. The pottery included 17 sherds from a black burnished ware jar dated to the late 3rd century.

The north-western end of the ditch terminated 2 m from ditch 158002, either to leave an opening wide enough to serve as an entrance into the enclosure or because this area was occupied by a bank associated with ditch 158002.

Near the angle in the ditch, it was cut by three pits. Pits 150887 and 150889 were both sub-rectangular in plan with steep sides and flat bases. Pit 150887 measured 1.2 m NW–SE by 0.85 m NE–SW and was 0.35 m deep, and pit 150889 measured 0.94 m NE–SW by 0.7 m NW–SE and was 0.5 m deep (Fig. 119). Pit 150549 was more circular in plan, with a diameter of 1.2 m and had sides with a moderate slope and a concave base. All three pits contained similar fills of mid-brown gravelly sand from which no artefacts were recovered. The pits were closely spaced, dug into the outer lip of the ditch at intervals of 0.5 m, and may have held the posts of a fence line that superseded the ditch.

Post-medieval

Pond 150268

A large oval feature, measuring 10.0 m by 5.25 m, at the eastern end of the site was interpreted as a pond. A machine-dug section across it revealed that it was 0.84 m deep with moderately sloping sides and a fairly flat base. It contained a sequence of five fills of homogeneous brown silty sands with varying amounts of gravel, which may have resulted from deliberate back-filling. It was cut by a post-medieval field boundary ditch (150085), and may have been backfilled as part of the general reorganisation of the landscape of which that ditch was a part.

Field boundaries 158005 and 150085

Two approximately parallel field boundary ditches (158005 and 150085) ran NW–SE across the eastern half of the site. They are likely to form part of a field system established *de novo* during the inclosure period of the late 18th and early 19th centuries, and both appear of the 1st edition Ordnance Survey map of 1887–8.

Ditch 150085, which cut the fills of pond 150268, was 0.95 m wide and up to 0.2 m deep. Its sides sloped gently to a concave base, which had clearly been truncated but is likely to represent the base of a feature that was originally relatively wide and shallow in profile. It was filled with a single deposit of brown silty sand. Toward the south-eastern end of the ditch two additional phases of this boundary were recorded. Ditch 152050, which contained a sherd of 19th century pottery, was up to 2.0 m wide and 0.12 m deep, with a similar wide, shallow profile to ditch 150085. It contained a single fill of greyish-brown gravelly sand and was cut by ditch 152052. The latter ditch was more narrow and steep-sided, but was similarly shallow. It was 0.65 m wide and 0.13 m deep and contained a fill of brown sandy silt with a high concentration of gravel.

Ditch 158005 was *c* 95 m south-west of ditch 150085. It cut the Romano-British northern and southern linear boundary ditches 158003 and 158006, and truncated the north-eastern corner of Enclosure 1. Like ditch 150085 it had a shallow profile and had been significantly truncated. It was up to 1 m wide with a maximum depth of 0.4 m. The depth decreased toward the north-western end until the ditch was completely truncated away in the northern part of the excavation. Its fill was a brown silty sand from which a sherd of pottery dating from the 18th century was recovered.

Roadside ditch 152147

Ditch 152147 was exposed in the northern part of the excavation. It ran north-south along the western edge of the excavated area and is likely to be a roadside drainage ditch alongside the A5127 Birmingham–Lichfield road. It was up to 3.3 m wide and 0.87 m deep with moderately sloping sides and a slightly concave base. and contained four fills of brown silty sand. A re-cut recorded in one of the two excavated sections was 2.3 m wide and 0.6 m deep and contained a single fill of red and grey mottled sand.

Boundary ditches in the northern part of the site

A ditch running NE–SW at the northern end of the site corresponds to a field boundary shown on the 1st edition OS map of 1887–8. In the same area, but on a slightly different alignment, was a boundary represented by a sequence of five successive ditches. One of the ditches (150631) had a ceramic drain running along its base and all were filled with similar deposits of dark, loamy soil similar to the topsoil, indicating that they are of recent date. Near the western edge of the excavation a boundary defined by four ditches branched off from the main NE–SW boundary and extended toward the north-west, continuing beyond the excavated area (158037). Ditch 152143 branched off the main ditch *c* 18 m from the northern edge of the excavation and similarly extended toward the north-west, extending beyond the western edge of the excavation north of roadside ditch 152147.

Ditches at the southern end of the site

Four ditches of probable post-medieval date, all aligned NW–SE, were recorded in the strip excavated extending southward from the main area, alongside the A5127. The most northerly, ditch 152078, corresponded approximately to a field boundary shown on the 1st edition OS map of 1887–8. It had a slightly curving form and measured 1.3 m wide and 0.55 m deep. It had fairly steep sides and a concave base and was filled with a single deposit of dark greyish-brown silty sand that may result from deliberate back-filling.

Ditch 152133 extended for 4.4 m from the western side of the excavated strip before terminating, and was 1.1 m wide and 0.35 m deep with a concave profile and contained a single fill of greyish-brown silty clay. Ditches 152132 and 152131 both had wide, shallow, flat-based profiles and were filled with similar deposits of grey clayey silt. The former was 1.5 m wide and 0.15 m deep, the latter 1.35 m wide and 0.28 m deep.

Tree-throws

A number of tree hollows may be of post-medieval date. Tree hollow 150013, near the north end of ditch 158005, contained a sherd of 19th century pottery. Tree hollow 150404 and 150415 were stratigraphically later than features securely dated to the Romano-British period, and three-throw hole 150037 contained Romano-British pottery which may be residual. The dating of the pottery from tree hollow 150013 suggests that these feature, and other undated examples, may result from an episode of tree clearance associated with the establishment of the post-medieval field system.

Table 71 Nail classification by context

Feature	*Type 10*	*Type 1*	*Unclass.*	*Total*
Ditch 158014	–	6	3	9
Ditch 150761	–	–	1	1
Ditch 158003	–	1	–	1
Ditch 158015	–	1	–	1
Pit 150259	13	–	–	13
Posthole 150104	–	–	2	2
Posthole 150720	1	–	–	1
Hollow 158018	–	–	1	1
Total	14	8	7	29

Finds

Metal finds, by Kelly Powell

The metalwork from this site consisted of three copper-alloy and 34 iron objects (Tables 70–1). Copper-alloy finds included a fragment of a broken, corroded and illegible coin (ON 154018), *c* 21 mm across but its original diameter probably greater, probably of 1st–2nd century AD date. It was recovered from the upper fill (150860) of the northern linear boundary ditch (158003, section 150861), north-east of Enclosure 1.

Table 70 Metal finds (exc. nails, see Table 71)

	Copper-alloy	*Iron*
Unstratified	1 coin	1 horseshoe
	1 *patera* handle	1 bar/strip frag.
	1 misc	
Ditch 158014		1 hook
		1 bar
		1 rod frag.

A flat fragment of a probable Romano-British bronze *patera* handle (ON 154004) (Fig. 120), was recovered, comparable in form to that recorded by Frere from *Verulamium* (Frere 1984, 48). Although this object was unstratified it was found in the vicinity of Romano-British posthole 150121, one of the group forming a possible entrance structure near the break in the northern linear boundary. It consisted of a short length of the fan-shaped butt end broken at the stem and retains maximum dimensions of 45 mm by 37 mm. The third copper-alloy find (ON 154006) was a modern object, also unstratfied and with no obvious relationship to any features.

The majority of the ironwork from this site consisted of nails or nail fragments (Table 71), 29 overall, of which three probable nails were too corroded to be firmly identified. All of the nails were recovered from Romano-British contexts, mainly boundary or enclosure ditches, with the exception of one example from post-medieval boundary ditch 158036 (cut 150761), though it is possible that this was also a residual Romano-British find. Twelve of the nails could be identified as having a probable structural function and eight were in good enough condition to be classified as Manning type 1, of which four complete examples were specifically classed as type 1b. The other examples were probably of this type.

The remaining 14 nails were identified as hobnails, Manning type 10. These were consistently 7–12 mm in length with a head diameter of 9 mm. With the exception of the single find from posthole 150720, they were recovered in two groups of nine and four from fills of pit 150259. The larger of the two groups notably came from context 150261, a dump of burnt material which formed the main fill of the pit. It is possible that these comprise the remains of entire shoes abandoned as refuse.

The remaining iron finds consisted of two bar or strip fragments (ONs 154005 and 154002), a hook from context 150835, a bent length of rod from context 150825, and an unstratified post-medieval horseshoe (ON 154017).

Find 154005 was also unstratified but spatially related to northern linear boundary ditch 158002. This bar was 190 mm in length and 6 mm thick; its true nature is uncertain due to heavy corrosion, but it is damaged at one end and may have possessed a small lip or similar feature above the damaged area. Find 154002 was recovered from Enclosure 3 ditch 158014 and was a tapered length of bar or strip, 66 mm in length. Its thickness and any clear features were not discernible due to heavy corrosion, however, it is possible that there was

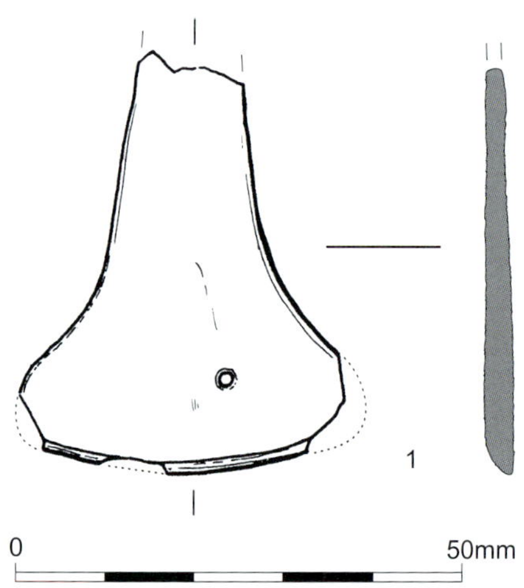

Fig. 120 Bronze *patera* fragment

a protrusion at the wider end. The hook, also from ditch 158014, was approximately 68 mm in length and appears to have been bent over at both ends. One end was damaged, but the undamaged end tapered to a sharp point. The function of this object is unknown, but it is likely to be Romano-British in date. Finally, the 30 mm bent length of rod was particularly round in section, with less corrosion than is typical of this assemblage and may be part of a relatively modern chain or similar object. Its location in the less secure upper fill of ditch 158014 may also indicate a later date.

Flint, by Kate Cramp

Eleven struck flints were recovered from the excavation (Table 150). Most of the flintwork was manufactured from locally available pebble flint from the gravels, with the single exception of a retouched piece of black chert, the source of which is unknown. The assemblage was spread across several contexts and is in variable condition. While much of the material is likely to be residual, technological indications suggest that some Mesolithic flintwork is present.

The assemblage was largely composed of unretouched types, including one flake, five blades/bladelets (one of which is crested) and one rejuvenation flake. An opposed platform blade core (Fig. 121, 1) was recovered from the fill of tree hollow 150474 (context 150476). Retouched tools include one trihedral pointed blade with deliberate proximal snap (Fig. 121, 2), one tanged bladelet (Fig. 121, 3) and the retouched chert artefact (Fig. 121, 4). The latter had been finely retouched along two convergent edges; it may have been a scraper when complete, but as a burnt fragment was unclassifiable. The tanged bladelet was recovered from ditch 158006 (context 150434) and was probably Mesolithic in date; a similar example was identified in the Early Mesolithic assemblage from Ascott-under-Wychwood (Cramp 2006), while another was associated with an Early Mesolithic ploughsoil collection from Higham Ferrers, Northamptonshire (Cramp and Lamdin-Whymark in prep.). It is possible that this example was also Early Mesolithic in date, although stray microliths from residual contexts cannot be securely dated.

The small group of three flints from context 150476 (tree hollow 150474) were in fresh condition and may have been contemporary with the deposit; a Mesolithic date is most likely for these pieces on technological grounds. Most pieces displayed platform edge abrasion and other traits reflecting the use of soft-hammer percussion; one of the blades had a faceted platform. Other pieces in the assemblage were techno-logically similar and possibly broadly contemporary, although these formed a more disparate spread and are more likely to be residual.

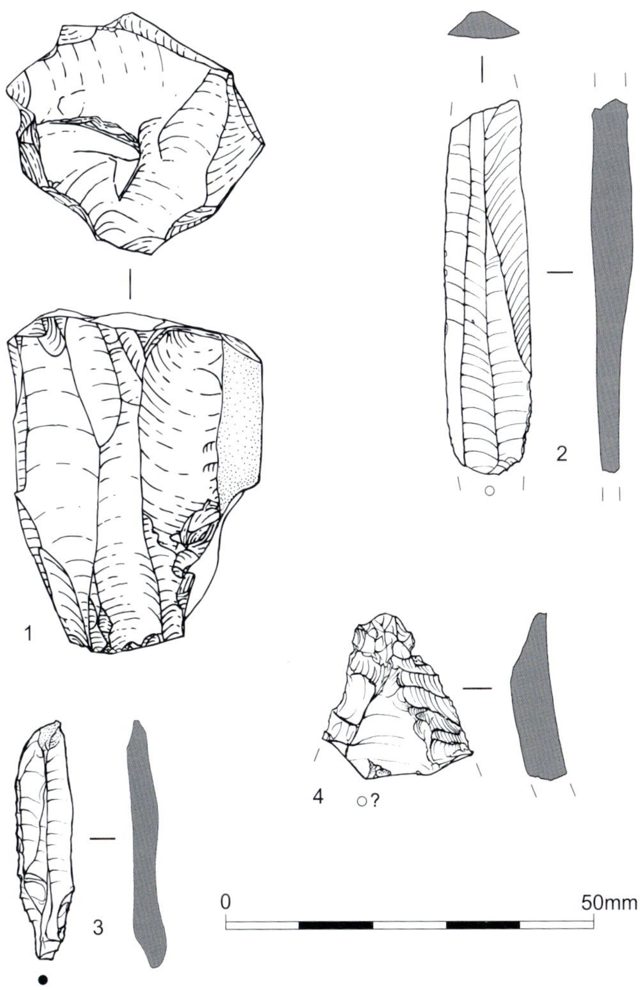

Fig. 121 Flints

List of illustrated flints (Fig. 121)

1. Bipolar (opposed platform) blade core, platform edge abrasion. Good quality flint with abraded cortex. Abandoned before exhausted. 52 g, context 150476, tree hollow 150474
2. Unclassifiable retouched tool, trihedral pointed blade, distal snap. Proximal end removed using microburin technique. Utilised. Mesolithic. ON 154015, unstratified
3. Unclassifiable retouched tool, tanged bladelet, bulb not removed. Utilised. Mesolithic, context 150434, ditch 158006, section 150432. ON 154014
4. Unclassifiable retouched tool, good quality, opaque black chert. Fine, semi-abrupt retouch to point. Possible scraper? Burnt and broken, unlocated posthole 150294. ON 154011

Glass, by H.E.M Cool

The only fragment of Roman vessel glass from this site (ON 150867) came from a square bottle of the type that was very common from the later 1st century into the 3rd century (Price and Cottam 1998, 194–8). That the only evidence for vessel glass use at this site is in the form of a bottle is unsurprising as these are often the only types of vessels present on rural sites of the 1st–3rd centuries (Cool and Baxter 1999, 84).

Early prehistoric pottery, by Carol Allen

A total of 42 sherds of Neolithic quartzite-tempered pottery was found, all in the subsoil (150031). The sherds were slightly to moderately abraded, and some of the decoration could only be seen vaguely. All the sherds appeared to come from one vessel and a partial profile can be reconstructed indicating that this was a Peterborough Ware vessel of Mortlake type. Activity of this period must have been taken place nearby, and possibly the pottery has been displaced from a pit during later ploughing.

Peterborough Ware, Mortlake pot

A simple rounded rim cabove a deep concave neck and part of a rounded body could indicate that this pot had a round base (Fig. 122). Decoration was apparent inside the neck and on the outer part of the rim, neck and upper body consisting of horizontal rows of impressed decoration possibly made with a small bone or piece of wood. The lower body had similar impressions in diagonal rows. Mortlake type of Peterborough Ware is known from Gonalston, Nottinghamshire (Allen 2000) and was also found within the ring ditches of Fatholme, near Barton-under-Needwood, Staffordshire (Losco-Bradley 1984), indicating that this type of pottery is known in this area, but rarely survives.

Radiocarbon dates have confirmed that all types of Peterborough Wares were in use by 3000 cal BC, and dates for Mortlake types range from 3600 cal BC to 2300 cal BC (Gibson and Kinnes 1997, 67; Gibson 2002, 80). It seems that most Mortlake types may have dated to about the middle of this period, possibly around 3000 cal BC.

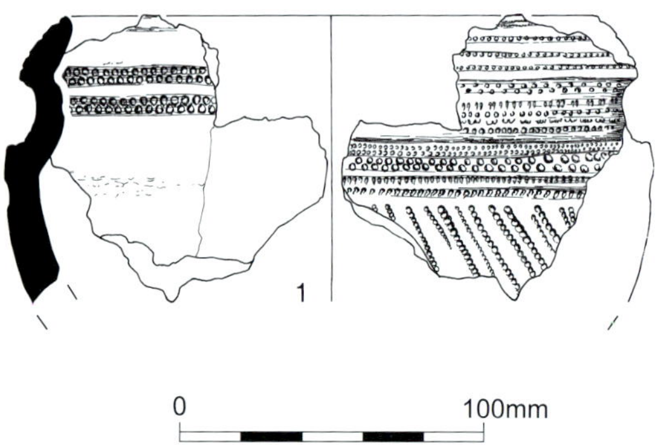

Fig. 122 Neolithic Peterborough Ware pottery

Pre-Roman Iron Age and Romano-British pottery, by Ruth Leary

There was a total of 3264 sherds (44875 g) of Iron Age and Romano-British pottery from the site. The sherds came principally from linear features, two structures and a pottery kiln. The average sherd weight was 14 g but this varied from feature to feature (Table 72). Soil conditions had resulted in poor surface preservation for much of the pottery, even where large sherds suggested little abrasion and redeposition. The nature of some of the larger groups, accumulations in ditches over a period of time, would be consistent with this kind of surface erosion. The overall date range for the assemblage was mid-/late 2nd–late 3rd/early 4th century with a small group (117 sherds, 1299 g) of pre-Roman Iron Age (PRIA) sherds of Middle Iron Age type (Fig. 123). The pottery dumped in the kiln was dated to the late 2nd–3rd centuries and archaeomagnetic dating gave a date of AD 125–175 for the final firing of the kiln. The site assemblage included sherds traceable to at least 16 different sources, including two Continental kiln groups in Central Gaul and in the region of the River Guadalquivir in southern Spain (Rodriguez Almeida 1989) and at least seven kiln groups outside a radius of 50 km from the site and, therefore, beyond the scope of local distribution in which producer and consumer might each travel *c* 15–25 km to a market (Peacock 1982, 85, 107, 112).

Table 72 Romano-British pottery: average sherd weight

Feature	*No.*	*Weight (g)*	*Av. weight*
Misc.	550	6500.4	11.82
150128	7	132.0	18.86
152121	37	613.8	16.59
158001	88	965.4	10.97
158002	31	351.5	11.34
158003	268	3119.9	11.64
158006	99	1271.8	12.85
158007	1	13.9	13.90
158008	4	16.2	4.05
158011	13	237.8	18.29
158012	1	14.6	14.60
158013	1	5.7	5.70
158014	1030	14,863.3	14.40
158015	89	1406.2	15.80
158016	1	7.9	7.90
158017	1	19.2	19.20
158018	182	2008.6	11.04
158019	45	306.9	6.82
158023	4	182.5	45.63
158025	1	3.3	3.30
158026	4	39.9	9.98
158027	58	376.5	6.49
158029	8	131.1	16.39

An archive catalogue was compiled for all the pottery according to the standard laid down by the Study Group for Romano-British Pottery (Darling 2004). Pottery was recorded detailing specific fabrics and forms, decorative treatment, condition, cross-joins/same vessel and was quantified by sherd count, weight and rim percentage values, giving estimated vessel equivalents. All the pottery from the site was catalogued in the archive and the stratified pottery was examined in order to date the features. Key groups are illustrated and catalogued below and unillustrated material is summarised. The fabric series (see Chapter 28) was cross-referenced with

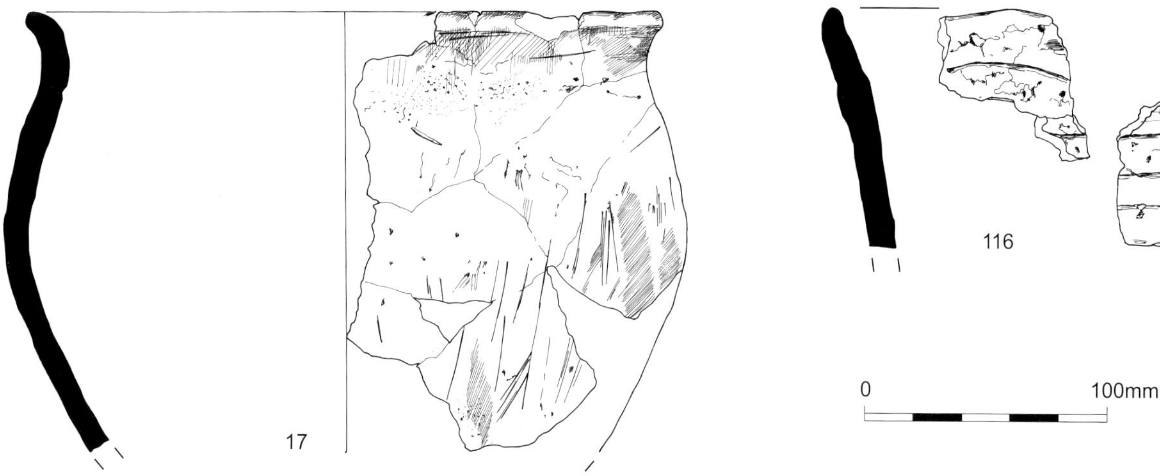

Fig. 123 Iron Age pottery

the Warwickshire fabric series and National Fabric Reference Collection codes (Tomber and Dore 1998) are included where appropriate.

Fabrics

The majority of the pottery was in fabrics made in the kiln or in a group of R fabrics amongst which waster sherds were found in other features on the site. These were used in the manufacture of the most prolific types of bowls, dishes and jars and were supplemented by BB1 medium-necked jars, plain and grooved-rim dishes and flanged bowls from Dorset, small numbers of wide-mouthed jars and one narrow-necked jar from the Severn Valley industry and small numbers of late shelly ware jars from the kilns at Harrold, Bedfordshire or related industries. The Derbyshire ware jars from the site may also have been traded but the presence of warped and distorted sherds, including a sherd from the kiln, raises the possibility of on-site production of this type. The small numbers represented do, however, fit the pattern of recovery of Derbyshire ware jars found on the periphery of its core distribution area where levels of *c* 2–5% of a site assemblage are commonly encountered.

The small proportion of oxidised wares may include material from kilns such as those at Mancetter as well as variants of Severn Valley wares. Most of the white wares may also come from Mancetter-Hartshill with a very small number comparable to *Verulamium* region products. Small amounts of fine ware from the Nene Valley kilns were identified with one red colour-coated flagon from Much Hadham and seven sherds of Oxfordshire red colour-coated ware from three vessels at the most.

Amphorae were also scarce contributing just over 2% of the total weight and 2% of the sherd count. Single sherds of grit-tempered wares G2, G3 and G5 were identified and three of G4. G2 is similar to pink grogged ware in some respects and also compares with the Warwickshire fabrics G12 and G43. One sherd was combed and the rather uneven surfaces suggest that it was handmade so it may belong to the 1st–2nd centuries rather than the later period. G3 looks like a reduced version of pink grogged ware and the single sherd came from a storage jar with similar decoration to that found on pink grogged storage jars. G4 is likely to be an early handmade fabric and may belong to the PRIA phase of activity. The eight sherds of pink grogged ware storage jars of late 3rd–4th century date are consistent with the chronological profile of the assemblage.

Vessel types

The majority of the assemblage was made up of jars (66%) with a relatively low number of bowls and dishes (*c* 18%) and very few beakers or cups. Flagons may have been represented by white ware body sherds but no forms were identifiable. The relative number of mortaria was relatively high (13%) and this may be due to ready access to supplies from the nearby kilns at Mancetter-Hartshill and/or manufacture on site. Compared with national trends, the make-up of the groups is entirely consistent with a rural settlement in the Midlands (Evans 2001, fig. 5) and lacks the high proportion of drinking vessels found on rural sites in the Severn Valley.

With regard to chronological change the bulk of the pottery groups dated to the mid–late 2nd–early 4th centuries but with only very small groups specifically isolated to the 2nd century. There was therefore little opportunity to examine changes in the make up of the assemblage over time. At Alcester the pattern of jar:bowls/dish ratio suggested that this area conforms to the southern pattern (Millett 1979), seeing an increase in the representation of bowls and dishes over time (Evans 2001, 53) contrasting with the rise in jars found on Romano-British sites of all kinds that has been identified in the north of the country (*cf.* Evans 1993, 102). The quantity of jars from Alcester, a Roman small town, is not unexpectedly much lower, *c* 40% in most cases, than at Shenstone.

Only body sherds and a handle from one or more Dressel 20 amphorae were present.

The bowls and dishes were made commonly in the locally produced reduced wares and BB1 with two oxidised types, one probably from Mancetter and the other a Severn Valley type (Nos 3 and 14), a Nene Valley colour-coated bowl (represented by a basal sherd) and samian vessels. The flanged bowls in reduced ware were mostly in fabric R2 and BB1 with small numbers in fabrics R3, R4, R7 and R12. Plain rim dishes were found in R2, R4, BB1 and one in R8, with grooved-rim dishes in BB1 only.

One GRA bead rim may have come from a carinated bowl of the late 1st–early 2nd centuries (context 150144, ditch 150083) but otherwise early bowl forms such as reeded rim bowls were absent. No flat-rim bowls such as are common in the Antonine period were found. One bead and flange hemispherical bowl of Antonine type was identified (No. 3). The assemblage was dominated by plain-rim dishes and grooved flat rim or bead and flange rim bowls. The types represented suggested a peak in activity in the late 2nd–3rd centuries with features silted up by the late 3rd or early 4th century. Apart from the moulded bead and flange bowls from the kiln the forms are well-known ones based on BB1 types traded from Dorset. A small number of samian bowls and dishes were present dating to the Hadrianic and Antonine periods. Only one dish in Oxfordshire red colour-coated ware was found, with up to two more represented by body sherds only.

Beakers were uncommon. Only one small jar or beaker with everted rim was identified in a local ware (R2), the remainder comprised two long necked bead rim beakers in CC1 and NV1 and a scale beaker in NV1. FLA body sherds may come from flagons but no diagnostic sherds were present.

Medium necked jars were found principally in the locally made reduced wares and BB1 with further types made in Derbyshire ware and shell-tempered ware. Jars with everted and near cavetto rims were the most numerous amongst the medium-necked jars in both local coarse wares and BB1. One jar with a short, everted rim resembled jars typical of the late 1st–early 2nd centuries, while two BB1 jars belonged to the Hadrianic-Antonine range with upright or slightly everted necks (cf. Gillam 1976, nos 2–3). The majority of the BB1 jars were of splayed rim types, commonly with obtuse lattice (dated *c* AD 235–45, Bidwell 1985, 174–6), three of which had a shoulder groove (dated after AD 240, Holbrook and Bidwell 1991, 96). The rim forms compared with vessels common in mid–late 3rd century groups (Gillam 1976, nos 8–10) although the development is known to be typologically uneven (Holbrook and Bidwell 1991, 95–6).

The local coarse ware medium necked jars had similar everted rims, probably copying the BB1 range. In addition to these, a group of Derbyshire ware jars with lid-seated rims was also present. These included several distorted sherds and may have been made locally, although no direct evidence for their on-site manufacture was obtained. A small number of shell-tempered jars with everted rims were also present. In fabric and form these compared with products of the Harrold kilns. These kilns achieved a more extensive distribution of jars like these in the late 3rd and 4th centuries (Brown 1994) although the precise forms were made earlier than this. In addition, similar forms in indistinguishable fabrics were made in the Nene Valley industries from the mid/late 2nd–4th centuries (Perrin 1999, fig. 70, nos 430, 440, 434 and 445). However, in view of the known distribution patterns, a date in the late 3rd century or later is favoured for these vessels.

Wide-mouthed jars were as numerous as the medium-necked jars. These were in local reduced wares and Severn Valley wares. The local reduced ware vessels were predominantly in fabric R2 with some vessels in R1, R4 and R7 and small numbers in R3, R5, R8, R10 and R13. Small numbers of wide-mouthed jars were also present in oxidised wares O3, O4. O7 and SV1, SV3 and SV4. All of these were either Severn Valley products or copied Severn Valley ware types. The locally produced wide-mouthed jars were similar to some of the Severn Valley vessels of the 2nd–3rd centuries but, since they lack the outbent neck feature so familiar in the Severn Valley range, were clearly following a local tradition. The typology contrasts with the later 'East Midlands burnished ware' tradition (Todd 1968b) characterised by thick-walled necked vessels with heavy beaded or hooked rims and the vessels are unlike the wide-mouthed jars found in the Derbyshire ware industries (Leary 2003). Unlike at sites such as Leicester, there seems to be no continuity between the Late Iron Age 'Belgic' tradition in Warwickshire and the Romano-British pottery kilns established by the army (Booth 1986, 24). It is from these military kilns that the later pottery industries developed and it is amongst their products that ancestral forms may be sought for these jars. At Leicester the wide-mouthed jar series develops apparently continuously from Late Iron Age wide-mouthed forms, and at centres like the 3rd century Derbyshire kilns relationships can be traced to necked jars produced in the Derby Racecourse kilns in the 1st and 2nd centuries (Leary 2003).

In Warwickshire ancestral forms for these wide-mouthed jars may be found at Mancetter in the 1st century (Scott 1981, fig. 15, no. 56 and fig. 16, no. 69). As in Derbyshire, wide-mouthed jars dated broadly on typological grounds to the late 2nd–early 3rd centuries at Mancetter are heavier with thicker walls (Hemsley 1959, fig. 7 no. 78). At Wappenbury the wide-mouthed jars in the 4th century kilns 1 and 2 are also of the thick-walled type with bead rim (Stanley and Stanley 1960–1 fig. 4, no. 1; fig. 5, no. 2A) and none was present in the earlier kiln 4, dated to the first half of the 2nd century. The kiln at Perry Barr was given a provisional date in the second half of the 2nd century but, as at Shenstone, dating was difficult due to the somewhat unremarkable nature of the products (Webster 1959, 38–9). The only truly wide-mouthed jar illustrated from Perry Barr (*ibid.*, fig. 3, no. 23) was not considered a kiln product but one vessel (*ibid.*, fig. 3, no. 4) might be considered an ancestral form. One wide-mouthed jar illustrated from the *mansio* at Wall is given a date in the mid-2nd century and compared to examples from *Verulamium* (Round 1990–1, fig. 19, no. 204). This vessel has the characteristic shoulder groove but a somewhat heavier everted rim than the Shenstone examples. More of similar types were found by Gould and dated to the 2nd century on somewhat unsatisfactory typological grounds (Gould 1963–4, fig. 17, no. 189).

A vessel from Greenfield's excavations compares well with the Shenstone series (Leary 1995–6, no. 60) and came from a posthole. This feature had no other pottery within it and the sherd was dated to the late 2nd century by reference to a sherd from a vessel with a similarly outbent rim found in a late 2nd century robber trench at the *mansio* excavations at Wall. Other material considered to be from the same structure included an unusual carinated sherd with rouletted decoration either from a copy of a castor box or a narrow necked jar, both of which belong to series of vessels made in the 3rd–4th century (Leary 1995–6, no. 61).

At *Tripontium*, wide-mouthed jars are rare in the late 2nd century groups published by Cameron and Lucas and the examples from 4th century groups are somewhat heavier and compare better with the 'East Midlands burnished ware' types of the late 3rd–4th centuries (Cameron and Lucas 1969, fig. 18 for a late 2nd century group and fig. 19, no. 199; fig. 20, no. 214; fig. 21, no. 238 and fig. 22, no. 250 for 4th century groups; Todd 1968b). Thus it would appear from these scraps of local evidence that the Shenstone jars may be transitional forms belonging in a period from towards the end of the 2nd until the late 3rd century. At Whitemoor Haye, Staffordshire, similar wide-mouthed jars were illustrated in local grey wares (Coates 2002, fig. 39, nos 9–10). These came from a single phase dated to the mid–late 2nd–early 3rd centuries and strengthen the evidence for the Shenstone wide-mouthed jars dating from an inception point in the second half of the 2nd century and declining in the later 3rd century when the heavier types developed.

The narrow-necked jars were less common than the medium- and wide-mouthed vessels but were made in a similar fabric range to the wide-mouthed jars, ie mostly in R2 with a good number in R8 and smaller amounts of R5, R10 and R13, O3 and SV1. Most of the vessels had simple everted rims of long lived form apart from a bifid rim vessel in SV1, a blunt, grooved rim in fabric R10 and a blunt ended everted rim in R13. Webster (1976) gives the bifid rim Severn Valley jars a 3rd century date (see No. 25). The grooved rim vessel (No. 95) compares with similar vessels from Derbyshire, one from kiln 2 at Lumb Brook, dated mid–late 2nd century (Leary 2003, no. 3), one from Roystone Grange (Leary forthcoming c), one from Rocester (Leary 1996, no. 95) and one from *Tripontium* in a context dating into the 3rd century (Cameron and Lucas 1969, fig. 16, no. 145).

Only one possible lid was recovered and this plain sherd was so distorted that it was difficult to decide if it was the rim of a lid or a plain rim dish.

The mortaria were predominantly hammerhead and reeded hammerhead types. The rims were mostly smooth or had less than four reeds. Smooth and reeded rim mortaria with four or fewer reeds were more common than multi-reeded mortaria. The latter were limited to five examples from late groups such as the fills 150825 (No. 80), 150536, 150524 (No. 107) and 150036 (No. 69) which also included types such as late shell-tempered vessels, fabric PNK GT and other late indicators. Hartley (2003) has suggested that multi-reed mortarium would be rare before *c* AD 230 but became the most common form by AD 260–280, while four-reeded vessels were being made before the end of the 2nd century and continued to be made thereafter. At Cramond a group dated to the early 3rd century has only one multi-reeded mortarium and is dominated by three- and four-reeded mortaria. On the basis of the Cramond evidence, the Shenstone mortarium assemblage suggests occupation in the early 3rd century but continuing later than at Cramond. The ratio of reeded mortaria to multi-reeded mortaria (more than four reeds) may indicate a decline in the late 3rd century with, perhaps, relatively little activity in the 4th century. This is borne out by the evidence of other categories of pottery. One spout fragment from gully 152121 came from an early Mancetter-Hartshill cream mortarium of early–mid-2nd century date.

A small number of other ceramic items was identified. Two spindle whorls had been made from potsherds of BB1 and grey ware and a sherd of R2 had been shaped into a roundel. An R4 curving D-sectioned rod was also found (No. 64); its function has not yet been established. Exceptional pieces were an almost complete grey ware lamp and a fragment of a 'pipeclay' Venus figurine (see below).

Chronology

The relative quantities of fabrics and forms on the site suggest that the focus of domestic and industrial activity on the site occurred from the mid–late 2nd century until the late 3rd century with the possibility of some activity, perhaps on the periphery of an adjacent domestic site, taking place as late as the early 4th century. There are some vessels belonging to the pre-Roman Iron Age but these have quite clearly come from much earlier features disturbed by later activity, including a post-medieval ditch. Very few features need be dated before the middle of the 2nd century. This is supported by the evidence of the samian ware. There was no South Gaulish material, and while, as a consequence of soil conditions, many sherds were not closely dated, only one vessel was (tentatively) assigned to the Hadrianic period, as opposed to 19 which were specifically Antonine or late Antonine in date and eight or nine for which no close dating was possible within the 2nd century.

Most of the larger groups came from accumulations within features which terminated in the late 3rd–early 4th centuries or from dumps of material discarded in partially silted up features dating from a similar period. The lack of stratification within the features with accumulation deposits precludes the isolation of groups within this rather broad chronological period. The kiln group is best dated to the late 2nd century but evidence from the settlement features in the form of discarded wasters and forms made in the fabrics found in the kilns (see below) strongly suggests that pottery production continued in the early–mid-3rd century outwith the limits of excavation.

The very small amounts of types characteristic of the 4th century such as late shell-tempered wares, late BB1 types, Oxfordshire and Nene Valley fine wares and pink grogged wares, all restricted to small numbers of sherds in the latest groups, suggest that occupation did not continue far into the 4th century, if at all.

Catalogue of illustrated sherds and discussion of stratified groups (Figs 123–7)

The Northern linear boundary ditch 158001

The pottery came principally from fills interpreted as layers of natural silting, except for a dump in 150878 (Table 73).

A small number of undiagnostic body sherds came from the secondary fill (150075) and included a small BB1 sherd from a dish or bowl giving a terminus post quem of *c* AD 120. Most of the pottery came from the later fills. Diagnostic sherds gave a date in the 3rd century and included sherds from a late BB1 jar

Table 73 Romano-British pottery from ditch 158001

Section	*Context*	*No.*	*Weight (g)*	*Av. weight*
150074	150075	2	29.9	14.95
150558	150556	4	17.6	4.40
150866	150876	8	177.2	22.15
150870	150871	1	37.4	37.40
150872	150872	1	9.5	9.50
150877	150878	64	555.3	8.68
Total		80	826.9	10.34

150878 fill of 150877

1. BB1 splayed rim jar with obtuse lattice burnish, *cf* Gillam 1976 no. 8 dated mid-3rd century
2. R13 narrow necked jar with blunt ended everted rim

An R2 plain rim dish and a cavetto rim jar were also present along with a samian sherd and body sherds of DBY, R2 and R7. A date in the mid 3rd century is consistent with these types.

Fills 150871 and 150872 yielded an incomplete rim sherd from a Mancetter-Hartshill reeded-rim mortarium of mid-3rd to mid-4th century date and a G2 body sherd respectively. Sherds of an MH2 mortarium base, an R2 wide-mouthed jar with flat everted rim as No. 29 from the kiln and body sherds of fabrics R13 and O4 were also found in late fill 150867. These sherds suggest that this ditch section was silting up during the second half of the 2nd century with dumping in the mid-3rd century in section 150877 and final infilling in the mid-3rd to mid-4th centuries.

Northern linear boundary ditch 158002

The small groups of pottery in this feature came from the uppermost layers of infilling and the ditch terminal (Table 74).

Table 74 Romano-British pottery from ditch 158002

Section	*Context*	*No.*	*Weight (g)*	*Av. weight*
150105	150107	14	232.5	16.61
150160	150161	9	59.8	6.64
150553	150551	8	59.2	7.40
Total		31	351.5	11.34

150107 uppermost fill of 150105

A small group of sherds included an R2 wide-mouthed jar of the type made in the kiln and an R4 plain-rim dish also the same as those made in the kiln. A sherd from a Mancetter-Hartshill mortarium dating after AD 130/40 and a G5 sherd with traces of combing probably dating to the 1st or 2nd century were also present. A date in the second half of the 2nd century would be consistent with the types present.

150161 fill of 150160

A group of nine sherds comprised body sherds of OAB, four abraded body sherds from a BB1 jar with traces of lattice burnish, probably obtuse, a feature appearing around *c* AD 223–225 (Bidwell 1985, 174–6), an incomplete reeded rim mortarium sherd of Mancetter-Hartshill type dating to the mid-3rd to mid-4th century and an R3 jar with short everted rim of a type more common in the late 1st–early 2nd centuries. Unfortunately the ditch fill was not stratified at this point but the early jar form provides some evidence for occupation earlier in the second century while the later mortarium and BB1 sherds agree with pottery types recovered from the late fill of other sections of the ditch.

150551 late fill of 150553

Eight sherds comprised three sherds from a BB1 bowl or dish with intersecting arcade burnish, a motif which grew in popularity in the late 2nd–early 3rd centuries (Gillam 1976, 68), four R2 body sherds and a Central Gaulish samian sherd from a form 18/31 dish. A date in the second half of the 2nd century would fit these vessel types.

The sherds from this section of ditch indicate infilling from the second half of the 2nd to the mid-3rd century or later.

Northern linear boundary ditch 158003

The character of the excavated fills suggested that the pottery from this ditch came from gradual infilling in contexts 150092, 150134, 150137, 150144, 150154 and 150367, dumps of material in context 150155 with late accumulation in 150860 (Table 75). The character of the pottery supports this with larger sherds coming from 150155 and small, abraded and fragmented sherds from 150144.

150089 late fill of 150092

3. O6 flanged, hemi-spherical bowl with groove at tip of rim. Common at Derby Little Chester in the Hadrianic-Antonine period (Birss 1985, 95 no. 36; *cf.* Booth 2006, no. 277, Antonine) and also at Mancetter-Hartshill. In the Severn Valley range, this form is dated to the mid-2nd to early 3rd centuries (Webster 1976, nos 65–6). The grooved rim is reminiscent of Rhaetian mortaria (*cf.* Lee

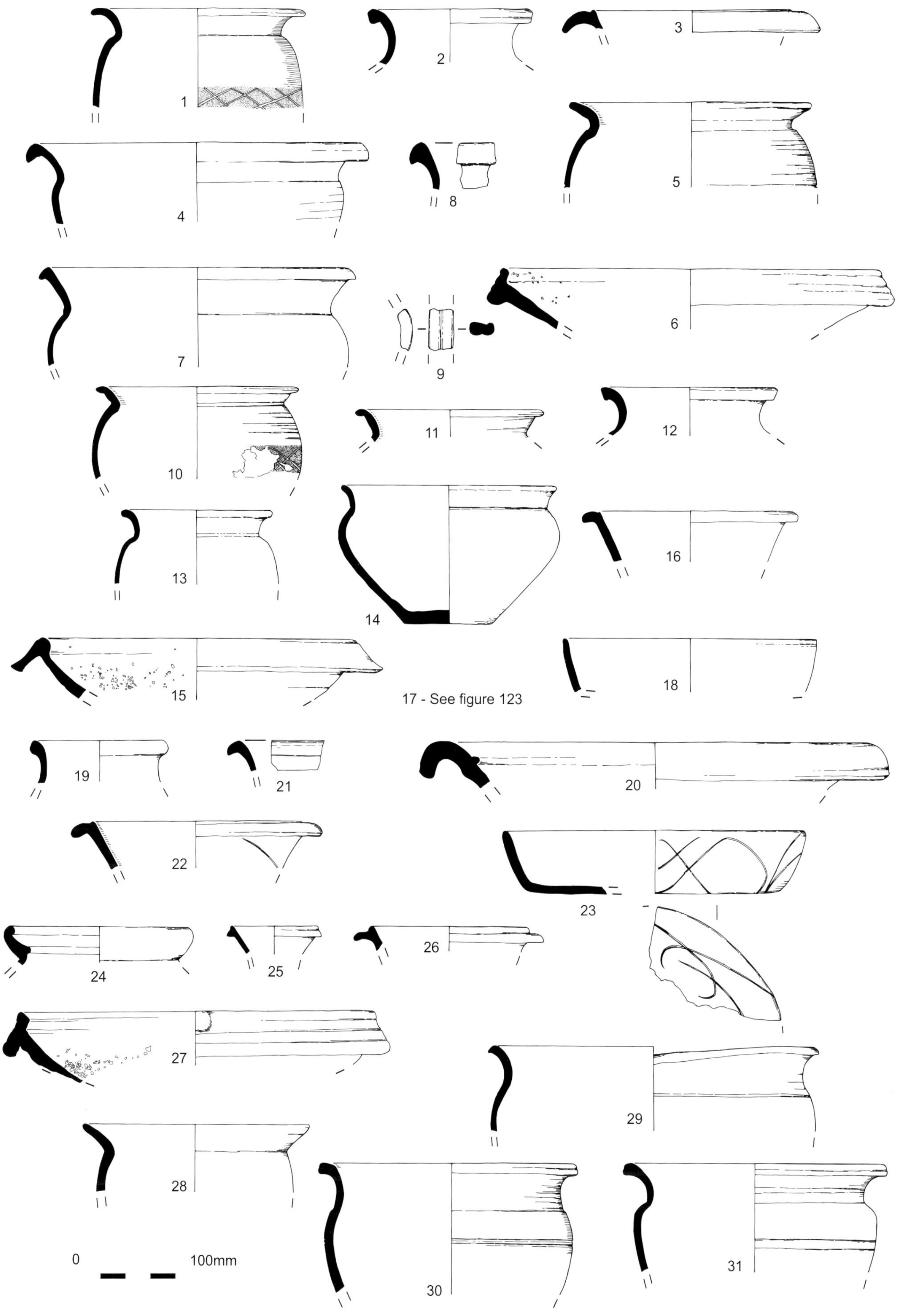

Fig. 124 Romano-British pottery

Table 75 Romano-British pottery from ditch 158003

Section	Context	No.	Weight (g)	Av. weight
150092	150089	26	428.7	16.49
150132	150134	2	10.6	5.30
150135	150137	20	398.8	19.94
150142	150144	106	440.2	4.15
150153	150154	42	366.6	8.73
	150155	69	1429.1	20.71
150366	150367	1	5.3	5.30
150861	150860	2	40.7	20.35
Total		268	3119.9	11.64

and Lindquist 1994, no. O381 dated mid-2nd–3rd century)

4. O7 wide-mouthed jar with outbent neck and hooked rim, *cf.* Severn Valley types dated mid-2nd–late 3rd centuries (Webster 1976, nos 23–4)
5. BB1 late splayed rim jar with grooved shoulder, mid-3rd century or later (Gillam 1976, no. 9; grooved shoulder dated from *c* AD 235–245 (Holbrook and Bidwell 1991, 96)

150134 and 150137 late fills

6. MH2 reeded rim mortarium with spout formed by pushing out upper rim. Three grooves. *Cf.* Evans 2002b, M83 dated 3rd century

Two SV3 body sherds and 12 sherds from an R1 wide-mouthed jar with everted, tapered rim as No. 34 indicate a date in the mid–late 2nd century.

150144 secondary fill in 150142

One hundred and three sherds (834 g, average sherd weight 8 g) from at least seven vessels. These comprised the five illustrated vessels, undiagnostic sherds from a grey ware jar and a R6 everted rim, probably from a carinated bowl of the 1st–2nd centuries. Around 49 sherds from the BB1 jars were present and also 35 from an R6 jar base and body. The latest Severn Valley ware vessel suggests that ceramic accumulation continued into the 3rd century but earlier sherds indicate activity from at least the early–mid-2nd century

7. SV3 wide-mouthed jar with wedge-shaped rim of Severn Valley type. 2nd–3rd centuries
8. SV3 hooked rim of wide-mouthed jar. Severn Valley ware type, 3rd–4th centuries
9. SV3 handle, probably of tankard
10. BB1 necked jar with everted rim, *cf.* Gillam 1976 no. 2, but the lattice decoration indicates a 3rd century date.
11. BB1 necked jar with everted rim, *cf.* Gillam 1976 no. 3, mid-2nd century

150154 lower fill of 150153

Forty sherds (295 g, average sherd weight 7.4 g). At least four vessels were represented; sherds from a W12 flagon, a BB1 bowl or dish base, a medium-necked, everted-rim jar in R8 and a narrow-necked jar with everted rim, slightly expanded at the tip, in R9. The medium-necked jar gives a date in the late 2nd or 3rd century. The narrow-necked jar rim was slightly distorted.

12.. R9 narrow-necked jar with everted rim, distorted
13. R8 smooth curving everted rim jar, copying black burnished types of the late 2nd–3rd centuries

150155 late fill 150153

14. O1 profile of everted-rim, wide-mouthed bowl, *cf.* Lee and Lindquist 1994, fig. 36, no O379 dated 2nd–3rd centuries; Webster 1976, no. 36
15. MH2 flanged mortarium with very slight groove demarcating bead rim. Nearly a hammerhead rim, *cf*, Darling 1999, nos 556–60. *c* AD 170–280

This fill also contained a BB1 plain rim dish with intersecting arcade burnish dating to the late 2nd–early 3rd centuries (Gillam 1976, no. 77), Central and possibly also East Gaulish samian ware with a date of AD 160 or later, body sherds of R3, R4, R9 and R10, SV4 and an R1 everted rim from a jar. These sherds suggest a date range in the late 2nd–early 3rd centuries.

150860 fill of 150861

16. R2 grooved, flanged rim bowl. This form is generally dated from the late 2nd to mid–late 3rd centuries (Holbrook and Bidwell 1991, 98)

This fill also contained a rim of an R2 everted rim jar common in the late 2nd to 3rd century. A small FLA2 sherd was recovered from fill 150367.

Southern linear boundary ditch 158006

Pottery came from seven sections of this ditch all of which seemed to be naturally infilled (Table 76). The larger group from 150168 comprised 58 sherds from an Iron Age pot and only three Romano-British sherds. The low numbers of sherds suggest that this ditch was further from the focus of domestic activity and dumping of domestic debris.

Table 76 Romano-British pottery from ditch 158006

Section	Context	No.	Weight (g)	Av. weight
150164	150167	11	137.8	12.53
	150168	61	860.7	14.11
150169	150171	1	25.3	25.30
	155027	1	34.0	34.00
150432	150437	3	5.0	1.67
150471	150486	1	14.3	14.30
150472	150488	2	1.7	0.85
150737	150738	16	188.1	11.76
155027	150193	4	38.9	9.73
Total		100	1305.8	13.05

150168 fill of 150164

Sixty-one sherds (861 g, average sherd weight 14.1 g). Three vessels were represented by sherds, a grooved-rim BB1 dish comparable to types dated to the late 2nd century (*cf.* Gillam 1976, no. 71), a grey ware jar of unknown type and a large percentage of a fragmented handmade P1 jar with everted rim of Middle Iron Age type. The pottery from the underlying layer 150167 gives a mid-3rd century date for this group. The Middle Iron Age jar presumably derives from adjacent layers which have fallen into the ditch at a late stage in infilling

17. P1 jar oxidised externally and grey internally. Neckless ovoid jar with everted rim. (Fig. 123)
18. BB1 grooved-rim dish dated to the late 2nd century (cf Gillam 1976, no. 71)

150167 fill of 150164

Eleven sherds (138 g, average sherd weight 12.5 g) from three vessels. A bead and flange Mancetter-Hartshill mortarium, two grey ware jar sherds and a Nene Valley colour-coated funnel necked beaker dating from around the mid-3rd century (Perrin 1999, 93).

Four further P1 Iron Age sherds were recovered from this ditch in context 150193. Further pottery sherds from this ditch included body sherds of BB1 and samian from 150437 and a post-medieval sherd, a BB1 basal sherd and FLA scrap from 150488, an R2 base and body sherds from 150738 and a R1 narrow-necked jar rim from 150486.

19. R1 everted rim sherd from narrow-necked jar. A long lived form, context 150486
20. MH1 morarium with low bead and flange rising above level of rim. Early 2nd century, context 150167

Linear boundary ditch 158006 seems, therefore, to have a phase in the Middle Iron Age or (more likely) to have cut an Iron Age feature, with further activity in the 2nd century and infilling in the 3rd century.

155027 fill of 150169

One sherd (34 g) from a handmade jar with simple everted rim in a sand-tempered fabric (PRIA). Iron Age.

Southern linear boundary ditch 158007 fill 150401

A much abraded sherd from a Mancetter-Hartshill reeded rim mortarium was found in this feature dating from the 3rd–mid-4th centuries. The rim had at least two reeds (and probably three) but was extremely abraded.

Southern linear boundary ditch 158008

This feature contained two SV4 sherds (context 150375) and two medieval sherds (contexts 150379 and 150467).

Enclosure 1

Ditch 158012

This ditch produced one sherd (15 g) from an O4 wide-mouthed jar in fill 150992.

21. O4 wide-mouthed jar with outbent neck and everted rim tip, *cf.* Webster 1976 types 23–4, mid-2nd–late 3rd centuries

Posthole 150099

Ten undiagnostic body sherds (60 g) of FLA1, R2 and R7. 2nd century or later.

Posthole 150104

Fifty-six sherds (868 g.) were found. Most sherds from fill 150103 were either abraded or very abraded, although this may be due to burial conditions. The majority of sherds were grey ware and at least two vessel forms were identified, a wide-mouthed jars with curving everted rims and one medium necked jar with a curving everted rim close to a cavetto rim. The wide-mouthed jars were similar to those found in the kiln in fabric and form but are of a long-lived form starting in the mid–late 2nd century and continuing into the 4th century. Examples in the 4th century tend to be thicker walled with chunkier rims and the more sinuous forms here suggest a date in the late 2nd or first half of the 3rd century. Oxidised sherds included a fine blunt ended, everted rim which was not closely datable. The presence of a samian dish form 31 and some white ware flagon sherds would support a date range in the second half of the 2nd century. Four sherds from a BB1 bowl/dish and a jar were too abraded and small to give anything more than a date after AD 120. Fill 150176 contained an undiagnostic R5 sherd and the rim of a late BB1 jar (*cf.* Gillam 1976, no. 10, late 3rd century).

Posthole 150121

The rim of a samian dish (3.6 g) was found in this posthole.

Roundhouse 1, posthole 150128

Five R11 body sherds (122 g) were found and one scrap (3 g) from a white ware base, similar to material from the Verulamium region. The grey ware was finer than that made in the kilns and was scorched and flaked. The tiny white ware scrap was also burnt to some extent and may have come from a flagon. A date in the late 1st or early 2nd century would fit this rather meagre dating evidence. There was also a single undiagnostic R4 sherd (7 g)

Roundhouse 1, posthole 150286

Two scraps of O4 (3 g) and samian ware (4 g), the latter of Antonine date.

Waterhole 150217 (Table 77)

22. BB1 grooved flanged bowl, *cf.* Gillam 1976 no. 42, late 2nd–early 3rd centuries
23. BB1 plain rim dish, with intersecting arcade burnish on the walls and intersecting lopped burnish outside the base, *cf* Gillam 1976, no. 81, late 3rd century
24. Derbyshire ware cupped rim jar
25. SV1 bifid rim jar *cf.* Webster 1976, no. 11, 3rd century
26. R12 bead and flange bowl

This group also included body sherds of CTA2, O4, R2, R4, R8, R12, R13 and samian ware, sherds from an SV1 wide-mouthed jar, a M1 mortarium base and a MH2 incomplete rim section of a reeded rim mortarium of mid-3rd to mid-4th century date. These types suggest a date in the late 3rd to mid-4th centuries. The primary fill 150408 contained four sherds: a distorted body sherd (37 g) from an R8 jar, two SV1 body

Table 77 Romano-British pottery from waterhole 150217

Context	No.	Weight (g)	Av. weight
150218	1	27.7	27.7
150219	20	465.5	23.28
150220	5	39.7	7.94
150221	9	268.4	29.82
150406	32	364.6	11.39
150407	4	82.9	20.73
150408	4	160.8	40.20
	75	1409.6	18.79

sherds probably from a narrow necked jar and a samian sherd (6 g) from a ?cup. A date in the second half of the 2nd century is likely.

Enclosure 2 (mid-Romano-British phase)

Enclosure ditch 158013

Only one small BB1 sherd (6 g) from a jar with lattice decoration was recovered from context 150978 in section 150977 giving a *terminus post quem* of *c* AD 120.

Ditch 158023 extension of Enclosure 2 ditch 158013: 150985 fill of 150984

A small group of four sherds from here included a body sherd of R2 (9 g) from context 150974 and a body sherd of R8 (6 g) and the rim (168 g) of an MH2 mortarium, both from context 150985.

27. MH2 reeded rim mortarium with fairly upright rim and spout formed by pushing out upper rim. The rim is quite upright suggesting a date *c* AD 200–230 (Hartley 2002, 51, nos 33 and 37)

Posthole 155012

An R2 base (15 g) and group of 13 sherds (66 g) came from an everted rim jar. This is similar to the wide mouthed jars from the kiln and may be of late 2nd–3rd century date.

Posthole 150296 fill 150297

One undiagnostic abraded R4 body sherd (14 g).

Posthole 150259 fill 150261

Twenty-two abraded sherds (132 g) were found in this fill including body sherds of R2, R5 and samian ware. Diagnostic sherds were from an R2 narrow-necked jar with neck cordon and upper body groove, a moulded bead and flange bowl of the type made in the kiln and a Central Gaulish samian ware bowl of 2nd century date. The kiln product would give a *terminus post quem* in the late 2nd–early 3rd centuries. A body sherd of R9 (18 g), and of an M1 mortarium base (56 g) were found with a medieval sherd in fill 150260

Ditch 152111

Three R2 sherds (20 g) and a MH2 sherd (20 g) were found in fill 150847 giving a date after AD 130/40.

Kiln

Some 769 sherds (12085 g) of pottery were recovered from the kiln firing chamber and stokehole and these were distributed through the kiln as shown in Tables 78–9.

The lowest fill of the firing chamber 150653 contained 31 badly flaked and fragmented R1 sherds probably all from a single wide-mouthed jar, the rim of which was missing, and two large sherds in R2 from a jar of unknown type. Two further small R2 sherds with a double horizontal groove may come from another wide-mouthed jar. These came from a layer possibly pre-dating the two clay piers. Their fabrics compare to waster vessels from the kiln and they presumably represent pottery made on the site either in an earlier kiln or in this kiln at an earlier phase. Three further sherds were found in layer 150746 and these comprised an R4 scrap and two small, much abraded sherds from an R2 plain rim dish.

The ashy layer 150697 and 150704 contained four body sherds from an R3 jar which bore no signs of misfiring. As this fabric was rare in the kiln, these may be domestic, non-kiln product debris or perhaps a variant of the common kiln fabric. An additional R2 jar base came from 150704.

Ashy layer 150704:

28. R2 wide-mouthed jar with everted rim, rather triangular rim tip. Distorted slightly
29. R2 badly overfired everted rim sherd of medium necked jar. Badly cracked and surfaces largely eroded. There is evidence for a slip or self-slip which has fired dirty white and some rare coarse soft grey inclusions, probably argillaceous. The fabric is hard to determine but it compares best with R2

Lower backfill layer 150702:

30. R2 wide-mouthed jar with curving everted rim and double groves on the shoulder. The rim has an irregular groove and is slightly warped. The surfaces are eroded, context 150702
31. R4 wide-mouthed jar with rather straight neck and rim everted to almost horizontal position. This vessel retains the burnishing on the upper body, defined by a shoulder groove, and inside the rim tip, context 150702
32. R2 very abraded rim of flanged bowl or dish with low bead rim, context 150702
33. R2 two rim sherds of flanged bowl or dish with low bead rim. The flange is wider than No. 32, context 150702
34. R2 wide-mouthed jar with curving everted rim with tapered tip and double shoulder grooves. Warped rim, context 150705
35. R2 two rim sherds of flanged bowl or dish with low bead rim, context 150705
36. R2 large rim and body sherd from wide-mouthed jar with curving everted rim and tapered rim tip. This vessel has many superficial cracks on the inside and further sherds from it were found in contexts 150705 and probably also one of the stokehole fills, contexts 150745, 150706
37. R2 rim and body sherd from wide-mouthed jar with curving everted rim and tapered rim tip. Joins sherds from stokehole fill 150571, context 150706
38. R2 rim and body sherd from wide-mouthed jar with curving everted rim and tapered rim tip, context 150706

Deposits in the stokehole also contained further pottery. Sherds from wide-mouthed jars in the same form as Nos 36–8 were present in layers 150586 (=150808) (one vessel), 150571 (four vessels, one joining No. 36), 150574 (=150571) (two wide-mouthed jars with grooved rim tips in fabrics R2 and R4) and 150814 (= 150571) (one R2 jar, as No. 36)

39. R2 abraded rim sherd of flanged bowl or dish with low bead rim, context 150571
40. R2 large sherd of flanged bowl or dish with low bead rim. Misfired and eroded, context 150571
41. R4 sherd giving profile of shallow plain rim dish, context 150571
42. R2 sherd giving profile of slightly deeper plain rim dish, context 150571

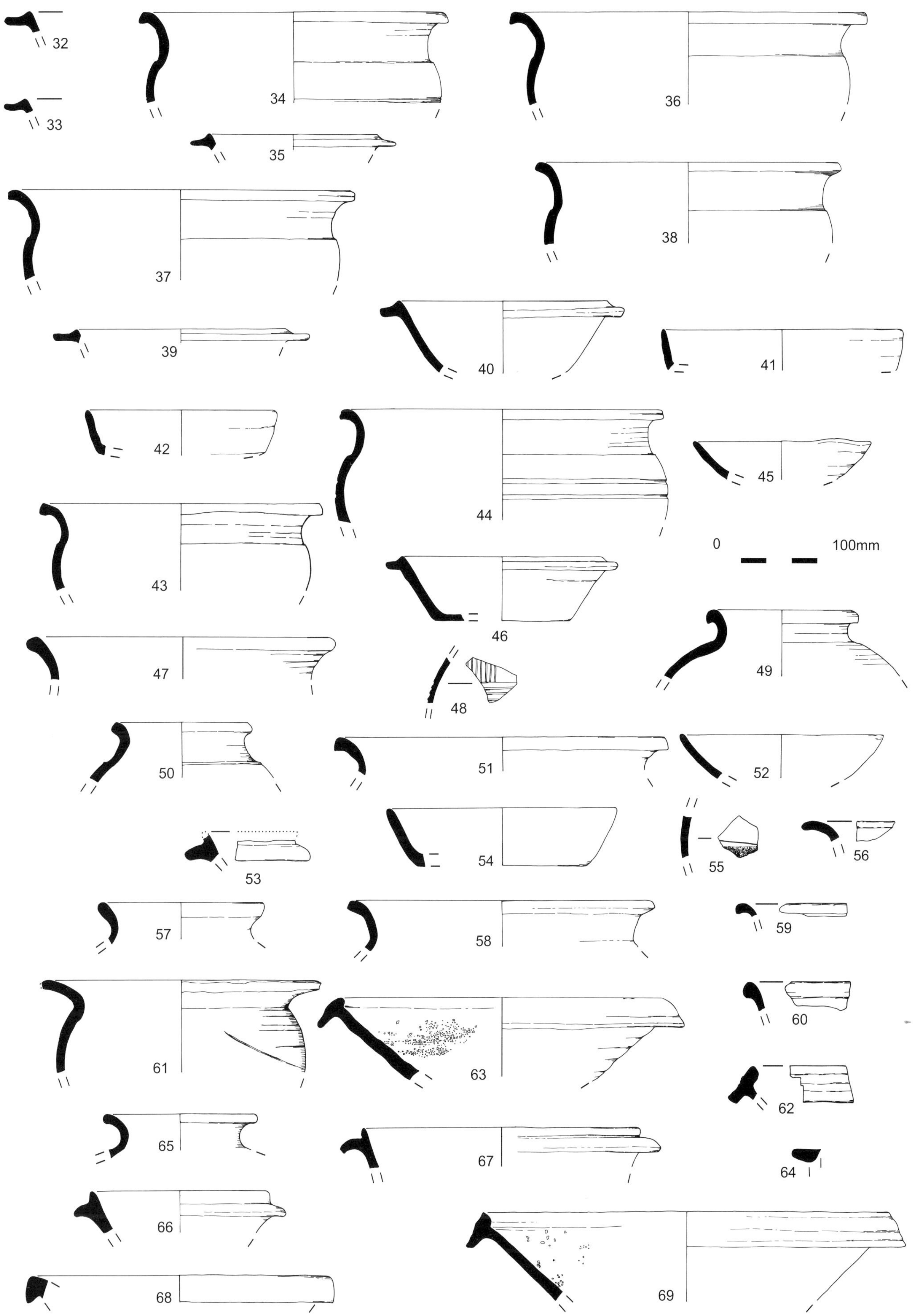

Fig. 125 Romano-British pottery

Table 78 Romano-British pottery: fabrics from the kiln fills by sherd count

Group	No.	BB1	DBY	NV1	PM	R?	R1	R1?	R2	R2?	R3	R3?	R4	R8	R8?	R10
Construction	48	–	–	–	–	–	31	–	7	9	–	–	1	–	–	–
Ashy layer	21	–	–	–	–	–	7	–	9	–	4	–	1	–	–	–
Backfill	534	–	1	–	–	–	66	1	318	1	–	–	144	1	1	1
Upper backfill	166	6	–	1	1	2	2	–	108	1	4	2	39	–	–	–
Total	769	6	1	1	1	2	106	1	442	11	8	2	185	1	1	1

Table 79 Romano-British pottery: fabrics from the kiln fills by sherd weight (g)

Group	Weight	BB1	DBY	NV1	PM	R?	R1	R1?	R2	R2?	R3	R3?	R4	R8	R8?	R10
Construction	722	–	–	–	–	–	437	–	265	18	–	–	2	–	–	–
Ashy layer	307	–	–	–	–	–	15	–	192	–	83	–	17	–	–	–
Backfill	9464	–	17	–	–	–	1224	5	7120	7	–	–	975	13	7	97
Upper backfill	1593	18		2		2	14	–	1139	33	38	8	337	–	–	–
Total	12,085	18	17	2		2	1690	5	8717	58	121	8	1331	13	7	97

Backfill layers

43. R2 abraded wide-mouthed jar with curving everted rim, context 150646
44. R2 wide-mouthed jar with curving everted, bifid rim. Large crack inside neck. Double groove on shoulder, groove on upper body and groove on neck, context 150646
45. R2 plain rim dish or lid. Overfired distorted sherd. The distortion makes it difficult to decide what this vessel is. As presented, it has a diameter of *c* 130 mm but this is likely to be due to severe warping and a dish is more likely, context 150646
46. R2 profile of flanged bowl with low bead rim, contexts 150647, 150648 (=150646)
47. R2 rim of wide-mouthed jar with upright neck and rounded, expanded rim. A form not otherwise found in the kiln, context 150603
48. R8? very hard sherd with row of at least three cordons next to zone of vertical burnished lines. The fabric is more like fabric R8 than R2 in colour, hardness and inclusion size range and abundance. The sherd shows no signs of burning or distortion so may not be a kiln product, context 150609 (=150569)
49. R10 constricted mouthed jar with expanded, curving, everted rim, The body is slightly discoloured, rather pink, presumably in firing. The fabric is similar to R2 but the clay pellets have fired reddish brown and are very distinctive. This may be due to the firing conditions and it may be an R2 fabric, context 150610.
50. R2 constricted neck jar with expanded, curving, everted rim and shoulder cordon. Slightly warped, context 150674

In addition to these vessels, sherds from three wide-mouthed jars came from fill 150745 (two everted rim examples in R2 and one bifurcated everted rim vessel in R4) along with a small everted rim sherd (possibly from a medium necked jar) and one from 150648 (R2).

Upper infill (eg, 150567):

51. R2 rim of wide-mouthed jar with blunt-ended, everted rim, context 150577
52. R4 abraded rim and body sherd of plain rim dish, context 150663
53. R4 abraded rim of bead and flange bowl of the mid 3rd century at the earliest, probably after AD 270 (Holbrook and Bidwell 1991, 98–9), context 150576
54. R2 plain rim dish, context 150664
55. BB1 jar body sherds with obtuse lattice decoration, context 150567
56. BB1 jar rim. The sherds are small but seem to be from a sharply everted rim of late type, probably the same jar as No. 55, context 150567
57. R2 sharply everted rim from constricted mouth jar, context 150567
58. R2 abraded rim from wide-mouthed jar. The vessel has quite a straight neck with a sharply everted rim, context 150567
59. R2 wide-mouthed jar with curving, everted, blunt-ended rim, context 150567

An abraded R2 bodysherd bore traces of rouletted decoration. A small glazed sherd of late medieval type was identified from layer 150666.

The sherds from the kiln predominantly displayed surface erosion or abrasion which varied in its extent. Compared to the material from the settlement some sherds were in fairly poor condition; this is to be expected if the pottery represented waster debris from the kiln cleared into the kiln at the end of its life. Not unexpectedly some fairly large sherds were present and the average sherd weight was just under 19 g. Sherds unequivocally not produced in the kiln are limited to the upper backfill layers, apart from a single sherd of Derbyshire ware from fill 150574 (=150571). As distorted DBY sherds were present on the settlement site, the production of Derbyshire ware jars locally cannot be discounted without fabric analysis.

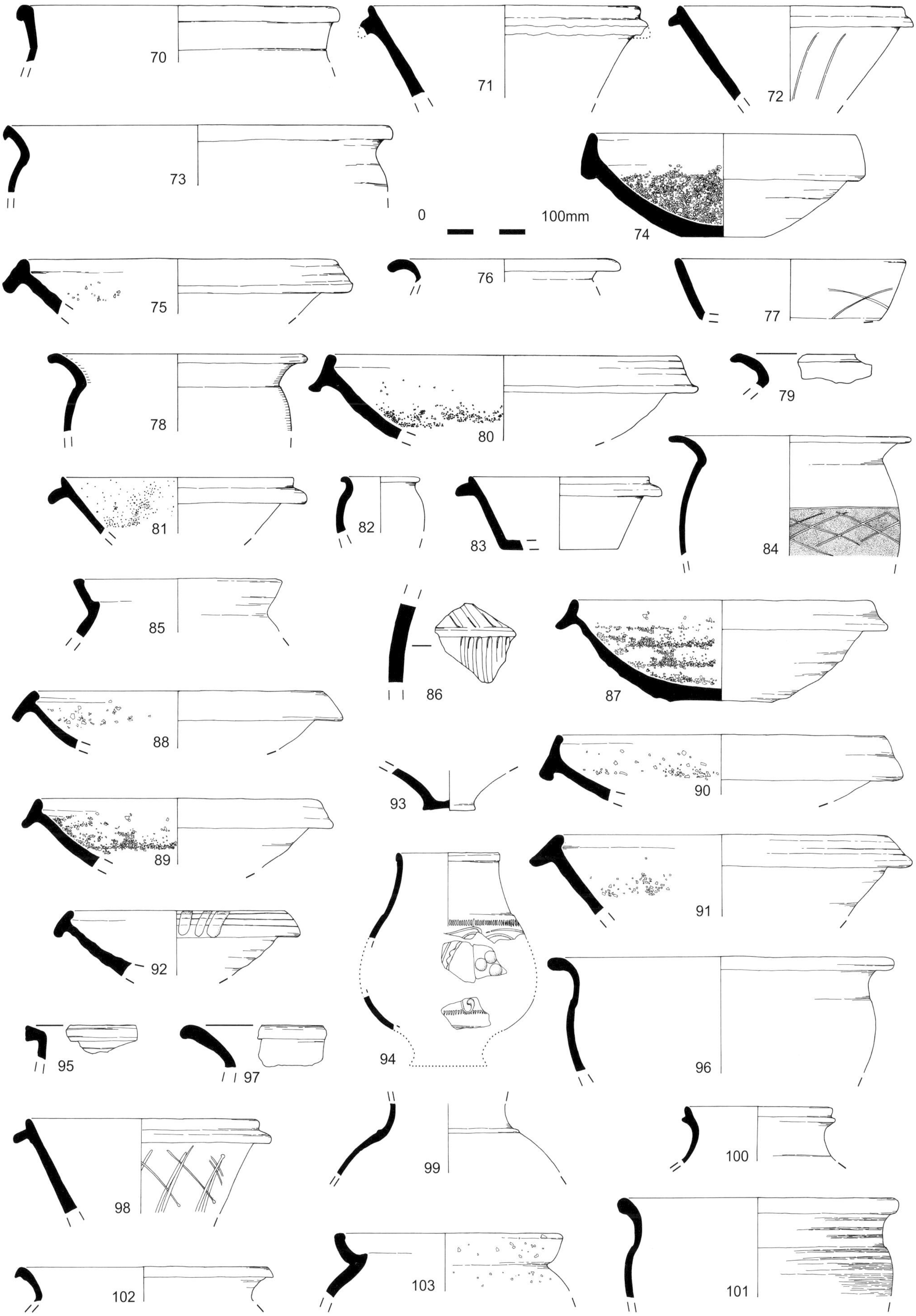

Fig. 126 Romano-British pottery

The range of vessels showing evidence for distortion and misfiring such as surface cracking, warping, overfiring and patchy reduction suggests that wide-mouthed jars, plain-rim dishes and flanged bowls with a distinctive low bead rim which joins the flange in a smooth curve were made in the kiln. An everted rim may indicate the production of medium-necked everted-rim jars and sherds from two constricted neck jars with a sharply everted rim and a curving everted rim (Nos 57–8) may be evidence of on-site production of this category also. The wide-mouthed jars were the most common type and were made in fabrics R2 and R4. Their diameter lay halfway between the medium-necked jar range and the generally wider mouthed jars of the 4th century. This group could be subdivided into at least five sub-groups based on the characteristics of the rim and neck but the forms were very similar. These sub-groups comprised examples with an upright neck and bead rim, curving neck and rim with tapering tip, curving neck with blunt, everted rim, curving neck with bifid, everted rim and curving neck with rim everted to the extent that it lies flat, at right angles to the neck.

Other variants from the settlement deposits were not found in the kiln but were not substantially different in type. Decoration was rare in the kiln and settlement groups, perhaps the result of burial conditions. Some sherds with good preservation indicated that this type was burnished on the shoulder in a zone demarcated by single or double horizontal grooves. Some of the rims were burnished just inside the rim tip. In no instance had the surfaces survived sufficiently to reconstruct the nature of the surface finish on the lower part of the body. Two body sherds, one in R2, the other in R8?, bore decorative motifs, the former vertical notch rouletting and the latter vertical burnished lines. The R8? sherd was not necessarily made in the kiln.

The bowls and dishes were very badly abraded and burnishing survived on only one, an R2 bowl or dish base. The bead and flange bowls were very distinctive and, unlike the usual form, they had a low bead which curved into a flange rather than forming a right angled junction with it. Where the profile survived the plain rim dishes were shallow.

The narrow necked jars survived as rim sherds but the example from 150674 retained a shoulder cordon (No. 50).

The non-local pottery included a sherd of Derbyshire ware, closely comparable to that made at the Belper kilns, Derbyshire (Leary 2003). Derbyshire ware occurs at Wall in mid-2nd century groups in small quantities (Round 1990–1, 68, no. 282) and is common at Rocester from the mid-2nd century and increases in quantity in the late 2nd–early 3rd centuries. A vessel was found in a context at Towcester dated to *c* AD 370 suggesting that Derbyshire ware was still being distributed further south in the late 4th century (Brown and Woodfield 1983, 80). Wall seems to be on the periphery of its core distribution zone and the possible copying of Derbyshire ware at the Mancetter-Hartshill kilns raises the possibility of a different source. The fabric of this sherd is, however, indistinguishable from Derbyshire ware produced in Derbyshire (but see below). The lack of development in the fabric means this sherd cannot be dated more closely. A small sherd of Nene Valley colour-coated ware appeared to come from the wall of an open vessel where some part, perhaps a flange, was about to come off. If this observation is correct a date in the later 3rd–4th centuries would be appropriate. This would agree with the dating of the BB1 jar or jars (Nos 55–6). These compare with the later BB1 jars with splayed rims of the 3rd century (*cf.* Gillam 1976, no. 10) and jars with obtuse lattice are now given a date after *c* AD 223–225 (Bidwell 1985, 174–6). The rim sherds are rather too small and fragmentary to be given anything more precise than a generally later date but the decoration provides a *terminus post quem* in the third decade of the 3rd century.

Sherds in fabrics R1, R2 and R4 were distorted, warped and badly flaked suggesting that these were being produced in the kiln. Several warped, overfired sherds of fabric R8, including a wide-mouthed jar with blunt ended everted rim, similar to examples from the kiln, were found in the fill of Enclosure 1 ditch 158014 suggesting that this fabric was also used in pottery production on the site. Fabric R10 is likely to be a variant of fabrics R2 or R4. No distorted sherds of R3 were found and this fabric was rare. It may be non-local or an unusual variant of R1 or R2.

The vessel types present in the kiln (Table 80) can be compared with products of other kilns in the region and occurring on settlement sites. The wide-mouthed jars have relatively small diameters and many are transitional from the medium- to wide-mouthed jar groups (see also above, Vessel types). The straight necked form No. 47 has some similarities to a vessel from Mancetter (Hemsley 1959, fig. 7 no. 78, from a kiln dated to AD 160–300 and a group dated to the late 2nd–early 3rd centuries) and the more curving rims of Nos 30 and 36–8 might be compared with the profile but not the diameter of one from Perry Barr, Birmingham (Hughes 1959, fig. 3, no 4), dated to the second half of the 2nd century. Rather better comparisons can be made with the Wappenbury group (Stanley and Stanley 1960–1) where some of the wide-mouthed jars have upright necks with expanded rims (*ibid.*, fig. 4, nos 1 and 11) and a flanged bowl from below kiln 1 (*ibid.*, fig. 4, no. 5b) has a low bead similar to the ones from the Shenstone kiln. The Wappenbury kilns were dated to the first half of the 4th century. On the domestic sites, similar wide-mouthed jars to those from the Shenstone kilns can be found at *Tripontium* dated to the late 2nd century and in a group said to be dating into the 3rd century (Cameron and Lucas 1969, fig. 14, nos 114–5 and fig. 10, no. 29 respectively). At Coleshill a wide-mouthed jar with grooved, everted rim similar to No. 44 was found in a context dated after the mid–late 2nd century (Booth 2006, no. 81).

However none of these comparisons is very close and recourse must be made to wider typological sequences and parallels. Non-local material gives a date range in the second half of the 2nd–4th centuries. The wide-mouthed jars are, in several respects, similar to Severn Valley ware wide-mouthed jars dated to the 2nd–3rd century (Webster 1976, nos 21–2). The rim form is typologically distinct from this series but can be better paralleled amongst the jars recovered from Newland Hopfields where it compares with types 1 and 2 dated to the mid–2nd–late 3rd centuries (Evans *et al.* 2000). The relatively upright character of the neck compares better with the earlier Severn Valley examples rather than the later ones and a mid-2nd–3rd century date would cover the more upright necked jars and the rather everted neck jars. Rather better sequences are available at Alcester, where the classic Severn Valley ware

Table 80 Romano-British pottery: forms present in the kiln using rim % values

Vessel type	*Form*	*Total of rim %*	*BB1*	*NV1*	*R1*	*R1?*	*R10*	*R2*	*R2?*	*R3*	*R4*	*R8?*
Bowl	bead & flange	5	–	–	–	–	–	–	–	–	5	–
	bead & moulded flange	78	–	–	–	–	–	70	5	–	3	–
		–	–	⋆	–	–	–	–	–	–	–	–
Bowl/dish	plain rim	3	–	–	–	–	–	3	–	–	–	–
	bead & moulded flange	20	–	–	–	–	–	20	–	–	–	–
Dish	plain rim	21	–	–	–	4	–	10	–	–	7	–
	plain rim	18	–	–	–	–	–	10	–	–	8	–
Dish/lid	plain rim	16	–	–	–	–	–	16	–	–	–	–
Medium-necked jar		–	–	–	⋆	–	–	–	–	⋆	–	⋆
	everted rim	34	–	–	–	–	–	23	–	–	11	–
	late splayed rim	–	⋆	–	–	–	–	–	–	–	–	–
	late splayed rim	5	5	–	–	–	–	–	–	–	–	–
	simple base	–	–	–	–	–	–	⋆	–	–	⋆	–
Medium/wide-necked jar	everted rim	8	–	–	–	–	–	8	–	–	–	–
Narrow-necked jar	everted rim	16	–	–	–	–	–	16	–	–	–	–
	everted rim	28	–	–	–	–	–	28	–	–	–	–
	outcurving rim	15	–	–	–	–	15	–	–	–	–	–
Wide-mouthed jar		17	–	–	–	–	–	–	–	–	17	–
	bifid everted rim	59	–	–	–	–	–	42	–	–	17	–
	everted rim, tapering tip	214	–	–	–	–	–	205	–	–	9	–
	necked, flat everted rim	37	–	–	–	–	–	37	–	–	–	–
	necked, flat everted rim	10	–	–	–	–	–	–	–	–	10	–
	necked, rounded expanded rim	6	–	–	–	–	–	6	–	–	–	–
	everted rim	7	–	–	–	–	–	5	–	2	–	–

⋆ = <0.1%

wide-mouthed jars with outbent necks are common from the late 3rd century. Before this date, wide-mouthed jars with straight and curving but fairly upright necks are present from the mid-2nd century (Ferguson 2001, fig. 129, no. 173; fig. 130, no. 208; fig. 131, nos 219 and 221). In the related sequence of wide-mouthed jars in south Wales a similar group of forms is dated to the 2nd–3rd centuries (Webster 1976; 1993, fig. 134, nos 12.1–3).

The bead and flange rim bowls mixed in with these jars seem to be contemporary with them and are not precisely paralleled locally. As far as national trends are concerned, a date in the mid-3rd century at the earliest, and more probably after AD 270, is preferred for bead and flange bowls (Holbrook and Bidwell 1991, 98–9). At Alcester, however, a close parallel is published from a phase dated AD 240–250/60 (Ferguson 2001, 32, no. 262). The low profile of the bead in these bowls may suggest that this is a variant of the incipient flanged or grooved flange bowl rather than the bead and flange bowl. Certainly the method of manufacture is quite different to that of the latter. This would permit the date range to be stretched back to the late 2nd to mid-/late 3rd centuries (Holbrook and Bidwell 1991, 99; Ferguson 2001, 47, no. B44). This dating would fit the date range of the wide-mouthed jars better and come closer to the archaeomagnetic date for the kiln. A BB1 bowl from Usk serves as an example of a possible prototype in BB1 for the form being made. Webster puts this in a flanged and ridged bowl category and it has a distinct curving sweep from the top of the rim to the tip of the flange similar to the moulded bead and flange bowls from the kiln (Webster 1993, fig. 128, 18.1).

One of the flanged rims from the kiln was of the normal bead and flange type (No. 53). This sherd certainly belongs to the second half of the 3rd century and is made in fabric R4. The sherd came from layers belonging late in the sequence of infilling and it does not necessarily belong to the period of kiln production. Vessels made in R4 include waster sherds from the kiln and this ware does seem to have been made there. However several of the later bead and flange bowls were found elsewhere on the site in this fabric and it is likely that production continued outside the area of the excavation as late as the early 4th century.

The plain rim dish form is current from the mid-2nd century until the 4th century. The forms at Shenstone compare with BB1 prototypes of the late 2nd–early 3rd centuries (Gillam 1976, nos 77–9) although none of the examples had any decoration surviving, so that aspect could not be taken into account. The sequence at Alcester is helpful here, showing very similar dishes appearing in the late 2nd–early 3rd centuries (Ferguson 2001, fig. 132, no. 269) while those in phases dated AD 240–250/60 appear more splayed in form (*ibid.*, fig. 134, nos 372–4).

The narrow-necked jars are long-lived simple forms (*cf.* Webster 1976, nos 1 and 2 in the Severn Valley range) and would not be out of place in the date ranges suggested for the other forms. The body sherds with burnishing (No. 48) and rouletting would tend to favour a date in the 2nd–3rd centuries rather than the 4th.

The kiln group, therefore, poses some dating issues, compounded by the early archaeomagnetic date. A date in the late 2nd century at the earliest is possible, with a late 2nd–early or mid-3rd century date preferred despite the conflict with the archaeomagnetic date. The final infilling includes sherds datable at least to the third decade of the 3rd century and perhaps as late as the late 3rd century. These, however, come from fill 150567 at the top of the feature, which may be considerably later than the main infill and the use of the kiln itself.

Further evidence for pottery production lay in groups found in the ditches and pits of the surrounding settlement. Two distorted sherds of Derbyshire ware were found in Enclosure 3, 158014 and unstratified levels. The former comprised a cracked and distorted jar base and the latter a cupped-rim jar typical of the Derbyshire ware industry. Given the possibility of production of Derbyshire ware at Mancetter-Hartshill, this is important evidence to consider. Buckland has suggested the production of Derbyshire type ware at Rossington Bridge, South Yorkshire in a fabric which can be distinguished from true Derbyshire ware by the presence of red ironstone inclusions and a reddish-brown colour (Buckland *et al.* 2001, 69). The distribution of this fabric is not known, but it has not been found by the author on rural sites around Doncaster and would seem to have been a minor product at Rossington. Links between Mancetter-Hartshill, Derby and the Doncaster industry are known from mortarium stamps (Hartley 1985, 124; 2001, 45–7) and include an example from Derby Little Chester in a form typical of G. Attius Marinus in a heavily overfired fabric similar to Derbyshire ware (Hartley 1985, 125, no. 71). Likewise at Rocester a fabric similar to Derbyshire ware was used for a mortarium stamped by Erucanus and thought to be from Mancetter-Hartshill (Ferguson 1996, 62). These strands of evidence suggest that variants of the hard, pimply fabric so typical of the Derbyshire ware industry may also have been produced in small quantities at other centres with links to Little Chester such as Mancetter-Hartshill and Doncaster. The possibility of production of this ware at Shenstone is increased by the presence of a sherd in the kiln.

Linked to this aspect of the ceramic range produced at Shenstone is a reeded hammerhead mortarium from Enclosure 3, ditch 158014. This vessel was exceptionally hard fired with an even orange-brown colour apart from one distorted grey sherd. The hard firing, coupled with the even coloration and the distorted sherd suggests that this vessel was produced on site. Its form indicates a date in the 3rd century, probably later than the excavated kiln, and is likely to indicate some later activity which included mortarium production.

In addition to the mortaria, an overfired R12 bead and flange bowl of at least late 3rd century date from Enclosure 3, ditch 158014 resembled waster material. This gives reasonable evidence for a potting industry on the site starting in the second half of the 2nd century and continuing into the 3rd century perhaps as late as AD 270 (Holbrook and Bidwell 1991, 98–9).

Enclosure 2 (later Romano-British phase) *Gully 158019 fill 150299*

A group of 43 sherds (294 g) from at least three vessels; one sherd from an R4 wide-mouthed jar, 25 sherds from an R2 wide-mouthed jar with thickened rim and 15 sherds from a BB1 jar(s).

60. R2 rim sherd from wide-mouthed jar with fairly upright neck and thickened rim
61. BB1 much fragmented BB1 jar or jars. The rim sherd is widely splayed (*cf.* Gillam 1976, nos 10–11) and the body sherds include one with a groove above the decoration and one with widely obtuse lattice decoration

The types indicated a date in the late 3rd or early 4th century. Fill 150304 contained a body sherd of BB1 and fill 150316 had two undiagnostic sherds of R2 and R6.

150412 layer of trample overlying cobbled surface 150411

Four body sherds of FLA2 (3 g), R2 (53 g) and SV1 (13 g). Probably mid-2nd century or later.

Table 81 Romano-British pottery from hollow 158018

Section	Context	No.	Weight (g)	Av. weight
	150373	81	496.7	6.13
	150386	1	1.0	1.00
	150387	14	449.2	32.09
150356	150359	48	629.5	13.11
150368	150370	38	432.2	11.37
150389	150388	5	17.0	3.40
Total		182	2025.6	11.13

158018 fill of hollow

The layers in this area seemed to have been deposited intermittently (Table 81).

62. MH reeded hammerhead mortarium with three grooves. Similar to No. 27. Rather grey–buff with paler grey core, possibly a waster. Context 150387
63. MH hammerhead mortarium. Similar to No. 69. Context 150387

Context 150388 also contained a scrap of BB1, a badly distorted DBY sherd and undiagnostic body sherds of R2, R5, R7 and R8. The mortaria give a date in the mid-3rd to mid-4th centuries. Context 150386 contained a scrap of R2.

64. R4 D section curving bar. Context 150373
65. R8 narrow necked jar. Context 150373

Context 150373 also contained scraps of BB1, CT, NV1, O4, O5, R4, sherds from an MH2 mortarium, and a much fragmented base and body of an R2 jar. Also present were footring sherds from a samian vessel and an Oxford red colour-coated vessel giving a date range extending into the late 3rd –4th centuries. A bodysherd in fabric R2 had been worked into a roundel.

Context 150370 included a rim from a late splayed rim BB1 jar (cf Gillam 1976 no. 10, late 3rd century), sherds of CT, DBY, a rim from a DBY cupped rim jar, a handle and body sherds from a Dressel 20 amphora, the base of a MH2 mortarium and sherds of O3, R2, SV3 and samian ware.

Context 150359 contained basal and body sherds from two R2 jars. These types indicate that infilling probably took place from the mid-3rd century, at the earliest, and continued into the 4th century.

Context 150388 contained five sherds (17 g) from a grooved flange rim bowl, *cf.* No. 16. This form is generally dated from the late 2nd to the mid–late 3rd centuries (Holbrook and Bidwell 1991, 98).

Context 150110 contained two sherds (6 g) from a BB1 jar with obtuse lattice, a MH2 hammerhead mortarium rim sherd (55 g), possibly reeded but too abraded to be sure, and three undiagnostic R5 sherds (13.5 g) indicate a date in the second half of the 3rd century

Posthole 150306 fill 150309

Sherds from an R2 wide mouthed jar with everted rim (36 g) similar to those made in the kiln, a scrap of BB1 (1 g) and a CT jar base (10 g), similar to the late shell-tempered wares from Harrold.

Hollow 150300

A sherd (57 g) of MH2 mortarium.

Hollow 150320, fill 150321

One O4 scrap (4 g).

Posthole 155012

Twenty-two sherds (162 g) came from an R8 narrow-necked jar with outcurving rim, a long lived form dating from the 2nd century onwards.

Hollow 150322, fill 150323

One sherd (10 g) of a BB1 grooved flange rim bowl, four sherds from an MH mortarium (9 g) and two sherds from an R2 jar (10 g), all abraded, were found and the BB1 vessel gives a date in the late 2nd–early 3rd centuries (see No. 20).

Posthole 150302 fill 150303

Six R4 jar body sherds (95 g).

Posthole 150333 fill 150336

Four scraps (2 g) of R2 pottery.

Hollow 150957, NE of Enclosure 1

The 37 sherds (413 g) from this feature included sherds from three reeded rim mortaria, one partially burnt, of mid-3rd to mid-4th century type with sherds of BB1, DBY, TS, including a Drag 31 dish, and R2 including a plain rim dish. These suggest a date range in the mid-3rd to mid-4th centuries.

Enclosure 3 ditch 158014

Most of the fills were interpreted as natural silting but two dumps of material including charcoal, brick and tile and pottery fragments were located in contexts in the northern section of the enclosure ditch, in 150819 (section 150821), and fills in sections 150828 and 150837 (Table 82). Only context 150827 in 150828 was considered a primary fill and this contained a sherd of PNK GT dating to the late 3rd–4th centuries. The concentration of debris in the northern area may result from activity centring on features 150037 and 150029 (context 150038 and 150029 respectively, see Nos 112–14) dating to the late 3rd–4th centuries.

Table 82 Romano-British pottery from ditch 158014

Section	Context	No.	Weight (g)	Av. weight
150034	150036	27	456.1	16.89
150078	150080	5	135.3	27.06
150185	150186	1	5.9	5.90
150196	150201	14	238.6	17.04
150538	150537	3	46.8	15.60
150543	150539	22	581.8	26.45
	150540	8	144.6	18.08
150821	150817	23	76.3	3.32
	150818	10	17.4	1.74
	150819	15	89.6	5.97
	150820	4	80.6	20.15
150828	150825	358	4339.8	12.12
	150826	481	7756.9	16.13
	150827	1	109.6	109.60
150837	150835	54	608.5	11.27
	150836	4	175.5	43.88
Total		1030	14,863.3	14.43

150036 fill of 150034

66. BB1 bead and flange bowl
67. BB1 bead and flange bowl
68. PNK GT squared hooked rim storage jar. *Cf.* Booth and Green 1989, fig. 1, no. 2. A fabric and form comparable to types produced near Stowe (Bucks) and distributed more widely in the late 3rd–4th centuries
69. MH2 abraded multi-reeded rim mortarium with at least four grooves. The rim is much abraded. See No. 80. Mid-3rd to mid-4th centuries

Body sherds of Dressel 20 amphora, O4, a BB1 jar, R2, R5, and SV3 were also present and the forms suggest a date in the late 3rd or early 4th century.

150201 fill of 150196

70. R7 wide-mouthed jar with straight neck and expanded rim. A form common in the 2nd–3rd centuries
71. R2/5 developed bead and flange bowl. The high bead suggests a date in the 4th century

An R5 everted jar rim was also present.

150537 fill of 150538

This fill contained sherds from a BB1 bowl or dish, a sherd from an open Nene Valley colour-coated vessel such as a dish or bowl and sherds from an R5 wide-mouthed jar. Nene Valley bowls and dishes tend to date to the late 3rd–4th centuries although the 2nd century samian may belong to an earlier stage in the infilling process.

150539 fill of 150543

72. BB1 profile of bead and flange bowl with burnished intersecting arcading, burnt. *Cf.* Gillam 1976, no. 44, dated mid–late 3rd century; Holbrook and Bidwell 1991. Probably after AD 270

73. SV1 wide-mouthed jar with hooked rim, *cf.* Webster 1976, no. 23, mid-2nd–late 3rd centuries
74. MH2 smooth, hammerhead mortarium

Two BB1 plain-rim dishes, a second BB1 bead and flange bowl, a Derbyshire ware sherd and body sherds of O4, R13 and R2 were also found.

150540 fill of 150543

75. MH2 reeded hammerhead mortarium with at least two very faint grooves. This is not abraded and the grooves must have been very faint originally. Cf. Evans 2002b M101–2, probably 3rd century

Also a burnt sherd from a BB1 plain rim dish, an R4 body sherd and a CT everted rim as No. 106

150186 fill of 150185

A sherd of Derbyshire ware; this ware dates from *c* AD 140 to the mid-4th century.

150817 fill of ditch terminal

Fill 15080 contained sherds of R1 and R5 and a fragment of tile.

150818 fill of ditch terminal 150821

Scraps of shelly wares, R2, O, CTOX and CTA2.

150819 fill of ditch terminal 150821

76. CTOX everted-rim jar. Probably from kilns at Harrold, Bedfordshire

Three sherds of G4 were also present.

150820 fill of terminal 150821

One burnt body sherd of BB1 and an MH2 reeded hammer head mortarium sherd.

150825 fill of 150828

77. BB1 plain rim dish with intersecting arcade burnish, *cf,* Gillam 1976, nos 77 and 79, late 2nd–early 3rd centuries
78. BB1 splayed rim jar, *cf.* Gillam 1976, no. 10, late 3rd century
79. BB1 splayed rim jar, *cf* Gillam 1976 no. 8, mid-3rd century
80. MH2 multi-reeded, hammerhead mortarium, slightly concave with four light grooves. *Cf.* Evans 2002b, M94 dated AD 200–280. Hartley 2002 has indicated that multi-reeded mortaria from Mancetter-Hartshill appear *c* AD 210/20–230 and were the most common type by AD 260–280. The concave profile of the rim rather than a true hammerhead form might suggest a date earlier in this period, perhaps in the mid-3rd century
81. R12 burnt developed bead and flange bowl. Late 3rd–4th centuries
82. R2/3 small jar or beaker with short everted rim
83. R2 bead and flange bowl with fairly low bead, late 3rd–4th centuries

In addition to the illustrated sherds a further two BB1 jars, one with an undiagnostic everted rim and one as No. 79, were identified with some 65 sherds from a BB1 jar(s) with obtuse lattice burnish and an incomplete rim from a bead and flange bowl. Fourteen sherds from the body and base of a CT jar were found with faint rilling. Given the rest of the assemblage these are more likely to belong to the late group of shell-tempered ware jars made at Harrold, Bedfordshire than an earlier group, and rilling is very common in the Harrold repertoire. However, comparison could also be made with an earlier fabric such as Warwickshire C41. Body sherds of Derbyshire ware, Dressel 20 amphora, FLA2 and FLA4, O1, O4, R12, R2, R4, R7, R8 and SV3 were present. Other diagnostic sherds included fragments from cavetto rim jars in R4 and R8, bead and flange bowls in R4 and R7, a wide-mouthed, bifid rim jar in R2 and a wide-mouthed jar with everted rim in R8 as well as a distorted body sherd from a beaker in R8, sherds from a narrow necked jar with grooved upper body in SV3 and three sherds from samian ware bowls and dishes, including one from a form 37. Sherds from two further Mancetter-Hartshill mortaria came from the same vessels as those in fill 150826. The joining sherds in these two layers suggest that this was a single deposit and the forms and fabrics present point to a date in the late 3rd century.

150826 fill of 150828

84. Over 110 sherds from a BB1 jar with splayed rim with obtuse lattice burnish and burnt matter adhering to the neck and upper body. Burnt. *Cf.* Gillam 1976, no. 10, late 3rd century
85. Derbyshire ware cupped-rim jar. A further 15 body and basal sherds of Derbyshire ware were also found from at least two jars
86. G3 storage jar body sherd with zones of lightly grooved oblique lines and vertical lines separated by horizontal grooves. Similar to PNK GT in fabric, apart from colour, and form (*cf.* Booth and Green 1989, fig. 1, no. 1). Late 3rd–4th centuries
87. M reeded rim, hammerhead mortarium with three grooves. Around half of this vessel was present. The fabric is an extremely hard orange with some grey streaks with moderate, well-sorted medium quartz and rare, medium rounded ferrous inclusions. It is pimply like a fine version of Derbyshire ware. The trituration grits are ill-sorted black grits, 1–4 mm with three slightly concentric lines of distribution. The grits sometimes have a bubbled appearance as slag but at other times have the appearance of severely overfired grog. The condition of the vessel suggests it was fired at very high temperatures which may have resulted in the grits sintering. One rim sherd had fired grey throughout and, although not joining, was identical in other respects and thought to be from the same vessel. In form the vessel compares with the products of the Mancetter-Hartshill kilns dated to the 3rd or early 4th century, *cf.* Evans 2002b, no. 98, AD 220–300; Darling 1999, no. 570, AD 230–240
88. MH2 smooth, hammerhead mortarium. Very small, *cf* Booth 1994, no. 25, mid-3rd to mid-4th centuries
89. MH2 hammerhead mortarium with traces of two grooves. *Cf.* Booth 1994, no. 25, mid-3rd to mid-4th centuries
90. MH2 hammerhead mortarium, small and probably originally reeded. Probably 3rd century
91. MH2 reeded, hammerhead mortarium with four grooves. Cf an unpublished mortarium from Derby Little Chester

dated by K Hartley to the 3rd–mid-4th centuries (Hartley archive report no. 126) and *cf.* Evans 2002b, M99, AD 230–320. The flange tip is singed black

92. MH2 reeded hammerhead mortarium with painted brown vertical stripes on flange. As Booth 1994, no. 25 but with very shallow grooves, more like three incised lines. Unabraded

An incomplete rim sherd from a bead and flange mortarium of Mancetter-Hartshill type was also present and compared with types made in the early 2nd century. A spindle whorl made from the body of a BB1 jar came from this context. One surface was burnished all over except around the central perforation where it has been chipped away in manufacture or use.

93. MHAD base of flagon
94. NV2 beaker with white painted scrolls, *cf.* Perrin 1999 no. 173, dated late 3rd–mid-4th centuries
95. R2 squared rim with two grooves on tip. Narrow-necked jar
96. R2 wide-mouthed jar with everted bifid rim, *cf.* Severn Valley ware type, Webster 1976, no. 11, dated 3rd century
97. R2 jar with sharply everted rim.
98. R2 developed bead and flange bowl with lattice burnish. *Cf.* Gillam 1976, no. 46 dated late 3rd–early 4th centuries, although the decoration may suggest an earlier date. Surface abraded or eroded overall inside body
99. R7 body sherd from cordoned narrow-necked jar
100. R8 narrow necked jar with bifid rim
101. R8 wide mouthed jar with everted rim, thickened at tip, slightly distorted. Possible waster

A further eight CT body and basal sherds came from 150826. These lacked the rilling of the jar in 150825 and came from a large jar. The fabric was similar to that of the jar in 150825 and may also be from Harrold, Bedfordshire. Body sherds in fabrics O1, O4, R2, R3, R4, R5, R6, R7, R8 and SV3 were also present. Other sherds were from an R1 wide-mouthed jar, several R2 and R8 everted rims from jars of uncertain form, an R3 bead and flange bowl, an R6 cavetto rim jar, an R8 plain rim dish, the rim of an Oxfordshire red colour-coated dish (Young 1977, C45 *c* AD 240–350 – for dating see Booth *et al.* 1993, 163), and samian ware types forms 18/31 and 36.

The presence of Much Hadham ware, Oxford red colour-coated ware, late BB1 jars and bowls, coarse ware types and the mortaria in 150825 and 150826 indicate a date range in the late 3rd–early 4th centuries. The presence of only one multi-reeded hammerhead mortarium would favour a date in the 3rd century (see Hartley 2002).

150827 primary fill of 150828

A sherd of PNK GT was recovered from the primary silt below the group in 150825 and 150826. This suggests a date in the late 3rd–4th centuries.

150835 fill of 150837

102. SV1 wide-mouthed jar with everted, slightly hooked rim. *Cf.* Webster 1976, no. 25, 2nd–3rd centuries

Sherds of BB1, a CT storage jar, an MH2 mortarium, an O3 wide-mouthed jar, an R11 body sherd, an R2 narrow necked jar, an R4 wide-mouthed everted rim jar, an R8 jar base, five samian sherds and a NV2 beaker were also present.

150836 fill of 150837

Sherds from an R8 wide-mouthed jar with everted rim and a large PNK GT sherd confirm the late 3rd–4th century date suggested for material found elsewhere in the ditch.

Enclosure 4 ditch 158016

A small burnt fine grey ware sherd (8 g) was recovered. This fine grey ware compares well with fabrics current in the late 1st–mid-2nd century, although in the absence of a diagnostic sherd certainty is elusive.

Table 83 Romano-British pottery from ditch 158015

Section	Context	No.	Weight (g)	Av. weight
150822	150824	9	172.5	19.17
150848	150850	78	1222.1	15.67
150895	150896	2	11.6	5.80
Total		89	1406.2	15.80

Ditch 158015, dividing Enclosures 3 and 4

A small group of pottery was recovered from three contexts in this feature (Table 83). 150824 contained a small group of body and base sherds, the high average weight being due to a basal sherd from a jar. The character of the fill suggested the gradual silting up of the secondary fill of this feature. The posthole 150896 contained undiagnostic abraded body sherds while 15850 contained a larger dump of domestic debris at the top of the silted up ditch.

150824 fill of 150822

A spindle whorl in a grey ware fabric, probably R2, was found with sherds from a R3 hooked rim wide-mouthed jar and sherds of BB1, R2, R3 R7 and R8.

150850 fill of 150898

103. Derbyshire ware cupped rim jar
104. R2 wide-mouthed jar with everted rim
105. R2 wide-mouthed jar with everted rim

This group also included sherds from a samian Form 31, two late BB1 jars (Gillam 1976, types 8 and 10), MH2 mortarium body and base sherds, two R4 and R7 wide-mouthed jars as Nos 104 and 105, sherds of Oxfordshire red colour-coated ware bowl and an SV3 sherd. These agree with the late 3rd–early 4th century date established for Enclosure 3 groups dumped in the ditch. Two undiagnostic sherds of R2 and R4 came from fill 150896.

Enclosure 3 features

Posthole 150720 fill 150833

Body sherds of R2 from a wide mouthed jar of uncertain type and another jar of undiagnostic form.

Gully 152121

Thirty-five sherds (454 g) from an R11 jar base and lower body with traces of curvilinear decoration outside the lower body. Also present was a R1 rim (20 g) from a wide-mouthed everted rim jar and an unusual fragment of spout (139 g) from a large bead and flange mortarium with a drab brownish slip. The latter is likely to be of early–mid-2nd century type and belongs to the more variable fabrics of this date from the kilns at Mancetter-Hartshill.

Ditch 158025

A single undiagnostic sherd (3 g) from a NV1 beaker was recovered from this ditch giving a mid–late 2nd century or later date.

Table 84 Romano-British pottery from ditch 158011

Section	Context	No.	Weight (g)	Av. weight
150064	150065	2	18.6	9.30
150066	150067	1	43.4	43.40
150070	150071	4	37.6	9.40
150523	150524	6	138.2	23.03
Total		13	237.8	18.29

Ditch 158011

The small group of pottery from this feature came from natural silting layers (Table 84). The average sherd weight is increased by the presence of a thick PNK GT sherd in 150067 and the multi-reeded mortarium sherd in 150524. These sherds also give a date range in the late 3rd to mid-4th centuries.

106. R2 narrow-necked jar with outcurving rim, context 150071
107. MH2 reeded hammerhead mortarium with spout formed by pushing out rim and four grooves. Mid 3d–mid 4th centuries, context 150524

A large PNK GT sherd came from context 150067, two R5 body sherds from 150065 and two SV1 body sherds from 150071.

Hollow 150533

Fourteen sherds (299 g) were recovered. These included an MH2 mortarium base, a NV1 bowl or dish base, an R13 wide-mouthed jar with hooked rim and body sherds of R1. The mortarium and late shell-tempered wares suggest a date in the late 3rd–4th centuries.

108. CTA2 everted rim jar with blunt end, *cf.* No. 114. Late 3rd–4th centuries, context 150534
109. R4 hooked rim, wide-mouthed jar, context 150534
110. R10 bead rim wide mouthed jar, context 150534
111. MH2 reeded, hammerhead mortarium with five grooves and a true hammerhead form. Probably late 3rd century, not unlike an example from Cramond dated AD 210/20–270 (Hartley 2002, no. 21). See No. 80, context 150825

158027 L-shaped ditch

Four scraps (9 g) of a BB1 plain rim dish of uncertain form were found in context 150560 and 17 sherds (68 g) from a late BB1 jar (Gillam 1976 no. 10, late 3rd century) with eight sherds (96 g) of R2, six sherds (55 g) of R4, one sherd (72 g) from a Dressel 20 amphora and 22 body sherds (77 g) of FLA2 were found in context 150890.

Hollow 150037

Twenty-nine sherds (241 g) were found in 150038 and three (260 g) in 150030. The greater average sherd weight from 150030 was due to the presence of one basal sherd from an R2 jar. The pottery was generally abraded.

112. CC1 necked beaker with everted rim tip. Although the source is uncertain, this general type should date to the late 3rd–4th centuries (*cf.* Perrin 1999, 96; Young 1977, C23)
113. CTA2 everted rim jar. *Cf.* examples at Harrold (Brown 1994). 723
114. CTA2 everted rim jar with blunt tip. *Cf.* examples at Harrold (Brown 1994). 722

CTA2 jars were distributed more widely in the late 3rd–4th centuries and these sherds probably belong to that period,

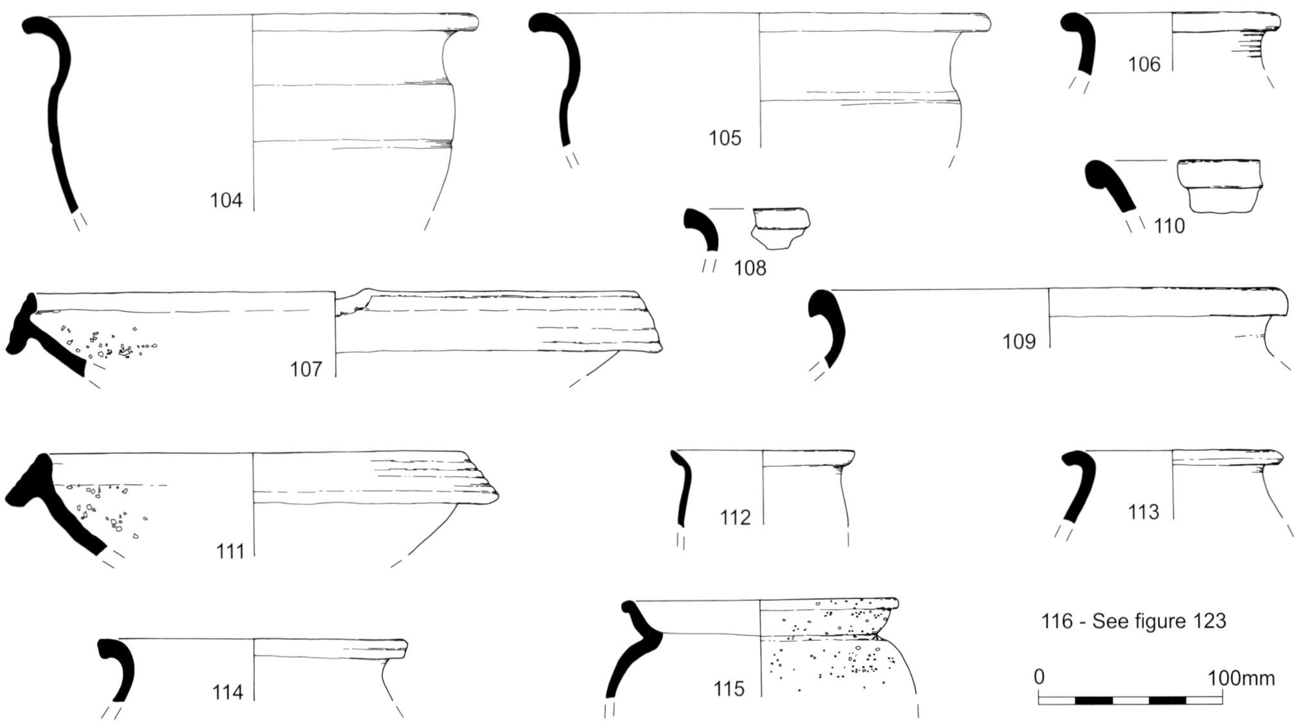

Fig. 127 Romano-British pottery

although it should be noted that similar forms appear at an earlier date (Brown 1994). There were also sherds of BB1, MH2, R3, R4, R8, including an incomplete rim sherd from an abraded MH2 smooth hammerhead mortarium, plus an R7 wide-mouthed jar with everted rim and a Central Gaulish Hadrianic Dr 37 bowl.

Sherds from two further vessels, a NV1 scale beaker and an R2 jar base, came from a possibly related feature 150030, giving a date in the mid–late 3rd century.

Unstratified or later features

115. DBY cupped rim jar with distorted rim and body

116. 55 sherds (434 g, average sherd weight 8 g) from a single P2 scored jar with slightly flaring rounded rim. The jar profile is difficult to reconstruct as the vessel was quite abraded and fragmented into fairly small sherds. It appeared to be bucket rather than barrel shaped. The scoring was quite shallow with *c* 6–7 mm spacing. Oxidised to brown/orange outside and reduced to grey brown inside, context 155000, post-medieval ditch 158009 (Fig. 123)

Spatial analysis, functional groups and site status

Although most of the pottery groups are either accumulations of ceramic debris or deliberate dumps of ceramic debris which has been accumulating nearby, the character of these differs from the normal assemblages from rural domestic sites in having more burnt, cracked, warped and distorted sherds, wasters from the pottery production being carried out on and near the site. Although the features were only sampled and therefore the nature of the distribution of sherds across the site was not fully recovered, some concentrations of both dumped and accumulated deposits of sherds were found in the northern part of Enclosure 3 and the adjacent section in ditch 158001 as well as in pits and hollows such as waterhole 150217. Only seven of the ditches (158001–3, 158006, 158015, 158027 and 152121); along with gully 158019 and hollow 158018, contained assemblages of 30–300 sherds with only the ditch of Enclosure 3 (158014) yielding over 1000 sherds. The ditch 158014 assemblage also had one of the largest average sherd weights (14 g). This evidence suggests that there may have been a focus of domestic activity in this area of the site with further domestic settlement to the north. The total sherd count from ditch 158006 was artificially increased by a redeposited Iron Age vessel fragmented within its fill. Ditches 158007, 158008, 158012, 158013, 158016, 158023, 158025 and 158026 contained fewer than ten sherds each. In addition to the concentration of ceramic debris around and adjacent to Enclosure 3 in ditches 158001, 158002, 158014, 1528027 and 152121, another focus of activity was located in and around gullies 158017 and 158019, including the fill of hollow 158018 within these ditches. This was less marked than around Enclosure 3 but was sufficient to suggest a second focus of domestic activity. Distorted and overfired sherds were found within both these areas of ceramic concentrations. No particular functional bias was found, except for a concentration of

Table 85 Romano-British settlement pottery (excluding kiln group): fabric quantification

Ware group	Fabric	No	Weight (g)	% total count	% total weight
A	DR20	7	762.3	0.28	2.32
B	BB1	441	3849.3	17.67	11.74
C	CT	63	1193.6	2.52	3.62
	CTA2	17	95.3	0.68	0.29
C total		*80*	*1288.9*	*3.20*	*3.91*
DBY	DBY	51	892.1	2.04	2.71
F	CC1	6	15.7	0.24	0.05
	MHAD	3	102.3	0.12	0.31
	NV	41	94.2	1.64	0.29
	ROX	7	58.6	0.28	0.18
F total		*57*	*270.8*	*2.28*	*0.82*
G	G2	2	34.5	0.08	0.11
	G3	1	41.8	0.04	0.13
	G4	3	48.2	0.12	0.15
	PNK GT	8	563.5	0.32	1.71
G total		*14*	*688*	*0.56*	*2.09*
M	LNV	3	207.4	0.12	0.63
	M	3	379.1	0.12	1.15
	MH	30	747.6	1.20	2.27
	MH1	3	286.5	0.12	0.87
	MH2	78	3862.4	3.12	11.73
M total		*117*	*5483*	*4.67*	*16.65*
O	O	9	10.7	0.36	0.03
	O1	33	487.9	1.32	1.48
	O2	4	24.0	0.16	0.07
	O3	8	29.3	0.32	0.09
	O4	32	242.3	1.28	0.74
	O5	2	5.2	0.08	0.02
	O6	1	43.3	0.04	0.13
O total		*89*	*842.7*	*3.57*	*2.57*
P	PRIA	117	1295.9	4.67	3.94
R	GRA	1	7.9	0.04	0.02
	R	3	13.4	0.12	0.04
	R1	42	1034.2	1.68	3.14
	R10	8	67.5	0.32	0.20
	R11	45	661.4	1.80	2.01
	R12	40	481.1	1.60	1.46
	R13	11	293.7	0.44	0.89
	R2	734	7231	29.32	21.96
	R3	19	237.9	0.76	0.72
	R4	73	907.8	2.92	2.76
	R5	83	1192.6	3.33	3.64
	R6	43	140.06	1.72	0.43
	R7	54	1330.8	2.16	4.04
	R8	92	1386.9	3.68	4.21
	R9	45	326.6	1.80	0.99
R total		*1293*	*15312.86*	*51.80*	*46.70*
S	TS	46	571.8	1.84	1.74
SV	SV1	41	672.7	1.64	2.05
	SV3	60	385.5	2.40	1.17
	SV4	31	162.4	1.24	0.49
SV total		*132*	*1220.6*	*5.29*	*3.72*
W	FLA	5	33.9	0.20	0.10
	FLA/NV1	1	0.3	0.04	*
	FLA1	26	110.5	1.04	0.34
	FLA2	17	134.5	0.68	0.41
	FLA4	3	32.8	0.12	0.10
W total		*52*	*312*	*2.08*	*0.95*
Total		2496	32790.26	100%	100%

mortaria in ditch 158014 in fill 150826 (Nos 87–92). Moderate amounts of pottery were also found discarded in hollow 150533 to the east of Enclosure 3, in waterhole 150217 and in posthole 150104.

Thus apart from the 'industrial' group from the kiln and the scatter of wasters across the site, the assemblage had a modest domestic character typical of rural settlement sites in the region (see above) (Table 85).

Comparison with earlier excavation

The nearby site of Shenstone (just west of the present Birmingham Road Nurseries establishment), excavated in the 1930s contrasted with the present assemblage in having far more samian ware; 52 decorated and stamped pieces were published, to which may be added more unpublished plain vessels (Hodgkinson and Chatwin 1944). The pottery was dated to the 2nd–4th centuries and was published by vessel form with little reference to context location. The fabric descriptions are not to current standards, being restricted to colour and overall impression or feel. This renders the group unusable from the point of view of dating the kiln products or for a detailed assessment of the fabrics present, but useful in providing a group characterised by higher status pottery.

The distinctive bead and flange bowl form was not illustrated from Shenstone but some of the jars compare with the kiln products (Hodgkinson and Chatwin 1944, nos 65, 68 and 71, everted and bifid everted rim forms). Several flanged hemispherical bowls in white ware are likely to have come from the Mancetter-Hartshill kilns (*ibid.*, nos 45 and 47) and several of the mortaria bear the names of potters from that industry. Derbyshire ware jars were also present (*ibid.*, no. 73). Two grey tankards are illustrated (*ibid.*, nos 87–8), in both cases with descriptions that might suggest misfirings or burnt condition. From the illustrated pottery, the Shenstone site would appear to have been occupied contemporaneous with the use of Site 15. Some of the descriptions of the pottery suggest the possibility that waster material was present and a crucible sherd together with some lead ingots (*ibid.*, no. 92) indicate that other industrial activities were being carried out there. The quantity of fine ware, particularly samian, indicates a site of higher status and this impression is strengthened by the presence of window

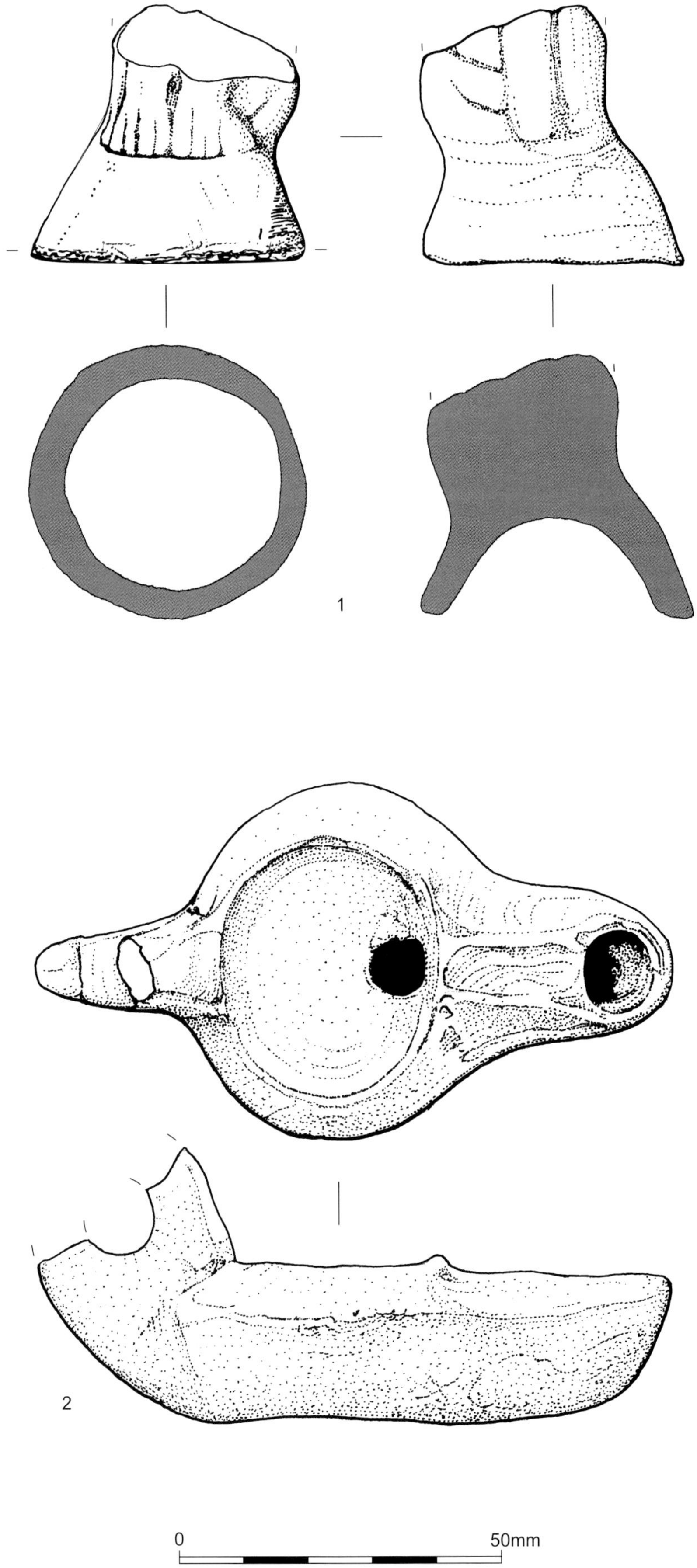

Fig. 128 Fragment of Venus figurine and ceramic lamp

Fig. 129 Fragment of Venus figurine and ceramic lamp

glass, roof and flue tile and *tesserae*. Study of the pottery assemblage from this site would allow an assessment to be made of the quantities of pottery from the Site 15 kiln reaching this settlement. Such work was not possible within the constraints of the present project.

Ceramic small finds, by Paul Booth

Two objects derived from 2nd–3rd century contexts in ditch 158003 adjacent to Enclosure 2.

1. Fragment of a white 'pipeclay' Venus figurine (Figs 128–9). Only the base, the feet and the lowest part of the drapery (visible at the rear) survive. The type is probably of Rouvier-Jeanlin (1972, 47) Type II, one of the commonest imported figurine types (Jenkins 1958), of which about 200 had been reported in Britain by 1993 (van Boeckel 1993, 247). Max base D 44 mm, surviving height 39 mm, context 150155. ON 154007
2. Lamp in sandy reduced ware (probably Shenstone pottery kiln fabric R2) (Figs 128–9). Complete except for top of handle. The simple, undecorated form is that of a Firmalampe of type Loeschke IX b (*cf.* Eckardt 2002, 190, 192), but the lamp is handmade and has no maker's mark. The form is comparable, but not identical, to that of a more fragmentary reduced ware lamp (in a different, but still fairly local fabric) from the temple site at Coleshill (Booth 2006, no. 590 in a context dated late 2nd–early 3rd centuries). Iron concretion obscures any internal sooting indicative of possible use. L: 100 mm, W: 54 mm, context 150367. ON 154012

Ceramic building material, by Cynthia Poole

A total of 389 fragments of ceramic building material weighing 32 kg was recovered from 75 contexts. Of this 38 fragments weighing 7933 g were post-Romano-British brick and roofing tile.

The collection was composed predominantly of *tegulae*, box flue tiles and bricks. No complete tiles of any form survived and the only complete dimension that could be measured was thickness. Quantification of the different forms is shown in Table 86.

Tegula

Tegulae were identified by the presence of the flange and/or an upper or lower cutaway at the corner. They ranged in thickness from 15 mm to 30 mm and were evenly distributed across this range. The largest surviving fragment had a width in excess of 225 mm.

Four flange types were present of which type A was the most common, followed in order of frequency by types D, B and E. Flange sizes ranged in width from 16 mm to 43 mm and in internal height from 34 mm. There was some hint of a preferred size for the Type A flanges, which mainly clustered at 23–26 mm in width. Some of the variations in size can occur along the length of a single flange, so no conclusions can be drawn from the small sample available from this site. A variety of cutaways was recorded. The most common was the lower cutaway type C1 (a triangular wedge cut from the lower angle), sometimes combined with A1 or A3 types. The only variety of upper cutaway identified was type A2, where the whole of the flange was sliced level with the body of the tile. In two cases the surviving flange end had been cut at a diagonal. A few had a distinct finger groove running along the basal angle and one had a groove along the top surface of the flange.

Imbrex

A few pieces were tentatively identified as *imbrex*, but they could equally be the plain sides of box flue. They ranged in thickness from 13 mm to 19 mm.

Box flue

Box flue tiles were identified on the basis of the combing on the surface of tile fragments, without the presence of other diagnostic features in most cases. It could therefore be argued that these were other types of tile or brick with a combed surface. Only two pieces had part of the side surfaces with evidence of vent holes – one rectangular and one triangular. Thicknesses ranged from 18 mm to 30 mm and the outer surface was sometimes slightly convex. It is this characteristic that suggests that the possible *imbrex* fragments may have been misidentified. Nearly all the box flue came from late Romano-British contexts, associated with Enclosure 3 and were all made in fabric S1. Only two fragments in fabric S2 came from a mid-Romano-British phase context (150958), where they occurred in the fill of a small oval oven base. Burning on the tile surfaces indicated that they formed part of the oven structure, possibly being used as supports for a drying floor or for lining the firing chamber.

Brick/flat tile

Approximately half of all Romano-British fragments fell into this category, which lacked any diagnostic characteristics. One fragment, 48 mm thick, could be designated a brick and four other pieces, measuring

Table 86 Quantification of ceramic building material

		Mid-Romano-British		Romano-British		Late Romano-British		Post-medieval		Total	
	Fabric	No.	Wt(g)	No.	Wt(g)	No.	Wt(g)	No.	Wt(g)	No.	Wt(g)
Tegula	S1, S2, S4	9	355	36	3626	31	4781	–	–	76	8762
Box	S2	2	307	1	73	32	3035	–	–	35	3415
Brick	S1	3	1405	–	–	2	330	–	–	5	1735
Imbrex	S1, S2	1	127	1	40	2	117	–	–	4	284
Flat/unid.	S1–4, S7, G1	10	533	30	1327	168	7112	9	518	217	9490
Disc	G1	–	–	–	–	1	35	–	–	1	35
Roof: flat	S3, S6	–	–	–	–	–	–	16	1040	16	1040
PM brick		–	–	–	–	–	–	17	6805	17	6805
PM unid		–	–	–	–	–	–	5	88	5	88
Total		25	2727	68	5066	236	15,410	47	8451	376	31,654

32–35 mm thick, were more likely than not to be from bricks, though other tile forms could not be excluded.

The majority of the flat tile ranged in thickness up to 31 mm, the same size range as for the *tegulae* and box flue tiles. Most of the fragments were similar in character to one or other of these categories and though some of the thinner fragments could have been *imbrex*, it is unlikely in the circumstances that they would represent more than a tiny proportion.

An oval disc made in fabric G1 and measuring *c* 50–55 mm long, *c* 20 mm wide and 28 mm thick had been chipped from a larger flat tile. It had no perforation drilled through it and may have been used as a counter or a weight.

Markings

Combing on the surfaces of the box flue tile was represented in most cases by a single straight band measuring 30–46 mm wide, using a wide coarse toothed comb of 6–9 teeth. The bands of combing were generally parallel or at right angles to any edge present. On one example there was a second band of combing running at a diagonal suggesting a saltire pattern.

A tally mark was partially preserved on the top surface of the flange of a *tegula*. It appeared to take the form to two incised lines forming a X, although only two arms of the cross survived. It is likely to represent the digit 10.

Three signature marks were observed. On the brick was a single finger groove forming a semicircle starting and ending at the brick edge. Two other fragments, one on a probable brick and one on a flat tile, likely to be a *tegula* fragment, had short remnants of curved finger groove, which could be parts of similar signatures.

Discussion

The primary source for the ceramic building material is not immediately apparent. The number of *tegulae* points to its possible use as roofing, but the lack of *imbrices* may imply that the *tegulae* were being used in some other manner. The presence of box flue and brick may indicate the presence of a heating system or hypocaust. *Tegulae* are on occasions used as cavity walling in place of box flues or in the construction of the flue walls for the firing chamber. In the absence of any structure of this sort or appropriate buildings on the site, it is necessary to look elsewhere for the primary source of the building material. A double ditched enclosure a few hundred metres to the west of this site has been suggested as the site of a villa and could be a potential source for the building material. It is clear that the building material found in the excavations was being used in a secondary situation and often finally discarded in yet a third place. The clear association of ceramic and stone building material with the pottery kiln (158022) and of the box tiles with the oven (150958) suggests that some material was being brought in for the construction of this type of structure. The tile may have been used as courses in the walls, to form arches over flues or as floors within such structures. Bricks or tiles are also commonly used as the surfaces of hearths. The heavy ploughing suffered by the site is likely to have destroyed the evidence for many such features.

Worked stone, by Ruth Shaffrey

Site 15 produced the largest assemblage of worked stone from the M6 Toll excavations. The largest artefact category was the rotary quern, of which eight fragments were retained. Six were types of Millstone Grit (Fig. 130), one lava and one was of a non-distinctive sandstone. The varied quern styles represented suggested use throughout the Romano-British period (see Chapter 28).

The most substantial worked stone (150964) was found in the collapsed kiln where six large tooled blocks adjoined to form a slab measuring 815 mm by 670 mm wide by 190 mm (Figs 131–2) and which had been used to roof the flue of the kiln. A number of other tooled pieces from the same context were likely to have been part of the slab although all were weathered. Of the remaining tooled pieces, at least three were definitely not part of the slab; while a number of others could not be assigned either way. The slab appeared to have had several notches on one side, the function of which is

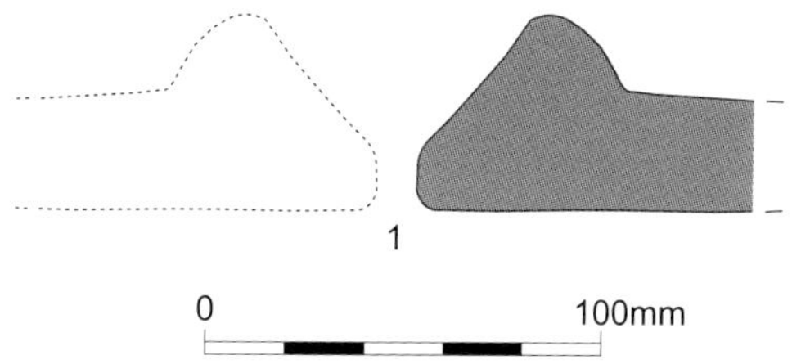

Fig. 130 Fragment of rotary quern

unknown. The original function of the slab is difficult to determine, as it was not clear whether the most damaged end indicated the original length of the slab. If half or less of the length survives, the possibility exists that the slab was originally a sarcophagus lid; width and thickness are certainly in keeping with this (Tufi 1983, 39–42).

Blocks of the same stone were recovered from three other contexts (150069, 150103 and 150956/ON 154019) (Table 87). The blocks were of a relatively uniform lithology – a fine to medium grained, well-sorted and well-rounded pale brown sandstone containing some mica and feldspar. This seemed most likely to be the Keuper Sandstone employed at Site 12 and at nearby Wall (Thorpe 1956, 28) (see Chapter 28, the worked stone). Large pieces of a greyish-blue to buff limestone were used as structural support for the roof of the flue (150801). These were probably taken from the flaggy beds of the Upper Wenlock Limestone at Walsall (Barrow *et al.* 1919, 11), a stone also known to have been used at nearby Wall (Thorpe 1956, 28). There was also a flat piece of stone that appeared to be a floor stone (150137, ditch 158003) and a fragment of roof stone complete with suspension hole was found in the uppermost fill of the Enclosure 3 ditch (150835, section 150837). This suggested that stone was used for roofing, if not on the actual site, then at a nearby structure.

Some 43 fragments of stone building material weighing just over 4 kg, originally recorded by Cynthia Poole, have been incorporated in this report.

Table 87 Worked stone, building blocks (excluding kiln)

Context	*ON*	*Notes*	*Size (mm)*	*Context type*
150069		Large chunk. 3 squared edges, clear traces tooling marks. Broken	180 x 110 x 90	fill of boundary ditch 158011
150103		Large, squarish chunk, no clear function	170 x 150 x 70	only fill posthole 150104
150956	154019	Large flat, squared chunk, not v. smooth on either face but squared edges	240 x 250 x 45	only fill hollow 150957

Catalogue of worked stone

1. Fragment of upper rotary quern. Probable medium grained Millstone Grit. Burnt on one edge. Pecked upper surface and edges. Straight edges and faces which are slightly curved but parallel. Centre missing. Grinding surface has worn so there is a slight lip round the edge suggesting pairing with smaller lower stone. D 390 mm, T 28 mm. Late Romano-British, context 150131, posthole 150127. ON 154009
2. Probable rotary quern fragment. Millstone Grit. Two worked surfaces but no centre or edges. T 55 mm. Late Romano-British, context 150826, ditch 158014 section 150828
3. Fragment of lower stone of rotary quern. Probable Millstone Grit. Straight vertical edges with slightly angled grinding surface and slightly convex under surface. Round cylindrical hole. D 370 mm, T 50 mm max at centre. Late Romano-British, context 150100, porthole 150099. ON 154010
4. Probable rotary quern fragments. Lava. Ten weathered fragments with slight evidence of worked surfaces but very friable. Late Romano-British, context 150827, ditch 158014 section 150828
5. Fragment of upper rotary quern (Fig. 130). Probable Millstone Grit. Small fragment of projecting hopper style quern with pronounced rim around a dished hopper and circular eye. T 44 mm to top of hopper rim. Late Romano-British, context 150201, ditch 158014 section 150196
6. Fragment of lower rotary quern. Millstone Grit. Very smooth upper surface, worked lower. Roughly straight edges leaning out slightly. Very steep profile. D *c* 450 mm, T 68 mm at centre (but not max). Late Romano-British, context 150488, ditch 158006 section 150472
7. Fragment of upper rotary quern. Probably Millstone Grit. Parallel surfaces but reasonably angled and curved. Pecked all over. Straight vertical edges. Large circular eye. Groove down one edge may be part of a handle fitting. D *c* 370 mm, T 37 mm. Late Romano-British, context 150100, posthole 150099. ON 154003
8. Fragment of upper rotary quern. Coarse grained pale brown quartzitic sandstone. Edge is very smooth suggesting reuse. T 75 mm (but not max). Late Romano-British, context 150560, ditch 158027 section 150599
9. Possible floor stone. Fine grained well-sorted pinkish micaceous sandstone, bedded. Two squared edges. L 100 mm, W 100 mm (not square), T 31 mm. Late Romano-British, context 150137, ditch 158003 section 150135
10. Fragments of the same stone type come from Romano-British contexts 150850 (T 30 mm, with two flat surfaces and straight edge at right angles), 150867, ditch 158015 seection 150848 (T 26 mm, with one worn flat surface, ?burnt) and from post-medieval context 150213 (L 75–95 mm, W >110 mm, T 42 mm, burnt)
11. Roof stone. Fine grained well-sorted grey slightly feldspathic sandstone. Edges are not clear but the suspension hole is half there. L 150 mm, W 95 mm, T 14 mm. Late Romano-British, context 150835, ditch 158014 section 150837
12. Twenty-seven fragments (four joining) forming about two-thirds of a diamond shaped or pentagonal roof stone. Nail hole 9 mm by 6 mm is set *c* 60 mm along from the head corner and 10 mm from the edge. L 368 mm, W

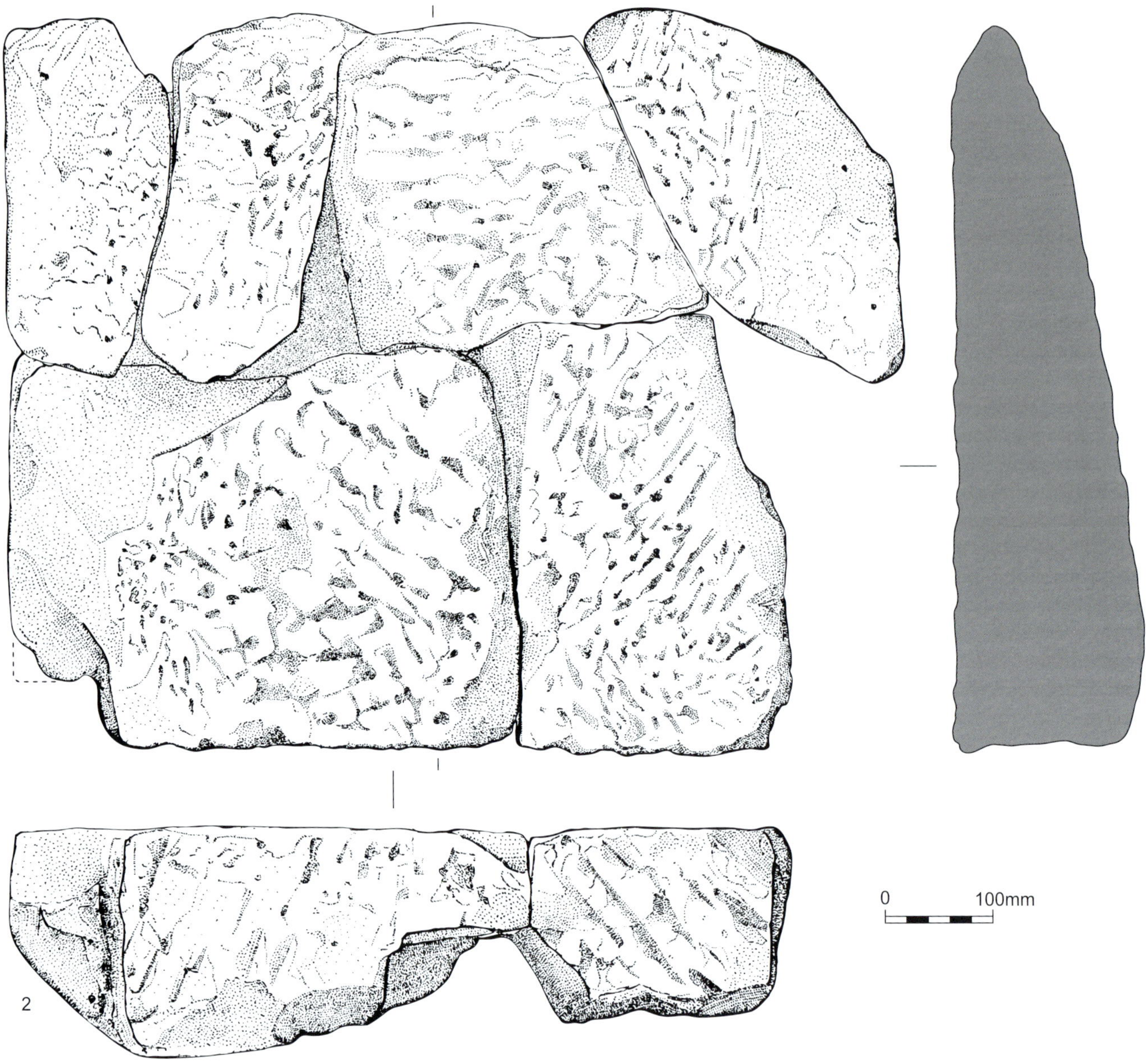

Fig. 131 Worked Keuper Sandstone slab used as roof for kiln flue

>250 mm, T 26 mm. Late Romano-British, context 150537, ditch 158014 section 150538

13. Further fragments of probable or certain roof stones of the same material were recorded from mid-Romano-British contexts 150567 and 150609 and from late Romano-British contexts 150825 and 150826. Like 150537 (above) the latter were all fills of late Romano-British ditch 158014
14. Flue support. Wenlock Limestone. Upright stone (one of four) used to line the kiln flue. L 300 mm, W 160 mm, T 20 mm. Late Romano-British, context 150801, kiln 158022
15. Large slab (Figs 131–2). Keuper Sandstone. In several pieces, of which six can be joined. The slab has been heavily weathered but is crudely tooled all over. In each corner of one long edge there is a notch (one measures 90 mm square; only a small portion of the other survives). These notches do not exist in the opposing corners. There is also a notch on the same side on the under surface. Slab L 815 mm, W 670 mm, T 19 mm thick. Roof of kiln flue. Late Romano-British, context 150964, Kiln 158022

Fig. 132 Worked Keuper Sandstone slab used as roof for kiln flue

Table 88 Charred plant remains from Romano-British ditches

		Feature S linear boundary ditch 158006		Enclosure 3 ditch 158014		
	Section	150187	150432	150543	150821	150828
	Context	150192	150434	150541	150818	150826
	Sample	153014	153060	153062	153096	153095
	Sample size (l)	18	20	20	20	20
	Flot size (ml)	30	36	75	50	90
Taxon	Common name					
Cereals						
Triticum spelta glume base	Spelt	–	–	1	–	1
Triticum cf. *spelta/dicoccum* grain	Hulled wheat	2	–	–	1	–
Triticum cf. *spelta/dicoccum* tail grain	Hulled wheat	–	–	–	–	1
Triticum sp. spikelet forks	Hulled wheat	–	–	–	1	–
Triticum sp. glume bases	Hulled wheat	–	–	–	1	–
Hordeum vulgare hulled grain	Barley	1	–	–	–	–
H. vulgare rachis frag. (6-row)	Barley	2	–	–	–	–
Secale cereale grain	Rye	1	1	–	–	–
Indet. cereal frag.		–	10	5	2	2
Culm internode		2	–	–	–	4
Culm base		–	2	6	–	4
Other crops						
Pisum sativum	Pea	–	1 cotyledon	–	–	–
Linum usitatissimum seed	Flax	–	–	1	–	–
Other species						
Chenopodium album	Fat-hen	1	–	1	1	–
Persicaria maculosa	Redshank	–	–	–	–	1+1f
Fallopia convolvulus	Black bindweed	3	–	–	–	–
Brassica nigra	Black mustard	2	–	–	–	–
Carex flacca	Glaucus sedge	2	–	–	1	–
Bromus sp.	Brome-grass	–	–	–	1	–
Small-fruited Poaceae	Wild grass	–	–	–	1	1

Environmental

Charred plant remains, by A.J. Clapham

One-hundred and twenty-nine samples averaging 20 litres were taken and assessed during the excavation, of which 110 were attributed to the Romano-British period. Thirty-one of these were analysed for charred plant remains from a variety of feature types including, enclosure ditches, semicircular gullies, pits, post holes, kiln/stoke holes and layers/spreads. The charred remains consisted of crop remains as well as weed seeds; there was enough variety in the species present to enable a reconstruction of the economic activity of the area. In general, the crop remains were poorly preserved whilst the weed species were in a better condition of preservation.

The majority of the samples were dominated by charcoal fragments, but only a few of the samples, those from kiln 158022 (sections 150564, 150597 and 150596) could be considered to be rich in plant remains (contexts 150698, 150702 and 150706). The results for each type of feature are presented below and in Tables 88–94.

Enclosure ditches

Five samples were analysed from the ditches, three were taken from Enclosure 3 (158014) and two from linear boundary ditch 158006 (Table 88). Overall, these samples contained very little in the way of plant remains and were dominated by charcoal fragments.

Southern linear boundary ditch 158006

Section 150187

A single sample was analysed from this feature, from middle fill, context 150192. Cereal remains were present and consisted of two grains of a hulled wheat, probably emmer or spelt (*Triticum dicoccum/spelta*) and a grain of hulled barley (*Hordeum vulgare*) which, from the rachis fragment recovered, could be identified as being of the 6-row variety. A single rye grain (*Secale cereale*) was also identified. Weed seeds identified include fat-hen (*Chenopodium album*), black bindweed (*Fallopia convolvulus*), black mustard (*Brassica nigra*) and glaucous sedge type (*Carex flacca*).

These remains suggested that the charred material was dumped into the ditch after an accident. The weed seeds could well have been associated with the crops, with the sedge growing at the edge of the field.

Section 150432

This sample was taken from context 150434 a middle fill of the ditch. This sample was again dominated by charcoal fragments and there were few plant remains present. These included a single rye grain, 10 fragments of indeterminate cereal grains, two culm bases and a cotyledon of pea (*Pisum sativum*). The presence of culm bases suggested that the roots of the cereals were uprooted either at harvest or after and then used as a fuel.

The charred plant remains from the linear boundary ditch 158006 have shown that several species of cereal (wheat, barley and rye) were grown locally. Another crop identified was pea. Culm nodes indicating the presence of straw or threshing waste were also found, it is most likely that this material resulted from the dumping of material that was charred by accident (as in the case of that from context 150192) or after being used as fuel (150434). The domination of charcoal in these samples suggests that the most likely source is fuel from domestic hearths.

Enclosure 3 ditch (158014)

Three samples were analysed from this feature group, and again the samples were dominated by charcoal fragments.

Section 150543

A single analysed sample from a lower fill of the ditch (context 150541) contained very few charred plant remains. A single find of a spelt glume base (*T. spelta*), along with five fragments of indeterminate cereal grains and six culm bases were recovered. A single seed of flax (*Linum usitatissimum*) was also present; the only weed species was a single seed of fat-hen.

Section 150821

Context 150818 was one of the upper fills of the northern terminal. Again this sample was dominated by charcoal fragments. Plant remains included glume wheat along with spikelet forks and glume bases and indeterminate cereal fragments. Other remains included fat-hen, glaucous sedge, brome-grass (*Bromus* sp.) and small-fruited grasses. Again, it is most likely that these remains represented the remains of crop processing which were used as fuel and then dumped into the ditch after use.

Section 150828

Context 150826 was the middle fill of the ditch. The plant remains included a tail grain of a glume wheat which was most likely to be spelt wheat as identified by the presence of glume bases. Fragments of indeterminate cereal grains along with straw nodes and culm bases were also recovered. Other remains recovered included redshank (*Persicaria maculosa*) and small-fruited grasses. It can be suggested that this assemblage represented the remains of crop processing.

From these samples it is possible to say that spelt wheat, 6-row hulled barley, rye, peas and flax were cultivated in the area. The presence of weed seeds and their size being approximate to that of the crops suggests that the remains are of the coarse sievings from crop processing.

Curved gullies

Roundhouse 1, gully 158020

Two samples were analysed from the semi-circular gully 158020 (Table 89).

Section 150275

Context 150274 at the base was yet again dominated by charcoal fragments but other plant remains were present and included two wheat glume bases and a grain of hulled barley. Seven fragments of indeterminate cereal grains were also found along with a culm base. Weed seeds present include a nut of redshank, a vetch seed and a caryopsis of rye-grass (*Lolium* sp.).

Section 150278

Context 150279 contained very little in the way of charred plant remains apart from nine fragments of indeterminate cereal grains and a culm base of onion-couch grass (*Arrhenatherum elatius* var. *bulbosum*).

The plant remains from this feature probably represent the dumping of the remains of domestic hearth.

Gullies 158017 and 158019

Four samples were analysed, two each from features 158017 and 158019 (Table 89).

Gully 158017

Context 150348 (section 150347) was dominated by charcoal fragments and contained few other charred plant remains except for four fragments of indeterminate cereal grain. Context 150365 (section 150364) contained three grains of a glume wheat and three fragments of indeterminate cereal grains. From the lack of remains found in these two samples it could be suggested that they represented a 'background flora'.

Gully 158019

Although context 150293 (the single fill in section 150292) was dominated charcoal fragments, other charred plant remains were recovered. These included spelt wheat glume bases and glume wheat grain, which were most likely to be of spelt wheat as were the spikelet forks and glume bases. Hulled barley grains were also present and were most likely to be of the 6-row variety as indicated by the rachis fragments. A single rachis fragment of rye was also identified. Indeterminate cereal grains and culm bases were also found. A single fragment of hazel nutshell (*Corylus avellana*) and one fat-hen seed were the only non-crop species present.

Context 150299 (section 150298) contained few charred plant remains including spelt glume bases and glume wheat grain. A single find of a 6-row barley rachis fragment along with seven fragments of indeterminate cereal grains and two culm nodes were identified. The only weed species recovered was a fragment of vetch (*Vicia* sp./*Lathyrus* sp.), two fragments of unidentified parenchyma were also present.

The plant remains from these two samples may represent the remains of crop-processing residues which may have been used as a fuel in a domestic hearth. The hazel nutshell fragment may be the remains of nuts gathered from the wild and then eaten, with the nutshells discarded onto the fire.

Table 89 Charred plant remains from Romano-British curved gullies

	Feature	Roundhouse 1 gully 158020		Gully 158017		Gully 158019	
	Section	150275	150278	150347	150364	150292	150298
	Context	150274	150279	150348	150365	150293	150299
	Sample	153019	153020	153033	153036	153022	152024
	Sample size (l)	15	18	20	20	20	20
	Flot size (ml)	20	50	62	20	44	50
Taxon	Common name						
Cereals							
Triticum spelta glume base	Spelt	–	–	–	–	2	1
Triticum cf. *spelta/dicoccum* grain	Hulled wheat	–	–	–	3	1	1
Triticum sp. spikelet fork	Hulled wheat	–	–	–	–	1	–
Triticum sp. glume base	Hulled wheat	2	–	–	–	2	–
Hordeum vulgare hulled grain	Hulled wheat	1	–	–	–	1	–
H. vulgare rachis frag. (6-row)	Barley	–	–	–	–	2	1
Secale cereale rachis frag.	Rye	–	–	–	–	1	–
Indet. cereal frag.		7	9	4	4	2	7
Culm node		–	–	–	–	–	2
Culm base		1	–	–	–	3	–
Other species							
Corylus avellana	Hazel	–	–	–	–	1	–
Chenopodium album	Fat-hen	–	–	–	–	1	–
Persicaria maculosa	Redshank	1	–	–	–	–	–
Vicia sp./Lathyrus sp. cotyledon frag.	Vetch/tare/vetchling/ pea	1	–	–	–	–	1
Lolium sp.	Ryegrass	1		–	–	–	–
Arrhenatherum elatius var. *bulbosum* tuber culm base	False oat-grass	–	1	–	–	–	–
Parenchyma frag.		–	–	–	–	–	2

Waterhole and pit

Four samples were analysed from a waterhole and pit (Table 90). In general, the plant remains were dominated by charcoal fragments although charred plant remains were present in varying quantities.

Waterhole 150217

Two contexts from this waterhole were analysed – context 150220 was an upper fill whilst 150408 is the primary fill. The sample from context 150220 contained few plant remains and included a single grain of hulled barley and fragments of indeterminate cereals. Other remains included a dock nutlet and a tuber of onion-couch grass. Again, context 150408 contained very few charred plant remains and these consisted of indeterminate cereal grain fragments. A fragment of hazel nutshell and seeds of black mustard were the only other finds in this context. The remains from the waterhole are most likely to represent crop processing waste which was used as a fuel with the charcoal and then dumped into the pit.

Pit 150259

Context 150260 was the lower of two fills of the pit, the charred plant remains present included spelt wheat glume bases, fragments of wheat grains (presumably spelt), two rye grains and chaff and a fragment of an oat grain (*Avena* sp.). Non-crop species present in this sample include hazel nutshell fragments, fat-hen, pale persicaria (*Persicaria lapathifolia*), knotgrass (*Polygonum aviculare*), sheep's sorrel, dock (*Rumex* sp.), vetches, clover (*Trifolium* sp.), black nightshade (*Solanum nigrum*), hairy sedge (*Carex hirta*), common sedge and small-fruited grasses.

Context 150261 has been interpreted as a deliberate dump of burnt material over context 152060, mixed with sand from the surrounding area, perhaps in order to fill the pit once it had gone out of use. Apart from the charcoal there was very little in the way of charred plant material. Wheat grains and some chaff were identified along with a sprouted barley grain and some rye chaff in the form of rachis fragments. Weed seeds identified include fat-hen, pale persicaria, sheep's sorrel and glaucous sedge. Fescue caryopses were also identified.

Both appeared to be the remains of dumping of crop-processing waste after is had been used as a fuel.

Postholes

Three contexts were analysed from three postholes (150104, 150306 and 155012) (Table 91).

Posthole 150104

Context 150103 is the main fill of posthole 150104 which cuts a tree hollow. 150103 contained pottery which has been interpreted as being deliberately deposited. The sample was dominated by charcoal fragments, although some charred

Table 90 Charred plant remains from Romano-British waterhole and pit

	Feature	Waterhole 150217		Pit 150259	
	Context	150220	150408	150260	150261
	Sample	153045	153053	152031	153016
	Sample size (l)	20	13	8	10
	Flot size (ml)	70	30	90	70
Taxon	Common name				
Cereals					
Triticum spelta glume base	Spelt	–	–	5	–
Triticum sp. spikelet fork	Hulled wheat	–	–	–	1
Triticum sp. glume base	Hulled wheat	–	–	–	–
Triticum cf. *spelta/dicoccum* grain	Hulled wheat	–	–	4f	1+2f
Hordeum vulgare hulled grain	Barley	1	–	–	–
H. vulgare hulled grain- sprouted	Barley	–	–	–	1
Secale cereale grain	Rye	–	–	2	–
S. cereale rachis frag.	Rye	–	–	3	1
Avena sp. grain	Oat	–	–	1f	–
Indet. cereal frag.		6	29	19	10
Culm node		–	1	3	–
Culm internode		–	–	2	–
Culm base		1	–	3	6
Other species					
Fumaria officinalis	Common fumitory	–	–	1 (modern?)	–
Corylus avellana	Hazel	–	1	1f	–
Chenopodium album	Fat-hen	–	–	1	4
Persicaria lapathifolia	Pale persicaria	–	–	2	1
Polygonum aviculare	Knotgrass	–	–	2	–
Fallopia convolvulus	Black bindweed	–	–	–	–
Rumex acetosella	Sheep's sorrel	–	–	10	2
Rumex sp.	Dock	1	–	1	–
Brassica nigra	Black mustard	–	1	–	–
Vicia sp./*Lathyrus* sp	Vetch/tare/vetchling/pea	–	–	2	–
Trifolium sp.	Clover	–	–	1	–
Solanum nigrum	Black nightshade	–	–	1	–
Carex hirta	Hairy sedge	–	–	9+2f	–
Carex flacca	Glaucus sedge	–	–	–	3+4f
Carex nigra type	Common sedge	–	–	1	–
Festuca sp.		–	–	–	1
Arrhenatherum elatius var. *bulbosum* tuber	False oat-grass	1	–	–	–
Small-fruited Poaceae			–	4	–
Parenchyma		–	1f	–	–

plant remains were present. These included chaff remains of spelt wheat as well as grain of a glume wheat (most likely spelt). The only other cereal remain was that of hulled barley grain. Weed seeds in this sample included sheep's sorrel, wild radish pod segments (*Raphanus raphanistrum*), vetches and common sedge nutlets. From the plant remains present it was difficult to determine if they were deliberately deposited. They most likely represented crop processing residue which had been used as a fuel along with the charcoal and then dumped into the pit. The presence of sheep's sorrel in the sample suggested that sandy, acid soils had been cultivated.

Posthole 150306

Posthole 150306 (secondary fill context 150309) was dominated by charcoal fragments but some charred plant remains were present. These include spelt wheat glume bases, wheat grains along with indeterminate cereal grain fragments and culm bases. The limited number of charred plant remains may represent a 'background flora' but it is possible that the remains represented crop-processing waste that was used as fuel which was then dumped and became redeposited in the posthole.

Posthole 155012

Context 155010 was richer in plant remains than posthole 150306. Although the sample was dominated by charcoal fragments, other plant remains were identified including spelt glume bases along with tail grain of hulled barley and grains of naked barley. Barley chaff (rachis fragments) was found as was chaff of rye. The only other significant inclusion was culm

Table 91 Charred plant remains from Romano-British postholes

	Feature	Posthole 150104	Posthole 150306	Posthole 155012
	Context	150103	150309	155010
	Sample	153011	153028	153115
	Sample size (l)	29	20	10
	Flot size (l)	110	36	50
Taxon	Common name			
Cereals				
Triticum spelta glume base	Spelt	6	3	8
Triticum spelta rachis frag.	Spelt	1	–	–
Triticum sp. glume base	Hulled wheat	–	2	5
Triticum cf *spelta/dicoccum* grain	Hulled wheat	1	–	–
Triticum sp. grain	Wheat	–	2	–
Hordeum vulgare hulled grain	Barley	4	–	–
H. vulgare hulled tail grain	Barley	–	–	1
H. vulgare naked grain	Barley	–	–	1
H. vulgare rachis frag. (6-row)	Barley	–	–	1
Secale cereale rachis frag.	Rye	–	–	1
Indet. cereal frag.		14	4	6
Culm base (non-cereal)		3	2	11
Other species				
Chenopodium album	Fat-hen	–	–	2f
Rumex acetosella	Sheep's sorrel	1	–	–
Raphanus raphanistrum pod	Wild radish	1	–	–
Vicia sp./*Lathyrus* sp.	Vetch/tare/vetchling/pea	2	–	–
Carex nigra type	Common sedge	1	–	–
Parenchyma		2f	–	–

bases. The only weed seeds identified from this context were those of fat-hen. The remains from this posthole again probably represented crop processing waste used as fuel and then dumped redeposited as part of the fill of the posthole.

Postholes 150286, 150127 and 150156 in Roundhouse 1

Context 150288 (Table 92) was the secondary fill of entrance posthole 150286, a part of Roundhouse 1, and contained few charred plant remains. Three grains of hulled barley were the only identifiable cereal remains. Several fragments of oak (*Quercus* sp.) cotyledons, redshank and onion-couch grass tuber were present and may represent a 'background flora'.

The deposits within internal posthole 150127 contained frequent charcoal flecks and Romano-British pot. A sample from context 150130 was found to consist mostly of charcoal fragments. Some charred plant remains were recovered including barley chaff in the form of rachis fragments, along with indeterminate cereal grain fragments, culm nodes and a culm internode. No weed seeds were recovered from this context.

Context 150157 is the fill of internal posthole 150156. This sample was again dominated by charcoal fragments with only a nutlet of black bindweed being found in the sample, possibly representing a 'background flora'.

Kiln 158022

Five samples were analysed from the stoke hole within kiln 158022 (Table 93). All of the contexts analysed were dominated by large amounts of charcoal fragments.

The plant remains in the top fill of the stokehole (context 150567) in the west quadrant consisted of spelt glume bases, wheat, barley, rye and oat grains. Other remains identified include pale persicaria, docks and hairy sedge nutlets.

Context 150571, another fill from the west quadrant of the stokehole, included wheat grains and chaff along with fat-hen, common chickweed (*Stellaria media*), sheep's sorrel, dock, mallow (*Malva* sp.), black medick (*Medicago lupulina*) and glaucous sedge.

Plant remains from context 150698 (=150697) include spelt wheat chaff (rachis fragments), wheat grains, barley grains and rye chaff. Fragments of non-grass stems are common in this context. Weed species identified include fat-hen, common chickweed, dock nutlets and flowers, mallow, clovers, selfheal (*Prunella vulgaris*), woodrush (*Luzula* sp.), common spike-rush (*Eleocharis palustris*), glaucous sedge nutlets, common sedge nutlets (*Carex nigra* type), heath grass (*Danthonia decumbens*) and small-fruited grasses.

Context 150706 and equivalent context 150702 are the richest contexts in terms of plant remains to be analysed from this site. In 150706 cereal and weed remains were common, especially the nutlets and flowers of dock which numbered in the thousands.

Cereal finds from 150706 included a single-grained spikelet of spelt wheat. Spelt wheat chaff (glume bases) were also found, along with other wheat chaff remains such as rachis fragments and spikelet forks, which due to

Table 92 Charred plant remains from postholes of Romano-British roundhouse 1

Taxon	Common name	Posthole 150127	Posthole 150156	Posthole 150286
	Context	*150130*	*150157*	*150288*
	Sample	*153003*	*153012*	*153023*
	Sample size (l)	*7*	*2*	*20*
	Flot size (ml)	*30*	*30*	*10*
Cereals				
Hordeum vulgare hulled grain	Barley	–	–	3
H. vulgare rachis frag. (6-row)	Barley	1	–	–
Indet. cereal frag.		2	–	3
Culm node		2	–	–
Culm internode		1	–	–
Other species				
Fallopia convolvulus	Black bindweed	–	1	–
Quercus sp. cotyledon	Oak	–	–	4f
Persicaria maculosa	Redshank	–	–	1
Arrhenatherum elatius var. *bulbosum* tuber	False oat-grass	–	–	1+1 culm base

their preservation condition could not be identified but were most likely to be of spelt wheat. Barley remains in the form of grain and chaff were also present. Weed seeds that were identified from this context include buttercups (*Ranunculus acris/repens/bulbosus*), fat-hen, blinks (*Montia fontana* ssp. *chondrosperma*), common chickweed, annual knawel (*Scleranthus annuus*), pale persicaria, knotgrass, charlock seeds and pod fragments (*Sinapis arvensis*), ribwort plantain (*Plantago lanceolata*), cornflower (*Centaurea cyanus*), cottongrass (*Eriophorum* sp.), glaucous and common sedge nutlets and small-fruited grasses. The most common finds were those of fat-hen, common chickweed, docks, charlock, glaucous and common sedge, and small-fruited grasses as well as many small non-grass stems which most likely belong to the dock remains.

Context 150702 contained similar types of plant remains to the preceding context but there were several differences. For example there is a greater number of rye rachis fragments. Some of the dock nutlets were better preserved and could be identified as being of either curled or broad-leaved docks (*Rumex crispus/obtusifolius*). Again, small stems, most likely that of dock were present in large numbers.

It is evident from the larger number of plant remains preserved along with the charcoal fragments that they were part of the fuel used to fire the kiln. From the large number and the variety of plant remains found within these contexts it is possible to build a picture of the economic activity of the occupants of the site (this will be discussed later). From the remains present it is possible to say that they originate from crop-processing activities and most likely are from the final sieving stages prior to storage.

Hollows and other layers

Four contexts were analysed from hollows (three from hollow 158018, one from amorphous hollow 150957) and one from a layer of burnt material on the edge of Enclosure 4 ditch 158015 (150897) (Table 94). Overall there were few charred plant remains identified from these contexts.

Hollow 158018

Three contexts were analysed from this hollow. Context 150369 was the primary fill and 150370 the upper fill. Very few charred plant remains were recovered from either and were very similar in composition. Both contained glume wheat and barley grains, whilst 150370 also contained wheat glume bases. Hazel nutshell fragments were present in both and a nutlet of black bindweed was found in the upper fill. The remains most likely represent the dumping of used fuel and a background flora.

Overall, the plant remains from the pits are most likely to represent the dumping of spent fuel as indicated by the high proportion of charcoal in the samples. The cereal remains and the associated weed seeds most likely were the remains of crop processing waste which was used as a fuel.

Context 150387, a middle fill, was a fairly thick layer containing some large rounded and sub-rounded flint gravel. As with other contexts analysed charcoal fragments dominated but cereal remains and other plant remains were recovered. Cereal remains included spelt wheat glume bases along with wheat grains and chaff, barley grains and rye rachis fragments. Other species found included hazel nutshell fragments, fat-hen, vetches, clover and corn mint (*Mentha arvensis*). It is most likely that the remains represent crop processing waste that had been dumped after being used as a fuel.

Hollow 150957

Context 150956 was the fill of an amorphous hollow and although dominated by charcoal fragments, some charred plant remains were present. These included spelt wheat glume bases along with wheat grains and other chaff remains such as spikelet forks. The only other cereal remains present included fragments of indeterminate cereal fragments. Culm bases of onion-couch grass were also identified. These remains most likely represent crop-processing waste which may have been burnt on a domestic hearth and then discarded.

Layer 150897

Spelt glume bases and other wheat chaff was recovered along with straw nodes. Weed seeds recovered include pale persicaria, sheep's sorrel, curled/broad-leaved docks, vetches, clovers, hedge-parsley, cleavers, glaucous sedge nutlets and onion couch grass tubers. It is most likely that these remains represent the dumping of crop-processing waste which was used as a fuel.

Discussion

Economic activity and the environments exploited at this site

Cereals were well represented at the site as both grain and chaff. The dominant cereal was spelt wheat which was represented by glume bases and rachis fragments. Wheat grains were present but due to the poor

Table 93 Charred plant remains from kiln 158022

	Feature	Romano-British kiln 158022				
	Section	150562	150562	150564	150596	150597
	Context	150567	150571	150698	150706	150702
	Sample	153067	153063	153111	153109	153110
	Sample size (l)	17	20	10	5	6
	Flot size (ml)	70	50	30	90	60
Taxon	Common name					
Cereals						
Triticum spelta grain spikelet fork	Spelt	-	-	-	1	-
T. spelta glume base	Spelt	7	-	-	7	15
T. spelta rachis frag.	Spelt	-	-	1	-	1
Triticum sp. spikelet fork	Hulled wheat	-	-	-	1	-
Triticum sp. glume base	Hulled wheat	-	1	-	-	-
Triticum sp. rachis frag.	Wheat	-	-	-	2	-
Triticum sp. basal rachis frag.	Wheat	-	-	-	1	-
Triticum cf. *spelta/dicoccum* grain	Hulled wheat	1	-	3	4	4
Triticum cf. *spelta/dicoccum* tail grain	Hulled wheat	-	1	-	-	-
Hordeum vulgare hulled grain	Barley	2	1	1	4	4
H. vulgare hulled tail grain	Barley	-	-	2	3	1
H. vulgare rachis frag. (6-row)	Barley	-	-	-	7	5
H. vulgare rachis frag. (2-row)	Barley	-	-	-	-	5
Secale cereale grain	Rye	1	-	-	-	6
S. cereale rachis frag.	Rye	-	-	1	1	33
Avena sp. grain	Oat	3	-	-	-	3+2f
Avena sp. awn frag.	Oat	-	-	-	1	1
Indet. cereal frag.	-	13	3	-	5	5
Cereal sprouts	-	-	-	1	-	-
Culm nodes	-	1	-	1 trigonous	-	-
Culm internode	-	-	-	23 (non-poaceae)	-	-
Culm bases	-	5 (non-cereal)	-	3	-	35
Other crops						
Pisum sativum	Field pea	-	-	1	-	-
Other species						
Ranunculus acris/repens/bulbosus	Buttercup	-	-	-	4	-
R. flammula	Lesser spearwort	-	-	-	-	1
Chenopodium album	Fat-hen	-	2	9+4f	47+28f	52+43f
Montia fontana ssp. *chondrosperma*	Blinks	-	-	-	1	4
Stellaria media	Common chickweed	-	1	31	153	275
Scleranthus annuus	Annual knawel	-	-	-	2f	-
Spergula arvensis	Corn spurrey	-	-	-	-	2
Persicaria lapathifolia	Pale persicaria	1	-	1f	3+9f	1
Polygonum aviculare	Knotgrass	-	-	-	2	3
Fallopia convolvulus	Black bindweed	-	-	-	-	1
Rumex acetosella	Sheep's sorrel	-	3	-	1	24
R. crispus/R. obtusifolius type	Curled dock	-	-	-	-	39
Rumex sp.	Dock	5	1	8 + 11flowers	1000s + flowers	-
Rumex sp. unfertilised flower	Dock	-	-	-	-	164
Polygonaceae indet		-	3	-	-	-
Malva sp.	Mallow	-	1	1	1	-
Sinapis arvensis seed	Charlock	-	-	-	78	-
S. arvensis pod frag.	Charlock	-	-	-	2	-
Raphanus raphanistrum pod	Wild radish	-	-	-	-	1+3f+1 seed
Medicago lupulina	Black medick	-	4	-	-	1
Trifolium sp.	Clover	-	-	1	1	2
Conium maculatum	Hemlock	-	-	-	-	3
Prunella vulgaris	Selfheal	-	-	1	-	-
Plantago lanceolata	Ribwort plantain	-	-	-	2	2
Galium aparine	Cleavers	-	-	-	-	3 (small)
Centaurea cyanus	Cornflower	-	-	-	1	1
Luzula sp.	Woodrush	-	-	2	1	-
cf *Eriophorum* sp.	Cottongrass	-	-	-	3	-
Eleocharis palustris	Common spike-rush	-	-	1	1	-
Carex hirta	Hairy sedge	2+1f	-	-	-	69
Carex flacca	Glaucous sedge	-	2	27+6f	145+60f	88+130f
Carex nigra type	Common sedge	-	-	4	20	29

Table 93 continued

	Feature	Romano-British kiln 158022				
	Section	150562	150562	150564	150596	150597
	Context	150567	150571	150698	150706	150702
	Sample	153067	153063	153111	153109	153110
	Sample size (l)	17	20	10	5	6
	Flot size (ml)	70	50	30	90	60
Taxon	*Common name*					
Cyperaceae culm node	Sedges	-	-	-	5	-
Bromus sp.	Brome-grass	-	-	-	3	-
Danthonia decumbens	Heath grass	-	-	1	-	-
Small-fruited Poaceae		1	1	4	52	35
Small stem (non-cereal)		-	-	-	183	335
Small culm node (non-cereal)		-	-	-	48	48
Unknown		-	-	-	1	-

preservation it was not possible to identify them to species – in all probability they were spelt. One interesting find of spelt was that of a single-grained spikelet with the grain still enclosed within the glumes. Most wheat spikelets tend to have two grains enclosed within the glumes, so the occurrence of a single-grained spikelet (in context 150706) is highly unusual. There are several possible explanations for this. It could be that the spikelet is the topmost one of the ear and so one of the last to develop, and therefore harvested before the second grain had a chance to mature; or the cereals were grown under stress conditions such as drought and the second floret in the spikelet was not fertilised or it could be a rare landrace which had spikelets with only one grain. One of the first two scenarios is the most likely. The presence of wheat chaff and tail grains suggests that the cereals were grown locally and that crop processing was taking place in the vicinity. This is also supported by the weed seeds found in the samples. The wheat was most likely grown on the more fertile soils within the area.

Barley was also found as indicated by the presence of hulled grains and chaff, especially rachis fragments. A single grain of naked barley was identified but this may have been present as a weed within the main crop. From the grain alone it is often difficult to tell if it is of the 6-row or 2-row variety but the presence of the rachis fragments has made it possible to identify, in the majority of cases, 6-row barley as the main crop, although some 2-row barley was also present and may have been sown as a mixed crop. Barley is a very tolerant crop and can be found on a variety of soils and in a wide range of conditions.

One other cereal of importance was that of rye. This was present in the form of some grains but in the majority of cases the chaff (rachis fragments) was found, especially from one context (150702) from the stokehole of the kiln (158022). It is well known that rye was part of Roman cereal cultivation on the continent but it is often considered to be an import in the British Isles at this period (see below). The finds of what may be considered a large number of remains at this site may then be of some importance as the presence of rachis fragments does not suggest importation but the local cultivation of the crop.

In general the soils probably utilised in the area for cultivation included both the light poor sandy soils and the heavier wetter clays. It is probable that all these crops were processed locally and the waste products were used to fire the kiln and in domestic hearths.

The only other crops that were identified from this site were peas and flax. Peas would have been grown as part of the staple diet in order to provide protein whilst flax is a dual purpose crop whereby the stems can be processed to produce fibre for textiles and the seeds can be crushed in order to provide oil.

Non-cultivated plants

The non-cultivated species identified can provide information on the types of habitat and soils exploited. The majority of the plants have been traditionally identified as crop weeds and are usually found associated with crops. Their presence along with the crops is usually interpreted as evidence for crop-processing activities and for local cultivation. At this site it is most likely to be true that the crops were grown and processed locally and the waste products were used as fuel to either fire the kiln or for domestic hearths. Some of the species recovered have specific habitat requirements (see below).

Some of the other species may have been gathered from the wild for food as indicated by the presence of the hazelnut shell fragments.

The weed seeds

As mentioned above the majority of the weed seeds are most likely to have been associated with the crop, either growing amongst it, such as black bindweed and cleavers which would have climbed up the stems of the crop, or low-growing, eg common chickweed. This suggests that the crop was harvested low down or even uprooted, as indicated by the numerous culm bases.

Also of interest are the large numbers of dock seeds found in context 150706; these represent either the

Table 94 Plant remains from Romano-British hollows and layer 150897

	Feature	Hollow 158018			Hollow 150957	
	Context	150369	150370	150387	150956	Layer 150897
	Sample	153039	153038	153048	153119	153117
	Sample size (l)	8	20	20	20	8
	Flot size (ml)	33	58	44	100	42
Taxon	Common name					
Cereals						
Triticum spelta glume base	Spelt	–	–	19	4	1
Triticum sp. spikelt fork	Hulled wheat	–	–	3	1	–
Triticum sp. glume base	Hulled wheat	–	1	8	5	–
Triticum sp. basal rachis frag.	Wheat	–	–	–	–	1
Triticum cf. *spelta/dicoccum* grain	Hulled wheat	1	1	3	5	–
Hordeum vulgare hulled grain	Barley	3	4	4	–	–
H. vulgare rachis frag. (6-row)	Barley	–	–	–	–	1
Secale cereale rachis frag.	Rye	–	–	4	–	–
Indet. cereal frag.		2	9	37	12	–
Culm node		–	–	6	–	–
Culm base		–	–	–	–	65
Other species						
Corylus avellana	Hazel	1f	1	2f	–	–
Chenopodium album	Fat-hen	–	–	3	–	–
Persicaria lapathifolia	Pale persicaria	–	–	–	–	2
Fallopia convolvulus	Black bindweed	–	1	–	–	–
Rumex acetosella	Sheep's sorrel	–	–	–	–	10
R. crispus/R. obtusifolius type	Curled dock	–	–	–	–	128
Vicia sp./*Lathyrus* sp.	Vetch/tare/vetchling/pea	–	–	1	–	1+3cot. f
Trifolium sp.	Clover	–	–	2	–	1
Torilis sp.	Hedge parsley	–	–	–	–	1
Mentha arvensis	Corn mint	–	–	2	–	–
Galium aparine	Cleavers	–	–	–	–	1
Carex flacca	Glaucous sedge	–	–	–	–	1+1f
Arrhenatherum elatius var. *bulbosum*	False oat-grass	–	–	–	3 culm bases	1 tuber f
Small-fruited Poaceae		–	–	–	–	1
Parenchyma		–	–	–	1f	–

deliberate clearing of docks from an overgrown patch of land which were then thrown into the kiln fire, or a particularly dock infested crop.

Some of the weeds can be used to indicate soil conditions; for example, the presence of annual knawel and corn spurrey indicate that sandy ground was cultivated, and may well be associated with the rye crop. Sheep's sorrel and heath grass also indicate that the sandy soils were most likely to have been acidic. Wetter soil conditions are indicated by the presence of blinks and pale persicaria, both of which prefer the heavier soils.

Some of the weeds can be found growing in all kinds of grassy places; these include the small-fruited grasses, glaucous sedge, selfheal, ribwort plantain, clover and black medick. Some of this grassland may have been damp as indicated by hairy sedge. It is likely that these species were growing at the edge of the fields and became incorporated with the crop at harvest time.

Other far wetter, if not boggy places are indicated by lesser spearwort, hemlock, possible cottongrass, common spike-rush and common sedge. These may have been located at the extreme edges of the cultivation where the water-table was far higher than that of the surrounding fields, producing boggy ground on which the crop could not grow.

Grain and awn fragments of oats were recovered from the samples. While oats can be present as either a crop or a weed, it is more likely in this instance that the remains represent the weedy species.

General observations on the arable economy during the Romano-British period

The assemblages from this site, along with those from Washbrook Lane (Site 5) and West of Crane Brook Cottages (Site 34) when considered together can provide information on agricultural practices for the region in general during the Romano-British period.

Cereal crops
The dominant cereal identified was wheat (*Triticum* sp.), represented by both grain and chaff. While spelt (*T. spelta*) was dominant there were some chaff remains of emmer (*T. dicoccum*). It is possible that the emmer remains are residual, as the dominant cereal grown in the Midlands and to the south in the Romano-British period was spelt (Greig 1991). However, it might be noted that emmer appears to have been grown in the region alongside spelt during the preceding Iron Age. As such it may be that either small amounts of emmer were still grown or that it survived as a contaminant or 'weed' of the spelt crop. Of interest is the find of a single grain spikelet of spelt wheat from Site 15 that may be evidence of a single-grained variant of the normally two-grained spikelet, or from the top of the spikelet.

Barley (*Hordeum vulgare*) was represented by both grain and chaff, and from the rachis fragments it was possible to distinguish both 2-row and 6-row varieties. The dominant variety was 6-row and it probable that the 2-row variety was growing as a contaminant of the main barley crop. A single grain of a naked variety of barley (*H. vulgare* var. *nudum*) was also found in a Romano-British posthole from Site 15, but is most likely a weed of the main barley crop. A single sprouted barley grain was also recovered from Site 15, but most likely represents spoiled grain rather than evidence for malting.

Rye (*Secale cereale*) was identified from Sites 15 and 34. At the former both grains and chaff were found, whilst at the latter only chaff was recovered. The presence of reasonable quantities of both grains and chaff suggest rye was cultivated locally and not growing as a weed, as suggested by Moffett (1996).

Rye is a crop well suited to the lighter sandy soils which dominate this area, providing a competitive advantage over the more nutrient demanding wheat crops (Robinson 2002a). It is often thought that rye became a dominant crop in the medieval period (Greig 1991), but there is growing evidence that it was cultivated on a wider scale in the Romano-British period.

Rye was part of Roman grain agriculture (Zohary and Hopf 2000) and charred grain has been retrieved from several Roman frontier sites along the Rhine and Danube (Hillman 1978; Behre 1992). Rye has also been recovered from Romano-British sites (Jessen and Helbaek 1944) but these were from Scottish sites and may well represent imports (Dickson and Dickson 2000). Since the early reports, rye has been recorded from other sites, especially on the lighter sandy soils of the Suffolk Brecklands (Murphy 1984). More recently significant finds of rye were made from a Romano-British waterhole at Melford Meadows, Brettenham, near Thetford (Robinson 2002a). Further west, Robinson (1995) had significant finds of rye associated with the sandy soils over the River Severn gravels at the Romano-British site at Ellesmere Road, Shrewsbury. A small number of remains were also identified from the Romano-British shrine at Orton's Pasture, Rocester (Monckton 2000). Moffett (1996) also found rye grains at the nearby New Cemetery site but considered them to be weeds rather than crops in their own right.

It has been hypothesised (Robinson 2002a) that rye did not become a major crop throughout much of England until the Late Saxon or medieval periods but in regions with large infertile free-draining sandy soils, rye may have been grown to a greater extent in the Roman period due its tolerance of poorer soils, as is the case in this area. The findings from this site and Site 34 appear to support this theory.

Non-cereal crops
Other crops identified included vegetables, such as beet (*Beta vulgaris*), most likely to represent leaf beet identified from Washbrook Lane (Site 5) and West of Crane Brook (Site 34), and peas (*Pisum sativum*) from Washbrook Lane. Flax/linseed (*Linum usitatissimum*) can be grown either as a fibre or oil crop depending on the sowing density of the seed. Densely sown fields are used for fibre production and those more widely sown are used for oil production. It is also possible that it was used as a dual crop producing both fibre and oil from the same plant.

The uncultivated species
The uncultivated species can be divided into several categories, although the division of the weed species into habitat type is artificial. Species associated with cultivated and open disturbed and waste ground were the main group represented. Low growing, tall and climbing habits were all present, as indicated by buttercups (*Ranunculus acris/repens/bulbosus*) and chickweed (*Stellaria media*) (low growing), common fumitory (*Fumaria officinalis*), black bindweed (*Fallopia convolvulus*) and cleavers (*Galium aparine*) (climbing) and redshank and pale persicaria (*Persicaria maculosa* and *P. lapathifolium*) and cornflower (*Centaurea cyanus*) (tall). This combination of habits suggests that some of the crops may have been harvested through uprooting.

Within this group of general weeds are four species indicative of acid/sandy soils: annual knawel (*Scleranthus annuus*), corn spurrey (*Spergula arvensis*), sheep's sorrel (*Rumex acetosella*) and heath grass (*Danthonia decumbens*). It is most likely that these species were all associated with crops, and more specifically rye. The majority of the soils in this area are light and sandy and therefore it is not surprising that there were some species present which indicate its cultivation. What is also interesting is that according to Cadbury *et al.* (1971) the modern distribution of heath grass is restricted to the north-west half of Warwickshire with a concentration in the Sutton Coldfield and Solihull areas; this shows that there is some continuity with the past flora of the area.

There were eight species indicative of several types of wetland. The majority of the species were found at Site 15, situated close to the Shenstone and Wall floodplain mires. It is likely that these species were growing within crops or at their edges, suggesting that marginal habitats were exploited for cereal production in the area. Lesser spearwort (*Ranunculus flammula*) and hemlock (*Conium maculatum*) are often associated with water-filled ditches, whilst the cottongrass (*Eriophorum* sp.), common spike-rush (*Eleocharis palustris*) and the sedges (*Carex hirta* and *C. nigra* type) would have grown within the Shenstone and Wall floodplain mires.

Aside from weed species, wild species associated with woodland were represented by three species, oak (*Quercus* sp.), hazel (*Corylus avellana*) and hawthorn (*Crataegus monogyna*). Oak was represented by several cotyledons of acorn, hazel by nutshell fragments and hawthorn by a seed. It is most likely that hazel was gathered from the wild and eaten as a supplement to the cereal diet. It is probable that these species indicate the presence of hedges which bordered the field systems. Hawthorn berries can be eaten and are a source of vitamin C, but they have a very astringent taste and it may be that the finds represent berries still attached to branches when burnt for fuel.

Conclusions

The Romano-British sites from the road corridor provide us with a considerable amount of information concerning the agricultural practices of this previously neglected region. The two principle assemblages, from Sites 15 and 34, indicate that crops were grown locally and in view of the proximity of Watling Street, the major market for the crops is likely to have been Wall (*Letocetum*). The evidence suggests that the crops were processed on site, and especially at Site 15 where crop-processing waste was probably used as fuel in the pottery kiln. At Site 34 the aisled building may have been used for the storage of crops prior to processing, or even the processing of crops after harvest.

The cereals grown in this area are the standard Roman cereals, spelt wheat and barley (Greig 1991), but the presence of rye is notable. The identification of rye expands our understanding of the range of crops exploited, for example in Romano-British Warwickshire (Booth 1996b). Its cultivation is consistent with the widespread presence of lighter, sandy, nutrient-poor soils, and some of the weed flora provides evidence of the exploitation of these as well as other marginal soils such as floodplain mires near Wall and Shenstone.

The evidence from Warwickshire (particularly the Avon valley) suggests that the environment was deforested, with open grassland with possible hedges (Bowker 1983; Booth 1996b). This also seems to hold true for at least some of the M6 Toll sites in south Staffordshire. Pollen evidence from Site 12 indicated an open landscape with some cereal production before the Romano-British period, and this impression is definitely supported for this period by the charred plant remains. With increasing evidence for rye cultivation in other areas of light sandy soils, it can no longer be suggested that it was a minor cereal or a weed of the major cereals, but a major crop in its own right (Murphy 1983a; 1984; Robinson 1995; 2002a). Apart from cereals there is evidence for other crops being cultivated in the area, these include beet, peas and flax.

Charcoal, by Rowena Gale

Bulk soil samples were collected from 110 Romano-British and nine undated contexts, from which 30 samples of charcoal (including one handpicked sample) from deposits of fuel debris were selected to represent various aspects of the social and economic life of the settlement, including domestic and industrial use, and the supply and management of woodland resources. Despite the frequent abundance of charcoal, it was mostly very degraded and often contaminated throughout with silty deposits. Charred plant remains were examined from the same suite of samples. The taxa identified are presented in Table 95.

Ditches

Samples from the second and third fills of sections 150169 and 150187, at the south-west end of the southern linear boundary ditch 158006, were located close to Enclosure 3. The charcoal included oak (*Quercus* sp.) heartwood, alder (*Alnus glutinosa*), birch (*Betula* sp.), hazel (*Corylus avellana*), ash (*Fraxinus excelsior*) and willow (*Salix* sp.)/poplar (*Populus* sp.). The character of these deposits suggests origins from domestic hearths.

Samples from the middle fills of sections 150821 and 151828 of Enclosure 3 ditch 158014 were also likely to represent domestic waste (as suggested by the remains of pottery and charred grain), although the inclusion of daub in the latter context could implicate burnt wattle. A 25% sub-sample was examined from the sample of context 150818 and identified as oak heartwood and roundwood, birch, hazel, the hawthorn/*Sorbus* group (Pomoideae) and gorse (*Ulex* sp.) or broom (*Cytisus scoparius*). The handpicked sample from context 150826 included four pieces of fast-grown oak roundwood measuring 10–15 mm in diameter, with four growth rings; one piece was bifurcated.

Curved gullies

Charcoal was examined from Roundhouse 1 gully 158020 (Enclosure 1), and curved gullies 158017 and 158019 (Enclosure 2). The charcoal from all three features almost certainly represented the dumped or accumulated remains of domestic hearth debris; charred grain was also present. There was a strong similarity in the overall character of the charcoal, which indicated the predominant use of narrow roundwood, although it was too degraded to assess the age and growth rates of the stems. The fuel consisted mainly of oak but with sporadic use of other species including birch, hazel, the hawthorn/*Sorbus* group, willow/poplar and gorse and/or broom.

Waterhole, hollows, pits and postholes

Pits associated with the settlement Enclosures 1 and 2 contained domestic refuse (charred grain, pulses, bone and pottery) and large deposits of fuel debris. The charcoal from waterhole 150217 (Enclosure 1), Roundhouse 1 entrance posthole 150286 and other postholes 150104, 150259, and hollow 158018

Table 95 Charcoal (no. frags)

Feature	*Section*	*Context*	*Sample*	*Alnus*	*Betula*	*Corylus*	*Ericaceae*	*Fraxinus*	*Ilex*	*Pomoideae*	*Prunus*	*Quercus*	*Salicaceae*	*Tilia*	*Ulex/Cytisus*
Ditches and gullies															
Southern linear boundary ditch															
158006	150169	150173	153013	8	-	-	-	-	-	-	-	18h, 4s	-	-	-
	150187	150192	153014	-	6	4	-	3	-	-	-	1h, 1s	1	-	-
Enclosure 3 Ditch															
158014	150821	150818	153096	-	4	1	-	-	-	3	-	24r,14s, 19u	-	-	1
	150828	150826	153123	-	-	-	-	-	-	-	-	3r	-	-	-
Curved gullies															
Enclosure 1															
158020	150275	150274	153019	-	-	-	-	-	-	-	-	3r, 1s, 6u	2	-	-
	150278	150279	153020	-	3	-	-	-	-	-	-	10h, 1r, 1s	-	-	1
Enclosure 2															
158019	150292	150293	153022	-	1	-	-	-	-	-	-	10r, 15u	-	-	2r
	150298	150299	153024	-	-	1	-	-	-	-	-	9r, 2s, 16u	*cf.* 1	-	-
158017	150347	150348	153033	-	-	*cf.*1r	-	-	-	4r	-	1r, 2s, 3u	-	-	1
	150364	150365	153036	-	-	-	-	-	-	2r	-	5r, 3s, 1u	-	-	1r
Waterhole, hollows, pits and postholes															
Enclosure 1															
Waterhole		150220	153045	-	6	2	-	1	-	-	1	24h/u, 17r	4	*cf.*1r	-
150217		150408	153053	3	*cf.*2	-	-	-	-	1	-	31r	3	-	-
North of Enclosure 1															
Hollow150957		150956	153119	-	-	4	-	-	-	-	-	19r, 3s	-	-	-
Enclosure 2 features															
Posthole 150104		150103	153011	-	2	2	-	-	-	-	-	10h, 22r, 2s	-	-	-
Pit 150259		150261	153016	-	2	-	-	-	-	10r	-	5h, 52r	-	-	4r
		150260	153031	-	-	-	-	-	-	3r	-	40r	-	-	11r
Hollow	150368	150370	153038	-	2	-	-	-	-	2	3	11h/u,5r,3s	-	-	-
158018		150369	153039	-	1	1	-	-	-	-	1	21h/u,4r, 6s	-	-	2
Roundhouse 1 postholes															
150127		150130	153003	-	13	-	-	-	-	-	1	5h/u, 1r	-	-	*cf.*1
150156		150157	153012	-	-	1	-	-	2	8	-	19h/u,4r, 12s	-	-	-
150286		150288	153023	-	*cf.*1	-	-	-	-	-	-	21h/u, 3r,2s	-	-	-
Other postholes															
150306		150309	153028	-	*cf.*1	-	-	-	-	-	-	21h/u,10r, 4s	-	-	-
155012		155010	153115	-	1	2	-	-	-	2	-	7h, 30r	-	-	-
Kiln stokeholes															
158022	150562	150571	153063	-	*cf.* 1	-	22r	2r	-	-	-	13r, 1s	-	-	85r
		150567	153067	-	1	1	-	-	-	7	-	10h/u,1s,3r	-	-	7
	150596	150706	153109	-	-	-	19r	-	-	-	-	11r	-	-	21r
	150597	150702	153110	-	-	-	18r	-	-	-	-	18r	-	-	17r
	150564	150698	153111	-	-	-	15r	-	-	-	-	11r	-	-	74r
Layer/spread															
		150387	153048	-	-	-	-	1	-	1r	-	23r	*cf.*1	-	-
		150897	153117	-	-	-	-	2r	-	-	19r	3h, 19r	-	-	-

Key: h = heartwood; r = roundwood (diam. <20 mm); s = sapwood (diam. unknown); U = maturity unknown (*quercus* only)

(Enclosure 2) closely resembled deposits from the curved gullies and indicated the predominant use of narrow roundwood from oak, interspersed with other species including alder (*Alnus glutinosa*), birch, hazel, ash (*Fraxinus excelsior*), the hawthorn/*Sorbus* group, blackthorn (*Prunus spinosa*), willow or poplar, gorse and/or broom and possibly lime (*Tilia* sp.). The preservation of this material was very poor and it was rarely possible to assess the age or growth rates of the stems, although fragments of fast-grown oak roundwood from context 150370, a fill of hollow 158018, included four growth rings. Twiggy material was also present in some contexts.

The irregular-shaped hollow 150957 (north of Enclosure 1) included oak roundwood and hazel.

Roundhouse 1 internal postholes

Large deposits of charcoal were associated with postholes 150127 and 150156. A 50% sub-sample was examined from sample 153003, from the top spit, context 150130, but proved to be mostly too degraded for identification. The taxa named included oak, blackthorn, birch and probably gorse or broom. The charcoal-rich fill 150157 of posthole 150156 was also 50% sub-sampled and identified as mostly oak heartwood and roundwood but also hazel, holly (*Ilex aquifolium*) and the hawthorn/*Sorbus* group. Charred grain was absent from both these features.

Other postholes

Charcoal from the fills of postholes 150306 and 155012 (Enclosure 1) clearly represented the remains of fuel debris. The taxa named include oak heartwood and roundwood, birch, hazel, willow or poplar, the hawthorn/*Sorbus* group, blackthorn, holly and possibly gorseor broom. Oak heartwood in posthole 155012 derived from largewood, some of which was fast-grown. Large amounts of charred grain were also present.

Kiln 158022

A well preserved pottery kiln was sited mid-way between Enclosures 2 and 3. Large amounts of fuel debris (charcoal) remained *in situ* in the basal levels of the oven and flue (contexts 150571, 150698 (=150697), 150702 and 150706. Charcoal from these contexts demonstrated the selective use of narrow roundwood and twiggy material from gorse/broom, heather (Ericaceae) and oak. Context 150567, the uppermost fill, included rather comminuted fragments, mostly from narrow roundwood but from a wider range of species and with less emphasis on gorse and heather (the latter was not apparently used) than in the other four samples. This would suggest that material in this context originated from a different event. The large quantities of charred grain, chaff and pulses recorded in all contexts may have been used as tinder or possibly to exploit the silica-rich properties of the cereal.

Layers/spreads

Context 150897 comprised a spread of charcoal near the north-west corner of Enclosure 3; probably from a domestic hearth; it consisted mainly of narrow roundwood from oak, ash and blackthorn.

The sample from layer/spread 150387 in hollow 158018, was similar in character to domestic hearth debris recorded from the nearby curved gullies and pits (see above). The large deposit of charcoal was 50% sub-sampled and identified as mostly narrow roundwood from oak but also the hawthorn/*Sorbus* group, ash and willow/poplar.

Discussion

Charcoal deposits (fuel debris) occurred in features throughout the site and provided the opportunity to compare the selection of fuel for different activities, for example, domestic cooking and heating and industrial use (pottery firing). Since fuel supplies would have been obtained from local sources, the current analysis also provides evidence of woodland composition and management.

Many of the 119 bulk soil samples were charcoal-rich but, unfortunately, most of this material was poorly preserved and degraded, and, in addition, silty sediments had seeped through the cellular structure, making it difficult to identify and to examine growth patterns and maturity. With the exception of the two internal postholes 150127 and 150156 (Round-house 1) and 150286, charred plant remains, including cereal grain and other foodstuffs, were frequent in contexts from which charcoal was examined.

Domestic fuel

Residues from domestic hearths were dumped with other domestic waste in enclosure ditches, curved gullies and pits. Deposits were particularly frequent in features associated with the middle Romano-British Enclosures 1 and 2. Charcoal was examined from the southern linear boundary 158006, ditch 150014 (Enclosure 3), curved gullies 158020 (Enclosure 1), 158017 and 158019 (Enclosure 2) and hollow 150957 (north of Enclosure 1), waterhole 150217 (Enclosure 1), postholes 150104, 150158, 150268, pit 150259 and hollow 158018 (Enclosure 2), postholes 150306 and 155012 (Enclosure 1) and internal postholes 150127 and 150156 within Roundhouse 1. These deposits indicated the consistent use of firewood composed of narrow roundwood, pre-dominantly oak but also incorporating a range of other species including gorse and/or broom, hazel, the hawthorn group, willow/poplar, blackthorn, alder, ash, birch and possibly lime. The narrow dimensions of the roundwood suggest the use of young stems, but owing to the poor condition of the charcoal it was not possible to assess the age range. A few fragments from hollow 158018 and ditch context 150826 (Enclosure 3) included fast-grown 4 year old oak stems. Roundwood from context 150826 is also likely to have originated from fuel debris, although the inclusion of daub material in this context could implicate the burnt remains of wattle.

Although the origin of charcoal in the burnt spreads/layers 150387 and 150897 is uncertain, the greater similarity of this material to domestic fuel debris than to industrial waste (see below) suggests domestic hearth debris as the more likely source.

Industrial fuel

The pottery kiln 158022 was probably in use from the late 2nd century onwards, producing sand-tempered coarse wares. Charcoal was examined from four basal deposits: contexts 150567, 150571, 150698, 150706 and 150702 and upper fill 150567. With the exception of context 150567, these deposits differed from those from domestic contexts and indicated the specific selection of gorse/broom, heather and oak, used as narrow roundwood and twiggy material. Heather and gorse have traditionally been used to fire ovens and kilns (gorse burns particularly fiercely) (Mabey 1996, 159; 231). As the springy stems of heather could also have provided packing material to support pots in the kiln chamber and for the fired ceramics, heather may have played a dual role at the kiln. In addition, the evergreen fronds of heather are easy to ignite and would have provided efficient kindling. The importance of heather in the firing process is underlined by its absence in other contexts. Charred cereal grain and chaff were also frequent in these deposits (Clapham, above), possibly as residues from tinder or kindling.

Environmental evidence

It is probable that by the Romano-British period the landscape was fairly open perhaps interspersed with areas of sparse oak woodland (possibly with hazel and holly as understorey) and heathland (birch, gorse and heather). Marginal woodland species included blackthorn, the hawthorn/Sorbus group and hazel. The presence of alder and willow are indicative of damp or waterlogged soils. Lime was provisionally named in a single context and, if present at the site, was probably rare.

Although it was difficult to obtain direct evidence of woodland management (owing to the degraded structure of the samples), the high incidence of narrow roundwood (<20 mm in diameter) and twiggy material provides convincing circumstantial evidence that most of the fuel used on site was obtained from a managed coppiced woodland. This suggestion is further supported by several pieces of 4 year old oak stem (from Enclosure 2, ditch 158014, context 150826 and 158018, context 150370) that included the fast growth often indicative of coppice. Although this can not be taken as conclusive evidence that oak coppice was grown on a four year rotation (the stems could have developed several seasons after the stool was initially cropped), the overall impression is that some areas of oak coppice were grown on a short cycle. Oak grown on longer cycles (to produce poles or timber) perhaps gave rise to the fast-grown largewood in the sample from posthole 155012. It is probable that most of the arboreal species in this neighbourhood were managed to some degree.

Most of the charcoal examined originated from domestic hearths and demonstrated that firewood consisted mainly of narrow oak stems, supplemented with roundwood from other species. In contrast, industrial fuel residues collected from the pottery kiln indicated the specific selection of roundwood from gorse/broom, heather and oak. This combination would have produced a particularly intense heat-source.

Discussion

The site produced limited evidence of Mesolithic, Neolithic and Iron Age activity, largely consistent with the more substantial evidence of these periods from Shenstone Linear Features (Site 13) and Shenstone Ring Ditch (Site 14), to the north and north-west, respectively.

Most of the features on the site, however, dated to the Romano-British period, when the site was the location of a rural settlement established during the middle part of the 2nd century and continuing into the late 3rd/early 4th centuries. The start date is interesting in itself as it may coincide with a regional phenomenon of dislocation of settlement patterns recognised in Warwickshire and the Upper Thames Valley (Booth 2002, 7; Henig and Booth 2000, 106–10). Usually this trend is identified from the abandonment of settlements, but here we may be witnessing the corollary of this, the establishment of new settlement. If this phenomenon relates to a change in the organisation of the agricultural landscape, possibly under the control of local landlords, this settlement may have been controlled by the occupants of the possible 'villa' site to the west.

The form of the settlement is unusual in that it appears to have been largely bounded by a pair of parallel ditches. However, the early development of the site is unclear. Although the pottery from the ditches is no earlier than that from other features, the adjacent fields, suggested by the arrangement of the northern linear boundary and ditch 158009 (and possibly also 158010), may represent the earliest elements of Romano-British activity on the site. However, Enclosures 1 and 2, which abut the northern linear boundary, are somewhat askew from its alignment, suggesting that they were not laid out respecting it. It is possible that they pre-dated it (in which case both would appear to have lacked north-western sides), but the small ceramic assemblages from their shallow ditches is not diagnostic enough to establish this relationship.

The details of the occupation within these enclosures, in terms of identifiable settlement features, are sparse, presumably because a large proportion of the evidence has been lost to truncation by later ploughing. The southern side of a possible roundhouse survived within Enclosure 1, and there are pairs of postholes within Enclosure 2. These could be the doorposts of stake-built roundhouses (cf examples of such structures at Danebury), drying racks, or something entirely different. Most of the mid Romano-British phase pottery came from the vicinity of these enclosures and the adjacent part of ditch 158003, and presumably this deposition of pottery indicates occupation in this area, even though no structural evidence survives. The ditch of Enclosure 3, the most substantial of the enclosure ditches, contained a much larger assemblage of domestic debris than any other part of the site. While this suggests that the occupation of Enclosure 3 was domestic in nature, the ditch around the Enclosure 4 was virtually devoid of artefactual material, apart from where it abutted Enclosure 3, and it clearly served a different function.

Some elements of the finds assemblage, however, appear at odds with the structural evidence, and it is possible that the features recorded do not represent the main focus of settlement activity in the vicinity. The assemblage of ceramic building material points to the presence nearby of more substantial buildings than anything suggested by the features recorded on the site, and the 'villa' site to the west is a possible source for such material, and for some of the other finds. The ceramic lamp and figurine, for example, and the *patera* handle from the surface of posthole 150121, are unusual finds in a rural context and would normally be associated with more Romanised sites such as towns, villas or temples.

Nonetheless, the non-kiln pottery assemblage from the site was characteristic of a relatively modest agricultural settlement, possibly on the margins of a higher-status villa. The agricultural character of the site is evident in the arrangements of fields, and the largest assemblage of worked stone, mostly quern fragments, found on the M6 Toll excavations. The location of industrial activity on the site, in the form of the pottery kiln, may also be viewed in this context, reflecting the wider organisation of the landscape in terms of high and low status settlement, industry and agriculture.

Both linear boundaries included later additions, extensions or re-cuts. The recutting of ditch 158006 and the consequent blocking of the wide gap through which ditch 158009 had passed, may represent the abandonment of the latter ditch as a field boundary. Over time, therefore, the boundaries appear to have become a way of dividing the domestic and industrial area from the agricultural land. This process may have preceded the replacement of Enclosures 1 and 2, in the later phase of the site's occupation, by the construction of Enclosures 3 and 4. The construction of ditches 158011 and 158025 during this phase, dividing Enclosures 3 and 4 from the area to the north-east and blocking access around the north-western side of Enclosure 3, may indicate a concern with preventing or controlling movement around the site, possibly connected with a need to restrict the movement of stock.

Chapter 18

East of The Castle, Shenstone (Site 32)

By Andy Simmonds

Introduction

A targeted watching brief was undertaken on land north-east of Shenstone, where cropmarks had been recorded indicating the presence of linear features in the western part of the site (Fig. 58). In addition, surface finds of coins, a bronze seal and a flint implement had been recorded in the same area. Post-medieval field boundaries were recorded and finds of Neolithic, Iron Age, Romano-British and Anglo-Saxon date were recovered from a number of tree hollows (Fig. 133).

The site, covering 2.2 hectares centred at NGR 411760 305350, was located east of The Castle Farm, between Streetway Road and the farm lane, both of which run from Shenstone to the A5 Watling Street. The geology over most of the site is mapped as Triassic Keuper Sandstone, with a small area of Boulder Clay at the north-west (Geological Survey of Great Britain 1954, Sheet 154, Lichfield). The topography of the site was almost level, sloping down very slightly at the east end towards Streetway Lane. The recent use of the site was for arable agriculture.

Fieldwalking and geophysical survey across the site yielded no significant additional information prior to topsoil stripping. Across the western part of the site stripping was halted at the top of a layer (320001/320063) initially thought to represent the natural subsoil. It was subsequently realised that this was not the case and the deposit was then sampled by trenching.

Results

Neolithic

A modest assemblage of Early Neolithic pottery, including a single Carinated Bowl, was recovered from a tree hollow (320065) exposed within one of the trenches excavated through subsoil layer 320001/320063 in the central part of the site. The feature measured *c* 1.4 m in diameter and 0.4 m deep and had a slightly bowl-shaped profile with irregular sides and a concave base. It was filled with a single homogeneous deposit of soft brownish-yellow sand (320066).

Romano-British

Pit 320043 was the only deliberately dug feature recorded pre-dating the post-medieval period. It was circular in plan with vertical sides and a flat base and measured 0.8 m in diameter and 0.6 m deep (Fig. 133). At the base of the pit was a layer of compact brown sand 0.1 m thick (320049), which contained a small concentration of quartz pebbles and was overlain by a deposit of reddish, charcoal-flecked brown sand (320044) that filled the remainder of the feature. Sherds of Romano-British pottery and a single fragment of ceramic roof tile were recovered from the upper fill.

Post-medieval

Two boundaries of probable post-medieval date were recorded, defined by ditches lying on parallel NW-SE alignments. One boundary was defined by ditch 325029, in the western part of the excavation. The south-eastern part of this ditch was cut into the subsoil layer (320001/320063, below), thus demonstrating the relatively recent date of the feature. It had an open, V-shaped profile and measured 1.5 m wide and 0.35 m deep. Its fill was a dark brown silty sand with frequent inclusions of gravel. To both the north-west and south-east the ditch petered out before reaching the edge of the excavation, most likely due to truncation from ploughing. Rutting from farm vehicles was observed along the north-eastern side of the ditch.

The second boundary was located near the eastern end of the excavation and was formed by a pair of parallel ditches. It is likely that they represent either drainage ditches on either side of a trackway or a field boundary formed by a bank and hedgerow between two ditches. The north-eastern ditch (325039) was exposed for a distance of 53 m, petering out at both ends due to truncation by modern ploughing. It was 0.8 m wide and 0.24 m deep with a concave profile. A thin primary fill of yellowish-brown silty sand (320024) was overlain by a lens of blackish-brown soil 20 mm thick (320025), above which was a main fill of greyish-brown silty sand (320026).

The south-western side of the trackway/boundary was recorded for a total length of 85 m and comprised ditches 325042 and 325049, which lay on the same alignment and had slightly off-set terminals 1 m apart. Ditch 325049 continued to the south-east beyond the edge of the excavation, and to the north-west ditch 325042 petered out. Both ditches were filled with deposits of reddish-brown silty sand and had been severely truncated, surviving to a depth of no more than 0.14 m.

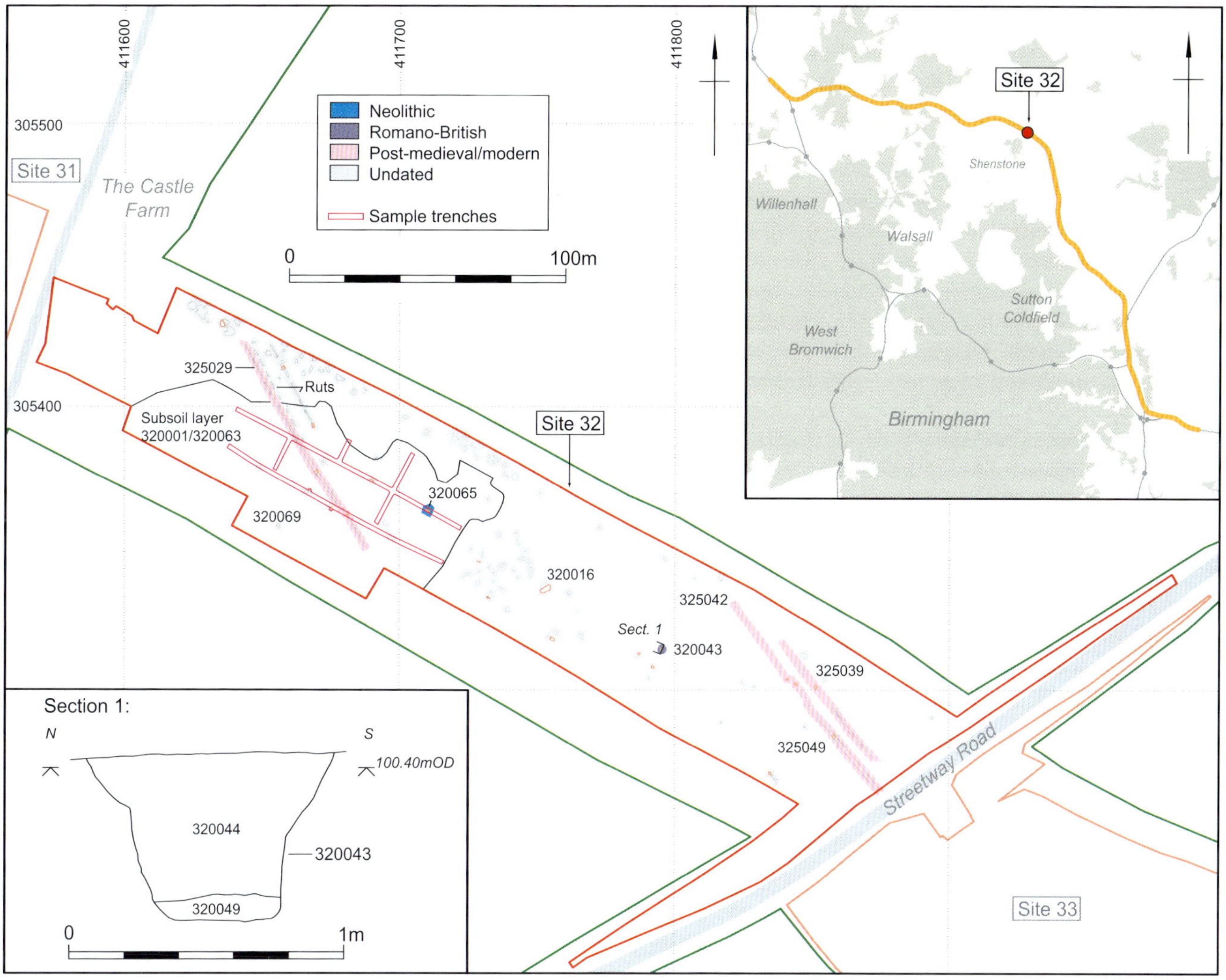

Fig. 133 East of The Castle Shenstone (Site 32) and section of pit 320043

Undated

Subsoil layer 320001/320063 was present across much of the western part of the site, sealing the natural sand, and was sampled by trenching. It was 0.2 m thick, composed of light reddish-brown silty sand with rounded flint gravel. The layer was sampled by the excavation of a series of trenches forming a grid pattern. A mixed assemblage of pottery was recovered, ranging in date from Iron Age to post-medieval. In addition to this ceramic material, metal detecting across the surface of the layer recovered two brooches and a pin of Romano-British date, a medieval bronze token, two lead weights, two iron nails and a total of seven unidentified pieces of iron. The mixed nature of the finds assemblage from this layer suggests that it had been substantially reworked, most likely by post-medieval cultivation.

Tree throw hole/hollow 320016 was the largest such feature excavated on the site, measuring 4 m by 3.2 m. It was approximately oval in shape with irregular sides and was only 0.2 m deep. Its fill was a dark reddish-brown silty sand from which a small mixed assemblage of artefacts was recovered, including a fragment of a ring-shaped ceramic loomweight typical of the Anglo-Saxon period. Also present were three sherds of probable Iron Age and one of Romano-British pottery and two small pieces of roof tile, probably of Romano-British date. It is uncertain whether this tree hollow was created during the Anglo-Saxon period and contained some residual material dating from earlier periods, or whether this mixed assemblage of artefacts was deposited together at some later, but unknown date.

Tree throw hole 320069 was situated at the south-western edge of the excavation (at a point where the subsoil layer 320001 had been present but had been removed by machining). It had an irregular shape in plan and measured 1.4 m by 0.7 m. Excavation revealed it to be 0.16 m deep with an irregular, undulating base. A fill of mottled brown sand (320070) was recorded along the southern edge of the feature, probably resulting from disturbance of the surrounding natural when the tree was upturned. This was overlain by the main fill of dark brown and black silty sand (320071) with a high concentration of charcoal and burnt material, which contained three undated iron nails and some burnt small mammal bones.

Finds

Metal finds, by Kelly Powell

This site produced four copper-alloy finds, two lead and 20 iron objects (Tables 96–7). The majority of the metal finds were recovered from the subsoil and are therefore limited in archaeological value. However, the unstratified assemblage included two copper-alloy Romano-British brooches (ONs 324002 and 324005). The first (ON 324002) was a Colchester-type bow brooch dating to the 1st century AD (Fig. 134, 1). The brooch was small and relatively bulky and could not be classified more closely. The second (ON 324005) was a penannular brooch of Fowler type Aa (Fig. 134, 2). Like the former this was also quite robust in form, with a rounded section. This form of penannular brooch persisted from the early 2nd century BC through to the mid-2nd century AD.

Table 96 Metal finds other than nails (unstratified)

Copper-alloy	*Lead*	*Iron*
2 brooches	2 weights	1 strip
1 pin frag.		1 strip/bar
1 token		1 sheet frag.
		2 misc. objects
		1 slag?

Later copper-alloy finds included a fragment of pin (ON 324003, ?post-medieval), and a Nuremburg token (ON 324007). The subsoil also produced two lead objects which may be identified as medieval? weights. Of particular note was a sub-circular pyramidal object with a central perforation measuring 10 mm in diameter. This had a flat bottom and was decorated with crude and irregularly spaced ridges. ON 324010 in contrast was a simple ring with D-shaped section.

The ironwork recovered from this site was particularly badly corroded and was all derived from the subsoil layer with the exception of four nails (Table 97). These nails, including ON 324008 and ON 324009, were recovered from an undated dump of burnt material within tree hollow 320069 and three may potentially be classified as Manning type 1b, if in fact Romano-British in date. Up to ten more nails were recorded, but the majority were very badly corroded and in light of their lack of contextual associations dating is difficult. Similarly, the remaining iron objects were generally unidentifiable in terms of function and undatable and of little archaeological value. They included a rectangular strip, a further corroded strip or bar, a fragment of sheet, two lumps or objects and a piece of metalworking slag.

Table 97 Nail classification by context

	Type 1b	*Unclass.*	*Total*
Unstratified	–	10	10
Tree hollow 320069	3	1	4
Total	3	11	14

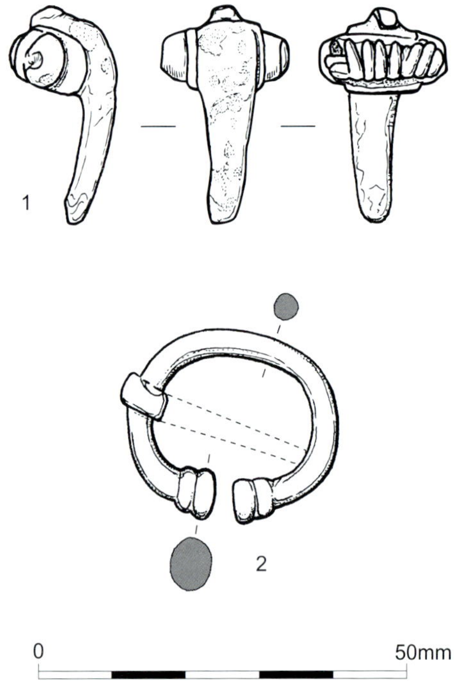

Fig. 134 Metal finds

Illustrated objects (Fig. 134)

1. Brooch. Copper-alloy. Colchester type bow brooch missing pin and catchplate. Plain D-sectioned bow and short, undecorated side wings. Copper-alloy spring coiled 6 times. L 30 mm, W 18 mm, context 320001. ON 324005
2. Brooch. Copper-alloy. Fowler type Aa brooch, missing part of pin. Circular section, flared terminals with a flattened end and central moulding. D 29 mm, T 3 mm, terminal D 5.5 mm, context 320063. ON 324002

Early prehistoric pottery, by Carol Allen

A total of 45 sherds of early prehistoric pottery were found on this site, all of which are Early Neolithic. The sherds were found in the fill (320066) of tree hollow 320065. Such early vessels are known elsewhere from tree hollows (Allen 2006) and it has been suggested that material was dragged into such contexts during a period of primary clearance and settlement of an area (Evans *et al* 1999, 244).

Early Neolithic pottery, Carinated Bowl and dating

Twenty-five of these sherds represented a single Carinated Bowl (Fig. 135). These sherds were undecorated and had a dark grey finish which had been abraded. The vessel wall was thick (10 mm) and the fabric coarse and tempered with granitic material. The rim was rounded and everted with a slight exterior lip and the body sherd appeared to be turning outwards, possibly towards a carination. Inside the rim and neck a number of horizontal finger smoothed ridges could be seen. Very similar material with angular quartz tempering has been found at Aston on Trent in south

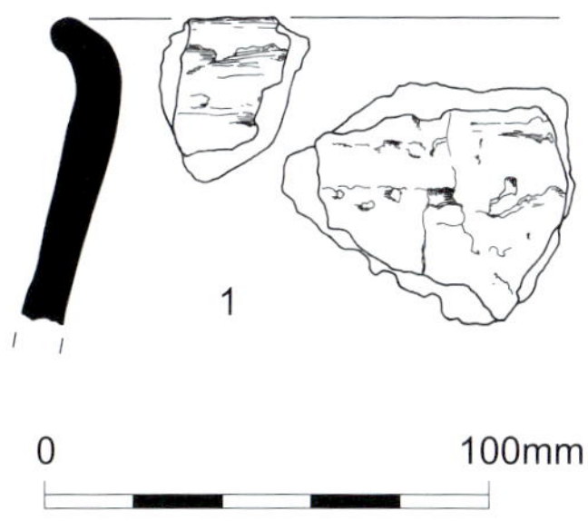

Fig. 135 Neolithic carinated bowl

Derbyshire in a pit within a ring ditch and dated to 3800–2900 cal BC (4700±150BP; Herne 1988, 19).

The second vessel (20 sherds) was probably a simple bowl of similar date; at Aston similar pottery was also found in the pit alongside the Carinated Bowl (Allen *et al.* in prep.), suggesting that these two types were in use together in this area.

Iron Age pottery, by Paul Booth

Three hand-made sherds, perhaps of Middle Iron Age date, were recovered from context 320015 in tree hollow 320016. Two (30 g) were in fabric AVQ3/4, but from different vessels as one sherd was noticeably thick (up to 13 mm). The third sherd (14 g), in a similar fabric (AV3), was a fragmentary slightly insloping rim from a simple jar with traces of burnishing on the shoulder and on the interior below the rim.

The date of these sherds is uncertain. Their character was generally consistent with that of the Middle Iron Age pottery from other M6 Toll sites and elsewhere in the area, although burnishing is not a common characteristic of this material. The sherds were, however, associated with a fragment of a probable annular loomweight in a (very different) fabric containing sand, common clay pellets and some iron oxides. Typologically this appears to be Anglo-Saxon, with a profile close to that of an example from Catholme (Carr and Losco-Bradley 2002, fig. 3.94, no. 1, but without the holes). In view of this an Anglo-Saxon date is possible for the pottery. The difficulties of distinguishing hand made sherds of these two periods are well-known, but were addressed usefully at Catholme (Kinsley 2002). Since context 320015 also included a sherd of Romano-British pottery and two fragments of (undated) ceramic building material it was clearly very mixed. On balance an Iron Age date is preferred for these sherds. Three sherds of Iron Age pottery are also noted from subsoil layer 320001/320063

Romano-British pottery, by Ruth Leary

Eleven sherds (205 g) of Romano-British pottery were found. Context 320044 in pit 320043 contained a large sherd from an MH2 mortarium with multi-reeded hammerhead rim (RE 8%, Evans 2002b, M96, AD 220–290). This vessel was singed along the flange. Context 320044 also contained two sherds (66 g) from a BB1 bowl or dish with intersecting loop burnish outside the base. Insufficient of the vessel was present for precise dating but BB1 did not appear in the region until after AD 120.

Subsoil layer 320001/320063 contained an MH2 mortarium body sherd (16 g) dating after AD 130/40, three undiagnostic R5 sherds, undiagnostic body sherds in fabrics R9 (18 g) and R8 (8 g) and three abraded R2 sherds from a wide-mouthed jar with bifid rim (9 g). This last vessel compares in fabric and form with vessels from the nearby Shenstone kiln dated mid/late 2nd–3rd century.

Discussion

The sparseness of the features recorded on Site 32 and the small size of the finds assemblage make interpretation very difficult. This is especially true as many of the finds, and in particular the metalwork, derive from subsoil layer 320001/320063 and are not associated with features. The mixed nature of the finds assemblage from the subsoil suggests that it had been reworked by post-medieval cultivation and this may have involved the importing of soil, with the result that artefacts may have been inadvertently introduced from elsewhere. It is therefore uncertain whether the material recovered from this layer should be taken at face value as derived from activities taking place on this site or regarded as redeposited. The presence of this material is, however, consistent with the record of earlier finds from the site.

The Romano-British metalwork is particularly problematic, as the assemblage, though small, contrasts sharply with the absence of such material from the excavation of Romano-British features to the immediate west at East of Birmingham Road Nurseries (Site 15). The presence of the Colchester-type brooch suggests that this group may date from as early as the 1st century AD, which would make it significantly earlier than the activity recorded on Site 15. If this material has not been introduced more recently, then the absence of associated features would suggest that it was derived from manuring or off-site disposal of refuse from the settlement on Site 15. The single pit recorded on this site indicates that activity associated with the settlement extended this far east, albeit on a small scale.

It is uncertain whether the same uncertainties attach to the derivation of artefacts recovered from the tree hollows. In the case of the Neolithic pottery from tree hollow 320065, the size of the assemblage and the fact that the feature was sealed beneath the subsoil layer suggest that it was an undisturbed *in situ* deposit. Ceramic evidence for a Neolithic presence has been recovered from both this site and Site 15, but in both cases the assemblage was small and was not associated with contemporary features, being derived from tree hollows and redeposited contexts.

The presence of a loomweight suggests the possibility of Anglo-Saxon domestic activity, particularly if the 'Middle Iron Age' sherds were in fact of Anglo-Saxon date. Settlement of this period has been recorded in the Trent and Avon Valleys, and so penetration into the Shenstone area would not be out of the question. However, the quantity of material recovered dating from this period was at best very small and derived from a tree hollow rather than a deliberately dug feature. The absence of further artefactual material or features of this date indicates that this was not the site of an Anglo-Saxon settlement, and these items may result from casual loss or disposal away from a contemporary settlement.

The two NW–SE aligned post-medieval field boundaries are depicted on the 1st Edition OS map of 1888 (sheet 58 NE) and are likely to have been associated with the nearby Castle Farm.

Chapter 19
Round Wood, Shenstone (Site 33)

By Carl Champness

Introduction

A geophysical survey, targeted watching brief and excavation were undertaken on land north of Round Wood, Shenstone, where a concentration of linear cropmarks to the south extended into the road corridor (Fig. 58), and where a Romano-British brooch, a ring and three medieval coins had reportedly been discovered by metal detector close to the western end of the site. The excavation revealed a curvilinear Romano-British ditch and a network of other field ditches and associated features, mostly poorly dated but probably of the post-medieval period.

The site, covering *c* 1.5 hectares, centred on NGR 412300 305200, lies to the south of the A5, immediately east of Streetway Road and about 1 km east of Shenstone (Fig. 136). The geology over most of the site is mapped as Triassic Keuper Sandstone, with First Terrace deposits towards the south-west (Geological Survey of Great Britain 1954, Sheet 154, Lichfield).

Results

Most of the features identified during aerial photographic and the geophysical surveys proved to be natural features and not archaeological in origin. Instead, the excavation revealed a series of large and small linear and curvilinear features concentrated towards the middle and eastern parts of the site. The smaller ditches were shallow and ephemeral in places, while the largest, which was associated with a network of linear drainage ditches and field drains that were probably later additions, was found to contain several overlapping cuts.

Mesolithic

A single Mesolithic flint blade (ON 336000) was recovered from an undated tree hollow (330323).

Romano-British

The earliest dated features were a curvilinear Romano-British ditch (330032) in the middle of the site, and a pit (330047) immediately south of the eastern terminal of the ditch.

Ditch 330032 ran north-east from the south-western edge of the site, before turning to the east and terminating near the north-eastern edge. It was *c* 0.5 m wide and up to 0.5 m deep, with moderately sloping sides into a concave base (Fig. 136). It is likely that this profile is the result of erosion of the ditch edges, and that the original profile would have been steeper, possibly V-shaped. Its basal fill was a light brownish-yellow silty sand, representing the initial stabilisation of the ditch profile. The secondary fill, concentrated towards the western/northern edge of the ditch, was a dark blackish-brown silty sand, and probably represents in-wash deposits of organic sediments, possibly indicating the practice of manuring with domestic rubbish. This layer contained three pieces of Romano-British ceramic building material (122 g) and a sherd of a 3rd–4th century Romano-British mortarium (54 g), as well as three moderately abraded reduced sherds (122 g). The upper fill of the ditch consisted of a gradual infilling with redeposited natural.

The pit (330047) was oval in plan, measuring 1 m long, 0.8 m wide and 0.45 m deep. It had moderately steep sides and a flat base, and was filled with mid-greyish-brown silty sand (331034) containing a single sherd (11 g) of 2nd century or later Romano-British pottery. The pit's function could not be ascertained.

Post-medieval, modern and undated

The remaining finds from the site comprised ten sherds of post-medieval pottery, 37 pieces of post-medieval ceramic building material, probably post-medieval slag and a piece of undated worked stone possibly used for building. The majority of the remaining features, therefore, were undated, although it is likely that most were post-medieval or modern in date, comprising field boundaries ditches and drainage ditches (the main curved ditch, 330029, for example, appeared on the 1st edition OS map of 1887–9).

It is possible, however, given the evidence of Romano-British activity on the site, that some of these features were contemporary with ditch 330032, although this cannot be demonstrated. Undated ditch 330315, for example, had a similar profile and fills to the Romano-British ditch (Fig. 136). It ran straight, west to east, at the south-western edge of site, for 42 m before being truncated. It was 0.6–0.8 m wide and up to 0.2 m deep, filled with a sequence of redeposited primary fills and slightly organic secondary fills.

The post-medieval/modern landscape was characterised by a large curvilinear field boundary (330029) running south-east to north-west before

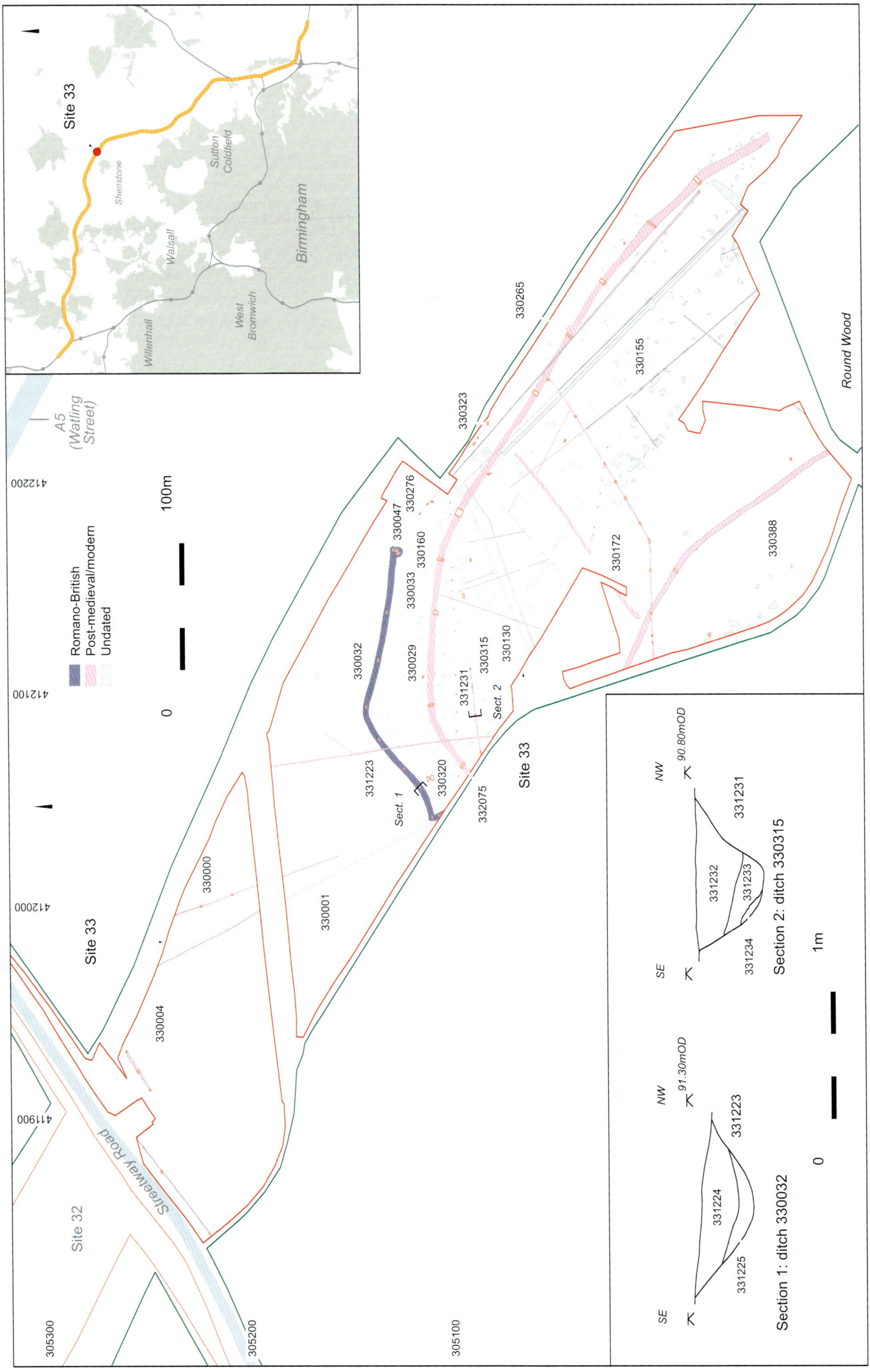

Fig. 136 Round Wood (Site 33) and sections of ditches 330022 and 330315

curving towards the south-west. Initially assumed to be a single wide ditch, excavation showed it to comprise a sequence of overlapping ditch cuts, one of which at the west contained a field drain. These produced sherds of post-medieval pottery, slag, and ceramic building material. Pollen from one of the recuts (cut 331245, in excavated section 332075) indicated an environment dominated by herbs with relatively few trees and shrubs, and with a strong indication of arable activity in the vicinity.

Five large tree hollows (330320, 330033, 330160, 330276 and 330265) were recorded along, or close to, this boundary ditch, two of which were excavated. They probably represent the mature trees shown on the 1st edition OS map, indicating the antiquity and longevity of the boundary.

A network of small drainage ditches and field drains were recorded in the area south-west of the boundary ditch, the most prominent being ditch 330388 which mirrored the orientation of the outer ditch. A third ditch (330172) ran NE–SW between the two curved ditches. In addition, over 100 other features, most of them tree hollows, were recorded, largely within the same area, of which 15 were excavated. They probably represent a phase of use of the site as woodland prior to the establishment of the post-medieval field system.

Two rows of undated postholes were found to cross the site on approximately east-west alignments. Every fourth or fifth posthole was excavated in order to characterise and date these features. They averaged 0.5 m in diameter and were 0.2–0.3 m deep, with vertical to near vertical sides and a sharp transition into a flat base. They were filled with greyish-brown sandy silt with rare pebble inclusions. Some of the postholes cut the post-medieval boundary ditches indicating a relatively recent date.

Three recent field boundary ditches, which previously divided the site into four rectangular arable fields, were recorded. The most westerly (330001) ran NW–SE, dividing the western part of site into two fields. The eastern part of the site was divided by ditches 330130 and 330155, that met towards the north-east edge of site.

Environmental

Charred plant remains, by A J Clapham

Twenty samples of 5–20 litres (averaging 7–8 litres) were taken during the excavations from largely undated features. Three of these samples were analysed for charred plant remains, all from undated (but probably post-medieval/modern) ditches (330000, 330004 and 330315). The number of remains in each sample was low and poorly preserved. The results are displayed in Table 98.

Charred plant remains were rare in these samples and in most cases were poorly preserved. The only cereal remains to be identified were found in ditch 330000 and consisted of a wheat grain (*Triticum* sp.), an immature wheat spikelet fork and a wheat glume base. It is most likely that the wheat represented by these remains is spelt (*Triticum spelta*). A fragment of hazel nutshell (*Corylus avellana*) was also identified from 330000 along with a vetch/tare seed (*Vicia*/*Lathyrus* sp.). The other two samples produced fragments of cereal grains.

Table 98 Charred plant remains from undated ditches

	Ditch	330000	330004	330315
	Section	331025	331027	331235
	Context	331026	331028	331164
	Sample	335000	335002	335016
Sample size (l)		9	10	10
Flots size (ml)		10	10	40
Taxon	Common name			
Cereals				
Triticum sp. grain	wheat	1	–	–
Triticum sp. immature spikelet fork	Wheat	1	–	–
Triticum sp. glume base	Wheat	1	–	–
Indet. cereal frag.		–	3	1
Other species				
Corylus avellana shell frag.	hazel	1	–	–
Vicia/*Lathyrus* sp.	Vetch/tare	1	–	–
Unknown		–	1	–

The three samples analysed from the post-medieval/modern ditches contained very few poorly preserved charred plant remains. As charred plant remains are very resilient to decay they may have been redeposited from the Romano-British activity at the site.

The presence of the vetch/tare may be associated with the cultivation of the cereals and the hazel nutshell may indicate a wild food component to the local diet. The wheat may have been cultivated locally as indicated by the pollen evidence.

Charcoal, by Rowena Gale

A single sample of charcoal was selected for detailed analysis to indicate the character of local woodland and the use of associated resources, and for comparative analysis with the pollen study. Sample 335000 came from the fill of undated (but probably post-medieval/modern) ditch 330000 and included a few fragments of oak (*Quercus* sp.) and gorse (*Ulex* sp.)/broom (*Cytisus scoparius*).

Environmental evidence

Although based on very slight evidence, the taxa named from the charcoal suggest that the environment supported oak woodland with areas of scrub, including gorse or broom.

This data accords with the preliminary results of the pollen analysis from post-medieval ditch 330029 (see below), which describes a mainly open landscape with areas of oak/hazel (*Corylus avellana*) woodland, with secondary components such as beech (*Fagus* sp.), hornbeam (*Carpinus* sp.), alder (*Alnus glutinosa*), birch (*Betula* sp.) and lime (*Tilia* sp.) and heathland species (heathers).

The paucity and poor condition of charcoal provided scant evidence either of the economic use of woodland resources or local woodland. The environmental requirements of the species named (oak and gorse/broom) accord with the type of landscape implicated by the pollen record, namely, sparsely wooded with some areas of heathland and arable cultivation.

Pollen, by Robert G. Scaife

Monoliths from the post-medieval boundary ditch 330029 (section 332075, cut 331245, contexts 331246 and 331247) were taken for pollen analysis with the aim of elucidating the land use of adjacent fields and, hopefully, the more regional vegetation and environment. Pollen was found in abundance in the fills of this post-medieval feature enabling pollen counts and construction of a pollen diagram (in archive). Analytical techniques are given in the report for Site 12 (Ryknield Street, Chapter 14).

The pollen data

Overall, the pollen assemblages are dominated by herbs (to 45% of total pollen) with relatively fewer trees (to 20%), shrubs (to 15%) and Ericales (to 20–5%). The pollen spectra are broadly similar throughout the profile although there appears to be a minor expansion of trees (*Betula* and *Quercus* upwards in the profile).

Trees and shrubs consist largely of *Corylus avellana* type (hazel; 20%) with lesser values of oak (to 8%), *Alnus* (alder; 10%), birch (to 10%). The latter becomes more important from 28 cm. *Tilia* (lime), *Fagus* (beech), *Carpinus betulus* (hornbeam) and *Ilex* (holly) are also present in small numbers. *Calluna vulgaris* (ling) is important (to 24%) with *Erica* (heather; to 5%).

Herbs are dominated by Poaceae (grasses; 45%) with cereal present throughout (to 6%). There is also a moderately diverse but sporadically occurring range of other herbs. These become more important in the upper half of the profile and include *Plantago lanceolata* (ribwort plantain; 1–2%), *Centaurea cyanus* (blue cornflower) and a range of other weeds of pasture, arable and waste ground.

Spores of ferns include a consistent but small presence of *Pteridium aquilinum*, monolete (*Dryopteris* type) and occasional *Polypodium vulgare*.

The inferred vegetation

The pollen catchment of the ditches is generally thought to be of restricted extent, that is, with pollen coming from on-site and/or very local sources. Whilst this may cause problems in interpreting the more regional environment such contexts can, by virtue of this local input, provide useful information on the land use adjacent to the sample site. This appears to be the case here. The local habitat was clearly of open character dominated by grassland and heathland environs, the latter being typical of sandy acidic substrates and podzolic soils developed on them. This is evidenced by the substantial numbers of *Calluna* (ling) and *Erica* (heath) pollen. In addition, however, there are also strong indications of local woodland and of some arable activity. Whilst the latter, cereal pollen and associated weeds (corn-flower) may have been liberated during local crop processing, it is perhaps more likely that they are an indication of arable activity in the adjacent fields. Small numbers of *Secale cereale* pollen indicate cultivation of rye along with wheat and barley. There is also evidence of grassland and pasture habitats with high values of non-cultivated Poaceae (grass) and other taxa of pastoral ground (eg *Plantago lanceolata*). The tree and shrub flora comprises largely taxa which are anemophilous and thus may represent the more regional woodland. Oak and hazel with some lime were most important on better drained soils while alder is more characteristic of damp soils. Birch becomes more important in the upper part of the ditch profile with values which suggest local growth perhaps as woodland regeneration.

Summary

The taphonomy of pollen recovered from the sediments of ditch fills can be complex given problems of over-representation of on-site pollen, a very local pollen catchment and the possibility of re-worked pollen incorporated in older sediments. Conversely, useful information may be obtained which pertains to the character of the local environment after construction of such features. This is the case here. The on-site and near local habitat was on of grassland/pasture with important areas of heathland. There is some evidence of arable activity which included cultivation of rye. Woodland also existed with birch ?scrub and more established oak, hazel with occasional lime and holly growing on the drier interfluves whilst alder probably formed important communities on the wetter floodplains.

Discussion

The single Romano-British ditch probably represents a fragment of a more widely organised landscape, possibly related to a nearby farmstead. The date of its initial establishment is unknown but, unless the limited associated finds are residual, it was filling up in the late Romano-British period.

The main boundary ditch may have defined part of a large subcircular enclosure, and although post-medieval maps suggest that the area within it was used as rough grazing rather than for arable cultivation, the large number of tree-throws suggests that it had originally been extensively wooded, possibly as an area of managed woodland. It is possible that the name 'Round Wood', which at the time of the excavation referred to the small copse immediately south of the site, is a reference to this. Examples of managed and enclosed woodland, used as a source of fuel and timber and for hunting, are known throughout the medieval period, and it is possible that this boundary is of greater antiquity than its dating suggests, with earlier evidence having been removed by its repeated recutting (it is noted, also, that the line of the ditch is roughly parallel to that of the Romano-British ditch). This woodland, however, must have been retreating through the post-medieval period (and possibly earlier) to its much reduced present-day limits.

SITES ALONG COLLET'S BROOK AND LANGLEY BROOK

Four sites – Collet's Brook Burnt Mound (Site 40), North of Langley Mill (Site 29), Langley Mill (Site 30) and Langley Brook (Site 39) – were excavated over a distance of *c* 1 km along the M6 Toll, east of Sutton Coldfield (Fig. 137), and their proximity means that the results at each site should be viewed in the light of contemporary features at the adjacent sites.

Three of the sites (Sites 40, 30 and 39) had stream-side locations along either Collet's Brook to the north or Langley Brook, of which the former is a tributary, both streams flowing in an easterly direction. Each of these sites contained features/deposits interpreted as either *in situ*, or material derived from, burnt mounds. Two of the sites (Sites 29 and 30) provided evidence of Iron Age settlement, including subrectangular enclosures, roundhouses and possible field boundary ditches. Their contrasting locations may explain in part some of the differences in the character of the Iron Age features uncovered, but these should be seen as indicative of the wider utilisation of the landscape.

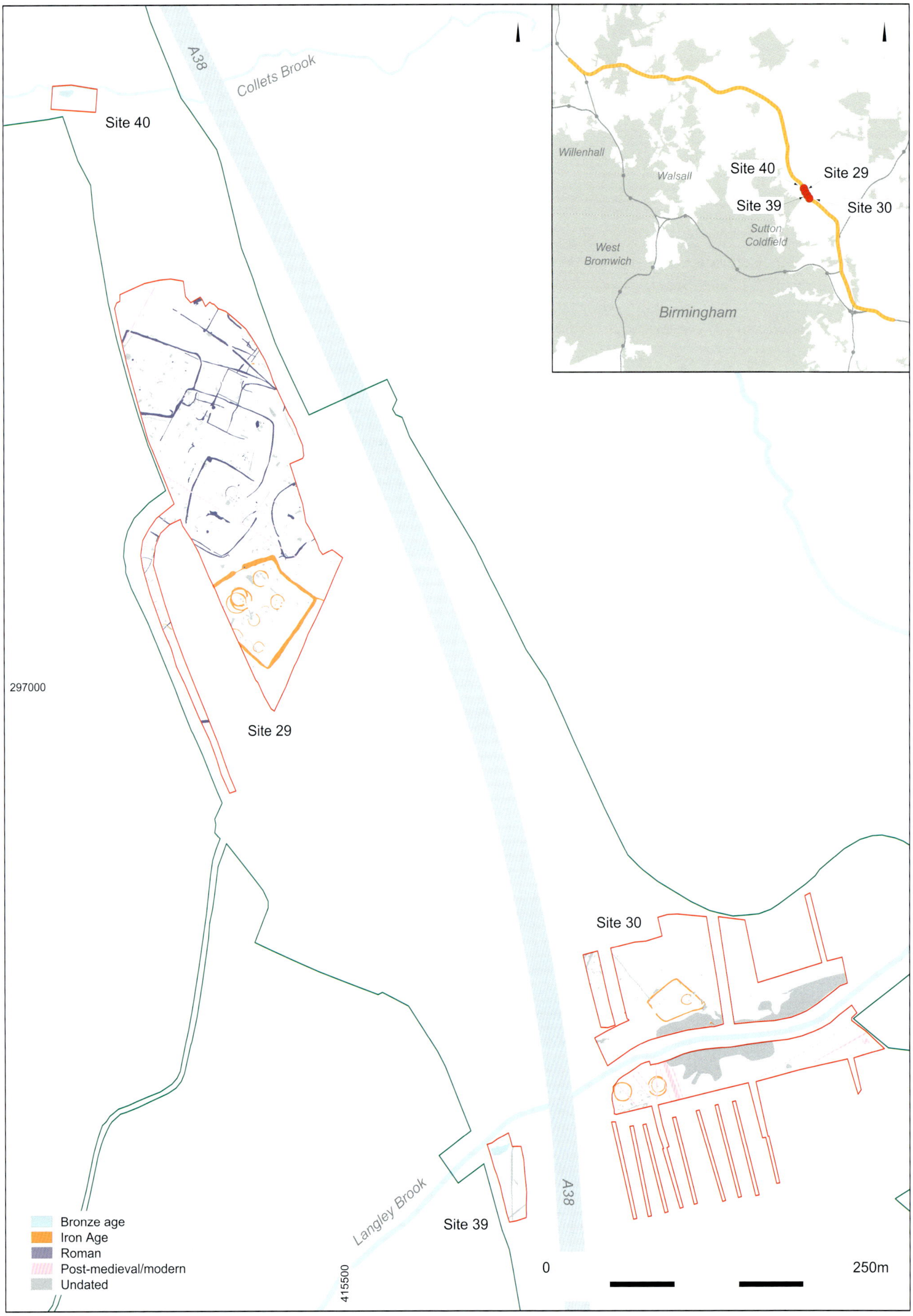

Fig. 137 Sites along Collet's Brook and Langley Brook

Chapter 20
Collet's Brook Burnt Mound (Site 40)

By Rebecca Devaney

Introduction

An archaeological excavation was undertaken at a site on the south side of Collet's Brook, where a dense, black spread of shattered stones and charcoal, which appeared to represent *in situ* burnt mound material, was exposed during topsoil stripping and identified during the general watching brief (Fig. 138). The excavation revealed the structure and extent of the mound which was radiocarbon dated to the Middle Bronze Age.

The site, centred on NGR 415300 297440, was located just west of the point at which the brook is crossed by the line of the A38 embankment. Collet's Brook flows west to east at this point. The geology is mapped as Triassic Keuper Marl (Mudstone), with alluvium along the brook (Geological Survey of Great Britain 1954, Sheet 154, Lichfield).

Results

The site consisted of a large spread of burnt mound material, possibly truncated at its northern edge by Collet's Brook. It was *c* 0.6 m deep overlying natural sands and gravels.

Mesolithic

A single broken flint blade of probable Mesolithic date was recovered from the natural, the heavy post-depositional damage indicating that it was residual.

Bronze Age

A layer of mid-grey silty sand with about 50% gravel inclusions (400005), identified beneath the north-

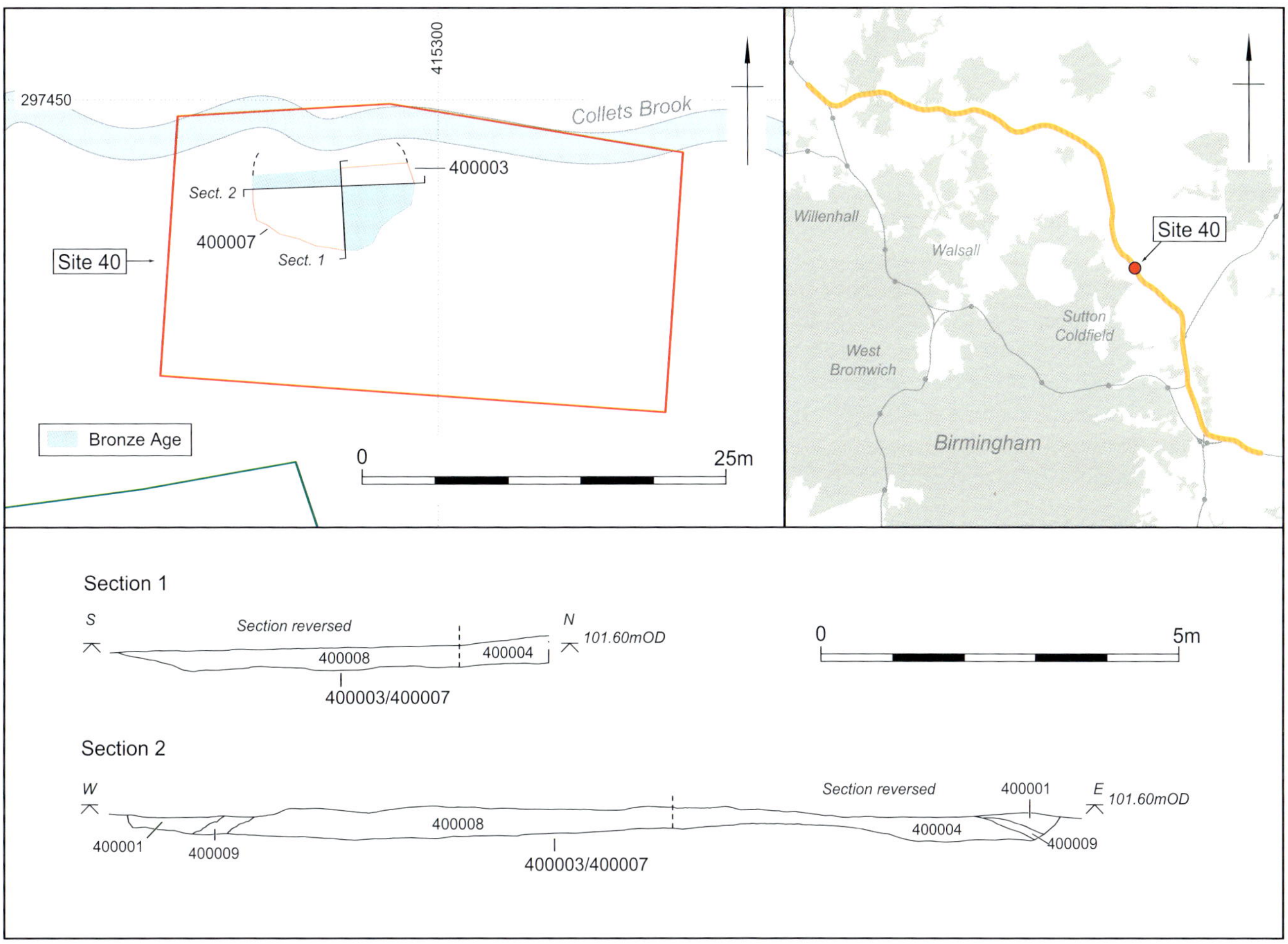

Fig. 138 Collet's Brook Burnt mound (Site 40)

Table 99 Radiocarbon dates from the burnt mound

Context	Material	Lab. No.	Result BP	Date cal BC at 2 σ
400004 (upper)	Alder	NZA-25069	3173±30	1520–1390
400008 (lower)	Hazel	NZA-25070	3185±30	1520–1400

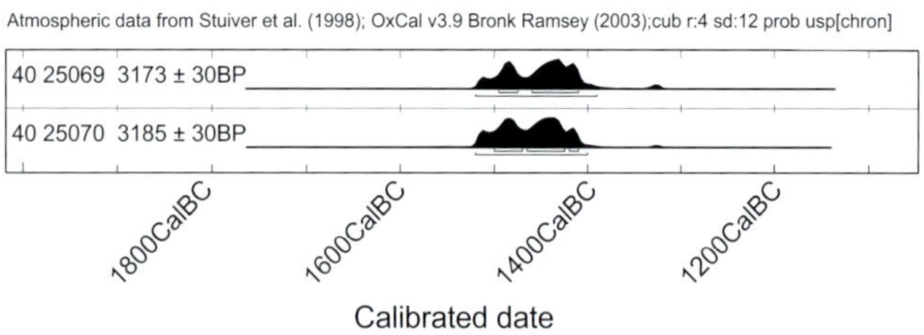

Fig. 139 Oxcal probability distributions of radiocarbon dates

eastern quadrant of the burnt mound, was interpreted as an alluvial deposit, possibly stained by the overlying burnt deposits. It was 2.1 m across and 0.25 m thick.

Cut 400003/400007 (in the NE and SW quadrants, respectively) formed a shallow hollow, *c* 7 m by 13 m, which represents the extent of the burnt mound material (Fig. 138). Its northern edge may have been truncated by the existing line of the stream, and it may have originally been more circular in shape. It is not clear if this feature was a deliberate cut, or if the burnt mound material simply overlay the pre-existing ground surface.

Deposit 400004 (NE)/400008 (SW) represents the body of the burnt mound, and consisted of a single layer, up to *c* 0.4 m thick, of charcoal rich, black silty sand with about 60% small burnt stones. The deposit appeared to be homogeneous and no individual dumping episodes were seen. However, in order to provided the greatest potential time depth for the burnt mound deposit, charcoal for radiocarbon dating was selected from samples collected from opposite ends of the mound, from the upper part of context 400004 and the lower part of context 400008. These produced radiocarbon dates in the Middle Bronze Age of 1520– 1390 cal BC (NZA-25069, 3173±30 BP) and 1520– 1400 cal BC (NZA-25070, 3185±30 BP), which are statistically indistinguishable (Fig. 139, Table 99).

The overlying deposit (400009), up to *c* 0.3 m thick and visible at the edge of the south-west quadrant, comprised a mid- to dark greyish-brown silty sand with about 60% burnt stone inclusions. This interface between the burnt mound and the topsoil (400001) may represent a trample zone caused by the action of delivering stones to and removing them from the mound. The site was sealed by a mid-greyish- brown sandy silt topsoil, 0.3–0.6 m thick, with about 20% small to medium sized sub-rounded pebbles.

Finds

Flint, by Kate Cramp

A single broken flint blade was recovered from the topsoil (context 400001) (Table 150). The blade had been soft-hammer struck and exhibited the scars of previous blade removals, indicating its position in a reduction sequence aimed at the production of blades. Technologically, the piece probably belonged to a Mesolithic industry although heavy recent damage to its edges confirmed that it had been redeposited.

Environment

Charred plant remains, by Lisa Gray

Four samples, each of 20 litres, were taken and processed from the burnt mound for the recovery of charred plant remains. Two samples were selected for analysis. Sample details and contents are given in full in Table 100. Preservation quality was generally poor and charred material was too fragmented for the survival of diagnostic features. High levels of root activity and many uncharred weed seeds were noted suggesting stratigraphic movement and the possibility of intrusive material (OWA 2003, 301).

The charred remains consisted of one fragment of poorly preserved cereal grain from the upper part of context 400004 and one fragment of hazelnut (*Corylus avellana*) shell from the lower part of context 400008. The cereal grain resembled barley or wheat (*Hordeum*/*Triticum* sp.). Samples from the lower part of context 400004 produced no plant remains. Very little can be gleaned from these remains. Far fewer plant remains were recovered from this site than from the similar features from West of Crane Brook (Site 9, Later Neolithic), Langley Mill (Site 30, Iron Age) and Langley Brook (Site 39, Early Bronze Age).

Table 100 Charred plant remains from the burnt monud

	Context	400004 (upper)	400008 (lower)
	Sample	404004	404003
	Sample size (l)	20	20
	Flot size (ml	500	750
Taxon	Common name		
Hordeum/*Triticum* sp. grain frag.	Barley/wheat	1	–
cf. *Corylus avellana* shell frag.	Hazel	–	1

Table 101 Charcoal from the burnt mound (no. frags)

Context	Sample	Alnus	Betula	Corylus	Prunus
400004	404002	21	–	–	1
400008	404003	34	3	3	–

Charcoal, by Rowena Gale

Four bulk soil samples were collected from the burnt mound and when processed yielded relatively large amounts of charcoal. Charcoal was examined from the upper part of context 400004 (NE quadrant) and from the lower part of context 400008 (SW quadrant). The taxa identified are shown on Table 101. Charcoal was frequent in both samples and consisted predominantly of alder (*Alnus glutinosa*) but also included small quantities of hazel (*Corylus avellana*), birch (*Betula* sp.) and blackthorn (*Prunus spinosa*).

Discussion

The burnt mound was composed of small pebbles that appeared to have accumulated fairly rapidly. There was no evidence of scorching or burning on the soil beneath. Charcoal was interspersed amongst the pebbles. The area in which the stone-heating activity took place is unknown but is likely to have been close to the burnt mound.

The heat-source was fuelled principally with alder, although other species including hazel, blackthorn and birch were also used; the charcoal was too fragmented to assess the use of narrow stems or coppiced growth. This implies that fuel was gathered mostly from the low-lying ground and floodplain in immediate vicinity of the site, which was probably colonised with alder carr. When burnt green (unseasoned), alder wood produces a rather sluggish fire but this performance can be improved through the use of narrow roundwood, which encourages a faster-burning and more intense heat source.

Since none of the other species named tolerate prolonged waterlogging, it is probable that small quantities of fuel were collected from drier land. With the abundance of alder, it could be anticipated that willow (*Salix* sp.), a frequent constituent of alder carr and damp or wet soils, would also have been used, there was, however, no evidence of such in the fuel debris.

Discussion

The burnt mound was relatively well-preserved and probably *in situ*. It was composed of quite small stones which may suggest that the material is more likely to derive from refuse disposal activity rather than indicating a place where stones were heated up. Moreover, the alluvial deposit beneath the burnt material does not show signs of burning, as would be expected if stones were burnt on the site. There are no obvious separate dumping or burning events, which suggests that the mound was in use for only a short period of time. The radiocarbon dates from contexts 400004 and 400008, of 1520–1390 and 1520–1400 cal BC, respectively, are statistically indistinguishable, and broadly contemporary with those from other Middle Bronze Age burnt mounds discussed by Hodder (2002). This burnt mound is not contemporary with any other dated examples within the M6 Toll, and although that from Langley Brook (Site 39) is also Bronze Age, it is slightly earlier, with little significant or no overlap.

Chapter 21
North of Langley Mill (Site 29)

By Andrew B. Powell and Kevin Ritchie

Introduction

The site, north-east of Sutton Coldfield, was first identified by a scatter of flints, including one fragment of Mesolithic type, during fieldwalking in 1992. Following a subsequent geophysical survey, which indicated a large number of roughly NE–SW aligned positive linear anomalies, and trial trenching, which revealed a number of cut features (although none containing diagnostic dating material), an excavation was carried out revealing a series of sub-rectangular enclosures, some containing evidence of structures. The enclosures date from the Middle Iron Age (400–100 BC) through the 2nd century AD with some minor evidence of 3rd and 4th century activity.

The site was an irregular rectangular parcel of land, covering *c* 3 hectares centred on NGR 415410 297150, and bounded to the east by the A38 (Fig. 140). It was located on the south facing slope of a hill at a height of *c* 111 m aOD. The geology is mapped as Triassic Keuper Red Marls with sandy bands (Geological Survey of Great Britain, Sheet 154, Lichfield).

Results

The pottery from the site spans the Middle Iron Age through the late Romano-British period. Within that sequence there appears to have been some continuity of occupation, although with a relatively low level of activity from the late 1st to mid-2nd centuries AD.

Middle Iron Age

Enclosure 1

An enclosed Iron Age settlement was recorded at the southern end of the site. This comprised a cluster of penannular ditches/gullies, marking the locations of a number of roundhouses (structures 1a–c and 2–6), and other features, bounded by a substantial ditch (291113) (Fig. 141). The sub-square enclosure, which had a 5.6 m wide entrance in the centre of its north-western side, measured internally 68 m front to back, by 60 m across. The rear part of the enclosure was regular in shape with right-angled corners at the east and south. The front part, however, was skewed slightly to the north, and the front side bowed slightly outwards.

In places, the ditch was over 4 m wide and 1 m deep with a generally shallow V-shaped profile, and more substantial, therefore, than any of the later enclosure ditches on the site (Fig. 142). The eastern terminal flanking the entrance had been substantially reworked over time. When the original wide U-shaped cut (293011) was approximately two-thirds filled, two parallel, steep-sided ditches (293014 and 293019), *c* 0.1 m apart, had been cut into its fill. No comparable recuts were recorded in the opposing terminal, or anywhere else around its circuit. When in turn these, and the rest of the ditch had silted up, a U-shaped gully (291114), 0.6 m wide and 0.3 m deep, was cut across the entrance gap between the two ditch terminals.

At least seven penannular ditches indicating probable roundhouses were recorded in this area, all but one of them having entrances facing to the south-east, a typical feature of Iron Age roundhouses. The three largest ditches overlapped indicating that one of the buildings (structure 1a–c), probably the settlement's principal residence, to the immediate right as one entered the enclosure, had been rebuilt in approximately the same location on at least two occasions (Figs 141–2).

In structure 1, the earliest ditch (292667, structure 1a) was 15.2 m in internal diameter, and averaged 0.8 m wide and 0.3 m deep. Although there were a number of small features, including pits and postholes within the general area of the entrances to the three overlapping ditches, two postholes (293459 and 293467), 0.6 m and 0.75 m in diameter, lay symmetrically within the 5.3 m wide entrance gap of ditch 292667, and appear to be associated with it. Posthole 293459 provided a radiocarbon date of 370–120 cal BC (NZA-25158, 2188±30 BP) (Fig. 143, Table 102).

The next ditch (292668, structure 1b), which was 14.9 m in internal diameter, and averaged 0.8 m wide and 0.5 m deep, appeared to have been recut on its south-western side, possibly indicating repair; there were no features clearly associated with its 4.6 m wide entrance. The final phase of construction (292666, structure 1c), was 12.3 m in diameter, and averaged 1.5 m wide and 0.6 m wide; a single stakehole was recorded in the base of the ditch, and a sandstone pebble used as a whetstone was recovered from the primary fill of the south-western entrance terminal. The ditch provided a radiocarbon date of 360–40 cal BC (NZA-25159, 2144±35 BP) (Fig. 143, Table 102).

Two pits, one (290734), possibly a large posthole *c* 1 m in diameter and 0.25 m deep, the other (292925) less regular in form and up to 1.6 m wide, appear to be positioned on either side of its 5.5 m wide entrance (although the edge of the latter, which produced fragments of amber bead, appeared to be cut by the gully of structure 1b).

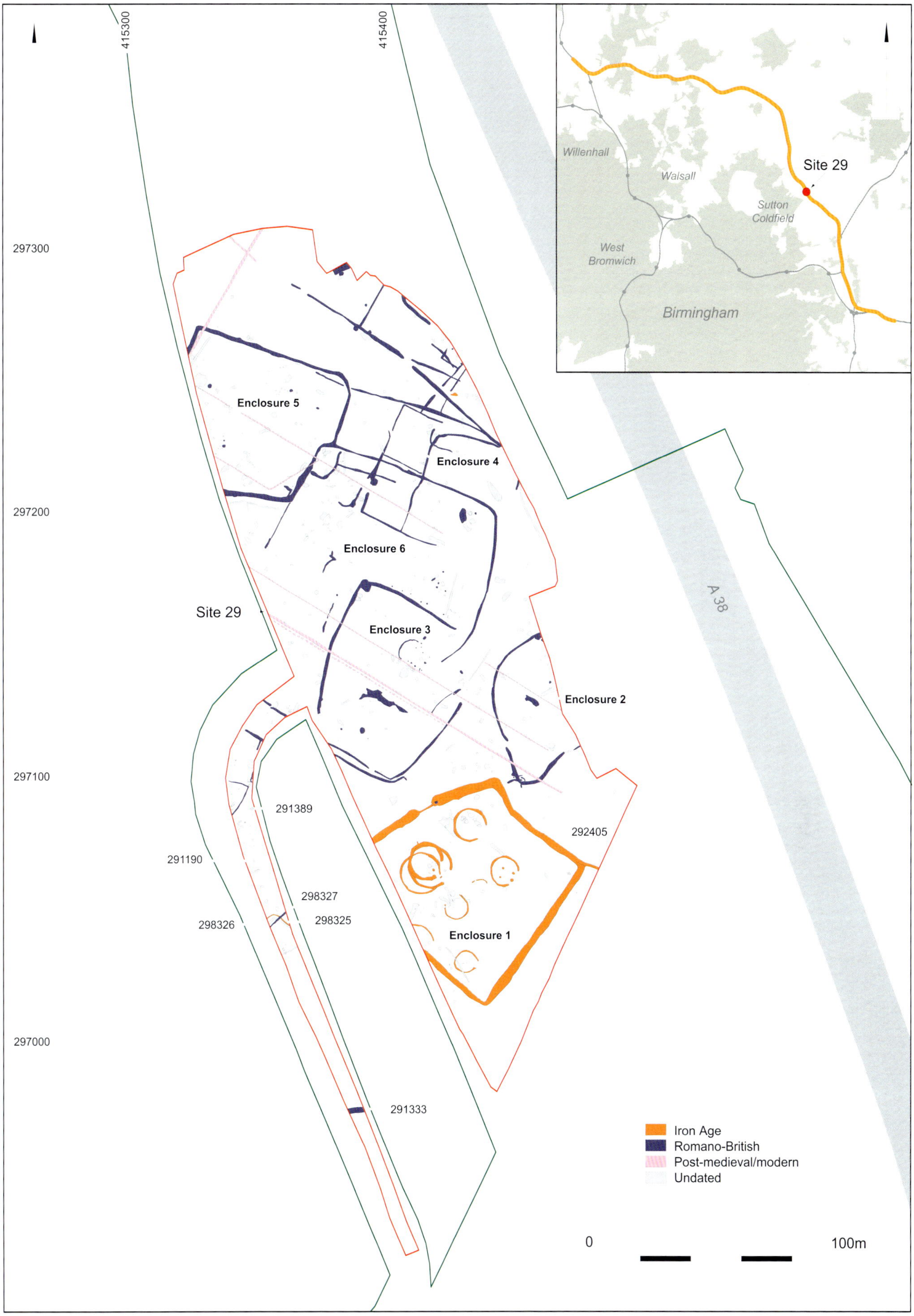

Fig. 140 North of Langley Mll (Site 29)

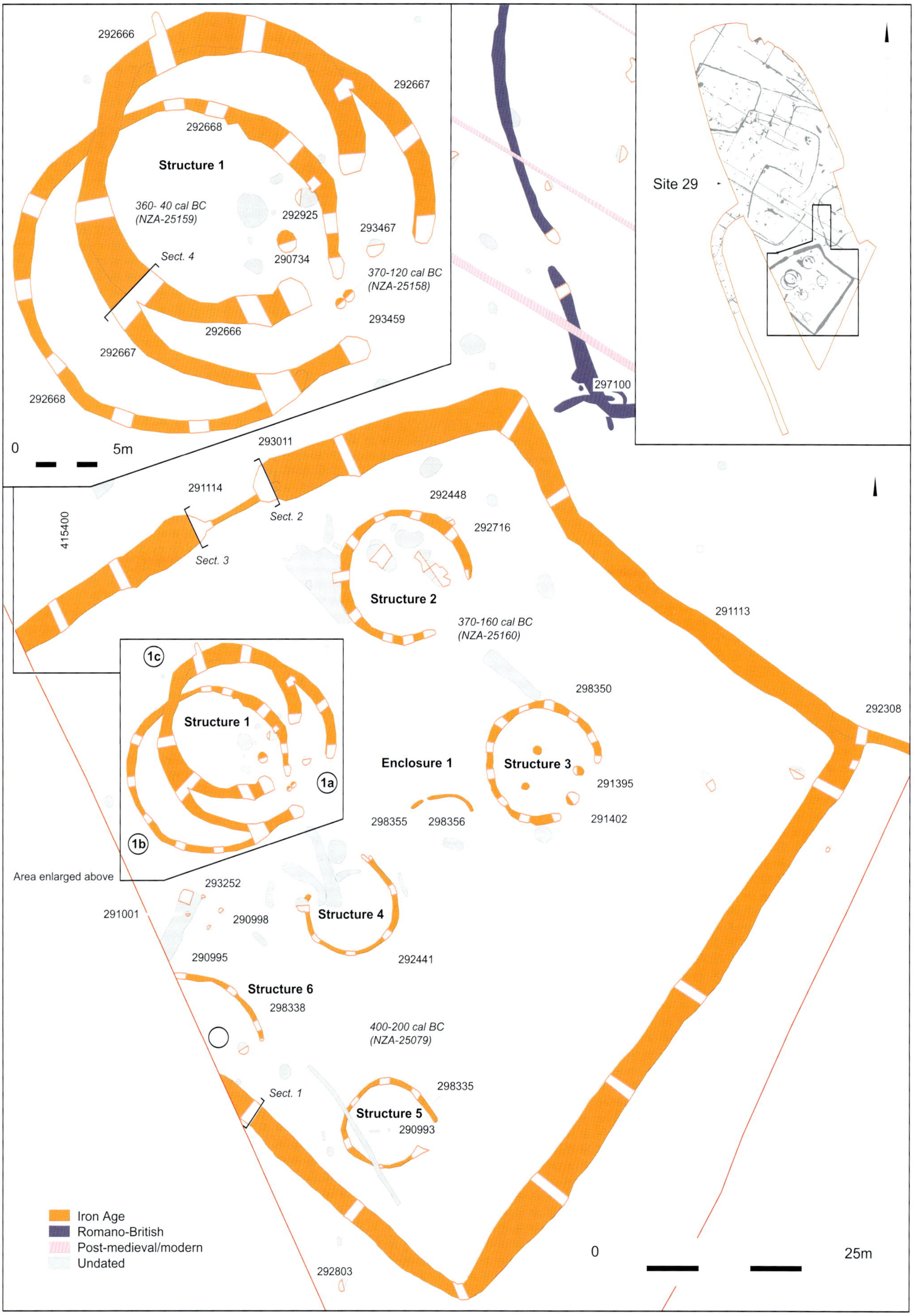

Fig. 141 Iron Age Enclosure 1

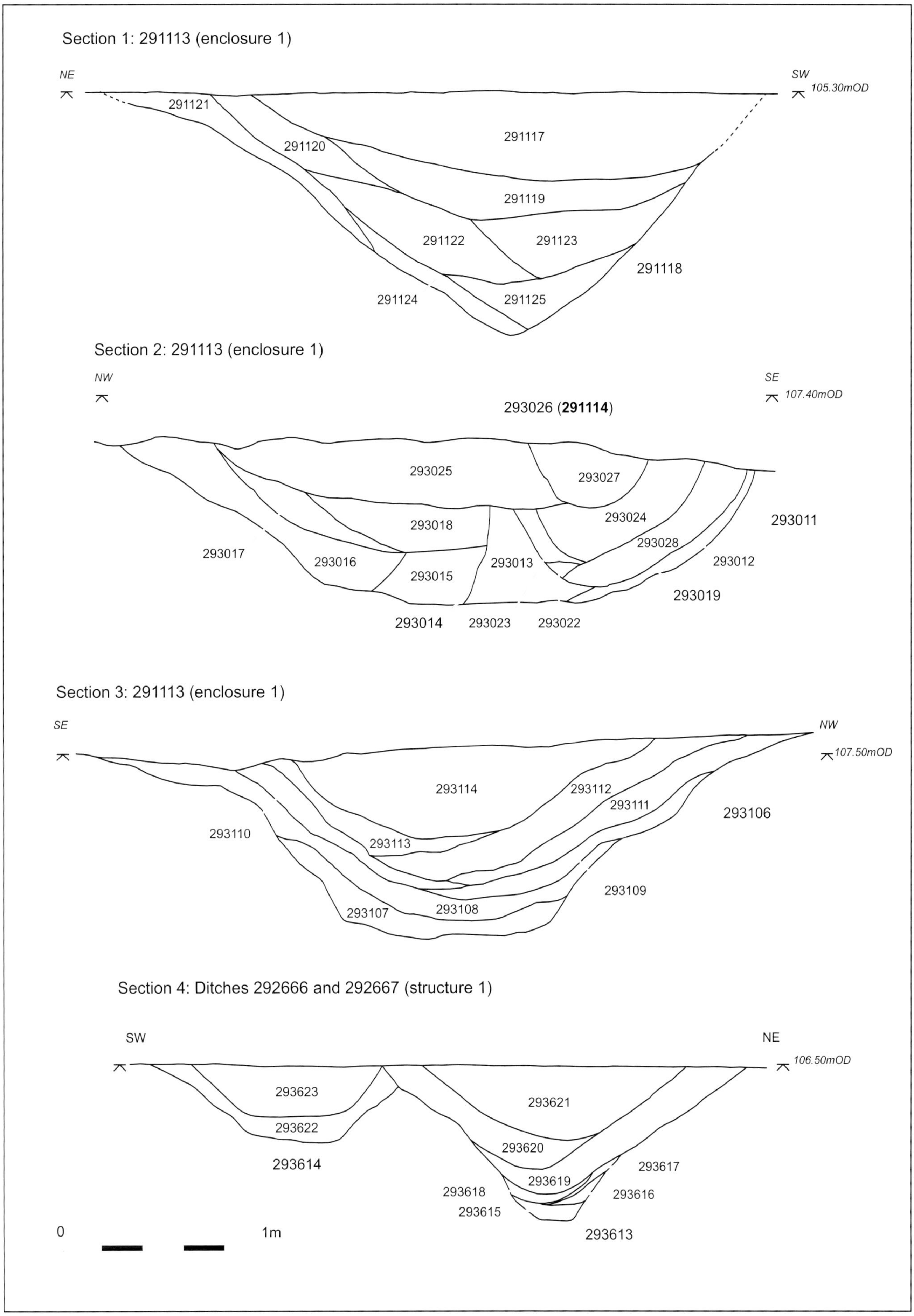

Fig. 142 Sections across enclosure ditch 291113

Table 102 Radiocarbon dates from North of Langley Mill

Feature	Context	Material	Lab. No.	Result BP	Cal BC at 2 σ
Roundhouse 298335	293243	Oak	NZA-25079	2274±35	400–200
Roundhouse 292716	292715	Birch	NZA-25160	2196±30	370–160
Posthole 293459	293461	Pomoideae	NZA-25158	2188±30	370–120
Roundhouse 292666	293636	Pomoideae	NZA-25159	2144±35	360–40
Enclosure 6, ditch 290801	290802	Oak sapwood	NZA-25081	1955±35	40 BC–AD 140
Hearth 290790	290791	Oak roundwood	NZA-25078	1833±30	AD 120–320

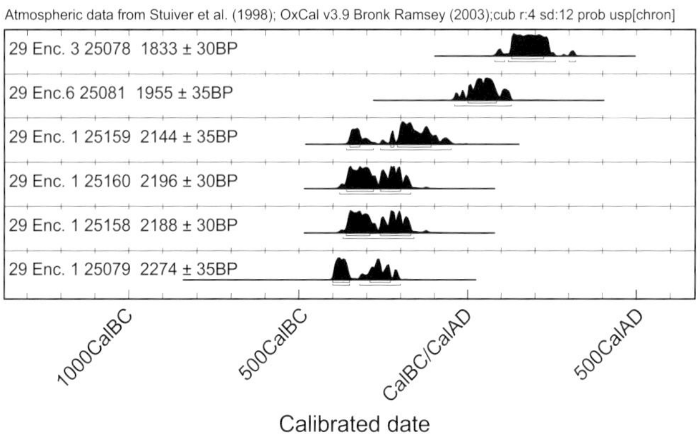

Fig. 143 Oxcal probability distributions of radiocarbon dates

Two other penannular ditches, although smaller than the phases of structure 1, may have enclosed secondary domestic structures. The ditch of structure 2 (292716), to the immediate left as one entered the enclosure, was 11.2 m in diameter, and averaged 0.9 m wide and 0.4 m deep, with a 5.8 m wide entrance; it had been re-cut on its north-east side. The ditch provided a radiocarbon date of 370–160 cal BC (NZA-25160, 2196±30 BP) (Fig. 143, Table 102). Although there were two groups of substantial intercutting pits inside the ditch, they produced no finds and it is unlikely that they were contemporary with the use of the structure. The ditch of structure 3 (298350), towards the rear of the enclosure, was 10.3 m in diameter, and averaged 0.7 m wide and 0.3 m deep. There were two pits (or possibly large postholes), set at a slight angle within the 6 m wide entrance, pit 291395 measuring 0.7–0.85 m wide and 0.4 m deep, and pit 291402 measuring 1.4 m in diameter and 0.2 m deep. These may have combined with two further unexcavated features, both *c* 0.8–0.9 m in diameter, towards the rear of the structure to form a roughly square four-post structure, probably part of the timber structure of the roundhouse, or possibly a separate structure not contemporary with it.

Two of the penannular ditches were significantly smaller and may represent non-domestic structures. The ditch of structure 4 (292441) was the only one not facing south-east, and it may be significant that it was located close to, and facing, the front of the principal roundhouse (structure 1). It was 8.4 m in diameter with a comparatively wide entrance (7.2 m), and averaged 0.5 m wide and 0.3 m deep. There were no internal features. Structure 5 (298335), the furthest from the enclosure entrance was 7.6 m in diameter, and less regular in shape with a slightly outward splayed terminal at the 2.7 m wide entrance. Its ditch averaged 0.5 m wide and 0.2 m deep. There was a single 0.25 m diameter posthole (290993) near its centre. A sample of charcoal from the ditch produced a radiocarbon date of 400–200 cal BC (2274±35 BP; NZA-25079) (Fig. 143, Table 102).

The north-eastern part of a possible eighth penannular ditch (298338, structure 6) averaging 0.7 m wide and 0.25 m deep, also potentially with a south-east facing entrance, extended beyond the western edge of the excavation. If it was a roundhouse, it would have had a diameter of *c* 15 m, extending beyond the boundary of the enclosure, and so apparently pre-dating its construction. This raises the possibility that some of the other structures may also have pre-dated the enclosure, so forming part of an open settlement.

There was a small square setting of four postholes (290995, 290998, 291001 and 293252), immediately south-west of structure 1. Such four-post structures are often interpreted as granaries, although the relatively slight nature of the resulting structure here might indicate some other function. The postholes averaged 0.5 m in diameter and 0.2 m deep and were spaced 2–2.5 m apart (centre to centre). A number of other pits and postholes, all undated, were recorded within and around the roundhouse ditches, as well as two short lengths of curved gully (298355 and 298356), neither excavated, in the centre of the enclosure.

All the pottery from features within the enclosure – the ditches of structure 1 and associated posthole 293459, and from posthole 291395 in the entrance of structure 3, is consistent with a date in the later part of the Middle Iron Age (see Booth, below). The lower fills of the enclosure ditch produced no pottery, but a secondary fill (the middle of five midway along the south-east side) contained three Iron Age sherds (83 g). The remaining pottery from the ditch came from its upper fills around its circuit and (apart from a further three Iron Age sherds) was all of Romano-British date (19 sherds weighing 85 g), including one sherd from a late 1st–mid-2nd century flagon.

Other features

No other ditches across the site can be confidently associated with the Iron Age settlement and Enclosure

1, although ditch 298325, *c* 50 m to the west, produced a single Iron Age sherd (Fig. 140). This ditch, the northern of two parallel features (298325 and 298326), each turning a near right-angled corner, was cut by another small ditch (298327), running towards the assumed position of the enclosure's western corner. Another small ditch (292308) was cut by the eastern corner of the enclosure.

A small quantity of Iron Age pottery was recovered from other contexts across the site (Fig. 144). Towards the north of the site, a steep-sided rectangular pit (293323), measuring 1.8 m by 0.5 m and 0.4 m deep, may also date to this period. There were signs of *in situ* burning on the compact natural in its flat base, and its lowest fill (293326) consisted almost entirely of charcoal and a number of large stones. The middle fill (293325), also rich in charcoal, produced a single sherd (7 g).

Romano-British

The remaining features across the site are not so easily distinguishable, nor so readily datable. They appear to represent at least a further five enclosures, paddocks, or fields (Figs 140 and 144). The pottery from the enclosure ditches provides little assistance in phasing these features, and while, towards the north of the site, the enclosures are increasingly overlapping so that stratigraphical relationships provide a degree of relative phasing, to the south there are no such relationships. Moreover, it is seldom possible to confidently associate any of the other features across the site with the enclosures within which they lie. The chronology of the site's occupation, therefore, is far from complete, and the following description is necessarily tentative, other interpretations of the evidence (some referred to below) being possible. None of the suggested enclosures is represented by the full circuit of a ditch, as they either extended beyond the edges of the excavation, had wide gaps in their circuits, or in some cases appear to have been completely open on one side.

Enclosure 2

Enclosure 2 was separated from the north-east corner of Enclosure 1 by a gap of just 4.5 m. It measured 44 m south-east to north-west, but extended beyond the eastern edge of the excavation, and had an irregular curved boundary on its south and western sides (298184 and 298525). There was a narrow entrance on the western side formed by a 2 m wide gap between slightly offset ditch terminals. There was also a possible entrance on the southern side, located at the edge of the excavation, represented by the ditch terminal at the west and two short lengths of gully (298537 and 298538), 2.6 m and at least 3.7 m long, separated by a 0.9 m wide gap. If the ditch terminal does represent one side of an entrance (which would have been at least 7 m wide), it may have held some form of gate or other structure, possibly to aid in the control and movement of livestock. The enclosure ditch was up to 1.1 m wide and 0.4 m deep (Fig. 145). The ditch and one of the 'entrance gullies' produced seven sherds of Romano-British pottery, but none sufficiently diagnostic to provide a date for the enclosure's construction.

There was a small number of features within the enclosure, predominantly isolated small pits and postholes, one of which, a small pit (293451) 1.2 m in diameter and 0.2 m deep, contained several layers of waste which appeared to have been dumped in rapid succession, including two sherds Romano-British pottery from its upper fill. Another pit (290987), measuring 0.6 m by 0.7 m and 0.25 m deep, produced the complete upper half of a rotary quern with metal spindle. There was also a short linear feature (290539) of uncertain function, measuring 5.5 m long, 0.8 m wide and 0.5 m deep with a charcoal-rich primary fill but no finds. Romano-British pottery was also recovered from three possibly natural features, most of it – a group of 26 sherds (416 g) dated to the late 3rd or 4th century – coming from irregular feature 293513. This was one of the largest assemblages from the site and given the apparently random distribution of late Romano-British pottery from the site, need not be associated with the use of the enclosure.

Enclosure 3

Immediately east of Enclosure 2 there was a subrectangular enclosure measuring 61 m by 54 m, narrowing to under 40 m at the south-west. Its north-east and north-west sides, both of which bowed out slightly, were defined by a single length of ditch (297983), up to 2 m wide and 0.35 m deep with a shallow V-shaped profile and up to two fills (Fig. 145). There was a 27 m wide gap at the eastern corner of the enclosure. The ditch on the south-eastern side (291338, a recut of ditch 291343), which also bowed outwards, continued around the southern corner, where there was a 2 m wide gap, beyond which a further length of ditch (298343) formed the south-western side. With a maximum width of just over 1 m, these ditches were less substantial that the ditch defining the northern side of the enclosure. At the south-western corner (which lay outside the excavation area), ditch 297983 stopped an estimated 6 m short of ditch 298343.

The three breaks in the enclosure circuit, of widely different sizes, clearly had different functions. A 14.5 m length of narrow ditch (291274) on a similar line to the south-east side of the enclosure, may have formed part of its ditch circuit, partly closing the large gap at the eastern corner, and narrowing the gap between Enclosures 2 and 3 to just less than 6 m, with a single posthole (290976) placed centrally within that gap. Two further linear features (292165 and 290973) inside Enclosure 3 may also have been associated with the entrance, perhaps having a role in controlling the movement of livestock in and out of the enclosure.

Also located within the entrance, but probably not associated with it, was a subrectangular feature (291270), possibly a hearth (or fire-pit) 1.3 m by 1.2 m and 0.25 m deep, displaying scorching on the base and

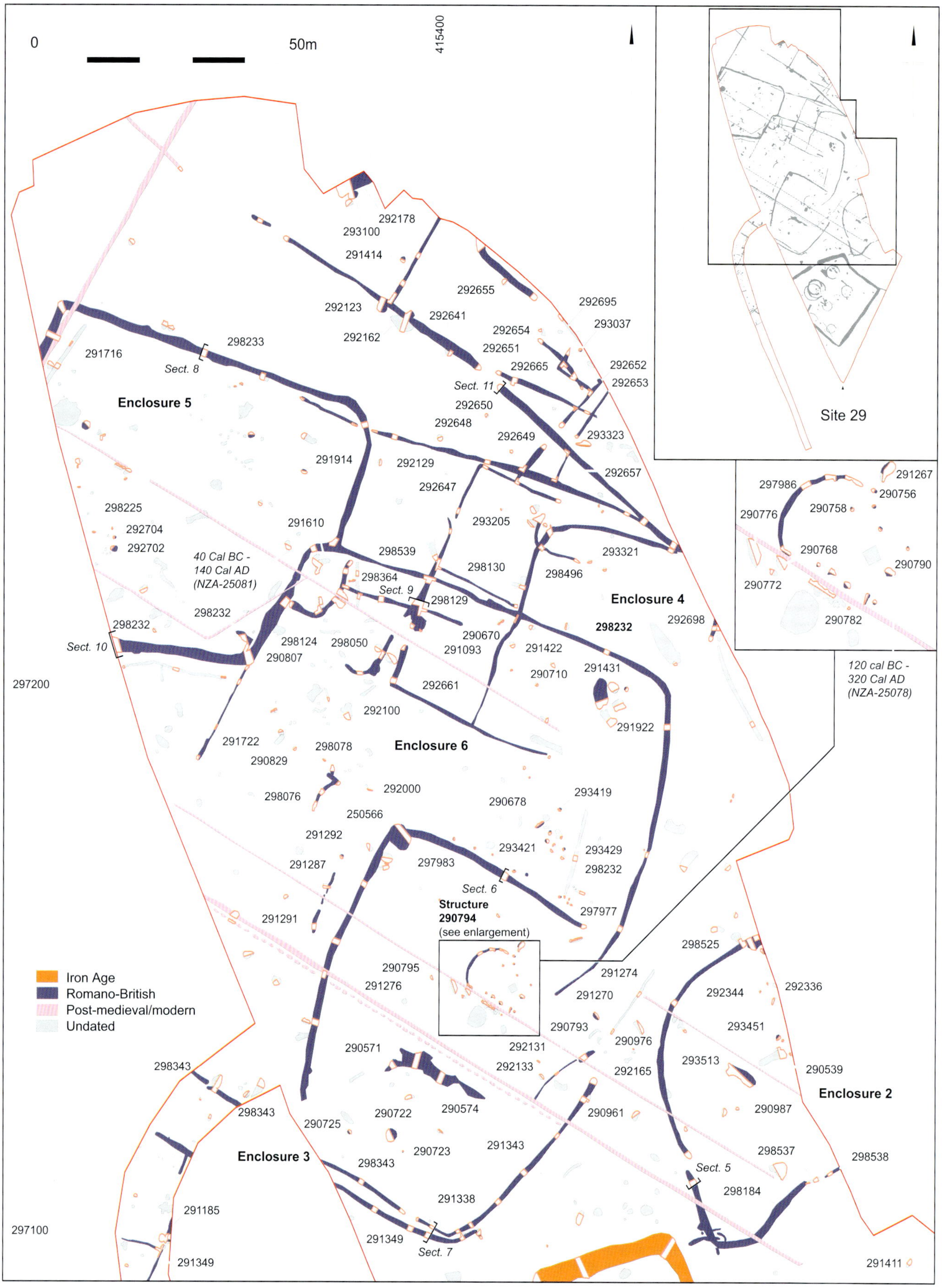

Fig. 144 Romano-British Enclosures 2–6

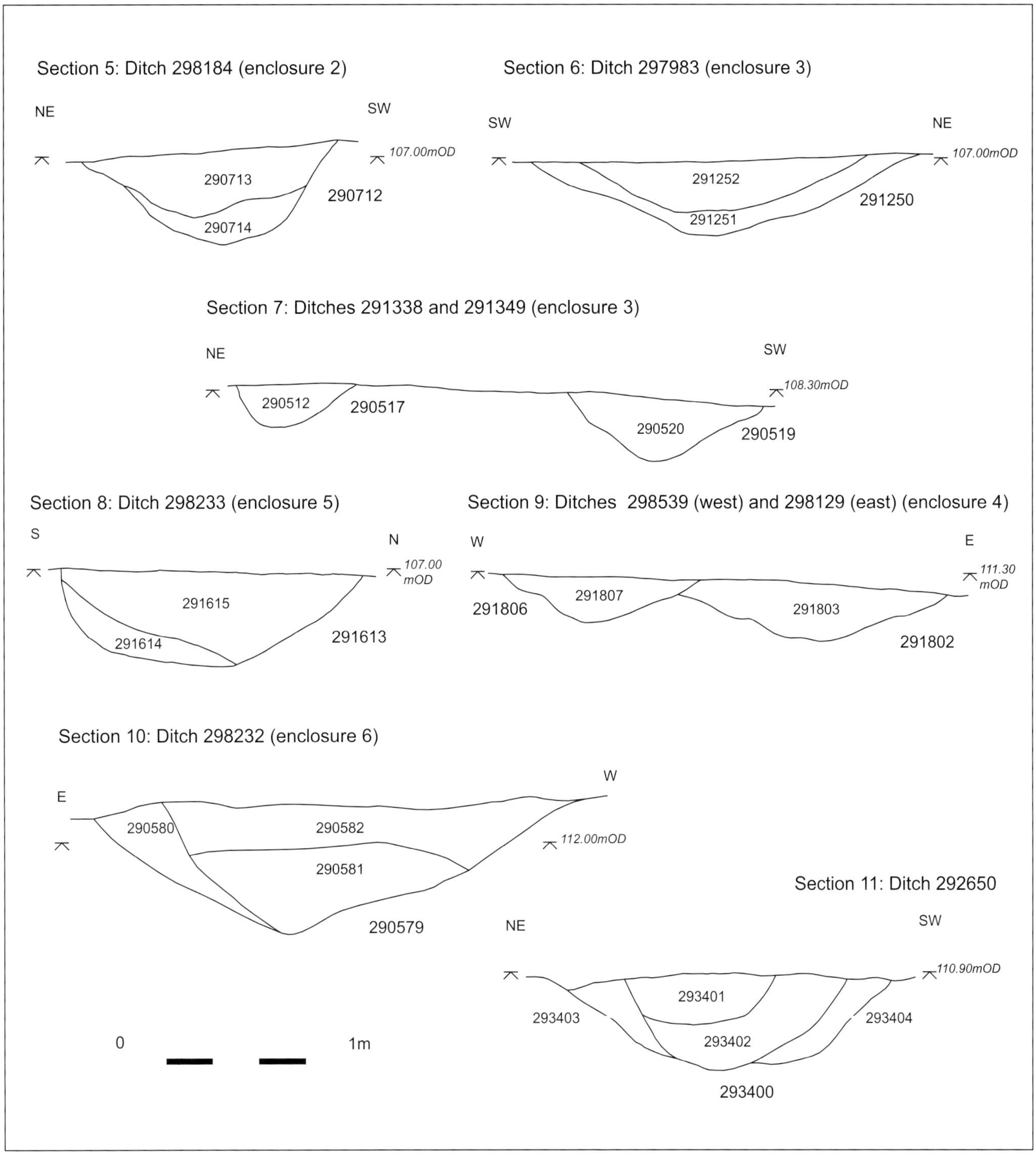

Fig. 145 Sections across enclosure and other ditches

with a charcoal-rich fill containing four sherds (36 g) of Romano-British pottery. There was a similar, but undated feature (292133) measuring 1.3 m by 0.8 m and 0.2 m deep, some 14 m to the south-east, also within the entrance area, with an adjacent posthole (292131) with the possible remains of an *in situ* post, and another more centrally within the enclosure (290795). (Although the various forms of fire-pit and features with *in situ* burning are of uncertain function, they are referred to below as 'hearths' for ease of reference).

A burnt deposit containing fire-cracked stones in the upper fill at the northernmost corner of ditch 297983 (section 250566) produced 29 sherds (2490 g) from the base and lower body of a Malvernian bucket jar. The ditch also produced a single sherd of late 1st–mid-2nd century pottery and a few undiagnostic Romano-British sherds. Quantities of burnt stone were recorded around the ditch circuit.

Ditch 298343 on the south-west side appears to have continued past the south-western corner and beyond the area of excavation, indicating that the enclosure was probably connected to a wider array of ditched features. Clearly associated with the enclosure was a further length of ditch (291349) that ran parallel to its south-western side and around its southern corner (Fig. 145). Just east of the corner, its eastern end turned sharply to the south-east towards the entrance of Enclosure 1, possibly indicating some relationship between them. At the corner the two parallel ditches were separated by no more than 0.3 m, widening to 2.5 m apart to the north-west. A length of ditch recorded further west may be the same feature, in which case the two ditches had separated to over 11 m apart, this latter section of ditch having a short offset to the south, possibly tying it into a series of further ditches and gullies to the south.

The main feature within Enclosure 3 was a structure (290794, structure 7) lying centrally toward the north-east end. The structure – possibly two overlapping structures, consisted of a rectangular setting of posts, bounded at north-west end by a semi-circular gully (Fig. 144). The post setting, comprising a line of five post holes up to 0.45 m in depth on the south-west side and a line of three on the north-east side, measured *c* 7 m long by 6.5 m wide. A very irregular linear feature (290772) *c* 2.6 m long and up to 0.2 m deep, outside and parallel to the south-west line of posts, may represent part of the same structure. The curved gully (297986 and 290756), which had a projected diameter of *c* 9 m, gave the structure an overall length of over 12 m. In one segment, a series of small holes in the base may have been stakeholes. There was an oval feature (290790), possibly a hearth, between the end posts at the south-east end of the structure, which produced a radiocarbon date of AD 120–320 (1833±30BP; NZA-25078) (Fig. 143, Table 102). Measuring 1 m by 0.5 m, it was surrounded by large stones. Its base, at a depth of 0.23 m, showed signs of scorching and it contained large quantities of charcoal, large pieces of burnt clay and numerous stones.

The function of this structure is uncertain. The curved gully at its north-west end is reminiscent of the native Iron Age tradition of roundhouse construction (which continued into the Romano-British period), while the rectangular setting of postholes would be more typical of the Romano-British period (although there are Iron Age parallels). For a single building to incorporate both techniques is unusual and it is possible that it represents overlapping buildings of two different phases, although their symmetrical relationship has the appearance of a physical association. If a single structure, it appears to have occupied an important position at the northern end of Enclosure 3, facing south-east towards the enclosure's wide entrance, but given the central position of the hearth where one would expect the entrance at its south-east end, a domestic function seems unlikely. It may have had some craft or industrial function requiring the use of fire, with the semicircular gully forming a wind break for the hearth. Alternatively, it may have had some religious function, perhaps as a shrine, its curved gully at the north-west giving an overall form comparable to a number of Romano-British apsidal shrines. Although a single BB1 sherd dated to after *c* AD 240, from part of the curved gully, would point to a mid-3rd century or later date for the structure, this could be intrusive; the rest of the pottery – from two of the postholes (290758 and 290782), the hearth and the gully – was consistent with a mid-/late 2nd century (or later) date, more in line with the phasing suggested here. A posthole (290768) outside the western end of the curved gully may also be associated with the structure, as may a large feature (290776) in the same area, measuring 3.2 m long and 0.6 m wide, and 0.7 m deep containing four naturally accumulated fills but producing no finds.

There was a range of other features including pits and postholes, both dated and undated, within the enclosure, although they were not necessarily associated with its use. Although some of the postholes were located relatively close together, they formed no recognisable structures.

A large feature (290571), *c* 20 m long, up to 1.6 m wide and 0.3 m deep, lay across the long axis of the enclosure, narrowing and curving towards the west at its west end. Above a thin primary fill the feature had been filled with a dump of material containing 15 sherds (272 g) of Romano-British pottery, including three mid-3rd to mid-4th century mortarium sherds, and a 3rd century Nene Valley beaker. The feature was cut by a similar feature (290574), up to 2 m wide and 0.2 m deep, which produced five sherds (90 g). These large irregular features, of uncertain function, would appear to be late within the occupation of the site; it may be significant that the large irregular feature (293513, above) in Enclosure 2, which also produced a large quantity of pottery, was also dated to the later 3rd–4th centuries.

A large pit (290722), 2.5 m in diameter and 0.4 m deep, towards the south-west of the enclosure, contained dumps of burnt material including 31 sherds (160) of Romano-British pottery. Two small adjacent pits (290723 and 290725) contained similar burnt material, the former producing six sherds (including one BB1 sherd dated to after AD 215/6), the latter producing ten sherds (185 g), one with a 2nd–4th century date.

Enclosure 4

The remaining enclosures, at the north end of the site, overlapped, and their identification in the following sequence is based on the recorded stratigraphical relationships between them (Figs 144 and 145).

A rectangular arrangement of ditches (292647, 292661 and 298129) towards the north-east of the site appeared to have been the earliest stratigraphically, although none produced any pottery. They appeared to form a small rectangular enclosure (Enclosure 4), possibly a field or paddock, 43 m long (aligned NE–SW) and 16 m wide with associated, partly bounded, areas to its north-east and south-east.

The ditch on the enclosure's south-western side (292661), which was *c* 1.5 m wide and no more than *c* 0.3 m deep, continued beyond its south-eastern corner, while the south-eastern side turned at the north and also continued towards the south-east, leaving a 4 m wide entrance gap at the north-east corner. Another ditch (292649/292652), itself with a 4 m wide break, extended north-east from the northern end of the enclosure. The north-west side of the enclosure was cut by a later ditch (Fig. 145), but it appeared to have had two further breaks, one *c* 3 m wide towards the enclosure's south-west corner, with a posthole (291093) just behind the northern ditch terminal, and another of indeterminate width towards the north-west corner. The enclosure contained a small number of pits, two of which (293205 at the north and 290670 close to the eastern side), had charcoal-rich fills.

Within the partly bounded area to the south-east of the enclosure (the eastern extent of which may have been represented by ditch 292698, which produced six sherds of Romano-British pottery) there was a number of isolated postholes and pits of varying dimension. Given the complex arrangement of enclosure and other ditches in this area it is not possible to determine any relationship between these features, or with the ditches. The majority of pits were 1–2 m wide and less than 0.2 m deep, and four (291422, 291431, 291922 and 293321) had charcoal-rich fills, the first two also producing pottery. Most of the pottery (over 100 sherds weighing 1377 g) came from a mid-/late 2nd century necked jar, recovered from the upper fill of pit 291431, which measured 1 m by 0.8 m and 0.43 m deep. One small feature (290710) contained two pieces of quernstone. There were no Romano-British features in the bounded area to the north.

Enclosure 5

At the north-west of the site, a number of ditches appear to form a subrectangular enclosure measuring 65 m by 50 m, widening to at least 54 m at the west. There was no visible entrance, although this may have been located towards its south-west corner which lay outside the excavation area. Its northern side was in approximately the same alignment as that of Enclosure 4, from which it was separated by a gap of *c* 18–20 m, possibly indicating a relationship between them (Fig. 146). An oval hearth (292129), measuring 1.2 m by 0.6 m and 0.2 m deep, lying in this gap, had a charcoal-rich upper fill (including a large quantity of charred grain) containing fire-cracked stones.

The identification, and indeed the phasing, of Enclosure 5, however, is problematic. In plan, it appeared to have been added onto, and therefore be later than, Enclosure 6 (below) to its south-east, as the ditch on the northern part of its circuit (298233) did not continue south beyond the ditch of Enclosure 6 (298232). Ditch 298233, which was *c* 1.3 m wide and 0.4 m deep with a shallow U-shaped profile (Fig. 145), was interpreted in the field as ending at a terminal at the point where it was subsequently cut by ditch 298232. Moreover, since ditch 298232 also formed what would be the southern side of Enclosure 5, the enclosure must originally have been open at the south-west, and therefore not, in fact, an enclosed space until the later ditch was constructed. Alternatively, if the enclosure had originally been fully bounded, there would have been a curious kink along its south-east side, fortuitously incorporated at a later date as the northern corner of Enclosure 6.

In fact, despite the recorded stratigraphical relationship between the two ditches, no clear margin between the fills of ditches 298233 and 298232 is indicated on the section drawn at their intersection; the recorded relationship between the ditches should therefore be treated with some caution; the possibility that Enclosure 5 was an addition to Enclosure 6 should be considered. The matter is not resolved by the ceramic evidence from the ditches. While a single rim sherd of a 3rd century mortarium recovered from the lower of two fills in Enclosure 5/6 ditch (section 290807) appears to provide a *terminus post quem* for the infilling of the ditch, ditch 298253, produced only two sherds from its upper fill, one of samian and another of possibly late 3rd or 4th century date.

The majority of features within the enclosure were postholes and pits of varying dimension, most of them undated. Pit 292702, measuring 1.3 m by 1.1 m and 0.15 m deep, produced a single late 1st–mid-2nd century sherd, while pit 291914, measuring 1.5 m by 1.2 m and 0.3 m deep, produced five sherds (345 g) of probable mid-/late 2nd century date and a further 50 *(c* 400 g) of less diagnostic form. The features were largely distributed in two loose clusters, towards the south-west and north-east, the latter group incorporating a line of small unexcavated features, possibly the postholes of a fence line. An undated linear feature (291716) running almost parallel to the north-west side of the enclosure was interpreted as the remains of a hedge-line.

Enclosure 6

Ditch 298232, which formed the east, north and part of the western sides of Enclosure 6, cut across the centre of Enclosure 4, and, as described above, was recorded as also cutting ditch 298233 of Enclosure 5 (Fig. 146). At the south-east it also encroached on Enclosure 3. As such it would appear to represent the final phase of enclosure construction on the site. This would be consistent with a sherd of 3rd century type mortarium found in the lower ditch fill (290808) on the north-west corner of the enclosure (section 290807). However, just 5 m to the north-east, at the north-west corner of the enclosure, the lower fill (290802) of ditch section 290801) produced a very early radiocarbon date of 40 cal BC–cal AD 140 (1955±35 BP, NZA-25081) (Fig. 143, Table 102).

The ditch varied considerably in its dimensions, being 1.5 m wide and 0.6 m deep with a V-shaped profile towards the west, but as little as 0.45 m wide and 0.2 m deep along the south-eastern side. The ditch bowed out slightly along the north-east side, which was over 70 m long; it bowed out more noticeably along the 60 m long south-east side, which ran south-south-west, before curving to the south-west, and narrowing significantly towards its apparent terminal. At the north-west corner,

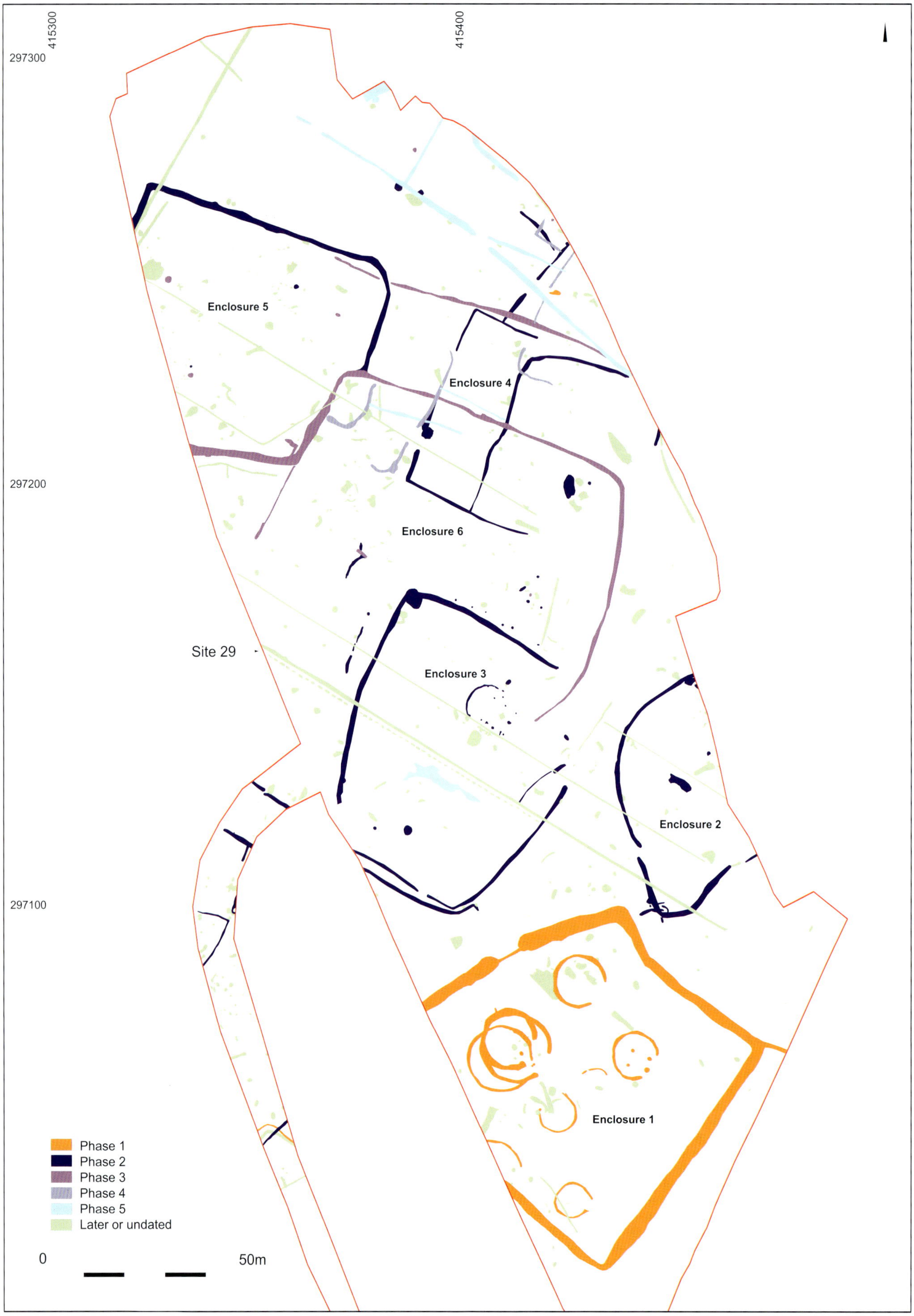

Fig. 146 Suggested phases of Romano-British enclosures

the ditch turned to the south-west for 25 m, then to the west, continuing beyond the area of excavation (Fig. 144), although a narrow gully (291722) continued its south-westerly line for a further 20 m from the corner, possibly forming an internal division. The enclosure, therefore, appeared to be open at the south and south-west.

An alternative interpretation is that the south-eastern corner of Enclosure 6 was formed by the south-eastern corner of Enclosure 3, which would make the latter an internal sub-division within a much larger, but possibly fully bounded enclosure (over 100 m in both directions). The westward continuation of ditch 298343 would represent its south-western side, extending beyond the area of excavation. Its wide south-east facing entrance, formed by the incurving end of ditch 298232 entrance and the northern terminal of ditch 291338, and possibly incorporating the other lengths of ditch (291274, 292165 and 290973), would have provided access into the sub-enclosure at a point immediately in front of the post-built structure.

As referred to above, a single rim sherd of a 3rd century mortarium recovered from the lower of two fills in ditch 298232 (along the section shared with Enclosure 5) may provide a *terminus post quem* for the infilling of the ditch. The remaining pottery was either of earlier date and (assuming the context of the mortarium sherd was secure) therefore residual, or of unspecific Romano-British date.

Some of the features in the north-eastern part of the enclosure also lay within the suggested boundaries of Enclosure 4, and have been described above. Within the rest of the enclosure, a short curvilinear feature (298124) in the northern corner may have enclosed a small subrectangular space measuring internally 12 m by 8 m. There was an irregular pit (291610) of unknown function, measuring 1.6 m by 1.2 m and 0.4 m deep, in the northern corner. There were also a number of isolated pits of no obvious function in the same general area, as well as a possible quarry pit (292100), 2.2 m in diameter and 0.4 m deep, with four naturally accumulated fills.

Further south was an arrangement of two short, possibly connected, linear features, their relationship obscured by a modern geotechnical trial pit. The longer feature (298076), at least 7 m long, produced 106 sherds (653 g) of pottery (from contexts 290815, 290817 and 290824) with a date range of late 2nd–4th century, suggesting a date for the infilling in the 3rd century. A shorter feature at the north (298078) produced a single Romano-British sherd. Again, a possible comparison may be drawn with the later features (293513 and 290571) in Enclosures 2 and 3 (above). Some 8 m to the north-west was an oval feature (290829), possibly a hearth measuring 0.8 m by 0.5 m, with a concave base 0.2 m deep burnt *in situ*, and filled with a deposit of burnt stones and charcoal. Also possibly associated was an alignment of three short ditch segments (291291), some 12 m to the south, with a combined length of 12 m. The northern segment was cut by a pit (291287), which produced two sherds (45 g) of pottery providing a date of mid-2nd century or later, and contained a large amount of charcoal of a wide range of wood species.

There was a tight cluster of features towards the eastern side of the enclosure, just north of Enclosure 3. It included at least six postholes within an area 8 m across, but forming no recognisable structure. One of the postholes (293421) produced a single sherd of Iron Age pottery, but posthole 293419 produced a mid–late 2nd century sherd and that from posthole 293429 was of general Romano-British date. Also in the group was a steep-sided pit (290678) measuring 1.1 m by 0.6 m and 0.3 m deep.

These features appear to have been bounded to the east by an undated ditch (298232) running approximately north, for over 16 m, from 2 m outside the north-east side of Enclosure 3. At its southern end there was a short right-angled gully (297977) extending 1.1 m to the south-east and 1.2 m to the north-east; it was 0.25 m wide and up to 0.18 m deep and is of unknown function. However, extending north-west from it, and possibly associated with it, there was an intermittent line of up to six probable postholes running parallel to the Enclosure 3 ditch, between 0.6 m and 1.7 m out from the edge of the ditch.

Two lengths of ditch (292648), with a combined length of over 70 m and a shallow and irregular U-shaped profile, lay *c* 23 m outside Enclosure 6 and parallel to its north-east side and may therefore be contemporary with the enclosure, occupying a similar stratigraphical position. Ditch 292648 cut across the ditch running north from Enclosure 4, and the ditch of Enclosure 5 passed through the 2.8 m wide break towards its north-west end.

Later features

A number of linear features towards the north of the site were stratigraphically later than the infilling of the Enclosure 6 ditch. Cutting across the north-east side of the enclosure (and also the north-west side of Enclosure 4) was a 20 m long curved ditch (298539) aligned approximately NE–SW, its north-east end narrowing and curving to the north (Fig. 145). Its upper fill (291080/291086) contained three sherds – two Romano-British and one Iron Age. At the south-west, after a 4 m break, a second ditch (298050) continued on the same alignment before curving to the north-west. Although it is notable that the break between the ditches corresponds to a break in the Enclosure 4 ditch, suggesting some functional relationship, the two features are clearly stratigraphically separate. It is possible that feature 298124 located in the northern corner of Enclosure 6 (described above) may be associated as it shared a similar orientation and form.

A similar arrangement of three ditch segments (298496, 292657 and 292653) lay *c* 15 m to the east, in a comparable stratigraphic position – again cutting Enclosure 4 as well as ditch 292648 (possibly contemporary with Enclosure 6, above). Combined, these ditch segments (which continued north-east beyond the excavation area), ran south-west for over 30 m before turning towards the south-east for a further 10 m. The segments had similar shallow and irregular U-shaped profiles. The two breaks between them were 6 m and 3 m wide, north and south respectively. They produced 31 sherds of Romano-British pottery, including one of 2nd century date.

The stratigraphically latest features on the site were a series of ditches in the north-east part of the site. They included two otherwise undated and almost parallel narrow ditches, both cutting ditch 298539, as well as across part of Enclosure 4. Ditch 298364 was 24 m, 1.3 m wide and 0.4 m deep with a shallow 'U' profile, and ditch 298130 was 17 m long.

Most of the features of this phase, however, lay over 40 m to the north and extended beyond the limits of the excavation. Ditch 292650 ran north-west for 46 m from the eastern edge of the excavation to a rounded terminal (Fig. 145), cutting across ditches 292648 and 292657. It was 1.4 m wide and 0.4 m deep, with a U-shaped profile and up to four fills possibly indicating a recut; among the four potsherds from the middle fill (293402) at the terminal was one of possible 3rd century date, providing some support for a relatively late date. A less substantial ditch (292651), 21 m long, up to 1 m wide and 0.3 m deep, converged with it on its north-east side, ending at an adjacent terminal. After an entrance gap (4 m from ditch 292657 and 3 m from ditch 292651), a third ditch (292641), up to 1.8 m wide, continued the same approximate line for a further 45 m, cutting pit 292123 containing three Romano-British sherds (150 g). From it an arm ran at a right-angle beyond the edge of the excavation. These ditches produced further Romano-British pottery. Two further undated lengths of ditch ran on approximately the same line as 292641 to the northern limit of excavation. Two sherds of medieval pottery found with two of Romano-British date in the single fill of a tree hollow (292162) cut by ditch 292641 are probably intrusive, although it is possible that this stratigraphically late field system is post-Romano-British.

A number of features lay to the north-east of this main ditch alignment. Among them was an irregular pit (293100), 2.6 m by 1.6 m, and 0.25 m deep, containing 13 sherds (288 g) of Romano-British pottery, and a piece of *tegula*. Its edge was cut by a large feature (292178), at least 7 m by 3 m, and 0.3 m deep and extending outside the excavation area, which produced a further 14 Romano-British sherds (212 g). Among the sherds from both features were a number dated to mid-3rd–4th centuries. The recurrence is again noted of late pottery within a large, generally unassociated and isolated feature. A nearby pit (291414), 1 m in diameter and 0.25 m deep, contained a single Romano-British sherd.

A number of other possibly associated linear features were also noted in this area (292654, 292655, 292665 and 292695). One gully (292665), forming a right-angle with arms 8 m and 4.6 m long, was up to 0.34 m wide and 0.2 m deep with a shallow U-shaped profile, its single fill producing 23 Romano-British sherds (118 g). It cut ditch 292652 (probably associated with Enclosure 4), as well as a slightly curved length of ditch (292654), the latter containing 30 Romano-British sherds (1784 g), most of which were from a storage jar, but including two sherds of a 3rd century BB1 jar. An adjacent posthole (293037) produced a sherd of samian.

Finds

Metal finds, by Kelly Powell

Eleven iron objects were recovered from this site (Tables 103–4). The most notable of these was a socketed knife from context 291345, in ditch 291349 (associated with Enclosure 3). Four of the remaining finds were certain nails or nail fragments with one further probable nail fragment. The nail from hearth 291270 (at the east of Enclosure 3) was too fragmentary for classification, but the remaining three complete examples from Romano-British contexts were classified by Manning type. Pit 290722 (Enclosure 3) produced a common type 1b. A hobnail (Manning type 10) was recovered from pit 291292 (Enclosure 6), whilst posthole 292704 (Enclosure 5) produced a less common type 2 nail. The remaining iron finds include a sub-rectangular length of bar of unknown function, broken at one end, from Iron Age enclosure ditch 291113 (upper fill 292605), and four unidentifiable lumps of heavily concreted iron.

Table 103 Metal finds excluding nails

Feature	*Iron object / misc. object*
Ditch 291349	1 knife frag.
Pit 291389	1 misc. object
Tree throw/hollow/pit 292448	3 misc objects
Enclosure 1 ditch 291113	1 bar frag.
Pit 292925	1 misc. object

Table 104 Nail classification by type

Feature	*Type 1b*	*Type 10*	*Type 2*	*Unclass.*	*Total*
Pit 290722	1	–	–	–	1
Hearth 291270	–	–	–	1	1
Pit 291292	–	1	–	–	1
Posthole 292704	–	–	1	–	1
Total	1	1	1	1	4

Worked stone, by Ruth Shaffrey

Four pieces of worked stone were recovered including one whetstone and three rotary querns. The whetstone was an unworked but utilised pebble and was recovered from the primary fill of the northern terminal of Iron

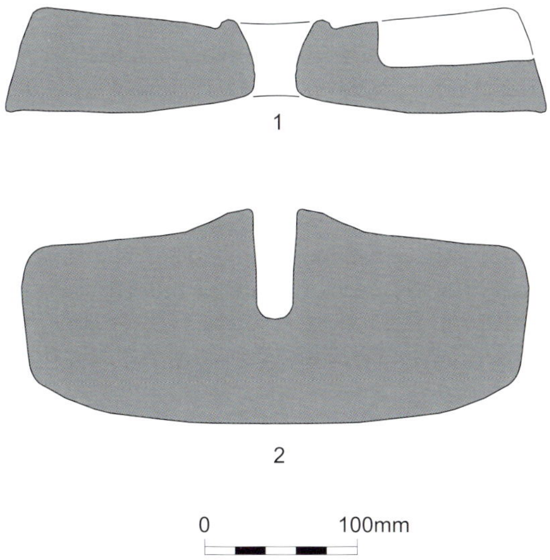

Fig. 147 Rotary querns

Age structure 1c 292666. The rotary querns (Fig. 147) all appeared to be made from Millstone Grit and included one upper stone of projecting hopper type (found during the evaluation) and two lower stones of thick beehive type (Enclosure 4, pit 290710 and Enclosure 2, pit 290987. The latter quern was complete and was recovered with the iron spindle still in the socket, and was the only find at the top of pit 290987. The deposition of querns in pits of Romano-British date is not unusual (Clarke 2000, 25) but the completeness of the quern and the lack of any other finds from the pit indicate that this was a deliberately placed deposit (Shaffrey 2003, 165).

Catalogue of worked stone

1. Natural whetstone, complete: slightly shelly grey sandstone elongate pebble used as a whetstone on two edges and one face; L 110 mm; W 30 mm, T 20 mm; probably Middle–Late Iron Age, context 292671, ditch 292666. ON 299950
2. Fragment of upper rotary quern: Millstone Grit; lateral handle slot measuring 90 mm long by 38 mm deep; biconical shaped perforation and slight projecting hopper; D 350 mm; T 60 mm max., evaluation context 290404 (Fig. 147, 1)
3. Lower rotary quern: Millstone Grit; two fragments joining; straight edges and convex base; slightly lipped towards central socket but otherwise flat grinding surface; grinding surface worn smooth; D *c* 310 mm; T 140 mm, context 290667, pit 290710 (Fig. 147, 2)
4. Complete lower rotary quern: probably Millstone Grit; iron spindle still attached in centre; convex base with flat grinding surface; pecked all over; D 410 mm; T 180 mm max., context 290988, pit 290987. ON 299952

Roman glass, by H.E.M. Cool

As on Sites 15 and 19 the only item of Roman vessel glass from this site was from an approximately rectangular body fragment from a blue/green prismatic bottle of the 1st–2nd centuries AD (ON 292705). This piece, which measured 36 mm by 30 mm, with a wall thickness 5 mm, was of additional interest as it had been deliberately flaked to produce a sharp edge. This type of re-use has been noted quite frequently on the glass from Roman sites, (Price and Cottam 1998, 9).

Amber bead, by Paul Booth

A single amber bead (SF 299951) came from context 292926, the fill of pit 292925 in Enclosure 1. Unfortunately, the bead was shattered (by a mattock blow) at the time of discovery and only some of the tiny fragments were recovered. It is possible, however, that the object was incomplete before it was found, as was the case, for example, with beads from Danebury (Cunliffe 1984, 396), where the rarity of such items in the Iron Age was also noted (see also Beck and Shennan 1991). Its presence here is one of few hints at wider contacts through exchange. The form of the bead was annular and its external diameter can be estimated at approximately 12 mm.

Iron Age pottery, by Paul Booth

Fourteen sherds (326 g) of hand-made Iron Age pottery were recorded. As with the Site 19 material (Chapter 24) a wide range of fabric types was noted, but these probably all belong to three or four fabric groups containing sherds in which the relative proportions

Table 105 Middle Iron Age pottery fabrics

Fabric group/ fabric	*No.*	*Weight (g)*	*Context*	*Comment*
Sand, organics/voids & iron oxides				
AV3	1	43	292605	Jar rim, burnished
AV13	1	6	291212	Jar rim
AIZ3	1	5	291086	Jar rim
AIZ4	1	27	291461	
AZ13	3	41	290873	
AZ14	1	25	291309	Rough vertical striations
Sand & clay pellets				
APV5	1	14	291075	
PA5	1	47	291396	Internal burnishing (*cf.* Warwickshire fabric P31)
Quartz/quartzite & sand etc				
QA5	1	33	293331	Scored
QAV5	2	62	292410	Base angle
?Organic voids & sand				
ZA3	1	23	293334	Jar rim, external burnishing (*cf.* Warwick-shire fabric C13)
Total	14	326		

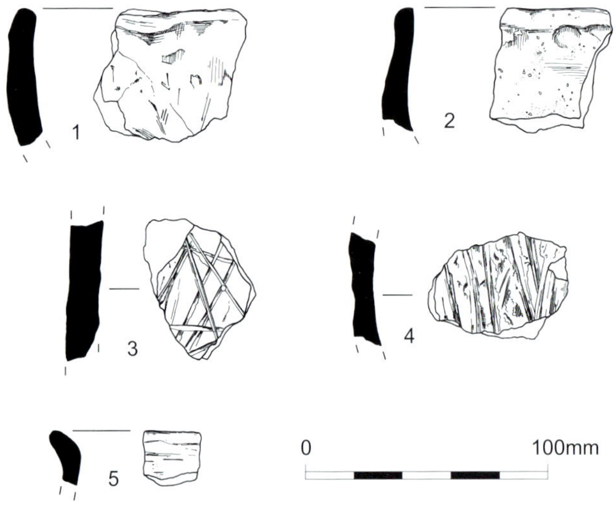

Fig. 148 Iron Age pottery

and/or size of the principal inclusion types were slightly variable (Table 105).

It is possible that fabric ZA3 was a component of the sand/organics/iron oxides group, but the predominance of the voids, regardless of their original nature, suggests that this was a distinct fabric. A notable characteristic of this small group, compared with others from the M6 Toll, was the relatively high incidence of surface treatments. Three of the sherds had been partly burnished. One (in fabric QA5) had deeply incised lines in the 'scored ware' tradition (Elsdon 1992) while a second sherd (in fabric AZI4), had distinct rough vertical striations which may also link it to this tradition. The M6 Toll sites lie very much at the western margin of the main distribution of scored ware (*cf. ibid.*, 84, 87), although occasional examples are known from considerably further west, for example at the Berth, Baschurch (Shropshire; Morris and Gelling 1991, 60–1). Locally there are further examples of the style from Coleshill (only two, Booth 2006) to the south and from Fisherwick to the north (eg Banks and Morris 1979, 48, fig. 12; curiously, although Elsdon refers to this site it does not appear on her distribution map). The scored ware tradition, originating perhaps in the 4th century BC, is thought to survive right up to the Roman Conquest in areas such as the lower Nene Valley (Elsdon 1992, 89; *cf.* Knight 2002, 133–4). In our area it can probably be regarded as an indicator of a Middle or Middle–Late Iron Age date.

Such dating is supported by the minimal evidence for vessel forms in this assemblage; simple, probably barrel shaped vessels with upright or slightly everted rims. These forms are consistent with those from the other M6 Toll sites, and with forms in the larger Coleshill and Fisherwick assemblages.

Eleven of the sherds (282 g) came from features within the Iron Age Enclosure 1. The sherd in fabric AZI4 came from the fill of a ditch (298325) to the west of the enclosure, and sherds in fabrics AIZ3 and APV5 were from the area of Enclosure 6. The quantities of material are inadequate to suggest a chronological sequence, but the association of the scored sherd No. 3 with the latest phase of the main roundhouse (1c) would be consistent with a date in the later part of the Middle Iron Age, confirmed by the radiocarbon date of 360–40 cal BC from another component of this structure.

Catalogue (Fig. 148)

1. Fabric AV3, dark brownish-grey. Abraded rim of simple upright jar. Patchy internal and external burnish, context 292605, fill of Enclosure 1 ditch cut 292604
2. Fabric ZA3, black. Simple upright jar rim, context 293334, Enclosure 1 roundhouse structure 1b
3. Fabric QA5, reddish-brown with black surfaces. Sherd of thick walled jar with deep scoring, context 293331, Enclosure 1 roundhouse structure 1c
4. Fabric AZI4, dark grey-brown. Scored ware type body sherd, context 291309, ditch 298325 west of Enclosure 1
5. Fabric AIZ3, dark grey-brown to black. Everted rim of ?jar, context 291086, fill of ditch 298539 in area of Enclosure 6

Romano-British pottery, by Ruth Leary

Some 745 sherds (11756 g) of Romano-British pottery were identified from the site (Table 106).

The illustrated sherds (Fig. 149) and discussion of stratified group

Enclosure 1

Ten sherds of Romano-British pottery were recovered from the enclosure ditch. These included the neck of a ring-necked FLA3 flagon with a fairly splayed neck typical of the early 2nd century and a samian sherd. Sherds from an SV3 tankard of 2nd century type (Webster 1976, no. 39) were present in context 292802 and a SV1 sherd from 292312. There were also undiagnostic body sherds of fabrics R9 and SV3 from 291910. These Romano-British sherds were scattered around the ditch circuit and all came from its upper fills. The sherds suggest that the ditch was still visible as a hollow in the 2nd century.

Enclosure 2

Only seven sherds of pottery (30 g) came from the enclosure ditch and these comprised undiagnostic body sherds of SV3, R7 and samian ware. Some sherds of a Central Gaulish samian form 31 of Antonine date came from entrance gully 298538 context 293067.

Within the enclosure, two undiagnostic R5 body sherds came from pit 293451 (context 293453), and an abraded sherd from a carinated O2 bowl was found in tree hollow 292336 (fill 292337), the latter probably belonging to the late 1st–2nd centuries. Feature 293513 (context 293516) contained 37 sherds of Romano-British pottery. Diagnostic sherds included a small body sherd from an ROX bowl dating to AD 270–400 (Young 1977, type C48), sherds from an SV3 wide-mouthed jar and an SV3 narrow-necked jar, the spout and body of a bead and flange MH2 mortarium broadly datable to the

Table 106 Quantities of Romano-British pottery wares and fabrics

Ware group	Ware	Count	Weight	Rel % count	Rel % weight
A	DR20	18	57.9	2.4	0.5
BB1	BB1	47	302.1	6.3	2.6
BB1	R18	4	7.5	0.5	0.1
BB1 total		*51*	*309.6*	*6.9*	*2.6*
C	CT	3	18.8	0.4	0.2
	CTA1	11	59.0	1.5	0.5
C total		*14*	*77.8*	*1.9*	*0.7*
DBY	DBY	4	39.9	0.5	0.3
E	E1	1	54.6	0.1	0.5
F	CC1	1	4.1	0.1	+
	NV	3	47.5	0.4	0.4
	ROX	6	103.7	0.8	0.9
F total		*10*	*155.3*	*1.3*	*1.3*
G	G2	23	1625.2	3.1	13.8
	MALV	34	2490.6	4.6	21.2
G total		*57*	*4115.8*	*7.7*	*35.0*
M	MH	19	907.4	2.6	7.7
O	O1	32	270.3	4.3	2.3
	O10	8	35.0	1.1	0.3
	O2	10	78.8	1.3	0.7
	O4	15	68.6	2.0	0.6
	O5	5	15.4	0.7	0.1
	O6	22	28	3.0	0.2
	O9	3	299.2	0.4	2.6
	SV4	2	16.3	0.3	0.1
O total		*97*	*811.6*	*13.0*	*6.9*
R	R	1	6.2	0.1	0.1
	R11	7	35.1	0.9	0.3
	R12	8	45.3	1.1	0.4
	R13	47	395.8	6.3	3.4
	R15	14	85.2	1.9	0.7
	R16	11	137.4	1.5	1.2
	R17	5	89.9	0.7	0.8
	R19	1	16.5	0.1	0.1
	R2	56	670.8	7.5	5.7
	R21	2	2.4	0.3	+
	R28	6	282.6	0.8	2.4
	R3	3	11.5	0.4	0.1
	R4	6	36.3	0.8	0.3
	R5	153	2182.3	20.5	18.6
	R7	23	134.0	3.1	1.1
	R8	7	70.0	0.9	0.6
	R9	7	45.0	0.9	0.4
R total		*357*	*4246.3*	*47.9*	*36.1*
S	TS	33	298.3	4.4	2.5
SV	SV1	26	237.5	3.5	2.0
	SV3	36	265.5	4.8	2.3
	SV4	10	34.4	1.3	0.3
	SV5	4	77.4	0.5	0.7
	SV6	5	24.8	0.7	0.2
SV total		*81*	*639.6*	*10.9*	*5.4*
W	FLA2	1	11.9	0.1	0.1
	FLA3	1	25.5	0.1	0.2
W total		*2*	*37.4*	*0.3*	*0.3*
WS	FLB2	1	4.3	0.1	+
Total		745	11,755.8		

2nd century, a scrap from an NV1 beaker and an ?East Gaulish Dr 31 or 31R of late 2nd century or later date. Overall, this group dates to the late 3rd or 4th century.

Enclosure 3

The enclosure ditch produced 55 sherds (2838 g) of pottery, but most came from the base and lower body of a Malvernian tubby jar (from context 290578) which seemed to be burnt. The remainder included an R12 jar with short everted rim of late 1st–early 2nd century type from context 290962 and an O9 storage jar from context 290557 (Fig. 149, 1). A samian sherd, probably from form 31 and of Antonine date, came from context 290971 in associated ditch 291349.

Cutting the enclosure ditch on the east side, pit 290961 produced sherds of R11, R15, O1 and a rim sherd from a bead rim bowl, probably a carinated bowl of the mid–late 2nd century, from its upper fill (290959).

Within the enclosure, gully 297986 (context 290753), in structure 290794, contained four sherds of pottery, three of fabric O1 and one R5 wide-mouthed jar with bifid rim, while context 290757 contained three sherds of pottery and these included sherds from a O6 wide-mouthed jar with an everted rim. These wide-mouthed jars compared with vessels from the Shenstone kiln in form, dating to the mid-/late 2nd–3rd centuries. A further body sherd from a BB1 jar with obtuse lattice decoration and shoulder groove from context 290757 gives a date in the 3rd century after *c* AD 240 (Bidwell 1985, 175). Body sherds of CTA1 and R21 came from fills 290759 and 290783 of the postholes, and hearth fill 290791 contained sherds of O4 and Antonine samian. All the sherds were abraded or very abraded. The wide-mouthed jars and BB1 jar suggest a date in the 3rd century after *c* AD 240 for the infilling of the gully. Feature 291267 context 291268 contained an undiagnostic R8 sherd.

Pit 290722 contained several early types, an R16 rusticated jar and a bead rim hemispherical bowl, an R7 jar with combed wavy line decoration, an R5 carinated bowl, an R5 narrow-necked jar and an R5 wide-mouthed jar. These vessels suggest activity in the early to mid-2nd century.

Sherds from an R17 jar, an O1 cup and an SV5 narrow necked jar came from pit 290725 (context 290726) (Fig. 149, 2–3). These are not well-dated forms but Evans notes the small bowl form in 3rd century contexts at Wroxeter and Alcester (Evans *et al.* 2000, bowl type 4.1). A date range in the late 2nd–3rd century would be possible.

Pit 290723 context 290724 contained a BB1 sherd from a jar with obtuse lattice dating from after AD 215/6 and a form 31R samian bowl dated after *c* AD 160. Only undiagnostic reduced ware sherds (R2, 12 and 15) were found in possible hearth 291270 context 291271.

Linear feature 270571 contained 17 sherds of pottery, including two multi-reeded MH2 mortaria of 3rd century, dating to AD 220–280 and 280–350 respectively, and a bead and flange MH2 mortarium of late 2nd–early 3rd century date. This group also included a Nene Valley colour-coated folded beaker of 3rd century date (Perrin 1999, fig. 61, no. 167), and an NV2 sherd from a funnel necked beaker of late 3rd–4th century type. A CT sherd was probably of Harrold type dating to the late 3rd–4th centuries. A samian ware form 31, had a rivet hole in the base. A date in the late 3rd century would fit these types (Fig. 149, 4–7).

Enclosure 5

Two sherds came from the upper fill of the enclosure ditch, an O1 bowl copying form 31 and a samian sherd. The O1 bowl may be a very abraded ROX sherd of Young 1977 type C45 dated *c* AD 240–400 (for the dating see Booth *et al.* 1993, 167). Unfortunately no pottery sherds came from the lower fills but this vessel gives a date in the late 3rd or 4th century for this enclosure.

Within the enclosure, modern posthole 292704 (context 292705) contained a scrap of 2nd century samian. An FLA3 body sherd from an open vessel, from pit 292702 (context 292703), is most likely to date to the late 1st–2nd centuries. Pit 291914 context 291915 contained 55 sherds of Romano-British pottery including sherds from an SV3 vessel with everted rim, an R13 wide-mouthed jar, an MH bead and flange mortarium and a R16 carinated bowl with bead rim. These suggest a mid–late 2nd century date (Fig. 149, 8–9). Tree hollow 290871 produced a BB1 sherd from a 2nd century flat-rim bowl/ dish.

Enclosure 6

The enclosure ditch produced 28 sherds (318 g) of pottery. The lower fill (290808) at the northern corner contained a sherd from an MH2 reeded hammerhead mortarium of 3rd century type (Fig. 149, 10). An R5 wide-mouthed jar may be contemporary with this or slightly earlier, while the CTA1 jar is likely to be residual (Fig. 149, 11–12). A samian bowl/dish dated to the early 2nd century came from fill 290451 and an intrusive post-medieval sherd was identified from context 292329. The mortarium from the lower fill gives a *terminus post quem* in the 3rd century for the infilling of the enclosure ditch.

Within the enclosure, short gully 291291 (context 291288) contained two sherds, an R7 rim from a wide-mouthed jar and an MH1 sherd from a bead and flange mortarium with the bead rising higher than the flange, suggesting a date in the mid to late 2nd century.

The pottery from gully 298076 (context 290817) included sherds of Derbyshire ware, BB1, R5, R18, an R2 narrow-necked jar (Fig. 149, 13), a plain-rim BB1 dish with traces of oblique linear burnish dating to the late 2nd–early 3rd century and the rim of a late BB1 jar with splayed rim, probably of 3rd century date (Gillam 1976, no. 10). Context 290824 contained body sherds of BB1, R5, R7 and samian and a Severn Valley hooked-rim jar of the late 2nd–4th century. These later sherds suggests a 3rd century date for the infilling of these features. The infilling layer 290815 above 298076 contained a BB1 bowl with flat grooved rim and burnished intersecting arcs of late 2nd–mid 3rd century date (*cf.* Gillam 1976, no 42) and an SV1 wide-mouthed jar of mid 2nd–mid/late 3rd century type (Fig. 149, 14) (Webster 1976, nos 27–9).

Pit 298078 (context 290826) may be earlier as it contained a small abraded FLB2 sherd, a fabric uncommon after the 2nd century.

Pit 291431 (context 291432) produced eight rather undiagnostic body sherds of fabrics R9, MH2 and G2, together with a large number of sherds (104) from an R5 wide-mouthed jar with blunt-ended everted rim (Fig. 149, 15). The mortarium sherd gives a date after AD 140/50 and the jar may belong to the mid–late 2nd century.

Posthole 293429 contained a very abraded reduced ware sherd, probably R19, posthole 293421 contained an Iron Age sherd, posthole 291078 contained an R5 sherd and posthole 293419 contained an R5 sherd from a bead rim bowl dating to the 2nd century, probably a carinated bowl of mid–late 2nd century.

The pottery from the internal features suggest activity during the mid–late 2nd century ending in the 3rd century, perhaps as late as the mid 3rd century on the basis of the BB1 jar from gully 298076. This is consistent with the pottery from the lowest ditch fill of Enclosure 6.

Field system to north and adjacent features

Four sherds of Romano-British pottery were found in gully 292655, including a wide-mouthed jar belonging to the mid–late 1st century AD in the middle fill (Fig. 149, 16). An undiagnostic sherd of SV3 was found in the fill 293415 below this vessel and dates from the 2nd century and a samian sherd from fill 293431 is dated AD 100–125.

Very little pottery was recovered from the field system ditches and most of it comprised undiagnostic sherds of Romano-British date. The ditches of Enclosure 4 produced no pottery, nor did later ditches 292648 or 298130.

Sherds of SV3 and an R7 bowl (Fig. 149, 17), probably of late 1st–early 2nd century date, were found in context 291080 of ditch 298539, and Iron Age sherds were found in context 291086 and two O1 scraps in 291083.

Ditch 292653 (context 293051) contained three R3 body sherds. An R5 neckless, everted rim jar, a late 1st–mid-2nd century type, was found in associated ditch 292657 (context 293216). Undiagnostic sherds of fabrics O6 and R5 were found in associated ditch 298496 (contexts 292420 and 293351) along with a small rim sherd from a BB1 flat rim bowl/dish of 2nd century type.

Ditch 292650 (contexts 293402, 293404 and 290527) contained a Derbyshire ware jar base, an R2 wide-mouthed jar, an O2 jar (Webster 1976, type 51) of 3rd–4th century date, SV6 sherds and a sherd from a Hadrianic or Antonine samian dish (Central Gaulish, 18/31R or 31R). An associated ditch 292641 (contexts 292124, 292174 and 291140) contained sherds from a bead rim R5 bowl, an SV4 everted rim jar, a sherd of modern pottery and four sherds of samian from at least 2 dish/bowl vessels also of Hadrianic or Antonine date. In addition, the ditch cut a tree hollow (292162) which contained two medieval sherds in its fill. Ditch 292651 (context 293503) contained sherds from an R5 wide-mouthed jar.

Gully 292665 (contexts 292710 and 292712) contained a larger group of pottery including a BB1 jar with obtuse lattice burnish of 3rd–4th century date, an R5 narrow-necked jar, an Iron Age jar rim, a very abraded samian sherd, a sherd from a Derbyshire ware cupped-rim jar and 18 small abraded Dressel 20 body sherds. An adjacent posthole, 293037 (context 293041) contained a sherd from a Hadrianic or Antonine samian dish/bowl (Central Gaulish form 18/31 or 31).

Other features
In the extension to the site at the south-west, ditch 291333 (context 291337) contained one scrap of fabric O2. Ditch 219349 (context 291173) contained a single CC1 scrap, and ditch 298325 (context 291309) contained an unabraded sherd of Iron Age pottery. Pit 291185 contained undiagnostic sherds of R8, R9 and O1.

At the north of the site, pit 291414 context 291415 contained an O1 body sherd of Romano-British type. Nearby pit 293100 (context 293101) contained 13 sherds including one from a reeded rim MH2 mortarium with six reeds, of the mid-3rd–mid-4th centuries, and an R28 wide-mouthed jar with everted rim. The adjacent large feature, 292178 (context 292179) contained sherds dating to the 3rd–4th centuries including an ROX bowl, an MH2 reeded rim mortarium (Fig. 149, 18–19), an R2 plain-rim dish and an O3 narrow-necked jar.

At the eastern edge of the site, ditch 292698 (context 290531) contained an O1 sherd from a carinated bowl of 2nd century date.

Chronology
Late 1st–mid-2nd centuries
The assemblage included very little pottery dating to the mid–late 1st century. One E1 jar was present in ditch 292655 and dated typologically to the mid–late 1st century but later sherds of 2nd century date were also present in this feature. Early types, such as rusticated ware, were recovered from pit 290722 with other types such as carinated bowls. This group is best dated to the early–mid-2nd century. The material from the Enclosure 1 ditch probably belongs to this early phase since it lacks BB1 sherds and includes an early ring-necked flagon and an SV tankard. The white ware bowl sherd from pit 292702 is most likely to belong to this phase as does the O2 carinated bowl from tree hollow 292336. An O2 carinated bowl from ditch 292698 may also be of early–mid-2nd date and an R7 carinated bowl from modern land drain 298539 may also belong here. A neckless jar with short everted rim came from ditch 292657 and compares with jars of the late 1st–mid-2nd century. The fills of the Enclosure 3 ditch included an early neckless everted rim jar of the late 1st–early 2nd centuries.

The Flavian–Trajanic forms of jars and bowls are rare on the site. Fabrics such CTA1, a common type in the late 1st–early 2nd centuries at sites such as Tiddington and Coleshill, the white and white-slipped wares and the earlier reduced wares such as R16 and R15 common on Site 12 are uncommon here. The samian ware includes no South Gaulish pieces; the earliest sherds are from Les Martres de Veyre and are dated *c* AD 100–125, but the majority of the material is Hadrianic and later.

Mid–late 2nd/early 3rd centuries
Rather more feature groups belong to the mid–late 2nd/early 3rd centuries. These include pit 298255, gully 291291, pit 298503, posthole 293419, pit 290961 and probable pit 290725. The pottery from these features was characterised by mortaria of mid–late 2nd type and a group of carinated bowls found at Tiddington and Coleshill in association with mid–late 2nd century pottery. Wide-mouthed jars with everted rims and Severn Valley ware vessels of 2nd–3rd century type also occur in these groups. The Enclosure 2 ditch may belong to this period although the small number of diagnostic sherds from its fill makes dating difficult. BB1 flat-rim bowls/dishes in ditch 298496 and context 290871 belong to this period.

3rd–4th centuries
The ditches of Enclosures 5 and 6 were both open to receive ceramic debris in the 3rd–4th century. Only two sherds were found in the ditch of Enclosure 5 so its date in uncertain. The 3rd century mortarium from the lower fill of the Enclosure 6 ditch indicates it was still being maintained up to this date. An earlier CTA2 rebated rim jar came from this ditch but the rest of the pottery dates from the mid–late 2nd century and a period of use from that period is likely.

Sherds from BB1 jars with splayed rims and obtuse lattice were present in gully 298076, gully 297986 and ditch 292665 while late pottery such as an MH multi-reeded rim mortarium, NV2 funnel necked beaker, Harrold shelly wares, Oxfordshire red colour-coated wares and later Severn Valley ware wide-mouthed jars with undercut rims came from feature 290571, ditch 292650 and pits 292178 and 293451. These indicate continued activity into the late 3rd century.

The absence of bead and flange bowls in grey ware or BB1 and oxidised bifid rim jars along with the small amount of late shelly ware indicates a decline in the later 3rd–4th century. The mortaria and BB1 vessels are predominantly of late 2nd–3rd century type and the reduced wide-mouthed jars compare with in form with those from the Shenstone kiln.

Spatial analysis, functional groups and site status
Seventy contexts contained less than ten sherds of pottery and many of these were undiagnostic body sherds. There were 11 contexts with more than 20 sherds and only two, in feature 298076 and pit 291431, with over 100 sherds. Pits 291914 and 290722, ditches 292665 and 298496 context 293351 and the ditches of Enclosures 1, 3 and 6 all contained over 20 sherds and of them only the groups from 292665 and Enclosure 3 had an average sherd weight over 13 g. The group from

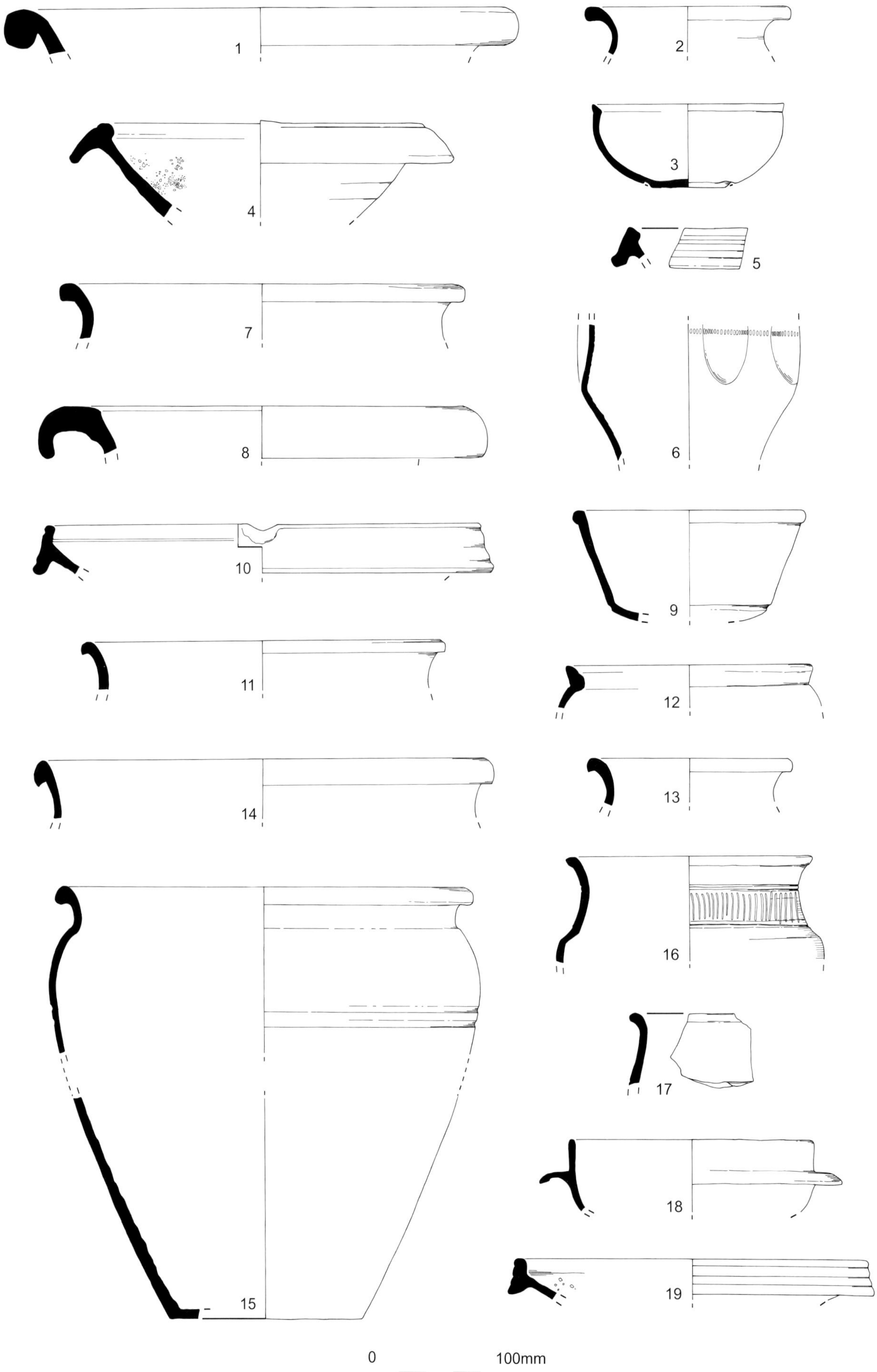

Fig. 149 Romano-British pottery

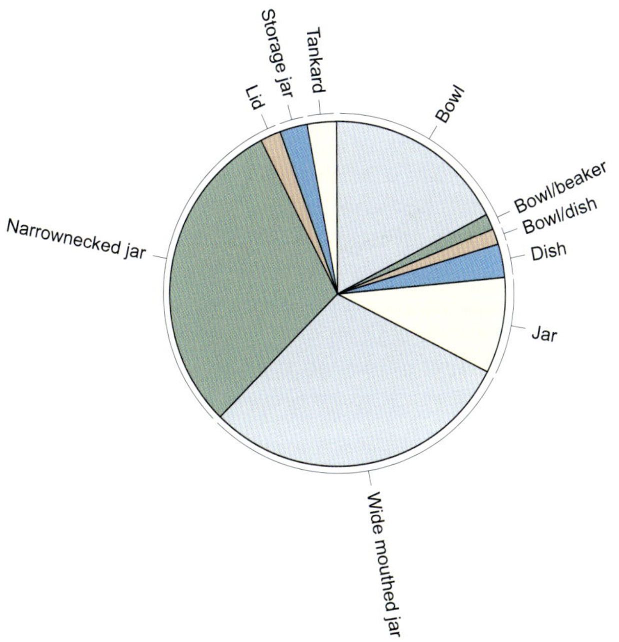

Fig. 150 Proportions of Romano-British vessel types

298076 was very abraded and fragmented with an average sherd weight of 6 g and the group from 298496 was even more fragmented with an average weight just over 1 g. The groups from 292665 and the Enclosure 3 ditch both included some large and heavy sherds from a MALV jar and the average sherd weight was inflated by these. The evidence suggests that large amounts of ceramic debris were not being deposited within the excavated area; what was discarded had been trampled and fragmented first, perhaps in a midden.

Analysis of the vessel types represented by estimated vessel equivalents (Fig. 150) contrasts with the group from Site 19 (see Chapter 24) in having considerably more wide-mouthed and narrow-necked jars, few flagons (none represented by EVES), only one amphora (not represented by EVES) and slightly less mortaria and tankards. The storage jars and lids at Site 29 may indicate storage of foodstuffs not encountered on Site 19. The level of bowls and dishes is indicative of a low status rural site, perhaps of lower status than Site 19. The greater number of wide-mouthed jars may be a chronological indicator since Site 19 had more BB1 jars and bowls and bead and flange mortaria of 2nd century type. Although the date ranges of the two sites overlap, Site 29 seems to have had a later emphasis.

Pottery supply

As suggested by the vessel type analysis the wares reaching the site indicate a modest settlement. The amphora percentage is low compared to Site 19, although the fine ware group is slightly larger, probably because of the later colour-coated wares reaching the site. Mortaria are relatively fewer in number and this may be linked with the function of the enclosures. Severn Valley wares were less common on Site 29 and reduced wares slightly more common. As these were dominated by the wide-mouthed jars and other types made at the Shenstone kiln this may reflect the ready availability of this type locally. At both sites fabrics R5 and R2 dominated the reduced wares. The fall in BB1 vessels compared with Site 19 is negligible. Both sites obtained small amounts of Derbyshire ware jars from Belper or locally. Malvernian ware jars and the early pink grogged ware G2 vessels were present on Site 29 but not at Site 19, whereas the latter had PNK GT jars, absent at Site 29. Both sites obtained Nene Valley and Oxfordshire colour-coated wares and early and late shelly wares CTA1 and CTA2. Site 29 had even fewer white and white-slip wares reflecting a relatively low level of occupation in the mid-1st–mid-2nd centuries.

List of illustrated pottery (Fig. 149)

1. O9 heavy rolled rim storage jar. 148 g. RE 10%, context 290557, Enclosure 3 ditch
2. SV5 narrow-necked jar, cf. Webster 1976, no. 5, 2nd–3rd centuries. 37 g. RE 25%, context 290726, pit 290725
3. O1? or SV1 cup/small bowl. *Cf.* Webster 1976, nos 34–5, 2nd–3rd centuries. 70 g, context 290726, pit 290725
4. MH2 bead and flange mortarium with bead just above sharply downbent flange, *cf.* Gillam 1970, no. 253, dated AD 180–230, a similar type post-dates the practice of stamping and is closely matched in mortaria found in Kiln 2 at Mancetter (unpublished), Evans 2002b, M81 AD 160–210. 24 g. RE 22%, context 290573, feature 290571
5. MH2 multi-reeded mortarium, *cf.* Hartley 2003, no. 21, at Cramond 210/20–270; Evans 2002b, M96 220–80. 36 g. RE 8%. A second mortarium of similar but rather later form (AD 280–350) was also present, context 290573, feature 290571
6. NV2 folded beaker on orange fabric with dark grey/brown colour coat and rouletted line across centre of indentation. Similar to indented beaker from Trier but the fabric is not of that type. The fabric compares with some folded beakers from the Nene Valley. Perrin 1999, fig. 61, no. 167, dated 3rd century. 40 g, context 290578, feature 290511
7. R2 wide-mouthed jar with blunt-ended everted rim. 56 g. RE 11%, context 290573, feature 290571
8. MH bead and flange mortarium, Evans 2002b, M77, AD 140–190. 106 g. RE 16%, context 291915, pit 291914
9. R16 bead rim bowl, probably a carinated bowl of 2nd century type. This vessel compares well with carinated bowls from Coleshill and Tiddington which were associated with mid–late 2nd century pottery. 72 g. RE 16%, context 291915 pit 291914
10. MH2 hammerhead mortarium with reed at top and bottom and shallow groove in the middle. Evans 2002b, M94 AD 200–260. 109 g. RE 16%, context 290808, Enclosure 6 ditch
11. R5 wide-mouthed jar with everted rim. 33 g. RE 9%, context 290694, Enclosure 6 ditch
12. CTA1 rebated-rim jar, a type current in the late 1st–early 2nd century at Derby (Birss 1985, table 3 CTA1). A similar vessel with organic temper occurs at Coleshill (Booth 1986, fig. 2, nos 1–2) in the 1st century associated

with Romano-British grey wares. 31 g. RE 11%, context 290694, Enclosure 6 ditch

13. R2 narrow-necked jar. 281 g. RE 5%, context 290817, gully 298076
14. SV1 wide-mouthed jar with hooked rim *cf.* Webster 1976, no. 26, mid-2nd–late 3rd centuries. 96 g. RE. 15%, context 290824, gully 298076
15. R5 necked jar with blunt-ended rather hooked rim. There were traces of oblique linear burnish on the shoulder zone. This vessel is similar to those made in the Shenstone kiln and it is distorted. A date in the mid–late 2nd century is consistent with the finer fabric and form. 1345 g. RE 99%, context. 291432, pit 291431
16. E1 carinated wide-mouthed jar with vertical spaced burnished lines decorating the upper body. This vessel compares with a group of vessels known to date to the mid–late 1st century, often in grog-tempered fabrics and in a 'Belgic' tradition (Booth 1986, fig. 4). Vessels in similar forms are known from Tiddington (Booth 1996a ;and unpublished) although the precise form and decoration is unparalleled there. At Leicester similarly decorated types can be found in a phase dated to AD 60–130 (Clay and Pollard 1994, fig. 51, no. 25 but this vessel lacks the sharp carination of No. 16). Vessels with more pronounced shoulders in similar fabrics to No. 16 occurred in phase 1 at Leicester (*ibid.*, fig. 52, nos 41–2, AD 1–70/80). However at Leicester the type continues to be made in gradually more Romanised fabrics into the 2nd century (Clarke 1999, fig. 62, no. 17). Typologically this vessel belongs to the group represented by Cam 218 and variants (Hawkes and Hull 1947). 55 g. RE 11%, context 293413, gully 292665
17. R7 everted rim bowl with median groove outside the body. 2nd century. Similar bowls are found at Tiddington and Coleshill associated with pottery of the mid–late 2nd century but the median groove suggests earlier vessels similar to those at Derby Racecourse in the late 1st–early 2nd centuries (Birss 1985, table 6, no. 65) so a date in the late 1st–early 2nd century date may be more likely. 30 g. RE 5%, context 291080, ditch 298539
18. ROX flanged hemi-spherical bowl, Young 1977, C51, AD 240–400. 110 g. RE 18%, context 292179
19. MH2 mortarium with four-reeded rim, Evans 2002b, M98, AD 220–300. 39 g. RE 9%, context 292179

Building material, by Cynthia Poole

Thirty fragments of ceramic building material weighing 702 g were recovered, of which four fragments (132 g) were medieval or post-medieval in date. Fabrics utilised for Romano-British material were, in order of frequency, S7, S1, S4, G1, S2 and S3. Fabric S6 was used for the post-Romano-British material. The only form identified was a *tegula* from pit 293100 (context 293101), at the north end of the site, with a very wide (40 mm) flange of type D/E. Another fragment assessed as a *tegula* flange is atypical of such an object and could in fact be part of a kiln firebar. All other pieces were unidentified or from unspecified flat tiles. One piece, 38 mm thick, may have been a brick fragment, but this too may have derived from an oven or kiln, possibly a fragment of plate or floor. Other fragments of fired clay with the building material included a possible kiln setter and small irregular firebar, as well as amorphous fragments probably from oven or kiln walls/lining.

The quantity and character of the building material was not indicative of its use in building construction on the site. The fragments were all relatively small and moderately to heavily abraded with an average fragment weight of 23 g. It is likely that the material was being obtained for use in ovens, corn driers or kiln structures, especially in view of the presence of some kiln or oven material.

Environmental

Charred plant remains, by Lisa Gray

One hundred and forty-nine samples were taken of 5–25 litres (averaging 15 litres) (Tables 107–10). Preservation was by charring and mineralisation. Preservation quality varied. One mineralised seed resembling hawthorn (*cf. Crataegus monogyna*) was observed in a sample from roundhouse gully 292666 (structure 1c) in Enclosure 1 (sample 291563, section 290595, context 290598). The charred remains consisted of wood and cereal grains, chaff and buds.

Mineralisation is the replacement of organic material by calcium phosphate and can occur by several means; the presence of calcium rich ground water, lime deliberately added to pits as sterilisation, fish bone and scales and human urine and faeces (Green 1979, 281).

The charred plant remains

The most interesting remains came from Enclosure 1, and pit 292129 (context 292127) east of Enclosure 5. Of the 15 samples analysed for Enclosure 1, nine produced grain and two produced chaff. The samples were dominated by wheat (*Triticum* spp.) grains. Some of these were identifiable as spelt (*T. spelta*). The most interesting sample was taken from a gully fill in roundhouse 2, sample 291560. This sample produced grain chaff and chickweed (*Stellaria media*) seeds.

Pit 292129 produced the richest charred assemblage of all the samples analysed. This sample was dominated by over 100 barley (*Hordeum sativum*) grains. These were mostly intact, hulled and four were twisted.

Feature function

Enclosure 1

Plant remains in most of these of these samples are scarce (Tables 107–8). No indication of human activities specific to this area was revealed by the macro-remains. There was no evidence of cess, refuse or storage.

The samples from Roundhouse 2 produced the richest charred assemblage in this enclosure. These included low quantities of chaff, spelt and barley grains and arable/waste ground plant seeds. Most of these

Table 107 Charred plant remains from roundhouse gullies in enclosure 1

		Roundhouse gullies											
	Structure no.	1a	1c		2		3			4		5	6
	Feature	292667	292666		292716		298350			292441		298335	298338
	Section	292696	290595	292433	292723	292429	292300	292402	291209	291209	291216	293241	293225
	Context	293600	290598	292435	292725	292430	292301	292403	291210	291212	291218	293240	293234
	Sample	291570	291563	291560	291569	291533	291503	291490	291586	291585	291588	291578	291550
	Sample size (L)	16	20	19	17	14	12	13	10	10	12	6	20
	Flot size (ml)	125	175	250	1000	400	500	100	10	30	60	60	60
Taxon	*Common name*												
Triticum spelta grain	Spelt	-	-	16	5	4	-	-	-	4	5	-	-
Triticum sp. spikelet base	Wheat	-	-	-	-	-	-	-	1	-	-	-	-
Triticum spelta glume base	Spelt	2	-	2	-	-	-	-	1	-	-	-	-
cf. *Triticum* sp. grain	Wheat	-	-	-	-	-	-	-	-	-	-	2	-
Triticum sp. grain	Wheat	-	-	29	16	-	-	-	-	-	-	-	-
cf. *Hordeum* sp. grain	Barley	-	-	-	-	2	-	-	1	-	-	3	-
Hordeum sp. grain	Barley	-	-	3	7	-	-	-	-	-	-	-	-
Hordeum/*Triticum* grain frag.	Barley/wheat	-	-	-	-	+	-	-	-	-	-	-	-
Avena sp. grain	Oat	1	-	-	-	-	-	-	-	-	-	-	-
Avena/*Hordeum*/*Secale*/*Triticum* grain	Indet. cereal	-	1	-	-	1	-	-	-	-	-	-	-
Stellaria media seed	Chickweed	-	-	16	-	-	-	-	-	-	1	-	-
Vicia/*Lathyrus*/ *Pisum* sp. seed	Vetch/tare/pea	-	-	1	-	-	-	-	-	-	-	-	1
Corylus avellana L nutshell frag.	Hazel	-	-	-	-	-	-	-	-	1	5	-	1
Bromus sp. seed	Brome	1	-	-	-	-	-	-	-	-	-	-	-
Avena/*Hordeum*/*Secale*/*Triticum* stem frag.	-	1	-	-	-	-	-	-	-	-	1	4	-
Indet. bud	-	1	-	-	1	-	-	-	-	-	-	-	-
Indet. wood frag. (>4 mm³)	-	+	++	+++	++	++++	++	++	+	++	+	+	+
Indet. wood fleck. (<4 mm³)	-	++++	+++++	+++++	++++	+++++	+++++	+++++	++	++++	++++	++++	+++++
Plant tissue - grain frag.	-	-	-	2	-	-	-	-	-	-	-	-	-

Key to estimated levels of abundance codes: + =1-10, ++ =11-50, +++ = 51-150, ++++ = 150-250 and +++++ = >250

Table 108 Charred plant remains from other features in Enclosure 1

	Feature	Ditch 291113		Pit 290734	Posthole
	Section	281904	293019		293459
	Context	291906	293024	290735	293461
	Sample	291503	291539	291557	291576
	Sample size (l)	20	20	15	16
	Flot size (ml)	60	60	60	250
Taxon	Common name				
Triticum spelta grain	Spelt	1	–	1	–
Stellaria media seed	Chickweed	1	–	–	–
Avena/Hordeum/Secale/Triticum stem frag.	Indet. cereal	2	–	–	–
Indet. wood frag. (>4 mm^3)		++++	+++	+++	++
Indet. wood fleck (<4 mm^3)		+++++	+++++	+++++	+++++

seeds were of chickweed. One poorly preserved vetch/tare/vetchling/pea (*Lathyrus/Vicia/Pisum* sp.) seed was identified. Small seeded legumes like this are common in cereal assemblages and could be evidence here of the weeds associated with any cereal crop. Assemblages of these are typical of sieving waste and could indicate that cereal processing or storage took place in this part of the enclosure.

The remaining samples in the enclosure produced few remains, consisting of low quantities of spelt and barley grains, and chaff (spelt glumes and cereal stem fragments). An oat (*Avena* sp.) grain was observed in context 293600 (roundhouse 1a), and could have been present as a crop weed or possible evidence of another arable crop.

Enclosures 2, 3 and 4/6

The samples from pits within the enclosures contained remarkably small amounts of charred remains (Table 109). Few cereal grains were present (wheat and wheat/barley) with the occasional weed seeds. This is not typical of domestic occupation which is either permanent or long lived.

In Enclosure 2, the field observation that the top fill of pit 292344 (context 292345) and secondary fill of pit 293451 (context 293453) were dump deposits of a hearth or fire is supported by the dominance of charred wood and the scarcity of other plant remains consisting of only a fragment of wheat and a vetch/tare (*Lathyrus/Vicia* sp.) seed.

In Enclosure 3, plant remains were scarce in both pits 290722 (context 290721) and 292133 (context 292132). Pit 290722 was dominated by charred wood and pit 292133 produced a few, poorly preserved charred wheat (*Triticum* sp.) grains and hazelnut shell (*Corylus avellana*) fragments. These remains do not give any indication of the function of the pits.

In Enclosure 4/6, the plant remains in pit 291922 (context 291923) consisted of a single charred seed of the grassland plant self-heal (*Prunella vulgaris*). Unfortunately this does not indicate any function and the field observation that this pit was the result of tree disturbance is very likely. In pit 291422 (context 291423) the presence of little more than one poorly preserved cereal grain resembling wheat/barley (*Hordeum/Triticum* sp.) confirms that this is more likely

Table 109 Charred plant remains from pits in Enclosures 2, 3 and 4/6

	Enclosure	2		3		4/6	
	Pit	292344	293451	290722	292133	291922	291422
	Context	292345	293453	290721	292132	291923	291423
	Sample	291592	291598	291470	291500	291532	291519
	Sample size (l)	7	20	20	10	20	10
	Flot size (ml)	40	250	750	250	500	120
Taxon	Common name						
Triticum sp. grain	Wheat	1	–	–	3	–	–
Hordeum/Triticum sp. grain	Barley/wheat	–	–	–	–	–	1
Vicia/Lathyrus sp. seed	Vetch/tare/vetchling	1	–	–	–	–	–
Prunella vulgaris seed	Self-heal	–	–	–	–	1	–
Corylus avellana nutshell frag.	Hazel	–	–	–	2	–	–
Indet. seed		+++	++++	–	–	–	–
Indet. wood frag. (>4 mm^3)		++	++	+++	+++	+++	+
Indet. wood fleck (<4 mm^3)		+++++	+++++	++++	+++++	++++	+++++

Table 110 Charred plant remains in other features

	Feature type	Hearth	Ditch	Pits				
	Feature	290790	291333	291190	291287	292129	292803	293321
	Context	290791	291217	291191	291288	292127	292804	293322
	Sample	291452	291487	291478	291467	291489	291516	291529
	Sample size (l)	20	20	18	9	7	10	20
	Flot size (ml)	1000	750	220	500	550	100	1000
Taxon	Common name							
Triticum spelta grain	Spelt	–	–	–	–	8	–	6
Triticum cf. *spelta* grain	Spelt	–	–	–	–	6	–	–
Triticum cf. *spelta* glume base	Spelt	–	–	–	–	–	–	2
T. spelta/aestivum grain	Spelt/bread wheat	–	–	–	–	–	–	2
Triticum sp. grain	Wheat	–	–	–	2	4	–	2
Hordeum spp. grain	Barley	–	–	–	–	–	–	4
H. vulgare grain	Barley	–	–	–	–	162	–	
Hordeum/Triticum sp. grain	Barley/wheat	–	–	–	–	1	–	
cf. *Avena* sp. grain frag.	Oat	–	–	–	1	2	–	12
Phalaris sp. seed	Reed-grass/canary grass	–	–	–	–	–	18	–
Avena/Hordeum/Secale/Triticum internode	Indet. cereal	–	–	–	–	2	–	2
Vicia cf. *hirsuta* seed	Hairy vetch	–	–	–	–	–	–	3
Vicia/Lathyrus/Pisum seed	Vetch/tare/vetchling/pea	–	–	–	1	–	–	17
Vicia/Lathyrus/Pisum seed frag.	Vetch/tare/vetchling/pea	–	–	–	1	–	–	–
Persicaria sp. seed	Redshank	–	–	–	–	–	–	4
Corylus avellana nutshell frag.	Hazel	–	14	–	2	–	–	–
Galium palustre seed	Marsh bedstraw	–	–	–	–	–	–	3
Indet. wood frag. (>4 mm^3)		++++	++++	++	+++	++++	+++	+++
Indet. wood fleck (>4 mm^3)		+++++	+++++	+++++	+++++	+++++	+++++	+++++

to be an ash pit as described in the field than a storage or refuse pit.

Other features (Table 110)
Hearth 290790 (context 290791) did produce abundant charcoal but no other charred plant macro-remains. Three pits produced moderate quantities of seeds and cereal remains. Pit 292129 (context 292127) produced the largest quantity of charred cereal on this site. These were dominated by hulled barley (*Hordeum sativum*). Four clearly twisted grains were observed. Lower quantities of spelt grains and poorly preserved wheat and oat grains were present. Pit 293321 (context 293322), produced a small but interesting assemblage containing a mixture of charred remains including grains of spelt and barley and fragments of oat grain along with seeds. The remaining seeds were of fairly typical arable weed species, bedstraw (*Galium palustre*) and redshank (*Persicaria* sp.).

Agricultural practices

Crops
Barley grains were the most frequent ones recovered from this site, mostly from pit 292129. Barley could have been used as food, fodder or for malting. None of the grains had sprouted so it can be assumed that these grains were originally destined for human or animal food in some form. Spelt wheat and poorly preserved wheat grains were present in slightly smaller quantities. Oat grains were present but rare and could have been a crop weed gathered in with wheat or barley. Both spelt and barley are common in Iron Age/Romano-British sites in Britain (Green 1981).

Cereal processing
Grains dominated the charred remains and small seeds and chaff were present in small quantities. These resemble the type of cereal waste produced by fine or coarse sieving as based on ethnographic studies of traditional cereal processing (Hillman 1981; 1984; Jones 1984). Charring of these remains could also have occurred by parching the grain prior to milling, use as fuel/tinder or, as observed ethnographically, have fallen out of a cooking pot and burnt (Bottema 1984, 209–10).

Other potential food plants
Many samples contained fragments of charred hazelnut shell. Hazelnuts would have been a freely available, highly calorific and easily portable food source. They have been found in Iron Age stomach contents where they formed a large part of a last meal (James and Rigby 1997, 28). The charred shells are probably from nuts roasted to crack the shells or to make the nuts more suitable for grinding (Mason 1996).

Context related variation in plant macro-remain assemblages by period and feature

One of the research aims for this site was to compare the Iron Age and Romano-British samples (OWA 2003, 267). This analysis has not revealed any clear temporal tends. Enclosure 1 was the only one definitely dated as Iron Age but the plant remains are similar to those from the other enclosures and features.

Charcoal, by Rowena Gale

Environmental samples were collected from 149 contexts throughout the site, a high percentage of which produced significant quantities of charcoal. The condition of the charcoal was generally very poor, probably partly due to the high water-table. Additional charcoal included four samples of handpicked material and two related to artefactual finds. Thirty-nine samples were selected for full analysis. One of the main objectives of the study was to assess spatial differences in fuel use between the enclosures, that might identify specific activities within the individual enclosure areas and, secondly, to compare these results with those from the settlement area to achieve an overall picture of the economic use of fuel resources at the site. On a broader scale, the study would also provide environmental data on local woodland.

The taxa identified are presented in Table 111.

Iron Age

Enclosure 1

Charcoal was examined from deposits associated with this large enclosure in the southern corner of the site, including the enclosure ditch (291113), roundhouse gullies, pits and postholes. Narrow roundwood predominated in samples 291503 and 291513 from the uppermost fills near the north-east and south-east corners of the enclosure ditch (sections 291904 and 291126 respectively); the taxa identified included oak (*Quercus* sp.), blackthorn (*Prunus spinosa*) and hazel (*Corylus avellana*).

Although charcoal was often abundant in the fills of the roundhouse gullies, preservation was so poor that it was frequently impossible to identify positively. The charcoal is likely to have originated from domestic hearth debris dumped or accumulated in the gullies. Samples were examined from gullies 292716, 292667, 292666, 298338, 298335, 292441 and 298350. Although oak was common to each sample, it was evident that firewood was supplied from a wide range of species including field maple (*Acer campestre*), alder (*Alnus glutinosa*), birch (*Betula* sp.), hazel, ash (*Fraxinus excelsior*), holly (*Ilex aquifolium*), the hawthorn/ *Sorbus* group (Pomoideae), blackthorn and willow (*Salix* sp.)/poplar (*Populus* sp.). Charred grain was frequent in gully 292716.

Charcoal was examined from adjacent pits 292925 and 290734, sited close to the entrance of the large roundhouse in the north-west corner of the enclosure. Both pits were shallow but, whereas the first appeared to be for rubbish disposal, a posthole within the second pit implicated a more structural role. Charcoal was frequent in both contexts but very degraded. The taxa identified from pit 292925 conformed in character to that from the roundhouse gullies (see above). Charcoal from pit 290734 was also consistent with fuel debris and the presence of both oak and birch, including roundwood, indicates that little, if any, of this material represents a structural post. The function of posthole 293459, located outside the entrance of the same roundhouse, was uncertain, although it may have supported a porch. Charcoal deposits from the fill of the feature were similar to those from the roundhouse gullies and probably represent domestic hearth debris. The taxa identified included oak, hazel, holly, the hawthorn/*Sorbus* group and blackthorn.

Romano-British

Enclosure 2

A small pit 293451 located within the enclosure contained several layers of waste which appeared to have been dumped in rapid succession. Charcoal was relatively sparse but consisted mainly of narrow roundwood from oak but also willow/poplar and *cf.* hazel.

Enclosure 3

Hearth 290790 was probably lined with stones and was located close to one end of a rectilinear structure, towards the centre of Enclosure 3. Scorching was recorded on the base of the hearth, and baked clay and fuel debris were abundant in its fill. Charcoal consisted mainly of roundwood from oak, ash, hazel, blackthorn and the hawthorn/*Sorbus* group but also included oak heartwood. Mixed species were also recorded from hearth 290795.

Waste material, probably from several phases of dumping, was also recorded in pit 290722, sited near the southern end of the enclosure. Charcoal here was abundant and consisted mainly of narrow roundwood. A 50% sub-sample was examined and identified as predominantly oak but also field maple, alder, birch, heather (Ericaceae), ash and blackthorn.

Towards the eastern entrance to the enclosure, hearth 292133 contained fuel debris consisting mainly of narrow roundwood from oak, although cf. hazel was also present. A possible posthole (292131), occurred close to hearth 292133; associated charcoal was degraded but included blackthorn and the hawthorn/ *Sorbus* group. Just outside the eastern entrance the charcoal-rich upper fill of pit 290961 (which cut into ditch 291338) probably included dumped domestic waste. Although the charcoal was mostly too degraded to identify, the taxa named included oak (narrow roundwood) and possibly blackthorn and field maple. Hearth 291270 was also sited within the entrance; fuel remains were comparatively sparse but indicated the use

Table 111 Charcoal (no. frags)

Feature	*Section*	*Context*	*Sample*	*Acer*	*Alnus*	*Betula*	*Corylus*	*Erica/ Calluna*	*Fraxinus*	*Ilex*	*Pomoideae*	*Prunus*	*Quercus*	*Salix/ Populus*	*Ulex/ Cytisus*
Iron Age															
Enclosure 1															
Ditch 291113	291126	291127	291513	-	-	-	1	-	-	-	-	1r	3h/u, 12r	-	-
	291904	291906	291503	-	-	-	-	-	-	-	-	12r	1r	-	-
Structure 1a	293696	293600	291570	*cf.* 1	*cf.* 5	-	-	-	-	-	*cf.* 1	-	8h/u, 1r	-	-
Gully 292667															
Structure 1c	293631	293636	291594	-	-	-	-	-	1	-	3	-	44h/u, 1s	-	-
Gully 292666															
Structure 2	292429	292430	291553	1	3	*cf.* 1	-	-	-	-	2	2	6h/u	-	-
Gully 292716	292723	292725	291569	-	*cf.* 1	-	-	-	-	-	*cf.* 1	*cf.* 1	12h/u	*cf.* 1	-
Structure 3	292300	292301	291484	-	-	-	-	-	-	-	-	-	4h, 1s	-	-
Gully 298350	292402	292403	291490	-	-	-	-	-	-	-	-	-	1u	-	-
Structure 4	291209	291212	291585	1	-	-	-	-	2	-	-	-	6u	-	-
Gully 292441	291216	291218	291588	*cf.* 1	*cf.* 2	-	-	-	1	*cf.* 1	-	2	6h/u, 5r	-	-
Structure 5	293241	293240	291578	-	-	10	-	-	1	-	-	2	2u	-	-
Gully 298335															
Structure 6	293235	293234	291550	-	-	-	-	-	-	-	*cf.* 1	-	5u	-	-
Gully 298338	293230	293231	291551	-	-	-	-	-	-	-	-	-	3u	-	-
Pit 290734		290735	291557	-	-	12	-	-	-	-	-	-	2s, 1r, 8u	-	-
Pit 292925		292926	291584	-	2	8	-	-	-	1	-	-	1r, 3u	-	-
Posthole 293459		293461	291576	-	-	-	1	-	-	2	5	2	10u	-	-
Romano-British															
Enclosure 2															
Pit 293451		293453	291598	-	-	-	*cf.* 6	-	-	-	-	-	4h/u, 12r	3	-
Enclosure 3															
Pit 290961		290959	291496	*cf.* 1	-	-	-	-	-	-	-	*cf.* 3	15r, 2u	-	-
Pit 290722		290721	291470	5r	2r	1	-	6r	1r	-	-	1	66r	-	-
Posthole 292131		292130	291495	-	-	-	-	-	-	-	2	1	-	-	-
Hearth 292133		292132	291500	-	-	-	*cf.* 2	-	-	-	-	-	47r, 2s	-	-
Hearth 290790		290791	291452	-	-	-	2	-	1r	-	1	1	21h/u, 9r, 6s	-	-
Hearth 290795		290796	291454	-	-	*cf.* 1	-	-	-	-	-	-	17h/u, 3s	1	-
Hearth 291270		291271	291461	1	1	-	-	4	-	-	1	-	5h/u, 1s, 1r	-	-
Posthole 291276		291277	291463	-	-	1	-	-	-	-	-	-	45h, 37s	-	-
Enclosure 4															
Pit 291422		291423	291519	-	-	-	1	-	-	-	1	1	2h, 38r	-	-
Pit 291922		291923	291532	1	-	-	1	-	-	-	1	-	4h, 37r	-	-
Pit 291431		291433	293705	-	-	-	-	-	-	-	-	-	1h, 29r, 5s	-	-
Pit 293321		293322	291529	-	-	-	-	-	-	-	-	-	74h/u, 12s	-	-
Enclosure 6															
Ditch 298232	290801	290802	293706	-	-	-	-	-	-	-	-	-	1s, 6u	-	-
Hearth 290829		290830	291468	-	-	2	-	-	-	-	-	-	95h/u, 2s	-	-
Hearth 292000		292001	291472	-	-	2	5r	-	-	-	-	-	55r, 2s	-	-
Pit 291287 e6		291288	291467	-	-	2	2	1	1	-	1	1r	2h, 49r	-	1

Feature	Section	Context	Sample	Acer	Alnus	Betula	Corylus	Erica/ Calluna	Fraxinus	Ilex	Pomoideae	Prunus	Quercus	Salix/ Populus	Ulex/ Cytisus
Other features															
Ditch 291333		291334	291487	-	-	-	-	-	-	-	-	-	77h, 2s	-	-
Pit 291190		291191	291478	-	-	-	-	-	-	-	-	-	33h	-	-
			293704	-	-	-	-	-	-	-	-	-	19h	-	-
Pit 292129		292127	291489	-	-	1	3r	-	3	-	-	-	15h, 36s	-	-
Pit 291411		291413	291505	-	-	-	-	-	-	-	-	-	59h/u, 1s		
Posthole 292405		292406	291494	-	-	-	-	-	-	-	-	-	59h/u, 2s	-	-

Key: h = heartwood; r = roundwood (diameter <20 mm); s = sapwood (diameter unknown); u = unknown maturity (*Quercus* only)

of oak, field maple, the hawthorn/*Sorbus* group, alder and heather.

A charcoal-rich deposit, concentrated in the centre of posthole 291276 may be from the remains of an oak post, although the presence of a small amount of birch indicated that material from other sources was also present.

Enclosure 4

Charcoal was examined from pit features 291422, 291922 and 291431 (which also lie within Enclosure 6); material from pit 291431 was collected by hand. In each feature the charcoal consisted principally of narrow roundwood from oak, although small amounts of oak heartwood were also present. Other taxa, minimally represented, included field maple, hazel, the hawthorn/*Sorbus* group and blackthorn. Small deposits of charred grain were present in the bulk samples. Although the origin of the charcoal is uncertain, the pits were probably constructed as ash/refuse pits. A large deposit of oak heartwood was also collected from the fill of pit 293321. This pit also contained a substantial amount of baked clay and charred grain and, thus, may have functioned as some type of hearth.

Enclosure 6

Charcoal was examined from two of the numerous hearths recorded within the enclosure, all of which included *in situ* scorching. Charcoal was particularly abundant in hearths 290829 and 292000, and a 50% subsample was examined from each. The former was lined with stones and fuelled almost entirely with oak heartwood, although birch was also present. Fuel debris in hearth 292000 differed in character to that from 290829, in that although oak predominated, it consisted mainly of narrow roundwood, some of which was fast-grown; birch and hazel roundwood were also named.

An extensive range of wood species was present in pit 291287: oak, birch, hazel, heather, blackthorn, the hawthorn/*Sorbus* group and gorse (*Ulex* sp.)/broom (*Cytisus scoparius*). This material mainly derived from narrow roundwood. The pit was located in an area where many of the features included charcoal-rich deposits.

Other features

Charcoal deposits from a number of other features across the site were also selected for this study.

A large quantity of charcoal (sample 291487) was collected from the basal fill of a substantial ditch (291333) running east-west on the southern edge of the site. The deposit was described during excavation as probably arising from repeated episodes of dumping, subsequently compacted by redeposited backfill of natural material. The character of the charcoal, however, suggests that it was more likely to have originated from a single event – or, if from repeated dumpings, then from an activity which utilised the same type of fuel. A 25% sub-sample of charcoal was examined and identified as exclusively oak largewood, with some fragments partially vitrified. The latter is indicative of high temperature burning and could implicate industrial or craft activities.

Although there was no evidence of a hearth structure, the shallow cut 292129 had clearly been used for burning. The function of the fire, which was sited just east of Enclosure 5, is unknown but the large quantity of charcoal that remained in the pit included fragments of oak, measuring up to 25mm in length, birch, hazel and ash. This pit also included a large amount of charred grain.

The lower fill of pit 291190, located on the western edge of the site, included a quantity of burnt ceramic material, possibly from the discarded lining of a hearth. Associated charcoal (samples 291478 and 293704) included large lumps of oak largewood. The function of the hearth is unknown but the evident selection of oak heartwood suggests that this was more likely to have been industrial or for craft activities than for domestic use. On the opposite side of the site, the secondary fill of the long ovoid pit 291411 contained a huge quantity of charcoal, of which a 25% subsample was identified. The sample consisted entirely of oak, mostly heartwood, some of which was fast-grown.

The lower portion of a burnt oak post remained *in situ* in posthole 292405, located in the south-east corner of the site. The post measured some 0.2 m in diameter.

Discussion

The excavation revealed an Iron Age/Romano-British farmstead and settlement. The excavated area included a number of ditched enclosures, the most southerly of which enclosed a group of dwellings and farm buildings. Evidence of features possibly for controlling livestock suggests that pastoral farming formed an important element of the economy. Hearths were recorded in several parts of the site but, although these sometimes included fragments of baked clay (possibly from hearth linings) and residual fuel debris, the function of these features is uncertain. Waste pits including dumps of fuel debris were also relatively frequent both within and outside the enclosures and associated with domestic contexts. Charcoal analysis was undertaken to determine differences in the type of fuel associated with possible industrial/craft activities and domestic hearths, and to assess spatial patterns of fuel use. Charcoal was often abundant but, owing to unstable soil conditions, preservation was poor and, consequently, the potential of the (often large) samples was frequently disappointing.

The selection and use of fuel

Evidence from hearths and waste pits indicated the use of two distinct categories of fuel. The most frequently used being narrow roundwood obtained from a broad range of species but predominantly oak. This formed the basis for domestic fuel as indicated by deposits in roundhouse gullies and associated pits and postholes within the Iron Age enclosure. Similar deposits were also collected from pits within Enclosures 2, 3 and 6, some of which may represent discarded domestic waste although some proportion of it is likely to have originated from fires and hearths situated within these enclosures. For example, evidence from hearths 290795, 292000 and 291270, indicated the use of narrow roundwood and was more or less consistent with fuel debris collected from pits 291422, 291922 and 291431 located within the same enclosure. Similarly, in Enclosure 3, fuel residues in hearth 292133 matched dumps of charcoal in posthole 292131 and pit 290722.

In contrast, charcoal debris in some hearth features indicated the selective use of oak largewood (including heartwood). Most, but not all, of these were peripheral to the enclosures. For example, hearth 290829 was located within Enclosure 6 on the western side; the hearth was lined with stones and may have differed in function from hearth 292000 in the same enclosure and hearth 291270 in Enclosure 3, from which narrow roundwood was identified (described above). The preferred use of oak largewood was also recorded from deposits in pit 291411 (on the eastern side of the site), pit 291190 and ditch 291333 (located on the western edge of the site), and pit 293321 (in Enclosure 4). Pits 291190 and 293321 also contained baked clay fragments.

Although there is some evidence to suggest a common link between the use of oak largewood and deposits of baked clay fragments (?hearth-lining), perhaps implicating industrial or craft activities, this was not always the case, as indicated by the deposits of baked clay mixed with fuel debris of narrow roundwood in hearth 290790 (structure 290794 in Enclosure 3) (the latter combination, however, does not necessarily preclude industrial use). More convincing evidence for industrial activity was provided by the large deposit of partially vitrified oak largewood in the fill of ditch 291333. Since vitrification is usually brought about through burning at temperatures exceeding 800°C (Prior and Alvin 1983), this suggests an activity producing/requiring extremely high temperatures.

The use of oak largewood including heartwood would have provided a high calorie heat source and would have been longer-lasting than that of narrow roundwood. The latter, however, has the capacity to produce an intensely hot fire very quickly and also offers the means of rapidly boosting the temperature of a dying fire. In the absence of artefactual evidence, it is impossible to specify the likely function of the roundwood fuelled hearths; some may even represent bonfires to dispose of hedge trimmings or scrub.

The procurement of fuel

A large assemblage of charcoal collected from contexts associated with enclosures and dwellings at the Iron Age and Romano-British farmstead and settlement indicated the use of fuel obtained from a wide range of species but predominantly from oak. The fast growth rates recorded in some fragments of oak wood roundwood (eg, in hearth 292000, Enclosure 6) and largewood (in pit 291411) suggest that some fuel, at least, was obtained from coppiced stems and poles. Although fast growth was not evident in the other species identified, it seems likely, given the great abundance of narrow roundwood present in most of the samples, that coppiced woodland provided most of the fuel used in domestic hearths and possibly also in some agricultural contexts. The rapid regeneration of the felled coppice stool can often be detected by wide growth rings in the young stems of some species, typically those of hazel (Morgan 1982) but detrimental external factors, such as shading, poor aspect and competitive vegetation may retard the rate of growth.

The absence of postholes parallel to the enclosure ditches suggests that these boundaries were marked by hedges rather than fences, probably using thorny stock-proof species, such as hawthorn and blackthorn. Hedgerows, therefore, may also have provided a source of narrow roundwood, although it is probably worth noting that blackthorn and the hawthorn group were not recorded in the samples significantly more frequently than other non-oak species.

Structural evidence

Structures recorded on site included several roundhouses (the largest of which appeared to have undergone several phases of rebuilding) and farm buildings (?granaries). In addition, a wooden structure aligned south-east/north-west was indicated by a line of postholes. Apart from the burnt base of a single oak post, still *in situ* in posthole 292405, scant evidence remained at the site to illustrate the type of timber used for construction. In view of the frequency of oak in the fuel deposits, it is probable that oak timber was also used extensively for construction work. The strength and durability of oak heartwood is particularly suited to outdoor and structural work (Edlin 1949).

Environmental evidence

The site was located on the south-facing slope of a hill, east of the Sutton Plateau. Within the site itself a series of enclosures suggests that agricultural land was dedicated to pastoral farming. Apart from boundary hedges adjacent to enclosure ditches, woodland trees and shrubs may have been fairly sparse in the immediate vicinity of the farmstead. This suggestion is supported by the presence of heathland taxa such as gorse/broom and ericaceous species in the fuel deposits. The charcoal analysis, however, indicated that the farming community had access to a diverse range of species – predominantly oak but also woodland species such as hazel, field maple, holly, birch and ash. Wetland species including alder and willow/poplar were also represented. It is also suggested that copses of managed woodland, in particular oak, were extant in the area (see above).

Discussion

The site produced evidence for intense and prolonged activity, from the Middle Iron Age through the Romano-British period, and given that the Iron Age activity is concentrated towards the southern, lower end of the site and the stratigraphically latest features are concentrated towards the higher, northern end, it was tempting to see the apparent series of similarly-sized enclosures as representing a sequence of activity whose focus shifted gradually uphill during the period of the site's occupation.

The actual sequence of development, however, is less clearly defined, and although a number of key stratigraphic relationships help elucidate the relative dating of some of the main components of that sequence, there remains a significant area of uncertainty both in its details and in its absolute dating, for which the ceramic evidence, a large proportion of which can be assigned only a general Romano-British date, provides only limited data. Nonetheless, six broad phases of activity are suggested (Fig. 146).

Phase 1

The possibility that the Iron Age settlement at the southern end of the site was initially unenclosed relies on the identification of feature 298338 as a roundhouse gully. It is quite possible, however, that it had some other function, perhaps defining and screening off a small area adjacent to the ditch. The relatively longevity of the settlement's occupation is indicated by the fact that the principal residence (structure 1) was rebuilt in approximately the same location on two occasions, with additional repairs to at least one of those phases, and by the repeated re-working of the enclosure ditch terminal. Because none of the other, relatively evenly spaced structures within the enclosure overlapped, it is possible that the settlement consisted, at any one time, solely of a principal residence (structure 1), a secondary residence (possibly structures 2, 3 or 6) and an ancillary structure (structures 4 or 5, and the four-post structure). The radiocarbon dates clearly indicate a Middle Iron Age date (possibly extending into the Late Iron Age) for its occupation. These are broadly contemporary with the radiocarbon dates from roundhouses at Langley Mill (Site 30, Chapter 22), *c* 400 m to the south-east (Fig. 137), as well as at Wishaw (Site 20, Chapter 25) and Shenstone Ring Ditch (Site 14).

The absence of pottery from the lower ditch fill, and the dearth of chronologically diagnostic pottery generally from the enclosure, means that it is not possible to suggest more than a Middle Iron Age date for its construction, with no evidence as to the date of its abandonment. The presence of Romano-British pottery, including a sherd of late 1st–mid-2nd century date from its upper fills, indicates that the ditch was not being maintained in the Romano-British period, probably no longer necessary in the new political climate, although the gully linking the infilled ditch terminals suggests that some activity was taking place, and it is possible that the enclosure, whose ditch was still visible as a hollow in the 2nd century, was adapted to some non-domestic use. The relative dearth of late 1st–mid-2nd century pottery from across the rest of the site also points to a significant reduction of settlement activity in the Early Romano-British period, although not its complete absence.

Phase 2

Features of this very broad phase extend across most of the site and include an additional four possible enclosures (Enclosures 2–5). Although the contemporaneity of these features cannot be proved, there is no reason why they should not all have been component parts of an integrated and organised agricultural landscape, both nucleated and focused within the site, and extending out from it, comprising enclosures, paddocks, fields and other fully or partly bounded areas.

There appears to have been no contemporary focus of settlement activity within the site associated with this array of ditches, although the numerous pits, postholes, hearths, short linear features and amorphous spreads of material, many containing evidence of burning, indicate the presence of domestic activity in the immediate vicinity, as does the presence of pottery and quern stones. Structure 7 is of uncertain function, but its peculiar form and its apparently prominent and isolated location in Enclosure 3, might support its interpretation as a religious shrine, as opposed to a domestic or industrial building.

The different forms of the enclosures may point to different functions. The enclosures varied in size, shape, contents, and in the width and the apparent numbers of their entrances. While some entrances were relatively narrow, in some cases incorporating entrance structures enabling them to be closed (Enclosures 1 and 2), others had associated ditches possibly designed to control the movement of livestock (Enclosures 3 and 4). In other cases the 'enclosures' were either open on one side (Enclosure 4, 5 and 6), or had wide breaks in their circuits (Enclosure 3).

Phase 3

It is possible that Enclosure 6 represented a modification of the phase 2 layout, incorporating and linking Enclosures 3 and 5 (subsuming the former within its more extensive bounds), and with only Enclosure 4, which it cut across, definitely going out of use. The sherd of reeded hammerhead mortarium, dated to *c* AD 200–260, from the lower ditch fill of Enclosure 6 provides a probable 3rd century date for the initial silting of the ditch. This would appear to be at odds with the very early Romano-British radiocarbon date 40 cal BC–cal AD 140 from a similar and adjacent context of the same ditch.

Although few other sherds from the site could be tied to the 3rd or 4th century, it may be significant that no such sherds were found in Enclosure 4, nor in Enclosure 1, which may also have gone out of use by this time. Further sherds of diagnostically 3rd and 4th century pottery were largely limited to a number of large but irregular features of uncertain function dispersed across the site, in Enclosure 2 (293513), Enclosure 3 (290571), and Enclosure 6 (298076/8), and at the northern edge of the site (adjacent features 292178 and 293100).

Phases 4 and 5

The phase 4 features, a comparatively localised group of gully segments sharing similar orientations, and some incorporating right-angled bends, would appear to form short boundaries of some kind, but without any obvious function. The fact that they clearly cut across the ditches of Enclosures 4 and 6 would suggest that these had gone out of use by this time, although there is nothing in the Romano-British pottery assemblage from these features to indicate a late date (in fact it included both residual Iron Age and late 1st–early 2nd century sherds).

Similarly, the pottery from the phase 5 features was also largely of indeterminate Romano-British date, although a single 3rd–4th century sherd was found in the middle fill of the terminal of ditch 292650. The single medieval sherd found in the fill of a tree hollow cut by the extension of this ditch (292641) raises the possibility that this latest phase post-dates the Romano-British period, although if so all the remaining sherds from these features, which apparently formed part of a field system, would have been residual – not impossible but perhaps unlikely.

Conclusion

It is probably no coincidence that the site of an enclosed Iron Age farmstead should have been subsequently occupied in the Romano-British period. Although the Iron Age settlement does not appear to have been large – perhaps no more than two or three structures at any one time – and no contemporary field boundaries were recorded (apart from possibly a single gully), it is possible that features of this period associated with the settlement lay beyond the limits of the site. Indeed, that the settlement was the focus of settlement and farming activity in the wide landscape, including possibly the features at Langley Brook (Site 30) which share a similar alignment (Fig. 137), is suggested by the substantial ditched enclosure built around it.

Following an apparent contraction of activity in the late 1st–early 2nd centuries, the site was extensively reoccupied in the period from the mid-2nd to the mid-3rd centuries, with an organised landscape being developed, involving the construction of a number of adjacent enclosures, each linked into a more extensive array of fields and other land boundaries. While this layout may have developed and been modified over time, with some elements supplanting outlived features, it seems that in the main many of these features were in use at the same time, rather than being a simple sequence of replacement enclosures. Despite the quantity of pottery and the frequent occurrence of burnt material from across the site, no obvious focus of settlement was identified, and the single identifiable structure, a rectangular building with what appears to be a semicircular 'apse' at its north-west end and some form of fireplace at the front, may have had a religious, rather than a domestic or industrial function.

Chapter 22
Langley Mill (Site 30)

By Rebecca Devaney

Introduction

Following geophysical survey and trial trenching, an archaeological excavation was undertaken on land adjacent to Langley Brook, east of Sutton Coldfield, some 400 m south-east of North of Langley Brook (Site 29) (Fig. 137). The site was centred on NGR 415800 296750, to the east of the A38, in an area now occupied by the more southerly of two adjacent M6/A38 junctions. Langley Brook, which flows approximately west-east and forms the boundary between the local authority areas of Birmingham (to the north) and Warwickshire (to the south), divides the site into northern and southern halves.

The geology is mapped as Triassic Mudstone, with alluvium along Langley Brook (Geological Survey of Great Britain 1996, Sheet 168, Birmingham).

Two possible burnt mounds, one on each side of the brook, had been identified during fieldwalking and a cropmark of a subrectangular enclosure just north of the brook had been identified from aerial photographs. A magnetic susceptibility survey undertaken as part of the geophysical survey, indicated the presence of three generalised concentrations of high readings, all at some distance from the brook, while the magnetometry showed four areas of 'magnetic debris/disturbance', all but one lying north of the brook and possibly relating to the remains of ploughed out burnt mounds.

During the topsoil stripping of the area on the north side of the brook, the spoil was arranged in north-south aligned bunds. Parts of these were subsequently removed to allow the examination of the underlying features. A range of features was recorded during the excavation, including the enclosure which was shown to be Iron Age in date, and the gullies of a number of Iron Age roundhouses (Fig. 151).

Results

The underlying geology consisted of naturally deposited sands and gravels (300003). Above this, a pale blue alluvial deposit (300002) was observed either side of Langley Brook. The extent of this deposit, varying in depth up to 0.8 m, is likely to delineate the floodplain. Concentrations of burnt stone, 1–2 stones thick, with approximate diameters of *c* 2 m, were recorded within the upper part of the deposit, possibly redeposited after eroding from a source upstream to the west. The sequence of deposition was sealed by a mid-greyish-brown clayey loam topsoil (300001) that contained sub-rounded stones. This material is very similar to that seen in the fills of many of the excavated features.

As there were almost no artefacts from the site, the phasing was determined largely on the basis of the limited stratigraphic evidence supplemented by the subsequent analysis of eight radiocarbon dates from selected features (Fig. 152, Table 112). Middle Iron Age features, including annular and penannular ditches, and a small sub-rectangular enclosure were recorded on opposite sides of the brook, at the west end of the site close to the embankment of the A38. Spreads of heat fractured stones, seen as discrete features and covering larger areas, were recorded along both banks. Few archaeologically significant features were identified in the eastern half of the site where a series of post-medieval and modern land drains was excavated.

Iron Age

South of Langley Brook

An annular ditch and two overlapping penannular ditches were recorded close together on an elevated gravel terrace on the south side of the brook (Fig. 153). Other smaller features were recorded within and around them, and although these were undated, it is likely that some were associated with the larger features, and they are therefore described in this section.

Annular ditch 300131 and adjacent features

The annular ditch (300131) lay at the western end of the excavated area. It had an external diameter of *c* 14.5 m with the width of the ditch varying from 0.8 m in the north-west (Fig. 154) to 1.5 m in the south. In general, the sides sloped at a 45° angle to a concave base. The depth of the ditch also varied, from 0.37 m in the east to 0.50 m in the south. It is suggested that the variation may have resulted from truncation caused by modern ploughing.

Three deposits were identified along the length of the ditch. The primary fill (eg 300315) was a mid-greyish-brown silty clay with frequent gravels, some sandstone pebbles and flecks of charcoal. The thickness of the deposit varied from 0.1 m to 0.23 m. The primary fill was overlain by a brown silty clay with frequent rounded pebbles (eg 300316). This deposit varied in thickness from 0.12 m to 0.4 m. The darker material may have derived from activity within the annular ditch. The final ditch fill was similar to the primary fill in terms of composition, inclusions and thickness and is likely to represent the abandonment of the earthwork (eg,

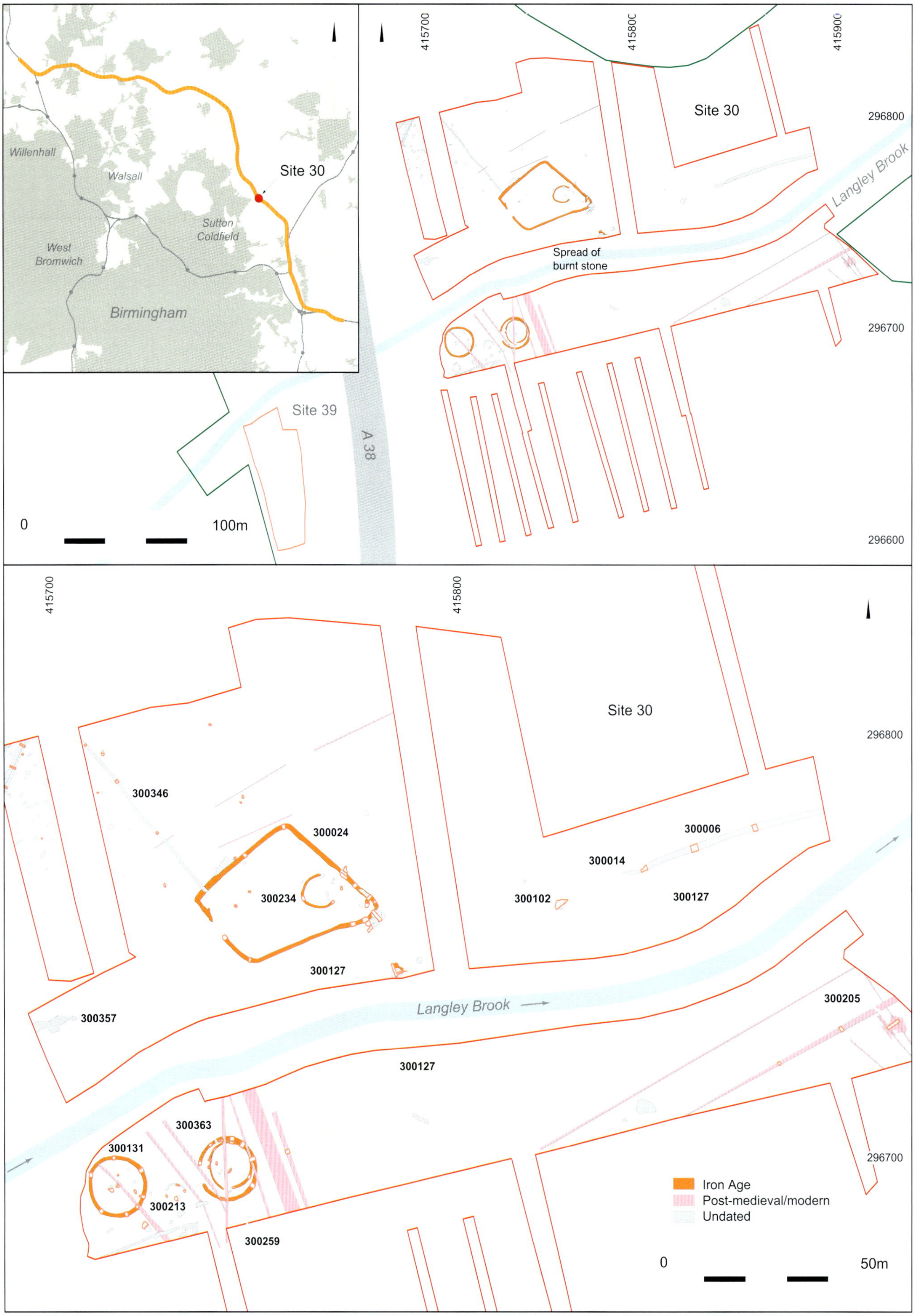

Fig. 151 Langley Mill (Site 30)

Table 112 Radiocarbon dates from Langley Mill

Feature	*Context*	*Material*	*Lab. no.*	*Result BP*	*Date cal BC at 2 σ*
Burnt stone spread	300127	Hazel	NZA-25066	2335±40	520–200
Penannular ditch 300234	300236	Hazel roundwood	NZA-25064	2308±30	410–200
Penannular ditch 300259	302014	Oak sapwood	NZA-25062	2288±30	400–200
Annular ditch 300131	300315	Birch	NZA-25061	2234±30	380–190
Pit 300285, oak slab	300286	Oak, sapwood	NZA-25240	2178±30	370–110
Pit 300053	300052	Pomoideae	NZA-25071	2125±30	200–40
Enc. ditch 300024	300026	Ash	NZA-25063	2095±35	200–1
Layer over enc. ditch	300121	Birch	NZA-25065	865±35	AD 1120–1250

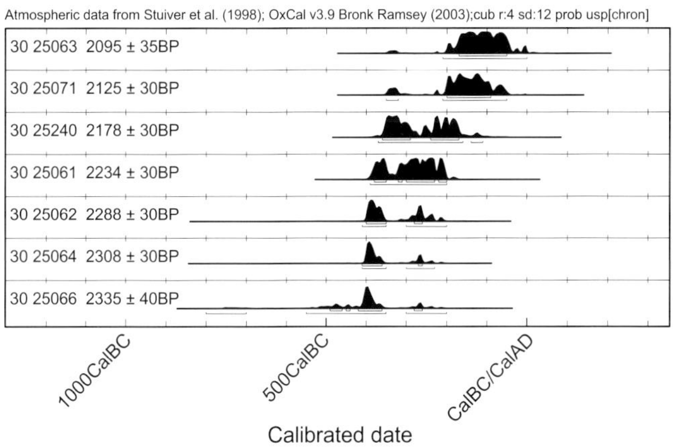

Fig. 152 Oxcal probability distributions of radiocarbon dates

300317). Fill 300145, the upper fill in the north-east quadrant of the ditch, produced a fragment of a probable quern stone, but this was not closely datable on typological or lithological grounds.

No other finds, datable or otherwise, were recovered either from the ditch or from any of the features within it, but its morphology and size, and the presence of a pit at its centre (300252, possibly a grave in which the acidic soil conditions had destroyed any bone), initially suggested that it was the ploughed out remains of a Bronze Age round barrow. However, a dump of charred remains in the primary ditch fill (300315) produced a Middle Iron Age radiocarbon date of 380–190 cal BC (NZA-25061, 2234±30 BP). If the ditch had had an entrance gap it would almost certainly be interpreted as an Iron Age roundhouse gully, but while the absence of an entrance does not rule out such an interpretation, there must remain some doubt (see Chapter 29).

The central pit (300252) was almost circular, with a diameter of 1 m and a depth of 0.4 m. Its sides sloped steeply and joined a concave base (Fig. 154). The first pit fill (300253) was a mid-brownish-yellow sandy silt containing large rounded stones up to about 0.1 m in size. The fill was approximately 0.2 m thick and was deposited on the east edge of the pit. Overlying this layer of was a fairly compact, mid-blackish-brown silty clay (300254) that contained small sub-angular stones. The deposit measured 0.1 m thick and was slightly slumped in the centre of the pit. The final deposit (300255) was an orangy-brown clay and contained slightly larger rounded stones. It was 0.15 m thick and sealed the pit.

Two smaller features within the interior of the annular ditch were interpreted as postholes, although no post-pipes were observed. Posthole 300149, north of the central pit, was roughly oval in shape and measured 0.35 m by 0.5 m. The sides were gently sloping at the top, but almost vertical below, with a total depth of 0.2 m. The base was concave and about 0.1 m in diameter. The primary fill (300150), a light brownish-red clay free from inclusions and up to 0.07 m deep, was overlain by a dark brown clay up to 0.12 m thick (300151) containing occasional small pebbles and one piece of probably intrusive post-medieval/modern ceramic building material. Posthole 300168, south-east of the central pit, was also oval in shape, measuring *c* 0.6 m by 0.2 m. It had steep sides and a concave base. The only fill (300169) was a mid-greyish-brown sandy silt with occasional small sub-angular gravel inclusions. The relationship of the postholes to each other, and to the annular ditch, was uncertain, and their layout does not suggest any obvious structure. Another posthole (300312) was located just outside the ditch on the north-west side. It was *c* 0.4 m in diameter and 0.2 m deep, with steep sides and a flat base, and a single fill (300313) of mid-greyish-brown silty clay with frequent gravel inclusions.

There were two pits on the eastern side of the interior. Pit 300152 measured 0.8 m by 1.1 m. It had a steep northern side whereas the southern side had a gradually breaking stepped edge, and a flat base. It was filled with a mid-greyish-brown silty clay (300153) containing approximately 50% large sub-rounded pebbles and frequent gravel inclusions. Pit 300302 was roughly circular, *c* 1.1 m in diameter and 0.5 m deep, with moderately steep sides and a flat base. The primary fill (300303), up to 0.1 m thick, was a mid-greyish-brown sandy clay with a small amount of gravel inclusions. The second fill (300304), up to 0.2 m thick, was a mid-grey silty clay with a small amount of gravel inclusions and larger rounded stones. The third fill (300305) was a mid-yellowish-brown silty clay with larger proportions of gravel and rounded stones than the previous fills. This fill was also more uneven, being thicker on the southern side of the pit. The upper fill (300306) was a light to mid-greyish-brown silty clay with a fair amount of gravel inclusions. Another pit

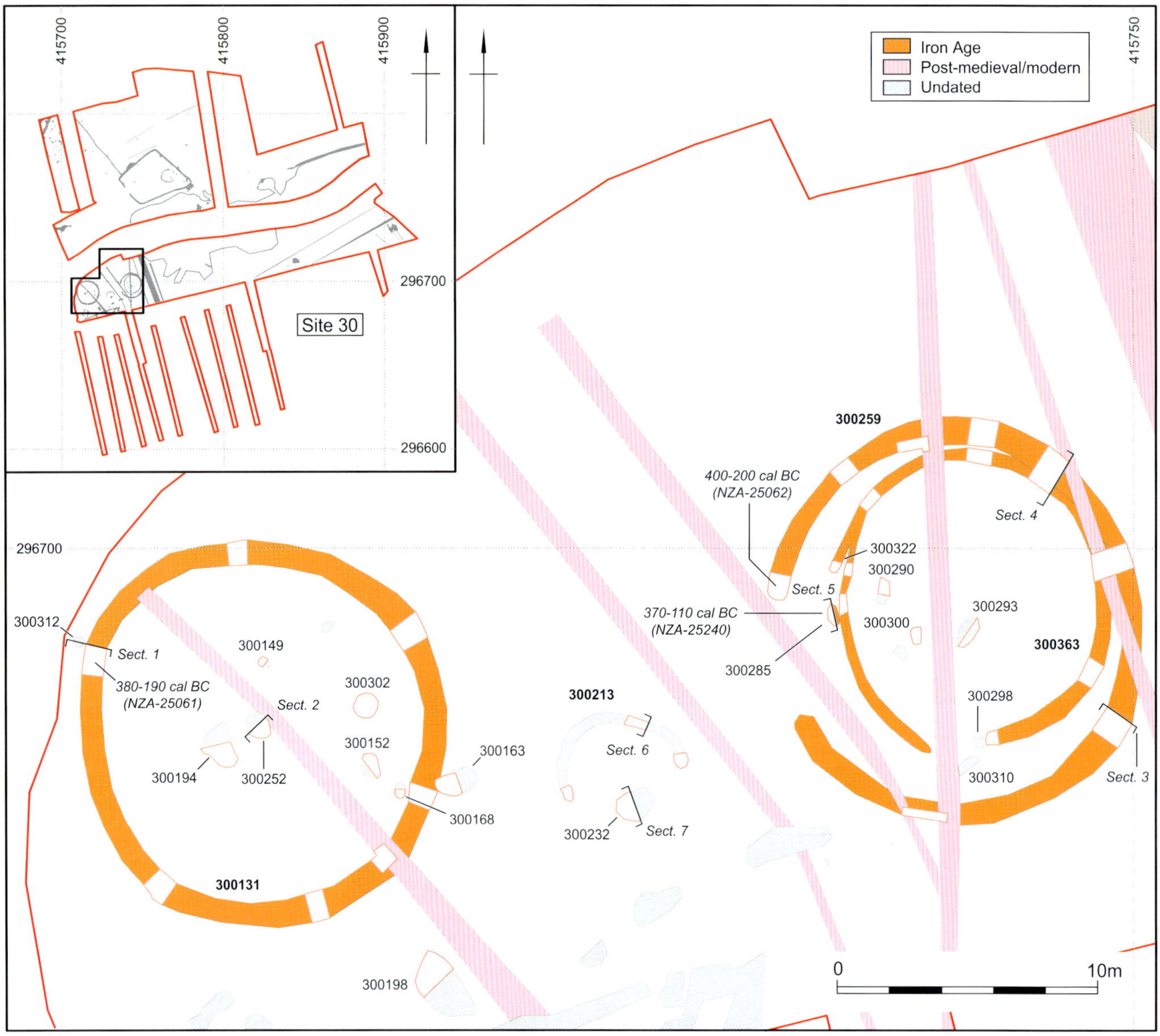

Fig. 153 The annular and penannular ditches south of Langley Brook

(300163) cut the annular ditch on its south-eastern edge. It was oval and measured 0.9 m in length and 0.3 m deep, with steep sides and a flat base. Its fill (300164) was a dark blackish-brown silty clay with frequent rounded stones and charcoal inclusions. Fragments of animal bone were recovered but the only identifiable pieces were two fragmentary cattle teeth. As with the postholes, the relationship between the pits was uncertain, and the fact that 300163 cut the annular ditch may indicate that that they were not directly associated with it.

Feature 300194, immediately west of the central pit, was irregularly shaped both in plan and section, measuring *c* 1.7 m by 1.3 m, interpreted as a tree hollow. Three fills were identified, all of which contained small sub-angular gravels and stones, but no finds. Similar features were recorded south of the annular ditch, one of which was excavated (300198).

Penannular ditch 300363 and gully 300322

Penannular ditch 300363 was 16 m east of annular ditch 300131 (and within the later penannular ditch 300259). A 2.3 m long spur (gully 300322) ran off it on its north-west side, and although the relationship between the two features is uncertain it suggests that the structure was modified at some time. The slightly irregular shape of ditch 300363 suggested that its south-western section may have been a later addition, almost closing what would originally have been a wide, south-west facing gap between the terminal of gully 300322 and the southern terminal of ditch 300363.

Together these features were *c* 11 m in diameter. The ditch varied in width from 0.6 m at the south-east to 0.25 m wide at the west, and had concave sides and a concave–flat base (Fig. 154). The depth also varied from 0.24 m in the north to 0.7 m in the west, probably due to truncation by modern ploughing. The basal fill, seen only in small patches in the east and west of the ditch and possibly deriving from activity within the enclosed area, was a dark brownish-grey to black silt with occasional small sub-angular pebbles and flecks of charcoal. The second fill, probably representing the abandonment of the feature, was a mid-greyish-brown silty clay with occasional sub-rounded pebbles. Gully

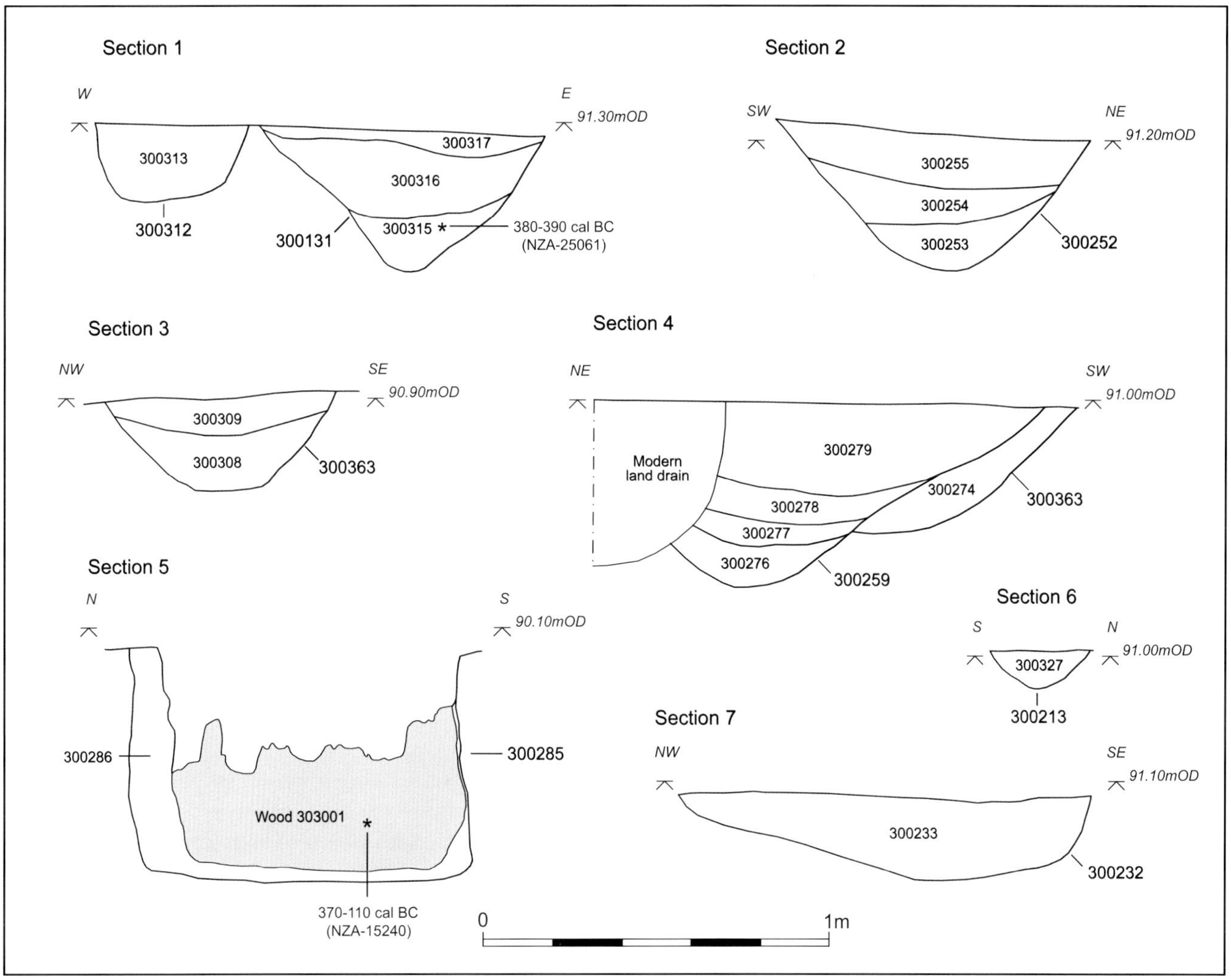

Fig. 154 Sections of features south of Langley Brook

300322 was filled with a dark greyish-brown clayey silt with occasional sub-rounded pebbles and charcoal flecks.

Penannular ditch 300259

Penannular ditch 300363 was surrounded by, and cut on its north-eastern edge by, another, larger penannular ditch (300259) (Fig. 154). Ditch 300259 was roughly circular with an external diameter of about 15 m and a west facing entrance 4.4 m wide. It had a U-shaped profile with a slightly pointed base, and its width varied from 1.3 m at the north-east to 0.7 m at the south, and its depth from 0.6 m at the south-east to 0.35 m at the north and west, again probably due to truncation by modern ploughing. The primary fill was a dark brownish-black silty sand with a high abundance of heat fractured angular quartzite pebbles and charcoal. The secondary fills differed only in the smaller quantities of heat fractured quartzite pebbles and charcoal. The uppermost fill was a thin layer of light yellowish-brown silty sand with occasional sub-rounded pebbles similar to the natural, and had probably accumulated after the abandonment of the ditch. Although no datable finds were recovered, charcoal from the primary fill produced a Middle Iron Age radiocarbon date of 400–200 cal BC (NZA-25062, 2288±30 BP) (Fig. 152, Table 112).

Both penannular ditches were interpreted as drainage ditches surrounding Iron Age roundhouses, although their west to south-facing entrances do not conform to the southerly to easterly orientations typical of Iron Age roundhouses. It is possible that the orientations related to the presence of the annular ditch to the west, comparable, for instance, to the anomalous orientation at North of Langley Brook (Site 29, above) of Iron Age structure 4, facing north towards structure 1.

Both penannular ditches were sealed by a light greyish-brown silty clay with occasional gravel deposits (300237). This material was similar to the natural deposits seen elsewhere on the site and may have derived from natural silting processes.

Features within the penannular ditches

There was a range of postholes/pits within the area define by the two penannular ditches, none of which produced any finds, and most of which were of uncertain relationship to the ditches, and of unknown function.

Pit 300285, which cut penannular ditch 300363 on its western edge was roughly oval in shape with almost vertical sides (Fig. 154). It was *c* 1 m long, 0.35 m wide and was excavated to a depth of 0.65 m before reaching the water table. It was filled with a dark grey silty loam with frequent mid- large sub-rounded cobbles (300286). Within the fill was a large slab of waterlogged squared oak (ON 303001), measuring 0.8 m long, 0.44 m wide and 0.2 m high, presumably the base of a substantial post. Its underside was flat, probably sawn, but the upper part was very degraded, and no other tool marks were observed on the timber. The slab was positioned against the southern side of the pit and packed around with medium sized sub-rounded cobbles. Its dendrochronological sequence was assessed but unfortunately the rings could not be matched against any dated sequences (OWA 2003, 278). However, a sample submitted for radiocarbon dating produced a Middle Iron Age date of 370–110 cal BC (NZA-15240, 2178±30 BP) which is contemporary with the result from the penannular ditch 300259 (Fig. 152, Table 112).

Pit 300290, in the western half of penannular ditch 300363, was oval and measured *c* 1 m long, 0.4 m wide and 0.3 m deep, with steep sides and a flat base. It was filled with a mid-greyish-brown silty clay, with medium sized rounded stones around the base and sides of the cut, similar to pit 300285 suggesting that these features could have been related.

Another oval pit (300293), near the centre of the penannular ditch 300363, measured *c* 1.3 m by 0.7 m and 0.1 m deep, with concave side and base. It had a thin primary fill (300294) of light grey sandy clay and an secondary fill (300295) of mid-greyish-brown silty clay with frequent gravel inclusions. Sealing the pit was a localised spread, approximately 0.08 m thick, of mid-brown silty clay (300292).

Pit 300298, cutting the southern terminal of penannular ditch 300363, was 0.5 m in diameter and 0.15 m deep with concave sides. It was filled with a dark brownish-grey silty clay with frequent small to medium sub-rounded pebbles and occasional charcoal flecks.

Pit 300300, located south of pit 300290, was *c* 0.6 m in diameter and 0.25 m deep with steep sides and a concave base. The single fill (300301) was a dark brownish-black silty clay with frequent gravel inclusions and occasional large pebbles.

Feature 300310, between the two penannular ditches at the south (and cut by a modern field drain), was sub-oval in shape with well defined, steep sides and a concave base. It was at least 0.8 m long, 0.4 m in width and 0.25 m deep. The single fill (300311) was a dark greyish-brown silty clay with occasional small sub-rounded pebbles and charcoal flecks.

Gully 300213 and pit 300232

Two possibly associated features, neither producing finds, lay between the annular ditch and the penannular ditches. Gully 300213 was defined as a semicircle 5 m across, being open to the south. It had moderately steep sides and a concave to flat base (Fig. 154), and was 0.3–0.55 m wide and up to 0.16 m deep (but only to 0.02 m at its eastern end, probably due to truncation by modern ploughing). Both ends of the gully appear to be genuine terminals and it is unlikely that it originally surrounded pit 300232. It had a single fill, a mid-dark grey-brown silty clay, with occasional inclusions of small stones and gravel. The pit was oval, measuring *c* 0.7 m by 1.3 m, and 0.3 m deep. It had fairly straight, gently sloping sides at the north, but almost vertical sides at the south (Fig. 154), and a concave base, and was filled with a mid-yellowish-brown silty clay with occasional large stone inclusions.

North of Langley Brook

The largest feature north of Langley Brook was a sub-rectangular enclosure, faintly visible on aerial photographs, with a main west-facing entrance and a smaller east-facing entrance that was subsequently blocked (Fig. 155). Within the enclosure was a penannular gully indicating the location of a roundhouse. As was the case south of Langley Brook, some of the undated features within and adjacent to the enclosure are likely to have been contemporary with it.

The enclosure

The enclosure was sub-rectangular in shape, with sides measuring 27 m, 29 m, 31 m and 20 m and enclosing a total area of *c* 670 m^2. The profile of the ditch (300024) varied throughout the perimeter of the enclosure. On the north side the ditch had steep sides and a concave to flat base, whereas on the south side (near the south-eastern corner) the sides sloped more gently (Fig. 156). Its depth was highly varied, probably due to truncation, with recorded depths from *c* 0.2 m to 0.6 m. The width at the surface was similarly variable, between 0.7 m and 1.2 m. The depositional sequence varied throughout the course of the enclosure ditch, although five distinct layers were identified.

A primary fill of light bluish-grey silt, up to 0.15 m thick with occasional rounded pebbles, was recorded at the north-west corner of the enclosure. It was similar in colour to the natural alluvial deposit seen elsewhere on the site (300002) and was likely to represent a natural inwash. It was overlain by a light to mid-greyish-brown silty sand, which formed the primary deposit along much of the northern and eastern sides of the enclosure. This layer contained frequent rounded pebbles and varied in thickness from *c* 0.1 m in the north to 0.4 m in the east. It was similar to the topsoil and probably represented the natural slumping of material into the ditch during its use.

Along the southern and western sides of the enclosure, the primary fill was a dark greyish-brown sandy silt/clay with rounded stones. It ranged in depth from *c* 0.1 m at the south-west corner to 0.5 m towards the east. This deposit contained more organic material than the other deposits and may have been deliberately dumped within the ditch. Overlying it was a light to mid-greyish-brown silty clay with frequent pebbles and gravel inclusions, and a consistent thickness of 0.2–0.25 m, which may represent natural slumping of material into the ditch. The uppermost fill recorded in a number of sections was a mid-orangy-brown silt, up to 0.2 m thick, containing occasional rounded stones and gravels, possibly redeposited natural.

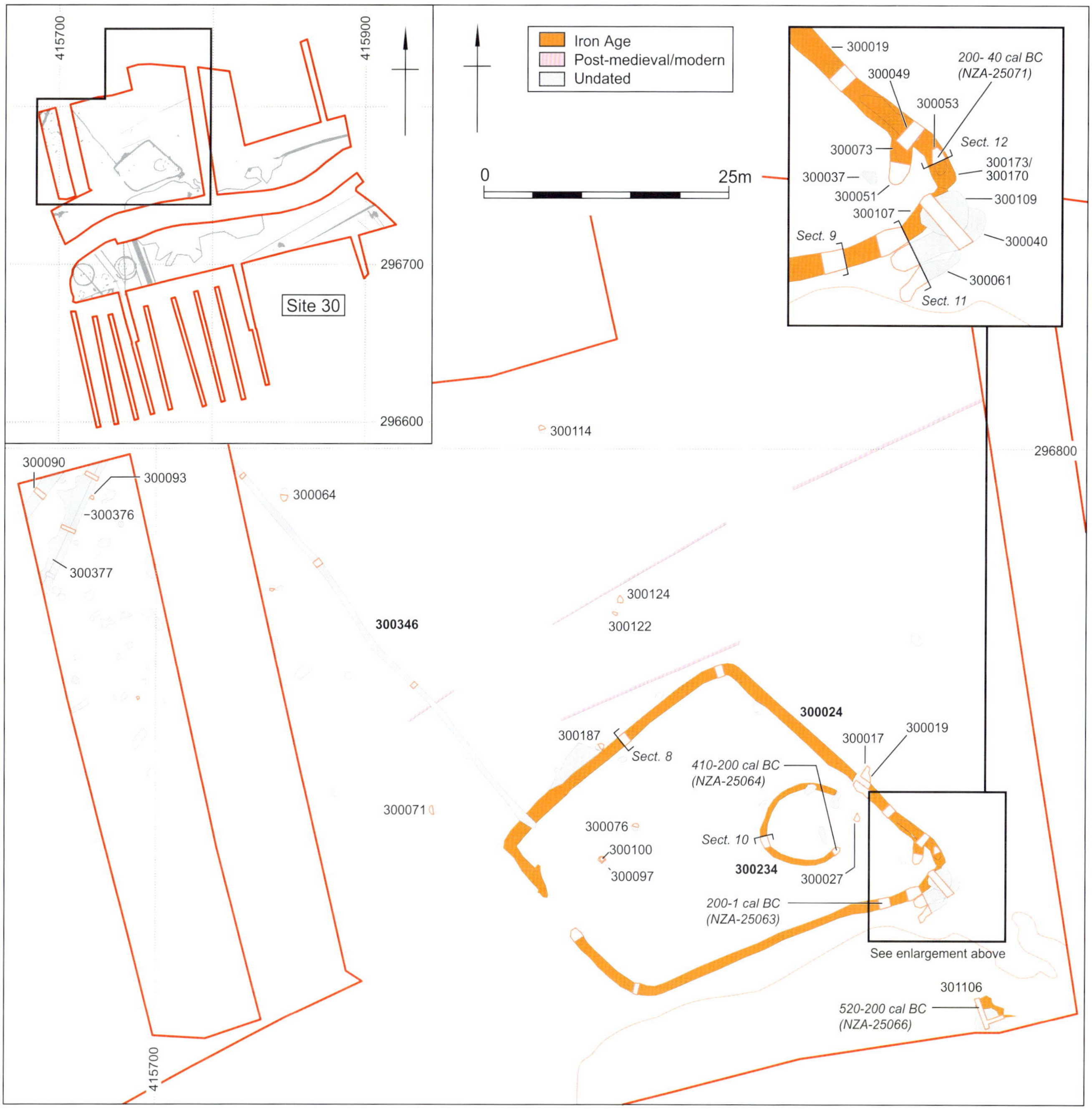

Fig. 155 The Iron Age enclosure north of Langley Brook

Charcoal associated with fire-cracked stones in the upper fill (300026) of ditch section 300025 (Fig. 156), located just west of the south-east entrance to the enclosure produced a radiocarbon date in the Middle-Late Iron Age of 200–1 cal BC (NZA-25063, 2095±35 BP) (Fig. 152, Table 112).

The main entrance to the enclosure, located approximately halfway along the short south-west side, was 4 m wide. The primary deposit in the southern terminal (300329) appeared to line the sides and base of the ditch and suggests that the ditch had been re-cut at some stage prior to the deposition of the secondary filling (300369).

There was a second, smaller entrance at the south-east corner of the enclosure, although this was later blocked (Fig. 155). Its northern terminal was formed by a short inward turning length of ditch (300073), with steep sides and a concave base. Its single fill (300074) was a light greyish-brown sandy silt/clay with occasional rounded stones probably representing the natural slump of topsoil into the ditch. This was truncated by a slightly wider re-cut (300051), extending further into the enclosure, containing a single fill (300050) of mid-greyish-brown sandy clay with frequent rounded stones. The southern terminal (300107) lay parallel to the northern terminal recut, to the immediate south-east, leaving a gap of just 1.3 m. The entrance was subsequently blocked by a short length of ditch (300173), filled with a dark greyish-brown sandy silt/clay with occasional rounded stones. A later re-cut (300170) contained two fills of greyish-brown sandy silt/clay with frequent rounded stones. The proximity of

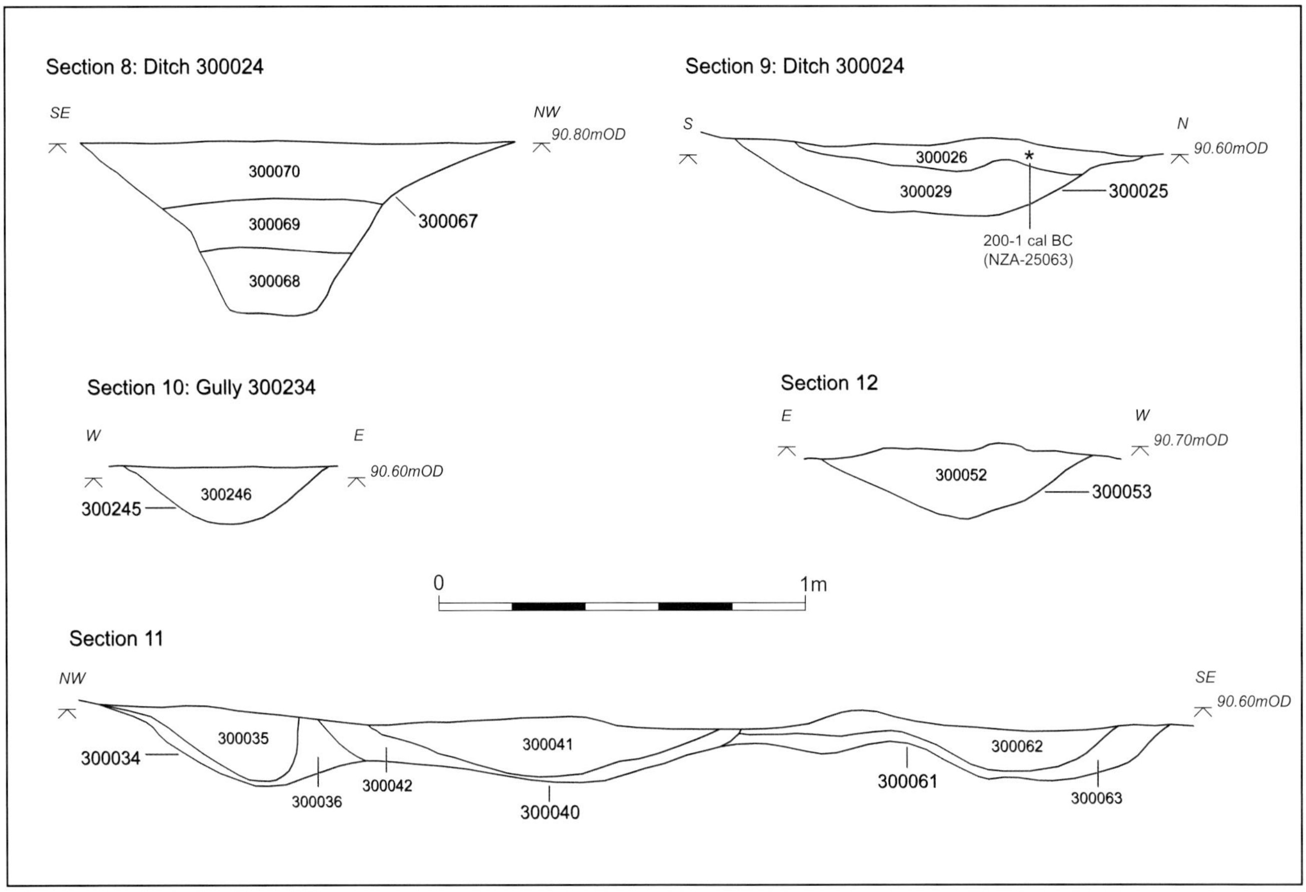

Fig. 156 Sections of features north of Langley Brook

the enclosure's south-eastern corner to the alluvial deposits alongside Langley Brook would have meant that cut features quickly silted up and would need re-cutting, and all the fills of the blocking ditch appear to have been the result of natural silting.

Features within the enclosure

A penannular ditch (300234) lay within the eastern half of the enclosure. It had an internal diameter of approximately 7 m and a wide (*c* 5.5 m) east facing entrance. The ditch was *c* 0.55 m wide and up to 0.2 m deep, with gently sloping sides and a concave base. (Fig. 155). It had a single fill of mid-greyish-brown sandy silt/clay with occasional rounded stones and charcoal flecks. Charcoal from the southern terminal (context 300236) produced a Middle Iron Age radiocarbon date of 410–200 cal BC (NZA-25064, 2308±30 BP) (Fig. 152, Table 112), contemporary with that from penannular ditch 300259 south of Langley Brook. Although this date is earlier than that obtained from the enclosure ditch (above), the latter was from the upper ditch fill, and it is possible therefore that the roundhouse and enclosure were contemporary. The penannular ditch's east-facing entrance conformed to the general pattern for Iron Age roundhouses, such as those recorded within the sub-rectangular enclosure, *c* 400 m to the north-west, at North of Langley Brook (Site 29), although its very wide entrance may indicate a non-domestic function.

Pit 300027 was situated just outside the entrance to the penannular ditch. It was oval and measured *c* 1.2 m by 0.7 m, and 0.3 m deep, with steep sides and a concave base. The earliest fill was a 0.2 m thick layer of mid-greyish-brown sandy silt containing about 10% large stones (300030), which filled the pit slightly higher on the north-eastern side. The pit was sealed by a layer of dark blackish-brown sandy silt with about 5% large stones, flecks of charcoal and patches of burnt clay (300028). Pit 300037 immediately west of the northern terminal of the enclosure's eastern entrance. It was kidney-shaped, measuring 1.2 m by 0.6 m and 0.2 m deep, with gently sloping sides and a concave base. On the base was a 0.1 m thick layer of mid-greyish-brown sandy silt with frequent large rounded pebbles (300038), above which was a 0.15 m thick fill of dark blackish-brown sandy silt with occasional rounded gravels and charcoal flecks (300039).

There were three features in the western half of the enclosure. Pit 300076 was *c* 0.6 m in diameter and 0.1 m deep with gently sloping sides sloped and concave base. The single fill was a dark blackish-brown silty clay with occasional rounded stones (300077). Posthole 300100 was 0.45 m in diameter and 0.4 deep with steep sides and a concave base, and a single fill of a mid-greyish-brown sandy clay with occasional sub-angular gravels (300101). The posthole was cut by oval pit 300097, measuring *c* 1.3 m by 0.6 m and 0.2 m deep. It had moderately sloping sides and a concave base. Filling the entire pit, apart from a hollow at its centre, was a layer of mid-orangy-brown silty clay with frequent rounded stones (300098), the hollow being filled with a dark blackish-brown charcoal rich deposit with frequent small rounded stones (300099).

Like most of the features at Site 30, finds were not recovered from any of the pits located within the enclosure. It was assumed that the function of the pits was related to the use of the enclosure, but the lack of dating evidence and other material means that this is not certain. The deposits in each of the pits were very similar. The greyish-brown and orangy-brown primary deposits were similar to the natural (300002 and 300003) and it is suggested that they derived from a natural silting process. The darker charcoal bearing secondary deposits may be the result of activity associated with the enclosure.

Ditch 300346

Undated ditch 300346 ran north-west to south-east for 48 m from the edge of the site to the north-west corner of the enclosure, terminating just within the enclosure and cutting its infilled ditch. Its was 0.6-0.8 m wide and up to 0.3 m deep, with steep sides and a concave base. It had an irregular and sinuous line that contrasted with the modern land drains recorded elsewhere on the site. A primary fill, only seen where the ditch was deepest, was a dark bluish grey silty clay with small sub-rounded pebbles. A secondary fill, recorded in all sections, was a mid-greyish-brown silty clay with occasional sub-rounded pebbles and gravel inclusions. The ditch probably formed part of a field system, and although its position and orientation parallel to the front of the enclosure suggests some relationship, it was clearly created after the enclosure ditch had silted up and so was not contemporary with the construction of the enclosure. The fact that the ditch appeared to continue for a short distance inside the enclosure supports this suggestion.

Features south-east of the enclosure

There was a series of irregular features situated just outside the south-east entrance of the enclosure (Figs 155–6). Feature 300061, a short, irregularly shaped linear feature, appears to be the earliest. It was 3.7 m long, 0.5 m wide and 0.14 m deep, with gently sloping sides and a flat base. A thick layer of orangy-yellow sand with sub-rounded stones (300063) spread over the base was interpreted as being slumped material. Filling the rest of the feature was a light to mid-grey sandy silt with rounded and sub-angular stones (300062), again interpreted as deriving from natural inwash. Both the enclosure ditch and feature 300061 were cut by another irregularly shaped linear feature (300040), 5.3 m long, 0.9 m wide and 0.24 m deep with a similar profile to 300061. Its primary fill (300042), a light to mid-grey sandy silt with sub-rounded and sub-angular stones, was up to 0.1 m thick. The upper fill (300041) was a dark grey sandy silt with abundant rounded stones and is likely to be a deliberate dump of material, possibly to level and stabilise the ground surface. A roughly circular shallow pit/hollow (300109) cut both feature 300040 and the southern ditch terminal of the enclosure's eastern entrance. It was 2.4 m in diameter and 0.2 m deep, with a 0.1 m thick primary fill of mid-dark grey sandy silt with occasional sub-rounded stones (300117), overlain by a 0.1 m thick layer of light brownish-grey sandy silt with sub-rounded stones (300110).

The function and sequence of these features was not clear. Feature 300061 could have been contemporary with the first phase of the enclosure prior to the blocking of the eastern entrance. Feature 300040 was clearly later than the first phase, but there was no evidence for its relationship with the blocking of the eastern entrance and the re-cutting of the ditches. Some of the fills appeared to result from natural silting but others represented deliberately dumped material, possibly placed to level and stabilise the ground surface. The features did not appear to result from trampling during the use of the entrance as they were in the wrong location and on the wrong alignment.

Other features cutting the enclosure ditch

A series of other features (300017, 300049 and 300053) cut the enclosure ditch on its eastern side. Pit 300017 was situated just beyond the eastern edge of the ditch and cut a tree hollow (300019). It was 0.6 m in diameter and 0.14 m deep, with gently sloping sides and a flat base. The only fill was a dark brown sandy silt with frequent rounded stones (300016). Feature 300049 was an elongated pit cutting the northern terminal of the enclosure ditch. It was 1.4 m wide and up to *c* 0.3 m deep. Its sides were moderately steep and the base slightly concave. The only fill was a dark brownish-grey sandy clay with occasional small to medium sized rounded stones, heat fractured stones and charcoal (300048).

Pit 300053, which cut into the fills of the blocking ditch re-cut (300170), was an elongated oval in shape, measuring *c* 1.5 m by 0.7 m and 0.2 m deep with gently sloping sides and a concave base (Fig. 156). Its single fill, a dark brownish-grey sandy clay with rounded stones, charcoal and occasional burnt stones (300052), contained a base sherd (21 g) of an Iron Age jar in a sand-tempered fabric; the base was flat and pinched out around the circumference. The charcoal produced a radiocarbon date of 200–40 cal BC (NZA-25071, 2215±30 BP), broadly contemporary with that from the upper ditch fill (above) (Fig. 152, Table 112).

Burnt stone spreads

A slot (301106), located between Langley Brook and the south-east corner of the enclosure, was excavated through an extensive spread of burnt stone (300127) that was recorded along both banks of the stream (Figs 151, 154). Charcoal from the deposit gave a radiocarbon date in the Early to Middle Iron Age of 520–200 cal BC (NZA-25066, 2335±40 BP) (Fig. 152, Table 112), broadly contemporary with the Iron Age settlement activity. Below the deposit was an alluvial deposit of mid-orangy-brown sandy silt with occasional rounded stones (300128); this was not fully excavated but was at least 0.15 m thick.

Another sampled deposit (300102), that had accumulated in a depression in the natural *c* 40 m to the north-east, comprised a dark brown sandy silt, up to 0.15 m thick, containing about 50% rounded pebbles (300104), overlain by a similar thickness of mid-orangy-brown clayey silt (300103) with occasional heat fractured pebbles at its upper surface.

There were further localised spreads of heat fractured stone and charcoal along both banks of Langley Brook. Spread 300247, situated in the south-east corner of the site (note surveyed), comprised a 0.1 m thick layer of heat fractured quartzite stones within the alluvial deposits. The majority of the stones had accumulated at the deepest part of an irregular, natural depression measuring about 2.2 m wide. Another spread (300372) was visible eroding out of the south bank of Langley Brook adjacent to annular ditch 300131. Its horizontal extent could not be established as it was not possible to excavate immediately alongside the brook. Surrounding the stones was a light greyish brown alluvial deposit, similar to 300002, about 0.2 m thick. The burnt quartzite stones were concentrated in the centre of the spread where they formed about 60% of the deposit, with the density gradually lessening to either side.

It is possible that these spreads were all approximately contemporary with the Iron Age occupation of the site. The 'clean' character of the stones and the relatively limited quantities of associated charcoal, however, suggest that this material had derived from nearby burnt mounds but had been redeposited as a result of flood action, consistent with the association of the stones with alluvial silts.

Medieval

A layer of a dark grey sandy silt with rounded stones and occasional lumps of charcoal (300121) was recorded lying above the infilled ditch of the Iron Age enclosure at its south-east corner and above feature 300109. Plant remains, including charred seeds and a fragment of a sloe stone were recovered, and charcoal produced a radiocarbon date in the medieval period of cal AD 1120–1250 (NZA-25065, 865±35 BP) (Fig. 152, Table 112). No other evidence for activity in the medieval period was recorded from the site.

Post-medieval and modern

Undated ditches with a variety of alignments were observed on the south side of Langley Brook (Fig. 151). Those with regular cuts are thought to be modern land drains while those with less regular cuts and, in some cases, abundant roots are interpreted as post-medieval or modern field boundaries. Some of the ditches could be seen to continue as linear depressions in the fields beyond the edge of the stripped area.

Three north-east to south-west aligned ditches (300090, 300376 and 300377) were located in the extreme north-west corner of the site (Fig. 155). The only find to be recovered from these ditches was a piece of post-medieval pottery.

An irregular shaped spread of dark greyish-black material (300205) lay at the extreme east end of the site. It measured approximately 4 m by 5 m and was 0.05 m deep. It was fairly compact and contained large pebbles and flecks of charcoal. No finds were recovered but it appeared to be a modern spread of burnt debris. It was cut by a modern field drain.

Other undated

Feature 300014 was a short length of gully aligned ENE-WSW and located towards the east end of the site north of Langley Brook (Fig. 151). It was *c* 4.8 m long, 0.3 m wide and 0.1 m deep, with variably sloping sides and a concave base, and had a single fill of mid-brown sandy silt with frequent sub-rounded pebbles (300015). It was truncated at its east end by ditch 300006 which ran east for 50 m beyond the site. The latter was 1.5 m wide and *c* 0.4 m deep, with gently sloping upper sides, which were steeper towards the U-shaped base. Its primary fill (300005) was a mid-greyish-brown sandy clay, *c* 0.3 m thick, with sub-angular and rounded stones. The secondary fill (300008) was a dark brown sandy silt with occasional rounded stones. This deposit was similar to the primary fill seen in the western terminal of the ditch (300013), although the latter also contained charcoal. Above 300013, lay two further fills (300012 and 300011) of mid-grey sandy silt with sub-angular and sub-rounded stones. The irregular line of this ditch suggested that it was not modern. As it was situated between natural alluvial deposits (300002) to the south and the natural gravels to the north it is possible that it could have been a boundary ditch separating the land susceptible to flooding from the higher and dryer land.

At the western margin of the site ditch 300357 was a shallow linear feature situated north of, and running parallel to Langley Brook with a comparable relationship to the brook to that of ditch 300006 (Fig. 151). It was 1.8 m wide and 0.2 m deep and continued beyond the edge of the excavated area. The sides sloped gently and joined a concave base. The only fill was a light greyish-brown sandy silt with frequent gravel inclusions (300358).

Pit 300064 was an oval pit in the north-west part of the site near the northern end of ditch 300346 (Fig. 155). It was 1.3 m by 0.8 m wide and 0.25 m deep, with moderately steep sides and a concave base. The earliest fill was a 0.15 m thick dark bluish-grey clay with occasional gravel inclusions (300065), overlain by a 0.1 m thick fill of mid-greyish-brown clay, again with occasional gravel inclusions (300066).

Table 113 Charred plant remains

	Period	Iron Age										Und.	Med.
	Feature type	Encl. ditch	Annul. ditch	Penannular ditches						Curved gully	Burnt stone spread	Burnt stone spread	Layer
	Feature	300024	300131	300234		300259				300213			
	Section	300025	300318	300235	300245	300165	300238	300165	300165	300326			
	Context	300026	300319	300236	300246	300167	300240	300166	300287	300327	300127	300247	300121
	Sample	302000	302033	302016	302018	392025	302012	302026	302027	302035	302008	302017	302011
	Sample size (l)	15	17	40	40	20	20	20	20	17	40	30	40
	Flot size (ml)	175	40	50	10	10	10	80	350	20	60	60	1000
Taxon	Common name												
Triticum dicoccum grain	Emmer	-	1	-	-	-	-	-	2	-	-	-	-
Triticum cf. *dicoccum* grain	Emmer	-	1	-	-	-	-	-	1	-	-	-	1
T.monococcum/dicoccum grain	Einkorn/emmer	-	1	-	-	-	-	-	-	-	-	-	-
cf. *T. monococcum/dicoccum* grain	Einkorn/emmer	1	-	-	-	-	-	-	-	-	-	-	-
Triticum spelta grain	Spelt	-	-	-	-	-	-	-	1	-	-	-	-
Triticum cf. *spelta* grain	Spelt	-	2	-	-	-	-	-	-	-	-	-	-
Triticum cf . *spelta* glume base	Spelt	-	-	-	-	-	-	-	1	-	-	-	-
Triticum sp. grain	Wheat	-	-	-	-	-	-	-	1	-	-	-	-
Triticum spp. grain	Wheat	-	-	5	-	-	-	-	-	-	-	-	-
Hordeum sp. grain	Barley	-	-	-	-	-	-	-	1	-	-	-	-
H. vulgare L. grain	Barley	-	-	-	-	-	-	-	1	-	-	-	-
cf. *Hordeum* sp. grain	Barley	-	-	1	-	-	-	-	-	-	-	-	-
Avena/Hordeum/Secale/ Triticum stem frag.	Indet. cereal	-	1	-	-	-		-	-	1	-	1	-
cf. *Vicia faba* seed frag.	Celtic bean/ horse bean	-	-	-	-	-	-	-	-	1	-	1	-
Brassica/Sinapis sp. seed	Wild cabbage/ mustard	-	-	-	-	-	-	-	-	1	-	-	-
Vicia/Lathyrus/Pisum sp. seed	Vetch/tare/ vetchling/pea	-	-	-	-	-	-	-	2	-	-	-	-
Prunus spinosa shell frag.	Sloe/blackthorn	-	-	-	-	-	-	-	-	-	-	-	2
cf. *Crataegus monogyna* seed	Hawthorn	-	-	-	-	-	-	-	-	-	-	-	1
Corylus avellana shell frag.	Hazel	-	1	-	-	-	-	-	-	-	-	-	-
Indet. bud	-	-	-	-	-	-	-	-	-	-	-	-	1
Indet. wood fleck (<4 mm^3)		-	++++	++++	-	++++	++	++++	+++++	-	-	-	-
Indet. wood frag. (>4 mm^3)		+++	-	-	+	++	++	+++	+	-	-	+	-
Indet. plant tissue poss. grain frag.		-	+	+	-	+	+	+	-	-	-	-	-

Key to estimated levels of abundance codes: + =1-10, ++ =11-50, +++ = 51-150, ++++ = 150-250 and +++++ = >250.

Oval pit 300071, located west of the enclosure (Fig. 155), measured *c* 1.1 m by 0.7 m and was 0.2 m deep, with gently sloping side and a concave base. The 0.14 m thick primary fill was a mid-grey clay with abundant gravel inclusions (300072), overlain by a 0.08 m thick secondary fill of mid-greyish-brown clay, again with gravel inclusions (300075).

Posthole 300093, truncated by post-medieval ditch 300376 in the north-west corner of the site (Fig. 155), was 0.5 m in diameter and 0.2 m deep, with gradually sloping sides and a concave base. The only fill was a light grey clay with abundant gravel inclusions (300094).

Pit 300114, near the northern edge in the central part of the site (Fig. 155), was *c* 0.8 m in diameter and 0.2 m deep, with moderately steep sides and a concave base. The only fill was a dark greyish-brown sandy clay with frequent sub-angular stones (300115).

Circular pit 300122, also situated north of the enclosure (Fig. 155), was 0.6 m in diameter and 0.1 m deep, with gently sloping sides and a concave base. The only fill was a mid greyish brown sandy clay with occasional small rounded stones (300123).

Oval pit 300124, adjacent to pit 300122, was 1.2 m long, 0.66 m wide and 0.1 m deep, with gently sloping sides and a concave base. The only fill was a dark greyish-brown sandy clay with frequent small rounded stones (300125).

Pit 300187, located just north of the northern side of the enclosure (Fig. 155), was roughly circular, with gradually breaking sides and a concave base. It was 0.6 m in diameter and 0.16 m deep, with a single fill (300188) of light grey silty clay with frequent gravel inclusions.

Environment

Charred plant remains, by Lisa Gray

Forty-eight samples were taken from a Middle–Late Iron Age settlement complex, from which 12 were selected for full analysis. Sample details and contents are given in full in Table 113.

Preservation was by charring. Preservation quality was generally poor. Monckton notes that high levels of root activity and uncharred weeds seeds could indicate stratigraphic movement and the possibility of intrusive material (OWA 2003, 276). Charred remains in these samples consisted of wood and cereal grains, seed and occasional cereal stem fragments and one bud.

Results

Iron Age features

Plant remains were scarce and generally poorly preserved. Grains of wheat (*Triticum* sp.) and barley (*Hordeum* sp.) were present in four samples and a fragment of chaff resembling a spelt wheat (*T. spelta*) glume was present in penannular ditch 300259 (context 300287). This sample produced the largest charred assemblage including two barley grains; one hulled and twisted (*H. sativum*) and one less well preserved (*Hordeum* sp.).

The grains varied in levels of preservation and characteristics. A certain spelt grain was observed in the sample from context 300287. Two particularly ridged grains were observed in samples from enclosure ditch 300026 and annular ditch 300131. These resembled the early cultivar einkorn but the preservation was too poor to be sure so a general identification of einkorn/emmer (*T. monococcum*/*dicoccum*) was given.

Medieval stone spread

Very little was recovered from this sample. Fragments of charred sloe/blackthorn (*Prunus spinosa*) and hawthorn (*cf. Crataegus monogyna*) were found.

Interpretation

Iron Age

These plant remains were too scarce and poorly preserved to provide any information about feature function. The finds of emmer, spelt and barley are common for this period. (Green 1981, 133) and for the region (OWA 2003, 13).

Medieval

The finds of fragment of sloe stone and an immature hawthorn berry could be traces of brushwood used as kindling.

Charcoal, by Rowena Gale

Significant quantities of charcoal were recorded in nine out of the 48 bulk samples but these were mostly poorly preserved. Eight samples of charcoal from well defined dumps of waste material were selected for analysis. Species identification was undertaken to indicate the character of local woodland and the use of woodland resources for domestic and ?ritual activities. The taxa identified are shown in Table 114.

Iron Age

Enclosure ditch 300024 and penannular gully 300234

A dump of fire-cracked pebbles mixed with charcoal was recovered from the upper fill 300026 of the southern ditch section 300025. The charcoal was very degraded and difficult to examine but produced a radiocarbon date of Middle-Late Iron Age (200–1 cal BC). The taxa identified included oak (*Quercus* sp.) heartwood, ash (*Fraxinus excelsior*) roundwood, blackthorn (*Prunus spinosa*) and alder (*Alnus glutinosa*) or hazel (*Corylus avellana*). The charcoal almost certainly represents fuel debris from heating the pebbles.

Penannular gully 300234 was within the enclosure close to the eastern boundary. Charcoal sample 302016 from context 300236, the fill of the southern terminal of the gully, was degraded and almost mineralised. The taxa named included oak heartwood, birch and hazel. This ditch may represent a drip gully from some type of structure, possibly a dwelling although the function of

Table 114 Charcoal (no. frags)

Feature	Section	Context	Sample	*Alnus*	*Betula*	*Corylus*	*Fraxinus*	*Pomoideae*	*Prunus*	*Quercus*
Iron Age										
Enclosure ditch										
300024	300025	300026	302000	–	–	cf. 2	1r	–	2	4h
Annular ditch										
300131	300318	300319	302033	–	2	–	1	–	–	12h
Penannular ditches										
300234	300235	300236	302016	–	1	2	–	1	1	12h
300259	300165	300287	302027	6	10	–	19	–	–	23h/u, 1s
	300175	300178	302014	32	3	–	1	–	–	5h
Burnt stone spread		300127	302008	–	–	3	–	–	–	4u
Other										
Und. burnt stone spread		300247	302017	–	–	–	1	1	–	2h, 1s
Medieval layer		300121	302011	–	2	–	–	–	–	69h

Key: h = heartwood; r = roundwood (diam. < 20 mm); s = sapwood (diam. unknown); u = unknown maturity (*Quercus* only)

the building is uncertain and could be either domestic or agricultural. The charcoal probably originated from a hearth associated with the building.

Annular ditch 300131 and penannular ditch 300259
Charcoal from context 300319, the basal fill of annular ditch segment 300318, was named as oak, ash and birch. Charcoal was examined from the ditch terminals 300165 and 300175 of penannular ditch 300259. That from the basal fill (300287) of terminal 300165 included oak and ash heartwood, alder, birch, blackthorn and the hawthorn/*Sorbus* group (Pomoideae); this sample also included of charred cereal grain. Context 300178, the primary fill of ditch terminal 300175, contained fire-cracked pebbles and a large amount of charcoal, of which a 50% sub-sample was examined. This consisted mainly of alder but also included oak, birch and ash. These deposits probably represent hearth debris.

Burnt stone spread 300127
Context 300127, an extensive spread of burnt stone on top of an alluvial deposit, contained only scant remains of charcoal - named as oak and hazel.

Burnt stone spread 300247
The date of the burnt stone spread 300247 was undetermined. It was located on the southern edge of the stream in the south-east corner of the site. Charcoal was relatively sparse but identified the use of oak, ash and the hawthorn/*Sorbus* group.

Medieval
Layer 300121
A layer of a dark grey sandy silt with rounded stones and occasional lumps of charcoal (300121) was recorded above the infilled ditch of the Iron Age enclosure at its south-east corner. The large amount of rather fragmented charcoal (sample 302011) consisted almost entirely of slow-grown oak heartwood, although a small amount of birch was also recorded. The charcoal is of unknown origin but produced a radiocarbon date of cal AD 1120–1250.

Discussion
Iron Age
Five samples of charcoal were examined from contexts which contained deposited material, as opposed to wind blown accumulations, and thus provide a more accurate picture of species selection related to function. Soil conditions, however, were not favourable for the long-term preservation of organic material and much of the charcoal was degraded. With the exception of deposits in the penannular ditch 300259, charred grain was rare.

Deposits from ditch segment 300025 (in the northern enclosure 300024) and penannular gully 300234 may have originated from a common source, for example, a domestic hearth associated with the building. Firewood was obtained from mixed species, including oak, hazel, ash and blackthorn. The charcoal was too comminuted to assess the use of coppiced wood.

South of the brook, a small quantity of well-preserved charcoal in sample 302033 from annular ditch 300131 was identified as oak, ash and birch. The terminals of the penannular ditch 300259, however, were more productive and contained charcoal from a wide range of species: alder, birch, ash, the hawthorn group, blackthorn and oak. While charred grain appeared to be absent from the northern terminal, some was recorded from context 300287 in the southern terminal, suggesting that food preparation was undertaken in this area. Associated charcoal probably originated from domestic hearth debris.

Charcoal from the burnt spreads 300127 and the burnt stone spread 300247 present direct evidence of the type of fuel used to heat the stones but, unfortunately, samples 302008 (context 300127) and

302017 (context 300247) were degraded and only a small amount of charcoal could be identified; this indicated the use of mixed species including oak, hazel, ash and the hawthorn group. Similar species were identified from fuel deposits from the burnt mound just upstream at Langley Brook (Site 39).

The overall picture suggests that oak usually formed the basic fuel, supplemented with the random use of other species. The additional and frequent use of alder wood associated with penannular ditch 300259 (not recorded from other contexts examined) may relate to the spatial distribution of alder and other species on the southern side of the brook.

Medieval

The charcoal-rich medieval sample 302011, from above the Iron Age enclosure ditch, was predominantly made up of oak heartwood, mostly obtained from slow-grown trees, supplemented with birch.

Environmental evidence

The charcoal assemblage illustrates an Iron Age landscape supporting a diverse range of woodland species: oak, ash, birch, hazel, the hawthorn/*Sorbus* group, blackthorn and alder. Oak probably formed the dominant woodland component although it is not known how widespread this was. Wetland species such as alder and willow (*Salix* sp.) (the latter not named in the charcoal examined) would almost certainly have grown on the damp soils alongside the course of Langley Brook (perhaps more densely on the southern side) and, where stream banks were better drained, ash may also have flourished.

Since the only sample available from medieval contexts was strongly biased in favour of oak, it is more difficult to comment on the character of the environment at this time. The slow growth of oak recorded in charcoal from layer 300121 could be indicative of trees growing in stressed habitats caused either by competitive woodland conditions or climatic/edaphic factors.

Owing to the fragmentation and poor condition of the charcoal, it was not possible to assess the use of managed woodland.

Discussion

The dearth of finds from the excavations at Langley Mill means that, had it not been for the radiocarbon dates, this site would have been very poorly dated. However, the dating to the Middle and Middle/Late Iron Age of the enclosure ditch, the annular and penannular ditches and the burnt stone spread on the north side of Langley Brook, makes it clear that the site represents a small Iron Age settlement. This settlement, spanning the brook, was therefore approximately contemporary with, and thus probably associated with, the larger settlement at North of Langley Brook (Site 29) *c* 400 m to the north-west. The contrasting hill-slope and stream-side locations may indicate functional differences between the two sites. It seems likely, however, despite the lack of material evidence, that parts of this site represent settlement activity, but the arrangement of the annular and pennanular ditches and the intervening semi-circular gully on the south side of Langley Brook appears less typically domestic than the enclosure north of the Brook. To the north of Langley Brook, ditches 300006 (with associated gully 300014) and 300357 were effectively on the same alignment as the south side of enclosure 300024 and while the ditches were not dated the overall layout is suggestive of broad contemporaneity and perhaps of a need to access the stream bank while remaining slightly separated from it. There appears to have no such attempt at demarcation south of Langley Brook.

Extensive spreads of heat-cracked stone were encountered on both sides of the brook. The initial identification of some of this material (300247) suggested that it represented a burnt mound, with the implication that a Middle Bronze Age date might be likely. Where dating was possible, it suggests that the deposits are of the Iron Age and broadly contemporary with the other features. The clean appearance of the heat cracked stones and the relatively low densities of associated charcoal, contrasting with the characteristic appearance of the material in the known burnt mound at Site 39, barely 100 m upstream, strongly suggest that the majority of the stones at Site 30 are probably redeposited burnt mound material, washed as a result of being waterborne, although some of them could represent activity of uncertain nature contemporary with the Iron Age settlement.

The association between Sites 29 and 30 suggested above may have taken a tangible form, perhaps in the Romano-British period. This is suggested by the alignment of ditch 300346, running uphill from the Iron Age enclosure, which it post-dated but the position of which seems to have been clearly understood when the ditch was dug. The projected line of this ditch runs almost exactly to the eastern corner of Iron Age Enclosure 1 in Site 29, where a short length of Romano-British ditch, albeit on a slightly different alignment, was indeed located. A long-term association between the two locations seems to be indicated.

The radiocarbon date obtained from charcoal over the enclosure ditch points to some form of activity in the medieval period, and it is possible that some of the undated features on the site belong to this period, although the main phase of historic activity appears to be represented by the array of post-medieval/modern ditches and land drains.

Chapter 23
Langley Brook (Site 39)

By Rebecca Devaney

Introduction

An archaeological excavation was undertaken on a site on the south side of Langley Brook, east of Sutton Coldfield, where probable *in situ* burnt mound material was revealed during the general watching brief phase (Fig. 157). Langley Brook flows approximately west to east and forms the boundary between the local authority areas of Birmingham (to the north) and Warwickshire (to the south). The site, centred on NGR 415620 296620, was located to the west of the A38, to the immediate east of which lay an Iron Age settlement site (Langley Mill, Site 30); to the north was a substantial Iron Age and Romano-British settlement (North of Langley Mill, Site 29) (Fig. 137). The geology is mapped as Triassic Mudstone, with Alluvium along the Langley Brook (Geological Survey of Great Britain 1996, Sheet 168, Birmingham).

Results

The site comprised a series of alluvial deposits, a spread of burnt mound material and a short, but relatively well defined linear feature, all sealed by a *c* 0.4 m thick topsoil. Five phases of activity at the burnt mound were identified, the first four of them bracketed by the four radiocarbon dates obtained from the site (Fig. 158, Table 115). Modern land drains were also identified and partly excavated, and the only find from the site was modern.

Early Bronze Age

Phase 1 – Tree growth and organic deposition

Feature 390018, an irregular shaped hollow measuring 1.38 m long, 0.83 m wide and 0.24 m deep, was cut into the natural sands and gravels beneath the north-east quadrant of the burnt mound (391006). At the base (390025, not shown in section) was the base of a tree and a small spread of roots. The secondary fill (390019) was a mid–dark brown sandy clay with about 8% gravel inclusions. The irregular nature of the cut and the presence of root material suggests that this feature was a tree hollow. Samples of waterlogged wood and charcoal from 390019 produced two radiocarbon dates falling within the Early Bronze Age. The waterlogged wood produced a date of 1880–1670 cal BC (NZA-25162, 3441±30 BP), contemporary with the charcoal of the burnt mound in the opposing (south-west) quadrant of the burnt mound (see phase 4, below). The charcoal from 390019 produced a date of 1680–1520 cal BC (NZA-25161, 3340±30), which the probability distribution indicates is significantly (probably about 100 years) later, but contemporary with that obtained from charcoal in the same (north-east) quadrant of the burnt mound (Fig. 158, Table 115).

Overlying the natural sand and gravels beneath the south-west quadrant of the burnt mound was a 0.15 m thick layer of dark brown peaty clay (390037), and the large amount of root material and frequent wood fragments present in the deposit suggests that it was associated with the tree hollow.

Phase 2 – Alluvial deposits 390021, 390022 and 390031

Filling a slight hollow beneath the north-east quadrant of the burnt mount and overlying the tree hollow, was an alluvial deposit of light greyish-yellow sandy clay (390021), with occasional charcoal and burnt stone inclusions in its upper horizon probably deriving from the burnt mound above. The deposit was *c* 4.6 m long, 0.9 m wide and 0.1 m thick. A deposit of mid–dark grey silty clay (390022), with frequent gravel inclusions, filled another slight hollow *c* 1 m to the north-east, measuring 1.7 m wide and roughly 0.07 m thick.

A layer of light yellowish-brown clay (390031) with occasional charcoal flecks and burnt stones within its upper horizon, was located beneath the south-west quadrant of the burnt mound. It was 0.06 m thick and extended across the base of the quadrant, and was probably the same as 390021.

Phase 3 – Hollow 390029

An irregular shaped hollow (390029), possibly a tree hollow, 1 m long, 0.8 m wide and 0.3 m deep, was cut into alluvial layer 390031 (and 390037) beneath the south-west quadrant of the overlying burnt mound. It was filled with a waterlogged, charcoal rich, black silty clay (390026) with abundant burnt stones.

Phase 4 – Burnt mound

The burnt mound lay in a very slight pear-shaped hollow, measuring approximately 15 m SW–NE by 7 m NW–SE. Deposits 390020 at the north-east and 390033 at the south-west comprised the burnt mound material identified in the excavated quadrants. They consisted of a black sandy clay that contained about 70% burnt stones and up to 8% charcoal flecks. Charcoal from these deposits produced radiocarbon dates, respectively, of 1680–1510 cal BC (NZA-25067, 3319±35 BP) and 1870–1620 cal BC (NZA-25068, 3426±30 BP), falling

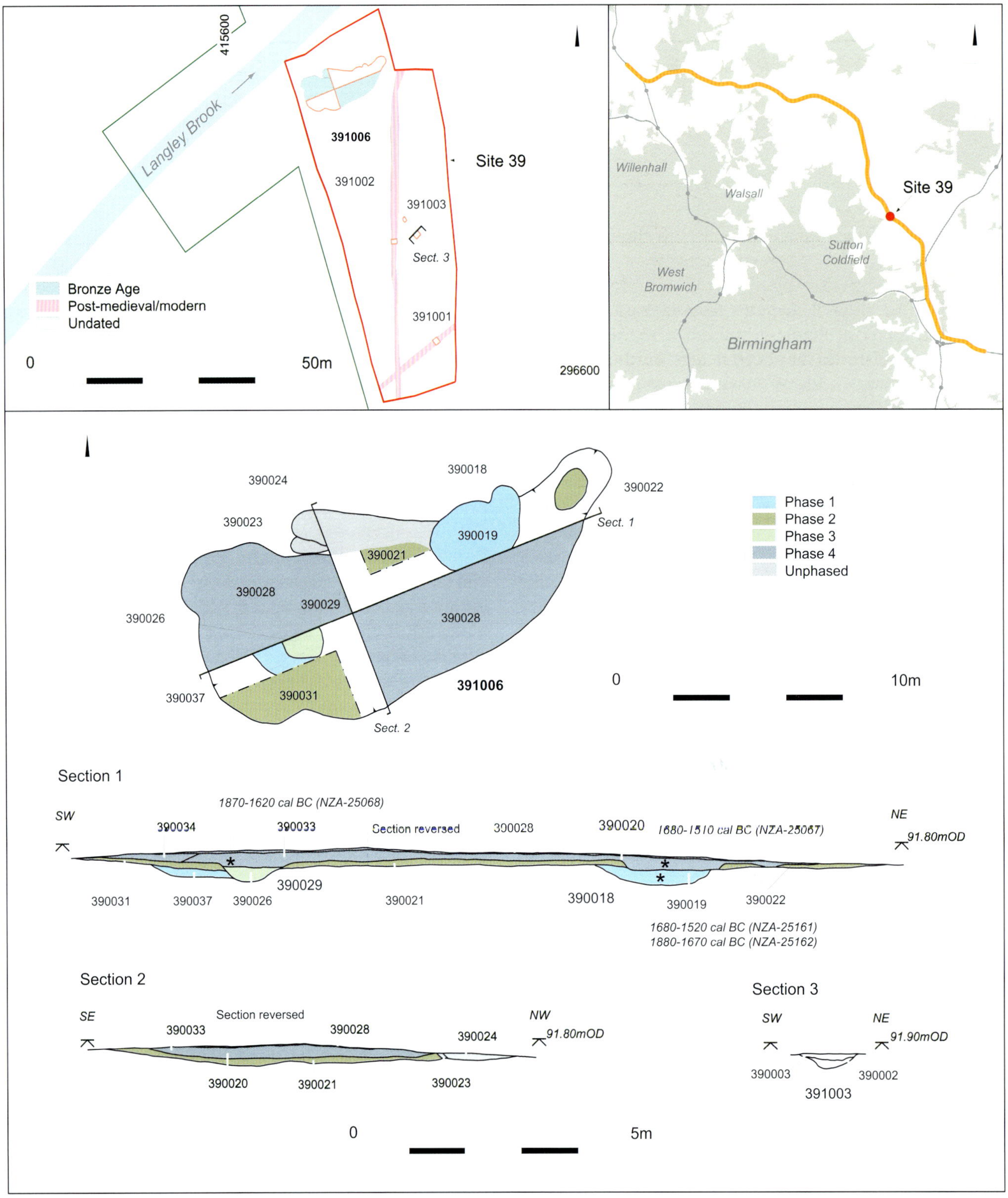

Fig. 157 Langley Brook (Site 39), plan and section of the burnt mound

within the Early rather than the Middle Bronze Age (Fig. 158, Table 115). Overlying the burnt mound was a thin layer (up to 0.04 m) of similar material (390028), although more disturbed, possibly by ploughing (or machining during the excavation).

Deposit 390034 was located over the western edge of the burnt mound. The material consisted of a mid–dark greyish-blue clay with common burnt stones and charcoal flecks. The deposit measured 0.1 m thick and extended beyond the area covered by the rest of the burnt mound. This material contained fewer burnt stones and charcoal than the main burnt mound material and may therefore represent a trample zone caused by the action of delivering stones to and removing them from the mound.

In general, the burnt stones were quite small, most measuring 0.02–0.04 m. This is characteristic of burnt mounds, as experiments suggest that they were hearths

Table 115 Radiocarbon dates

Feature	Context	Material	Lab. no.	Result BP	Date cal BC at 2σ
NE quadrant of burnt mound	390020	Pomoideae	NZA-25067	3319±35	1680–1510
SW quadrant of burnt mound	390033	Hazel	NZA-25068	3426±30	1870–1620
Tree-throw hole/hollow 390018	390019	Alder charcoal	NZA-25161	3340±30	1680–1520
		Alder wood	NZA-25162	3441±30	1880–1670

at which stones were heated for use off the feature, and so consist of those fragments that were left behind because they were too small to pick up (Hodder 1998; 2004, 39–40). Nonetheless, the alluvial deposits beneath the burnt material were not burnt or scorched as would be expected if stones had been heated on the site. There were no apparent separate dumping or burning events and no alluvial silting deposits between the three layers of material. This suggests that the burnt mound was in use for only a short period of time.

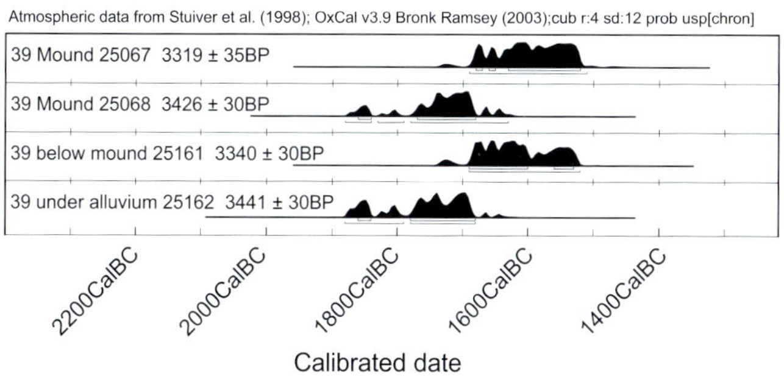

Fig. 158 Oxcal probability distributions of radiocarbon dates

Phase 5 – Post-burnt mound deposits

A series of deposits (390036, 390023, 390024 and 390013) post-dated the burnt mound. Spread 390036, a natural alluvial deposit that overlay layer 390034 at the western edge of the burnt mound, was a mid-bluish-grey silty clay with occasional small pebbles (not shown in section). It was 0.08 m thick and extended further west than the area covered by the burnt mound. Spread 390023, which overlay the northern edge of the burnt mound, was a mid brown sandy clay with few gravel inclusions. It was *c* 0.1 m thick and extended *c* 0.75 m north of the burnt mound, and may relate to some form of disturbance, possibly ploughing. Overlying this was a 0.12 m thick layer of mid orange silty clay (390024) that extended a further 1 m north. Overlying all the features in this area of the site was a 0.02 m thick light yellowish-brown sandy silt with occasional small rounded stones (390013).

Undated and modern

An short linear feature (391003), aligned NW–SE, was located in the centre of the site. It was 5 m long and up to 1 m wide, and 0.3–0.4 m deep (Fig. 157). The primary fill (390002), a light yellowish/bluish-grey clay with abundant small to large sub-rounded and sub-angular pebbles and cobbles, was overlain by a mid- to dark bluish-grey clay with occasional darker patches (390003). The function of the feature and its relationship to the other features on the site are unknown.

The site was crossed by two modern land drains (391001 and 391002).

Environment

Charred plant remains, by Lisa Gray

Seven samples of 20 litres and one of 5 litres were taken from features associated with the burnt mound. Five samples were selected for analysis of charred plant remains; two came from phase 1 features predating the mound, while the remainder came from phase 4 deposits associated with the burnt mound itself. Sample details and contents are given in full in Table 116.

Preservation quality and type

The preservation quality of the charred remains was generally poor with many remains in fragments and too poorly preserved for the survival of diagnostic features. The site was close to a stream and exposed to long-term wet conditions (OWA 2003, 297). The charred remains were rare and consisted of fragments of nutshell, fragments of wood and indeterminate plant tissue.

The charred remains

Single fragments of hazelnut (*Corylus avellana*) were recovered from contexts 390020 and 390026 (samples 392002 and 392004). A fragment of non-woody plant tissue was observed in context 390020, although it was too poorly preserved to allow identification. Sample 392001 (context 390019) from a phase 5 deposit post-dating the mound was not fully analysed but a grain of barley (*Hordeum* sp.), immature or wild, was observed during the assessment along with a partially charred terminal culm/basal rachis fragment (OWA 2003, 298). These are the only cereal remains observed in the samples from this site.

Charcoal, by Rowena Gale

Compared to the charred plant remains, charcoal was reasonably abundant in the seven bulk samples. Three samples from the burnt mound were selected for

Table 116 Charred plant remains from the burnt mound

Taxon	Common name	Phase 3	Phase 4	Phase 4
	Context	390026	390020	390034
	Sample	392004	392002	392006
	Sample size (l)	20	20	20
	Flot size (ml)	1000	625	1000
cf. *Mercurialis perennis* seed	Dog's mercury	–	–	1
Corylus avellana nutshell frag.	Hazel	1	1	–
Indet. plant tissue		–	1	–

analysis to indicate the selection of fuel and to provide material for radiocarbon dating. The samples of waterlogged wood represented debris that had accumulated naturally in these deposits, thus providing background evidence of the local environment. Three samples of waterlogged wood were selected for analysis, with particular reference to the charcoal deposits.

Although fairly large amounts of charcoal were recovered, its condition varied from very poor and comminuted (sample 392005) to reasonably well preserved (sample 392002). The wood, however, although waterlogged on excavation, had subsequently dried out and as a result the cellular structure had undergone total collapse. Although it was evident that these samples included both narrow roundwood and fragments from more mature wood and bark, it was impossible to identify this material to species owing to the absence of diagnostic features. The taxa identified are shown in Table 117.

The burnt mound

Charcoal was examined from pre-mound hollow fill 390026 (sample 392004), and burnt mound contexts 390020 (sample 392002) and 390033 (sample 392005). Charcoal was frequent in all three samples; samples 392002 and 392005 were 50% and 25% sub-sampled, respectively. The three samples were more or less similar in species content and indicated the use of fuel obtained mainly from alder (*Alnus glutinosa*), birch (*Betula* sp.), hazel and ash (*Fraxinus excelsior*), with less emphasis on the hawthorn/*Sorbus* group (Pomoideae), blackthorn (*Prunus spinosa*), oak (*Quercus* sp.) and elm (*Ulmus* sp.).

Discussion

Evidence from the charcoal suggests that firewood used to heat the stones was gathered from a range of trees and shrubs but predominantly from those growing in the area around the stream edge and thus close the hearth (and mound). Alder was probably present on the damp/wet soils in the immediate vicinity of the mound, possibly as alder carr. Birch and hazel also tolerate damp (but not waterlogged soils). Ash was also quite frequent and may have colonised the steam banks where soils were better-drained. Elm typically grows on rich alluvial soils and, although present, did not appear to have been much used – perhaps due either to the difficulty of cutting the wood or to its poor performance as firewood. It may not have been common in the area. The comparatively infrequent use of oak, blackthorn and member(s) of the hawthorn group could suggest that these species were not so readily available.

Owing to the desiccation of the waterlogged wood samples, it was not possible to use this material as a means of assessing the range of arboreal species that grew close enough to the stream for fallen debris to become entrapped in the surrounding boggy soils, although hand picked material was available (see Chisham below)

Waterlogged plant remains, by Chris J. Stevens

Three samples were examined from well-sealed, deposits associated with tree hollows preserved under the Early Bronze Age burnt mound (Table 118). As the samples came from underneath the mound and were close to Langley Brook, they provided some possibility for preservation of plant material through waterlogging. Waterlogged material has been recovered previously from tree hollows excavated within the Nene and Thames Valleys (Lambrick and Moore 1987; Moore and Jackson 1990; Robinson 1992), where it has helped provide evidence for the nature of the environment after Neolithic clearance (Robinson 1992; Brown 1997). However, the samples contained very little waterlogged material, and generally little that could shed light on the environment following the loss/removal of the trees and prior to the formation of the mound itself.

The species present are those commonly associated with scrub and patches of wet rough grassland, eg

Table 117 Charcoal and desiccated wood from the burnt mound (no. frags)

Phase	Feature	Context	Sample	Alnus	Betula	Corylus	Fraxinus	Pomoideae	Prunus	Quercus	Ulmus
1	390018	390025	392003	Dessicated wood too collapsed to identify							
		390037	392007	Desiccated wood too collapsed to identify							
3	390029	390026	392004	11	16	4	8	–	1	–	–
4	391006	390020	392002	24	16	1	8r	1	–	3s	1r
		390033	392005	–	6	10	21	1	1	4u	–
		390034	392006	Dessiccated wood too collapsed to identify							

Key: r = roundwood (diam. <20 mm); s = sapwood (diam. unknown); u = maturity undetermined (*Quercus* only)

Table 118 Waterlogged plant remains

	Phase	1	1	3
	Feature	Tree-hollow 390018	?Tree-hollow	Tree-hollow 390029
	Context	390019	390037	390026
	Sample	392001	392007	392004
	Flot size (ml)	250	500	250
	Residue size (ml)	100	35	60
Taxon	*Common name*			
Bryophyte	Moss	–	+	–
Ranunculus acris/repens/bulbosus	Buttercup	1	1	–
Rosaceae	Thorn	–	1	–
Urtica dioica	Common nettle	5–10	–	–
Rubus sp.	Bramble	5–10	1	–
Viola sp.	Volet	5–10	–	1
Carex sp.	Sedge	–	–	1
Waterlogged wood frag.		5–10	–	–
Bud indet.		–	1–5	–

+ present

bramble (*Rubus* sp.), common nettle (*Urtica dioica*), sedge (*Carex* sp.) and buttercup (*Ranunculus acris/repens/bulbosus*). The remains of violet were of larger seeded species and so more probably of hairy or sweet violet (*Viola hirta* or *V. odorata*; *cf.* Turner 1968; Kelly 1964). The former is more associated with pastures and open woodland and scrub, the latter with woodland and scrub, but both are found on generally dry to moist, base rich soils. The evidence from the wood analysis (below) suggests the existence of some stands of woodland at the channel edge comprising elm, birch, and hazel, as well as possible alder. The species recorded from the samples might be seen as colonisers of woodland clearance or open woodland growing at the channel edge, but given the presence of nettle and sweet and/or hairy violet, such activity is likely to have been associated with a more stable drier riverside edge rather than one which was subject to flooding.

Waterlogged wood, by Catherine Chisham

The large timber recovered from the tree hollow below the Bronze Age burnt mound (context 390025) is of mature *Ulmus* sp. (elm) (Table 119). The waterlogged wood fragments from context 390037 were of mature roundwood and twigwood of *Corylus avellana* (hazel) and a single twigwood fragment *cf. Betula pendula/pubescens* while those from hollow 390029 (context 390026) were all roundwood (likely branch) of *Betula pendula pubescens* (silver or downy birch) It is notable that despite these wood fragments having been found beneath a burnt mound none were charred.

Discussion

The excavation showed a sequence of tree growth and alluvial activity prior to the formation of a burnt mound in the Early Bronze Age. Further extensive spreads of burnt stone were recorded on both sides of Langley Brook *c* 150–250 m to the north-east at Langley Mill (Site 30). Although charcoal from one of these spreads produced a radiocarbon date in the Middle Iron Age (contemporary with the settlement on that site), it is possible that some of this material could have derived from, and in origin been contemporary with, the Early Bronze Age burnt mound recorded on this site.

Table 119 Waterlogged wood identifications from the burnt mound

Feature	*Context*	*Sample*	*Ident.*	*No. frags. ident.*	*Comments on sample*
390018	390025	392003	Mature *Ulmus* sp.	3	3 v. large frags. (largest 280 x 180 x 180 mm), prob. from 1 timber
390029	390026	392004	*Betula pendula/pubescens* roundwood	12	Frags all >30 mm, some partially rounded (by degradation), several distorted/twisted
	390037	392007	Mature *Corylus avellana*	6	In total >20 frags > 30 mm including roundwood with bark
			Corylus avellana young roundwood	3	
			cf. *Betula pendula/pubescens* twigwood	1	
			cf. *Corylus/Alnus* twigwood	1	

SITES AT WISHAW

Two adjacent sites (Wishaw Hall Farm, Site 19, and Wishaw, Site 20) were investigated to the north-west and south-east, respectively, of Grove Lane, Wishaw (Fig. 159). They were largely bisected by a stream flowing eastwards into the River Tame Valley. The general archaeological background relating to these two sites is described here.

A small ploughsoil assemblage of Mesolithic flintwork comprising a flint core, scraper and blades was known from the area south-east of Grove Lane (Hodder 1992) and, more widely, from near Wishaw Church, Over Green, Grounds Farm and Lower Green, providing significant evidence of Mesolithic occupation in the area. Prehistoric occupation was also suspected from Wishaw Hall Farm after a scatter of fire cracked quartzite pebbles similar to a 'burnt mound' (Hodder and Welch 1990) was found adjacent to the stream. Other sites of this type have been found elsewhere in the area.

Romano-British occupation debris (WCC SMR 6393) was recorded during a metal detector survey by the South Staffordshire Archaeological and Historical Society immediately north-east of Wishaw Hall Farm indicating the location of a farm or settlement associated with metal working (OAU 1994d, 3). A ploughed-out Roman coin hoard is also attested (Seaby 1992). Romano-British pottery has been reported from around Site 20 (Hodder 1988), and from land north of Well Cottage. Medieval pottery has been found adjacent to Grove Lane and also north of Well Cottage (OAU 1994d). An area of post-medieval settlement remains was noted north-east of the site (OAU 1994b).

An archaeological evaluation undertaken in 1993, as part of the assessment of archaeological impact of the M6 Toll (OAU 1994b), concentrated on land south of Grove Lane, but trenches also investigated land immediately south and east of Wishaw Hall Farm. No evaluation was undertaken within the area of Site 19.

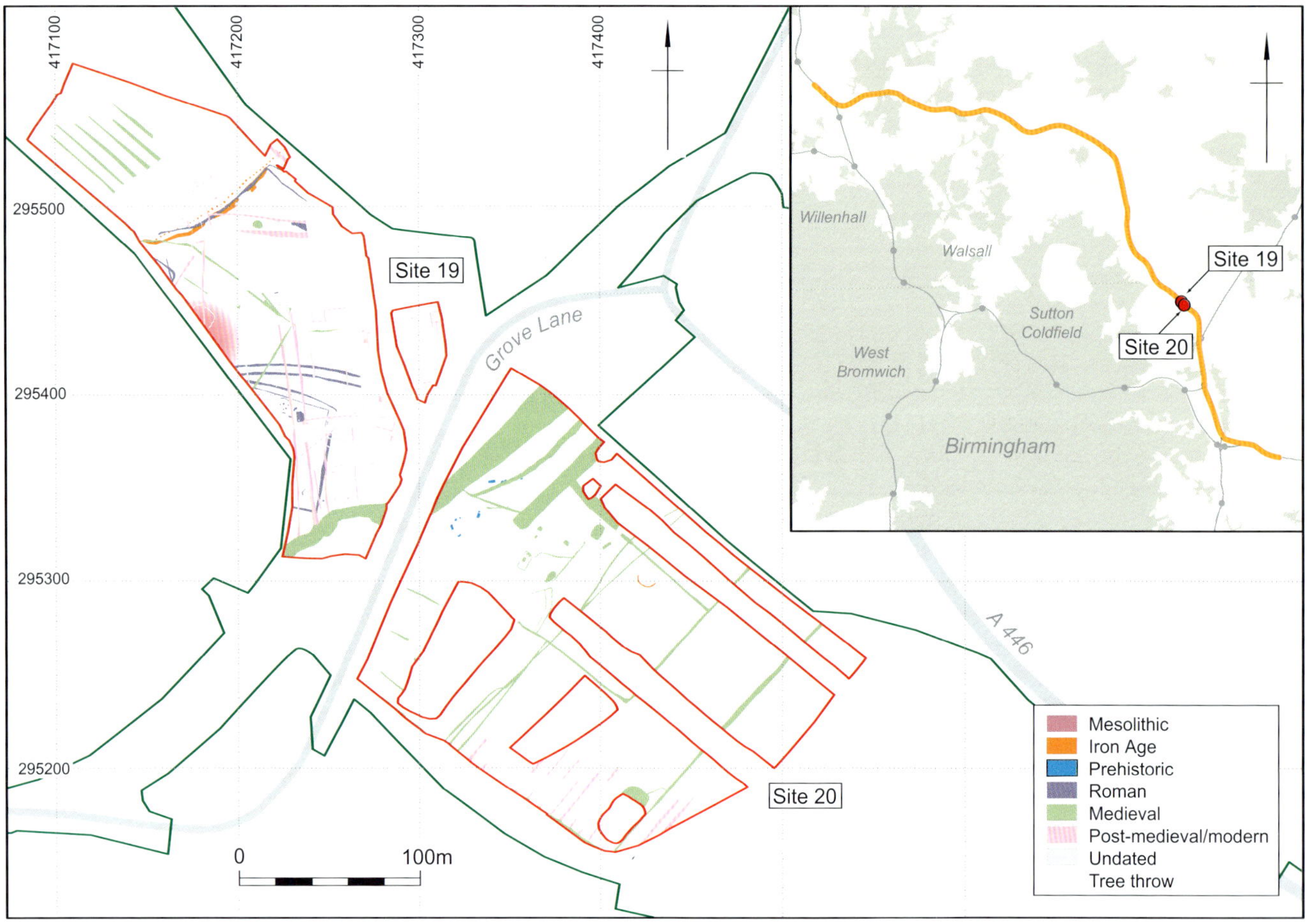

Fig. 159 Sites at Wishaw

Chapter 24
Wishaw Hall Farm (Site 19)

By *Mike Trevarthen*

Introduction

An excavation was undertaken on land immediately north-west of Grove Lane (B379) near its junction with the A446 at The Belfry, adjacent to the site of the recently demolished Wishaw Hall Farm. The fieldwork began as a targeted watching brief, but in light of the significant archaeological remains discovered, it was upgraded to a full excavation. The excavation revealed Iron Age features, including a pit alignment, and a Romano-British enclosure, as well as a number of medieval and post-medieval features (Fig. 160).

The site, centred at NGR 417190 295430 occupied the gentle, south-facing slope of a low hill, between *c* 99 m aOD at the northern end and *c* 85 m aOD near Grove Lane.

South-eastern parts of the site were formerly occupied by the buildings and yards of Wishaw Hall Farm, demolished as part of the M6 Toll construction work. Several areas of concrete hardstanding within the former farm were removed under archaeological supervision, but the ground here had been subject to substantial disturbance and some truncation, and no additional archaeological remains were seen.

The underlying geology is mapped as mudstones of the Triassic Mercia Mudstone Group. To the north, the low hill incorporates a bed of 'skerry' (bedded siltstones and sandstones within the Mercia Mudstone Group) and, beyond the site boundary, is capped by Pleistocene glaciofluvial deposits. The southern part of the site overlay head deposits of Pleistocene–Holocene date (British Geological Survey 1996). The weathered upper exposure of natural strata varied across the site, but was typically stiff, sometimes slightly loamy, mottled red-grey clays. These were marked by innumerable poorly defined hollows and tree hollows, often filled with paler grey clay-silt. At the southern end of the site, head deposits gave rise to markedly more stony ground.

A small unnamed stream adjacent to Grove Lane was exploited in medieval times to supply water to a complex of fishponds (Chapter 25, Fig. 179). Part of the backfilled tail of the valley pond was located at the southern end of the excavation but not excavated. In this area groundwater was encountered just below the machined surface. More recently the stream had been culverted via a buried pipe south of Grove Lane. The majority of the site was better drained, although there was a network of artificial land-drains.

Results

Mesolithic

A total of 1583 items of struck flint, as well as 38 pieces of burnt unworked flint, were found, comprising over 90% of the total flint assemblage from the M6 Toll. This material included cores, flakes, blades, microliths and microburins, and other debitage. All diagnostic elements of the group point to a late Mesolithic date, with no Neolithic or Bronze Age component noted.

The flint was recovered mainly from the weathered machine-stripped surface of the site, although lesser amounts were recorded as residual or intrusive finds in excavated features. The greatest concentrations lay near to the site's western edge, and its distribution clearly continues beyond the limits of excavation (Fig. 160). A wider spread of flint was also observed, but decreasing in intensity with distance from the main concentration (see Cramp below).

One area initially suspected to be an *in situ* concentration of flint was subject to controlled excavation, using a grid of 1 m squares, with individual flints being three-dimensionally surveyed. However, this material was shown to be redeposited in a series of tree hollows, and/or had migrated down through the soil profile into secondary settings through long-term biological activity. A small component of the overall assemblage was clearly redeposited after excavation of the site began, either by (sometimes considerable) rainwater surface run-off or, in the case of the smallest fragments, by wind action whilst the site was dry.

Iron Age

During the Iron Age, a sequence of WSW–ENE aligned boundaries was established, indicating large-scale division of the landscape.

Pit alignment

Part of a slightly sinuous ENE–WSW pit alignment was investigated. It was discovered at a late stage in the excavation, after selective remachining had been undertaken to clarify the extent of other features. By this time, a number of deeper machine-cut sampling trenches had already been excavated, and these account for some of the gaps in the alignment. Other perceived gaps result from truncation by later archaeological

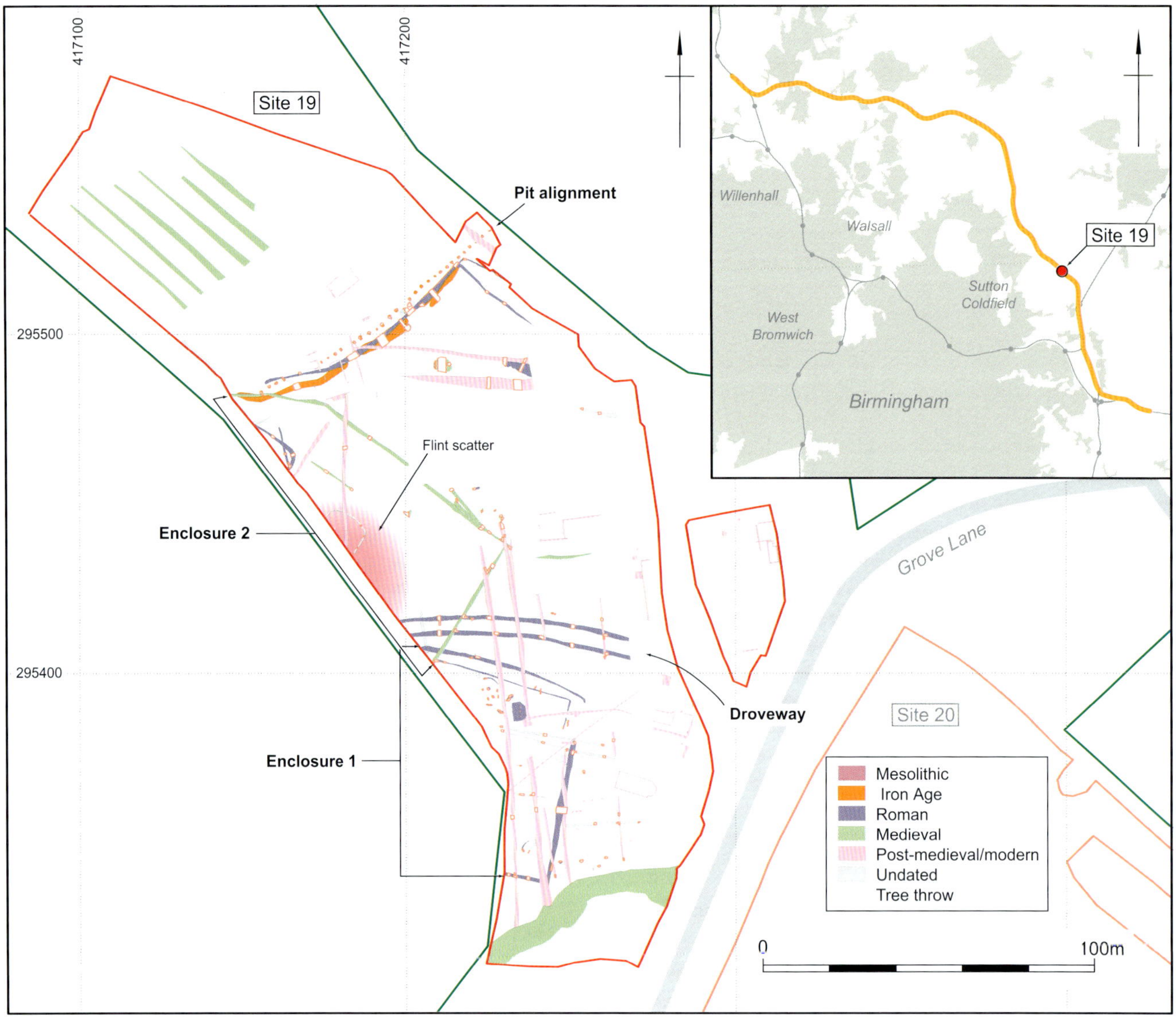

Fig. 160 Wishaw Hall Farm (Site 19)

features and masking by 19th–20th century building remains. Precise location details for a small number of pits were lost after the theft from site of a laptop computer holding survey data (see also Cramp, Chapter 28), although these have been reconstructed, where possible, from plans and photographs.

Some 30 pits were fully or partially exposed during excavation (Fig. 161), although taking into account the factors above, the actual number may have been as high as 40. The alignment was probably originally continuous within the site, and almost certainly continued beyond its eastern and western boundaries. Individual pits varied in shape from near-circular to oval, and square or rectangular, and were up to *c* 0.7 m deep, with concave or tapering profiles and flat or gently concave bases. The pits ranged from 0.65–1.4 m across, although the majority lay in the range of *c* 0.75–1.0 m. The most significant variations in pit dimensions clearly reflected differential truncation during remachining. One pit (191388) was recorded as triangular in plan, but this should be regarded with some caution since the definition of individual features was often poor, and partial truncation of a square pit by an unrecognised modern land-drain remains a possibility.

The linear spacing of pits was consistent, with their centres set, on average, *c* 2.5 m apart. There were no obvious changes of direction within the alignment, or of pit-shape, such as might indicate sectional or 'gang' working during construction. All of the pits displayed simple sequential infill sequences, and there was no evidence for recutting or cleaning out of individual pits, nor indeed of any effort to maintain the boundary after it had been created.

Pit alignments typically produce only small finds groups (Pollard 1996, 111). Artefacts from these pits were similarly scarce, although a single distinct deposit (191238/191239) comprising stones, two sherds of Middle Iron Age pottery and the partial remains of an inverted human skull appeared to have been deliberately placed at the base of pit 191221, probably immediately (or shortly) after the alignment was created (Figs 162–4). Two radiocarbon dates were obtained from the placed deposit. One, from a carbonised residue on a sherd of pottery, fell within the Middle Iron Age:

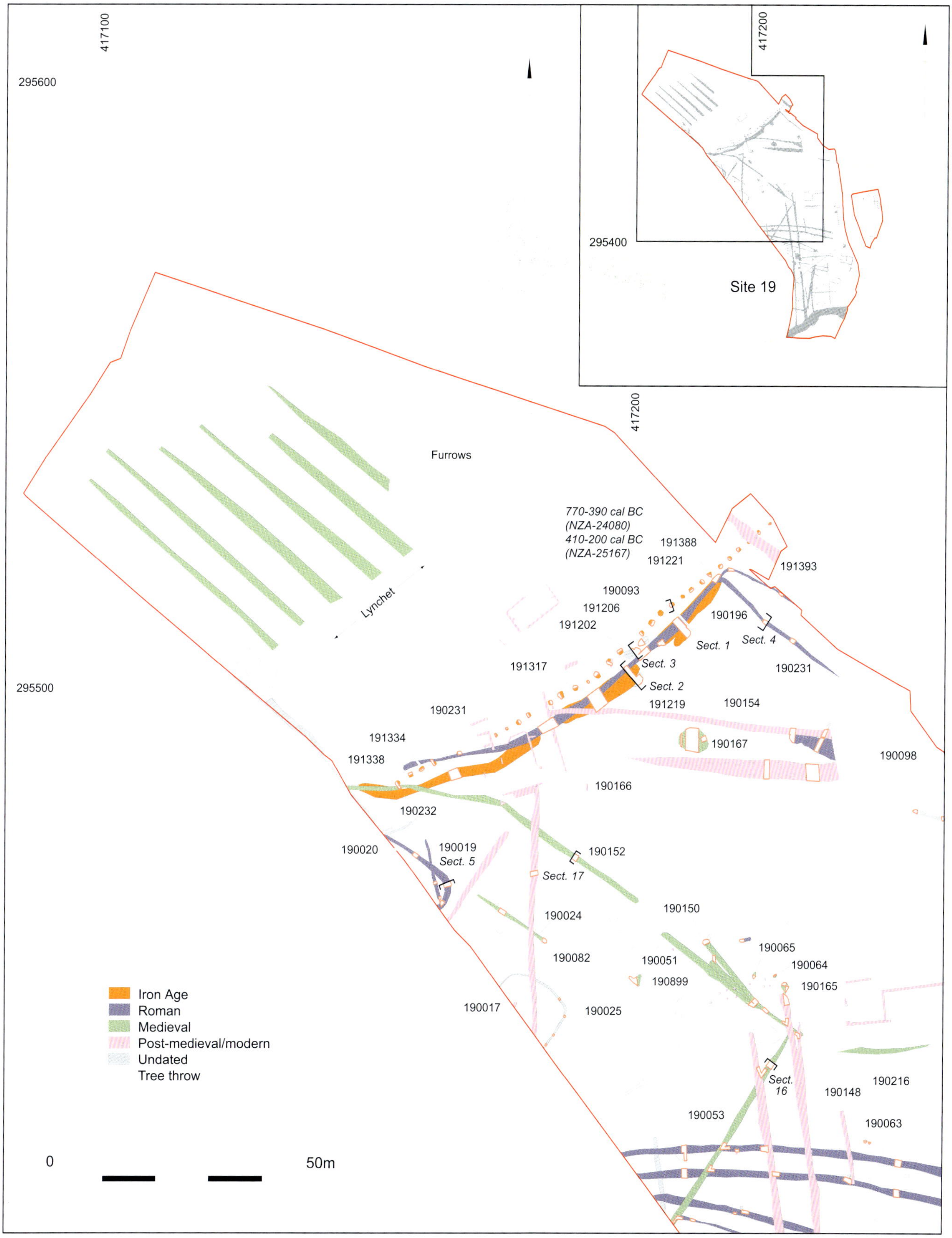

Fig. 161 The north-western part of the site

Fig. 162 Placed deposit in pit 191221

Fig. 163 Excavation of placed deposit in pit 191221

410–200 cal BC (2313±30 BP, NZA-25167). This may reasonably be taken as indicative of the period within which the pit alignment was constructed, and is statistically indistinguishable (at the 95% confidence level) from the date of 380–190 cal BC from a narrow semi-circular ditch to the south at Wishaw (Site 20) (Harding, this volume). The other determination was on a piece of the human skull. This was Early Iron Age in date (770–390 cal BC, 2429±35BP, NZA-24080) indicating that the skull was significantly older than its deposition in a Middle Iron Age context might otherwise suggest (Fig. 165, Table 120).

Segmented ditch

Whilst the pit alignment was not maintained in the long-term, the landscape division it established remained of sufficient importance to be redefined by several large co-aligned ditches, interpreted as elements of a single segmented boundary (Fig. 161). Three individual segments of ditch (190196, 191219, 190232) were located, although the central ditch (191219) had been recut on at least one occasion (Fig. 164). These were of variable dimensions and profile, but probably originally steeply V-shaped, up to 1.5 m deep and eroded up to 3 m wide. The western segment (190232) was the longest of the three (*c* 36 m) and also the most sinuous, turning slightly northward at its western end, as if following the contour of the hillslope. Other segments of ditch may lie to the west, beyond the area of excavation, but no eastern extension of the monument could be defined where the site was extended to expose more of the pit alignment. As with the earlier boundary, only slight dating evidence was recovered, but the pottery which was present suggests a Middle Iron Age date. The upper fills of all three segments were cut by a Romano-British ditch (190231, see below), indicating it was substantially infilled by this time.

The discontinuous form of the segmented ditch and its close spatial co-alignment with the older boundary suggest both monuments served broadly similar roles. The two phases of the central segment remain problematic, however. The original cut (191219) had become infilled to a depth of at least 1.5 m before being recut (190199) and there was no evidence that it had been deliberately backfilled. The paucity of finds denies the possibility for close chronological dating for the two ditch cuts, but a purely intuitive interpretation might see recutting of the central segment as the partial re-instatement of a mature or obsolescent boundary feature. Here it is also tempting to attribute pits 190093, 191202 and 191206 (below) to any such later prehistoric phase of activity.

Pits 190093, 191202 and 191206

Three vertically sided and flat-based sub-oval pits lay immediately north of the eastern causeway in the segmented ditch. Although two of the pits were sequentially cut (Fig. 164), there was no stratigraphic relationship between them and the ditch. The presence within them of deposits of burnt stone, and the paucity of artefacts, again pointed to a non-domestic function, and it may be that they were positioned to constrict or to block the eastern causeway of the segmented ditch.

Romano-British

Field-boundaries

The alignment of the Iron Age segmented boundary was perpetuated by a sinuous Romano-British field boundary ditch (190231). Near the eastern edge of the site, this ditch turned abruptly to the south-east, where it was traced for a distance of *c* 30 m. At its maximum excavated extent the ditch was 1.2 m wide and up to

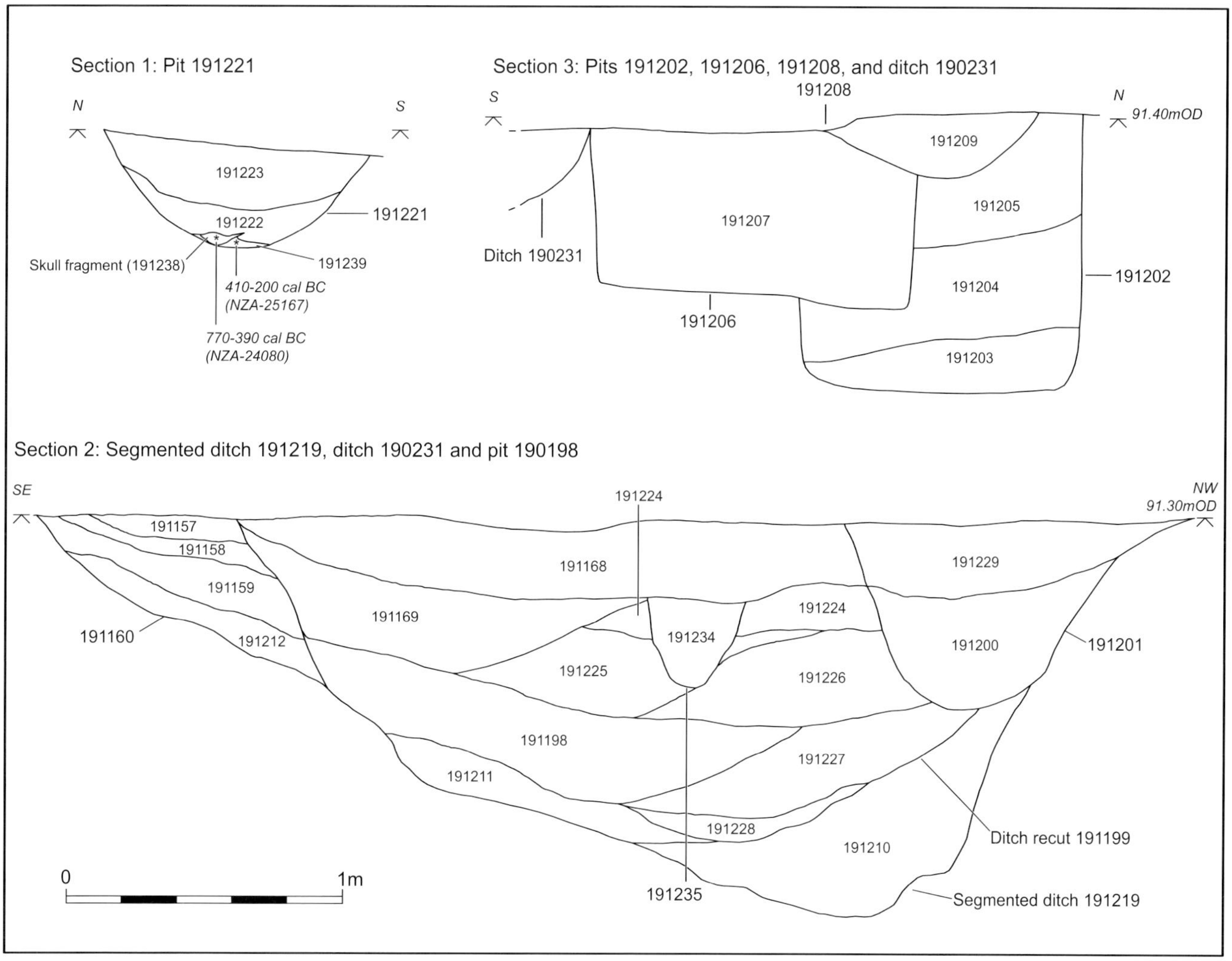

Fig. 164 Sections of Iron Age ditches

Table 120 Radiocarbon dates

Feature	Context	Material	Lab. no.	Result BP	Date cal BC at 2σ
Pit 191221	191239	Human skull	NZA-25080	2429±35	770–390
	191239	Residue on pot	NZA-25167	2313±30	410–200
Hollow 190098	191096	Maple	NZA-25059	1980±30	40 BC–AD 120
Burnt 'trough' 190043	190860	*Prunus* or Salicaceae	NZA-25058	1922±35	AD10–220

0.65 m deep, although it was rather more truncated to the east (Fig. 167). An earlier ditch (191393), also of Romano-British date, followed a similar course to the east and may have enclosed a slightly larger area.

A length of curvilinear ditch (190020) (Fig. 161) situated near the site's western edge may represent another component of this field system, possibly the opposing side of an entrance-way (Fig. 167). Its relationship to north–south ditch 190019, which it intersects with, was not established. Ditch 190019 was 11.2 m long, 0.6 m wide and 0.2 m deep, with a rounded concave profile. Its single undifferentiated fill produced 29 sherds of pottery, comprising bodysherds of a Dressel 20 amphora, an MH2 mortarium, SV1, and an SV5 narrow-necked jar of 2nd–3rd century type. A possible waster and conjoining sherd were noted, although no other evidence for pottery production has been found locally. The finds from this feature seem to represent a deliberate dump of ceramic material (Leary, below).

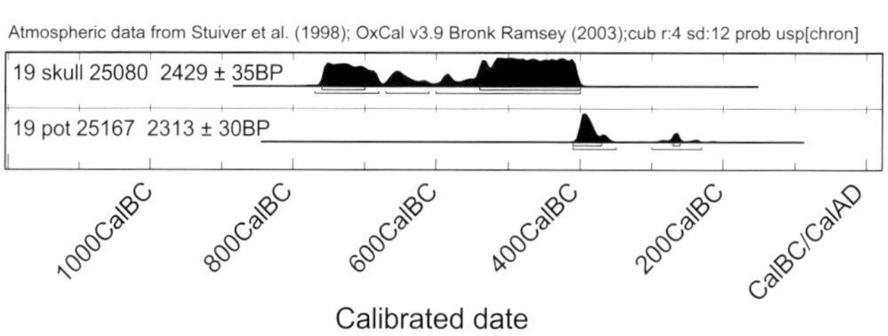

Fig. 165 Oxcal probability distributions of radiocarbon dates from the pit alignment

Enclosure 1 ditches

Some 85 m to the south-east, part of a rectilinear ditched enclosure (Enclosure 1) was identified (Fig.

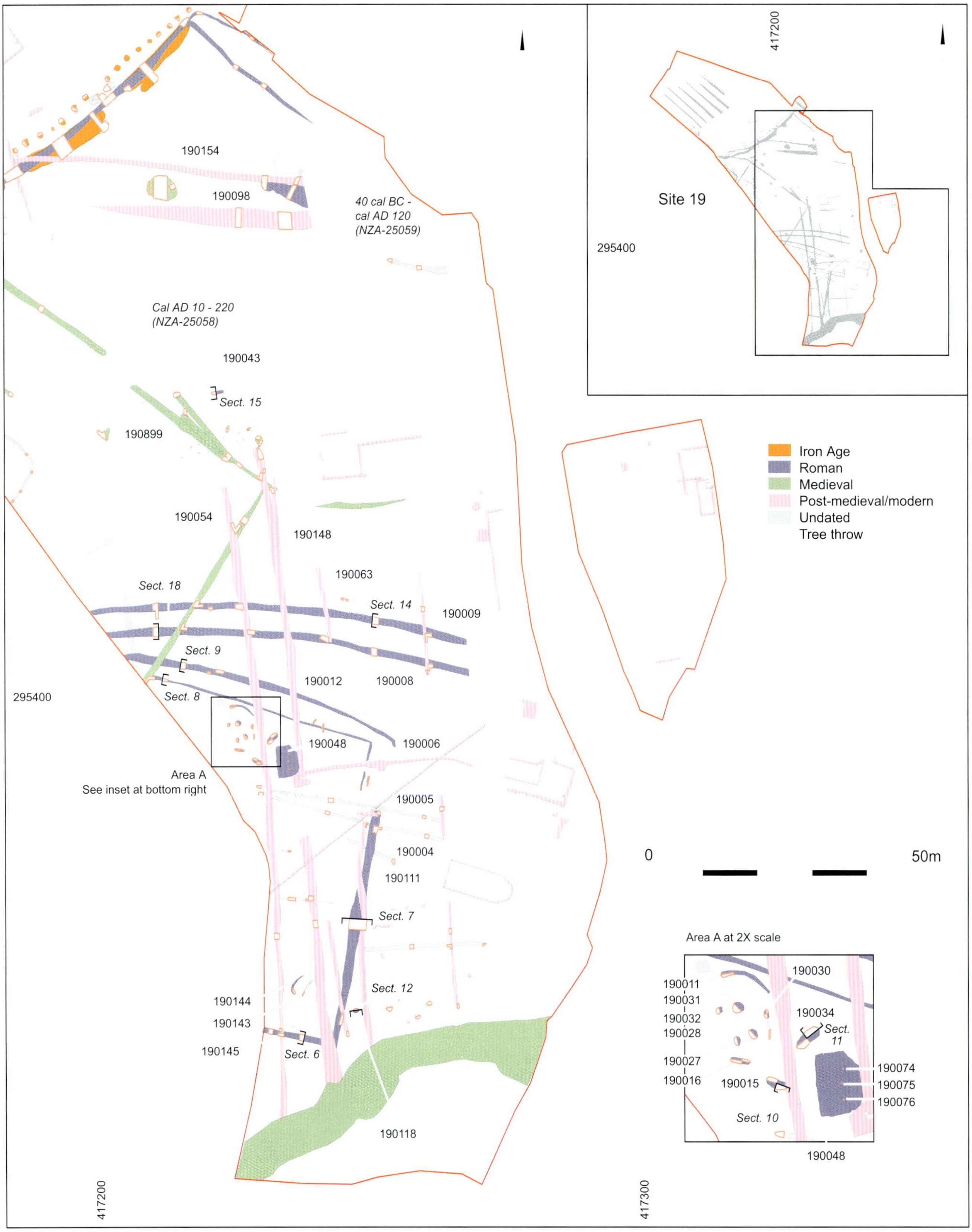

Fig. 166 The central and south-eastern parts of the site

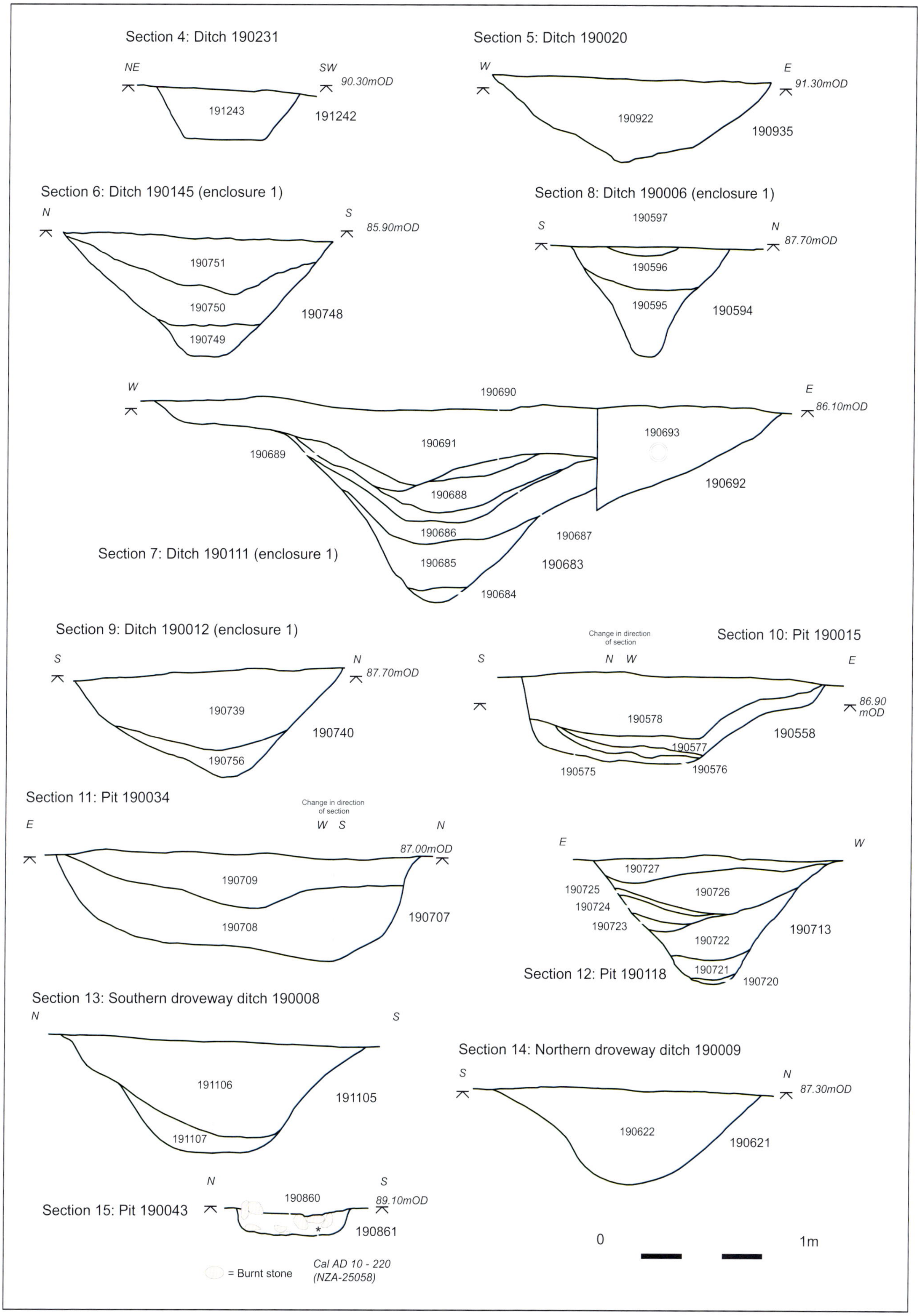

Fig. 167 Sections of Romano-British features

166). Measuring 59 m north–south, its full extent could not be defined, as any western boundary lay outside the excavated area. However, both of the northern boundary ditches appeared to start turning southward at the far-western edge of the site, hinting at a square, or sub-square plan which would have enclosed an area of *c* 0.25 hectares.

The southern and eastern arms of the enclosure were formed by a single broad V-shaped ditch (190111/190145) up to 0.9 m deep, and commonly *c* 1.1–1.8 m wide (Fig. 167). The northern edge of the enclosure was defined by two parallel ditches. The inner, straight ditch (190006) was up to 0.8 m wide and 0.5 m deep, with a V-shaped profile (Fig. 167), whilst the outer, slightly bowed, ditch (190012), was up to 1.3 m wide (narrower to the east) with a U-shaped profile (Fig. 167). It is not known whether these ditches were directly contemporary, or if they indicated a phase of remodelling in this area. An entrance near the enclosure's north-east corner is indicated by a rounded butt-end terminal at the northern end of ditch 190111. This was aligned on the western end of outer northern ditch 190012, although the termini of both northern ditches seemed to have been truncated.

Enclosure 1 (internal features)

A localised cluster of truncated features lay near the northern edge of Enclosure 1 (Fig. 166). Among these was a sub-rectangular hollow (190048), probably representing a former hollow or sunken area of external surface. This had been crudely metalled in places with patches of small, closely packed pebbles (190703), set directly into the exposed natural clay subsoil. The hollow measured *c* 5.5 m by 4.5 m but was only 0.05 m deep. A north–south alignment of three possible circular stakeholes (190074, 190075 and 190076) set 1.3 m apart survived within the hollow, which was sealed beneath a remnant dark soil (190702) containing burnt stone, charcoal and pottery of 3rd–4th century date.

Three sub-oval pits were of unknown function. One of these (190016) was only *c* 0.1 m deep, but pit 190015, 2.3 m to the south-south-east, was better preserved, 0.45 m deep with steep to near-vertical sides and a flat base (Fig. 167). Four fills contained 15 sherds (102 g) of Romano-British pottery, including two of late 3rd–4th century date. Just over 3 m to the north-north-west, pit 190034 was of a similar profile and depth (Fig. 167), with two fills producing 13 sherds of Romano-British pottery (133 g). Four sub-circular pits (190027, 190028, 190030 and 190031) and a posthole (190032) lay just north of the elongated features, but only 190028 was of any significant depth (*c* 0.25 m). Pit 190027 contained four sherds (53 g) from the handle of a late 2nd–3rd century vessel, and pit 190031 produced a single Romano-British sherd (911 g).

Three short lengths of irregularly curvilinear ditch (190011, 190143 and 190144) within Enclosure 1 might indicate eaves-drip gullies associated with circular structures, but far too little survived to be confident of any such interpretation.

Enclosure 1 and its internal features all have ceramic sequences suggesting construction in the mid–late 2nd century, with activity continuing through the 3rd century. That some local occupation persisted into the first half of the 4th century is indicated by the presence of later Romano-British ceramics, usually in upper feature fills, but only one coin (ON 193021) was found, a *dupondius* of Antoninus Pius (AD 138–161). This was unstratified and is of little value for dating; it could have remained in circulation until the mid-3rd century and been redeposited even later. Coinage post-dating the mid-3rd century was notably absent.

Pit 190118

Sub-oval pit 190118 lay immediately outside the south-east corner of the enclosure. It measured 1.2 m by 0.85 m, and was 0.6 m deep, with a narrow rounded base (Fig. 167). Of eight successive fills, only the upper two contained any pottery – 48 sherds dated from the mid-1st–2nd centuries AD.

Droveway 1

North of Enclosure 1, two parallel, east–west aligned and slightly curvilinear ditches (190008 to the south and 190009 to the north) were recorded for *c* 70 m before their eastern ends were lost beneath the remains of the modern farmyard. Ranging from *c* 1.0 m to 1.7 m wide and up to 0.55 m deep (Fig. 166), the ditches lay 3–4 m apart and may have originally have flanked a local trackway or agricultural droveway. Pottery from these features suggested that they originated in the mid-2nd century, with infilling through the later 2nd–3rd centuries, and some material dumped as late as the 4th century.

'Trough' 190043 and feature 190098

A vertically-sided and flat-based elongate sub-rectangular 'trough'-like pit (190043) measuring *c* 2.2 m by 0.65 m and 0.1 m deep lay in isolation near the centre of the site (Fig. 166). A single fill deposit of dark, stiff charcoal-rich silty clay with abundant heat-crazed and fractured quartzite pebbles and cobbles was believed to be *in situ*, or represent a single dump of burnt material. No other finds were recovered but radiocarbon dating of *Prunus* or Salicaceae charcoal from the feature indicated that it was of Late Iron Age or early–middle Romano-British date, within the period cal AD 10–220 (1922±35, NZA-25058) (Fig. 168; Table 120).

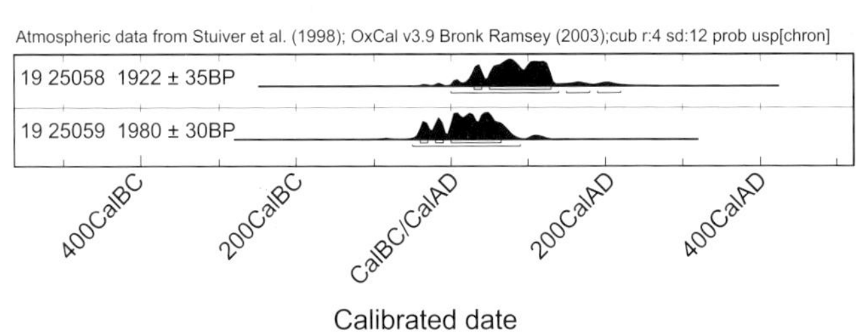

Fig. 168 Oxcal probability distributions of radiocarbon dates from Romano-British burnt features

Another less well-defined deposit of similar charcoal-rich soil and burnt stone lay in an irregular linear hollow (190098) nearly 40 m to the north. Here, a sample of *Acer* charcoal provided a radiocarbon date of 40 cal BC–cal AD 120 (1980±30, NZA-25059) (Fig. 168; Table 120), confirmed that activity involving heating of local stone was taking place in the Late Iron Age or early Romano-British period.

Feature 190017

Feature 190017, situated against the western edge of the excavation (Fig. 161), represents the butt-end of a NNE–SSW aligned feature, up to 0.40 m deep, with moderately sloping sides and a narrow, flattish base. Five separate fill deposits were recorded, producing a large quantity of Romano-British pottery.

Medieval

Limited medieval remains attest to an agricultural landuse, and a ditched enclosure (Enclosure 2) may have marked the edge of a landholding (Fig. 161).

Enclosure 2

A number of ditches (190053, 190150 and 190151) shared a common date, while others (190024, 190152 and 190216), although they contained no dating evidence, have been assigned to this phase on the basis of their similarity of alignment and form. These features were all shallow (none was more than 0.4 m deep) with generally rounded, concave profiles (Fig. 169), and form what may have been an enclosure, possibly around a building to the south-west of the site. The sparse pottery from the enclosure belonged mainly to the mid-13th–early 14th centuries, although a small component may be of 14th or possibly even 15th century date.

Within the enclosure was a 16 m long ditch (190024), possibly forming an internal division parallel to its north-western side, and an undated shallow gully (190025), also appearing to be aligned on the enclosure. The gully, cut by a post-medieval/modern ditch and extending beyond the excavation, formed three sides of what may have been a slightly rounded subrectangular feature, 13 m wide and at least 9 m long.

Pits

Three small features were recorded near the north-eastern corner of the enclosure. Feature 190165 was shallow and sub-circular, measuring 1.45 m wide and 0.3 m deep. The association of what may have been a narrow (0.4 m) flue, and the presence of charcoal-rich fills containing grain fragments suggest it may have been a truncated oven-base. Sherds of cooking pot in Coventry-type ware indicate a general date range of *c* 1150–1250 (Rátkai, below), the earliest medieval pottery from the site.

Two small sub-oval pits lay immediately to the north-west, although they were later in date. Pit 190065

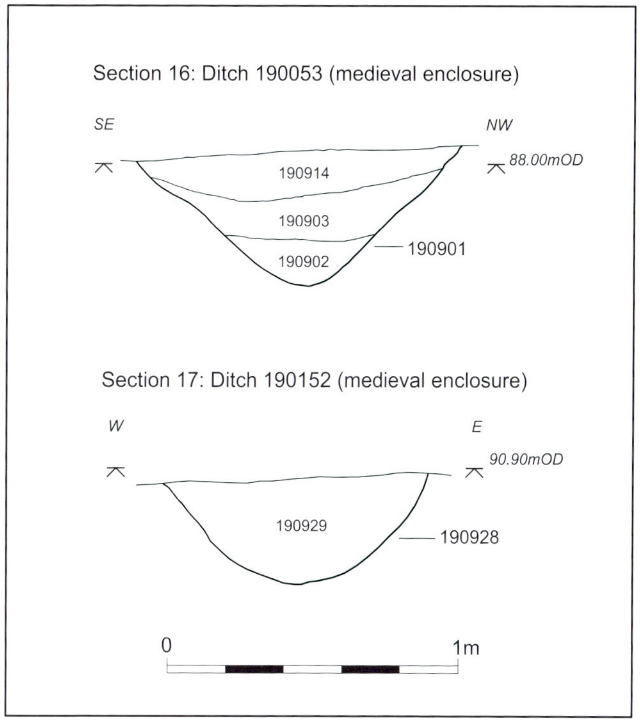

Fig. 169 Sections of medieval ditches

measured 1.3 m by 0.5 m, with a shallow concave profile 0.08 m deep. Forty-two sherds of 13th–early 14th century pottery came from half-excavation of its single fill. Pit 190064, measuring 0.75 m by 0.6 m and was 0.05 m deep, produced two sherds of mid-13th–14th century date.

Pond/watering hole

Sub-oval hollow 190167 measured *c* 5.8 m by 4.3 m, and was up to 0.3 m deep. It was most probably a small pond, or hollow for watering livestock. An homogeneous grey clay-silt filled the feature, with abundant cobbles concentrated near its outer edges, where they may have been deliberately dumped to improve access to the water. Nearly 100 sherds of late medieval (15th century, and some possibly 16th century) pottery were found, particularly amongst the cobbles.

Strip-fields and lynchet

A NE–SW aligned (cross-slope) lynchet lay on, and had exaggerated a slight natural break in, the hillslope. Whilst intrinsically undated, this feature is most likely to have developed from a medieval land boundary, and may originally have defined the southern limits of the strip fields that formerly lay immediately to the north-west. Evidence for these was observed in the form of at least six truncated furrows. The fills of these merged into a deep wedge of homogeneous colluvial clay-silt above the lynchet. Much of this material is likely to have accumulated whilst the strip fields were under arable cultivation in the medieval period, with erosion and transport of soils exacerbated by their downslope orientation. It is also probable that colluvial deposition continued here into the post-medieval period.

Post-medieval/modern

Some evidence for the layout of the post-medieval and recent landscape was noted, including several approximately north–south aligned field boundary ditches and a very poorly defined and crudely metalled east–west aligned trackway, following the foot of the medieval lynchet. Other more recent remains relate to the development and operation of Wishaw Hall Farm, its outbuildings and environs.

Undated

A number of features cannot presently be assigned a phase, either through a paucity or absence of datable finds, or because they have no clear structural or stratigraphic associations.

Finds

Coin, by Paul Booth

A single coin, in poor condition, certainly of Antoninus Pius (AD 138–161), was recovered. It was damaged and partly corroded. The reverse legend was problematic. It was just about possible to suggest ALEXAND[RIA COS II S C], (RIC III, 593, AD 139), but the S (of S C) is in the field and not part of the legend. The details of the standing figure were also not very clear.

Dupondius.Obv: ANTONINUS AUG [poss PIU., radiate head r
Rev:?]IILE....(4 uncertain letters) [, with S in left field, figure standing left

Metal finds, by Kelly Powell

This site produced a small but varied group of 13 copper-alloy objects, in addition to 11 iron and 12 lead objects (Fig. 170). The majority of the copper-alloy and lead assemblages were unstratified and contain a large proportion of medieval and post-medieval artefacts (Table 121).

Table 121 Metal finds other than iron nails

Feature	Copper-alloy	Lead	Iron
Unstrat.	1 beaded torc frag.	1 disc	
	1 stud	1 cloth seal?	
	1 knob handle	7 rolled sheet frags	
	1 ring		
	1 buckle		
	1 hook tag		
	2 misc.		
	1 coin		
Enclosure 1 ditch 190012, section 190740	1 ring		
Late med. pond 190167, fill 191172	1 misc.	3 strips	
	1 buckle		
Post-med/modern ditch 190163, section 191001	1 misc.		
Modern feature 190830			1 misc.
Tree-throw/hollow 190627			1 misc.

Romano-British

Several of the unstratified copper-alloy finds have been identified as Romano-British. The most notable of these, and possibly the most significant single metal object recovered from the M6 Toll, was a section from a beaded torc of 1st–2nd century AD date (ON 193011) (Fig. 170, 1; 171) (see Hunter, below). The additional unstratified probable or certain Romano-British finds included a circular conical-headed stud (ON 193009) (Fig. 170, 2). This is comparable to that recorded by Allason-Jones and Miket from South Shields Roman Fort (1984, 246–7, no. 3.965). A knob handle of probable Romano-British date (ON 193016) (Fig. 170, 3) was composed of a single piece of copper-alloy shaped into three circular elements decreasing in size vertically. The underside indicated a missing square or rectangular shaft with possible evidence of solder and it is therefore loosely comparable to a knob handle from *Verulamium* (Frere 1972, no. 106). Functional classification of this object is unfortunately not possible, though it is likely to be a furniture fitting. Finally, two copper-alloy rings were identified as Romano-British, one unstratified and one from Enclosure 1, ditch 190012 (section 190740, fill 190739; ON 193017) (Fig. 170, 4). The unstratified ring was the larger of the two, with an external diameter of 23 mm. Both were generally circular with a slightly irregular D-shaped section the unstratified ring was less corroded. These items may have had a range of functions and are broadly comparable with examples reported from Uley (Woodward and Leach 1993, fig. 114, no.12) and from Colchester (Crummy 1983, 162, no. 4397).

Most of the ironwork from this site was of probable Romano-British date and consisted mainly of nails or nail fragments (Table 122) with one unidentifiable object. Overall, nine probable nails or fragments were recovered, three of which, from pit 190015, appeared to be complete or almost complete hobnails of Manning type 10. Three examples from post-medieval/modern

Table 122 Nail classfication by context

	Type 1b	Type 10	Unclass.	Total
Ditch 191074	1	–	–	1
Ditch 190663	–	–	1	1
Pit 190015	–	3	2	5
Pond 190167	2	–	–	2
Total	3	3	3	9

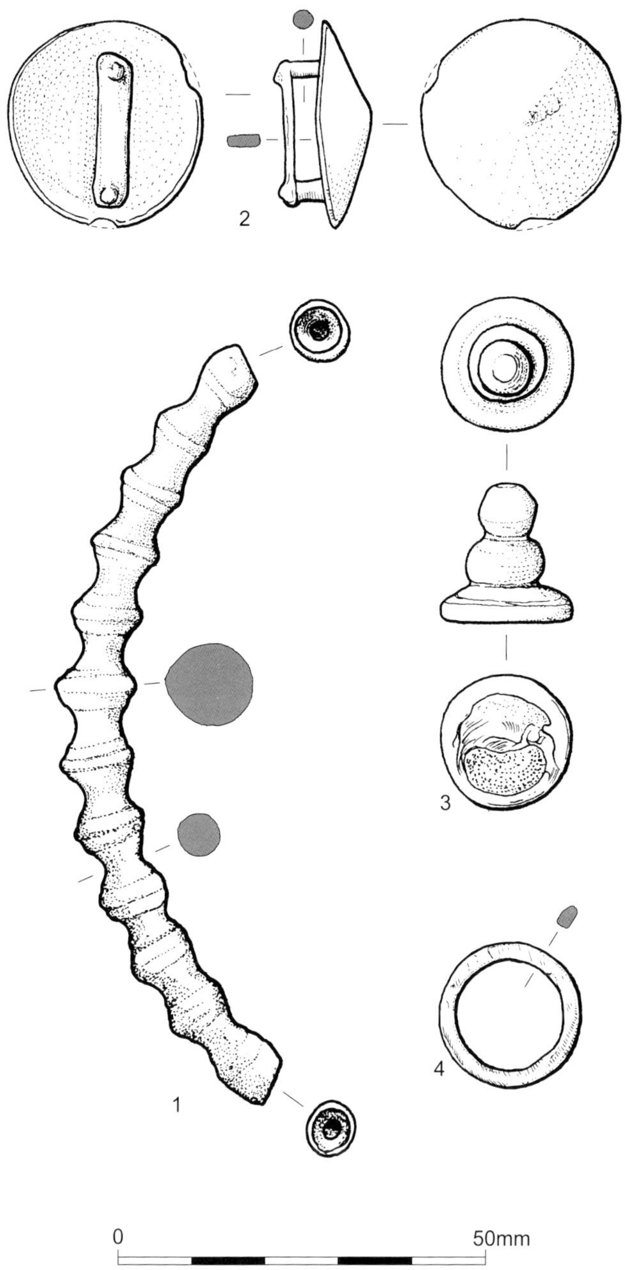

Fig. 170 Metal objects

ditch 190063 (context 191073) and layer 191172 in late medieval pond 190167 could be classified as Manning type 1. Two remaining examples from pit 190015 (context 190578) and a find from Romano-British ditch 190019 (context 190664) could not be classified, and the former could not firmly be described as nails due to their poor condition. A small fragment of iron, 27 mm long, from tree hollow fill 190628 may have been a damaged nail but it appeared to taper at either end.

Post-Romano-British

Unstratified copper-alloy finds of presumed post-Romano-British date included a post-medieval buckle, a hook tag and an unidentified flower-shaped object. Additionally a 15th century double loop buckle was recovered from layer 191172 (pond 190167) which also contained 15th century pottery. This context also produced three fragments of narrow copper-alloy strip of varying length. The lead finds were unstratified and included a small flat disc with a central perforation (ON 193010), a possible cloth seal (ON 193013) and seven short lengths of rolled sheet. Comparable objects to these have been identified as fishing net weights, as at Sandwell Priory (Egan 1991, 94, fig. 33). Such an identification (and a likely medieval date) is possible given the association of the site with the adjacent fish ponds at Wishaw (Site 20). No comparable objects were found there, however, though two pieces of lead sheet were recovered. A substantial fragment of a post-medieval carthorse shoe was recovered from a modern context (190831).

Additionally, three miscellaneous copper-alloy objects of unknown date were recovered from unstratified material: a broken and irregularly-shaped sheet fragment (ON 193001), a possibly burnt object and an unidentifiable flat, curving piece, 34 mm long, 3 mm thick, which is clearly broken at one end and appears to taper at the other.

List of illustrated metal objects (Fig. 170)

1. Beaded torc. Incomplete. Copper-alloy (from surface X-ray fluorescence analysis): brass with a little lead. L 100 mm; int D 120–130 mm; bead D 7.5–10.5 mm, socket D 6 mm, depth 4–6 mm, unstratified. ON 193011
2. Stud. Copper-alloy. Circular stud with conical head and a loop of rectangular shape and section on the reverse. Some edge damage to the head. D 22 mm, T 0.5 mm, loop L 20 mm, W 4 mm, unstratified. ON 193009
3. Knob handle. Copper-alloy. Possibly missing rectangular shaft at base. Small knob terminal above two further concentric circular elements. Base D 17 mm, top D 7 mm, L 18 mm, unstratified. ON 193016
4. Ring. Copper-alloy. Complete. Regular D-shaped section. D 19 mm, context 190739. ON 193017

A Romano-British beaded torc fragment, by Fraser Hunter

A portion of beaded torc was found by metal-detecting during site stripping (Figs 170, 1 and 171); it came from the surface of a medieval ditch, near the north-west corner of the Romano-British enclosure. It is a complete beaded section, cast in a single piece with mortised ends (one end slightly damaged) for the missing hoop to fit into. There are 12 bead motifs, each comprising a broad central disc with two narrower flankers, the size increasing towards the centre. The surface condition is poor, but there is no sign of decoration.

Beaded torcs are typical of central Britain in the first two centuries AD. They have been studied and summarised most recently by MacGregor (1976, 97–9), but recent finds (including this one) have expanded the distribution and raised some questions which make it worth revisiting the type.

Beaded torcs are in two parts, with a hoop to the rear of the neck and a separate beaded portion to the front, joined in a mortice and tenon fixing. They fall into two types: those with a bar-like or girder-like hoop and separately-cast beads threaded onto a rod of iron or, less

Fig. 171 Beaded torc fragment

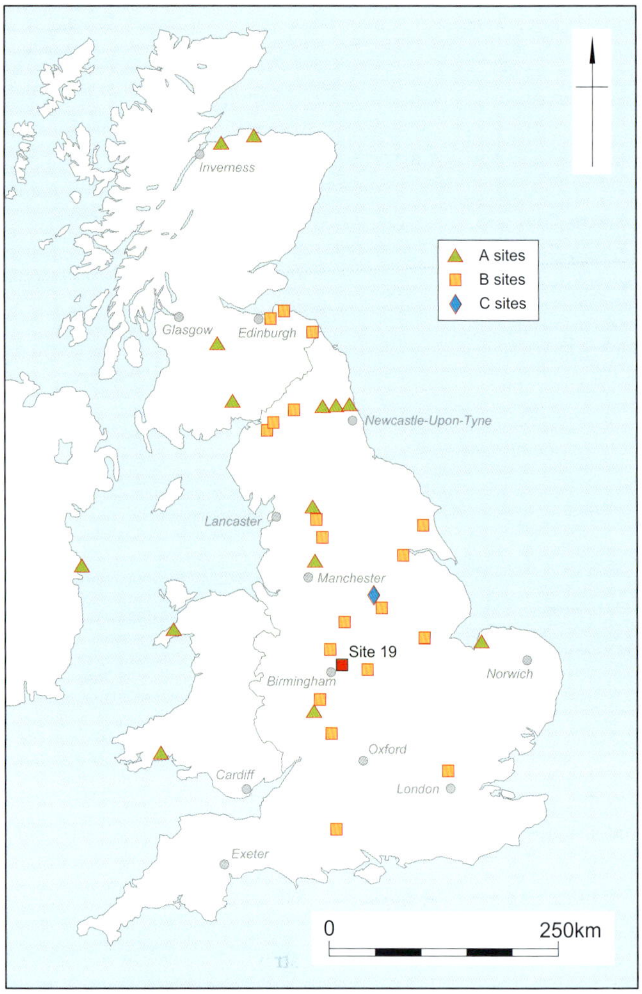

Fig. 172 Distribution of torcs

commonly, copper-alloy (here type A); and those with a rod-like hoop, often decorated, where the beaded section is cast in one (type B). One unusual example is a hybrid with other torc types. Within the broad types there is a range of decorations. The type A torcs are more elaborate, but the type B ones do show a variety of decoration; the Wishaw Hall Farm example is notably plain. Its tripartite bead form is typical of type B torcs; they often bear some decoration, although any surface detailing may have been lost in this case.

MacGregor (1976, 113–5) listed 14 examples (see notes to Table 123). From recent finds and re-identification of older examples this has now expanded substantially to 37; the additional examples are listed in Table 123, with an updated distribution in Figure 172. The source of the new finds is interesting, as it shows the importance of the Portable Antiquities Scheme (PAS) to our knowledge of such finds: four are from recent excavations, a further five were identified from old publications or in museum stores, while nine come from the Portable Antiquities Scheme or the Treasure Act and a further four from pre-PAS metal-detecting or Scottish Treasure Trove, with one casual find. It is notable that the finds reported from the PAS scheme are all of the more recognisable type B, suggesting that single finds of type A beads may be slipping unrecognised through the net.

These new examples lead to a significant shift in our understanding of the type. The distribution is now markedly broader, with many of the new finds coming from central England; rather than from Forth to Humber, the core distribution now runs south to the Severn-Wash line.

While many of the new examples are stray finds, those with associations confirm the 1st–2nd century AD date which MacGregor suggested; indeed the quantity from Hadrian's Wall and from Antonine contexts elsewhere suggests a 2nd century floruit. There is nothing to corroborate MacGregor's suspected typological development from type A to type B.

This firmly Romano-British dating leads to a number of questions. Torcs are seen as a quintessentially Iron Age object: what are we to make of these apparently late examples? It is intended to publish the recent finds and consider these questions more fully, but here a couple of points may be raised. There is a general problem with dating metalwork of this period, especially in northern Britain where datable associations tend inevitably to be Romano-British; this has the effect of pulling earlier material into a Romano-British bracket. However, here the quantity of Romano-British associations make the dating secure. The type's origins could be argued as pre-Romano-British, but this is much harder to trace on current evidence. While the decoration on most is simple geometric patterning, the example from Lochar Moss (MacGregor 1976, 204) is ornamented with a typical late Celtic broken-back scroll motif. However, much of this late Celtic art in northern Britain is Romano-British period in date (Dungworth 1996, 407–10), so this does not demonstrate any earlier origins. In truth the type now looks very Romano-British – a development from and transformation of the earlier indigenous idea of torcs. Rather than the elite examples, primarily in gold, known from the Late Iron Age, the use of copper-alloy (and the fairly mundane decoration) suggests that these beaded torcs were rather more socially widespread, although their occurrence in hoards indicates that they were still valued. Much like the development of types such as dragonesque brooches, they are a development of local styles in the Romano-British period, creating a distinctively Roman-British object.

This tradition of Iron Age-derived metalwork is strongest in central Britain, from Humber to Forth (eg

Table 123 Finds of beaded torcs since the listing in MacGregor (1976, 113–5)

Site	County	Site Type	Torc type	Details	Dating ev.	Reference
Carmarthen	Carmarthen	Roman town	B	beaded frag.	late 2nd c	Webster 2003, 322–3, fig. 8.6, no. 77
Coygan Camp	Carmarthen	RB reuse of Iron Age hillfort	A	bead	late 3rd c context	Wainwright 1967, 91, fig. 23, no. 7; Jope 2000, 293, pl. 259e
South Shields	C. Durham	Roman fort	A	3 separate beads	Antonine	Croom 1997–8
Inveresk	E. Lothian	Roman fort	B	beaded portion	Antonine	Bishop 2004, 152, fig. 100, no. 3
Chigwell	Essex	stray	B	beaded frag.		Major 1996, 308, fig. 6, no. 4
Dumbleton	Gloucs.	stray	B	beaded frag.		PAS GLO-41CEA6
Huncote	Leics.	stray	B	beaded portion		PAS LEIC-DD6041
Adlingfleet	Lincs.	stray	B	beaded frag.		PAS NLM4339
Folkingham	Lincs.	stray	B	beaded frag.		PAS LIN-65A032
Urquhart	Moray	stray	A	bead		Hunter 2006, 153, fig. 18a
Culbin	Moray	Iron Age site	A	enamelled bead		Hunter 2006, 153–4, fig. 18b
NW Norfolk	Norfolk	?Votive	A	frag. beads on bars		J.D. Hill pers. comm. (treasure find)
Caw Gap	Northumb.	?Roman wall	B	beaded portion		Allason-Jones 1984
Corbridge	Northumb.	Roman fort/town	A	bead	late Antonine	Croom 1997–8, 62
Mansfield	Notts.	stray	B	beaded portion (in 2 pieces)		PAS DENO-304F42 & 306A31
Dinnington	S. Yorks.	stray	*	hybrid	RB	Beswick *et al.* 1990
Clay Mills, Burton-on-Trent	Staffs.	stray	B	beaded portion		Leahy 1979, 52–4
Wall, Lichfield	Staffs.	stray	B	beaded frag.		PAS WMID5241
Wishaw Hall Farm	Warwicks.	RB site	B	beaded portion	?RB	this volume
Victoria Cave, Settle	W. Yorks.	RB site	A	bead only	RB	Croom 1997–8, 62
Durnford	Wilts.	stray	B	beaded frag.		PAS WILT-DAA276
Droitwich Spa	Worcs	stray	B	hoop & some beads		PAS WMID3118
Unprov.		?	B	beaded portion		Mills 1995, 18–19

PAS = Portable Antiquities Scheme. The example from Dinnington* is a hybrid between beaded torcs and hinged collars. MacGregor's no. 209 should be dismissed (see Leahy 1979, 54). Her records of 2 type B torcs from the Settle caves (nos 197 & 201) are probably duplicates; published sources only record 1, from Attermire (Raistrick 1939, 139) whose description correlates with no. 201. However, Croom (1997–8, 62) identifies a bead from a type A torc from 'a cave near Settle'; this is Victoria Cave (also known as King's Scarr; Roach Smith 1848, pl. xxvii, 3; Branigan and Dearne 1991, 111, no. 4.58)

Hunter 2007), correlating broadly with the military zone, but these torcs indicate a more complex picture. They are not found across Roman Britain, being all but unknown in the south; but equally they are clearly not solely a product of the developing culture of the military zone. Their distribution is broadly complementary to the more restricted spread of hinged neck collars of Wraxall type (MacGregor 1976, map 15) which are primarily found in south-west England; these are poorly dated but may be seen as broadly contemporary. This suggests that there was a series of regional types of neck ornament across and indeed beyond Roman Britain, but absent from the south-east. To consider the implications of these questions would take us beyond the confines of a specialist report, but it raises intriguing questions about the regionality reflected in artefact distributions and what lies behind them.

It is not clear who was wearing such items. Where the internal diameter is recorded, most are small, suggesting they were predominantly female ornaments, although the overall range (from 100 mm to 135 mm) would allow use by males, females and youths. Further work on the recent finds may clarify this.

Glass, by H.E.M. Cool

The only fragment of Roman vessel glass from this site was a rim fragment of a blue/green bottle of the 1st–2nd centuries (ON 190739), the outer edge of which is folded out, up, in and flattened. That the only evidence for vessel glass use at this site was in the form of a bottle is unsurprising as these are often the only types of vessels present on rural sites of the 1st–3rd centuries (Cool and Baxter 1999, 84).

Flint, by Kate Cramp

Introduction

This site produced the largest single assemblage of flintwork from the M6 toll excavations, providing over 90% of the route-wide assemblage. The collection comprised 1583 struck flints and 38 pieces (71 g) of burnt unworked flint, which derived almost entirely from a subsoil scatter of flintwork, adjacent to and extending beyond the western limit of the excavated area (Fig. 160). Approximately 400 flints, including one microlith, four microburins and 249 chips, were retrieved from the sieved residues of samples taken from the main cluster of the flint scatter (sample numbers 193508 and 193512).

The flintwork represented an accomplished blade-based industry, characterised by the use of soft hammer percussion and careful core preparation. A full range of knapping products was present, from preparatory flakes, chips and cores to finely-retouched and utilised tools. The microlith component was dominated by scalene microtriangles and rod-like backed bladelets, suggesting a later Mesolithic date for the collection (Jacobi 1978, 19). Other tools included retouched and truncated flakes and blades, scrapers, various piercers, notched and serrated flakes, and one fabricator. Flaked axes and burins were, perhaps significantly, entirely absent from the collection. The assemblage is summarised in Table 150.

Excavation methods

The flints were recovered from a subsoil layer below the ploughsoil and from the fills of numerous artificial and natural features cutting this layer. The flint scatter extended for approximately 220 m by 60 m, but the majority of material was recovered within a 100 m by 40 m area truncated by the western limit of the excavated area.

The majority of the flintwork from the scatter was three-dimensionally recorded (1166 flints), although point and context information was lost for 262 small finds. A discrete cluster covering an area approximately 4 m by 4 m, was subjected to detailed grid-excavation, with full recovery of material from alternate 1 m² collection units. This exercise demonstrated that the flintwork had been deposited in natural features/tree-throw holes. The fact that the cluster was grid excavated clearly emphasised the density of flints within it.

The absence of naturally occurring flint on the site made identification of even tiny struck flakes comparatively easy. The flints were mainly recovered from the weathered machine-stripped surface of the site, with a lesser amount being recorded as residual or intrusive finds in excavated features. By far the greatest concentrations of flint lay adjacent to the western edge of the site, and the distribution of material clearly continues to the west, beyond the limits of excavation. A wider distribution of flint was also observed, but this decreased in intensity with distance from the main concentration.

Taphonomy

While there may be elements of the assemblage which were *in situ*, these were so comprehensively masked by redeposited finds, or by the majority of material which lay in secondary contexts, that the former cannot now be recognised. Much of the flint was redeposited in tree hollows, and/or had migrated down through the soil profile into secondary settings through long-term biological activity.

Individual flints were three-dimensionally surveyed where they were found, but a small component of the assemblage was clearly redeposited after excavation of the site began, either by (sometimes considerable) rainwater surface run-off or, in the case of the smallest pieces, by wind action while the site was dry.

Condition

The condition of the flints was generally very fresh, with minimal post-depositional edge damage observed on the majority of flints. While it may not have been *in situ*, the flintwork was thus unlikely to have been significantly disturbed since its original deposition. A few rolled and damaged flints were recorded, but these exceptional pieces probably belonged to a different phase of occupation.

A light, incipient cortication was noted on the majority of flints. The occasional piece exhibited a dense white discoloration, while uncorticated flints were also present in small quantities. A significant proportion of the assemblage displayed a light orange iron-staining, the development of which appeared to have been a post-depositional process rather than a characteristic of the raw material. Although formal analysis was not undertaken, no patterning was observed in the distribution of these various surface conditions.

Raw material

The raw material used on site was entirely flint, although large quantities of burnt quartzite pebbles were recovered from the scatter (see Shaffrey below). The colour of the flint varied from light grey through light beige to mid-brown. Iron-stained pieces tended to be slightly orange or pinkish-tinged. Where present, the cortex was thin, abraded and occasionally pitted; it varied in colour through greys, browns and creams to white. In some cases, the surface of the cortex had a distinctive glossy sheen. Thermal fractures and other imperfections were often present, and it seemed that the flint was probably of an unpredictable knapping quality. From the shape and form of the flake removals, they appeared to originate from sub-rounded pebbles or small cobbles. No removal exceeded 50 mm in length, which may be directly related to the size of the parent nodule. The condition of the cortex and the quality of the flint indicated a secondary source, and it is unlikely that any of the material has been obtained directly from chalk deposits. Approximately 1 km to the south-east of the site, the underlying geology includes extensive areas of Pleistocene sands and gravels that may have provided flint nodules of workable size and condition for most knapping purposes; river gravel or similar deposits may also have been exploited.

The assemblage

The assemblage comprised 1583 struck flints, including 534 chips, and was spread across an area measuring approximately 220 m by 60 m, although most of the material was recovered from the dense central cluster. A further 38 pieces (71 g) of burnt unworked flint were also recovered (Table 150).

The assemblage represented a careful, blade-based industry, involving considerable investment in platform preparation and maintenance. Excluding chips (<10 mm^2), the collection was dominated by unretouched flakes (481 pieces), although blades were well represented and their abundance supports the Mesolithic origin of the collection. The shift from blade production in the Mesolithic to flake production in the later Neolithic and Bronze Age period has been well documented elsewhere (eg Pitts 1978; Pitts and Jacobi 1979; Ford 1987). A blade is here defined as a long narrow removal, conventionally described as a flake whose length is at least twice its breadth (Bordes 1961, 6). A total of 274 blades, bladelets and bladelike flakes were recorded which, as a group, provided 35% of all unretouched removal types (excluding chips and irregular waste). This figure falls comfortably within the range predicted for Mesolithic collections (Ford 1987, 79), despite any bias caused by the high proportions of breakage, particularly of blades, in the assemblage.

The scars of previous blade removals could be seen on the dorsal surfaces of both flakes and blades. A total of 185 flints (22.8%) with dorsal blade scars were recorded in a sample of 811 pieces (see Attribute analysis methodology, Chapter 28), indicating their position within a reduction sequence aimed at the production of blades. Plain platforms predominated (148 pieces or 34.2%) in a sample of 433 assessable (ie intact) pieces, although platforms of linear type were also well represented (135 pieces or 31.2%). Numerous removals, along with the parent cores, displayed platform edge abrasion. This technique, which involved grinding or chipping the edge of an overhanging striking platform to encourage a more regular and predictable removal, was present on 167 flints (20.6%) in the sample. Numerous chips also displayed remnants of platform edge abrasion, but this component was not quantified in detail.

An analysis of bulb morphology revealed a preference for soft hammer percussion (eg Onhuma and Bergman 1982). A total of 201 flints in the sample were recognised as soft hammer products, compared to 20 hard hammer flakes; a further 590 flints were either unassessable or of indeterminate hammer mode. Soft hammer struck pieces thus outnumbered hard hammer removals in a ratio of 10:1. Soft density percussors, made from antler, wood or bone for example, are thought to diffuse the force of the blow and result in finer, more laminar removals. The low numbers of hinge- and step-terminated flakes (94 pieces), which are associated with the use of hard hammer percussion, compared to feather terminations (374 pieces), was consistent with this observation.

All elements of the reduction sequence were represented in the assemblage, from cortical preparation flakes (43 pieces or 5.3%) and trimming flakes (224 pieces or 27.6%) to non-cortical flakes (65.9%); ten pieces (1.2%) were unassessable, usually owing to the severity of burning or breakage. The relatively low number of preparatory flakes suggested that cores were being decorticated elsewhere, perhaps at source, as a way of reducing their weight for transportation while simultaneously testing their quality.

Numerous chips were also recovered, both by hand (285 pieces) and from sieving (249 pieces). Some represented broken (and often burnt) fragments of larger flakes, but many genuine pieces of microdebitage from knapping were also retrieved, including core front chips (Newcomer and Karlin 1987, 35, fig. 4.3). No retouch chips (*ibid.*, fig. 4.4) were identified, but the material was not analysed in detail. The presence of these chips strongly suggests that knapping activity and/or tool retouch was performed in the immediate area. The presence of numerous pieces of a related flint type, distinguished by visual similarities in colour and cortex (see Refitting analysis methodology, Chapter 28), implies the presence of material originating from the same core, although no refits were found to confirm this. Two fragments of a bladelike flake conjoined on an old break, but the fragments were found together.

A total of 35 cores and eight tested nodules were recovered from the site, although interestingly only one core (Fig. 173, 1) was recovered from the central cluster. Both flake and blade cores were present, but the former dominated the assemblage; multi-platform flake cores alone accounted for 15 (42.9%) of the total number. Blade cores, including examples of the opposed platform variety (eg Fig. 173, 2), are present in smaller numbers. However, many of the flake cores displayed the scars of earlier blade removals. It seems that, in many cases, the cores started out as blade cores and were worked as flake cores only in the later stages as they neared exhaustion. The assemblage contained numerous blades struck from opposed-platform blade cores, which clearly showed that this core type was under-represented; perhaps many were last worked to yield flakes as part of an economical approach to core reduction.

The cores had been carefully worked at all stages of the reduction sequence: in initial preparation, during flaking with platform edge abrasion to strengthen the platform edge, and by rejuvenating faces and platforms between flaking episodes. Core faces were regularly refreshed, as witnessed by 14 face/edge rejuvenation flakes, but only two platform rejuvenation tablets were recorded. Crested flakes and blades, mainly of the uni-directional variety, were also common (ten pieces).

The retouched component consisted of 107 tools (10.2% excluding chips) which, while including a wide range of types, was heavily dominated by simple edge-retouched flakes and blades (37 pieces) and scrapers (21

Table 124 Classification of microliths from the Mesolithic scatter (after Jacobi 1978, 16, fig. 6)

Microlith	*Total(% total microlith assemblage)*
1a	1 (6.7)
1bc	1 (6.7)
Unclass. Early Meso. form	1 (6.7)
5	2 (13.3)
7a1	4 (26.7)
7a2	3 (20.0)
Unclass. Late Meso. form	2 (13.3)
Unclass.	1 (6.7)
Total	15

Table 125 Classification of microburins from the Mesolithic scatter

Microburin	*total (% of total microburin assemblage)*
Proximal, left-hand notch	11 (37.9)
Proximal, right-hand notch	3 (10.4)
Medial	1 (3.5)
Distal, left-hand notch	5 (17.2)
Distal, right-hand notch	7 (24.1)
Unclass.	2 (6.9)
Total	29

pieces). Thin, broad blanks seem to have been preferred for the manufacture of retouched flakes and blades, which usually displayed light direct retouch to one or more edges (eg Figs. 173, 3–4); inverse retouch was occasionally present on these pieces (eg Fig. 173, 5). Scrapers, on the other hand, tended to be abruptly retouched on thick, often plunging, flakes or blades (eg Figs 173, 6–8). One of the scrapers (Fig. 173, 9), apparently made on a re-used core, displayed exceptionally heavy rounded use-wear from scraping soft density materials.

The collection of 15 microliths was dominated by late Mesolithic types (Table 124), including narrow scalene microtriangles (class 7; Fig. 173, 10–12) and rod-like backed bladelets (class 5; Fig. 173, 13). Simple obliquely-blunted points (class 1; Fig. 173, 14–15) featured in much smaller numbers. When dominant in a collection, obliquely-blunted microliths indicate a date in the pre-Boreal or very early Boreal period (perhaps 8th millennium cal BC); their presence in later Mesolithic assemblages may often be a residual one (Jacobi pers. comm.). Four unclassifiable microliths, one probably an early shape (Fig. 173, 16) and two fragments from narrow-blade microliths, were also present. Specialised geometric forms, such as microlunates, microrhomboids and micro 'tranchets', perhaps significantly, were absent from the assemblage. Given that the latter two forms are not usually found in assemblages pre-dating 5000 BC (Jacobi 1978, 19), a date early in the Late Mesolithic is tentatively suggested for the collection from Wishaw Hall Farm.

The assemblage contained significantly more microburins than microliths. A total of 29 microburins were identified (Table 125), outnumbering microliths by a ratio of nearly 2:1 and perhaps indicating more production on site than use. Proximal, distal and medial examples were all represented, with the most common form being the proximal microburin notched on the left-hand edge (eg Fig. 173, 17–18). This is, perhaps, unsurprising given the shape of the finished microliths (eg Fig. 173, 10–12). Distal microburins were also well represented by a total of 12 pieces (eg Fig. 173, 19), which seemed to have been notched on either edge. In general, simple notches and snaps were the most common form of manufacture, the 'normal' form described by Clark (1934, 68–9), although two examples bore simple edge retouch prior to a deliberate snap. Several of the notched blades in the assemblage probably represented unfinished attempts at microlith manufacture using the microburin technique (see Inizan *et al.* 1992, 69, fig. 24).

Other retouched forms include backed bladelets (eg Fig. 173, 20), truncated flakes and blades (eg Fig. 173, 21), spurred tools and piercers (eg Fig. 173, 22), notched blades and flakes (eg Fig. 173, 23), and serrated flakes (eg Fig. 173, 24). Both serrated flakes have been made on bladelike blanks, with serrations on one of the longer edges; neither piece displays any silica gloss. The fabricator (Fig. 173, 25) has been minimally retouched on a mostly cortical blade. A single removal has been made each side of the bulb on the ventral surface, and the abrasion typical of this artefact class can be clearly seen on the proximal end of the tool.

Low-power use-wear analysis was performed on a sample of 190 flints from the scatter that were given ON numbers (see Use-wear analysis methodology, Chapter 28). Use-wear was detected on 78 pieces (Fig. 174a), while 103 flints showed no evidence of use; a further nine pieces were unassessable, in most cases due to burning or breakage. The flints were being used to work a variety of materials, ranging from soft density substances such as meat and hide, to hard materials such as seasoned antler (Fig. 174b). An emphasis on medium density materials is apparent, although given that this category encompasses the widest range of substances, this may not necessarily reflect any particular task specialisation. These materials were being worked with a scraping, cutting and/or whittling action (Fig. 174c). Only six instances of piercing damage were recorded, which is perhaps to be expected from an assemblage of tools dominated by edge-retouched flakes and scrapers to the near-exclusion of piercers. There are also indications of intra-site assemblage variation in the spatial patterning of utilised pieces, primarily between the cluster and the surrounding scatter, with a far greater density of flints used for soft cutting/whittling activities in the central cluster.

Proportions of burning and breakage are particularly high in the assemblage: a total of 319 (20.2%) struck flints are burnt and 715 flints (45.3%) are broken. If pieces broken as a result of burning (accounting for 157 pieces or 22% of all broken flints) are excluded, the total

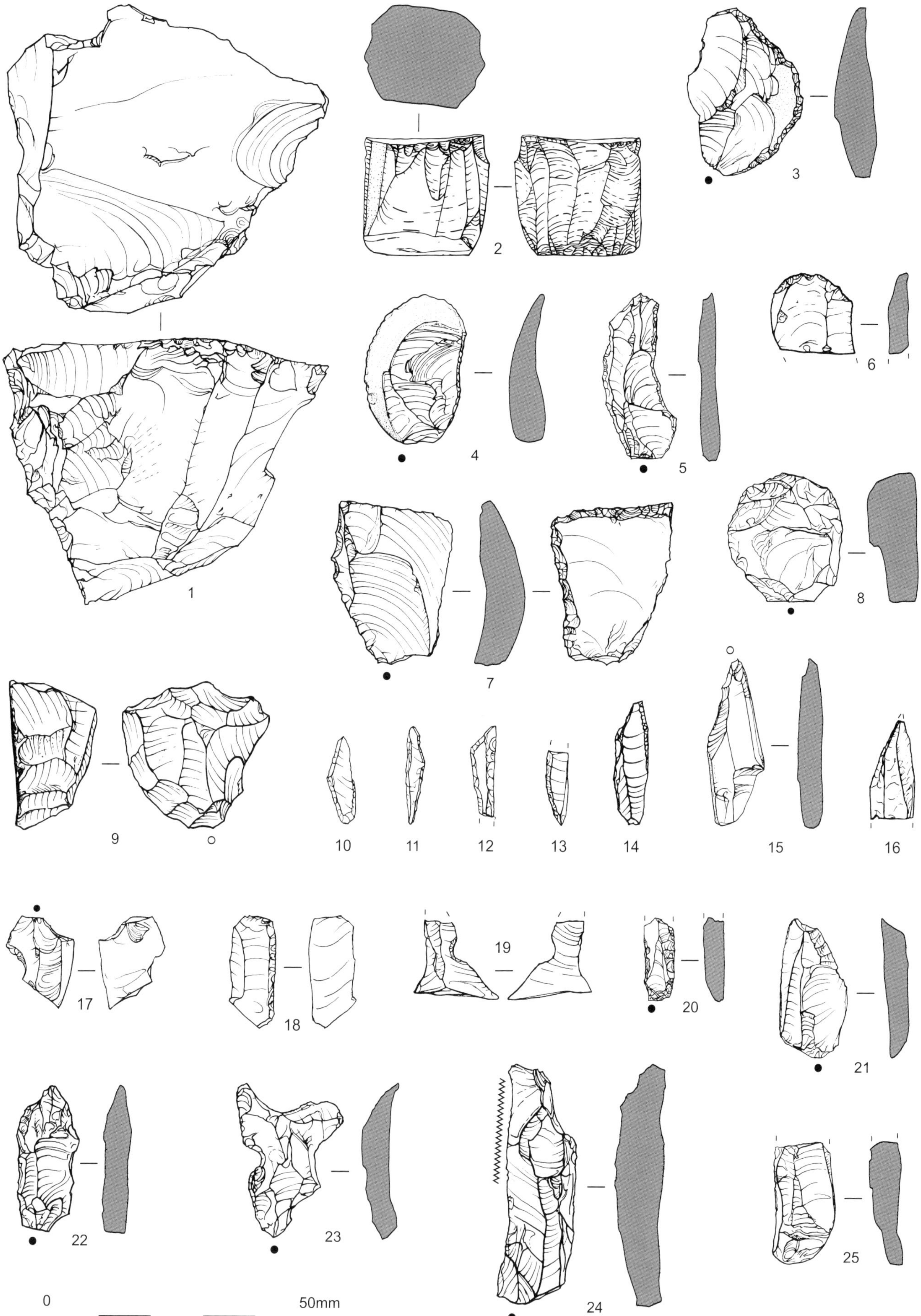

Fig. 173 Flints

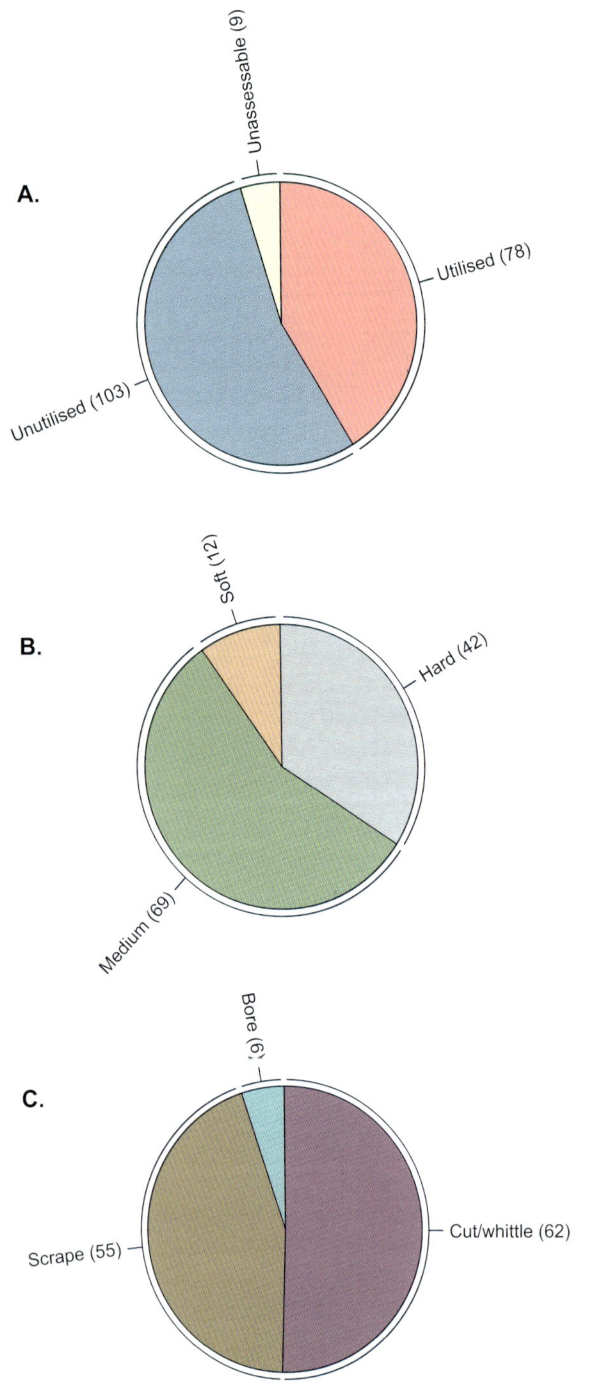

Fig. 174 Results of use-wear analysis performed on sample of flint from the Mesolithic scatter

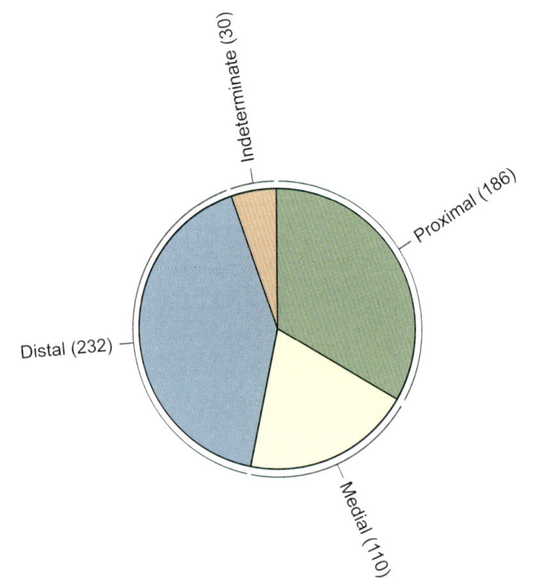

Fig. 175 Classification of broken flake fragments resulting from non-burning breaks (mostly deliberate snaps) from the Mesolithic scatter

falls to 558 pieces or 35.3% of the assemblage. This is nonetheless exceptionally high, and results from the deliberate snapping of blades for further adaptation or use in composite tools. An analysis of the remnant fragments in the assemblage shows that proximal and distal elements are more frequently represented that medial pieces (Fig. 175), suggesting that the medial section was preferred for the manufacture of microliths and other tools and was thus more likely to be removed from the scatter. It seems that proximal and distal pieces were treated as unwanted by-products in much the same way as microburins. Indeed, at nearly 4:1, the ratio of proximal and distal fragments to medial fragments is higher than that of proximal and distal microburins to microliths (1.7:1).

Discussion

The flintwork forms a coherent assemblage which, through its technological appearance and the presence of chronologically distinctive artefacts, can be dated to the late Mesolithic. While it is accepted that the flint scatter has probably not been preserved in its primary context, the fresh condition of the vast majority of flints implies that lateral or downslope post-depositional movement has often been relatively slight.

The shape and size of the scatter, which is defined by a dense cluster *c* 100 m by 60 m against a more general spread of material, is fairly typical of sites identified in the region (Saville 1981b, 51). The extent of such scatters suggests that these locations were of considerable importance and probably represent campsites. The assemblage cannot easily be characterised according to Mellars's (1976) settlement typology, as the retouched component contains exceptionally low numbers of both microliths (14%) and scrapers (20%), while burins and tranchet axes, along with axe sharpening and thinning flakes, are entirely absent. The size of the scatter and the fairly balanced representation of microliths and scrapers in the tool inventory align it most closely with Type B settlements, thought to represent predominantly winter occupation (Mellars 1976, 389–94). Several similar sites have previously been identified in Warwickshire, the closest only 8 km to the south-east, but all represent disturbed surface scatters (Saville 1981b).

The assemblage contains several microburins and is marked by high proportions of breakage, much of it probably deliberate. A certain proportion of the scatter, therefore, almost certainly derives from microlith production. Most of the microburins are proximal examples that have been notched on the left-hand edge (Table 125), which corresponds with the predominance of left-hand blunted microliths and is the normal microburin form (Clark 1934, 68). Proximal microburins with left-hand notches are well represented in three surface assemblages from Warwickshire examined by Saville, where they form 86% of the total (1981b, 57). The ratio of microburins to microliths at these sites is, however, significantly lower than at Wishaw Hall Farm and might indicate that methods other than the microburin technique were being used to produce the geometric forms from these sites (*ibid.*, 57–8).

The collection contains very few cortical flakes, indicating that core preparation was not undertaken to any great extent at this location, although the cores themselves are present in reasonable number. Indications of other activities, including cutting, scraping and piercing, are implied by the repertoire of retouched tools and borne out by the results of the low-power use-wear analysis.

The focus of Mesolithic occupation appears to have been on, and beyond, the western limit of the excavated area, making a full reconstruction of the area of occupation impossible. Struck flints were present only in low densities on the slightly steeper ground to the north, but the amount of material recovered from the medieval and post-medieval colluvium that lay above the lynchet suggests that there a greater assemblage had been eroded. Localised sub-concentrations within the main scatter almost certainly indicate accumulations of flintwork within tree hollows that were not individually recorded.

There are no palaeoenvironmental data from the excavation from which to reconstruct the late Mesolithic landscape, and no comparative data are available from nearby sites.

List of illustrated flint (Fig. 173)

1. Unclassifiable blade core, multiple platforms. Several faults and hinge-terminated scars; nonetheless abandoned prematurely. Grey flint with white weathered cortex, from secondary source. Good quality but with occasional frost shatters. 151 g. Mesolithic scatter, context 190778. ON 193038
2. Opposed platform blade core, small (*c* 25 mm) cylindrical core for production of narrow bladelet removals. Simple opposed platforms with abraded edges. High platform angle. 16 g. Mesolithic scatter. ON 193216
3. Retouched flake, plunging flake with light, semi-abrupt retouch on distal and right-hand edges. Mesolithic scatter. ON 193066
4. Retouched flake, side-trimming flake with slight abrupt retouch on right-hand edge, Mesolithic scatter. ON 196252
5. Retouched blade, bladelike flake with continuous edge retouch on left- and right-hand edges; some inverse retouch also present on left-hand edge. Mesolithic scatter. ON 196075
6. End scraper, thin tertiary flake (probable blade) with shallow, curving distal retouch. Burnt and broken. Mesolithic scatter. ON 196228
7. End and side scraper, straight, semi-abrupt inverse retouch on distal and right-hand edges; light direct retouch combined with heavy use-wear on left-hand edge. Mesolithic scatter. ON 193361
8. End-and-side scraper, small disc-like scraper with abrupt distal retouch. Mesolithic scatter, context 191241. ON 196436
9. Unclassifiable scraper, possible small flake core reused as scraper. Very rounded use-wear from soft-scraping activity. Mesolithic scatter. ON 193469
10. Microlith, class 7a1 (Jacobi 1978, 16, fig. 6). Mesolithic scatter. ON 196103
11. Microlith, class 7a1 (*ibid.*). Mesolithic scatter, context 191200. ON 196432
12. Microlith, class 7a2 (*ibid.*). Extreme part of tail lost. Mesolithic scatter. ON 196186
13. Microlith, incomplete, but probably class 5 (*ibid.*). Tip lost. Mesolithic scatter. ON 196095
14. Microlith, class 1bc (*ibid.*). Mesolithic scatter. ON 196367
15. Microlith, possibly heat-treated? Very large microlith on side-trimming blade with hinge termination. Oblique proximal retouch, comparable to class 1a (*ibid.*). Sample 193512, Mesolithic scatter, context 190772. ON 193512
16. Microlith, unclassifiable early Mesolithic shape. Probably derives from an obliquely blunted point, with class 1a most likely (*ibid.*). On relatively broad blade, *c* 10 mm wide. Tail lost. Mesolithic scatter. ON 196438
17. Microburin, proximal, left-hand notch. Mesolithic scatter. ON 193246
18. Microburin, proximal, left-hand notch. With continuous edge retouch. Mesolithic scatter. ON 196185
19. Microburin, distal, right-hand notch. Mesolithic scatter. ON 193846
20. Backed bladelet, backed bladelet with abrupt retouch on right-hand edge; some retouch also present on proximal left-hand edge. Bulb not removed. Mesolithic scatter. ON 193895
21. Truncated flake, distal truncation, 45°. Left-hand edge utilised. Mesolithic scatter. ON 193481
22. Piercer, abrupt retouch along both lateral edges of blade to form distal point. Mesolithic scatter. ON 193181
23. Notch, 7 mm wide by 4 mm deep, on left-hand edge of flake. Some edge retouch. Mesolithic scatter. ON 196454
24. Serrated flake, serrated flake on unifacially crested blade from opposed platform core. Irregular, bifacial serrations on left-hand edge, *c* 8 teeth per 10 mm. No edge gloss noted. Mesolithic scatter. ON 193888
25. Fabricator, no retouch: proximal end exhibits rounded use-wear usually associated with fabricator tools. Mesolithic scatter. ON 193414

Iron Age pottery, by Paul Booth

Some 30 sherds (405 g) of hand-made Iron Age pottery were recovered. In addition, four sherds (51 g) of wheel-thrown pottery in a Late Iron Age ceramic tradition came from context 191139, which also produced handmade material.

Much minor variation was observed in the fabrics present, but these seem to represent slightly varying proportions of the same range of inclusion types and all the sherds probably belonged to one of four fabric groups (Table 126).

Diagnostic characteristics other than the fabric inclusions were scarce. There was no identifiable surface treatment or decoration and the only feature sherds were two rims. The first of these, in fabric AM3, was from a simple barrel-shaped jar, the second, in fabric AVP4, with an everted rim tip, was perhaps from a similar form but only the rim itself survived (Fig. 176, 1). Similar rather undiagnostic forms are characteristic of the Iron Age pottery from Coleshill, only *c* 6 km distant to the SSE and the everted rim tip finds an exact parallel in a fabric (P31) very similar if not identical to sherds recorded in the present assemblage as fabric APV4 (Booth 2006, 117). P31 was the commonest Iron Age fabric at Coleshill (by sherd count). The other principal Iron Age fabric there was the sand-tempered P11. Fabrics AM3 and AN3 at Site 19 were both very similar to P11. In view of these similarities of fabrics and forms it is likely that at least some of the Wishaw pottery was derived from the same sources that provided the majority of the Iron Age pottery to the pre-temple settlement at Coleshill.

These analogies provide some indication of the chronology of the Site 19 material, Coleshill being fairly firmly dated to the Middle–Late Iron Age. Further support comes from the radiocarbon date derived from carbonised residue on a sherd in fabric QAPM5, one of two found associated with human skull fragments in one of the pits of the pit alignment. This fabric is not paralleled in the Coleshill assemblage. The date, 410–200 cal BC, nevertheless confirms the Middle Iron Age character of the hand made assemblage as a whole.

Table 126 Middle Iron Age pottery fabrics

Fabric group/ fabric	*No.*	*Wt (g)*	*Context*	*Comment*
Sand, no other significant inclusions				*cf.* Warwickshire fabric P11
AM3	3	73	191214	jar rim
AN3	1	8	191169	
Sand, organics & clay pellets				
APV3	8	40	191068	
APV4	1	65	191303	v. hard fired, *cf.* Warwickshire fabric P31
AVP3	3	9	191072	
AVP4	3	28	191139	jar rim
VAP4	1	8	191233	thick walled (17 mm)
Sand & quartz/quartzite etc				
AQM4	2	8	191387	thin walled sherds
QAPM5	2	126	191239	Radiocarbon date
QAZM4	5	30	191139	
Sand & unident. inclusions				
ARM3/4	1	10	190922	poss. related to above group
Total	30	405		

Seventeen sherds (203 g) certainly came from components (contexts 191068, 191072, 191169, 191214, 191233 and 191303) of the segmented ditch adjacent to the pit alignment. All of these were in sand or sand/organic/clay pellet fabrics. Further sherds came from context 191139, the fill of ditch section 191138, which may also have been a component of the segmented ditch. This small but significant group contained sherds of fabrics QAZM4 and AVP4 and in addition was the only one on the site to produce Late Iron Age material. The hand-made sherds could, but need not, have been residual. The Late Iron Age sherds, two each in grog-tempered GA3) and sand-tempered (AV3) 'Belgic type' fabrics (13 g and 38 g respectively), were from wheel-thrown vessels, one an everted rim jar with a cordoned shoulder (Fig. 176, 2).

The remaining material came from features of uncertain or Romano-British date.

List of illustrated sherds (Fig. 176)

1. Fabric AVP4, black. Everted tip of jar rim, context 191139
2. Fabric AV3, black. Everted rim jar with cordoned shoulder as Thompson (1982) type B3. Vestigial burnish on neck and shoulder, context 191139

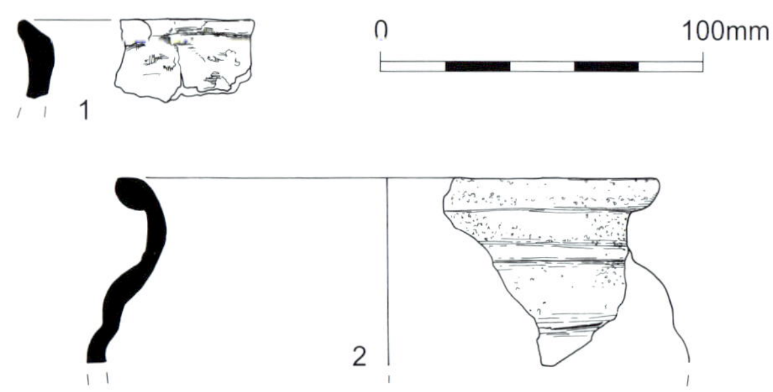

Fig. 176 Iron Age pottery

Romano-British pottery, by Ruth Leary

In total, 823 sherds (11,825 g) of Romano-British pottery were found. An archive catalogue was compiled for all the pottery according to the standard laid down by the Study Group for Romano-British Pottery (Darling 2004). Pottery was recorded detailing specific fabrics and forms, decorative treatment, condition, cross-joins/same vessel and was quantified by sherd count, weight and rim percentage values, giving estimated vessel equivalents. All the pottery from the site was catalogued in the archive and the stratified pottery was examined in order to date the features. Key groups are illustrated and catalogued below (Fig. 177) and unillustrated material is summarised (see Chapter 28 for the detailed fabric descriptions).

Table 127 Romano-British pottery from the enclosure ditches

Ware group	*Ware*	*Form*	*Count*	*Wt (g)*	*Rim%*	*Rel % count*	*Rel % wt*	*Rel % EVEs*
BB1	BB1		3	4.0		1.11	0.20	
	BB1	plain rim jar	7	149.6	25	2.58	7.36	10.78
	BB1	jar	19	77.5		7.01	3.81	
	BB1	necked jar	2	41.0	22	0.74	2.02	9.48
	BB1	splayed rim jar	2	28.3	16	0.74	1.39	6.90
BB1 total			*33*	*300.4*	*63*	*12.18*	*14.78*	*27.16*
DBY	DBY		1	4.1		0.37	0.20	
F	NV	rouletted beaker	1	1.6		0.37	0.08	
M	ROX/RSOX	Young 1977, C100 or WC7	1	23.3	7	0.37	1.15	3.02
NP	NP		1	40.8		0.37	2.01	
O	O		6	50.4		2.21	2.48	
	O1		1	2.8		0.37	0.14	
	O2		1	4.8		0.37	0.24	
	O4		1	1.7		0.37	0.08	
	O5	n-necked jar	3	26.7	15	1.11	1.31	6.47
O total			*12*	*86.4*	*15*	*4.43*	*4.26*	*6.47*
R	R12		5	34.7		1.85	1.71	
	R13		1	9.5		0.37	0.47	
	R2		3	19.4		1.11	0.95	
	R2		1	65.9		0.37	3.24	
	R2	w-mouthed jar	1	38.9	8	0.37	1.91	3.45
	R2/5		1	10.5		0.37	0.52	
	R2/5	flat rim bowl	1	25.1	8	0.37	1.23	3.45
	R21	bowl	2	24.3	9	0.74	1.20	3.88
	R21	w-mouthed jar	2	7.5	1	0.74	0.37	0.43
	R22		3	107.9		1.11	5.31	
	R25		1	4.3		0.37	0.21	
	R4		2	3.0		0.74	0.15	
	R4	bead-rim small jar	18	12.2	11	0.37	0.60	4.74
	R5		63	83.3		2.95	4.10	
	R5		3	374.7		23.25	18.43	
	R7		1	13.3		1.11	0.65	
	R8		2	10.8		0.37	0.53	
	R8		6	25.9		0.74	1.27	
	R9		10	13.5		2.21	0.66	
	R9	handled beaker	117	74.8		3.69	3.68	
R total				*959.5*	*37*	*43.17*	*47.20*	*15.95*
S	TS		5	5.7		1.11	0.28	
	TS		3	102.6		1.85	5.05	
S total			*8*	*108.3*		*2.95*	*5.33*	
	SV1		6	77.7		2.21	3.82	
	SV1	n-necked jar	5	80.7		1.85	3.97	
	SV1	tankard	1	15.2	12	0.37	0.75	5.17
	SV3		5	3.5		1.85	0.17	
	SV3	tankard	2	29.9		0.74	1.47	
	SV4	tankard/beaker	70	222.2	79	25.83	10.93	34.05
	SV4	n-necked jar	7	69.4	19	2.58	3.41	8.19
SV total			*96*	*498.6*	*110*	*35.42*	*24.53*	*47.41*
W	FLA3		1	9.8		0.37	0.48	
Total			271	2033	232			

List of illustrated sherds (Fig. 177) and discussion of stratified groups

Enclosure 1

Ditches

A total of 271 sherds (2033 g) was recovered from the Enclosure 1 ditches (Table 127). The average sherd weight was only 7 g and many were undiagnostic scraps. The most closely dated sherd from this part of the site, a mortarium rim made at the Oxfordshire kilns and dated to the 4th century, came from modern disturbance above ditch 190006 (section 190714). BB1 sherds from late jars with obtuse lattice burnish came from ditch 190145 (fill 190750, section 190748) and ditch 190012 (fill 190739, section 190740), and rim sherds from two jars with splayed rims came from ditch 190145 (fill 190749, section 190748). This type has been dated at *Vindolanda* to before AD 223–225 and can now be dated as early as AD 215/6 from evidence at Cramond, and it continued in use through the 4th century (B. Ford 2003, 59). A colour-coated sherd from a rouletted beaker dating to the late 2nd–early 3rd centuries (*cf.* Perrin 1999, 93) was present in ditch 190145 (fill 190662, section 190659) and probably came from the Nene Valley potteries.

An SV4 jar (Fig. 177, No. 2) may be contemporary with the BB1 jar while the cordoned bowl belongs to an earlier phase in the occupation. An R9 body sherd with the stump of a handle may come from a locally made tankard but not enough of the vessel survived to reconstruct the form. Samian ware from the ditches was dated to the mid–late Antonine period and the remaining body sherds were not closely datable. The absence of the finer reduced wares such as R15 and R16 and any early forms such as Flavian–Trajanic jars suggests that infilling took place after the mid-2nd century. The large proportion of Severn Valley wares, in later fabric types, would support this date range while the BB1 sherds indicate activity in the late 2nd–early 3rd centuries and perhaps extending later into the mid-3rd century. Most of the datable sherds indicate activity in the mid–late 2nd or early 3rd century.

1. R21 bowl with upright rim and cordon outside upper body. May be a cordoned, carinated bowl of type common in late 1st–early 2nd centuries, *cf.* Green 2002, fig. 38 B3 from a 1st century phase. Fabric and form suggest date early in this period. Although plain examples with upright rims are common in the published assemblages from Wall (Round 1990–1, no. 20; 1981–2, nos 44, 53 and 161) examples with cordons seem less so. 24 g RE 9%. This is earlier than most of the datable sherds from the enclosure ditches. Ditch 190006, s. 190594, fill 190597
2. SV4 rim and neck of narrow-necked jar with hooked rim, *cf.* Webster 1976, no. 4, dated 2nd–4th centuries. This is a long-lived form but given the coarser fabric, unlike the fine vesicular Severn Valley ware of the 1st and 2nd centuries, a date in the second half of the 2nd century or later is likely. 69 g RE 19%. Ditch 190145, s. 190836, fill 190838
3. SV1 tankard, *cf.* Webster 1976, no. 42, 2nd–3rd centuries. 15 g RE 12%. Ditch 1900012, s. 190740, upper fill 190739
4. Very fragmented and abraded SV4 carinated bowl with bead rim. Not readily paralleled in the Severn Valley repertoire. Carinated tankards are known from Gloucester, dated late 1st–2nd centuries and it is noted that they continue to be made later in the 2nd century (Rawes 1982, type 152–4). Quite a small diameter, *c* 140 mm, which is large for a tankard but too small for the type of carinated bowls found in reduced wares on Site 12 (see above). A similar vessel in a reduced ware from Tiddington came from a late 2nd century group (Booth 1996a, fig. 27, no. 450). 222 g RE 79%. Ditch 190012, s. 190740, upper fill 190739
5. BB1 plain rim dish. This appears to be undecorated except for all over burnish and in profile is similar to those of late 2nd–early 3rd century type. Holbrook and Bidwell have demonstrated that plain dishes such as this were produced from the 2nd century although they became more common in the 3rd–4th centuries (1999, 99–100, *cf.* fig. 32, no. 56.1b, late 2nd–early 3rd centuries). 111 g RE 15%. Ditch 190012, s. 190740, upper fill 190739
6. BB1 plain rim dish with intersecting arcade decoration, *cf.* Gillam 1976, nos 77–9, late 2nd–early 3rd centuries. 39 g RE 15%. Ditch 190012, s. 190740, upper fill 190739
7. R12 flat-rim bowl, copying 2nd century BB1 types. 25 g RE 8%. Ditch 190012, s. 190740, upper fill 190739
8. BB1 necked jar, mid–late 2nd century, *cf.* Gillam 1976, nos 3 and 4. 41 g RE 22%. Ditch 190012, s. 190740, upper fill 190739
9. O5 narrow-necked jar with blunt-ended, everted rim, slightly bifid suggesting 3rd century date in comparison with the Severn Valley ware types (see No. 28). 27 g RE 15%. Ditch 190145, s. 190659, top fill 190662
10. R2 wide-mouthed jar with thickened everted rim. Similar to forms from the Shenstone kiln. Probably late 2nd–early 3rd centuries. 39 g RE 8%. Ditch 190145, s. 190659, top fill 190662
11. BB1 small jar with bead rim, *cf.* Gillam 1976, no. 24, probably 2nd century. 12 g RE 11%. Ditch 190012, s. 190757, fill 190758
12. BB1 jar with splayed rim with burnt matter on the neck. A late form, *cf.* Gillam 1976, no. 8, mid-3rd century. 12 g RE 6%. A second rim of this type was present. Ditch 190145, s. 190749, fill 190749

Other material from ditch 190012 (section 190930, fill 190931) included R8 sherds from a wide-mouthed jar with bead rim, a sherd from a BB1 lid or possibly a plain rim dish, an R2 jar in a form copying a BB1 jar of the early–mid 2nd century, sherds from two MH2 mortaria bases and much of a late 2nd–early 3rd century MH2 mortarium similar to No. 30. Infilling during the second half of the 2nd century to early 3rd century would be consistent with these types.

Hollow 190048, layer 190702

A group of 26 sherds (717 g) were found in layer 190702. The diagnostic sherds give a consistent date in the late 2nd–early 3rd century. A samian ware sherd of Hadrianic or Antonine date was also recovered.

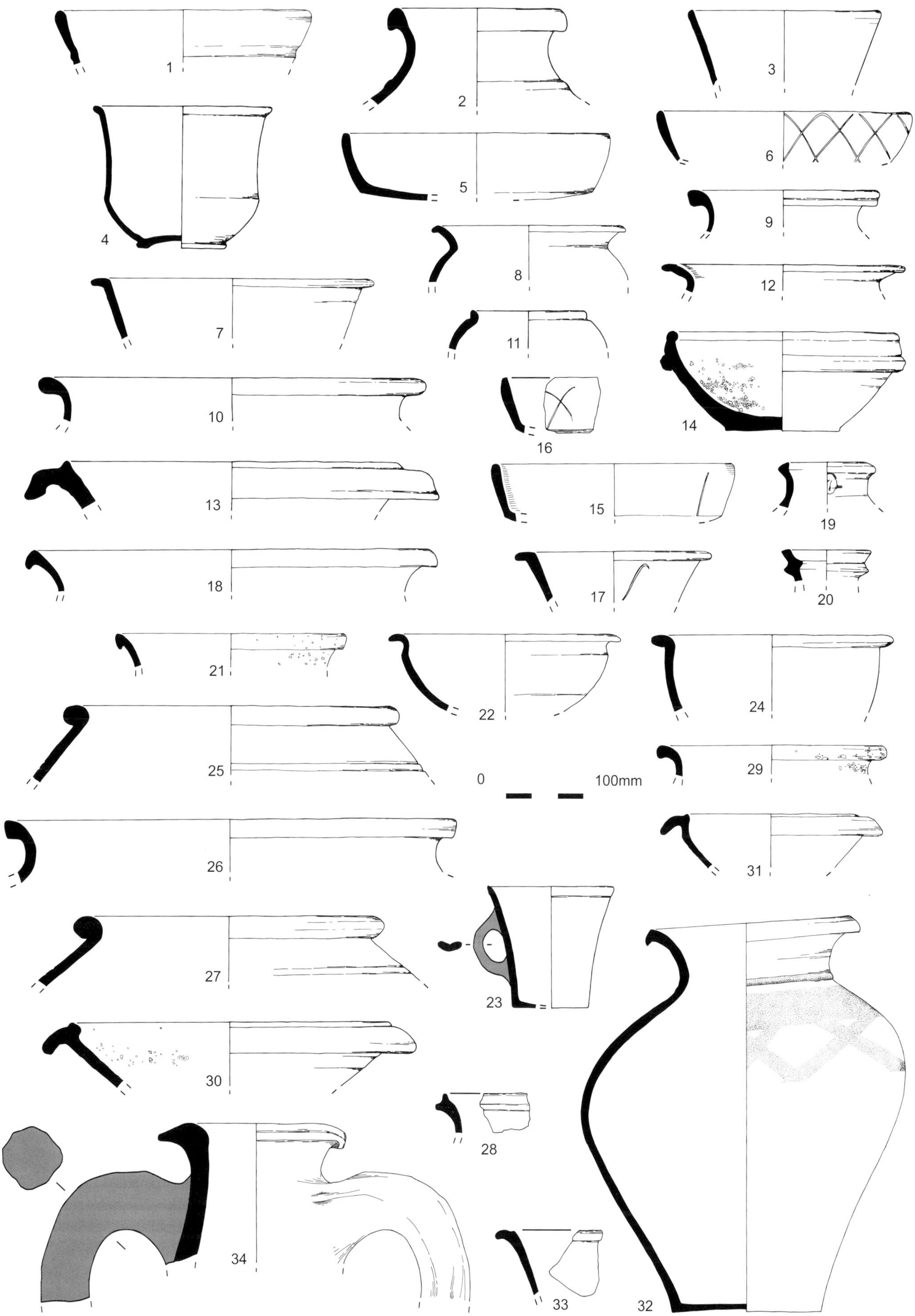

Fig. 177 Romano-British pottery

13. MH1 bead and flange mortarium, mid–late 2nd century, *cf.* Evans 2002b, M72 dated AD 140–80. 126 g RE 6%
14. MH2 collared mortarium. This form is not readily matched but it seems to be a variation on the collared mortaria of the late 2nd–mid-3rd centuries. Probably late 2nd–early 3rd, *cf.* Evans 2002b, M 85 dated AD 170–220. 187 g RE 9%
15. BB1 profile of plain rim dish with traces of burnished lattice decoration, *cf.* Gillam 1976, nos 77–8, late 2nd–early 3rd centuries. 27 g RE 6%
16. BB1 profile of plain rim dish with burnished intersecting arcs on the walls, *cf.* Gillam 1976, nos 77–8, late 2nd–early 3rd centuries. 24 g RE 4%. A second dish of this type came from this context
17. BB1 flat rim bowl or dish with very faint traces of burnished intersecting arcs on the walls, a feature dating to the late 2nd century (Gillam 1976, 68). 21 g RE 3%
18. SV1 wide-mouthed jar with outbent neck and hooked rim, *cf.* Webster 1976, no. 24 dated late 2nd–early 3rd centuries. 50 g RE 9%
19. FLA3 splayed rim flagon with triangular rim and slightly internal rebate. *Cf.* at Catterick, Evans 2002b, type F8.4 dated 2nd century. This type is present at Mancetter-Hartshill and probably came from there. As a general form, triangular rim flagons seem to be particularly common in late 2nd century groups and similar vessels are present in a late 2nd century group from Tiddington (Booth 1996a, fig. 28, nos 494–5) and Coleshill (Booth 2006, 152, fig. 43, no. 281). 19 g RE 32%
20. FLA3 pulley rim flagon with internal cup, *cf.* Evans *et al.* 2000 F2.61 and 62; Gillam (1970) no. 6 dated AD 120–200 and no. 16 dated AD 175–250. *Cf.* also at Catterick, Evans 2002b, type F6 L2–E3. 24 g RE 50%

Pit 190015 (quadrants 190558/569)

This feature produced 15 sherds including the neck of an R5 wide-mouthed jar, seven CT sherds, two FLA3 sherds, one R13 sherd, a scrap of a NV1 beaker with barbotine decoration of the mid-/late 2nd century or later and two sherds of a CTA2 hooked-rim jar of late 3rd–4th century date.

21. CTA2 hooked-rim jar. Rilled body sherds from this feature probably belong with this rim. Brown 1994, nos 248–9, 302 15 g RE 10%, context 190583

Pit 190034 (SW quadrant 190710, and NE quadrant 190707)

Thirteen sherds were recovered from this feature: two BB1 sherds from a jar and bowl or dish, an R9 sherd and the flange of a MH2 mortarium of mid–late 2nd century form (*cf.* Gillam 1970, no. 253) from 190712 and a Severn Valley type bowl of 2nd–3rd century type; the eight sherds of fabrics R2, R13, O2, SV1 and FLA3 from context 190709 were abraded and undiagnostic.

22. SV4 abraded sherd from a bowl with curved out rim, cf Webster 1976, no. 36, dated 2nd–3rd centuries, *cf.* Lee and Lindquist 1994, O379. Similar vessels were made at Wilderspool (Hartley and Webster 1973, nos 49 and 51). 36 g RE 8%, context 190711

Pit 190027

23. SV1 very abraded sherds from a tankard with 2 ribbed handle, *cf.* Webster 1976, nos 42–3, late 2nd–3rd centuries; *cf.* Lee and Lindquist 1994, O267. 53 g RE 6%, context 190557

Posthole 190032

Sherds from a MH bead and flange mortarium (198 g RE 13%) in the same form as No. 13, mid–late 2nd century, were recovered from the post packing, context 190537, as were 31 sherds from a Dressel 20 amphora

Pit 190031

Samian ware sherd from a form 37 or 38 bowl, Hadrianic or Antonine.

Curved gully 190011 (section 190542)

An abraded rim sherd from a Nene Valley colour-coated flanged bowl (13 g RE 8%) of late 3rd–4th century date came from context 190543. This vessel was burnt.

Curved gully 190144 (section 190679)

An abraded scrap of rim (3 g RE 5%) came from fill 190680. This was similar to that found on carinated bowls of 2nd century type but was too small for precise dating.

Pit 190118

One handmade CT sherd came from upper fill 190726. This was partially oxidised and had traces of combing or rilling. The fabric compared well with a CTA1 rebated-rim jar from Site 29 and the handmade character of the sherd suggests it belongs to this group, dating to the late 1st–mid-2nd centuries.

Forty-three sherds of Romano-British pottery from uppermost fill 190727 included undiagnostic sherds in fabrics R5, R12, and R13. The forms present (Nos 24–7) suggest a date perhaps in the second half of the 2nd century. The wide-mouthed jar is similar to those made in the Shenstone kiln. The two narrow-mouthed jars/storage jars compare with some jars from Tiddington in late 2nd century groups (Booth 1996a, fig. 71, nos 1478 and 1489) made in a distinctive vesicular grey ware unlike the fabrics of Nos 25 and 27. It is difficult to date this form, but very similar types were made in the East Midlands and South Yorkshire characterised by Buckland (*et al.* 2001) as type F. These are made with or without handles or lugs. The Yorkshire examples were present in the Antonine kilns at Rossington Bridge, Doncaster and continued in use into the 4th century. The flat-rim bowl seems to be copying the well-known BB1 bowls and dishes in both form and fabric. A date in the second half of the 2nd century or early 3rd century is likely for this form.

24. R12 flat-rim bowl with rounded body 206 g RE 50%, context 190727
25. R5 narrow-necked jar with bead rim and double groove on the shoulder. The rim is distorted. 350 g RE 13%, context 190727
26. R24 wide-mouthed jar with blunt-ended everted rim. 72 g RE 8%, context 190727
27. R11 narrow-mouthed jar with bead rim and double grooves on the shoulder. 146 g RE 6%, context 190727

Droveway ditches

Fifty-seven sherds (596 g) of Romano-British pottery came from the ditch fills of the droveway. This material was predominantly late in date including Oxfordshire red colour-coated ware, pink grogged ware and late shell-tempered ware. A fine white sherd from the primary fill appeared to have a dark colour coat although the identification of this sherd was compounded by the presence of post-burial deposits adhering to the surface. The fabric was exceptionally fine and unlike Nene Valley wares. If colour-coated it is likely to be an import such as Cologne ware but the condition precludes certainty. A PNK GT body sherd from uppermost fill 190548 (section 190544) gives a date in the late 3rd–4th centuries and this is supported by sherds from an Oxfordshire red colour-coated ware bowl type C46 of 4th century date which was burnt along the broken edge. Another badly burnt vessel, a BB1 plain rim dish similar to Nos 15 and 16 dated to the late 2nd–early 3rd centuries, came from uppermost fill 191038 (section 191034). This fill also contained 24 abraded R5 sherds from the body, rim and base of a wide-mouthed jar with simple everted rim. This compared well with the products of the Shenstone kiln but was in a finer fabric and probably dated to the mid 2nd century. The diagnostic sherds suggest infilling during the late 2nd–3rd centuries with material reaching the ditches as late as the 4th century.

28. R2 narrow-necked jar with bifid rim with slight internal rebate. Narrow-necked jars with bifid rims date to the 3rd century in the Severn Valley ware range (Webster 1976, nos 10–11). 78 g RE 25%. Ditch 190008, s. 191034, fill 190138
29. CTA2 everted-rim jar, *cf.* Brown 1994, nos 178, 248 and 299–318, from late 3rd–4th centuries. 19 g RE 10%. Ditch 190008, s. 191105, 191106
30. MH2 mortarium with bead slightly above the flange, which is curved, going down quite steeply with thicker distal end, *cf.* Gillam 253 dated AD 180–230. The type post-dates the practice of stamping and is closely matched in mortaria found in Kiln 2 at Mancetter (unpublished), *cf.* Evans 2002b, M81 AD 160–210. 83 g RE 8%. Ditch 190008, s. 191105, 191106

Field boundaries

In total, 93 abraded sherds of Romano-British pottery were retrieved from field boundary ditch 190231 (section 190201). These included very abraded fragments from a fine oxidised vessel, from lower fill 191200, in fabric SV1. The small diameter, upright walls and bead rim suggest a Severn Valley tankard of fairly early date, in the 2nd century. The only other sherd from this fill was an undiagnostic R4 sherd. A dump of material in fill 191243 (section 191242) included sherds from a BB1 flat-rim bowl or dish, a type common in the Antonine period, an R2 jar with wavy line combed decoration and body sherds of R3 and SV1. The jar, decorated with combed wavy lines, was too fragmentary for its form to be sure but comparable decorative zones are found on conical jars of the late 1st–early 2nd centuries at Alcester (Lee and Lindquist 1994, R148). Upper fill 191372 (section 191370) contained a neck sherd from an SV3 wide-mouthed jar of 1st–2nd century type (Webster 1976, nos 19–20). These few sherds suggest a date range in the 2nd century.

Only 19 sherds (254 g) were found in ditch 190020 to the west, but these included a second SV3 tankard of similar type to that found in ditch 190231 (but too fragmentary to aid dating) as well as the rim of an O5 tankard or bowl, the base of a CTA1 jar, an R2 jar base and undiagnostic body sherds of FLA3 and R2. A flanged hemispherical bowl was also present and dates to the 2nd century.

31. R16 flanged, hemispherical bowl. 26 g RE 20%. Ditch 190020, s. 190643, fill190644

The 29 sherds (851 g) from ditch 190019 came from single rapid fill 190937 (section 190736) and comprised body sherds of a Dressel 20 amphora, an MH2 mortarium, SV1, and an SV5 narrow-necked jar of 2nd–3rd century type.

32. SV5 narrow-necked jar with everted rim. Cf. Webster 1976, type 5. Seventeen sherds. The rim was distorted and looked overfired. This compared well with a large group of sherds from 190931 and 190932 which were also distorted and looked overfired. A rim sherd from 190932 joined that from 190937 and all are used in the illustration. 295 g RE 18%

Other pottery

33. BB1 grooved flanged rim bowl, *cf.* Gillam 1976, no. 42 dating to the late 2nd–mid//late 3rd century (Holbrook and Bidwell 1999, 98 type F). 23 g RE 3%. Unphased ditch 190004, s. 190502, fill 190503
34. Dr20 amphora rim and handle section. 776 g RE 45%. Unphased ditch 190005, s. 190512

The assemblage suggests occupation centred on the second half of the 2nd century and the first half of the 3rd century with continued ceramic deposition as late as the 4th century. Unstratified finds included an abraded, incomplete rim sherd which seems to be from an Oxfordshire red colour-coated ware bowl dating to the mid–late 4th century (Young 1977, C93). Fragments of two more late BB1 jars with splayed rims were also found in unstratified levels and an MH2 reeded rim mortarium with four reeds came from unlocated ditch segment 191117, fill 191125. This vessel may be compared with mortaria dated elsewhere to the 3rd century (eg Cramond, Hartley 2003, nos 34–5, 200–260).

Pottery distribution

Of 87 contexts, 67 had ten or fewer sherds and 57 had an average sherd weight of less than 10 g. Larger sherd groups in the Enclosure 1 ditches, from feature 190017, field boundary ditch 190231 and droveway ditch 190009 were all abraded with an average sherd weight of less than 10 g. Pit 190118, hollow 190048, and post hole 190032 had larger sherds with an average sherd weight of 20 g, 28 g and 29 g respectively, the last being due to the robust mortarium and amphora sherds. The Enclosure 1 outer ditch (190012, section 190930) included very well preserved sherds weighing an average of 40 g.

Many of the features contained small groups of abraded pottery which had fallen into accumulation deposits in earth dug features. The group from ditch 190019 was larger and seemed to represent a deliberate deposit of ceramic material (fill 190937). This group included a possible waster and conjoining sherd.

Droveway ditch 190009 also contained a group of some 40 sherds (section 191034, fill 191038) and a similar sized group was found in field boundary ditch 190231 (section 191242, fill 191243). A larger group of around 190 sherds came from an upper fill (190739, section 190740) of Enclosure 1 ditch 190012. The material from the field system ditch and the enclosure ditches seem to be deliberate dumps. A similar pattern of relatively clean earth dug features with discrete dumps of domestic debris was encountered on Site 15 (Shenstone, East of Birmingham Road Nurseries).

Other features had concentrations of ceramic debris, such as surface 190702 in hollow 190048, and posthole 190032. The former seems to consist of domestic debris preserved in the hollow above the cobbling, while the latter comprises sherds of amphora and a mortarium which may have been used as post packing, being the most robust ceramics of the range available. Amphora sherds were used as a post-pad in a posthole excavated at High St, Doncaster (context 699, Leary 2004). Pit 190118 had a group of some 40 sherds in the final fill and pit 190015 had a small deposit of 13 sherds in the top fill. No pattern was detected in the make-up of these groups or those from the ditches, and they are interpreted as discrete deposits of domestic rubbish.

Functional groups and site status

Site 19 had relatively high numbers of bowls, dishes and flagons (Table 128). Compared with Midlands sites examined by Evans (2001, fig. 3) the assemblage falls on the border of rural sites with villa and urban sites. However, Booth has noted that a partiality for carinated bowls in north Warwickshire may distort the evidence of vessel types in use on sites in this region (Booth 1991, 8). The proportion of drinking vessels is also inflated by the number of tankards. This, however, may not reflect status as much as the local availability of tankards at this time. A similarly disproportionate number of drinking vessels was identified as a regional characteristic by Evans on Severn Valley rural sites (2001, 30 and fig. 7) for the same reason. The relatively high proportion of mortaria on the site may be a similar phenomenon – mortarium wasters from Sites 12, 13 and 15 suggest some local manufacture and this may have resulted in greater numbers of these vessels being readily available locally.

Table 128 Romano-British pottery: relative quantities of vessel types (RE)

Vessel type	*Rel %*
Amphora	4.4
Bowl	23.0
Bowl/dish	1.3
Dish	4.7
Flagon	8.1
Jar	10.8
Small jar/beaker	1.1
Mortaria	12.3
N-necked jar	21.8
Tankard/beaker	6.0
W-mouthed jar	7.0

This impression of relatively high status for a rural settlement was confirmed by the presence of several amphorae on the site as well as fine wares such as Oxfordshire red colour-coated ware, Nene Valley colour-coated wares and samian ware (Table 129). The numbers of fine wares were relatively low but fine and specialist wares combined (as Booth 1991) total just over 13% of the site assemblage, a figure which is higher than other rural Warwickshire sites (*ibid.*, fig. 2) such as Wasperton with only 4.9%, Stretton-on-Fosse at 8% and Tiddington at 7.9%. The amphora contribution is particularly notable as are the numbers of mortaria. The latter may however be linked with a ready supply of this specialist item at nearby potteries. The small size of the assemblage must also be taken into account when considering the amphora. The sherds seem to represent only two or three vessels. Although the number of amphora sherds is inflated as many came from a single vessel, this site, nonetheless, had more individual amphorae represented than any other site on the M6 Toll. This is the more notable given that Site 19 was further from the market centre of Wall than any of the other main M6 Toll Romano-British sites.

Pottery supply

In addition to locally produced coarse wares, Site 19 obtained pottery from several other sources including imported samian and amphora from Gaul and Baetica and possible colour-coated ware from Cologne (Table 129). British fine wares were acquired from the Nene Valley and Oxfordshire potteries and mortaria from Oxfordshire were also identified. Traded coarse wares include jars, bowls and dishes in BB1 from Dorset, jars from the Bedfordshire kilns at Harrold, Derbyshire ware jars probably from the Belper area in Derbyshire (if not locally produced), pink grogged ware from Buckinghamshire and Severn Valley ware vessels. The white wares compare with samples identified as from the Mancetter-Hartshill kilns and the white ware mortaria from the site compare with the products of that industry.

In addition some of the oxidised and reduced wares were probably obtained from local kilns such as those at Mancetter-Hartshill, Perry Barr and Sherifoot Lane, whereas much may have been made locally in kilns including and preceding the Shenstone kiln. The fabrics produced at the Shenstone kilns accounted for over a third of the reduced wares and the form of the wide-mouthed jar made in R5, the most common reduced ware on the site, demonstrates a close typological link with the products of the Shenstone kiln, suggesting that this may be an earlier fabric or a finer variation. A small number of sherds with charcoal inclusions may come from the Severn Valley industry (fabrics R11 and R21) and one vessel with a very distinctive pale grey, almost white fabric, with dark grey surface is very similar to Nene Valley grey ware and may come from that pottery.

Table 129 Romano-British pottery: quantification of fabrics and wares

Ware group	Ware	Fabric	Count	Wt (g)	Rel % count	Rel % wt
A	DR20	DR20	35	1188.7	4.25	10.05
BB1	BB1	BB1	93	731.5	11.30	6.19
C	CT	CT	2	1.1	0.24	0.01
	CT	CTOX	3	6.5	0.36	0.05
	CTA1	CTA1	4	58.7	0.49	0.50
	CTA2	CTA2	6	33.9	0.73	0.29
	CTB1	CTB1	5	22.4	0.61	0.19
C Total			*20*	*122.6*	*2.43*	*1.04*
DBY	DBY	DBY	2	9.3	0.24	0.08
F	KOL	KOL?	4	9.4	0.49	0.08
	NV	NV	1	1.6	0.12	0.01
	NV	NV1	2	13.4	0.24	0.11
	ROX	ROX	2	31.5	0.24	0.27
F total			*9*	*55.9*	*1.09*	*0.47*
G	G	G	1	55.0	0.12	0.47
	PNK GT	PNK GT	1	45.6	0.12	0.39
G total			*2*	*100.6*	*0.24*	*0.85*
M	M	M	1	198.0	0.12	1.67
	MH	MH	3	168.7	0.36	1.43
	MH	MH2	37	2034.6	4.50	17.21
	ROX/RSOX	ROX or WSOX	1	23.3	0.12	0.20
M total			*42*	*2424.6*	*5.10*	*20.50*
O	O	O	6	50.4	0.73	0.43
	O1	O1	3	29.0	0.36	0.25
	O2	O2	3	9.3	0.36	0.08
	O4	O4	10	44.3	1.22	0.37
	O5	O5	5	38.2	0.61	0.32
	O6	O6	7	25.8	0.85	0.22
O total			*34*	*197*	*4.13*	*1.67*
R	R1	R1	1	8.1	0.12	0.07
	R11	R11	5	149.8	0.61	1.27
	R12	R12	25	340.0	3.04	2.88
	R13	R13	4	22.8	0.49	0.19
	R16	R16	1	26.1	0.12	0.22
	R2	R2	91	1023.5	11.06	8.66
	R2	R2?	5	99.8	0.61	0.84
	R2/5	R2/5	2	35.6	0.24	0.30
	R21	R21	4	31.8	0.49	0.27
	R22	R22	5	336.4	0.61	2.84
	R24	R24	1	72.2	0.12	0.61
	R25	R25	1	4.3	0.12	0.04
	R26	R26	1	11.2	0.12	0.09
	R27	R27	1	12	0.12	0.10
	R3	R3	12	77.9	1.46	0.66
	R4	R4	6	28.2	0.73	0.24
	R5	R5	120	1154.3	14.58	9.76
	R7	R7	23	222.6	2.79	1.88
	R8	R8	8	117.2	0.97	0.99
	R9	R9	45	253.3	5.47	2.14
R total			*361*	*4027.1*	*43.86*	*34.06*
S	TS	TS	12	169.1	1.46	1.43
SV	SV1	SV1	50	541.2	6.08	4.58
	SV3	SV3	9	58.1	1.09	0.49
	SV3	SV3?	1	16.4	0.12	0.14
	SV4	SV4	78	328.0	9.48	2.77
	SV5	SV5	62	1694.0	7.53	14.33
SV total			*200*	*2637.7*	*24.30*	*22.31*
W	FLA2	FLA2?	1	3.7	0.12	0.03
	FLA3	FLA3	12	156.9	1.46	1.33
W total			*13*	*160.6*	*1.58*	*1.36*
Total			823	11824		

A large number of vessels were in oxidised fabrics comparable to Severn Valley or Severn Valley type wares in the Warwickshire fabric series. These were either of the fine, almost inclusionless type or had charcoal inclusions. Production of tankards of Severn Valley ware type is known at Perry Barr and some of the coarser examples on Site 19 may have come from there. A waster in distinctively hard orange ware, SV5, which compares with a Warwickshire fabric thought to be from the Severn Valley, raises the possibility that some of the oxidised wares may have been made in the vicinity of Wall. This fabric has also been identified by the author at Rocester in later phases (Leary forthcoming a) and this only serves to highlight the difficulties encountered in distinguishing the coarser Severn Valley wares from local oxidised wares.

If, for example, fabrics SV4 and 5 are local wares, the Severn Valley ware contribution to the ceramics shrinks to only 7%. In addition two vessels in SV4 and SV5 accounted for 70 and 38 sherds respectively and if these are counted as a single sherd each, this reduces the overall proportion of SV wares to *c* 13% by count. This contrasts with Coleshill (less than 1% in group 3539, 3rd–4th century) but compares well with Tiddington where oxidised wares made up 12–18% of the site assemblages and of these oxidised wares, Severn Valley wares totalled over 70%. The low numbers of Severn Valley wares at Coleshill are balanced by the oxidised wares attributed there to the nearby Mancetter-Hartshill kilns, and it may be that competition from the local kilns resulted in the Severn Valley potteries being disadvantaged. At Tiddington, a similar phenomenon is observed during the period when the Tiddington kiln produced oxidised ware and the Severn Valley ware contribution concomitantly dropped. At Metchley, Severn Valley oxidised wares make up 43% of the total assemblage from the site (Hancocks 2004, 48–9) and in the later phase 4 27% of the group was oxidised Severn Valley ware.

Table 130 Medieval pottery: quantification of total assemblage

Fabric	*No.*	*wt(g)*	*%no.*	*% wt*
MP02	2	19	0.60	0.38
MP10	44	1531	13.10	30.70
Roman	2	7	0.60	0.14
RS01	5	63	1.49	1.26
Sg12	1	2	0.30	0.04
SLM10	4	78	1.19	1.56
SLM12.1	2	25	0.60	0.50
SLM13	1	8	0.30	0.16
SLM13.4	5	96	1.49	1.93
SLM20	16	465	4.76	9.32
Sq04	10	262	2.98	5.25
Sq08	2	17	0.60	0.34
Sq11	19	94	5.65	1.88
Sq20	2	5	0.60	0.10
Sq20.2	12	55	3.57	1.10
Sq20.3	4	33	1.19	0.66
Sq20.4	12	75	3.57	1.50
Sq30	28	1003	8.33	20.11
SV40	1	8	0.30	0.16
TG	2	1	0.60	0.02
WW01.1	44	446	13.10	8.94
WW01.4	106	644	31.55	12.91
WW01.5	8	36	2.38	0.72
WW04	3	13	0.89	0.26
Modern glazed ware	1	1	0.30	0.02
Total	336	4987		

Medieval pottery, by Stephanie Rátkai

A small medieval assemblage consisting of 336 sherds was recovered from numerous, mainly linear, cut features (Tables 130 and 131). The disuse of these features has been dated by the pottery present but with the caveat that the excavated sections from which the pottery was drawn represent only a very small sample of the contents of that feature. The overall average sherd weight was 14.9 g. However, for all but three features the average sherd weight was under 15 g and for most features under 10 g. This is fairly consistent with general pottery scatters being incorporated into ditch and other feature fills. The three features with above average sherd weights were post-medieval/modern ditch 190148 and pond 190167, the material from the latter found among the cobbles at its edge.

Three dating criteria were used. First what could be termed the 'whiteware horizon'. Whitewares are a particularly distinctive feature of north Warwickshire and south Staffordshire assemblages. As yet there is no firm dating for when they were first manufactured but a date around the middle of the 13th century is generally accepted. By the later 13th and 14th centuries these wares were dominant. Therefore features containing over 50% of whitewares were given a later 13th–14th century date. Features containing a smaller proportion of whitewares were dated *c* 1250–1275 and features without whitewares to before *c* 1250. The presence of Chilvers Coton C wares has been taken as indicating a 14th or 15th century date and features with Midlands Purple or late oxidised wares were dated to the 15th–16th centuries. Using the above criteria three tentative time frames could be established for activity on the site.

The earliest feature appeared to be a pit 190165 which contained cooking pot sherds in Coventry-type ware (WCTS Sq 20.4) and WCTS Sq11, giving a general date range of *c* 1150–1250. The residual occurrence of further Coventry-type ware sherds confirmed activity of this date on the site, although overall they only made up 9% by sherd count (3.4% by sherd weight) of the entire medieval assemblage. The earliest significant post-Romano-British occupation would therefore seem to have dated to the same period as that at Wishaw (Site 20) to the south. Coventry-type

Table 131 Medieval pottery: quantification by sherd count and context

Feature	Context	MGW	MP02	MP10	Roman	RS01	Sg12	SLM10	SLM12.1	SLM13	SLM13.4	SLM20	Sq04	Sq08	Sq11	Sq20	Sq20.2	Sq20.3	Sq20.4	Sq30	Sv40	TG	WW01.1	WW01.4	WW01.5	WW04	Total
Ditch 190008	190886	–	–	–	–	–	–	–	–	–	–	–	–	–	–	–	2	–	–	–	–	–	–	–	–	–	2
Ditch 190008	191037	1	–	–	–	1	–	–	–	–	–	–	–	–	3	–	1	–	1	–	–	–	–	1	–	–	8
Ditch 190009	190939	–	–	–	–	–	–	–	–	–	–	–	–	–	–	–	–	–	1	–	–	–	2	–	–	–	3
Ditch 190019	190937	–	–	–	–	–	–	–	–	–	–	–	–	1	–	–	–	–	–	–	–	–	–	1	–	–	2
Ditch 190019	190982	–	–	–	–	–	–	–	–	–	–	–	–	–	–	–	–	–	–	–	–	–	–	1	–	–	1
Ditch 190053	190903	–	–	–	–	–	–	–	–	–	–	–	–	–	–	–	–	–	–	–	–	–	–	1	–	–	1
Ditch 190053	190914	–	–	–	–	–	–	–	–	–	–	–	–	–	–	–	–	–	–	–	–	–	–	1	–	–	1
Ditch 190053	190972	–	–	–	–	–	–	–	–	–	–	–	–	–	–	–	–	–	1	–	–	–	–	6	–	–	7
Ditch 190053	190973	–	–	–	–	1	–	–	–	–	–	–	–	–	3	–	–	–	–	–	–	–	1	–	–	–	5
Ditch 190063	191073	–	–	–	–	–	–	–	–	–	–	–	–	–	1	–	–	1	1	–	–	–	1	1	–	–	5
Pit 190064	190878	–	–	–	–	–	–	–	–	–	–	–	–	–	–	–	–	–	–	–	–	–	2	–	–	–	2
Pit 190065	190868	–	–	–	–	3	–	–	–	–	–	–	–	–	–	–	–	–	–	–	–	–	–	38	–	–	41
Ditch 190082	190729	–	–	–	–	–	–	–	–	–	–	–	–	–	1	–	–	–	–	–	–	–	2	2	–	–	5
Ditch 190082	190730	–	–	–	–	–	–	–	1	–	–	–	–	–	–	–	–	–	–	–	–	–	–	1	–	–	2
Feature 190098	190675	–	–	–	–	–	–	–	–	–	–	–	–	–	–	–	–	1	–	–	–	–	–	10	–	–	11
Feature 190098	190676	–	–	–	–	–	–	–	–	–	–	–	–	–	–	–	–	–	–	–	–	–	–	2	–	1	3
Ditch 190145	190699	–	–	–	–	–	–	–	–	–	–	–	–	–	–	–	–	–	–	–	–	–	–	1	–	–	1
Ditch 190148	191002	–	–	–	–	–	–	–	–	–	–	–	–	–	–	–	–	–	–	2	–	–	–	7	–	–	9
Ditch 190150	190954	–	–	–	–	–	–	–	–	–	–	–	–	1	–	–	–	–	–	–	–	–	1	–	–	–	2
Ditch 190150	190966	–	–	–	–	–	–	–	–	–	–	–	–	–	–	–	2	–	–	–	–	–	–	1	–	–	3
Ditch 190150	191056	–	–	–	–	–	–	–	–	–	–	–	–	–	–	2	–	–	–	–	1	–	–	–	–	–	3
Ditch 190150	191092	–	–	–	–	–	–	1	–	–	–	–	–	–	1	–	–	–	–	1	–	–	1	–	–	–	4
Ditch 190150	191109	–	–	–	–	–	–	1	–	–	–	–	–	–	–	–	–	–	–	–	–	–	–	–	–	1	2
Ditch 190152	191362	–	–	–	–	–	–	–	–	–	–	–	–	–	–	–	–	–	–	–	–	–	1	–	–	–	1
Feature 190165	190898	–	–	–	–	–	–	–	–	–	–	–	–	–	–	–	–	–	1	–	–	–	–	–	–	–	1
Feature 190165	190915	–	–	–	–	–	–	–	–	–	–	–	–	–	2	–	–	–	–	–	–	–	–	1	4	–	7
Feature 190165	190951	–	–	–	–	–	–	–	–	–	–	–	–	–	7	–	–	–	–	–	–	–	–	–	–	–	7
Pond 190167	191171	–	–	23	–	–	–	–	–	–	2	–	–	–	–	–	–	–	–	7	–	2	–	1	–	–	35
Pond 190167	191172	–	2	21	–	–	–	2	1	1	3	16	–	–	–	–	–	–	2	16	–	–	1	1	–	–	66
Pit 190899	190900	–	–	–	–	–	–	–	–	–	–	–	10	–	–	–	–	–	–	–	–	–	6	–	1	–	17
Treethrow 190983	190984	–	–	–	–	–	–	–	–	–	–	–	–	–	–	–	–	–	–	–	–	–	–	1	–	–	1
Treethrow 191008	191007	–	–	–	–	–	–	–	–	–	–	–	–	–	–	–	–	–	2	–	–	–	3	–	–	–	5
Treethrow 191009	191010	–	–	–	–	–	1	–	–	–	–	–	–	–	–	–	–	–	–	1	–	–	–	15	–	–	17
Treethrow 191091	191090	–	–	–	–	–	–	–	–	–	–	–	–	–	–	–	–	–	–	–	–	–	2	–	–	–	2
Treethrow 191111	191110	–	–	–	–	–	–	–	–	–	–	–	–	–	–	–	–	–	–	1	–	–	3	1	2	1	8

Table 131 continued

Feature	Context	MGW	MP02	MP10	Roman	RS01	Sg12	SLM10	SLM12.1	SLM13	SLM13.4	SLM20	Sq04	Sq08	Sq11	Sq20	Sq20.2	Sq20.3	Sq20.4	Sq30	Sv40	TG	WW01.1	WW01.4	WW01.5	WW04	Total
Ditch ?190876	190876	–	–	–	–	–	–	–	–	–	–	–	–	–	–	–	–	–	–	–	–	–	–	2	–	–	2
Ditch ?191011	191012	–	–	–	–	–	–	–	–	–	–	–	–	–	–	–	–	–	–	–	–	–	–	1	1	–	2
Ditch ?191133	191134	–	–	–	–	–	–	–	–	–	–	–	–	–	–	–	–	–	–	–	–	–	2	–	–	–	2
Ditch ?191138	191139	–	–	–	–	–	–	–	–	–	–	–	–	–	–	–	–	–	–	–	–	–	–	5	–	–	5
Ditch ?191140	191141	–	–	–	–	–	–	–	–	–	–	–	–	–	1	–	–	–	–	–	–	–	–	2	–	–	3
Ditch ?191199	191168	–	–	–	2	–	–	–	–	–	–	–	–	–	–	–	–	–	–	–	–	–	–	–	–	–	2
Ditch ?191218	191220	–	–	–	–	–	–	–	–	–	–	–	–	–	–	–	–	–	–	–	–	–	–	2	–	–	2
Ditch ?191218	191280	–	–	–	–	–	–	–	–	–	–	–	–	–	–	–	–	–	–	–	–	–	4	–	–	–	4
Layer	191387	–	–	–	–	–	–	–	–	–	–	–	–	–	–	–	7	2	3	–	–	–	12	–	–	–	24
Total count		1	2	44	2	5	1	4	2	1	5	16	10	2	19	2	12	4	12	28	1	2	44	106	8	3	336
Total weight		1	19	1531	7	63	2	78	25	8	96	465	262	17	94	5	55	33	75	1003	8	1	446	644	36	13	4987

? = context information lost

ware sherds tended to be found to the west of ditch 190053. Those outside the focal distribution were in ditch 190063 slightly to the east of 190053, in ditch 190154 and pond 109167.

Pit 190899 (fill 190900) and a ditch 190019 (fill 190937/190982) may have dated to *c* 1250–1275 but most of the remaining features contained a high proportion of whitewares and would therefore be more or less contemporary with activity associated with the disuse of the fish ponds on Wishaw (Site 20).

Features dated to the 15th–16th centuries only occurred in the northern part of the site. Ditch 190150 contained sandy late oxidised ware sherds (WCTS SLM10) dating to the 15th or 16th centuries (fills 191092 and 191109). The small proportion (by percentage of sherd weight) of the group taken up by Chilvers Coton C sherds may indicate that they were residual and hence the date of the disuse of the feature would lie in the 16th century rather than the 15th century. Pond 190167 (fills 191171 and 191172) appeared to contain deliberately dumped material (see above). The average sherd weight of Chilvers Coton C, and Midlands Purple ware and other late medieval wares (37.7 g and 46.7 g respectively) was in marked contrast to that of the residual whitewares and Coventry-type ware from the pond. The sherd size and relative proportion of the Chilvers Coton C sherds suggested that they were contemporary with the Midland Purple wares etc which would date this feature to the (probably later) 15th century.

The functional composition of the pottery was examined (Table 132). Four main categories of vessel form were present; cooking pots, bowls, jugs and jars/cisterns. Overall, cooking pots were best

Table 132 Medieval pottery: functional analysis (by no.)

Vessel type/function	*No.*
Food preparation/consumption	
bowl	45
Cooking/some food storage	
cooking pot/jar	139
pipkin	1
Liquid consumption	
jug	32
drinking vessel	2
Liquid storage	
cistern	4
jar/cistern	20
jug/jar/sistern	14
Storage	
jar	11
Unknown	71
Total	339

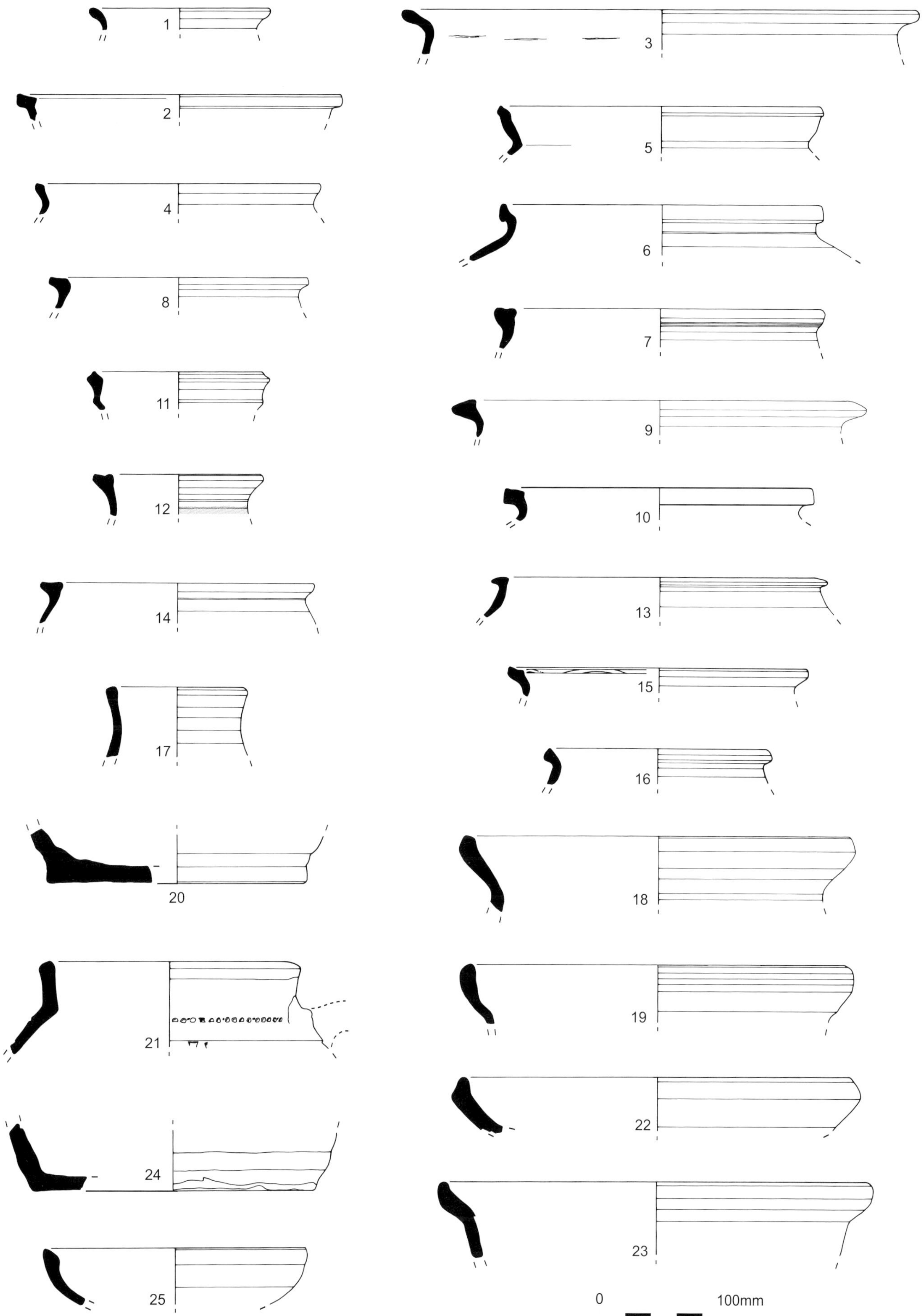

Fig. 178 Medieval pottery

represented, with a greater number of whiteware than iron-rich sherds. Whiteware bowls and jugs were equally represented and far outnumbered contemporary iron-rich wares. However, bowls were almost equally well represented amongst the 15th–16th century material whereas jugs were not. The preponderance of whiteware cooking pots was not seen at Wishaw (Site 20), where jugs and bowls were much better represented. The best represented late medieval form was the jar or cistern. The absence of Cistercian ware cup sherds, a normal find with cisterns, particularly, but not exclusively, on urban sites, was notable and the only ceramic drinking vessel was represented by two Tudor Green cup sherds. Tudor Green is not a common find in the West Midlands and certainly not on rural sites. This may reflect rather low socio-economic status of rural settlements or may reflect rather more 'old-fashioned' ceramic usage, where wooden drinking vessels were still the accepted norm. The absence of Cistercian ware may also be due to chronological factors, in which case activity on the site may have largely ceased before the end of the 15th century. A small assemblage of post-medieval pottery, mostly poorly-stratified, was collected on the site, but this was not examined by the writer.

List of illustrated vessels (Fig. 178)

1 Coventry-type ware, WCTS Sq20.3, cooking pot, sooted on exterior and on inner face of rim, internal and external abrasion, unstratified
2. Coventry-type ware, WCTS Sq20.3, bowl, exterior soot, unstratified
3. Coventry-type ware, WCTS Sq20.2, cooking pot, internal and external abrasion, unstratified
4. Coventry-type ware, WCTS Sq20.4, cooking pot, interior and exterior abrasion, unstratified
5. CPJ01 WCTS Sq11, cooking pot, interior and exterior abrasion, context 191037, ditch 190008, s.91036
6. Reduced Deritend ware, WCTS RS01, cooking pot, context 190868, pit 190065
7. WW01, WCTS WW01.4, cooking pot, context 190676, feature 190098
8. WW01, WCTS WW01.4, cooking pot, context 190675, feature 190098
9. WW05, WCTS WW01.4, cooking pot, context 190868, pit 190065
10. WW05, WCTS WW01.4, bowl/pipkin sooted on exterior and on inner face of rim, interior and exterior abrasion, context 191010, tree hollow 191009
11. WW01, WCTS WW01.4, jug, burnt, context 190699, ditch 190145, s.190695
12. WW04, WCTS WW01.5, jug, trace of exterior olive glaze and red slip decoration, context 190915, pit 190165
13. WW03, WCTS WW01.1, cooking pot, context 190878, pit 190064
14. WW03, WCTS WW01.1, cooking pot, exterior soot, context 191110, tree hollow 191111
15. WW03, WCTS WW01.1, cooking pot/pipkin heavy soot on exterior rim, glaze spots on interior rim surface, possibly incised wavy line on rim, unlocated context 191387
16. WW03, WCTS WW01.1, cooking pot, pinkish-brown surfaces, exterior sooting, unlocated context 191387

Pond 190167

17. Chilvers Coton C, WCTS Sq30, jug/jar, context 191172
18. Chilvers Coton C, WCTS Sq30, bowl, context 191172
19. Chilvers Coton C, WCTS Sq30, bowl, pale olive glaze spot on exterior, context 191172
20. Chilvers Coton C?, WCTS Sq30?, crude jar or bowl base, straight-wired base, thin, patchy, abraded olive-brown glaze on interior, context 191172
21. Midlands Purple ware WCTS MP10, jar, internal and external purple-brown slip, trace of crude roller stamping on exterior, context 191172
22. Midlands Purple ware, WCTS MP10, bowl, context 191171
23. Midlands Purple ware, WCTS MP10, bowl, context 191172
24. Midlands Purple ware, WCTS MP10, ?jar base, very crude, interior brown slip, reddish exterior wash or slip, interior purple glaze spots, some exterior soot, context 191171
25. LMT01, WCTS SLM20 bowl, abraded, context 191172

Worked stone, by Ruth Shaffrey

The site produced one flat piece of worked stone (from context 190583), measuring 66 mm by 65 mm and 21 mm thick, with well but unevenly worn faces suggesting use as a palette; the wear on both sides rules out its use as a floor stone and it is not even enough to be a wall veneer. The one surviving edge has also been worn down and appears to have been used as a whetstone. It was recovered from the fill of a probable late Romano-British pit 190015 (190583). This palette is made from Quartz Conglomerate of the Old Red Sandstone from the Forest of Dean, a lithology unknown in the area around the M6 Toll sites. It was widely used for Romano-British rotary querns further south in the area around Alcester and Tiddington but the nearest known find spots are 15 km away at Grimstock Hill and Bubbenhall (Shaffrey 2006) placing this on the periphery of known use. In addition to being an unexpected material in the region, the object is also unique because the use of Quartz Conglomerate for anything other than querns (and occasionally mortars) is unknown (Saunders 1998), irrespective of whether it started out as a quern and was reused.

Building material, by Cynthia Poole

A total of 105 fragments of ceramic building material weighing 6183 g was recovered from 19 contexts together with fragments of sandstone weighing 148 g. Of this over half was post-Romano-British in date. The forms are summarised and quantified in Table 133. *Tegulae* were the most common form and all had type D flanges, most being of above average width, between 27 mm and 36 mm. One also had a lower cutaway

Table 133 Quantities and forms of building material

	Fabric	No.	Wt(g)
Tegula	S1, S4	3	741
Brick	S7, S1, S2	3	725
Flat	S4, S1, S2	6	443
Tessera	S1, S2	42	680
Unid.	S1, S2, S4	5	24
Post-RB	S6 & ?	45	3681
Roof, floor	Sst	2	148

combining types C2 and D1 on one corner. Three fragments of brick, 36–>42 mm thick, were the only other identifiable form.

A group of small fragments from context 190739 (Enclosure 1, ditch 190012, section 190740) associated with one of the *tegulae* may be interpreted as crudely made *tesserae* chipped from a *tegula*. Evidence of flange sizes and fabrics indicate that more than one *tegula* was utilised in their production. Some pieces were very rough, but a few were quite carefully shaped and a variety of shapes was present including rectangular, triangular, trapezoidal and some more irregular polygonal shapes. They divide into four size groups: small: 15–20 mm, medium-small: 15 mm by 20 mm by 30 mm, medium–large: 25–30 mm and large: 25 mm by 40 mm by 50 mm. These pieces may have been left over from manufacturing *tesserae* from *tegulae* or rejected as too crude. Their presence may indicate the preparation of materials rather than the actual existence of a tessellated pavement within the settlement.

The fragments of sandstone are from split slabs in two thicknesses (10 and 16 mm) that could have been used for either roofing or flooring. They are likely to be Romano-British, but there were no diagnostic characteristics on which to assign a date to the pieces. However, they were also from context 190739 and could have been collected for production of *tesserae*.

Environment

Charred plant remains, by Lisa Gray

A total of 41 samples of 5–40 litres was taken and assessed during the excavation phase. Many contained little to no material and only 12 were chosen for analysis. Preservation quality was generally poor with many remains in fragments and too poorly preserved for the survival of diagnostic features. High levels of root activity and many uncharred weeds seeds were noted and it was suggested that this indicated stratigraphic movement and the possibility of intrusive material (OWA 2003, 247). Many uncharred seeds were observed during the analysis of these samples. Sample details and contents are given in full in Tables 134–6.

Results

Middle Iron Age pits 191221, 191334, 191338 and 191317

Plant remains were scarce and generally poorly preserved in these samples (Table 134). They consisted of a few cereal grains and fragments of possible hazelnut (*Corylus avellana*) shell. Some cereal grains resembled free-threshing wheat (*Triticum aestivum*), while two grain fragments were too poorly preserved to distinguish between barley or wheat (*Hordeum*/*Triticum*).

Romano-British pits 190015, 190118 and burnt feature 190098

Both pits produced very little charred material (Table 135). Pit 190118 produced virtually nothing other than a small number of fragments of plant tissue, possibly grain fragments, but with no diagnostic features. Pit 190015 produced four poorly preserved grains of bread wheat (*cf. Triticum aestivum*) and an unidentified wheat grain. Also present were five fragments of hazelnut shell.

Two samples from burnt feature 190098 also yielded very little charred material. Context 191098 produced one wheat grain, one poorly preserved barley/wheat grain, an oat (*Avena* sp.) grain and a large legume resembling celtic bean/horse bean (*cf. Vicia faba*).

Medieval oven 190165

The few plant remains from this feature were poorly preserved and fragmentary. One grain fragment resembled bread wheat and another oat. A small number of seeds of orache (*cf. Atriplex* sp.) and one domestic pea (*Pisum sativum*) were also recorded.

Post-medieval/modern ditches 190148 and 190154

The sample from ditch 190148 was the most productive seen from this site (Table 136). The assemblage was dominated by grains of bread wheat type and seeds of peas, beans and a variety of arable weed seeds. Two fragments of chaff (culm nodes from stems) and two fragments of hazelnut shell were also recovered.

Ditch 191054 produced thirteen seeds of legumes; many were intact and resembled horse/broad bean (*Vicia faba*) or domestic pea (*Pisum sativum*) (Table 136). The remaining assemblage from ditch 190148 included smaller quantities of bread wheat, one of possible spelt wheat and others too poorly preserved to identify to species or genus (ie rye/wheat *Secale*/*Triticum*). This sample produced the only find of rye (*Secale cereale*) for this site.

Interpretation

Middle Iron Age pits

The plant remains shed little light on agricultural practices for this period at the site. It has been argued that as free-threshing wheats are generally absent from Iron Age and Roman sites such finds are more likely than not to be intrusive (van der Veen and O'Conner 1998). Monckton noted the possibility that these remains may have been introduced into the deposit through bioturbation (OWA 2003, 248).

Romano-British pits

The plant remains in these samples are sparse compared with sites in the West Midlands region (Monckton 2003, 16–18). The absence of weeds or large quantities of chaff or weed seeds means that the information these samples

Table 134 Charred plant remains from Middle Iron Age pits

Taxon	Common name							
		Feature	*191221*		*191334*		*191317*		*191338*
		Context	*191240*	*191241*	*191318*	*191320*	*191337*	*191335*	*191339*
		Sample	*193527*	*193528*	*195537*	*193538*	*193532*	*193534*	*193535*
		Sample size (l)	*10*	*10*	*20*	*20*	*20*	*8*	*20*
		Flot size (ml)	*15*	*30*	*10*	*25*	*5*	*5*	*5*
Triticum aestivum grain	Bread wheat	–	–	2	–	–	–	–
cf. *T. aestivum* grain frag.	Bread wheat	–	–	–	–	–	–	1
cf. *Triticum* sp. grain	Wheat	1	–	–	–	–	–	–
Hordeum/Triticum sp. grain frag. (distal end)	Barley/wheat	–	–	–	–	–	1	1
cf. *Corylus avellana* nutshell frag.	Hazel	–	–	–	–	1	1	2
Indet. wood frag. (>4 mm^3)		++++	+	+++	++	–	++	++
Indet. wood fleck (<4 mm^3)		++	++	+++++	++++	–	–	+++
Indet. plant tissue (?grain frag.)		–	–	–	+	+	–	–
Indet. plant tissue		+	+	+	–	–	–	1

Key to estimated levels of abundance codes: + = 1–10; ++ = 11–50; +++ = 51–150; ++++ = 151–250; +++++ = >250

Table 135 Charred plant remains from Romano-British contexts and undated spread

Taxon	Common name					
	Period	*Romano-British*				*Undated*
	Feature	*Pit 190015*	*Pit 190118*	*Burnt feature 190098*		*Stone spread 190166*
	Context	*190578*	*190727*	*191098*	*191097*	*191108*
	Sample	*193502*	*193502*	*193523*	*193524*	*193522*
	Sample size (l)	*8*	*5*	*20*	*10*	*20*
	Flot size (ml)	*250*	*40*	*60*	*40*	*60*
Triticum cf. *spelta* grain frag.	Spelt	–	–	–	–	–
cf. *T. aestivum* grain	Bread wheat	4	–	–	–	–
Triticum sp. grain	Wheat	1	–	1	1	–
cf. *Secale cereale* grain	Rye	–	–	–	–	–
Triticum/Secale sp. grain	Wheat/rye	–	–	–	–	–
cf. *Triticum/Secale* sp. grain	Wheat/rye	–	–	–	–	–
Hordeum/Triticum sp. grain frag. (distal end)	Barley/wheat	–	–	1	–	–
Avena sp. grain	Oat	–	–	1	–	–
Avena/Hordeum/Secale/Triticum culm node	Indet. cereal	–	–	–	–	–
Vicia faba/Pisum sativum seed	Celtic bean/horse bean/pea	–	–	–	–	–
cf. *Vicia faba* seed	Celtic bean/horse bean	–	–	1	–	–
Vicia/Lathyrus sp. seed	Vetch/tare/vetchling/pea	–	–	–	–	–
cf. *Corylus avellana* nutshell	Hazel	5	–	–	–	–
Indet. wood frag. (>4 mm^3)		++++	–	–	–	–
Indet. wood fleck (<4 mm^3)		+++++	–	–	–	–
Indet. plant tissue (?grain frag.)		–	+	–	+	–
Indet. plant tissue		–	–	+	–	+
Indet. shell frag.		–	–	–	–	3

Table 136 Charred plant remains in medieval and post-medieval/modern samples

	Period	Medieval	Post-medieval/modern	
	Feature	Oven 190165	Ditch 190148	Ditch 190154
	Section		191001	190695
	Context	190950	109002	190696
	Sample	193516	193521	193506
	Sample size (l)	3	9	10
	Flot size (ml)	5	8	2250
Taxon	Common name			
Triticum cf. *spelta* grain frag.	Spelt	–	–	1
cf. *T. aestivum* grain	Bread wheat	–	1	1
T. aestivum grain	Bread wheat	–	52	–
cf. *T. aestivum* grain frag.	Bread wheat	1	–	–
Triticum sp. grain	Wheat	–	1	1
cf. *Secale cereale* grain	Rye	–	–	1
Triticum/Secale sp. grain	Wheat/rye	–	–	2
cf. *Triticum/Secale* sp. grain	Wheat/rye	–	–	1
Avena sp grain frag.	Oat	1	5	–
Avena/Hordeum/Secale/Triticum culm node	indet. cereal	–	2	1
Silene sp. seed	Campion/catchfly	–	15	–
cf. *Atriplex* sp. seed	Orache	4	–	–
Vicia faba seed	Celtic bean/horse bean	–	8	–
Vicia faba/Pisum sativum seed	Celtic bean/horse bean/pea	–	7	10
Pisum sativum seed	Pea	1	–	–
Vicia/Lathyrus sp. seed	Vetch/tare/vetchling/pea	–	13	2
Fabaceae indet. seed	Legume	–	1	–
Polygonum mite seed	Tasteless waterpepper	–	2	–
Rumex cf. acetosella seed	Sheep's sorrel	–	5	–
Rumex acetosella type seed	Sheep's sorrel	–	2	–
Rumex sp. seed	Dock	–	3	–
cf. *Corylus avellana* nutshell frag.	Hazel	–	2	1
Anthemis cotula seed	Stinking mayweed	–	5	–
Chrysanthemum segetum seed	Corn marigold	–	4	–
Indet. wood frag. (>4 mm^3)		++	–	+++
Indet. wood fleck (<4 mm^3)		+	–	+++++
Indet. plant tissue (?grain frag.)		+	++	++

could give about the ecology of the fields and agricultural practices in general is limited.

Medieval oven

The sample from oven 190165 was dominated by wood charcoal, probably the remains of fuel, with only a small number of grains and a pea, that may relate to its use for cooking or baking.

Post-medieval/modern ditches

Ditch 190148 produced an assemblage resembling sieving waste from final cleanings, becoming charred as a result of being thrown into a fire as fuel. The species represented within the assemblage have quite different habitat preferences. Stinking mayweed (*Anthemis cotula*) is common on heavy soils and is an indicator of the cultivation of waterlogged loams and clay soils (Hanf 1983, 235), while corn marigold (*Chrysanthemum segetum*) and sheep's sorrel (*Rumex acetosella*) are weeds of crops grown upon drier sandy, acidic soils (Clapham *et al.* 1964, 394; Hanf 1983, 403). The assemblage would then appear to represent either crops grown upon different soils or possibly fields that crossed both sandstone and clay geology.

Charcoal, by Rowena Gale

Forty-one bulk soil samples were taken from contexts relating to all periods of activity. Of those containing charcoal, 10 were selected for detailed analysis. The quantity and condition of the charcoal varied from abundant and well preserved in the Romano-British pit 190015 and 'trough' 190043, to sparse and degraded in

Table 137 Charcoal (no. frags)

Feature	*Cut*	*Context*	*Sample*	*Acer*	*Betula*	*Corylus*	*Fraxinus*	*Pomoideae*	*Prunus*	*Quercus*	*Salcaceae*
?Mesolithic/Neolithic Flint scatter											
		190762	193508	–	–	–	–	–	–	6h	–
		190772	193512	–	–	–	–	–	–	13h	–
Middle Iron Age pits											
191221		191241	193528	–	–	–	–	–	3	1h, 1s	–
191317		191320	193538	–	–	–	–	–	–	3u	–
Romano-British											
Pit											
190015	190558	190578	193502	–	1	5	15	19r	8r	1h, 3r	–
Burnt 'trough'											
190043	190861	190860	193526	–	–	–	86	–	4r	5u	cf. 1
Burnt feature											
190098	191096	191097	193524	cf. 1	–	–	–	–	–	12h/u, 1s	–
Medieval oven											
190165		190951	193517	–	–	cf. 1	–	–	–	8h, 1s	–
Post-medieval/modern ditches											
190148	191001	191002	193521	–	1	cf.1	1	6	1	8h, 3r, 1s	–
190154	190695	190696	193506	–	–	–	–	–	1	30u	–

Key: h = heartwood; r = roundwood (diam. <20 mm); s = sapwood (diam. unknown); u = maturity undetermined

contexts 190762 and 190772 (spatially associated with the flint scatter) and in the medieval oven 190165. Species identification was undertaken to indicate the character and use of local woodland. The taxa identified are shown in Table 137.

Late Mesolithic

Charcoal recovered during the sampling of the large flint scatter on the central western boundary of the site (contexts 190762 and 190772) consisted of oak (*Quercus* sp.) heartwood. However, the presence in the latter context of small amounts of charred grain and a small fragment of possible coal suggests that some, it not all of the organic deposits could be intrusive, deriving from later agricultural and domestic use.

Middle Iron Age

Charcoal samples 193528 and 193538 were collected from the top fills of pits 191221 and 191317 of the pit alignment. Although mostly too degraded for identification, some fragments were named as oak and blackthorn (*Prunus spinosa*). Both contexts included small amounts of charred cereal grain.

Romano-British

The preservation of organic material in waste pit 190015 was markedly better than that from other contexts from which charcoal was examined. The charcoal-rich sample from the top fill of the pit included a high proportion of narrow roundwood from hawthorn/*Sorbus* group (Pomoideae) and blackthorn; other taxa identified included oak, ash (*Fraxinus excelsior*), hazel (*Corylus avellana*) and birch (*Betula* sp.). This layer also contained charred hazel nutshell and cereal grain, burnt bone, pottery and burnt clay and stone.

'Trough' 190043 was roughly in the centre of the site. The feature was shallow and contained burnt pebbles and a large quantity of charcoal. This material may represent burning *in situ* or have been dumped shortly after burning nearby. A 25% sub-sample of the largest fraction was identified as ash, sapwood from fast-grown trees, but also oak, blackthorn and willow (*Salix* sp.)/poplar (*Populus* sp.).

Burnt feature 190098 was close to the stream. Degraded charcoal from the basal layer included oak and *cf.* field maple (*Acer campestre*). Cereal grain was sparse.

Medieval

Charcoal obtained from the basal fill (context 190951) of pit/oven 190165, located on the central eastern boundary of the site contained a small quantity of degraded oak and *cf.* hazel. This layer represents the remains of *in situ* firing in an oven or furnace; the absence of lining material or slag suggests an oven as the more likely.

Post-medieval/modern

Ditch 190154 was aligned east–west on the eastern edge of the site. Several layers of infilling had occurred and sample 193506 was taken from the topmost fill (context 190696). This contained a huge amount of well-preserved charcoal, of which a 25% sub-sample was examined. Many fragments were quite large with some measuring 45 mm in length. A few fragments were partially vitrified and probably indicative of burning at temperatures exceeding 800°C (Prior and Alvin 1983). The sample consisted almost entirely of oak largewood, although blackthorn was also present. Large quantities of charred cereal grain and pulses were also identified.

Fuel debris from the top fill of ditch 190148 contained a wide range of taxa: oak, the hawthorn/*Sorbus* group, blackthorn, ash, birch and *cf.* hazel. The inclusion of pottery and charred food remains (cereals, pulses and hazel nutshell) suggests domestic origins.

Discussion

Charcoal was recovered from numerous features across the site but often in insufficient quantity to warrant detailed examination. Although there was no certain evidence of settlement within the excavated area, the frequent association of charred food stuffs (cereal grain and sometimes pulses and nutshell) and occasionally pottery and bone suggests that, in most instances, the charcoal originated from domestic fuel debris. There is some doubt, however, as to the authenticity of charcoal associated with the earliest deposits (190762 and 190772), relating to the scatter of Mesolithic worked flints, since this could be intrusive. The two Middle Iron Age pits (191221 and 191317), formed part of a pit alignment (a series of pits running east–west) and although viable charcoal was rather sparse, it indicated the use of oak and blackthorn.

Domestic refuse, including fuel debris, was particularly abundant in the Romano-British pit 190015. Evidence from the charcoal indicated that fuel was collected from a wide range of species, particularly from the narrow stems (roundwood) of shrubby species such as blackthorn, the hawthorn group and hazel but also making use of ash, oak and birch. The frequency of shrubby species could suggest that some fuel was sourced from hedgerows or scrub.

Two contexts more certainly related to agricultural or craft activities were: the Romano-British burnt 'trough' 190043, which appears to have been used essentially to heat pebbles, possibly as a pre-treatment prior to crushing, and the medieval oven/pit 190165, for which no particular function has been assigned, although metal-working is unlikely. The activities associated with the 'trough' employed firewood consisting predominantly of ash but also blackthorn, oak and possibly willow/poplar. Ash provides high calorie firewood and has the advantage that it does not need to be as well seasoned as other woods.

Charcoal was less frequent in the oven/pit and consisted of oak and possibly hazel. Although it is suggested that deposits in the adjacent ditch 190148 may also have related to activities in the oven, this seems more likely to have been an independent deposit of domestic waste from elsewhere.

A large deposit was obtained from the uppermost fill of the post-medieval ditch 190154. This deposit differed from that in most other contexts in that it consisted almost entirely of oak and appeared to have been burnt at temperatures high enough to have caused some vitrification; although this deposit may have originated from a non-domestic activity, the presence of cereal grain and pulses suggests otherwise.

The frequency of oak throughout (apparently) domestic deposits suggests that oak was specifically sought out for domestic firewood/fuel, possibly in favour of other species, although it would be necessary to examine larger samples than were available to get an accurate overall picture of fuel selection/ preference.

Environmental evidence

Site 19 was situated on a hillside sloping down to a stream in the valley bottom. Underlying soils at the site were basically sandy. The abundance of oak in the charcoal samples suggests widespread distribution at the site and thus it is likely that oak formed the major woodland constituent in the area from the Neolithic to the medieval period. Within the Romano-British period it is probable that ash, field maple and hazel grew in association with oak. Shrubby species such as blackthorn and the hawthorn group may have colonised parts of the hillside as scrub, marginal woodland or grown in hedgerows in both the Iron Age and Romano-British periods. Woodland was probably confined to areas less suited to farming. Despite the proximity of the stream, there was scant evidence of wetland species. The similarity of these results from the Romano-British period to the prehistoric features from Wishaw (Site 20) suggests that firewood was obtained from the same type and indeed possibly the same area of woodland.

Ash sapwood from the Romano-British burnt trough included both slow and fast growth, the latter reflecting optimal/stress-free growing conditions. There was no secure evidence to implicate the use of managed woodland.

Discussion

The focus of late Mesolithic occupation appears to have lain on, or beyond the western edge of the site, making any reliable estimation of its area impossible. Flint was also present in low densities on the slightly steeper ground to the north, and additional material came from the medieval and post-medieval colluvium that lay above a lynchet in this area. Localised sub-concentrations within the main assemblage almost certainly indicate tree hollows that had not been individually recorded. The low ratio of microliths and scrapers to retouched pieces, and the absence of tranchet axes, axe sharpening flakes or burins mean that the site cannot easily be classified by Mellars' (1976) settlement typology, but it bears closest comparison with Type B settlements, believed to represent predominantly winter occupation (Mellars 1976, 389–94, see Cramp, above). There are, however, no palaeoenvironmental data from the excavation upon which to reconstruct the late Mesolithic landscape, and no comparative data are available from other sites nearby.

The Iron Age activity represents the establishment of an important land-division, probably originally in the

Middle Iron Age, in the form initially of a pit alignment which in most respects is of typical form (Pollard 1996; Luke forthcoming). Its single-phase and possibly short-term nature and the presence of square and rectangular pits bears comparison with other excavated examples across Britain (eg Miket 1981; Barber 1985; Gurney *et al.* 1993; Pollard 1996; Ellis 2004; Luke forthcoming). However, the alignment was slightly unusual in that a number of the pits were constructed with their long axes perpendicular to the axis of the alignment as a whole.

Pit alignments are a comparatively common monument type, particularly in the Midlands and Yorkshire Wolds, but also elsewhere in the British Isles. In Warwickshire other excavated alignments are known from Wasperton (Palmer 2002a) and Ling Hall Quarry, Church Lawford (Palmer 2001a; 2004) and further examples have been plotted by Warwickshire Museum from cropmarks at Old Milverton, Hampton Lucy, Wolston, Kings Newnham, Weston under Wetherley and Ryton-on-Dunsmore (Hingley 1996, 13). In south Staffordshire, there are examples near Wall and Shenstone (Whitehouse 1960–1).

The discontinuous nature of pit alignments was clearly intentional, and examples commonly display a morphological consistency which suggests a very distinct, and widely acknowledged set of meanings. They may have been 'permeable' boundaries intended to filter access according to contemporary social rules, or even to make explicit the act of transition between defined 'spaces'. In view of their sometimes close relationship to natural landscape features (Pollard 1996), to older monumental landscapes (Ellis 2004; Last 2005) or to land defined by river-meanders (Luke forthcoming), there is no certainty that alignments were ever even intended as boundaries for the corporeal world. Pollard has observed that use of pit lines 'was clearly satisfactory, with the form carrying a commonly understood meaning related to the character of the boundary or area being defined' (1996, 110). The consistently observed lack of evidence for maintenance has been taken to imply that it was the act of their construction which was of significance, rather than their longevity, perhaps as a means of re-enforcing group identity in relation to a location (*ibid.*). The spatial relationship between an alignment and its audience may also have been important: Taylor has noted that perceptions of the permeability or impermeability of pit alignments might have changed according to the proximity of an observer. Utilising analysis by Higuchi (1983) he has estimated that the individual elements of an alignment at Plants Farm, Maxey, Cambridgeshire, would have been evident at distances of less than *c* 200 m but appeared as a continuous barrier from further away (Taylor 1997). Some low-lying alignments may not even have been visible at all times of year: the two successive riverside alignments at Meadow Lane, St Ives, Cambridgeshire, were almost certainly occasionally submerged beneath winter flood-waters (Pollard 1996 110).

The Iron Age activity on the site should be viewed in the context of the Middle and Middle/Late Iron Age enclosed settlements excavated at Langley Mill (Site 30) and North of Langley Mill (Site 29), respectively, *c* 2 km to the north-west and, closer to hand, the Middle Iron Age activity 300 m to the south-east at Wishaw (Site 20) where a curvilinear gully, probably representing a roundhouse, points to settlement activity.

Pit alignments often represent primary landscape-divisions, superseded by ditched field-systems and enclosures (Pollard 1996, 111), and that was the case here, replaced first by the segmented ditch, also of probable Middle Iron Age date and possibly with a broadly similar role, but also by the Romano-British field ditch, lying to the north of the rectangular enclosure. The function of the enclosure remains uncertain. Few of its internal features were securely dated, and none could be ascribed to a specific activity. No building traces were found, although finds including mortaria and occasional ceramic roof tiles came from the enclosure ditches, suggesting proximity to domestic buildings. However, these need not have lain within the enclosure, as previous survey work has identified a concentration of Romano-British settlement remains in the field immediately east of the site (OAU 1994a). A small assemblage of what may be ceramic *tesserae* came from ditch 190012, although these are not thought to indicate the immediate presence of a tessellated floor: the group appears to represent unused tesserae blanks, or discards from *tesserae* production (see Poole, above). There is also no immediately apparent context for the fragment of beaded torc.

The widespread occurrence of sometimes large amounts of 'clean' redeposited thermally cracked quartzite cobbles across (and beyond) the site remains unexplained. Some of this material was residual in feature-fills, but considerable quantities also had no recognised context, occurring as sporadic pieces or very shallow, loosely associated 'drifts' on, or in, the upper exposure of natural deposits (such as spread 190166). Redeposited burnt stone was noted in the fills of the Iron Age segmented ditch, but was also seen in features of all subsequent phases.

Only a single feature containing potentially *in situ* burnt stone was identified – early–middle Romano-British 'trough'-like pit 190043 (Fig. 167). However, the presence of this feature does not explain either the quantity of thermally altered stone, nor its occurrence on the hillslope to the north. It is possible that former prehistoric burnt mound sites have been completely eroded from the site and their stone component extensively spread downslope (a phenomenon commented upon elsewhere in Warwickshire by Barfield and Hodder 1989), but there is no surviving archaeological evidence from which the position, or extents of these hypothetical deposits might be reconstructed. Burnt stone is not intrinsically datable, and it remains likely that local stone has been heated for various purposes over several millennia.

Most of the medieval activity from the site dates from the mid 13th–early 14th centuries. It must, therefore, be taken as broadly contemporary with the fish ponds excavated at Wishaw (Site 20) to the immediate south-east and which extended (unexcavated) into the southern part of this site, although, unlike Wishaw, the site also yielded limited ceramic evidence for later medieval activity (14th–16th century). No medieval structural or settlement remains were found on the site, and the range of features on the site – enclosure, ridge and furrow, lynchet, and waterhole – indicate a wholly agricultural land use on the north side of the stream, distinctly different to that on the south side (Wishaw, Chapter 25).

Chapter 25
Wishaw (Site 20)

By Phil Harding

Introduction

An excavation and targeted watching brief were undertaken on land at Wishaw, where an archaeological evaluation in June 1993 examined a probable medieval moat and fish ponds that had been extensively damaged by levelling in the 1970s (OAU 1994b).

The site, covering *c* 5.15 hectares centred on NGR 417400 295280, lay at the mouth of one of several small tributary valleys which drain eastwards into the flood plain of the River Tame (Fig. 159). The stream itself rises approximately 1.25 km west of Wishaw Hall Farm at 107 m aOD and falls to the site at 84 m aOD. The area of former fishponds lay partially within a small paddock of permanent pasture where traces of earthworks were still visible although most of the excavated area lay to the south in an arable field (Fig. 179).

The underlying geology is mapped as Triassic Mercian Mudstone although the lower slopes on which the fish ponds lay were covered by a thin veneer of Pleistocene Glaciofluvial Deposits (Geological Survey of Great Britain 1996, Sheet 168, Birmingham).

Historical background

Wishaw comprises an area of dispersed settlement, with three small concentrations of settlement around Over Green, Grove End and Wishaw Hall Farm (Fig. 219). The farm lies *c* 1 km north-west of Wishaw Church with Moxhull, an additional medieval hamlet immediately to the east in what is now the Belfry Golf Centre. Documentary sources (*VCH* 1947, 258–61) provide accounts of the estates at Wishaw and Moxhull from Edward the Confessor onwards.

References (Dugdale 1730, 934) indicate that land at Wishaw passed to the Knights Templar, possibly as a gift from one of the major landholders, the Corbucions, in the late 12th–early 13th century. It seems likely that this transfer occurred after 1185, when a major survey of Templar landholdings was undertaken. The Knights Templar was a military order that had become established in England by 1128 from origins in the Holy Land. It functioned to protect pilgrims and followed a rule based on that of St Benedict.

It is unclear exactly how much land was initially gifted to the Templars; in 1227 they granted land to Margery de Lisle, a family which later owned Moxhull Manor. By 1275 the Templars held 4.5 *virgates* (55 hectares) in Wishaw and 1.5 *virgates* (18 hectares) in Moxhull. Their overlordship was confirmed in 1287 and the manor had passed to the Hospitallers by 1326 following the suppression of the Knights Templar in 1312.

None of the documentary sources describes the precise location of the manor. However, in 1675 Ogilby mapped an area as 'Wisshaw Green' immediately north of Wishaw Hall Farm, a farm that is located in the centre of the parish. The tithe maps (1847) also record Hall Meadow and Hall Orchard in fields adjacent to the earthwork site.

Archaeological background

The medieval earthworks and fish ponds at Wishaw Hall Farm (WCC SMR 55 and 6124) were first recorded by the Ordnance Survey (1st edn 6 in Survey), where they were marked as an L-shaped 'moat'. They lie immediately east of Moxhull Old Hall (WCC SMR 192) (the Belfry Golf Club) which also retains traces of a moat (WCC SMR 194) and a fishpond (WCC SMR 193), now an ornamental lake for the golf course. C J Bond surveyed the entire earthwork complex at Wishaw including channels and ponds in 1969 on a 'rough and ready' plan (Bond pers comm.) during a study of deserted medieval villages in the area (Fig. 180). He concluded that, although the earthworks were shown 'as a moat':

> '...on closer inspection this is nothing like a moated enclosure. One side (SE) is completely absent, another (SW) is negligible, and a third (NE) elongated to a ridiculous length for a moat. Immediately north of the L-shaped pond are traces of another pond system: a low dam across the stream, and a damp square depression between the L-shaped pond and the stream which could have been a take-off leat to drive a mill. The stream is culverted in a couple of places, and large sandstone blocks are built into the culvert mouths together with much later bricks' (Bond 1969).

He later postulated that the square shallow pond might provide a shallow water habitat for ducks. Beyond the 'moat' he plotted a system of old field boundary ditches, aligned approximately NE–SW, to the south and east of which one was shown on the 1895 6 in Ordnance Survey map. Bond considered that the earthworks most closely resembled fish ponds at Washford, Redditch, on

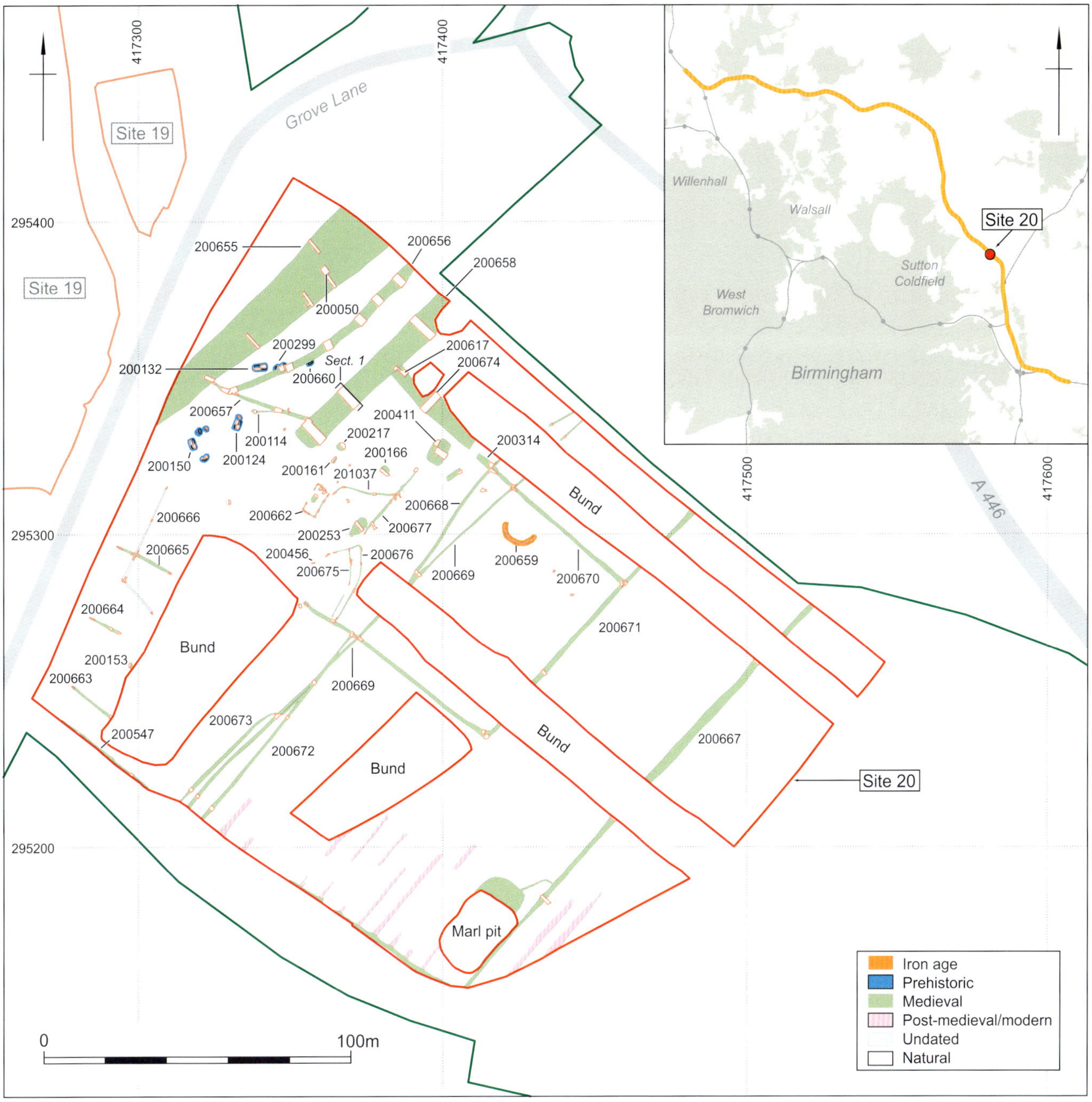

Fig. 179 Wishaw (Site 20)

the Warwickshire–Worcestershire border, a parish that coincidentally also contained land that had been owned by the Knights Templar.

Outflow from the site ran eastwards along the A446 to the former fish ponds in the grounds of the Belfry Golf Course. This course is likely to follow more closely the drainage although the stream is likely to have been artificially modified more than once; an estate survey of 1843 maps the flow as north along the present A446, parallel to the contour and into an adjacent tributary valley.

Bond's survey, although not measured accurately, fortuitously provided the only record of the earthworks before they were levelled in 1972 to improve the land for agriculture. This survey, which has been subsequently 'rubber-sheeted' and draped over the accurate site grid (Fig. 180), illustrates the value of even the most rudimentary sketch plan to record upstanding field monuments. The topsoil was removed, the stream culverted underground through a concrete pipe to the road, the ponds back-filled with clay and the topsoil reinstated. A subsequent field walking survey (Hodder 1992) noted the presence of dressed sandstone blocks within the area of the 'moat' that might represent the residue from robbed structures, although it is possible that they were derived from the former culvert. A concentration of medieval pottery was also noted with other pottery found on the rising ground to the south and on land running north from Wishaw Hall Farm parallel to the present A446.

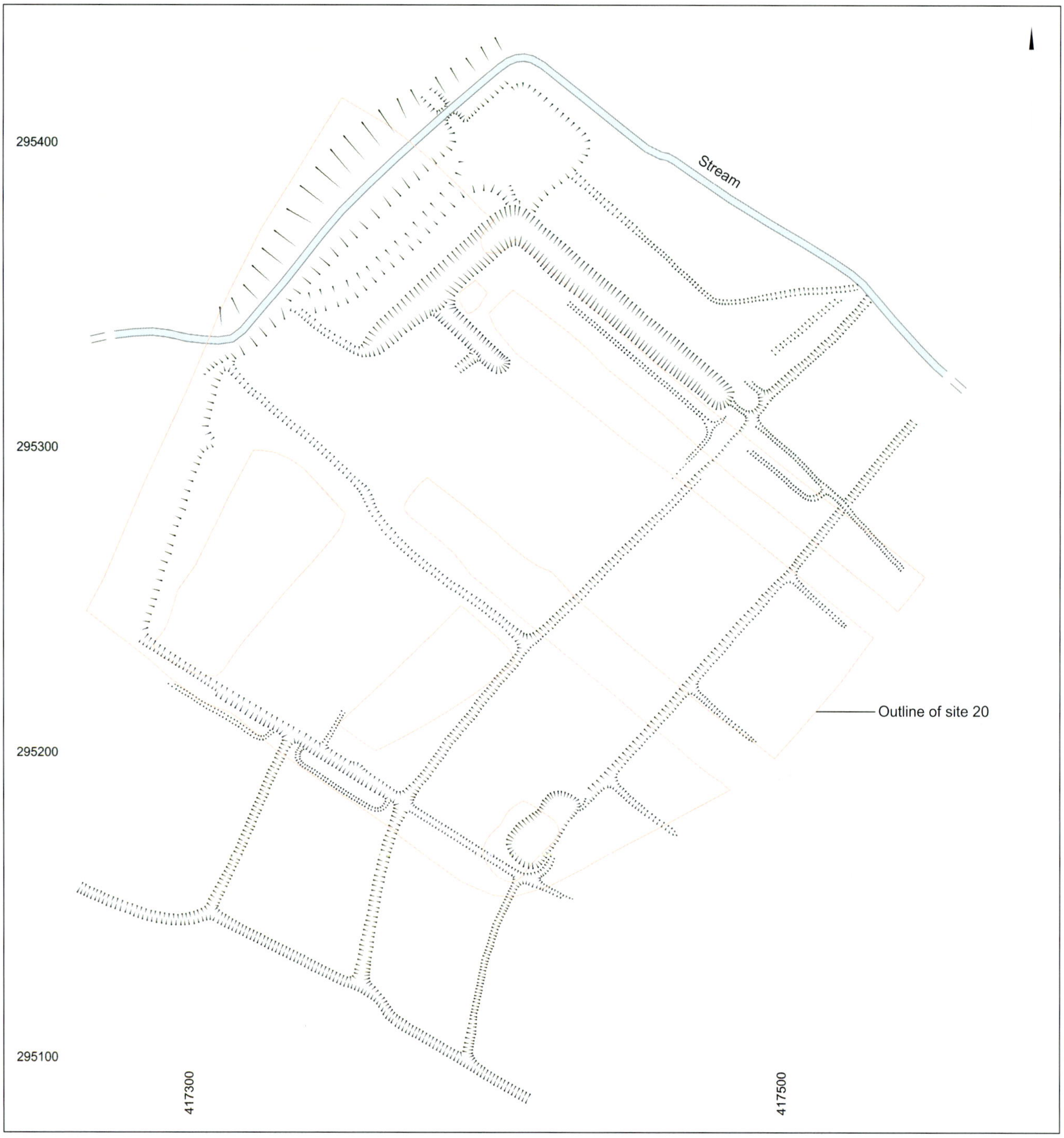

Fig. 180 Earthwork Survey (after C.J. Bond)

Methodology

The results of the evaluation and other data were used to define the scope of additional work. Although the site had been severely damaged by the levelling, it was considered that sufficient archaeological deposits remained intact to make it possible to clarify the exact extent, relationships and date of all archaeological remains on the site but especially those representing medieval activity within the road easement. Additional work was considered necessary to resolve the possibility that 'burnt mound' material might be present on the site but was primarily aimed at retrieving sufficient information to provide an understanding of the layout and function of the individual components of the fish ponds, their relationships to the area of possible settlement on the east side of Grove Lane and the field system south of the fish ponds. An area of 1 hectare centred on the former earthworks and medieval settlement was identified for sample excavation, which aimed to establish key stratigraphic relationships, basic dating and a general characterisation of palaeo-environmental deposits. The remaining 4.15 hectares of the site, primarily the field systems, were treated as a targeted watching brief where excavation and recording were undertaken to ensure compatibility with the fish ponds and place them in their broader archaeological landscape.

All overburden was removed under constant archaeological supervision using tracked 360° excavators fitted with toothless grading buckets. The brief required that this material should be removed from the site to an adjacent field for storage. However, it proved impossible in the weather conditions and underlying geology to transport spoil across the site without destroying the underlying archaeological deposits. It was agreed with the Local Authority Archaeologist that this material should be stored on site in linear bunds.

Results

Iron Age/prehistoric

A north facing arc of ditch (200659), which described a semicircle 11 m in diameter, was located 40 m from the eastern edge of the medieval fish pond complex (Fig. 179). It measured 0.6 m wide and 0.25 m deep with sloping sides and a flat base 0.2 m across. The east terminal was well cut with a flat base 0.4 m across and contained a lens of sandy silt at the base with charcoal, fragments of burnt quartzite pebbles and eight sherds of Middle Iron Age pottery from a single vessel. The adjacent bedrock was unmodified suggesting that the material had been placed in the ditch as ash. The overlying mid-light grey sandy silt included occasional charcoal flecks and rounded pebbles and filled the remainder of the ditch. The Middle Iron Age date was confirmed by a radiocarbon result of 380–190 cal BC (NZA-25060, 2239±30 BP) from charcoal in the ditch (Fig. 215, Chapter 29). The feature probably represents the remains of a ring gully around an Iron Age roundhouse, its eastern terminal (containing the deposit of ash, stones and pottery) forming the southern side of a south-east facing entrance (*cf.* the possibly placed deposit at Shenstone Ring Ditch, Site 14). However, there were no traces of any post positions, and other functions for the feature are possible.

Although there was no other dated prehistoric material on the site, deposits of burnt stones of possible prehistoric date were detected along the south bank of the stream filling a scatter of nine rectangular and irregular pits. Three of the pits (200124, 200132 and 200150) were sub-rectangular or oval in plan with well cut moderately sloping sides and flat bases. They ranged from 1.3 m to 4.1 m long, and averaged 1.5 m wide and 0.18 m deep. The reminder were less well cut with irregular oval or circular outlines and concave sides and bases, and measuring 1.1–2.8 m long, 0.8–1.20 m wide and averaged *c* 0.1 m deep. Most contained charcoal and burnt or unburnt quartzite pebbles in varying quantities; pit 200150 was filled almost exclusively with burnt material. The underlying natural clay was unmodified suggesting that the contents had not been burnt *in situ*.

Pits 200660 and 200299 were truncated by medieval channel 200656 and fragments of heavily burnt quartzite pebbles derived from the latter pit were found on the base of the channel, suggesting that the features containing burnt stone predated the construction of the fish ponds. However, one pit (200124) contained pottery – 26 fragments of abraded mid-13th–14th century pottery – and iron nails, which is a large assemblage to be considered intrusive. In all other respects, including the stratigraphical relationship to the channel, the pits are most closely related in location and contents to prehistoric burnt mound features from the area (Langley Brook, Site 39, and Collett's Brook Burnt Mound, Site 40) that are discussed in more detail elsewhere in this volume.

There is evidence from elsewhere along the M6 Toll to indicate that features comprising or containing burnt stone concentrations may be multi-period, including of medieval date, such as the burnt pebbles associated with two medieval drying ovens recorded at Shenstone Linear Features (Site 13, Chaper 15). While the balance of established opinion considers it likely that most such burnt stone features are of prehistoric date, it cannot be discounted that here they may relate to the processing of fish from the ponds.

Medieval

The excavation was focused on the complex of large and small ponds, and the channels that fed them with water from the stream. Other features in the southern part of the site included a series of ditches apparently forming part of a rectangular field system, or property boundaries probably unrelated to the fish ponds.

The valley pond

Water for the fish pond complex was supplied via a natural stream that had been dammed to form a valley pond (200655) (Fig. 180), the western extension of which was recorded but not excavated at the southern end of Wishaw Hall Farm (Site 19) (Fig. 159). This pond served as a reservoir for additional ponds that were dug off the line of the stream and were supplied with water through a network of channels from the valley pond. The drainage pattern away from the fish pond complex lay beyond the easement of the road and had been destroyed by agriculture; however it was possible to reconstruct this aspect of the drainage pattern from the results of Bond's survey of 1969 (Fig. 181). Flow of water away from the valley pond was undoubtedly regulated via a weir in the dam and excess water allowed to drain downstream, possibly in a ditch, towards Moxhull Manor. Additional outflow channels, which are otherwise indistinguishable from a network of field boundaries that lay to the south of the fish pond complex, drained water away from the off-stream fishponds. The dam lay just north of the road easement and therefore beyond the scope of the excavation. The valley pond extended approximately 112 m south from the dam, covered an estimated *c* 1720 sq m, of which *c* 1420 sq m lay within the excavation area. Calculations

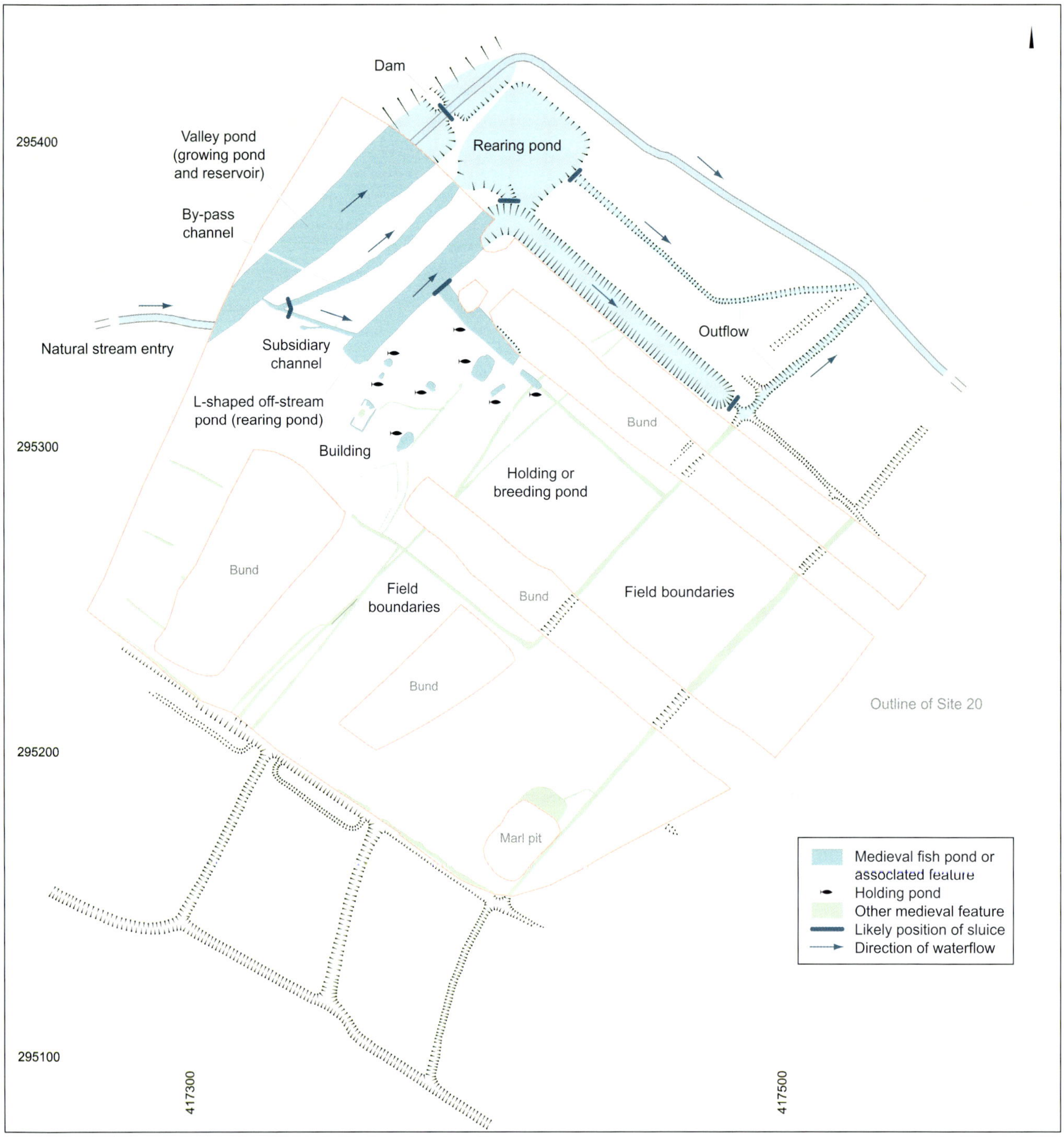

Fig. 181 Interpretive plan of the fish ponds

suggest that it may have contained in the region of a million litres of water.

The stream lay in a valley 19 m wide where the gradient is approximately 1:100. It occupied a channel with a shallow sloping north side and a steeper slope on the south. Part of the north edge of the valley pond had been truncated by the foundations of a former brick-built post-medieval cottage, which were accompanied by 18th and 19th century pottery in that part of the pond. It seems unlikely that the valley profile had been modified artificially to create the pond; indeed the surface of the natural clay at the base of the pond was indented with irregular hollows, which are likely to represent scour features. The clay was covered with coarse, fluvial quartzite gravel, *c* 0.3 m thick, in a red-brown sandy matrix, which is likely to have been laid down when the valley was first eroded by a high energy current. The basal gravel was overlain by mid orange-brown silty clay, probably also fluvial in origin and deposited as the water flow was arrested by the dam. Two isolated wooden stakes and a plank were embedded in the silty clay in a trench (200050) cut through the pond. The larger stake measured 0.88 m long, 0.1 m in diameter and was sharpened to a point which penetrated the underlying gravel. The other stake which was 0.6 m long and 0.3 m in diameter could not be traced below the silty clay. The plank measured 1.6 m long, 0.2 m wide and was 0.03 m thick. It lay in the lower part of the

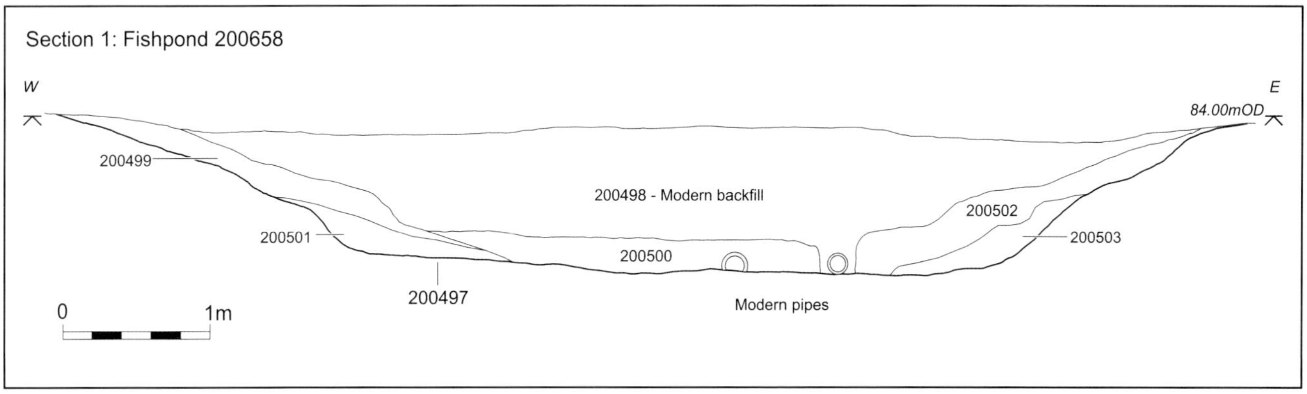

Fig. 182 Section of the off-stream pond

silty clay and had become incorporated in the pond fill after the initial stages of sedimentation. A tip of a further stake was found in the bed of the pond *c* 32 m to the south-west of the others. These timbers formed no coherent or continuous structure although they were considered to have been connected with the use of the pond rather than a later fence line.

Fish ponds frequently required routine maintenance and it is most likely that the basal silt accumulated after the pond went out of use. Molluscs characteristic of those living in stagnant water were present in the valley pond but not in other ponds at the site.

Stream water was diverted away from the valley pond into a by-pass channel (200656) that ran parallel to the former stream course to supply water to a square pond at the north end of the site and to take floodwater from the valley pond. The channel also helped to reduce the rate of sedimentation in the valley pond; silting is more prevalent at the tail of this type of pond where the natural flow of water is slowed as it enters the main body of water. Excavations confirmed that the silts in the valley pond at this point were interspersed with lenses of reworked quartzite pebbles which may have been deposited by floodwater and reflect sedimentation as the flow of the stream was deflected into the channel. The channel was cut from 0.25 m above the base of the valley pond, a point at which a constant supply of water could probably be maintained to other ponds, even during drought, but sufficient to cope with floodwater preventing overspill in the valley pond. The by-pass channel fell from 83.70 m aOD in the south to 82.75 m aOD in the north, a gradient of 1:67. It measured from 0.6 m deep in the south to 1.3 m in the north and ranged from 1.2 m to 2.7 m wide. It was cut with steep sloping sides and a narrow rounded base and was filled by a series of red-brown or grey-brown silty clays with rounded pebbles. Sherds of 13th–14th century pottery and occasional charcoal flecks were present in the primary silts of most sections excavated through the feature.

A subsidiary channel (200657), 1.4 m wide, 0.6 m deep with regular sloping sides and a narrow flat base, 0.3 m across, diverted water from the by-pass channel to the large L-shaped, off-stream pond that had for long been interpreted as a moat. This smaller channel ran 34 m along the slope at a gradient of 1:200, possibly deliberately engineered to deflect a steady flow of water from the by-pass channel and ensure a more controlled, less sediment laden, rate of supply to the pond. This was also confirmed by the presence of horizontally bedded silts and cross-bedded sands that had subsequently blocked the mouth of the subsidiary channel at its junction with the by-pass channel. There were no other clearly defined primary silts although a thin lens of dark grey clay was observed at the base of a section through the feature. The secondary fills comprised grey-brown silty clay which was capped by bulldozed material. A small spur channel (200114), 8 m long with no apparent water source or function, joined the subsidiary channel 23 m south-east of the valley pond and with it drained into the off-stream pond. The subsidiary channel entered the south-west corner of the off-stream pond approximately 0.65 m above its base at 83.75 m OD.

The off-stream pond

A portion of the L-shaped, off-stream pond (200658), *c* 65 m long and covering 545 sq m, was included in the excavation area; the remainder, calculated from Bond's earthwork survey, comprised approximately 964 sq m and lay beyond the easement. It ranged from 7.7 m wide near the terminal to 9.6 m wide to the north (Fig. 182). It was well cut with regular moderately sloping sides and a flat base, 4.6 m across, with a gradient which fell from 83.04 m OD to 82.75 m OD (1:165). Similar dimensions, profile and base level were recorded in an evaluation trench located 10 m beyond the road easement, immediately east of the corner of the pond, where the base level was 82.64 m OD. The primary fill comprised poorly laminated dark grey sandy silt with gravel which had weathered from the ditch sides near the edges. The quantity of gravel at the terminal was enhanced in the south-west corner by material introduced from the subsidiary channel (200657). There were also increased quantities of gravel on the opposite side of the pond where tips of material including burnt quartzite fragments and charcoal appear to have been thrown in from the edge. The basal silts at this point contained fragments of 14th century pottery, refuse that is likely to have originated from activity connected to a structure, 20 m south of the pond.

The secondary silts comprised mid grey-brown silty clays which probably accumulated slowly once the water management systems had decayed, although the feature is likely to have been waterlogged for long periods after the abandonment of the site. The former topsoil was heavily truncated by the landscaping of the 1970s. Traces of a thin turf line of dark friable loam, 0.02 m thick, were observed in the terminal *c* 0.55 m above the base of the pond. All other sections (eg Fig. 182) showed a sharp contact between the underlying deposits and the backfilled material which comprised redeposited unleached yellow-orange clay, 0.75m thick, with festoons of dark brown silty clay topsoil.

Holding pond

A rectangular pond (200674) extended from the south-east edge of the off-stream pond. It measured 35 m long, covered 232 sq m and was 1.05 m deep with sloping sides and a flat base 3.2 m across. The two ponds were connected by a shallow, concave overflow channel with a base 0.4 m above the floor of the off-stream pond which allowed water to enter the holding pond. The basal light grey clay primary silts contained gravel towards the edges which had weathered from the sides. This was particularly noticeable below the mouth of the overflow channel where the water had entered the pond. A well decayed stump of a wooden post, 0.27 m long and 0.07 m in diameter, was found in a posthole (200617) 0.3 m in diameter and 0.27 m deep which was cut in the pond base at the north corner. This may relate to a timber frontage or, more probably, a sluice to regulate the water supply; as such it represents the only evidence found at the site for a structure to control the water supply although equipment of this type would have been necessary throughout the pond system. There was no apparent method by which to empty the pond. The overlying deposits alternated between bands of well sorted more and less gravelly grey-brown silty clay which had entered from the south-west edge of the pond. This material contained a sherd of 17th century slipware and a clay pipe stem in the upper fill of the overflow channel and may relate to post medieval ploughing or deliberate backfill which pre-dated the activity in the 1970s.

Small ponds and associated features

A number of isolated, smaller features lay south of the off-stream pond and holding pond. They were between 15 m and 20 m apart, but were of differing dimensions and form and showed no coherent pattern, although the similarities of their primary fills suggested that they had originally functioned as ponds. The largest was a sub-rectangular feature (200411) that was visible on the 1969 earthwork survey apparently connected to the southern edge of the holding pond. The excavation showed it to be separated from the pond by a strip of natural clay 2.5 m across. It was 8.5 m long, 5.5 m wide and 1.1 m deep with steep sides and a flat base. The primary laminated, dark grey clay, 0.4 m thick, was overlain by two lenses of sandy clay, possibly deliberate backfill, which originated from the east side. The overlying grey sandy clay silt and loam included waterborne, colluvial and organic material which was oxidised towards the surface and probably represents silting of a low-lying hollow which remained damp at certain times of the year.

Feature 200217 measured *c* 2.5 m in diameter with steep sides and was 0.95 m deep with a flat base. There was a ring of stakeholes, averaging 0.12 m apart and 0.1 m in diameter, around the base with another possible stakehole in the centre, probably to support nets to deter herons and other predators from the developing fish. The stakeholes were filled with blue-grey clay identical to the primary pond fill which suggests that the stakes were removed when the site was abandoned. The overlying bands of orange-red clay were interleaved with charcoal rich layers, containing large quantities of 13th century pottery which suggested that this feature had been backfilled deliberately. Feature 200217 lay only 4 m east of the terminal of the off-stream pond and close to pit 200161 which also both contained large amounts of charcoal. Their proximity to structure 200662 (below) indicates that this area was the principal zone of human activity at the complex and that feature 200217 provided a convenient receptacle for rubbish disposal when fish production ceased. The area also coincided with the southern extent of a surface scatter of medieval pottery collected by Hodder (1992), possibly material that had been disturbed by the landscaping and further spread by ploughing.

Two oval features, 200166 and 200253, had silted naturally and may also have been dug as breeding ponds (see below). The former, *c* 3.5 m long, covered 7.6 sq m and was 0.7 m deep with moderate sloping sides and a flat base. It was filled with light grey-brown silty sand 0.2 m thick and was overlain by deposits of mid red-brown silty clay. Four sherds of 13th–14th century pottery were found in the tertiary fill. Feature 200253 was *c* 7.8 m long, 22.3 sq m in area and 1.6 m deep with steep sides and a narrow rounded base. The primary silt was overlain by bands of grey and red-brown silty loam which included small quantities of mid-13th–early 14th century pottery.

The west end of rectangular feature 200314, which covered 17.7 sq m, lay immediately east of the holding pond and cut through the junction of ditches 200668 and 200670. It was 8.4 m long and was 0.5 m deep with moderate sides and a flat base 1.8 m across. The basal grey sandy clay which was 0.15 m thick and probably water laid was overlain by grey sandy clay loam. Pottery also confirmed a 13th–14th century date.

There is nothing to indicate how these isolated ponds were filled with water. A series of shallow ditches was recorded close to features 200411 and 200253, but none drained directly into either of them and they are unlikely to have supplied, at the most, any more than periodic rainwater run-off. One of the ditches (201037) drained from the north-east corner of structure 200662 into a second ditch (200677) which was aligned towards but stopped 4 m south of feature 200411. An associated pair of insubstantial, discontinuous, curving gullies (200675,

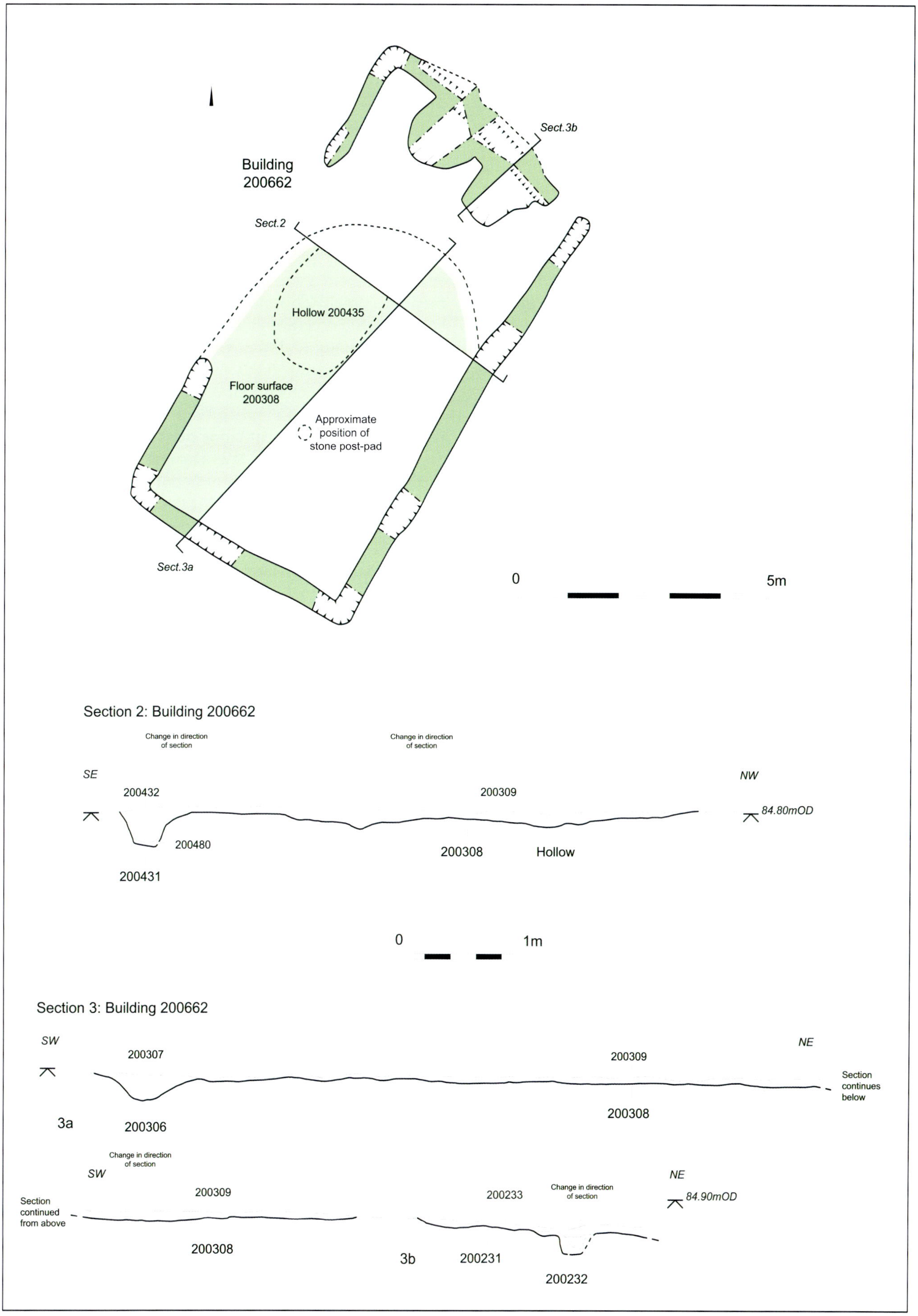

Fig. 183 Plan and sections of structure 200662

200676), 1.8 m apart at the south and 3.8 m apart at the north, extended from feature 200253 to link with the adjoining medieval field system. They averaged 0.4 m wide and 0.2 m deep and were filled with light grey sandy silt and large quartzite pebbles at the base which may have assisted drainage or functioned as a shallow foundation for boundary walls. A short slot (200456) west of gully 200675, may have been associated with it.

Structure 200662

The foundation trench for a rectangular building aligned north–south was located approximately 10 m south of the terminal of the off-stream pond. It was 9.7 m long and 4.7 m wide with a doorway 4.4 m wide on the west side and another 0.8 m wide at the east end of the north gable (Fig. 183). The foundation trench averaged 0.4 m wide and 0.2 m deep with steeply sloping irregular sides and a flat base and was filled with fine grey-brown sandy silt which was similar to the adjacent bedrock. There were no postholes at the trench terminals or at the corners of the building suggesting that it was probably of timber-framed cruck or box-frame construction in a beam slot with a timber-framed thatched roof. The local clay is likely to have been sufficient to clad wattle panels and infill the framing.

A red sandstone post-pad, 0.4 m square and 0.15 m high, was located 2 m from the south wall of the building along the central axis and may have supported a timber for a hipped roof. Additional sandstone fragments were found in the terminals of the main doorway and in the foundation trench north of the door where quartzite pebbles were also present.

A spread of occupation debris lay on the bare earth floor which had been heavily trampled, especially inside the doorway where an irregular hollow (200435) 3 m long, 1.5 m wide and 0.1 m deep had been worn. Although material was found throughout the floor area of the building it seems likely that some objects were placed against or possibly hung from the wall. A cluster of sherds, which may have been from the same pot, lay against the north wall of the building, while two lead strips, possibly unfinished net sinkers, were found in the south-west corner with fragments of poorly preserved iron (a number of possible lead sinkers were found at Wishaw Hall Farm (Site 19) to the immediate north-west). The iron was primarily from the upper fill of the foundation trench and, lacking more positive identification, it is likely that these represent no more than nails from the fabric of the building lost during its destruction or collapse.

Field and property boundaries

At the west of the site, three ditches (200663, 200664, 200665), approximately 24 m apart, with a fourth (200547) 10 m south of 200663, ran eastwards from Grove Lane and possibly represent medieval tenement boundaries south-west of the fish pond complex. The ditches were set back approximately 40 m east from the present lane and could be traced for at least 20 m. Ditches 200663, 200665 and 200547 averaged 0.9 m wide and 0.4 m deep with steep sides and a slightly rounded base. Ditch 200664 was less well preserved and heavily truncated at the east end. The ditches were filled with grey sandy clay which had silted down slope from the south. Medieval pottery, contemporary with that from the fish pond complex, was present in all three ditches with iron working slag in ditch 200665.

Ditch 200665 cut through an earlier ditch (200666) which ran for 15 m SE–NW before turning 34 m to the north, parallel to Grove Lane, where it was truncated by ploughing. The ditch, which was filled with light grey sandy silt, averaged 0.5 m wide and 0.3 m deep with steep sides and a flat base. It does not conform to the medieval field boundaries and, apart from its stratigraphic relationship with ditch 200665, was undated making it difficult to place within the general layout and chronology of the site. It may relate to an earlier phase of medieval land use on the site, or possibly to the undated but presumed prehistoric activity represented by the burnt stone deposits.

An oval pit (200153) was located at the east end of the plot defined by ditches 200663 and 200664. It measured *c* 1.6 m by 1.4 m but could not be excavated below 0.6 m due to the water table. It was filled with mid-grey-brown sandy silt and contained large quantities of mid–late 13th century pottery and charcoal.

A rectangular enclosure, probably a paddock of approximately 0.3 hectares, lay south-east of the fish pond complex. The north-west side was defined by a pair of ditches (200668 and 200669) which averaged 0.9 m wide and 0.16 m deep with shallow or moderately sloping sides and a flat base. Ditch 20670 formed the enclosure's north-east side and ditch 200671 the south-east and south-west sides, these being 1.2 m wide and 0.3–0.5 m deep with moderately sloping sides and a flat bases. Ditch 200669 was traced beyond ditch 200671 to the south-west, and although the various ditches on this line (including ditch 200668, and ditches 200672 and 200673 at the south-west) were insubstantial, together they probably formed a significant boundary dividing the fish farm complex and probable settlement facing onto Grove Lane from the agricultural land to the south-east. The line of this boundary was apparently redefined several times and may have formed part of an initial land division which become incorporated into the layout of the paddocks at a later stage.

The ditches were filled with grey silty clay and sandy silts which provided few opportunities to observe stratigraphic relationships between individual ditch fills. It was possible, however, to demonstrate that ditches 200673, 200669 and 200672, which may have been recut, were dug consecutively. The relationship of ditch 200671 and 200672 suggests that they were contemporary although variations in depths suggest that they may have undergone maintenance or alterations at different times. Ditch 200671, which also showed a marked change in depth at the intersection with ditch 200672, may have been extended at some stage, across the twin parallel ditches (200675, 200676).

A number of other earthworks plotted on the 1969 earthwork survey were not visible/detected on the ground.

Ditch 200667 ran NE–SW at the south-east end of the excavated area. It measured 1.8 m wide and 0.9 m deep on the clay slopes to the south but was only 0.55 m deep in the north. It had steep sides and a rounded base and had silted naturally with grey-brown mottled silty clay. A tree hollow at the edge of the ditch towards the southern end suggests that it was a major field boundary. It drained surface run-off from the high ground to the south, and the overflow from an adjacent marlpit. The ditch was shown on the Ordnance Survey 1895 6 in map although its alignment with the medieval field systems suggest that its origins may be much earlier. It is therefore likely that it was cleaned out and maintained frequently.

Finds

Post-Romano-British metalwork, by Ian Scott

This site produced 17 iron objects and two pieces of lead. The iron included 12 nails and various miscellaneous pieces. One of the latter comprised large numbers of sheet and/or strip fragments recovered together from the foundation trench of structure 200662 (context 200307). The pieces are broken and quite heavily concreted. They varied in size, many of the larger pieces having rivet, or nail, holes (visible on X-ray plates). The original object, or objects, could not be reconstructed. These could have been parts of single large object, or mixed broken fragments. A smaller number of similar pieces were recovered from the same feature (context 200370). One recognisable iron object was a tanged awl, or bradawl, with tapering circular section point. This could not be closely dated but could be quite modern.

The two lead objects were neatly cut pieces of quite thick sheet, one a trapezoid, the other a long rectangle. Overall the assemblage was very limited and of minor significance.

Flint, by Kate Cramp

Six flints were recovered, comprising two flakes, one blade, one bladelike flake, one end scraper and one retouched flake. None was corticated, although a light orange iron-staining was present on two pieces. The raw material was of the same flint type as that represented by the Late Mesolithic assemblage from Wishaw Hall Farm (Site 19), to the immediate north-west. Most pieces had been carefully struck and were of narrow proportions. The technology employed suggested that the flint from this site was probably contemporary with that from the adjacent site. A struck flake of quartzite was identified in the stone assemblage and suggested that materials other than flint were being knapped.

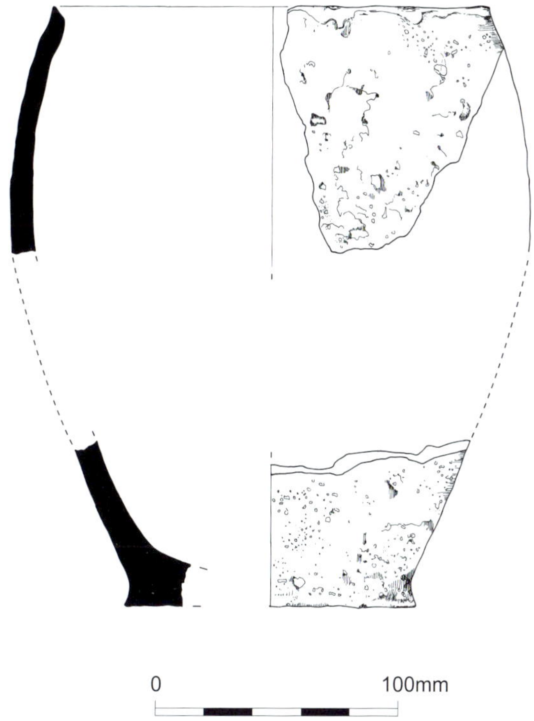

Fig. 184 Iron Age jar

Iron Age pottery, by Paul Booth

Seven Iron Age sherds (390 g) came from a single context, 200337, the eastern terminal of the semicircular gully (200659). The sherds, in a distinctive clay pellet fabric PVA5 (see Later prehistoric pottery fabrics), with oxidised or irregularly fired surfaces, were probably all from a single vessel, a simple barrel-shaped jar with a gently insloping rim, bevelled on the interior, and a slightly splayed, flat base (Fig. 184). Although generally large, the sherds were rather abraded, but this was probably a consequence of soil conditions rather than of repeated deposition. Their location in the gully terminal was comparable to that of sherds from Shenstone Ring Ditch (Site 14) and may indicate a placed deposit.

The fabric was not closely paralleled amongst the Iron Age material from other M6 Toll sites, nor in the larger collection from Coleshill, only *c* 5.5 km distant to the SSE. The Middle Iron Age date assignable on typological grounds is, however, confirmed by a radiocarbon determination on charcoal associated with the sherds, giving a date of 380–190 cal BC (NZA-25060, 2239±30 BP).

Medieval pottery, by Stephanie Rátkai

The medieval pottery was examined at x 20 magnification and divided into fabric groups. These were later cross-referenced to the Warwickshire County Pottery Type Series (WCTS, Rátkai and Soden 1998). Fabrics which were recorded for the first time at this site were given a new WCTS code. Details of all the medieval fabrics found on the M6 Toll sites are given in

Table 138 Quantification of the total medieval pottery assemblage

Fabric	*No.*	*Wt(g)*	*%no.*	*%wt*
chaff	1	3	0.15	0.03
?Roman	3	47	0.45	0.50
RS ems	1	9	0.15	0.10
RS01	14	130	2.08	1.38
Sg12	16	117	2.38	1.24
Sg40	4	33	0.60	0.35
Sg50	1	7	0.15	0.07
slpw	1	19	0.15	0.20
Sq05	1	9	0.15	0.10
Sq08	3	39	0.45	0.41
Sq11	50	526	7.44	5.57
Sq20	1	7	0.15	0.07
Sq20.2	7	86	1.04	0.91
Sq20.3	17	147	2.53	1.56
Sq20.4	37	312	5.51	3.30
Sq25.1	1	8	0.15	0.08
Sq30	6	105	0.89	1.11
SV40	3	43	0.45	0.46
SV40?	1	14	0.15	0.15
SV41	4	59	0.60	0.62
WW01.1	192	3463	28.57	36.68
WW01.4	272	3729	40.48	39.49
WW01.5	5	72	0.74	0.76
WW01.6	16	345	2.38	3.65
WW03	11	99	1.64	1.05
WW04	4	14	0.60	0.15
Total	672	9442		

Chapter 28. The pottery was quantified by sherd count and weight and minimum rim count (Table 138). Details of vessel form, decoration, glaze, sooting and wear were noted.

Three-quarters of the medieval assemblage by sherd count (*c* 82% by sherd weight) was made up of whitewares which were divided into six fabric groups. Of these fabrics only two, WCTS WW01.1 and WW03, were represented in the type series

The assemblage overall contained only a small number of fabrics which comprised one per cent or greater of the assemblage. These were in descending order of importance: Coventry type wares (WCTS Sq20.2–4), a coarse, sandy cooking pot ware (WCTS Sq11), reduced Deritend ware (WCTS RS01), glazed Deritend ware (WCTS Sg12), Chilvers Coton C ware (WCTS Sq30), a coarse cooking pot fabric with mixed inclusions, possibly derived from Boulder Clays (new fabric WCTS SV41) and a glazed gritty ware (new fabric WCTS Sg40).

There were three possible Romano-British sherds found in pit 200161, in the primary fill of off-stream pond 200658 and in the secondary fill of slot 200456. These presumably represent part of a 'manuring scatter' incorporated into later features. A small burnished chaff-tempered sherd of Early-Middle Saxon date was found within the upper fill (200236) of the wall trench of structure 200662. A simple rim sherd from the fill (200022) of by-pass channel 200656 could also have been of Anglo-Saxon date or maybe Iron Age.

The contexts or features from which the pottery was derived could be divided into three main groups; ditch and channel fills, fills of ponds and associated features, and contexts associated with structure 200662. The pottery has therefore been tabulated (Tables 139–41) according to these groupings in order to facilitate the comparison of the pottery groups. It was immediately apparent that the relative proportion of all whitewares associated with structure 200662 and with the pond fills was much the same, at 75% and 78% respectively. All but two of the backfilled ponds contained whiteware sherds as did every context associated with structure 200662. Whitewares were dominant in the fills of pond 200217 and off-stream pond 200658 which could suggest that they were the latest to be backfilled, with pond 200253 being perhaps the earliest since it has a much higher proportion of cooking pot sherds in Coventry-type ware (dating to the 12th–13th centuries). It is therefore possible that pond 200253 was beginning

Table 139 Medieval pottery from structure 662 (quantification by sherd count)

Context	*chaff*	*Sg12*	*Sg50*	*Sq05*	*Sq08*	*Sq11*	*Sq20*	*Sq20.2*	*Sq20.3*	*Sq30*	*WW01.1*	*WW01.4*	*WW01.5*	*WW03*	*WW04*	*No.*	*Wt(g)*
200233	–	–	–	–	–	44	–	1	–	–	–	40	–	–	–	85	925
200236	1	–	–	–	–	–	–	–	–	–	2	11	–	–	3	17	201
200239	–	–	–	–	–	–	–	–	–	–	–	1	–	–	–	1	76
200242	–	–	–	–	–	3	–	–	–	–	2	15	–	–	–	20	450
200309	–	1	–	–	–	–	–	–	–	–	–	1	–	1	–	3	92
200422	–	–	–	–	–	–	–	–	–	–	–	1	2	–	–	3	24
200423	–	–	–	–	–	1	–	1	–	–	–	1	–	–	–	3	20
200425	–	–	–	–	–	–	–	–	–	–	–	4	–	–	–	4	25
200427	–	–	1	–	–	–	1	2	1	1	–	2	–	1	–	9	72
200429	–	–	–	–	1	–	–	–	1	–	2	30	1	–	–	35	659
200430	–	–	–	1	–	1	–	–	–	–	–	54	–	2	–	58	729
200482	–	–	–	–	–	–	–	–	–	–	–	7	–	–	–	7	32
Total	1	1	1	1	1	49	1	4	2	1	6	167	3	4	3	245	3305

Table 140 Medieval pottery from ditches (quantification by sherd count)

Feature	*Context*	*RS ems*	*Sg12*	*Sq08*	*Sq11*	*Sq20.2*	*Sq20.3*	*Sq20.4*	*Sq30*	*SV40*	*SV41*	*WW01.1*	*WW01.4*	*WW01.5*	*WW01.6*	*No.*	*Wt(g)*
200547	200549	–	–	1	–	–	–	–	–	–	–	–	–	–	–	1	15
200656	200022	1	–	–	–	–	–	–	–	–	–	–	1	–	–	2	72
	200066	–	1	–	–	–	–	–	–	–	–	–	–	–	–	1	1
	200068	–	–	–	–	1	–	–	–	–	–	1	–	–	–	2	43
	200071	–	–	–	–	–	–	–	–	–	–	–	19	–	–	19	262
200657	200100	–	–	–	–	–	–	–	1	–	–	–	–	–	–	1	27
200664	200107	–	–	–	–	–	–	–	–	–	–	–	1	–	–	1	17
	200109	–	–	–	–	–	–	–	–	–	–	1	5	2	–	8	159
	200111	–	–	–	–	–	–	–	–	–	–	–	9	–	1	10	128
200667	200173	–	–	–	–	–	–	1	–	–	–	–	–	–	–	1	27
	200224	–	–	–	1	–	–	–	–	–	–	–	–	–	–	1	3
	200228	–	–	–	–	–	–	–	–	–	–	–	3	–	–	3	40
	200243	–	–	–	–	–	–	–	–	–	1	1	–	–	–	2	20
	200244	–	–	1	–	–	–	–	–	1	–	–	–	–	–	2	24
	200288	–	–	–	–	–	–	–	–	–	–	1	–	–	–	1	45
200669/ 200670	200346	–	–	–	–	–	1	1	–	–	–	–	–	–	–	2	19
200670/ 200671	200115	–	–	–	–	–	–	–	1	–	–	–	–	–	–	1	22
	200452	–	–	–	–	–	–	1	–	–	–	–	–	–	–	1	20
200673	200635	–	–	–	–	–	4	–	–	–	–	–	–	–	–	4	4
200675/ 200676	200538	–	–	–	–	–	–	29	–	–	–	–	–	–	–	29	146
200676	200579	–	–	–	–	–	1	–	–	–	–	–	–	–	–	1	4
	200581	–	–	–	–	–	–	–	–	–	–	1	1	–	–	2	32
	200584	–	–	–	–	–	1	–	–	–	–	–	–	–	–	2	49
Total		1	1	2	1	1	6	32	1	1	1	4	33	2	1	83	1179

to be neglected around the mid-13th century. The much larger quantity of pottery from pond 200217, in contrast, and the absence of any Coventry-type wares suggested a deliberate backfilling or dumping of material in the later 13th or 14th centuries.

The ditch and channel fills could be divided between those that have no whitewares (200547, 200657, 200669, 200670, 200671, 200673 and 200675), those with some whitewares (200667, 200676 and 200677) and those where whitewares were dominant (by-pass channel 200656 and ditch 200664). Although it is always difficult to draw firm conclusions from what are small ditch fill samples, it does appear that the absence/presence of whitewares and their relative proportions within ditches may be chronologically significant. If this is so, a possible pattern emerges when the relative proportion of whitewares within all features is plotted. To the south-east of structure 200662, whitewares were either not present or comprised a lesser component of the feature fills, suggesting that earlier activity was focused in this area. However, single sherds of Chilvers Coton C ware (WCTS Sq30) were found in ponds 200253 and 200314, the junction of ditches 200670 and 200671 and in context 200620 in the marl pit. The sherd from fill 200115 of 200670/200671 (see below) may have been intrusive, although it was comparatively large at 22 g, but the two sherds from pond 200253, weighing 2 g and 3 g respectively, almost certainly were. The sherd from 200620, which weighed 34 g, the only pottery recovered from the slot, strongly suggested that the marl pit represented later activity in the 14th or 15th centuries.

In the north-west and far west of the site whitewares were dominant in the various feature fills and in structure 200662. A number of the features (eg by-pass channel 200656, ditch 200664 and pond 200217) had average sherd weights of 15 g or more which suggested primary or near primary deposition. Pit 200153, also with a preponderance of whitewares, at the far west of the site, had the highest average sherd weight at 17.8 g. The average sherd weight for all the contexts associated with structure 200662 falls below 15 g, at 13.5 g. Generally speaking, however, the contexts with a predominance of whitewares had greater quantities of pottery within them, made up of larger sherds. Cross-join information, albeit very limited, linked floor surface contexts 200427 and 200430 in structure 200662 and fills 200219 and 200293 of pit 200217. This is further

Table 141 Medieval pottery from ponds

Feature	Context	Roman?	RS01	Sg12	Sg40	slpw	Sq20.2	Sq20.3	Sq20.4	Sq30	Sv40	Sv40?	Sv41	WW01.1	WW01.4	WW01.6	WW03	WW04	Total no.	Total wt (g)
200161	200159	1	–	–	–	–	–	–	–	–	–	–	–	–	–	–	–	–	1	5
200166	200169	–	–	–	2	–	–	–	–	–	–	–	–	2	–	–	–	–	4	36
200217	200219	–	–	–	–	–	–	–	–	–	–	–	–	24	2	4	–	–	30	871
	200282	–	–	10	2	–	–	–	–	–	–	–	–	9	1	–	–	–	22	128
	200293	–	–	3	–	–	–	–	–	–	–	–	–	34	27	–	–	–	64	919
200253	200254	–	–	–	–	–	–	–	1	–	–	1	–	–	–	–	–	–	2	24
	200255	–	–	–	–	–	1	–	–	–	1	–	1	1	–	–	–	–	4	65
	200256	–	–	–	–	–	–	1	–	–	–	–	–	–	2	–	–	–	3	45
	200258	–	1	–	–	–	–	1	–	1	–	–	–	–	1	–	–	–	4	48
	200259	–	–	–	–	–	–	2	1	–	–	–	–	1	1	–	4	–	9	22
200314	200317	–	–	–	–	–	–	1	–	–	–	–	–	–	–	–	–	–	1	14
	200318	–	–	1	–	–	–	3	–	1	–	–	–	–	1	–	–	–	6	27
200411	200165	–	–	–	–	–	–	–	–	–	–	–	–	1	–	–	–	–	1	13
200658	200438	1	–	–	–	–	–	–	–	–	–	–	–	1	11	–	3	1	17	184
200674	200621	–	–	–	–	1	–	–	–	–	–	–	–	–	–	–	–	–	1	19
Total		2	1	14	4	1	1	8	2	2	1	1	1	73	46	4	7	1	169	2420

evidence to suggest that dominance of whitewares is linked to dumping of material rather than gradual accumulation.

Single sherds of Chilvers Coton C ware were found in subsidiary channel 200657 and floor surface context 200427 of structure 200662. The distribution of Chilvers Coton wares in this area of Warwickshire is still somewhat uncertain. They form a dominant group in Coventry but do not seem to penetrate much, if at all, into Birmingham. Wishaw may lie on the edge of their distribution and Wishaw Hill Farm (Site 19) which produced much more later pottery than this site, contained a reasonably high proportion of Chilvers Coton C sherds (Rátkai, Chapter 24). It is probably fair, therefore, to say that the very small numbers of Chilvers Coton C sherds from this site are chronologically significant. Chilvers Coton C ware was dated by Mayes and Scott (1984) to the late 13th–15th centuries with a 14th–15th century floruit. Its paucity at this site and the high number of whitewares suggest that most of the contexts in the north-west and west of the site dated to the late 13th or early 14th centuries.

A group of 27 medieval sherds (283 g) was recovered from pit 200124, one of several associated with possibly prehistoric deposits of burnt stone. Only whitewares were present, mainly fabric WCTS WW01.4, but six sherds of fabric WCTS WW01.6 were also found. One cooking pot rim was present and the remainder of the sherds which could be assigned to form came from jugs, with at least two red-painted whiteware jugs represented by body sherds. The mixture of prehistoric and medieval material in one pit is not easy to explain. As Harding noted above, the quantity of medieval pottery makes intrusion unlikely. The abraded nature of the pottery, which links it with material found within structure 200662 and the fills of pond 200217 (see discussion below) and the presence of several sherds from single vessels also seem to rule intrusion out. Although there seems little doubt that the other pits were associated with possible 'burnt mound' material perhaps 200124 was different. Burnt pebbles were noted for example in a secure medieval feature oven/pit 133066 at Shenstone Linear Features (Site 13, Chapter 15) associated with two drying ovens.

Vessel form and function

By sherd count 37.8% of the assemblage comprised cooking pots/jars, 27.4% bowls or pipkins, and 19.0% jugs (Table 142). The remainder of the assemblage was unclassifiable. The assemblage was also quantified by minimum rim count and minimum base count. These produced similar proportions of vessel types to the sherd count.

Several Coventry-type ware cooking pot rims were found, two from floor surface contexts 200423 and 200427 of structure 200662, four from the fills of pond 200253, one from the junction of ditches 200669/200670 and one from ditch intersection 200675/200676. The latter was heavily sooted externally. A cooking pot from 200253 was also sooted

Table 142 Functional analysis of medieval pottery (quantification by sherd count)

Vessel type/function	*No.*
Food preparation/cooking	
bowl	87
Food consumption	
platter (post-med.)	1
Cooking	
cooking pot/jar	251
cooking pot/jar?	3
pipkin	61
bowl/pipkin	36
Liquid consumption	
jug/pitcher	1
jug	127
Unknown	105
Total	672

externally. Single rim sherds in fabric WCTS SV40 and SV41 were recovered from pond 200253 and pit 200153 respectively.

As would be expected the greatest number of rim sherds was found among the whitewares. Fifteen cooking pot/jar sherds were present in fabrics WW01.1 and WW01.4. Only four of these vessels were sooted, although roughly half were heavily abraded. There was no correlation between deposition site and the amount of abrasion present. Bowls and/or pipkins were the next best form represented by rim count. Two pipkin rim sherds were found within the floor of structure 200662, as was a bowl with an incised wavy line along the rim, an internal green glaze and an externally sooted base. Two bowls were found within the fill of pond 200217, one burnt and the other with a sooted rim, decorated with an incised wavy line. Two further whiteware bowls were found in by-pass channel 200656 and ditch 200677. Whiteware jug rims were found in ditches 200677 and 200664, floor surface context 200430 of structure 200662 and within burnt stone pit 200124.

An examination of the base sherds revealed a similar picture to the foregoing, with cooking-pot/jars predominating, followed by bowls/pipkins and the least well represented form being jugs. However quantification by minimum base count indicated that bowls were more frequently found in the pond backfills, particularly in pond 200217. It was also apparent that it was the lower sections of the bowls which were sooted as most bases were sooted externally, one internally and externally and one externally above the base angle, suggesting that it may have sat within another vessel or on a stand during the cooking process. Most of the bowl bases were heavily abraded. Three bowl bases and one ?pipkin base were found within structure 200662, again heavily abraded. Some of the bowl bases from pond 200217 and structure 200662 had patches of brown discoloration or decay on the interior glazed surface. This discoloration has been seen on other glazed whiteware bowls, from Lichfield (Rátkai 2004b) and Minworth Greaves (Rátkai 2001a) for example, but the cause is as yet unknown. The overall similarity of the bowl bases from pond 200217 and structure 200662, in terms of wear and discoloration, is perhaps rather odd, given the rather different depositional situations in which they were found, one presumably open and waterlogged and the other on dry land and roofed over.

Deritend ware jug sherds were found mainly in pond fills or from structure 200662 floor. White slip decoration was visible on two vessels but, as on so much of the pottery from the site, abrasion had removed much of the surfaces. Ten very heavily abraded sherds from a Deritend ware jug were found in the uppermost fill of pond 200217. Precise dating for Deritend ware has not yet been established, despite recent work on pottery from the Bull Ring Birmingham (Rátkai forthcoming b). However, Sherlock's (1957) original suggestion of early 13th–early 14th centuries seems to be broadly correct. If so the dating fits well with the proposed abandonment of the site in the early 14th century.

Jugs in whiteware fabric WCTS WW01.1, although glazed (olive or pale green), were largely undecorated. One jug from pit 200153 had combed decoration and there was one sherd from a 'red-painted whiteware' jug from pond 200217. As with many of the sherds there was abrasion, often heavy, and two jugs had patches of brown discoloration in the glaze, like those seen on the bowls. Fabric WCTS WW01.4 had rather more examples of decorated sherds, the techniques comprising combing, stabbing and the use of red slip; ie further examples of red-painted whiteware. Several red-painted whiteware sherds were found associated with burnt stone pit 200124. Jug glazes varied from bright, apple green to olive.

Three jugs were represented in WCTS fabric WW01.6, one with applied strip and tear-drop decoration, similar to North French decorative schemes of the late 13th–early 14th centuries. Jug sherds (and one bowl sherd) were found in fabric WCTS WW03. Examples of combed, stabbed and comb impressed decoration were noted. Jugs were found in three other fabrics: WCTS Sg40, WCTS Sq25.1 and Chilvers Coton C (WCTS Sq30). The WCTS Sg40 jug was represented by two very heavily abraded joining handle sherds from pond 200166 and two tiny flakes less than 1 g in total from pond 200217. Warwickshire fabric WCTS Sq25.5 is typified by a light bodied sandy clay containing rounded clay pellets and is normally associated with pitchers.

The small heavily abraded sherd from pit 200153 had been decorated with an applied strip and had an opaque yellowish-green glaze. The glaze and decoration seem consistent with the sherd coming from a pitcher, suggesting a late 12th or early 13th century date. The sherd therefore would be roughly contemporary with the Coventry-type wares from the site and together these indicate that medieval activity on the site probably began *c* 1200.

The remaining jug sherd was in a hard-fired Chilvers Coton C fabric. It was one of two sherds from the intersection of ditches 200670/200671 (see above) and may be intrusive. On the basis of comparison with Chilvers Coton wares from Burton Dassett in the south-east of Warwickshire (Rátkai forthcoming e) the jug probably dates to the later 14th or even 15th centuries.

Discussion

The date of the construction of the fish ponds is difficult to deduce from the ceramic evidence, since, clearly, while operational, they would have been kept clean and well maintained. However, the earliest medieval pottery from the site, mainly the Coventry-type wares and the possible pitcher fragment, suggests that there was probably occupation on the site from the early 13th century or even the late 12th century. Fabrics with mixed inclusions, possibly derived from Boulder Clays, such as WCTS SV40 and SV41, are also likely to have a similar date range to the Coventry-type wares. Much of the pottery from the ponds and ditches and from the floors of structure 200662 seems to be roughly contemporary and is consistent with dumping and/or accumulation when the fishponds were abandoned. This probably occurred in the early years of the 14th century, in view of the absence of any significant quantities of Chilvers Coton C wares. For once, therefore, the pottery evidence seems to tie in remarkably well with the documentary evidence. The documented tenure of Wishaw by the Knights Templar (surely the group with the means and reason for the construction of a series of fish ponds), from the late 12th century to the early 14th century, is exactly matched by the proposed pottery dating. The link between the Knights Templar and the fish ponds also perhaps provides the most valid reason why the fish ponds, an expensive and time consuming venture, were so abruptly abandoned and fell into disuse. The downfall of the Templars effectively removed the driving force from the management of the land. It is probably significant that one of the latest sherds from the site was associated with the marl pit, itself an indicator of a different type of land use from fish farming.

The happy coincidence between the pottery dating and the ownership of the land by the Knights Templar, does not, unfortunately, remove several problems associated with the pottery assemblage. The most salient of these is where did all the dumped material come from? There is little doubt that the pottery from the floor contexts identified in structure 200662 is ostensibly the same as that recovered from the fills of certain ponds and ditches. Pottery is seldom found within domestic medieval floor surfaces, which were usually kept rigorously clean. This can be clearly seen, for example, at Burton Dassett, a deserted settlement in south-eastern Warwickshire (Rátkai forthcoming e). The presence of large quantities of pottery within buildings can be attributable to several factors; building collapse, dumping of material after building abandonment, or the accidental incorporation of smaller pot sherds into clays brought into buildings for use as flooring (or to patch existing floors). An example of the latter was noted at The Explosion Site, Alcester (Rátkai 2001b). This could be the reason for the pottery found within structure 200662. Having said that, some of the sherds are really a little too large to be entirely consistent with this explanation. Harding (below) observes that a cluster of sherds from the same vessel may represent a pot which was suspended from the wall of the structure and this is an attractive conjecture. Several groups of sherds of this sort were noted during the recording of the pottery and represent a cooking pot (fabric WCTS Sq11) and a pipkin (fabric WCTS WW01.4) from wall trench fill 200233, the base and lower part of a bowl (fabric WCTS WW01.4) from wall trench fill 200236, a bowl (fabric WCT WW01.4) from wall trench fill 200242, a bowl or pipkin base (fabric WCTS WW01.4) from fill 200429 of hollow 200435 and a bowl or pipkin (fabric WCTS WW01.4) from fill 200430 of the hollow. It is quite possible that these vessels were suspended or shelved within the building, since they represent ordinary functional items of pottery, of the sort which may well have been used by someone maintaining the fish ponds. In addition, if the sherds making up the 'cluster' are removed from the quantification of the pottery, that leaves a maximum (bearing in mind that some of these sherds could be unrecognised parts of the sherd 'clusters') of 57 sherds spread through the floor surfaces, many of which are quite small and could have found their way into the building by a variety of routes. In fact the presence of a chaff-tempered sherd from the upper fill of the wall north trench (context 200236) indicates that some extraneous material has found its way into the building.

The 'clusters' of sherds from the structure may be quite significant in terms of highlighting the range of pottery likely to be used by an ordinary person in the medieval period. Whether this represents pottery used for culinary purposes – the greater number of sherds were unsooted – or was in part connected with the upkeep of the fish ponds is impossible to say. There are however, two caveats to the preceding. Not one complete vessel was found within the structure, which either indicates that there has been later disturbance or that the pots were never complete when deposited. The latter would, of course, effectively demolish the conjecture of suspended pots within the building. Secondly all the bowl/pipkin sherd clusters were very heavily abraded internally and externally. Did this occur whilst they were in use? The high incidence of abrasion on the pottery assemblage in general seems to refute this. The incidence of abrasion on the sherds from within the structure seems to suggest that the pottery had been exposed to the elements for some period of time. Coincidentally, similar high levels of abrasion and heavy abrasion were found in pottery recovered from the fills of adjacent pond 200217 which strongly argues for the pottery coming from the same source. However, there

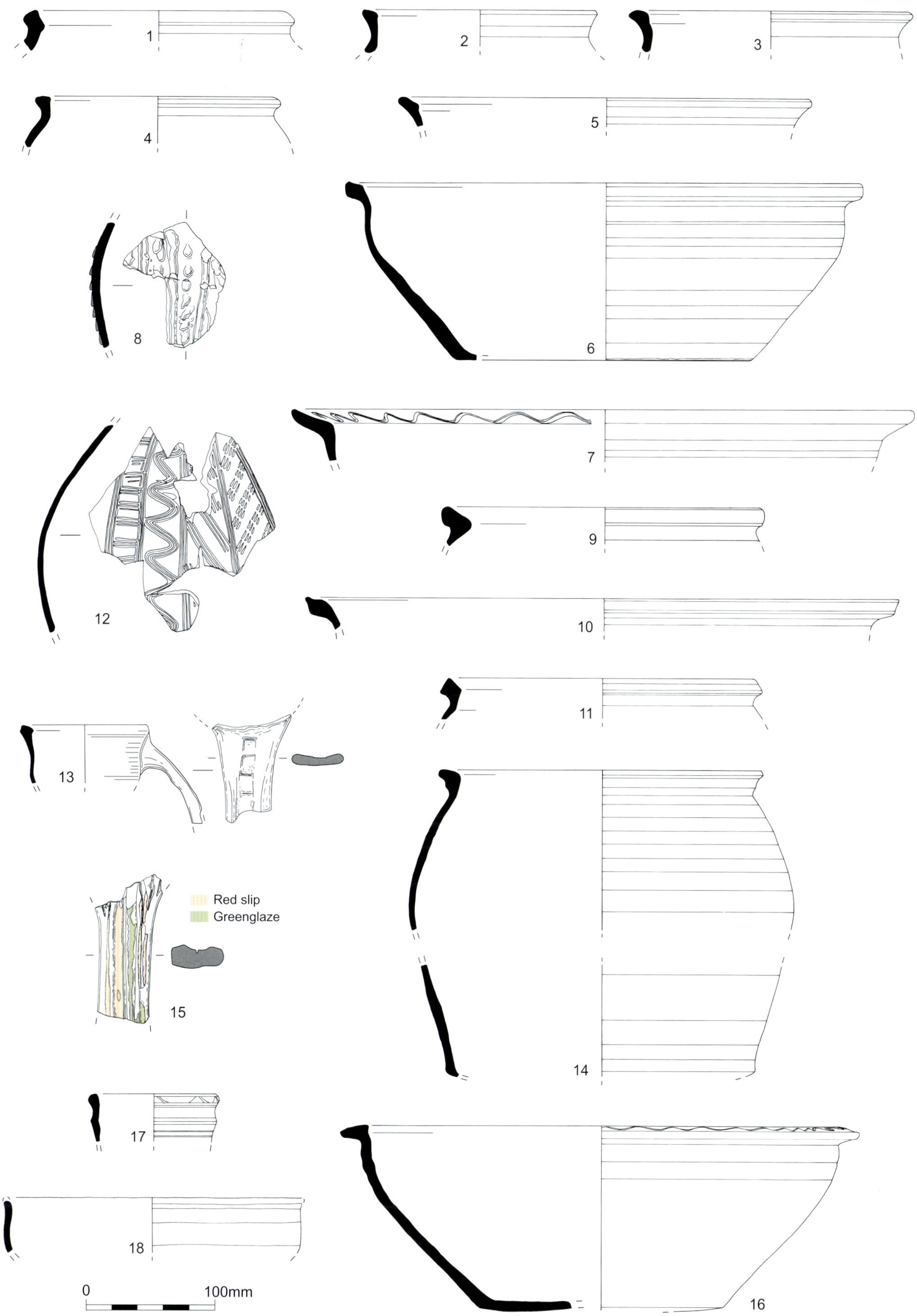

Fig. 185 Medieval pottery

are no cross-joins between the structure floor contexts and the fills of pond 200217 although there are plenty between the various floors and, separately, between the fills of pond 200217. In addition, there seems just too much pottery overall for it to have been derived from structure 200662, especially if the latter was only seasonally occupied. Also, the presence of at least three highly decorated jugs, and indeed a rather higher proportion of jugs overall, does not sit well with the presumed life-style of the occupant or occupants of the structure. In short, the pottery evidence from structure 200662 and pond 200217 is tantalising and contradictory.

The following facts can be deduced from the pottery from structure 200662 and pond 200217. The abrasion evident on both groups is indicative of exposure to the elements and therefore suggests that the pottery had been in the open for some time. It seems unlikely that pottery would have been dumped within the abandoned structure, particularly as an abandoned pond was so close by. It is not impossible, on the other hand, that some material from the structure was removed and dumped in the pond. This could explain the lack of complete vessels in the structure, and the heavily trampled nature of the floors (above) is not inconsistent with some process of demolition and clearance within the structure. A cross-join (Fig. 185.14) between wall trench fill 200233 and floor context 200430 also hints at disturbance. The abraded nature of the pottery in pond 200217 would most closely match that of midden material. Was there perhaps a dwelling or dwellings somewhere in the vicinity, traces of which were removed during 1970s levelling? Harding (above) notes:

> 'The area also coincided with the southern extent of a surface scatter of medieval pottery collected by Hodder (1992), possibly material that had been disturbed by the landscaping and further spread by ploughing'.

So the evidence really does seem to indicate rather more occupation in this area of Wishaw in the past than is now apparent.

Illustrated vessels (Figs 185–6)

Ponds

1. CPJ06 WCTS Sv40. Cooking pot, context 200254, pond 200253
2. Coventry-type ware WCTS Sq20.4. Cooking pot, context 200254, pond 200253
3. Coventry-type ware WCTS Sq20.2. Cooking pot, some abrasion, context 200255, pond 200253
4. Coventry-type ware WCTS Sq20.3. Cooking pot, patch of external soot, abraded, context 200256, pond 200253
5. Coventry-type ware WCTS Sq20.3. Cooking pot, abraded, context 200258, pond 200253
6. WW03 WCTS WW01.1. Bowl, heavily abraded, trace of interior light green glaze, trace of external soot, context 200219, pond 200217
7. WW03 WCTS WW01.1. Bowl, sooted, possibly burnt, incised wavy line on rim, very gritty fabric, context 200219, pond 200217
8. WW06 WCTS WW01.6. Jug body sherd, abraded, applied self clay 'scales' and ribs, some external olive glaze remaining, context 200219, pond 200217
9. WW03 WCTS WW01.1. Cooking pot/jar, abraded, context 200219/200293, pond 200217
10. WW03 WCTS WW01.1. Cooking pot/jar, abraded, context 200219/200293, pond 200217
11. WW01 WCTS WW01.4. Cooking pot jar, abraded, context 200219/200293, pond 200217
12. WW005 WCTS WW01.4. Jug, heavily abraded, complex combed and comb impressed decoration, trace of external apple-green glaze, context 200293, pond 200217
13. Deritend ware WCTS Sg12. Jug rim and handle sherds, very heavily abraded, context 200293, pond 200217

Structure 200662

14. WW01 WCTS WW01.4. Pipkin, heavily abraded, trace of green glaze on lower interior of vessel, context 200233/200430
15. WW01 WCTS WW01.4. Red-Painted whiteware jug handle, abraded, bands of red slip and olive glaze along handle, context 200309
16. WW03 WCTS WW01.1. Bowl, incised wavy line on rim, abraded, very heavy abrasion on external base, sooting on exterior base/base-angle, trace of green glaze on interior base, internal brown deposit or ?glaze decay, context 200242
17. WW02 WCTS WW02. Jug, external olive-green glaze, trace of horizontal combing around neck, context 200430

Ditches

18. Early–Middle Saxon sherd. Bowl, abraded, context 200022, channel 200656
19. WW03 WCTS WW01.1. Bowl, channel 200656
20. WW05 WCTS WW01.4. Cooking pot, abraded, some external soot, single apple-green glaze spot on exterior, context 20071, channel 200656
21. WW05 WCTS WW01.4. Cooking pot, small patches of light internal and external soot, possibly post-breakage, context 200109, ditch 200664
22. WW05 WCTS WW01.4. Small ?jar, context 200109, ditch 200664
23. WW05 WCTS WW01.4. cooking pot/jar, context 200111, ditch 200664
24. Coventry-type ware WCTS Sq20.4. Cooking pot, heavy external soot, context 200538, ditch 200676
25, WW01 WCTS WW01.4. Jug, external splash of yellowish-brown glaze, context 200228, ditch 200677

Miscellaneous features

26. WW03 WCTS WW01.1. Jug, abraded, trace of pale olive glaze on exterior, blue-grey mottling on surface where glaze has worn away with patches of brownish discoloration or decay, context 200458, slot 200456
27. CPJ05 WCTS Sv41.Cooking pot, abraded, external soot, context 200154, pit 200153

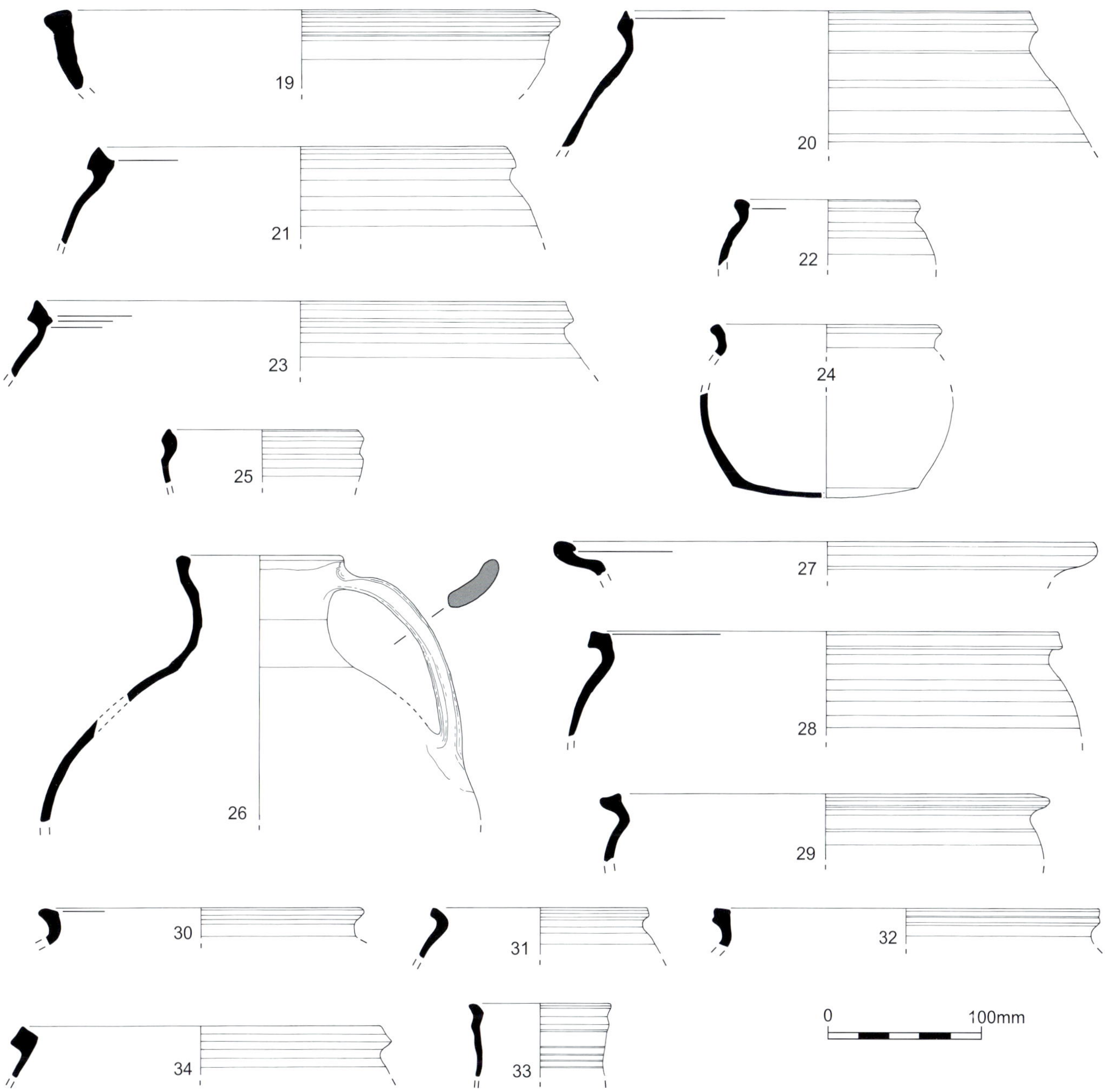

Fig. 186 Medieval pottery

28. WW03 WCTS WW01.1. Cooking pot, abraded, trace of some internal and external soot, context 200154, pit 200153
29. WW03 WCTS WW01.1. Cooking pot, heavy internal abrasion, heavy external soot, context 200154, pit 200153
30. WW03 WCTS WW01.1. Cooking pot, cooking pot, trace of external sooting, context 200154, pit 200153
31. WW03 WCTS WW01.1. Cooking pot, heavy external sooting and over rim, context 200154, pit 200153
32. WW03 WCTS WW01.1. Cooking pot, abraded, trace of sooting on rim, context 200154, pit 200153
33. WW03 WCTS WW01.1. Jug, heavily abraded, trace of yellowish-olive glaze on exterior, apple-green glaze spot on rim, context 200125, burnt stone pit 200124
34. WW03 WCTS WW01.1. Cooking pot/jar, abraded, context 200125, burnt stone pit 200124

Environment

Charred plant remains, by Lisa Gray

Ten samples, averaging 10–20 litres, were taken and assessed during the excavation, of which three could be dated to the prehistoric and two to the medieval period, the remainder were unphased. Three samples were chosen for analysis, two from a prehistoric pit and ditch and the third from a medieval rectangular building. Sample details and contents are given in Table 143.

Preservation quality and type

Preservation quality varied. Most uncharred seeds were well preserved but many of the charred remains were fragments. Relatively few charred remains were

Table 143 Charred plant remains

	Period	Prehistoric		Medieval
	Feature	Pit 200150	Ditch 200659	Building 200662
	Context	200152	200337	200242
	Sample	207509	207539	207520
	Sample size (l)	20	2	15
	Flot size (ml)	450	500	100
Taxon	*Common name*			
Triticum aestivum grain	Bread wheat	–	–	7
Triticum cf. *dicoccum* grain	Emmer	–	2	–
Triticum sp. grain	Wheat	3	–	–
Hordeum vulgare grain	Barley	–	–	1
Hordeum sp. grain	Barley, naked	1	1	–
cf. *Hordeum* sp. grain	Barley	2	–	–
Avena sp. grain	Oat	–	1	+
Secale cereale grain	Rye	–	–	1
Avena/Hordeum/Secale/Triticum coleoptiles	indet. cereal	–	–	1
Vicia faba seed	Celtic bean/horse bean	–	–	6
Pisum sativum seed	Field pea	–	–	4
Vicia/Lathyrus/Pisum sp. seed frag.	Vetch/tare/vetchling/pea	–	–	+
cf. *Vicia* sp. seed	vetch	1	–	–
Indet. wood frag (>4 mm^3)		++	+++	+++
Indet. wood fleck (<4 mm^3)		+++++	+++++	–
Indet. bud		–	–	1

Key to estimated levels of abundance codes: + = 1–10; ++ = 11–50; +++ = 51–150; +++++ = >250

recovered from these samples other than wood charcoal, and this comprised cereal grains and legumes and single finds of a coleoptile and a bud. Uncharred root fragments and seeds were observed in the samples, indicative of bioturbation.

Prehistoric features

Both samples, from semicircular Iron Age ditch 200659 and ?prehistoric pit 200150, produced charred grains and no chaff. One charred seed vetch (*cf. Vicia* sp.) seed and three wheat (*Triticum* sp.) grains were observed in pit 200150. The cereal grains were too poorly preserved to allow any further identification. Two poorly preserved wheat grains were recovered from ditch 200659. They resembled each other in size and general shape and the straight sides allowed a tentative identification of emmer (*Triticum cf. dicoccum*).

Three charred barley (*Hordeum* spp.) grains were recovered from pit 200150 and one from ditch 200659. All were too poorly preserved to establish whether they are straight or twisted (two or six rowed) but they did appear to be naked.

Medieval building 200662

The sample from wall trench fill 200242 produced a small but well preserved charred assemblage dominated by grains and legumes. A coleoptile fragment was present and was the only chaff fragment observed. The most frequent grains were bread wheat (*T. aestivum*). Single grains of rye (*Secale cereale*) and barley (*H. sativum*) were present. Low quantities (<10) of oat type (*cf. Avena* sp.) fragments were also preserved.

Six Celtic/horse beans (*V. faba*) were recovered along with six peas (*Pisum sativum*) and low quantities of fragments of vetch/tare/vetchling/pea (*Vicia/Lathyrus/Pisum* spp.) seeds. A charred ovoid bud was recovered but charring has made the diagnostic features unclear so identification was not possible.

Feature function

Prehistoric features

Little could be inferred from the samples because they were so small and poorly preserved. It is likely that they were not a true reflection of the archaeobotanical record and the absence of chaff could be an indication of poor preservation rather than the use of clean prime grain.

Medieval rectangular building

The remains were well preserved, and the absence of chaff and weed seeds might indicate general waste from cooking (Bottema 1984, 209–10), or the final cleaning of grain. A further possible source was observed during experimental work reconstructing Saxon and medieval bread ovens (Cane and Cane, unpublished, cited in Moffett, 1994, 61) who noted the use of a layer of uncleaned grain to keep the bread from sticking. However, in this case, the lack of chaff or weed seeds seemed to indicate that this was a store or waste from cooking.

Table 144 Charcoal (no. frags)

Feature	Context	Sample	Alnus	Betula	Corylus	Fraxinus	Pomoideae	Prunus	Quercus
?Prehistoric pit									
200150	200152	207509	–	6	–	–	–	13	3h, 17r, 1s
Semicircular Iron Age ditch									
200659	200337	207539	–	–	2	6	3	–	15h
Medieval rectangular building									
200662	200242	207520	cf. 1	3	–	–	–	3	6h/u, 5r. 1s

Key: h = heartwood; r = roundwood (diam. <20 mm); s = sapwood (diam. unknown); u = maturity undetermined (*Quercus* only)

Economy and diet

The grains from prehistoric features are typical of those found in pre-Romano-British assemblages (Green 1981). Little else can be determined about cereal processing or consumption because the samples are so small and poorly preserved. The mixture of crop plants present in the medieval building is typical of the mixed crops sown in the medieval period. Rye was sometimes grown as part of a mixed crop, 'maslin', which included rye and wheat (Hammond 1993, 2). The pulses present could also have been part of a mixed crop such as 'pulse' – peas and beans or 'bervechicorn' – dredge and vetches (Hammond 1993, 2). The oats present could have been part of a mixed crop or barley and oats, 'dredge' (Greig 1988, 111).

Charcoal, by Rowena Gale

Bulk samples produced large quantities of charcoal, mostly in rather poor condition. Two prehistoric samples and one medieval sample (each interpreted as fuel debris) were selected for species identification. Analysis was undertaken to indicate the character of local woodland and the use of wood resources. The taxa identified are presented in Table 144.

Prehistoric period

Pit 200150

It was not clear whether the heat-affected clay in the base of this sub-rectangular pit had resulted from *in situ* burning or from the dumping of intensely hot material. The sample, from the fill (context 200152) of the pit, included charred cereal grain and charcoal; the latter consisted of oak (*Quercus* sp.), blackthorn (*Prunus spinosa*) and birch (*Betula* sp.).

Semicircular ditch 200659

Sample 207539, from the fill of the Middle Iron Age curved ditch 200659, contained a large quantity of charcoal, much of which was too degraded to identify. The taxa named included oak, hazel (*Corylus avellana*), ash (*Fraxinus excelsior*) and the hawthorn/*Sorbus* group (Pomoideae). Charred cereal grain was also present.

Medieval

Rectangular building 200662

A small rectangular building associated with the use of the fish ponds dated roughly from the mid-13th to early 14th centuries. Sample 207520 probably represented the remains of fuel used within this structure for domestic purposes. The charcoal consisted of small fragments from oak, blackthorn, birch and possibly alder (*Alnus glutinosa*).

Discussion

The site was located close to the present day course of a small stream, which appears to have been the focus of activity around the formation of 'burnt mound' features, of putative prehistoric date, and for the construction of fish ponds in the medieval period. The small rectangular structure erected close to the fish ponds probably served as shelter for local workers.

The combination of charcoal and charred cereal grain (see Gray, above) in the prehistoric features would be consistent with the dumping of domestic waste and fuel debris; the latter demonstrates that firewood was collected from oak, birch, blackthorn, the hawthorn group, hazel and ash. Domestic origins also seem likely for charcoal deposits from the medieval building and indicate the use of oak, blackthorn, birch and probably alder. None of the charcoal fragments examined was large enough to assess the use of managed woodland.

Environmental evidence

The site was based on sandy gravels in the Tame Valley close to a small stream, which suggests that the area was low-lying and possibly prone to flooding. Wetland species such as willow (*Salix* sp.), poplar (*Populus* sp.) and alder were almost totally absent in the charcoal examined from both the prehistoric and medieval features (although alder was tentatively identified from poorly preserved material in the medieval deposit, 200242). This may, however, have more to do with species selection related to function, than species distribution in the environment. The species identified (oak, hazel, birch, ash, blackthorn and the hawthorn group) more typically grow in moist to dry conditions. Alternatively, it may be that the well-drained soils at the site ensured that waterlogging was infrequent. These

Table 145 Waterlogged plant remains

Taxon	Common name	By-pass channel 200656	Valley pond 200655	Pit 200161
	Context	200068	200381	200160
	Sample	207505	207531	207513
Urtica dioica	Common nettle	1	–	–
Rubus sp.	Bramble	1	–	–
Sambucus nigra	Elder	–	1	–
cf. *Salix* sp.bud	Willow	–	–	1
Poaceae spikelet	Modern grass	–	1	cf. 2

results correlate with those from prehistoric and medieval contexts on Site 19.

Waterlogged plant remains, by Chris J. Stevens

Four samples were examined for waterlogged plant remains from features associated with the medieval fish ponds – the valley pond (200655), the by-pass channel (200656), pond 200217 and pit/pond 200160. The samples were sorted for identifiable material under a low-powered stereo-binocular microscope. The material was identified and recorded using the nomenclature of Stace (1997).

None of the samples examined contained significant quantities of waterlogged material. Only three species were identified as possibly waterlogged; pit 200217 contained none. These came from the channel and the valley pond (Table 145). The species are all common components of scrub or hedgerow environments: bramble type (*Rubus* sp.), elder (*Sambucus nigra*) and common nettle (*Urtica dioica*). This material was only recovered from two of the samples and, at least in the case of seeds of bramble and elder, survived by virtue of their highly resistant seed coats.

The absence of waterlogged material from pond 200217 itself suggests that the feature had dried out in antiquity after being infilled, or beforehand. The paucity of waterlogged remains from the other features also suggests these features had ceased to be waterlogged, the limited amount of material within them probably relating to the period following their abandonment.

Molluscan evidence, by Michael J. Allen

The watery environment

Twenty samples were examined from the by-pass channel (200656), valley pond (200655), off-stream pond 200658, pit 200161 and three possible breeding ponds: 200166, 200217, and 200253. Samples of 1500 g were processed by standard methods (Evans 1972) for land snails. Rapid scanning of the flots showed that most features were devoid of shells; only the three samples from the valley pond contained any. This distribution of

Table 146 Mollusca from the valley pond

Feature	Valley pond 200655		
Section	200050	200080	
Context	200072	200381	200084
Sample	207506	207532	207533
Depth (cm)	spot	20–30	10–20
Weight (g)	1500	1500	1500
Terrestrial			
Acanthinula aculeata (Müller)	–	–	1
Discus rotundatus (Müller)	–	+	1
Freshwater			
Lymnaea truncatula (Müller)	7	–	4
Lymnaea cf. *truncatula* (Müller)	–	2	–
L. peregra (Müller)	10	–	6
Lymnaea spp.	20	–	13
Gyraulus albus (Müller)	11	–	3
G. crista (Linnaeus)	1	–	1
Ancylus cf. *lacustris* (Linnaeus)	1	–	–
Pisidium valves	31	6	126
Ostracods	+++	1	++++
Terrestrial total	0	+	2
Aquatic total (Nos valves ÷2)	59	5	90
Total	59	5	92

shell survival may be significant. The shells from the valley pond probably reflect post-use, that is, the immediate disuse environment, rather than that when the valley pond was in use and stocked with fish.

The species present were predominately aquatic, and included a range of taxa that tend to indicate stagnant or slow-moving, poorly-oxygenated water with some reedy vegetation (Table 146). In particular, the more difficult to identify, but more niche-specific *Pisidium* species are particularly useful. These are one of the more common taxa preserved.

Many of the species were tolerant of drying out (*Gyraulus albus* and many of the *Pisidium* spp.), or even amphibious (*Lymnaea truncatula*). Although the *Pisidium* species were not fully identified and quantified, they included largely species of poor water that can tolerate desiccation (*P. personatum*, *P. casertanum*) and those common in reedy and swampy waters (*Sphaerium cornuim cf. Musculium lacustre*). There was a lack of species enjoying well-oxygenated clean and flowing water; for example there was only one specimen of *Ancylus lacustris*.

The terrestrial assemblage is small, but the presence of two obligatory shade-loving species, may suggest mesic and shaded habitats in or surrounding the pond.

The valley pond environment

The assemblages were devoid of many of the species commonly found in very clear well managed ponds and lakes, and indicated a reedy, muddy swampy environment with the body of water subject to drying out. This indicates an overgrown, neglected, but water-fed pond, rather than a well managed and maintained fish or ornamental pond. The sampled sediment was more than 0.3 m of mud that had accumulated through the rotting of vegetation.

Discussion

The evidence of Iron Age activity, in the form of a probable roundhouse gully, can be viewed in the context both of the long-term Iron Age boundary – pit alignment and segmented ditch – recorded 300 m to the north-west at Site 19, and of the other Iron Age settlement structures, both open and enclosed, located close to a stream at Langley Brook (Site 30) as well as at North of Langley Brook (Site 29). The radiocarbon dates from these sites (Table 162, Chapter 29) are broadly comparable within the Middle Iron Age. The undated pits containing evidence of burning may be associated with the Iron Age activity on this site, as similar deposits of burnt stones were found at the other Iron Age sites.

The focus of the excavation, however, was on the medieval activity, particularly on the fish pond complex contructed on the south side of the stream. While the fish ponds would have been a valuable resource within the economy of the Knights Templar's estate at Wishaw, they would have formed only one component of a wider, predominantly agricultural landscape. The economic diversity of that landscape is suggested both by the other features recorded on this site, including the array of rectangular ditched fields or paddocks flanking the fish pond complex, as well as by the enclosure, watering hole/pond, ridge-and-furrow and lynchet recorded north of the stream at Wishaw Hall Farm.

Fish formed a major ingredient of the medieval diet, providing an essential feature of the economy for both the landed gentry and the Church; however it remained primarily a luxury item appearing at the table of those able to afford it (Dyer 1988, 27). Consumption was closely linked to the Christian faith, which required that meat, especially from four-footed species, was avoided on Fridays and Saturdays, throughout Lent and during important festivals, with which the medieval calendar was well provided. The Knights Templar who held land at Wishaw took their code loosely from the Rule of St Benedict (Upton-Ward 1992), which prohibited strictly the eating of meat. However, not only was this rule frequently overlooked by the Knights Templar to enable them to undertake their strenuous military duties, but fish was not regarded as meat and formed a suitable alternative source of protein. Apart from its religious links fish also provided means of displaying wealth at lavish feasts along with animal and avian flesh. Consumption within a high class household may have reached a pound or two (up to about a kilogram) per person by weight per day (Dyer 1988, 28) with large quantities needing to be purchased to meet demand. Sea fish were consumed in larger quantities than freshwater fish, even in areas that involved long distance transport from the coast (*ibid.*, 30). However, freshwater fish, both from rivers and ponds, commanded much higher prices by weight than salt water species, a fact that restricted its consumption to royal, aristocratic and ecclesiastical menus. This may, to some extent, relate to the labour intensive nature of fish farming.

Well-stocked fish ponds therefore provided an appropriate method by which to supplement the demand for fresh fish, primarily for private consumption but exceptionally for sale. Fish ponds needed to be located not only with special attention to the local water supply but were frequently, though not always, located in relation to the heart of the estate itself. Some fish ponds were located in open country (Aston and Bond 1988, 430), but Goody (1982) drew attention to the frequent location of ponds within the immediate confines of the household or monastery, where they provided symbols of social status, landscape features and deterrents to poachers. The evidence suggests that the fish ponds at Wishaw lay close to medieval settlement. Wishaw Hall Farm may have contained a significant medieval house and relatively large quantities of medieval pottery were found from adjacent fields. The ponds are also linked to those immediately to the east surrounding Moxhull Manor (The Belfry).

Very little documentary evidence survives to testify to the labour force that was involved in the day-to-day running of fish ponds. The most comprehensive descriptions were documented by Prior William More of Worcestershire who recorded details of fish pond maintenance related to the cathedral between 1518 and 1535 (Aston 1982). Documentary references relating to 'royal' fishermen are also known (Steane 1988, 46), although these represent the king's representatives rather than those charged with the day-to-day maintenance. Bailiffs or keepers were more likely to be responsible for fish ponds at a local level, as for example at Stafford (Steane 1988, 63) where the Wymer family, during the late 12th and 13th centuries, was granted 'custody' of the king's pond for a rent of half a mark. In return for managing affairs, but not undertaking capital repairs, the Wymers were entitled to take certain fish from the king's pond. Again it is more likely that the Wymers delegated routine menial duties to un-named individuals that lived locally. Illustrations (Steane and Foreman 1988, fig. 12) also draw attention to the fact that labour was needed to drag nets when the ponds were fished. In the absence of detailed records of day-to-day labour it is impossible to be sure of the staffing levels.

However, if comparisons with present day commercial fish ponds are remotely relevant, it is estimated (Shears pers. comm.) that fish ponds similar to those at Wishaw would require one person to undertake routine maintenance/feeding each day throughout the year. Harvesting using nets could be achieved with a minimum of two people, while a team of 4–6 would have been sufficient to completely drain, aerate and restock an individual pond.

The excavation produced no evidence to indicate what species of fish might have stocked the ponds. The failure to recover fish remains from pond sediments is a strange but recurring feature of excavations that have been undertaken of such features. However, documentary references of 1380 indicate that monastic ponds at Cryfield, Warwickshire were stocked with perch, roach, bream, tench and pickerel (pike) (Hilton 1960, 220–1), a breeding list that is repeated from elsewhere in Britain.

Documentary sources from both monastic (Bond 1988, 95) and royal (Steane 1988, 45) sources record transactions for stocking and restocking fish ponds. These records indicate that fish would probably have been readily available from other fish ponds within 20–30 km of Wishaw, although it was possible to transport stock in barrels over larger distances, if it was necessary to do so. Using these records with reference to current fish pond practice (Scott and Shears pers. comm.) it is possible to speculate on the way in which the ponds at Wishaw might have operated. Fishing and stocking/restocking undoubtedly occurred throughout the year to accommodate the Christian calendar; however, for many ponds restocking may have occurred in the spring following a period in winter when a pond was more likely to be routinely drained, cleaned, aerated to release nutrients and reflooded. This procedure was necessary in the barrage pond (created by a dam and filling the main stream course), every 3–4 years (Scott pers. comm.). The general design of the pond system at Wishaw, like other medieval fish ponds, suggests that, by operating a sluice network, it would have been possible to maintain stock in adjacent ponds while others were undergoing maintenance.

Construction of fish ponds

Chambers (1988, 122) noted that fish ponds often survived into the later medieval period but in a considerably altered state as a result of modifications which masked earlier ponds. The fish pond system at Wishaw was abandoned in the early 14th century and therefore represents a design that is probably much as it was originally laid out, although it is possible that even at Wishaw the off-stream ponds were developed from an initial barrage pond. This pond, the valley pond, comprised the most important feature of the pond layout, functioning both as a large breeding pond and as a reservoir for supplying water to the adjacent off-stream ponds.

The design of the pond complex undoubtedly made it possible to stock all ponds at the same time but also, by closing sluices, to drain individual ponds in rotation while still maintaining a supply of fish. It is likely that not only the barrage pond but also the square pond east of the dam and the L-shaped off-stream pond functioned as breeding ponds for the maintenance of fish supplies.

Smaller ponds, including that adjoining the off-stream pond, are more likely to have functioned to hold brood stock, to store fish for short periods immediately following harvest when species may have been separated, or as spawning ponds for species that could be released into breeding ponds stocked with carnivorous pike. Taverner (1600) specifically mentioned bream, which spawn freely, as an appropriate species that could be kept with pike to sustain the food chain. Individual water-filled pits, which are well represented at Wishaw, are also likely to have served as holding ponds for short term storage of fish for the table, for breeding or for separated stock. When lined with a net, possibly supported on wooden posts, or a woven rush basket (skep), as at Washford (Gray 1968), these pits provide a ready container in which relatively large numbers of fish can be confined and retrieved easily.

Associated buildings

Chambers (1988), in discussing the requirements for successful fish pond construction also noted the relatively small number of sites that had been excavated. In most instances this work was no more than rescue work directed towards recording details of dam or sluice construction and pond profiles. Few fish pond sites had been subjected to area excavation on the scale of that at Wishaw which demonstrated the value of work on this scale by exposing traces of subsidiary ponds or more importantly structural remains. The distribution of buildings at fish pond sites has been deduced primarily from the results of earthwork surveys where building platforms are apparent; at Llanddew (Nenk *et al.* 1992) fish ponds belonging to a 12th century estate of the Bishop of St David's were associated with a large platform representing one or possibly two building plots with a small house platform close by.

Traces of four building platforms were visible at the fish pond site thought to be associated with the Knights Templar at Washford. One, of daub walled construction, was excavated (Gray 1968) and considered to represent a smokehouse. The excavations at Wishaw exposed the remains of a previously undetected, single storey open fronted building that was found with relatively large quantities of domestic refuse. This material included pottery of 13th and early 14th century date, which was also found in adjacent pits and fish ponds. In addition, charred bean and pea fragments, with wheat grains, also suggested material that had been raked from a domestic hearth as food preparation remains. This may indicate that the structure served a domestic function providing possibly seasonal accommodation for a fish keeper, when domestic refuse was discarded into the ponds as they went out of use. Refuse from earlier activity may have been spread on the open fields. The dimensions place it within the size range of domestic structures excavated at Burton Dassett Southend (Dyer 1996, 126). However, the absence of a clearly defined hearth and the presence of a broad doorway suggests the structure is more likely to represent an agricultural building where equipment was repaired or stored, fish processed and other related activities (wildfowling, gathering reeds etc) associated with the site were undertaken. It is possible that the structure served both functions, providing accommodation for both fish keeper and equipment, and represents a timber-framed Midlands 'fish house' similar to that of the early 14th century Meare Fish House, Somerset (Aston 2000). This rather more luxurious stone built structure, with a first floor hall, is of similar dimensions (Wood 1965, 33) to that at Wishaw and provided accommodation and storage for staff employed at fish ponds of Glastonbury Abbey.

The excavation at Wishaw was partially initiated by the prospect that the site represented a 'moated' site. Aston and Bond (1988) noted that, especially in the Arden district of north-west Warwickshire, manorial complexes, often associated with moats, were the most common site type with fish ponds. Moated sites may be, but are not always, associated with manor buildings; Rahtz (1959, 1–32) excavated a moat site at Humberstone, Leicestershire which he concluded was more probably a fish pond of 13th century or later date. The results of the excavation at Wishaw found no additional dressed stone fragments, structural remains, foundations or increased quantities of domestic refuse to suggest that a 'manor' house had stood within the area enclosed by the 'moat' – the L-shaped pond. The report of the 1993 evaluation (OAU 1994b) noted that the ground surface may have been reduced by the landscaping of the 1970s; however the shallow linear ditches that cross this area are of a consistent depth across the entire site, suggesting that there was minimal reduction of the ground level beyond the pond edges. It remains a remote possibility that buildings of a similar size and construction to that found at the southern edge of the fish pond complex were located beneath the bund of stored topsoil in that area and were not sampled in the evaluation.

It is impossible to be sure whether the Knights Templar holdings at Wishaw ever included the fish pond site. However, in view of the fact that documentary evidence confirms that they held land at both Moxhull and Wishaw with the manor, presumably Wishaw, there is a strong case for thinking that they did. The recorded area of their estates translates to 15% of the present parish of Wishaw and the manor is likely to have occupied a dominant, central location in the parish. Wishaw is not alone in Warwickshire in having connections with the Knights Templar – the preceptory at Temple Balsall was equipped with three large ponds and an additional fishery is thought to have existed at Wolvey. The design of one of the principal features of the complex at Wishaw, the L-shaped pond, is reminiscent of that at the Knights Templar manor at Washford, Redditch (Bond 1988, 103) on the Warwickshire–Worcestershire border at the southern edge of Arden. This 13th century fish pond complex covered over 1.5 hectares and also included an L-shaped pond. It may be no more than coincidental that this repeated design appeared at a time when moats were being constructed in large numbers in the Arden region of north Warwickshire.

Dyer (1996) examined the development of rural settlement in Warwickshire and challenged the idea that the Arden represented an area of woods, moors and heaths that had been subjected to internal colonisation during the 12th and 13th centuries. Citing the evidence for Romano-British occupation at several locations in Wishaw, principally near Wishaw Hall Farm, he postulated that the area may well have witnessed some woodland regeneration after the Romano-British period but that thin, patchy occupation had continued nevertheless. This settlement was of sufficient density at Wishaw to register a manor at the time of Edward the Confessor (*VCH* 1904, 333) and a priest and seven households, comprising three *villani* and four *bordarii* by the *Domesday* Survey of 1086. Harvey (1976) considered that this represented scattered rather than nucleated occupation, a description echoed by Dyer (1996, 120) for North Warwickshire in the 9th or 10th century, as one of irregular field systems, enclosed crofts and mixed land use. One certain and one possible sherd of Saxon pottery from the site have provided valuable archaeological evidence confirming that settlement was present at Wishaw by this date. Settlement had expanded continuously from this base throughout the 12th and 13th centuries.

An extensive survey of Wishaw undertaken by Hodder (1992) listed four possible centres of medieval occupation based on parish records of open field systems and surface artefact collections; the church, Over Green and Grove End with additional settlement centred on Wishaw Hall Farm, Moxhull and Lower Green. The church building was first recorded in 1240, 13 years after the first reference to the Knights Templar in Wishaw, and still contains fragments of 13th century architecture, although the *Domesday* Survey makes it clear that a church had already existed in the parish before 1086. Hodder (1992, 44) could find no firm evidence for medieval occupation around the church but argued that it had been constructed on a virgin site over an existing open field system and that the road system had been realigned around it. Concentrations of pottery at Over Green and Grove End and two 'moat' sites at Over Green provided firm evidence for 13th and 14th century settlement there; however, these sites both lie at the western edge of the parish and now straddle the parish boundary of Sutton Coldfield. Concentrations of medieval pottery were also present in the area of the earthwork site at Wishaw Hall Farm and adjoining land, which he considered may relate to activity at Moxhull Manor. Hodder concluded by speculating that the earthwork site at Wishaw Hall Farm may have represented the manor site complete with its own chapel or church, which was later relocated to its present location on a virgin site.

The 13th century appears to have been one of considerable activity within Wishaw. Not only was the church relocated to a new site but an entire planned fish pond complex with associated field system was laid out at Wishaw Hall Farm. Traces of an open field system, with traces of ridge-and-furrow agriculture, are present on the rising ground to the south of the site, although it is impossible to be certain whether this pre-dates the newly planned complex, as at the church, or post-dates it. Expansion at this time, from an existing settlement pattern, has been detected (Dyer 1996) across most of north and west Warwickshire in documentary and place name evidence as former woods and waste lands were colonised by additional isolated houses and hamlets. Dyer (*ibid.*) emphasised that one characteristic feature of this expansion in the Arden landscape was the adoption of 'moated' sites, of a similar size to that at Wishaw.

Two hundred and nine examples are known in Arden (Dyer 1996), by far the greatest density in Warwickshire, where they frequently coincided with parishes that contained well documented 13th century expansion. The construction of a moat, often with associated fish ponds, represented a major outlay of capital; however this would have been within the scope of 'people of superior rank' (Dyer (1996, 122) including the Knights Templar, who would have enjoyed patronage from the wealthy or profits from local pastoral or woodland products. Unlike Wishaw, most 'moated' sites were likely to be furnished with a hall, kitchen and domestic buildings (Dyer 1996, 124) and were often detached from other settlement (Smyth 1994), features that strengthen the argument that the moat site at Wishaw was not occupied. Research (Roberts, 1973; Skipp 1981; Hooke and Marshall 1987) has concluded that the surrounding landscape comprised areas of open fields, enclosed pastures, with cattle, sheep and pigs, and woodland providing raw materials for charcoal burning, ash burning, woodcutting, turning and tanning (Watkins 1993).

The fish pond complex at Wishaw Hall Farm appears to have been in use for a relatively short period of time, spanning the mid-13th–early 14th centuries when the Knights Templar were at their most successful, then closed down and replaced by the Knights Hospitallers, an order that followed similar rules; ownership of the manor had been transferred to them by 1326 (*Cal. Inq. p.m.* vi, 469). Any transfer of ownership combined with a destabilisation of population is likely to have had a profound effect on the fish ponds at Wishaw. It seems improbable that, had the complex been maintained, new owners would have neglected what was probably a very profitable, working establishment. It is possible that this relatively isolated complex suffered from a shortage of labour to operate it and funds to finance its maintenance especially after the Black Death of 1349. It is equally possible that problems related to the water supply, including drought, or recurring disease within the stock made a sufficiently large impact on the pond complex that it no longer became viable to continue breeding fish at the site.

The history of the Arden region, indeed of the entire county was one of economic and population decline throughout the 14th and 15th centuries when many villages and hamlets were 'deserted' or shrank in size (Dyer 1996). Surface scatters of medieval pottery (Hodder 1992; OAU 1994b) indicate that settlement at Wishaw contracted dramatically at this time while the excavated material confirms that there was no prolonged activity at the fish pond complex into the mid 14th century. The likelihood is that once it was abandoned, and possibly drained to harvest the last crop of fish, its condition deteriorated. The limited environmental evidence suggests that the ponds became overgrown, were uneconomical to level for ploughing until the introduction of heavy machinery and remained as upstanding earthworks. The immediate environs may well have reverted to pasture as did most of south Warwickshire from the 14th century onwards (M. Aston pers. comm.).

Fish ponds in Warwickshire

Aston and Bond (1988) reviewed the distribution, form, date, and social and economic role of fish ponds in Warwickshire using a large corpus of material collected from extensive field and documentary survey. They pointed out that Warwickshire, which straddles the main watershed of England, contained not only a major river, the Avon, but was also characterised by numerous small, relatively low gradient streams and rivers. These were not only suited for holding stocks of river fish but could be dammed easily to create artificial ponds and lakes. In addition large parts of north Warwickshire, an area which included Wishaw, were characterised by impervious Mercian Mudstone. Aston and Bond included Wishaw at the north end of their zone 8, The Forest of Arden. This linear strip of land encloses the drainage of the Rivers Arrow and Alne, which flow south into the River Avon and the Rivers Tame and Colne, which flow north to the Trent. Of these the southern part is by far the most densely populated part of Warwickshire for fish ponds. The northern band, which includes Wishaw, contains a lower density of sites; however they pointed out that north Warwickshire was characterised by a greater range of ponds from a greater variety of sites, including royal palaces, castles, monastic sites, villages (both extant and deserted), manor houses, parks and others in the open country.

The most common form of pond throughout Warwickshire was, as at Wishaw, the valley pond. Excess water from low energy streams could be regulated by a spill way at the side of the dam or a sluice beneath it, which could be opened when necessary to drain the pond. Streams prone to flooding were frequently diverted via a by-pass channel, a feature also present at Wishaw, with sluices at the tail of the pond. A by-pass channel also provided a greater range of options for water to be supplied to other linked ponds and enabled others to be closed for maintenance.

The dam itself was frequently not large, but of sufficient size to create a large expanse of relatively shallow water. Survey of a monastic fish pond complex at Cryfield, Warwickshire (Aston and Bond 1988, 425) recorded a dam that measured 1.5 m high, while the earliest dam revealed during excavations at Kenilworth

Castle (Thompson 1965) was only 0.74 m high, although it was later raised to 3.7 m in height. Currie (1990) stressed that dams were frequently well-made, multi phase, complex features constructed of carefully rammed material. The dam itself at Wishaw lay beyond the easement so that it was not possible to study this aspect of the fish pond complex; however calculations from excavated sections in the valley pond showed that a dam approximately 1 m high would have been sufficient to retain water in the valley pond without overflowing the valley sides. Shallower water would have prevailed at the tail of the pond where the floor lay approximately 0.24 m below the base of the by-pass channel and 0.5 m below the maximum water level nearer the dam. The depth of the artificial off-stream pond also measured approximately 1.2 m to the level of the surrounding land surface, although it is likely that the sides of this pond were originally raised with spoil from its construction.

The presence of fish ponds at Wishaw Hall Farm and Moxhull Manor raises the possibility that two sets of fish ponds may be present on the same stretch of river. Aston and Bond (1988, 423) noted that this was frequently the case; at Kenilworth a large complex of fish ponds at the castle were also separated by a road from others belonging to the Augustinian abbey but otherwise formed an unbroken chain.

Detailed survey (Bond 1988) showed that the pond at Washford also had an additional long rectangular pond on the third side and a small tank on the fourth side. The entire complex was connected by an elaborate system of leats that demonstrate how the flow of water may have been directed away from the ponds at Wishaw.

SITES AT THE SOUTH-WESTERN END OF THE ROUTE

Chapter 26
Curdworth Top Lock (Site 21)

By Andrew B. Powell

Introduction

A programme of archaeological building recording was undertaken at the Curdworth Top Lock and the lock-keepers cottage at Dunton Wharf, on the Birmingham and Fazeley Canal north-east of Curdworth. The aim of the work was to provide a record of the observable fabric and structure of the building and lock prior to their demolition. The cottage, built in the late 18th century, had undergone a number of alterations and extensions during its lifetime and had been converted into two dwellings. The adjacent lock, the first in a flight of eleven locks at Dunton, was of typical construction similar to others on the canal, with single, manually operated gates at each end.

The site, covering 0.42 hectares centred on NGR 418450 293720, comprised the Curdworth Top Lock, a brick-built overflow spillway and the remains of a small wharf, as well as the adjacent lock-keeper's cottage (Figs 187 and 188). It also included (although outside the specific archaeological area affected by the road scheme) a channel leading to the Dunton Basin (now infilled) on the south side of the canal, and a brick bridge, which has now been substantially extended, over the A446 Lichfield Road. The canal remains in operation and the lock has been moved as part of the M6 Toll construction.

The geology is mapped as Pleistocene Glacio-lacustrine Deposits (Geological Survey of Great Britain 1996, Sheet 168, Birmingham).

The Birmingham and Fazeley Canal, built between 1783 and 1790, was an important early canal and of great significance in the industrialisation of the West Midlands, Warwickshire and south Staffordshire, being a link in James Brindley's celebrated 'Silver Cross' of waterways linking the Severn with the Humber, and the Mersey with the Thames.

Methodology

A search of historic maps was undertaken at the British Waterways Archive in Gloucester in order to clarify the date of the cottage and any phases of development.

The archaeological survey was undertaken in two phases. Although the recording of the lock-keeper's cottage was intended to be part of the programme of archaeological works, demolition commenced in January 2001 before the interior could be photographed, or the exterior elevations surveyed. Nonetheless, rapid recording of a substantial part of the building was undertaken before the demolition was completed. This consisted of a photographic survey and a hand drawn plan (1:20) of the ground floor, supplemented by an external digital survey of the ground floor using a Topcon GTS 211D Total Station. Written notes were made of materials and methods of construction and evidence for changes, additions and alterations.

The recording of the lock and spillway, carried out in November 2001, consisted of a photographic survey, a hand drawn plan and elevations (1:100) of the lock chamber, a profile of the lock chamber and overflow/spillway (1:20) and detailed drawings of the lock gates (1:50) and a tie beam (1:10); these were supplemented by a digital survey.

A cross-section was then cut through the lock using a 30 ton 360° mechanical excavator fitted with a toothed bucket, assisted by a mechanical breaker used to break through the lower walls. The section was positioned to allow examination of one of the *in situ* tie beams. Due to the depth of the lock (nearly 4 m) it was necessary to step the excavation to allow access; however, after recording the beam, this was abandoned due to the presence of a fibre optic cable close to the south wall. As the ground was unstable, recording continued from the surface.

Results

Cartographic evidence

The earliest known plan of the site is on the 1791 survey of the Birmingham and Fazeley Canal by James Sherriff, produced three years after its opening. It shows a single dwelling (the lock-keeper's cottage) south-west of the lock, with no outbuildings. The 1st edition OS 25 in map of 1873 shows the now extended cottage with a number of small outbuildings. To the north-east, adjacent to the south side of the lock, was a terrace of three properties.

In 1880, plans and elevations were drawn up showing proposals for a further two-storey extension to the rear of the cottage and several internal alterations, although these are not shown on an 1884 survey by William Cottrell (Fig. 189), nor on an 1896 survey, both of which show the buildings in greater detail than the earlier maps.

The cottage

The two-storey brick-built building, gabled at either end under a slate roof, showed three main phases of

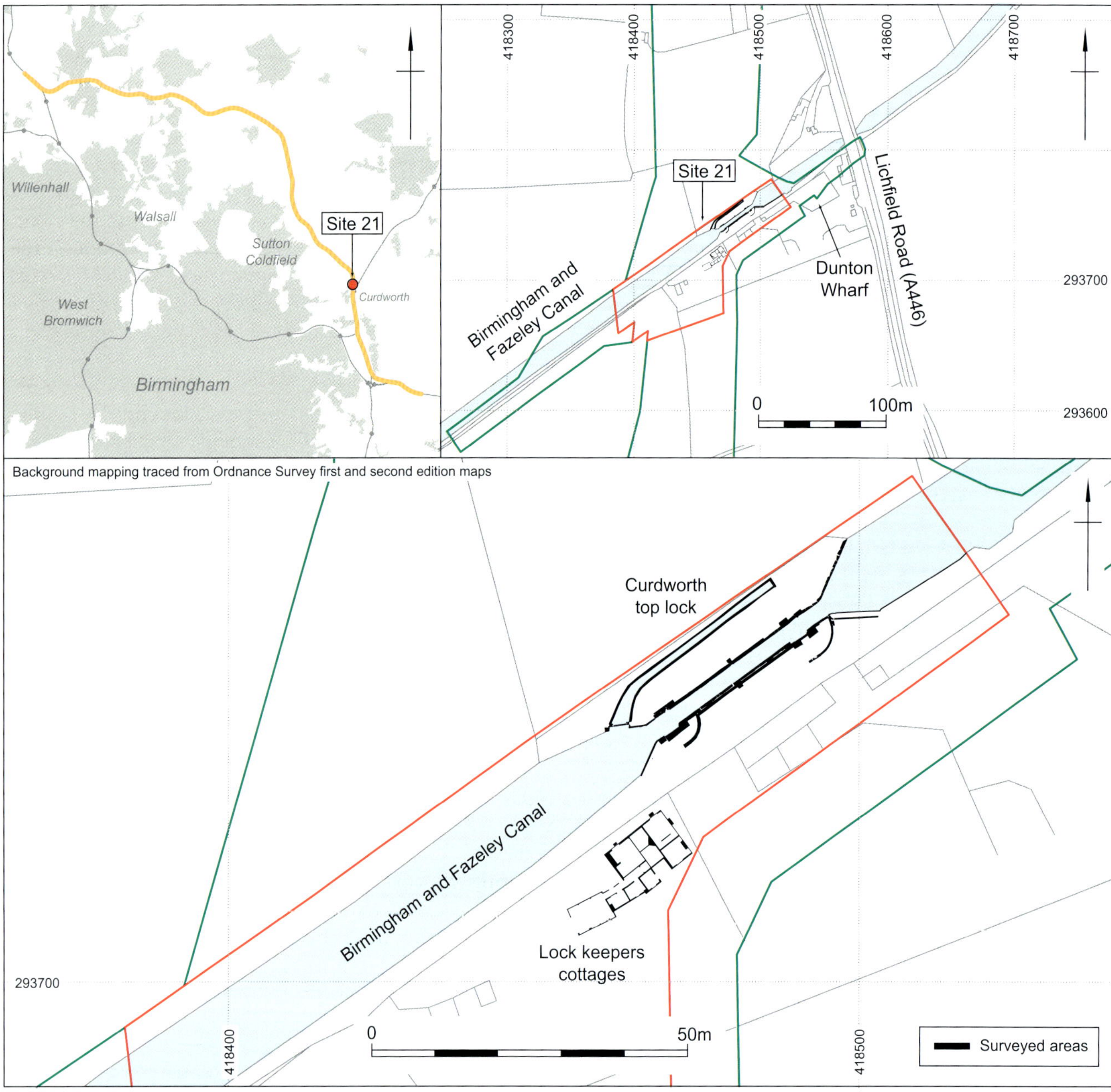

Fig. 187 Curdworth Top Lock (Site 21)

Fig. 188 View of the lock and cottage from the north-east

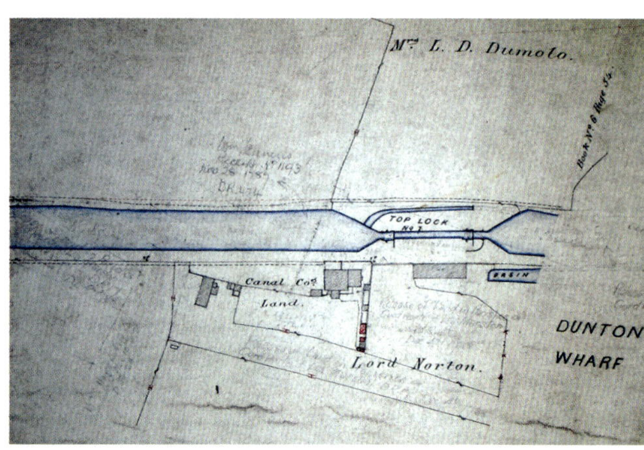

Fig. 189 1884 survey by William Cottrell (British Waterways Archive No. 829.94)

construction. The original single dwelling, provided for the lock-keeper, was twice extended in the 19th century, on the first occasion creating two separate dwellings (Nos 252 and 253) (Fig. 190); it was converted back a single house in the 20th century.

Phase 1

The original cottage had three principal ground floor rooms, identified on the 1880 building plans. The largest was the parlour accessed directly from the front door. It contained a fireplace on the south-west wall, and had a staircase in the south-west corner leading down to a vaulted cellar, and up to the first floor main bedroom. There was a cellar light outside its front window.

The rest of the ground floor was divided largely into two smaller rooms, each with fireplaces in adjacent corners and sharing the same chimneystack. The front room, possibly used as the office where the lock-keeper collected the tolls, had one door from the parlour and another leading to the kitchen to its rear. There was probably a door in the rear wall of the kitchen (later replaced by a large window). The door would have provided access to an external, single storey, wash house that was entered from the north-east; the wash house had a window in its gable end.

A single storey roofed passage, accessed through an exterior door on the south-west side, ran behind the parlour giving access to both it and the kitchen, its lean-to roof visible in the building's rear elevation. The 1880 plan also shows a small pantry on the south side of the passage.

The first floor had three rooms. The main bedroom, above the parlour, also had a fireplace on the south-west wall, and at the north-east gave access to a smaller room with a fireplace in its south-east corner, both these rooms having windows at the front. The smaller room led into a similar sized room at the rear. The latter may have had a window in its north-east wall (although this would have been blocked by the Phase 2 extension).

The front elevation, which had a central door opening and two sash windows on the ground floor and a further two sash windows on the first floor, was constructed using Flemish stretcher bond. The south-west elevation did not have any window openings and showed only the phase 1 gable, which had a two-flued internal chimneystack for the parlour and main bedroom fireplaces, and the access to the ground floor passage. The gable end of the north-east elevation was concealed behind the later extensions.

Phase 2

The second phase of construction saw the creation of two separate dwellings – the original cottage, No. 252 at the west, occupied by an outside tenant, and No. 253 at the east occupied by the lock-keeper – by the addition of a two-storey extension on the north-east side. No. 252 comprised the parlour and kitchen on the ground floor and the two forward-facing bedrooms of the first floor.

No. 253 comprised the two rooms of the extension, as well as the former ground floor office and the rear upstairs room of the original cottage; there was also a cellar. The former office was accessed by a new doorway inserted in the wall from the extension, its other doorways, to the parlour and kitchen of No. 252, presumably being blocked. The first floor was accessed by a flight of stairs rising from the north-east corner of the ground floor room, at the top of which a door was inserted in the wall of the small rear room at the point where there had probably been a window. Although the 1880 plans indicate that a replacement window was to be inserted in the rear wall of this room, it appears that instead a narrow window was inserted in its south-west facing wall.

The front elevation of the two dwellings was now symmetrically proportioned, having a second door and a third ground floor sash window, and a third window on the first floor. The new phase of construction was evident in the keyed join between the two styles of brickwork, the extension being constructed using Chequered bond incorporating flared header bricks for decorative effect.

All the windows in the building's front elevation were of similar six-lighted sash design, although the reveals of the four windows in the phase 1 building had been rendered, in contrast to the two on the extension. A possible explanation for this is that, when the building was extended, the facade may have been redesigned, and new six-lighted sash windows inserted, to give the frontage a symmetrical appearance. If the original windows had fitted flush with the outside face of the wall, the rendered reveals would have formed a fillet or covering concealing any damage that may have been done when moving them back, while those in the extension were built into the brickwork and so had neater brickwork surrounding them.

The extension's north-east gabled elevation was of Flemish stretcher bond, with a single decorative stringcourse following round from the front elevation at eaves height. It had an external chimneystack with two flues, the rooms on both floors containing fireplaces. The 1880 plans give no indication of an existing door to the cellar on the north-east elevation of the extension, and instead suggest that access may have been on its south-east side, with steps running down the inside of north-east wall. There was a cellar light below the front window.

Probably at the same time, a new wash house was built at the south-west corner of No. 252, accessed from immediately outside its rear passage. The external property boundaries, as shown on Cottrell's 1884 map, indicate that the original washhouse at the rear was transferred to No. 253. This would have made the back door from the kitchen of No. 252 superfluous, and it may have been at this time that it was replaced by a wider window, there being traces of infilled brickwork around it.

Phase 3

It was the addition of a further two-storey extension, comprising ground floor kitchen and first floor

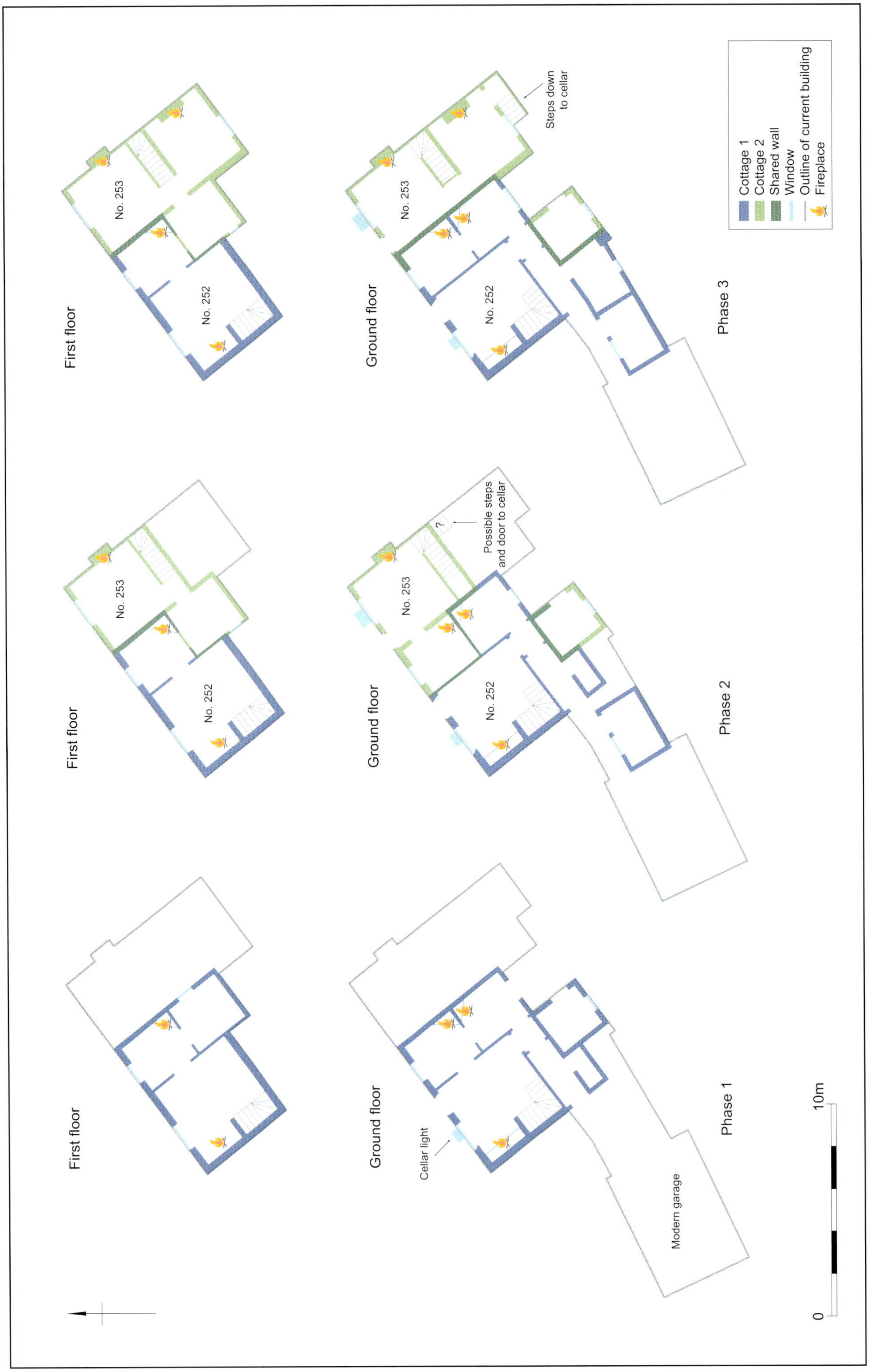

Fig. 190 Cottage phase plans

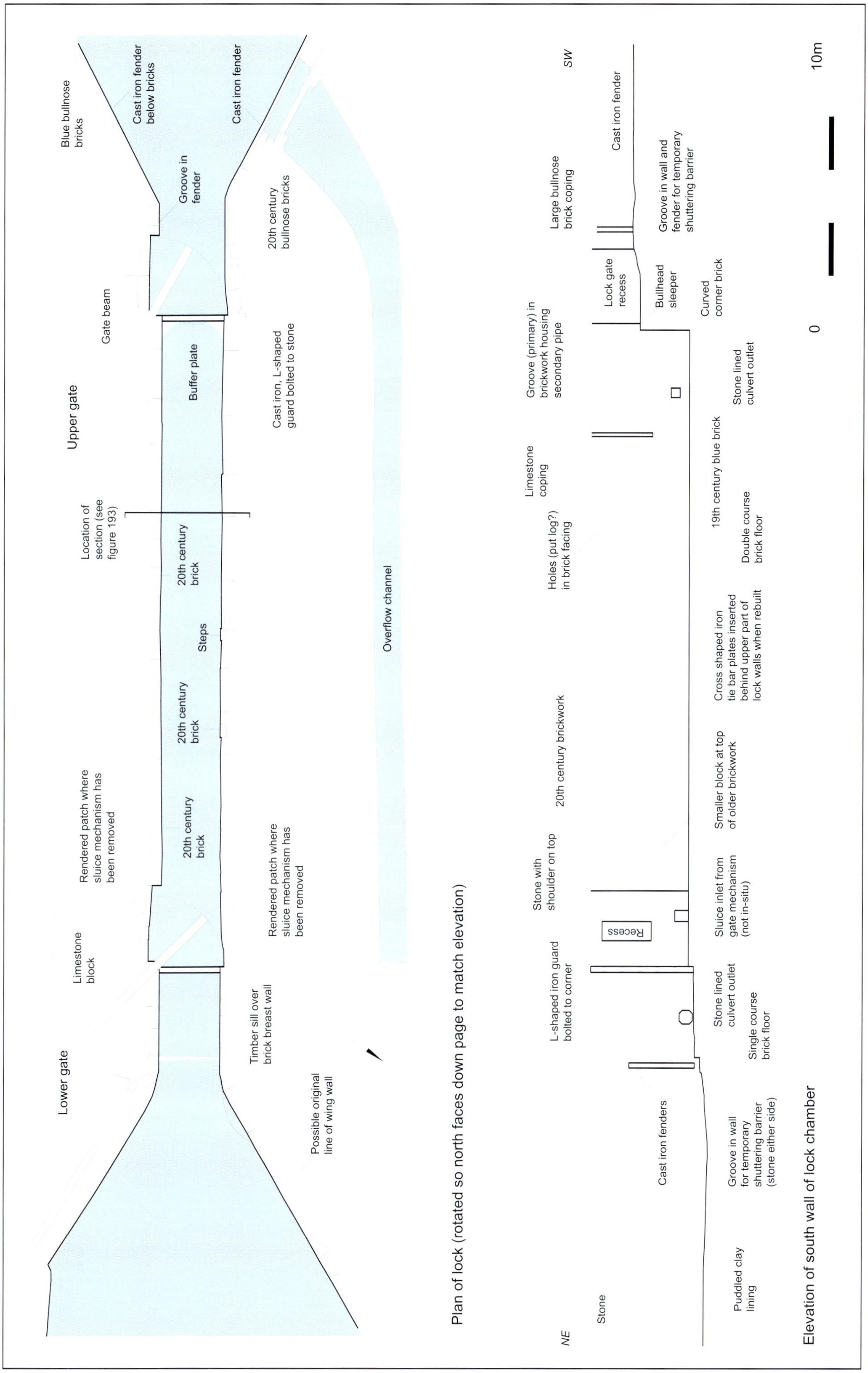

Fig. 191 Plan of the lock and elevation of the south wall of the lock chamber

bedroom, at the rear of No. 253, for which the 1880 plans were drawn up. This extension, which resulted in a double gabled north-east elevation (Fig. 188), was block bonded to the rear of No. 253.

According to the plans, the central front room (the phase 1 lock-keeper's office) was to be transferred back to No. 252, the door from No. 253 being blocked and the original door from No. 252's parlour being re-opened. This would have meant that No. 253 now comprised a front living room and rear kitchen on the ground floor, and three bedrooms on the first floor. In fact, it is uncertain whether this division of rooms between the two dwellings was realised, since, when surveyed, the central front room was linked by doors both to No. 253 and to the kitchen of No. 252 to the rear, with the door to the parlour remaining blocked. This suggests either that the Phase 3 plans were not followed through in all their details, or that there had been further internal changes, probably at some time in the 20th century.

The north-east wall of the phase 3 extension had an internal chimneystack with two flues, both of the new rooms having fireplaces. As the new extension would have blocked any access to the cellar on the south-east side of the phase 2 extension, the plans show a proposed new door below the north-east corner of the new kitchen. In fact, a new doorway to the cellar, accessed by an external set of steps, was inserted at the base of the wall below the internal staircase.

The south-east elevation of the extension had windows on both floors, and a door from the kitchen leading down a flight of steps to ground level, running towards the phase 1 wash house. In addition, the original pantry in No. 252 may have been enlarged at this time, with a chimney in its rear wall which linked the old and new wash houses, although this is not shown on the 1880 plan.

The lock

The chambered lock had single gates at each end and was of typical construction, broadly similar to others on the canal (Fig. 191). The gates were manually operated by balance beams (Fig. 192), with semi-circular raised brick tread patterns in the ground. The chamber walls were brick-lined and the copings were largely of limestone (Fig. 193). The brick overflow/spillway had a U-shaped profile, part of its length running in a culvert to the lower end of the lock.

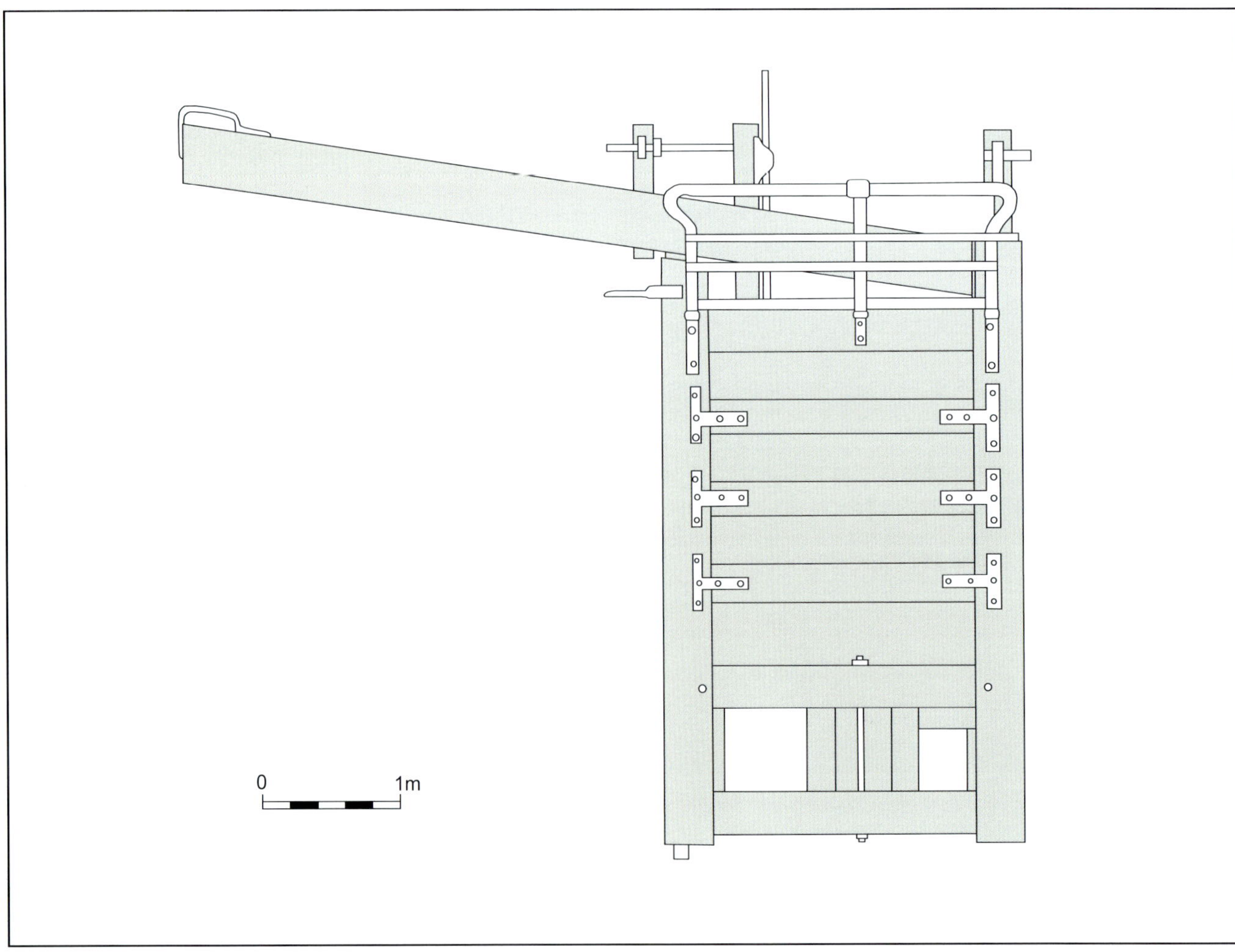

Fig. 192 The lower lock gate

The lock chamber

Wing walls opened out to the full width of the canal at both ends of the lock. Outside the lower gate, the single coursed brick invert on the floor of the chamber mouth was separated from the puddled clay canal lining by a brick breast wall, with a timber sill beam fixed to its upper surface, built across the end of the chamber.

The lock chamber was 24.5 m long, 2.3 m wide and 3.9 m deep, its walls built of brick topped by limestone copings, and its floor lined with two courses of bricks. The entire construction was set into the underlying marls without any foundation. The principal brick used was red and laid in English bond, although parts of the chamber walls had been re-lined using Staffordshire blue bricks.

The section through the lock showed that the walls were 1 m thick, with only a minor widening at their bases (Fig. 193). The south wall was strengthened by a series of tie beams, spaced 4.2–4.8 m apart and 1.6–2.0 m above the floor, linked to brick buttresses behind the wall. The opposite lock wall had only two narrower brick buttresses with lighter wooden ties running through them.

The tie beam

One of the tie beams on the south side, of a composite iron and timber construction, was examined in detail in the section cut across the lock (Fig. 193). It had an iron cruciform bracing plate located on the inside face of the lock chamber and flush with the inside face of the brick lining. The plate was attached to a square-sectioned iron rod, 1.75 m long and 40 mm wide, with a threaded end, that passed back through the wall. At the back of the wall the rod passed through a 0.2 m long V-shaped groove cut

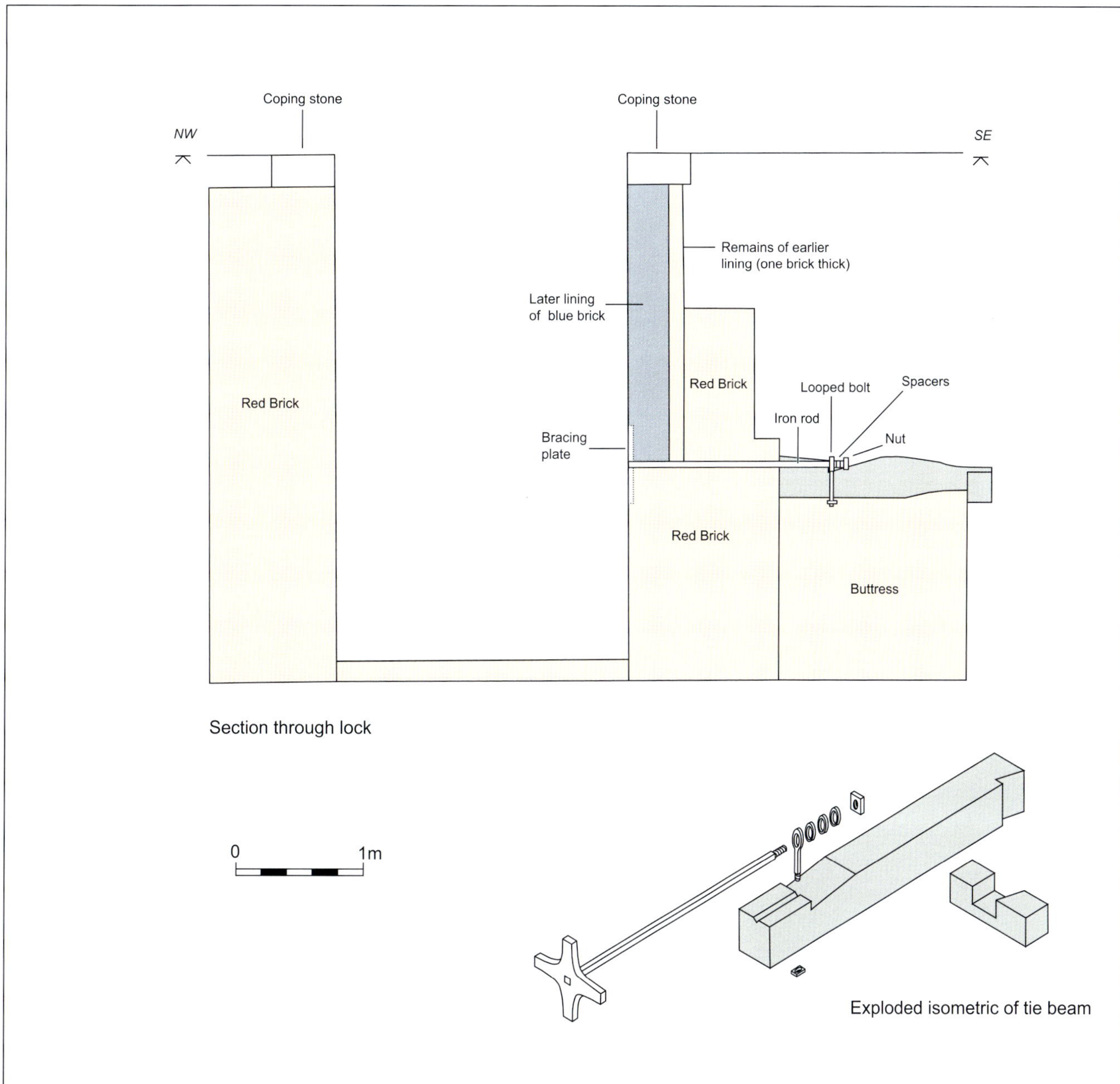

Fig. 193 Cross-section of the lock chamber and tie beam, and exploded isometric of the tie beam

in the upper surface of a squared-sectioned beam, 0.25 m square and 1.7 m long, laid horizontally behind the wall (possibly on the original ground surface), with one end abutting the wall. At the end of the groove was a shallow notch, with its vertical side towards the wall against which lay the eye of a looped bolt that passed down vertically through the beam and was fixed underneath by a square nut. The iron rod passed through the eye of the bolt, then three iron spacers, before being secured by a square nut on its end, so attaching the two parts – iron and timber – of the tie beam. The whole of the joint assembly was covered with a cement capping. The other end of the timber beam was connected, by means of an un-pegged, half-lapped notch, over a smaller piece of timber, 0.75 m long and 0.2 m square, forming a 'T' piece, one arm of which was laid tightly behind the adjacent brick buttress. The buttress, which stood proud of the rear of the lock wall, was 1.4 m deep and 0.9 m wide.

Evidence for change

The principal evidence for change or development within the lock was the replacing of the lower lock gate with one of a different design. The original system had employed culverts with sluice gates within the lock wall, but this had been replaced by a gate with two door paddles and two sets of winding gear on the gate itself. The earlier winding gear at the top of each sluice or culvert had been removed and the recess cut into the coping stone had been filled in. The old shutters were left *in situ* to maintain the water seal. The upper lock gate had not been changed and the winding gear and sluice gates remained *in situ*.

Discussion

The recording of the two aspects of this site – the construction and development of the lock-keeper's cottage and the construction of the Curdworth Top Lock – combine to provide not only detailed information about the canal's construction and operation, but also a glimpse into the domestic life of an official employee of the canal company.

Although the lock-keeper's cottage could not be examined in as much detail as had been hoped, observation of its structure and fabric during demolition, supplemented by the examination of maps and building plans, have allowed the main phases of construction to be identified. The continuing extension and changing layout of the cottage may reflect the need for additional manpower to service the increasing traffic along the canal and the consequent expansion of the canal facilities at Dunton.

Fig. 194 Reclamation of the lower lock gate

The lock itself was of a standard design, although there was evidence for changes to the design of the lock gates. These changes may have been in response to the failure of two of the Curdworth locks in 1789. The unreliability of the locks at both Curdworth and Dunton remained a continuing problem until 1823 when the faults in their original design were finally rectified (Broadbridge 1974).

Postscript

Following the recording of the lock, fixtures such as the stone copings, lock gates, sluice assemblies, winch gear and the sill beam buffer plate from below the upper lock gate were salvaged so that British Waterways could reclaim any useful components (Fig. 194); the buffer plate, for example, was to be re-used in the new lock being constructed to the south.

Chapter 27

Hawkeswell Farm, Coleshill (Site 24)

By Andrew B. Powell

Introduction

An excavation was undertaken on land immediately north of the historic hamlet of Hawkeswell, where a previous evaluation (OAU 1993) had indicated medieval activity. The excavation produced significant quantities of medieval pottery from features of uncertain function. It also revealed the remains of possible garden features probably of later medieval date, and post-medieval hedge lines.

The site, an approximately rectangular parcel of land covering 1.38 hectares centred on NGR 421580 286740, was located 2.4 km south-east of Coleshill (Fig. 195). It was bounded to the east by the cutting for the now dismantled Whitacre and Hampton branch of the Birmingham and Derby Junction Railway, and to the south by the M6 motorway.

The site lay between 80.6 m and 85.7 m aOD on poorly drained land sloping south and east towards the River Blythe, within the Upper Trent Valley drainage system. The geology is mapped as Triassic Mudstone and Arden Sandstone Formation (Geological Survey of Great Britain 1992, Sheet 168, Birmingham). The recent land use had been predominantly arable, although substantial parts of the surrounding area (now under pasture) have been used in the past for landfill.

Archaeological and historical background

The medieval hamlet of Hawkeswell, south-east of Hawkeswell Farm, survived as part of Coleshill parish until the 19th century, although it appears not to have been an important settlement and was not one of the subsidiary manors of Coleshill (OAU 1994d, 46). A 1783 plan of the parish (by J Snape, WRO (U) Z115) shows 14 buildings associated with the hamlet, most of which stood in the area now occupied by the M6 motorway and the former railway line. The Ordnance Survey Old Series 1 in map of 1814–17 shows a large building at the north-east of the village, possibly Hawkeswell Hall, with an enclosed area of ground to its north possibly representing part of its grounds. To the east was a lane, running north from Hawkeswell before turning to the west towards Coleshill; this survived as a hollow-way cutting across the eastern part of the Site. Hawkeswell Farm, to the north of the site, is locally said to have replaced the original Hall when the railway was built (opened in 1839 and closed in 1917) (VCH 1964).

The 1st edition OS map of 1889–91 shows a single building in Hawkeswell, at the same location south of the site as that shown on the Old Series map (now under the south side of the M6 motorway). The line of the hollow-way is shown as a trackway now flanked to the east by railway cutting. The area to the north of the building is shown as farmland with a field boundary lying immediately west of the trackway, and a pond and winding boundary or ditch in the south-west part of the site.

The 1993 evaluation (OAU 1993) indicated a sequence of medieval and post-medieval ditches and pits, and cobble spreads associated with the hollow-way. There was evidence of medieval domestic activity dating from the 12th–14th centuries but no *in situ* traces of buildings. In addition, possible enclosures or field boundaries were identified on the site from amorphous linear cropmarks visible on aerial photographs.

Results

Medieval

The hollow-way

The hollow-way, which may be medieval in origin, existed as a substantial depression. A section across it, near its mid-point within the site, showed that it was 6.2 m wide and *c* 0.3 m deep, with a firm sandy clay surface (240115) on its base containing pebble cobbles 0.03–0.15 m in diameter. This surface was cut on the east side by a U-shaped ditch (240100), 0.7 m wide and 0.45 m deep, containing dark brown silt, possibly for drainage purposes. Some 13 m north of the section, there was a small area of unmortared post-medieval brickwork (240013), subsequently much disturbed, overlying the cobbled surface on the eastern side of the hollow-way. This may mark the point where a subsidiary path joined the hollow-way from the south-east, possibly to join up with a 'substantial building' that was destroyed when the railway was constructed (OAU 1994d, 46).

Within the remaining medieval features, two main phases of activity were identified of the basis of the pottery, the majority of which was of 12th–13th century date, but with a small proportion also of 14th–16th century date.

Medieval phase 1

Approximately three-quarters (by weight) of the pottery of this phase came from a small group of features cutting an irregular spread of disturbed natural (240010) in the centre of the site. One of these features, a sub-rectangular cut (240401) of unknown purpose, pro-

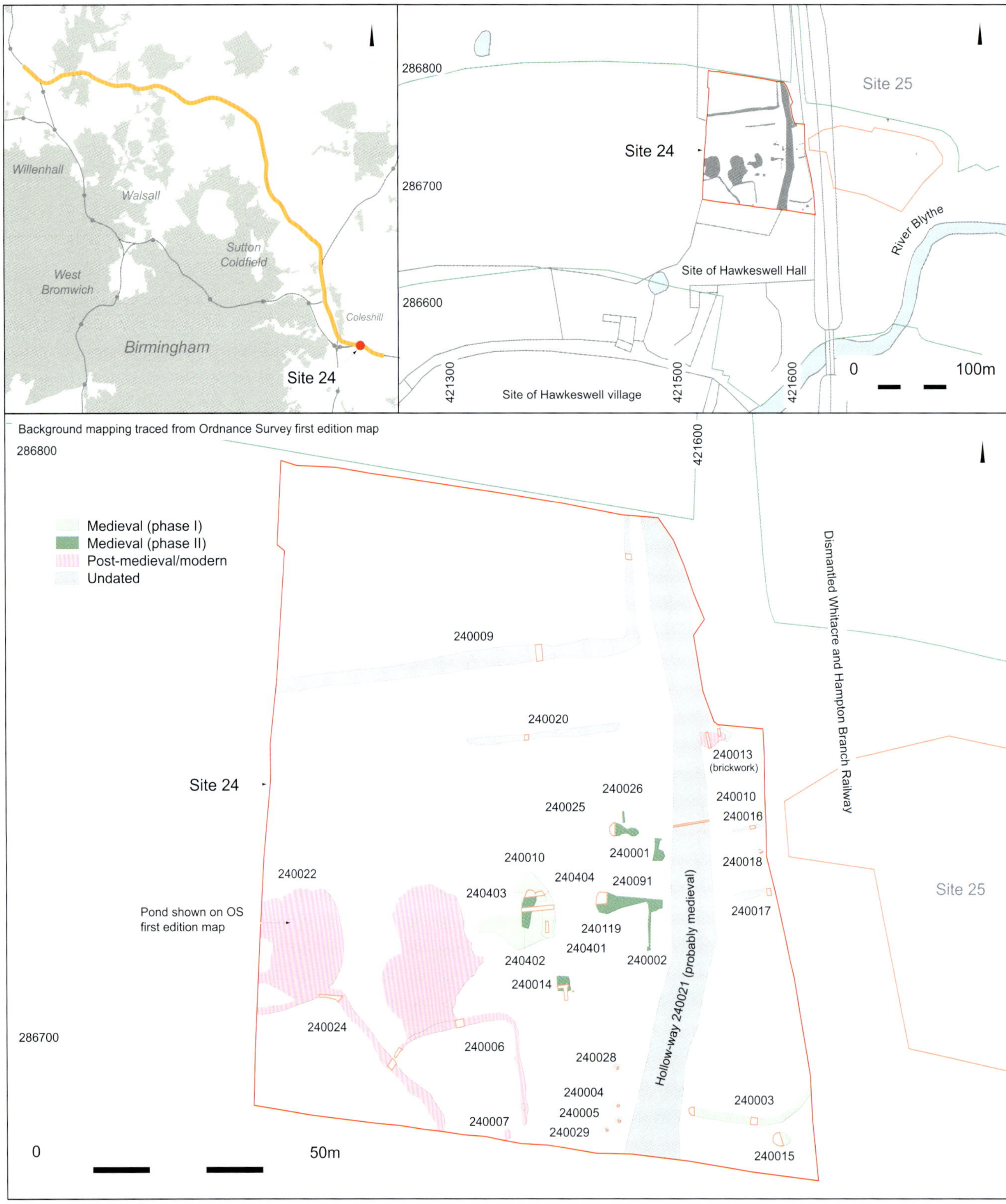

Fig. 195 Hawkeswell Farm (Site 24)

duced over 11 kg of medieval pottery (Fig. 196). The cut, which was 5.1 m long and up to 1.1 m wide aligned north–south, was up to 0.6 m deep at the north, where it had a near-vertical end and moderately steep sides, but it became shallower to the south. Its primary fill (240148), a 0.2 m thick layer of silty sand filling a depression in the base of the cut at the north end, produced 41 sherds (910 g) of 13th century pottery. Above this, lying largely against the edges of the cut, was a loose, 0.25 m thick deposit of pieces of sandstone averaging 0.2 m across (240147), capped by a 0.1 m thick layer of pebble gravel (240159). All these layers were sealed by a uniform, and clearly backfilled layer of loose silty sand loam (240117) filling the rest of the cut. This contained 674 sherds (10,169 g) of pottery of 12th to early 13th century date and a fair amount of charcoal. The section drawing also shows a significant quantity of ceramic building material from contexts 240117 and

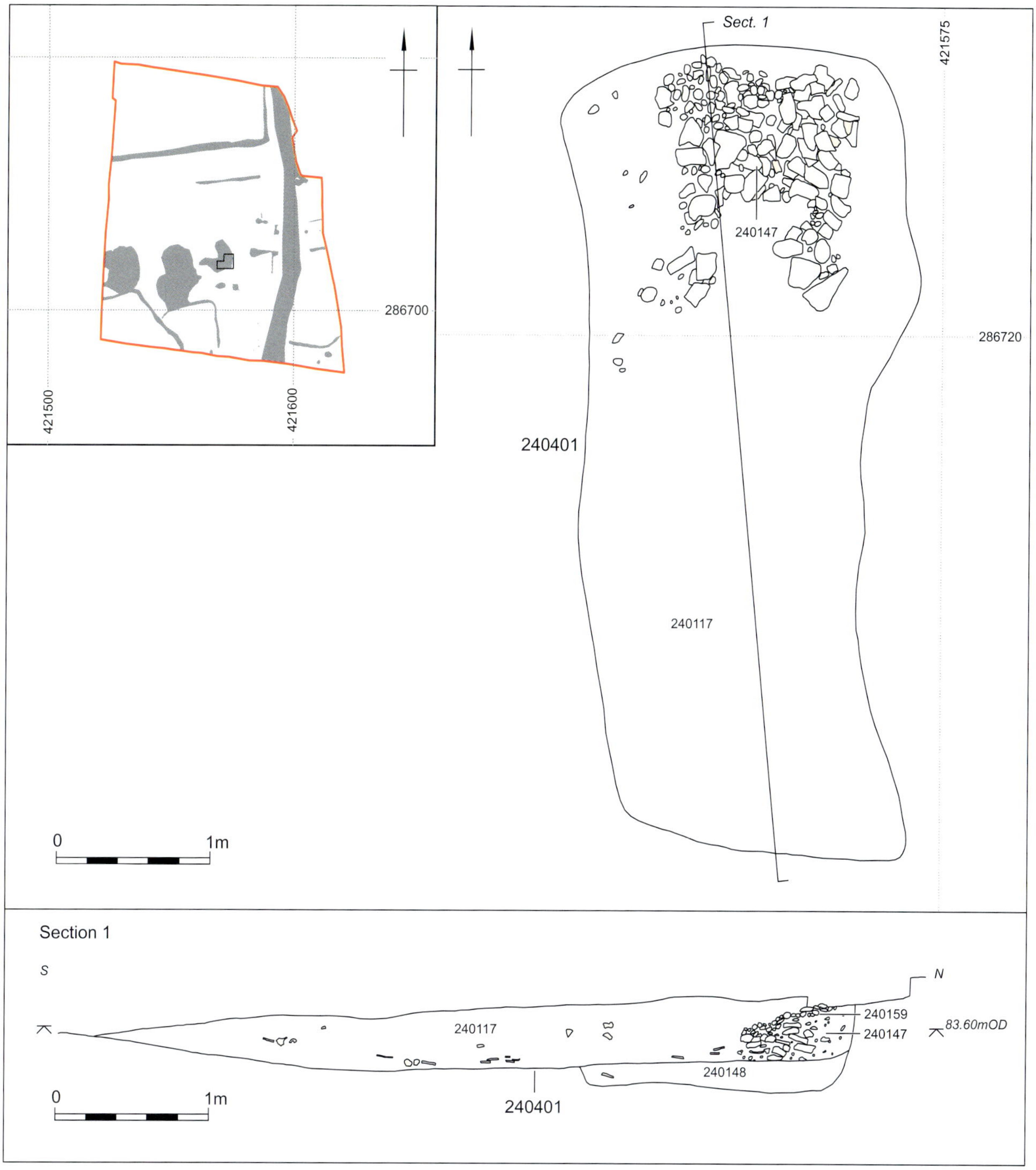

Fig. 196 Feature 240401

240147. Unfortunately, most of this material was not retained.

To the immediate north-west of feature 240401 was a series of intercutting features (Fig. 197), the earliest of which was shallow sub-rectangular scoop (240404), *c* 1.8 m across with moderately steep concave sides and a flat base *c* 0.1 m deep. It contained large cobbles in a sandy clay matrix, but produced no finds. It was cut on its west side by an irregular rounded pit (240403), *c* 1.8 m wide with moderately steep sides, and *c* 1 m deep (although its base was not quite reached). Its lowest recorded fill (240154) comprised lenses of silty clay, sand and charcoal, suggesting episodes of dumping and natural silting. Above this was a layer of collapsed natural (240153) on the west side then a charcoal-rich dump of clayey sand (240152) on the eastern side, producing four sherds of mid-13th–14th century pottery and ceramic building material. The rest of the pit was filled by a dump of burnt clay and charcoal in a reddish-brown sandy clay (240146) that spread east from the pit; this material contained no finds. It was cut by a later stone-lined trench (240402, below)

Two other features – a pit and a ditch east of the hollow-way, in the south-eastern corner of the site – can also be assigned to this period (Fig. 195). Pit 240015 measured 3.4 m by 2.2 m, and was 0.8 m deep with a shallow U-shaped profile. Its primary fill (240128), a layer of clayey silt up to 0.25 m thick, was overlain by a

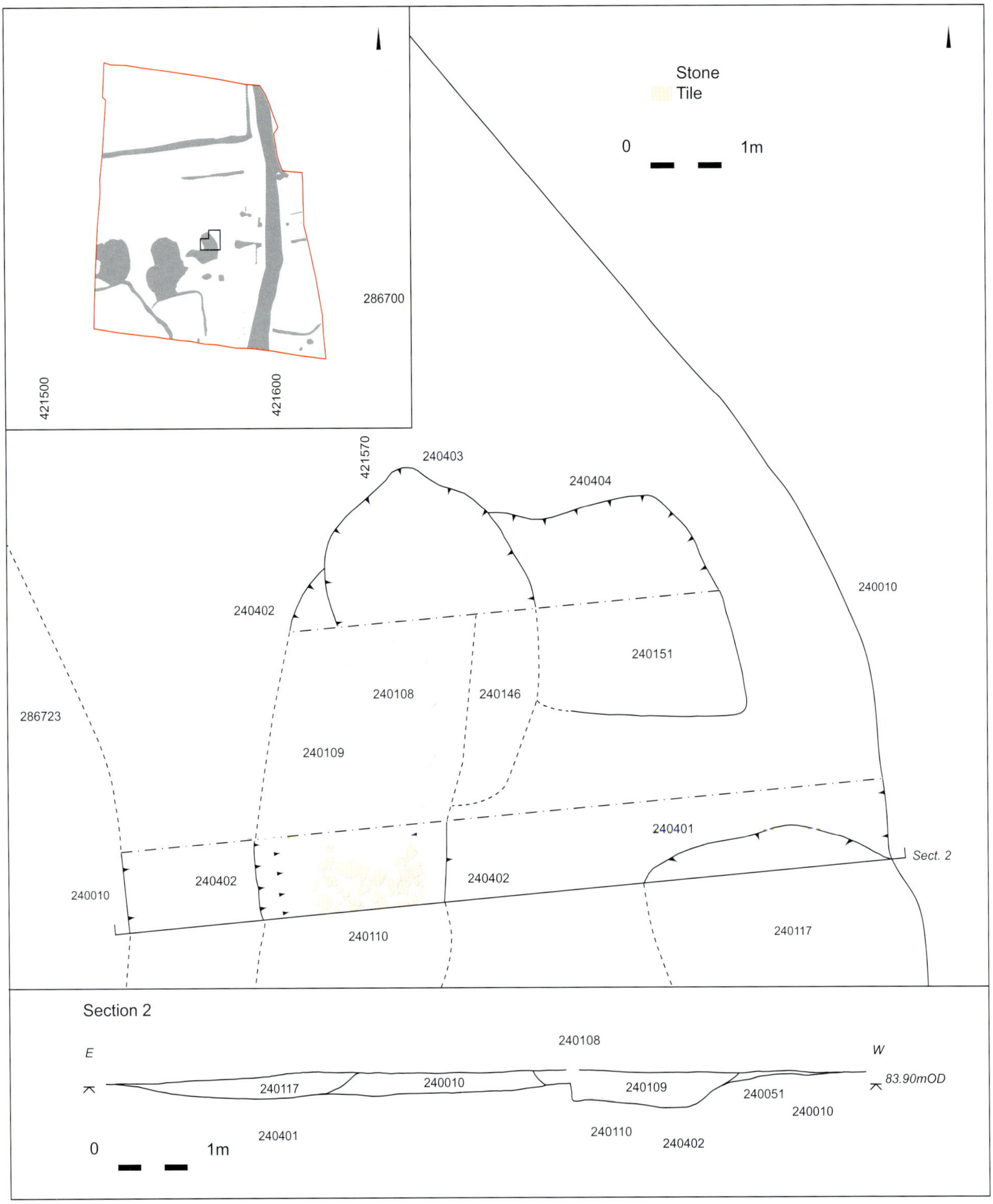

Fig. 197 Features 240404, 240403 and 240402

loose silty sand (240106) containing some charcoal and producing 61 sherds (1452 g) of 12th–13th century pottery, two whetstones (Fig. 203) and part of a barb-spring padlock. Immediately to its north was a 23 m long ditch (240003) running east from a rounded terminal 0.4 m from the edge of the hollow-way before turning to the north-east and continuing beyond the edge of the site. This was up to 1.7 m wide and 0.5 m deep with a variable profile but a generally flat base. It appeared to have been recut at one of the two excavated sections, with the single fills of both the original cut and the recut containing between them 30 sherds (391 g) of 13th century pottery (as well as a residual flint flake of probable Mesolithic date).

Medieval phase 2

Continued occupation in the vicinity of the site is indicated by quantities of late medieval and early post-medieval pottery from a range of features. Some of this material was of 14th–15th century date although the majority was dated to the 15th–16th centuries. Although the ceramic sequence could indicate a significant

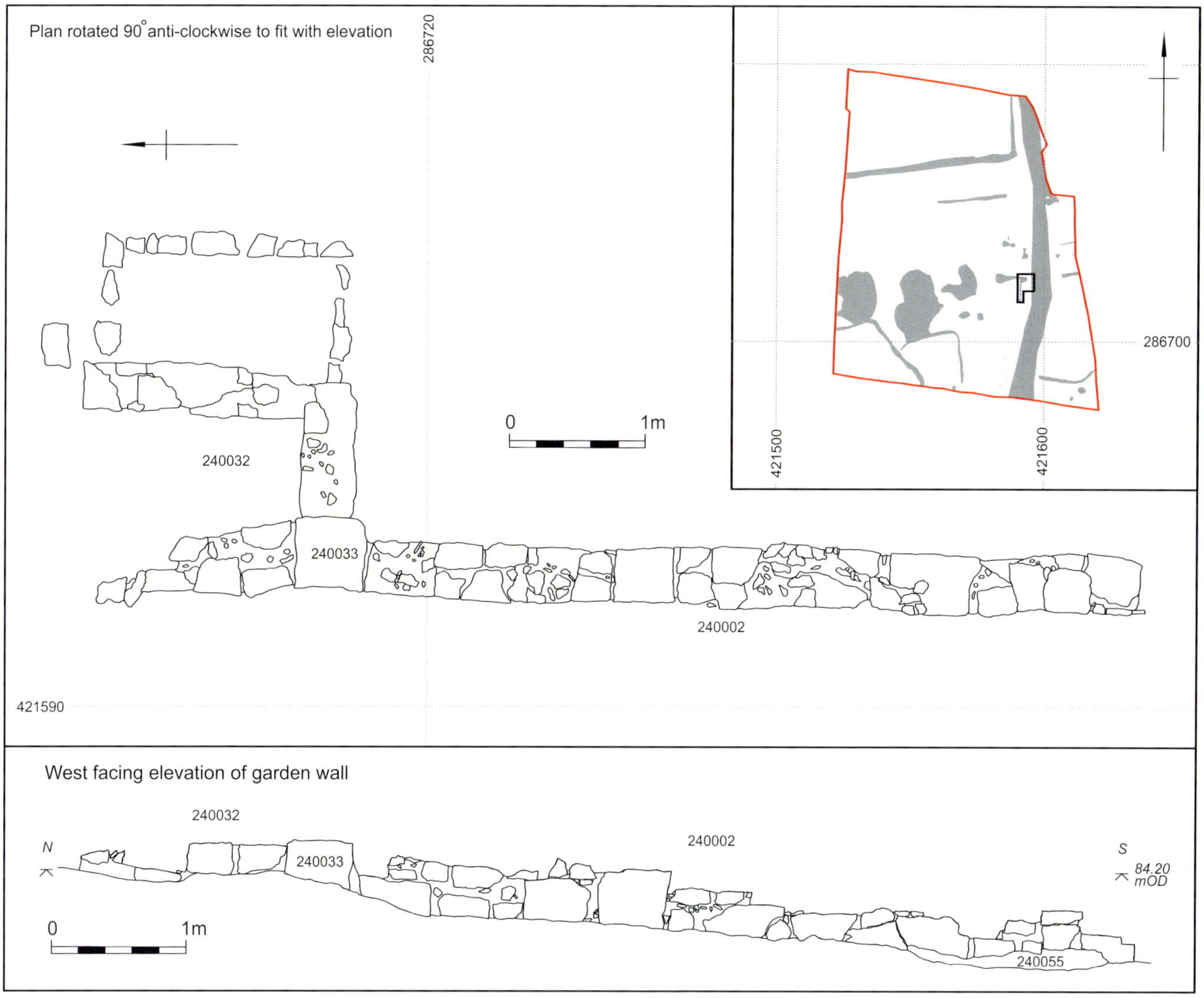

Fig. 198 Plan and elevation of garden wall

contraction of settlement at Hawkeswell from the late 13th century, with population gradually increasing again into the late medieval/early post-medieval period, such an interpretation must be treated with caution, as other factors, such as changes in landuse and manuring regimes, would also affect the relative concentrations of materials recovered.

The most prominent feature was a stone wall (240002), perhaps a garden wall (possibly associated with a house pre-dating the construction of Hawkeswell Hall), running north–south for 7.8 m on the west side of the hollow-way. It consisted of roughly dressed sandstone blocks interspersed with smaller stones and bonded with mortar. It was *c* 0.45 m wide and survived up to two courses (0.4 m) high (Fig. 198). Although the ground sloped to the south, the stones were laid level, having at one point been laid on a levelling layer of stony sandy clay (240055) (containing 29 sherds of 13th century pottery). Elsewhere the wall had been laid directly on the natural. A large (0.54 m square) sandstone block (240033), near the northern end of the wall, formed the south-west corner of a hollow square pier (240032), 1.6 m wide and 2 m long, marking the end of the wall. A less substantial rectangular arrangement of stones extended 0.8 m east from the pier, up to the edge of the hollow-way. Demolition rubble from the subsequent levelling of the wall, comprising pieces of sandstone and mortar and a large amount of tile, was recorded on its east side (240035) and within the interior of the pier (240043) where it produced five sherds (341 g) of 15th–16th century pottery. Layers of redeposited natural (240034) and soil (240036), lying against its east side of the wall, produced ten sherds of 15th–16th century pottery and two sherds of 17th century pottery, respectively.

Some 6 m north of the pier, a spread of sandstone blocks (240001), a number of them apparently *in situ*, also on the edge of the hollow-way, may be the demolished remains of a matching pier, the two features appearing to form an entrance through the wall. The spread produced 19 early 13th century sherds and 16 late 17th–early 18th century sherds. There was an associated layer of mixed demolition rubble and topsoil (240042).

The line of the wall corresponds approximately to the eastern boundary of the enclosed area shown on the 1814–17 map, and to the field boundary shown on the 1889–91 OS map. As a result, a post-medieval date was

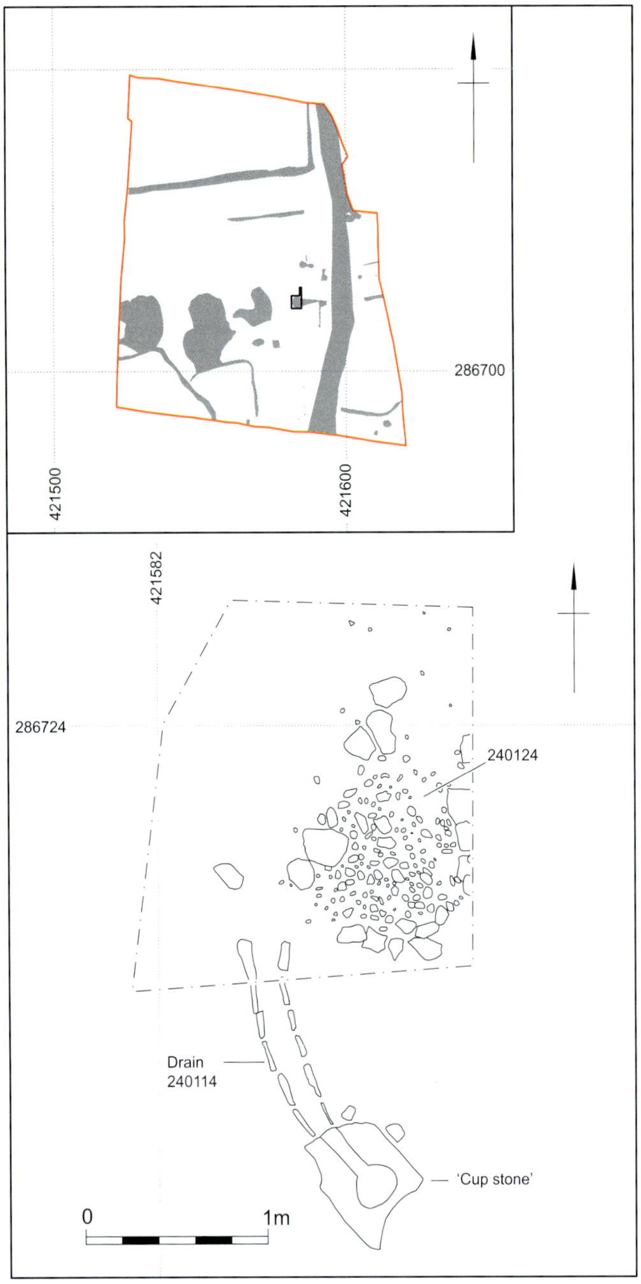

Fig. 199 Plan of circular setting, drain and cup stone

considered likely for the construction of this feature. However, the pottery assemblage from the various contexts associated with the wall suggest a medieval date, although it was possibly demolished in the post-medieval period (see Rátkai, below).

A flat-based cut (240091) ran west for *c* 4.5 m from the southern pier. It was 0.7 m wide and 0.1 m deep, steep on the north (uphill) side and shallow on the south side. A spread of sandstone rubble and a few post-medieval tile fragments in its fill (240105) suggest that it may have been the foundation trench of a demolished and/or robbed wall, probably flanking the approach to the entrance. At the western end of the trench were the disturbed remains of a circular setting (240119), *c* 1 m in diameter, of sandstone blocks surrounding a cobbled surface of small rounded pebbles), overlying a layer of compact silty clay (240124) (Fig. 199). To its south a

Fig. 200 Cup stone

further rough spread of cobbles (240099), produced four sherds of 15th–16th century pottery, as well a pieces of ceramic building material. Also south of this feature was a short (1.1 m), slightly curved length of 'drain' (240114), its sides (but not its base) lined with small sandstone slabs. At its south-east end, this fed into an approximately rectangular sandstone block, 0.47 m by 0.57 m and 0.1 m thick, in the top surface of which had been carved a 0.1 m wide and 0.05 m deep channel running to a circular 'cup', *c* 0.25 m in diameter (Fig. 200). The original form of this feature, clearly designed to collect water in the 'cup', is unclear, although it is possible that the circular stone setting, perhaps the foundation for a garden ornament, was associated with it.

Further to the west, cutting the western edge of phase 1 pit 240404 within the area of disturbed natural, was the rounded terminal of a 6.5 m long trench (240402), 2 m wide and 0.3 m deep aligned north–south. South of its terminal, the trench had a moderately steep side to the west, but the profile of the eastern side was unclear, due in part to a 2.6 m long line of substantial sandstone blocks and slabs (240108), between *c* 0.2 m and 0.5 m across, lying against or close to the eastern side. Across the flat base of the cut was a spread of broken tiles (240110). The trench fills (240139 and 240139 in the terminal, and 240109 to the south) produced sherds of predominantly 12th–13th century date. However, a number of sherds of 15th–16th century pottery suggest that this stratigraphically latest features in this area was contemporary with the other stone or stone-lined features of phase 2.

North-west of the possible entrance in the wall (Fig. 195), was an irregular feature (240025), 5.2 m long and 2.2 m wide, aligned east–west. It had a maximum depth of 0.14 m, and a single sandy clay fill, on the surface of which was a small quantity of sandstone rubble, possibly associated with the feature but perhaps more likely deriving from the demolished wall to the east. To its immediate north, aligned north–south, was a small linear feature (240026), 2 m long by 0.4 m wide and 0.2 m deep, with moderate to steep sides and a flat base. Its silty sand fill (240127), which produced ceramic building material as well as ten small sherds of presumably redeposited 12th–early 13th century pottery, contained abundant small stones, possibly to aid drainage of a planting bed or other garden feature.

Towards the south of the site, a small, three-sided stone structure (240014) (Fig. 201) also dates to this period. The structure appeared to have been open to the west, measuring 1.8 m north–south and up to 1.2 m east–west, and comprised a single course of roughly squared, unmortared sandstone blocks interspersed with smaller stones (240039). Underlying the stones was a cut (240040), suggested in the field to be a foundation trench, although due to the small area excavated the functional relationship between the cut, its loose loam fill (240044) and the stone structure is hard to determine. Within the interior of the structure and to its south was a 0.2 m thick spread of dark loam (240047) containing frequent pebbles and small pieces of sandstone, and producing 29 sherds of 15th–16th century pottery. This layer also contained, in the area immediately west of the structure, numerous pieces of tile. Layer 240047 was cut to the south by a 1.2 m wide feature (240048), 0.3 m deep with a U-shaped profile whose single silty clay fill (240049) produced two further 15th–16th century sherds. Although interpreted in the field as an east–west ditch, it was not traced outside the 0.3 m wide slot in which it was recorded. In addition, there was a small circular feature (240027), possibly a truncated posthole, 0.3 m in diameter and 0.1 m deep with a concave profile, cutting the natural some 0.5 m south-east of the stone structure, and therefore possibly associated with it.

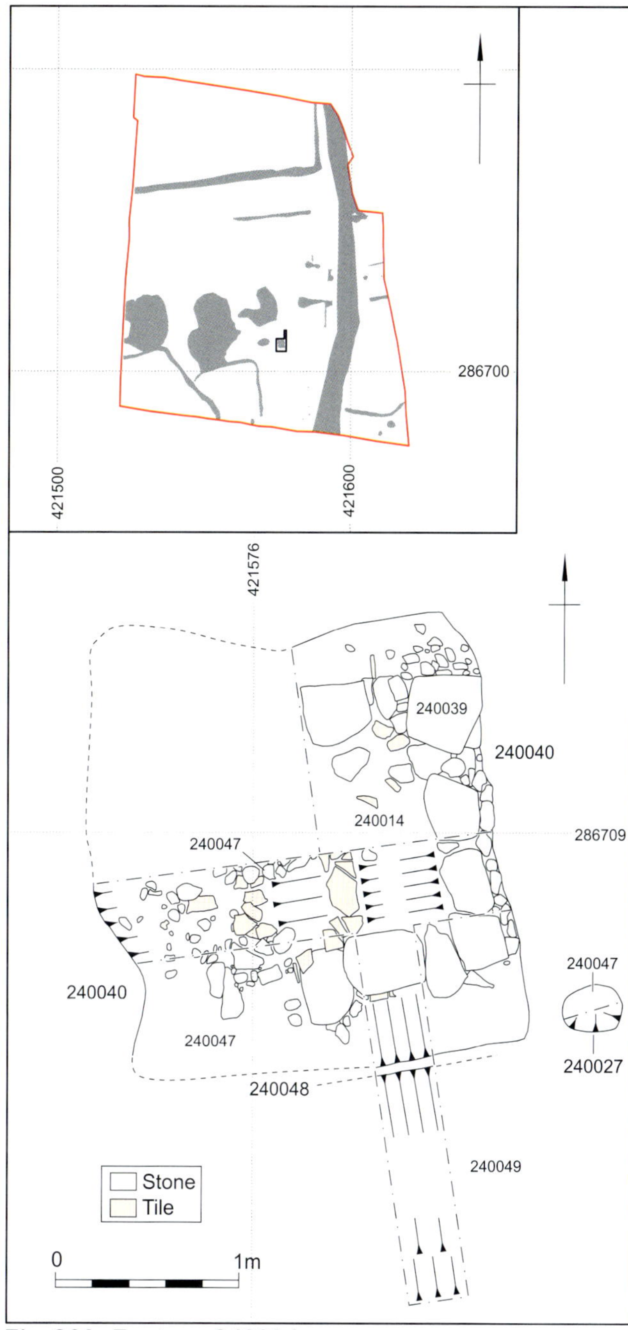

Fig. 201 Feature 240014

Post-medieval/modern

The date of construction of the building shown on the Old Series OS map of 1814–17 is not known, but the post-medieval pottery from the site suggests a late 17th century date. The map indicates a possible walled area to the north of the house at that date, although the land had reverted to farmland by the time of the 1st edition OS map in 1889–91.

Post-medieval features were concentrated towards the south of the site. They included a curious feature (240007), with a concave surface made up of large (0.1–0.2 m diameter) rounded cobbles (240130), extending beyond the southern edge of the site (Fig. 202). The cobbles had been laid on a bed of fine sand (240131), in turn overlying a 0.3 m thick layer of dark grey soil (240133) containing five sherds of late 17th–early 18th century pottery, as well as post-medieval tile and brick. Six sherds of late 17th–early 18th century pottery, came from an accumulation of soil (240129) over the cobbles. The partially excavated cut (240132) containing these layers was 1.8 m wide and at least 0.4 m deep with moderately steep sides. Some 0.4–0.7 m outside the feature was a concentric cut (240135), comprising a very steep-sided V-shaped slot of a similar depth, with a loose gravel fill containing further tile and brick (240136). The nature of this probably ornamental feature is unknown.

There were also two winding linear features (240006 and 240024), either ditches or hedge lines,

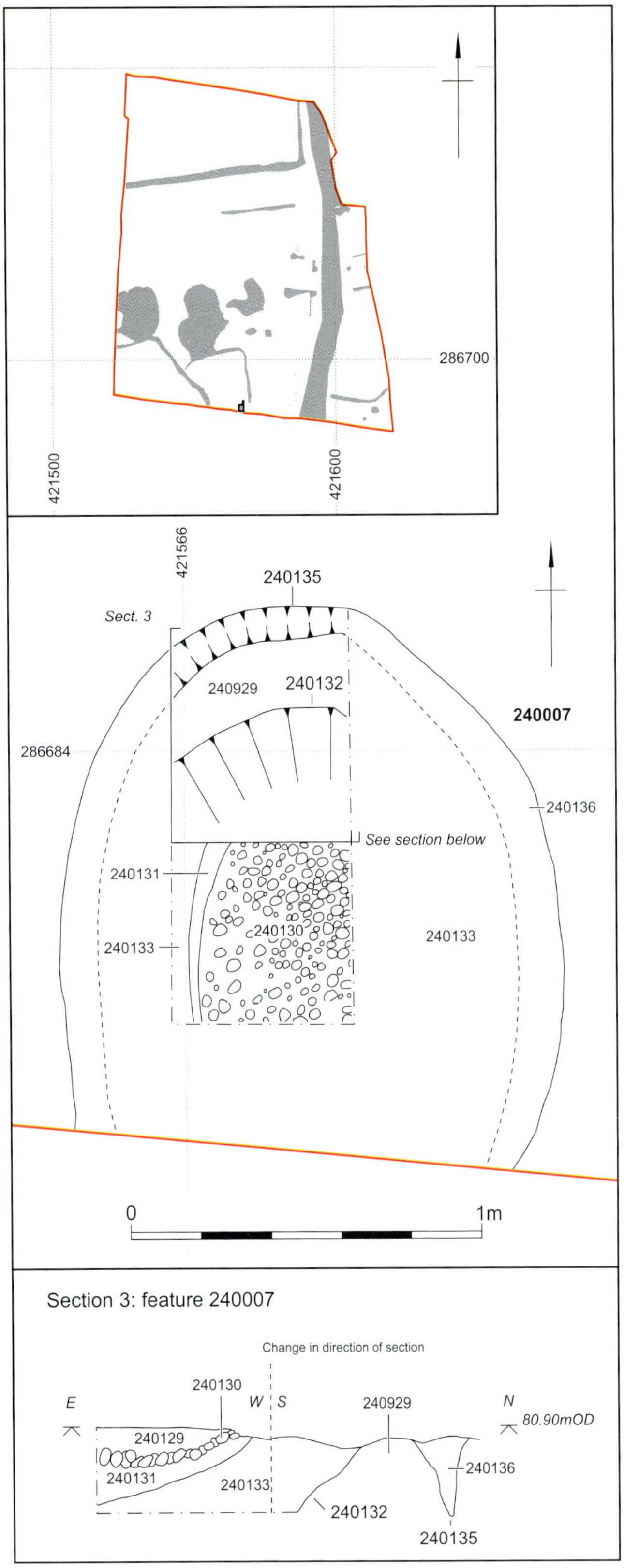

Fig. 202 Feature 240007 plan and section (A4 240929, 290930, 240524)

corresponding closely to a feature shown on the 1st edition OS map running south-east from a pond on the western edge of the site (itself corresponding to feature 240022, below). Feature 240006, which was 1.2 m wide and 0.25 m deep with moderately steep sides and a flattish base, ran north from near the south edge of the site before turning to the west then south-west towards feature 200024. Although it appeared to end just short of feature 200024, this may be due to its truncation by ploughing, the OS map showing the two features as connected. It was filled with a dark organic soil (240038/240070) which produced 12 sherds of 17th and 18th century pottery, post-medieval tile, charcoal, metal and pieces of clay pipe, the finds being concentrated towards the base. Feature 200024 was recorded running north-west from the southern edge of the site to the edge of feature 200022, then turning to the south-west. It was up to 1.8 m wide and 0.3 m deep, with a shallow irregular profile possibly resulting from the grubbing out of a hedge. It had up to two fills, the lower fill (240095) producing four sherds of 17th century pottery.

The northern side of feature 240024 was encroached upon by the southern edge of a large amorphous spread of brown sandy clay almost 20 m across and extending beyond the western edge of the site. A machine slot dug into this layer revealed that it sealed a layer of grey-brown sandy silt containing post-medieval and modern rubbish. Because the feature containing these layers (240022) was not identified as a former pond during the excavation, the layers was interpreted only as a rubbish dump, with the result that the feature was not recorded nor further investigated. Consequently, the date of the pond, which could feasibly have been of medieval origin, or which may have been associated with the post-medieval landscaping at Hawkeswell Hall, was not established. There was a further extensive spread of modern rubbish east of the pond.

Undated

Two undated parallel ditches, 10 m apart, ended at terminals *c* 4 m east of the hollow-way, continuing east beyond the eastern edge of the site (Fig. 195). That to the north (240016) was 0.55 m wide and 0.1 m deep, while that to the south (240017) was 1.2 m wide and 0.2 m deep. Both had shallow concave profiles, and single fills producing no finds. Between them there was a small circular feature (240018), possibly a truncated posthole, *c* 0.55 m in diameter and 0.15 m deep. It seems likely that these two ditches were associated, perhaps flanking an approach across the hollow-way towards the entrance in the garden wall, or framing a view from the entrance across the valley below. The view east from this point would have afforded good views of the ruins of Maxstoke Priory east of the River Blythe. Alternatively they may have been unrelated to the entrance, and it may be significant that they shared the same orientation as features 240009 and 240020, west of the hollow-way.

Feature 240020, recorded running approximately east-west for *c* 27 m, was 0.8 m wide and 0.15 m deep with a single sandy clay fill. Parallel to it, *c* 12 m to its north, feature 240009 ran from the west side of the site to within 3 m of the hollow-way before turning at a right angle to the north. This feature was 2.3 m wide and 0.3 m deep, with a silty sand primary fill and an organic rich upper fill. Although very shallow in profile, and therefore probably not effective as drainage ditches, these appear to have marked boundaries, possibly being the remains of hedge lines. Neither feature produced any dating evidence, although their position would appear to correspond approximately to the northern boundary of the property shown on the Old Series OS map of 1814–17. These undated feature (and ditches 240016 and 240017) may relate to the suggested landscaping in the 17th–18th centuries.

An irregular north–south line of four very shallow circular features (240028, 240004, 240005 and 240029), possibly truncated postholes, on average 0.4 m in diameter and 0.02–0.1 m deep, was recorded west of the hollow-way at the southern end of the site. These are also undated.

Finds

The metalwork, by Ian Scott

This site produced 16 iron objects, including six nails and five miscellaneous pieces. There were two bindings or corner reinforcements (feature 240006, fill 240038), and an unidentified object formed from strongly curved strip with at least two nails, or nail holes (topsoil). The other finds included a post-medieval horseshoe (context 240038) and part of a barb-spring padlock with a cylindrical case (pit 240015, fill 240106). Only part of the case, with the bolt *in situ*, survived. The latter could be Romano-British, medieval or early post-medieval in date, but in view of the associated finds, a medieval date seems certain. The assemblage is limited in its range of objects, with only the padlock fragment being of particular interest.

Flint, by Kate Cramp

A single bladelike flake was recovered from ditch 240003 (context 240086) (Table 150). The flake had been struck from a simple platform, the edge of which had been abraded. The heavily damaged condition of the flint indicated its residuality, and technologically it could belong with an industry of Mesolithic date.

Worked stone, by Ruth Shaffrey

Two whetstones and three other possible building stone blocks were recovered from the site. All three probable building stone fragments utilised the local Triassic sandstones and none was exceptional (Chapter 28). The whetstones were made of Norwegian Ragstone and Blue Phyllite. The Blue Phyllite example (ON 240601 context 240106, Fig. 203), which measured 85 mm by 9 mm by 6 mm, was of the sort that probably belonged to a personal tool kit, being a well made thin rectangular whetstone pierced at one end. It was only lightly used on edges and faces but the unpierced end had been worn into a tip from each wide face The Norwegian Rag example, which measured 85 mm by 27 mm by 10 mm, appeared to have made use of a piece of the raw material, rather than being a neatly finished whetstone. Both were recovered from the upper fill of pit 240015 (240106) dating to the 12th–13th century and they may suggest the presence of some sort of industrial activity.

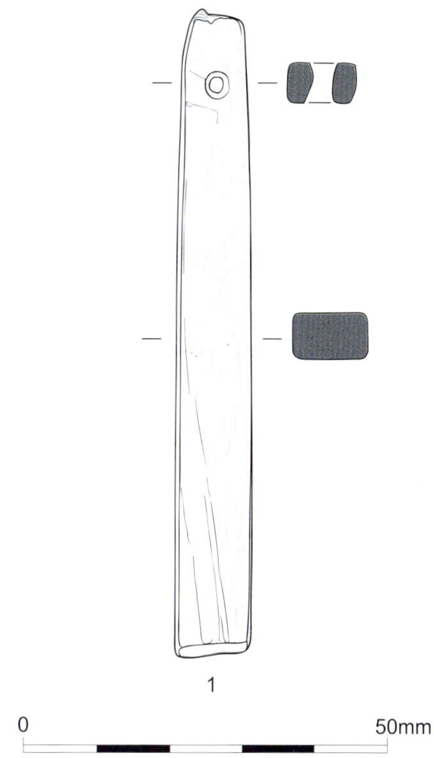

Fig. 203 Blue phyllite whetstone

Blue Phyllite was available from a number of sources including Scotland, Wales, the Lake District and Scandinavia (Margeson 1993, 197), but it has been suggested that Norway is the most likely source given that Phyllite and Norwegian Rag are often found together, as here (Pritchard 1991, 135). The Norwegian Rag whetstone is of interest because of its use of a piece of the raw material. Blocks of the raw material were imported into London from the 11th century (*ibid.*, 155) so it is perhaps unsurprising to find unfinished pieces being utilised, but it does indicate that the raw material was distributed further afield than London and was not all for manufacture in workshops there.

Medieval and later pottery, by Stephanie Rátkai

The medieval pottery from the site was intriguing since, in effect, the assemblage constituted a series of ceramic 'snap-shots', the earliest belonging to the 12th–mid-13th centuries, the second to the end of the medieval period, ie the 15th or 16th centuries, and the third to the 17th (probably second half) or early 18th centuries (see Tables 147–8). Unlike at Wishaw (Site 20) and Shenstone Linear Features (Site 13), whitewares did not form any significant part of the assemblage. They were mainly present in the topsoil, with odd sherds occurring in the pits associated with the area of disturbed natural (240010), possible wall demolition layer 240001, garden feature 240014 and in layers 240088 (a cleaning layer of wall 240002), 240099 (a cobbled layer to the south of feature 240119), and 240120 (a layer overlying stone setting 240119).

Nearly all the pottery pre-dated *c* 1300 and the majority pre-dated *c* 1250. Late medieval pottery accounted for only *c* 4.6% and post-medieval pottery *c* 3.4% of all the pottery recovered. This clearly suggested that there was minimal activity on the site in the latter two periods and that this was restricted to the area to the west of the hollow-way. This would be in keeping with this area being enclosed or park land associated with Hawkeswell Hall to the south. In some respects, however, if this was the case then it is difficult to explain why there was any late medieval or post-medieval pottery at all, especially since the pottery comprised mostly large sherds and, although there were variable degrees of abrasion, the sherds were not typical of ploughsoil scatters or garden soils. In fact it was striking that the average sherd weight for pottery from the topsoil was 19.8 g and, for the unstratified material, 21.31 g. The overall average sherd weight was 16.2 g. In effect this suggests very little disturbance, but this is wholly at odds with the stratigraphic data.

The cartographic evidence seemed to indicate that by 1814–17 the excavated features were no longer extant, with the exception of the pond 240022 and associated gullies, possibly hedge lines, 240024 and 240006. The latest pottery from 240006 was a white salt-glazed stoneware sherd. White salt-glazed stoneware had a *floruit* of *c* 1720–1760/70. This may indicate that the feature dated to the second quarter of the 18th century. The remainder of the pottery from 240006 was consistent with this date since it belonged to the late 17th–early/ mid-18th century, apart from three residual medieval sherds. Fill 240095 of 240024 contained 17th century coarse ware and a Midlands Purple jar or cistern base, suggesting a deposition date in the later 17th century. It is possible, therefore, that pond 240022 was a pre-existing feature and that 240024 was subsequently constructed, to be followed by 240006. Feature 240007, which lies a short distance to the south-west of the southern end of 240006, contained six sherds in fill 240129 and five sherds in fill 240133 The former comprised one blackware mug sherd and five coarse ware bowl sherds, the latter contained three coarse ware bowl sherds, a feathered slipware platter sherd and one yellow ware bowl sherd. Again these sherds were comparatively large with an average sherd weight of 30 g. A deposition date for the pottery appears to lie in the later 17th or early/mid-18th century. It is possible that feature 240007 went out of use at about the time that 240024 and/or 240006 were being constructed since topsoil over 240007 contained coarse ware, yellow ware and tin-glazed earthenware sherds consistent with its disuse in the late 17th or early 18th century.

Another putative garden feature, 240014, lay to the north east of 240006. Pottery was recovered from contexts 240047 and 240049 and a small piece of daub or fired clay from posthole fill 240046. Layer 240047 contained six large Midland Purple Ware WCTS MP02 (fabric MP02) jug, jar or cistern sherds, a small Tudor Green sherd and an admixture of generally much smaller earlier medieval sherds comprising whitewares, Coventry-type wares, an iron-poor jug sherd (fabric WCTS Sg04 (IP03), a reduced Deritend ware cooking pot sherd and a fabric cpj18 (WCTS RS03) cooking pot sherd. Fill 240049 of ditch 240048, which cut 240047, contained part of a Midlands Purple WCTS MP02 (fabric MP02) cistern bung-hole and a small Coventry-type ware sherd. It is possible that these two sherds were disturbed from 240047. From the ceramic evidence it is very difficult to believe that this structure is post-medieval and a 15th or 16th century date seems the most likely.

There was a spread of tile to the west of the structure which may have been connected with it. Another possible garden feature, 240026, adjacent to 240025 further north, contained 10 sherds of fabric CPJ15 WCTS Sq09, which represented at least two cooking pots (Fig. 205, 38–9) and more ceramic building material. The pottery sherds were quite small with an average sherd weight of 9.1 g, which would be consistent with redeposition or disturbance, and the two garden features 240014 and 240026 could therefore be contemporary.

The putative garden walls and entrance way leading into the grounds (240002 and possibly 240001) contained sherds of a mixed date range. In stone spread 240001 the earliest sherds comprised Coventry type wares and fabric CPJ15. A whiteware (WCTS WW01.4) jug sherd and an elaborately decorated Lyveden-Stannion B sherd WCTS CO04 (Fig. 205, 40) are likely to date to the second half of the 13th or 14th centuries. There were two late oxidised ware WCTS SLM14, SLM21 (LMT05, LMT06) sherds dating to the 15th or 16th centuries and a feathered slipware pie-crust platter rim of later 17th–mid-18th century date. The sherds were generally fairly large and unabraded, so nothing looked obviously residual. Demolition/topsoil layer 240042 associated with the wall only contained Coventry-type ware cooking pot sherds and mudstone tempered ware WCTS Sq25.1 (fabric MUDST02) pitcher sherds but no later material. The pottery was slightly more fragmentary than that from 240001 and slightly more abraded. There were no rim sherds. This demolition pottery seems to be more or less contemporary with that from linear feature 240026 to the north-west (see above). Again stone spread 240001 makes little sense as a 17th century feature and makes more sense as a medieval feature perhaps demolished in the 15th–16th centuries or possibly in the later 17th–18th centuries. If the former then it would have gone out of use at more or less the same time as 240014, if the latter, at the same time as 240007.

Table 147 Medieval pottery: quantification of total assemblage

Fabric	*No.*	*Wt(g)*	*%no.*	*%wt*
cbm	3	69	0.26	0.37
CO04	1	54	0.09	0.29
Crucible	1	13	0.09	0.07
MP10	8	308	0.68	1.66
MUDST	165	2304	14.04	12.39
RS01	7	55	0.60	0.30
RS03	11	44	0.94	0.24
RS03.1	5	11	0.43	0.06
Sg04	3	25	0.26	0.13
Sg12	1	18	0.09	0.10
Sg40	9	367	0.77	1.97
SLM12.1	18	733	1.53	3.94
SLM14	4	91	0.34	0.49
SLM20	3	94	0.26	0.51
SLM20?	1	9	0.09	0.05
SLM21	8	247	0.68	1.33
SLM40.1	1	8	0.09	0.03
Sq08.2	6	57	0.51	0.31
Sq09	53	599	4.51	3.22
Sq09.1	2	136	0.17	0.73
Sq20.1?	11	49	0.94	0.26
Sq20.2	464	7113	39.49	38.25
Sq20.3	118	2145	10.04	11.30
Sq20.5	142	2142	12.09	11.52
Sq20.5?	1	15	0.09	0.08
Sq22	23	171	1.96	0.92
Sq23.1	5	51	0.43	0.27
Sq23/23.4	15	458	1.28	2.46
Sq30	1	13	0.09	0.07
Sq30?	1	6	0.09	0.03
STR40	2	15	0.17	0.08
FG	4	15	0.34	0.08
WW01.1	12	169	1.02	0.91
WW01.4	17	233	1.45	1.25
WW01.5?	1	1	0.09	0.01
WW01.7	1	29	0.09	0.16
WW05	2	22	0.17	0.12
WW06	5	48	0.43	0.26
Post-medieval				
blackware	3	2	0.26	0.01
coarseware	25	566	2.13	3.04
slip-coated ware	2	24	0.17	0.12
slipware	2	56	0.17	0.30
tin-glazed earthenware	2	4	0.17	0.02
white salt-glazed stoneware	1	2	0.09	0.01
yellow ware	5	31	0.43	0.17
Total	1175	18,622		

Garden wall 240002 was associated with contexts 240034, 240036, 240043, and 240055. Pottery from 240034 comprised late oxidised wares WCTS SLM12.1 jug, jar or cistern sherds and WCTS SLM21 bowl sherd (Fig. 205, 41), a Tudor Green type bowl, probably lobed (not illustrated) and a residual unglazed whiteware (WW01.4) body sherd. Pottery from 240043 was similar and was made up of five WCTS SLM12.1 (MP03) jug/jar or cistern sherds and a fabric LMT05 (WCTS SLM14) bowl sherd. A levelling layer below a section of wall 240002 (240055) contained only early medieval pottery, ie Coventry-type ware (very heavily abraded), and fabrics CPJ18 and CPJ19 (WCTS RS03, RS03.1). There were 29 sherds in total. Context 240036 was the only one to contain post-medieval pottery – a single coarse ware sherd weighing 78 g – and a medieval cooking pot sherd. This group of contexts was rather similar to those forming stone spread 240001. Each contained a context with only early medieval pottery, both contained late medieval sherds, although better represented in 240002, and both contained a single post-medieval sherd.

The interpretation of features 240001 and 240002 as walls flanking an entrance way is not unreasonable. However, the pottery evidence is difficult to interpret. In general terms the formalisation of a park associated with Hawkeswell Hall and the attendant laying out of a sandstone wall and entrance way would fit with developments in the 16th century and there is sufficient pottery of that date to support this, although it does not adequately explain the preponderance of medieval pottery. The post-medieval sherds could then conceivably have been associated with the destruction of this entrance arrangement and could be seen as part of an early–mid-18th century remodelling which would have been more or less contemporary with the construction of 240024 and 240006 and the disuse of 240007.

A further series of contexts, 240088, 240089 and 240099, contained late medieval pottery. The former two were cleaning layers over wall 240002, while 240099 was associated with feature 240119. Layer 240088 contained a fabric LMT07 (WCTS SLM20) bowl (Fig. 205, 43) possibly cross-joining with sherds from 240089, a fabric LMT06 bowl (Fig. 205, 42) and a further three sherds from a second bowl possibly cross-joining with sherds from 240034, wall 240002. There was, in addition, an 18th century coarse ware bowl sherd, possibly intrusive, and a residual fabric WW03 (WCTS WW01.1) green-glazed jug base with a drilled hole, possibly part of a riveted repair, above the base angle. Layer 240089 contained two joining fabric LMT07 (WCTS SLM20) bowl sherds and an undiagnostic fabric LMT08 (WCTS SLM20?) sherd. Cobbled surface 240099 contained two fabric MP03 (WCTS SLM12.1) jug/jar or cistern sherds, one probably a cross-join with 240043, wall 240002, and a jug sherd in the same fabric, probably a cross-join with 240034, also wall 240002. There was one residual whiteware sherd (WCTS WW01.7, fabric WW09), a green-glazed rod handle with herringbone slashing. Although these layers did not produce a large amount of pottery the sherds were quite large, with average sherd weights of 25.6 g, 17.3 g and 30.5 g respectively, which again suggests little disturbance and is unusual for

Table 148 Medieval pottery: quantification by sherd count by context/feature group

	12th-13th centuries					15th-16th centuries								17th-18th centuries				
Fabric	*240003*	*240015*	*240401*	*240402*	*240403*	*240001*	*240002*	*240014*	*240026*	*240088*	*240089*	*240099*	*240119*	*240006*	*240007*	*240024*	*240031*	*Total*
C004	–	–	–	–	–	1	–	–	–	–	–	–	–	–	–	–	–	1
crucible	–	–	1	–	–	–	–	–	–	–	–	–	–	–	–	–	–	1
MP02	–	–	–	–	–	–	–	7	–	–	–	–	–	–	–	–	–	7
MP10	–	–	–	–	–	–	–	–	–	–	–	–	–	–	–	1	–	1
RS01	–	–	–	2	–	–	–	1	–	–	–	–	–	–	–	–	4	7
RS03	–	–	–	–	–	–	10	1	–	–	–	–	–	–	–	–	–	11
RS03.1	–	–	–	–	–	–	5	–	–	–	–	–	–	–	–	–	–	5
SLM12.1	–	–	–	–	–	–	11	–	–	–	–	3	–	–	–	–	4	18
SLM14	–	–	–	2	–	1	1	–	–	–		–	–	–	–	–	–	4
SLM20	–	–	–	–	–	–	–	–	–	1	2	–	–	–	–	–	–	3
SLM20?	–	–	–	–	–	–	–	–	–	–	1	–	–	–	–	–	–	1
SLM21	–	–	–	–	–	1	1	–	–	4	–	–	–	–	–	–	2	8
Sg04	–	–	–	1	–	–	–	1	–	–	–	–	–	–	–	–	1	3
Sg12	–	–	–	1	–	–	–	–	–	–	–	–	–	–	–	–	–	1
Sg40	–	–	–	–	–	–	–	–	–	–	–	–	–	–	–	–	9	9
Sq08.2	4	–	–	–	–	–	–	–		–	–	–	–	–	–	–	2	6
Sq09	5	–	14	4	4	9	–	–	10	–	–	–	1	–	–	–	6	53
Sq09.1	1	1	–	–	–	–	–	–	–	–	–	–	–	–	–	–	–	2
Sq20.1?	4	–	–	–	–	7	–	–	–	–	–	–	–	–	–	–	–	11
Sq20.2	–	–	449	12	–	3	–	–	–	–	–	–	–	–	–	–	–	464
Sq20.3	9	41	–	–	–	11	1	18	–	–	–	–	–	3	–	–	34	128
Sq20.5	1	17	93	4	–	5	14	–	–	–	–	–	–	–	–	–	8	142
Sq20.5?	1	–	–	–	–	–	–	–	–	–	–	–	–	–	–	–	–	1
Sq22	2	–	19	–	–	–	–	–	–	–	–	–	2	–	–	–	–	23
Sq23.1	–	–	–	2	–	–	–	–	–	–	–	–	–	–	–	–	3	5
Sq23/23.4	–	–	14	–	–	–	–	–	–	–	–	–	–	–	–	–	1	15
Sq25.1	7	2	138	5	1	3	–	–	–	–	–	–	2	–	–	–	7	165
Sq30	–	–	–	–	–	–	–	–	–	–	–	–	1	–	–	–	1	2
Sq80.1	–	–	–	–	–	–	–	–	–	–	–	–	–	–	–	–	1	1
StR40	2	–	–	–	–	–	–	–	–	–	–	–	–	–	–	–	–	2
TG	–	–	–	–	–	–	2	2	–	–	–	–	–	–	–	–	–	4
WW01.4	–	–	2	2	2	1	1	–	–	–	–	–	1	–	–	–	8	17
WW01.1	–	–	1	1	–	–	–	1	–	1	–	–	–	–	–	–	8	12
WW01.5?	–	–	–	–	–	–	–	1	–	–	–	–	–	–	–	–	–	1
WW05	–	–	–	1	–	–	–	1	–	–	–	–	–	–	–	–	–	2
WW01.7	–	–	–	–	–	–	–	–	–	–	–	1	–	–	–	–	–	1
WW06	–	–	–	–	–	–	–	–	–	–	–	–	–	–	–	–	5	5
Post-medieval																		
Blackware	–	–	–	–	–	–	–	–	–	–	–	–	–	2	1	–	–	3
Coarseware	–	–	–	–	–	–	1	–	–	1	–	–	–	6	13	4	–	25
Mottled ware	–	–	–	–	–	–	–	–	–		–	–	–	1	–	–	–	1
Slip-coated ware	–	–	–	–	–	–	–	–	–	–	–	–	–	2	–	–	–	2
Feathered slipware	–	–	–	–	–	1	–	–	–	–	–	–	–	–	1	–	–	2
Tin-glazed earthenware	–	–	–	–	–	–	–	–	–	–	–	–	–	–	2	–	–	2
White salt-glazed stoneware	–	–	–	–	–	–	–	–	–	–	–	–	–	1	–	–	–	1
Yellow ware	–	–	–	–	–	–	–	–	–	–	–	–	–	1	4	–	–	5
Total	36	61	731	37	7	43	47	33	10	7	3	4	7	16	21	5	104	1172

pottery found within layers. It would certainly suggest that the later medieval material was not part of a manuring scatter nor had been subjected to plough action. The cross-joins demonstrate that the features 240001, 240002 and 240091, part of the presumed entrance arrangements, and features to the south are associated. The most likely interpretation is that they were demolished at the same time. If this is so then the coarse ware bowl sherd from 240088 may not be intrusive and may date the demolition.

A series of features, some intercutting, within 'disturbed natural' 240010, lay roughly due west of the putative entrance arrangement. Three of these features, 240402, 240403 and 240404, appeared to extend into the path of the presumed entrance arrangements and must surely pre-date them. Pit 240401 lay slightly to their south-east. The pottery from all four features, especially 240401, was extremely problematic. Over 65% by sherd count, 60% by sherd weight of the pottery from the site was from these features. Pit 240401 alone contained 737 sherds. A substantial quantity of roof tile was associated with the features within the disturbed natural 240010.

Five roof tile fragments, accidentally included within the pottery from 240117, the upper fill of pit 240401, and were treated as a sample representing the fabrics

Table 149 Medieval pottery: functional analysis (quantification by sherd count)

Vessel type/Function	240003	240015	240401	240402	240403	240001	240002	240014	240088	240089	240099	240121	240006	240007	240024	240026	240031	Total
Food preparation/consumption																		
bowl	–	–	5	–	–	–	1	–	6	2	–	1	3	14	–	–	2	34
bowl?	–	–	–	1	–	–	–	–	–	–	–	–	–	–	–	–	–	1
Food consumption																		
platter	–	–	–	–	–	1	–	–	–	–	–	–	–	1	–	–	–	2
Cooking/some food storage																		
cooking pot/jar	22	58	605	21	4	35	29	20	–	–	–	5	2	–	–	10	60	871
cooking pot/jar?	5	1	–	1	–	–	–	–	–	–	–	–	–	–	–	–	1	8
pipkin	–	–	7	–	–	2	–	–	–	–	–	–	–	–	–	–	–	9
Liquid consumption																		
pitcher	–	–	7	1	–	–	–	–	–	–	–	–	–	–	–	–	–	8
jug/pitcher	–	–	59	–	–	1	–	–	–	–	–	–	–	–	–	–	5	65
jug	–	–	5	5	2	1	–	2	1	–	2	–	–	–	–	–	22	40
drinking vessel	–	–	–	–	–	–	–	1	–	–	–	–	1	2	–	–	–	4
Liquid storage																		
cistern	–	–	–	–	–	–	–	1	–	–	–	–	–	–	1	–	–	2
jar/cistern	–	–	–	–	–	–	–	1	–	–	–	–	–	–	–	–	–	1
jug/cistern	–	–	–	–	–	–	6	–	–	–	–	–	–	–	–	–	–	6
jug/jar/cistern	–	–	–	1	–	–	5	2	–	–	2	–	–	–	–	–	5	15
Storage																		
jar	–	–	3	–	–	–	–	–	–	–	–	–	–	1	–	–	–	4
Miscellaneous																		
jar/bowl	–	–	–	–	–	–	–	–	–	–	–	–	–	1	–	–	–	1
crucible	–	–	1	–	–	–	–	–	–	–	–	–	–	–	–	–	–	1
Unknown	9	2	39	7	1	3	6	6	–	1	–	1	10	2	4	–	9	100
Total	36	61	731	37	7	43	47	33	7	3	4	7	16	21	5	10	104	1172

present. Two fabric groups were noted. The first comprised tiles with a sandy, mudstone tempered fabric akin to pottery fabric MUDST (Sq25.1). The tiles were fired to buff, pale brown or grey-brown and as such were rather different from the orange or red tones seen in many medieval and post-medieval tiles. One of the sandy mudstone tempered tiles had traces of a greenish glaze and there was evidence to suggest that the tiles had had a central nib. There is no reason to assume that this tile fabric was anything but contemporary with the pottery. The second group had fabrics similar to the Coventry-type wares and were fired orange or dull red-brown. This group too seemed to be contemporary with the pottery from the fill of 240401.

The primary fill of 240401 (240148) contained a mix of Coventry-type ware cooking pots and mudstone tempered wares (Sq25.1, Sq22) and four iron-rich sandy ware sherds (ir01 WCTS Sq23/Sq23.4). Just over 63% of the sherds could definitely be categorised as coming from cooking pots. One Coventry-type ware cooking pot rim was the same form as, and probably the same vessel as, a cooking pot (Fig. 204, 18) from 240117, the upper fill of pit 240401. Another Coventry-type ware cooking pot was decorated with an applied thumbed strip. A Coventry-type ware jar (Fig. 204, 6) with combed decoration was a unique form from the site. Although the combed decoration is typical of some of the earlier Coventry wares (*cf.* Redknap 1996) the vessel form is not paralleled in the extensive illustrations from Broadgate East, Coventry. Three mudstone-tempered ware cooking pot rim sherds were present. These comprised a small rim diameter jar (Fig. 204, 7, MUDST02), with a form which looked almost Romano-British, a cooking pot with a slightly dished rim (Fig. 204, 8, MUDST03) and an everted rim cooking pot (Fig. 204, 9, MUDST04). Five MUDST03 body sherds from a jug or pitcher were present. The pitcher had an under-glaze white slip and yellowish glaze but was otherwise undecorated. The mudstone-tempered wares were by and large heavily abraded but abrasion was not particularly apparent amongst the Coventry-type wares. The date range of the pottery would seem to fall into the mid-12th–early 13th centuries.

The upper fill of cut 240401 (240117) also contained mainly Coventry-type wares and mudstone tempered wares. Fourteen sherds from a CPJ15 cooking pot were present along with oxidised iron-rich sherds (IR01 WCTS Sq23/Sq23.4) and three whiteware sherds and a crucible fragment (not illustrated). As far as could be determined just over 81% of the sherds were from cooking pots. The Coventry-type cooking pots (Fig. 204, 10–23) had rounded profiles, sometimes with a slight ridge on the shoulder (eg Fig. 204, 10–11, 13, 20) and, occasionally, applied vertical thumbed strips. The minimum rim count indicated that at least 31 cooking pots were present. There was a disproportionately large number of base sherds, some 60 in total. Unfortunately it was not possible to estimate how many vessels they represented.

Four variants of mudstone tempered ware were initially identified (MUDST01-04) but these were subsequently merged under the codes Sq25.1 (fabrics MUDST01-03) and Sq22 (MUDST04). Nearly every sherd was very heavily abraded, making it difficult to determine the original colour and condition of glazed sherds. The most common fabrics were MUDST02 and MUDST03. A small diameter cooking pot or possible pipkin was noted in fabric MUDST01 (Fig. 205, 26). The vessel was very abraded but there were traces of a thin external glaze and under-glaze white slip and possibly traces of an interior white slip. Sherds in fabric variant MUDST02 seemed to be primarily from jugs or pitchers (Fig. 205, 30–1) which often had an under-glaze white slip. Two handles were present (Fig. 205, 32–3), one (Fig. 205, 32) rather unaccountably completely lacking in abrasion. The latter had a copper-mottled, olive green glaze. There was one possible foot from a tripod pitcher. At least one cooking pot, which had a rounded profile and a finger impressed rim, was represented in this fabric (Fig. 205, 25). At least two bowls were present, one with an internal and external white slip and circular impressions along the rim (Fig. 205, 28) and the other with traces of a finger impressed rim (Fig. 205, 29) and internal and external white slip. Both vessels share the same sloping-sided form and both were presumably originally glazed. Two further rim sherds were recorded in this fabric although they were so heavily abraded that it was impossible to assign them with any certainty to form. A pipkin was also represented (Fig. 205, 27) again with an internal and external white slip and traces of glaze. The vessel form is rather curious, having a disproportionately large and heavy handle. A similar pipkin form in Chilvers Coton A fabric was recorded on Site 1, kiln 8 at Chilvers Coton (Mayes and Scott 1984).

Three possible jugs or pitchers were represented in variant MUDST03, all with under-glaze white slip and olive, yellowish or clear, copper speckled glazes. One very fragmentary cooking pot/jar rim sherd was recorded and a number of body sherds, one with an applied thumbed strip, presumed to have come from cooking pots/jars. A pitcher with a corrugated neck (Fig. 205, 35) and a cooking pot with a finger impressed rim (Fig. 205, 34) were recorded in fabric MUDST04.

Other sherds from 240117 represented a whiteware cooking pot (fabric WW03, WCTS WW01.1) and two jugs (fabric WW05), a crucible and a pitcher with applied vertical thumbed strip (fabric IR01 WCTS Sq23/Sq23.4).

The whiteware sherds and some of the forms of the mudstone tempered wares (eg pipkin Fig. 205, 27), suggest that some of the material dates to the second half of the 13th century. The absence of large quantities of whitewares would, however, tend to indicate that the group had accumulated before the 14th century, indeed probably early in the second half of the 13th century. The average sherd weight for primary fill 240148 was 20.4 g, which is consistent with the material being undisturbed and *in situ*, whereas the average sherd weight for later fill 240117 was 14.3 g which suggests that some disturbance is likely.

Fills 240138 and 240139, the lower and upper fills of the terminal of trench 240402 which was stratigraphically later than pit 240403, contained the familiar mix of Coventry type wares, including a pitcher handle (Fig. 205, 36), and mudstone tempered wares. In addition 240138 contained sherds from a glazed Deritend ware jug and three whiteware sherds. Fill 240139 also contained two reduced Deritend ware cooking pot sherds, a whiteware base sherd and an iron-poor (IP03, WCTS Sg04) jug sherd. Fill 240109 (the single fill south of the terminal) contained only one sherd, in fabric IR02, (WCTS Sq23.1), and a further IR02 sherd was found in 240139. All this is consistent with a 13th century deposition date. However a jug and a jug, jar or cistern sherd in fabric LMT05 WCTS SLM14 in 240139 date to the 15th or 16th centuries. It is tempting to see these two sherds as intrusive but the presence of tile fragments at the base of the cut links the trench fills to those recovered from features 240014 and 240026 (see above) which seem to date to the 15th or 16th centuries. The sherds in the fills of 240402 were quite large and although some were heavily abraded, the majority were not, which is rather inconsistent with the pottery being residual. The presence of late medieval pottery, even though it is poorly represented, also ties this fill to 240001 and 240002, and 240402 is on roughly the same north–south alignment as them.

Trench 240402 cut feature 240403 which contained seven sherds in its upper fill (240152). These comprised four sherds from a CPJ15 (WCTS Sq09) cooking pot, a mudstone tempered ware sherd, possibly ceramic building material, and two sherds from a whiteware (WW05 WCTS WW01.4) jug (not illustrated). This suggests a pottery deposition date in the mid–later 13th century. There were further fragments of roof tile in this feature which were probably more or less contemporary with the pottery, although this would be quite an early date for the use of ceramic roofing tile in a rural context.

The average sherd weights of the fills of 240402 and 240403 were 14.6 g for 240403, which is more or less the same as that for the secondary fill of pit 240401, but for the three fills of 240402 average sherd weights ranged from 12.1 g (fill 240138) to 22.3 g (fill 240139) and 26 g (fill 240109). The latter two figures are relatively high and tend to suggest that these two fills have not been particularly disturbed.

A small group of sherds was found in layer 240120 overlying circular feature 240119 which lay between wall 240002 and the central pits (above). The group contained only medieval material which was rather fragmentary with an average sherd weight of 8.6 g and may therefore be redeposited. It comprised a possible Chilvers Coton C sherd (WCTS Sq30), a whiteware (fabric WW01 WCTS WW01.4) bowl sherd with an internal apple green glaze, four mudstone-tempered cooking pot sherds (fabrics MUDST03 WCTS Sq25.1 and MUDST04 WCTS Sq22) and a fabric CPJ15 WCTS Sq09 cooking pot sherd. An additional small (7 g) fragment may have been daub.

Two features to the east of the hollow-way, pit 240015 and ditch 240003, contained early medieval pottery, similar to that found to the west of the hollow-way. Here, however, there was no ceramic building material recorded in the fills and therefore a degree of certainty that there had been no contamination or disturbance. There was no pottery in the primary fill of pit 240015 (240128), but the secondary fill (240106) contained Coventry type wares (Fig. 204, 2–4) CPJ16 (Fig. 204, 1) and mudstone tempered wares. Many of the sherds were fairly large and all the sherds appeared to be from cooking pots. An applied thumbed strip was present on a mudstone tempered sherd (MUDST02 WCTS Sq25.1) and on a Coventry type ware sherd (COVT04 WCTS Sq20.5) and bands of horizontal combing were noted on another COVT04 sherd, very similar to sherds found in the fills of 240003 (see below) and in 240042, associated with the possible demolished wall 240001. The absence of any whitewares, jug sherds or glazed wares of any sort would tend to suggest a date before *c* 1250 for the deposition of the material. Two COVT04 WCTS Sq20.5 cooking pots were of the same form as ones recovered from 240117 (Fig. 204, 20) but otherwise the cooking pot forms were not recorded elsewhere on the site.

The long ditch (240003) to the north of pit 240015 also contained only cooking pot sherds (fills 240059 and 240086), although in a greater number of fabrics than from pit 240015. A rather crude cooking pot rim sherd (Fig. 204, 5) oxidised orange-brown throughout may have been a Coventry-type ware variant. In addition to Coventry type wares, other cooking pot fabrics were present – CPJ15, CPJ16, CPJ17 and CPJ20, MUDST02, MUDST04 and two very abraded iron-poor sherds, with a pale pinky-brown fabric, IP04 (WCTS fabrics Sq09, Sq09.1, Sq08.2, Sq25.1, Sq22 and STR40 respectively). There were further examples of Coventry type wares with applied thumbed strips and with bands of horizontal combing.

The sherds from ditch 240003 were often heavily abraded and smaller (average sherd weight 9.2 g from fill 240059 and 13.3 g from fill 240086) than those from pit 240015 (average sherd weight 23.6 g). The pottery from the ditch fills therefore looks more like surface or manuring scatters accidentally incorporated into the fill of the ditch rather than deliberate dumping/primary disposal.

Over half the pottery from topsoil 240031 dated to the 12th or 13th centuries and was broadly similar to that found for example in pit 240401. Included amongst this were a number of cooking pot rims in forms not hitherto recorded amongst the Coventry-type ware cooking pots (Fig. 205, 44–6), one of which (Fig. 205, 44) had a drilled hole, possibly part of a repair, in the shoulder, or paralleled amongst the material from pit 240401. Also present was a Coventry-type ware cooking pot, the same form as Figure 204, 10, which had an applied, vertical thumbed strip. Whitewares formed a higher proportion of the group at *c* 20% than anywhere else on site. Both cooking pots (Fig. 205, 47) and green-glazed jugs were represented. A new fabric, only recorded in 240031, was fabric IP05, (WCTS Sg40). Two vessels were represented. One, a large hand-formed jug or pitcher (Fig. 205, 48) had a ridge at the neck shoulder junction, a deep vertical thumbed strip and a slightly opaque olive-tan glaze on the exterior. Olive glaze had also covered the interior of the vessel neck. The rim appeared to have been decorated with small circular impressions. Vessel form and manufacture suggested a date no later than the 13th century. The second was another jug sherd with olive glaze spots and a ridge at the neck-shoulder junction. A small amount of late medieval or early post-medieval pottery occurred in the topsoil consisting of two bowls (fabric LMT06, WCTS SLM21) and three jug, jar or cistern sherds (fabric MP03, WCTS SLM12.1). Another new fabric, fabric IP06 (WCTS Sg41) seemed to belong to this period. The fabric had few inclusions and was oxidised throughout. A single vessel was represented, a jug or possibly cistern with a broad plain strap handle and a patchy olive-tan glaze. Post-medieval pottery was only found in topsoil from above garden feature 240007 (see above).

Several features are noticeable about the pottery from the topsoil. Firstly the sherds are large with an average sherd weight of just under 20 g. Secondly the pottery was rather less abraded that that found in the feature fills, particularly those in the central area of the site. The absence of any post-medieval pottery, with the exception of that from over 240007, would seem to suggest rather limited activity on the site after the 16th century at the latest. One sherd, a fabric IR02 (WCTS Sq23.1) body-base sherd, appeared to be from the same vessel as one found in 240117 in pit 240401 and some of the mudstone tempered sherds also looked to be parts of vessels recorded 240117. The topsoil pottery therefore may provide some corroboration for the idea that the pits 240401–4 in 'disturbed natural' 240010 may have been dug or contaminated in the 15th–16th centuries.

Discussion

The pottery evidence indicates that quite considerable activity took place in the 12th–13th centuries. The pottery seems to be consistent with normal domestic occupation, apparently concentrated in the centre of the site (Table 149). The condition and sheer volume of pottery indicates that it must be more or less *in situ*, ie the sherds do not represent a dump of material brought in from elsewhere. The amount of pottery suggests that there must have been at least one building in the vicinity, which presumably lay partly or wholly in the area of 'disturbed natural' 240010. Traces of any building were presumably removed by the digging of features 240401, 240402, 240403 and 240404 and the formation of 240010. The absence of any other evidence for concentrated medieval occupation in the area of excavation is puzzling, the exceptions being ditch 240003 and pit 240015 to the east of the hollow-way, although the quantity of pottery from these two features is in no way commensurate with that recovered from 240010 and associated features. The question remains, therefore, what was the nature of and reason for the small area of occupation in otherwise open unoccupied land, well away from Hawkeswell Hall and the settlement of Hawkeswell hamlet. One possibility is that this area marks the site of an large house subsequently replaced by Hawkeswell Hall. This might explain the presence of ceramic roof tile which would be more likely to be encountered (in a rural setting) on a higher status building in this period.

Whatever the reason for occupation in the 12th–13th centuries the paucity of whitewares and other types of pottery one might reasonably expect to find in the 14th century indicates that abandonment of this area, or general settlement contraction, occurred in the 14th century. This would hardly be surprising given the combination of worsening climatic conditions, poor harvests and the continuing predations of plague in that century.

A second period of activity occurred in the 15th or 16th centuries. The following interpretation is speculative but not inconsistent with the pottery evidence. It is possible that the land to the west of the hollow-way was 'improved', gentrified or formalised into parkland or garden. This would explain the putative entrance way and associated walls and one or two garden features. The pottery cannot pin down accurately when exactly this might have occurred but in a broader setting this type of gentrification can be paralleled in the Elizabethan period. The origin of the pottery is difficult to explain. Manuring scatters seem unlikely. The pottery is fairly basic and utilitarian, of a type routinely encountered in deposits of the late medieval or early post-medieval period. However, the near absence of drinking vessels is interesting and it is possible that the pottery may represent remains of vessels used by those labouring on the 'new' garden.

A third period of activity appears to have occurred in the later 17th–18th centuries. The garden or park may well have had an overhaul with the planting of hedges and perhaps the demolition of the entrance way. This may reflect the vogue for 'landscaped' gardens or may indicate a change in land use.

Illustrated vessels (Figs 204–5)

Pit 240015 and ditch 240003

1. CPJ16 WCTS Sq09.1 cooking pot, abraded, some ext soot, context 240106 pit 240015
2. COVT WCTS Sq20.3 cooking pot, black throughout, context 240106 pit 240015
3. COVT WCTS Sq20.3 cooking pot, external soot, context 240106 pit 240015
4. COVT WCTS Sq20.3 cooking pot, abraded, context 240106 pit 240015
5. COVT? WCTS Sq20.3 cooking pot, abraded, context 240059 ditch 240003

Pit 240401

6. COVT WCTS Sq20.3 jar?, black throughout, combed decoration, context 240148
7. MUDST02 WCTS Sq25.1 small cooking pot, heavy abrasion, ext soot, context 240148
8. MUDST02 WCTS Sq25.1 cooking pot, context 240148
9. MUDST04 WCTS Sq22 cooking pot, external soot on rim, context 240148
10. COVT WCTS Sq20.3 cooking pot, external soot, context 240117
11. COVT WCTS Sq20.3 cooking pot, abraded, external soot, context 240117
12. COVT WCTS Sq20.3 cooking pot, abraded, external soot, context 240117
13. COVT WCTS Sq20.3 cooking pot, heavy external soot, abraded, context 240117
14. COVT WCTS Sq20.3 cooking pot, ?trace of combed decoration, external soot, abraded, context 240117
15. COVT WCTS Sq20.3 cooking pot, context 240117
16. COVTYM WCTS Sq20.5 cooking pot, context 240117
17. COVT WCTS Sq20.3 cooking pot, context 240117
18. COVT WCTS Sq20.3 cooking pot, context 240117
19. COVTWCTS Sq20.3 cooking pot, context 240117
20. COVT04 WCTS Sq20.5 cooking pot, heavy abrasion, trace of external soot, context 240117
21. COVT04 WCTS Sq20.5 cooking pot, heavy abrasion, trace of external soot, context 240117
22. COVT04 WCTS Sq20.5 cooking pot, heavy abrasion, trace of external soot, context 240117
23. COVT04 WCTS Sq20.5 cooking pot, context 240117
24. IR01, Sq23/Sq23.4 cooking pot, context 240117
25. MUDST02 Sq25.1 cooking pot, thumbed rim, heavily abraded, context 240117
26. MUDST01 Sq25.1 cooking pot, heavily abraded, possible trace of external white slip, trace of external soot, context 240117
27. MUDST02 Sq25.1 pipkin, heavily abraded, white slipped surfaces, trace of external soot, context 240117
28. MUDST02 Sq25.1 bowl, abraded, stabbing on rim, white slipped surfaces, context 240117
29. MUDST02 Sq25.1 bowl, abraded, trace of internal white slip, ?thumbed rim, context 240117
30. MUDST02 Sq25.1 jug, heavily abraded, context 240117
31. MUDST02 Sq25.1 jug base, ?trace of external white slip, context 240117
32. MUDST02 Sq25.1 jug handle, under-glaze white slip, bright green glaze with darker (copper) green mottles, context 240117
33. MUDST02 Sq25.1 jug handle, heavily abraded, stabbed decoration, context 240117
34. MUDST04 WCTS Sq22 cooking pot, context 240117
35. MUDST04 WCTS Sq22 pitcher, corrugated neck, unglazed, context 240117

Feature 240402

36. COVT WCTS Sq20.3 handle, stabbed decoration, context 240138

Pit 240403

37. WW05 WCTS WW01.4 jug, abraded, context 240152

Garden features

38. CPJ15 WCTS Sq09 cooking pot, context 240127, feature 240026
39. CPJ15 WCTS Sq09 cooking pot, some abrasion, context 240127

Fig. 204 Medieval pottery

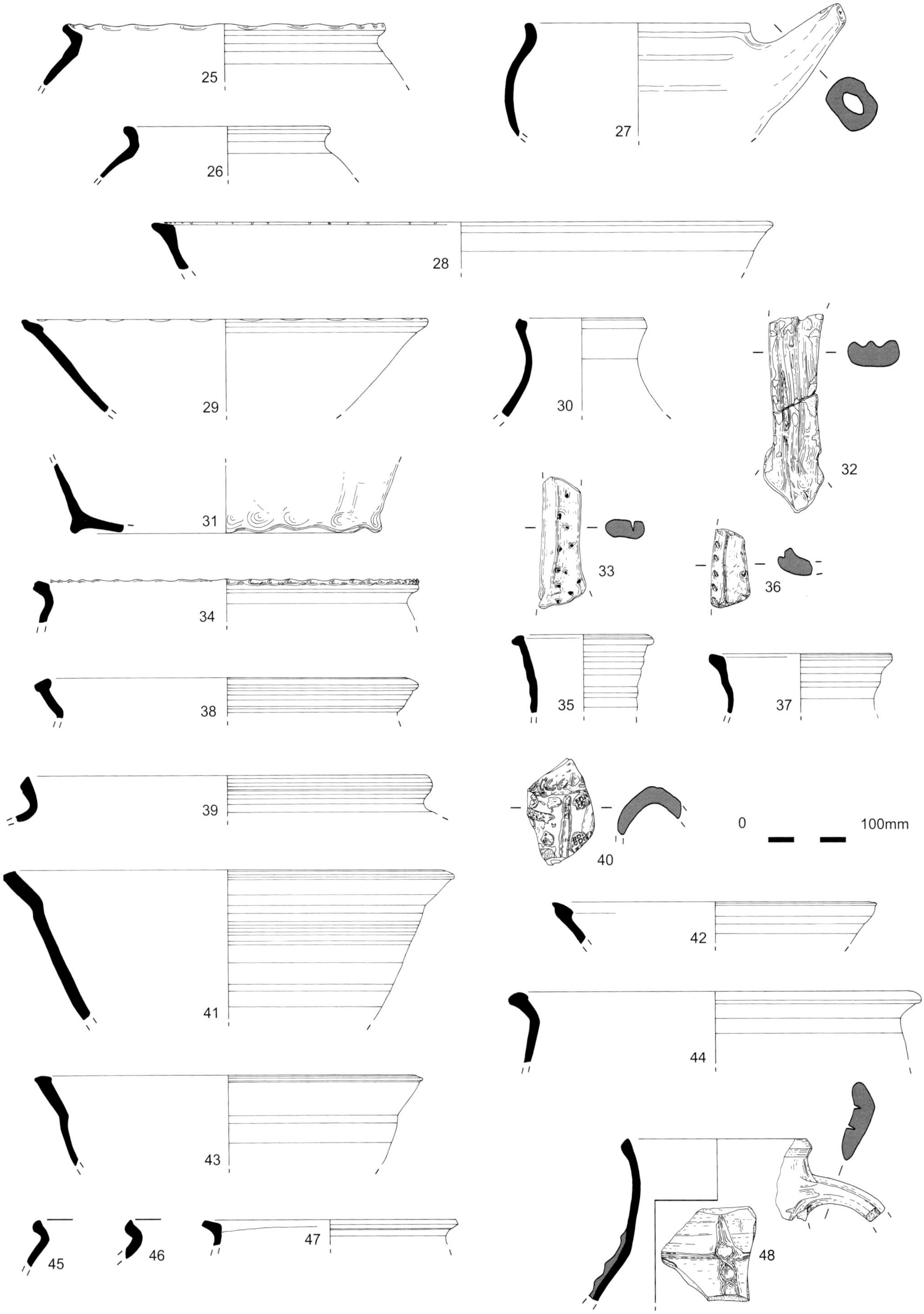

Fig. 205 Medieval pottery

40. Lyveden-Stannion B ware WCTS CO04 ?form, applied and stamped white clay decoration, context 240001
41. LMT06 WCTS SLM21, bowl, external soot, context 240034,
42. LMT06, WCTS SLM21 bowl, external soot, internal olive green glaze run, context 240089
43. LMT07 WCTS SLM20, bowl, external soot, context 240088, possible cross-join with 240089

Topsoil

44. COVT WCTS Sq20.3 cooking pot, heavily abraded
45. COVT WCTS Sq20.3 cooking pot
46. COVT WCTS Sq20.3 cooking pot
47. WW05 WCTS WW01.4 cooking pot, external soot
48. IP05 WCTS Sg40 jug, external yellowish-olive glaze, applied decoration

Discussion

The range of features on this site clearly reflects the long span and changing nature of the occupation at Hawkeswell, starting in the medieval period. However, not only may the suggested creation and maintenance of a formal garden on the site in the later medieval phase have disturbed earlier deposits, but their subsequent demolition and the possible 17th–18th century landscaping of the site would have further mixed materials of different periods; all these deposits will have been further reworked by more recent cultivation.

The medieval features in the centre of the site are of unknown function, although they suggest a range of different activities. This appears to begin with a high level of traffic, human or animal, possibly in the location a building, resulting in the localised disturbance of the natural. This was followed by activity involving burning, with deposits of burnt clay and charcoal-rich soil being dumped in and around pit 240403 while the large quantities of pottery and ceramic building material dumped in feature 240401 further point to the proximity of settlement activity.

The intermittent nature of the pottery sequence, with other main phases of activity in the 15th–16th and the late 17th–mid-18th centuries, may reflect the location of the site on the northern margins of the settlement, making it subject to periods of expansion and contraction. However, in the absence of data about the history of Hawkeswell Hall (and any predecessors), the nature and dating of the later medieval and post-medieval features are not certain.

The phase 2 medieval features, however, are interpreted as relating to the creation of a formal garden on the site, perhaps associated with a large house predating Hawkeswell Hall. They comprise a range of stone or stone-lined features, such as the garden wall with its substantial gateway framing a vista across the Blythe valley, the possible 'water feature' represented by the circular stone setting and its associated drain and cup-stone, the rectangular stone setting, possibly the foundation for an ornamental feature, and the stone-lined trench.

Further changes occurred in the late 17th century, possibly involving the landscaping of the site (over the now, possibly long since, demolished garden features) associated with Hawkeswell Hall. The pond on the west side of the site, possibly a medieval feature, may have been incorporated within the arrangement of both the garden and the later landscaping.

SYNTHESES

Chapter 28

Environmental and Material Culture Studies

Environment and agricultural economy, by Chris Stevens

Introduction

While previous work in Shropshire and Stafford has provided the basis of a detailed off-site environmental history of the region (Leah *et al.* 1998), the excavations along the M6 Toll provided a unique opportunity to investigate evidence for the agricultural economy, as well as the utilisation and management of local natural resources that took place within these ancient environments. Environmental evidence from the sites covered the Neolithic to the medieval period, and the discussion that follows discusses aspects of the environment and agricultural economy within each major period.

Neolithic

While Mesolithic flints were recovered from some of the sites, no environmental evidence was directly associated with them. Pollen evidence from King's Pool, Stafford, suggests that between 6000–5000 cal BC the later Mesolithic forests were dominated by pine with an expansion of alder, and with high amounts of microscopic charcoal indicating burning. By the Early Neolithic it is probable that pine forests had given way to those on the drier soils dominated by oak, elm, hazel and probably lime in the south Midlands (Bartley and Morgan 1990), with birch and alder fen carr within the lowland river valleys. It is within this forest that the earliest evidence for agriculture is found. A single grain of barley from Shenstone Linear Features (Site 13, Chapter 15) yielded a radiocarbon date of 3710–3530 cal BC (4846±30 BP, NZA-25898), and in addition to a few cereal remains there were large quantities of hazelnuts shells. A further deposit pre-dating 2920–2660 cal BC (4230±35 BP, NZA-25076) from West of Crane Brook also yielded some evidence for the exploitation of hazelnut (Site 9, Chapter 13).

The remains sit well with a picture of Neolithic Britain in which a diverse subsistence strategy is practiced, seeing the utilisation of wild foods and cultivated cereals which, with barley, probably included emmer wheat (Moffett *et al.* 1989; Robinson 2000; Stevens 2006). While such a lifestyle suggests a mobile strategy in which cereals were not necessarily grown in the region, it might be noted that cereal pollen has been identified from a sequence at Lammascote Road, Stafford, dating to 3800–3500 cal BC (Pearson 2002; Pearson *et al.* 1999). The Early Neolithic date for the grain is broadly contemporary with some of the earliest other dated cereal grains from both the north (Jones 2000; Hedges *et al.* 1991, 279–96) and south (Wilkinson and Murphy 1995), suggesting that cereal agriculture spread across the country relatively rapidly reaching this and most regions within 200–300 years.

Charcoal from two of the sites (Sites 9 and 13) suggests the exploitation for fuel of a fairly diverse range of species from local woodlands, including oak, ash, hawthorn/Sorbus, alder and birch. Of some interest is that both these sites produced evidence for pine which is only subsequently found within Romano-British cremation related deposits. Pine charcoal probably associated with Early Neolithic activity was also recovered from Whitemoor Haye Quarry (Gale 2002). While pine forest is likely to have been diminished within the local woodland it is probable that some stands survived into the Neolithic, at least to the elm decline (Gale 2002). To the west pine pollen is seen in Late Mesolithic–Early Neolithic deposits, declining prior to 2460–2130 cal BC (Leah *et al.* 1998). However, at Perry Barr, north Birmingham, deposits dating to the later Neolithic 2890–2580 cal BC (Beta-219914) yielded evidence for pine, along with alder, lime, elm and hazel (Tetlow and Gearey 2006).

Investigations of deposits under Watling Street at Wall revealed evidence for pine woodland in peat deposits, with whole stumps recovered from the underlying sand (Godwin and Dickson 1964–5), while pine stumps were also recorded below peat deposits at Sutton Park (Bloomer 1923).

Bronze Age

Environmental evidence from this period is slight and relates to burnt mound and associated deposits dating from the Early to the Middle Bronze Age. At most of these sites (Sites 20, 39, 40, Chapters 25, 23, 20) the charcoal suggested that very local woodland resources were exploited growing in wetter areas adjacent to the river floodplain yielding charcoal of alder, hazel, ash and birch. At Langley Brook deposits dated to around 1880–1670 cal BC (NZA-25162, 3441±30 BP) even yielded waterlogged remains suggesting a woody scrubland of such a composition that included elm, hazel, birch and probably alder (Site 39). Similar evidence for the exploitation of local riverside resources, alder, alder buckthorn and willow, was also recovered from a burnt mound at Cob Lane, Birmingham (Hodder 2004, 33–5).

For the region as a whole a shift from oak dominated woodland to that dominated by hazel is noted (Bartley and Morgan 1990), occurring in the Early Bronze Age and perhaps continuing into the Iron Age (see below).

There is a small amount of evidence for cultivation from the end of the Early Bronze Age to the start of the Iron Age, and cereal remains include wheat and barley from Wishaw (Site 20), Colletts Brook (Site 40) and Langley Brook (Site 39), while the presence of hazelnut shells at the latter two sites indicate the continued use of wild resources.

Iron Age

The Iron Age sees an increase in evidence for cereal agriculture, associated with the appearance of more permanent, planned settlements. Although the evidence for some sites is slight, spelt and emmer wheat appeared to have been farmed alongside 6-row hulled barley (Sites 14, 19, 29, 30, Chapters 16, 24, 23, 21), and several other sites in the region have produced similar evidence (Park Farm, Barford, Moffett 1993–4, table 5; Whitemoor Haye Quarry, Ciaraldi 2002; Marsh Farm, Pearson in preparation; Midsummer Hill, Colledge 1981). There is little evidence for the cultivation of pulses in the region during the Iron Age, although Greig (1979) has tentatively identified pollen of *Vicia faba* from Fisherwick.

It is probable that spelt appears in the general region in the Middle–Late Iron Age as seen within areas on the periphery of the region (Monckton 2006). The continued cultivation of emmer in the Iron Age is of some interest as the species is largely absent from sites to the south within Wessex (G. Campbell 2000) and the Thames Valley (Robinson and Wilson 1987). It has been noted that emmer fares well on lighter, drier soils (Percival 1921, 188; Jones 1981), and while varieties no doubt exist that are capable of exploiting wetter soils (Davies and Hillman 1988), there is increasing evidence to suggest the continued cultivation of emmer in parts of the country in which sandier soils are quite prolific, such as around Birmingham, within parts of Cambridgeshire (Murphy 2003; Stevens 2003), Kent and north-east Britain (van der Veen 1992).

In comparison with other parts of the country there is little evidence of a weed flora, suggesting that grain was stored relatively clean (for hulled wheats probably in the spikelet), while the general low density of such remains is consistent with processing for the needs of the core family, as might be conducted on small, largely self-contained farmsteads. Other evidence for cereal agriculture is scant; a saddle quern dated to the Early–Middle Iron Age was recovered from Shenstone Ring Ditch (Site 14), while North of Langley Mill (Site 29) had a four-poster granary. A probable saddle quern was also recovered from Marsh Farm near Hamden-in-Arden (N. Palmer, in prep.), and such querns are consistent with small scale processing operations. It might however be noted that both saddle querns and rotary querns appear to have been used simultaneously within the Middle–Late Iron Age at Fisherwick (Samuels 1979) and Whitemoor Haye Quarry (Bevan and Ixer 2002).

The local environment in which these crops were grown would still appear relatively forested from the pollen evidence, comprising alder, birch, hazel and oak woodlands, with hazel as noted earlier becoming increasingly dominant (Site 12, Chapter 14). There is some evidence for the increase of heathland probably associated with clearance during the later part of the Iron Age. This is seen in pollen sequences under the Roman Roads at Ryknield Street (Site 12) and Watling Street at Wall (Godwin and Dickson 1964–5), while a podzol was recovered from under Ryknield Street at Sutton Park (Hodder 2004, 47–8). It might be noted that evidence from King's Pool near Stafford to the north indicates quite large scale deforestation in the period *c* 800–400 cal BC (Bartley and Morgan 1990), while at Fisherwick, as at Ryknield Street, there is also some indication that holly becomes more important along with ash, associated with increased clearance. While lime appears at both these sites Scaife (Site 12) suggests it is largely a remnant from the Bronze Age, although small quantities of lime have also been recovered from the top of a sequence dated to cal AD 240–420 (Beta-219913) in north Birmingham (Tetlow and Gearey 2006).

The charcoal evidence showed no indication of management of these woodlands during the Iron Age, but that wood from most of these species, including in addition to birch, hazel, alder and oak, wood of blackthorn, ash, hawthorn/sorbus, yew, field maple and poplar (Sites 14, 19, 29, 30) was collected for fuel. While no evidence for the exploitation of heathland was found at any of the M6 Toll sites, such evidence is recovered from other sites in the region during the Iron Age (Whitemoor Haye, Gale 2002).

No evidence for animals was found for this period from any of the excavations, although other sites have yielded a small amount of evidence for cattle, sheep/goat and horse (Startin 1979; Hammon in prep.), while insect evidence from Fisherwick yielded many species associated with grassland and with the dung of large herbaceous mammals (Osborne 1979).

Romano-British

The Romano-British period sees several changes both in the environment, as well as agricultural practices. Alongside the laying out of new field systems, the range of crops seen is much larger with spelt becoming the predominant crop (Site 15, Chapter 17; *cf.* Greig 1991), with lesser amounts of barley, rye and emmer cultivated (Site 15). In addition some sites also produced evidence for the cultivation of pea, bean, flax and beet (Sites 5, 12, 15, 29, 34).

As also seen within both Kent and Cambridgeshire, there is some suggestion within the Midlands that during the Romano-British period emmer is largely replaced by spelt, although it might be noted that remains of emmer were recovered not only from the Romano-British sites along the M6 Toll, but also from Coulters Garage, Alcester (Colledge 1985–6) and to the south from Deansway, Worcester (Moffet 1995).

It is possible that new varieties of spelt were introduced with similar ecological preferences as emmer. However, unique to this part of the country, rye, which is absent from most of Roman Britain, appears to have been cultivated in the region during this period. It is notable the crop also appears in Romano-British deposits from Whitemoor Haye Quarry (Ciaraldi 2002) and Hanbury Street, Droitwich to the west (Straker AML Report 2812, cited in Greig *et al.* 1987). The evidence from the M6 Toll is more substantial than previously, however, and would seem to confirm its status as a crop rather than a weed (*cf.* Moffett 1996) during this period (Site 15). Unlike the Iron Age sites some ecologically diagnostic weed seeds are present at the M6 Toll sites and also are seen at Whitemoor Haye Quarry (Ciaraldi 2002) indicating the cultivation of drier sandier soils, perhaps associated with rye and barley, and wetter soils, perhaps associated with spelt (Site 15).

For other evidence of agricultural change along with the appearance of field systems and possible agricultural buildings (Site 34), it is interesting to note that while rotary querns are present on several of the sites (Sites 15, 29, 34) there is not a single find of saddle quern dated to this period. Such evidence may hint at larger family groups for which such querns are more suited.

There is some suggestion of increased deforestation during this period (Site 12) and certainly the evidence from King's Pool, Stafford suggests major clearance probably within the late Roman period (Bartley and Morgan 1990). While the basic forest composition remains largely the same, charcoal evidence at a number of sites suggests the management of woodland, in particular the coppicing of oak on both long and short cycles, perhaps in response to declining woodland resources and increased demand for activities such as pottery production (Sites 12, 15, 19, 34). There is also the suggestion of the increased expansion of heathland seen within the evidence for its exploitation for fuel from the appearance of charcoal of heather, gorse and/or broom (Sites 12, 15, 34).

Romano-British cremation burials

The evidence from the cremation burials is unusual in that, unlike many Romano-British examples but in common with many of a Bronze Age date, tubers of false-oat grass are reasonably common (Site 12). The most likely explanation for the presence of such tubers relates to the creation of a fire-break, a necessity when building a pyre in long grassland, and the subsequent use of this material cleared from the broken turf as tinder for the pyre. Such tubers are usually absent from Romano-British deposits, for instance, the East London Cemetery (Davies 2000) implying the use of formalised areas for cremations that were largely kept clear of such vegetation. However, at the more rural cemetery at Ryknield Street, it appears that, between cremations, grassland grew back within the areas of former pyres so that clearance of vegetation was required before the next was constructed.

The high presence of cereal grains and remains of legumes, including lentil, as well as wild foods, such as sloe, bramble and hazelnut, can be associated with ovens and the preparation of funerary feasts (Site 12). McKinley (Site 12) suggests that some of the enclosures may have functioned as funerary gardens, perhaps linked with such banqueting (Toynbee 1971, 94–100). It might be noted that such remains were common at the Eastern Cemetery in London (Davies 2000), as well as from Roman cemetery sites on the continent (Preiss *et al.* 2005; Šoštaric *et al.* 2006). Further it might be noted that the unusual find of lentil occurring at Ryknield Street and many of the other sites can be directly associated with certain funeral rites (Megaloudi 2004). In addition to these feasts it would appear that pine wood was deliberately used in the pyres (Site 12). By this time we may assume that pine was either absent or rare within the region, raising the possibly that it was specifically brought in or that surviving stands were sought out for cremations. In addition the cremations provided the only evidence for animal remains, in particular pigs, their abundance more likely representing their importance within funeral feasts and as ritual deposits within the cremations (Site 15), than their general dietary status.

Saxon and medieval

As in most parts of Britain the medieval period sees important changes in agricultural practices that probably have their roots within the Saxon period (*cf.* Moffett 1994). Alongside the continued cultivation of barley, we see at the M6 Toll sites the appearance of free-threshing wheat and increased evidence for the cultivation of rye, peas and beans (Sites 13, 19, 20; Chapters 15, 24, 25). While some remains of spelt were recovered it is probable these are residual and that certainly by the medieval period it was no longer widely if at all cultivated within this country. The significance of free-threshing wheat is that it is more easily processed than spelt, yielding free-grain rather than grain still enclosed in spikelets (Green 1981).

It would appear that rye became a major crop within the late Saxon and medieval period, and investigations at Shenstone Linear Features clearly demonstrated how differences in its harvesting and processing could be detected in the archaeobotical record (Site 13). That rye rachises are so abundant may suggest that the crop was stored in the ear after the straw had been removed perhaps for use as thatch or within the preparation of malt. In terms of the final processing of the grain, unlike in the Romano-British period, when the evidence suggests grain was ground in the household, by the medieval period it would be taken to the miller. Certainly watermills and even a possible windmill have been recorded from the manor of Sutton and Manley from the 10th–15th centuries (VCH 1947, 230–45). A larger medieval millstone probably associated with a watermill was recovered from Shenstone Linear Features (Site 13 and below), while historical records indicate the presence of at least two watermills associated with Shenstone Manor (Chapter 30).

Ecological evidence from both Shenstone Linear Features (Site 13) and Wishaw Hall Farm (Site 19) suggest the exploitation both of sandier soils, but also of heavier clay soils. It is probable that the use of the mouldboard plough would have facilitated the cultivation of at least the latter soils. In general it is probable that the period sees the expansion of arable fields onto previously unworked land and with it further clearance of forest. Indeed the evidence at King's Pool, Stafford indicates an almost complete clearance of local forest, associated with cereal production (Bartley and Morgan 1990; Leah *et al.*1998). Associated with such clearance we see further evidence for woodland management and the use of heathland species, eg gorse or broom, for fuel, with similar species to those seen in the Roman period occurring comprising oak, hazel, holly, birch and blackthorn (Sites 13, 20).

The metal finds, by Kelly Powell

The Romano-British sites on the M6 Toll produced 1117 metal objects overall, the majority of which came from Ryknield Street (Site 12, Chapter 14) (999 or 89%). The remaining sites produced scattered metal finds totalling no more than 40 each. Notably 1022 of the objects are iron and the majority of these are nails. In general most copper alloy and lead finds were from unstratified contexts and many of these are post-Roman. The objects were recorded individually and classified using accepted typologies; comparative examples were consulted where appropriate.

With the exception of Site 12 the Romano-British sites on the M6 Toll produced a surprisingly small number of metal finds. The potential for preservation of metal objects is illustrated by the large number of nails from Site 12. This may indicate that material culture was not rich in this region during the Romano-British period. The only objects of particular note not found at Site 12 were the two unstratified brooches from East of The Castle, Shenstone (Site 32, Chapter 18) which seem to indicate activity dating to the 1st century AD, and the beaded torc from Wisham Hall Farm (Site 19).

The greater number of metal objects from Site 12 is unsurprising considering the existence of a Romano-British cemetery. However, the apparent lack of pyre/grave goods is somewhat unexpected. Only a single fragment of copper alloy bracelet, a coin and a possible iron bow brooch survived as recognisable pyre/grave goods. Other finds from this site which were not nails mainly represent fittings from wooden objects. One coffin with lead binding is clearly recognisable in the archaeological record. The other fittings considered alongside the small size of nails in general may indicate a tradition of making cremation burials in small boxes, as seen at Skeleton Green (Partridge 1981).

The flint, by Kate Cramp with Hugo Lamdin-Whymark

A total of 1711 struck flints and 39 pieces (72 g) of burnt unworked flint was recovered from 12 sites along the M6 Toll (Table 150). Around 98% of this total was provided by the material from just two sites: Shenstone Linear Features (Site 13, Chapter 15) and Wishaw Hall Farm (Site 19, Chapter 24), which together produced a total of 1681 struck flints. The remaining sites on the route produced very small quantities of flintwork, rarely exceeding ten pieces and usually consisting of single stray finds in later contexts. All of the flint came from sites along the eastern stretch of the route – between West of Crane Brook Cottage (Site 34) and Hawkeswell Farm (Site 24); none was recovered from any of the sites at the western end.

Methodology

The struck flint was recorded using a series of defined categories that break down into three broad groups: debitage, cores and retouched forms. A separate category of burnt unworked flint was used to describe burnt pieces with no struck surfaces or obvious signs of use. This material was quantified by piece and by weight and, where possible, the source of the nodules was identified (eg chalk flint or bullhead flint).

Debitage

Debitage was divided into flakes, blades, bladelets, bladelike flakes, irregular waste and chips. Irregular waste is here defined as shattered pieces, frequently non-bulbar, which are produced during knapping. Particular unretouched flake types, such as core rejuvenation flakes and crested blades, were recorded separately.

Chips were defined as pieces whose broadest surface was less than 10 sq. mm, including small flakes or fragments of flakes (Newcomer and Karlin 1987, 33). In order to avoid any sampling bias, a distinction was made in the database between chips that were excavated by hand and those that were recovered by sieving.

Cores

Cores were recorded on the basis of removal type and the number of platforms present (eg multi-platform flake core or single platform blade core). All complete cores were weighed.

Retouched tools

The terminology for retouched forms follows standard morphological descriptions, for example Bamford (1985, 73–7), Healy (1988, 48–9) and Saville (1981a, 7–11). Microliths were classified according to Jacobi

Table 150 Quantification of struck and burnt unworked flint assemblages by site

Category:	*Site 34*	*Site 9*	*Site 12*	*Site 13*	*Site 14*	*Site 15*	*Site 40*	*Site 19*	*Site 20*	*Site 24*	*Total:*
Flake	1	–	2	43	–	1	–	481	2	–	530
Blade	–	–	1	16	1	4	1	109	1	–	133
Bladelet	–	–	–	3	–	1	–	101	–	–	105
Bladelike flake	–	–	–	4	–	–	–	64	1	1	70
Core face/edge rejuvenation flake	–	–	–	–	–	–	–	14	–	–	14
Rejuvenation flake tablet	–	–	–	–	–	–	–	2	–	–	2
Crested flake/blade	–	–	–	–	–	1	–	11	–	–	12
Unclassifiable waste	–	–	–	6	–	–	–	88	–	–	94
Microburin	–	–	–	2	–	–	–	29	–	–	31
Chip	–	–	–	13	–	–	–	534	–	–	547
Single platform flake core	–	–	–	–	–	–	–	4	–	–	4
Multi-platform flake core	–	–	–	2	–	–	–	15	–	–	17
Core on a flake	–	–	–	2	–	–	–	–	–	–	2
Single platform blade core	–	–	–	1	–	–	–	3	–	–	4
Opposed platform blade core	–	–	–	–	–	1	–	2	–	–	3
Unclass. blade core	–	–	–	1	–	–	–	6	–	–	7
Unclass./frag, core	–	–	–	–	–	–	–	5	–	–	5
Partially-worked nodule	–	–	1	–	–	–	–	8	–	–	9
Retouched flake	–	–	1	2	–	–	–	27	1	–	31
Retouched blade	–	–	1	–	–	–	–	10	–	–	11
End scraper	–	1	–	1	–	–	–	4	1	–	7
Side scraper	–	–	–	–	–	–	–	2	–	–	2
End-and-side scraper	–	–	–	–	–	–	–	10	–	–	10
Scraper on non-flake blank	–	–	–	–	–	–	–	1	–	–	1
Unclass. scraper	–	–	–	–	–	–	–	4	–	–	4
Microlith	–	–	1	–	–	–	–	15	–	–	16
Truncated flake	–	–	–	–	–	–	–	2	–	–	2
Truncated blade	–	–	–	–	–	–	–	4	–	–	4
Backed blade(let)	–	–	–	–	–	–	–	7	–	–	7
Burin	–	–	1	–	–	–	–	–	–	–	1
Piercer	–	–	–	–	–	–	–	6	–	–	6
Spurred piece	–	–	–	–	–	–	–	1	–	–	1
Notch	–	–	–	–	–	–	–	8	–	–	8
Serrated flake	–	–	–	–	–	–	–	2	–	–	2
Fabricator	–	–	–	–	–	–	–	1	–	–	1
Chisel arrowhead	–	–	–	1	–	–	–	–	–	–	1
Unclass. retouch	–	–	–	1	–	3	–	3	–	–	7
Total:	1	1	8	98	1	11	1	1583	6	1	1711
No. (%)burnt struck flints	–	–	–	1 (1.0)	–	1 (9.1)	–	319 (20.2)	1 (16.7)	–	322 (18.8)
No. (%)broken struck flints	–	–	–	22 (22.5)	–	3 (27.3)	1 (100.0)	715 (45.3)	3 (50.0)	–	744 (43.5)
No. (%*) retouched pieces	–	1 (100.0)	4 (50.0)	5 (5.9)	–	3 (27.3)	–	107 (10.2)	2 (33.3)	–	122 (10.5)
No. burnt unworked flints	–	–	1	–	–	–	–	38	–	–	39
Wt (g) burnt unworked flints	–	–	1	–	–	–	–	71	–	–	72

(1978, 16, fig. 6); the length, breadth and width of complete examples were recorded following the metrical methodology outlined below.

Attribute analysis

Further analysis was performed on all small find numbered flints from the scatter on Site 19, excluding chips and burnt unworked flint. Non-small find numbered retouched flints from sieving were also included in the technological assessment, bringing the total number of analysed flints to 811 pieces. Attributes recorded included platform type (after Tixier *et al.* 1980, fig. 47), termination type (Cotterell and Kamminga 1987), hammer mode (eg Onhuma and Bergman 1982) and extent of dorsal cortex. The presence or absence of platform edge abrasion and dorsal blade scars was also recorded.

Metrical analysis

Metrical analysis was performed on all retouched tools from the scatter on Site 19, and involved recording the length, breadth and thickness to the nearest millimetre, using standard methods (Saville 1980). Metrical analysis was not performed on unretouched pieces due to the high proportion of breakage in the assemblage and the obvious bias towards high rates of breakage among blades.

Refitting analysis
Following the recommendations of the assessment, the assemblage from Site 19 was subjected to refitting analysis. The refitting exercise involved laying out all the flintwork from the scatter and grouping the material according to visual similarity in raw material type. With the exception of one conjoining blade, very few refitting pieces were found within the assemblage although there were many instances where it was possible to suggest that the same nodules, or very similar ones, were used on the appearance of the flint alone.

Use-wear analysis
Low power use-wear analysis was performed on a randomly selected sample of 190 small find numbered flints from the scatter on Site 19, drawing on the results of experimental work published by Tringham *et al.* (1974), Cotterell and Kamminga (1979), Odell (1981), Odell and Odell-Vereecken (1980) and Brown (1989). Each assessable flint was scanned using a binocular microscope at 10x magnification to determine the presence or absence of use-wear. A higher magnification (20x) was used to provide more information on the distribution and morphology of the damage scars, from which the density of the contact material (hard, medium or soft) and the action type (cutting/whittling, scraping or boring) could be inferred.

The results of all these analyses were recorded directly on to an MS *Access* database, a print out of which will be made available in the archive.

Overview

To date, no sites or individual artefacts of Early Mesolithic date have been recovered from the region (Saville 1981b), and no demonstrably Early Mesolithic flintwork came from the M6 Toll investigations. However, the Late Mesolithic is well represented and accounts for most the lithic assemblage from the route. The distribution of this material is quite distinct. In general, the scatter of flintwork is sparse, with very little or none at all recovered from most sites. Most of the sites around Shenstone and Wall contained one or more flints, two contained eight and 11 flints (Ryknield Street, Site 12, and East of Birmingham Road Nurseries, Site 15 respectively) and 98 flints were recovered from Site 13. While the numbers are still comparatively low, the scatter indicates a reasonable background late Mesolithic presence, perhaps relating to one or more settlement areas beyond the limits of the project. The excavation of Site 19 revealed an extensive scatter of late Mesolithic flintwork, the remains of a probable campsite, covering an area c. 100 m in length and of unknown width (the scatter extends beyond the limits of the road).

The Neolithic and Bronze Age periods are very poorly represented by the lithic record from the M6 Toll. A single diagnostic artefact, a Middle–Late Neolithic chisel arrowhead (Fig. 100, 3) was recovered from Site 13. With the exception of this piece, only a couple of undiagnostic flakes may belong to a post-Mesolithic industry. Scattered features suggest Neolithic and Bronze Age activity, yet the virtual absence of flint despite the existence of relatively local sources, indicates that flint was not an important element of the material culture in this region during these periods.

The worked stone, by Ruth Shaffrey

A total of 72 pieces of worked stone was retained during the excavations for the M6 Toll; these were all examined with the aid of a x10 magnification hand lens. The assemblage encompasses a broad variety of object types including rotary and saddle querns, whetstones, polishing and fire stones, a gaming counter and building stone including structural blocks, floor and roof stones and an architectural piece. No evidence for domestic activities such as spinning and weaving was found amongst the stone artefacts.

Structural

Large pieces of probable Wenlock Limestone from Walsall (Barrow *et al.* 1919, 11) were used as structural support for the roof of the flue in the pottery kiln at East of Birmingham Road Nurseries (Site 15, Chapter 17) but otherwise all the building stone recovered is Triassic Keuper Sandstone. This underlies much of the area and, being largely free from drift (Barrow *et al.* 1919, 143), would have been easily available. This stone was used extensively at Wall, although no evidence for quarrying the stone was found on site (Thorpe 1956, 28), and a substantial number of tooled blocks of it were recovered, principally from Ryknield Street (Site 12, Chapter 14) and Site 15. None of it was found *in situ* but all provide evidence for substantial stone structures in the vicinity. The easy availability of sandstone suitable for building explains its very singular use and the absence almost entirely of any other stone types (for structural purposes).

Of most interest are the massive slab reused as the kiln roof at Site 15 and the architectural piece from Site 12. Both may have been related to funerary monuments – the latter as a wall corner feature and the former as a possible sarcophagus lid (see individual site descriptions). Other evidence for the structural use of stone is limited although an enclosure ditch at Site 15 produced a single roof stone indicating the use of stone for roofing somewhere nearby the site and a slab of Keuper Sandstone used for paving.

Querns

In total, there are ten identifiable rotary querns, almost all made from Millstone Grit – from Site 15, North of Langley Brook (Site 29, Chapter 21) and West of Crane

Brook Cottage (Site 34, Chapter 12) – with three contexts (from Sites 12 and 15) producing small fragments of lava. The Millstone Grit used for the querns is of varying types but all are pinkish medium to coarse-grained feldspathic quartz cemented sandstones. The M6 Toll sites are within reasonably close proximity to the Derbyshire Millstone Grit and although a specific source has not been identified, it seems likely that all the querns are from this region. It is interesting that the Keuper Sandstone seems not to have been exploited for rotary querns. Presumably it was deemed unsuitable in comparison to the hardwearing Millstone Grit querns which must have been readily available.

An unusually broad range of styles is represented amongst the rotary querns including projecting-hopper (two examples), disc (two examples), flat-topped (one example) and beehive (two examples). The remaining items are too fragmentary for type to be accurately determined. The range in styles is likely to be due to the different chronologies at each site. Site 29, which has evidence for Late Iron Age activity, produced the two beehive querns, both of a type similar to those from Fisherwick of Late Iron Age date (Samuels 1979, 65 and fig. 17). Sites 15 and 34 meanwhile, do not have significant Iron Age components and produced only Romano-British style querns.

Three querns are of particular interest. The first is a medieval millstone fragment from Shenstone Linear Features (Site 13, Chapter 15), which indicates the presence of a watermill on, or near the site. The second quern of interest is a complete quern with the iron spindle still in the socket (ON 299952) from North of Langley Mill (Site 29, Chapter 21). Rotary querns with surviving iron fittings are reasonably common finds over much of the East Midlands (Samuels 1979, 65), but this was deposited as a lone find at the top of a pit (290987) of probable 1st–2nd century AD date. The completeness of the quern and the lack of any other finds from the pit indicate that it was a deliberately placed deposit. It sits alongside a saddle quern from Shenstone Ring Ditch (Site 14, Chapter 16) that also appears to have been part of a structured deposit in the uppermost fill of a pit. The saddle quern is from a Middle Iron Age context and so they do not represent activity in the same period but they do suggest a focus on querns as items of special significance in the area. The deliberate or placed deposition of querns in pits on sites of all periods is becoming increasingly well known (Shaffrey 2003, 165) although no regional surveys of occurrences have yet been carried out.

These two examples will add to a growing number being published and will continue to raise awareness so that more examples may be identified and recorded on site. This saddle quern may well have been selected as being of special significance because of its unusual stone type, which although probably collected from the glacial deposits nearby, would not have been commonly available (see Chapter 16, Site 14).

Other artefacts

The range of other artefacts of worked stone is very small and includes only three whetstones, two of medieval date (Hawkeswell Farm, Site 24, Chapter 27) and one of Romano-British date (Site 29, Chapter 21). None of these is unusual and all are discussed in the relevant site sections. In addition, there is one palette of an imported Quartz Conglomerate (see Wishaw Hall Farm, Site 19, Chapter 24), a polished gaming counter (Site 13, Chapter 15) and three unworked stones used as processors (all from Site 12, Chapter 14).

The earlier prehistoric pottery, by Carol Allen

Quantification and catalogue

The earlier prehistoric pottery originated from four sites along the route of the road. These were Ryknield Street (Site 12, Chapter 14), Shenstone Linear Features (Site 13, Chapter 15), Birmingham Road Nurseries (Site 15, Chapter 17) and East of the Castle, Shenstone (Site 32, Chapter 18). All lie just north of Shenstone and east of Wall.

A total of 186 sherds of pottery were found on these sites weighing 1213 g (including some fragments). The pottery sherds represent approximately eight separate vessels of prehistoric date. Some of the sherds cannot be identified to a date with any certainty and these are designated as prehistoric type. All the sherds are detailed in the attached catalogue (Table 151).

Of these sherds four vessels are represented which have form or decoration and these can be identified to a specific type. These sherds have been illustrated (above).

Methodology

The pottery has been recorded and described according to the guidelines of the PCRG (1997). In addition, this report conforms to the standards and guidance of the IFA (2001). All the sherds were counted and weighed and are detailed in the catalogue. The fabric type and abrasion level of the sherds are also given and the part of the pot remaining, rim or body, is recorded. There were no complete profiles and no base sherds were apparent.

All the sherds were examined by use of a x2 binocular microscope in order to allow the fabric types to be summarised.

Fabrics

Six different fabric types were recognised by examination of all the sherds. The division of the fabric types was made based upon the apparent tempering materials and the appearance, colour and firing of the sherds. This assumes that the potters were aiming to produce pots with a distinctive appearance and tempering.

Table 151 Catalogue of earlier prehistoric pottery

Feature	Context	No. pots	No. sherds	Wt (g)	Fabric	Abrasion level	Date	Pot part	Description
Ryknield Street (Site 12)									
RB grave 122376	122377	1	2	14	QUCV	S	Preh	B	
	122379	–	2	3	QUCV	V	Preh	B	
RB grave 122405	122406	2	2	20	GRMV	U	EBA	B	collar of Collared Urn, herringbone decoration
	122521	–	1	4	GRMV	S	Preh	B	undecorated orange sherd
RB pit 122534	122407	3	10	55	GRMV	S	EBA	R,B	upper collar of Collared Urn & body sherds
	122495	–	1	1	QUMM	S	Preh	B	undecorated
RB grave 122609	122609	–	1	22	QUCV	S	Neo?	B	coarse, thick undecorated body sherd, large angular white inclusions
RB grave 122675	122676	–	1	5	QUCV	S	Preh	B	undecorated
	122723	–	1	4	QUCV	V	Preh	B	coarse
Total Site 12			21	128					
Shenstone Linear Features (Site 13)									
Pit 133089	133659	1	37	214	QUCC	M/A	Neo	B	undecorated, also hazelnuts & grain. Radiocarbon date 3940–3700 cal BC (NZA-25056)
Pit 133090	133091	–	1	10	QUCC	U	Neo?	B	undecorated
	133662	2	29	153	QUCC	U/S	Neo?	B	undecorated, also hazelnuts
	133672	2	11	29	QUCC	U/S	Neo?	B	undecorated, also fire-cracked pebbles
Total Site 13			78	406					
E. of Birmingham Road Nurseries (Site 15)									
subsoil	150031	1	42	412	QTSV	S/M	Neo	R,B	Peterborough Ware Mortlake pot, partial profile, impressed decoration in horizontal rows on ext. & neck, also inside neck, & diag. rows on lower body. Simple rounded rim
E of The Castle, Shenstone (Site 32)									
tree hollow 320065	320066	1	25	150	GTMV	S/M	Neo	R,B	undecorated black burnished ext., horizontal smoothing inside rim & neck, rounded everted rim, poss. carinated bowl of grimstone type. Other sherds & frags
		2	20	117	GTMV	S	Neo	B	undecorated, brown ext.
Total Site 32			45	267					
Total			186	1213					

Fabric: see text. *Abrasion level*: U = unabraded, S = slight (5–25% surface affected), M = moderate (25–50%), A = abraded (50–75%), V = very abraded (>75%)
Pot part: B = body, R = rim

Full details of the six types are provided below, where the coding, quantity and sizes are shown. The six types and the sites where they were found are summarised below on Table 152 by weight.

The fabrics are designated by a four letter code. The first letter indicates the type of inclusion, QU=quartz, GR=grog (crushed fired pottery), QT=quartzite and GT=granitic type. The third letter indicates the quantity of the inclusions, S=sparse (3 to 9%), M=moderate (10–19%) and C=common (20–30%). The modal inclusion size is indicated by the fourth letter, M=medium (0.25–1.00 mm), C=coarse (1.00–3.00 mm) or V=very coarse (>3.00 mm).

Fabric 1, QUCV, contains a common amount of moderately sorted large white angular pieces of quartz, and is orange on the exterior and has a grey interior and brown core. The white quartz is clearly visible on the surface of the sherds.

Fabric 2, GRMV, has a moderate amount of moderately sorted subangular pieces of grog (crushed fired pottery) which is orange in colour. The large pieces are clearly visible on the surface. The colour of the sherds is orange to buff throughout.

Fabric 3, QUMM, has a moderate amount of well sorted subrounded quartz, some of which is white and some is clear. The sherds are orange to brown throughout.

Table 152 Summary of earlier prehistoric fabric types by weight for each site

Fabric	*Code*	*Description*	*Total pottery by weight (g) per site*				
			Site 12	*Site 13*	*Site 15*	*Site 32*	*Total*
1	QUCV	Quartz, v. coarse, angular & white	48	–	–	–	48
2	GRMV	Grog, orange & large	79	–	–	–	79
3	QUMM	Quartz-tempered ware, medium	1	–	–	–	1
4	QUCC	Quartz, coarse & angular	–	406	–	–	406
5	QTSV	Angular quartzite	–	–	412	–	412
6	GTMV	Granitic inclusions	–	–	–	267	267
Total			128	406	412	267	1213

Fabric 4, QUCC, has a common amount of moderately sorted angular mainly white quartz, of coarse to very coarse size, some clear, with very few pieces visible on the surface. The exterior is smoothed and orange to brown, the interior and core are black.

Fabric 5, QTSV, contains a sparse amount of moderately sorted angular quartzite which is angular and mainly white in colour. The exterior is pale brown, the interior is black and the core grey.

Fabric 6, GTMV, has a moderate amount of granitic tempering, with some mica and feldspar apparent, and these inclusions are poorly sorted and angular, suggesting the material was crushed and added. The exterior is black to brown and interior brown to grey and the core is grey.

Each fabric type is unique to a particular site although Site 12 has three separate fabric types. Changes in fabric types used in prehistoric pottery through time are commonly seen even on the same site (Allen 1991, 4–5; Chowne *et al.* 2001). Traditions of pottery manufacture often are seen to change with each period and the tempering materials varied according to the region (Allen and Hopkins 2000, fig. 8; Cleal 1995).

The sites lie on Triassic Sandstones with Boulder Clay nearby and it is likely that the tempering materials in the sherds at each of these sites could have been found fairly locally, so there is no suggestion of pots being traded. The nearby Bunter Pebble Beds contain sandstone, quartz and quartzite pebbles which could be crushed for addition as tempering (Hains and Horton 1969, 66), and granitic material may have been found in the Boulder Clay of the Midlands glacial deposits (*ibid.*, 89–90). Petrological analysis and further study would be required to clarify the type of granitic material and its origin (Knight *et al.* 2003).

Later prehistoric pottery fabrics, by Paul Booth

Later prehistoric pottery was recorded using elements of the Oxford Archaeology recording system for later prehistoric and Roman pottery, which is in line with the recommendations of the Prehistoric Ceramics Research Group (PCRG 1997). Characteristics of fabric and manufacture, and form and decoration where present, were recorded using standard codes. Quantification was by sherd count and weight, and also by vessel count (based on rims) and rim percentages (REs) for vessel types.

Fabrics were coded with regard to inclusion types (defined by alpha codes), listed in descending order of importance, followed by a numeric indicator of coarseness on a scale of 1 (very fine) to 5 (very coarse). Most of the M6 Toll prehistoric fabrics were at 3 or 4 on this scale, ie with typical inclusion sizes in the range 0.4–1 mm and 1–2 mm respectively. Inclusion types identified were:

A	quartz sand
G	grog
I	oxide minerals, mainly Iron oxides
M	mica
N	none visible
P	clay pellets
Q	large angular Quartz(ite)
R	rock – various (includes igneous etc)
V	vegetable/organic
Z	indeterminate voids

None of the material examined was subject to detailed fabric analysis as the quantities of material recovered (and in some cases their poor contextual associations) were such that the value of such work appeared to be limited at this stage.

Romano-British pottery fabrics, by Ruth Leary

Fabric descriptions

The fabric of the pottery was first examined by eye and sorted into fabric groups on the basis of colour, hardness, feel, fracture, inclusions and manufacturing technique. A sample of the sherds was further examined under a x30 binocular microscope to verify these divisions. The size of the sample was as large as was felt necessary for each fabric group. Equivalents to fabric codes in the Warwickshire County Museum Series are given where relevant.

Colour: narrative description only

Hardness: after Peacock (1977)
soft - can be scratched by finger nail
hard - can be scratched with penknife blade
very hard - cannot be scratched

Feel: tactile qualities
smooth - no irregularities
rough - irregularities can be felt
sandy - grains can be felt across the surface
leathery - smoothed surface like polished leather
soapy - smooth feel like soap

Fracture: visual texture of fresh break, after Orton (1980).
smooth - flat or slightly curved with no visible irregularities
irregular - medium, fairly widely spaced irregularities
finely irregular - small, fairly closely spaced irregularities
laminar - stepped effect
hackly - large and generally angular irregularities

Inclusions:
type: after Peacock (1977)
frequency: indicated on a 4-point scale: abundant, moderate, sparse & rare where abundant is break packed with inclusion & rare is break with only 1–2 examples of an inclusion.
sorting: after Orton (1980)
shape:angular - convex shape, sharp corners
subangular - convex shape, rounded corners
rounded - convex shape no corners
platey - flat
size:
sub-visible - only just visible at x30 and too small to measure
fine - 0.1-0.25 mm
medium - 0.25-0.5
coarse - 0.5-1 mm
very coarse - over 1 mm

The fabrics

A: amphorae

A10 Probably Dressel 20

A11 Dressel 20, Peacock and Williams 1986, class 25. Globular-shaped amphora used to carry olive oil from the Roman province of Baetica in southern Spain in use from the mid-1st century until just after the mid-3rd century AD. Known from over 100 kilns operating in the region of the River Guadalquivir (Rodriguez Almeida 1989). Warwickshire fabric series A21.

B: Black-burnished ware

BB1 as Tomber and Dore 1998, South-East Dorset BB1 (DOR BB1).

R18 medium grey, hard, sandy with hackly fracture. Abundant, well-sorted, medium sub-rounded quartz and sparse medium rounded white inclusions. Similar to Warwickshire R12 except for white inclusions. Very likely to be burnt BB1 on the basis of some of the forms recovered.

C: calcareous fabrics

CT these are brown vesicular wares and are best considered as belonging to group CTA2. This is borne out by the jar forms and by their generally late associations.

CTA1 orange-brown with grey core. Soft with soapy feel and laminar fracture. Abundant, ill-sorted, fine to coarse, long thin vesicles, occasionally shell surviving. Rare, coarse rounded black pebbles. Warwickshire C41

CTA2 brown-grey with grey core. Hard, fairly smooth feel and laminar fracture. Abundant, ill-sorted, platey vesicles. These compare well with pottery from the Harrold kilns, Bedfordshire. Warwickshire C11.

CTOX as CTA2 but oxidised surfaces. A small number of bodysherds were identified from Wishaw Hall Farm (Site 19). These are likely to be oxidised wares from the kilns at Harrold or nearby kilns producing similar vessels.

CTB1 brown, fairly hard and smooth with laminar fracture. Moderate, ill-sorted fine to medium platey vesicles. Less vesicular than CTA1 and 2. Only five rilled sherds of this fabric were recovered from Site 19 context 190578, pit 190015. These were associated with late material including a CTA2 jar. It is very likely that this is a variant of CTA2

E: Late Iron Age-Early Roman 'Belgic type' wares

E1 Hard dark grey with brown margins. Slightly sandy where unburnished. Irregular fracture. Sparse/moderate, well-sorted, medium, sub-rounded quartz, rare, rounded, coarse dark inclusions, iron oxides, and sparse fine gold mica. The fracture has elongated voids which seem to be caused by poor clay preparation rather than dissolved or burnt out material.

F: fine wares

This category includes fine fabrics with surface treatments such as glazing, mica-dusting and colour coats.

CC1 local? Orange with black colour coat. Soft with powdery feel. Rare, fine, rounded quartz and black inclusions. The single form is from a beaker with appears to have a long neck and everted rim tip so an Argonne source is unlikely. This is likely to be the product of a small, perhaps local, kiln making colour-coated ware.

CC2 Argonne or locally produced roughcast ware. Orange with brown coat. Hard, smooth fabric with fairly smooth fracture. Sparse, ill-sorted fine quartz and ill-sorted, medium to fine red-brown inclusions. These may be imported (Tomber and Dore 1998, ARG CC) or a finer local roughcast ware

NV Nene Valley colour-coated ware. Tomber and Dore 1998, LNV CC NV1 Nene Valley colour coated ware, white with dark grey/brown colour coat. NV2 Nene Valley colour coated ware, orange/brown with dark grey/brown or red/orange colour. Warwickshire F52

KOL? Cologne? Fine white colour coated ware with dark colour coat. Tomber and Dore 1998, KOL CC. Identified as likely to be from Cologne. Warwickshire F37.

MG1 mica-dusted ware. Medium orange throughout. Hard with smooth feel and fracture. Rare, fine, sub-rounded quartz and rounded black inclusions. Mica is rare in the break but abundant on the surfaces. This may be a worn mica-dusted ware or a mica-rich slip. The form, an indented beaker, is a common form in this fabric group throughout Roman Britain. This is likely to be made by a military potter, perhaps at Wall or another nearby military pottery.

MHAD Hadham red ware. Tomber and Dore 1998, HAD OX.

ROX Oxfordshire red colour-coated ware. Tomber and Dore 1998, OX CC. Warwickshire F51.

G: coarse gritted fabrics

G2 early pink grogged ware. Hard pinkish buff with grey core. Bumpy feel and irregular fracture. Sparse medium quartz and sparse to moderate coarse grey, brown and white inclusions – grog? Early pink grog type fabric, or possibly pink grogged ware. Warwickshire G12.

G3 pink grogged ware variant? Light grey but otherwise like PNK GT. Fairly smooth apart from protruding inclusions. Hard with smooth matrix and coarse inclusions protruding. Sparse-moderate, very coarse, ill-sorted sub-angular, grey-buff inclusions, grog or argillaceous cognates, rare fine mica, some ferrous staining/inclusions, rare, medium, sub-rounded quartz. Warwickshire G11?

G4 reduced brown dark grey fabric. Hard with smooth leathery feel. Possibly hand made. Sparse-moderate well sorted, sub-rounded medium quartz, sparse, ill-sorted, coarse to medium ferrous brown inclusions and buff-grey angular inclusions, sparse coarse charcoal. Warwickshire group G.

G5 buff, hard sandy fabric with harsh feel. Irregular fracture. Moderate, fairly well-sorted, medium, sub-rounded quartz and abundant ill-sorted medium to very coarse rounded, argillaceous inclusions – orange brown and buff, up to 4–5 mm across. Most similar to PNK GT but with more quartz. Warwickshire G12?

PNK GT Pink grogged ware. Tomber and Dore 1998, PNK GT. Booth and Green 1989. Warwickshire G11.

MALV Malvernian ware. Tomber and Dore 1998, MAL RE A. Peacock 1967. Warwickshire G44.

M: mortaria

MH Mancetter-Hartshill. Fine-textured, cream fabric, varying from softish to very hard, sometimes with pink core; self-coloured or with a self-coloured slip. Inclusions usually moderate, smallish, transparent and translucent white and pinkish quartz with sparse opaque orange-brown and rarely blackish fragments; rarely white clay pellets (or re-fired pottery). The range in fabric is, in fact, quite wide, from that with virtually no inclusions to fabrics with a fair quantity and fabrics with hard, ill-sorted black inclusions. The trituration grit after AD 130–140 (MH2) consisted of hard red-brown and/or hard blackish material (probably refired pottery fragments), with only very rare quartz fragments. Earlier mortaria (MH1) usually have mixed trituration grit in which quartz and sandstone are normal components and some early 2nd century mortaria probably have entirely quartz trituration grit.

Mancetter-Hartshill mortaria of AD 130/140 onwards are usually easy to recognise, but Mancetter-Hartshill fabrics of AD 100–130 are more variable. During this period it can be difficult distinguishing Mancetter-Hartshill, Little Chester and Wroxeter fabrics. A further difficulty is that a few potters were active at both Mancetter-Hartshill and Little Chester. One vessel from Ryknield Street (Site 12) had a pinkish-cream fabric with substantial grey core, soft with powdery feel and fracture. The inclusions were abundant fine well-sorted quartz with rare coarse grey inclusions and sparse medium-fine, rounded brown inclusions. The trituration grits were quartz 1–4 mm, mostly 1–2 mm. As the vessel was burnt it was harder to identify its fabric. This is likely to be a Mancetter-Hartshill fabric dating before AD 130/40 but it could be local and also has some similarities to vessels from Little Chester, Derby. Warwickshire M22.

M1 Local ware. Cream/yellowish-cream, hard, smooth with irregular fracture. Moderate, sub-angular medium quartz, rare, ill-sorted coarse to medium rounded black and red/brown inclusions. Trituration grits, black argillaceous grits, 1–2 mm.

This fabric occurred on Site 12, Shenstone Linear Features (Site 13), Site 19, North of Langley Brook (Site 29) and East of Crane Brook Cottage (Site 34). Many of the examples appeared to be burnt or misfired so that the slip had fired to a light grey hue. As examples from Sites 12, 13 and 19 were distorted, it is likely that this fabric was being produced locally. The distorted vessels were unabraded, whereas those which were not distorted, from Sites 19 and 34, had suffered abrasion. The example from Site 19 seemed to be burnt from use rather than having the misfired nature of the distorted sherds with their greyish slips.

M2 Local ware. Brown/orange colour with grey core. Extremely hard, pimply feel like a fine Derbyshire ware fabric. Abundant, ill-sorted sub-angular medium quartz and ill-sorted coarse-medium, rounded brown/black inclusions (iron oxides?). Trituration grits, black argillaceous grits 2–3 mm.

This fabric is extremely hard and a base from East of Birmingham Road Nurseries (Site 15) appears to have been misfired to a greyish colour on the inside which is quite unworn. Although the mortaria are not distorted, the degree of overfiring suggests they may be wasters from a local kiln.

MWS1 Uncertain source, perhaps Wroxeter. Orange with white slip. Soft with sandy feel and irregular fracture. Moderate, well-sorted, medium-fine, sub-rounded quartz, sparse, fine mica and rounded, grey inclusions. Sparse trituration grits surviving, 2–4 mm quartz and sparse red/brown and grey grits.

ROX/WSOX Oxfordshire mortarium. Red colour-coated or white slip oxidised. Tomber and Dore 1998, OXF RS and OXF WS. Warwickshire M71 and M43.

O: oxidised wares

DBY Derbyshire ware. As Tomber and Dore 1998, DER CO. This ware is commonly oxidised both on the M6 Toll sites and in Derbyshire. The sherds present were compared with samples from Holbrook and Lumb Brook and were not significantly different at x30 magnification. However, several distorted vessels were present and a local source cannot be ruled out, particularly since a DBY sherd was recovered from the Site 15 kiln (not a waster). The distorted sherd comprised a base with a cracked base and surface flaking and a warped bodysherd, both from Site 15. Warwickshire R23.

O1 orange, fine, soft and powdery ware with smooth fracture. Moderate, well-sorted, very fine quartz and rare, fine rounded black inclusions. Warwickshire O11.

O2 orange, soft, powdery feel with fairly smooth fracture. Moderate, very fine quartz with less common medium, sub-rounded quartz and rounded black/brown inclusions. Warwickshire O11.

O3 orange, soft with sandy feel and irregular fracture. Moderate, well-sorted, medium quartz and coarse, rounded brown, argillaceous inclusions. Similar to SV4 but with no charcoal. Warwickshire group O.

O4 dark orange-red. Hard, sandy feel and irregular fracture. Moderate, well-sorted, medium quartz with sparse, coarse-very coarse, rounded brown, red and buff inclusions, probably clay pellets/siltstones. Warwickshire group O.

O5 orange sometimes with grey core. Hard and smooth with irregular fracture. Moderate, ill-sorted, medium-coarse, sub-rounded quartz, sparse fine mica and medium-coarse red/brown inclusions. Warwickshire O12.

O6 pale orange, soft with powdery feel. Finely irregular fracture. Abundant, well-sorted, fine, sub-rounded quartz, sparse, fine mica, and ill-sorted, medium-coarse red/brown inclusions. Warwickshire O11.

O7 medium-pale orange with paler core. Hard and smooth with finely irregular fracture. Moderate, medium sub-rounded quartz, sparse medium-fine rounded red/brown inclusions and vesicles. Similar to Warwickshire O12.

O8 orange hard, very rough with irregular fracture. Moderate. Well-sorted, coarse. Sub-rounded quartz, Rare, ill-sorted, fine-medium red/brown inclusions. Warwickshire O51.

O9 orange, hard, rough feel and hackly fracture. Moderate, well-sorted, medium, sub-rounded quartz and abundant, ill-sorted, rounded and rather angular grey and buff inclusions, argillaceous. Warwickshire G12.

O10 orange, hard and sandy feel. Irregular fracture. Moderate, medium, sub-rounded quartz, sparse. ill-sorted black, inclusions, burnt organics. Some voids are present. Warwickshire O32?

SV1 orange often with buff core, soft, powdery with smooth fracture. Sparse, very fine quartz. Closely comparable to Severn Valley ware. Warwickshire O23.

SV2 as SV1 but with sparse to moderate voids. Warwickshire O21.

SV3 as SV1 but with sparse to moderate fine to medium charcoal inclusions. Warwickshire O21.

SV4 orange with darker core. Hard, rough and irregular fracture. Moderate, medium, sub-rounded quartz and coarse-medium, rounded brown inclusions, sparse voids, some with black remains, probably charcoal. Warwickshire O32.

SV5 orange with buff core. Hard, smooth with fairly smooth fracture. ?sub-visible quartz. Common, medium voids, some retaining burnt organics, and white inclusions. Warwickshire O27.

SV6 orange with grey core. Hard with rough feel and irregular fracture. Fine with abundant, ill-sorted, medium to coarse elongated burnt organics and voids, rare medium quartz and white inclusions. Warwickshire O32.

P: prehistoric fabrics

P1 brown, patchily oxidised. Hard with slightly rough feel where not smoothed. Irregular fracture. Sparse-moderate, ill-sorted, medium, angular quartz, sparse, ill-sorted, coarse igneous inclusions with large mica flakes in them – granite, sparse, ill-sorted, coarse medium, rounded red/brown inclusions, iron oxides.

P2 grey-brown with grey core. Soft, smooth with irregular fracture. Sparse, fine quartz., rare, fine mica and possibly long thin voids where organic matter has been used as temper.

P3 black-dark grey. Hard, smooth with fairly smooth fracture. Rare ill-sorted medium quartz, mica and brown inclusions. ?Igneous inclusions – granite. Variant of P2, not like any of the P Warwickshire samples.

R: reduced coarse wares

R1 Shenstone kiln R1. Light grey, soft with irregular fracture and fine sandy feel. Sparse, well-sorted, medium, sub-angular quartz, moderate, well-sorted very fine/sub-visible quartz, rare coarse–very coarse grey rounded inclusions, probably igneous, sparse, well-sorted fine mica, some rare, coarse rounded argillaceous inclusions, cognates.

This fabric is characterised by being finer than R2, lacking the quantity of quartz and having rare very coarse inclusions. It tends also to be lighter in colour, in the region of 10YR6/1.

R2 Shenstone kiln R2. Medium brownish-grey or grey sometimes with darker grey surface. Hard, sandy feel with irregular fracture. Sparse, ill-sorted, coarse, subrounded opaque quartz, moderate, well-sorted, medium-sized, sub-rounded, opaque quartz, sparse, ill-sorted rounded, soft, dark grey inclusions, sparse, ill-sorted, fine mica, rare, coarse, rounded ferrous inclusions, rare, sparse grey, ?igneous inclusions, sparse, coarse black inclusions.

This fabric is characterised by moderate to common quartz inclusions at two fractions, the coarse ones being rare, the medium being common. The feel is generally harsher than R1 and the colour mostly browner in the region of 10YR 5/1–4/1. There is evidence that surfaces may have been a darker colour, 10YR 4/1, when fired successfully but most of the kiln examples were similar in colour throughout. Those outside the kiln were generally a good grey with darker surface so it is suggested this was the intended colour.

R3 Shenstone kiln R3. Light grey with darker surfaces. Soft and sandy to powdery with irregular fracture. Sparse, ill-sorted, medium to coarse sub-angular to sub-rounded, soft grey inclusions, clay cognates or grog, moderate, well-sorted medium, sub-rounded quartz and sparse fine mica.

This fabric is characterised by the sub-rounded grey inclusions visible on the abraded surface and has finer quartz than R2 but more numerous than R1. It grades into R2. The colour is a light grey, less brown than R2 in the region of 2.5Y6/1 with darker surface 2.5YR 5/1. Like Warwickshire R22, tentatively identified as Wappenbury at Tiddington.

R4 Shenstone kiln R4. Dark grey with brown margins and brown or buff core. Hard, smooth or slightly sandy with irregular fracture, sometimes slightly laminar. Moderate, ill-sorted, coarse to medium sub-rounded quartz, sparse, fine mica and rare, ill-sorted, rounded argillaceous inclusions. Some elongated fine–coarse voids but there are no organics visible and these may be due to poor clay preparation rather than burnt out organics. This fabric is similar to Warwickshire O14 but differs in having no organics and being rather coarser. Warwickshire R42 is also similar but finer. This fabric is characterised by the darker grey surfaces in the region of 2.5Y 4/1 and the reddish–brown core 5YR 4/3.

Of the fabrics found in the kiln, R2 and R4 were similar to samples from Tiddington kiln 2, Warwickshire R21, but the Tiddington fabrics had more quartz and tended to be coarser and harder.

R5 pale grey as R3. Soft and powdery feel with finely irregular fracture. Sparse, well-sorted, medium, sub-rounded quartz, sparse, ill-sorted, soft rounded grey inclusions (clay pellets), sparse, ill-sorted, long thin voids fine to coarse. Possibly a sub-group of R3 or a finer version of R2. Slightly coarser than R16. Three distorted vessels in this fabric suggest local production. Warwickshire R01.

R6 dark grey surfaces, 2.5Y 5/1 with light grey core 2.5Y 7/1–7/2. Soft, powdery with irregular fracture. Sparse, medium, sub-rounded quartz, rare fine–coarse brown ferrous inclusions, rare, medium, rounded grey argillaceous inclusions, rare irregular voids. A fine fabric unlike Shenstone kiln products. Warwickshire R01.

R7 light grey (2.5Y 7/1 to 7/2) with orange/brown core (7.5Y 5/3 to 4/3). Soft, powdery feel with slightly irregular fracture. Sparse, medium, sub-rounded quartz. Characterised by colour and fine fabric. Warwickshire R01 with brown core. Similar to Sherifoot Lane.

R8 medium grey in region of 7.5YR 6/1–5/1. Very hard with quite smooth feel. Hackly fracture. Abundant ill-sorted medium–coarse rounded quartz. Characterised by hard fabric and abundant rather coarse quartz. Very commonly distorted, warped and overfired on Site 15 suggesting this is a local fabric. *Cf.* Warwickshire R21/22 from Tiddington and Wappenbury kilns respectively.

R9 grey with buff/brown core, in region of 10YR 6/2–5/2, core 10YR 5/3 probably darker surfaces. Very hard, sandy with irregular fracture. Abundant, well-sorted, medium sub-rounded quartz. Sparse grey and brown inclusions – ?clay pellets and ferrous inclusions. Unidentified source. Warwickshire group R.

R10 grey often with brown core. Fairly soft with sandy feel and irregular slightly laminar fracture. Sparse to moderate, well-sorted, medium sub-rounded quartz, moderate, ill-sorted, coarse–medium orange rounded argillaceous inclusions, ill-sorted coarse rounded ferrous inclusions/ cognates. Possibly variant of R4 or R2, misfired? Characterised by hard fabric and abundant medium quartz. Rare, *cf.* Warwickshire R44.

R11 hard smooth grey with brownish–grey core. Fairly smooth fracture with sparse, medium, sub-rounded quartz, rare, ill-sorted, elongated black inclusions, burnt organics. No wasters, possibly Mancetter-Hartshill or Sherifoot Lane. Similar to Warwickshire R18, R44 and O14.

R12 grey with brown core or margins. Hard and harsh feel. Irregular fracture. Abundant, sub-angular quartz. ?Mancetter-Hartshill. Warwickshire R15?

R13 light grey with brown margins. Hard, smooth feel and irregular fracture. Moderate well-sorted, medium, sub-rounded quartz. Similar to R4 and R2 except for colour but paler grey and brown margins. One possibly distorted sherd. Warwickshire R42?

R14 grey-black, rarely red-brown. Core can be darker or lighter, very rarely oxidised. Soft to very hard, usually smooth, rarely slightly rough. Sparse rounded soft grey, argillaceous lumps. Sparse sub-rounded soft off-white inclusions, and sparse black ?iron ore specks. Warwickshire R11.

R15 light grey with brown core and dark grey surfaces. Hard with smooth feel and fracture. Sparse, medium, sorted, sub-rounded quartz, rare fine rounded white inclusions and sparse elongated voids and burnt organics, rare, coarse rounded red/brown inclusions. *Cf.* Warwickshire fabric R41 but sample of R41 lacks organics. Also similar to Warwickshire R18, ?Mancetter-Hartshill or Sherifoot Lane.

R16 medium grey. Probably most had darker grey surfaces originally. Soft and powdery with smooth fracture. Sparse well-sorted very fine quartz, sparse fine mica, rare, coarse, rounded grey inclusions, argillaceous, rare coarse, rounded irregular, rounded white inclusions, sometimes partially eroded, all voids therefore calcareous. *Cf.* R6. Two distorted vessels. Probably made in the Wall area. Warwickshire R01.

R17 pale grey. Hard, smooth with smooth fracture. Moderate, fine burnt organics and/or voids. Sparse coarse rounded white inclusions and sparse medium, sub-rounded quartz. *Cf.* R16. Waster suggests local product. Warwickshire R01.

R18 see under BB1.

R19 grey, sometimes with brown/grey core. Soft with smooth powdery feel and smooth fracture. Sparse, medium, sub-rounded quartz, moderate/sparse, fine vesicles and sparse ill-sorted, coarse-medium rounded grey/red/brown inclusions. Similar to R16 but finer with no white inclusions. Like Warwickshire R01.

R20 grey very hard fabric with conchoidal fracture. Micaceous, sparse, medium, rounded brown and grey inclusions, rare quartz. Similar to R19. Mancetter-

Hartshill? *Cf.* Warwickshire Mancetter-Hartshill grey ware R11.

R21 grey with brown/grey core. Hard, sandy with hackly fracture. Moderate/sparse, well-sorted, medium, rounded quartz, moderate, ill-sorted, fine to medium, rounded and long thin black inclusions, burnt organics and coarse rounded red/brown and grey inclusions, argillaceous? *Cf.* Warwickshire O14.

R22 light grey with darker grey core. Soft with sandy or smooth feel depending on condition. Smooth fracture. Sparse, well-sorted medium, sub-rounded quartz, abundant ?sub-visible quartz. Micaceous. Occasional voids. Like R16 but with sub-visible grains. Warwickshire R11 Mancetter-Hartshill grey ware.

R23 medium-pale grey. Sandy rather granular feel with hackly fracture. Abundant, well-sorted, medium, sub-angular quartz. Very similar to R18 but rather finer quartz. *Cf.* Warwickshire R15, ?Mancetter-Hartshill.

R24 pale grey with pale core. Hard, smooth with smooth fracture. Very like sample from Mancetter. Sparse fine quartz and fine white speckles, rare medium sub-rounded quartz and sparse fine and medium voids. Warwickshire R11.

R25 grey with darker grey surfaces. Soft smooth with irregular fracture. Sparse, medium sub-angular quartz, rare, medium, rounded white inclusions. Sparse/moderate, ill-sorted, elongated voids and black inclusions and streaks in clay. Possibly sub-visible quartz also. Similar to R7 but slightly coarser and with black and white inclusions. Warwickshire R21?, Tiddington kiln 2.

R26 grey white with dark grey surfaces. Probably Nene Valley grey ware.

R27 orange with traces of grey surface, grey core. Hard and rough. Irregular fracture. Sparse-moderate, well-sorted, medium sub-rounded quartz, rare medium, rounded reddish-brown inclusions. Warwickshire group R.

R28 light grey with darker grey margins and brown core. Sandy feel and finely irregular fracture. Sparse/moderate, well-sorted medium, sub-rounded quartz, sub-visible fine quartz, rare, coarse, rounded off white inclusions and brown inclusions. *Cf.* Warwickshire O14.

Q: white slipped wares

FLB1 pale orange with white wash. Soft, smooth with smooth fracture. Sparse, medium sub-rounded quartz and fine burnt organics. Warwickshire group Q.

FLB2 as O6 with white slip but brighter orange. Warwickshire group Q.

No sources were identified for this small group.

W: white wares

FLA1 cream, sometimes dirty cream with pinkish interior. Hard with smooth surfaces and finely irregular fracture. Sparse, well-sorted, fine, sub-rounded quartz and sparse, ill-sorted, rounded, fine–medium red inclusions. Warwickshire W12, Mancetter-Hartshill.

FLA2 cream, sometimes dirty cream with pinkish interior. Hard with smooth surfaces and irregular fracture. Abundant, well-sorted, medium, sub-rounded quartz and rare, ill-sorted, rounded, fine–medium orange and black inclusions. Warwickshire W12.

FLA3 cream. Soft, very smooth fabric with smooth, almost conchoidal fracture. Rare, medium, sub-rounded quartz and rare, ill-sorted, fine–medium, rounded, red/brown inclusions. Warwickshire W21, probably Mancetter-Hartshill.

FLA4 *Verulamium* region white ware. Tomber and Dore 1998, VER WH. Warwickshire M21.

FLA5 hard, rough cream fabric. In Site 12 grave 122780 this fabric has a grey slip – possibly burnt self slip? Irregular fracture. Sparse, medium sub-rounded clear and pink quartz, rare, fine rounded orange inclusions. Warwickshire group W.

The samian ware, by J. M. Mills

The majority of the samian ware is in poor, eroded, condition due to the acidity of the soil. The aggressive burial conditions have resulted in a change of appearance of the pottery making the production centre (fabric) difficult to identify. In addition the sherds are very abraded with little or no surface surviving; this not only adds to the difficulty in identifying form and fabric, but also denudes the moulded decoration which, in all but one case, makes it impossible to identify particular potters. Only two vessels are stamped, one stamp is too incomplete to read, the other is made uncertain by surface etching.

All the samian was examined macroscopically and with a hand lens in an attempt to identify form and

Table 153 Samian: summary of forms identified

Form	Site 5	34	12	13	15	19
SG 18	–	–	4	–	–	–
SG 27	–	–	1	–	–	–
SG 36	–	–	1	–	–	–
SG 18 or 18R	–	1	–	–	–	–
SG 15/17 or 18	–	1	–	–	–	–
SG dish/bowl	–	1	–	–	–	–
Les M 18/31	–	–	–	3	–	–
Les M dish/bowl	–	–	–	1	–	–
CG 37	–	–	5	–	2	–
CG bowl	1	–	1	3	4	3
CG 27	–	–	1	–	–	–
CG 18/31	–	–	–	–	1	–
CG 18/31 series	1	1	1	5	5	–
CG 31R	–	1	–	1	4	1
CG 31	–	–	–	4	2	–
CG dish/bowl	–	–	–	3	–	–
CG 38	–	–	–	–	2	–
CG 36	–	–	–	–	1	–
CG Curle 23	–	–	–	–	1	–
CG 33	–	1	–	–	–	1
CG?	–	–	–	1	4	4
?EG 36	–	–	–	–	1	–
?EG 33	–	–	–	–	1	–
CG or EG 37	–	–	–	–	1	–
?EG ?cup	–	1	–	–	–	–
?EG 31 OR 31R	–	–	–	1	–	–

fabric and thus assign a date. The condition of the material coupled with the small sherd size in many instances has resulted in a very low level of positive identification and hence very broad date ranges being assigned.

The overall impression is of a low level of samian ware consumption. The range of forms is very limited, each group being dominated by bowls and dishes often of the Dragendorf form 18–18/31–31 series (Table 153). Very few cup forms are present. There are few decorated bowls (form 37) perhaps suggesting a rural settlement of limited sophistication. Both Ryknield Street (Site 12, Chapter 14) and West of Crane Brook Cottage (Site 34, Chapter 12) have significant quantities of vessels from south Gaul (probably La Graufesenque) of Flavian and Flavian–Trajanic date. On all sites samian use continued to the end of the 2nd century AD (mostly indicated by the presence of bowls of form 31R) and it seems most likely that most vessels date from the mid–late Antonine period (or more simply to the second half of the 2nd century AD). The latest vessels are those of possible eastern Gaulish manufacture – identified on the basis of strong orange coloured fabrics; these date to the end of the 2nd century, perhaps extending into the 3rd century.

Romano-British pottery, industry and trade, by Ruth Leary

An archive catalogue was compiled for all the pottery according to the standard laid down by the Study Group for Romano-British Pottery (Darling 2004). Pottery was recorded detailing specific fabrics and forms, decorative treatment, condition, cross-joins/same vessel and was quantified by sherd count, weight and rim percentage values, giving estimated vessel equivalents (EVES). All the pottery from the site was catalogued in the archive and the stratified pottery was examined in order to date the features. Key groups are illustrated and catalogued below and unillustrated material is summarised. The fabric series was cross-referenced with the Warwickshire fabric series and National Fabric Reference Collection codes (Tomber and Dore 1998) are included where appropriate.

Quantification is predominantly by sherd count for wares and fabrics and estimated vessel equivalents for vessel forms because these are the most commonly used values in published reports of site assemblages in the region. Full details of fabrics by sherd weight are given for all the M6 Toll sites in Table 158.

Pottery production

The excavations discovered a kiln at East of Birmingham Road Nurseries (Site 15, Chapter 17) and study of the pottery from the other sites has suggested further evidence for pottery manufacture. Warwickshire is renowned for the large kiln complex at Mancetter-Hartshill, covering over 3 km, developing in the early 2nd century and becoming a major supplier of mortaria, and probably flagons, to the northern military market and the Midlands. In addition to this large-scale production, Booth (1986; 1991) has discussed several other small potteries in the region of local importance. These include two kilns of the 1st and early 2nd centuries respectively at Tiddington (Booth 1986; 1996a), four kilns at Wappenbury (Stanley and Stanley 1960–1), comprising one of the 2nd century and three of the 3rd–4th centuries, 2nd–3rd century kilns at Ryton-on-Dunsmore (Bateman 1976–7) and Bubbenhall (Jones and Palmer 1994), a 2nd century kiln at Perry Barr (Hughes 1959) and 2nd century kilns at Lapworth and Sherifoot Lane, Sutton Coldfield (both unpublished, but see Booth 1996b, 50, fig. 14).

At military sites, locally produced ceramics have been suggested at Metchley in the mid-1st–early 2nd centuries (Green 2002, 105), including mortaria and flagons. The pottery from the Lunt included distorted vessels (Webster 1973, fig. 18, nos 211–2) which may indicate local kilns and certainly, as Booth has pointed out (1986, 24), the early pottery from both Mancetter and the Lunt bears little relationship to preceding 'native' potting traditions and implies the arrival of potters with the army. At Wall, everted-rim jar wasters in a fine grey ware were found amongst the pottery excavated by Greenfield (Leary 1995–6, 36, nos 18, 19 and as 25) and these, together with distorted waster material from Ryknield Street (Site 12, Chapter 14) suggest that late 1st–early 2nd century kilns existed at Wall to serve the fort. This local industry may have continued in the Hadrianic–Antonine period but some coarse ware has been identified as identical to that from Mancetter-Hartshill (Gould 1963–4, 33), implying that coarse ware products from there were obtained by the inhabitants of nearby forts and associated settlements. At Metchley local wares were supplemented by regionally traded Severn Valley wares which dominated the assemblage by phase 3 (AD 60–75, Hancocks 2004, 65–6). At the Lunt Webster identified a 3rd or 4th century product of the Wappenbury kilns amongst his 'post-1st century wares' (1975b, 33).

To these may be added probable kilns serving the major settlement at Alcester (Ferguson 2001, 49). At *Tripontium* at least two possible wasters have been published (Cameron and Lucas 1969, 156, no. 164, 163 no. 239), associated with 3rd and late 4th century pottery which may relate to kilns serving that settlement.

The Shenstone kiln and pottery production around Wall

Evidence for pottery production at Shenstone indicated manufacture of a range of bowls, dishes and jars in rather coarse grey wares, one of which was similar to a fabric from Tiddington kiln 2. The forms comprised plain-rim dishes and bead and flange bowls, everted-rim medium-necked jars, wide-mouthed jars with everted, bifid and bead rims and everted-rim narrow-necked jars.

These were most commonly made in fabrics R2 and R4 but the evidence of waster sherds from the kiln indicated that a finer grey ware fabric, R1, was also used to make plain-rim dishes and medium-necked jars. The presence of wasters and overfired sherds in fabric R8 suggests that this was also made at the kiln and fabric R10 may be a variant of R2 or R4. The vessels from the kiln together with the additional wasters in kiln fabrics from Site 15 suggest that the kiln or kilns producing the vessels were active in the late 2nd–early or mid-3rd century. This extends rather later than the archaeomagnetic date of AD 125–175 but the evidence of wasters in other fabrics and of the full range of vessels made in the kiln fabrics, which includes developed bead and flange bowls, clearly shows that potting activity continued in the vicinity as late as the second half of the 3rd century.

Production is limited to a narrow range of coarse ware vessels suitable for the kitchen. Comparisons with the products of other local kilns, where the details are published or available, were not close and tended to be rather generalised. The distinctive bead and flange bowl type in particular was virtually unmatched and remains unusual. The common wide-mouthed jars were not closely paralleled and the closest matches typologically were at the 3rd–4th century kilns at Wappenbury. The distinctive bead and flange bowl made at the kiln was only found on Site 15 and Shenstone Linear Features (Site 13, Chapter 15), both sites associated with pottery production. The wide-mouthed jars were more commonly found outside the immediate environs of the pottery kiln. These were present on Sites 12 (cremation grave 122568), 19 (top fill of Enclosure 1 and ditch 190009, Chapter 24), 29 (ditch 292650 and feature 290571, Chapter 21) and 32 (layer 320063, Chapter 18). The kiln fabrics R1, R2, R4 and R8 were relatively uncommon except at Site 15 (Table 154). The assemblages from Washbrook Lane (Site 5, Chapter 7) and East of the Castle, Shenstone (Site 32, Chapter 18) were small (70 and 11 sherds respectively). The narrow-necked jar in R4 from Site 5 was the only vessel from the context and the bifid rim wide-mouthed jar came from a context with medieval and post-medieval sherds. The small amount of local kiln wares from West of Crane Brook Cottage (Site 34, Chapter 12) came from pit 340121 (33 sherds from a single vessel found with an R14 sherd) and ditch 348008, pre-dating the aisled building. These were not typologically diagnostic but illustrate the distribution of the wares in the mid-2nd century. Similarly the vessel from cremation grave 122568 on Site 12 was a wide-mouthed jar in kiln fabric R4.

Table 154 Relative proportions of site assemblages made up of Shenstone Site 15 kiln fabrics (based on sherd count)

Fabric Site	*5*	*12*	*13*	*15*	*19*	*29*	*32*	*34*
R1	–	–	–	4.7	0.1	–	–	–
R2	–	1.9	6.3	37.7	11.7	7.5	18.2	8.7
R4	7.1	0.9	–	8.2	0.7	0.8	–	–
R8	–	0.1	–	3.0	1.0	0.9	9.1	–
Total	7.1	2.9	6.3	53.6	13.5	9.2	27.3	8.7

The scarcity of kiln wares on Site 12 may reflect their chronological span which centres on a period after the main period of ceramic deposition at the cemetery in the early–mid-2nd century. The more frequent incidence of the wares at sites occupied in the later 2nd–3rd centuries such as Site 19 and Site 29 (Site 32 had only 11 sherds in total) indicates that the potters supplied at least 10% of the ceramics during this period to local sites. At Site 13 one vessel, a flanged bowl with low bead/groove like those made at the Shenstone kiln, was found in the only substantial group, pit 133154, which included pottery dating from the late 2nd–early 3rd to the mid-3rd to mid-4th centuries with a deposition date around the middle of the 3rd century accommodating most of the types.

Derbyshire ware sherds were present in the kiln and three waster sherds were identified from Site 15, including a cupped-rim jar. The degree of warping and cracking of these sherds rather argues against them being seconds and, despite the lack of any fabric characteristics distinguishing them from true Derbyshire ware when examined at x30 magnification, it seems likely that the pottery operating at Shenstone was producing this ware, albeit in small quantities. Small scale production of Derbyshire ware type jars is known at Rossington Bridge, Doncaster in the Antonine period and has been suspected at the Mancetter-Hartshill kilns (Leary 2003, 103). At Rocester a distorted cupped-rim jar in Derbyshire ware has recently been identified amongst the pottery from the Northfields excavations (Leary in prep.) which may extend the evidence for small scale manufacture of this type to another military pottery linked to the group of potters who are known from mortarium stamps to be moving between Mancetter-Hartshill, Little Chester and Rocester and later to Doncaster.

Mortarium stamps of Septuminus, Aesticus and possibly G. Attius Marinus and Victor are known at Mancetter-Hartshill and Little Chester; a semi-illegible stamp and a second stamp, possibly of Vitalis 4, occur at Rocester, Mancetter-Hartshill and probably also at Little Chester, and stamps of Sarrius, Setibogius and Secundua at Mancetter-Hartshill and Doncaster (Hartley 1985; 2001; Bevan and Hartley 2000). Such close links demonstrated by the mortarium makers' stamps may well have involved the movement of potters and/or ideas, making or influencing the coarse ware types being made at these potteries.

Certainly the occurrence of wasters of a distinctive type such as Derbyshire ware at all these sites can best be explained as another manifestation of such links between the potteries. Although mortarium stamp links have not yet been found at Wall, the type of the Shenstone kiln certainly compares well with Mancetter-Hartshill kilns and the mortarium wasters from the excavations, particularly in fabric M1, show typological links with the Mancetter-Hartshill potters both in fabric and form.

Production was small scale in character and seems to have been no more than a local concern. The evidence for mortarium production relies on the presence of wasters, both misfired and distorted. Wasters from Sites 12, 13, 15 and 19 suggest that cream self-slipped bead and flange mortaria (M1) and hammerhead, reeded-rim mortaria (M2) were also made in the vicinity. It remains a possibility that these are seconds from Mancetter-Hartshill but the establishment of a mortarium maker in the vicinity of Wall during the first half of the 2nd century would have been in keeping with the attested small scale production at sites such as Rocester and Derby Little Chester (see above).

Mortaria in fabric M1 would not be readily distinguished from Mancetter-Hartshill products if fired normally and it is not clear if the excessive hardness of M2 is due to overfiring or is a deliberate effect. Similar reeded rim mortaria in a more orthodox 'Mancetter-Hartshill' fabric on Site 13 may have been the desired result for the potters and this implies that an unknown proportion of the Mancetter-Hartshill mortaria from M6 Toll sites may, in fact, be locally made. Production in the style of Mancetter-Hartshill mortaria is well-known from Little Chester, where local products can be very difficult to distinguish from Mancetter mortaria (Hartley 1985, 125–6). Some evidence for this small scale activity continuing into the 3rd–4th centuries at the Derbyshire ware kilns at Holbrook near Belper was recovered by Brassington (1980, 45–6, nos 572–4, reeded hammerhead mortaria in Derbyshire ware including distorted examples).

Hartley identified an unreeded hammerhead mortarium in a very hard fired fabric at Little Chester dating later than AD 240. This vessel seemed to be an unused waster with red-brown painted decoration and was found with a high proportion of mortaria in the same form, raising the possibility of later mortarium production at Derby (Hartley 2002, 221, nos 44, 225). The similarity of the M2 mortaria from Site 13 to Derbyshire ware in its very hard character and rather pimply fabric invites comparison with the Derbyshire ware mortaria from Holbrook. Similarly at Rocester (Ferguson 1996, 62; Bevan and Hartley 2000, 34–5) a distorted and unusable waster from excavations at Orton's Pasture together with the presence of distinctive fabrics indicates production of mortaria there in the early 2nd century, and it is possible that potters moved between Rocester and Little Chester. No later mortarium production is known from Rocester.

At Wall Hartley recorded that most of the mortaria from the rescue excavations of 1980/81 were from the Mancetter-Hartshill kilns (1985, 25). On the *mansio* site (Hartley 1992, 34–6) Mancetter-Hartshill products were common, but vessels generally attributable to the Midlands, with one specifically from Little Chester, were also identified and may come from minor potters such as those working at Shenstone. At Coleshill most of the mortaria were from Mancetter-Hartshill, while at Tiddington one mortarium in a local reduced kiln fabric R21 suggested some small scale mortarium production on site (Booth 1996a). None of the other small Warwickshire kilns are recorded as making mortaria.

Earlier potting activity is suggested by waster vessels of late 1st–early 2nd century type. These are uncommon but include a neckless everted rim jar from cremation grave 122780, Site 12, in a fine grey ware R17. This vessel had a clearly distorted rim but did not show signs of burning. To this may be added distorted narrow-necked jars in fabric R16 from Site 12 (unburnt vessel from pyre related deposit 122083, early 2nd century) and Site 34 (from the ditch cut by the posthole building and from one of the postholes). Although not tightly dated, the fabric and general form as well as the associated datable material in both cases suggest an early 2nd century date. Wasters have also been found on other excavations at Wall (fine grey ware jars and a white ware beaker, Leary 1995–6, nos 18, 19 and one as no. 25). These may indicate kilns which were the precursors of the Shenstone kiln as implied by the fabric M1 mortaria.

A narrow-necked jar from Site 19 in fabric SV5 compared with Severn Valley ware forms but was misfired and distorted (as Webster 1976, no. 5). This vessel came from a group with types dating to the second half of the 2nd–early 3rd century and implies production of this fabric locally. The fabric compared well with Warwickshire fabric O27, identified as a probable Severn Valley fabric at Tiddington (Booth 1996a). At Alcester comparison with fabrics from Great Buckman's Farm and Newlands kilns at the Malvern Links site suggested a Malvernian source (Booth and Evans 2001, microfiche). The evidence from Site 19 raises the possibility of local production of oxidised ware in the Severn Valley tradition.

Thus the evidence of the wasters points to kiln activity around Wall from the early 2nd century with close ties to the potteries at Mancetter-Hartshill, Rocester and Little Chester. The earliest production seems to be of Flavian-Trajanic types common at military sites in the region. Activity on Site 15 may have commenced in the mid–late 2nd century but this clearly extended into the 3rd century and the developed form of the bead and flange bowls indicates activity in the second half of that century. The overfired reeded hammerhead mortarium supports this dating.

The probable manufacture of Derbyshire ware jars implies the continuation of links with the Mancetter-Hartshill/Derby/Doncaster group of potters in the mid–late 2nd century or later. The waster jar in fabric SV5, previously identified as Severn Valley ware, perhaps indicates the influence of Severn Valley potters, an influence perhaps also manifested by the 2nd century tankards made at Perry Barr (Hughes 1959), Tiddington (Booth 1996a) and Mancetter-Hartshill (unpublished), although of limited duration (Booth 1986, 32). The products of the Shenstone kiln, although belonging to general typological classes found in neighbouring industries, are not typologically close to the products of the Severn Valley ware industries.

The wide-mouthed jars, for example, contrast both with the typical Severn Valley ware examples with their classic wedge-shaped rims and with the East Midlands burnished ware group to the north (Todd 1968b) with their heavy bead or hooked rims and burnished surfaces. Local parallels for details of the form are not numerous but this may be a result of chronology since the published groups are of slightly different date ranges to the Site 15 kiln group. It appears that as the military moved on, potteries which continued in use developed idiosyncrasies of form which, while equivalent to those developing in neighbouring industries, were distinctive and particular to quite a small area of the country. This can be seen in the related Derbyshire ware industry to the north where a different and distinctive wide-mouthed jar was also developed (Leary 2003, 104–5).

Thus although the different industries produced a similar range of vessel types with comparable features, the angle of the neck, the form of the rim and the nature of the surface treatment all served to create distinctive and at times highly individual responses to the same needs. This local industry incorporated influences derived from a huge industry supplying large tracts of the country, including the northern frontier zone, with mortaria, while still maintaining the character of a stylistic zone which may have covered only north Warwickshire. This latter zone may have corresponded to ancient ethnic boundaries and certainly can be glimpsed in the distribution of traded wares such as Severn Valley ware, Derbyshire ware, East Midlands burnished ware, Malvernian wares and pink grogged wares (see below).

Trade and exchange

Consideration of the trade in ceramics over time is limited in two respects. Regionally produced wares were not always distinctive, so fabrics such as R5, R7, R15 and R16 are similar to fabrics from Mancetter-Hartshill, wasters from Wall and fabrics from the kilns at Sherifoot Lane, Sutton Coldfield. This means that production of these common wares at Wall itself cannot be ruled out, and it is difficult to trace the distribution of products of local kilns in the absence of other distinctive features such as vessel type or treatment. In addition many of the assemblages came from ditch accumulations which had been formed over a period of 100 years or more. Where different fills were not detected within these the resulting ceramic groups span a rather broad date range. Thus the chronological precision available is somewhat restricted and the inter-relationship of the local kilns cannot be easily established.

Nonetheless the pottery from Site 34 provided an assemblage of fairly short duration and some of the pottery from Site 12 could be given a narrow date range and thus sheds light on the character of pottery obtainable around Wall in the early–mid-2nd century. The later groups are much more mixed and do not provide groups assignable to narrow date ranges. They do, nevertheless, demonstrate changes in trade networks during the late Romano-British period and the dating of individual vessel types helps to pinpoint when some of the changes are likely to have occurred.

Late 1st–early 2nd centuries (Flavian–Trajanic)

Sites 34 and 12 are the most informative regarding trade and exchange during the Flavian–Trajanic period, although most of the vessels belong to the early 2nd century rather than the 1st century. While Iron Age pottery is present on several of the sites, very few sherds belonging to fabric group E, the late Iron Age ware group (Warwickshire fabric series group E, Booth 1986, 24) were found: a few fragments from Site 19 and a single sherd from a later Roman feature on Site 29. Similarly there is very little Roman pottery belonging to the early years of occupation and types which are restricted to the pre-Flavian or early Flavian periods were not identified. The early phase at Site 12 can yield useful information but is, naturally, not representative of the full range of pottery types used by the living and has a heavy bias towards vessels considered appropriate for use as pyre goods and/or burial urns (Table 155).

The vessels are predominantly jars in fairly fine grey ware fabrics made either at an early kiln near Wall or at the potteries known at Mancetter-Hartshill and Sherifoot Lane, Sutton Coldfield. The incidence of samian is high compared with other sites but as this is a cemetery, the significance of this is limited since table wares were common elements in the accompanying burial rites and memorial feasts. Similarly the large amount of white ware and white-slipped ware flagons were needed for libations and drink at these occasions.

Trade with the *Verulamium* region in the late 1st–early 2nd centuries was indicated by the presence of the FLA4 flagon. The mica dusted indented beaker from Site 12 was a common type at Rocester (Leary 1996, 42 MG1; Bevan 2000, 16 MG1) but was much rarer at the related fort at Derby (Birss 1985, table 123). The indented beaker form is common and is made in Britain (Marsh 1978, type 21). At Rocester it was suggested that the coarser mica dusted ware may have been locally produced and there is evidence that at both Rocester and Derby Little Chester the potters produced a specialist fine ware range, mica-dusted at Rocester and glazed ware at Derby (Leary 1996, 49). Mica dusted ware was also a very minor component of production at Mancetter-Hartshill. Fabric MG1, however, compared better with a finer fabric found at Rocester which may be imported or traded from an unknown British source. The cemetery white wares are likely to be from Mancetter-Hartshill although, as there may be mortaria production at Wall in a cream ware, it follows that local flagon production would also be possible.

The CTA1 rebated-rim jar is a type found at Coleshill (*c* 3%, Warwickshire fabric C41) used to make jars of 1st and 2nd century date and is present in similar quantities at Barton-under-Needwood to the north of Wall (Table 159). This vesicular ware was identified as organic tempered, but sherds from these excavations retain fragments of shell suggesting that some, if not all of the vesicles are from dissolved shell temper. A similar

Table 155 Fabrics and forms used in the early 2nd century groups at Site 12, by vessel count

Ware group	*Fabric*	*Samian Form 18*	*Samian Form 27*	*Samian Form 36*	*Everted rim beaker*	*Folded beaker*	*Ring-n flagon*	*Neckless everted rim jar*	*Rebated-rim jar*	*Rusticated jar*	*Closed vessel*
C	CTA1	–	–	–	–	–	–	–	1	–	–
F	MG1	–	–	–	–	1	–	–	–	–	–
MALV	MALV	–	–	–	–	–	–	–	–	–	1
O	O4	–	–	–	–	–	–	–	1	–	–
R	R12	–	–	–	1	–	–	–	–	–	–
	R14	–	–	–	1	–	–	–	–	1	–
	R15	–	–	–	–	–	–	–	–	1	1
	R16	–	–	–	1	–	–	–	–	1	3
	R2	–	–	–	1	–	–	–	–	–	–
	R22	–	–	–	1	–	–	–	–	–	1
	R23	–	–	–	–	–	–	1	–	–	–
	R4	–	–	–	–	–	–	–	–	–	2
	R5	–	–	–	–	–	–	3	–	–	3
S	TS	4	2	1	–	–	–	–	–	–	–
W	FLA	–	–	–	–	–	–	–	–	–	1
	FLA2	–	–	–	–	–	–	–	–	–	2
	FLA3	–	–	–	–	–	–	–	–	–	2
	FLA4	–	–	–	–	–	–	–	–	–	3
WS	FLB2	–	–	–	–	–	1	–	–	–	–

fabric and form is present at Wall (Leary 1995–6, no. 1; Gould 1966–7, nos 57–8) and Rocester (less than 1%, Leary 1996, 42 CTA1). Vessels in a comparable fabric and form are published from *Tripontium* (Cameron and Lucas 1969, no. 37; 1973, no. 348 in an early 2nd century pit). A very similar ware was found at the Derby Racecourse kilns and Little Chester fort, Derby (Brassington 1971, nos 137–42; Birss 1985, 90, 3% in the late 1st–early 2nd century) where Swan suggested it was from the Nene Valley or Northamptonshire (1984, 125). Vessels of this type are common at sites such as Brixworth (Woods 1970) and have been more widely studied in the Nene Valley by Friendship-Taylor (1999). These wares also occur in some quantity at *Margidunum* used for storage jars and rebated-rim jars (Oswald 1952, pl. viii, no. 1 and pl. xv, no. 4), where they contrast with the native shell-tempered wares of Nottinghamshire and Lincolnshire which are invariably in reduced fabrics in a different range of forms. If these vessels are all from the same source then they represent an important and widespread trade centring on military sites, perhaps of a perishable commodity contained within the jars rather than the jars themselves. The Northamptonshire source suggested by Swan has been further supported by the publication of very similar vessels from the early kilns at Harrold (late 1st–2nd centuries, Brown 1994, fig. 24, nos 37–40 for the rebated rim jars and fig. 22 for the storage jars). These early jars were commonly oxidised in colour. Locally the fabric accounts for 3% of the assemblage at Coleshill and less than 1% at Tiddington (Booth 1996a). At Princethorpe the shell-tempered ware is entirely made up of a fabric in an Iron Age tradition (Evans 1998, 62) and further south in the Arrow Valley and at Alcester it is similarly absent (Evans 1996–7, 101; Ferguson 2001, 183) its place being taken perhaps by Malvernian ware. Analyses of these jars would be desirable to ascertain if they are indeed likely to be from the same source and to determine where that might be. If these CTA1 jars are from Northamptonshire they are represent a small scale but significant distribution on the periphery of their core market area.

Other fabrics (G2, G3, G5, PNK GT see below) indicate trade/exchange with western Buckinghamshire. The primary distribution zone for fabric PNK GT lies south-east of Wall and only quite small quantities have been found in Warwickshire (Taylor 2004), particularly in this early period.

Further information regarding this period may be gleaned from the small amount of early pottery from the features predating the aisled building on Site 34. This group included pottery dating to the mid-2nd century but some vessels are stylistically closer to the early 2nd century range. The CTA1 group identified in Site 12 group 1 was present in the form of a combed storage jar, and an R15 jar wide-mouthed cordoned jar compares well with early 2nd century types at Derby and Rocester. A distorted narrow-necked jar in fabric R16 adds weight to the suggestion that pottery production was established at Wall during this period. The small group of features of this date on Site 29 yielded a rusticated and an undecorated jar with short everted rims in R16 and R5, CTA1 jars, carinated bowls in R5, O1 and O2, white ware ring-necked flagons, a white ware bowl and an early Severn Valley type tankard (SV3). These occurred in contexts lacking BB1 sherds, perhaps implying a pre-Hadrianic date. A group of G2 sherds from Site 29 may also belong to this phase. A diagnostic G2 vessel came from a context with 3rd century BB1 but at Tiddington the fabric was generally thought to belong in the 1st and 2nd centuries and the form here, a storage jar with horizontal and oblique combing, is typical of the 1st–early 2nd century. A vessel in a similar fabric but in a different form, a channelled-rim jar, was identified at Wall (Leary 1995–6, 29, no. 9). This fabric was also identified at Tiddington (Booth 1996a, Warwickshire fabric G12) and may be related to early pink-grogged ware from Buckinghamshire.

The oxidised and white wares are also likely to be from Mancetter-Hartshill since at present there is no evidence for production of these around Wall. There were three waster sherds in fabric R5 – a bead-rim neckless jar with constricted mouth, a wide mouthed jar with everted rim and a jar basal sherd. These suggest manufacture in the area of Wall. The range of forms – neckless everted rim jars with rustication or shoulder grooves, carinated bowls with bead, everted and bifid rims, wide-mouthed jars including those with upright necks and everted or bead rims (but not those with the everted bifid rims similar to those at the Site 15 kiln) – in R5 suggests a date range from the early 2nd probably continuing until the second half of the 2nd century.

No diagnostic bowls and dishes other than the carinated bowls were present in R5. The jars and carinated bowls are similar to those found at Mancetter-Hartshill and Sherifoot Lane kilns (unpublished) and the wide-mouthed jars may be precursors of those from the Site 15 kiln. Quantification of the reduced wares at Sites 19 and 29 compared with Site 12 shows that fabric R5 was more common on these sites and R16 was more common on Site 12. This suggests that although fabric R5 may have been in use in the early 2nd century it continued and became the dominant fabric in the second quarter of the 2nd century onwards until the Site 15 kiln wares became more common. The forms made support this view.

The early 2nd century assemblages seem to be dominated by local reduced wares with small amounts of oxidised and white wares probably coming from the Mancetter-Hartshill kilns and regionally traded wares from the Severn Valley region and Northamptonshire. Imported samian was present in small quantities and there may have been some mica-dusted ware from the Continent or an unknown British source. There are very small amounts of *Verulamium* region white ware and coarse ware jars from Northamptonshire, but the contribution of non-local sources is generally very restricted.

2nd century (Hadrianic-Antonine)

Rather more pottery groups are attributable to this period although the problem of gradually accumulating ditch fills on many of the sites continued to preclude the separation of quantified groups from later material from the same contexts. The characteristic fabric of this period, BB1, was not prolific at any of the sites except the cemetery (18%) where jars and beakers were selected both for use as urns and as pyre goods. Otherwise the relative quantity of BB1 ranges from under 2% to around 14%. The larger groups compare well with quantities at Coleshill (10%) and Tiddington (14%) and contrast with Princethorpe, where BB1 barely reaches 1% of the assemblage from a site with much Antonine samian (Evans 1998, 62). Groups from local military sites indicate that between 13% and 20% of the total assemblage of this period in the area could be made up of BB1 (Fig. 210, below).

The take-up of this ware on hinterland sites would be affected by the availability of alternatives. In the Arrow Valley sites, for example, Evans found that the rural population acquired far less BB1 than that at nearby Alcester and, in addition, only obtained vessels such as cooking bowls and dishes not available locally. Surprisingly the kiln site, Site 15, has the most BB1 after Site 12. From the analysis of the forms in kiln fabrics it is clear that production continued in and around Sites 13 and 15 until the second half of the 3rd at least. The BB1 forms include medium-necked jars, dishes and bowls with more jars than bowls and dishes (76% of all the BB1 from the site). The kiln group did not include many medium-necked jars (Table 156) and this type may thus have still been in demand. Rather more bowls and dishes were in local supply but the group from the kiln was dominated by wide-mouthed jars. On other sites the vessels in the kiln fabrics were more frequently narrow-necked jars and small jar/beakers (Table 156). However if Site 12 is excluded (since small jars were particularly selected for use in the burial rites) medium-necked jars and bowls and dishes remain fairly low numerically and the narrow-necked jars still outnumber the wide-mouthed jars. This would tend to imply that although the kiln group may have a bias in the vessels represented related to the nature of individual firings, medium necked jars were never very common and this vessel type would have to have been obtained from elsewhere if it was needed. Some supplementary source of bowls and dishes would probably also have been required, including that category represented by the BB1 repertoire.

The BB1 forms divide relatively evenly between the Hadrianic–Antonine period and types belonging to the 3rd century, suggesting that supply was even throughout the 2nd and 3rd centuries, although there is little evidence for the 4th century pattern.

Table 156 Site 15 kiln group and groups outside of Sites 15 & 12: vessel composition using EVES

Vessel	Rel % total EVES from kiln	Rel % total EVES outside Site 15	Rel % total EVES outside Sites 15 & 12
Bowl	13.5	1.0	1.6
Bowl/dish	3.7	2.0	3.2
Dish	6.3	2.0	3.2
Dish/lid	2.6	3.3	–
Medium-necked jar	6.3	5.0	7.9
Small jar/beaker	–	37.0	5.8
Narrow-necked jar	9.6	38.7	58.4
Wide-necked jar	57.0	11.0	14.7

This period also sees a contribution from Severn Valley ware. Although groups uncontaminated with later material are difficult to identify, most of the assemblage from Site 34 belongs to this period and some 5% of the group was probably from the Severn Valley ware industries. These sherds were in a later fabric SV1 rather than the early vesicular Severn Valley ware and may have all come from a wide-mouthed jar of a type given a mid–late 2nd century date range (Evans *et al.* 2000, JWM5). This vessel is likely to be the precursor of greater trade with the Severn Valley kilns from the mid–late 2nd century onwards. The quantities at Sites 19 and 29, where datable pottery concentrated in the late 2nd–3rd centuries, were noticeably higher than at Sites 34 and 12 (Table 157). The higher representation of Severn Valley ware at Site 19 relates to a larger number of tankards from that site and this may in turn be linked with the status and ethnicity of the inhabitants (see below). Site 15 produced relatively little Severn Valley ware; this is completely consistent with the presence of a kiln producing the principal export forms of the Severn Valley kilns, namely narrow-mouthed and wide-mouthed jars. Nevertheless the most numerous form in Severn Valley ware from the M6 Toll sites were wide-mouthed jars (37% of the Severn Valley ware types) and these were mostly of late 2nd–3rd century types, suggesting that these were desirable despite local production of this form.

The SV fabrics are markedly finer than the local products and the oxidised colour may have been thought more attractive. Narrow-mouthed jars were also popular (22% of the ware group) and tankards and bowls made up *c* 15% and 19% each of the SV group. The narrow-mouthed jars were also competing with local products in the same way as the wide-mouthed vessels, but the tankards and bowls were in forms not apparently made at Wall (Webster 1976, types D, E and H). Although tankards were found at Mancetter-Hartshill, Tiddington kiln 2 and Perry Barr (and a reduced tankard was part of the repertoire at Sherifoot Lane), the fabrics of the tankards on M6 Toll sites (mostly SV1 and some SV3) suggest a Severn Valley source.

Fabrics SV4 and 5 were only common on Site 19 and the SV5 vessel from there was a distorted waster suggesting local manufacture. The status of SV4 is not certain but it compared with Warwickshire fabric O32 which has been assigned to the Severn Valley group and the forms, a bowl with everted rim, an early carinated bowl, a narrow-mouthed jar with outcurving rim and a wide-mouthed jar (Webster 1976, nos 36, type H, type A and nos 19–20 respectively) compare well with Severn Valley products. Severn Valley ware forms do not seem to have been copied closely in the region, with the exception of the tankards.

Other oxidised wares reached *c* 13% of the site assemblages on sites where special circumstances did not apply, *viz* kiln and burial sites with assemblages heavily related to site function. Ten different fabrics were distinguished. The fine fabric O1 was principally used to make Severn Valley ware types (Webster 1976, nos 36 and 50) and a small number of samian copies, Form 31 and possibly Form 27. Fabrics O2 and O3 have a similar range of Severn Valley type wide-mouthed jars but fabric O4 was used to make wide-mouthed jars like those from the Shenstone kiln with bifid rims, as well as a rebated-rim jar. O5 forms included a narrow-necked jar with blunt ended, everted rim and a possible tankard and O6 included an early 2nd century carinated bowl and a bead and flange hemispherical bowl in forms common at Mancetter-Hartshill, Derby, Rocester and Wall, as well as wide-mouthed jars like those at the Shenstone kiln with bifid and everted rims. No typologically diagnostic sherds were found in fabrics O7, O8 and O10, but O9 included three storage jars and may better belong with group G, perhaps being a variant of the pink grogged ware group. There was no firm dating evidence for these wares. The use of various oxidised wares clearly spans the 2nd and 3rd centuries and was influenced by types such as the carinated bowls and flanged hemispherical bowls common at the early military potteries, and by Severn Valley ware types. The contribution to the assemblages seems small, *c* 10%, the higher proportion at Site 34 being due to the fragmentation of a single vessel into over 30 sherds. It would appear that oxidised wares were produced in small numbers, perhaps at several different centres.

The proportion of mortaria in the assemblages averaged just under 4% with an exceptional 21% at Site 13 where they may have been produced. Despite the possibility of local production the majority have fabrics macroscopically indistinguishable from Mancetter-Hartshill fabrics, both amongst the 2nd century and the 3rd–4th century types. However, the existence of wasters in similar forms to vessels in fabrics more like Mancetter-Hartshill white wares demands caution since 'successful' firings may have resulted in vessels indistinguishable from the products of the larger concern. These vessels should be included in any future programme of fabric characterisation. Local production seems to have been a short lived effort in the first half of the 2nd century, with another try possibly in the 3rd century.

By the late 2nd century white and white-slipped wares were very rare and account for less than 2% at Sites 15 and 19 and less than 1% at Site 29. Group C wares also drop to around 2%. On Sites 15 and 19 these are predominantly late Harrold products belonging to the 3rd–4th centuries and on Site 29 the group C sherds are largely from a late 1st–early 2nd century rebated-rim jar, redeposited in a 3rd century layer. It appears, therefore, that there is little group C material belonging to this period. Group G is rare except at Site 29 where over 7% of the assemblage belonged to this group. However these came from the G2 jar mentioned above dating to the earlier period, and from a Malvernian jar from the same ditch which may belong to this or the preceding period. Malvernian ware was generally scarce but was present on Site 5 associated with a Severn Valley ware jar of mid–late 2nd century type and also in cremation grave 120202 in Site 12, where it was

Table 157 Relative percentages of ware groups and fabrics by site, based on sherd counts

	Sites (W-E)	5	34	9	12	13	15	32	29	19	All
Ware group	Ware										
A	A10	–	0.5	–	–	–	–	–	–	–	*
	DR20	1.4	0.5	–	0.1	–	0.2	–	2.4	4.3	1.1
A total		*1.4*	*1.0*	–	*0.1*	–	*0.2*	–	*2.4*	*4.3*	*1.1*
BB1	BB1	4.3	6.1	85.7	23.8	1.6	14.2	18.2	6.3	11.3	13.6
	R18	–	–	–	4.7	–	–	–	0.5	–	0.8
BB1 total		*4.3*	*6.1*	*85.7*	*28.5*	*1.6*	*14.2*	*18.2*	*6.8*	*11.3*	*14.3*
C	CT	–	–	–	0.1	–	2.0	–	0.4	0.6	1.2
	CTA1	–	5.6	–	0.2	–	–	–	1.5	0.5	0.6
	CTA2		–	–	–	–	0.5	–	–	0.7	0.4
	CTB1	–	–	–	–	–	–	–	–	0.6	0.1
C total		–	*5.6*	–	*0.3*	–	*2.5*	–	*1.9*	*2.4*	*2.2*
DBY	DBY	–	–	–	–	–	1.7	–	0.5	0.2	1.0
E	E1	–	–	–	–	–	–	–	0.1	–	*
F	CC	–	–	–	0.4	–	–	–	–	–	*
	CC1	–	–	–	–	–	0.2	–	0.1	–	0.1
	CC2	–	1.0	–	–	–	–	–	–	–	0.1
	KOL	–	–	–	–	–	–	–	–	0.5	0.1
	MG1	–	–	–	0.1	–	–	–	–	–	*
	MHAD	–	–	–	–	–	0.1	–	–	–	*
	NV	–	–	–	–	–	1.3	–	0.4	0.4	0.8
	ROX	–	–	–	–	–	0.2	–	0.8	0.2	0.3
F total		–	*1.0*	–	*0.5*	–	*1.8*	–	*1.3*	*1.1*	*1.4*
G	G2	1.4	–	–	–	–	0.1	–	3.1	–	0.4
	G3	–	–	–	–	–	*	–	–	–	*
	G4	–	–	–	–	–	0.1	–	–	–	*
	G5	–	–	–	–	–	–	–	–	0.1	*
	MALV	1.4	–	–	–	–	–	–	4.6	–	0.6
	PNK GT	–	–	–	–	–	0.3	–	–	0.1	0.1
G total		*2.9*	–	–	–	–	*0.4*	–	*7.6*	*0.2*	*1.2*
M	M1		0.3	–	0.2	–	0.1	–	0.1	0.1	0.2
	M2	–	–	–	–	4.8	0.1	–	–	–	0.1
	M3	–	–	–	–	–	*	–	–	–	*
	MH	2.9	–	–	2.1	9.5	3.5	18.2	2.4	4.9	3.2
	MWS	–	0.3	–	–	–	–	–	–	–	*
	ROX/RSOX	–	–	–	–	–	–	–	–	0.1	*
M total		*2.9*	*0.5*	–	*2.3*	*20.6*	*3.7*	*18.2*	*2.5*	*5.1*	*3.5*
MALV	MALV	–	–	–	0.1	–	–	–	–	–	*
O	O	2.9	–	–	–	1.6	0.3	–	–	0.7	0.3
	O1	24.3	–	–	3.2	–	1.0	–	4.3	0.4	1.8
	O10	–	–	–	–	–	–	–	1.1	–	0.1
	O2	–	–	–	–	–	0.2	–	1.3	0.4	0.3
	O3	–	–	–	–	–	0.3	–	–	–	0.1
	O4	2.9	11.5	–	1.3	3.2	1.0	–	2.0	1.2	1.9
	O5	5.7	–	–	–	–	0.1	–	0.7	0.6	0.3
	O6	–	1.3	–	0.3	–	*	–	2.9	0.9	0.7
	O7	–	0.8	–	–	3.2	–	–	–	–	0.1
	O8	–	–	–	–	–	–	–	0.1	–	*
	O9	1.4	–	–	–	–	–	–	0.4	–	0.1
O total		*37.1*	*13.5*	–	*4.8*	*7.9*	*2.9*	–	*12.9*	*4.1*	*5.6*
R	R	–	–	–	–	–	0.2	–	0.1	–	0.1
	R1	–	–	–	–	–	4.7	–	–	0.1	2.4
	R10	–	–	–	0.3	–	0.3	–	–	–	0.2
	R11	–	–	–	–	–	1.5	–	0.9	0.6	0.9
	R12	–	0.3	–	0.2	–	1.3	–	1.1	3.0	1.2
	R13	–	0.8	–	0.1	–	0.3	–	6.3	0.5	1.1
	R14	–	0.3	–	0.9	–	–	–	–	–	0.1
	R15	8.6	18.9	–	3.0	1.6	–	–	1.9	–	2.0
	R16	21.4	30.6	–	11.6	–	–	–	1.5	0.1	4.1
	R17	–	1.0	–	0.2	–	–	–	0.7	–	0.2

Table 157 continued

Ware group	Sites (W-E) Ware	5	34	9	12	13	15	32	29	19	All
	R19	–	–	–	0.7	–	–	–	0.1	–	0.1
	R2	–	8.7	–	1.9	6.3	37.7	18.2	7.5	11.7	22.6
	R2/5	–	–	–	0.7	–	*	–	–	0.2	0.1
	R20	–	–	–	0.4	–	–	–	–	–	0.1
	R21	–	–	–	0.1	6.3	–	–	0.3	0.5	0.2
	R22	–	–	–	3.3	–	–	–	–	0.6	0.6
	R23	–	–	–	0.3	–	–	–	–	–	*
	R24	–	–	–	–	–	–	–	–	0.1	*
	R25	–	–	–	–	–	–	–	–	0.1	*
	R26	–	–	–	–	–	–	–	–	0.1	*
	R27	–	–	–	–	–	–	–	–	0.1	*
	R28	–	–	–	–	–	–	–	0.8	–	0.1
	R3	–	0.3	–	–	–	0.9	–	0.4	1.5	0.7
	R4	7.1	–	–	0.9	–	8.2	–	0.8	0.7	4.6
	R5	–	–	14.3	3.0	7.9	2.6	27.3	20.5	14.6	6.4
	R6	–	0.3	–	–	–	1.4	–	–	–	0.7
	R7	–	–	–	4.3	–	1.7	–	3.1	2.8	2.2
	R8	–	–	–	0.1	–	3.0	9.1	0.9	1.0	1.8
	R9	7.1	0.3	–	0.3	31.7	1.4	9.1	0.9	5.5	2.1
R total		*44.3*	*61.2*	*14.3*	*32.3*	*54.0*	*65.3*	*63.6*	*47.9*	*43.9*	*54.7*
S	TS	2.9	2.3	–	4.7	1.6	1.5	–	4.4	1.5	2.4
SV	SV	–	0.8	–	–	–	–	–	–	–	*
	SV1	4.3	3.6	–	1.2	1.6	1.3	–	3.5	6.1	2.3
	SV2	–	–	–	–	–	0.1	–	–	–	*
	SV3	–	–	–	–	1.6	1.8	–	4.8	1.2	1.7
	SV4	–	0.5	–	0.3	–	1.0	–	1.6	9.5	2.0
	SV5	–	–	–	–	–	–	–	0.5	7.5	1.1
	SV6	–	–	–	–	–	–	–	0.7	–	0.1
SV total		*4.3*	*4.8*	–	*1.5*	*3.2*	*4.2*	–	*11.1*	*24.3*	*7.3*
W	FLA	–	–	–	0.2	–	0.1	–	–	–	0.1
	FLA1	–	3.1	–	–	–	0.8	–	–	–	0.6
	FLA2	–	–	–	4.6	4.8	0.5	–	0.1	0.1	1.0
	FLA3	–	0.3	–	14.0	6.3	–	–	0.1	1.5	2.3
	FLA4	–	–	–	4.4	–	0.1	–	–	–	0.7
	FLA5	–	–	–	0.3	–	–	–	–	–	*
	W1	–	–	–	–	–	0.1	–	–	–	*
	W12	–	–	–	–	–	*	–	–	–	*
W total		–	*3.3*	–	*23.6*	*11.1*	*1.6*	–	*0.3*	*1.6*	*4.8*
WS	FLB	–	–	–	0.1	–	–	–	–	–	*
	FLB1	–	0.3	–	–	–	–	–	–	–	*
	FLB2	–	0.3	–	1.0	–	–	–	0.1	–	0.2
WS total		–	*0.5*	–	*1.1*	–	–	–	*0.1*	–	*0.2*
Total sherd count		70	392	7	908	63	3149	11	746	823	6158

* = <0.1%

associated with late 1st–early 2nd century types. It is known at Tiddington, Coleshill and in the Arrow Valley sites at levels of *c* 1% and was most common in the late 1st–2nd centuries. At the earlier site at Metchley nearly 3% of the assemblage is Malvernian ware (Hancocks 2005, 49, from phase 3, AD 60–75) but it has not been previously published at Wall and the SGRP bibliography details as displayed on Potsherd (http/www.potsherd.uklinux.net/atlas/ware/MALV) do not record any instances to the north of Wall.

Fine ware levels were extremely low. One scrap possibly from a Cologne roughcast beaker was found on Site 19 and sherds of a roughcast ware with orange core and dark grey colour coat were present on Sites 12 and 34 and are likely to belong to this period. These may be local versions of imported vessels, perhaps from the Mancetter-Hartshill kilns. None of the other group F vessels belongs to this period.

This period is therefore characterised by a wide range of pottery suppliers with several local sources suggested by the number of different coarse wares occurring in fairly small numbers. There is evidence for exchange/trade with neighbouring regions to the south and west and to the east and north, and for rather small numbers of imported wares and of fine table wares of any kind. The sites seem to lie on the edge of the

Table 158 Relative percentages of ware groups and fabrics by site based on sherd weights

	Sites (W-E)	*5*	*34*	*9*	*12*	*13*	*15*	*32*	*29*	*19*
Ware grp	*Ware*									
A	A10	–	0.6	–	–	–	–	–	–	–
	DR20	13.1	1.2	–	0.3	–	1.7	–	0.5	10.1
A total		*13.1*	*1.7*	–	*0.3*	–	*1.7*	–	*0.5*	*10.1*
BB1	BB1	2.5	5.7	27.8	10.8	0.8	8.9	32.2	2.6	6.2
	R18	–	–	–	0.4	–	–	–	0.1	–
BB1 total		*2.5*	*5.7*	*27.8*	*11.2*	*0.8*	*8.9*	*32.2*	*2.6*	*6.2*
C	CT	–	–	–	*	–	2.7	–	0.2	0.1
	CTA1	–	5.6	–	1.0	–	–	–	0.5	0.5
	CTA2	–	–	–	–	–	0.2	–	–	0.3
	CTB1	–	–	–	–	–	–	–	–	0.2
C total		–	*5.6*	–	*1.0*	–	*3.0*	–	*0.7*	*1.0*
DBY	DBY	–	–	–	–	–	2.1	–	0.3	0.1
E	E1	–	–	–	–	–	–	–	0.5	–
F	CC	–	–	–	0.2	–	–	–	–	–
	CC1	–	–	–	–	–	*	–	*	–
	CC2	–	0.1	–	–	–	–	–	–	–
	KOL	–	–	–	–	–	–	–	–	0.1
	MG1	–	–	–	0.1	–	–	–	–	–
	MHAD	–	–	–	–	–	0.2	–	–	–
	NV	–	–	–	–	–	0.2	–	0.4	0.1
	NV1	–	–	–	–	–	*	–	–	–
	ROX	–	–	–	–	–	0.1	–	0.9	0.3
F total		–	*0.1*	–	*0.3*	–	*0.6*	–	*1.3*	*0.5*
G	G2	0.5	–	–	–	–	0.1	–	13.8	–
	G3	–	–	–	–	–	0.1	–	–	–
	G4	–	–	–	–	–	0.1	–	–	–
	G5	–	–	–	–	–	–	–	–	0.5
	MALV	6.5	–	–	–	–	–	–	21.2	–
	PNK GT	–	–	–	–	–	1.3	–	–	0.4
G total		*7.0*	–	–	–	–	*1.6*	–	*35.0*	*0.9*
M	M1	–	1.0	–	0.3	20.2	0.3	–	0.2	1.7
	M2	–	–	–	–	19.1	1.0	–	–	–
	M3	–	–	–	–	–	0.3	–	–	–
	MH	12.8	–	–	1.7	7.9	10.9	42.7	7.5	18.6
	MWS	–	3.9	–	–	–	–	–	–	–
	ROX/RSOX	–	–	–	–	–	–	–	–	0.2
M total		*12.8*	*4.9*	–	*2.0*	*47.2*	*12.6*	*42.7*	*7.7*	*20.5*
MALV	MALV	–	–	–	1.3	–	–	–	–	–
O	O	1.9	–	–	–	1.2	*	–	–	0.4
	O1	7.5	–	–	0.4	–	1.1	–	2.3	0.2
	O10	–	–	–	–	–	–	–	0.3	–
	O2	–	–	–	–	–	0.1	–	0.7	0.1
	O3	–	–	–	–	–	0.1	–	–	–
	O4	1.6	6.6	–	0.1	1.5	0.5	–	0.6	0.4
	O5	5.2	–	–	–	–	*	–	0.1	0.3
	O6	–	2.1	–	*	–	0.1	–	0.2	0.2
	O7	–	0.3	–	–	6.8	–	–	–	–
	O8	–	–	–	–	–	–	–	*	–
	O9	16.1	–	–	–	–	–	–	2.5	–
O total		*32.3*	*9.0*	–	*0.5*	*9.4*	*2.0*	–	*6.8*	*1.7*
R	GRA	–	–	–	–	–	*	–	–	–
	R	–	–	–	–	–	*	–	0.1	–
	R1	–	–	–	–	–	6.3	–	–	0.1
	R10	–	–	–	*	–	0.4	–	–	–
	R11	–	–	–	–	–	1.6	–	0.3	1.3
	R12	–	0.5	–	*	–	1.1	–	0.4	2.9
	R13	–	0.6	–	*	–	0.7	–	3.4	0.2
	R14	–	5.8	–	3.5	–	–	–	–	–
	R15	1.5	16.7	–	6.0	1.1	–	–	0.7	–
	R16	7.2	6.3	–	15.1	–	–	–	1.2	0.2
	R17	–	0.3	–	1.6	–	–	–	0.8	–
	R19	–	–	–	1.4	–	–	–	0.1	–
	R2	–	29.4	–	6.1	3.9	36.7	4.3	5.7	9.5
	R2/5	–	–	–	*	–	0.1	–	–	0.3
	R20	–	–	–	*	–	–	–	–	–

Table 158 continued

Ware grp	*Sites (W-E)* / *Ware*	5	34	9	12	13	15	32	29	19
	R21	–	–	–	0.1	6.8	–	–	*	0.3
	R22	–	–	–	5.4	–	–	–	–	2.8
	R23	–	–	–	*	–	–	–	–	–
	R24	–	–	–	*	–	–	–	–	0.6
	R25	–	–	–	–	–	–	–	–	*
	R26	–	–	–	–	–	–	–	–	0.1
	R27	–	–	–	–	–	–	–	–	0.1
	R28	–	–	–	–	–	–	–	2.4	–
	R3	–	0.4	–	–	–	0.8	–	0.1	0.7
	R4	8.2	–	–	2.1	–	5.1	–	0.3	0.2
	R5	–	–	72.2	11.6	4.1	2.7	8.1	18.6	9.8
	R6	–	0.1	–	–	–	0.3	–	–	–
	R7	–	–	–	9.2	–	3.0	–	1.1	1.9
	R8	–	–	–	*	–	3.2	3.7	0.6	1.0
	R9	8.6	0.4	–	6.6	12.6	0.7	9.0	0.4	2.1
R total		*25.5*	*60.5*	*72.2*	*68.9*	*28.5*	*62.9*	*25.1*	*36.1*	*34.1*
S	TS	2.2	4.7	–	1.8	0.2	1.3	–	2.5	1.4
SV	SV	–	0.1	–	–	–	–	–	–	–
	SV1	4.6	1.0	–	0.2	0.1	1.5	–	–	4.6
	SV2	–	–	–	–	–	0.2	–	–	–
	SV3	–	–	–	–	0.2	0.7	–	2.3	0.6
	SV4	–	1.5	–	0.1	–	0.4	–	0.4	2.8
	SV5	–	–	–	–	–	–	–	0.7	14.3
	SV6	–	–	–	–	–	–	–	0.2	–
SV total		*4.6*	*2.5*	–	*0.3*	*0.3*	*2.8*	–	*5.6*	*22.3*
W	FLA	–	–	–	*	–	*	–	–	–
	FLA1	–	3.2	–	–	–	0.2	–	–	–
	FLA2	–	–	–	4.1	11.6	0.3	–	0.1	*
	FLA3	–	0.8	–	4.9	2.1	–	–	0.2	1.3
	FLA4	–	–	–	0.5	–	*	–	–	–
	FLA5	–	–	–	1.0	–	–	–	–	–
	W1	–	–	–	–	–	*	–	–	–
	W12	–	–	–	–	–	*	–	–	–
W total		–	*4.0*	–	*10.6*	*13.6*	*0.7*	–	*0.3*	*1.4*
WS	FLB	–	–	–	*	–	–	–	–	–
	FLB1	–	0.2	–	–	–	–	–	–	–
	FLB2	–	0.9	–	1.7	–	–	–	*	–
WS total		–	*1.2*	–	*1.7*	–	–	–	*	–
Total weight		1262.3	2691.6	41.7	42,843.6	1458.0	43,650.0	205.5	11,759.8	11,824.7

* = <0.1%

distribution zone of much of the regionally traded material. Malvernian ware and Severn Valley ware were rare to the north and east while the distribution of Derbyshire ware peters out to the south. Thus in the Antonine groups at Barton-under-Needwood, *c* 19 km to the north of Wall, 9% of the group is made up of Derbyshire and pre-Derbyshire wares and much of the common coarse ware compares with products of the kilns at Derby Little Chester (Table 159) whereas at Coleshill, a similar distance to the south, only single sherds have been identified. The group G early pink grogged wares are virtually absent to the north where quite a different coarse ware is found relating to Todd's Trent Valley ware and its successors (1968a), while the earlier shell-tempered ware CTA1 seems to be more common to the north and east (3% at Barton-under-Needwood and Derby in late 1st–early 2nd century contexts) and absent to the south and west. This ware was common on Site 34 (5.8%) but was otherwise scarce. It was also present at Coleshill (3.1%) and Crewe Farm, Kenilworth (1.6%) and further north at Barton-under-Needwood (3%) but was otherwise less than 1% and absent in the south at Alcester and the Arrow Valley sites and under 0.5% at Tiddington. At Derby a similar fabric was present in the Flavian-Trajanic phase (3%, Birss 1985, table 10). This ware seems on present evidence to be distributed from Northamptonshire into north Warwickshire, south Derbyshire and south Nottinghamshire

The early and late pink grogged wares were present in very small numbers at most of the sites from Wall southwards but were extremely rare to the north (Taylor 2004, fig. 1).

That these zones may reflect tribal boundaries has been raised elsewhere (Evans 1988) and locally (Evans 1994, 149). The fall off in Severn Valley ware Evans noted to be coincidental with the putative border between the Dobunni and the Corieltauvi. Derbyshire

Table 159 Comparison of relative quantities of ware groups using sherd count values

Ware / Site	A	BB1	C	DBV	E	F	G	M	O	R	S	SV	W	WS
All Tiddington Sites														
All sites	1.1	14.3	2.2	1.0	*	1.4	1.2	3.5	5.9	54.7	2.4	7.3	4.8	0.2
TG	0.2	12.6	4.3	–	1.2	1.7	10.3	1.3	5.2	51.2	4.1	3.8	1.5	0.2
TD	0.4	10.1	3.3	–	5.4	2.6	2.9	1.1	5.6	53.7	4.6	7.8	1.2	0.4
TR	0.4	2.1	2.2	–	55.6	0.1	3.8	0.3	9.2	21.1	1.5	4.6	0.7	0.2
TK	*	13.0	–	–	–	2.5	2.5	–	7.7	39.2	8.9	23.3	–	1.9
TM	0.1	0.5	1.8	–	81.7	0.1	1.8	0.1	1.4	6.0	0.7	2.6	0.2	–
TW	0.7	2.2	1.8	–	11.3	1.8	2.5	0.5	18.0	53.9	4.2	*	1.2	0.3
Coleshill	1.3	9.6	3.3	*	*	0.6 (NV)	2.3	11.9	14.5	47.1	4.9	0.7 (in M)		0.2
Greensforge	–	16.0	–	–	–	*(NV& ROX)	3.0	3.0	–	–	3.0	74.0	1.0	–
Avon Valley														
D: 1st	–	–	–	–	30.0	–	7.7	–	0.1	19.6	0.6	8.6	–	1.0
C1: 2nd	0.3	2.3	0.2	–	3.8	0.2	8.1	2.3	0.3	22.8	2.7	37.7	0.3	0.2
C2: L3–4	0.1	13.5	7.7	–	0.8	8.2	2.8	1.9	–	17.4	2.1	42.1	0.4	–
C3: L3–4	1.0	3.3	1.0	–	0.4	4.1	1.6	1.0	0.6	12.5	4.1	68.5	0.4	–
Princethorpe Antonine	–	0.1	0.7	–	0.1	–	–	0.3	15.7	75.2	2.2	0.3	1.6	1.0
Barton-under-Needwood	1.9	20.5	3.7	9.1	–	–	0.6	2.8	26.5	25.9	2.2	1.6	3.4	0.6
Metchley	6.9	0.1	–	–	–	0.5	11.3	0.5	–	12.0	4.6	49.1	6.3	9.7
Rochester NC	4.3	14.3	–	8.8	–	1.4	–	2.5	6.2	35.5	10.0	–	8.4	0.9
Rochester Orton's	11.8	12.8	*	4.4	–	3.0	–	1.8	5.8	34.2	10.5	–	7.9	*
Derby														
2: 120–140	8.7	4.7	1.2	–	–	0.6	–	0.4	5.8	45.1	4.2	–	26.4	2.7
3: 140–180	16.2	11.5	0.3	10.6	–	3.3	–	6.6	14.5	16.1	11.8	–	16.8	8.6
4: 180–200/10	13.1	11.5	0.5	25.9	–	2.6	–	3.5	6.9	9.4	9.7	–	16.4	0.2
5: 200–240	21.8	20.6	–	20.2	–	6.3	–	*	9.9	–	6.7	–	5.5	–
6: 230–280	10.0	16.3	–	20.6	–	6.7	–	8.1	0.9	0.5	13.4	–	13.4	2.4
7: 270+	2.1	14.0	1.4	39.8	–	15.9	–	0.2	0.6	6.3	7.8	–	4.2	–

* = <0.1%

References: Tiddington (Booth 1996a); Coleshill (Booth 2006); Greensforge & Arrow Valley (Evans 1996–7); Metchley & Barton-under-Needwood (Leary 1995); Rochester New Cemetery (Leary 1996); Rocester Orton Pastures (Bevan 2000); Derby (Martin 2000)

ware, the main source of which lies in Corieltauvian territory, is noticeably scarcer in the regions of the Cornovii and Dobunni while none of the characteristic types from the Trent Valley potteries of the 2nd century and very little from the Nene Valley kilns was present around Wall.

Ware groups C and G perhaps illustrate the existence of regional and/or trading zones on a smaller scale than Derbyshire and Severn Valley wares, both of which had extensive distribution zones extending to the northern frontiers. The M6 Toll sites seem to have lain on the edges of the distribution networks used by the purveyors of jars in ware groups C and G and only acquired small amounts of them. These jars were generally lid-seated medium necked jars or larger storage jars and may well have been distributed for their contents rather than usefulness alone. Together with Derbyshire ware cupped-rim jars, these vessels are rarely found with sooting in the author's experience. In the case of Derbyshire ware, unlike BB1, the vessels distributed were only one or two forms from a wider range which included bowls and dishes, wide-mouthed jars and narrow-necked jars. Some of these jars may have been distributed outside their core market because of the desirability of their contents. Handmade native jars found at the site of the Rhine fleet in Köln-Alteburg have been interpreted as just such packaging, although in this case distribution was limited to the military areas and absent from the civil zones (Carroll 2002). A similar explanation for small amounts of native pottery (5%) was put forward at the Roman fort at Velsen on the lower Rhine frontier (Brandt 1983, 135 cited in Carroll 2002, 903). Several vessels at *Vindolanda* bear graffiti itemising the contents in some way suggesting the possibility that vessels were distributed on account of the value of their contents. A dark grey storage jar bears the legend 'vessel 8½ Roman pounds, filled 43½ Roman pounds' (Birley *et al.* 1993, 97). Another jar, with a post-firing inscription reading '*Cors...1884*' (Hassall and Tomlin 1988, 503, no. 79), implies the careful counting of the content rather than measurement by volume, suggesting the value of the individual pieces. Although the jar could merely have been utilised by the quartermaster in the army stores, it may alternatively have been a vessel marked up for the transportation of some precious content, carefully counted. The freight of luxury goods to individuals on the northern frontier is well documented in the *Vindolanda* writing tablets. Recent residue analysis by Hamer on Derbyshire ware suggested the possibility of oil or honey storage (Hamer 2002). Honey and 'wine and honey' is mentioned in the *Vindolanda* tablets in a list of foodstuff and in a letter (Bowman 1994, 118–9). At York an increase in the numbers of North African amphorae at a time when North African reinforcement probably arrived suggests that the troops may have brought or obtained supplies familiar to them (Williams and Carreras 1995, 237–8). It may be that other containers less obviously related to specific commodities in the way that amphorae are, may also have been distributed primarily because of the commodity they contained. This would explain the distribution of specific vessels, suitable for storage of foodstuffs, outside the core market in areas where other locally made vessels were available as store jars if such were required.

These distributions may in addition have reflected ethnic groupings within the larger tribal areas. The CTA1 group was common in Northamptonshire and present at a consistent level of *c* 1–2% in Warwickshire, Staffordshire, south Derbyshire and south Nottinghamshire, but rare in north Derbyshire and north Nottinghamshire suggesting a difference in the distribution patterns there.

Although some regional barriers may have existed based on tribal considerations, other wares such as BB1 seem to be widespread, transcending any regional groupings. BB1 was obtained in different amounts depending on the availability of local substitutes as well as on overall availability. Exchange of ideas can be seen in the range of vessels made at the local kilns with vessel types such as tankards, common in the Severn Valley potteries, being copied at kilns in the area, perhaps first adopted at Mancetter-Hartshill, but other types being made with local typological idiosyncrasies. Mancetter-Hartshill clearly continued to be a source of ideas and/or manpower and potteries linked to that industry, such as that in Derbyshire, may have continued to exchange ideas and techniques such as the extremely hard firing of Derbyshire ware as late as the 3rd century. Some ideas seem to cross the boundaries respected by the regionally traded items. Mortarium potters moved freely between Mancetter, Rocester, Derby and Doncaster and on to Scotland, crossing Cornovian, Corieltauvian and Brigantian territory. Furthermore at least one link across these territories survived into the Antonine period and possibly the 3rd century, with versions of Derbyshire ware appearing at Mancetter-Hartshill, Wall, Doncaster and the Derbyshire ware kilns around Belper.

These distributions and stylistic links suggest a complex network of contacts based on ancient tribal zones interplaying with imposed communication networks of military origin with additional commercial possibilities opening up as road systems and local government facilitated both far flung and small-scale trade.

3rd–4th centuries

The proportion of late to early BB1 ware suggested that the level of supply remained fairly static throughout the 2nd and 3rd centuries. Severn Valley wares were predominantly of types dating to the mid/late 2nd–3rd centuries (see above), implying an increase in trade during this period amounting to *c* 5% on Site 34 and rising to 24% on the later Site 19. This pattern has also been found at other sites in Warwickshire (Tiddington, Booth 1996a; Alcester, Evans 1994, 145; Arrow Valley sites, Evans 1996–7, 105). Local grey ware production continued in the 3rd century, and perhaps in the early 4th century. The later forms such as the bead and flange bowls, jars with late splayed rims and the range of wide-mouthed jars were principally in the coarser wares, R2, R4, R8 and R12, suggesting that much of the everyday pottery was locally made.

The incidence of Derbyshire ware, possibly produced locally, is very low except at Site 15. The small quantities of Derbyshire ware rather suggest that either this type was not locally produced or that its production was a short-lived venture. The dating of contexts on Sites 15, 19 and 29 containing Derbyshire ware is consistently late, falling in the 3rd century. The ware is associated with late BB1 jars with splayed rims (Gillam 1976, nos 8–11), BB1 jars with obtuse lattice burnish, bead and flange bowls and reeded hammerhead mortaria dating to the mid-3rd to mid-4th century. Wall is on the edge of the distribution of Derbyshire ware

There were more fine wares dating to the 3rd–4th centuries than previously, but the numbers were still very small. These include Nene Valley colour coated ware beakers of 3rd–mid-4th century type and late 3rd–4th century bowl fragments, a Hadham flagon, as many as four Oxfordshire red colour-coated bowls and one mortarium and a funnel neck beaker in an unsourced colour-coated ware. These come from different tribal areas but, like the samian ware they replaced, may represent a similar level of trade which crossed such boundaries in all periods.

The connection represented by the early pink grogged wares was continued by the presence of late pink grogged ware in small numbers but the early group CTA1 wares were superseded by south Midlands shelly wares. Their presence here and in Leicestershire contrasts with relative scarcity to the north in the Trent Valley and Nottinghamshire where their place is taken by Dales ware, Derbyshire ware and locally produced grey ware lid seated jars. This distribution pattern contrasts with that of the earlier fabric CTA1 which was found in similar quantities in Nottinghamshire. At

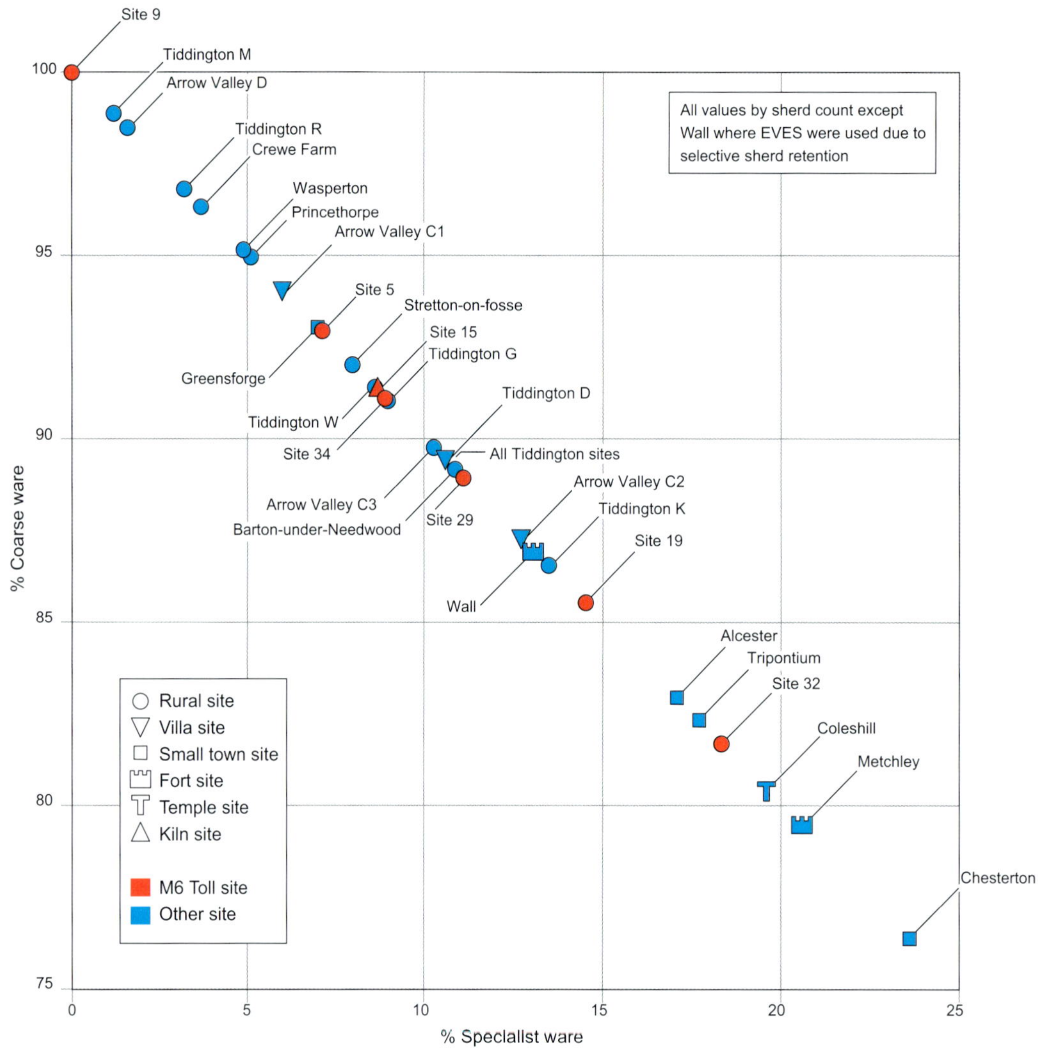

Fig. 206 Ratio of coarse wares to specialist and fine wares on M6 Toll sites (except Sites 12 and 13) and other Warwickshire, Staffordshire and Derbyshire sites

Coleshill and site C2 in the Arrow Valley this fabric was considered one of the most important late fabrics (9.3% and over 7% respectively) and the relatively low numbers on the M6 Toll sites reflect the absence of very late Roman groups. The very small numbers of late shell-tempered fabrics at Site 19 compared with Site 29 were consistent with the earlier date range, in the late 2nd–3rd centuries, of most of the groups on the former site. The mortaria in this period came from local kilns and from Mancetter-Hartshill although it is difficult to distinguish how many came from each source (see above).

Compared with 3rd century groups from Alcester, the sites around Wall lack the large Severn Valley and Oxfordshire kiln contributions. Nene Valley vessels are twice as common as Oxfordshire vessels, whereas at Alcester and the Arrow Valley sites this situation is reversed and the fine wares were further augmented with brown slipped fine wares from the south-west (Ferguson 2001, 47 and table 124; Evans 1996–7, table 14). At Coleshill, Oxfordshire fine wares were only present in very small quantities, possibly with some of the south-western brown slip ware, and were found only in 4th century groups, whereas rather more Nene Valley fine ware was identified (Booth 2006). To the north and east sites were dominated by pottery belonging to the umbrella group of East Midlands burnished ware (Todd 1968b), with a large Nene Valley contribution and small amounts of Oxfordshire colour-coated wares in the 4th century. To the north-west Derbyshire ware was used for coarse ware jars and to the east Dales ware and south Midlands shelly wares occurred. Thus the sites around Wall retain the frontier characteristics observable in the 2nd century in the later Roman period, with the difference that large scale fine ware manufacturers, now situated within the province, supplied colour-coated table wares replacing the earlier imported samian ware.

Status and function – regional patterns

Pottery wares

Booth (1991) has examined the character and status of sites using the ratio of coarse wares to fine and specialist wares with some success in Warwickshire while Evans has carried our similar analyses using the ratios of

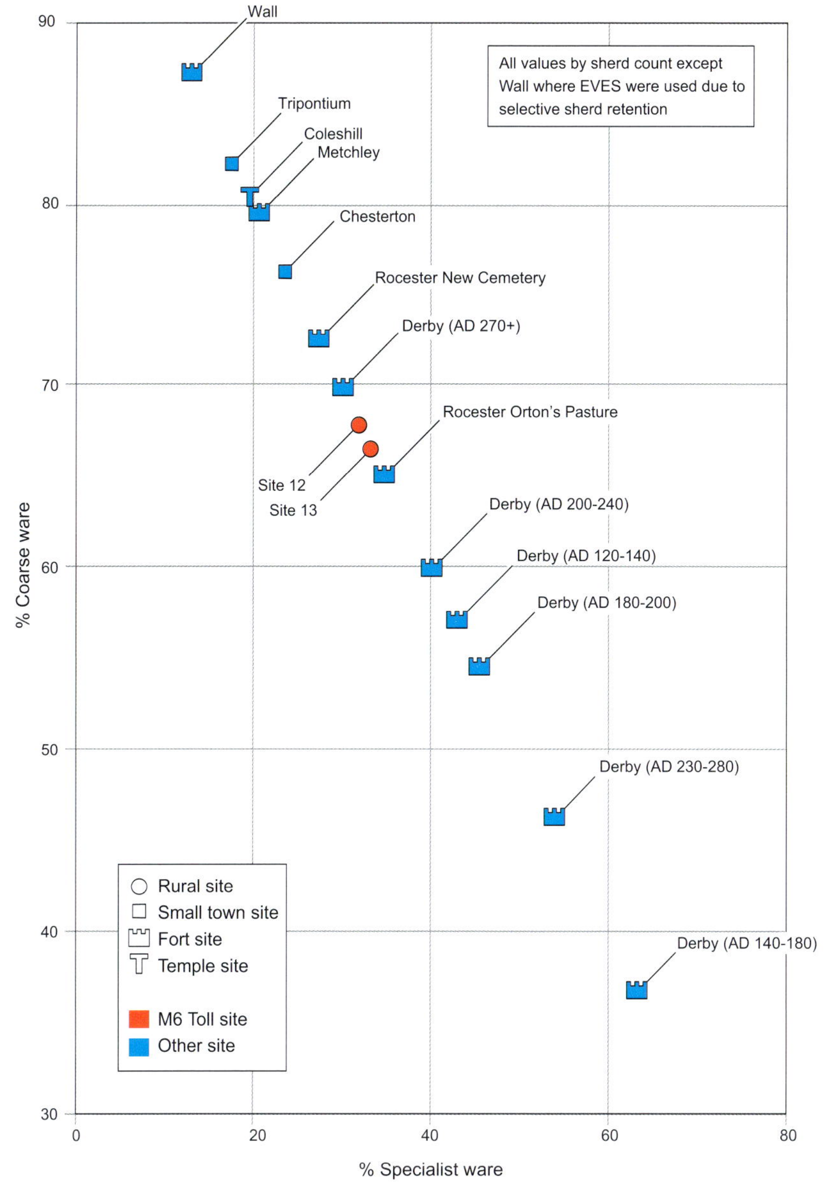

Fig. 207 Ratio of coarse wares to specialist and fine wares on M6 Toll Sites 12 and 13 and small towns and forts in the region

different vessels types such as table ware and kitchen ware (1993; 2001). Both methods have been examined here with significant results.

Booth's fine and specialist wares comprise samian, fine wares, amphorae, mortaria and white and white-slipped wares. Combining data from the present sites with his data and evidence from more recently excavated sites, some 30 groups were plotted using the ratios of coarse to fine/specialist wares (Figs 206–7). The distribution of sites shows a near continuum of sites with rural sites ranging from 0–14% fine and specialist wares, small towns at *c* 15–18% and military based sites *c* 23–63%. It should be noted that the data from Wall fort rely on a group in which selective retention was clearly practised by Greenfield (Leary 1995–6, 26). The quantification was, therefore, limited to estimated vessel equivalents since rejection of undiagnostic body sherds by the excavator made any other method of quantification meaningless. In addition the samian from this excavation was not quantified and therefore could not be included in the quantification.

Although the spread of sites forms a continuum (Fig. 206), fine and specialist wares are significantly more common on the fort sites (Fig. 207). The large numbers of the fine and specialist ware group at Derby Little Chester may reflect the production of mortaria, probably flagons and also fine wares such as glazed ware vessels at the kilns there. Derby seems to have acquired more colour-coated wares than the Warwickshire and Staffordshire forts. This is principally due to the influx of Nene Valley wares in the mid/late 2nd century onwards, a period not included in the assemblages shown for the Warwickshire and Staffordshire forts and a ware not well represented in Warwickshire until the late 3rd–4th centuries (Booth 1996a). However even in the early–mid-2nd century groups Derby had *c* 2% more colour-coated ware, from Gaul or the Rhineland, than the groups from Rocester, Staffordshire.

It is noticeable that in this analysis, Site 12, the cemetery, and Site 13, a site yielding mortarium wasters, lie closest to the fort sites, with more fine and specialist wares than the small towns and the temple site at Coleshill (Fig. 207). The concentration of this group on Site 13 is largely explained by the mortaria wasters and may be dismissed in terms of indicating anything other than a specialist function for the site.

The cemetery group has functional aspects that would tend to increase the fine/specialist ware component, particularly reflecting the heavy use of flagons and table wares such as samian in funerary rites and memorial meals. Whether the larger proportion of these fine wares on the site also indicates the higher status of those being buried is difficult to determine in the absence of comparable data from the fort and *vicus* at Wall itself. It may be that the rural population were prepared to give of their best ceramics to the funerary rituals. White wares amounted to a mere 3% of the assemblage from Site 34 during the period in which its use was at its height.

The relative quantity of samian on Site 12 is similar to that on Site 29 although nearly twice that on Site 34. It is generally half that from the fort sites except Metchley, a group which Hancocks notes lacked high status wares and was not distinctively military in character (2004, 66). The low level at Derby during phase 2 has been identified as part of a widespread shortage of Hadrianic samian in groups from Derby (Dickinson 1985, 79; 2000, 161). Certainly the Site 12 cemetery has considerably less samian than was recorded in the grave fills and cremations pits at Derby Racecourse at a similar period (Birss 1985, table 20, full quantification of the samian not carried out). At Derby burnt samian sherds incorporated into later inhumation graves were common and ranged in date from the Flavian–Trajanic period to the late 2nd or early 3rd century. Without contemporary quantified material from the Wall fort and *vicus* it is difficult to evaluate the status of the mourners and the dead on Site 12. The group has some similarities with the rural settlements around it and some marked contrasts with the cemetery at the neighbouring fort at Derby.

The group from Wall (excluding the samian, see above) lies very close to the M6 Toll group when considered all together. This may indicate that the non-samian pottery from sites in the surrounding hinterland was very close in character to that from the fort site. This would in turn suggest that in some areas of the *vicus* and fort, samian might be the only ceramic element which would characterise the area as military. When the samian is excluded from the other fort site quantifications (Fig. 208) Wall still has a relatively low level of fine and specialist wares, although it now lies closer to fort sites at Rocester and Metchley. While the group from the fort annexe at Metchley was not considered distinctively military in character, the Rocester R1 group from the New Cemetery came from the area of the fort and together with Wall these may indicate that military installations in the region had less access to fine and specialist wares than the fort at Derby to the north. By contrast, the temple site at Rocester, Orton's Pasture yielded a similar ratio of fine and specialist wares to coarse wares as found at Derby, suggesting that the function of this site, like that of Site 12, demanded the procurement of a greater quantity of fine and specialist wares than was available at the New Cemetery site.

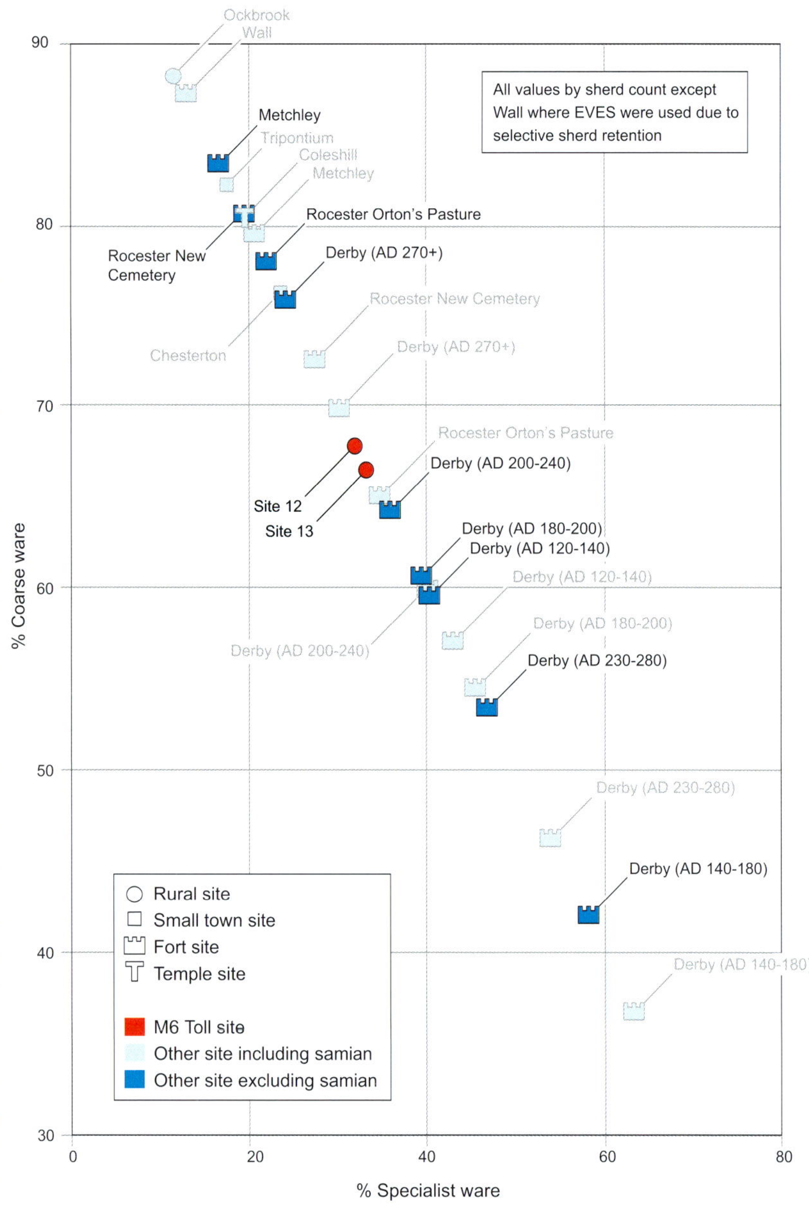

Fig. 208 As Fig. 207 but with fort assemblages shown excluding samian

The small towns at Alcester, Chesterton and *Tripontium* along with the Coleshill temple site lie between the fort group and the rural settlements. Site 19 lies nearest these in overall terms but Site 29 had more than twice as much samian ware as Site 19, whereas the latter had more white wares, amphorae and mortaria. The greater quantity of samian ware at Site 29 is likely to reflect the earlier phase of occupation there, lacking on Site 19. It could be argued that Site 19 had an inflated number of mortaria because of the ready availability of such vessels. However, the relative quantity of amphora sherds on the site was the highest for any M6 Toll site. Although probably deriving from a handful of vessels, most of the sherds coming from a single feature, these represent contact with a commodity that was clearly very important to the Romans, for both cooking and bathing. Its presence in contexts dated to the late 2nd–mid-3rd centuries, a time when the military character of Wall is certainly in doubt and when, therefore, amphorae were perhaps not being delivered there, suggests either some effort on the part of the inhabitants of Site 19 to obtain amphorae, or a high degree of curation of the large and useful containers long after their contents had gone. None of the amphorae show signs of secondary usage and although it has been suggested that the amphora sherds on some rural sites may have come as empty containers (Evans 2002a, 27), this is not necessarily the case. The putative higher status of Site 19 is further supported by the larger number of bowls and dishes there compared with Site 29.

Sites 19, 29, 34, 5 and 15 form a cluster of sites with *c* 6–13% of their assemblages made up of fine and

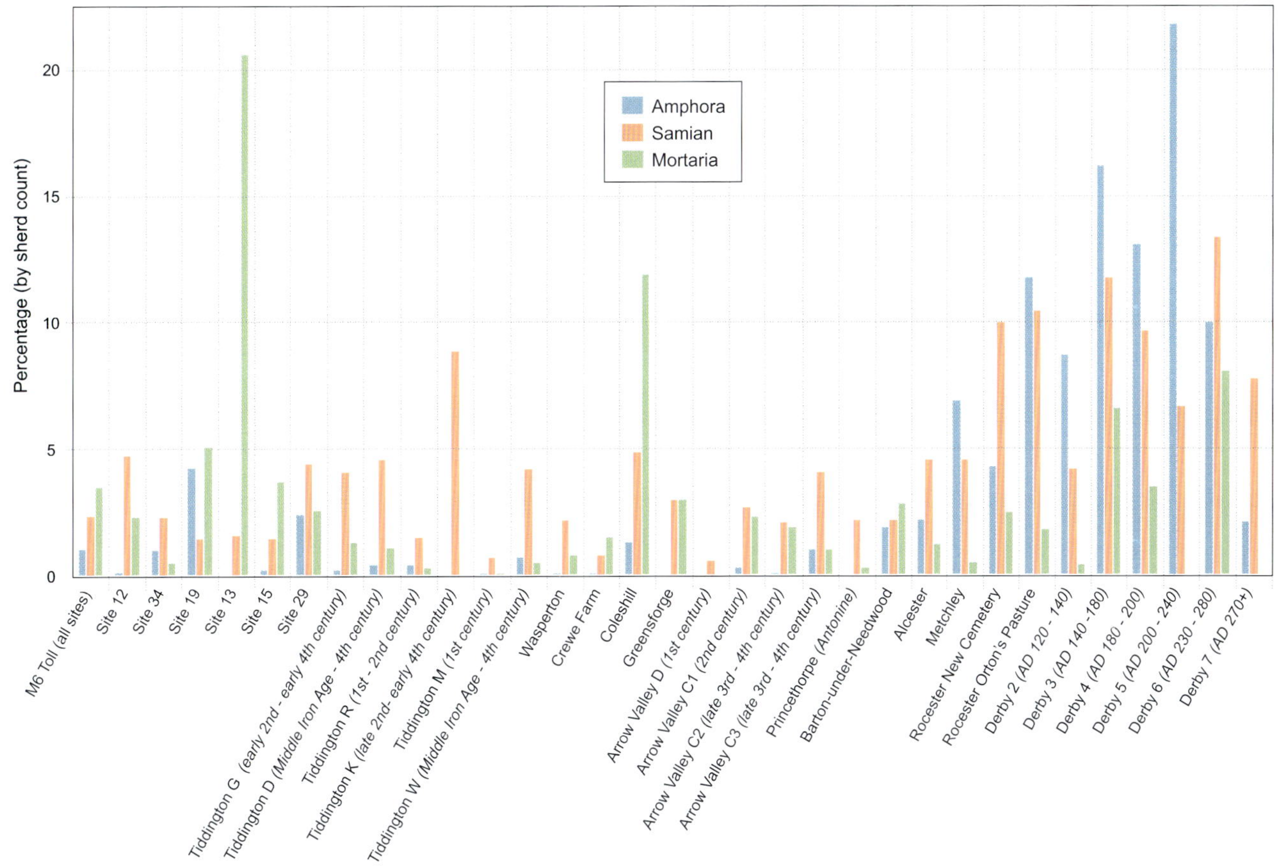

Fig. 209 Quantities of amphorae, samian and mortaria sherds, quantified by sherd count as common to all sites

specialist wares. Other sites in this group include the Salford Priors villa site in the Arrow Valley, Tiddington, Barton-under-Needwood and Stretton-on-Fosse. A group of sites characterised by a more restricted range of wares with fewer specialist and fine wares seems to be represented by rural settlements at Wasperton, Princethorpe, Tiddington sites TR and TM (both intensively occupied in the 1st century) and the 1st century site of Arrow Valley site D.

Differences within ceramic groups from civilian settlements were partially linked to changes on the site. For example the construction of more romanised buildings in the Arrow Valley was accompanied by an increase in fine and specialist wares. Sometimes chronology is a determining factor (*cf.* Booth 2004, 39–40); for example at Tiddington the sites with predominantly 1st century occupation fall outside this group. Wasperton and Princethorpe lie on the border of the civilian group with moderate amounts of fine and specialised wares. At Princethorpe the fine and specialist ware group is made up of white ware, mortaria and samian; amphorae and fine wares were scarce or absent. Similarly Wasperton lacks amphorae and both fine wares and white wares were scarce (Booth 1991, fig. 2). The 'middle' group had consistently large quantities of samian ware, and amphora sherds were usually present as were a small number of fine wares.

By separating out some of the fine and specialist wares, amphorae can be seen as a good status indicator as has been observed elsewhere (Fig. 209, Evans 2001, fig. 11; Booth 2004, 49). It is noticeable that the rural settlement at Barton-under-Needwood, Staffordshire, with nearly 2% of its assemblage made up of amphora sherds, has nearly as high a representation of these as the small town of Alcester. Compared with figures for sites in Nottinghamshire and Lincolnshire, this is as high as several forts and small towns. The amphora content of the M6 Toll site assemblages is low, under 1.5%, except on Site 19 and 29, with over 4% and 2% respectively. This places Site 19 higher than sites such as the Arrow Valley villa, Alcester and all the rural sites. The concentration of over 30 sherds from one vessel on Site 19, however, means that this percentage has been artificially inflated.

Relative quantities of samian ware clearly divide military from civilian sites, although the group from Metchley is towards the low end of the range (Fig. 209). Rural sites with larger quantities of samian include the villa site C in the Arrow Valley, Coleshill temple, and several sites at Tiddington. The small size of the group from Tiddington site TK renders this result suspect, but at sites TG, TD and TW samian makes up over 4% of the assemblages. Early sites with a concentration of 1st century activity have very little samian while the remainder range from *c* 2% to *c* 4%. Sites 12 and 29 can be placed at the high end of this range. It is to be expected that the function of Site 12 would result in a larger amount of fine table ware being deposited there, but the result from Site 29 may indicate a difference in status and character.

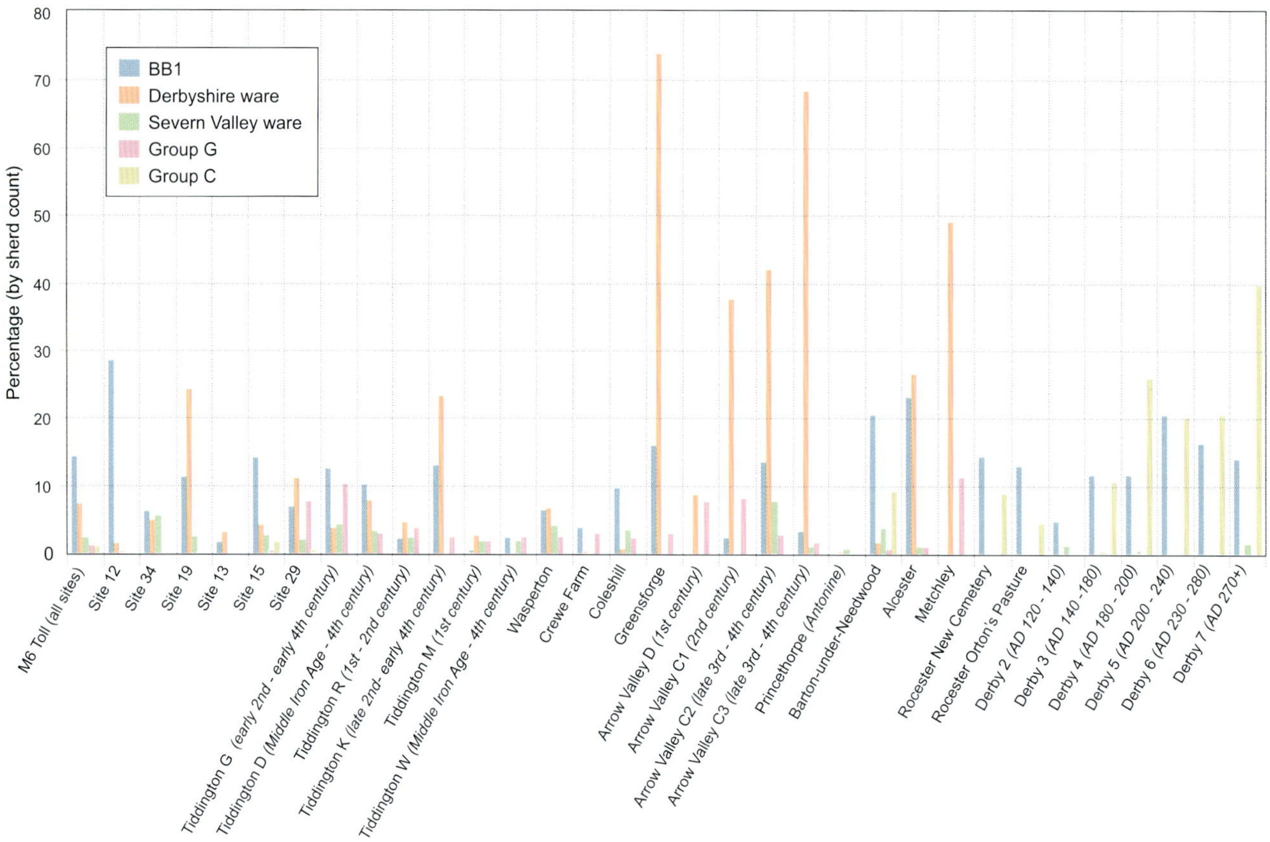

Fig. 210 Relative quantities of traded coarse wares, BB1, Derbyshire ware, Severn valley ware, groups G and C sherds quantified by sherd count as common to all sites

By contrast the variations in quantities of mortaria seem random in parts. Booth suggested that the large number at Coleshill may reflect local availability due to the proximity of the Mancetter-Hartshill industry (Booth 1991, 7). The percentage of mortaria was high at Site 13 and included several wasters. A similar explanation may be put forward here. However, at other settlement sites within a short distance, the mortarium component was modest suggesting that the large amount at Coleshill is either due to mortarium production nearby and/or to some specialist use at the temple site.

Further light on the character of the sites can be gained from analysis of the principal traded wares (Fig. 210). These present contrasting patterns, some perhaps due to local circumstances and others linked to the presence of forts in their vicinity. The distribution of BB1 in the province has a strong link with military establishments and is thought to be in procuratorial control to some extent (see Allen and Fulford 1996 for a full discussion). Apart from Site 12 and the small group from Tiddington site TK, the Warwickshire rural sites do not acquire quantities of this ware comparable to those from similar sites in Derbyshire near the fort at Derby (over 20% at Barton-under-Needwood and 15% in the aisled building at Ockbrook, both in Antonine phases, Leary 1995; 2001) but rather more than the quantities from rural sites in the Trent Valley, Nottinghamshire (5% at Holme Pierrepont and 1% at Hoveringham, Leary unpublished reports for TPAT). Apart from the inflated quantity from the cemetery Site 12, where BB1 vessels were used both as urns and pyre goods, the quantities of BB1 ranged from 6% to 14% except at Site 13 where the large mortarium component distorts the figures. There is some indication at Tiddington that BB1 increased in importance from the late 2nd century onwards and this may explain the small amount at Site 34 (with a mainly early–mid-2nd century date range). However in terms of datable forms, the quantities on the M6 Toll sites seem to be largely constant. In the Arrow Valley Evans noted that a restricted range of BB1 vessel types was selected for purchase and suggests that local products met needs for any other vessel types. At Site 15, despite being a coarse ware production site, BB1 was more common than on any other M6 Toll site except the cemetery. This suggests that these wares were especially valued, more than at Princethorpe, for example, and may reflect access to Roman trade networks related to military supplies and perhaps military style cooking habits.

The other traded wares, by contrast, show a distinct geographical distribution pattern with Severn Valley ware and Malvernian wares to the south, Derbyshire wares to the north and Northamptonshire calcite gritted wares in Warwickshire and some in Derbyshire. These wares contrast with the previous imported and military based BB1 ware in having distributions related to geography and chronology rather than status, and the low quantities on the M6 Toll sites may indicate that there was an adequate supply of equivalent wares from

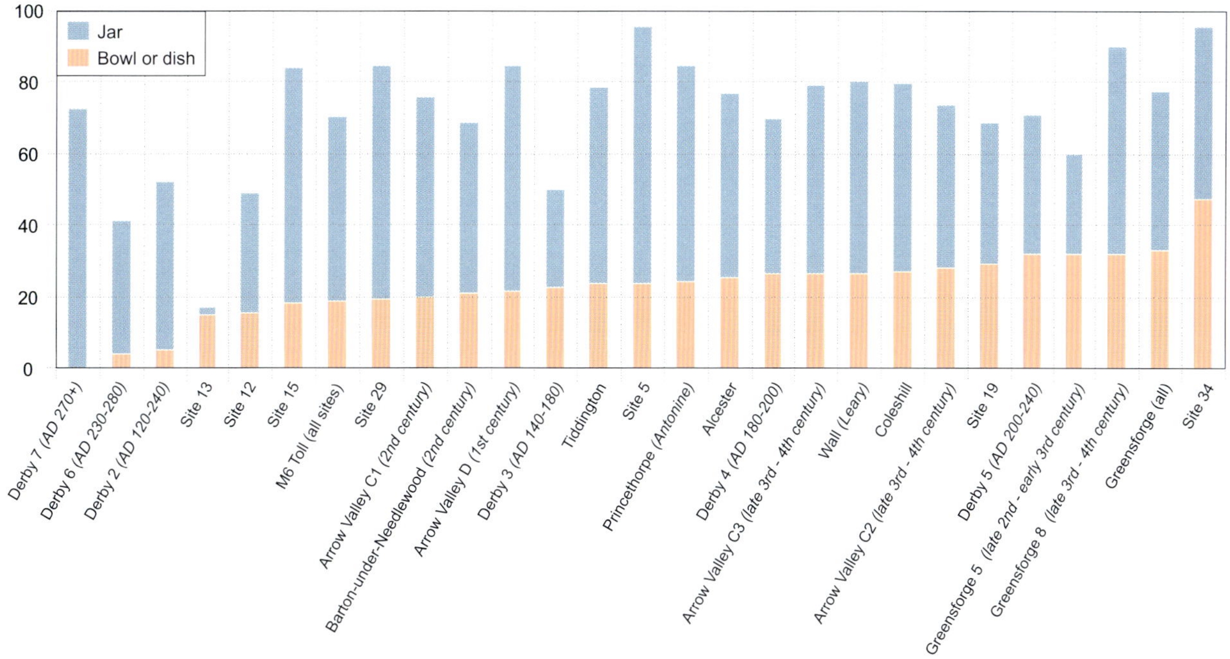

Fig. 211 Comparison of proportions of jars to bowls and dishes (Wall and Derby exclude samian), quantified by EVES

nearby kilns. The rather larger quantities of Severn Valley ware from Sites 19 and 29 compared with Coleshill and Crewe Farm are partially inflated by a number of tankards from these sites and, in the case of Site 19, fabric SV5 which may be a local product. The predominantly 1st–2nd century date range may explain the low levels of Severn Valley ware at Crewe Farm. At Coleshill great difficulty was encountered distinguishing later Severn Valley wares from local oxidised wares, including Mancetter-Hartshill products, and it may be that the overall total of Severn Valley wares should be increased. On the basis of the easily identifiable early Severn Valley fabric O21, levels of some 2–3% were found in the 2nd century at Coleshill and this may more accurately reflect the overall importance of Severn Valley wares at this site. The Malvernian ware from Site 29 was unusual. Apart from Metchley with nearly 3% of its assemblage identified as Malvernian ware and Arrow valley site C1 (8%), there is commonly none or only *c* 1% and less.

Pottery forms

Consideration of the vessel types present on the sites can also shed light on their function or status. Evans has found that the ratio of jars to bowls and dishes can be an index of status and the adoption of Roman eating habits (1993; 2001). Site 34 had the highest proportion of bowls/dishes, more than Alcester and the villa in the Arrow Valley. The fort sites at Wall and Derby would undoubtedly have had a far higher proportion of bowls and dishes had the samian been quantified, but it is interesting to note that in the latest periods (6 and 7), when samian would not have been readily available to make up the shortfall, there were very few bowls and dishes, following a northern pattern (Fig. 211) (Evans 1993). The other sites yielded a range of *c* 15–33% with most of the M6 Toll sites towards the low end except Site 19. Sites such as the temple at Coleshill, the settlement at Greensforge, Wall itself, Alcester and the Arrow Valley villa and Princethorpe have over 20% bowls and dishes. At Princethorpe, however, most of the other vessels were jars, whereas on other sites a wider range of other vessels was present. Site 29 has both a small number of bowls and dishes and a large number of jars despite some indications of higher status suggested by the large number of samian sherds (see above).

A consideration of drinking vessels and flagons highlights several characteristics of the region, some relating to function and some related to geography and perhaps ethnicity (Fig. 212). In this analysis Sites 5, 15, 29 and 34 all have a low level of this vessel type as do rural settlements at Barton-under-Needwood, Staffordshire, and the latest group from Derby. This analysis agrees with the jar/bowl analysis except in the case of Site 34 which falls unexpectedly short. The result for Site 13 is misleading as this represents a single flagon rim. The group from Site 10 is too small for consideration but the beaker, a late import from Trier, may indicate relatively high status. The Site 19 assemblage consistently seems to suggest higher than average status for a rural site. Site 12 showed a large proportion of vessels related to drinking and would have had an even larger percentage had the small jar/beaker group been included. These vessels were not always quantified separately from other beakers or jars on other sites in the region so they were not counted as beakers here for the sake of consistency.

The villa site in the Arrow Valley, the small towns and the forts obtained greater numbers of vessels related to drinking, with the forts obtaining the greatest numbers. Site 19 can be placed with these groups as can the temple site at Coleshill. Princethorpe was not far behind

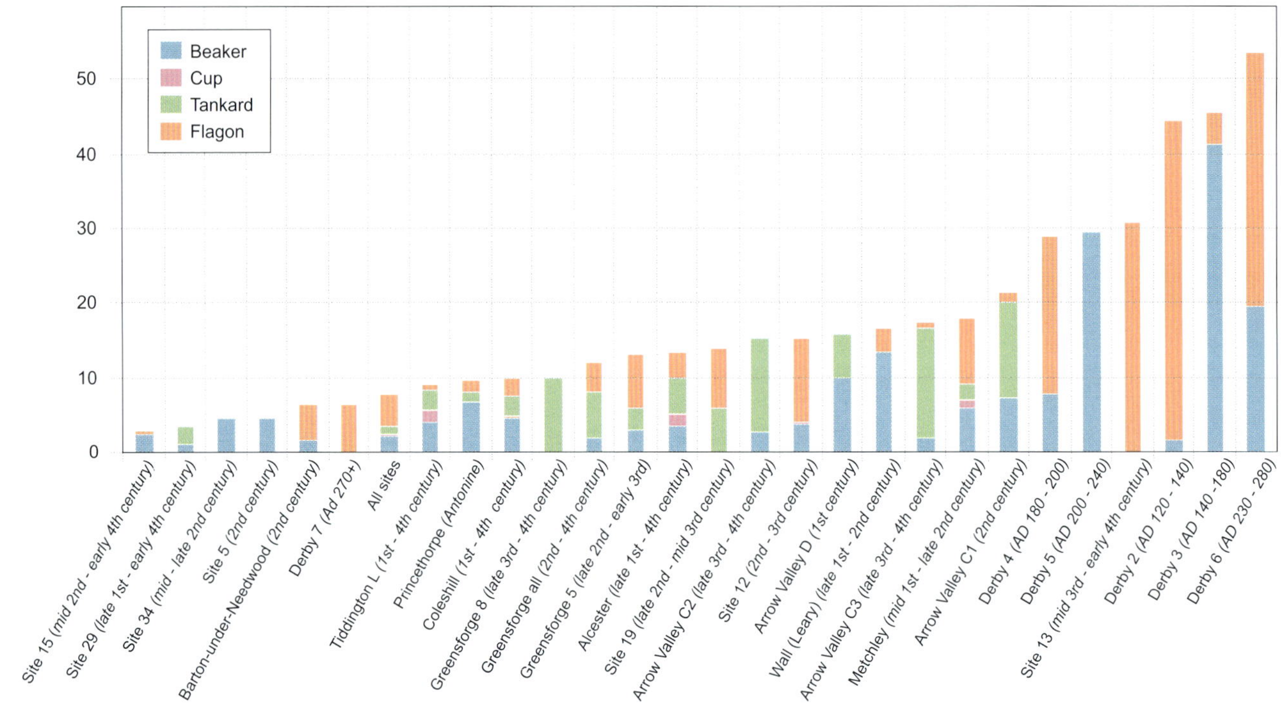

Fig. 212 Comparison of drinking vessel types (Wall and Derby exclude samian), quantified by EVES

these sites. It may be noted that relative differences in the numbers of flagons are, of course, partially dependent on the site chronology since these were most common in the 1st and 2nd centuries. Although not necessarily equivalent in functional terms, smaller flagons may have functioned as drinking vessels in some instances. On Site 12 the coarse ware beakers/small jars seemed to replace the earlier flagons in Hadrianic–Antonine features.

Evans has previously noted that sites in the south and east of Warwickshire and in the Severn Valley were characterised by high levels of drinking vessels (Evans 2001, fig. 7) in the form of tankards and that this may be linked with societal characteristics (Evans 1996–7, 119) with an Iron Age ancestry. Thus the distribution of tankards may be directly linked with a pre-Roman ethnic group living in the Severn Valley where, Evans suggested, 'the consumption of drink, was deeply embedded in social relations and where … drink was a means of acquiring and/or maintaining social standing.'

This is an attractive suggestion but more prosaic functions are possible. Jane Evans has suggested the tankards were used as a measure for dry or wet foodstuff (Hancocks 2004, 55). The sites in south Warwickshire clearly belong to this tankard-using group and tankards become increasingly less common moving northwards. However, at Tiddington, Princethorpe and Coleshill, the numbers of drinking vessels were maintained by the acquisition of beakers in the place of tankards or in addition to the small numbers of tankards. Tankards appeared on Sites 19 and 29, both lying in the southern part of the road scheme, and the quantities on Site 19 may suggest stronger links with the Severn Valley group. At the fort sites at Metchley (despite a large Seven Valley contribution to the site ceramics), Wall and Derby beakers were much more common. The Metchley group may indicate that military personnel actively eschewed the use of tankards there.

At the early fort at the Lunt, Baginton, Webster noted a tankard in dark grey ware of Durotrigan type and commented on it being uncommon (Webster 1973, fig. 15, no. 155). The illustrated pottery from the Lunt gives the impression that flagons were common and small coarse ware beakers and jars may have been the drinking vessel of choice. Beakers normally have a rather smaller capacity than tankards and are predominantly imported or traded fine ware types, or local copies of these. It is noticeable that at sites near Derby, such as Barton-under-Needwood, the number of beakers had not increased to make up for the lack of tankards. It would appear that the high drinking vessel count at Coleshill, Princethorpe and Tiddington could reflect similar societal characteristics to those found in the Severn Valley.

The need for suitable drinking vessels, however, was made up with a mixture of beakers and tankards to a level slightly below the total drinking vessels from Severn Valley sites. By contrast, further north on Sites 15, 34, 5 and at Barton-under-Needwood, the numbers fell. At Site 29 the low numbers may also be due to lower status. Compared with rural sites to the north along the Trent Valley such as Newark (2.2%, Timby 2005, table 2), Hoveringham (1.9%, TPAT unpublished) and Barrow-on-Trent (0.6%, TPAT unpublished), the number of drinking vessels are high, approaching those found at the small town Brough-on-Fosse (9–16% in the 3rd–4th century, Leary forthcoming) and the civitas capital of the Corieltauvi, Leicester (9–16 % in the late 1st to early–mid-3rd centuries, Clarke 1999, tables 12, 15 and 22). This analysis indicates interplay of factors relating to both ethnicity and status, particularly complicated by the marginal position of the northern sites in terms of putative tribal boundaries.

The medieval pottery, by Stephanie Rátkai

In order to reduce repetition in the medieval pottery texts the methodology and details of pottery fabrics have been combined here in one section. After this there is an overview of the similarities and differences in the site assemblages, evidence for dating and the possible significance of the pottery in a wider regional and socio-economic setting.

All the medieval pottery was examined under x 20 magnification and divided into fabrics. These were given generic alpha-numeric codes eg WW01, WW02 etc for whitewares, CPJ01, CPJ02 for cooking pots, IP01 etc for iron poor wares other than whitewares, IRG01 etc for iron rich glazed wares etc. Known fabrics were given an acronym eg Deritr = reduced Deritend ware, Derit = Deritend ware, CCC = Chilvers Coton C ware, Covt = Coventry type ware. In this way all four medieval sites – Shenstone Linear Features (Site 13, Chapter 15), Wishaw Hall Farm (Site 19, Chapter 24), Wishaw (Site 20, Chapter 25) and Hawkeswell Farm (Site 24, Chapter 27) – could be directly compared. The pottery fabrics from the Warwickshire sites (Sites 19, 20 and 24) were then matched to the Warwickshire County Type Series (WCTS) set up by Rátkai and Soden (1998) (Table 160). Those fabrics which could not be paralleled were given new codes and a sample of the fabric retained for integration into the type series held by Warwickshire Museum. At present there is no County Type Series for Staffordshire, although Ford (1995) produced an overview of Medieval Staffordshire pottery. Recent work by Rátkai (2002; 2004b; forthcoming c) produced a type series for southern Staffordshire. Given the proximity of Lichfield to Shenstone, pottery from the latter has been compared with the Lichfield type series. There were insufficient resources allocated in the project to use the Birmingham Bull Ring pottery type series (Rátkai forthcoming b).

Lack of resources has also meant that lengthy, detailed fabric descriptions have been avoided in the overview. For fabrics already found in the Warwickshire County type series the reader is referred to Rátkai and Soden (1998) although this is now in need of some revision. Fabrics not in the type series have been given a general description. Fabrics from Shenstone not previously recorded in Staffordshire have been described in more detail since there is no Staffordshire County Type Series. Fabrics which are very minor components of the respective assemblages have not been discussed in depth. A reference collection of the Staffordshire fabrics and Warwickshire fabrics has been boxed with the respective sites.

To further ease comparison of the four sites, a continuous fabric/form sequence was adopted. However, generally speaking, each site produced a different range of vessel forms.

Possible Early–Middle Saxon pottery

There were a few possible Early–Middle Saxon sherds. A small (3 g) chaff-tempered sherd was found within one of the floor surfaces of structure 200662 on Site 20. A more substantial sherd (Fig. 185, 18) was found within a ditch fill on the same site. The sherd was hard, black throughout and tempered with sparse subrounded quartz and ?quartzite <0.25 mm and a very small amount of fine organic material. A small group of ten sherds (fabrics described in the Site 13 pottery report) was found, unstratified, at Shenstone.

Pottery from Early–Middle Saxon occupation is extremely elusive in the West Midlands. The westernmost counties of the region were aceramic in this period but sites such as Catholme in Staffordshire (Losco-Bradley and Kinsley 2002) and Wasperton (Ford 1996) in Warwickshire show that sites further east were using pottery. Although Catholme and Wasperton demonstrate the importance of the Trent and Avon river systems on settlement, it is not unreasonable to expect other settlements, probably small scale and dispersed, similar to that seen at Grange Park, Northampton (Rátkai forthcoming a) along the line of the M6 Toll. There is no evidence, to date, in Warwickshire of a site with continuous occupation from the Early–Middle Saxon period through to the post-Conquest period. That is to say that the historic villages of Warwickshire do not appear to have early antecedents although there is a case to be made for many of these villages having begun in the Late Saxon period. There therefore appears to be a change in settlement pattern between the Early–Middle Saxon period and the later. This is particularly interesting in regard to Shenstone, since the excavated area is presumed to lie on land marginal to the main settlement, which appears to have been brought into use for a comparatively brief period. The Anglo-Saxon sherds discovered here may therefore be the only tantalising evidence of a change of focus in the settlement pattern.

Post-conquest pottery

The most striking aspect of the pottery fabrics was how few were shared by all three locations ie Hawkeswell Farm, Wishaw and Shenstone. Reduced Deritend ware (Rátkai forthcoming b), Coventry-type wares, and whitewares WW01/WW05 and WW04 (WCTS WW01.4 and WW01.5 respectively) were the only fabrics common to them all. The whiteware fabrics were not in the Warwickshire County Type Series. Effectively, the whitewares formed a regional tradition whereas cooking

Table 160. Medieval pottery fabric concordance and descriptions

Name/Description	*BNRR Code*	*Type Series Code*	*Site 13*	*Sites 19, 20*	*Site 24*
Chaff-tempered ware	**A/S chaff**	**E-MS01**		x	
Early–Middle Saxon ware?	**A/S CPJ07**	**E-MS02?**		x	
Early–Middle Saxon ware	**A/S**	**E-MS03**	x		
Sandy cooking pot	CPJ14	LTS CPJ3	x		
Reduced sandy cooking pot ? Igneous & mudstone inclusions	CPJ10/CPJ12	LTS CPJ4	x		
Reduced sandy cooking pot	CPJ10?	LTS CPJ8	x		
Midlands whiteware	WW07	LTS WW2	x		
Oxidised sandy ware	**CPJ11**	**SH CPJ11**	x		
Sandy cooking pot	**CPJ13**	**SH CPJ13**	x		
Iron-poor glazed ware	**IP02**	SH IP02	x		
Lyveden Stannion B ware	LYST B	WCTS C004			x
Midlands Purple Ware	MP02	WCTS MP02		x	x
Midlands Purple Ware	MP01	WCTS MP10		x	x
Reduced Deritend ware	DERITr	WCTS RS01	x	x	x
Reduced sandy cooking pot	CPJ18	WCTS RS03			x
Reduced sandy cooking pot	CPJ19	WCTS RS03.1			x
Iron-poor glazed ware	**IP03**	**WCTS Sg04**			x
Oxidised glazed Deritend ware	DERIT	WCTS Sg12		x	x
Oxidised glazed Deritend ware ?	IRG02	WCTS Sg12?	x		
Iron-poor glazed ware	**IP05**	**WCTS Sg40**			x
Iron-poor glazed ware	**IP06**	**WCTS Sg41**			x
Sandy glazed ware	**IRG01**	**WCTS Sg50**		x	
Late medieval oxidised ware	LMT02	WCTS SLM10		x	
Late medieval oxidised ware	MP03	WCTS SLM12.1		x	x
Late medieval oxidised ware	LMT04	WCTS SLM13		x	
Late medieval oxidised ware	LMT03	WCTS SLM13.4		x	
Late medieval oxidised ware	LMT05	WCTS SLM14			x
Late medieval oxidised ware	LMT01/LMT07	WCTS SLM20		x	x
Late medieval oxidised ware	LMT08	WCTS SLM20?			x
Late medieval oxidised ware	**LMT06**	**WCTS SLM21**			x
Sandy cooking pot	CPJ09	WCTS Sq04?		x	
Sandy cooking pot	CPJ02	WCTS Sq05		x	
Sandy cooking pot	CPJ08	WCTS Sq08		x	
Sandy cooking pot	**CPJ17**	**WCTS Sq08.2**			x
Sandy cooking pot	**CPJ15**	**WCTS Sq09**			x
Sandy cooking pot	**CPJ16**	**WCTS Sq09.1**			x
Coarse sandy cooking pot	CPJ01/CPJ03	WCTS Sq11		x	
?Warwick sandy cooking pot	F119	WCTS Sq20		x	
Warwick/Coventry-type ware	COVTYM	WCTS Sq20.1?			x
Coventry-type ware	COVT02	WCTS Sq20.2		x	x
Coventry-type ware	COVT	WCTS Sq20.3		x	
Coventry-type ware	**COVT03/CPJ04**	**WCTS Sq20.4**	x	x	
Coventry-type ware?	**COVT04**	**WCTS Sq20.5**			x
Coventry-type ware?	CPJ20	WCTS Sq20.5?			x
?Mudstone-tempered ware	MUDST04	WCTS Sq22			x
Oxidised sandy ware	IR02	WCTS Sq23.1			x
Sandy oxidised ware	IR01	WCTS Sq23/Sq23.4			x
?Mudstone-tempered ware	MUDST	WCTS Sq25.1		x	x
Chilvers Coton C ware	CCC	WCTS Sq30		x	x
Iron-rich gritty ware	**GRITTYW01**	**WCTS Sq80**		x	
Iron-poor gritty ware	**GRITTYW02**	**WCTS Sq80.1**			x
Cooking pot ?igneous inclusions	**CPJ05**	**WCTS STR12**		x	
Cooking pot ?igneous inclusions	**CPJ06**	**WCTS STR13**		x	
Cooking pot ?igneous inclusions	**IP04**	**WCTS STR40**			x
Tudor Green/Tudor Green-type ware	TG	WCTS TG		x	x
Midlands whiteware	WW03	WCTS WW01.1		x	x
Midlands whiteware	**WW01/WW05**	**WCTS WW01.4**	x	x	x
Midlands whiteware	**WW04**	**WCTS WW01.5**	x	x	x
Midlands whiteware	WW06	WCTS WW01.6		x	
Midlands whiteware	**WW09**	**WCTS WW01.7**			x
Midlands whiteware	WW02	WCTS WW03		x	
Midlands whiteware	**IP01**	**WCTS WW04**	x	x	
Midlands whiteware	**WW08**	**WCTS WW05**			x
Midlands whiteware	**WW10**	**WCTS WW06/LTS WW1**			x

References: WCTS Warwickshire County Pottery Type Series (Ratkai and Soden 1998); LTS Lichfield Type Series (Rátkai 2004b); SH Shenstone Type Series Ratkai (this volume, Chapter 15)

Fabrics in bold are previously unrecorded fabrics

pots, with the exception of the Coventry-type wares, seemed to have had a more circumscribed and local distribution. A total of 61 fabrics were identified from the four sites which could be divided into the following groups.

Whitewares

A number of fabric variations within the whitewares were apparent. Fabric WW01/WW05 (WCTS WW01.4) had virtually no iron impurities in the clay and hence fired to a consistently white, very occasionally cream, colour. The clay body contained rare-moderate, reasonably well-sorted, rounded quartz (WW01 was less sandy than WW05 but the difference almost certainly represents a continuum rather than two separate fabrics). Fabric WW03 (WCTS WW01.1) was a much more gritty fabric with abundant subrounded quartz. The surface of the sherds was noticeably more gritty than WW01/WW05 and the fracture hackly. There was also a tendency for WW03 to have an often thick, blue-grey core. Further along the spectrum was fabric WW07, only found at Site 13, which shared many of the characteristics of WW03 but had rather less-well sorted quartz grains and a tendency to fire cream rather than white. This may suggest that different clay sources were used, the one for WW07 having rather more iron impurities in the clay resulting in a less pure white. Also the WW07 sherds were often patchily fired or burnt, so the overall look of what was there was quite different. Nevertheless WW03 and WW07 are clearly in the same sandy whiteware tradition. There is clearly some sort of overlap between WW03 and WW07. WW03 has rather larger but sparser grains but one or two sherds put into the Wishaw Type Series as WW03 are very close to WW07. The basic point is that they are gritty, with a greater tendency to reduced grey cores or indeed reduced throughout the sherd, with only light coloured surfaces. Fabric WW07 seems to be the same fabric as Lichfield Fabric WW2 (Rátkai 2004b) and as a red-painted whiteware sherd from Minworth Greaves (Rátkai 2001a). Fabric WW03 is the same as WCTS fabric WW01.1 and Birmingham fabric WW1 (Rátkai forthcoming b)

Other whitewares, which formed a minor component of the assemblages were as follows:

WW02 (WCTS WW03) Sparse-moderate ill-sorted rounded iron-stained quartz, sparse iron oxide

WW04 (WCTS WW01.5) Ill-sorted, often iron-stained quartz grains, rare red ferrous inclusions, pale pink surfaces, white core, occasionally thin, pale blue-grey core. This fabric was found at Sites 24, 20 and 13 where it formed less than 1% except at Site 19 where it formed just over 2% of the assemblage

WW06 (WCTS fabric WW01.6) This fabric only occurred at Site 20. It contained ill-sorted sub-angular quartz, sparse white ?clay pellets or possibly mudstone and numerous organic voids or partly combusted organic material. Surfaces were white or cream and the core pale grey

WW08 (WCTS fabric WW05) This is a very hard fired, reduced gritty ware, generally firing pale grey with moderate black iron inclusions. The firing and the rather 'grubby' nature of the sherds suggest that they are part of the 'late whiteware tradition', found in Staffordshire, although WW08 was only found at Site 24. Products of the Sneyd Green kilns in northern Staffordshire are part of this tradition and the purplish colour of the glaze on one sherd suggest a date in the 15th century

WW09 (WCTS fabric WW01.7) This fabric was represented by a single sherd from Site 24, a rod handle with oblique 'herringbone' slashing. The fabric is white–pale pink with abundant fine quartz grains *c* 0.1 mm and is paralleled by a sherd from Solihull (Rátkai 2003)

WW10 (WCTS fabric WW06) Again this fabric was only found at Site 24. It is a fine white fabric with sparse, ill sorted quartz grains and sparse rounded reddish-brown ferrous inclusions. The surfaces have a very smooth feel. The interior surface generally fires white but the external surfaces are more likely to be yellowish with reddish patches where the glaze or glaze medium has burnt away. Glazes are thin copper speckled green or olive. The fabric is similar to Lichfield fabric WW1 (Rátkai 2004b)

Vessel forms

Fabric WW01/05 cooking pots/pipkins tended to have angular squared rims (eg Figs 178, 9; 185, 11; 186, 21, 23) sometimes with a grooved upper face (Fig. 186, 20), or squared sometimes undercut flat-topped rims (eg Fig. 178, 7). Similar forms were found in Fabric WW03 (eg Figs 178, 14; 186, 28–9, 32). The same angular qualities were apparent in the WW07 rims (Fig. 102, 2, 8, 12–13). A sharply angled everted rim was common to WW03 and WW01/05 (Figs 185, 9 and 178, 8). More rounded rim forms were found in WW03 (Figs 178, 15–16; 186, 31) and more upright thickened rims were found on pipkins (Figs 185, 14 and 178, 10).

The cooking pot rim forms can be paralleled at Drayton Bassett (Ford 1995, fig. 14, 75–84) and Lichfield (Rátkai 2004b, figs 6.2, 7.7 and 8.16; Rátkai forthcoming c) but are also similar to whiteware (fabric A) cooking pots from Chilvers Coton (Mayes and Scott 1984) eg from site 1, kiln 8 and site 1, feature 4 (*ibid.*, fig. 65) and site 3, kiln 15 (*ibid.*, fig. 70).

Jugs in fabric WW01/WW05 usually had a carinated neck and squared everted rim (eg Figs 178, 11; 186, 25 and 205, 37). A red-painted whiteware jug (Fig. 178, 12) had an expanded, slightly dished rim. Decoration consisted of combed horizontal bands (not illustrated but similar to WW03 jug, Fig. 186, 33) or more elaborate designs (eg Fig. 185, 12). The other main class of decorated jugs were the red-painted whitewares with vertical painted bands of thin red slip (eg Fig. 185, 15), as on baluster base (Fig. 102, 11). Strap handles were the norm and an unillustrated example from Site 24 had deep slashing at the base of the handle and around the junction of the handle to the body. A sherd from Site 19 (feature 190098) was from a carinated jug with incised decoration on the lower section and applied red clay strips and possibly red slip bands on the upper section. Only a small portion of the jug survived but it looked very much like an imitation of a Boarstall-Brill jug (eg Mellor 1994 fig. 60, 3–4). A whiteware imitation of a

Boarstall Brill jug was noted by Rátkai (1990, 46 and fig. 18.129).

One rather plain jug was found in fabric WW03 (Fig. 186, 26) with a plain strap handle. The glaze had originally been a light green but the glaze had discoloured or deteriorated into a thin, mainly blue-grey covering. Odd examples of red-painted decoration or combing were noted but generally speaking the grittier WW03 fabric was more likely to be used for cooking pots, pipkins and bowls than for jugs.

A highly decorated jug was found in WW06 (Fig. 185, 8) which had a design of alternate applied self clay strips and scales. Sherds from a WW02 jug (Fig. 186, 17) show it to have not only had combed decoration but also bands of impressed decoration, possibly made with the points of the comb teeth. Unfortunately the two decorated sherds were small and did not join to the illustrated rim sherd so it was not possible to work out the full decorative scheme on the vessel.

Jugs sherds in WW07 formed only a small proportion of the fabric which was mostly used for cooking pots and some bowls. There were only four rim sherds in WW07 and these were from cooking pots (see above). However, many of the jug sherds were from red-painted whiteware vessels.

There was a single example of a small rod handle with oblique 'herringbone' slashing (unillustrated) from Site 24 (fabric WW09) similar to a handle illustrated by Perry (Redknap and Perry 1996, fig. 39, 579).

The jug rim forms can be paralleled in south Staffordshire (eg Ford 1995, fig. 16, 109, from Drayton Bassett) but unlike the cooking pot rims cannot be closely matched with whiteware jugs from Chilvers Coton. Red-painted whiteware jugs are widely distributed in south Staffordshire and have been found for example at Drayton Bassett, Dudley Castle, Lichfield, Walsall and Stafford Castle. They are also found in north-west Warwickshire, for example at Minworth Greaves and Birmingham. Their most southerly distribution point seems to be Weoley Castle, in the suburbs of Birmingham (see below). No red-painted whitewares have been reported from Coventry and there is no evidence of them having been amongst the output of the Chilvers Coton industry.

A number of sloping sided bowls (Fig. 185, 6–7, 16; Fig. 186, 19) usually with horizontal rims were found in fabric WW03. Other bowls sherds recognisable by glazing on the interior base were noted in fabrics WW01/WW05 at Sites 19, 20 and 24 and in WW07 at Site 13. Whiteware bowls were most numerous at Site 20. Parallels for Figure 185, 6 can be found in Lichfield (Rátkai 2004b, fig. 7.6; forthcoming c) and Minworth Greaves (Rátkai 2001a). The bowl type illustrated as Figure 185, 7 has parallels at Chilvers Coton (Mayes and Scott 1984, site 1, kiln 8, fig 18.10) and similar rims to Figure 186, 19 can be seen in Mayes and Scott (1984, figs 82 and 83 from site 13 kiln 32a–c). One bowl (Fig. 185, 16) is very similar to one from Drayton Bassett (Ford 1995, fig. 18.139)

In Lichfield, whitewares formed the dominant part of the 13th–14th century assemblages. On Sandford Street (Rátkai 2004b; forthcoming c) and at Greenhill (Rátkai 2001c) up to 70% of the assemblage comprised whitewares. Whitewares were an important component of pottery assemblages in Walsall (Wrathmell and Wrathmell 1974–5) and Drayton Bassett in south Staffordshire and Minworth Greaves, lying between Coleshill and Wishaw, in Warwickshire. Sandy whitewares including red-painted whitewares were found at Stafford Castle (Rátkai forthcoming i), although it is not possible to say with any certainty what their relative frequency was, since the deposits in which they occurred were very mixed and disturbed with a high residual component. Whitewares were also present but not in any great quantity at Brewood, Staffordshire (Rátkai 2004a) and at Wolverhampton. At Old Hall Street Wolverhampton (Rátkai forthcoming h) a red-painted whiteware handle was identical in form to Figure 185, 15 and also paralleled by a handle from Drayton Bassett (Ford 1995, fig. 16 113).

At the Bull Ring, Birmingham (Rátkai forthcoming b), in Phase 1 (predominantly 13th–14th centuries) the proportion of whitewares across three sites and seven areas varies considerably, from just under 2.5% to 15.5%, but generally forms *c* 5–8% of the assemblages. Most of the town's ceramic needs seem to have been met in this period by Deritend wares, which were made in the historic centre of Birmingham. A small proportion of the whitewares was made up of red-painted whiteware jugs.

At Weoley Castle, a defended moated site in what is now the southern suburbs of Birmingham, whitewares, especially whiteware jugs formed a much higher proportion of the assemblage (pers. obs.). Both highly decorated and red-painted whiteware jugs were present. However, the evidence from Weoley should be treated with a certain amount of caution since a substantial amount of the material was recovered before the Second World War, by workmen during clearance activities, so the highly decorated pieces and particularly the lighter bodied fabrics were more likely to be seen and retained. At Kings Norton (Rátkai 2000), a prosperous village, now part of the southern suburbs of Birmingham, whitewares were not an important component of the assemblage, suggesting that there was some bias operating which made the whitewares a feature of the Birmingham and, in particular, Weoley Castle assemblages. Weoley Castle was a demesne site of the de Somerys, barons of Dudley in the 13th and 14th centuries (J. Hunt, pers. comm.) and Birmingham came under the lordship of the de Birminghams, a cadet branch of the family of the lords of Dudley. Dudley itself lies in southern Staffordshire where there is a strong likelihood that some whitewares were manufactured. The marked presence of whitewares at Weoley Castle is therefore rather interesting and suggests that, in this case at least, pottery supply was in part influenced by seigneurial factors. The de Birminghams, despite familial and tenurial links with the Barons of Dudley, seemed not to have maintained particularly close connections with them (J. Hunt, pers. comm.). However, Birmingham did have important industrial ties with the Black Country, in southern Staffordshire, which supplied raw materials, particularly iron, to the medieval town. In addition, glazed Deritend ware, made in the historic heart of Birmingham, often had white slip decoration. It is thought that the white clay for the slip also came from the Coal Measure Clays of the Black Country. The presence, then, of whitewares in Birmingham and at Weoley Castle illustrates some of the different factors involved in the supply of pottery in the medieval period.

At Coventry exact figures are not easily available regarding the proportion of whitewares present. As far as can be ascertained no red-painted whitewares have been found here and the majority of the whitewares are thought to derive from Chilvers Coton. However, there has been a tendency to ascribe all Coventry whitewares to Chilvers Coton, leading to the obvious circular arguments. Some of the whitewares illustrated by Perry (Redknap and Perry 1996) are not described as having a white fabric and the majority of illustrated examples are in forms unparalleled at Chilvers Coton. It is possible that some of the whitewares, then, are not from the Nuneaton area and may more closely match the whitewares found on the M6 Toll sites.

The heartland for red-painted whitewares seems to lie in an area bounded by Lichfield to the north, Walsall or possibly Wolverhampton (to date there have been insufficiently large assemblages to deduce the relative importance of whitewares) to the west and Minworth Greaves (or possibly Coleshill) to the east. The less sandy whitewares such as WW01/WW05 seem to be most frequent in the Wishaw-Minworth Greaves area. Although whitewares are an important component of Coventry assemblages, the absence of red-painted whitewares would seem to indicate a different source of supply, almost certainly Chilvers Coton, for most of its whiteware.

Coventry-type wares

The terms 'Coventry' and 'Coventry-type' wares have been used in this report primarily to denote sandy, wholly black, wholly dark grey or brown with dark grey core cooking pots with clearly visible soft brown, red-brown or red inclusions. Coventry wares were first discussed in detail by Wright (1982, Much Park Street, fabrics 3 and 4) and Redknap (1985). Wright and Redknap describe the fabric in differing terms with Wright's 'dark red clay pellets' becoming in Redknap 'reddish-brown sandstone', a description which does not alter in the later Broadgate East report (Redknap 1996). The red-brown inclusions noted by this author do not have the appearance of sandstone, since they have an earthy consistency with no obvious granular structure which one would expect to find in a sandstone. They may be clay pellets, but if so some of them seem rather amorphous with an ill-defined structure. In the absence of any petrological research the true nature of these inclusions has yet to be established.

Redknap (*ibid.*) dates Coventry ware to the mid-12th–mid-13th centuries. However, this dating rests mainly on Coventry wares being found at Brandon Castle (constructed mid-12th century and destroyed *c* 1266) with no well stratified sequence from Coventry itself. At Broadgate East, Phases 1 and 2 did not contain Coventry Ware cooking pots sherds although Coventry tripod pitcher sherds were present in Phase 2. The Coventry ware cooking pots in Phase 3 were found associated with varying amounts of Chilvers Coton A ware and sometimes with Cannon Park ware. In short, there appears to be a hiatus at Broadgate East between early ceramic groups which contained calcareous-tempered wares, amongst others, and the later groups with Chilvers Coton A, since there were no groups where Coventry ware cooking pots were the dominant fabric and Chilvers Coton A was not present. Wright (*op. cit.*) suggests that Coventry ware is early at Much Park Street and dates it 12th–mid-13th centuries.

Moreover, although Coventry wares were certainly the dominant pottery type in Coventry, there is, as yet, nothing to tie their manufacture to Coventry itself, the nearest possible site being Potters Harnall to the north of the city. However, the preponderance of this ware in Coventry does indicate a fairly local source of production. Fabrics which are very similar to Coventry wares have been found in Warwick (Rátkai 1990; 1992a) and it seems quite possible that a number of production sites existed to the south of Coventry (where later the Cannon Park industry was located) which would have been ideally placed to supply both Coventry and Warwick. In short the term 'Coventry ware' implies a great deal more than we actually know about its production and the term 'Coventry-type ware' has been used throughout in this report.

Some credence to the idea that there were several Coventry-type ware production sites is given by the variations detectable in the group as a whole, a fact also noted by Wright (1982) and Redknap (1996). At Site 20 three main types were identifiable COVT01-03 (WCTS Sq20.2-20.4) with COVT03 (WCTS Sq20.4) not previously present in the county type series. At Site 24, due to exigencies of time it was not possible to examine all the Coventry-type ware sherds under the microscope. A random sample of these sherds examined under x20 magnification seemed most closely to resemble COVT02 (WCTS Sq20.2). However there were two further sub-groups at Site 24. The first, coded COVT04 (WCTS Sq20.5), had quite light surfaces (although these had been heavily abraded) fired to pale grey or light reddish-orange or pinkish-orange. These usually had very abundant red (or black/dark grey in the case of reduced sherds) ?ferrous/argillaceous inclusions. However the vessel forms in COVT04 were for the most part paralleled among the other Coventry-type wares from the site. The second group was characterised by a grey fabric with quite broad yellowish margins (fabric COVTYM possibly WCTS fabric Sq20.1, eg Fig. 204, 16). This fabric has been recovered from early contexts at Warwick. These differences in fabric are interesting not least because there is a very real chance that some of the earliest material from all the four sites was found at Site 24 and these two variants may be early Coventry-type ware products. Many of the Coventry-type ware sherds from Site 24 were characterised by an oxidised exterior surface and a reduced dark grey interior surface. This may indicate that they were fired stacked one above another, thus preventing the circulation of oxygenated air to the interior of the vessels during firing.

Nearly every sherd of Coventry-type ware was from a cooking pot. The rim forms from Sites 19 and 20 could all be paralleled by illustrations in the Broadgate East report. However, this was not so with some of the cooking pots from Site 24. The forms which could not be paralleled were Figures 204,10, 12–13, 19–20, 23 and 205, 44. Forms illustrated as Figure 204, 10, 12–13 and 20 were the most common at Site 24. In general the main rim forms at Broadgate East (see Redknap 1996, 38, fig. 11) tend to have thickened or expanded rim terminals. This is not the case with most of the cooking pots from Site 24 where the shoulder-neck-rim is all of a similar thickness. In addition the external profile from shoulder to rim is a continuous curve, a feature not seen on the Coventry ware from Broadgate East. Another characteristic of the Site 24 cooking pots is a slight ridge or facet at the shoulder. A single example of this is illustrated by Wright (1982, fig. 60, 2). The jar form (Fig. 204, 6) is also unparalleled, although the combed decoration is quite typical of early Coventry wares on both cooking pots and pitchers (see Redknap 1996, figs 21 and 33). The jar had a clay body which was black throughout. Cooking pots (Fig. 204, 14 also possibly with combed decoration and Fig. 204, 2) both had completely black fabrics. The black fabric together with the vessel forms may indicate that these vessels are early.

Two sherds from Coventry Ware tripod pitchers, a handle and a tripod foot, were found on Site 24. No other site produced pitcher sherds in any fabric. Coventry-type wares form a minor component of the Birmingham Bull Ring assemblages at 1–2%. They have not been recognised to the south or west of the city.

Mudstone-tempered wares

The term 'mudstone-tempered ware' has been used here (and in later discussions) in the absence of any petrological work to denote fabrics which contained rounded, often ovoid, inclusions with no clearly discernible structure or grain size under x20 magnification. They could be mudstone or siltstone or even clay pellets.

Along with the whitewares and the Coventry-type wares, mudstone-tempered wares formed an important class of fabrics, although they were only mainly found at Site 24. Two fabrics were identified although the main difference between them was the final fired colour of the clay body and it is possible that the two fabrics represent variations in the same basic ware, especially as the clay does not seem to have been particularly well prepared. The use of white slip beneath the glaze suggests that the pottery was produced in an area with easy access to a white-firing clay.

The fabric fires buff, pale pink or pale brown to orange, salmon pink or brown and contains sparse-moderate ill sorted sub-rounded quartz, up to 0.5 mm and sparse-moderate pale brown, brown or reddish-brown rounded mudstone up to 2 mm in length. The mudstone fragments are clearly visible on the abraded surfaces of the sherds. Both glazed and unglazed sherds were present, glazed vessels usually having an under-glaze white slip.

The mudstone-tempered sherds were for the most part heavily abraded. However, odd sherds which had escaped wear or weathering showed that originally the pottery was fairly well made and glazes were a good, strong, glossy green, usually with copper mottling or speckling.

Cooking pots were rounded with angular rims (Fig. 204, 9) which were sometimes thumbed (Fig 205, 25 and 34) or slightly dished (Fig. 204, 8). Cooking pots (Fig. 205, 9 and 34) had finer fabrics than usual and flecks of mica were visible on the surface. This fabric seems to be the same as WCTS fabric Sq22 which has been found in Warwick (Warwick fabric 125, Rátkai 1990; 1992a). There was a small diameter upright rim jar (Fig. 205, 26) which had possible traces of an external white slip. The fabric contained some organics in the clay body and the form is much more Roman than medieval. The sherd was from a medieval context (240148) pit 240401 and the absence of any Roman material from the site tends to suggest that the jar must be post-Roman. The rather simple rim form is similar to that of a pipkin (Fig. 205, 27) from the same pit. The pipkin had a disproportionately large handle which was hollow throughout most of its length. The vessel had originally had an overall white slip coating and presumably was also glazed. The form of the pipkin is similar to a whiteware pipkin from Chilvers Coton (Mayes and Scott 1984, site 1, kiln 8, fig. 18.9). A second sherd may have been part of a hollow pipkin handle (not illustrated).

Two sloping-sided bowls were present (Figs 205, 28–9). These too had the remains of a white slip covering and both had decoration on the rim. Two very heavily abraded rim sherds may also have come from bowls.

Pitchers were also made (Fig. 205, 30–3, 35). The fabric of a pitcher with a corrugated or ribbed neck (Fig. 205, 35) was finer than usual and similar to that of the two cooking pots described above (WCTS fabric Sq22). One pitcher (Fig. 205, 30) had originally been glazed but all that remained was a pale grey patchy shadow on the surface. This was one of the few glazed vessels which did not appear to have had an under-glaze slip. Both handles (Fig. 205, 32–3) had been slipped before glazing. One of these (Fig. 205, 33) was very heavily abraded but the other was in good condition and had a glossy olive glaze with some dark green copper mottles. A pitcher sherd was also recovered from Site 20.

The mudstone-tempered ware was found with Coventry-type ware and four fabric IR01 sherds in what is probably an undisturbed medieval context, 240148, the primary fill of pit 240401. This suggests a general date range of *c* 1150–1250. The pitcher sherds could date to the late 12th–early 13th centuries but the pipkin is more likely to date to *c* 1250–1300. Unfortunately, because of the heavily abraded condition of the sherds it was impossible to determine whether the vessels were hand formed or wheel-thrown, which would have helped with their dating.

The fabric is paralleled by WCTS fabrics Sq25.1 and Sq26. Fabric Sq25.1 was recovered from waster pits on School Road, Alcester and was used for pitchers (Cracknell and Jones 1985–6). Fabric Sq26 was found at Stratford (Rátkai 1992b) and Worcester (pers. obs.). There is very little difference between the fabrics, although the Stratford example had an under-glaze white slip. Further under-glaze slipped mudstone-tempered ware sherds were found at Goldicote near Stratford (Rátkai 2006) where they were recorded as fabric Sq25.1. Fabrics Sq26 and Sq25.4, another mudstone-tempered ware variant, were also recorded at Goldicote. A distribution pattern encompassing Stratford and Alcester seems sensible, but Site 24 would seem too far away to fit comfortably into a normal distribution pattern. However, nearby Coleshill was an important market. A regular medieval market there became the biggest specialised market in north Warwickshire and was known for its sophistication. It specialised in harness and tack, shoes, clothing, cooking utensils, spices and wines (pers. comm. Iain Soden; Soden 2005, 218). Such a market may have proved a magnet in attracting ceramics for sale from further afield.

A sherd of an under-glaze slipped ware with 'pink ?clay pellets' was recovered from pre-Friary levels at the Whitefriars, Coventry (Rátkai 2005). Fabrics 21–2 from Much Park Street (Wright 1982) contained sedimentary rock and fabric 22 sounds very similar to the Site 24 mudstone-tempered ware. Wright suggests that these two fabrics are Nuneaton products (Chilvers Coton fabrics B-Bi variants). However, several factors make a Nuneaton source for the Site 24 ware unlikely (but not impossible). Firstly, the sherds are indistinguishable from those from Stratford, Alcester and Goldicote. Secondly, the use of white slip is not paralleled in the Chilvers Coton report and although the angular rims on the cooking pots are found in fabrics B-Bi and the pipkin can be paralleled by a whiteware pipkin, the pitchers and bowls and the small jars are not paralleled. Thirdly, the petrological description of Chilvers Coton fabrics B and B1 (Williams 1984, 196) does not seem to match the mudstone-tempered ware from Site 24, most notably the absence, in the latter, of mica, sandstone and felspathic rock. However, a Nuneaton source would make more sense regarding distribution.

Cooking pots

Site 24

A further five cooking pot fabrics were identified; CPJ15, CPJ16, CPJ17, CPJ18 and CPJ19. These fabrics formed a minor component of the assemblage.

Fabric CPJ15 was an ill-sorted sandy fabric with sparse ill-sorted quartz up to 0.5 mm, sparse organics, rare sandstone and rare mudstone, the latter two probably occurring as detrital grains. The inclusions suggest that there has been little preparation of the clay before use. The sherds were all from cooking pots. The two rim sherds were from rounded cooking pots with either an everted rim with thickened terminal (Fig. 205, 38) or an everted thickened rim (Fig. 205, 39). Fabric CPJ15 was the best represented cooking pot fabric after the Coventry-type wares. There is no reason to believe that it is anything other than a local ware, possibly imitating Coventry-type ware forms. The fabric was not present in the County Type Series and was coded WCTS Sq09.

A large rim-body sherd (Fig. 204, 1) was found in fabric CPJ16. This was heavily abraded on the interior with a patchy external surface ranging in colour from grey to orange to brown. The vessel form and the firing indicate that this cooking pot must be quite early, certainly no later than the 12th century. The fabric contained abundant subrounded yellow-grey quartz *c* 0.25 mm with rare larger grains up to 2 mm, sparse sandstone generally *c* 0.5 mm but sometimes up to 5 mm, and sparse burnt-out organics. No match for this was found in the County Type Series and it was coded WCTS Sq09.1.

Fabric CPJ17 could not be exactly matched in the County Type Series. The fabric contained abundant well-sorted sub-rounded quartz <0.25 mm and rare-sparse, burnt-out organics. The fabric was coded WCTS Sq08.2.

Ten fabric CPJ18 sherds, from one vessel, came from a levelling layer (below wall 240002). The sherds were black throughout with a fine fabric containing a scatter of sub-angular quartz grains up to 0.25 mm, rare organics and with numerous small flecks of mica visible on the surfaces. The sherds appeared to have been wiped and had slightly lustrous surfaces. There were traces of internal sooting and a shiny black deposit visible on some of the sherds. There were no form sherds, although the vessel was clearly quite small. A further sherd with a thin pale brown surface was found in a layer interpreted as a ground surface. Everything suggests that this fabric is early. The ten sherds were found together with 14 Coventry-type ware sherds which came from the base of one cooking pot and five fabric CPJ19 sherds. The latter had a brown fabric with sparse sub-rounded quartz *c* 0.25 mm, sparse rounded red (?iron oxide) inclusions and sparse burnt-out organics. The sherd surfaces were dark grey with some mica flecks visible. The absence of form sherds makes it very difficult to date CPJ18 and CPJ19. They appear early but the associated Coventry-type ware sherds suggest a 12th century date.

Fabric CPJ18 is similar to although slightly less sandy than WCTS fabric RS03 which appears to be a 12th century fabric in Warwick. There is no exact parallel for fabric CPJ19, although it is similar to fabric CPJ18. It has therefore been coded WCTS fabric RS03.1.

Sites 19 and 20

Six cooking pot fabrics were identified: fabrics CPJ01, CPJ02, CPJ05, CPJ06, CPJ08 and CPJ09, of which

CPJ01, CPJ02 and CPJ09 have been found in Warwick. A somewhat elaborately modelled rim in fabric CPJ01 (Fig. 178, 5) is typical of this fabric and a similar rim is illustrated from Bridge End, Warwick (Rátkai 1990, fig. 15, 64) in fabric 113 which was coded Sq11 in the County Type Series. Fabric CPJ08, a rather standard brown-grey sandy ware, was matched with a Worcester-type ware cooking pot sherd in the County Type Series. As the fabric contains nothing which could be said to be very diagnostic and as there was only a single body sherd the suggestion of a source in Worcestershire should be treated with caution.

Fabrics CPJ05 and CPJ06 were not present in the Warwickshire County Type Series, although similar to WCTS STR11, and were coded STR12 and STR13 respectively. The former was a coarse sandy ware with brown surfaces and dark grey core. Inclusions comprised rare sub-rounded lumps of sandstone up to 2 mm, rare sub rounded quartz up to 1 mm, rare sub-rounded mudstone up to 2 mm, rare igneous inclusions up to 2 mm and very rare golden mica. This fabric is very similar to Lichfield fabric CPJ9, which is thought to derive from the area of the Caldecote Volcanic Series. Rátkai (forthcoming c) states:

> 'The fabric [Lichfield fabric cpj9] is the same as Fabric J11 from Stafford Castle (Rátkai forthcoming i) which is directly paralleled by granitic-tempered sherds from Wolvey, Warks (Rátkai 1998). Sherds from both Stafford Castle and Wolvey were examined petrologically by Dr David Williams who writes:- "Only one of the Stafford sherds has a fabric which resembles the Wolvey material. This ... contains frequent inclusions of a quartz-diorite or granodiorite rock and closely resembles Wolvey (fabric A). Wolvey is situated a few miles to the south east of the Pre-Cambrian and Cambrian igneous formations around Nuneaton [Geological Survey 1in Map of England Sheet No. 169; Eastwood, 1923]. A local source in the Nuneaton area is suggested and it is worth noting that the nearby medieval kilns at Chilvers Coton produced pottery whose fabric contained diorite [Williams 1984]. The remaining two sherds from Wolvey, (fabrics B and C), also contained distinctive inclusions of shale. It is possible that these derive from the Stockingford Shales which outcrop around Nuneaton [*ibid.*]. Inclusions of shale were also a feature of some of the Chilvers Coton fabrics [*ibid.*]."'

Further examples of this fabric have been found at Coventry (Wright 1982), Bascote (Rátkai forthcoming d) and Cotton Park (Denham 2001). One rim sherd was recorded in this fabric (Fig. 186, 27), from what looked like a straight-sided cooking pot with an in-turned rim, similar to those found on 12th–13th century Malvernian cooking pots (Vince 1985). There is no question, however, that fabric CPJ06 is quite different from that of the Malvernian cooking pots.

Fabric CPJ06 is another fairly crude fabric with rare sub-angular and sub-rounded quartz grains up to 3 mm, rare rounded mudstone, rare ?quartzite up to 3 mm, rare rock fragments, possibly igneous in origin and sparse elongated voids caused by the burning out of organic matter and sparse flecks of golden mica visible on the surfaces. The sherds tended to have brown surfaces and a grey core and the fabric is hard. A rim tip was recorded which looked to be from a simple everted rim form. A second rim sherd (Fig. 185, 1) had a slightly angular everted form.

Site 13

The dominant cooking pot fabric at Site 13 was fabric CPJ10 which represented *c* 24% of the assemblage by sherd count and sherd weight. The fabric usually has reduced dark grey surfaces, a grey or brown core and on some sherds yellowish-grey margins. The clay body is poorly sorted. Inclusions are infrequent and comprise rounded quartz grains *c* 0.5 mm, sometimes stained yellow, sparse rounded mudstone/siltstone up to 0.5 mm, rare ?sandstone and rare miscellaneous dark rock fragments, some granular, all *c* 0.5–1 mm. Cooking pots were rounded with angular rims (Fig. 102, 1 and 5) or squared rims (Fig. 102, 3–4, 10). There was one rounded slightly dished rim too small for illustration.

The fabric is very similar to Lichfield fabric CPJ4 where there were exact parallels for Figure 102, 1 and 5 (Rátkai forthcoming c, illustrated vessel no. 1). There are also certainly points of similarity between Deritend ware and fabric CPJ10 in terms of vessel form, particularly the angular rims and the light rilling or combing on the exterior of the vessels. Two sherds originally recorded as CPJ10?, which were characterised by dark grey surface and core and pale buff margins, were matched to Lichfield fabric CPJ8.

The remaining cooking pot fabrics CPJ11-14 were a minor component, forming in total no more than 7% by sherd count or 9% by sherd weight. Fabric CPJ12 is probably a slightly sandier variant of CPJ10. There were no fabric CPJ12 form sherds. Fabric CPJ14 is the equivalent of Lichfield fabric CPJ3. Only three rather fragmentary rims were found in this fabric (Fig. 102, 6–7, 9). There are no illustrated examples of this ware from Lichfield. There were only four fabric CPJ13 sherds and these probably represent a slightly coarser variant of fabric CPJ14.

Fabric CPJ11 could not be matched in the Lichfield type series. It was oxidised pale brown with a slightly more orange core. Inclusions comprise sparse, ill sorted, sub-rounded quartz *c* 0.5 mm and sparse red rounded inclusions *c* 0.25–0.5 mm, probably iron oxide. Seven of the sherds may have come from a jug and a further five came from a cooking pot with a rather angular everted rim. The vessel was too fragmentary for illustration.

The cooking pot fabrics were largely very different from those found in Warwickshire and with several parallels or close similarities with pottery from Lichfield a south Staffordshire source is likely for most of them.

The one exception to this was a single Coventry-type ware sherd.

Minor fabric components

The following fabrics are represented by very few, or, in some cases, only single sherds. For most fabrics there were no form sherds, sometimes the sherds were very small and often very abraded. In view of this, the fabrics are only cursorily described and the appropriate County Type Series reference given.

Fabric IR01 was similar to fabric WCTS Sq23.4 which was first recorded at Solihull (Rátkai 2003) and to fabric WCTS Sq23 which was recorded in Warwick. Two vessel types were present; a cooking pot with a thumbed rim and applied thumbed strip (Fig. 204, 24) and a jug represented by a body sherd with olive glaze spots, decorated with an applied thumbed strip.

Fabric IR02 appeared to be paralleled by WCTS fabric Sq23.1, previously recorded in Warwick. All the sherds were very abraded, so it was not possible to tell if it was a wheel-thrown ware or hand formed. The base of a small diameter jug or cooking pot was present and an elaborately modelled everted rim which was too fragmentary and abraded for illustration. The form is similar to ones from the Bull Ring, Birmingham.

An iron-rich olive glazed sherd, fabric IRG01, weighing 1 g was found at Shenstone. The highly micaceous nature of the fabric suggests that it might be glazed Deritend ware. In addition glazed Deritend sherds were found at Sites 24, 19 and 20. Reduced Deritend cooking pot sherds were recorded at Sites 24, 19 (see Fig. 178, 6), 20 and 13.

A single salmon pink glazed jug sherd with an applied 'crinkled' strip painted over with red iron oxide (fabric IP02) was found at Site 13. Similar fabrics and decoration are known from south Staffordshire.

Two coarse gritty ware fabrics were recorded, an iron-rich sherd from Site 20 and an iron-poor sherd from Site 24. They were coded WCTS fabrics Sq80 and Sg80.1 respectively. A third gritty ware, fabric IP04, with mudstone and other rock fragments was found at Site 24 and recorded as WCTS fabric STR40.

Three further iron-poor sandy sherds were identified at Site 24 fabric IP03, an olive-glazed ware which was reduced a pale grey with moderate-abundant quartz <0.25 mm and sparse-moderate reduced grey ferruginous inclusions; fabric IP05 which had a clean fabric with a scatter of rounded quartz grains 0.25–0.5 mm, occasionally stained red, and a scatter of rounded red (?iron oxide) inclusions; fabric IP06 which had few inclusions and was oxidised pinkish-buff throughout. Fabric IP03 may be a Chilvers Coton C variant and has been coded WCTS Sg04. Fabric IP05 has been coded WCTS Sg40 and fabric IP06 WCTS SLM42. The upper section of an olive glazed jug (Fig. 205, 48) was found in fabric IP05, which typologically should date to the late 12th or more probably the early 13th century.

A highly decorated Lyveden-Stannion B sherd (WCTS fabric CO04) was found at Site 24 (Fig. 205, 40). It was the only calcareous-tempered sherd from the four sites.

Late medieval/post-medieval transitional wares

These wares fall mainly into two overlapping categories. The first consists of wheel-thrown oxidised red, orange or buff wares of varying degrees of sandiness, the second of Midlands Purple wares. However in many cases the distinction between the two depends not so much on fabric type but on the firing. In effect most of the oxidised wares have the potential to be Midlands Purple. This makes the distinction between the two groups a little arbitrary and somewhat subjective. The other fabric in this group is Tudor Green or Tudor Green-type ware. One vessel, probably a lobed bowl, of Tudor Green-type ware (not illustrated) was found at Site 24 and two tiny sherds weighing 1g in total, probably from a cup, were found at Site 19. The sandy nature of the fabric suggests that it was probably a product of the Chilvers Coton kilns.

Late medieval/post-medieval transitional wares were only found at Sites 24 and 19. Three Midlands Purple fabrics were identified which were present on both sites. All three were matched in the Warwickshire County Type Series, with MP03 lying somewhere between a late oxidised ware and true Midlands Purple. Fabric MP01 was a particularly crude gritty brownish fabric with harsh purple or purple-brown surfaces. An identical fabric was noted at the Cross Keys car park, Lichfield (Marches Archaeology, site code CKL05, pers. obs.). Form sherds were only found at Sites 19 and 20. Vessels consisted of jugs or jars (Fig. 178, 21 and 24) and sloping sided bowls (Fig. 178, 22–3). The jug/jar was decorated with crude roller stamping. A very similar vessel with a same fabric but harder-fired with a more purple fabric and glaze was recorded at Sandford Street, Lichfield (Rátkai 2004b, fig. 11, 36).

Fabric MP01 is almost certainly the same as Chilvers Coton fabric D and it was notable that a small number of sherds identified as late Chilvers Coton C ware from Site 19 were a less well fired version of MP01. These too were from a jug or jar (Fig. 178, 17) or bowls (Fig. 178, 18–19). The forms seem compatible with the output of the Chilvers Coton kilns and even the rather odd form (Fig. 178, 19) is perhaps paralleled there (Mayes and Scott 1984, fig. 86, 738.443.204). A particularly thick base was also found in this fabric (Fig. 178, 20).

The contrast between the coarse lumpen look of the late Chilvers Coton wares and the quality of the pottery from the previous two or three centuries is really quite striking. Functionality appears to have driven away all aesthetic considerations. The contrast between the utilitarian bowls, jug/jars and cisterns and contemporary table wares such as Tudor Green Ware and Cistercian Ware could not be more pronounced.

The remaining late medieval or early post medieval fabrics were fired orange or red-brown. All of the fabrics could be matched to the Warwickshire County Type Series apart from LMT06, a very sandy, coarse fabric with abundant well-sorted rounded quartz *c* 0.5 mm, sparse fine-grained pale sandstone and rare, coarser, red sandstone.

Rim sherds were from bowls, two different types of which were represented. The first consisted of sloping sided bowls with slightly everted rims with expanded or thickened terminals (Fig. 205, 41–2). The second group of bowls had distinctive curving rims (Fig. 178, 25). The latter are paralleled at Much Park Street, Coventry (Wright 1982, fig. 63.99–100), where they are illustrated as lids. The subsequent finding of more complete examples shows them to have been bowls, usually with an internal glaze on the base and lower section of the vessel. This vessel form is known from West Bromwich (Hodder 1988–9b, fig. 1.21), Wednesbury (Hodder and Glazebrook 1985–6), Dudley Castle (pers. obs.), Birmingham (Rátkai forthcoming b) and Lichfield (Rátkai 2004b, fig. 15.58), amongst others in the region. The bowl type is always found in a sandy orange-red fabric with rounded quartz and burnt-out organic voids (WCTS fabric SLM20).

It is therefore hard not to believe that all the examples of this type were made in one place and that is likely to be one of the many forms made as part of the extensive late medieval and early post-medieval Wednesbury industry. It therefore seems probable that Wednesbury was supplying a large market. At the Whitefriars, Coventry WCTS fabrics SLM13 and SLM20 (Whitefriars fabrics A23 and A25) were recorded in levels dating to the late 15th and 16th centuries and a Wednesbury source suggested for them (Rátkai 2005, 318). In fact there is a very strong possibility that Wednesbury was supplying the greater part of the ?later 15th–16th century wares found in south Staffordshire and central-northern Warwickshire. It is possible that the Wednesbury industry was able to expand its market as the Chilvers Coton one declined.

At Site 24 there was a tendency for bowls to be made in the sandy oxidised fabrics and jugs/jars/cisterns were found in the Midlands Purple ware fabrics. Roughly similar numbers of bowl and jug/jar/cistern sherds were found here. The greater number of bowl sherds were sooted externally (eg Fig. 205, 41, and 43) with two bowls having heavy internal and external soot (eg Fig. 205, 42). The picture was more mixed at Site 19 with no clear divide between fabric and form. At Sites 19 and 20 jug/jar/cistern sherds were better represented; the bowl sherds were rarely sooted, although five jar/cistern sherds, representing two vessels, were partially sooted externally. The absence of Cistercian ware or blackware drinking vessels is worthy of note. Certainly, on urban sites such as Lichfield the utilitarian bowl and jar/cistern combination is leavened by the addition of table wares, particularly drinking vessels. Even outside the urban sphere, the final occupation of House D2, Burton Dassett (Rátkai forthcoming e) in south-eastern Warwickshire, a declining rural settlement by the late 15th century, was associated with a number of Cistercian ware cups as well as utilitarian wares. However, Bascote, a small village finally deserted in the 18th century (Rátkai forthcoming d) had a late medieval or early post-medieval pottery assemblage much more like those seen at Sites 19, 20 and 24.

> 'In the later medieval material there is a lack of "table wares" eg salts, chafing dishes and cups and "fashionable" pottery such as Cistercian ware and Tudor Green-type wares are rare or in the case of Tudor Green non-existent. The limited range of forms suggests that the inhabitants of Bascote were not especially prosperous, an impression which continues into the post-medieval period.' (*ibid.*).

The impression given by the late medieval/early post-medieval pottery from these sites is that both groups are utilitarian and low status. The late pottery from Site 19 is in marked contrast to the earlier pottery associated with the fish ponds of Site 20 and may suggest a decline in fortunes.

Summary

The site with the earliest pottery assemblage was Site 24. Here the pottery consisted predominantly of cooking pots with only a small number of other forms represented. Sites 20 and 13 seem to have been roughly contemporary and both have a high incidence of whitewares. Site 19 is contemporary with Site 20 but also has pottery of the 15th–16th centuries, which is similar to the later pottery component from Site 24. At Site 24 there was certainly a hiatus between the earliest occupation and the latest and this may also be true of Site 19. It is often difficult to pick out groups of 14th–early/mid-15th century pottery. Under the circumstances it is convenient to relate this to worsening climatic conditions, poor harvests and plague which characterised the 14th century and which were certainly responsible for the contraction or disappearance of settlements nationwide.

Shenstone would seem to be a case in point, with expansion of the settlement in the more favourable conditions of the 13th century followed by retraction and abandonment of the area excavated, in the following century. The situation at Site 20, however, appears to have been rather different, where the unavoidable impression is that the change in ownership of the land after the dissolution of the Templar order adversely affected the site. Without them, there simply appears to have been no impetus and just as importantly, no money, to continue the fish pond complex. Worsening conditions in the 14th century may well have been decisive in preventing the re-establishment of the fish ponds but are unlikely to have been the primary cause of their decline.

Pottery supply in the 12th–mid-13th centuries seems to have been dominated by Coventry-type wares. Sites 19, 20 and 24 seem to form a line marking the western-most extent of an area where Coventry-type wares were important. At Birmingham, further to the west, although Coventry-type wares are found, they are a very minor component. The socio-economic focus of Site 24 seems then to have been on Coventry in the 12th and early 13th centuries. However, this pattern does not seem to continue during the second half of the 13th century and later.

The similarity of assemblages from Minworth Greaves, Wishaw, Drayton Bassett, Shenstone, Walsall and Lichfield in terms of quantity of whitewares, the presence of red-painted whitewares and the vessel types represented is striking and suggests a very distinct socio-economic zone, distinct from Birmingham to the west and Coventry to the south-east. This zone may have extended as far south as Barston (Rátkai forthcoming g) Knowle (pers. obs.), and Solihull (Rátkai 2003), although only very small assemblages of pottery have been recovered from these areas. Why the whitewares seem largely unlike those from the Chilvers Coton kilns is odd, especially as the latter are a major component of the Coventry assemblages. The inescapable conclusion is that there must be at least one other whiteware production site located in the triangular area bordered by Lichfield, Walsall and Minworth Greaves or Coleshill.

The M6 Toll sites, Lichfield, Sutton Coldfield, Minworth Greaves, Solihull and Barston all had mudstone/siltstone-tempered wares and further work is needed on this class of fabrics in terms of their petrology, relationship to each other and their likely source or sources. At face value they suggest yet another north–south link between these north Warwickshire and south Staffordshire sites, but this may be illusory since mudstone/siltstone-tempered wares are known from Birmingham, Stafford, Warwick, Chilvers Coton, Wolvey and Dunchurch also (Rátkai forthcoming f). The source and distribution of those fabrics with igneous rock fragments constitutes another fabric class which needs to be explored in more detail.

The paucity of Chilvers Coton C wares is also of interest. Since they have been found in Solihull, Barston and Minworth Greaves, their near absence on the M6 Toll sites is probably influenced by the chronology of the sites and suggests little activity on these sites in the 14th and 15th centuries.

By the 15th–16th centuries very similar fabrics and vessel forms are seen throughout north Warwickshire and south Staffordshire. This may reflect the growing homogeneity in pottery output or may reflect the wider distribution of products made by large scale concerns such as Wednesbury, which may have stifled competition and put smaller less economic pottery manufacturers out of business.

Building material, by Cynthia Poole

Introduction

The Roman ceramic and stone building material has been examined from five of the excavated sites, where the quantity of material or character of the site suggested this would further our understanding of the settlements. Seven other sites – West of Crane Brook (Site 9, Chapter 13), Shenstone Linear Features (Site 13, Chapter 15), Shenstone Ring Ditch (Site 14, Chapter 16), East of the Castle, Shenstone (Site 32, Chapter 18), Round Wood (Site 33, Chapter 19), Wishaw (Site 20, Chapter 25) and Hawkeswell Farm (Site 24, Chapter 27) – produced only a few fragments each of Roman building material. These were noted in the post-excavation assessment but are not reported on here.

All the material has been recorded by site on an Excel file, together with detailed descriptions of the fabrics. Diagrams of the *tegulae* flange and cutaway types are also illustrated on a worksheet within this file. The fabrics were characterised using a binocular light-incident microscope at magnifications from x25 to x40, though having established the major fabric categories the majority of the material was scanned with a x10 hand lens to enable it to be assigned to a fabric group.

The fabrics

Eight ceramic building material fabrics were identified, one (S5) of which appears to have been exclusively used for fired clay. All were sandy to some extent and types S1–S4 may in fact be gradations or variations of a single fabric or variations in the same geological deposit exploited at different sites.

Fabric S1: Orange, fine silty slightly micaceous clay, slightly laminated, containing a low density of fine quartz sand, red or buff clay pellets *c* 2 mm and very rarely mudstone or quartzite grits up to 10 mm. The soft powdery character of this fabric may reflect the effect of the acidic soils on it

Fabric S2: Reddish-brown, containing moderate-frequent medium and coarse quartz sand; hard

Fabric S3: Orange or red, micaceous clay containing fine and medium quartz sand and red clay pellets <2 mm

Fabric S4: Reddish-brown, maroon, cream streaks, sometimes laminated clay containing frequent sand, fine-coarse including quartz and distinctive white sand, dark red clay pellets, rare sandstone grits, voids of organic impressions often filled with black mineral deposits. Fairly porous and generally hard

Fabric S5: Maroon red, sand laminated clay containing frequent quartz sand and small hard concretions or grits of sand or sandstone and ?ferric deposits

Fabric S6: Red, brownish-red, with high density of medium and coarse quartz sand

Fabric S7: Yellowish-red, light brown with a high density of medium and coarse quartz sand with diffuse poorly defined yellowish red clay pellets up to 5 mm

Fabric G1: Light reddish-yellow, fine silty micaceous clay containing common fine and medium quartz sand and frequent subangular quartzite grits and pebbles mostly 1–5 mm, sometimes up to 10 mm

Variations in the pattern of fabric distribution were not apparent on an individual site basis, largely because of the small quantities of material from some of the sites (Table 161). Fabric S1 is the dominant fabric at all sites except Site 12, where it was not present, but otherwise

Table 161 Quantification in grammes of fabrics by site

Site (W–E)	*34*	*12*	*15*	*29*	*19*	*Total*
Fabric						
S1	218	–	17,823	131	1307	19,479
S2	–	279	2418	5	11	3713
S3	–	4	123	1	1	129
S4	–	248	2177	37	179	2641
S5[FC]	[145]	–	[1100]	[149]	[20]	1414
S6	NK	NK	215+	132	NK	347+
S7	–	68	483	381	417	1349
G1 (CBM &[FC])	–	–	44	[191]	–	235

little could be concluded. However, by grouping the sites into a north-westerly group around Wall (Sites 12, 15 and 34) and a south-easterly group (Sites 19 and 29) a broad pattern is apparent (Fig. 213). The finer fabrics (S1–S4) dominate around Wall whilst the coarser fabrics (S7 and G1) become commoner, although not dominant, in the south-east group. This may indicate the presence of one centre of production in the Wall area and a second to the south. It is unfortunate that too little Roman ceramic building material was obtained from the most westerly and southerly sites excavated on the scheme to be able to test this pattern further.

Discussion

The ceramic and stone building material appears to have been of minor importance at all the sites in terms of actual buildings. There is no evidence to suggest it was being used in any quantity that would be compatible with the construction and use of either domestic or agricultural buildings. At most of the sites there appears to be a preference for *tegulae* and/or bricks, with additionally box flue at Site 15. The absence of *imbrex* indicates that roofing was not a requirement. It is likely that the majority of the building material was acquired for re-use in structures such as hearths, ovens, kilns or corndriers. Brick and tile are commonly found built into the walls, flues, arches and floors of such structures. Most Roman rural sites have at least a few such structures and apart from the *in situ* kiln and oven identified on Site 15, fired clay has been found at all the sites implying the presence of similar structures. In particular at Site 29 there is evidence from the fired clay for the existence of a kiln in the area and at Site 12 a row of six ovens was found.

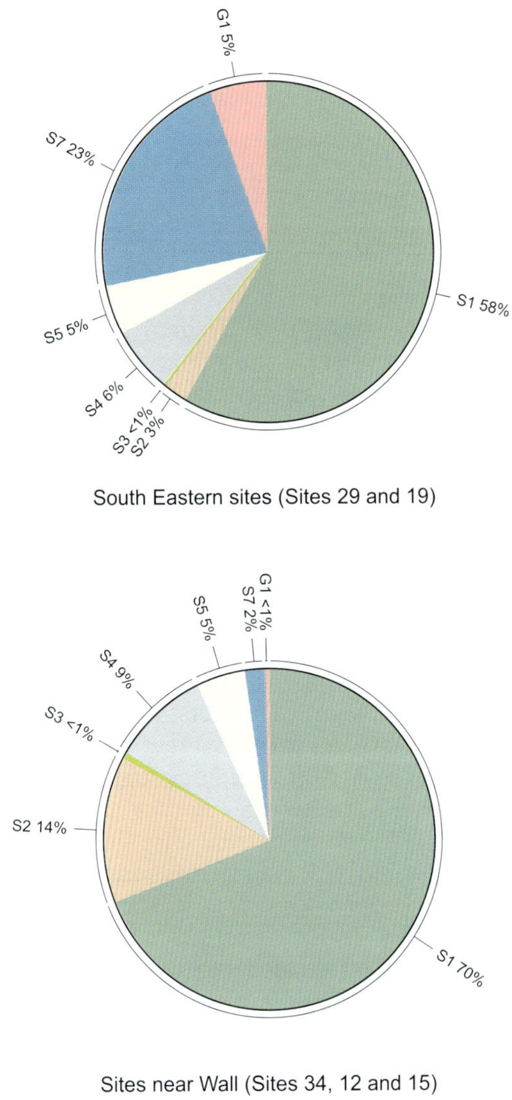

Fig. 213 Comparison of fabric proportions at the Wall sites and SE sites

At Site 19 a different activity is implied by the group of crude *tesserae* suggesting either casual production on site or perhaps less likely the presence of an artisan's workshop.

The analysis of the fabrics has suggested that tile was being sourced from at least two production centres, one possibly centred on Wall and one to the south-east. The forms of the *tegulae* also hint at differences between the south-eastern area and sites around Wall. Sites 19 and 29 produced *tegulae* with flanges of type D, whilst at Sites 12 and 15 a greater variety of flange types was in evidence.

Chapter 29
Prehistoric Discussion

By A.P. Fitzpatrick

Sites and finds of prehistoric date were found across much of the route of the new road. These discoveries range in date from the Mesolithic to the Iron Age; a span of perhaps 6000 years. Their distribution, both geographically and chronologically, is, however, far from even.

Mesolithic

The earliest evidence from the scheme is represented by two groups of Late Mesolithic material from Shenstone Linear Features (Site 13, Chapter 15) and Wishaw Hall Farm (Site 19, Chapter 24).

The largest and most significant of these was from Site 19 where an assemblage of over 1500 flints was recovered, representing one of the largest found in the West Midlands (Saville 1981b). It dates to early in the late Mesolithic, perhaps the 6th millennium BC.

The scatter clearly extended beyond the road corridor. Within the corridor it covered an area of *c.* 100 m by 60 m. The flints were found on a gentle slope on which medieval and later lynchets had been created. Because of this, it is likely that parts of the assemblage had been transported downhill as well as migrating though the soil horizons. However, the fresh condition of many of the flints suggests that any displacement had been minimal.

The slope on which they were discovered overlooked low ground and the course of a stream. The few flints (6) from the adjoining site, Wishaw (Site 20, Chapter 25), may well be related to activities undertaken from this camp as may be material found at Wishaw Hall Farm in an earlier survey (Hodder 1992, 42–3). The single find from Colletts Brook Burnt Mound (Site 40, Chapter 20) to the north might be viewed in a similar light, though it is one of several finds of Mesolithic material identified in a systematic survey of the area (*ibid.*).

Assessment of the lithic assemblage from Site 19 against suggested types of Mesolithic sites, for example a base camp or hunting camp, is hampered by the low numbers of microliths and scrapers. However, in general terms the assemblage may be compared to what was characterised as a winter campsite (Mellars 1976; *cf.* Saville 1981b). Tools were manufactured at the camp and microware analysis of a sample of the flints shows that they were used to work soft substances such as meat and hide and also harder materials such as antler.

In contrast to the large and clearly defined scatter on Site 19, the 98 flints from Site 13 were largely recorded during surface cleaning of the site, from an area *c* 100 m across. The quality and integrity of this assemblage is clearly not as good as that from Site 19 but it seems likely that it also dates to the Late Mesolithic. Some elements of the assemblage, flake cores and squat flakes are likely to be later in date and in view of the Early Neolithic date of two pits on the site, it is quite possible that these elements should be associated with that activity. Whether there was much, if any, overlap between these activities cannot be established.

In addition, small numbers of Mesolithic flints were found at the adjoining sites – Ryknield Street (Site 12, Chapter 14), Shenstone Ring Ditch (Site 14, Chapter 16) and East of Birmingham Road Nurseries (Site 15, Chapter 17). Those at Site 12 also formed a small cluster not dissimilar to that from Site 13. These finds all seem likely to relate to the exploitation of the higher ground to the north and east of what is today called the Wall and Shenstone wetlands, a mire to the south into which Site 13 projected as a slight promontory. Such a position forms a classic ecotonal location for Mesolithic camps and the number of flints of various dates found around Wall (Gould 1966–7, 10; Round 1969–70, 25–7) would also be consistent with this.

Few Mesolithic assemblages have been recorded in primary or closely related contexts in modern excavations in the region (Cane and Cane 1986; Saville 1981b). The emphasis of the most recent syntheses has therefore been placed on material from rock shelters on the higher grounds of northern Staffordshire (Saville 1976), or assemblages found some time ago, such as Bourne Pool, Aldridge, a site that also overlooks low lying wetlands (Gould and Gathercole 1956; Saville 1972–3; *cf.* also Purchase 1972). Some of these finds may be early Post-Glacial in date (Jacobi 1987).

However, as the finds from Site 13 show, material still continues to be discovered in the course of excavations of later sites such as Sandwell Priory, which has yielded over 800 pieces (Hodder 1989–90, 11–21) and Tutbury Castle, Staffordshire (Barrett and Hislop 2004, 59). A large assemblage from Kisses Barn, Polesworth, has also been excavated, though not yet published in full (S.C. Palmer 1992).

However, despite the absence of material recorded in fieldwalking related to the M6 Toll, systematic surveys indicate a consistent scatter of material in lowland areas (Birmingham and Warwickshire Archaeological Society 1998; Deakin and Deakin 2000; King *et al.* 1980; Barfield *et al.* in prep.). It is noteworthy that in the survey of Wishaw and Middleton, many of these finds were discovered close to streams and the largest assemblage of 25 pieces came from Wishaw Hall Farm (Hodder 1992, 42–3) pointing to the major assemblage excavated subsequently at Site 19.

The difficult conditions of recovery during the scheme wide watching brief mean that it is not possible to see how extensive this pattern of lowland activity close to streams and wetlands in the Mesolithic was. The finds from the excavated sites on the M6 Toll are, however, consistent with the pattern.

Neolithic

Features of Neolithic date were found on three sites, all of which were near to modern Wall, which might hint at wider activity in this area.

Two Early Neolithic pits were found on Site 13 (Shenstone Linear Features, Chapter 15). Pit 133090 contained hazelnut shells, indeterminate cereal grains, heat shattered stone, and early Neolithic bowl pottery. Pit 133089 also contained hazelnut shells, charcoal, similar pottery and four cereal grains identified as barley, emmer/spelt and indeter-minate cereal. Oak sapwood from pit 133089 yielded a date of 3940–3700 cal BC (NZA-25056; 5004±30 BP) and the barley grain (*Hordeum vulgare*) a date of 3710–3530 cal BC (NZA-25898; 4846±30). Other similar sherds were found in a tree hollow and further sherds found in the watching brief also seem likely to derive from either small pits or tree hollows.

The occurrence of isolated Neolithic pits is well attested (Thomas 1999, 64), as is the presence of Neolithic finds in tree hollows and it has been suggested that this reflects tree clearance (Evans *et al.* 1999). As is the case here, such features are usually found in the course of examining sites of later date.

Other Early Neolithic pottery was found to the east at East of The Castle, Shenstone (Site 32, Chapter 18) where part of a carinated bowl was found in a tree hollow. This pottery is likely to be slightly earlier than that from Site 13 (Herne 1988), before 3700 cal BC.

Closer to Wall on Site 15 (East of Birmingham Road Nurseries, Chapter 17), part of a Peterborough Ware bowl was found. The type of feature – if any – from which it derived is not clear. The bowl is of the Mortlake variety, which dates to 3350–2900 cal BC.

Other finds include flint that might be of Neolithic date from West of Crane Brook (Site 9, Chapter 13), a chisel arrowhead probably of this date from Site 13, the finds from around Shenstone and Wall (Gould 1966–7, 10; Round 1969–70, 25–7), to which may be added a flint sickle blade, probably of Neolithic date, from Shenstone (Watson 1994).

Despite the rarity of material of Neolithic and Bronze Age date from the fieldwalking surveys, these finds are quite localised in the context of the scheme as a whole – within a few kilometres of each other – and they suggest extensive if not intensive activity around the Wall and Shenstone wetlands. It is in this context that the burnt deposit at Site 9 (west of Crane Brook) which yielded a later Neolithic radiocarbon date of 2920–2660 (NZA-25076; 4230±35) should be viewed. The fractionally later determination of 3970±100 BP (Birm-799) from the Ridgeacre, Birmingham burnt mound may be noted, but this is a marked outlier from the main group and there is little to suggest that the feature at Site 9 was a burnt mound.

Work on the earlier Neolithic in the West Midlands has understandably concentrated on monuments, complexes of which are often visible on aerial photographs (eg Barclay *et al.* 2003, 222–4). Cursuses and mortuary enclosures have been examined near Warwick at Barford Sheds (Loveday 1989) and Charlecote (Ford 2003), as has a possible causewayed enclosure at Wasperton (Hughes and Crawford 1995). Part of a ditched enclosure has also been excavated at The Grange, Church Lawford (S.C. Palmer 1999a; in prep. a). Other possible causewayed enclosures are known in the region, either from cropmarks (Oswald *et al.* 2001, 155) or from concentrations of finds, such as those from Warwick (Thomas 1974, 39).

Only a few Early Neolithic features that pre-date these monuments and enclosures have been published. In addition to the carinated bowl from Site 32, there are two examples from different sites at Kings Newnham, Warwickshire (i: S.C. Palmer 2003, 58–60, fig. 11; and ii: Area C on the Churchover to Newbold Pacey gas pipeline; S.C. Palmer 1999b; in prep. a).

Peterborough Ware, which was found on Site 15, is as might be expected more frequent and has been recorded at several sites in southern Staffordshire: Fatholme, Fisherwick, Lichfield, and Whitemoor Haye (Miles 1969; Barfield 1980–1; Coates 2002, 44–5; Hewson 2004). As with the bowl from Site 15, some of these finds may be associated with occupation sites. Finds from Warwickshire include several from the Barford sites (Oswald 1966–7b, 37), Charlecote (Ford 2003, 24, 26), Church Lawford (Area D, with variant radiocarbon dates) (S.C. Palmer in prep. a), Kings Newnham (Area C)(*op. cit.*), Warwick, and Wasperton (Hughes and Crawford 1995, 19–21, 31–3).

However, the most significant result from the current project is the early date for cultivation provided by the pits on Site 13. The two radiocarbon dates from pit 133089 are not contemporaneous. The date of 3710–3530 cal BC from the barley falls within the currently accepted date range for the associated early Neolithic bowls of 3650–3350 BC. However, the date from the charcoal is earlier, suggesting that it may be residual. Although only a few grains are present, they nonetheless offer what may be the earliest clear evidence for Early Neolithic cultivation in the West Midlands, dating to the first half of the 4th millennium BC. Although the date is early, there are earlier dates and more extensive evidence from Lismore Fields, Buxton, Derbyshire (Jones 2000).

In common with many Neolithic finds in England, both cultivated and wild foodstuffs are present in the pits on Site 13 in small quantities. How important cereals

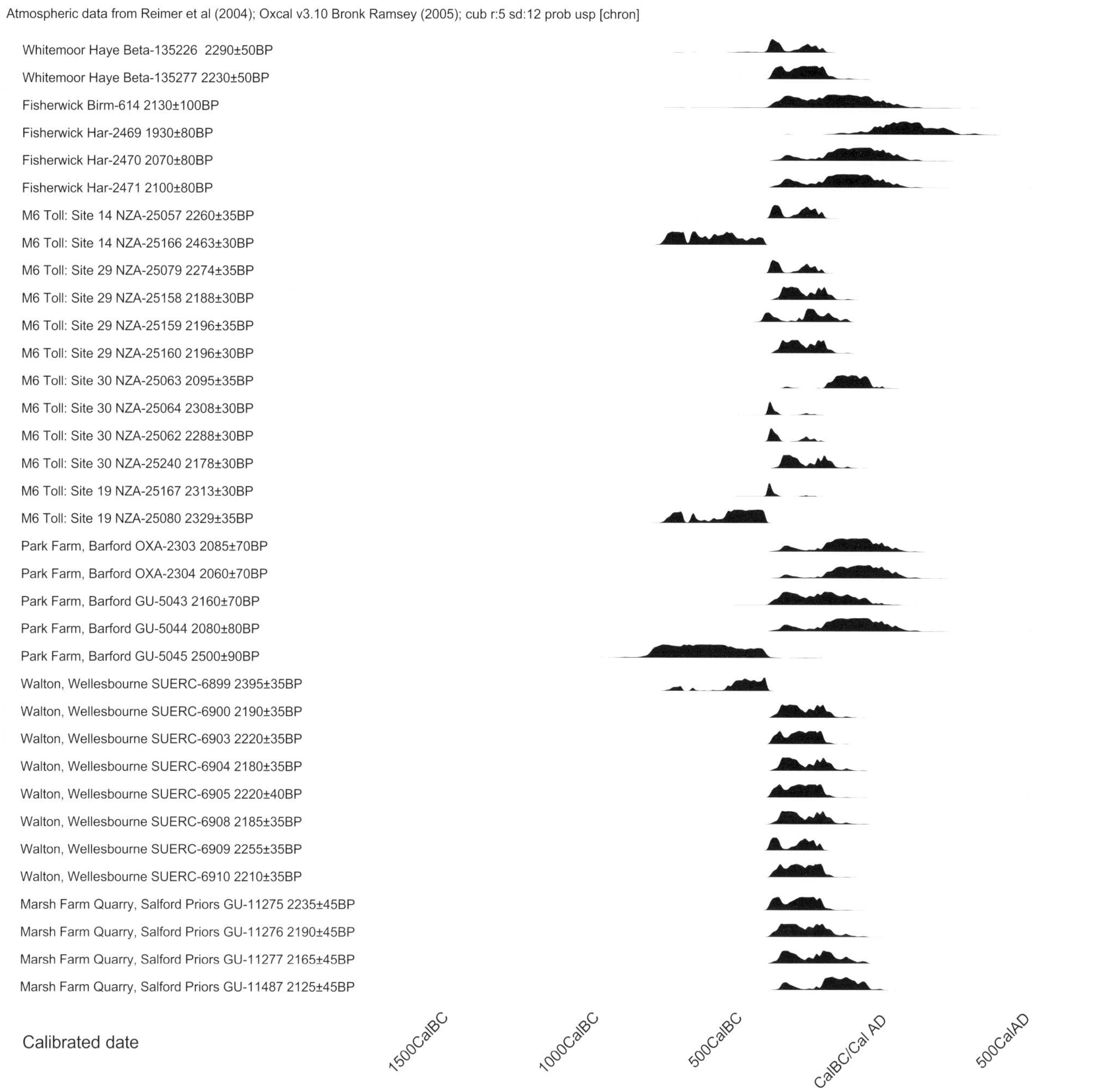

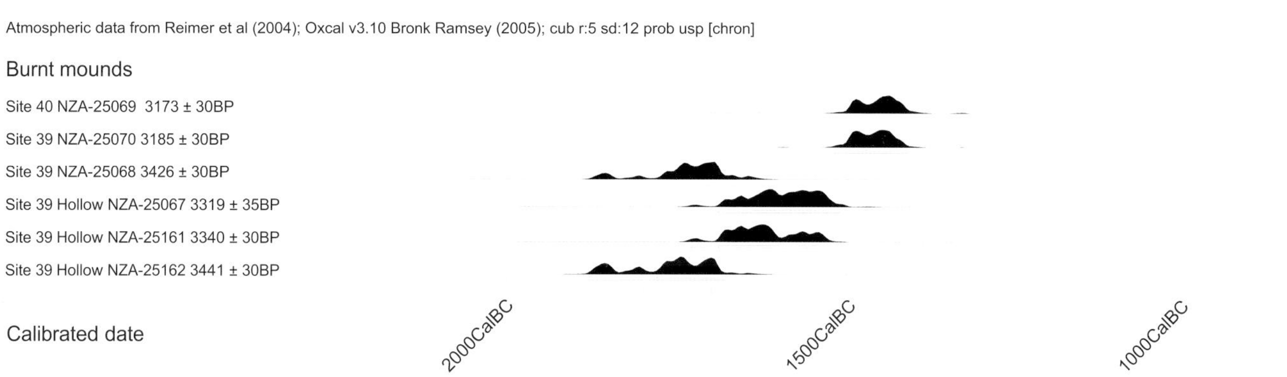

Fig. 214 (Top) Radiocarbon dates from Iron Age settlements in Staffordshire and Warwickshire; (bottom) radiocarbon dates from the M6 Toll burnt mounds

were in relation to other types of food and the implications of this for the adoption of agriculture have been matters of considerable debate (Moffet *et al.* 1989; Jones 2000; Robinson 2000; Whittle 2000; Stevens 2007) to which the M6 Toll finds can make only a modest contribution. Interestingly though, this combination of cultivated and wild foods is seen again on the M6 Toll, on the sites of Iron Age date.

Bronze Age

In contrast to the modest but significant finds from the Mesolithic and Neolithic, the Bronze Age evidence from the M6 Toll is notable primarily for its rarity.

Some redeposited pottery on Site 12 (Ryknield Street, Chapter 14) and the two burnt mounds found in the watching brief, Langley Brook (Site 39, Chapter 23) and Site 40 (Chapter 20), provide virtually the only evidence. To this might be added some of the flints found in the watching brief and perhaps also the small, but poorly dated, flint scatter from Coleshill Hall Walk (unreported Site 35, in archive).

The earliest Bronze Age activity may be represented by the redeposited fragments of Collared Urn found in Romano-British features on Site 12. The vessel probably dates within first half of the 2nd millennium BC (Needham 1996, 131; Allen and Hopkins 2000, 307). Collared Urns usually, but not invariably, come from funerary contexts (Longworth 1984) and this is the most likely source of these finds. More recent finds remain rare in both Staffordshire (Coates 2002, 47) and Warwickshire, where there are finds from Boteler's Castle (Jones *et al.* 1997) and Charlecote (Ford 2002, 206).

The locations of the burnt mounds found at Sites 39 and 40 are typical. Both lay next to streams, Langley Brook and Collett's Brook, and they were only *c* 850 m apart. Although the characteristic spread of heat shattered stone was found at both sites, neither yielded any evidence for the pits or stone or timber lined troughs found at some sites. This might be as a result of their discovery in a watching brief but as there was little sign of *in situ* burning, it is also possible that both sites contain primarily dumped material.

Burnt mounds nearby include Middleton New Park and Middleton Hall (Hodder 1990; Hodder and Welch 1990, 17–18) but despite the number of these sites known in the West Midlands (Hodder and Welch 1990; Barfield 2002), few have been excavated in modern times.

The dating of burnt mounds is relatively well established (Hodder 1990, 108, fig. 47) with many falling between 1300 and 800 BC. The mound at Milwich, Staffordshire yielded radiocarbon dates that suggest that the sites may have been used for some time. A sample from low in the mound gave a date of 1880–1400 cal BC (3290±100 BP; GU-5096) and one from higher in the mound gave a date of 1510–1170 cal BC (3080±60 BP; GU-5095) (Welch 1994–5).

In this situation, the radiocarbon dates from Sites 39 and 40 are useful additions, and they also extend the dating slightly earlier within the Middle Bronze Age (Fig. 214). Site 40 is dated to 1520–1390 cal BC by two statistically indistinguishable dates of 1520–1400 cal BC (3185 ±30 BP; NZA-25070) and 1520–1390 cal BC (3173±30 BP; NZA-25069). Charcoal from Site 39 yielded dates of 1870–1620 cal BC (3426±30 BP; NZA-25068) and 1680–1510 cal BC (3319±35 BP; NZA-25067), suggesting that, as at Milwich, burning took place over several centuries. The fragments of Collared Urn from Site 12 could be contemporary with these burnt mounds.

Dates from a hollow beneath the mound on Site 39 yielded dates from alder wood of 1880–1670 cal BC (3441±30 BP; NZA-25162) and from alder charcoal of 1680–1520 cal BC (3340±BP; NZA-25161). Given the nature of the site and what is presumed to be the extensive use of charcoal from a variety of sources, not too much emphasis should be placed on the slightly earlier dates from this site, essentially towards the end of the early Bronze Age and the beginning of the Middle Bronze Age or the variation between them. They do, however, indicate that these sites were built and used in similar locations over several centuries and the changing periods of use may reflect a shifting pattern of settlement. The recent discovery of burnt mounds nearby at Springfield Road and Withy Hill Road (M. Hodder pers. comm.; see Fig. 215) may also hint at this.

The debate as to whether burnt mounds represent cooking sites or saunas (Barfield 1991; Barfield and Hodder 1987; Hodder 1998; Hodder and Barfield 1991) need not be rehearsed here. More relevant is their importance in indicating Bronze Age settlement for which there is otherwise scant evidence. A number of the burnt mounds have been found in systematic surveys in Birmingham, Staffordshire and Warwickshire so the recorded distribution may be taken to be reliable (Barfield and Hodder 1989; Hodder 1990; Hodder and Welch 1990; Barfield 2002) (Fig. 215).

This shows widespread Middle Bronze Age activity and this is borne out by the regular reporting of metalwork (eg Gunstone 1964; Thomas 1974; Hodder 1980–1; Mullin 2003, 115–16) and the less common excavation of Early–Middle Bronze Age barrows in lowland settings (Garwood 2002). Recent burial and barrow excavations include Charlecote, Kings Newnham, Ryton-on-Dunsmore and Wasperton in Warwickshire (S.C. Palmer 2003; Hughes and Crawford 1995; Ford 2003, 15–22, 28–9) and Fatholme and Tucklesholme Farm in Staffordshire (Losco-Bradley 1984, 402; Martin and Allen 2001). Undated ring ditches known from aerial photography are numerous (eg Hodder 1980–1), but few flat graves have been recorded (eg Harbury on the Churchover-Newbold Pacey gas pipeline; S.C. Palmer in prep. a).

The relationships of burnt mounds, metalwork and settlements have been addressed (Ehrenberg 1991; Dunkin 2001) but this has been based on the presumption that settlements were permanent, an idea

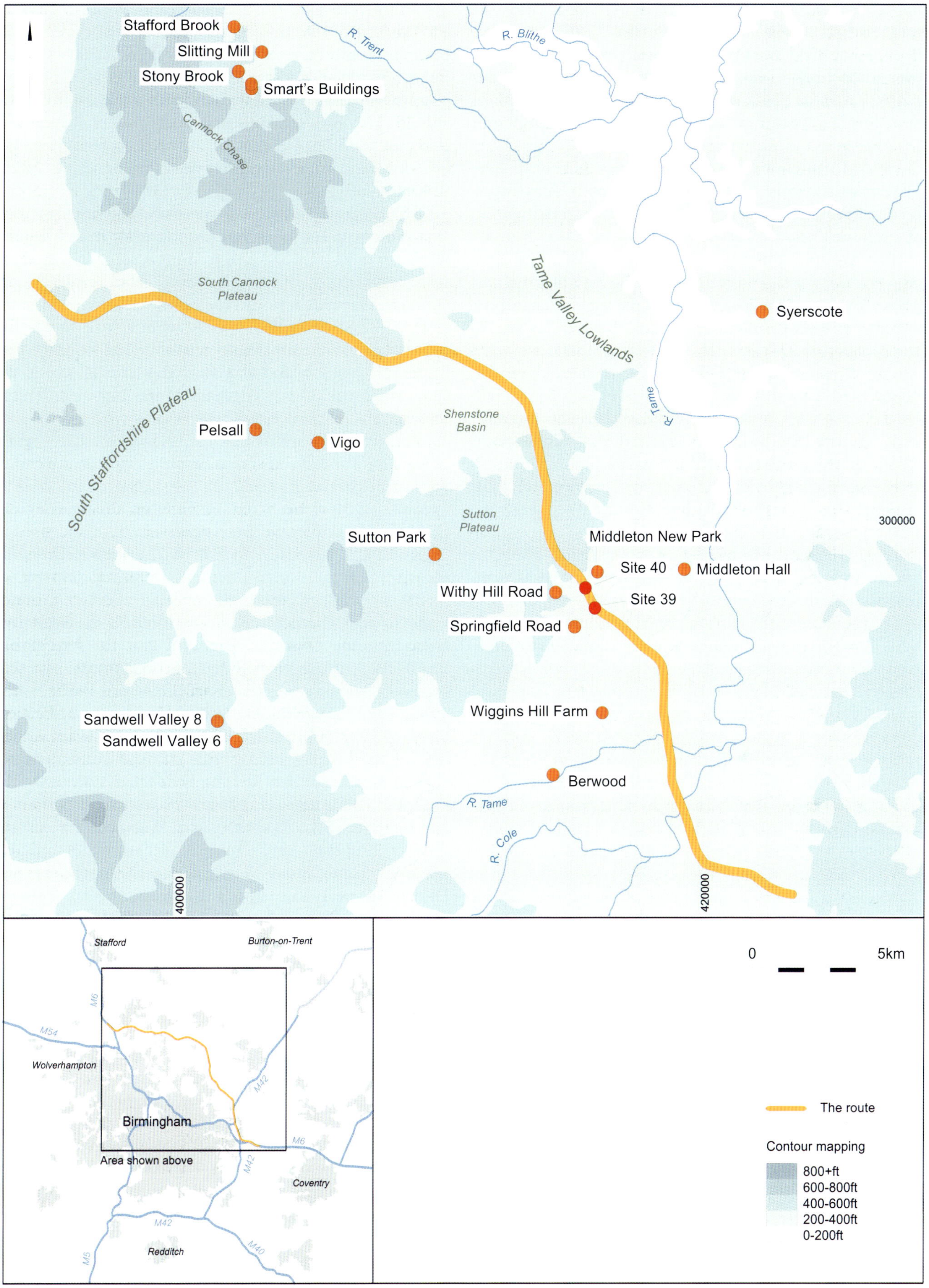

Fig. 215 Distribution of burnt mounds

that has been challenged for the Early Bronze Age at least (Brück 1999b; Mullin 2003, 80–1). The Middle Bronze Age field systems that are increasingly apparent over some parts of southern England (Yates 1999) are not common in the West Midlands (Dalwood 2002, 5) and are apparently absent from Birmingham, Staffordshire and Warwickshire.

What fragmentary evidence there is for Bronze Age settlement suggests that it was not enclosed. A possible post built roundhouse next to the Iron Age settlement at at Meriden Quarry, Warwickshire, was undated but lay close to group of pits dated to 1800–1600 BC. The Iron Age buildings were, in contrast, defined by penannular gullies (Stevens 2005). Other Middle Bronze Age pits groups are known from Rugby (S.C. Palmer 2002a, 2) and Wasperton (Hughes and Crawford 1995, fig. 11). There is also evidence from Warwickshire for an unenclosed Late Bronze Age settlement at Ling Hall Quarry (Area AB) where penannular gullies are present (S.C. Palmer 2001a; 2006a), Barford, and Whitchurch where there is also an extensive midden site (Hingley 1996, 12, fig. 8). Evidence from Staffordshire is slight but includes a possible Middle Bronze Age house at Fisherwick (Smith 1974–5).

If Middle–Late Bronze Age settlements do prove to be unenclosed they will be difficult to detect in prospection and evaluation, and even harder to identify in a watching brief during construction. The small quantities of pottery that are often difficult to date compound the situation. Late Bronze Age settlements have proved difficult to identify over much of England; where the West Midlands appears to differ on the evidence currently available, however, is in the current rarity of Early Iron Age settlements. Apart from a single isolated feature at West of Crane Brook Cottage (Site 34), most of the evidence for the Iron Age along the M6 Toll dates from the Middle Iron Age.

Iron Age

Introduction

The bulk of the evidence for prehistoric activity on the M6 Toll dates to the Iron Age. Until relatively recently, it was thought that Iron Age settlements were rare in the West Midlands. This perception was transformed in the 1990s by a series of excavations, particularly in southern and central Warwickshire, that yielded extensive evidence. The M6 Toll sites add to this emerging picture.

Settlements were excavated at Site 14, Site 29 (North of Langley Brook, Chapter 21) and Site 30 (Chapter 22), and part of a pit alignment was recorded at Site 19 (Chapter 24). Another Iron Age structure and small pits were found at Wishaw (Site 20, Chapter 25) and there were also finds of Iron Age pottery from Sites 15 and 32 (Chapters 17 and 18). It has been suggested that such is the rarity of pottery of later prehistoric date in Warwickshire that its presence may indicate settlement nearby (S.C. Palmer 2002a). Given the relatively large quantities recovered in Romano-British contexts at Site 15 and the extensive cropmark evidence, this interpretation may apply there. Less clear is the interpretation of the small amount of possible Iron Age pottery from Site 32 where there are very few features. It should also be remembered that the enclosure at Saredon (Site 26, Chapter 2) whose morphology might be compared with later prehistoric examples, is quite undated.

The potential of the river gravels of Warwickshire was first demonstrated by aerial photography in the 1960s (Webster and Hobley 1964; Whimster 1989) and a systematic study of this evidence from central and southern Warwickshire by Hingley (1989) demonstrated a wide range of farms, mainly within compounds or enclosures, whose morphology was typical of Iron Age settlements on lowland England. Similar evidence from cropmarks was already apparent in the Tame and Trent Valleys (Smith 1979; Knight 1984).

Recent excavations in both Staffordshire and, especially, Warwickshire have begun to demonstrate the regional characteristics of the Iron Age. Most excavations have been on settlements, amongst which considerable variety has been revealed.

Perhaps because of their susceptibility to identification in aerial photography, enclosed settlements have been the type of site excavated most frequently in Warwickshire. In addition to the evidence from Brandon Grounds, Brandon and Bretford; Park Farm, Barford; Rollright; Ryton-on-Dunsmore; and the series of enclosures at Wasperton (Crawford 1981; 1982; 1983; 1984) available at the time of Hingley's reviews (1989; 1996), a number of other enclosed settlements have been excavated recently. These sites include substantial excavations at Ling Hall Quarry Areas F, Z, and AB (S.C. Palmer 1994a; 2001a; 2004; 2006a); Marsh Farm (S.C. Palmer 1994b; 2000c) and Meriden Quarry (Stephens 2005), and smaller ones at Frankton (Area E: Churchbold-Newnham Pacey pipeline; S.C. Palmer in prep. a), King's Newnham (S.C. Palmer 2003); and Rugby Cement Works (Harvard 2004). There is also evidence of an Iron Age settlement that spans the Iron Age–Romano-British transition beneath the Romano-Celtic temple at Coleshill (Magilton 2006). Uniquely to the region, for the present at least, the Meriden Quarry enclosure is polygonal in plan.

Several settlements have been found to be associated with major landscape boundaries, either linear ditches or pit alignments, and these include Ling Hall Quarry, Church Lawford Area AB (S.C. Palmer 2004; 2006a), and Area Z (S.C. Palmer 2001a), Walton (S.C. Palmer 2000b; 2006b), and Coton Park (Chapman 1998). Some elements or these settlements are unenclosed while others are within a series of often small enclosures, the so-called 'ladder' or 'clothesline' settlements

Many of these settlements have, as with the earlier excavations, been found in work ahead of gravel quarrying (Fig. 216). Open, or unenclosed settlements have been identified much less frequently but one has been identified recently at Wood Farm Quarry (C. Jones

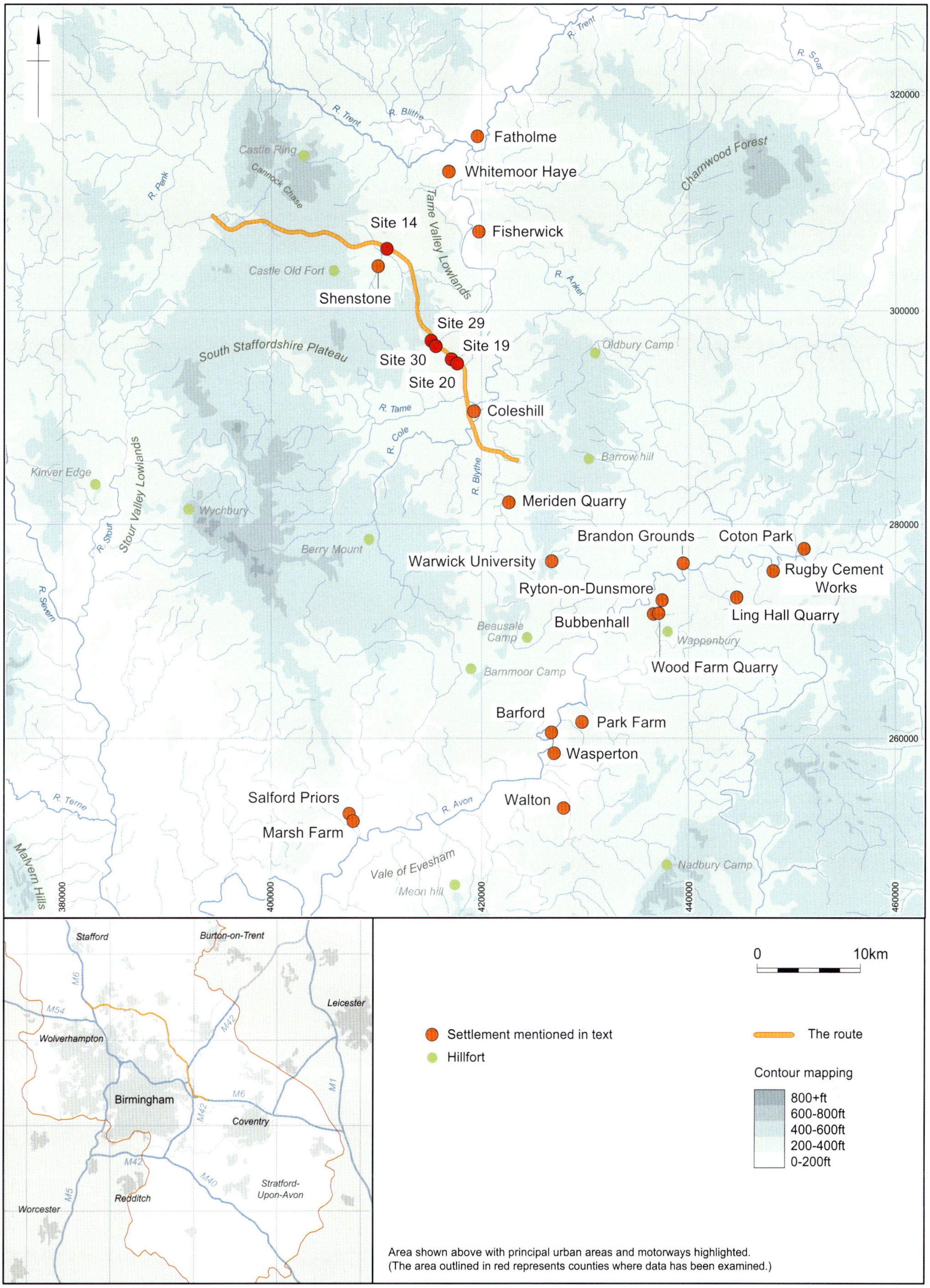

Fig. 216 Distribution of selected Iron Age sites

2004) as has an extensive settlement at Warwick University, Coventry (Hill 2002).

There has been less work in Staffordshire but most of it comes from the south-east of the county, including the programme of excavations at Fisherwick (Smith 1979) and the extensive excavations at the nearby Whitemoor Haye Quarry (Coates 1997; 2002). At Whitemoor Haye two settlements were enclosed (Areas A and B) and a third (Area C) may also have been, though the enclosure ditch is slight.

While it is clear that collectively these excavations provide a major data set that can stand comparison with any region in Britain (Fig. 216), only a few have yet been fully published: Meriden Quarry (Stevens 2005) and Park Farm, Barford (Cracknell and Hingley 1993–4) in Warwickshire, and Fisherwick (Smith 1979) and Whitemoor Haye Quarry (Coates 2002) in Staffordshire. Even so what may prove to be a number of regional characteristics can be tentatively discerned.

Chronology

It is clear that many settlements in the Midlands have been dated to the Middle and sometimes the Late Iron Age often on the basis of the scored ware pottery. This is the case for Warwickshire and the same is true of the smaller number of settlements known from Staffordshire, at Whitemoor Haye Quarry (Coates 2002) and Fisherwick (Smith 1979), though both these sites have a small number of radiocarbon dates.

The distribution and chronology of scored ware is still emerging (Elsdon 1992; Beamish 1998; Knight 2002, 133–4). Its dating is complicated by the difficulties of radiocarbon calibration between *c* 800–400 BC and of the standard deviation of luminescence dating (Barnett 2000; Willis 2002, 14–15). However, it seems increasingly likely that this long lived decorative treatment was in use from at least the 4th, and maybe 5th century BC, to the 1st century AD. The subtleties of the regional variation that might be anticipated in such a widespread and long lived type are not yet apparent.

It is also likely that as scoring provides one of the few diagnostic traits in Iron Age assemblages its presence in assemblages largely dominated by plain wares, often in the form of simple ovoid jars, has been over-emphasised.

However, the dating is borne out by an increasing number of radiocarbon dates with which the evidence from the M6 Toll sites is consistent. Scored ware was only found at Langley Mill, Site 29. Only a few sherds of Late Iron Age pottery were found at Site 19.

Settlements

The settlements from the M6 Toll are of different types (Fig. 217) and occupy a range of topographical locations. The enclosed settlement at Site 29 is typical of many of Iron Age date, a rectilinear enclosure with several circular buildings, perhaps as many as six, one of

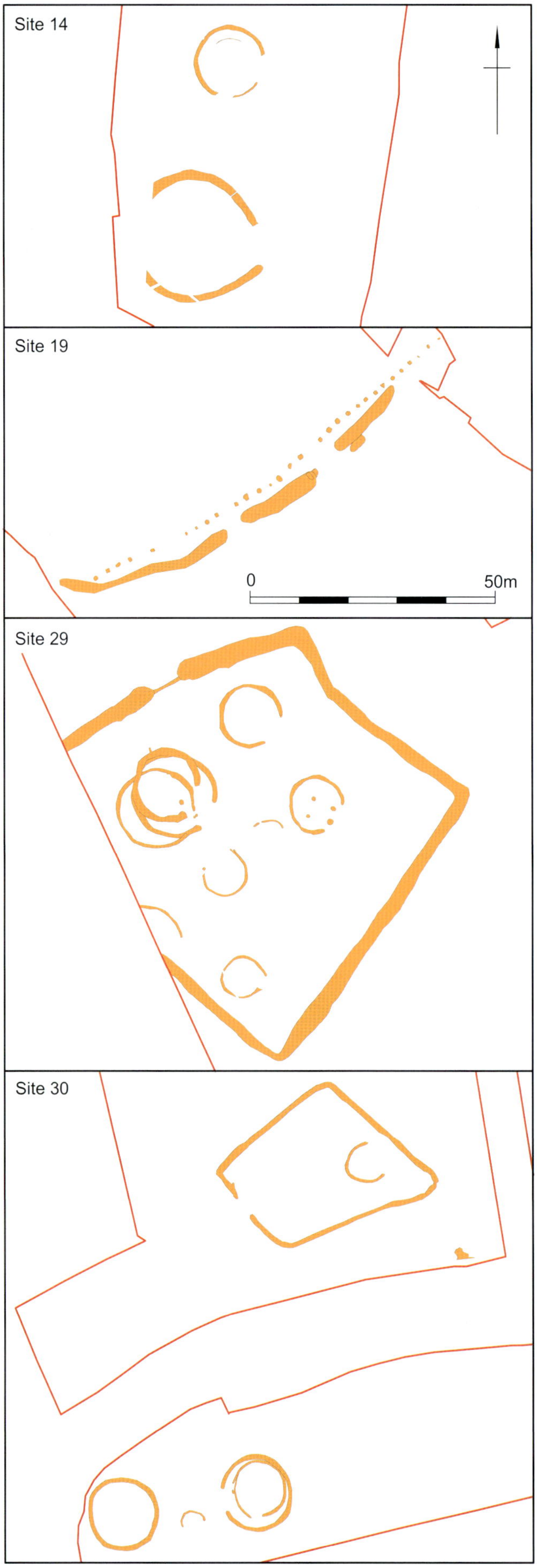

Fig. 217 Comparative plans of Iron Age sites

which was rebuilt at least three times. Four radiocarbon dates indicate a 4th–2nd century BC occupation and they are consistent with the stratigraphic evidence.

Site 14 has, within the excavated area, a single roundhouse and a small compound. The radiocarbon dates suggest that these two features were not contemporary. Oak charcoal from the penannular gully yielded a date of 400–200 cal BC (2260±35 BP; NZA-25057), while residue on a pot from the compound yielded a date of 770–410 cal BC (2463±30 BP; NZA-25166). However, as the date from the compound falls within the Early Iron Age radiocarbon calibration plateau, little weight can be attached to the difference.

Site 30 is more complex, with activity straddling either side of Langley Brook. To the north of it there is a small compound with a single circular building. There is little evidence for domestic activity from the enclosure and as Sites 29 and 30 are only 500 m away, and virtually contemporary, the enclosure in Site 30 might have had a different purpose from the settlement at Site 29. Alternatively the enclosure at Site 29 may have succeeded that at Site 30.

To the south of the enclosure on Site 30 are a ring ditch, a penannular gully and part of a small penannular gully. The radiocarbon dates indicate that the penannular gullies either side of the brook are contemporaneous, dating to 410/400–200 cal BC. The other dates from the enclosure ditch: 200–1 cal BC (2095±35 BP; NZA-25063): a pit cutting it: 200–40 cal BC (2125±30 BP; NZA-25071), and the ring ditch: 380–190 cal BC (2234±30 BP; NZA-25061) form a tight grouping. As the features to the south of the brook are so close to the stream and prone to being waterlogged or flooded, there is some question as to whether they could have been used for domestic purposes.

These dates suggest that there was a mixture of enclosed and unenclosed or open elements in these settlements. Although the importance and date of enclosure varied throughout the British Iron Age (Bowden and McOmish 1987; 1989), a general trend for more settlements to be enclosed through the course of the Middle Iron Age can be identified. As many of the excavated sites have been identified because of their large and prominent enclosure ditches, the apparent chronological grouping of Middle Iron Age sites may be a product of the patterns of recognition and excavation rather than reflecting an increase in settlement. While the evidence from the M6 Toll sites is consistent with this, it should be noted that it is not yet possible to examine whether open and unenclosed settlements display a similar trend or how sites were open or enclosed at different times. At Wood Farm Quarry there are hints of both open and enclosed settlements (C. Jones 2004, 68) and there is a hint at Site 29, as there is at Areas AB and F at Ling Hall Quarry, Church Lawford, that an unenclosed phase preceded the building of the enclosure. The settlement at Warwick University appears to have both unenclosed and enclosed phases (Jones 2001).

Within individual settlements there are a number of recurrent traits. Pennanular gullies are common but few have evidence for posts within the areas enclosed, prompting Palmer to suggest that the buildings were mass walled. Such buildings would have had walls of turf or cob (Allen *et al.* 1984, 94), which also took the considerable weight of the conical thatched or turf roof. In view of the apparent emphasis on pastoralism suggested by the botanical evidence (see below), buildings with grass walls, and perhaps roofs also, may have had a particular symbolism.

Many of these buildings are likely to have been houses, but others might have been outhouses or byres, a point emphasised by the identification of stable manure in one the penannular gullies in the enclosed settlement A at Whitemoor Haye (Coates 2002, 63). Many settlements such as Wood Farm Quarry, Bubbenhall (C. Jones 2004) and Ling Hall Quarry, Church Lawford, Area Z (S.C. Palmer 2006a) show evidence for the re-building of buildings on the same site, sometimes two or three times, and there is similar evidence from Site 29.

Large storage pits are not common on these settlements (Hingley 1996, 16). Often they are completely absent. However, clusters of pits do occur on some sites, for example Walton (S.C. Palmer 2000b; 2006b) and Ryton-on-Dunsmore (S.C. Palmer 2006c). Small pits that occur on some sites, for example at Marsh Farm Quarry (S.C. Palmer 2000c; in prep. b); Park Farm, Barford; and Wasperton (Hingley 1996, 16), may have had a special purpose, either in manufacturing or storage.

Evidence for four or more post structures that are usually interpreted as granaries appears on the evidence currently available to be rare. They are known at Ling Hall Farm Quarry, but away from the settlements, (S.C. Palmer 2002b; 2006a), and possibly at Site 29. Pairs of posts occur on some sites, for example Ling Hall Quarry, Church Lawford (S.C. Palmer 1994a), but they could have supported many different types of structure. All the M6 Toll sites have small quantities of chaff and seeds of cultivation that are typical of sieving waste from crop processing, and there is a quern from Site 14, but none of the sites yielded any direct evidence for the storage of grain.

The semicircular structure at Site 20 is noteworthy. It lies on low ground with higher ground close by. While it could be the remains of a pennannular gully, it is possible that it represents a different sort of structure. Two of the structures at Meriden Quarry, one of which (RH 2) is semi-circular gully, contained exceptional quantities of heat shattered stone, as did a dumb-bell shaped feature (Stevens 2005, 10–11) and Palmer notes a number of other possible examples (2002b, 6). At Walton, a Middle–Late Iron Age semi-circular gully enclosed a rubble platform that overlay spreads of fuel ash slag and charcoal. It has been suggested that the structure was involved with cremation (S.C. Palmer 2000b; 2001b, 95; 2006b; in prep. c). The structure at Site 20 does not, however, contain the very large quantities of burnt material reported from these two sites.

Across Warwickshire, charcoal, burnt bones and heat cracked pebbles are ubiquitous on settlements, and pits containing burnt stone also occur on some Staffordshire sites (Smith 1979, 42). It is possible that these materials represent debris from cooking troughs or other uses, for example such as parching crops. If the structure at Site 20 was originally semi-circular, its proximity to the group of nine pits or troughs containing heat shattered stone 100 m to the north could suggest that it had a special purpose, but perhaps in this case a domestic one, perhaps associated with cooking. The context of the isolated hollow on Site 34 that contained heat cracked pebbles and yielded a radiocarbon date of 800–520 cal BC (NZA-25164; 2515±30 BP) is not clear. Although the nearby Crane Brook may originally have flowed closer to the site, the quantities of burnt material from the feature do not compare with those from the Bronze Age burnt mounds at Sites 39 and 40.

Pit alignments

The pit alignment at Site 19 is an example of a type of landscape division well known in the area (Hingley 1996; S.C. Palmer 2001a; 2001b; 2004). Dating is often sparse so that some alignments such as that at Catholme, Staffordshire can only be tentatively dated as later prehistoric (Losco-Bradley and Kinsley 2002, 15–20, fig. 2.1–2). The only dating evidence for one of the alignments between Shenstone and Wall was a sherd of abraded Roman pottery (Whitehouse 1960–1). However, some examples are clearly dated to the Iron Age, for example at Ling Hall Quarry, where several examples, and some post alignments have been excavated (eg S.C. Palmer 2000a). Two of the alignments have radiocarbon dates in the Early Iron Age (S.C. Palmer 2001b, 94). A parallel pit alignment at Whitemoor Haye produced Iron Age pottery and a radiocarbon date of 400–150 cal BC from a recut pit (2230±60 BP; Beta 135227; Coates 1997, 68; 2002, 15).

The three excavated Ling Hall Quarry settlements are adjacent to pit alignments (in Areas F, AB and Z). Little direct evidence for settlement was found at Site 19 and while the presence of pottery from one of the pits might suggest the proximity of settlement, the presence of what is probably a placed deposit of a fragment of human skull could equally point to the marking of a boundary. The radiocarbon dates from the residue on one of the pieces of pottery of 410–220 cal BC (2313±30 BP; NZA-25167) and that from the skull of 770–390 cal BC (2429±35 BP; NZA-24080) do not overlap. The skull is older and while this might suggest that it had been curated, the fact that the date falls within the Early Iron Age radiocarbon plateau means that this possibility should be considered cautiously. As is typical of the area (S.C. Palmer 2006a) but also more widely (Thomas 2003), the pit alignment at Site 19 boundary was later reworked to take the form of a series of elongated pits and this alignment was maintained into the Romano-British period.

Farming

Evidence for the agricultural basis of these settlements is slight. At Meriden Quarry a small quantity of cereals was present but could not be identified to species (Stevens 2005, 23). At Park Farm, Barford charred plant remains were sparse though it could be said that, quite typically for the Iron Age, emmer, spelt and barley were cultivated, but that wild foods such as hazelnuts and sloes, were also gathered. However, the quantities are so small that it has been suggested that they have been brought to the settlements from elsewhere. The same is true of the settlements at Marsh Farm Quarry (S.C. Palmer in prep. b) and Ling Hall Quarry, Church Lawford (S.C. Palmer 2006a).

There is similar evidence from Whitemoor Haye Quarry. Here, however, the small quantity of charred plant remains included stable manure from the penannular gully of a building in one of the enclosed settlements (Coates 2002, 63). Although considerable evidence for the local, low lying, environment at Fisherwick was obtained from waterlogged remains, most evidence for the wider landscape came from pollen. Only a small proportion of this was from cereals though impressions of threshed emmer and spelt were preserved in oven daub and querns were found. Given the proximity of the settlement to the River Tame this may reflect an essentially pastoral basis, as has been suggested in a similar location at Mingies Ditch, Oxfordshire (Allen and Robinson 1993). A similar picture is evident at Whitemoor Haye, although the evidence may post-date the Iron Age settlement (Coates 2002, 68, 74).

The evidence from the M6 Toll sites is also modest, but it is consistent with this pattern. North of Langley Mill (Site 29) yielded the largest assemblage in which spelt and barley were present, as were weeds of cultivation, mainly chickweed. An oat grain could be a weed or slight evidence for another crop of cultivation, and the same is also true of a single vetch or pea. The barley could have been used for food but also for animal fodder. Wild foods are also represented by hazelnuts. Much of this small and light material is likely to have been used as tinder to light fires.

At Site 30 wheat and barley and a single fragment of chaff were present, while the pit alignment on Site 19 contained a few cereals, probably wheat, and also hazelnuts. Site 14, located close to the Wall and Shenstone wetlands, also produced few charred plant remains. Those that were present were again emmer and spelt, with occasional seeds of wild species presumably harvested as weeds amongst the cereals. Fragments of chaff and also stem fragments are, like the weeds of cultivation, likely to derive from the sieving of crops to clean them. This rarity of cereals is widespread in the West Midlands at sites that have been sampled systematically for environmental evidence, and at which querns have also been found (S.C. Palmer 2002a, 7). Iron Age fields are all but absent. There is no question, however, that cereals were cultivated (*cf.* van der Veen 1992). It is not yet clear, though, whether the small quantities of charred plant remains and the rarity of pits and granaries that could have been used to store grain, reflect a greater emphasis on pastoralism than in some areas further to the south.

It is clear from work further north in Britain, for example, that cereals were cultivated but that pits were not commonly used to store seed grain (eg Harding 2004). Different methods of processing and storing cereals may also be relevant. If stored in a quite clean condition, less grains of barley are likely to be wasted than grains of hulled wheats during processing as the lighter hulls are easier to separate from the grain than glume bases. In addition, unlike the hulls of emmer and wheat, barley hulls generally do not survive charring. However, neither of these possibilities seems able to account entirely for such a low level of cereals.

The pollen from an old ground surface at Site 12 not far from Site 14 shows a change from a dominant woodland of alder, oak and hazel to a more open environment. It is thought that this change is likely to have occurred in the Iron Age. In the more open landscape hazel was more important and there is some evidence for cereal cultivation, or at least the use of cereals. This evidence is consistent with that from Site 14. Iron Age fields, however, are notably absent.

Charcoals from all the sites indicate that many types of wood including hazel, field maple, birch and ash were used for fuel with variations due to the local geology and soils. At all of them, however, oak seems to have been the preferred firewood. There is little evidence from the Iron Age to suggest whether, as might be anticipated, woodlands were managed for example by coppicing. There are, however, some hints that coppicing was practised by the Romano-British period.

Animal bone was absent from the M6 Toll sites and this has also been the case on many of the sites recently excavated in Warwickshire which are sited on acidic gravel soils. Only at Coton Park, Rugby and Walton, have large faunal assemblages yet been noted. At Coton Park cattle, sheep/goat, pig and also horse and dog are present (Chapman 1998), while at Walton, Warwickshire, cattle were the dominant species followed by sheep/goat, pig with horse and small passerine also present (S.C. Palmer 2006b; in prep. c). These compositions are typical of many Iron Age sites. The small assemblage from Fisherwick was dominated by cattle (70% by number) with pig, sheep/goat, horse and deer also present (Smith 1979, 79).

Although the Iron Age settlements on the M6 Toll, and generally elsewhere in the West Midlands, date from the Middle Iron Age onwards, it is uncertain what emphasis should be placed on the evidence seen at Site 12 for a change to a more open environment. The evidence from Site 12 is not well dated, and it may reflect localised rather than systemic change.

Material world

There were few finds from the settlements on the M6 Toll. The few diagnostic pottery sherds from Sites 19, 20 and 29 suggest barrel shaped jars with upright or everted rims. These simple forms appear typical of the range of pottery known from the area (Hingley 1989, 130–1, fig. 9:5; Cracknell and Hingley 1994; Smith 1979, 43–52; Coates 2002, 50–1, fig. 36–7). Two sherds of scored ware were found at Site 19 and this surface treatment is present amongst a number of Warwickshire sites, which appear to form the western extent of its distribution.

None of the settlements had any evidence for craft activities; there were few tools, only a quern from Site 14 and a whetstone from Site 29. There were no certain loom weights or any other evidence for manufacturing that could be compared with the working of metal, bone and antler found at Coton Park, Rugby (Chapman 1998) or the apparent ironworking at Warwick University (Hill 2002).

The very small quantities of finds appear typical and preclude a discussion of the use of space within settlements such as that undertaken, for example, in Northamptonshire (Gwilt 1997). However, the marking of the terminals of building gullies and enclosure ditches by the placing of objects and other offerings is well attested in the British Iron Age. This has been noted nearby in the quantities of material placed in the ditch terminals of the enclosed settlement at Marsh Farm, Salford Priors. It has also been suggested that the large pieces of pottery in a pit alignment at Whitemoor Haye, Staffordshire were placed deposits (Coates 2002, 48–9). All the pottery from Site 14, representing a single vessel, came from the southern enclosure terminal. At Site 20 the pottery also came from the terminal of the semicircular gully and this is commonly the case at the settlements at Ling Hall Quarry, Church Lawford (S.C. Palmer pers. comm.). However as the quantities are so small it is, as yet, difficult to place much emphasis on this and similar distributions at Fisherwick were interpreted in terms of domestic discard (Smith 1979, 98).

Perhaps more persuasive as placed deposits are the saddle quern from the pit that was cut into the southern enclosure terminal at Site 14, and perhaps the whetstone from the enclosure terminal at Site 29. However, a cautionary note is sounded by the fragment of quern in the terminal of a semicircular gully (RH 2) at Meriden Quarry, Solihull, which joins with another fragment in a pit outside the enclosure (Stevens 2005, 10).

Too much emphasis should not be placed on the frequently small quantities of material culture. The size of the pottery assemblages may only indicate that greater use was made of wooden or leather containers. Two separate finds nearby of gold torcs, from Needwood Forest (Leeds 1933; Jope 2000, 84, 254, pl. 118) and Glascote (Painter 1969–70; Jope 2000, 84, 254, pl. 119) which can be compared to finds from Snettisham, Norfolk (Stead 1991a), indicate a wealth and status that is not apparent in the settlement record. It may be that wealth was displayed in other ways instead, perhaps for example, in the ownership of cattle.

The exchange of materials and objects is well documented in the West Midlands through currency bars (Hingley 1990; 1996, 20) and Group A–E and Droitwich/Cheshire Plain briquetage. These types of briquetage had been rare in Warwickshire (Morris 1994) but both types have recently been identified at Meriden Quarry, and Marsh Farm, Salford Priors (Hancocks 2002, 13–14; Stevens 2005, 21) to which may be added the small groups of Droitwich/Cheshire briquetage from Fisherwick and Whitemoor Haye (Coates 2002, 52), and the single sherd from Site 14 on the M6 Toll, all in Staffordshire.

Querns made from millstone grit or granite, perhaps from Derbyshire, have been found at sites in the West Midlands, for example Fisherwick and Meriden Quarry, Solihull, but the example from Site 14 seems likely to be made from a glacial erratic from the deposits that overlie the South Staffordshire Coalfield and so be from a relatively local source. In contrast, the amber bead from Site 29 is certainly from a distant source, either the east coast of England or northern Europe. Such finds are rare in Iron Age Britain (Beck and Shennan 1991), with beads and rings known only from Middle–Late Iron Age burials in Yorkshire (Stead 1979, 81, 86; 1991b, 93) and occasionally from settlements, such as the two beads from the Bredon Hill hillfort, Worcestershire (Hencken 1938, 86, fig. 12, 4–5).

Burial and religion

The presence of part of a human skull in one of the pits in the alignment at Site 19 is in many ways typical of the Iron Age (Whimster 1981; Wilson 1981). The selection of particular parts of the body, especially skulls and long bones, for burial within settlements and related contexts is clear (Wait 1985, 92–8). The find from Site 19 is, along with a jaw from an enclosure ditch on the Barford Bypass (S.C. Palmer pers. comm.), one of the first examples of this common practice yet recorded from the area.

These finds emphasise how infrequent formal Iron Age burials are in the West Midlands (Whimster 1981, fig. 167–71, fig. 53). Three crouched inhumations from pits at Walton are Middle–Late Iron Age in date (S.C. Palmer 2000b/c; 2001b, 95; 2006b; in prep. c). Four crouched inhumations at Wasperton are also apparently of the Early Iron Age (Crawford 1983, 19), and some older finds, such as that from Stretton-on-Fosse might possibly also be Iron Age (Thomas 1974, 40).

Possibly also associated with funerary or religious practices are some small ring ditches found in Warwickshire. At Ling Hall Quarry, Church Lawford Area Z, a square enclosure that stood apart from the settlement enclosures contained a small ring ditch. The possibility has been raised that it may have been a mortuary and/or ceremonial enclosure (Palmer 2001a; 2002b, 7; 2006a). Although larger in size, the ring ditch (300131) at Site 30 may be comparable. This ditch forms a complete circle and this presents some difficulties in interpreting it as a penannular gully, not least because there are examples immediately adjacent to it. The low lying location of this part of Site 30, adjacent to a stream, makes it an unlikely location for settlement or even a byre. It may also be no coincidence that the entrances to the two overlapping penannular gullies adjacent to 300131 face west, and not east as is usual in the West Midlands. A large timber, perhaps a post, was also set upright in a pit (300285) in the entrance to the penannular gullies.

Between the two large circular features is a small semi-circular gully, whose size recalls the mini-ring ditches of Late Bronze Age–Iron Age date found at Salford Priors (S.C. Palmer 1999a), Ryton-on-Dunsmore (Bateman 1976–7), and Ling Hall Quarry, Church Lawford (S.C. Palmer 1999b; 2006a). A related gully has been excavated recently at Ryton-on-Dunsmore (S.C. Palmer 2006c).

Some circular ditches are thought to have encircled houses or provided drainage for them; a nearby example is at Meriden Quarry, Solihull. But in this instance there were also substantial postholes that probably represent a porch. However, such examples are rare. It seems unlikely that ring ditch 300131 represents a barrow. Examples of Iron Age date are very rare (Whimster 1981, 31–4; Hughes 1994, 400; Hill *et al.* 1999, 265, 270, n.9) and although there is a central feature within ring ditch 300131, there is no evidence that it was a grave. On the evidence presently available it is not possible to determine the uses of ring ditch 300131 and the associated features; but it is questionable whether they represent a settlement.

Conclusion

Part of the importance of the Iron Age sites from the M6 Toll is that they were largely unexpected. It is salutary to recall that the cropmark from which Site 14 was identified was initially thought to be a Bronze Age barrow. Site 30 was also known from a cropmark but the date and extent of activity was unknown. Site 29 was only recognised during the programme of works reported here.

As the majority of the sites so far investigated in the West Midlands have been both enclosed and also sited on river gravels, with notable concentrations in the valleys of the Arrow, Avon and Tame rivers, the locations of Site 14 next to a wetland and Site 29, on a low hill of Red Marl, provide a glimpse into the range of other environments being used in the Iron Age. They also suggest that other settlements should be anticipated in similar locations.

Clearly, the full complexity of the region in the Iron Age has yet to be discerned. Little is known of the hillforts such as Castle Ring and Castle Old Fort that lie close to the M6 Toll (Wardle 2002b), or indeed of other types of site. The final reports on the settlements at Park

Farm, Barford and Meriden Quarry in Warwickshire and Fisherwick and Whitemoor Haye Quarry, Staffordshire are the only ones on recent excavations to have been published. Partly because of this it is not clear whether some features such as the semi-circular building at Site 20 or the apparent ring ditch at Site 30 are typical or atypical. However, the clear dating of all the sites to the Middle and Late Iron Age and the presence of only small quantities of cereals seems typical. The correlation, if any, between these traits and also the hint from Site 12 for a change to a more open landscape in the Iron Age, is yet to be explored fully.

However, much of the evidence from the Iron Age sites on the M6 Toll can, at this stage, be seen in many regards to be typical of the emerging evidence from the West Midlands. The settlements at Sites 14, 29 and 30 and the pit alignment at Site 19 are all characteristic of the region (Hingley 1989; Smith 1977; 1978; O'Brien 1979) and indeed of much of central England (Knight 1984; 1992; Clay 1992; 2001; Kidd 2004; Challis and Harding 1975; Wheeler 1979; Haselgrove 1999).

Chapter 30
Romano-British Period Discussion

By Paul Booth

Introduction

The evidence for activity of the Romano-British period revealed by the M6 Toll project is of considerable importance for understanding the development of the region at this time (Fig. 218). While avoiding the Roman military establishments and 'small town' of Wall the project has revealed significant evidence for settlement and other activity in the hinterland of that site and in the vicinity of Watling Street to the west of Wall. This is not the full story, however, because additional settlement has been revealed away from the line of the major Roman road in the very poorly-understood area between Wall and the major settlement and temple complex at Coleshill, some 19 km distant to the SSE. The sites examined were presumably for the most part involved in agriculture, although the nature of that activity is not always well-defined. Evidence for pottery production was also revealed, as well as an important cemetery located on Ryknield Street just south-east of Wall.

The imposed infrastructure

The Roman army is thought to have reached this part of the West Midlands area by about AD 48 (eg Frere 1987, 60–2) and a series of military sites was established at about that date or shortly thereafter. Major bases of so-called 'vexillation fortress' type – ie probably including a legionary component in their garrison – were established at Mancetter in north Warwickshire (Scott 1981; 1998), and perhaps also at Wall (Gould 1997) where there was certainly a series of forts, and were supplemented by a further sequence of forts at Metchley, some 24 km south of Wall (A. Jones *et al.* 2002; 2004). The earliest elements of other complexes of military sites were also established, as at Greensforge to the south-west, *Pennocrucium*, 20 km west of Wall, where there was another probable vexillation fortress and, rather later, Rocester, over 30 km north of Wall and probably not established until *c* AD 100 (Esmonde Cleary and Ferris 1996). These sites were linked by major roads – in particular Mancetter, Wall and *Pennocrucium* were all adjacent to Watling Street, the principal east–west road into the West Midlands, while Ryknield Street ran from Metchley (connected by other roads to sites further south and ultimately to the Fosse Way) to Wall, crossing the line of Watling Street just to the east of the complex of military sites and later civilian settlement and heading to Little Chester (Derby) and beyond.

The date of construction of the roads is less clear than that of the forts, but the earliest military establishments will have preceded the formalisation of the road alignments. The first metalling of Watling Street at Wall has been dated *c* AD 70 by Gould (1964–5; 1997, 351). Neither at Ryknield Street (Site 12, Chapter 14), where the line of Ryknield Street was intersected, nor at Watling Street, Hammerwich (Site 41, Chapter 10), 3 km west of Wall, where Watling Street was examined, was close dating of the primary road construction obtained. Indeed at Site 12 the surfaces of Ryknield Street had been completely removed by ploughing, except where they survived in fragmentary condition beneath a later field boundary, although a section examined in 1965 just north of Site 12 revealed a cambered gravelled surface 7.3 m wide and up to 0.37 m thick (Oswald 1966–7, 39) and immediately north of this a width of *c* 8.4 m was recorded (Gould 1964–5).

At Site 41 the earliest identified road surface of Watling Street was about 5.5 m wide. Its construction had been preceded by tree clearance, but this may not have occurred immediately prior to the building of the road. The construction of both roads employed local gravel and quartz cobbles, but there were no traces of more substantial stone components, either for bedding or as top surfaces. This is also true of the much better preserved length of Ryknield Street in Sutton Park, some 7–10 km south of Wall. Here the road is up to 9 m wide and 0.4 m thick, with discontinuous ditches (Hodder 2004, 60–3).

The military sites at Wall have been the subject of numerous excavations, mostly small scale (for a convenient, concise summary see Ellis 1999, 15–18). The earliest military activity may date from the late AD 40s, the presumed date of a probable marching camp located from the air lying south of the modern village and immediately north-east of the West of Crane Brook site (Site 9), while a further possible camp of *c* 2.5 hectares lay to the west, north of Watling Street (Welfare and Swan 1995, 175–6). The putative vexillation fortress, straddling the line of Watling Street to the north of the first marching camp, was probably established in the early 50s and abandoned by the end of that decade. Subsequent forts, the earliest perhaps established in the aftermath of the revolt of Boudicca, lay on the high ground to the north. The latest of the sequence of three forts in this location was abandoned early in the 2nd century, by which time the civilian settlement was developing on the lower slopes south-west of the Flavian military sites.

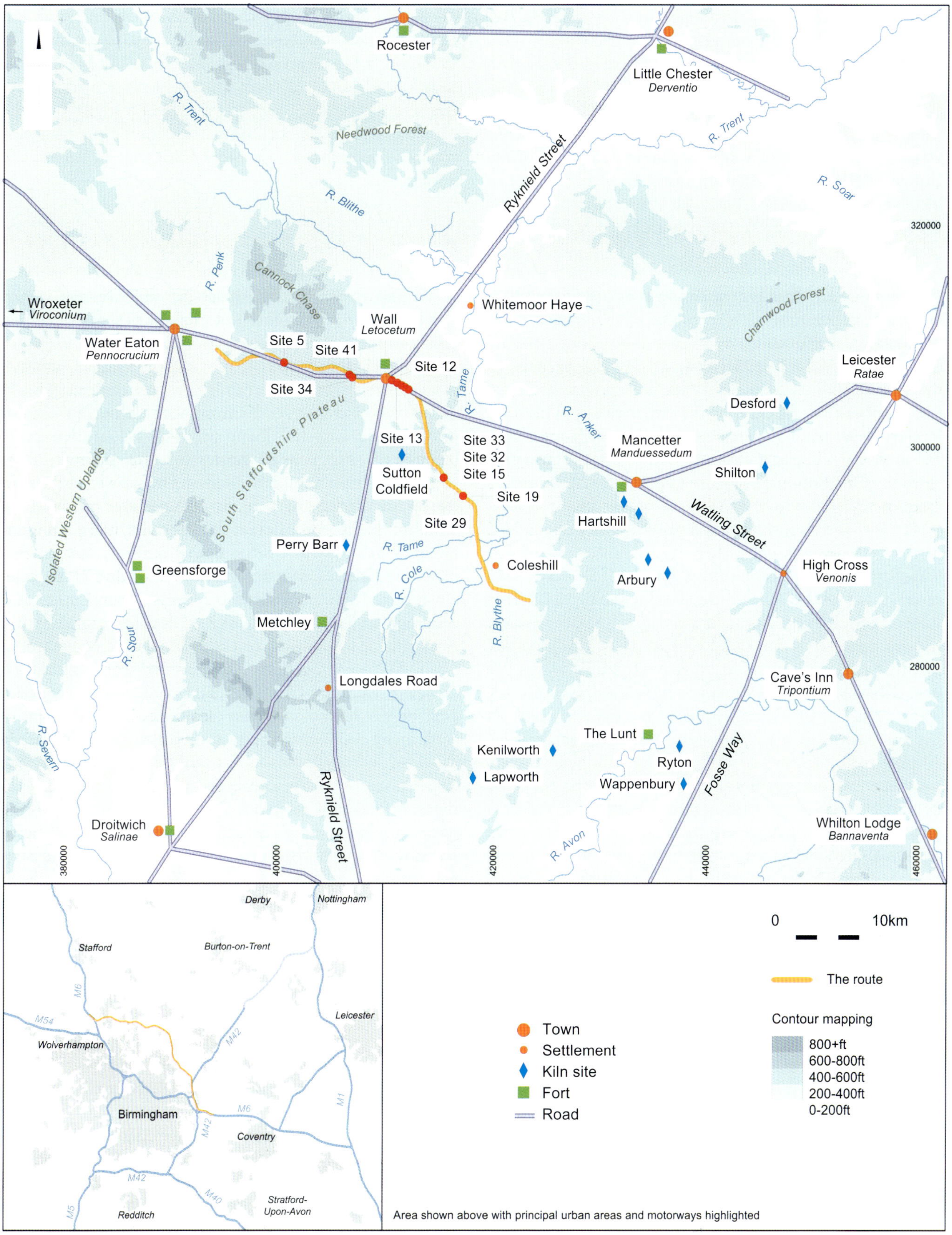

Fig. 218 Distribution of Romano-British sites mentioned in the text

The two principal extant structures, the bath house and the slightly later building interpreted as a *mansio* (initially built in timber), lying close to the line of Watling Street, were probably both built while the uphill military site remained in use, but presumably served both military and civilian communities at this time. These were by no means the only significant buildings at Wall, which eventually developed a mainly linear form, stretching along Watling Street perhaps for as much as *c* 1.5 km, including cemeteries that presumably lay beyond the limits of settlement (the figure of 3 km given by Burnham and Wacher (1990, 276) is based on the account of Oswald (1966–7a); some of the discoveries listed by him seem more likely, in the light of recent work, to relate to activity beyond the eastern limit of the Roman roadside settlement rather than forming part of it). Nevertheless, the focus on these buildings has resulted in a view of Wall as primarily a posting station (exemplified by Gould 2001). Both bath house and 'guest house' had several major structural phases, though there are divergent views on the date of the 'third guest house/*mansio*', the first phase of this structure to be built in stone, which is assigned by Gould (2001, 40–1) to about 130 and by Ellis (1999, 21) perhaps to the 170s. Either way, the building was probably out of use by about the middle of the 3rd century. The bath house survived in use longer, but had ceased to function as such by the end of the 3rd century, possible subsequent occupation being apparently of domestic character.

At Wall the continued importance of the main roads in the later Romano-British period is indicated by the fragmentary milestone of Claudius II (268–70) reportedly found built into the bath house in 1912 (RIB 2246), and is reflected in a single major late Roman development. This was the construction of a substantial fortified enclosure of 2.1 ha, surrounded by a wall *c* 2.7 m thick with a contemporary rampart and triple ditches, astride the line of Watling Street at the highest point on the line of this road, in the eastern part of the settlement. A date in the late 3rd or early 4th century seems likely for this enclosure, the function of which continues to be debated, although its likely origin as one of a series of comparable enclosures along Watling Street, from *Uxacona* (Red Hill) in the west to *Bannaventa* (Whilton Lodge; Dix and Taylor 1988), has long been recognised (eg Webster 1971; 1974, 55–7; Gould 1999). Such limited evidence for 4th century activity as there is from Wall seems mainly to concentrate within the enclosure (Gould 2001, 67; Ellis 1999, 24), although excavation there has been only on a small scale. The status of the settlement in the later 4th century and later is speculative (see further below).

Elsewhere the road system prompted the development of related settlements with no military antecedents. A significant example of this is seen at Longdales Road, at Kings Norton in south Birmingham, *c* 6 km south of Metchley on the road to Alcester, where some ditches and minor roads were laid out at right angles to the line of Ryknield Street, although not all features shared this alignment. A multiple-ditched enclosure lay some 200 m west of Ryknield Street. Timber buildings, including possible circular structures, are indicated both within this enclosure and elsewhere (Hodder 2004, 64–8; pers. comm.) and the settlement appears to have been more extensive than a simple farmstead (see also below). A similar sort of site may have existed at Coleshill, immediately adjacent to the south-east end of M6 Toll, where very recent work has added to the evidence of settlement examined in 1979–80 (Magilton 2006; Nicholas Palmer pers. comm.). Although a road (probably on a north–south alignment) has yet to be positively identified the character of the site, including its major temple complex, appears increasingly consistent with that of a roadside settlement.

Settlement origins and early chronology

It is unsurprising that there are differences in the trajectories of development of those sites that are closely linked to the imposed pattern of Roman roads, forts and towns and those which are less obviously directly associated with such features. These associations broadly divide the evidence for Romano-British period activity into two halves, the north-western and south-eastern parts of the M6 Toll. In the former area, activity of the Romano-British period appears to be consequent upon the construction of Watling Street and the establishment of Wall. Field systems at Washbrook Lane (Site 5, Chapter 7) and a major Romano-British building at West of Crane Brook Cottage (Site 34, Chapter 12) are both close to the line of Watling Street. Neither site has any evidence of pre-Romano-British activity, except for a single burnt stone feature at Site 34, likely to be of broad Early–Middle Iron Age date. It must be admitted, however, that the Site 34 building was probably only part of a larger complex and pre-Romano-British settlement could perhaps have underlain another part of this site, which was probably centred south of the M6 Toll. At Site 12, the cemetery just south-east of Wall, there is minimal evidence for prehistoric activity and none is convincingly associated with a pre-Romano-British origin for the cemetery itself, a fact which is unsurprising given that the layout of the cemetery is dependent upon the line of the other major Roman road in the area, the roughly north-south aligned Ryknield Street.

South-east of Wall the position is more equivocal. Although the focus of the users of the East of Birmingham Road Nurseries (Site 15, Chapter 17) was surely the adjacent small town, this area was certainly one with earlier settlement (most clearly seen at Shenstone Ring Ditch, Site 14, only 250 m distant from the early Romano-British Enclosure 1 on Site 15, although some Middle Iron Age pottery was also recovered from Site 15 itself), even if it is not certain that there was continuous activity in this general location. Unfortunately the character of Romano-British activity at East of the Castle, Shenstone (Site 32, Chapter 18) and Round Wood, Shenstone (Site 33, Chapter 19) is very poorly defined and its relationship to any possible earlier activity in those areas is completely speculative.

Further south-east, however, more removed from the direct influence of Wall, a much more direct link between Iron Age and Romano-British settlement is seen. At North of Langley Brook (Site 29, Chapter 21) and Wishaw Hall Farm (Site 19, Chapter 24) there were close spatial relationships between linear features of both periods, even if at Site 19 the Romano-British enclosure lay a short distance from the boundary complex where continuity of alignment from the Middle Iron Age (starting with a pit alignment) seems certain.

The demonstration of direct continuity of settlement from the Iron Age into the Romano-British period is much more difficult than demonstration of adjacent locations. A major part of this problem is caused by the absence of a 'Late Iron Age' that is well defined ceramically. The presence of wheel-thrown pottery in a 'Belgic' tradition is well-established in the Avon valley, but such material is very poorly represented north of the valley, and at Coleshill comprised only seven sherds out of a site total of 16,881, the latter figure including a significant handmade 'Middle' Iron Age element (Booth 2006). The conclusion drawn there (based on evidence from the site sequence as well as simply that of the ceramics) was that the handmade material continued in use up to the time of the arrival of 'Romanised' pottery fabrics at some time after the middle of the 1st century AD, and was only very rarely supplemented by wheel-thrown pottery before that time. A similar situation seems to prevail on the M6 Toll sites. A tiny handful of 'Belgic type' sherds (two each in sand- and grog-tempered fabrics) was present at Site 19 and a single sherd came from Site 29, but such material was otherwise absent.

If the Coleshill scenario is followed here it can be suggested that at Sites 19 and 29 there may have been a continuous sequence of occupation from the Middle–Late Iron Age into the Romano-British period, although the quantities of handmade 'Middle' Iron Age material at these sites were very much smaller than at Coleshill. In addition, the Middle Iron Age radiocarbon dates from Enclosure 1 at Site 29 do not seem to suggest activity through to the end of the 1st millennium, but the dating programme did not emphasise the latest deposits in the Enclosure 1 sequence, so this may not be conclusive. Continuous activity, albeit at slightly different locations, is also possible in the Site 14/15 area, for example, but cannot be demonstrated there, and the radiocarbon dates from Site 14 perhaps indicate an absence of activity there in the later part of the Middle Iron Age/Late Iron Age.

Overall, therefore, the evidence suggests some continuity of settlement location in the region traversed by the M6 Toll, particularly away from the vicinity of Wall. Around Wall itself, where later prehistoric activity was relatively well-established (eg Whitehouse 1960–1), and adjacent to the line of Watling Street to the west, the existing pre-Conquest settlement pattern was either disrupted and/or supplemented by the establishment of new sites whose location was determined by that of the road and sites directly upon it. There is as yet insufficient evidence from the area to allow the conclusion that the former pattern was normative, although the data appear to point that way. There seems to be no compelling reason why established settlement patterns need have been disrupted at the time of the Conquest except in locations closely adjacent to foci of military activity, as at Wall, or elsewhere where individual or group circumstances (not usually identifiable from archaeological evidence) led to instances of dispossession and expropriation.

However they were established, all the Romano-British settlements show an apparent concentration of occupation in the 2nd century, with more varied evidence for later activity. Some sites seem to have gone out of use during the 3rd century. This can be seen particularly clearly at sites such as Site 34, while in some other cases the evidence is less certain. Elsewhere occupation continued into the 4th century (see further below). In all cases the dating is dependent, usually exclusively, upon the pottery evidence, with differences in the size and character of assemblages accounting in large part for the variation in definition of the chronological range at individual sites.

Settlement form

The settlement sites with probable or possible pre-Romano-British origins, Sites 19, 29 and 15, all incorporated enclosure elements in their plans. It is likely that such elements were the most significant component of these sites, as was the case with most (but not all) of the pre-Conquest settlements. None of the enclosure ditches on any of these sites was particularly substantial, however, and at Site 29, for example, they contrasted with the Iron Age enclosure ditch, which was rather deeper and wider than any of the comparable Romano-British features. The latter did not all form complete circuits. This may have related to their function, but may also suggest the inclusion of less readily detectable elements such as hedges or even removable fences in their circuits.

An extreme form of this arrangement may be seen at Saredon (Site 26, Chapter 2) where a roughly U-shaped enclosure, unfortunately completely undated but perhaps most likely to have been of late prehistoric or Romano-British date, was defined by quite a substantial ditch on three sides. The open northern side is likely to have been at least 100 m long. While some particular functional characteristic may be indicated by this arrangement, it is more likely that the enclosure was completed by an organic barrier such as a substantial hedge or a patch of woodland. At Site 15 it is noticeable that the ditches of Enclosures 1 and 2 were significantly slighter than that of the later Enclosure 3 to the south-west. The latter was also the most completely-enclosed of these features (except that its southern corner lay outside the limit of excavation), with a well-defined entrance in the western corner. All the enclosures were defined by single ditches, with the partial exception of Site 19, where there were two ditches, perhaps contemporary, on the northern side. This form contrasts with that of multiple ditched enclosures at Shenstone just west of Site 15 (Gould 1972, 1–3, see also below) and that at Longdales Road (Hodder 2004, 64–5, see also above), but such strongly defined sites are relatively uncommon in the area.

The Site 19 enclosure lay adjacent to a ditched trackway (although the two features were on slightly different alignments and are not likely to have been established at the same time), but was otherwise not directly linked to a more extensive arrangement of boundaries. At Site 29 the enclosures varied considerably in their degree of completeness (not simply as a result of differential preservation) but most were irregularly linked, either directly or by overlapping of some parts, even though not all were thought to be contemporary. It is not clear if there were more widespread boundary systems beyond the enclosures at Site 29, although this is possible.

A rather different arrangement prevailed at Site 15. Here, as at Site 29, there were multiple enclosures, two pairs of which were linked, but all of these, plus the pottery kiln and the majority of other Romano-British features, were contained between two parallel ditches roughly 60–65 m apart, with only occasional late Romano-British features extending beyond these ditches. The significance of this arrangement is unclear. It is particularly striking because the alignment of the two principal ditches reflects neither that of any known pre-Roman features, nor that of Watling Street, only *c* 200 m distant to the north, nor that of the north–south and east–west aligned double ditched cropmark enclosure which lies some 200 m to the west (Hodgkinson and Chatwin 1944; Gould 1972, site A). This last was certainly contemporary in part with the use of Site 15 and indeed is likely to have been closely related to it.

In contrast, at Site 5, what seems to have been a relatively straightforward field system was clearly aligned directly upon Watling Street and presumably therefore post-dated the establishment of that road. Elsewhere there is little or no indication of extensive systems of field boundaries of Romano-British date, although occasional features at Shenstone Linear Features (Site 13) and particularly Site 33, for example, might have been surviving fragments of such systems, nor is there much indication of the chronological depth of these systems (*cf.* eg Chadwick 1999, 160–2). The ditched boundaries at Site 34 might also have included field system components as well as enclosures forming part of the settlement layout. Just east of the M6 Toll area, however, work in 2004 on the improvement of the Weeford to Fazeley stretch of the A5 revealed ditches of probable or certain Romano-British date aligned approximately perpendicular to the north side of Watling Street at four separate locations over a distance of *c* 1500 m (Cramp and Brown forthcoming). These probably formed part of one or more field systems broadly analogous to that seen at Site 5.

The evidence from Sites 15 and 29 makes it clear that enclosures were a recurring element in settlement layout, ie that they were constructed throughout most of the Romano-British period, as far as can be seen from the dating evidence, although there are no certain examples of enclosures that originated in the 4th century. They were also used in the very particular context of the cemetery alongside Ryknield Street at Site 12. Here ditches defined roadside zones *c* 45 m deep west of Ryknield Street and *c* 40 m deep on the east side. It is not clear if the eastern zone was defined from the beginning with the specific purpose of accommodating the cemetery, but this is possible. Elsewhere, a roadside ditch was seen on the north side of Watling Street at Site 41.

Only at Site 29 is it likely that the majority of the settlement lay within the excavated area. This makes establishment of the character of the individual settlement sites particularly difficult, especially in the case of Sites 15 and 34. The possible relationship of the former site to the nearby double ditched enclosure west of Birmingham Road Nurseries has already been mentioned, but lack of detailed understanding of that site (or of the intervening area) precludes further analysis. However, the finds from there suggest that it had a high status component and if it is assumed that it formed the principal domestic focus of the wider complex the Site 15 features may be seen as accommodating a series of subsidiary activities. Their nature is, however, poorly defined, with the obvious exception of pottery production, although the area of this particular activity was not closely delimited. At Site 34 the situation is, if anything, more problematic because of the complete lack of meaningful information about other likely components of this settlement outside the road corridor. Extremely ephemeral cropmark evidence suggests that these probably lay to the south of the excavated site. At present it is assumed that the major aisled building was not the principal domestic structure at this site, but this is based largely upon the relative absence of domestic debris associated with this building, and in view of the general paucity of such material across the M6 Toll sites such an assumption may be invalid. It is notable, however, that while a probable hearth structure was located outside the building there were no traces of any comparable features within it. Such an absence might support the view that this was not a domestic building, but given the general level of preservation on this as on many other M6 Toll sites cannot be conclusive.

The alignment of features at Site 34, as at Site 15, noticeably bore no relationship to the line of Watling Street, only *c* 200 m distant to the north. In this instance topographical factors including the relationship of the site to the (now straightened) course of the Crane Brook may have been influential. It is possible, however, that at both Sites 15 and 34 some elements of the layout of the pre-Romano-British landscape, now undetectable, resulted in the observed orientations of the Romano-British settlements in the same way that the Romano-British features of Sites 19 and 29 were more obviously related to previous activity.

The almost exclusive concentration of the settlement evidence on sites incorporating enclosures may present a misleading impression of the wider character of settlement form. The potential for location by aerial photography or geophysical survey of sites that did not include significant ditched components was low, and while it is most unlikely that significant Roman sites escaped undetected (see Concluding Remarks below) it is possible that locations of relatively ephemeral activity were not identified. Such sites could perhaps have constituted an additional component in a pattern of settlement that was particularly concerned with pastoralism. By virtue of their probably more temporary character in comparison with the enclosed settlements they could also have constituted a more dynamic component within local settlement patterns. The paucity of structural and artefactual material even at the better-defined settlements suggests that more temporary sites might have been very difficult to identify in anything less than ideal conditions. The existence of unenclosed settlement components in the Iron Age is demonstrated at Sites 14 and 30, and for the early Romano-British period is suggested elsewhere in the area at Coleshill, where circular structures in successive phases were related to ditches which may have formed field boundaries rather than settlement enclosures (Magilton 2006). The existence of such settlement components in the M6 Toll area in the Romano-British period must be considered a possibility, therefore, although their likely numbers and consequent importance are impossible to judge.

Settlement components: buildings

Buildings can be difficult to identify in rural settlement contexts in a number of areas of Roman Britain, and this region is no exception. The obvious exceptions are high status buildings usually associated with villa sites, but no such structures were identified in the present project. The most spectacular building, the substantial aisled structure on Site 34 (see further below), might indeed have formed part of a villa complex, but was entirely of timber and, unless the material had been very comprehensively recycled, did not even have a tiled roof. Sandstone was readily available for building and was widely used in the region, for example at Wall and at Sites 34 (the well lining) and 12 (see below), while at Site 15 reused elements were employed in the kiln and were found elsewhere, most likely derived from the nearby double-ditched enclosure to the west. From this and the published evidence (Hodgkinson and Chatwin 1944) it is clear that at least one building within that enclosure probably had stone walls, glazed windows and a stone-tiled roof, although no *in situ* structural traces were identified. It is therefore uncertain whether the enclosure contained only one or several buildings, although Gould (1972, 3; 2001, 53, 55) has suggested that a (possibly subsidiary) structure can be seen on aerial photographs in the northern part of the enclosure.

Within Site 15 structural traces were ephemeral, but a potential circular structure of middle Romano-British date, incorporating vertical posts and defined in part by a curvilinear gully, was identified within Enclosure 1. At a slightly later date a group of features within Enclosure 2, again including lengths of curving gully, possible postholes and an irregular cobbled surface, may have related to a second structure. The exact plan and dimensions of this are very uncertain but it may still have been of roughly circular form. The finds from Site 15 included, by the standards of the project, relatively large quantities of ceramic building material and stone roofing material, but none of this appears consistent with the structural evidence as currently understood, and it is likely that all this material was reused for other purposes, as may have been the case with ceramic building material at Sites 19 and 29 (see further below).

The structural evidence from Site 29 was equally exiguous, but suggests a progression from circular to rectilinear building traditions, a sequence certainly observed in rural settlement contexts in Warwickshire at Crewe Farm, Kenilworth, where a circular structure was replaced by a rectilinear posthole building (Ford 1971), and at Bidford Grange (Booth 1996b, 45). It is possible that the adjacent elements at Site 29 – part of a ring gully and a rectilinear arrangement of postholes – were components of a single structure, but this seems improbable and, although there is no direct stratigraphic evidence to confirm the interpretation, it seems more likely that the circular structure was the earlier of the two. This would have represented a continuation of the Iron Age building tradition seen in Enclosure 1 of this site. The succeeding posthole structure, *c* 7 m by 6.5 m, equally represented continuity of use of the chosen, probably domestic location, also seen in Enclosure 1, but with the difference that the renewal of this location eventually involved a change in construction type. Continuity of tradition was also maintained in respect of building orientation, the Enclosure 1 Iron Age structures and both the Enclosure 3 Romano-British ones having a south-easterly aspect (*cf.* Oswald 1997).

The absence of other structures of Romano-British date at Site 29 may indicate that there was only one domestic unit amongst a series of broadly contemporary enclosures, but it is also possible that other building traditions, such as mass-wall (eg cob) construction which involved no significant use of intrusive subsoil features, were in use. They may even have been in use in this region in the Iron Age if the limited structural evidence from Site 14 is any guide. That such traditions were also found in Warwickshire in the Iron Age has been suggested by S.C. Palmer (2006a) for Ling Hall, Church Lawford, and might be inferred from the drainage gullies with no internal features at Wasperton (Crawford 1984; see also Fitzpatrick above), while in the early Romano-British period some of the penannular gullies at Coleshill contained internal features, but few if any of these were clearly structural, with the exception of probable door posts in at least one instance (Magilton 2006, 18). Such traditions were probably quite widespread in the Romano-British period, particularly (but not exclusively) for construction on lower status rural settlement sites, as has been argued for the Upper Thames valley, for example (Allen *et al.* 1984). Construction in a mass-wall tradition is therefore a distinct possibility at a number of sites in the region. The small sub-enclosure in the north corner of Enclosure 6 at Site 29 could have accommodated a structure of this type and of the size of the posthole building in Enclosure 3, although other uses for the sub-enclosure are of course possible.

The only clearly 'Romanised' building encountered in the M6 Toll sites was therefore the aisled building from Site 34. This is a good example of the type, although at ten bays length, with an overall length to width ration of just over 3:1, it is towards the top end of the size range of known examples, particularly of those entirely built in timber. Comparable structures in terms of dimensions include the timber phases of the buildings at Denton, Lincolnshire (Smith 1964) and Landwade, Suffolk (Greenfield 1960), of 8 and 9 bays respectively. Both of these, however, were succeeded by stone built structures and clearly incorporated domestic elements. There are, however, some slightly unusual aspects of the Site 34 building plan.

First, the aisles are notably narrow, and do not conform to the typical proportions of aisled buildings in which the 'aisles' are half the width of the 'nave'. Secondly, at the north-west end of the building an intermediate post was placed between the main aisle posts of the gable end. In addition, the outer wall line, often interpreted as forming aisles, was also carried round the north-west end of the building. This feature almost certainly means that a principal entrance to the building was in the south-east gable end. It is less clear if there were entrances in the long sides of the building, but this is quite likely. Not only were the 'aisles' quite narrow, but it was notable that the posts supporting the outer wall, though less substantial than the main 'aisle' posts, were rather larger than is sometimes the case with buildings of this type. The implications of this for the appearance of the building are not clear; the reconstruction of this building type as typically having a 'basilican cross-section' has been challenged, for example by Smith (1963, 1, 25–7), to the extent that a single roof has become the standard reconstruction (King 1996, 66), as seen for example in the context of the buildings at Orton Hall Farm (Mackreth 1996, 69).

At Site 34 the relatively substantial size of the outer wall posts might, however, suggest that this was a separate structure independent of the main roof, the weight of which would have been carried on the principal roof trusses and would not require significant support only *c* 1.5–2 m outside the ends of those trusses. This might in turn suggest that the building did in fact have a basilican cross section, ie that the 'nave' walls were higher than the aisle roof level and contained clerestory openings, but this is speculative. That such a building form did exist in Britain is demonstrated unequivocally by the Meonstoke façade (King and Potter 1990; King 1996), albeit that that building was entirely of stone and substantially wider (though not longer) than the Site 34 structure.

The most striking parallel to the Site 34 building comes from Somerford Keynes in the upper Thames Valley (Miles *et al.* 2007, 236–8). This was an entirely timber structure, of nine bays, with two posts in one of the short ends. The only significant difference from the Site 34 building was the absence of structural components for the outer walls (presumably removed by plough truncation), though the likely extent of the building can be estimated on the basis of adjacent ditch lines. It was *c* 23 m long with a nave width of *c* 5.5 m (from centre to centre of the post pits), from which a total width of up to *c* 10 m may be estimated (and a total length of up to 27 m is suggested by Miles *et al.* (2007), based on Mackreth's reconstruction of Orton Hall Farm). The building was constructed in the early 2nd century or slightly later, when a Late Iron Age–early Romano-British settlement was radically reconfigured, and may not have survived in use much past the end of the 2nd century. The suggested context of this phase of activity may have involved official intervention in the organisation of the landscape and its component settlements (*ibid.*), a situation that might possibly have been paralleled at Site 34.

Physical and agricultural landscapes

As discussed above (Chapter 29), pollen evidence from below the Roman road in Site 12 indicates declining levels of woodland and the development of a relatively open landscape with some evidence for arable agriculture. The extent to which this can be regarded as typical of the situation across the region by the time of the Roman conquest is uncertain, but the combined environmental evidence from Site 15, in particular, reveals a diverse landscape by the 2nd century. The charcoal remains suggest a fairly open landscape with areas of sparse oak woodland (perhaps with hazel and holly understorey), while marginal woodland species included blackthorn, hawthorn (and related species) and hazel. Charred hazel nutshells were found at Site 15 and at several other sites as well. There are hints that some at least of the woodland might have been managed (Gale, Chapter 17). Pine charcoal from Site 12 suggests the presence of these trees, if not of pine woods, on some of the local sandy acidic soils, a suggestion supported by the presence of increasing quantities of pollen of heathland plants (ling and heather), as well as of pine, in the upper part of the profile from beneath Ryknield Street at this site. The same association of pine and heather (and birch), indicative of heathland, was noted in the charcoal from Site 34, less than 4 km distant to the west, alongside evidence that 'oak formed the dominant woodland component in that area' (Gale, Chapter 12).

Wetter ground was near at hand in the valley of the Crane Brook (the Shenstone wetlands) – probably no more than a few hundred metres away to the south of Site 12 and just west of Site 15. Alder and willow were found here; other plants (spike-rush, cotton-grass and sedges) may have reached Site 15 with fuel, or they may indicate that the very margins of the wetland were cultivated for arable. In contrast, heathland was again found relatively close by, indicated by charred remains of heather and gorse or broom, and birch probably grew here. A similar range of environments is seen at Site 29. Heathland plants (gorse/broom and heather) recall the historically attested use of this site, while alder and willow indicate exploitation of the adjacent stream valley. Again, some managed woodland may have lain nearby.

Hedges are likely to have been a recurring landscape component, both adjacent to settlements and perhaps further afield. Appropriate taxa (blackthorn, hawthorn/*Sorbus* etc) are widely seen in the charcoal records, although they could have been growing in other contexts. The existence of hedges associated with enclosures was, however, specifically suggested for example at Site 29 (Gale, Chapter 21), and while the evidence is no more compelling there than for other M6 Toll sites, the suggestion is plausible and the likely association of hedges with 'incomplete' enclosures has already been considered.

The prevailing soil types in the region are so acidic that animal bone did not usually survive, thus precluding any assessment of the character and importance of animal husbandry in the agricultural regime. This is particularly unfortunate since the absolute quantities of charred plant remains recovered from a number of the settlement sites are such as to suggest that arable production may not always have been particularly important, and that many communities therefore had an emphasis on pastoralism. Quantities of charred remains recovered will have varied depending on the location of the sampled areas, so that the limited plant remains from Site 5, for example (and perhaps the even more limited remains from undated features at Site 33), may reflect the location of the site within the (presumably arable) fields some short distance removed from likely locations of crop processing and domestic activity, rather than indicating that cereal production was of little importance here.

This explanation is unlikely to be valid, however, at Site 29, where again only very small amounts of charred cereal remains were recovered, but much more of the settlement was examined. The inference that arable production was a low level activity here may be supported by aspects of the layout of the enclosures, which can be argued as suggesting concern with stock control. Less of the likely settlement focus was examined at Site 19, but here again the overall quantities of cereal remains were very small, and the ditched trackway north of the main enclosure might again have been intended to control the movement of animals in the vicinity of the settlement. At Fisherwick, in the Tame valley some 13 km north of Site 19, the juxtaposition of a farmstead enclosure and trackway formed part of the basis for interpreting the site as having a stock-rearing function (Miles 1969) and a similar stock-rearing emphasis may have prevailed at Whitemoor Haye, just north of Fisherwick, though the evidence there was considered insufficient to form a firm conclusion (Coates 2002, 88).

The main concentrations of cereal remains were therefore recovered from sites located in the vicinity of Wall and relatively close to the line of Watling Street, particularly from Site 15. The principal cereal crops were wheat and barley. Spelt was the likely majority component of the former category and was recorded at all the principal settlement sites, except perhaps Site 19, but emmer wheat was also present at Site 34 and free-threshing bread wheat (*Triticum aestivum*) was noted at Site 19 in pits of both Iron Age and Romano-British date (but in such small quantities that one wonders if the grains could have been intrusive). Oats occurred at Site 29 but only in small quantities, like all the other cereals at this site, and has generally been regarded as a contaminant or an accidental component of the cereal crops considered here, rather than a deliberately cultivated crop.

Another cereal crop was rye. This may have been present at Site 19 but was certainly recorded at Sites 15 and 34, where the character of the remains is consistent with its cultivation in the vicinity. At both Site 15 and Site 34 rye was less well-represented than spelt wheat or barley, but the quantities were nevertheless such that it is most unlikely to have been an accidental component of other crops. Widely regarded as particularly indicative of post-Romano-British agricultural practice, rye is being increasingly recognised on Romano-British sites in the region, albeit generally in small quantities, as at Rocester (Monckton 2000, 67–8) and Whitemoor Haye (Ciaraldi 2002, 63, 65) and in the Arrow valley to the south (Moffet and Ciaraldi 1999, 163, 165), although at Metchley its occurrence in the pollen record does seem to be of post-Romano-British date (Greig 2005, 78–9).

The general dominance of spelt and barley is in line with evidence from much of lowland Roman Britain as a whole as well as from the region, particularly in Warwickshire. The significance of rye, given its relative rarity, is hard to assess at present, though its tolerance of poor (acidic) soil conditions is a plausible explanation for its occurrence in this area. It is notable, however, that at Ling Hall Quarry, Church Lawford, in the upper Avon Valley, the presence of significant quantities of barley was interpreted as perhaps reflecting the suitability of that crop for the acidic soils of the area (S.C. Palmer 2002b). Whether rye was favoured in the region for a similar reason remains to be established. A simple correlation of its occurrence with acidic soils may not follow, however, as the soils of the Arrow valley, for example, are not particularly acidic. The widespread use of barley (and also spelt) for malting in Roman Britain is not reflected in the M6 Toll evidence; occasional sprouted grains are insufficient in quantity to indicate such a use.

Overall, the plant remains suggest arable production in the immediate vicinity of Sites 5, 34 and 15, with associated processing activities. The situation is less clear at Sites 29 and 19, where thc quantities of cereal remains are such that significant cereal production seems unlikely. At Site 29, it is notable that only grains were present amongst the very small cereal assemblage from the Romano-British enclosures, in contrast with the preceding Iron Age settlement, in which both grain and chaff were found. This may indicate that grain was already processed by the time it reached the Romano-British enclosures, suggesting that it was not produced there (meal clearly was, however, on the basis of the quern stones found). Chaff was similarly absent at Site 19. In both cases the overall quantities of charred remains were such that the significance of the absence of processing waste should not be over-emphasised, but it is certainly suggestive of an agricultural regime in which cereal production was at best a minor component.

Weed seeds, in addition to giving an impression of the appearance of the fields, also provide evidence about the nature of cereal harvesting. Both the presence of low growing plants (including buttercups and particularly chickweed) in a range of weed types, and of cereal culm bases (at Sites 15 and 34), suggest the possibility that crops were harvested by uprooting (Clapham, Chapters 17 and 12).

The principal cereals may have been supplemented by pulses – peas, for example, were recorded at Sites 5 and 15 and pulses were also noted at Site 19. Beet, perhaps a Roman introduction as a cultivated species, occurred at Sites 5 and 34 and was probably deliberately cultivated there, but is more likely to have been leaf beet than a root plant. Flax or linseed remains were found at Site 15, but it is unclear whether this was grown as an oil crop or for fibres, or both. Damp conditions relatively close to this site, clearly indicated by aspects of the uncultivated plant assemblage, might have been suitable for flax retting, but there is no direct evidence for this activity.

More specific plant uses may be implied by finds from the Site 12 cemetery. These included lentils, from a number of contexts. While these could have been in general use as foodstuffs their unique occurrence in an M6 Toll context in the cemetery suggests that such commodities were confined to the community at Wall, as might indeed be expected, and moreover that they perhaps had a very specific ritual association (see further below).

Other economic activities

Pottery production

The most obvious non-agricultural activity was pottery production. This was directly evidenced at Site 15 and may have been practised elsewhere in the vicinity of Wall. The evidence from other M6 Toll sites suggests that the products of Site 15 achieved a relatively limited distribution; they reached all the significant Romano-British sites, from Site 5 in the west to Site 19 in the south-east, but while they amounted to 13.5% of sherds at the latter site, elsewhere they comprised less than 10% of the pottery in all the sites with meaningful assemblages, except at Site 15 itself. The chronological range of production suggested by the archaeomagnetic date for the kiln and the typological characteristics of the pottery itself together indicate that this activity was undertaken over a considerable period, perhaps from the mid-2nd century until as late as the second half of the 3rd century (see Leary, Chapter 28), though not necessarily continuously through this period and not necessarily only in the excavated kiln. Such production, principally of reduced coarse wares but also occasionally of oxidised coarse wares, is in a well-established regional tradition (Booth 1986; 1996b, 47–50). The evidence of nearby consumer sites suggests that, despite being quite long-lived, the scale of production at Site 15 was not particularly intensive. In the context of a wide range of possible economic activities perhaps associated with an estate based west of Site 15 this could be seen as relatively low level and seasonal, though sufficiently well organised to merit the construction of at least one substantial kiln.

More unusual is the limited but suggestive evidence for the production of both Derbyshire-type ware and of mortaria in the style of the Mancetter-Hartshill industry. Sherds of the former were present at Site 15, including in kiln contexts. Mortarium 'wasters' were more widely distributed, at Sites 12, 13, 15 and 19. Site 19 seems unlikely to have been a location of pottery production. Vessels at the other sites could have all derived from a single source, although production at more than one place close to Wall is possible. The typological variation of the vessels concerned suggests that, as with coarse ware production, this activity took place over an extended period covering much of the 2nd century and extending into the 3rd. The connection with the Mancetter-Hartshill industry implied by the mortaria is supported by the form of the Site 15 kiln. With its two substantial pedestals this is strongly reminiscent of later Mancetter-Hartshill kiln types (eg Swan 1984, 73, fig. xiii), an association that supports the later 2nd century and later dating of the associated pottery, rather than the mid-2nd century archaeomagnetic date.

The possibility of mortarium production close to Wall raises the question of where the necessary clay was obtained. The success of the Mancetter-Hartshill industry was based in large part on its access to a significant source of iron free white firing clay obtainable from coal measure outcrop deposits at Hartshill. No such deposits are known to exist in the vicinity of Wall and although coal measures occur east of Wall near Tamworth and at Walsall Wood only 6 km to the south-west, there is at present no evidence for the exploitation of any associated clays in antiquity. That iron free clays were available in the area, however, is also suggested by the popularity of medieval white wares in the north Warwickshire/south Staffordshire area commented upon by Rátkai (Chapter 28). Unfortunately, specific sources of these are not known. A widely-quoted anthropological study (Arnold 1981; 1985, 50–4) showed that a majority of potters dug their clays from within 1 km of their communities. Nevertheless, many potters were prepared to travel further if necessary, on the basis of which a typical maximum 7 km radius from the production site was identified for clay procurement. For the Romano-

British period, at least, it seems likely that clays would have to have been imported to the Wall area for white ware production to have been achieved. *In extremis* they could perhaps have been brought from Hartshill, some 26 km distant along Watling Street, but exploitation of a closer source is more likely. The generally yellowish colour of the probable local pieces might suggest the clay in this source was not of the highest 'pipeclay' quality associated with many Mancetter-Hartshill mortaria. It may be the same material that was also used for possible production in the Derbyshire ware tradition at Shenstone.

These hints of specialist aspects to pottery production in the vicinity of Wall, perhaps even at Site 15 itself, do not necessarily invalidate the low intensity/seasonal production model already suggested. The key factor is the volume of the relevant productions, and nothing in the present evidence suggests that the possible specialist potting in or around Shenstone was at anything other than a low level.

Stone extraction

Stone quarrying must have been a significant activity in the vicinity of Wall, where both raw material (Bromsgrove (formerly Keuper) sandstone) and a focus of consumption occurred. The precise location of Roman stone quarries around Wall is not known (Thorpe 1956, 28), but possible locations include Quarry Hills, Lichfield (only 2.2 km to the north), and Hopwas, some 5 km to the east (Gould 2001, 65; Ellis 1999, 19). Sandstone was encountered for example at Sites 34 (well lining), Site 12 (where it was used for at least one probable mausoleum or enclosure feature in the roadside cemetery) and Site 15 (re-used building material – see also above and below). The way in which this activity was organised is unclear. It was perhaps centred on Wall itself, but building material may have been worked on site to specific requirements. Whether this applied to more elaborate pieces is less certain. The interpretation of the large slab from Site 15 re-used in the pottery kiln is unfortunately uncertain, but if it was part of a coffin or sarcophagus lid it is perhaps more likely that this would have been prepared in the workshop than at the point of use, although decorated stone coffins were often transported in a roughed-out state (eg Walker 1990, 9).

Other craft activities

Evidence for other operations is extremely slight, even at the level of site-specific activity in support of domestic or agricultural functions. Indications of textile preparation or working were minimal at best; no stone objects associated with spinning or weaving were found; two triangular 'loomweights' from Site 19, quite possibly of early Romano-British date, may more likely have been used in a hearth or oven than for their traditionally-assigned purpose (Poole, Chapter 24) and only two pottery spindle whorls were found, both from Site 15.

There was no evidence for non-ferrous metal-working, and only minimal quantities of iron slag and related material from Sites 12, 13, 15, 19, 29 and 33, much of which was from poorly-dated contexts not necessarily of Romano-British date (report in assessment archive). At most 600 g of undiagnostic slag came from Romano-British contexts in Site 19, while 93% (by weight) of the 'slag' from Site 15 consisted of a single piece of vitrified clay lining, perhaps from nothing more than a domestic oven, found in a ditch fill. At best this material indicates very low level smithing activity. Other occasional activities are suggested by small amounts of reworked artefactual material – a fragment of glass from Site 29 flaked to produce a sharp edge, and *tegula* fragments from Site 19 apparently cut to form *tesserae*. The latter operation presumably took place on site and appears to have involved the use of recycled tile, but it can hardly be regarded as a routine part of day to day life here.

A further example of artefact re-use may have been the production of an unusual palette/whetstone from a fragment of Old Red Sandstone – just possibly a re-used quern fragment – also at Site 19. Any other craft activities, whether for household purposes or aimed at distribution by sale or other means beyond the individual settlement, presumably involved organic materials and have left no archaeologically recoverable trace.

Trade

The generally small numbers of non-ceramic artefacts (see also below) mean that consideration of trade is largely confined to the evidence from pottery. This has been discussed by Leary (above) and need only be summarised here. The quantities of non-ceramic material are in any case such that it may be questioned how many of these were acquired through purchase, rather than by gift or other socially-determined distribution mechanisms. It is presumed, although it is not directly demonstrable, that much of the trade to sites in the vicinity of Wall will have been channelled through that settlement. The occupants of Sites 34, 13 and 15, for example, will have been within easy reach of market facilities at Wall, while Site 5 was 10 km distant but with an easy journey along Watling Street if required. Site 29 lay a similar distance south-east of Wall but with a less obvious direct line of communication to it. Site 19, the most remote of the significant Romano-British settlements in terms of access to Wall (*c* 12 km), was, however, only 7 km from the major settlement at Grimstock Hill, Coleshill, and may have looked to that site as a local market centre.

Despite the modest size of the pottery assemblages they did contain a range of fabrics that are typical of the region, although generally the 'exotic' end of the range was limited in variety and quantity. Samian ware and amphorae, however, were consistently present at all the main sites (5, 12, 34, 15, 19 and 29), even if amphorae, in particular, occurred in small quantities and the mechanism for their distribution remains uncertain. Samian ware was best represented at Site 12, a consequence of the cemetery function of the site, which also explains the minimal quantity of amphora sherds there. Imported colour-coated wares were scarce, with single examples of vessels from Trier (Site 10), Köln (Site 19) and perhaps the Argonne (Site 34).

Extra-regional British wares fall into two main groups. Fine and specialist wares included a single Much Hadham sherd from Site 15 and Nene Valley and Oxford colour-coated wares from Sites 15, 19 and 29. Nene Valley sherds were usually slightly more common than Oxford ones, but the latter industry also supplied the only extra-regional mortarium sherd recorded, from Site 19. Non-local coarse wares were more abundant. Black-burnished ware was the most important of these and although its overall importance may be slightly exaggerated by its occurrence in the Site 12 cemetery it was still a significant component of the assemblages at Sites 15 and 19 and comprised more than 5% of sherds at Sites 34 and 29 as well (this fabric is, however, consistently better-represented by sherd count than by weight). Less remote but still relatively distant sources of coarse wares included north Bedfordshire (Harrold shell-tempered ware), Buckinghamshire (pink grogged ware) and probably Northamptonshire (fabric CTA1) to the south-east and Malvern to the south-west. The Severn Valley ware from M6 Toll sites cannot be assigned to specific production sites; some of it could therefore have travelled a considerable distance, for example from the Malvern area, or it could have come from more nearly adjacent (though unknown) sources.

The difficulties of distinguishing between the output of relatively local coarse ware producers, even when individual production sites are known, have been discussed by Leary (above), and make assessment of the relative importance of these sources very difficult. For example, the role of the major Mancetter-Hartshill industry in supplying the M6 Toll sites cannot be quantified precisely. Although it is likely to have been significant, the situation even with regard to well-known products of this industry, such as its mortaria, is considerably complicated by the suggestion of multi-centre localised production in the same style, and presumably by some of the same potters. Overall, however, it is likely that the majority of mortaria from M6 Toll sites did derive from Mancetter-Hartshill (Leary estimates approximately 90% by sherd count) and this industry was probably a significant coarse ware supplier as well, notwithstanding the contributions of the known Shenstone and Sherifoot Lane kilns and other possible but as yet unlocated kilns in the Wall/Shenstone area.

The way in which the distribution of the products of these kilns was organised remains uncertain. The inhabitants of sites adjacent to Wall could have obtained basic household objects like pottery vessels from a market within the small town – and it is most probable that imported pottery would have been distributed in this way. Whether the occupants of Site 19, for example, used the same networks is less certain. Equally, while the potter(s) using the Shenstone kiln might have sent all or at least a majority of their wares to market in Wall, it is unlikely that the Sherifoot Lane (Sutton Coldfield) potters would have operated in the same way. The archaeological evidence does not allow us, however, to distinguish between several different possible distribution mechanisms, whether by the potters themselves or by intermediaries (*cf* eg Peacock 1982, 156–8).

Very few other artefact types can be assigned to sources in the same way as pottery and therefore used to assess the range of economic contacts of individual sites. Glass may have been obtained through market centres, quite likely in close association with a range of higher status ceramics (Evans 2005, 147). While it was not made locally, there is good evidence of its production as close as Mancetter (Price and Cool 1991, 25–7; Price 2005, 170–1). Ceramic building material was probably produced within a similar framework to pottery; known pottery and tile kilns in the region occupied a broadly similar geographical location (Booth 1996b, 49–50). There is at present no evidence of local tile manufacture, but a source in the vicinity of Wall may be suggested for at least some of the excavated material on the basis of the requirement for building material there, and this suggestion receives some support from the distribution of fabrics, which suggests one grouping (of finer fabrics) at sites close to Wall and the possibility of a second centre of production providing at least some of the tile reaching sites to the south, such as Site 19 (Poole).

The one clear indicator of non-ceramic trade connections is the quernstones, which reveal a simple but interesting pattern (Shaffrey) (Table 162). With the exception of a single stone of an unsourced sandstone, from Site 15, all the stones are of Millstone Grit, the majority source (Sites 34, 15 and 29), or of imported lava. Fragments of stones in the latter material were found only at Sites 12 and 15, and their distribution presumably emanated from Wall, and evidently concentrated in the immediate vicinity of the market. (Unfortunately there are no useful data on stone types from Wall itself). The absence of querns in Old Red

Table 162 Numbers of querns from Romano-British contexts by stone type (frags certainly from same object count as 1)

Stone type / *Site*	*Lava*	*Millstone Grit*	*Old Red Sandstone*	*Other*
34	–	1	–	–
12	2	–	–	
15	1	6	–	1 uncert. sandstone
29	–	3	–	
Coleshill	–	25	13	2 ?Charnwood Forest
Metchley	1	10	–	1 uncert. sandstone

Sandstone (Shaffrey 2006 and Chapter 28) is notable. The M6 Toll sites lie at, and apparently help to define, the limits of the distribution of this stone type. At Coleshill, just to the south, Millstone Grit stones comprised 60% of the quern fragments, as opposed to 35% of Old Red Sandstone (N Palmer 2006), while querns from Metchley were almost entirely of Millstone Grit (Turner 2001, 86; Bevan and Ixer 2005) although, unsurprisingly in a military context, a lava quern was also present there (Bevan and Ixer 2005, no. 2).

Material culture

A striking characteristic of the Romano-British sites of the M6 Toll, as with those of other periods, is their relative 'poverty' in terms of material culture, particularly when compared with areas further south. This comparison can be made most easily with relation to the pottery evidence, but it is apparent in other classes of material as well. It is important not to overstate the case, particularly since variations in the level of sampling between comparative sites and M6 Toll cannot be quantified, but on the basis that the M6 Toll transect resulted in significant excavated samples from at least four settlement sites (from west to east Sites 34, 15, 29 and 19), some comparisons can be made with other sites from the region. The overall quantity of metal objects is small and the great majority derived from the Site 12 cemetery; in any case this and all the smaller metalwork assemblages were dominated by iron nails.

Coins were almost absent, although a hoard of 156 radiates with a closing date of *c* AD 273 (Seaby 1992) was found in 1988 very close to Site 19 and almost certainly originated from it, and a small but very similar hoard (more than 20 coins, of which the latest identified were five issues of Tetricus: AD 270–273) is known from near Wiggins Hill, *c* 2 km south of Site 19 (Chattock 1884, 235; this hoard is not listed in Robertson 2000). Further hoards, most notably one of 3237 coins up to AD 353 from Coleshill (King 1992), are also known from the near vicinity of the M6 Toll corridor.

Only three brooches were recovered from the entire project, two from Site 32 and unstratified, the third an iron pyre-good from Site 12; individually significant items were a probable vessel handle from Site 15 and the beaded torc fragment from Site 19, but with the exception of the latter such pieces are remarkable for their rarity value rather than any other characteristics.

The excavations carried out in the Arrow valley (S.C. Palmer 1999c) in advance of the construction of the A435 (now A46) south of the Roman small town of Alcester in Warwickshire may not provide a precise parallel for the M6 Toll project, but in terms of distance from a major nucleated settlement and the fact that structures relating to a villa site (but excluding the main domestic unit) were examined, comparisons with Sites 34 and 15 may be valid. The Arrow valley evidence contrasts notably with that from the M6 Toll, particularly with regard to metal objects; 141 coins and a wide variety of copper alloy objects including 29 brooches were amongst the material recovered (Mays 1999; Lloyd-Morgan 1999). In contrast, the quantity of pottery (5135 sherds, Evans 1999) was more nearly matched by that from Site 15 (3271 sherds), although the latter group did of course include waste material from the pottery kiln. Although pottery was universally present on the M6 Toll sites the amounts in use seem to have been modest.

Other comparative material from rural settlements in the region is relatively scarce. As an indication, however, the relatively small scale excavation of a settlement enclosure at Crewe Farm, on the Kenilworth Bypass (Ford 1971) produced 1835 sherds of pottery (Booth 1991, 4–5), well over twice as many as from broadly comparable (and more extensively excavated) M6 Toll sites such as 19 and 29, while a relatively low status rural settlement at Wasperton in the Avon valley produced over 21000 sherds (*ibid.*). These figures suggest a distinct difference in the use of pottery on rural settlements between the Avon valley and the area to the north-west. Ceramic building material also appears rare in the latter area, despite the fact that it included known production sites. As already observed, its absence from the Site 34 aisled building is particularly notable. Only at Site 15 is it possible that ceramic building material may have derived from structures on the site, although even here its use could have been secondary. At Site 29 the quantities and condition of the fragments are such that limited secondary use alone seems likely, and the same may have been true of the slightly larger quantities from Site 19, where the disproportionate number of *tegulae* in relation to *imbrices* is not consistent with the use of the material on roofs – they were again perhaps recycled for other purposes, including, rather bizarrely, the production of *tesserae*.

Glass is another widely occurring and distinctive Romano-British artefact type but again was rare on most M6 Toll sites. Fragments from Site 12 derived principally from vessels placed on funeral pyres but perhaps occurring in other contexts as well. Elsewhere, however, only single fragments were found at Sites 15, 19 and 29. All of these were from bottles, the most common glass vessel class found in Roman Britain, and the Site 29 fragment had been reused. In the Arrow valley, in comparison, where 15 vessel glass fragments were recovered (plus four of window glass), Palmer (1999) noted the poverty of the assemblage in contrast with those from villa sites further south – and by way of extreme contrast it may be noted that about 10,000 glass fragments were recovered from the baths basilica at Wroxeter (Pretty 1997, 319).

A number of indicators therefore suggest that the inhabitants of the Romano-British rural settlement sites of M6 Toll experienced a level of use of a range of artefacts that contrasted with practice in areas to the south, even as close as the Avon valley, some 35 km from Wall. It is important to note that the situation in the major nucleated settlements and in sites with military associations would always have been different, but the small quantities of material even from a probable high status site like Site 34, relatively close to Wall and to Watling Street, are notable. The M6 Toll sites therefore belong with other minor settlements in the region, such as Whitemoor Haye (Coates 2002, 88–9), although not all such sites necessarily show the same pattern of artefact use, since at Catholme, a site just north of the confluence of the Tame and Trent and *c* 1 km east of the line of Ryknield Street, Leary (2002, 21) records over 200 sherds of Romano-British pottery from field-walking. This is a remarkable quantity compared to the minimal amounts of pottery recovered in fieldwalking of the M6 Toll sites and one that may derive from a relatively substantial assemblage.

The M6 Toll levels of pottery and other finds appear to relate to a pattern of artefact use widely seen further north, for example at sites such as Great Woolden Hall, Cheshire, where minimal quantities of Romano-British pottery and other material were recovered (Nevell 1998, 58–9; more generally, Matthews 1997), and west, for example in Shropshire, where even villa sites, although architecturally impressive, appear materially 'quite impoverished' (White and van Leusen 1997, 140; for general remarks see White and Gaffney 2003, 221–3). Unfortunately, quantified data that would allow more local comparison of these questions do not exist for Staffordshire villa sites (Wardle 2002a). In the case of the Shropshire villas, however, it is hard to see that their 'impoverished' character was a consequence of lack of economic clout or difficulties of access to markets, and it seems more likely to have reflected a long-established cultural tradition that was shared by the inhabitants of a wide range of settlement types in that region (eg Booth 2000, 136–7), the only significant exceptions being places such as Wroxeter itself and the roadside settlement of Meole Brace (Ellis *et al.* 1994). More locally, Hodder (2004, 68) has drawn attention to the contrast in finds quantities between the site beside Ryknield Street at Longdales Road, Kings Norton (see above) and sites 'in the north of Birmingham', such as those of M6 Toll and others identified through fieldwalking (eg Hodder 1992, 42, 49; Birmingham and Warwickshire Archaeological Society 1998; 1999), and suggested that Longdales Road may have been a local market centre, therefore having some similarity with sites like Meole Brace.

On the basis of the scale and character of artefact use seen on most of the M6 Toll sites therefore, the area seems to be associated with a north-western tradition of low level usage, contrasting with areas such as the Avon valley relatively close by to the south-east. The reasons for this difference are not altogether clear but are characterised here as broadly cultural and social, rather than economic, and are considered further below.

Funerary and ritual landscapes

Romano-British cemeteries are very poorly represented in the archaeological record of the West Midlands. The Site 12 cemetery, in a classic roadside location, is thus a significant addition to the evidence for burial across the region as well as to understanding of the urban morphology of Wall. The relationship of the site to Wall is, in fact, curious as the cemetery lay spatially some distance from the nucleated settlement and was not on the road leading directly from it. It is possible, as has been discussed above (McKinley), that the cemetery was not intended primarily for the inhabitants of Wall itself, but it is not clear that the occupants of the surrounding rural communities would have felt the need to use a cemetery which was both in a very typically 'Roman' location and incorporated evidence for very typically 'Roman' rites and practices. Although it is possible that the excavated sample is simply one unrepresentative end of a much more extensive cemetery, the overall character of the burials and of the layout of the site as seen is much more indicative of an association with the town than with its rural hinterland.

If this is the case, why was the cemetery located where it was? The earliest burials, as (most probably) in the Watling Street cemetery partly examined to the west of Wall, were of later 1st century date and were therefore contemporary with continuing military occupation of the area, although a significant civilian community was presumably in existence by this time. There is, however, nothing overtly military about any of the burials from either cemetery, and the mixed community buried in Site 12 may well have been entirely civilian.

Communities which might have buried their dead at Wall include the military, the direct families of the military, other occupants of the burgeoning *vicus*/roadside settlement and inhabitants of the surrounding rural area, although these last seem unlikely contributors. The extent to which different cemeteries might have been preferred by these groups (if at all) is unknown, but present evidence suggests that a major roadside location was the overriding factor, indicating that these communities were integrated into mainstream Roman practice (via the prevailing traditions of the north-west provinces). In considering the logic of cemetery location the topography of Wall is very important. By the later 1st century it is possible that the majority of the length of Watling Street from the lower part of the hill to the west as far as its crest, if not even further east, was already occupied in one way or another. It is also likely that there was a concentration of settlement around the junction of Watling Street and Ryknield Street still further east, although it is uncertain if this was continuous with activity along the Watling Street frontage to the west. In this general scenario, the obvious places for burials were along Watling Street beyond the limits of settlement both to the west and east. This is what is seen to the west of Wall, but east of the crossroads was an area where Watling Street was carried across poor, peaty ground. This may have been considered unsuitable for use as a cemetery, with the result that attention was turned to the line of Ryknield Street, which in the Site 12 stretch was on ground which was well drained but, because of its location marginal to the lower lying ground, may have been of limited value for agricultural purposes. The margins of Ryknield Street north of the Watling Street crossroads may also have been used for burial, but there is no evidence for this.

It is arguable, therefore, that the location of a cemetery for the inhabitants of the eastern part of Wall, and perhaps particularly for those settled in the vicinity of the Watling Street/Ryknield Street crossroads, was decided principally on topographical criteria. The space available seems to have been adequate for the purpose since there is no significant evidence for expansion of the area of burials beyond the defined southern limit of the cemetery, nor for excessive crowding within it, although the internal evidence for lack of intercutting of graves may additionally indicate the use of markers.

The layout of the cemetery took advantage in part of an already existing roadside zone defined by a ditch west of the original westerly road-zone ditch of Ryknield Street. A corresponding ditch on the east side seems to have been a later addition, however, and did not extend further south than the east–west cemetery limit on this side of the road, itself defined by a ditch that was secondary to the original easterly road-zone ditch (the primary road-zone being *c* 17–18 m wide between these ditches). Internal features of the cemetery east of Ryknield Street included four ditched enclosures, but only one of these certainly contained a burial; two of the others surrounded probable tree hollows while the fourth contained a small 'mortuary house'.

The physical characteristics of the cemetery therefore included not just grave mounds (and their possible markers) but also enclosures, almost certainly trees, and a small timber structure within one of the enclosures. West of Ryknield Street a relatively substantial ditch subdivided the cemetery area, though the significance of the division is unknown. Also west of Ryknield Street, and perhaps originally located north of the excavated area, was a more imposing stone structure, the evidence for which derives entirely from building material redeposited in a ditch. Of unknown size, it may have been broadly comparable to the ditched enclosures in function, but this is not certain and is based on the assumption that the squared sandstone blocks walled an unroofed enclosure.

Whether this was a mausoleum or a walled cemetery enclosure is unknown, but both types of structure could have stood side by side as in the Watling Street cemetery in Southwark (Mackinder 2000, 14–19) and, more locally, at Derby Racecourse, where the mausolea were lined up alongside a road while the walled cemetery stood some little distance back from the road behind the mausolea (Wheeler 1985, 222–30). That the Site 12 structure was intended to make a visual impact is demonstrated by the one decorated sandstone piece recovered in association with the squared blocks. While it cannot be certain that all the stones belonged to the same structure it is most economical to assume that this was the case. The function of the decorated piece is unclear as it is not readily paralleled, but it was ridged on all four sides and may therefore have stood proud of one of the corners of the walled enclosure as a finial-like ornament. It seems unlikely to have been a capital; much more probably the walled enclosure was unroofed, although fragments of *tegulae* were also found with the worked stone.

Other component features of the cemetery would have been one or more *ustrinae*. In addition a series of hearth-like features aligned on the western boundary of the cemetery may have been associated with the preparation of funerary feasts. These features are suggestive of spatial organisation of activity within the cemetery, but this is not particularly borne out by evidence from other types of feature such as pyre debris deposits, which occurred in almost equal numbers both east and west of Ryknield Street. Nevertheless, while those to the east appeared to be fairly randomly distributed amongst the other features, some of those to the west were grouped, perhaps around a pyre location. The latter need not have involved the existence of a defined above-ground structure.

The occurrence of imported lentils in the cemetery has already been mentioned, and their significance could have been specifically ritual in character. Evidence from Mainz (Zach 2002, 105) is particularly valuable for demonstrating a direct association in a ritual context between lentils and pine nuts (*pinus pinea*), the latter more widely found with religious associations in Britain, with recent evidence eg from London (Giorgi 2000, 12), from a shrine at Westhawk Farm, Ashford, Kent (Booth 2001b, 18–19) and locally from the shrine at Orton's Pasture, Rocester (Ferris *et al.* 2000, 77). The use of pine wood in some of the funeral pyres may also have been a deliberate choice (for its aromatic qualities), but the Site 12 pollen evidence indicates that these trees were present in the local environment, so there is no reason to suppose that pine was specially imported to the site for use in cremation pyres.

The overall layout of the site, with its hints of apparent planning and zoning of activity alongside less systematic disposition of some burials and (for example) pyre debris deposits, appears fairly typical of the relatively small number of cremation cemetery sites from Britain in which consideration has been given to the wide range of different activities that would have occurred as successive stages of the burial ritual (*cf* McKinley above). On present evidence, however, parallels for the rectilinear enclosures seem too scattered and disparate for their significance to be clear.

Early Romano-British examples are notable at *Verulamium* both at the St Stephens and particularly the King Harry Lane cemetery, where they are Late Iron Age in origin. It is debatable if the late Romano-British examples seen at sites such as Lankhills and Poundbury, and suggested as ancestral to a post-Romano-British tradition of burial enclosure (Webster and Brunning 2004, 78), should be seen as growing out of the early Romano-British tradition or as something distinct, in the absence of evidence that clearly joins the two together.

There was only a single Romano-British burial from the other M6 Toll sites, a cremation from Site 34. The soil conditions of course very largely precluded the survival of unburnt bone (the skull fragments from the Iron Age pit alignment at Site 19 are a notable exception). Generally therefore, isolated inhumation burials would have to have been identified on the basis of the feature shape, and isolated burials of neonates or small children, typically in small, shallow and sometimes irregular graves, would usually be impossible to identify without the survival of bone.

The Site 34 cremation burial, of an unsexed adult or sub-adult, was heavily truncated. Its placement (probably) in a ceramic urn, and the presence of an associated find of an iron hobnail, presumably a pyre good, are significant because they imply the performance of a cremation ritual of recognisably Roman provincial character rather than in a 'native' tradition. This in turn has implications for the character of the site and its occupants. Unfortunately the burial could not be closely dated. The surviving pottery sherds were chronologically undiagnostic, but there was nothing to suggest that they and the burial did not fall within the main period of occupation of the site (principally the 2nd century), although the sequence of any relationship with the aisled building, roughly 20 m distant to the south-east, is speculative.

It is likely that the occupants of rural settlements would have been buried in the vicinity of these settlements, but there is effectively no surviving evidence from the area for this nor, unsurprisingly, is there any indication of local pre-Romano-British burial traditions that might inform understanding of Romano-British practice. The only location where burial activity might be indicated in addition to Site 34 is Site 15, and the suggestion is largely based on the interpretation of the large sandstone block from the Site 15 kiln as part of a coffin or sarcophagus lid. This interpretation is uncertain, so the entire argument is tentative at best. It is not impossible, however, as the potential villa enclosure just west of Site 15 is one of the few places where a family burial plot incorporating such features might conceivably have occurred. Moreover, since the Site 15 features were very likely part of the same estate complex it is possible that the putative burial plot lay between it and the settlement enclosure. It is rather less likely that the lid, if correctly interpreted, was salvaged and brought to Site 15 from Wall. Two further objects from Site 15 may also be relevant in this context. The pottery lamp and pipeclay figurine, recovered from the same area of the site, roughly 60 m NNE of the kiln, are both types of object commonly encountered in graves, indeed lighting equipment of all types occurs more commonly in burials than in any other context type in Roman Britain (Eckardt 2002, 115). It is therefore possible that these pieces derived from a disturbed burial, perhaps even from the coffin whose lid was reused in the kiln, but other interpretations are also possible (see below).

If correctly understood, the extremely limited evidence suggests that detectable burials were associated with higher status settlement sites. It goes far beyond the evidence to infer that burial practices associated with other rural settlement sites were radically different – this simply cannot be known at present. In broader terms, however, the following outline can be set out. The regional pre-Romano-British burial rite is not generally archaeologically recoverable; it may or may not have involved excarnation or analogous processes (see Fitzpatrick above), but it is most unlikely to have involved widespread use of cremation, since such burials have a chance of being recognised, even if not placed in ceramic containers.

The 'standard' early Romano-British rite of cremation was an alien introduction; evidence for its occurrence is therefore confined largely to 'alien' settlement forms – forts, towns and occasional high status (villa or similar) rural settlements. Inhabitants of lower status settlements may have continued to use an 'invisible' rite or rites; as was observed some years ago of the early Romano-British period 'we simply do not know how most Romano-Britons were buried at that time' (Jones 1991, 117). This remains true, and it remains true of other areas, such as the upper Thames valley, where late Romano-British rural burial traditions are much better understood than is the case in the area around Wall (Booth 2001a, 36–7).

The chronology of the introduction of inhumation is uncertain. In the Site 12 cemetery this did not happen before the late 2nd century (McKinley above), but this is likely to have been the earliest possible date. Two cremation burials were dated late 2nd–3rd century, but whether these preceded or were contemporary with the earliest inhumation burials is of course unknown. The dating from Derby Racecourse provides a useful comparison, however. There the walled cemetery, perhaps established by the mid 2nd century, contained both cremation and inhumation burials, some of the latter certainly in place by the later 2nd century (eg Wheeler 1985, 243), while cremation burials diminished in number during the 3rd century (*ibid.*, 235). Other inhumation burials from the region, for example at Alcester (Langley 1994), Tiddington (Palmer 1982, 14, 16) and Wasperton (Crawford 1983, 25–6) in Warwickshire, tend to be dated to the 3rd–4th centuries, but in some cases at least this may depend more on general perceptions of the expected date than on chronological reality. At these sites, however, the general lack of earlier cremation burials (with the exception of a few scattered examples from Alcester and Tiddington) is in notable contrast to the situation at Site 12 and at Derby. The apparent lack of inhumations from the Watling Street cemetery at Wall may not be significant as it is almost certain that the early excavators would not have located such burials (*cf.* McKinley above).

Other religious activity

An alternative interpretation of the pottery lamp and figurine from Site 15 (see above) is that they derived from a shrine, whether domestic or more widely accessed. The best local parallel for the lamp is from the temple site at Coleshill (Magilton 2006) and two ceramic lamps of different form were amongst the material from the shrine at Orton's Pasture, Rocester (Bevan 2000, 53–4). The Rocester finds also included a *patera* handle (*ibid.*, 55–6, no. 10). Although of a very simple form compared to the elaborate imported Rocester piece, a probable copper-alloy *patera* handle was also found at Site 15. The findspot of this object was *c* 25 m from that of the lamp and figurine, but all were associated with Enclosure 2, with its enigmatic stone surface and structural traces. The evidence does not amount to the compelling picture assembled by Ferris (2000, 74–82) for Rocester, and it is of course possible that all the Site 15 objects were redeposited from original locations of use far from Enclosure 2, but their relative proximity is striking, particularly in the complete absence of comparable material from any other M6 Toll site.

As Ferris (*ibid.*, 82) has noted, there is little formal evidence for religious 'sites' in the region. Temples and shrines do occur, however, in the context of nucleated settlements, most obviously at Wroxeter, but also at Rocester, Coleshill and presumably at Wall itself. That the occurrence of one or more temples was a typical feature of many 'small towns' is well known (Burnham and Wacher 1990, 40) and should be expected without leading to the characterisation of these sites as primarily religious in character (Booth 1998, 616). Evidence from Wall consists primarily of the well known group of carved stones found built into the walls of the *mansio*. These presumably derived from a shrine, albeit of unknown form (Round *et al.* 1978–80; Round 1990–1; Henig 2004, 35–7).

Other potential or actual indications of religious activity are scarce. The possibility that the Romano-British structures in Enclosure 3 at Site 29 might represent a shrine was considered, but this idea was based principally on the unusual form of a building with curving and rectilinear elements. If these are seen as two successive structures they appear more ordinary and a domestic function seems likely. More widely, the alignment of these and the adjacent Iron Age buildings, with entrances facing south-east, is indicative of the role of the broad structure of belief systems within the patterns of everyday life (eg Fitzpatrick 1997; Oswald 1997; Giles and Parker Pearson 1999). Another manifestation of these concerns is the placement of special or structured deposits, with human and animal bone, pottery and querns amongst the material types that can occur in such deposits. At Site 29 it is suggested that the burial of the complete lower stone of a rotary quern should be interpreted in this light (Shaffrey above; *cf* Shaffrey 2003, 163–5; Clarke 2000, 25). Such patterns of activity have a greater chance of detection in areas with an abundant material culture (see above). The relative paucity of evidence for activity of this kind on M6 Toll sites may therefore reflect these issues rather than the absence of such activity. Special deposits of animal bone, for example, could have been relatively common, perhaps particularly amongst communities where stock raising was the principal economic activity, but have simply not survived.

Wider landscapes

Some points of similarity and contrast with a variety of sites beyond the area of the M6 Toll transect have already been discussed, and are treated more extensively, for example with relation to pottery, above (Leary). It is uncertain how far the inhabitants of the M6 Toll settlements were concerned with affairs beyond the ambit of their local centres of Wall and Coleshill, but the location of these centres is itself of some interest because they appear marginal to the territories of two Romano-British tribal groupings, the Cornovii to the west and the Corieltauvi to the east. Simply in terms of distance from the adjacent tribal capitals, Wroxeter and Leicester respectively, Wall lies almost exactly at the mid point of a west–east line drawn between the two. Such a position is consistent with the hypothesis (Hodder and Hassall 1971; Millett 1990, 148–9) that a number of important 'small towns' developed at economically favourable points at the margins of tribal territories, ie furthest away from direct control of the large towns and most able to exert a local influence as market centres, particularly in the later Romano-British period.

To the south it is possible that sites such as Droitwich, Alcester and Chesterton developed in this way at or close to the northern margins of Dobunnic territory (*cf.* Booth 1996b, 53), which is likely to have covered much of the Warwickshire Avon valley. Nearer to hand the association of some temple sites with tribal boundaries or meeting places proposed by Stevens (1940, but not well-supported by the Gallic evidence; S Esmonde Cleary pers comm) has been used to suggest that Coleshill might have lain at such a location (Magilton 2006, 101), more likely on the boundary of the Corieltauvi with the Cornovii than with the Dobunni (Booth 1996b, 53). These pointers do not define the Cornovian/Corieltauvian boundary with precision, however. Whitwell (1982, 59) summarised the different assessments of this question and eventually concurred with Webster (1975a, 21) in placing Wall with the Cornovii, a view followed by the majority of subsequent authorities.

The exact location of the tribal boundary, which is unknowable, is not as important as the possible consequences of relatively marginal locations in social and economic terms. Is it possible that the variations in artefact use discussed above had any correlation with tribal territories? The problem here is to identify the factors that constrain distributions, particularly the relative importance of economic and social factors and their potentially complex interrelationships, and to be aware of the extent to which the arguments about distributions defining boundaries can become circular. Nevertheless, the present evidence can be used in two different ways.

The first relates to the distribution of particular pottery traditions. Leary (Chapter 28) has drawn attention to the fact that the M6 Toll sites appear to lie at the margins of a number of major regional distributions. While a number of ceramic distribution patterns (particularly those of imported wares) always transcended local and regional boundaries and some (for example of black-burnished ware) seem to have been linked at least in part to military activity, others were perhaps determined by different factors. The location of the region at the outer limit of the distribution of 'Belgic' type pottery has already been mentioned. On the Warwickshire evidence it is possible to see this distribution as effectively confined to the Dobunni and perhaps also to the Corieltauvi. This pattern suggests the possibility that the approximate coincidence of other distributions of pottery emanating from centres south and east of the region may reflect the continuation of the earlier ('Late Iron Age') tradition. It is also possible, however, that north-westerly distributions from these centres faded out here simply because they ran into the 'low-level artefact use' area, regardless of whether this correlated with tribal territories. More useful, therefore, is the evidence of pottery deriving from centres located north and particularly west of the M6 Toll area.

The southerly distribution of Derbyshire ware clearly does not extend beyond north Warwickshire, and the distribution of Severn Valley ware appears to be very limited to the east of Wall, as well as having a fairly well-defined easterly limit further south (Booth 1986, 35–6; Evans 1994, 149). In both cases the presence of local and significant regional industries may have been a constraining factor, but it did not inhibit the distribution of black-burnished ware, for example, and it is arguable that a genuine pattern is detectable, though with distribution networks that were not entirely mutually exclusive. A comparable readjustment of patterns of stylistic zoning of pottery from the Iron Age to the Romano-British period has been suggested in relation to the Trent valley, with less clear definition of these zones in the later Romano-British period (Knight *et al.* 2004, 144–6). The Trent is seen as a potentially significant social boundary in both periods, but this analysis does not focus on the upper part of the valley, though it does reinforce a long-established view of ceramic and therefore potential social distinction north and south of the river (*ibid.*).

The other aspect of this question relates to the issue of material culture use discussed above. Relatively 'wealthy' assemblages may be seen as a Dobunnic characteristic, but is it possible to distinguish between Cornovian and Corieltauvian patterns of material culture use, and is it even valid to try? Sparse artefact assemblages are demonstrably a rural Cornovian characteristic (see above), and may correlate with a view of Cornovian society as 'decentralised and egalitarian' (Millett 1990, 100), but they did not necessarily stop abruptly at the margins of Corieltauvian territory, wherever those may have been. There are simply insufficient data from rural settlements in Staffordshire to permit assessment of the variation in their artefact assemblages in relation to this or other questions, although general indications are that the pattern of limited finds assemblages prevails across much of Staffordshire (Wardle 2002a, 21), with the obvious exception of the principal nucleated and military sites.

Even the significance of the existing evidence for settlement distribution is uncertain. The few known Staffordshire villas are, in broad terms, associated with the major roads (*ibid.*, 18), a pattern which is given limited support by the M6 Toll evidence for sites such as 34, if it can be categorised in this way. Cropmark evidence of prehistoric and Romano-British date concentrates almost exclusively in the river valleys, and in particular those of the lower Tame and the adjacent parts of the Trent in eastern Staffordshire, but even here work has generally been at a low level compared to the middle parts of the Trent valley (see eg Knight *et al.* 2004, 145, fig. 6.20).

The only other notable cluster of aerial photographic evidence of later prehistoric and Roman settlement is that on the relatively light soils in the vicinity of Wall (*ibid.*, 21), where the apparent association with the Crane Brook is less likely to have been important. The M6 Toll evidence for location of settlement away from 'obvious' locales such as the major river valleys is presumably of wider relevance for the region, but given the potential problems of site identification even with systematic fieldwork, increasing understanding of the wider Romano-British rural settlement pattern will not be easy. Overall, therefore, more evidence is required for the distribution and type of rural settlement in the region before firmer conclusions can be drawn about the character of such settlement with regard to cultural associations. Nevertheless, the distinct 'Cornovian' pattern provides a model of such associations which can be examined with new data.

The end of the Romano-British period

Evidence for late Romano-British activity across the M6 Toll sites is scarce. Fourth century features and deposits are identified solely on the basis of pottery evidence as there is a complete absence of the normally ubiquitous copper alloy coinage of this period.

Local production of reduced coarse wares may have continued into the early 4th century, but did not certainly continue beyond this time. Fine wares, particularly from the Nene Valley and Oxfordshire kilns, were more common from about the middle of the 3rd century onwards, but their date ranges are typically broad and do not usually allow a distinction to be made between late 3rd century and 4th century examples. A range of non-local coarse wares in the later period includes black-burnished ware and Harrold-type shell-tempered wares, but the quantities are modest. Overall, there is very little if any material that needs post-date the middle of the 4th century. This is about the time when the Mancetter-Hartshill industry seems to have been in decline (eg Tyers 1996, 124), although the chronology of its later phases is not well understood and depends largely on the pattern of mortarium loss in better dated northern military sites. At Coleshill the occasional appearance of Oxfordshire mortaria (Booth 2006, 163) may indicate a ceramic phase subsequent to the demise of the Mancetter-Hartshill industry, but any analogous phase on the M6 Toll sites is represented only by a single Oxfordshire mortarium sherd, which may not be significant. A general absence of late 4th century pottery seems clear, but it is less clear how far this reflects a cessation of settlement activity.

There are potentially two distinct groups of settlement to consider. The first relates to the imposed network and the second to the wider rural landscape. The imposed network is represented by Wall, with ramifications in the immediately adjacent settlements. The alien character of the early Roman military complex was reasserted by the construction of the late defended enclosure at about the end of the 3rd century. This was surely not for the benefit of the local populace, but was a military/administrative installation, with a wider purpose than simply securing a line of communication in the specific historical scenario envisaged by Webster (1974, 57). On present, admittedly limited, evidence activity within the enclosure was at a fairly low level, and 4th century activity beyond it almost non-existent. The chronology of the Site 12 cemetery appears to mirror that of the settlement, with very little evidence for 4th century burial, and no evidence at all for burial in the later 4th century. Such burials could of course have occurred elsewhere, perhaps closer to the defended enclosure if the overall extent of settlement had contracted substantially by this time.

The latest coin from Wall is one of Gratian, dated AD 381 (Gould 2001, 72). The comparable installations may have had broadly similar chronologies, but there is no meaningful evidence for *Uxacona* and *Pennocrucium*. At Mancetter unstratified coins extend the date range to Maximus (AD383–388; Oswald and Gathercole 1956, 50). At *Tripontium* at least three coins of Arcadius are known (Besly 1981, 50) and there are other indications of very late or even early post-Romano-British activity there, while at *Bannaventa* the latest coin mentioned was dated 388–392 (Dix and Taylor 1988, 314). The evidence from these sites may be consistent with the suggestion that north Wales and the West Midlands fall into an area which was not supplied with the latest coinage to reach Britain, after *c* AD 392 (Brickstock and Casey 1994, 160). *Tripontium* and *Bannaventa* are likely to have been too far east to have fallen within the relevant area, although the coins of Arcadius at *Tripontium* have a wide date range (388–402) which does not resolve the question either way. If this interpretation is relevant at Wall, however, as seems likely, the absence of the latest coinage will not necessarily reflect an absence of occupation or other activity, although such an absence is possible. A local comparison may be seen at Coleshill, where a list of 64 coins terminated with six issues of Valens and Gratian, none later than *c* AD 375 (Seaby 2006). This pattern contrasts with that seen a little further south, where coins of the House of Theodosius are tolerably well-represented, as for example at Alcester (Brickstock and Casey 1994, 160).

If the loss of coin issues later than those of the House of Valentinian was generally minimal in the nucleated settlements of the region it is unsurprising that such material did not occur in the adjacent countryside. Equally, if a corollary of this is that the markets of the nucleated centres were also in decline, the absence of extra-regional later 4th century pottery, the distribution of which probably relied on such markets, is easily explained. As such pottery constituted an increasing proportion of later 4th century assemblages (Going 1992, 101–2; *cf.* Symonds 1997, 317–8), however, its general absence is probably still significant for places like Wall. What happened at the rural settlements of the hinterland of Wall is another question altogether since, as discussed above, there was a regional tradition of a low level of artefact use which might have revived in the late Romano-British period. However this may be, the earlier pottery evidence suggests that occupation had already ended at Site 5 and at Site 34 by about the mid-3rd century (at latest), while Sites 19 and 29, though continuing later, saw only quite low level activity even in the first half of the 4th century. Even at Site 15 there was no compelling ceramic evidence for activity of the second half of the 4th century.

Ostensibly, therefore, the archaeological evidence suggests that there was no activity at any of the M6 Toll sites by the later 4th century, and that this might have been the case as early as the mid-4th century. The interpretation of this evidence is difficult. It seems inconceivable that the landscape was empty at this time, but without significant early 'Anglo-Saxon' settlement features, which would at least allow assessment of their relationship to earlier Romano-British settlement, it is difficult to judge what was happening. To the north, at Catholme, the survival of a long-established linear boundary through the Romano-British period and into the Anglo-Saxon is likely (Losco-Bradley and Kinsley 2002, 20). This evidence may suggest, but does not prove, the survival of a community at this time. At Wasperton in the Avon valley a much-discussed cemetery sequence indicates continuity of burial function and perhaps of population from late Romano-British to Anglo-Saxon (Booth 1996b, 45). Such evidence is lacking from the M6Toll area – perhaps for want of definable later settlement, as already mentioned. In view of the general scarcity of evidence for early Anglo-Saxon activity in the region, however, even the occasional fragments of pottery at Site 32 are of some significance, although unfortunately there were no recognisable associated features. It is generally thought that Lichfield replaced Wall as the focus of settlement in the early post-Romano-British period (see Chapter 31); certainly the name seems to derive directly from *Letocetum*, the Roman name (meaning 'grey wood') for Wall (Gelling 1992, 59–60), and a sunken featured building of two phases has recently been found there, but is as yet not closely dated (S. Dean pers. comm.).

A change of local centre would not necessarily have resulted in the demise of individual farmsteads. It is possible, however, that with a declining framework of Romano-British local centres these farmsteads, which had probably tailored their agricultural output to meet the requirements of taxation and of local markets, even if such developments are not clearly identified in the archaeological record, became unviable. It is perhaps not a coincidence that the possible evidence for 'continuity' mentioned above comes from sites in the valleys of the Trent and Avon, locations with a long-developed tradition of settlement and perhaps with land of better quality than the particularly acidic soils of the south Staffordshire/north Warwickshire border area.

In Birmingham, pollen evidence from the vicinity of Metchley indicates the development of woodland and a significant reduction in any evidence of human activity (Greig 2005, 78), presumably consequent upon the abandonment of the site by about AD 200 (Jones 2004, 87). This pattern may of course have been quite localised, but it does suggest the possibility of a very real reduction in the overall extent of Romano-British settlement in the region in the later part of the period. Hodder (2004, 78) argues that those sites that did survive in the later Romano-British period in the Birmingham area were often at locations which became foci of later medieval activity. Whether the environmental determinism implied by these suggestions represents the main reason for the demise of identifiable late Romano-British settlement in the area can only be tested with further evidence.

Summary and conclusions

The area around Wall has long been thought to show a reasonable density of later prehistoric activity, even if that activity has tended to be poorly characterised. The M6 Toll excavations have improved definition of a number of sites and identified new ones, thus providing a more complete picture of the settlement pattern and landscape impacted upon by the Roman army from about AD 48. Direct physical impacts of the Roman conquest are not recorded in any of the M6 Toll sites, except insofar as the construction of Watling Street at Site 41 may have involved tree clearance. The consequences of the imposition of a series of forts at Wall must have been considerable, and were continued by the civilian settlement which grew up alongside and then survived the forts. Even if this community was only a few hundred strong its requirements in terms of provisioning might, at least in the short term, have imposed a strain on nearby settlements which had no tradition of production of a significant agricultural surplus. It is generally agreed, however, that in lowland Britain the capacity to meet increased demand, particularly for cereals, was present (eg Matthews 1998, 28). A response to this challenge appears to be seen in the development of field systems and settlements at Sites 5 and 34 and at Site 15 and the related ditched settlement to its west. It is particularly unfortunate that we have no certain knowledge of the origins of these sites: do they represent a local response to the needs of the new community or were they established by incomers with a developed eye for the opportunities presented by the growth of Wall? Either way, aspects of architecture and religious/funerary practice at Sites 34 and 15 indicate that these people shared at least some of the cultural background of the small town community.

As already noted, the agricultural emphasis of these sites was probably on cereal production, amongst which rye was a component in addition to the more common spelt wheat and barley. Although the function of the aisled building at Site 34 is not certain, its likely use as a barn suggests the potential of such sites to store, and therefore to produce, a significant surplus, and the location of the site was presumably also deliberately intended to take advantage of Watling Street for distribution.

The concern with cereal production at the sites with ready access to Wall and/or to Watling Street does not seem to have been matched elsewhere. Although the loss of animal bone evidence makes it impossible to be certain, it seems likely that at Sites 19 and 29 the principal activity was pastoralism. It is not certain if the need for animal products was as clearly defined as that for cereal, but the requirements of the Roman army for all the secondary products of cattle, as well as for meat, are well known. While the absence of evidence for textile manufacture might simply indicate that sheep were driven to market and processed there, it may also be a slight hint that the principal concern was with cattle raising, a suggestion supported, for example, by the (admittedly small) faunal remains assemblages from Iron Age Fisherwick, which were dominated by cattle bones (Greig *et al.* 1979, 98). These too would have been delivered to the local market centre on the hoof. Whether stock raising increased in intensity from the early Romano-British period onwards is not clearly demonstrable, but if the provision of the aisled building at Site 34 is seen as evidence of intensification of arable production there in the 2nd century it may be reasonable to interpret the proliferation of enclosures at Site 29 in a comparable way, particularly if, as is possible, several of them were contemporary.

It is possible to summarise the principal M6 Toll settlements in terms of a series of basic oppositions; Sites 34 and 15 with arable based economies plus (in Site 15) additional economic diversification, the presence of some Roman architectural forms and building material, hints of adoption of recognisable Roman provincial practice with regard to burial and other religious activity; Site 29 and 19 with pastoral economies, little indication of developed building types and no clear evidence for the nature of religious practice. This opposition must be too simplistic, but the differences do seem to be real. In terms of the organisation of society and the status of the occupants of these sites there may have been fewer distinctions, particularly if the heads of households were all drawn from the same local landholding class, which is possible but not demonstrable.

Perhaps, for example, the enclosure at Site 19 should be seen as approximately equivalent to the possible villa site west of Site 15, regardless of whether, as Gould (2001, 53–6) has suggested, the latter held the key to understanding of the settlement pattern immediately around Wall. The artefactual evidence, for example, contains hints that the Site 19 settlement was not of particularly low status. As well as being (presumably) the source of the late 3rd century coin hoard found close by (see above) the pottery included a more than accidental quantity of amphora (what the people did with these sherds or their contents is another matter) and, although too much should not be based on a single object, the presence of the beaded torc suggests the existence of contacts beyond the purely day to day. Such hints are missing at Site 29, but this was probably the most important of the excavated settlements in the Iron Age. Whether this status changed in the Romano-British period, or was manifested in another way – for example through cattle herds, is impossible to say.

The question of the relationship of the rural sites to Wall could perhaps be reversed. Was Wall in fact an alien establishment throughout the Romano-British period? As a sequence of military sites it was clearly imposed by interests far removed from those of local communities, at least in the short term. Did the later settlement then become integrated into the wider rural community and if so, in what ways and to what extent? The answers to these questions are perhaps most clearly seen in relation to the evidence for the people of Wall; the evidence of the Site 12 cemetery suggests a community distinct from that of the region – subjectively it has the feel of the northern military, rather than the southern civil – even after the end of the military period. It is arguable that the community remained largely self-contained, that its focus was on Watling Street and places, institutions and functions connected by it, and that it took what it needed from the surrounding countryside without providing much that was archaeologically tangible, at least, in return. This trend may be seen right up to the end of the Romano-British period, with the identification of potential evidence for Christian activity at Wall itself (Symons 1992–3), but with little likelihood that its effects were felt beyond the settlement.

Chapter 31
Medieval Period Discussion

By *John Hunt*

Introduction

The sites with significant medieval phases excavated during archaeological work on the M6 Toll run south-eastwards from the Staffordshire site at Shenstone Linear Features (Site 13, Chapter 15), in the northern part of the route, through to the Warwickshire sites at Wishaw Hall Farm (Site 19, Chapter 26) and Wishaw (Site 20) and Hawkeswell Farm (Site 24, Chapter 27) in Coleshill. The ceramic evidence from the Warwickshire sites suggests that they were at their most active from the 12th to the early 14th centuries, at which time the landscape of north Warwickshire was characterised by two influential features. The first was its natural setting, as the area lay within the woodland 'pays' that is known in Warwickshire as the Arden, although this woodland character is typical of much of the medieval West Midlands, so that woodland landscape, and the society and economy that it supported, was similarly characteristic of parts of Staffordshire.

Secondly, in the area between Birmingham, to the south, and Tamworth, to the north-east and focused on Sutton Coldfield, Henry I permitted the Earls of Warwick to establish Sutton Chase, carved out of the royal forest of Cannock (Fig. 219). Such private forests were a rare distinction, 26 having been created around medieval England at various times, but that at Sutton was among the earliest established. The greater part of the Chase fell within north Warwickshire, through which much of the modern road now passes. The sites at Wishaw are situated in the heart of the Chase. However, the bounds also took in about 12 sq. miles (*c* 31 sq. km) of land in south-east Staffordshire, so that it impinged on Staffordshire manors such as Drayton Bassett, Hints, Weeford and Shenstone, although in the case of the latter, the excavated site appears to have lain just to the north of the boundary (Hodder 1988, 4, 296; Hunt 1997, 110, 112; Cantor 1982, 70–2; Cantor 1968, 50; Stokes and Wellstood, 1932, 27, no. 135; Wrottesley 1885, 290; Midgley 1947, 235–6).

The Warwickshire portion of the area, the upland country of the county, is drained by the Tame-Blythe system of streams lying mostly between 60 m and 120 m above sea level, but rising to above 150 m in the East Warwickshire Plateau and on the Staffordshire border. This is an area where soils are mixed in character and quality, derived from a wide variety of drift deposits overlying Mercia Mudstone. More specifically, Wishaw and Hawkeswell are situated on slowly permeable seasonally waterlogged reddish fine loams, over clayey soils, and suited to winter cereals and stock raising on short-term grassland (Kinvig 1954, 307; Soil Survey, 1983). The Staffordshire part of the study area falls within the southern upland of the county, Shenstone being situated in the Lichfield area sub-region, lying at 75–110 m, with generally light soils derived from Triassic sandstones, sometimes modified by small patches of Boulder Clay.

Shenstone is situated in an area dominated by well drained sandy and coarse loamy soils over soft sandstone, suited to cereals, grassland and woodland. Site 13, however, is located within an area of deep permeable sandy and peaty soils suited to cereals and rough grazing (Wheatley 1954, 212–3; Soil Survey 1983). Well-wooded in 1086, this was an area that was generally characterised by a dispersed settlement pattern, with only low levels of nucleations, themselves often small (*cf.* Roberts and Wrathmell 2000, 55).

The absence of any pre-Conquest charters or deeds relating to the manors in question makes inevitable a reliance upon *Domesday Book* as the departure point for reconstructing the character of the area in the medieval period. In the discussion below the manors of Wishaw, Coleshill and Shenstone are first reviewed in turn, placing the archaeology in its historical context, followed by a discussion of the general themes and an examination of the issues raised, and contributions made through the work described in this volume.

The manors of Wishaw, Coleshill and Shenstone

Wishaw

In 1086 the manor of Wishaw was held by Orderic, who before the conquest had held the manor freely, but who now held it as a tenant of William fitz Corbucion. A relatively modest manor, it was assessed at two hides with land for two ploughs. The fall in the manor's value between 1066 and 1086, from 30 shillings to 10 shillings, may have been the result of the disturbances attendant upon the conquest itself, or more closely related to estate re-organisation. However, the fact that the manorial tenant had not changed and that, of William fitz Corbucion's 18 Warwickshire manors, only eight (44%) showed a decline in value (only four (22%) showed an actual increase in value), it seems unlikely to simply be a reflection of estate re-organisation. However, *Domesday Book*, while fundamental to any appreciation of the medieval manor, is nonetheless only a 'snapshot' at a particular point in time.

The population on the manor was recorded as three *villani* and four *bordarii*, together with a priest. This likely represents a population in the region of 35 people, most of whom were living as smallholders or cottagers, most probably dispersed across the landscape of the manor, and typically holding 5–10 acres (*c* 2–4 hectares) of land (Harvey 1986, 254). Harvey (1976, 197) has drawn attention to the potential significance, and impact, of bordars within the manorial economy and its associated landscape, highlighting the integral role that they might have played, as a class, in agricultural expansion. As she comments, they were not just a symptom of expansion, but also its personnel. While the villeins held integral parts of the vill and its arable land, cottars and bordars tended more towards the 'edge' or margins, particularly of cultivation (*ibid.*, 198). Harvey perhaps works to a rather centralised or nucleated concept of settlement in this model, and it is the case that working at the margins of cultivation does not necessarily also imply living at the margins of settlement. However, it seems probable that a preponderance of bordars in a population points to a dispersed settlement pattern as more likely. Harvey also argued that where large numbers of bordars occurred in county populations, at 40% or more, this suggested 'fullish' population levels and active expansion, particularly in woodland contexts (*ibid.*, 193). Warwickshire, at 29%, falls short of this suggested level (Darby 1977, 20), but a clearer indicator is to apply this notion at the level of the vill, or locality. Thus, in the case of Wishaw, some 57% of the population may be described as bordars.

Hodder's work on Wishaw between 1979 and 1982 further underscores the impression of a manor characterised by hamlets and dispersed settlement, with medieval occupation at Wishaw Hall Farm, Over Green, Grove End and Lower Green (Hodder 1992). The isolated location of the church at Wishaw led Beresford to conclude that it perhaps represented the site of a deserted settlement, and Hodder considered that the anomalies in the road and field pattern around the church might mark such a settlement area but, when fieldwalking was conducted, the amounts of medieval pottery produced was not consistent with a likely settlement site – in short, there is no persuasive evidence of medieval settlement in the immediate vicinity of the church (*ibid.*, 43–4). The church itself poses some issues. Although *Domesday Book* records the presence of a priest in 1086, it is a matter of debate as to whether this necessarily implies a church in Wishaw itself.

However, if there was a church here at this date it does not appear to have been on the site occupied by the present church dedicated to St Chad. The architectural evidence points to a 13th century date for this church, and there is a documentary reference of 1240 to Henry, the rector of Wishaw; references to the rights of advowson here occur on several occasions in the 14th century (Stokes and Drucker 1939, 117, no. 1586; Drucker 1943, 15, no. 2026, 105, nos 2391, 2392; Hubbard 1947, 260–1; Hodder 1992, 42–3). Furthermore, as Hodder observed, the church was built on top of former strips in the field system, confirming both that any earlier church, if present, was located elsewhere, and that the present, 13th century, church represents a 'later phase' in the history of the settlement (Hodder 1992, 44). Bond's comment, that seemingly isolated churches might arise when built to serve generally dispersed settlement, seems appropriate here (Bond 1985, 117), although this example is not located central to the parish.

Although the overlordship of the fitz Corbucion fee was transferred to the earls of Warwick by William II during the 12th century, the family retained their interests in Wishaw and it was perhaps their gift of land that established the Templars in the parish. Following Dugdale's lead, Coss has noted the large number of alienations made by this family, and the implications that this ultimately had for the decline of their lordship by the 14th century (Coss 1991, 300–1). Patronage of the Templars was seemingly popular in Warwickshire. Earl Roger of Warwick (d. 1153) founded a Templar house at Warwick, and while not particularly generous thereafter, it established a precedent that the fitz Corbucions might well have felt inclined to support. Overlords apart, however, Roger de Mowbray's support established Balsall, which later became the *caput* of the Templars in the West Midlands, and Robert Marmion, baron of Tamworth, gave them the manor and mill at Barston.

The Templars therefore emerged in Warwickshire as lords of three large manorial estates, at Sherborne, Balsall and Barston, together with an urban centre and a number of smaller rural properties granted by a number of lesser lords in the region. The fitz Corbucions were among this latter group, giving a mill at their manor of Studley, and lands in Wishaw and Moxhull (Lees 1935, cv, cvi, cviii, cix). The fact that Wishaw is not specifically mentioned in the 1185 inquest suggests that this grant was made after that date. In 1274–5, Guy de Foresta, Master of the Templars in England was at law defending his rights to 8d of rent in Wishaw (Stokes and Wellstood 1932, 199, no. 925) while, in the Hundred Courts of 1275–6, the Templars of Balsall were accused of withdrawing services due on land in Wishaw, Moxhull and elsewhere. Their holdings here were recorded as 4½ virgates in Wishaw, together with 1½ virgates and three cottages in Moxhull (Gooder 1995, 82; Illingworth 1812–18, ii, 227), from which in 1227 they were granting lands to Margery de Lisle, the family that subsequently held Moxhull Manor and tenements in Wishaw (Hubbard 1947, 259, 260).

The Templars were to hold land in the parish until their dissolution, after which their lands at Wishaw passed to the Knights Hospitaller in 1326 (Hubbard 1947, 259; Maxwell Lyte 1910, no. 748). The manorial sub-tenancy was most probably held in the 13th century by the de Castello family, but the de Berefords were clearly rising to prominence, as Walter de Bereford and his son are found dealing with lands in the manor by 1257, and in 1287 Osbert de Bereford settled lands here on his brother, William. By the early 14th century the

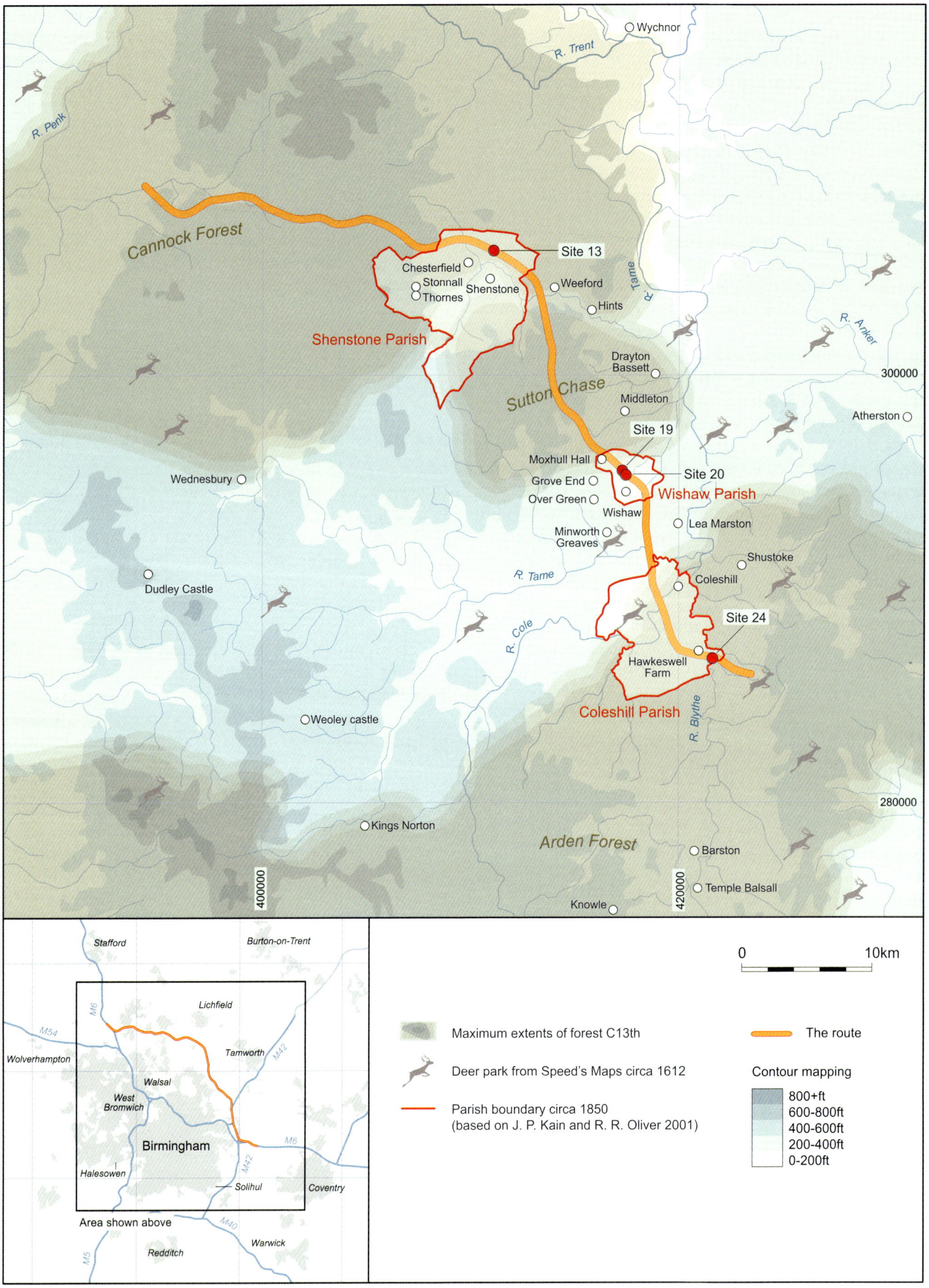

Fig. 219 Distribution of medieval sites

Bereford family had accumulated lands in no fewer than nine counties, and William de Bereford was among the most distinguished lawyers of his generation (*cf.* Hunt 1997, 71–2; Maxwell Lyte 1910). However, it is interesting to note that in 1256 Hugh de Bereford, Walter de Bereford and William de Castello were all fined for respite of knighthood (Coss 1991, 263), suggesting that they were claiming to be unable to bear the costs associated with the dignity of knighthood.

The decline in the number of knights is a well-known and much discussed phenomenon of 13th century England. While many families sought to avoid this expense, there may be some grounds here for supposing that de Castello's circumstances were more serious than those of the de Berefords. The de Castello family seems to have managed to sustain itself at Wishaw into the 14th century. A case of 1323–4 between William de Bereford (plaintiff) and William, son of George de Castello (deforciant) regarding a messuage, a toft and a carucate of land in Wishaw, together with the advowson of the church, demonstrates that de Castello, who held the advowson in 1306, had by 1323 acknowledged this to be the right of de Bereford, of his gift and held of him. Although not invariably the case, the advowson of the church often followed the descent of the manor, suggesting that the de Castellos, and then the de Berefords, held the 'terre tenancy' of the manor.

At his death in 1326, William de Bereford held the manor and advowson of Wishaw of the Prior of the Hospital of St John of Jerusalem in England by service, or rent, of 17d a year; his son Edmund received a charter of free warren in 1335 (Maxwell Lyte 1910, no. 748; Hubbard 1947, 259, 260; Stokes and Drucker 1939, 117, no. 1586; Drucker 1943, 15, no. 2026).

A brief glimpse of the 14th century vill is afforded through the short extent in the *Inquisition post mortem* of 1326 (TNA C134/102/6 mem.4; CIPM 1904–70), the Subsidy Roll of 1332 and the Poll Tax of 1379 (Carter 1926, 73; Fenwick 2001, 654, 655). The 1326 survey describes a manor worth a little more than £5 a year with 88 acres of arable land, valued at only 3d per acre yearly – a poor valuation even by the standards of the West Midlands. In the honor of Tutbury, for example, 8d per acre seems to have been about average for arable land, while some of the land in the honor of Dudley, noted for its poor arable land, was valued at 6d per acre (Hunt 1997, 79–80). The contribution of the arable to the demesne economy of the manor, worth 22 shillings, had more to do with the amount of land brought into cultivation than it did with the scale of productivity per acre.

However, Campbell has demonstrated that, in the area under discussion, the mean arable acreages of demesnes were relatively low, as was their value (*cf.* B.M.S. Campbell 2000, figs 3.05; 3.11; 7.13). However, valuations apart, the demesne illustrates that arable land was a noticeable feature in the landscape of this woodland manor. The extent also recorded 12 acres of meadow, valued at 12d per acre, and a 'foreign' wood which was common pasture. There was a *capital messuage*, or manor house, valued at 18d a year, but for the manorial lords their greatest assets were the rentals of their tenants, worth £3 16s 8d, and the accompanying pleas and perquisites of the court, worth one shilling annually. The tenants are described as freemen, bondmen and cottars, but unfortunately there is no indication of either their numbers or of their relative proportions in the demographic profile of the manor. However, the rental valuations could easily represent a population of 50 or more, and it seems probable that the freemen and cottars represented the assarters of the vill.

The Subsidy Roll of 1332 offers some support for the impression gained from the 1326 survey. The subsidy names only four taxpayers, headed by Sir Edmund de Bereford, which arguably represents a population of around 50, which if so suggests a population increase of less than 50% since the late 11th century, a surprisingly modest rate of increase. Rather curiously, the Poll Tax lists distinguish between the vill of Wishaw and the rest of Wishaw, so that there are two entries recorded, without any duplication of the names recorded. The vill listed 31 named taxpayers, while the other list gave 23 named taxpayers.

The names are only modestly informative. Robert Mason, and a widow named Margery Mason, may reflect one local occupation, as might William Wrythe, and Richard Walse was described as a 'taillour'. John Ryhtyng's name suggests his family's involvement with assarting, while names such as de Blythe, Attehurst and Othehull are topographical in nature and commonly found among dispersed populations. Names such as Aldebryton and de Waruyk point to some migration into the area. More striking than these details, however, is what this suggests about the size of the population as a whole. These lists point to a probable population in Wishaw well in excess of 200, significantly larger than that suggested by the 1332 taxation. The dangers of applying statistical estimates too closely are well known, but such approaches are generally indicative of trends, which in the case of Wishaw suggests one of two possibilities. Either that the 1332 subsidy under-represents to a greater degree than normal the size of the local population, or that the 47 years between the two lists did genuinely see, as a minimum, a fourfold increase in the population of Wishaw, a phenomenon that would have run contrary to the prevailing trends of the time. Elements of both may apply; certainly the demographic history of the West Midlands is not necessarily always one of discernable population decline in the 14th century.

The two adjacent sites, on either side of Grove Lane in Wishaw, appear to develop and decline within the timescales discussed above. Site 19, north-west of the former site of Wishaw Hall Farm, reflects the agricultural land use that might be expected of such a community, although the precise functions are not always clear, and no structural remains were certainly seen. A number of commonly aligned and dated shallow ditches, producing small quantities of mid-13th–early 14th century pottery, have been interpreted as a ditched enclosure, to which has been added the possibility that this had previously enclosed a building. The interpretation of this feature as an enclosure is not without question, and there is certainly no evidence of a structure associated with it. However, enclosures formed from banks and ditches were commonplace in woodland landscapes, a normal means of dividing and managing the land, creating defined areas of cultivation, and therefore naturally associated with processes such as assarting or small intakes of land. The two small sub-oval pits serve mainly to confirm the dating of the main phases of activity on this site, while the lynchet and truncated furrows again underscore the essentially agrarian nature of the activity on this site. The pottery from this site is consistent with the possibility of some activity by the late 12th or early 13th century, but the majority of the pottery, associated particularly with the linear cut features, points to the period *c* 1250–1325 as being that with which the excavated features are primarily associated.

Site 20 is rather different in nature, and had been marked by earthworks opposite Wishaw Hall Farm until they were levelled in 1972. The earthworks, previously thought to represent a moated site, were identified as a fish pond and associated features by Bond when he surveyed the earthwork complex in 1969, at the heart of which was an L-shaped pond, with traces of another pond system to the north. Bond concluded that the earthworks most closely resembled fish ponds at Washford (Redditch), held by the Knights Templar. Hodder's fieldwalking further emphasised medieval activity on the site, which the most recent excavations have more closely defined.

Together with holding and breeding ponds, and water management features, the excavation provided evidence of an associated structure, a rectangular building aligned north–south with doors on the western side, and at the east end of the north gable. The absence of postholes may indicate a timber framed cruck building, or a box frame construction in a beam slot. There was also some indication that objects had been placed against, or hung from, the wall. In addition, field and possible property boundaries were observed on the site. It has been suggested that the four ditches running eastwards from Grove Lane might represent tenement boundaries to the south-west of the fish pond complex while, to the south-east of the complex, a number of ditches define an enclosure, described as a possible paddock. Although the excavated evidence for tenements here is slender, the possibility seems a real one in view of the pottery scatter and observed activity on the site, confirming Wishaw Hall Farm as one of the medieval settlements within the parish.

Therefore, the most significant features on Site 20 are the fish ponds, features that generally related to seigneurial lifestyles, that is, to the gentry or to the church, and for whom they represented a significant asset within a manor. The ownership of the Wishaw ponds is not certainly known, although they are likely to have been the possession of either the Templars or their tenants. The morphological similarity between the ponds at Wishaw and those of the Knights Templar at Washford, where the presence of at least four buildings has been postulated (Bond 1988, 103), may be seen as lending weight to a Templar association at Wishaw. But morphology is not necessarily, of itself, a diagnostic indicator. Fish ponds vary greatly in their form, from single small ponds to more extensive and complex systems, capable of managing a greater number and variety of fish, and of regulating their breeding and storage (*ibid.*, 95). Furthermore, all fish ponds required arrangements for a custodian and for maintenance, and for a workforce to operate them, the scale of which must have varied according to the nature of the ponds in question. Thus, the complexity of the system at Wishaw, its capacity, and the likely labour and maintenance requirements, all tend towards suggesting the association of the ponds here with the needs and resources of the Templars, rather than with the lords of the manor. It is also the case that no reference is made to the fish ponds in the 1326 de Bereford extent, an omission that lends further weight to this suggestion. The comparison with Washford also suggests that the one building represented at Wishaw by structure 200662 is unlikely to have fulfilled all the needs associated with working these ponds. It is feasible to suggest that some of the postulated tenements may also have had a direct functional relationship with this activity.

Although fish ponds are referred to in *Domesday Book* and occur also in the 12th century, they seem to have proliferated particularly during the 13th and 14th centuries (Bond 1988, 92–3). Rátkai has concluded that the dominance of whitewares, but more particularly the paucity of Chilvers Coton C ware, dates Site 20 to the 13th–early 14th centuries. That is, that medieval occupation on the site can be shown by the late 12th or early 13th century, but that the discarding of material in the ponds and ditches, together with material from structure 200662, indicate dumping and abandonment in the early 14th century, a dating profile that is broadly consistent with the neighbouring Site 19.

As Harding remarks (Chapter 25, Site 20), the 13th century appears to have been a period of considerable activity in Wishaw. As was the case throughout the West Midlands and, indeed, throughout much of England, this was a period of major demographic growth. For example, in Warwickshire, the northern part of Stoneleigh hundred at least lies within the Arden. In the Forest of Arden it has been suggested that, in the two centuries following 1086, the population growth ran at some 375%, while in most parts of England population increase has been estimated in the region of around 250% (Hallam 1981, 151). Hilton's comparison of the Bishop of Worcester's estate in 1182 and 1299 suggested at least a 65% increase in the tenant population, although he recognised that this was likely to be a significant underestimate (Hilton 1983, 75), while Halesowen, between 1086 and 1315, saw a population increase of around 200% and, in Staffordshire, the population in the woodland parish of Wombourne increased between 1086 and 1327 by around 294% (Hunt 1997, 132).

More generally, population growth in Staffordshire has been calculated as running at some 933% between 1086 and *c* 1290 (Hallam 1981, 151). The problems related to using the taxation rolls are well known and have been discussed above but, while it would be unwise to place too much reliance on precise figures, the basic trend of population growth in the manor is evident, arguably in excess of 400% by the 14th century. This expansion in population clearly had implications for settlement and land use in the countryside, as population pressure drove colonisation and cultivation of woodland and heath. The Forest of Arden was no exception to this process of assarting and clearance during the 12th and 13th centuries. The *Domesday* description of Wishaw arguably suggests that the process was already underway before the end of the 11th century, but more generally the process intensified over subsequent centuries, and deeds survive that illustrate this process across the Arden in the 12th and 13th centuries (*cf.* Watkins 1993, 20). Although Wishaw is not specifically mentioned, near neighbours such as Middleton, Lea Marston, Shustoke and Coleshill are, and there can be little doubt that the population in Wishaw was similarly engaged. Thus, more land was brought into cultivation, and new settlement created, although the latter tended not to obscure the characteristics of dispersed settlement patterns where they were present.

The increase in the numbers of tenants was a profitable opportunity for landowners, for most of whom, on average, rentals represented the largest single source of their income, often heavily supplemented by customary payments, tallages, pleas and perquisites, frequently ranging between 40% and 70% or more of a lord's income. Wishaw was no different. In 1326 the manor was valued at £5 13s 2d, of which 67%, that is, £3 16s 8d, was drawn from rentals alone (TNA C134/102/6 mem 4). However, there were also difficulties for landowners at this time, as many aristocratic families found themselves under significant financial strain, a situation that has been explained as arising from the impact of inflation, and from greater ambition and extravagance on the part of lords, whose expenditure was linked to emphasising their political and social position. Anxiety over incomes generally led landowners to review and reorganise the management of their estates, and of their tenants, often turning to direct exploitation of their demesne, a trend which Coss detected around Coventry from the 1220s, gathering pace by the 1230s. Those who failed to recognise the problem, or to understand how to respond to it were often vulnerable to the failure of their lordship. Concomitant to these trends was increased competition between neighbours to secure resources of all kinds, and thereby to enhance and maximise their assets (*cf.* Hunt 1997, 79).

The upturn in activity observed on the sites in Wishaw finds its context against these regional trends. An expanding population within the parish generated more settlement and an extension of the cultivated area. The features on Site 19 may reflect assarting; they certainly reflect the agricultural activity that characterised the economic basis of the manor. As Hodder observed (1992, 44, 46), the building of the church on a new site in the 13th century may be understood within the context of expanding population and settlement. That it was built over previously cultivated land runs contrary to what one might expect, and may hint that the more marked 'upward trend' in population growth within the manor came a little later within the 13th century. However, it may be that the location of this site in relation to the pattern of settlement present in the parish at that time was regarded as a more critical factor. There is also the question of who might make this previously cultivated land available for a church at a time of increased financial difficulties for most landowners. The likelihood is that this grant lay with the lord of the manor, particularly since the lords retained the advowson. It is not certain whether this grant is to be associated with the Castello family, but it seems probable, despite the apparent financial pressures that the Castellos appear to have found themselves in during the 13th and early 14th centuries. However, such generosity might often be a cause for later regrets within the donor family.

Templar interests in the manor were established between 1185 and the early 13th century, and it is with the Knights Templar that the fish ponds seem most probably associated. The fish pond complex represented a significant manorial asset, and in this sense reflects the intensification of resources that landowners looked to during the challenges of the early 13th century – in this case, in the wider context of the Warwickshire estate of the Knights Templar. The dating from the excavation suggests that it was precisely during this period that the fish pond complex came into existence.

More problematic are the closing phases of Site 20. The dumping or accumulation of material in the ponds and ditches, particularly marked by the early 14th century, reflects the abandonment of the fish ponds, although Rátkai has demonstrated that the process was not an abrupt one. Pond 200253 was among the first to fall into neglect by the mid-13th century, and it is not improbable that the process of neglect ran through the second half of the 13th century to reach its climax in the early 14th century. This profile suggests that a direct association between the abandonment of the site and the fall of the Knights Templar is perhaps too simplistic, although the latter may well have sealed the fate of the complex. (It should be observed that this chronological profile is also one that would be consistent with an alternative interpretation of the ownership of the complex, held by the Castello lords of the manor; the picture of gradual neglect from the mid-13th century might be seen as accompanying the family's probable financial difficulties, while the final abandonment of the complex in the early 14th century would be consistent with the family leaving the manor and transferring the lordship to the Bereford family.) It may be that the complex was becoming too costly to maintain, and that the gathering neglect of the site actually reflected a longer term decline in the fortunes of the Knights Templar in Warwickshire. Gooder's survey of Temple Balsall highlighted the gradual decline of the Order, with an increasingly aged and infirm brotherhood, a severe drop in the numbers of the Order, and an increasingly serious and slack situation in the condition of their estates. Decline on this scale ran over several decades, certainly since the later 13th century. Gooder has calculated that by 1308 there were, across England, 123 men to manage at least 57 estates. Consequently, lay bailiffs and reeves must have run many properties, with only occasional supervision (Gooder 1995, 82–5).

Although the 14th century brought difficulties to the English countryside, the chronology of Sites 19 and 20 should not be regarded as necessarily representing the onset of decline in Wishaw. In the mid–late 13th century, a north aisle was added to the nave of St Chad's Church, and the south aisle was added *c* 1330. The chancel dates to the earlier 14th century, *c* 1310–20 (Hubbard 1947, 260). It is difficult to determine whether these phases of build were prompted by the pressures of population growth or the motivations of patronage; the probability is that they were a combination of the two. Whatever the circumstance, it was clearly possible to find the necessary resources within the parish to undertake building works of relatively good quality, not all of which can be associated with the transfer of lordship to the Bereford family by 1326. Whether such expenditure was always wise within the context of wider family fortunes is another matter.

The enlargement of the church in the late 13th and early 14th centuries is therefore contemporary with the closing phases on the two Wishaw sites, highlighting the need to interpret such matters with caution. Furthermore, we have seen that there is some reason to suppose a fairly large population at Wishaw well into the 14th century, while Rátkai has observed that the abraded nature of the pottery in pond 200217 recalls midden material, suggesting that there was once more occupation in this area of Wishaw than is now apparent, the evidence for which was perhaps lost in the 1970s levelling of the site. This seems highly probable, at least in the later 13th and 14th centuries.

Hawkeswell Farm, Coleshill

Coleshill, in north Warwickshire, was a large woodland parish which, in addition to Coleshill itself, also contained four other settlements and a number of scattered homesteads (Watkins 1982, 2). At the time of *Domesday* the king held the manor of Coleshill, assessed at three hides, as had been the case before the Conquest. The manor had a recorded population of 30 *villani* and 13 *bordarii*, perhaps representing around 200 people, while there were also 10 burgages in Tamworth that belonged to the manor and some 7560 acres of woodland. The manor appears to have been purchased from Henry I by the Clintons, with whom it directly remained into the second half of the 14th century. However, when John de Clinton died in 1353 or 1354, he left a daughter as his only heir, which brought the manor into the hands of the Montforts of Beaudesert (Boston and Midgley 1947, 50).

Together with Gilson, Kingshurst and Alcott, Hawkeswell was one of the other settlements in the parish. Located in the south-east of the parish, by the time it was recorded on the 1843/4 Parish Map (WCRO Z436U) it was little more than an extended farmstead or a shrunken hamlet. In Dugdale's time only three houses were noted there (Dugdale 1730, 1021). Now represented by Hawkeswell Farm, the place-name, meaning 'spring of the hawk', or 'spring of a man named Heafoc', is recorded in the 1260 Assize Rolls and on a number of subsequent occasions although it does not appear as a separate entity in the Warwickshire Subsidy Rolls of 1327 or 1332 (Glover *et al.* 1936, 44).

However, the place-name suggests, and the archaeology of Site 24 confirms, that the medieval hamlet was in existence well before the date of this reference. The 1993 evaluation indicated a sequence of ditches and pits, and cobble spreads, associated with a hollow-way of probable medieval origin. Excavation demonstrated the most intensive medieval activity towards the centre of the site, but the nature of this activity is unclear. However, the pottery of 12th and 13th century date is consistent with normal domestic activity, an impression that is reinforced by finds that include whetstones and the fragment of a possible barrel lock. Deposits of burnt clay and charcoal-rich soil are also suggestive of such activity, while the presence of a linear stone lined trench may represent the remains of a structure. Therefore, while the precise nature is unclear, medieval settlement activity in close proximity to the excavation is the most coherent interpretation that may be applied to the site.

As Dugdale noted (1730, 1021) Hawkeswell was not an independent manor, but a member of Coleshill, and therefore held of the Clintons. However Dugdale noted in particular the family of Simon de Blithe de Hawkeswell, whose descent he traced from late in Edward I's reign to that of Henry VI in the 15th century. They were not the only family with interests in Hawkeswell. In the mid-13th century, for example, the Mordak or Murdac family, most closely associated with Compton Murdac (Verney) had interests here. They were a prominent Warwickshire knightly family, Henry Murdac being a tenant of, and within the affinity of, the Beauchamps, and also sheriff of Warwickshire (Mason 1980, nos 58, 59, 308). In 1267–8, as part of an agreement relating to Stockerston in Leicestershire, Henry Mordak granted to William Mordak and Isolda, his wife, lands and tenements in several places in Leicestershire and Warwickshire, the latter including

Packington, Shelton, Baddesley, Coventry and Hawkeswell, to be held of Henry and the chief lord (Stokes and Wellstood 1932, 184, no. 854). Subsequently, in 1307, Alice de Bouyle, widow of Sir Thomas de Bouyle, son and heir of Sir William Murdac, quitclaimed all her rights in her lands of Coleshill and Hawkeswell, to Walter de Omylly (WDM, no. 131).

Nearly all the medieval pottery from Site 24 predates *c* 1300, and most of it is earlier than *c* 1250, within a range running from the mid-12th to early in the second half of the 13th century. The lesser quantities of late medieval and post-medieval pottery might be interpreted as being consistent with much reduced activity on the site by the 14th century, until there was a revitalisation of activity in the 15th or 16th century. However, if so, it is an interpretation to be applied to this specific site rather than extended to Hawkeswell as a whole. What medieval documentary evidence there is for the place is at its fullest by the 14th and 15th centuries, indicating on-going activity.

Land transfers do not, of themselves, necessarily inform on such as settlement form or population trends, but they can suggest something on the economy of the vill, and certainly the decline or changing priorities of some families, or the growing prosperity of others. They do not appear, however, to suggest an obviously declining settlement at Hawkeswell. By 1305 Hawkeswell had a common field called 'Ruyecroft', close to waste land that John de Clinton was granting to John de Collesley at a rent of 1s 8d, presumably to be assarted (WDM, no. 128). It has been suggested that the de Clinton family effectively had an assarting policy, encouraging and supporting such activity (Watkins 1982, 13), although the main thrust of this came in the mid-13th century; activity did continue into the mid-14th century, but it was more sporadic in nature, and there was a tendency in the 14th century for assarts to be incorporated into the common field system (Watkins 1982, 16, 17, 19).

By the 15th century Hawkeswell had a field system that in 1455 included 'Hawkeswellfield', 'Meadowfield' and 'Longmeadowfield', and there was also a quarry called 'Cellesleypit'. As Watkins observed, it seems likely that this field system had emerged long before it was mentioned in the mid-15th century (WDM, nos 621, 623; Watkins 1982, 11). 'Hawkeswellfeld', for instance, was specifically referred to by this name in 1376 (WDM, no. 412). Reference was also made in 1438 to 'Hawkyswellgrene', presumably a focus for some settlement (WDM, no. 588). A number of deeds relating to Hawkeswell date to the time of Edward III and Richard II, recording grants and quitclaims, a number of which reference the holdings that Walter Cuyly (or Culy) had here (WDM, nos 377, 412, 417), another Warwickshire knightly family.

Following the pattern in the rest of the Arden, the dominant social class in Coleshill was the free peasantry, but villein tenure did also occur, and on the basis of a rather late charter, dating to 1451, it would seem that Hawkeswell was one of the places where it did occur (WDM, no. 614; Watkins 1982, 27–8). Apart from livelihoods derived from working the land, the surviving deeds offer only fleeting glances of the community in Hawkeswell, and for the most part they are those who were granting or receiving land – names such as William le Reve (Reeve) of Hawkeswell, or Thomas le Fisshere, and Thomas Eddirsley, described as a husbandman (WDM, nos 381, 412, 416, 465, 614). A number of people from Hawkeswell clearly migrated to the town of Coleshill itself between 1200 and 1350 (Watkins 1982, 62). Unfortunately, in the material that does survive, there is nothing that indicates the size of the medieval population in Hawkeswell, the level of its prosperity, or the demographic trends affecting the vill. Rather, at best, we see in such as the 1332 Subsidy Roll the names of people listed under Coleshill who likely had lands in Hawkeswell, based on the evidence of later deeds, such as Roger de Edresle, Thomas le Fysshere, Richard de Edresle and John de Collesleye (Carter 1926, 62). Thus, it seems that archaeology may ultimately have more to offer in this respect, should future opportunities arise.

Shenstone

Before the conquest a free man named Godwin held the manor of Shenstone, probably as a retainer of the earls of Mercia, and with lands in all five hundreds of the shire (Hunt 1991–2, 16–17). By 1086 it was a part of the Staffordshire honor of Earl Roger de Montgomery, with Robert d'Oilly holding the manor as his tenant. Assessed at three hides with land for 12 ploughs, the manor was valued at 100 shillings.

Most probably before 1135, the de Bray brothers, Richard and Tanetin were enfeoffed with land in Shenstone by Robert d'Oilly. Tanetin's son, William, inherited the manor as a minor, Henry d'Oilly selling the wardship, *c* 1156–62, to Ralph the King's Clerk. However, in *c* 1164, Henry d'Oilly confirmed to William de Bray the lands in Shenstone which had been held by his father and uncle, held by the service of one-third of a knight's fee, a tenure confirmed by an entry in the Pipe Rolls of 1166–7, together with the scutage of Swinfen. The vill of Swinfen came to William by his marriage to Isabel, the daughter of Richard de Vernun and his wife, Avicia. William had at least two sons, Roger and Philip, the former becoming a priest and holding the benefice at Shenstone, paying annually 5 marks rent from the church to his brother (Eyton 1880, 47; 1881, 197, 198, 199; Grazebrook 1896, 240, 241, 242, 252).

The church of Shenstone had been given in 1129 to Oseney Abbey, founded by Robert d'Oilly (Grazebrook 1896, 240), and consequently the Abbot and Convent of Oseney also had interests in the parish. Around 1190 they permitted William de Bray a chantry in his *curia* of 'Calewenhulla', an unknown location although there is a tradition of a chapel formerly located in Nether Stonnall (Grazebrook 1896, 244, 245). Abbot Hugh also conceded to William the right to do justice over thieves caught in the abbot's manor of Stonnall, but there were instances of dispute between William and the abbot, as in the case of *novel disseisin* in the manor of Shenstone in 1203. A Fine of 1209 addressed at least some issues when it allowed to the abbot and his men of Stonnall rights of common of pasture in Shenstone, certain easements, conceded the church of Shenstone to be the right of the abbot and his successors, and acknowledged that the charter which the abbot held, granted by William de Bray, was lawful and true (Wrottesley 1882a, 2, 77; 1882b, 175; Grazebrook 1896, 250).

William de Bray apparently survived his sons, as he made arrangements for the fee and manor of Shenstone, the appurtenances of which included at least two mills, and parts of Swinfen, to be transferred to Robert de Grendon with his marriage to William's daughter, Avicia. Henry d'Oilly gave his assent, and received homage for the manor from Robert. After Avicia died, survived by her husband and an heir, Robert de Grendon successfully negotiated his retention of the manor and the wardship and marriage of his son, on which William de Bray could have made a claim. The fact that Robert's son was in any case William de Bray's heir must have facilitated any such arrangements (Grazebrook 1896, 250, 252).

Thus the manor of Shenstone passed to the Grendon family, Robert de Grendon being recorded as holding the fee in 1235–6 and 1242–3 (Maxwell Lyte 1920, 544; 1923, 970), and in the Hundred Rolls of *c* 1255, where he held of the heirs of d'Oilly (Wrottesley 1884, 108). Robert remarried and seems to have lived until 1272, to be succeeded by his son Ralph (Wrottesley 1885, 61). Ralph was dead by 1280, but before his death he demised the manor for a term of four years to Robert Burnel, the bishop of Bath and Wells. Demises are often indications that those granting them were facing financial difficulties, although in this case other motives may have been present. Whatever the truth of this, the bishop held both the manor and wardship of Ralph's son, also named Ralph, whom he married to Joan Burnel, and who in turn inherited the manor (*ibid.*, 103; Wrottesley 1890, 77–8). Their son, Robert, followed them in 1337 but he died childless about 28 years later (*ibid.*) and by a deed that his father had arranged, Grendon's Staffordshire property was destined subsequently to pass via Robert's sister to the Rochfords, while their Warwickshire estate went to the Chetwynds (Wrottesley 1891a, 7, 108; 1891b, 292, 296).

The recorded population of Shenstone at the time of *Domesday* was 21 *villani* and four *bordarii*, perhaps representing a population in the order of 125 people. By the early 14th century, the subsidy rolls of 1327 and 1332–3 suggest a population in the order of 460–510 people, that is, a fourfold increase since the late 11th century (Wrottesley 1886b, 227–8; 1889, 103–4). As previously discussed in the context of Wishaw, such demographic trends inevitably had a significant impact upon the landscape of manor and parish.

At the time of *Domesday*, the manorial survey of Shenstone included around 4536 acres of woodland. An obvious consequence of such population growth was the promotion of assarting, cutting into woodland and heath, bringing new areas into cultivation and settlement. This process is readily detected, particularly as Shenstone lay within the Forest of Cannock, and partially within Sutton Chase. In 1235 it was reported that Robert of Grendon was felling oaks in order that he might build a stable and enclose his park, having been licensed by the earl of Warwick to empark his wood of Shenstone as it lay within the bounds of Sutton Chase (Hodder 1988–9a, 46–8; Birrell 1999, 23).

By 1271 there are numerous references to assarting, both old and new. For example, Robert of Grendon had himself newly assarted 4 acres in Stonnall and sown it with oats, while Robert of Gresbrok had newly assarted 2 acres in Stonnall, sowing it once with rye and once with oats. William the reeve of Lynn took half an acre, which was sown with oats. Among the old assarts men such as Elias of Lynn had 1½ acres, in Lynn, sown twice with winter corn and four times with oats, and William at the elm of Stonnall whose half-acre assart had been sown three times with winter corn, and three times with oats (*ibid.*, 90, 91). Similarly, in 1286, several more references occur. Amongst these mention is made of William Athelyn in Little Stonnall for 4 acres in Shenstone, sown twice with winter corn and three times with spring corn. Walter the forester had 2 acres, of which one lay fallow while the other had been sown once with winter corn and three times with spring corn. Robert Burnel, bishop of Bath and Wells, as custodian, also appears holding Robert of Grendon's 4 acres, sown twice with winter corn and three times with spring corn. Geoffrey of Thornes appears, alongside others, including the abbot of Oseney, who had enclosed their assarts with ditches and dead hedges (*ibid.*, 165–8).

The names recorded on the subsidy lists similarly reflect both assarting (eg Ralph atte rudinge) but still more so a population dispersed across a varied manorial landscape, having moved into all types of land. Thus, we find such as William Otheheth (and William del Heeth), John del Hethe, William ad boscum (also William Attewode) and Richard del Haselwode (*op. cit.*). From those mentioned in the Forest Pleas we may add Geoffrey on the hill and Robert de Rudyng (*op. cit*, 166), and from the Plea Rolls, names such as Henry, son of Richard de Gorsthull (1278/9), Geoffrey de Gorsthill (1299/1300) and William atte Rudyng (1335) (Wrottesley 1885, 143; Wrottesley 1886a, 72; Wrottesley 1890, 55). All of these names are found alongside others referring to hamlets across the manor, such as Thornes, Stonnall and Chesterfield, which reinforce the impression of settlement extending across the Grendon fee.

Site 13 reflects this expansive local community of the 13th and 14th centuries, apparently representing a previously unknown (and unpredicted) medieval settlement site situated at the northern margins of the manor, just beyond Sutton Chase and Shenstone Park, and to the north of Chesterfield, this latter settlement certainly being in existence by 1324 (Wrottesley 1888,

101). Comprising a rectangular post-built structure interpreted as a byre or barn, together with a sub-rectangular enclosure that may have been used for stock control, two clay-lined ovens and several pits, this complex may be readily associated with a medieval farmstead. Regrettably the excavated area did not reveal any habitations, leaving open the question of whether these features are to be associated with a farmstead(s), or with a more substantial settlement. There is no pressing reason to assume that this represents more than one or two farmsteads. In addition to animal husbandry, the ovens indicate cereal production and processing, being used to dry grain, while Feature 133066, containing charcoal, charred cereal grains, seeds and nutshell, also had some form of drying, smoking or curing function.

The documented presence of two mills in Shenstone may explain the fragment of a single large worn millstone from Site 13. While the ten unstratified sherds of Early Anglo-Saxon pottery give cause for some interest and concern, their presence on the site may be explained in various ways, and may well have more implications for the environs of Site 13 rather than for Site 13 itself. This apart, the pottery from the enclosure and ditch, and from the ovens, is suggestive of a site not fully utilised before the middle years of the 13th century, a dating that is consistent with the impact of assarting activity and population expansion within Shenstone. The high proportions of cooking pot fabrics, the limited range of fabrics, and the distinct preponderance of locally produced wares, are all suggestive of a relatively low status settlement functioning within a modest socio-economic context. The presence of a few sherds of Deritend ware does not detract from this impression; direct and indirect links with Birmingham are to be expected.

The sampling of charcoal and plant remains, while confirming that the site was indeed agrarian in nature, also produced results that resonate closely with some aspects of the documentary record. The presence of oak, alder, birch, hawthorn, hazel, gorse, broom, blackthorn and holly is sometimes reflected directly and indirectly in such as the Forest Pleas, and in personal names, like those reflecting heathland locations, or more specific names, such as Richard del Haselwode. A medieval provenance for finds of hazelnuts clearly fits the local environment, and confirms the observation that hazel was common locally. The presence of hedgerows is also consistent with a managed agrarian landscape; the Forest Pleas noted the use of hedges and ditches to enclose assarts in Shenstone (discussed above).

Finally, the charred plant remains demonstrated the importance of rye in the pit and oven samples, while other taxa recovered represented plants closely associated with arable or cultivated ground. Difficult soils meant that barley, oats and rye were widely cultivated across parts of the region (*cf.* Hunt 1997, 79–80, 177). A hardier and more tolerant grain, rye was apparently well suited to assarted and cleared land, as seems to be the case in Shenstone. The Forest Pleas relating to Shenstone and Stonnall in 1271, although making reference to rye on the assart of Robert de Gresbrok in Stonnall, leave no doubt as to the local importance of oats and winter corn as the staple crops at this time. Interestingly, in the pleas for 1286, there appears to have been a shift in emphasis, and perhaps of practice. While there are occasional references to oats, the prevalent practice was one of sowing winter corn and spring corn; in fact, if the references to sowing these respective crops are totalled in the 1286 record, it is found that 68% refer to spring corn. Although caution is clearly necessary, the presence of spring-sown rye at Site 13 might suggest a dating in the 1280s or later for the samples.

The pottery evidence suggests a contraction or abandonment of settlement at Site 13 during the course of the 14th century, after *c* 1310, an impression that the absence of 15th century pottery perhaps reinforces, and the possibility of linking this to the impact of the Black Death mid-century onwards cannot be overlooked. However, settlement can shift or contract for many different reasons, often highly localised, perhaps related to individuals or their tenures. It is possible that the growing adversities in the first half of the 14th century did pose difficulties for some Shenstone settlements, particularly those farmsteads located on poorer lands, but it is difficult to demonstrate in this instance. Furthermore, in so far as can be seen, there does not appear to have been a catastrophic fall in population at this time. When Shenstone was assessed for the Poll Tax in 1377, some 236 people were taxed, rendering £3 18s 8d (Fenwick 2001, 460). Of 48 vills within Offlow Hundred, Shenstone had the sixth highest assessment, surpassed only by Burton-on-Trent, Walsall, Marchington, Barton-under-Needwood and Tutbury. Allowing for evasion and exemptions, it will be immediately evident that this list of taxpayers still represented a very substantial population within the manor, certainly not fewer than 500 people.

Overview

Settlement origins and early chronology

The Anglo-Saxon evidence

Evidence for the Anglo-Saxon predecessors of the later medieval settlements, particularly archaeological evidence, is notoriously difficult to identify. This *lacuna* is well understood in the West Midlands, where the question of village origins remains a key issue in research strategies on rural settlement (Hunt forthcoming). Not only is there a lack of material from the earlier phases of Anglo-Saxon settlement, there is also a dearth of material from the late 9th–early 11th century period. The M6 Toll sites have proven to be no exception to this pattern. Although all of the manors are clearly of pre-Conquest origin, the excavated sites are notable for their paucity of Anglo-Saxon pottery.

Shenstone (Site 13) produced ten sherds of unstratified pottery of Early to Middle Anglo-Saxon date, while Wishaw (Site 20) produced a small chaff-tempered sherd within a floor surface of structure 200662, and a more substantial sherd in a ditch fill on the same site, also of Early–Middle Anglo-Saxon date (Rátkai, Chapter 25). This is tantalising material, especially in the case of Shenstone since it is not very distant from important Early and Middle Anglo-Saxon sites in the Trent Valley, particularly the cemetery at Wychnor and the settlement at Catholme (Losco-Bradley and Kinsley, 2002), and nor are these sites far from the important Mercian centre at Tamworth, and one as yet undated sunken floored building (two phases) at the Cross Keys site in Lichfield (S. Dean, pers. comm.). This area was held by the Tomsaetan, whose territory ran through the lands on the eastern side of the Staffordshire watershed, into northern and western Warwickshire (Hooke 1985, fig. 3, 12). The Warwickshire sites, however, are more remote from the known early archaeology associated with the Avon valley, the closest cemetery sites being Alcester, and Baginton to the south of Coventry (*cf.* Ford 1996, 61, fig. 1).

Anglo-Saxon settlement or land use in the vicinity of both Shenstone and Wishaw might be suspected, but unfortunately the ceramic evidence does little to elucidate its nature. While there is too little evidence to make much of, it does tend to support the possibility that often what perhaps differed pre- and post-conquest was not so much the absence of settlement, but rather its intensity and sense of independent 'identity'. Arguably, in the case of pre-conquest settlement patterns, what we should be examining more closely is the context of the manor or estate rather than the 'cores' of historic villages, in which case both the Shenstone and the Wishaw sites have made a contribution. However, there remains the unresolved issue of the general absence of 10th and 11th century pottery from medieval settlement sites, despite some encouraging results from Coton on the Wolds (Warwickshire) where 10th and 11th century occupation has been demonstrated, lasting until the late 13th or 14th century (Hunt forthcoming; Maull 1998a, 47; 1998b, 95).

Medieval settlement

The sites excavated at Wishaw, Hawkeswell and Shenstone are all rural in context. Notwithstanding agreement with Roberts and Wrathmell's observation that the construct, opposing models of dispersed and nucleated settlement, tends to be an over-simplification (Roberts and Wrathmell 2002, 173), these sites are nonetheless located within an area that is largely characterised by a woodland landscape and a dispersed settlement pattern. They are of varying size. If we follow Dyer's 'rule of thumb' that a place with ten or more taxpayers in 1332 may be judged as large (Dyer 1996, 121), then we may certainly regard Shenstone as large and Wishaw, and most probably Hawkeswell, as small, although concerns regarding the population of Wishaw have been discussed, putting at question the guidance offered by the 1332 subsidy. However, whatever their size, the archaeology of these places finds a ready context in the expansion of rural society that occurred in the late 12th and 13th centuries, where population growth was accompanied by assarting, expanding settlement and cultivable land. Irregular field systems and enclosed crofts are typical of north and west Warwickshire, while south-eastern Staffordshire sees a transition from this towards field systems in the lower Tame valley that might be more readily described as champion (Roberts 1973, 212–3; Dyer 1996, 121).

It is clear that the expansion of settlement into this woodland landscape was not a uniquely medieval phenomenon. Prehistoric and Romano-British settlement is evident across the area, as at Wishaw (both at Wishaw Hall Farm, (Site 19) and where Hodder's fieldwalking produced Romano-British material). Here, the greatest quantity of this material came from Grounds Farm rather than in the proximity of the medieval hamlets (Hodder 1992, 46), which may be interpreted as suggesting some shift in settlement sites, but within the same locality, and perhaps estate.

Dyer has suggested that the medieval expansion into the Arden was based on existing pre-conquest patterns, and that this was effectively recolonisation, following a period of woodland regeneration between *c* AD 400 and 1000 (Dyer 1996, 119). However, a phase of woodland regeneration does not imply that this was necessarily marginal land, or that this was an unpopulated, uncultivated and unworked landscape during this period. Rather we know that there was a thinly scattered population across this area, most evidently demonstrated by the record of *Domesday Book*. In this sense of continuity it is possible to speculate that where 12th and 13th century pottery appears, it may not so much reflect 'new' farms and hamlets, but rather settlement reorganisation, which may have included the first emergence of some places as independent manors (*ibid.*). The model of multiple and changing settlement foci within an estate over time, and of settlement fluidity, is a well-established one (*cf.* Taylor 1983, 112, 113, 116) and the prominence of *bordarii* within the population of a vill like Wishaw may be seen as a reflection or agent of such reorganisation within the landscape.

Economy

The apparent absence of early settlement in specific locations should not necessarily be taken to imply that this was 'marginal' land, even if these were sites that were taken up in the 12th and 13th centuries, and then seemingly 'abandoned' in the 14th century. As Bailey illustrated, there has been in the past a tendency to identify land as marginal or otherwise in relation to its capacity to grow grain (Bailey 1989, 3–5). It was this concept that gave birth to the notion of a 'journey to the margin', but in woodland areas especially, it should not be assumed that poor arable land was necessarily marginal. Land that was marginal for arable cultivation was not necessarily marginal economically, and where the extension of arable occurred, this may have never been seen as anything more than a temporary diversification. 'Margins' were never static, but constantly moving in line with changing conditions

(Bailey 1989, 15). The changes in land use highlighted by excavation therefore do not necessarily indicate 'success' or 'failure' on sites, but rather, transitions.

Taken together, Wishaw and Shenstone illustrate something of the complexity and diversity of woodland manors, their settlements and economy. Earthwork surveys have revealed the high density of fish ponds in the Arden – large numbers of ponds on all sorts of sites and varying greatly in their form, very different from the south of Warwickshire where there are fewer ponds, and these mostly linked to village sites (Aston and Bond 1988, 421). Such ponds, as at Wishaw, reflect one aspect of the varied woodland economy (*cf* Dyer 1996, 126). Above all, of course, these were agrarian communities utilising, or reutilising, previously 'undeveloped' land as effectively as circumstances allowed. At Wishaw and Shenstone traces were revealed relating to land management and property divisions, reflective of possible stock control and certainly of cultivation. Shenstone further illustrates the particular challenges of the woodland environment in confirming, alongside the documentary record, the use of hardy cereals – a practice that was actually widespread throughout Staffordshire.

Although Hawkeswell is a little earlier in date, the sites at Wishaw and Shenstone also share a similar chronological profile, all three sites (19, 20, 13) apparently seeing a change in their patterns of activity by the mid-14th century. It is tempting to presume that such changes in the English countryside at this date arise from the well rehearsed litany that affected Europe during this period – deteriorating weather, failing harvests and famine, animal disease, and then the impact of the plague, all of which combined to initiate a demographic downturn. Such explanations for change in the countryside are reinforced, such as by Postan's view on the nature of marginal land, and the associated notion of the retreat from the margin. However, convenient as such explanations may be, there is a need to approach this matter with caution.

Our understanding of 'marginal' land is now more sophisticated, and the possibilities of normal review or reorganisation of land use, as opposed to retreat from the land, has to be taken into account. While it would be unreasonable to ignore the possibility of some impact between *c* 1310 and 1350, neither Wishaw nor Shenstone offer convincing evidence of a drastic downturn in population numbers by the mid-century. In the case of Wishaw Site 20, more specific factors also need to be taken into account related to the declining fortunes of the landowners. It is probable that similar trends affected other rural sites as well, even those currently under discussion, but such information related to issues of tenure, particularly at levels below that of manorial lordship, is generally very difficult to come by. Dyer has given consideration to the decay in rural settlement in Warwickshire *c* 1350–1520, dating that runs a little later than the sites currently under discussion, asking to what extent the Arden shared the fate of the Feldon in this regard (Dyer 1996, 129, 130). There is a need for more work on woodland communities, but it would seem that while they were affected by these trends of decline, there does not seem to be shrinkage on the same scale in the Arden as elsewhere in the county. Hallam also observed that evidence for a 14th century population decline in the West Midlands is hard to come by, particularly in the period 1280–1350 (Hallam 1981, 151). It may be that the mixed economic basis of woodland communities added to their resilience, Dyer observing that the leading county taxpayers were actually to be found in this part of Warwickshire by the 16th century. Such observations are clearly true of communities such as Shenstone and Wishaw, underscoring the need to avoid simplistic assumptions.

Trade

The very small numbers of non-ceramic medieval artefacts recovered from the M6 Toll sites mean that, as with the Romano-British period, the evidence for trade and craft activities is almost entirely confined to that from the pottery. (The only possible exceptions are two imported whetstones – one of Norwegian Ragstone and one of Blue Phyllite – from Hawkeswell Farm; Shaffrey Chapter 27). The ceramic material is among the most consistent and abundant of the evidence drawn from the four medieval sites, and apart from providing the basis by which the sites have been dated, the material has also raised questions in its own right (Rátkai Chapter 27). Particularly striking is the similarity that Rátkai has observed in the assemblages of whitewares and vessel types from Minworth Greaves, Wishaw, Drayton Bassett, Shenstone, Walsall and Lichfield (Fig. 219) datable to the period *c* 1250–1325. More generally, there are 13th century whitewares from Tamworth, and while they may be found across the county, they are most common in mid and south Staffordshire (Ford 1995, 34, 35).

But what is significant here is the similarity that may be observed in this particular assemblage of whitewares, sufficient in Rátkai's view to suggest that they may have formed a distinct zone, readily distinguished from that of Birmingham to the west and of Coventry to the south-east. Similarly, Wishaw and Coleshill mark the westernmost extent of the area in which Coventry-type wares were important, Coleshill, itself a flourishing market, apparently looking primarily to Coventry in the 12th and early 13th centuries, although this changed in the second half of the 13th century. This being so, what factors are likely to have played a part in creating this situation? What might such a distribution pattern represent?

The formation of a 'market zone' responding to the prompts of supply and demand will inevitably be one factor in shaping the scene; the supply of ceramics, like any manufacture, responded in part to the opportunity presented by a market. Best known of the production sites is Chilvers Coton at Nuneaton, a location that would give access to the markets of north Warwickshire and south Staffordshire, but it seems unlikely that this production centre would prompt such a well defined and 'compact' zone as is suggested here.

A production centre closer to hand, near the Staffordshire–Warwickshire border, seems highly probable, and it might be expected that such a centre would be stimulated by markets like those at Tamworth and Lichfield, boroughs where the demand for ceramics would have been an influential factor, as were the distribution networks that focussed on them (*cf.* Hunt 1997, 121, fig. 8.1). If this distribution was based on Nuneaton, the convenience of Watling Street as a link to both boroughs is difficult to overlook. Indeed, Chilvers Coton wares were also an important element in the ceramics found at Leicester, suggesting that another Roman road, the Fosse Way, was also a part of the network by which this pottery was distributed (Rátkai, pers comm.).

Lichfield was larger than Tamworth, expanding to surpass the county town itself in size (*cf.* Dyer 2002, 8, 13), and its growing population must have made significant demands of local pottery producers. The bishop's survey of 1298 recorded 286½ burgages in Lichfield, which could easily represent some 1400 people, an estimate broadly confirmed by the 1327 lay subsidy assessment. By 1377 Lichfield's population may be estimated to be in excess of 2000 people (*ibid.*, 12; Slater 1985, 123–4). Significant normal domestic usage aside, Lichfield was not only a major trading and commercial centre, but also an important ecclesiastical centre and community. These roles ensured that Lichfield was provided with inns, taverns and hostelries of various kinds, and the occupations that supported them, all of which again likely made heavy demands of the pottery industry. By the 15th century it is possible to show a 'potter' living in Lichfield, although it seems unlikely that they were not a part of Lichfield's occupational profile well before this time (Dyer 2002, 19). As always with potters, their likely social and economic standing probably left most of them invisible in the medieval records, particularly in the taxation lists. The question is left open as to the extent to which pottery production here was urban and/or rural. A primarily rural production in the vicinity of Lichfield seems an attractive notion.

Therefore, it is not difficult to associate the distribution of this pottery with both the demands of a major commercial, social and religious centre like Lichfield itself, and the market that it provided for the surrounding area, together with the activities of itinerant pedlars or middlemen (*cf.* McCarthy and Brooks 1988, 87). There is a need for more research related to the hinterlands of boroughs and markets, and also on the production and distribution of items such as ceramics (*cf.* Hunt forthcoming). This may challenge the current impression that no other products can be cited to parallel the evidence given by the pottery, although this might not be expected if at heart we are dealing with a production centre operating within a localised distribution network.

However, the distribution of pottery may well have been the composite result of many factors of varying complexity, rather than a simple reflection of supply and demand, these also contributing to the impression of specific zones associated with particular wares; for the most part, in the West Midlands, these approaches require development to take them beyond accusation of speculation. Nonetheless, one possible illustration may be drawn from north-eastern Staffordshire, where at Wychnor the dominant fabric, dating to the 14th and 15th centuries, was found to be gritty ware. Although this ware has been found on sites south of the River Trent, such as Lichfield, it is more familiar from sites further north. Staffordshire sites that have produced this fabric include Croxden, Rocester, Uttoxeter, Tutbury and Catholme, and possibly Burton-upon-Trent.

This gritty ware tradition also occurs in Derbyshire. Apparently of local manufacture, although the precise location is unknown, the pottery was primarily geared towards meeting the basic needs of cooking and storage. There will always be concern as to how representative a selection of find spots actually are, but an observation that may be made of those noted in association with gritty ware are the number that have direct links with the honor of Tutbury, or might be expected to fall within some of the networks related to it. Tutbury was the *caput honoris*, held in the early 14th century by the earls of Lancaster, and Uttoxeter was a borough within the honor, where the earls held demesne.

Wychnor was part of the honor, the Somervilles being tenants of the earls, while the Verdun family, tenants of the earls at Crakemarsh and Combridge, were patrons of Croxden Abbey, as were their successors, the Furnivals. Combridge is located within Rocester parish. Catholme is located no great distance from Wychnor, while Burton-upon-Trent neighbours Tutbury and was an important local centre. Thus, coincidence aside, it is not difficult to consider how a network of contacts within the honor of Tutbury, as much reflecting the interaction of neighbouring families and affinities as any 'business cycle' within the honor, could play a part in explaining the distribution of this particular fabric. Clearly much more research is needed to test this particular case, but the potential influence of such networks should not be overlooked.

Social as well as economic factors may therefore have a role to play. Furthermore, aside from direct pottery production for a market, further explanations include the use of pottery as containers for other products being traded, direct purchase from the kiln sites by those who could afford it, and the speculative trading of some merchants to accompany their main commodity, or perhaps to avoid an outward or return journey with empty carts or pack animals. Therefore, if pottery is moved around an area because of social interaction, use as containers and storage, or because of a response to speculative trading opportunities, it follows that to some degree the distribution of pottery may reflect social and economic contacts within an area. Where clear patterns may be detected, based on distinctive geographical distributions, then they likely preserve something of the imprint left by activity and interchange within the locality, and reflect another dimension on how community and locality functioned.

While recognising the potential complexities that might shape a distribution pattern, demand must remain one of the factors to be considered. The influence of any social factors, at least of the kind explored above in connection with gritty wares, is much more difficult to discern here. The sites concerned are not united by relationship to another network or socio-political structure within the local landscape. Rather, they seem more likely to be linked by geography and the impact of neighbourhood, and by relative proximity to Lichfield and its hinterland.

When we think of 'demand', whose demand do we mean? It is natural to consider the possibility of the gentry as key customers, and developing gentry culture brought with it a sense of association and identity, and also of purchasing power. The likely importance of an urban centre like Lichfield again highlights the probable significance of this place in helping to define the zone in question. The pottery represents the normal domestic range of items, from everyday peasant contexts. There are no status connotations here, at least not as we would normally understand them, and no apparent reason to associate this distribution pattern with the needs of the local gentry. Rather, we appear to be witnessing, for the most part, the demand articulated by local peasant consumers in town and countryside. Rátkai has emphasised within this pottery not only the similarities within the fabric groups, but also their similar functional composition, most obviously the use of internally green glazed bowls for cooking (Rátkai, pers. comm.). To what extent can we infer from this consumer preference, and beyond that, localised cultural affinities?

Undoubtedly the peasant consumer would exercise a preference where he had the ability and opportunity to do so, but it remains uncertain as to what extent the whitewares distribution represents active consumer preference as opposed to selection of the most readily accessible product. The distribution pattern is most probably a combination of two factors – ready availability through local production, together with social and economic 'networking' within the neighbourhood. The latter may have done something to reinforce choice as well.

Why does the use of whiteware bowls for cooking stand out in this group of sites, but is not found, for instance, at Birmingham, or in Coventry? The fact that it does occur in Lichfield means that it is not simply a rural phenomenon. Is this a reflection of a localised cultural affinity, or the result of the nature and type of local production? These are questions about which, for the present, it is difficult to do more than speculate. It remains difficult however to dismiss the impact that production and distribution networks *per se* must have had. In this sense we are seeing a market zone as well as the 'footprint' of social and economic interaction, and perhaps of some cultural affinity.

The question of what influences manorial links might have played in patterns of production, consumption and distribution in south-eastern Staffordshire and north-western Warwickshire, if any, remain as yet unsatisfactorily addressed. Certainly many of the Warwickshire gentry held land in Staffordshire, and vice versa. The de Grendons took their *nom de terre* from their Warwickshire manor, north-west of Atherstone, but they also held Shenstone. What was true of the gentry was even more so of the greater aristocracy. For example, the differences between the pottery assemblages from Birmingham and Weoley, despite their geographical proximity, are likely to be a reflection of both the status of Weoley Castle, one of the principal residences of the de Somery barons of Dudley (Hunt 1997, chaps 4 and 5), and perhaps of seigneurial and family links to south Staffordshire, where much of the honor was located, including the *caput honoris* at Dudley Castle; links which certainly reached, at various times, the area around Walsall and Drayton Bassett (Hunt 1997, chaps 2 and 3). However, since the de Birminghams also had seigneurial and family links with south Staffordshire, the question might be asked to what extent the Birmingham assemblages reflect these?

However, with regard to this particular 'pottery zone', there is nothing to suggest socio-political or tenurial links rooted in the manors *per se*. If there was any pottery production within these manors, it might be expected that those profiting from the activity would seek to promote their market among their neighbours. Such promotion might well involve the encouragement of local lords, but there is no reason to assume that they should take any closer interest in this than in any other of the activities that made up the manorial economy. However, such discussion is, at present, nothing more than speculation. It remains unclear to what extent pottery production was manorially based, although it seems probable that much of it was. Furthermore, despite a reference to a Robert le Potter in the Plea Rolls for 1269 at Drayton Bassett (Wrottesley 1883, 175), any pottery production sites within this area have as yet to be identified. Manorial links aside, such localised patterns of distribution almost certainly reflect not only a source of production, but also the action of the informal links, the dynamic of locality, where friends and neighbours influence each other, in this case to be reflected in the local market and choices in the pottery that was favoured.

Conclusion

The evidence from the four sites above demonstrates the exciting nature of the transition and expansion period of the 12th–early 14th centuries. As noted above, an area at first characterised by small hamlets and dispersed settlements saw an enormous population increase: perhaps as much as 933% in some parts between the years 1086–1290. In many ways the post-medieval period, discussed in detail in the next chapter, showed a similar pattern of establishment followed by spectacular growth.

As will be discussed in the next chapter, the earlier stages of the post-medieval period showed widespread but dispersed use of the natural resources of the region, for example wood coal and iron. Later, as the infrastructure of turnpikes, canals and latterly railways and tarmacadam roads improved distribution networks, the expansion of the post-medieval industrial economy reached its zenith. Interestingly, the population of Staffordshire between 1801 and 1971 rocketed from 242,693 to 1,856,550 and likewise, in Warwickshire from 206,798 to 2,155,930. This was a similar percentage growth to that of the medieval period. (Mason and Windrow 1972, 38–42).

Chapter 32
Post-medieval Period Discussion

By Jonathan Gill

Introduction

It is clear that the post-medieval development of the landscape through which the M6 Toll passes relates to the wider development of Birmingham, the Black Country and the whole West Midlands region. Therefore a general account of the industrialisation of this wider region is of relevance and has been included in this study even though this means that some places which are several kilometres away from the M6 Toll are mentioned (Fig. 220).

Apart from the obvious geographical relationship between the West Midlands conurbation and the route of the M6 Toll skirting around its edge there are other more direct relationships which also mean that a study of this larger area is of relevance. This is partly because each of the main post-medieval sites which have been studied – Hawkins Canal Basin (Site 1, Chapter 3), Hatherton Reservoir (Site 2, Chapter 4), Gilpin's Basin and Wharf (Site 3, Chapter 5) Churchbridge Complex (Site 4, Chapter 6), Cannock Extension Canal (Site 6, Chapter 9), Wyrley and Essington Canal (Site 8, Chapter 11) and Curdworth Top Lock (Site 21, Chapter 26) – are canal or related features that form part of a waterways network covering the West Midlands which was of great importance in the post-medieval development of the whole region. Another important relationship is how the Cannock Chase coalfield, through which the M6 Toll passes, developed in the later 19th century partly to meet the demand for coal which the older Black Country field could no longer supply. The very necessity for the M6 Toll itself, which was constructed to ease congestion on the M6 which passes through Birmingham and the Black Country, is also clearly directly related to the great expansion of the West Midlands in the 20th century.

Other than the industrial sites mentioned above, few post-medieval sites were included in the project. However brief mention will be made of two sites where non-industrial features of post-medieval date were recorded. One, Swan Farm (Site 36, Chapter 8), was one of the limited building recording works specified in the project. The other, Hawkeswell Farm (Site 24, Chapter 27) contained possible landscaping features of 17th–18th century date which may have been associated with Hawkeswell Hall. These sites too might be seen as exemplars of economic and social trends known to have occurred in the West Midlands. Small numbers of artefacts of post-medieval date were recovered during the course of the project but the assemblages of pottery and ceramic building material were too small or too poorly stratified to warrant detailed analysis.

In a study of this nature there is a need for a summary background of the wider area and a more detailed discussion of the post-medieval development of the immediate landscape through which the road passes. It is also necessary to be selective in covering certain themes, such as transport, which have been particularly important in the development of the region. There is inevitably a heavy bias in this section towards the industrialisation of the region, partly because the post-medieval sites examined were mainly industrial, partly because in this general area post-medieval development closely equates to industrialisation and partly because the wider area of the West Midlands becomes of national significance as a result of the industrial revolution.

Industrialisation of the West Midlands region

The West Midlands region, around which the M6 Toll skirts, has for much of the post-medieval period been one of the country's most important industrial centres. In the early post-medieval period both Birmingham and the area that later became known as the Black Country had a relatively large number of small-scale industries, particularly ironworks, and the region then developed very rapidly from the mid-18th century. This industrialisation was partly based on the south Staffordshire coalfield which divides into two principal areas: the Black Country to the south, where the coal was exploited extensively prior to the later 19th century and the Cannock Chase area to the north though which the M6 Toll passes and where large scale mining did not start until the mid-19th century.

Birmingham

For much of the post-medieval period Birmingham has been England's second city in terms of its size and economic importance. It had grown during the later medieval period into both a modest sized market town and a manufacturing centre which produced a wide range of goods from textiles and jewelled ornaments to forged tools and swords. The town is located on a raised plateau which acts as a watershed and although this results in the waterways being frequently too fast flowing for easy navigation (detailed further below) it ensured a good supply of water to drive the many mills which became established in the area.

By the end of the medieval period the town's trade had started to concentrate particularly on the manufacture of various metal products such as cutlery, swords, nails and a wide variety of trinkets and 'toys'. Wrought iron was largely supplied from the Black Country works and this was then worked up in Birmingham. Writing in 1538, John Leland comments of Birmingham that 'a great part of the town is maintained by smithies, who have their iron and sea-cole out of Staffordshire' (Cattell *et al.* 2002).

Birmingham expanded greatly during the 18th century together with the scale and productivity of its existing manufactures. Its metal industries were increasingly supplied with iron from the gradually expanding number of coke-fired blast furnaces within the general region. These included furnaces within the Coalbrookdale area, *c* 50 km to the west of Birmingham, where coal (in the form of coke) was famously first used to smelt iron in 1709 as well as many closer ironworks in the Black Country. This expansion was initially despite poor transport links with distant markets, but the construction of a network of turnpike roads, and then more crucially a dense network of canals from the 1760s provided a huge stimulus to the local manufacturers (detailed below in section on transport).

The organisation of Birmingham's industry appears to have been quite different to that of many of the other great industrial cities such as Liverpool and Manchester in that, rather than being based on the factory system, it was largely based on the small-scale workshop operated by individuals or small teams of artisans. There were, of course, exceptions, such as Matthew Boulton's Soho works, but as a general rule this remained true until towards the middle of the 19th century. As a result of this the layout of the town developed differently to other cities. The workforce was relatively skilled and well paid and, although Birmingham had a great many back-to-back houses, it avoided the worst of the desperate overcrowding that blighted many cities in the 19th century. Space for the expansion of the city in the later 18th and early 19th centuries was created by large estates being developed by families such as the Colmore family to the north and west of the city centre and the Holt family of Aston Hall *c* 10 km west of the M6 Toll.

Black Country

The *Black Country* has been the name used since the 19th century to describe the heavily industrialised area between Birmingham and Wolverhampton. The area is not precisely defined so that sometimes it can be used to describe a large area which extends north as far as Brownhills, immediately adjacent to the M6 Toll, but it more usually refers to an area further south with Dudley as its unofficial 'capital'. Even by a conservative definition the northern part of the Black Country extends to within a few kilometres of the M6 Toll and the large scale industrialisation of this area has played a part in the development of the area through which the northern half of the road now passes.

The key factor in the industrialisation of this area is the fact that it lies on a coalfield and in particular that in this part of south Staffordshire the coal outcrops at the surface in many areas and could be easily reached from early times with crude holes or bell pits. This area also contained a seam of coal known as the 'thick coal' or the '10 yard seam' (although technically it was a series of separate, immediately adjacent seams) which was easily accessible and which allowed large quantities of coal to be rapidly extracted. Iron ore is also found in the area which could be smelted to create iron initially using charcoal as a fuel.

Similarly to Birmingham the Black Country was already an important manufacturing centre of some consequence well before the main phase of the Industrial Revolution. There are references to iron mining in the medieval period in Walsall and Wednesbury and there was a forge in Walsall by the mid-16th century. A lock making industry is believed to have been established in Wolverhampton by the turn of the 17th century and nail making was of importance in several parts of the Black Country by the same period.

The industrialisation and post-medieval development of the Black Country landscape followed a distinct pattern with large areas of common land gradually being enclosed in the 17th and early 18th centuries by small scale squatter encroachment. Semi-permanent squatting in hastily erected dwellings on common ground was a common occurrence during the early industrial revolution in many parts of the country and it appears to have been widely accepted or even, sometimes, encouraged by landowners if labour was needed locally. A great many of these squatters in the Black Country would either earn a living extracting coal in the local pits or where it outcropped at the surface, or they would have a small workshop or smithy where they could produce iron goods. The types of goods that were manufactured in the Black Country tended to be more utilitarian than the generally finer items produced in Birmingham, such as nails, chains and a wide range of other goods. Different areas tended to specialise in certain products, such as saddlery goods in Walsall, locks in Wolverhampton, scythes at Belbroughton and tubes at Wednesbury. Alongside this industry agriculture continued to be widely practised in the form of a dual economy.

Much of the iron for the many local blacksmiths was supplied from furnaces outside the area but in the mid-18th century the first coke-fired Black Country blast furnaces were constructed and John Wilkinson's ironworks at Bradley, which was blown in 1766, was one of the largest and most complex in Britain.

In the second half of the 18th century the industrial nature of the Black Country developed dramatically with the increased availability of wrought iron swelling the numbers of metal workers in the area and the growing demand for coal increasing the number and

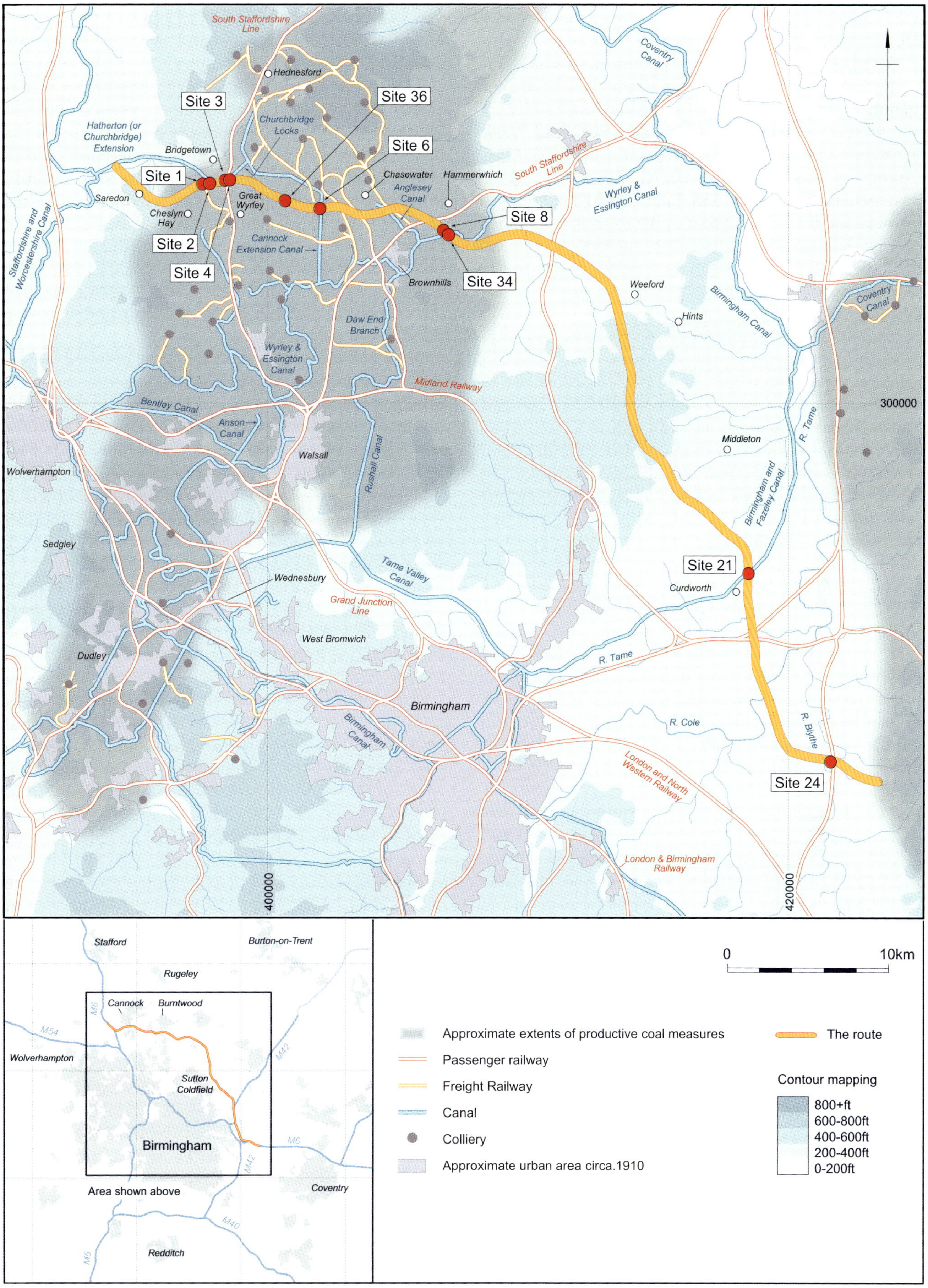

Fig. 220 Distribution of post-medieval sites

productivity of the local collieries. In 1776 the road between West Bromwich and Wolverhampton was described as 'one continued village of nailers' and that 'About Wednesbury the whole country smoaks with coal-pits, forges, furnaces &c.,' (Trinder 1987, 75). By the early 19th century the area was the second most important iron working area in the country (after south Wales) and the number of blast furnaces in the whole of Staffordshire had risen from six in 1788 to 90 in 1820 (Trinder 1987, 111). This development was closely tied to the development of the canal network in the area allowing coal to be transported to the furnaces and forges and the finished goods to be distributed to markets.

Unlike the other major iron working areas, the principal characteristic of the Black Country's industrial landscape continued to be that of the small, independent concern either operating a mine, a forge or a furnace, rather than a large scale integrated works, and distinct areas continued to specialise in particular iron products. The mines tended to be of a much smaller nature than in other coalfields and well into the 19th century the winding drums were frequently operated by horse gins rather than steam engines.

Early industry within the Cannock Chase area

The industrial development of the area through which the northern half of the M6 Toll passes, immediately to the south of Cannock Chase, follows a different pattern from that of Birmingham and the Black Country. For geological reasons the main coal measures in this area are much less easily accessible than in the rest of the south Staffordshire field and they were therefore not extensively exploited until the second half of the 19th century when the Black Country collieries were becoming less able to meet local demand. Therefore, although this area did have a number of important ironworks and other industrial concerns prior to the 18th century it did not see the great expansion in the iron industry, based on coal, which occurred in Birmingham and the Black Country at the start of the industrial revolution.

The early ironworks were based on using charcoal as a fuel, for which Cannock Chase provided a plentiful supply of trees. Among these were an iron forge in Hednesford built by William Colmore in 1472, a forge in Brereton opened in 1533 and two forges operated by William Fletcher in Rising Bridge (Rising Brook) and Beaudesert Park.

Perhaps the most important of these early works was a group operated by the Paget family initially developed in the second half of the 16th century. Sir William Paget was granted extensive manors in the Cannock Chase area in 1546 and in 1560 the family was granted a licence to fell trees on the chase for iron making. The Paget's main works were between Cannock and Rugeley (*c* 6 km north of the M6 Toll) and they were clearly relatively extensive and well developed for the period. The family's industrial concerns in this period included two forges and two furnaces, one of which it has been suggested may have been the earliest in the Midlands (*VCH* 1959, 110) as well as coal mines in Cannock Wood, and ironstone mines. Due to this iron industry Cannock Chase is reported to have been substantially stripped of timber by the early 17th century (*VCH* 1959, 111). By 1623 the Pagets owned the earliest known slitting mill in the Midlands for nail making.

Among various other ironworks of relevance to the current study is a forge on the north-east side of Cannock which was operated by the Foley family. In a national context the Foleys were among the great pioneers of the iron industry, particularly nail making, in the 17th and early 18th century and they owned a number of works throughout the Midlands.

Several early manufacturing centres developed in the general Cannock Chase area including Burntwood, the historic centre of which is now *c* 3 km north of the M6 Toll. The *Victoria County History* reports that in the mid-17th century there are known to have been a locksmith, a pinmaker and more than one nailer in Burntwood. The local nail making industry developed substantially in the following century, partly based on domestic production, and brick making is known to have been undertaken in Burntwood in the early 18th century.

As well as those on Cannock Chase there were also a number of other significant early ironworks relatively close to the southern half of the route of the M6 Toll. One of these was in Middleton, Warwickshire (*c* 3 km east of M6 Toll) where a furnace was constructed in 1592 to replace a previous hammer mill which itself had been constructed in 1570. The Middleton blast furnace, which produced cast iron, operated in conjunction with a forge at Hints (2 km east of M6 Toll) which is known to have been in operation by 1592 and where the iron was refined and drawn out into bars.

In the later 19th and 20th century the extensive industrialisation of the Cannock Chase region was heavily centred around the mining industry but even prior to this period there was small scale extraction of coal for both domestic use and those processes of the iron industry which could use coal as a fuel.

In the Cannock Chase area most of the seams of coal were very deeply set (detailed further below) but in certain locations coal measures could be relatively easily reached and mining is first recorded in this general area at the very end of the 13th century. There are numerous references to mines and coal pits around Cannock Chase pre-dating the industrial revolution including the mines operated by the Pagets in the 16th century at Beaudesert Park as well as mines at Cheslyn Hay in the 1630s, Great Wyrley by 1642 and in Burntwood in the 1650s (*VCH* 1959). These would have presumably been bell pits or very small scale 'open cast' mines if the coal was sufficiently shallow, but the quantity of this accessible coal was very limited in the Cannock Chase area and this extraction does not appear to have significantly expanded as the wider demand for coal exponentially increased during the initial stages of the industrial revolution.

In the first half of the 19th century there are reported to have been several pits in the Cannock Chase area with shafts of over 70 yd (*c* 64 m) deep (*VCH* 1959) including one at Walk Mill, Cannock from where William Gilpin was raising coal for his edge tool factory at Churchbridge, part of which has been investigated at Site 3 (detailed further below). However these shafts would have been nothing like deep enough to reach the main coal seams which were worked, and which proved so profitable, in the later decades of the 19th century.

Nineteenth century exploitation of the Cannock Chase Coalfield

South Staffordshire contains one of the most historically important and, relative to its modest size, productive coalfields in the country. The field continues for 25 km in a roughly north–south direction between Stourbridge on the southern edge of the Black Country to Cannock Chase and Brereton in the north. As detailed above, in many parts of the Black Country the coal outcropped or was easily reached using bell pits and this has been used in the industry of the area for many centuries. Partly as a result of wasteful practices in extracting the apparently plentiful coal, the Black Country collieries became less profitable and less able to meet the ever expanding local demand for coal. The industrial-scale exploitation of the Cannock Chase coalfield in the second half of the 19th century was based largely on meeting this demand.

In contrast with much of the southern part of the south Staffordshire coalfield the majority of the coal in the northern part (or the Cannock Chase coalfield), through which the M6 Toll passes, is located in deeply-set seams which are not easily reached. The dramatic geological division between the northern and southern areas is caused by a series of faults which have forced the coal measures in certain areas many metres below those in other areas. The main fault is the east–west Bentley Fault, north of Walsall and Wolverhampton, but the geology is further complicated by a series of other faults within the Cannock Chase area further dividing the coal measures. Another distinction between the two areas is that the Cannock Chase coal generally had a relatively high bitumen content and was more suited to domestic use rather than coking for industrial use.

The first trial bore to attempt to locate the deep coal seams in the Cannock Chase area was dug in 1849 by the Marquis of Anglesey (a descendent of William Paget; see above) on his land to the east side of Norton Pool (Chasewater). This revealed four seams of coal and soon afterwards a deep mine (the Hammerwich Colliery) was established in this area. There was a steady increase in the number of pits in the Cannock Chase field during the 1850s and 1860s as well as a boom in the first half of the 1870s which saw a series of large new collieries. A major economic slump towards the end of the 1870s saw coal prices fall, thus affecting the profitability of the newly constructed pits, and no new shafts were sunk in the area in the 1880s. By the end of the decade the economic cycle had turned once again and several pits opened during the 1890s so that by 1900 there were 33 pits in the Cannock Chase field. In contrast with those surviving collieries in the rest of the south Staffordshire coalfield the Cannock Chase pits were deep, modern, highly productive pits and the first three decades of the 20th century can be seen as the heyday of the coalfield. Production in the area peaked, as it did nationally, just before the First World War.

After nationalisation of the coal industry in 1947 several pits closed and mining in the area was concentrated in the more productive collieries in which mechanisation was employed. Overall production in the field remained largely static for most of the third quarter of the century (*c* 4.5–5 million tons annually) and a small number of new pits opened in this period but, by the later 1970s and 1980s, both the local and national coal industry was in rapid decline and in 1993, Littleton Colliery, the last major pit in the Cannock Chase coalfield ceased production.

The second half of the 20th century also saw substantial programmes of open-cast mining in the Cannock Chase field including a large area between Norton Canes and Bridgtown through which the M6 Toll now passes. Among the features removed by this open-cast extraction was much of the northern half of the Cannock Extension Canal, a part of which has been investigated at Site 6.

Development of the transport network in the region

Among the most important themes of this study and of the development of the area in the post-medieval period is that of transport. This is partly due to the fact that six of the seven post-medieval sites investigated during the construction of the M6 Toll were canal features but it is also a more general reflection of the great importance that transport developments played in the industrialisation of the region in the 18th and 19th centuries. It is also perhaps appropriate because the whole study itself is of course being undertaken due to a modern transport development (the M6 Toll).

Turnpike roads and pre-canal transport links

Although the industrial development of southern Staffordshire was considerably advanced prior to the 'take off' of the industrial revolution in the second half of the 18th century this was despite, rather than because of, its transport connections. There was, of course, a network of roads in southern Staffordshire from well before the 18th century but the type of heavy industry for which the geology of the region was perfectly suited is not well suited to road transport. Coal could only be transported economically short distances by road and, indeed, in the late 17th century the roads around Wednesbury, Sedgeley and Dudley in the Black Country were described as being poor due to them being 'uncessantly [*sic*] worn with the carriage of coal' (*VCH* 1967, 279).

The heavy industry required water transport but unlike the great north-east coalfield of Northumberland and Country Durham, which flourished in the 18th century by carrying coals by sea down the east coast to London, the south Staffordshire coalfield was a long way from the coast. The area was also not blessed with convenient navigable inland waterways, partly due to it being set on a plateau with relatively steep sides frequently rendering the rivers too fast flowing, and this was a major hindrance to large scale industrial development prior to the second half of the 18th century.

The new system of turnpike roads which had started to develop nationally in the second half of the 17th century significantly improved the quality of many roads, particularly those between towns. This saw the responsibility for financing the maintenance (and occasionally construction) of roads transferred from local parishioners, who had limited vested interest in maintaining the principal through roads, to the road users themselves in the form of tolls. The network of turnpike roads in south Staffordshire and in the area of the M6 Toll appears to have developed relatively slowly.

One of the main early developments came in 1729 with the turnpiking of the entire Staffordshire section of the Roman Watling Street (A5) the route of which the M6 Toll follows relatively closely. In the same year the Lichfield to Shenstone road and the Lichfield to Walsall road (as far as Muckley Corner), were also turnpiked. Each of these now passes over the M6 Toll: the Walsall road at a point east of Brownhills, and the Shenstone road, at a point to the east of Wall. Between 1766 and 1793 the road between Walsall and Stafford, which crosses the M6 Toll at Churchbridge, was turnpiked and there was a toll gate close to this point.

Canals

The large scale industrial development of south Staffordshire could only occur with a new system of transport and the canal network, which dramatically developed in the second half of the 18th century, provided the perfect catalyst. The development of the national network of canals began in Lancashire in the late 1750s and 1760s with several relatively short routes, including the Bridgewater Canal, which was constructed to carry coal from the Duke of Bridgewater's mines at Worsley to Manchester. Longer routes of wider significance followed and by 1790 the famous Grand Cross (or Silver Cross) of canals had been completed which linked the four main estuary navigations of southern Britain: the Thames, the Mersey, the Severn and the Humber. The key elements of the cross were the Trent and Mersey Canal, completed in 1777, the Staffordshire and Worcestershire, which opened in 1772 and which linked the Trent and Mersey to the Severn, and the Coventry Canal and Oxford Canal which linked to the Thames. The Birmingham and Fazeley Canal also formed part of the final link in the Grand Cross, linking Birmingham to the Coventry Canal, and this is of particular relevance to the current study as Curdworth Top Lock on the Birmingham and Fazeley has been investigated at Site 21.

Birmingham and the Black Country were close to the centre of the Grand Cross but the main new canals skirted around Birmingham plateau due to its situation, which would have necessitated a complex and expensive system of locks. Even before the completion of the Grand Cross it was clear to industrialists and investors that linking Birmingham into the canal network would provide a stimulus to local trade and plans were quickly prepared to connect the town to the Staffordshire and Worcestershire Canal. The campaign for the new canal started in 1767 and among those promoting the venture was Matthew Boulton, one of Birmingham's greatest industrialists. At that time he owned a silversmith and buckles business in the town but his significance grew when he opened the Soho Foundry on the north side of the town and entered into partnership with James Watt.

James Brindley, the renowned canal engineer, was placed in charge of the project and construction was completed in 1772. The canal ran north-west from the centre of Birmingham, via Wolverhampton to a junction with the Staffordshire and Worcestershire at Aldersley. The circuitous route of the canal served many collieries and it was a great success, bringing dividends to shareholders and reducing the price of coal to manufacturers in the area. As a result of the success of this line a dense network of branch canals developed within this area during the following years, linking manufacturing and mining districts. The Dudley and Stourbridge Canals were early additions, being constructed by rival companies and being completed in 1779 to further link the Black Country to the trunk canal network. After a protracted and acrimonious phase of planning the Birmingham and Fazeley Canal was constructed in the 1780s to extend the network eastwards. Although this was initially promoted by a rival company to the Birmingham Canal the two companies amalgamated before it was opened and, in 1796, they adopted the title of The Birmingham Canal Navigations (BCN).

The 1790s saw a huge number of new canals proposed in many parts of the country and this boom has been dubbed the 'canal mania'. The clear success of the early routes prompted many new schemes, some of which were less viable than the previous ones, and there were a number of extensions to the network in Birmingham and the surrounding area. These included routes to Warwick and Worcester (though that to Worcester was not fully completed until 1815) as well as the Selly Oak extension and the Wyrley and Essington Canal.

The Wyrley and Essington is of relevance to the current study in two related ways. First it has been archaeologically investigated at Site 8 but also, more generally, its circuitous route (nicknamed the 'curley Wyrley') passed through many settlements close to the road and played an important part in their 19th century development. The initial application for an Act for the Wyrley and Essington Canal was made in 1791 with the original route being from Wyrley to the Birmingham Canal at Wolverhampton. Even before completion of the original modest line applications had been made for the substantial extension of the canal, to link with the Coventry Canal at Huddlesford, as well as for a new branch line (the Hay Head branch). These were completed in 1797. The Wyrley and Essington was profitable and during the 1820s and 1830s there was a series of proposals for a merger or union between it and the BCN. This was finally realised in 1840 when the Wyrley and Essington became part of the BCN and, a year later, a cut was made between the two canals near Walsall.

The investigation at Site 8, where a trench was cut through an embanked section of the canal, revealed the basic nature of its initial construction comprising simple embankments without internal structure, reinforcement or lining. Unsurprisingly the investigation also found much evidence of the repeated repairs required in the following decades. The fact that the canal has such a basic structure implies that speed of construction was of greater importance than quality and this may be a reflection of the 'canal mania' when it was felt there were huge fortunes to be made in their construction.

The early decades of the 19th century saw many new short arms and basins added but the main work of this period was that of improving the existing lines. Thomas Telford, the eminent engineer, was commissioned to undertake various alterations to the BCN and, between 1827 and 1838, the main line from Birmingham to Aldersley was shortened by 7 miles (*c* 11.3 km) through straightening the route. These improvements may have been undertaken directly as a result of foresight by BCN of the threat to their trade posed by the embryonic railway system (see below). Also, presumably due to this, the second quarter of the 19th century saw a consolidation of the regional canal companies and along with the Wyrley and Essington, the Dudley Canal Company was also amalgamated into the BCN in 1846.

Two other significant developments of this period of relevance to the current study were the construction of the Anglesey Branch Canal and the Hatherton Branch Canal (sometimes called the Churchbridge Extension Canal). The Anglesey Branch was constructed in 1850 to connect the Wyrley and Essington with the Cannock Chase reservoir (or Norton Pool) at Norton. The M6 Toll now truncates the line of this canal below the reservoir (now known as Chasewater). This branch canal was constructed by the Marquis of Anglesey both to supply water to the Wyrley and Essington and to provide a transport link for his new colliery adjacent to the reservoir. The Hatherton Branch Canal, which was constructed in 1841 as a branch of the Staffordshire and Worcestershire Canal, particularly reflects the importance of the industrial complex which William Gilpin had developed in Churchbridge and of his mines in Great Wyrley and Cheslyn Hay that were also connected to the canal.

Four of the seven post-medieval sites investigated in the current study are grouped in this area and the work here has enhanced the understanding both of the individual features and the wider industrial landscape. These sites comprise part of a reservoir for the Hatherton Canal (Site 2), a colliery basin and aqueduct connected to the Hatherton Canal, a further basin and wharf for Gilpin's Churchbridge Edgetool Manufactory, again connected to the Hatherton Canal and a bridge. The work on these structures illustrates the industrial nature of the canal and the relationship between the industrial complexes and local transport connections, as well as providing a more detailed understanding of the detailed construction and use of the structures.

In a national context the middle and later decades of the 19th century saw a clear decline in the relative importance of the canal network often exacerbated by the fact that many railway companies bought or operated local canal companies. To some extent the Birmingham network was no different as an agreement was reached in 1846 by which the BCN was leased by the London and Birmingham railway.

However the Birmingham canal network bucked the national trend by remaining viable as an industrial freight carrier and it continued to expand into the second half of the 19th century at a time when in most areas investment into new canals had all but ceased due to competition from the railways. The relative economic strength of the Birmingham Canal Navigations meant that they they reacted to various proposals for new railway lines, particularly in the emerging Cannock Chase Coalfield, with extensions to their canal network.

The most important of these, and directly relevant to the current study, was the Cannock Extension Canal, proposed in 1853 and completed in 1863, connecting the Wyrley and Essington Canal to the collieries of the new coalfield. This canal has been truncated by the construction of the M6 Toll at Site 6. Another important related piece of canal engineering of this period was a set of 13 locks at Churchbridge which was constructed in 1860 to connect the new Cannock Extension to the Hatherton Branch. The M6 Toll passes through the site of the base of these locks, although they were sadly removed between 1952 and 1972 by open cast mining. Another important new canal construction of this period in the wider West Midlands region was the 3000 yard (*c* 2750 m) Netherton tunnel on the Dudley Canal, constructed in 1856–9, the last canal tunnel to be constructed in the country.

As well as the substantial new additions to the network stimulated by the exploitation of the Cannock Chase Coalfield there are also many smaller examples of how canals remained important industrial freight carriers. Among these are a number of basins or transport interchanges where goods could be transferred from canal to railway, showing that the two systems co-existed for a period in the second half of the 19th century. One example of this has been investigated in the current study at Site 3.

Although the canals around Birmingham continued to flourish much longer than in most parts of the country the last quarter of the 19th century did see a significant decline in their fortunes, relative to the railways, and this was exacerbated in the early decades of the 20th century by the reduced economic viability of the older parts of the south Staffordshire coalfield. Parts of the canal network continued to be important carriers of freight longer than in many parts of the country, largely due to short haul coal traffic to local works, but even in the active Cannock Chase coalfield the proportion of coal carried by canal reduced from 24% in 1935 to 16.7% in 1947 and to 10.3% in 1952. Despite this reduction in trade, the BCN was unusual in that the network remained virtually intact until it was nationalised in 1948.

The canal landscape, and the importance which the canal network played in the development of the West Midlands region, is unique in the United Kingdom. Nowhere else did the canals provide quite such a stimulus to industrial development and nowhere else was there such a density of lines or so many fine examples of canal engineering such as the flights of locks. As a result, the surviving canal network has a particular significance within this region.

Railways

Although the canal network remained important longer in the West Midlands than in many parts of the country, the great expansion of the railways from the second quarter of the 19th century was hugely significant in the development of this region, as with all the main industrialised (or industrialising) parts of the country.

Its central location between London and the great manufacturing centres of the north meant that Birmingham was always going to be a key hub of the train network and, during the 1830s, the Grand Junction Railway connected Birmingham with the Mersey and the London and Birmingham Railway connected it with the capital. In addition to these main lines of national importance there developed, in the mid-19th century, a dense network, particularly around the Black Country, of other shorter lines between towns and branches or extensions from existing lines. The network around the Black Country was stimulated by, and acted as a stimulus to, the flourishing iron industry and its extension was further assisted by great competition in this area between the lines of rival rail companies.

In the area further north, around the Cannock Chase coalfield, although there was a series of proposals in the 1850s for new rail lines to cross this area most of these were not constructed and it was not until the 1870s that the network of new railway lines developed significantly in this area. As detailed above, the large scale exploitation of the Cannock Chase coalfield in this period saw the relatively late extension of the canal network and the collieries initially relied largely on canals to transport their coal. A number of short feeder railway lines were constructed but these were principally to carry coal from the pit to the canal for carriage to local works and the wider Birmingham canal network. One such feeder line was constructed to connect collieries at Wyrley Bank to the Hatherton Branch Canal at Churchbridge. The M6 Toll now crosses this tramway although the site was not specifically investigated in the current works.

One relatively early exception to this trend for rail lines in the Cannock Chase area to be merely canal feeders was the Norton Branch of the South Staffordshire Railway which was constructed in 1858 from Ryders Hayes on the main line to Norton Canes, with the express purpose 'to convey mineral products of the locality to the South Staffordshire towns and works and to Birmingham' (*VCH* 1967, 318). The route of the M6 Toll crosses this line a short distance east of the Cannock Extension Canal (and Site 6). The development of the rail network in the area allowed the expansion of the Cannock Chase coalfield by allowing collieries to be located further from the canals.

As the coalfield developed and became more productive in the 1860s the need for greater and more flexible transport links became more apparent and the boom in new collieries of the early 1870s in the Cannock Chase area also saw a significant shift towards railways acting as principal carriers of coal rather than merely acting as feeders for the canals. A number of new branch lines connected new collieries with the Norton Branch railway and, in 1879, the Norton Branch was itself extended northwards.

Further expansions in production in the coalfield saw further branch rail lines constructed towards the end of the 19th century and into the 20th. One short line of relevance here was the construction of a new connection between Conduit No 3 Colliery and the Midland Railway in *c* 1895. This colliery was to the east of Norton Canes and the line adjoined the Midland Railway immediately south of the A5 Road on the north-west side of Brownhills.

A further branch line was constructed from the colliery of TA Hawkins & Sons Ltd (also known as Cannock Old Coppice Colliery) to the Cannock Line near Churchbridge. This line is shown on the 2nd edition 25 inch OS map with a tramway extending north-east as far as a canal basin (investigated in the current works as Site 1) and separate tramways extending eastwards, skirting beneath the Hatherton Reservoir (Site 2) towards the Cannock line of the South Staffordshire Railway. Neither the tramway to the canal basin nor to the railway are shown on the 1st edition OS map of 1884 although an earlier tramway link between the colliery and the canal is shown. The fact that these tramways post-date 1884 confirms that, at the very end of the 19th century, colliery owners still considered the canals to be important carriers of coal and that was necessary to provide links to them. It is known that the tramway to the railway was constructed in 1901 (*VCH* 1967) but it is not known whether the tram to the canal basin was a contemporary improvement or an earlier development.

The route of the tramway to the canal basin has been truncated by the M6 Toll and evidence of the former tracks was recorded in Site 1, but the tramway to the railway appears to have been entirely (or virtually entirely) to the south of the works relating to the construction of the Toll road. At its very western end the tramway may have been impacted by the construction of the road but this was not within one of the sites of archaeological investigation.

The 2nd edition 6 inch OS map shows at least five railway lines crossing the future path of the M6 Toll, all of which are in the northern half of the study area. These include three passenger carrying lines of the London and North Western Railway (L&NWR): the South Staffordshire line which opened in 1849 and which now crosses the M6 Toll just north-east of Brownhillls; the Cannock Branch (opened in 1858) crossing it at Churchbridge; and the Sutton Coldfield to Lichfield line (opened in 1884) crossing the road just north of Shenstone.

In addition to these principal lines the map also shows the Norton Branch of the L&NWR, which was a freight carrying line opened in 1858, the route of which is now crossed by the M6 Toll to the east of Norton Canes. Two further short freight branches are also shown immediately east of the Norton Branch, the line of each of which is now truncated by the M6 Toll, and one of these is the link constructed in 1895 (referred to above) to connect Conduit No 3 Colliery with the Midland Railway. Yet another short freight branch line is shown on the 2nd edition OS map a relatively short distance to the east which links a colliery in Chasetown to the South Staffordshire line of the L&NWR. This freight line is again now crossed by the M6 Toll.

In addition to these lines there are likely to have been a great many other tramways or tracks, some very short lived, in the general vicinity of the M6 Toll which would have been used to carry coal or various other raw materials either to a principal transport network or to a site for processing. It is likely that a number of these will have crossed the route in the areas not specified for archaeological investigation but the remains from one such tramway survived at West of Crane Brook Cottage (Site 34). This site was principally targeted to investigate cropmarks which were found to be Romano-British in origin but the site also uncovered the remnants of sleeper settings of a rail/tramway that appear to have related to a nearby sand quarry. It is interesting to note that no evidence for such a tramway is shown on the 1st or 2nd edition OS maps, suggesting that the feature may have been very short lived, unless it was constructed well into the 20th century.

The post-medieval landscape along the M6 Toll

The 1 inch Ordnance Survey map of 1902 has been used to describe the landscape at the turn of the 20th century when the main initial development of the industrial revolution had occurred but before 20th century urbanisation had hidden many older features.

At a basic level, the post-medieval landscape of the M6 Toll divides into two distinct halves and the 2nd edition OS map reflects this. The northern half of the route passes through an industrial landscape dotted with collieries and criss-crossed by mainline railways, smaller freight rail branches and canals which connected the pits and manufacturers to the wider transport network, while the southern half of the route has a quite different character. This section only crosses one canal, towards its southern end, and one railway. In this area the 1902 OS map shows that, at the turn of the 20th century, the future route of the Toll road passed through, or adjacent to, a series of country houses or parks, surviving fragments of woodland and numerous farms.

Saredon to Great Wyrley

The study corridor surrounding the northern 3 km of the M6 Toll, from Saredon to Churchbridge, contains some of the most historically important industrial sites or features of the whole route. Among these is Wedges Mill, the former site of which is located *c* 300 m north of the M6 Toll, to the west of Bridgtown, between the Wyrley and Essington Canal and the A5 Watling Street.

Although there appear to have been earlier mills at this site the factory for which Wedges Mill is most important was an edge tool works established in 1790 by William Gilpin who went on to become the most important figure in the important edge tool industry of southern Staffordshire. Gilpin had been apprenticed in the edge tool trade in Wolverhampton before he established his own works at Wedges Mill, a mill site that he had acquired through marriage. The site had a water driven hammer and was developed into a significant and highly successful industrial complex. Its success led to Gilpin expanding his interests in the early 19th century by purchasing land at Great Wyrley, Pelsall and Essington to provide him with his own sources of coal, ironstone and limestone. In 1806 the Gilpin's edge tool works expanded to another site *c* 0.6 km to the east in Churchbridge and this site, which was provided with a steam engine, was gradually developed so that by 1817 it had largely superseded the original Wedges Mill. The importance of Gilpin's works and the more general development of Churchbridge in the first half of the 19th century is reflected by the construction of the Hatherton Branch (also sometimes known as the Churchbridge Extension) of the Staffordshire and Worcestershire Canal in 1841. The canal and related features have been investigated at Sites 1–3 in the current investigation.

The Edge Tool Manufactory in Churchbridge is clearly shown on the 1st and 2nd edition OS maps (1884, 1902) as a well developed complex with many buildings and a network of tramways providing links to the Cannock Branch of the South Staffordshire railway and to the adjacent canal basin and wharf (Site 3). The complex was immediately to the south of Site 4 and the main works were immediately to the south-east of Site 3. Several of the tramways from the edge tool works extended into Site 3 and evidence of these, as well as other related structures, were recorded. By the date of the first edition OS map the wagons on these tracks would have been shunted by a steam train but it is known that when the complex was first constructed it had horse drawn tramways linking it with Gilpin's pits and with the canal.

William Gilpin's importance to the edge tool industry extended beyond the success of his own enterprise as a number of other edge tool manufacturers were trained in his works. These included Cornelius Whitehouse who established an edge tool factory in Bridgtown, immediately north of the M6 Toll, in 1869 and his brothers then opened another works in the same town. Bridgtown was an industrial settlement of the second half of the 19th century which was laid out with a regular plan in the 1860s and 1870s on former wasteland to provide housing for the miners and workers from other industries, such as brick and tile works, which were expanding rapidly in this period.

Clearly the chosen location of the settlement of Bridgtown was heavily influenced by the important transport intersection adjacent to it at Churchbridge and through which the M6 Toll now passes. Considering the importance of transport in the industrialisation of the region and in this study Churchbridge is clearly a key site. At this point there was an intersection between two turnpike roads (Watling Street and the Walsall to Stafford road) close to which was a toll house. In addition the Hatherton Branch of the Staffordshire and Worcestershire Canal passed through this same point (now truncated by the M6 Toll) and it connected to the Churchbridge locks which were constructed in 1860 and which provided a link to the Cannock Extension Canal. In addition the L&NWR South Staffordshire Line (Cannock Branch), which was constructed in 1849, also passes over the same intersection. The importance of this intersection is demonstrated by the development immediately around it shown on the 1st and 2nd edition 25 inch OS maps. As detailed above these show Gilpin's edge tool works immediately to the south, a brickworks immediately to the north and the new settlement of Bridgtown to the north-west

Immediately to the south of the northernmost section of the M6 Toll are the neighbouring settlements of Great Wyrley and Cheslyn Hay which were small pre-existing settlements which have each spread into a single built-up area in the 20th century. Great Wyrley has medieval origins and Cheslyn Hay had ten people chargeable for the hearth tax in 1666. Although these settlements grew substantially with the main development of the Cannock Chase coalfield in the second half of the 19th century, this area, to the south of Watling Street and extending down towards Landywood, was one of the main parts of the Cannock Chase Coalfield where seams were accessible relatively close to the surface. There were many small pits in this vicinity prior to the mid-19th century including several that were probably at least partially located beneath the current route of the M6 Toll. Deane *et al.* (2005) report that, in the early 19th century, there were four shafts in the Churchbridge area which are now overlain by the M6 Toll.

The *Victoria Country History* reports that before its inclosure in 1797 Cheslyn Common had been occupied by a series of squatters in 'mud huts' and presumably many of these squatters worked in the local pits. As discussed above, people squatting on common land while working in local industries was a common and important feature of the early stages of the industrial revolution in many areas.

Other than mining the only other industry of importance in this area has been the manufacture of bricks and tiles, particularly the famous Staffordshire Blue engineering bricks which were used to construct a wide range of structures including many canals and canal features in this area. The 1st edition OS map of 1884 shows the Rosemary Tile Works a short distance to the south-west of Hatherton Reservoir as well as the brickworks in Churchbridge referred to above.

To the north of the M6 Toll in this area, beyond Bridgtown, is the larger town of Cannock which expanded dramatically in the second half of the 19th century due to the growth of the local coal industry. In 1851 it was no more than a large village which had developed somewhat in the 18th century as a spa town but it then grew substantially from a population of 3000 in 1861 to 24,000 in 1901 (Palliser 1976). Unlike those a short distance to the south in the Great Wyrley and Cheslyn Hay area, the coal measures around Cannock are much more deeply set and the exploitation of these minerals was only possible with the larger scale mining of the later 19th century, mainly to the north of the town.

Great Wyrley to Brownhills

Approximately 4 km to the east of Churchbridge and the northern edge of Great Wyrley is Norton Canes which is immediately north of the M6 Toll and is another small mining settlement which expanded greatly in the later 19th and 20th centuries. The main collieries in this area were owned by the Conduit Colliery Company and were mainly developed from the 1860s. They were each deep mines with tramway links to the Cannock Extension Canal or to the developing railway network. Norton Green Colliery (Conduit No. 4) and Conduit No. 3 Collieries were located just to the north of the current route of the M6 Toll and Coppice Colliery (or Conduit No. 2) appears to have been immediately to the south of the current location of the M6 Toll. None of these collieries was within the specified sites for archaeological investigation and thus they have not been recorded in the works on the M6 Toll.

Building recording was undertaken of the brick-built house of probable 18th century date at Swan Farm, Norton Canes (Site 36). The multi-storey building with cellar and tiled gabled M-shaped roof had been much modified and had suffered from subsidence due to mining activities. The house was of double pile plan, with an extension of the ground floor by means of an outshut at the rear. The double-pile house plan came in to use in the late 17th century, was universally used in the 18th century and lasted though much of 19th (Brunskill 1997, 48). It had begun to be used for farmhouses from the early 18th century (Brunskill 1997, 82–3). The post-medieval period was one in which there were many changes in the design of vernacular houses for various reasons which include rebuilding of earlier houses in more durable materials, or to cope with population growth between the 16th and 19th centuries (Newman *et al.* 2001, 63). It was noted that that one of the farm outbuildings had a large chimney and boiler. This might have been a later adaptation of a forge, suggesting that the building may once have been a smithy.

Immediately to the north of the M6 Toll is the large reservoir which, since 1956, has been called Chasewater but which was previously known as the Great Pool, Norton Pool and simply Cannock Chase Reservoir. This was constructed in *c* 1798 when the Crane Brook was dammed to provide a reservoir for the newly constructed Wyrley and Essington Canal. The M6 Toll cuts through the former location of the Anglesey Branch Canal which extended south-east from the reservoir to feed the Wyrley and Essington. It was on the eastern side of this reservoir that the first trial bores for the deep coal in the Cannock Chase area were made in 1849 and the first deep mine was subsequently established here. Many other deep pits were also dug in the area surrounding the reservoir, largely belonging to the Cannock Chase Colliery Company. To the east of the company's main pits the new mining settlement of Chasetown was laid out, initially in the 1860s, with a regular, partially radial plan and the 1st edition OS map shows that, typically for the period, the small town was provided with a Church (St Ann's), a Methodist Chapel (Wesleyan), a Primitive Methodist Chapel and a school.

To the south of this part of the M6 Toll is Brownhills, the northern edge of which now extends beyond Watling Street and close to the modern Toll road. The origins of Brownhills lie in the fact that this is another of the few areas around Cannock Chase where some coal measures are sufficiently shallow to be relatively easily extracted and mining is known to have been relatively extensively undertaken on Brownhills Common long before the 19th century. Brownhills Common is north of the main modern town of Brownhills and extends north towards the current route of the M6 Toll. During the 18th century a small settlement developed at this point either side of the existing roads and in the mid- and later 19th century a much more substantial settlement was laid out to the east of the new railway line which bisected the area, to accommodate the many new workers in the large, deep mines being established. The industry of Brownhills was not solely based on coal mining and the 1st edition OS map shows a substantial chemical works to the north of the main town (but south of Watling Street) as well as a flour mill and a gas works.

Brownhills to Shenstone

Brownhills, to the south of the M6 Toll, and Chasetown, to the north, provide an indication of the eastern extent of the Cannock Chase coalfield and the character of the landscape through which the toll road passes is quite different to the east of this area.

The land here remains today largely agricultural with small settlements that did not see dramatic expansion in the later 19th century as did those on the adjacent coalfield. There are obviously no collieries or associated features such as tramways and there are no other substantial industrial concerns such as the brick or tile works further west. The Wyrley and Essington Canal extends through this area in a north-easterly direction towards Lichfield, as does the South Staffordshire railway line (L&NWR), but other than some minor structures such as lime kilns in Muckley Corner, significant industrial plants have not been established alongside the canal banks. The M6 Toll cuts through the Wyrley and Essington Canal in this area (Site 8).

To the north of the M6 Toll is the settlement of Hammerwich that appears to have had something of a nail making industry, in common with Burntwood a short distance to the north (see above). The *Victoria County History* records that a nailer was living in Hammerwich in 1774 and there was a nailer's shop in the township in 1824. Numerous nailers are recorded on the censuses of 1841 and 1851 but only two in 1861, which suggests that local labour may have transferred at this time to the new mines a short distance to the west.

To the east of Hammerwich is the parish of Wall with Pipehill, created from the two formerly separate townships. These were both small settlements with 12 people in each assessed for the hearth tax in 1666. Their populations each grew slowly to *c* 100 people by around 1800 and then fluctuated slightly for much of the 19th century. The land continued to be used largely for pastoral farming although the 1st edition OS map shows a smithy in Wall.

To the east of Wall the M6 Toll diverges towards the south-east and continues through largely agricultural land between various small settlements. The only township in this area which has developed into a larger settlement is Shenstone which is less than 1 km to the south-west of the Toll road and which appears to have developed alongside the main historic Lichfield to

Birmingham road. The 1st edition OS map shows a flour mill, with mill pond and a smithy.

Shenstone to Curdworth

The historic landscape of the southern half of the M6 Toll is distinctly different from that of the northern half and the 1902 OS map shows that, at that date, it consisted largely of farmland, surviving woodland and parkland from several modest estates in the area. Indeed, whereas the dominant feature interspersing the general landscape surrounding the northern half of the route is the colliery, in the southern half it is the country house.

Towards the northern end of this section, the OS map shows Manley Hall and Shenstone Park to the west of the M6 Toll route and, in the same general area, Swinfen Hall is to the north-east and beyond this is Packington Hall. These were clearly each significant houses set in parkland. Slightly to the south of these, at the southern edge of Staffordshire, is Canwell Hall, through the parkland of which the M6 route passes.

In the same general area there are several small settlements such as Weeford and Hints that had small scale or nascent industries which, unlike the similar sites in the northern half of the route, did not develop into major complexes or industrial sites. As referred to above, Hints had a forge in the 16th century which operated in conjunction with a blast furnace in Middleton, several km to the south, and the 1902 map shows a smithy in Weeford.

Over the county border into Warwickshire, Ashfurlong Hall and Moor Hall are to the west of the M6 Toll and further to the south, although still close to the route, are Langley Hall, Moxhull Hall and Dunton Hall. During investigations at Hawkeswell Farm, Coleshill (Site 24) a number of possible garden and landscaping features of late medieval to post-medieval date were excavated – possibly related to Hawkeswell Hall. There have not been many opportunities to excavate garden features of this date in the region, although the much better preserved multi-phase gardens at Castle Bromwich Hall of possible 16th–18th or 19th century date have been extensively studied (Currie and Locock 1993). The 16th century had seen a change in the composition of the country's elite, with many new gentry building a distinct class of houses by the mid-17th century (Mercer 1954). In the 18th century many houses and gardens were remodelled and others become 'old fashioned' as the fortunes and status of their owners rose or fell.

By far the largest settlement in this general area shown on the 1902 OS map is Sutton Coldfield which now extends east almost as far as the M6 Toll although its historic centre is further to the west. Sutton Coldfield was an old settlement which developed considerably in the post-medieval period more as a residential area for people working in other areas rather than as an industrial centre itself. In the 17th and 18th centuries there was small scale industry in the area, particularly mills powered by pools formed in what is now Sutton Park, producing a wide range of items, but this manufacture based on water power was soon overtaken by the much larger industrial enterprises developing in Birmingham and the Black Country.

It is somewhat ironic that, although the historic character of the southern half of the M6 Toll is much more rural and less industrialised than the northern half, perhaps the most important industrial feature that the road passes through, at least in terms of its preservation, is close to the southern end of the route. The construction of the M6 Toll truncated and necessitated considerable alterations to Dunton Wharf and Lock of the Birmingham and Fazeley Canal in Curdworth. This was the only one of the post-medieval features investigated that remains as a working canal at the point where it is crossed by the M6 Toll. However, although the canal is the best surviving industrial feature impacted by the M6 Toll it is not a reflection of an industrial landscape in the way that the canals in the northern half of the route are. The banks of this canal were never lined with industries (at least in the general vicinity where the M6 Toll has now been constructed). This canal was constructed to link two relatively distant places and the landscape remained largely rural. Indeed this is perhaps one of the principal reasons why this waterway has remained viable into the 21st century for pleasure cruisers, unlike the less conventionally picturesque landscape which surrounds the other canals further north along the M6 Toll around the Cannock Chase Coalfield.

Conclusion

In any major study involving individual sites from a number of different periods, such as that of the M6 Toll, it is likely that the investigations at the post-medieval sites will answer different types of questions than the older sites and will serve a slightly different function. At each of the seven post-medieval sites (particularly the six canal-related sites) we have several maps which show us the overall layout of the features when they were still fully operational and a great deal was already known of the sites prior to the start of archaeological works. It was known in some detail what types of structures were at each site and indeed many of the structures were already at least partially visible above ground. In addition, at some sites, other similar structures still survive relatively close by, such as at Curdworth lock (Site 21) which formed part of a flight of 11 locks, ten of which survive.

At the start of the project it was much less likely that the investigations at the later sites would uncover anything particularly unexpected, with the potential to significantly alter our understanding of the post-medieval period, than the earlier sites and this has proved to be the case.

This is not to say that the intrusive investigation of the later sites has not been worthwhile as it has indeed enhanced our understanding of the construction of the individual features as well as their development and use. Perhaps the most successful sites, which revealed the greatest quantity of new information, were the two canal basins (Sites 1 and 3) and the lock. The main components of both Hawkins Basin and Gilpin's Basin survived and this allowed detailed recording programmes at each site. The features at Site 3 (Gilpin's Basin) included the remains of a goods shed and the base from a crane adjacent to the goods shed while among the features revealed at Site 1 were nudging stones in the aqueduct to protect the main aqueduct walls and evidence of former rails which ran along each side of the basin.

The overall study has enhanced our understanding of canal construction in this area and a number of common themes have been raised at different sites. Among these is the simplicity of the embankments and dams. Both the dam at Site 1 and the substantial embankment at Site 8 appear to be nothing more than an earth mound incorporating no structural element or reinforcing. Another feature of several sites is the number of phases of repair and rebuild which were necessary after the structures' initial construction. This is true of both the canal walls, the embankments and the other structures and it is probably a good reflection of the considerable strain placed on any canal structure. Most of the structures appear to have been originally constructed of red brick and then partially rebuild with stronger Staffordshire Blue engineering bricks in the later 19th century. The work has also clarified our understanding of the use of clay to line of the bottom and sides of the canal features.

As well as the detailed understanding of each individual site the overall study has also been of value in illustrating more general points. These relate to the history, expansion and significance of the canal network in this area as well as its relationship to the development of the wider area in the post-medieval period.

The sites have provided a series of snapshots of sites illustrating the development of the canal network in this area and many of the key themes in understanding its history. The four canals which the M6 Toll cuts through and which have been investigated illustrate well the 'story' of the canal network in north and east of Birmingham. The Birmingham and Fazeley Canal (of which Site 21 forms a part) was a relatively early canal which formed part of the important 'Grand Cross' of waterways linking the country's four estuary navigations; the Wyrley and Essington (including Site 8) was constructed during the peak period of canal construction in the 1790s; the Hatherton Branch of the Staffordshire and Worcestershire canal (including Sites 2 and 3) was a late construction having been opened in 1841 while the Cannock Extension Canal (Site 6) was completed in 1863 and represents one of the country's last significant developments of the canal network. In addition, to a lesser extent the sites have also illustrated the more modern history of the canal network as elements from two sites (Site 21 and 1) have been recovered to allow their reuse in canal restoration works.

One of the main themes that the sites illustrate is the wide range of structures associated with the canal network. The most fundamental of course is the canal itself but there are also a great many subsidiary features which demonstrate different functions of a canal and the ways in which it operated. Site 21 allowed a detailed investigation of the form and operation of a lock and the same site included a study of the lock-keepers cottage. Features at other sites included reservoirs (Site 2), wharfes (Sites 3 and 6), an aqueduct (Site 1), a dam (Site 2), works basins (Sites 1 and 3), embankments (Sites 6 and 8) and various bridges (Sites 3 and 4).

Another theme that the sites illustrate is how the original construction of the canals was driven by industry and how its relatively late expansion in the mid-19th century dovetailed with the exploitation of the Cannock Chase coalfield. Several of the sites are also illustrative of the period in the second half of the 19th century in which canals and the railway network dovetailed and co-existed, particularly in the carriage of coal and other industrial products. The clearest example of this is Site 3 which included an interchange basin to allow the transfer of goods from canal to railway.

Chapter 33

The M6 Toll: Closing Remarks

The main results of the M6 Toll archaeological works programme have been set out above and then discussed in terms of broad chronological periods, the latter following the revised framework of major period-based research themes identified in the post-excavation assessment report (OWA 2003) (see Chapter 1). In this section it is proposed to indicate some of the more important aspects of the project, refer briefly to a number of themes which have cross-period relevance, and make some general observations about the archaeology of the region and of major projects of this nature based on the experience of M6 Toll project.

At the outset of the project it was anticipated that its principal contributions were likely to be in relation to later prehistoric and Romano-British rural settlement and in providing archaeological detail relating to the industrial sites. To a large degree this proved to be true, though the extent to which wider understanding of the canals and other 19th century monuments of the area has been improved may be less than was hoped.

The Mesolithic flint scatter of Wishaw Hall Farm (Site 19), the burnt mounds of Langley Brook and Collet's Brook (Sites 39 and 40), the Iron Age settlements of Shenstone Ring Ditch, Wishaw, North of Langley Brook and Langley Mill (Sites 14, 20, 29 and 30), boundaries at Wishaw Hall Farm (Site 19) and possible non-settlement features at Langley Mill (Site 30) have all contributed to a much enhanced understanding of the diversity of prehistoric activity in the area. For the Romano-British period, the unexpected discoveries of the major aisled building at West of Crane Brook Cottage (Site 34), the Ryknield Street cemetery (Site 12) and the pottery kiln at East of Birmingham Road Nurseries (Site 15), amongst a mass of other features, have shed important light on aspects of the impact first of the military and then of the civilian community of the small town of Wall on the surrounding area. In the post-Roman period the evidence from Shenstone Linear Features, Wishaw and Hawkeswell Farm (Sites 13, 20 and 24) arguably reveals something of the reality of the dispersed settlement patterns of the region that is both known from and enhanced by comparison with documentary evidence.

The M6 Toll project has undoubtedly produced important archaeological results. It is debatable, however, whether the archaeological potential of the area traversed by the new road was fully realised. There are many reasons for this, the most important of which is probably the longevity of the project.

When fieldwork began in December 2000, in the middle of the (then) wettest winter since records began, it was as part of a programme of work the outlines of which had been effectively established six years earlier, in the recommendations made in the archaeological report adopted as part of the findings of the public enquiry that approved the proposed route of M6 Toll. In turn, based largely on data gathered (very thoroughly, it should be said) in the early 1990s, the approach to the mitigation of certain parts of the archaeological resource, particularly in relation to what were collectively termed 'industrial sites', fell short of what would generally be regarded as desirable today. In particular, the belief that significant evidence could be recovered through watching brief operations may seem, with hindsight, somewhat optimistic. In relation to the industrial sites, however, it is perhaps difficult to know what else could have been done. The cutting of a section through the Cannock Extension Canal (Site 6), for example, was a significant engineering operation in its own right, and not a task that would normally fall to archaeologists to manage. Recording of the canal had perforce to be undertaken within the engineering programme, and access to other sites would always have been dependent upon preliminary engineering tasks. The key to success in these circumstances is always the fullest communication between all the parties concerned, and an understanding by each of what the others have to do, and why.

Standing buildings constituted a further aspect of the post-medieval landscape which was under-valued in the early stages of the project, although in fact remarkably few buildings were directly impacted by the new road and none of these was listed. No building recording was specified in the original project design and the recording that was eventually undertaken, at Swan Farm and Curdworth Top Lock (Sites 36 and 21), was carried out more hurriedly than was desirable. The principal building complex affected by the route, at Wishaw Hall Farm, was completely demolished well before the start of the archaeological programme and even before the appointment of the archaeological contractor. While there were valid (non-archaeological) reasons for this the fact that no provision had been made for recording at any stage represents a lapse in 'joined up thinking'. In contrast, the fact that most post-medieval ceramics were not reported in detail was a positive outcome of the post-excavation assessment process, based on the small quantities and poor contexts of most of this material, which were considered to render it of minimal analytical value.

A wider area of recent development which might have impacted upon the planning of M6 Toll archaeological works is the general approach to landscape. The 1994 archaeological report pre-dated widespread work on historic landscape characterisation (HLC), but a number of significant categories of historic land use, such as ancient woodland, common land and greens, extent of inclosure (distinguishing between 18th/19th century and earlier episodes), deer parks and other parkland etc, were mapped. While falling short of comprehensive HLC (yet to be completed in Staffordshire and Warwickshire) this mapping provided valuable information and, in the context of M6 Toll, it is doubtful if more detailed HLC would have altered the programme of archaeological works, let alone the planning of the route.

The factors which had the most significant effect on the recognition of archaeological sites and features of most periods as encountered along the M6 Toll were soils and artefact quantities. In terms of the effectiveness of site location the two are intimately connected. The former produced cropmark evidence of reasonable quality in the vicinity of Wall (although by no means all the archaeological features examined there appeared on the aerial photographs), but elsewhere the quantity and quality of this evidence was variable.

Some significant sites (eg Site 29) were not revealed by cropmark evidence at all. In other cases, the quality of the evidence was such that in many parts of the country it might have been disregarded as revealing no meaningful archaeological features. Fortunately in the case of Site 34, where the traces were so unclear that a very experienced practitioner could not plot them but only indicate their presence, the latter was taken as justification for intrusive work which led to the discovery of the only major Romano-British structure in the entire project. Nevertheless, because of the paucity of other evidence, the indications of cropmarks were one of the primary means of identification of sites for further work. Reservations about the significance and interpretation of cropmarks inevitably surface in these circumstances. As already mentioned at the beginning of this volume, a number of the examined sites not reported here were identified on the basis of diverse cropmark features. A possible ring ditch (or at least, a very clear circular mark) at Brownhills (Site 27, in archive) was discounted in the original desk-based assessment and in the aerial photographic review (Babtie 2000). On examination at the request of the Local Authority Archaeologist, no archaeological features were identified. Conversely at Weeford (Site 16, in archive) a linear boundary was identified as a potential pit alignment (*ibid.*). On excavation it was clear that some kind of boundary was present, but it was certainly not a pit alignment, and the features were ephemeral and undated.

Geophysical survey, a standard 'next step' in many archaeological projects, was mostly unrevealing and generally added little to the aerial photographic evidence where that was present. It is unclear if the poor geophysical survey results were a consequence of generally unresponsive soil types, perhaps exacerbated by the unusually wet conditions. Fieldwalking, also, was for the most part equally ineffective in site location, principally as a consequence of low base level incidences of most artefact types. Despite some success in the area, eg in the Birmingham and Warwickshire Archaeological Society's work in the Sutton Coldfield area (1998; Jones 1999), and Mike Hodder's work at Wishaw (1992) the technique was unproductive on M6 Toll. The earlier work, however, was based on very closely-spaced transects (typically *c* 3 m; M. Hodder pers. comm.) as opposed to the commonly deployed 20 m transect spacing used in 2000.

Large quantities of 18th century and later material were recovered from fieldwalking the route of M6 Toll, but almost nothing of earlier periods. The identification of Site 29, initially on the basis of three pieces of flint, in an earlier local fieldwalking project, followed by trenching based on very slight indications of linear features recovered in the intervening geophysical survey, is a story that has lost nothing in the telling (Hodder 2004, 45) but which equally contains many lessons. In that case, however, the association of flints with later features was almost certainly fortuitous. At Coleshill (Site 23, in archive), a small flint scatter located in fieldwalking was examined by test pitting and in the subsequent watching brief and yielded nothing – here the scatter was entirely contained within the ploughsoil, a not uncommon situation with such material. A 'one size fits all' approach to projects of this type clearly will not do, and methodologies may need to be varied more widely than is generally the case in order to accommodate the particular characteristics of regional archaeological resources.

The problem of site location by fieldwalking was not related to soil type and site conditions; artefact visibility in the relatively light soils of much of the route was usually good. The prevailing soil types therefore lend themselves to arable agriculture (while their acidity resulted in the loss of much key evidence, particularly human and animal bone) and the relative ease of cultivation once drainage issues have been addressed was undoubtedly a factor in the condition of many of the excavated sites.

Repeated reference is made in the site narratives to truncation of features by ploughing, and the effective absence of vertical stratigraphy across most sites is also a consequence of destruction through arable agriculture, though typical of sites in this situation. In every one of the principal excavations reported here (excluding the industrial sites) erosion of features by ploughing was clearly seen, and in many cases the resulting damage was extensive. That it is ongoing is indicated by occurrences such as that of large sherds of Neolithic pottery, in a recent ploughsoil context at Site 15. The potential complexity resulting from different campaigns of ploughing was illustrated particularly at the Ryknield Street cemetery at Wall (Site 12), where three successive stages of machine stripping were undertaken in order to ensure that no burials had been missed – the features did not show consistently at the same level. What is less clear is whether plough truncation had removed complete sites. This is possible in the case of the earlier prehistoric period, as for example at archive Site 23 (above), but the Mesolithic flint assemblage of Site 19 was mostly encountered at the interface between ploughsoil and natural subsoil, rather than entirely within the former. For later, characteristically 'artefact poor' periods, there were no instances on the M6 Toll where it was possible to use the existing surface evidence to suggest the location of sites which had left no additional trace. In such circumstances the significance of one or two sherds, while conceivably substantial, will always remain uncertain.

The widespread distribution of broadly similar soil types, related to a relatively narrow range of underlying geologies, means that there was little indication of variation in site recovery (through techniques such as field walking and geophysics) that correlated with soil type. The same was broadly true of the aerial evidence; the fact that cropmark sites appear to concentrate in the vicinity of Wall may indeed reflect a genuine concentration of ancient, particularly later prehistoric and Romano-British, activity in this area. It does not simply reflect the existence of more responsive soils there; comparable soils were widely distributed across the route.

Equally there is no clear indication of correlation between the effectiveness of site location techniques and topography, principally because the range of topographical locations on M6 Toll sites was relatively limited. Most of the M6 Toll sites were located on fairly level ground or on gently sloping stream valley sides, while stream-edge locations were favoured for burnt mounds and occasionally for settlement and other sites. Even in the latter locations there was no masking of sites by significant alluvial deposits; although such deposits were present (particularly at Site 30) their extent generally seems to have been quite restricted. More extensive and deeper alluvial deposits might have existed in the valleys of the more substantial rivers Tame and Cole in the south-eastern part of the route, but here the M6 Toll was sited along the line of the existing M42 and there were no opportunities to examine this possibility. Colluvial deposits on the valley sides were also of limited extent and seem unlikely to have had a marked impact on site detection. The most significant 'masking' deposit identified, apart from the problems at Site 12 mentioned above, was seen at Site 32, near Shenstone, where a localised probable former ploughsoil was located on relatively high and level ground. It may be that the absence of a slope here had reduced the degree of erosion of this deposit by subsequent ploughing, although there was no indication of the survival of comparable deposits in an identical topographical position at the adjacent Site 15.

One type of material that can be recognised in fieldwalking is heat-shattered stone. Such stone is widely found in the area and is particularly characteristic of burnt mounds, generally dated to the Middle–Late Bronze Age. The M6 Toll evidence, however, has expanded that from some earlier work in demonstrating that this type of material can occur in contexts with a wide variety of type and period, certainly including features of later prehistoric and Romano-British and possibly even medieval date, although the evidence for the latter from Site 20 is not conclusive. The variety of contexts, and of physical locations, including a low hilltop setting at Site 29, raises questions about the interpretation of the use of heated stones, which may have varied through time if not within a specific period. The M6 Toll evidence has shed little light on the 'sweat lodge or cooking' debate which has engaged those studying burnt mounds in the West Midlands and elsewhere for some time. What it does do, however, is draw attention to the variety of possible burnt stone contexts. The occurrence of such material in stream-side locations is probably indicative of the presence of burnt mounds, whatever their function, but in some cases, as at Site 30, this material seems to have been redeposited. Elsewhere on the same site and at Site 34 such material, still in a stream-side setting, was associated with Iron Age radiocarbon dates. Away from streams, occurrences of heat cracked stones might have quite different meanings and simple 'burnt stone equals burnt mound' assumptions need to be avoided unless supported by additional evidence.

The occurrence of only modest, and in some cases minute, quantities of artefacts of many periods has been emphasised (and the lack of material associated with burnt mounds is a classic regional example). It is probably fair to say that this characteristic, while not unexpected, was more pronounced than had been anticipated. In essence, on the present M6 Toll evidence, fieldwalking, particularly with a transect spacing of less than 20 m, would stand a reasonable chance of locating sites of Mesolithic date, and some (but not all) Romano-British and medieval sites, but little else. Site 34, for example, was not identified in fieldwalking. It is impossible to say if the low artefact levels in the Neolithic and especially the Bronze Age and Early Iron Age simply reflect low level activity across the region in these periods (nevertheless, such activity was present, but was revealed in the stripping of sites targeted on remains of other periods), but for the Iron Age and Romano-British periods, where the evidence is stronger, there seems little doubt that a genuine pattern of cultural activity is being observed. It contrasts with evidence from relatively close by to the east and south, and suggests that much of the M6 Toll area had affinities, at least in terms of the response of its inhabitants to the use of certain types of 'typical' archaeological material, such as pottery, with areas to the north and west. That such a pattern probably persisted into the Anglo-Saxon period is perhaps unsurprising. How far it survived into the medieval period is less clear.

A further consequence of what from the perspective of the fieldworker, rather than the interpreter of the results of fieldwork, can be called the 'artefact problem', may be seen with regard to the general watching brief phase of the project. In such circumstances, particularly when, as is quite typical, archaeologically unfriendly machinery is in use, location of features relies on two main characteristics; the distinctiveness of fills and the presence of artefacts as a warning signal. In circumstances in which the general level of feature visibility is quite low, as on M6 Toll, the importance of artefacts is enhanced, and their general absence will exacerbate the difficulties of site identification. It is probably no coincidence that the only two sites located during the general watching brief were burnt mounds (Sites 39 and 40), both readily identified by their distinctive composition and colour, which could not have been missed in any circumstances (Fig. 221). It is highly unlikely that major sites of any period escaped without notice at this stage of the project, but there can be no such confidence in relation to minor sites.

The factors already discussed also raise the question of how effective speculative evaluation trenching across the entire route might have been. That this was not done was largely another consequence of the age of the project. Trenching was only undertaken as a means of establishing the character and potential of sites already indicated by other means, and even here it was not done systematically but tended to be targeted on known 'features'. Perhaps more important, however, is the timing of the programme of work – by the time trenching was carried out the project had developed a momentum which did not allow for detailed reconsideration of the overall strategy in the light of new information. Had trenching been undertaken along the whole of the M6 Toll transect at an early stage (although in practice, this rarely happens anywhere even today, a notable exception being recent work on motorways in Ireland and now in Northern Ireland) it is likely that some features would have been identified which were never seen in the project as it was actually carried out.

The difficulty, however, because of the 'artefact problem', would have been to determine the date and therefore the potential significance of the features concerned. An example of this difficulty even in excavation can be seen at Site 26. This site has featured relatively little in the general discussions of the project, for the simple reason that the excavated enclosure is completely undated; estimates of its date ranged from prehistoric to post-medieval. Clearly confirmation of the presence of (for example) a late prehistoric site in this part of the route would be an important addition to local knowledge, but as it is the significance of the excavated enclosure remains quite uncertain. Identification of such features (undated ditches) in evaluation presents substantial difficulties in assessment of significance (with room for widely divergent views, perhaps dependent upon the role of the particular archaeologist concerned) and therefore in determination of further mitigation strategies.

Questions of sample levels arise directly from this point. These are of wider concern and some, such as the appropriateness of the 2% evaluation sample, have been widely discussed (eg Hey and Lacey 2001). In an excavation context, the level of sampling of features is one that needs to be reconsidered in relation to regional characteristics such as variability in artefact levels. A sample size which might produce assemblages that are perfectly adequate to allow dating and characterisation of other aspects of features on sites in other parts of lowland England may be quite inadequate to achieve these ends in south Staffordshire. Again this is hardly a novel conclusion, but still requires further consideration, as does the question of achieving more precision in comparative characterisation of sites, particularly through artefact analyses. This can only really be achieved by comparison of assemblage sizes with the volumes of earth removed in the excavated sample, calculation of which should be increasingly simple to do with digital technology, but which would add enormously to the value of our still broadly judgmental assessments of issues such as site status based on comparison of (for example) pottery assemblages. Much (rightly) has been made of such comparisons above, but more precise data on sample volumes and percentages in relation to overall feature density would put these comparisons on a more secure footing.

Fig. 221 General view of Collet's Brook Burnt mound (Site 40)

Linear projects are often problematic when it comes to presenting the results in wider landscape terms. This is particularly so with M6 Toll because of the scarcity of comparative archaeological data in the immediate vicinity, especially from substantial excavation, for almost any period. The M6 Toll data themselves are too few to allow the development of detailed models of landscape development, though some very broad generalisations may be attempted. Neolithic and Early Bronze Age finds were made entirely fortuitously in the course of work on sites of other periods. These discoveries may support the view that locales considered suitable for later prehistoric and Romano-British settlement had already long been favoured in this way, but it is impossible to be certain that the extent of Neolithic and Early Bronze Age activity was as limited as this might imply. Nevertheless, the concentration of all of the known activity around the Wall and Shenstone wetlands (finds from Sites 12, 13, 15 and 32; see Fitzpatrick, Chapter 29) is probably significant. The location of burnt mounds near Langley Mill (Sites 39 and 40) may indicate a broadening of scope in terms of landscape exploitation by the Middle Bronze Age, but this is not reflected in detectable activity in the area where Neolithic and Early Bronze Age finds were concentrated. There is a much closer correlation between Iron Age and Romano-British sites, but this does not necessarily mean that there was continuity of settlement location over a period of a millennium; there is far too little precision in the Iron Age chronology for this to be demonstrable.

Nevertheless, the majority of the Iron Age radiocarbon dates, and probably of the pottery as well, suggest an emphasis on the Middle to Late rather than the Early Iron Age, with an increased likelihood, albeit no certainty, that this activity could have been continuous with that of the Romano-British period. At almost every significant location of Middle Iron Age activity (Sites 14, 15, 29, 19 and 20) Romano-British settlement is identified within a few hundred metres at most, and within 500 ms at Site 30. In this last case, however, the possibility that the Iron Age enclosures at Sites 29 and 30 were linked by a ditch of Romano-British date supports the view that the stream-side location of Site 30 may have retained some significance in this period, despite the lack of direct supporting evidence. Although the evidence is insufficient for certainty, it appears that the lowest lying locations of Iron Age settlement, at Site 30 and Site 20, were not used in this way in the Romano-British period, but whether this reflects environmental factors such as an increased risk of flooding in the stream valleys, or a change in functional emphasis which did not require exploitation of these locations, is unknown.

This exception apart, utilisation of the landscape is at its most intensive in the Romano-British period, at least as expressed in terms of numbers of sites with archaeologically detectable activity, but this still does not necessarily indicate a densely occupied landscape, but rather one with concentrations of activity in areas that were favoured for a variety of reasons, including ease of communication and access to markets, access to a variety of natural resources and the availability of suitable agricultural land. These factors seem to have coincided in the vicinity of Wall and perhaps explain a concentration of activity here across periods, with the communication/market factor of added importance in the Romano-British period.

Even in periods when this was of little or no significance, the Wall area remained a focus for settlement. The exiguous traces of Anglo-Saxon activity in the area can be seen in this way, but are so slight that assessment of their long term associations, whether as developing from residual Romano-British communities or indicating the early phases of what would become the medieval settlement pattern, is impossible. The principal medieval sites appear to reflect a variety of landscape use patterns; utilisation of the varied resources of the Wall area (Site 13), specific exploitation of a stream for fish farming (Site 20) and a new form of nucleated village development (Site 24) having no clear connection with earlier patterns of settlement.

In national terms, few if any of the sites examined were intrinsically remarkable. It was perhaps this which led to a loose characterisation of the area, in a national publication, as 'an empty landscape' (*British Archaeology*, June 2002, 5), a view that was promptly and rightly rebutted by the regional curators (*British Archaeology*, August 2002, 25). What is important about the sites revealed is not so much what they are but that, in several cases, they represent the first significant examples of their type and date to have been examined in the area. The Iron Age and Romano-British rural settlements, for example, may have parallels for many of their characteristics elsewhere in the country, but currently have rarity value as sites of their specific types in the region. The extent to which they will retain their status as type sites depends on the exigencies of future development. It can at least be hoped that the M6 Toll project has made a substantial contribution not only in the recovery of these sites but also in highlighting some of the issues involved in their detection and examination.

Bibliography

Adams, J C, 1987 *Outline of Fractures*, London

Allason-Jones, L, 1984 A first-century bronze torc from Caw Gap, *Archaeologia Aeliana* (5th series) 12, 227–8

Allason-Jones, L and Miket, R, 1984 *The Catalogue of Small Finds from South Shields Roman Fort*, Soc Antiqs Newcastle upon Tyne Monogr 2

Alcock, J P, 1980 Classical religious belief and burial practice in Roman Britain, *Archaeol J* 137, 50–85

Allen, C S M, 1991 Thin sections of Bronze Age pottery from the East Midlands of England, in *Recent Developments in Ceramic Petrology* (eds A Middleton and I Freestone), British Museum Occas Pap 81, 1–15, London

Allen, C, 2000 *Holme Dyke, Gonalston, Notts, Report on Prehistoric Pottery*, unpublished report for Trent & Peak Archaeological Unit

Allen, C, 2006 *Holbeck Park, Barrow, Cumbria, Report on Neolithic Pottery*, unpublished report for Oxford Archaeology North

Allen, C S M, Harman, M and Wheeler, H, 1987 Bronze Age cremation cemeteries in the East Midlands, *Proc Prehist Soc* 53, 187–221

Allen, C and Hopkins, D, 2000 Bronze Age Accessory Cups from Lincolnshire: Early Bronze Age pot?, *Proc Prehist Soc* 66, 297–317

Allen, C, Garton, D and Priest, V, in preparation, Hickens Bridge, Aston on Trent, Derbyshire, Neolithic, Bronze Age, Iron Age and Romano-British sites – 1994–5

Allen, J R L and Fulford, M G, 1996 The distribution of south-east Dorset black-burnished category 1 pottery in south-west Britain, *Britannia* 27, 223–81

Allen, M J, 1986 Magnetic susceptibility as a potential palaeoenvironmental determinant, *Circaea* 4, 18–20

Allen, M J, 1995 Land molluscs, in *Balksbury Camp, Hampshire, Excavations 1973 and 1981* (G Wainwright and S Davies), English Heritage Archaeol Rep 4, 92–100, London

Allen, M J, 1998 *The Development of Prehistoric Land-use in the Guiting Power Landscape; the Land Snail Evidence*, unpublished report for Guiting Power Estate

Allen, M J, 2001 Land snail evidence for landscape and land-use change, in Excavations at Balksbury Camp, Andover 1995–97 (C J Ellis, and M Rawlings), *Hampshire Stud* 56, 54–67

Allen, M J forthcoming Land snails, in *Battlesbury Bowl, Warminster and Sites Along the Southern Range Road* (C J Ellis), Wessex Archaeology, Salisbury

Allen, M J and Bayliss, A, 1995, Appendix 2: the radiocarbon programme, in *Stonehenge in its Landscape: Twentieth Century Excavations* (R M J Cleal, K E Walker and R Montague), English Heritage Archaeol Rep 10, London

Allen, M J, Rhodes, E, Beavan, N and Groves, C, 2004, Absolute chronology, in *A Prehistoric Ritual Complex at Eynesbury, Cambridgeshire* (C J Ellis), E Anglian Archaeol Occas Pap 17, 60–8, Salisbury

Allen, M J and Macphail, R I, 1987 Micromorphology and magnetic susceptibility studies: their combined role in interpreting archaeological soils and sediments, in *Soil Micromorphology* (eds N Fedoroff, L M Bresson and M A Courty), Plaisair: Association Française pour l'Etude du Sol, 669–76, Paris

Allen, T G and Robinson, M A, 1993 *The Prehistoric Landscape and Iron Age Enclosed Settlement at Mingies Ditch, Hardwick-with-Yelford, Oxen,* Thames Valley Landscapes: the Windrush Valley Volume 2, Oxford

Allen, T, Miles, D and Palmer, S, 1984 Iron Age buildings in the Upper Thames Valley, in *Aspects of the Iron Age in Central Southern Britain* (eds B Cunliffe and D Miles), Oxford Univ Comm Archaeol Monogr 2, 89–101, Oxford

Archaeological Investigations, 2005 *Oxley Park (West) Milton Keynes Excavation of an Iron Age Settlement and further trenching (interim report)*, Hereford Archaeol Ser 659

Arnold, D E, 1981 A model for the identification of non-local ceramic distribution: a view from the present, in *Production and Distribution: a Ceramic Viewpoint* (eds H Howard and E L Morris), Brit Archaeol Rep S120, 31–44, Oxford

Arnold, D E, 1985 *Ceramic Theory and Cultural Process*, Cambridge

Aston, M, 1982 Aspects of fishpond construction and maintenance in the 16th and 17th centuries with particular references to Warwickshire, in *Field and Forest: an Historical Geography of Warwickshire and Worcestershire* (eds T R Slater and P J Jarvis), 257–80, Exeter

Aston, M (ed), 1988 *Medieval Fish, Fisheries and Fishponds in England*, Brit Archaeol Rep 182, Oxford

Aston, M, 2000 *Monasteries in the Landscape*, Stroud

Aston, M and Bond, C J, 1988 Warwickshire fishponds, in Aston (ed) 1988, 417–34

Babtie 2000, *Birmingham Northern Relief Road Aerial Photographic Assessment: Archaeology: Rectified Mapping*, unpublished report (August 2000)

Bagnall, J N, 1874 The recent excavations at Etocetum, *Birmingham and Midland Institute, Archaeological Section Transactions, Excursions and Reports* 4, 38–42

Bailey, M, 1989 The concept of the margin in the medieval English economy, *Econ Hist Rev 2nd ser* 42(i), 1–17

Baker, A R H and Butlin, R A (eds), 1973 *Studies in Field Systems in the British Isles*, Cambridge

Ball, F and Ball N, 1983–4 'Rescue' excavation at Wall (Staffordshire) 1980/81 (Wall excavation report no. 13) *Trans Staffordshire Archaeol Hist Soc* 25, 1–29

Bamford, H M, 1985 *Briar Hill excavation 1974–1978*, Northampton Development Corporation Archaeol Monogr 3, Northampton

Banks, P J and Morris, E L, 1979 Iron Age pottery and briquetage, in C Smith (ed) 1979, 45–57

Barber, B and Bowsher, D, 2000 *The Eastern Cemetery of Roman London, Excavations 1983–1990*, MoLAS Monogr 4, London

Barber, J, 1985, The pit alignment at Eskbank Nurseries, *Proc Prehist Soc* 51, 149–66

Barclay, A, Lambrick, G, Moore, J and Robinson, M, 2003 *Lines in the Landscape. Cursus Monuments in the Upper Thames Valley: Excavations at the Drayton and Lechlade Cursuses*, Thames Valley Landscapes 15, Oxford

Barfield, L, 1980–81 Neolithic material, 42–3, in M O H Carver, Excavations south of Lichfield Cathedral, 1976–77, *Trans Staffordshire Archaeol Hist Soc* 22 (1982), 35–69

Barfield, L H, 1991, Hot stones: hot food or hot baths?, in Hodder and Barfield (eds) 1991, 59–67

Barfield, L H, 2002 The West Midlands burnt mound survey, *W Midlands Archaeol* 45, 15

Barfield, L, Deakin, M and Deakin, T, in preparation, Avon Valley field survey: second preliminary report on the surface flint collected in the upper Avon Valley, in S C Palmer, in preparation a

Barfield, L H and Hodder, M, 1987 Burnt mounds as saunas, and the prehistory of bathing, *Antiquity* 61, 370–9

Barfield, L H and Hodder, M A, 1989 Burnt mounds in the West Midlands: surveys and excavations, in *Midlands Prehistory: some Recent and Current Researches into the Prehistory of Central England* (ed A Gibson), Brit Archaeol Rep 204, 5–13, Oxford

Barrett, G and Hislop, M, 2004 Tutbury Castle, *W Midlands Archaeol* 47, 58–60

Barrow, G, Gibson, W, Cantrill, T C, Dixon, E E L and Cunnington, C H, 1919 *The Geology of the Country Around Lichfield Including the Northern Parts of the South Staffordshire and Warwickshire Coalfields: Explanation of Sheet 154*, Norwich

Barnett, S, 2000 Luminesence dating of pottery from later prehistoric Britain, *Archaeometry* 42, 431–57

Bartley, D D and Morgan, A V, 1990 The palynological record of the King's Pool, Stafford, England, *New Phytol* 116, 177–94

Bass, W M, 1987 *Human Osteology*, Missouri

Bateman, J, 1976–7 A late Bronze Age cremation cemetery and Iron Age/Romano-British enclosures in the parish of Ryton-on-Dunsmore, Warwickshire *Trans Birmingham Warwickshire Archaeol Soc* 88, 9–47

Beales, P W, 1980 The Late Devensian and Flandrian vegetational history of Crose Mere, Shropshire, *New Phytol* 85, 133–61

Beamish, M, 1998 A Middle Iron Age site at Wanlip, Leicestershire, *Trans Leicestershire Archaeol Natur Hist Soc* 72, 1–91

Beck, C, and Shennan, S, 1991 *Amber in Prehistoric Britain*, Oxford

Beckett, J H, 1925 Archaeology, *Trans North Staffordshire Fld Club* 59, 184–6

Beek, G C van, 1983 *Dental Morphology: an Illustrated Guide*, Bristol

Behre K.E, 1992 The history of rye cultivation in Europe, *Vegetation Hist Archaeobot* 1, 141–56

Beijerinck, W, 1947 *Zadenatlas der Nederlandsche*, Flora Veenman and Zonen, Wageningen

Bennett, K D, Whittington, G and Edwards, K J, 1994 Recent plant nomenclatural changes and pollen morphology in the British Isles, *Quat Newslet* 73, 1–6

Besly, E, 1981 Coins, in J Lucas, *Tripontium*, third interim report, *Trans Birmingham Warwickshire Archaeol Soc* 91 (1984), 49–51

Beswick, P, Megaw, M R, Megaw, J V S and Northover, P, 1990 A decorated late Iron Age torc from Dinnington, South Yorkshire, *Antiq J* 70, 16–33

Bevan, L, 2000 Small finds, in I Ferris *et al.* 2000, 53–9

Bevan, L and Ixer, R, 2002 Worked stone, in Coates (ed) 2002, 60–1

Bevan, L and Ixer, R, 2005 Stone objects (Area 7), in A Jones 2005, 46

Bevan, L and Hartley, K F, 2000, The mortaria, in Ferris *et al.* 2000, 30–5

Bidwell, P T, 1985 *The Roman Fort of Vindolanda at Chesterholm, Northumberland*, English Heritage Archaeol Rep 1, London

Birbeck, V and Moore, C, 2004 Preservation and investigation of Roman and medieval remains at Hyde Street, Winchester, *Proc Hampshire Fld Club Archaeol Soc* 59, 77–110

Bird, J and Young, C 1981 Migrant potters – the Oxford connection, in *Roman Pottery Research in Britain and North-West Europe* (eds A C Anderson and A S Anderson), Brit Archaeol Rep S123, 295–312, Oxford

Birley, E, Birley, R and Birley, A, 1993 *The Early Roman forts: Reports on the Auxiliaries, the Writing Tablets, Inscriptions, Brands and Graffiti*, Vindolanda Res Rep New Ser 2, Hexham

Birmingham and Warwickshire Archaeological Society 1998, The 'East of Sutton' survey, *W Midlands Archaeol* 41, 109–11

Birmingham and Warwickshire Archaeological Society 1999, The 'East of Sutton' Survey, *West Midlands Archaeol* 42, 146–8

Birrell, J (ed), 1999 *The Forests of Cannock and Kinver: Select Documents 1235–1372*, Staffordshire Hist Collect

Birss, R S, 1985 Coarse pottery, in J Dool *et al.* 1985, 90–124 and 259–67

Bishop, M C, 2004 *Inveresk Gate: Excavations in the Roman Civil Settlement at Inveresk, East Lothian, 1996–2000*, STAR Monogr 7, Edinburgh

Black, E W, 1986 Romano-British burial customs and religious beliefs in south-east England, *Archaeol J* 143, 201–39

Bland, R (ed), 1992 The Chalfont hoard and other Roman coin hoards, *Coin hoards of Roman Britain* 9, London

Blay, W R, 1925 *Letocetum*, Wall, Walsall

Bloomer, H H, 1923 The presence of Scots pine (*Pinus sylvestris*) in Sutton Park, Warwickshire, *Proc Birmingham Natur Hist Phil Soc* 15(1), 23–9

Boardman, S and Jones, G, 1990 Experiments on the effects of charring on cereal plant components, *J Archaeol Sci* 17, 1–11

Boekel, G M E C van, 1993 Terres cuites du Centre dans les Pays-Bas, le Luxembourg et la Grande-Bretagne, in *Les Figurines en Terre Cuite Gallo-romaines* (eds C Bémont, M Jeanlin and C Lahanier), 240–52, Paris

Bond, C J, 1969 *Wishaw, Warwickshire*, unpublished field notes
Bond, C J, 1985 Medieval Oxfordshire villages and their topography: a preliminary discussion, in Hooke (ed) 1985, 101–23
Bond, C J, 1988 Monastic fisheries, in Aston (ed) 1988, 69–112
Booth, P, 1982 Recent work on Ryknield Street at Alcester, *Trans Birmingham Warwickshire Archaeol Soc* 92 (1985), 136–43
Booth, P, 1986 Roman pottery in Warwickshire – production and demand, *J Roman Pottery Stud* 1, 22–41
Booth, P, 1991 Inter-site comparison between pottery assemblages in Roman Warwickshire: ceramic indicators of site status, *J Roman Pottery Stud* 4, 1–11
Booth, P, 1994 Mortaria, in Cracknell and Mahany 1994, 132–43
Booth, P, 1996a *Tiddington Roman Settlement: Iron Age, Roman and Anglo-Saxon Pottery*, rep for Warwickshire County Council
Booth, P, 1996b Warwickshire in the Roman period: a review of recent work, *Trans Birmingham Warwickshire Archaeol Soc* 100 (1999), 25–57
Booth, P, 1998 Defining small towns in Roman Britain, *J Roman Archaeol* 11, 613–623
Booth, P, 2000 The pottery, in J R Hunn, Hay Farm, Eardington, Shropshire, in R J Zeepvat (ed) *Three Iron Age and Romano-British Rural Settlements on English Gravels*, Brit Archaeol Rep 312, 134–7, Oxford
Booth, P, 2001a Late Roman cemeteries in Oxfordshire: a review, *Oxoniensia* 66, 13–42
Booth, P, 2001b The Roman shrine at Westhawk Farm, Ashford: a preliminary account, *Archaeologia Cantiana* 121, 1–23
Booth, P, 2004 Quantifying status: some pottery data from the Upper Thames Valley, *J Roman Pottery Stud* 11, 39–52
Booth, P, 2006 Pottery and other ceramic finds, in Magilton 2006, 103–65
Booth, P, Boyle, A and Keevill, G D, 1993 A Romano-British kiln site at Lower Farm, Nuneham Courtenay, and other sites on the Didcot to Oxford and Wootton to Abingdon water mains, Oxfordshire, *Oxoniensia* 58, 87–217
Booth, P, and Evans, J, 2001 *Roman Alcester: Northern Extramural Area Excavations 1969–1988*, Roman Alcester Ser 3, Counc Brit Archaeol Res Rep 127, York
Booth, P and Green, S, 1989 The nature and distribution of certain pink, grog tempered vessels, *J Roman Pottery Stud* 2, 77–84
Bordes, F, 1961 *Typologie du Palaeolithique Ancien et Moyen*, Bordeaux
Boston, N and Midgley, M M, 1947 Coleshill, in VCH 1947, 47–57
Bottema, S, 1984 The composition of modern charred seed assemblages, in *Plants and Ancient Man: Studies in Palaeo-ethnobotany* (eds W van Ziest and W A Casparie), 207–11, Rotterdam
Bowden, M and McOmish, D, 1987 The required barrier, *Scottish Archaeol Rev* 4, 78–85
Bowden, M and McOmish D, 1989 Little boxes: more about hillforts, *Scottish Archaeol Rev* 6, 12–16
Bowker, C H, 1983 Environmental research at Wasperton: 2nd interim report, *West Midlands Archaeol* 26, 28–35
Bowman, A K, 1994 *Life and Letters on the Roman Frontier*, London
Braithwaite, G, 1984 Romano-British face pots and head pots, *Britannia* 15, 99–131
Brandt, R, 1983 A brief encounter along the northern frontier, in Roman and native in the Low Countries, in *Spheres of Interaction* (eds R Brandt and J Slofstra), 129–43, Brit Archaeol Rep S184, Oxford
Branigan, K and Dearne, M J, 1991 *A Gazetteer of Romano-British Cave Sites and their Fnds*, Sheffield
Brassington, M, 1971 A Trajanic kiln complex near Little Chester, Derby, 1968, *Antiq J* 51, 36–69
Brassington, M, 1980 Derby Racecourse kiln excavations 1972–3 *Antiq J* 60, 8–47
Brickstock, R, and Casey, P J, 1994 Coins, in Cracknell and Mahany 1994, 157–62
Broadbridge, S R, 1974 *The Birmingham Canal Navigations Volume 1, 1768–1846*, Newton Abbot
Bronk Ramsey, C, 2003 *OxCal Program v3.9*, Oxford
Brothwell, D R, 1972 *Digging Up Bones*, London
Brown, A, 1994 A Romano-British shell-gritted pottery and tile manufacturing site at Harrold, Beds, *Bedfordshire Archaeol* 21, 19–107
Brown, A E and Woodfield, C, 1983 Excavations at Towcester, Northamptonshire *Northamptonshire Archaeol J* 18, 43–140
Brown, A G, 1989 Use-wear analysis of surface material – can it really be done? *Lithics* 10, 33–6
Brown, T, 1997 Clearances and clearings: deforestation in Mesolithic/Neolithic Britain *Oxford J Archaeol* 16(2), 133–46
Brück, J, 1999a Houses, lifecycles and deposition on Middle Bronze Age settlements in southern England, *Proc Prehist Soc* 65, 145–66
Brück, J, 1999b, What's in a settlement? Domestic practice and residential mobility in Early Bronze Age southern England, in *Making Places in the Prehistoric World* (eds J Brück and M Goodman), 52–75, London
Brunskill, R W, 1997 *Houses & Cottages of Britain*, London
Buckland, P C, Hartley, K F and Rigby, V, 2001 The Roman pottery kilns at Rossington Bridge excavations 1956–1961, *J Roman Pottery Stud* 9
Buckley, V (ed), 1990 *Burnt Offerings. International Contributions to Burnt Mound Archaeology*, Dublin
Buikstra, J E and Swegle, M, 1989 Bone modification due to burning: experimental evidence, in *Bone Modification* (eds R Bonnichsen and M Sorg), 247–58
Buikstra, J E and Ubelaker, D H, 1994 *Standards for Data Collection from Human Skeletal Remains*, Arkansas Archaeological Survey Research Series 44
Burnham, B C and Wacher, J S, 1990 *The 'Small Towns' of Roman Britain*, London
Butterfield, B G and Meylan, B A, 1980 *Three-Dimensional Structure of Wood: An Ultrastructural Approach*, London
Cadbury, D A, Hawkes, J G and Readett, R C, 1971 *A Computer-Mapped Flora: A Study of the County of Warwickshire*, London
Campbell, B M S, 2000 *English Seigniorial Agriculture 1250–1450*, Cambridge

Campbell, G, 1994 The preliminary archaeobotanical results from Anglo-Saxon West Cotton and Raunds, in *Environment and Economy in Anglo-Saxon England* (ed J Rackham), Counc Brit Archaeol Res Rep 89, 65–82, York

Campbell, G, 2000 Plant utilisation:the evidence from charred plant remains, in B Cunliffe, *The Danebury Environs Programme, The Prehistory of a Wessex Landscape Volume 1: Introduction*, English Heritage and Oxford Univ Comm Archaeol Monogr 48, 45–59

Campbell, G, 2004 Charcoal and other charred plant remains, in Cool 2004, 267–71

Cameron, H and Lucas, J, 1969, *Tripontium*: first interim report, *Trans Birmingham Warwickshire Archaeol Soc* 83, 130–79

Cameron, H and Lucas, J 1973, *Tripontium*: second interim report, *Trans Birmingham Warwickshire Archaeol Soc* 85, 93–144

Cane, C and Cane, J, 1986 The excavation of a Mesolithic cave-site near Rangeley, Staffordshire, *Staffordshire Archaeol Stud* new ser 3, 1–12

Cantor, L, 1968 The medieval forests and chases of Staffordshire, *North Staffordshire J Fld Stud* 8, 39–53

Cantor, L (ed), 1982 *The English Medieval Landscape*, London

Carr, M and Losco-Bradley, P, 2002 Loom-weights, in Losco-Bradley and Kinsley 2002, 110

Carroll, M, 2002 Native pottery, food packaging and the supply lines of the German fleet (*Classis Germanica*), in *Limes XVIII Proceedings of the XVIIIth International Congress of Roman Studies*, (eds P Freeman, J Bennett, Z T Fiema and B Hoffmann), 901–5

Carter, W F (ed), 1926 *The Lay Subsidy Roll for Warwickshire of 6 Edward III (1332)*, London

Cattell, J, Ely, S and Jones, B, 2002 *The Birmingham Jewellery Quarter: an Architectural Survey of the Manufactories*, London

Chadwick, A, 1999 Digging ditches but missing riches? Ways into the Iron Age and Romano-British cropmark landscapes of the north midlands, in *Northern Exposure: Interpretative Devolution and the Iron Ages in Britain* (ed B Bevan), Leicester Archaeol Monogr 4, 149–71, Leicester

Challis, A J and Harding, D W, 1975 *Late Prehistory from the Trent to the Tyne*, Brit Archaeol Rep 20, Oxford

Chambers, R A with Gray M, 1988 The excavation of fish ponds, in Aston (ed) 1988, 113–36

Chapman, A, 1998 Coton Park, Rugby, *W Midlands Archaeol* 41, 95–7

Charles, M, 1984 Introductory remarks on the cereals, *Bull Sumerian Agric* 1, 17–31

Chattock, C, 1884 *Antiquities*, Birmingham

Chowne, P, Cleal, R M J and Fitzpatrick, A P, with Andrews, P, 2001 *Excavations at Billingborough Lincolnshire, 1975–8: a Bronze–Iron Age Settlement and Salt-working Site*, E Anglian Archaeol 94, Salisbury

Ciaraldi, M, 2002 Plant macroremains, in G Coates 2002, 62–6

CIPM (1904–70) *Calendar of Inquisitions Post Mortem and other Analogous Documents in the Public Record Office, (Henry III–7 Richard II)* 15 vols, London

Clapham, A R, Tutin, T G and Warburg E F, 1964 *Excursion Flora of the British Isles*, Cambridge

Clark, J G D, 1934 The classification of a microlithic culture: the Tardenoisian of Horsham, *Archaeol J* 90, 55–77

Clarke, G (ed), 1979 *Pre-Roman and Roman Winchester: Part II The Roman Cemetery at Lankhills*, Winchester Stud 3, Winchester

Clarke, R, 1999 The Roman pottery, in *Roman and Medieval Occupation in Causeway Lane, Leicester* (A Conner and R Buckley), Leicester Archaeol Monogr 5, 95–164, Leicester

Clarke, S, 2000 In search of a different Roman period: the finds assemblage at the Newstead military complex, in *TRAC 99 Proceedings of the Ninth Annual Theoretical Roman Archaeology Conference* (eds G Fincham, G Harrison, R Holland and L Revell), 22–9, Oxford

Clay, P, 1992 An Iron Age farmstead at Grove Farm, Enderby, Leicestershire, *Trans Leicestershire Archaeol Hist Soc* 66, 1–82

Clay, P, 2001 Leicestershire and Rutland in the first millennium BC, *Trans Leicestershire Archaeol Hist Soc* 75, 1–19

Clay, P and Pollard R, 1994 *Iron Age and Roman Occupation in the West Bridge Area, Leicester Excavations 1962–1971*, Leicester

Cleal, R M J, 1995 Pottery fabrics in Wessex in the fourth to second millennia BC, in *'Unbaked Urns of Rudely Shape'* (eds I Kinnes and G Varndell), Oxbow Monogr 55, 185–94, Oxford

Coates, G, 1997 Alrewas, Whitemoor Hayes, *W Midlands Archaeol* 40, 66–9

Coates, G (ed), 2002 *A Prehistoric and Romano-British Landscape Excavations at Whitemoor Haye Quarry, Staffordshire 1997–1999*, Brit Archaeol Rep 340, Oxford

Colledge, S, 1981 Charred grain and other seeds, in S C Stamford, *Midsummer Hill: An Iron Age Hillfort on the Malverns, 1965–70*, 160–2, Leominster

Colledge, S, 1982 Organic material from pits F246 and 247, in S C Stanford, Bromfield, Shropshire, Neolithic, Beaker and Bronze Age Sites, 1966–1979, 286–7, *Proc Prehist Soc* 48, 279–320

Colledge, S, 1985–6 Alcester, Coulter's Garage, the carbonised remains, 88–91, in P Booth, Roman store buildings in Alcester, *Trans Birmingham Warwickshire Archaeol Soc* 94 (1989), 63–106

Collingwood, R G and Taylor, M V, 1925 Roman Britain in 1924, *J Roman Stud* 14, 206–51

Colyer, C, Gilmour, B J J and Jones, M J, 1999 *The Defences of the Lower City Excavations at the Park and West Parade 1970–2 and a Discussion of Other Sites Excavated up to 1994*, Counc Brit Archaeol Res Rep 114, York

Cool, H E M, 2004 *The Roman Cemetery at Brougham, Cumbria: Excavations 1966–1967*, Britannia Monogr 21, London

Cool, H E M, 2006 *Eating and Drinking in Roman Britain*, Cambridge

Cool, H E M, and Baxter, M J, 1999 Peeling the onion; an approach to comparing vessel glass assemblages, *J Roman Archaeol* 12, 72–100

Cool, H E M, Lloyd-Morgan, G and Hooley, A D, 1995 *Finds from the Fortress*, Archaeol York 17/10, York

Cooper, J C, 1978 *An Illustrated Encyclopaedia of Traditional Symbols*, London

Cooper, N J (ed), 2006 *The Archaeology of the East Midlands: An Archaeological Resource Assessment and Research Agenda*, Leicester Archaeol Monogr 13

Cordie, R in press (2006) Zu den latènezeitlichen Grabgärten von Wederath/ Belginum, in - (ed.) *Studien zur Lebenswelt der Eisenzeit Reallexikon der Germanischen Altertumskunde* 53, Berlin

Cordie-Hackenberg, R and Haffner, A, 1997 *Das keltisch-römische Gräberfeld von Wederath-Belginum*, Mainz am Rhein

Cornish, V, 1946 *The Churchyard Yew and Immortality*, London

Coss, P, 1991 *Lordship, Knighthood and Locality. A Study in English Society c. 1180–c. 1280*, Cambridge

Cotterell, B and Kamminga, J, 1979 The mechanics of flint flaking, in *Lithic Use-wear Analysis* (ed B Hayden), 97–112, London

Cotterell, B and Kamminga, J, 1987 The formation of flakes, *Amer Antiq* 52, 675–708

Cracknell, S and Hingley, R, 1993–4 Park Farm, Barford: excavation of a prehistoric settlement site, 1988, *Trans Birmingham Warwickshire Archaeol Soc* 98, 1–30

Cracknell, S, and Jones, M, 1985–6 Medieval kiln debris from School Road, Alcester, *Trans Birmingham Warwickshire Archaeol Soc* 94 (1989), 107–22

Cracknell, S and Mahany, C, 1994 *Roman Alcester: Southern Extramural Area, 1964–66 excavations, Part 2, Finds and Discussion*, Counc Brit Archaeol Res Rep 97, York

Cramp, K, 2006 *The flint, in Building Memories: the Neolithic Cotswold Long Barrow at Ascott-under-Wychwood, Oxfordshire* (eds D Benson and A Whittle), 289–314, Oxford

Cramp, K and Brown, R, forthcoming Excavations on the A5 Weeford to Fazeley Road Improvement Scheme, Staffordshire, *Trans Staffordshire Archaeol Hist Soc*

Cramp, K and Lamdin-Whymark, H, in preparation Higham Ferrers flint report

Crawford, G, 1981 Wasperton, Warwickshire: excavation of gravel site, *W Midlands Archaeol* 24, 121–9

Crawford, G, 1982 Excavations at Wasperton: 2nd interim report, *W Midlands Archaeol* 25, 31–44

Crawford, G, 1983 Excavations at Wasperton: 3rd interim report, *W Midlands Archaeol* 26, 15–27

Crawford, G, 1984 Excavations at Wasperton - 4th interim report, *W Midlands Archaeol* 27, 43–53

Croom, A T, 1997–8 Torc beads from South Shields Roman fort, *Arbeia J* 6–7, 60–3

Crowe, N, 1994 *The English Heritage Book of Canals*, London

Crummy, N, 1983 *The Roman Small Finds from Excavations in Colchester 1971–9*, Colchester Archaeol Rep 2, Colchester

Cunliffe, B, 1984 *Danebury: an Iron Age Hillfort in Hampshire Vol 1, the Excavations, 1969–1978: the Finds*, Counc Brit Archaeol Res Rep 52, London

Cunliffe, B, 1991 *Iron Age Communities in Britain* (3rd edn), London

Currie, C K, 1990 Southwick Priory Fishponds: Excavations 1987, *Proc Hampshire F Club Archaeol Soc* 46, 53–72

Currie, C K and Locock, M, 1993 Excavations at Castle Bromwich Hall Gardens 1981–91, *Post-Medieval Archaeol* 27, 111–99

Dallimore, W, 1908 *Holly, Yew and Box*, London

Darby, H C and Terrett I B (eds), 1954 *The Domesday Geography of Midland England*, Cambridge

Darby, H C, 1977 *Domesday England*, Cambridge

Darling, M J, 1999 Roman pottery, in Colyer *et al.* 1999, 52–123

Darling, M J, 2004 Guidelines for the archiving of Roman pottery, *J Roman Pottery Stud* 11, 67–75

Dark, K and Dark, P, 1997 *The Landscape of Roman Britain*, Stroud

Davies, M S and Hillman, G C, 1988 Effects of soil flooding on growth and grain yield of populations of tetraploid and hexaploid species of wheat, *Annals of Botany* 62, 597–604

Davis, A with Moulins, D de, 2000 The plant remains, in Barber and Bowsher 2000, 368–9

Davis, S, 1989 Animal remains from the Iron Age cemetery, in Stead and Rigby 1989, 250–9

Deakin, M and Deakin, T, 2000 Recent flint finds in the Upper Avon Valley, Warwickshire: an interim report, *W Midlands Archaeol* 43, 41–5

Dean, A, Drury, M and Lucas, M 2005 *The Cannock Chase Coalfield and the Coal Mines*, Cannock Chase Mining Hist Soc

Decker, K V and Scollar, I, 1962 Iron Age square enclosures in Rhineland, *Antiquity* 36, 175–8

Denston, C B, 1994 Human skeletal remains, in Cracknell and C Mahany (eds) 1994, 215–16

Dickinson, B R, 1985 Samian, in Dool *et al.* 1985, 79–90 and 256–8

Dickinson, B, R, 2000 Samian, in Langley and Drage 2000, 160–85

Dickson, C and Dickson, J, 2000 *Plants and People in Ancient Scotland*, Stroud

Dix, B, and Taylor, S, 1988 Excavations at Bannaventa (Whilton Lodge, Northants) 1970–71, *Britannia* 19, 299–339

Dool, J, Wheeler, H, Birss, R, Annable, R and Mackreth, D, 1985 Roman Derby: excavations 1968–1983, *Derbyshire Archaeol J* 105

Down, A and Welch, M, 1990 *Chichester Excavations 7: Apple Down and The Mardens*, Chichester

Drucker, L (ed), 1943 *Warwickshire Feet of Fines, Volume 3, (1345–1509)*, Warwick

Dugdale, W, 1730 *The Antiquities of Warwickshire, Illustrated from Records, Leger Books, Manuscripts, Charters, Evidences, Tombes and Armes*, 2 edn, Vol 2 (rev William Thomas), London

Dunkin, D J, 2001 Metalwork, burnt mounds and settlement on the West Sussex Coastal Plain: a contextual study, *Antiquity* 75, 261–2

Dungworth, D B, 1996 The production of copper alloys in Iron Age Britain, *Proc Prehist Soc* 62, 399–421

Dyer, C C, 1988 The consumption of fresh water fish in medieval England, in Aston 1988 (ed), 27–38

Dyer, C, 1996 Rural settlement in medieval Warwickshire, *Trans Birmingham Warwickshire Archaeol Soc* 100, 117–32

Dyer, C, 2002 The urbanizing of Staffordshire: the first phases, *Staffordshire Stud* 14, 1–31

Eastwod, T, Cantrill, T C and Whitehead, T H, 1923 *The Geology of the County Around Coventry*, London

Eckardt, H, 2002 *Illuminating Roman Britain*, Monographies Instrumentum 23, Éditions Monique Mergoil, Montagnac

Edlin, H L, 1949 *Woodland Crafts in Britain*, London

Egan, G, 1991 Other small finds, in M A Hodder, Excavations of Sandwell Priory and Hall 1982–88, *Trans Staffordshire Archaeol Hist Soc* 31, 88–97

Ehrenberg, M R, 1991 Some aspects of the distribution of burnt mounds, in Hodder and Barfield (eds) 1991, 41–58

Ellenberg, H, 1988 *Vegetation Ecology of Central Europe*, 4 edn, Cambridge

Ellis, C J, 2004 *A Prehistoric Ritual Complex at Eynesbury, Cambridgeshire: Excavation of a Multi-Period Site in the Great Ouse Valley, 2000–2001*, E Anglian Archaeol Occas Pap 17, Salisbury

Ellis, P, 1999 *Wall Roman Site, Staffordshire*, London

Ellis, P, Evans, J, Hannaford, H, Hughes G and Jones, A, 1994 Excavations in the Wroxeter hinterland 1988–1990: the archaeology of the A5/A49 Shrewsbury bypass, *Trans Shropshire Archaeol Hist Soc* 69, 1–119

Elsdon, S M, 1992 East Midlands scored ware, *Trans Leicestershire Archaeol Hist Soc* 66, 83–91

Esmonde Cleary, A S and Ferris, I M, 1996 *Excavations at the New Cemetery, Rocester, Staffordshire, 1985–1987*, Stafford

Evans, C, Pollard, J and Knight M, 1999 Life in woods: tree-throws, 'settlement' and forest cognition, *Oxford J Archaeol* 18(3), 241–54

Evans, C J, 1996–7 Coarse wares and mortaria, in A Jones, Greensforge: investigations in the Romano-British civilian Settlement 1994, *Trans Staffordshire Archaeol Hist Soc* 38 (1999), 19–25

Evans, C J, 2000 Form series, in *The Roman Baths and Macellum at Wroxeter, Excavations by Graham Webster 1955–85* (ed P Ellis), English Heritage Archaeol Rep 9, 195–245, London

Evans, C J, Jones, L and Ellis, P, 2000 *Severn Valley Ware Production at Newland Hopfields*, Brit Archaeol Rep 313, Oxford

Evans, J, 1988 All Yorkshire is divided into three parts: social aspects of later pottery distribution in Yorkshire, in *Recent Research in Roman Yorkshire* (eds J Price and P R Wilson), Brit Archaeol Rep 193, 323–37, Oxford

Evans, J, 1993 Pottery function and finewares in the Roman north, *J Roman Pottery Stud* 6, 95–118

Evans, J, 1994 Discussion of the pottery in the context of Roman Alcester, in Cracknell and Mahany (eds) 1994, 144–50

Evans, J, 1998 The Roman pottery, in R Cuttler and J Evans, A section through the Fosse Way and the excavations of Romano-British features at Princethorpe, Warwickshire, 1994, *Trans Birmingham Warwickshire Archaeol Soc* 102 (2000), 61–8

Evans, J, 1999 Roman pottery, in S C Palmer 1999c, 101–25

Evans, J, 2001 Material approaches to the identification of different Romano-British site types, in S James and M Millett (eds) *Britons and Romans: Advancing an Archaeological Agenda*, Counc Brit Archaeol Res Rep 125, 26–35

Evans, J, 2002a Iron Age and Roman pottery, in *Iron Age and Romano-British Settlement Enclosures at Moss Carr, Methley* (I Roberts and J Richardson), W Yorkshire Archaeol Services Publ 2, 26–30, Leeds

Evans, J, 2002b Pottery from the CFA excavations, in Cataractonium: *Roman Catterick and its Hinterland Excavations and Research, 1958–1997* (ed PR Wilson), Counc Brit Archaeol Res Rep 128, 352–496, York

Evans, J, 2004 The pottery vessels, in Cool 2004, 333–63

Evans, J, 2005 Pottery in urban Romano-British life, in *Roman Working Lives and Urban Living* (eds A MacMahon and J Price), 145–66, Oxford

Evans, J G, 1972 *Land Snails in Archaeology*, London

Eyton, R W (ed), 1880 *The Staffordshire Pipe Rolls of 31 Henry I (AD 1130) and of 1 to 35 Henry II (AD 1155 to 1189)*, Staffordshire Hist Collect 1

Eyton, R W (ed), 1881 *The Staffordshire Chartulary, Series I and II of Ancient Deeds*, Staffordshire Hist Collect 2(i)

Farwell, D E and Molleson, T I, 1993 *Excavations at Poundbury 1966–80. Volume II: The Cemeteries*, Dorset Natur Hist Archaeol Soc Monog 11, Dorchester

Fenwick, C C (ed), 2001 The Poll Taxes of 1377, 1379 and 1381, Part 2. Lincolnshire–Westmoreland. *Rec Social Econ Hist* new ser 29, Oxford

Ferguson, R, 1996 The mortaria, in Esmonde Cleary and Ferris 1996, 61–3

Ferguson, R, 2001 Roman pottery, in Booth and Evans 2001, 28–66

Ferris, I M, 2000 Discussion, in Ferris *et al.* 2000, 72–83

Ferris, I M, Bevan L and Cuttler, R, 2000 *The Excavations of a Romano-British Shrine at Orton's Pasture, Rocester, Staffordshire*, Brit Archaeol Rep 314, Oxford

Fitzpatrick, A P, 1997 Everyday life in Iron Age Wessex, in *Reconstructing Iron Age Societies* (eds A Gwilt and C Haselgrove), Oxbow Monogr 71, 73–86, Oxford

Ford, B, 2003 The coarse pottery, in Holmes 2003, 58–85

Ford, D A, 1995 *Medieval Pottery in Staffordshire, AD 800–1600: A Review*, Staffordshire Archaeol Stud 7, Stoke on Trent

Ford, S, 1987 Chronological and functional aspects of flint assemblages, in *Lithic Analysis and Later British Prehistory* (eds A Brown and M Edmonds), 67–81, Brit Archaeol Rep 162, Oxford

Ford, W J, 1971 Crewe Farm, Kenilworth, Warws, *W Midlands Archaeol Newslett* 14, 14

Ford, W J, 1996 Anglo-Saxon cemeteries along the Avon Valley, *Trans Birmingham Warwickshire Archaeol Soc* 100 (1999), 59–98

Ford, W J, 2002 The Romano-British and Anglo-Saxon settlement and cemeteries at Stretton-on-Fosse, Warwickshire, *Trans Birmingham Warwickshire Archaeol Soc* 106, 8–114

Ford, W J, 2003 The Neolithic complex at Charlecote, Warwickshire, *Trans Birmingham Warwickshire Archaeol Soc* 107, 1–40

Ford-Lloyd, B V, 1995 Sugarbeet and other cultivated beets, in *Evolution of Crop Plants* (eds J Smartt and N W Simmonds) 2 edn, 35–40, New York

Frere, S S, 1972 *Verulamium Excavations, Volume 1*, Rep Res Comm Soc Antiqs London 28, Oxford

Frere, S S, 1984 *Verulamium Excavations, Volume 3*, Oxford Univ Comm Archaeol Monogr 1, Oxford

Frere, S S, 1987 *Britannia*, 3 edn, London

Friendship-Taylor, R M, 1999 *Late La Tène pottery of the Nene and Welland valleys, Northamptonshire; with Particular Reference to Channel-rim Jars*, Brit Archaeol Rep 280, Oxford

Gale, R, 1997 Charcoal, in A P Fitzpatrick *Archaeological Excavations on the Route of the A27 Westhampnett Bypass, West Sussex, 1992, Vol 2: the Cemeteries*, Wessex Archaeol Rep 12, Salisbury, 77–82

Gale, R, 2002 Charcoal, in Coates 2002, 74–8

Gale, R, 2005 *Baldock Bypass: Charcoal from Cremations and Domestic Contexts in Areas 1 and 4*, unpubl rep for Environmental Archaeology Consultancy

Gale, R and Cutler, D, 2000 *Plants in Archaeology*, London

Gejvall, N G, 1981 Determination of burned bones from prehistoric graves: Observations on the cremated bones from the graves at Horn, *OSSA Letters* 2

Gelling, M, 1992 *The West Midlands in the Early Middle Ages*, Leicester

Gibson, A, 2002 *Prehistoric Pottery in Britain and Ireland*, Stroud

Gibson, A and Kinnes, I, 1997 On the urns of a dilemma; radiocarbon and the Peterborough problem, *Oxford J Archaeol* 16(1), 65–72

Giles, M and Parker Pearson, M, 1999 Learning to live in the Iron Age: dwelling and praxis, in *Northern Exposure: Interpretative Devolution and the Iron Ages in Britain* (ed B Bevan), Leicester Archaeol Monogr 4, 217–31, Leicester

Gillam, J P, 1970 Types of Roman coarse pottery vessels, in *Northern Britain* 3 edn, Newcastle

Gillam, J P, 1976 Coarse fumed ware in northern Britain and beyond, *Glasgow Archaeol J* 4, 57–89

Giorgi, J, 2000 The plant remains in Mackinder 2000, 10–12 and 65–6

Glover, J E B, Mawer, A and Stanton, F M, in collaboration with Houghton, F T S, 1936 *The Place Names of Warwickshire*, Cambridge

Godwin, H, 1956 *A History of the British Flora*, Cambridge

Godwin, H and Dickson, J H, 1964–5 Report on plant remains in organic deposits below Roman road (Watling Street) at Wall, monolith cut and examined, in Gould 1964–5, 17–18

Going, C J, 1992 Economic 'long waves' in the Roman period? A reconnaissance of the Romano-British ceramic evidence, *Oxford J Archaeol* 11(1), 93–117

Gooder E 1995, *Temple Balsall. The Warwickshire Preceptory of the Templars and their Fate*, Chichester

Goody, J, 1982 *Cooking, Cuisine and Class: a Study in Comparative Sociology*, Cambridge

Gould, J P, 1963–4 Excavations at Wall, Staffordshire, 1961–3 on the site of the Early Roman forts and of the Late Roman defences, *Trans Staffordshire Archaeol Hist Soc* 5, 1–50

Gould, J P, 1964–5 Excavations in advance of road construction at Shenstone and Wall (Staffordshire), *Trans Staffordshire Archaeol Hist Soc* 6, 1–19

Gould, J P, 1966–7 Excavations at Wall (Staffordshire), 1964–6, on the site of the Roman forts, *Trans Staffordshire Archaeol Hist Soc* 8, 1–38

Gould, J P, 1972 Romano-British farming near Letocetum (Wall, Staffs), *Trans Staffordshire Archaeol Hist Soc* 18, 1–8

Gould, J P, 1991–2 Further thoughts on *Letocetum*, *Trans Staffordshire Archaeol Hist Soc* 33, 1–3

Gould, J, 1997 *Letocetum*, an early vexillation fortress?, *Britannia* 28, 350–2

Gould, J P, 1998 Letocetum: *the Rise and Decline of a Roman Posting Station*, Walsall

Gould, J P, 1999 The Watling Street *burgi*, *Britannia* 30, 185–97

Gould, J P, 2001 Letocetum: *the Rise and Decline of a Roman Posting Station*, privately published (rev edn)

Gould, J P and Gathercole, P W, 1956 Flint implements from near Bourne Pool, Aldridge, *Trans Birmingham Warwickshire Archaeol Soc* 74 (1958), 53–5

Grant, A, 1989 Animals in Roman Britain, in *Research on Roman Britain 1960–1989* (ed M Todd) Britannia Monogr Ser 11, 135–46, London

Gray, L, 2003 The plant remains, in *An Excavation in the Western Cemetery of Roman London, Atlantic House, City of London* (S Watson), MoLAS Archaeol Stud Ser 7, 63–4, London

Gray, M, 1968 Washford, Worcs, *West Midlands Archaeol Newslett* 11, 30

Grazebrook, H S (ed), 1896, *The Shenstone Charters, copied from the Chartulary or Great Coucher Book of the Duchy of Lancaster in the Public Record Office*, Staffordshire Hist Collect 17

Green, F J, 1979 Phosphatic mineralization of seeds from archaeological sites, *J Archaeol Sci* 6, 279–84

Green, F J, 1981 Iron Age, Roman and Saxon crops: the archaeological evidence from Wessex, in *The Environment of Man: the Iron Age to the Anglo-Saxon Period* (eds M Jones and G Dimbleby), Brit Archaeol Rep 37, 129–53, Oxford

Green, F J, 1994 Cereals and plant food: a reassessment of the Saxon economic evidence from Wessex, in *Environment and Economy in Anglo-Saxon England* (ed J Rackham), Counc Brit Archaeol Res Rep 89, 83–8, York

Green, S, 2001 Coarse wares, in A Jones *et al.* 2001, 90–106

Greene, K T, 1993 The fortress coarsewares, in *Report on the Excavations at Usk 1965–76. The Roman Pottery* (W H Manning), 3–121, Cardiff

Greenfield, E, 1960 Note on the aisled building at Exning, Landwade, Suffolk, with plans, *J Roman Stud* 50, 228–9

Greep, S, 2004 Bone and antler veneer, in H E M Cool 2004, 273–82

Greig, J R A, 1979 Seeds and pollen from site SK187082, in C A Smith (ed) 1979, 81–4

Greig, J R A, 1988 Plant resources, in *The Countryside of Medieval England* (G Astill and A Grant), 108–15, Oxford

Greig, J R A, 1990 Practical ecology: experiments in growing traditional cornfield weeds and a comment on their archaeological records in Britain, in *Experimentation and Reconstruction in Environmental Archaeology (Symposia of the Association for Environmental Archaeology 9 Roskilde, Denmark 1988)* (ed D Robinson), 41–62, Oxford

Greig, J R A, 1991 The British Isles, in *Plants and Ancient man: Studies in the Palaeoethnobotany*, (eds W van Zeist, K Wasylikowa and K Behre), 299–334, Rotterdam

Greig, J, 2005 Pollen and waterlogged seeds, in A Jones 2005, 75–80

Greig, J R A, Colledge, S M and Limbrey, S, 1987 A review of environmental archaeology, in *Environmental Archaeology: a Regional Review* 2 (ed H C.M Keeley) HBMC Occas Pap 1, 101–24, London

Greig, J R A, Osborne, P J, Smith, C and Williams, P, 1979 Part IV – the landscape of the Fisherwick area during the Iron Age, in C Smith (ed) 1979, 93–103

Gunstone, A J H, 1964 An archaeological gazetteer of Staffordshire. Part I. Chance finds and sites, excluding barrows and their contents, *North Staffordshire J Fld Stud* 4, 11–45

Gurney, D A, Neve, J and Pryor, F M M, 1993 Excavations at Plants Farm, Maxey, Cambridgeshire, in *The Fenland Project No 7: Excavations in Peterborough and the Lower Welland Valley 1960–1969* (W G Simpson, D A Gurney, J Neve and F M M Pryor), E Anglian Archaeol 61, Cambridge

Gwilt, A, 1997 Popular practices from material culture: a case study from the Iron Age settlement at Wakerley, Northamptonshire in *Reconstructing Iron Age Societies: New Approaches to the Iron Age* (eds A Gwilt and C Haselgrove), 153–66, Oxford

Haffner, A, 1989 *Gräber-Spiegel des Lebens*, Mainz am Rhein

Hains, B A and Horton, A, 1969 *British Regional Geology, Central England*, Norwich

Hallam, H E, 1981 *Rural England 1066–1348*, London

Hamer, A, 2002 *A Study of the Use and Origins of Derbyshire Ware Pottery with a Case Study of the Romano-British Site of Kniveton*, unpublished dissertation, University of Liverpool

Hammon, A, in preparation Animal bone, in S C Palmer in preparation b

Hammond, P W, 1993 *Food and Feast in Medieval England*, Gloucester

Hanf, M, 1983 *The Arable Weeds of Europe*, Ipswich

Hancocks, A, 2004 Romano-British pottery, in A Jones, Roman Birmingham 2, Metchley Roman Forts excavations 1998–2000 and 2002, the eastern and southern annexes and other investigations, *Trans Birmingham Warwickshire Archaeol Soc* 108, 47–66

Harding, D W, 2004 *The Iron Age in Northern Britain: Celts and Romans, Natives and Invaders*, London

Harman, M, 1985a The mammalian bones, in H Wheeler, The Racecourse Cemetery, in Dool *et al.* 1985, 274–80

Harman, M, 1985b Appendix 4: The cremations: Derby Racecourse Cemetery, in Dool *et al.* 1985, 332–9

Hartley K F, 1985 Mortaria, in Dool *et al.* 1985, 124–30

Hartley, K F, 1992 The mortaria, in Round 1992, 34–6

Hartley, K F, 1996 Mortaria stamps, in Esmonde-Cleary and Ferris, 64–70

Hartley, K F, 2001 Mortaria, in Buckland *et al.* 2001, 39–47

Hartley, K F, 2002 The mortaria, 213–24, in C Sparey-Green (ed) Excavations on the south-eastern defences and extramural settlement of Little Chester, Derby 1971–2, *Derbyshire Archaeol J* 122, 1–328

Hartley, K F, 2003 The mortaria, in Holmes 2003, 49–58

Hartley, K F and Webster, P V, 1973 The Romano-British kilns near Wilderspool, *Archaeol J* 130, 77–104

Harvard, T, 2004 Rugby, Rugby Cement Works, *W Midlands Archaeol* 47, 77

Harvey, S P J, 1976 Evidence for settlement study: *Domesday Book*, in Sawyer (ed) 1976, 196–7

Harvey, S P J, 1986 Taxation and the economy, in Holt (ed) 1986, 249–64

Haselgrove, C, 1999 Iron Age societies in central Britain: retrospect and prospect, in *Northern Exposure: Interpretive Devolution and the Iron Ages in Britain* (ed B Bevan) Leicester Archaeol Monogr 4, 253–78, Leicester

Hassall, M W C and Tomlin, R S O, 1988 Inscriptions, in Roman Britain in 1987, *Britannia* 19, 485–508

Hawkes, C F C and Hull, M R, 1947 *Camulodunum First Report on the Excavations at Colchester 1930–1939*, Rep Res Comm Soc Antiq London 14, Oxford

Healy, F, 1988 *The Anglo-Saxon Cemetery at Spong Hill, North Elmham, Part VI: Occupation During the Seventh to Second Millennia BC*, E Anglian Archaeol 39, Gressenhall

Hedges, R E M, Housley, R A, Bronk Ramsey, C and Klinken, G J van, 1991 Radiocarbon dates from the Oxford AMS system: Archaeometry Datelist 13, *Archaeometry* 33(2), 279–96

Hemsley, R, 1959 A Romano-British pottery kiln at Manduessedum, *Trans Birmingham Warwickshire Archaeol Soc* 77, 5–17

Hencken, T C, 1938 The excavation of the Iron Age camp on Bredon Hill, Gloucestershire, 1935–37, *Archaeol J* 95, 1–111

Henig, M, 2004 *Roman Sculpture from the North West Midlands*, Corpus Signorum Imperii Romain, Great Britain Volume 1, Fascicule 9, London

Henig, M and Booth, P, 2000 *Roman Oxfordshire*, Stroud

Herne, A, 1988 A time and place for the Grimston Bowl, in *The Archaeology of Context in the Neolithic and Bronze Age* (eds J C Barrett and I A Kinnes), 9–29, Sheffield

Hewson, M, 2004 Alrewas, Whitemoor Haye Quarry, *W Midlands Archaeol* 47, 51

Hey, G and Lacey, M, 2001 *Evaluation of Archaeological Decision-making Processes and Sampling Strategies*, Oxford Archaeol Unit and Kent Co Counc

Higuchi, T, 1983 *The Visual and Spatial Structure of Landscapes*, London

Hill, J D, Evans, C and Alexander, M, 1999 The Hinxton rings – a Late Iron Age cemetery at Cambridgeshire, with a reconsideration of the northern Aylesford Swarling Culture, *Proc Prehist Soc* 65, 243–73

Hill, S, 2002 *Archaeological Work at Westwood Running Track, University of Warwick, Coventry*, Univ Warwick unpubl rep

Hillman, G, 1978 On the origins of domestic rye – *Secale cereale*: the finds from aceramic Can Hasan III in Turkey, *Anatolian Stud* 28, 157–74

Hillman, G, 1981 Reconstructing crop husbandry practices from charred remains of crops, in *Farming Practice in British Prehistory* (ed R Mercer), 123–82, Edinburgh

Hillman, G, 1984 Interpretation of archaeological plant remains: the application of ethnographic models from Turkey, in *Plants and Ancient Man: Studies in Palaeo-ethnobotany* (eds W van Ziest and WA Casparie), 1–41, Rotterdam

Hingley, R, 1989 Iron Age settlement and society in central and southern Warwickshire, in *Midlands Prehistory* (ed A Gibson), Brit Archaeol Rep 204, 122–57, Oxford

Hingley, R, 1990 Iron Age 'currency bars': the archaeological and social context, *Archaeol J* 147, 91–117

Hingley, R, 1996 Prehistoric Warwickshire: a review of the evidence, *Trans Birmingham Warwickshire Archaeol Soc* 100 (1999), 1–24

Hilton, R H (ed), 1960 *The Stoneleigh Leger Book*, Warwick

Hilton, R H, 1983 *A Medieval Society. The West Midlands at the End of the Thirteenth Century*, Cambridge

Hodder, I R and Hassall, M W C, 1971 The non-random spacing of Romano-British walled towns, *Man* 6, 391–407
Hodder, M A, 1980–1 The prehistory of the Lichfield area, *Trans Staffordshire Archaeol Hist Soc* 22, 11–23
Hodder, M A, 1988 *The Development of Some Aspects of Settlement and Land use in Sutton Chase*, unpubl PhD thesis, Univ Birmingham
Hodder M A, 1988–9a, Medieval parks in Drayton Bassett, Shenstone, and Weeford (Shenstone), *Trans Staffordshire Archaeol Hist Soc* 30, 39–52
Hodder, M, 1988-9b Medieval and post-medieval pottery from West Bromwich Manor House, *Trans Staffordshire Archaeol Hist Soc* 30, 35–8
Hodder, M A, 1990 West Midlands: burnt mounds in the English West Midlands, in Buckley (ed) 1990, 106–11
Hodder, M A, 1989–90 Excavations at Sandwell Priory and Hall 1982–88, *Trans Staffordshire Archaeol Hist Soc* 31
Hodder, M A, 1992 The development of the North Warwickshire landscape: settlement and landuse in the parishes of Wishaw and Middleton, *Trans Birmingham Warwickshire Archaeol Soc* 97, 41–56
Hodder, M, 1998 Reconstructing burnt mounds, *W Midlands Archaeol* 41, 27–9
Hodder, M, 2004 *Birmingham: The Hidden History*, Stroud
Hodder, M A and Barfield, L H (eds), 1991 *Burnt Mounds and Hot Stone Technology. Papers from the Second International Burnt Mound Conference, Sandwell, 12th–14th October 1990*, Sandwell
Hodder, M A and Glazebrook J, 1985–6 Excavations at Oakeswell Hall, Wednesbury, 1983, *Trans Staffordshire Archaeol Hist Soc* 27, 64–77
Hodder, M A and Welch, C, 1990 Burnt mounds in the south Staffordshire area, *Staffordshire Archaeol Stud* new ser 4, 15–24
Hodgkinson, H R, 1927 Notes on excavations in the Roman cemetery at Wall, October 1927, *Trans Birmingham Archaeol Soc* 52, 308–11
Hodgkinson, H R and Chatwin, P B, 1944 The Roman site at Shenstone, Staffordshire, *Trans Birmingham Archaeol Soc* 63, 3–32
Hodgson, J M, 1976 *Soil Survey Field Handbook*, Soil Survey Technical Monogr 5, Harpenden
Holbrook, N and Bidwell, P T, 1991 *Roman Finds from Exeter*, Exeter Archaeol Rep 4, Exeter
Holden, J L, Phakley, P P and Clement, J G, 1995a Scanning electron microscope observations of incinerated human femoral bone: a case study, *Forensic Sci Int* 74, 17–28
Holden, J L, Phakley, P P and Clement, J G, 1995b Scanning electron microscope observations of heat-treated human bone, *Forensic Sci Int* 74, 29–45
Holmes, N, 2003 *Excavation of Roman Sites at Cramond, Edinburgh*, Dundee
Holt, J C (ed), 1986 *Domesday Studies. Novocentenary Conference, Royal Historical Society and Institute of British Geographers, Winchester 1986*, Woodbridge
Hooke, D, 1983 *The Landscape of Anglo-Saxon Staffordshire: The Charter Evidence*, Keele
Hooke, D (ed), 1985 *Medieval Villages, A Review of Current Work*, Oxford Univ Comm Archaeol Monogr 5, Oxford
Hooke, D and Marshall, D, 1987 *The Arrow Valley Project. 1 Morton Bagot, A Parish Survey*, Univ Birmingham Dept Geogr Occas Publ 24, Birmingham
Hubbard, C, 1947 Wishaw, in VCH 1947, 258–61
Hughes, E G, 1994 An Iron Age barrow burial at Bromfield, Shropshire, *Proc Prehist Soc* 60, 395–402
Hughes, G and Crawford, G, 1995 Excavations at Wasperton: part 1. Neolithic and Early Bronze Age, *Trans Birmingham Warwickshire Archaeol Soc* 99, 9–45
Hughes, H V, 1959 A Romano-British kiln site at Perry Barr, Birmingham, *Trans Birmingham Warwickshire Archaeol Soc* 77, 33–9
Hunt, C, 1996 Plant macrofossils, in *Barrows in the Peak District: Recent Research* (eds J Barnatt and J Collis), 158–60, Sheffield
Hunt, J, 1991–2 Land tenure and lordship in tenth and eleventh century Staffordshire, *Staffordshire Stud* 4, 1–20
Hunt, J, 1997 *Lordship and the Landscape: A Documentary and Archaeological Study of the Honor of Dudley c. 1066–1322*, Brit Archaeol Rep 264, Oxford
Hunt, J, forthcoming The Medieval Period, West Midlands Regional Research Framework for Archaeology
Hunter, F, 2006 New light on Iron Age massive armlets, *Proc Soc Antiq Scot* 136, 135–60
Hunter, F, 2007, Artefacts, regions and identities in the northern British Iron Age, in C Haselgrove and T Moore forthcoming, *The Later Iron Age in Britain and Beyond*, 286–96, Oxford
IFA (Institute of Field Archaeologists), 2001 *Standard and Guidance for the Collection, Documentation, Conservation and Research of Archaeological Materials*, Reading
Illingworth, W (ed), 1812–18 *Rotuli Hundredorum temp. Hen III et Edw I, Records Commission*, Volume II, London
Inizan, M–L, Roche, H and Tixier, J, 1992 *Technology of Knapped Stone*, Cercle de Recherches et d'études préhistoriques, Meudon
Jacobi, R, 1978 The Mesolithic of Sussex, in *Archaeology in Sussex to AD 1500* (ed P L Drewett), Counc Brit Archaeol Res Rep 29, 15–22, London
Jacobi, R M, 1987 On some flint and chert artefacts from Ossoms Cave, Staffordshire, *Staffordshire Archaeol Stud* new ser 4, 86–93
Jacomet, S, 1988 *Prähistorische Getreidefunde*, privately publ, Basel
James, H, 2003 Roman Carmarthen Excavations 1978–1993, *Britannia* Monogr Ser 20, London
James, S and Rigby, V, 1997 *Britain and the Celtic Iron Age*, London
Jarrett, M G, 1994 Non-legionary troops in Roman Britain: part one, the units, *Britannia* 25, 35–77
Jenkins, F, 1958 The cult of the 'pseudo-Venus' in Kent, *Archaeologia Cantiana* 72, 60–76
Jessen, K and Helbaek, H, 1944 Cereals of Great Britain and Ireland in prehistoric and early historic times, *Kongel Danske Vidensk Selsk Biol Skrifter* 3(2), 68
Jones, A, 2004 Roman Birmingham 2. Metchley Roman forts: excavations 1998–2000 and 2002, The eastern and southern annexes and other investigations, *Trans Birmingham Warwickshire Archaeol Soc* 108

Jones, A, Bevan, L, Dodds, N, Steiner, M, Dickinson, B, Evans, J, Ferris, I M and Green, S, 2001 Roman Birmingham 1. Metchley Roman forts: excavations 1963–4, 1967–9 and 1997, *Trans Birmingham Warwickshire Archaeol Soc* 105

Jones, C, 2004 Bubbenhall, Wood Farm Quarry, *W Midlands Archaeol* 47, 66

Jones, C, Eyre-Morgan, G, Palmer, S C and Palmer, N, 1997 Excavations in the outer enclosure of Boteler's Castle, Oversley, Alcester, 1992–93, *Trans Birmingham Warwickshire Archaeol Soc* 101, 1–97

Jones, C and Palmer, S, 1994 *Excavations of a Romano-British farmstead and pottery kiln at Glebe Farm quarry, Bubbenhall, Warwickshire, interim report*, unpubl Warwickshire Mus rep

Jones, D M (ed), 2002 *Environmental Archaeology – A Guide to the Theory and Practice of Methods, from Sampling and Recovery to Post-Excavation*, London

Jones, G, 1984 Interpretation of archaeological plant remains: ethnographic models from Greece, in *Plants and Ancient Man: Studies in Palaeoethnobotany* (eds W van Zeist and W A Casparie), 43–61, Rotterdam

Jones, G, 2000 Evaluating the importance of cultivation and collecting in Neolithic Britain, in *Plants in Neolithic Britain and Beyond* (ed A S Fairbairn), Neolithic Stud Group Seminar Pap 5, 79–84, Oxford

Jones, G, forthcoming, Evidence for the importance of cereals in the Neolithic: charred plant remains from the Neolithic settlement at Lismore Fields, Buxton, in *The Excavation of a Mesolithic and Neolithic Settlement Area at Lismore Fields, Buxton, Derbyshire* (ed D Garton)

Jones, M K, 1981 The development of crop husbandry, in *The Environment of Man, the Iron Age to the Anglo-Saxon Period* (eds M K Jones and G Dimbleby), Brit Archaeol Rep 87, 95–127

Jones, M K, 1988a The arable field: a botanical battleground, in *Archaeology and the Flora of the British Isles* (ed M K Jones), Oxford Univ Comm Archaeol/Oxbow Monogr 14, 86–92, Oxford

Jones, M K, 1988b The phytosociology of early arable weed communities with special reference to southern England, in *Der prähistorische Mensch und seine Umwelt* (ed H Küster), Forschungen und Berichte zur Vor- und Frühgeschichte in Baden-Württemberg 31, 43–51, Stuttgart

Jones, R F J, 1991 Cultural change in Roman Britain, in *Roman Britain: Recent Trends* (ed R F J Jones), 115–20, Sheffield

Jones, T, 1999 Birmingham, the 'East of Sutton' survey, *W Midlands Archaeol* 42, 146–8

Jope, E M, 2000 *Early Celtic Art in the British Isles*, Oxford

Kelly, M R, 1964 The middle Pleistocene of north Birmingham, *Phil Trans Roy Soc London* 247(741), 533–92

Kenyon, D, 2001 Finmere, Foxley Fields Farm (Finmere Quarry), *S Midlands Archaeol* 21, 41

Kidd, A, 2004 Northamptonshire in the first millennium BC, in *The Archaeology of Northamptonshire* (ed M. Tingle), 44–62, Northampton

King, A, 1991 Food production and consumption, in *Roman Britain: Recent Trends* (ed R F J Jones), 15–20, Sheffield

King, A, 1996 The south-east facade of Meonstoke aisled building, in *Architecture in Roman Britain* (eds P Johnson and I Haynes), Counc Brit Archaeol Res Rep 94, 56–69, York

King, A, 1999 Animals and the Roman army: the evidence of animal bones, in *The Roman Army as a Community* (eds A Goldsworthy and I Haynes), J Roman Archaeol Supp Ser 34, 139–49, London

King, A C and Potter, T W, 1990 A new domestic building-facade from Roman Britain, *J Roman Archaeol* 3, 195–204

King, C E, 1992 Coleshill, Warwickshire, in Bland (ed) 1992, 242–78

King, L E, King, J W, King, P W and Fisher, R, 1980 Kinver Edge Area, *W Midlands Archaeol* 23, 97

Kinsley, G, 2002 Characterisation of the handmade pottery, in Losco-Bradley and Kinsley 2002, 100–1

Kinvig, R H, 1954 Warwickshire, in Darby and Terrett (eds), 1954, 270–308

Kislev, M E, 1988 *Pinus pinea* in agriculture, culture and cult, in *Der prähistorische Mensch und seine Umwelt* (ed H Küster, 73–79, Stuttgart

Knight, D, 1984 *Late Bronze Age and Iron Age Settlement in the Nene and Great Ouse Basins*, Brit Archaeol Rep 130, Oxford

Knight, D, 1992 Excavations of an Iron Age settlement at Gamston, Nottinghamshire, *Trans Thoroton Soc* 96, 16–90

Knight, D, 2002 A regional ceramic sequence: pottery of the first millenium BC between the Humber and the Nene, in *Prehistoric Britain: the Ceramic Basis* (eds A Woodward and J D Hill), Prehist Ceram Res Group Occas Publ 3, 119–42, Oxford

Knight, D, Howard, A J and Leary, R, 2004 The Romano-British landscape, in *Trent Valley Landscapes; the Archaeology of 500,000 Years of Change* (eds D Knight and A J Howard), 115–51, King's Lynn

Knight, D, Marsden, P and Carney, J, 2003 Local or non-Local? Prehistoric granodiorite-tempered pottery in the East Midlands, in *Prehistoric Pottery, People, Pattern and Purpose* (ed A Gibson), Prehist Ceram Res Group Occas Publ 4/Brit Archaeol Rep S1156, 111–25, Oxford

Lambrick, G H and Moore, J P, 1987 Drayton Cursus, *S Midlands Archaeol* 17, 85–6

Langer, R H M and Hill, G D, 1991 *Agricultural Plants*, 2 edn, Cambridge

Langley, R S, 1994 Birch Abbey burials, in *Roman Alcester: Southern Extramural Area, 1964–1966 Excavations Part 1: Stratigraphy and Structures* (ed C Mahany), Counc Brit Archaeol Res Rep 96, 144–7

Langley, R and Drage, C, 2000 Roman occupation at Little Chester, Derby: salvage excavation and recording by the Trent & Peak Archaeological Trust 1986–1990, *Derbyshire Archaeol J* 120, 123–287

Last, J, 2005 Life by the river: a prehistoric landscape at Grendon, Northamptonshire, *Proc Prehist Soc* 71, 333–60

Leah, M D, Wells, C E, Stamper, P, Huckerby, E and Welch, C, 1998 *The Wetlands of Shropshire and Staffordshire*, NW Wetlands Survey 5, Lancaster

Leahy, K, 1979 Some prehistoric finds from the Burton upon Trent area, *Derbyshire Archaeol J* 99, 52–57

Leary, R S, 1995 The Romano-British pottery, in Martin 1995

Leary, R S, 1996 Roman coarse pottery, in Esmonde-Cleary and Ferris 1996, 40–60

Leary, R S, 1995–6 Roman pottery in A Jones, Excavations at Wall (Staffordshire) by E Greenfield in 1962 and 1964 (Wall Excavation Report no 15), *Trans Staffordshire Archaeol Hist Soc* 37 (1998), 26–37

Leary, R S, 2001 Romano-British pottery, in A Palfreyman, Report on the excavation of a Romano-British aisled building at Little Hay Grange Farm, Ockbrook, Derbyshire 1992–95, *Derbyshire Archaeol J* 121, 95–130

Leary, R, 2002 Romano-British pottery from excavations and fieldwalking, in Losco-Bradley and Kinsley 2002, 20–23

Leary, R S, 2003 The Romano-British pottery from the kilns at Lumb Brook, Hazelwood, Derbyshire *Derbyshire Archaeol J* 123, 71–110

Leary, R S, 2004 *The Romano-British Pottery from excavations on High St Doncaster*, unpubl rep for W Yorkshire Archaeol Services

Leary, R S, forthcoming a The Romano-British coarse pottery, in P J Ellis, The Old Shops excavations, Mill St, Rocester, Staffordshire, *Trans Staffordshire Archaeol Hist Soc*

Leary, R S, forthcoming b The Romano-British pottery, in M Williams, Results of an Archaeological Excavation at the Roman Settlement at Middlewich, Cheshire

Leary, R S, forthcoming c The 1988–1992 pottery report from Farm 2 and the 1978–1992 revised pottery report, in R Hodges *Roystone Grange: The Formation of a Roman Community*

Leary, R S, forthcoming d The Romano-British and Iron Age pottery, in B E Vyner (ed) The Archaeology of the A46 Fosse Way Upgrade: Newark–Lincoln

Leary, R S, in preparation The Roman pottery from excavations at Northfield Avenue, Rocester

Lee, F and Lindquist, G, 1994 Romano-British coarse pottery, in Cracknell and Mahany 1994, 3–92

Leeds, E T, 1933 Torcs of the British Iron Age, *Antiq J* 13, 466–7

Lees, B A, 1935 *Records of the Templars in England in the Twelfth Century. The Inquest of 1185*, London.

Letts, J, 1999 *Smoke Blackened Thatch: A Unique Source of Late Medieval Plant Remains from Southern England*, London

Lines, R, 1984 Man's use of birch – past and present, *Proc Roy Soc Edinburgh* 85B, 203–13

Lloyd-Morgan, G, 1999 Copper alloy, in S C Palmer 1999c, 134–42

Longworth, I H, 1984 *Collared Urns of the Bronze Age in Great Britain and Ireland*, Cambridge

Losco-Bradley, S, 1984 Fatholme, Barton-under-Needwood, Staffs, *Proc Prehist Soc* 50, 402

Losco-Bradley, S and Kinsley, G, 2002 *Catholme: An Anglo-Saxon Settlement on the Trent Gravels in Staffordshire*, Nottingham Stud Archaeol 3, Nottingham

Loveday, R, 1989 The Barford ritual complex: further excavations (1972) and a regional perspective, in *Midlands Prehistory* (ed A Gibson), Brit Archaeol Rep 204, 51–84 Oxford

Lovell, J, 2005 Excavation of a Romano-British farmstead at RNAS, Yeovilton, *Proc Somerset Archaeol Natur Hist Soc* 148, 7–70

Luke, M, forthcoming, The Biddenham Loop: a Prehistoric and Romano-British Landscape

Lucy, S, 2000 *The Anglo-Saxon Way of Death*, Stroud

Mabey, R, 1996 *Flora Britannica*, London

MacGregor, M, 1976 *Early Celtic Art in North Britain*, Leicester

Mackinder, A, 2000 *A Romano-British Cemetery on Watling Street*, MoLAS Archaeol Stud Ser 4, London

Mackreth, D F, 1996 *Orton Hall Farm: A Roman and Early Anglo-Saxon Farmstead*, E Anglian Archaeol 76, Manchester

Magilton, J, 2006 A Romano-Celtic temple and settlement at Grimstock Hill, Coleshill, Warwickshire, *Trans Birmingham Warwickshire Archaeol Soc* 110

Major, H, 1996 Roman and medieval metal finds from north and west Essex, *Essex Archaeol Hist* 27, 307–10

Manning, W H, 1985 *Catalogue of Romano-British Iron Tools, Fittings and Weapons in the British Museum*, London

Margary, I D, 1948 *Roman Ways in the Weald*, London

Margary, I D, 1973 *Roman Roads in Britain*, 3 edn, London

Margeson, S, 1993 *Norwich Households: The Medieval and Post-Medieval Finds from Norwich Survey Excavations 1971–1978*, E Anglian Archaeol 58, Norwich

Marsh, G, 1978 Early second century fine wares in the London area, in *Early Fine Wares in Roman Britain* (eds P Arthur and G Marsh), Brit Archaeol Rep 57, 119–223, Oxford

Martin, A, 1995 *Report on an Archaeological Evaluation at Tucklesholme Farm, Barton under Needwood*, unpubl Gifford rep

Martin, A and Allen, C, 2001 Two prehistoric ring ditches and an associated Bronze Age cremation cemetery at Tucklesholme Farm, Barton-under Needwood, Staffordshire, *Trans Staffordshire Archaeol Hist Soc* 39, 1–15

Martin, T S, 2000 Coarse pottery, in Langley and Drage 2000, 186–221

Mason, E (ed), 1980 *The Beauchamp Cartulary, Charters 1100–1268*, London

Mason, F K and Windrow M, 1972 *Know Britain*, London

Matthews, K J, 1997 Immaterial culture: invisible peasants and consumer subcultures in north-west Britannia, in *TRAC 96: Proceedings of the Sixth Annual Theoretical Roman Archaeology Conference, Sheffield 1996* (eds K Meadows, C Lemke and J Heron), 120–32, Oxford

Matthews, K J, 1998 Rural settlement in Roman Cheshire: a theoretical view, in Living on the edge of Empire: Models, Methodology and Marginality (ed M Nevell), *Archaeol North West* 3(13), 27–34

Maull, A, 1998a *Rugby, Coton Park*, Medieval Settlement Res Group Annu Rep 13, 47

Maull, A, 1998b Rugby, Coton Park, deserted medieval village, *W Midlands Archaeol* 41, 95

Maxwell Lyte, H C (ed), 1910 *Calendar of Inquisitions Post Mortem and Other Analagous Documents* VI, Edward II, London

Maxwell Lyte, H C (ed), 1920 *Book of Fees, commonly called Testa de Nevill, Part 1, 1198–1242*, London

Maxwell Lyte, H C (ed), 1923 *Book of Fees, commonly called Testa de Nevill, Part 2, 1242–1293*, London

Mayes, P and Scott, K, 1984 *Pottery Kilns at Chilvers Coton, Nuneaton*, Soc Medieval Archaeol Monogr 10

Mays, M, 1999 Roman coins, in S C Palmer 1999c, 126–34

McCarthy, M and Brooks, C M 1988 *Medieval Pottery in Britain AD 900–1600*, London

McKinley, J I, 1991 *Cremated Bone from the Area 15 Cemetery, Baldock, Hertfordshire*, unpubl rep for Letchworth Mus

McKinley, J I, 1992 *Cremation and inhumation burials from St. Stephen's cemetery, St. Albans*, unpubl report for Verulamium Mus

McKinley, J I, 1993 Bone fragment size and weights of bone from modern British cremations and its implications for the interpretation of archaeological cremations, *Int J Osteoarchaeol* 3, 283–7

McKinley, J I, 1994a *The Anglo-Saxon cemetery at Spong Hill, North Elmham Part VIII: The Cremations*, E Anglian Archaeol 69, 78–120, Gressenhall

McKinley, J I, 1994b Bone fragment size in British cremation burials and its implications for pyre technology and ritual, *J Arch Sci* 21, 339–42

McKinley, J I, 1997a The cremated human bone from burial and cremation-related contexts, in *Archaeological Excavations on the Route of the A27 Westhampnett Bypass, West Sussex, 1992* Vol 2 (A P Fitzpatrick), Wessex Archaeol Rep 12, 55–72, Salisbury

McKinley, J I, 1997b Bronze Age 'barrows' and the funerary rites and rituals of cremation, *Proc Prehist Soc* 63, 129–45

McKinley, J I, 2000a The analysis of cremated bone, in *Human Osteology* (eds M Cox and S Mays), 403–21, London

McKinley, J I, 2000b Cremated human remains, cremation burials and cremated remains, in Barber and Bowsher 2000, 61–7, 264–77, 360–5

McKinley, J I, 2000c Phoenix rising; aspects of cremation in Roman Britain, in Pearce *et al.* (eds) 2000, 38–44

McKinley, J I, 2004a Compiling a skeletal inventory: disarticulated and co-mingled remains, in *Guidelines to the Standards for Recording Human Remains* (eds M Brickley and J I McKinley), BABOA/IFA Pap 7, 13–16, Southampton

McKinley, J I, 2004b The human remains and aspects of pyre technology and cremation rituals, in Cool 2004, 283–309

McKinley, J I, 2004c Aspects of the cremation ritual as evidenced by the animal bones, in Cool 2004, 331–2

McKinley, J I, in press, In the heat of the pyre: efficiency of oxidation in Romano-British cremations – did it really matter? in Beyond Recognition: The Analysis of Burned Human Remains (eds C W Schmidt and S Symes), 23–40, Oxford

McKinley, J I and Smith, P, 1997 Cremated animal bone from burials and other cremation-related contexts, in *Archaeological Excavations on the Route of the A27 Westhampnett Bypass, West Sussex, 1992* Vol 2 (A P Fitzpatrick), Wessex Archaeol Rep 12, 253, Salisbury

McWhirr, A, Viner, L and Wells, C, 1982 *Romano-British Cemeteries at Cirencester*, Cirencester Excav 2, Cirencester

Megaloudi, F, 2004 Funeral plant offerings from historical sites: a preliminary study, in *Spatial Analysis of Funerary Areas* (eds L Smejda and J Turek), 109–14, Plzen

Mellars, P, 1976 Settlement patterns and industrial variability in the British Mesolithic, in *Problems in Economic and Social Archaeology* (eds G de G Sieveking, I H Longworth and K E Wilson), 375–99, London

Mellor, M, 1994 Oxfordshire pottery: a synthesis of middle and late Saxon, medieval and early post-medieval pottery in the Oxford region, *Oxoniensia* 59, 17–217

Mercer, E, 1954 The Houses of the Gentry, *Past and Present* 5, 11–72

Midgley, M, 1947 The Borough of Sutton Coldfield, in VCH 1947, 230–45

Miket, R, 1981 Pit alignments in the Milfield Basin and the excavation of Ewart 1, *Proc Prehist Soc* 47, 137–46

Miles, D, Palmer, S, Smith, A and Jones, G P, 2007 *Iron Age and Roman Settlement in the Upper Thames Valley: Excavations at Claydon Pike and other sites within the Cotswold Water Park*, Thames Valley Landscapes 26, Oxford

Miles, H, 1969 Excavations at Fisherwick, Staffs. – a Romano-British farmstead and a Neolithic occupation site, 1968, *Trans Staffordshire Archaeol Hist Soc* 10, 1–23

Millett, M J, 1979 An approach to the functional interpretation of pottery, in *Pottery and the Archaeologist* (ed M J Millett), Inst Archaeol Occas Publ 4, 35–47, London

Millett, M, 1990 *The Romanization of Britain*, Cambridge

Mills, N, 1995 *Roman Artefacts found in Britain: Catalogue and Price Guide*, Witham

Moffett, L, 1994 Charred cereals from some ovens/kilns in late Saxon Stafford and the botanical evidence for the pre-burh economy, in *Environment and Economy in Anglo-Saxon England* (ed J Rackham), Counc Brit Archaeol Res Rep 89, 55–64, York

Moffett, L, 1995 *Botanical Remains from Worcester Deansway*, Anc Monum Lab Rep 19, 39/95

Moffett, L, 1996 Charred plant remains, in Esmonde Cleary and Ferris 1996, 35

Moffett, L, 1999 The prehistoric use of plant resources, in *Excavations at Barrow Hills, Radley, Oxfordshire. Vol I: the Neolithic and Bronze Age Monument Complex* (A Barclay and C Halpin), Thames Valley Landscapes 11, 243–7, Oxford

Moffett, L and Ciaraldi, M, 1999 Charred plant remains, in S C Palmer (ed) 1999, 32–4, 162–71

Moffett, L and Smith, D, 1996 Insects and plants from a late medieval and early post-medieval tenement in Stone, Staffordshire, UK, *Circaea* 12(2), 157–75

Moffett, L, Robinson, M and Straker, V, 1989 Cereals, fruit and nuts: charred plant remains from Neolithic sites in England and Wales and the Neolithic economy, in *The Beginnings of Agriculture* (eds A Miles, D Williams and N Gardner), Brit Archaeol Rep S496, 243–61, Oxford

Monaghan, J, 1997 *Roman Pottery from York*, Archaeol York Fasc 16/8, York

Monckton, A, 2000 Charred plant remains, in Ferris *et al.* 2000, 67–71

Monckton, A, 2006 Environmental archaeology, in Cooper (ed) 2006, 259–286

Mook, W G, 1986, Business meeting: recommendations/resolutions adopted by the twelfth International Radiocarbon Conference, *Radiocarbon* 28, 799

Moore, J and Jackson, D A, 1990 Stanwick, Redlands Farm, *S Midlands Archaeol* 20, 55–6

Moore, P D and Webb, J A, 1978 *An Illustrated Guide to Pollen Analysis*, London

Moore, P D, Webb, J A and Collinson, M E, 1991 *Pollen Analysis* 2 edn, Oxford
Morgan, R A, 1982 *Tree-ring Studies in the Somerset Levels; the Examination of Modern Hazel Growth in Bradfield Woods, Suffolk, and its Implications for the Prehistoric Data*, Anc Monum Lab Rep 3839
Morris, E L, 1985 Prehistoric salt distributions: two case studies from western Britain, *Bull Board Celtic Stud* 32, 336–79
Morris, E L, 1994 Production and distribution of pottery and salt in Iron Age Britain: a review, *Proc Prehist Soc* 60, 371–93
Morris, E L and Gelling, P S, 1991 A note on The Berth, in Prehistory in Lowland Shropshire (ed M Carver), *Trans Shropshire Archaeol Soc* 67, 58–62
Mould, Q, 2004 The miscellaneous items of metal, in Cool 2004, 402
Mudd, A, Williams, R J and Lupton, A, 1999 *Excavations Alongside Roman Ermine Street, Gloucestershire and Wiltshire: The Archaeology of the A419/A417 Swindon to Gloucester Road Scheme Volume 1: Prehistoric and Roman Activity*, Oxford
Mullin, D, 2003 *The Bronze Age Landscape of the Northern English Midlands*, Brit Archaeol Rep 351, Oxford
Munsell, 1992 *Munsell Soil Charts*, New York
Murphy, P, 1983a Iron Age to late Saxon land use in the Breckland, in *Integrating the Subsistence Economy* (ed M Jones), Brit Archaeol Rep S181, 177–209, Oxford
Murphy, P, 1983b Plant macrofossils, 121–8, in D G Buckley and D Priddy, The excavation of a Bronze Age ring-ditch, Clacton, Rush Green, Essex Archaeol Hist 15
Murphy, P, 1984 Environmental archaeology in East Anglia, in *Environmental Archaeology: a regional review* (ed H C M Keeley), Anc Monum Hist Build Occas Pap 6, London
Murphy, P, 2003 Plant macrofossils and molluscs, insects and pollen, in *Power and Island Communities Excavations at the Wardy Hill Ringwork, Coveney, Ely* (C Evans), E. Anglian Archaeol 103, 84–114, Cambridge
Needham, S P, 1996 Chronology and periodisation in the British Bronze Age, *Acta Archaeologia* 67, 121–40
Nenk, B S, Margeson, S and Hurley, M, 1992 Medieval Britain and Ireland in 1991, *Medieval Archaeol* 36, 305
Nevell, M, 1998 Great Woolden Hall: a model for the material culture of Iron Age and Romano-British rural settlement in north west England, in *Living on the Edge of Empire: Models, Methodology and Marginality* (ed M Nevell), Archaeol North West 3(13), 48–63, Chester
Newcomer, M H and Karlin, C, 1987 Flint chips from Pincevent, in *The Human Uses of Flint and Chert* (eds G de G Sieveking and M H Newcomer), 33–6, Cambridge
Newman, R, Cranston, D and Howard-Davis, C, 2001 *The Historical Archaeology of Britain c. 1540–1900*, Stroud
Niblett, R, 1999 *The Excavation of a Ceremonial Site at Folly Lane, Verulamium*, *Britannia* Monogr 14, London
Nielsen-Marsh, C, Gernaey, A, Turner-Walker, G, Hedges, R, Pike, A and Collins, M, 2000 The chemical degradation of bone, in *Human Osteology in Archaeology and Forensic Science* (eds M Cox and S Mays), 439–54, London
O'Brien, C, 1979 Iron Age and Romano-British settlement on the Trent Basin, in *Invasion and Response: the Case of Roman Britain* (eds B C Burnham and H B Johnson), Brit Archaeol Rep 73, 299–313, Oxford
Odell, G H, 1981 The mechanics of use-breakage of stone tools: some testable hypotheses, *J Field Archaeol* 8, 197–209
Odell, G H and Odell-Vereecken, F, 1980 Verifying the reliability of lithic use-wear assessments by 'blind tests': the low power approach, *J Field Archaeol* 7, 87–120
Onhuma, K and Bergman, C, 1982 Experimental studies in the determination of flake mode, *Bull Inst Archaeol London* 19, 161–71
Orton, C R, 1975 Quantitative pottery studies, some progress, problems and prospects, *Science Archaeol* 17, 30–5
Orton, C R, 1980 Introduction to the pottery reports, in Excavation at Billingsgate Buildings 'Triangle', Lower Thames Street, 1974 (D M Jones), *Trans Middlesex Archaeol Soc Spec Pap* 4, 37–8
Osborne, P J, 1979 Insect remains, in C A Smith (ed) 1979, 85–7
Oswald, A, 1966–7a Observation on the construction of road to by-pass Wall, Staffs, *Trans Staffordshire Archaeol Hist Soc* 8, 39–41
Oswald, A, 1966–7b Excavations for the Avon/Severn Research Committee at Barford, Warwickshire, *Trans Birmingham Warwickshire Archaeol Soc* 83 (1969), 1–64
Oswald, A, 1997 A Doorway on the past: practical and mystic concerns in the orientation of roundhouse doorways, in *Reconstructing Iron Age Societies* (eds A Gwilt and C Haselgrove), Oxbow Monogr 71, 87–95, Oxford
Oswald, A and Gathercole, P W, 1955 Observation and excavation at *Manduessedum* 1954–6, *Trans Birmingham Archaeol Soc* 74 (1958), 30–52
Oswald, A, Dyer, C and Barber, M, 2001 *The Creation of Monuments: Neolithic Causewayed Enclosures in the British Isles*, London
Oswald, F, 1952 *Excavation of a Traverse of* Margidunum, Nottingham
Oxford Archaeological Unit (OAU) 1993 *Birmingham Northern Relief Road: Hawkeswell Farm, Archaeological Evaluation*, unpubl rep
Oxford Archaeological Unit, 1994a *Birmingham Northern Relief Road: Shenstone Hall Farm, Lichfield District, Staffordshire, Archaeological Evaluation*, unpubl rep
Oxford Archaeological Unit, 1994b *Birmingham Northern Relief Road: Wishaw Hall Farm, Wishaw, Warwickshire, Archaeological Evaluation*, unpubl rep
Oxford Archaeological Unit, 1994c *Birmingham Northern Relief Road: Crane Brook, Wall, Staffordshire, Archaeological Evaluation*, unpubl rep
Oxford Archaeological Unit, 1994d, *Birmingham Northern Relief Road Inquiry: Archaeological Report (Deposit Document 34A)*, unpubl rep for Dept of Transport and Midland Expressway Ltd
Oxford Archaeological Unit and Babtie Group, 2000 *Birmingham Northern Relief Road Archaeological Project Design: Revised General Strategy and Methodology*, unpubl OAU/Babtie rep
Oxford Wessex Archaeology (OWA), 2003 *M6 Toll (Birmingham Northern Relief Road) Staffordshire, Birmingham and Warwickshire 2000–2, Proposals for Post-excavation Analysis and Publication of Results*, unpubl rep for CAMBBA

Paget-Tomlinson, E, 1993 *The Illustrated History of Canal and River Navigations*, Sheffield

Painter, K S, 1969–70 An Iron Age gold-alloy torc from Glascote, Tamworth, Staffordshire, *Trans Staffordshire Archaeol Hist Soc* 11, 1–6

Palliser, D M, 1976 *The Staffordshire Landscape*, London

Palmer, N, 1982 *Roman Stratford: Excavations at Tiddington 1980–81*, Warwick

Palmer, N, 1999 Vessel and window glass, in S C Palmer 1999c, 151

Palmer, N, 2006 Domestic stonework, in Magilton 2006, 194–201

Palmer, N, in preparation Other finds, in S C Palmer, in preparation b

Palmer, S C, 1992 Polesworth, Kisses' Barn Farm, *W Midlands Archaeol* 35, 57–8

Palmer, S C, 1994a Church Lawford, Ling Hall Quarry, *W Midlands Archaeol* 37, 79–82

Palmer, S C, 1994b Salford Priors, Marsh Farm, *W Midlands Archaeol* 37, 95–7

Palmer, S C, 1999a Church Lawford, Churchover to Newbold Pacey Transco gas pipeline Area D, *W Midlands Archaeol* 42, 103–5

Palmer, S C, 1999b Church Lawford, Churchover to Newbold Pacey Transco gas pipeline Area G, *W Midlands Archaeol* 42, 109

Palmer, S C, 1999c Archaeological excavations in the Arrow Valley, Warwickshire, *Trans Birmingham Warwickshire Archaeol Soc* 103 (2000), 1–231

Palmer, S C, 2000a Church Lawford, Ling Hall Quarry, *W Midlands Archaeol* 43, 92

Palmer, S C, 2000b Wellesbourne, Walton, Transco Newbold Pacey-Honeybourne Pipeline Areas A–E, *W Midlands Archaeol* 43, 107

Palmer, S C, 2000c Marsh Farm Quarry, Salford Priors, *W Midlands Archaeol* 43, 99

Palmer, S C, 2001a Church Lawford, Ling Hall Quarry, Area Z, *W Midlands Archaeol* 44, 159

Palmer, S C, 2001b Any old Iron Age? Recent work on the Iron Age in Warwickshire, *W Midlands Archaeol* 44, 93–5

Palmer, S C, 2002b *Ling Hall Quarry, Church Lawford, Warwickshire, Archaeological Investigations 1989–1999*, unpubl Warwickshire Mus Fld Archaeol Projects Group Rep 0210

Palmer, S C, 2003 King's Newham, Warwickshire: Neolithic, Bronze Age and Iron Age excavations along a gas pipeline in 1990, *Trans Birmingham Warwickshire Archaeol Soc* 107, 41–75

Palmer, S C, 2004 Church Lawford, Ling Hall Quarry, Area AB, *W Midlands Archaeol* 47, 66–70

Palmer, S C, in preparation a, Neolithic, Bronze Age, Iron Age, Romano-British and Anglo-Saxon excavations on the Churchover to Newbold Pacey gas pipeline in 1999

Palmer, S C, in preparation b, Iron Age and Romano-British settlement at Marsh Farm Quarry, Salford Priors: further excavations in the Warwickshire Arrow Valley (1991–2000), Warwick

Palmer, S C, in preparation c, Excavations within an Iron Age settlement at Walton, Wellesbourne, Warwickshire, on the Newbold Pacey to Honeybourne Transco gas pipeline in 2000

Partridge, C, 1981 *Skeleton Green: A late Iron Age and Romano-British Site, Britannia* Monogr 2, London

PCRG, 1997 *The Study of Later Prehistoric Pottery: General Policies and Guidelines for Analysis and Publication*, Prehist Ceram Res Group Occas Pap 1 and 2, Salisbury

Peacock, D P S, 1967 Romano-British pottery production in the Malvern district of Worcestershire, *Trans Worcestershire Archaeol. Soc* 3 ser 1, 15–28

Peacock, D P S, 1977 Ceramics in Roman and medieval archaeology, in *Pottery and Early Commerce* (ed D P S Peacock), 21–34, London

Peacock, D P S, 1982 *Pottery in the Roman World: An Ethno-archaeological Approach*, London

Peacock, D P S and Williams, D F, 1986 *Amphorae and the Roman Economy*, London

Pearce, J, Millett, M and Struck, M (eds), 2000 *Burial, Society and Context in the Roman World*, Oxford

Pearson, E, in preparation, Charred plant remains assessment in (ed.) S C Palmer in preparation b

Pearson, E, Greig, J and Jordan, D, 1999 *Environmental remains from a watching brief at Lammascote Road, Stafford*, Worcester CC Archaeol Service internal rep 767

Pelling, R and Robinson, M, 2000 Saxon emmer wheat from the Upper and Middle Thames Valley, England *Environ Archaeol* 5, 117–9

Percival, J, 1921 *The Wheat Plant*, London

Perrin, J R, 1990 *Roman Pottery from the Colonia 2: General Accident and Rougier Street*, Archaeology of York 16/4, York

Perrin, J R, 1999 Roman pottery from excavations at and near to the Roman Small Town of *Durobrivae*, Water Newton, Cambridgeshire, 1956–58, *J Roman Pottery Stud* 8

Philpott, R, 1991 *Burial Practices in Roman Britain*, Brit Archaeol Rep 219, Oxford

Pitts, M W, 1978 On the shape of waste flakes as an index of technological change in lithic industries, *J Archaeol Sci* 5, 17–37

Pitts, M W and Jacobi, R M, 1979 Some aspects of change in flaked stone industries of the Mesolithic and Neolithic in southern Britain, *J Archaeol Sci* 6(2), 163–77

Polfer, M, 2000 Reconstructing funerary rituals: the evidence of *ustrina* and related archaeological structures, in Pearce *et al.* (eds) 2000, 30–8

Pollard, J, 1996, Iron Age riverside pit alignments at St Ives, Cambridgeshire, *Proc Prehist Soc* 62, 93–115

Pope, E J, O'Brian, M A and Smith, C, 2004 Identification of traumatic injury in burned cranial bone: an experimental approach, *J Forensic Sci* 49, 431–40

Porter, V, 1990 *Small Woods and Hedgerows*, London

Pretty, K, 1997 Appendix 5: vessel glass, in *The Baths Basilica, Wroxeter: Excavations 1966–90* (P Barker, R White, K Pretty, H Bird and M Corbishley), English Heritage Archaeol Rep 8, 319–23, London

Preiss, S, Matterne, V and Latron, F, 2005 An approach to funerary rituals in the Roman provinces: plant remains from a Gallo-Roman cemetery at Faulquemont (Moselle, France), *J Vegetation Hist Archaeobot* 14(4), 363–72

Price, J, 2005 Glass working and glassworkers in cities and towns, in *Roman Working Lives and Urban Living* (eds A MacMahon and J Price), 167–90, Oxford

Price, J and Cool, H E M, 1991 The evidence for the producton of glass in Roman Britain, in *Ateliers de Verriers de l'Antiquité à la Periode Pré-industrielle* (eds D Foy and G Sennequier), Actes de 4èmes Rencontres (Rouen 1989), Association Française pour l'Archéologie du Verre, 23–30, Rouen

Price, J and Cottam, S, 1998 *Romano-British Glass Vessels: a Handbook*, Counc Brit Archaeol Pract Handbk in Archaeol 14, York

Prior, J and Alvin, K L, 1983 Structural changes on charring woods of *Dichrostachys* and *Salix* from Southern Africa, *Int Assoc Wood Anat Bull* 4(4), 197–206

Pritchard, F, 1991 Stone artefacts, in *Aspects of Saxo-Norman London: 2 Finds and Environmental Evidence* (ed A Vince), London Middlesex Archaeol Soc Spec Pap 12, 120–279, London

Purchase, A, 1972 A collection of Mesolithic flints from Coton Hill, Stafford, *Staffordshire Archaeol* 1, 30–1

Rackham, O, 1986 *The History of the Countryside*, London

Rackham, O, 2003 *Ancient Woodland: its History, Vegetation and Uses in England*, Kirkcudbright

Rahtz, P A, 1959 Humberstone earthwork, Leics, *Trans Leicestershire Archaeol Hist Soc* 1, 1–32

Raistrick, A, 1939 Iron-Age settlements in West Yorkshire, *Yorkshire Archaeol J* 34, 115–50

Rátkai, S, 1990 The medieval pottery, in S Cracknell, Bridge End, Warwick: Archaeological excavation of a medieval street frontage, *Trans Birmingham Warwickshire Archaeol Soc* 95, 17–72

Rátkai, S, 1992a Medieval pottery, in S Cracknell and M W Bishop, Excavations at 25–33 Brook Street, Warwick 1973, *Trans Birmingham Warwickshire Archaeol Soc* 97, 1–40

Rátkai, S, 1992b Medieval pottery in S Cracknell, 'Bards Walk', Wood Street, Stratford-upon-Avon: medieval structures excavated in 1989, *Trans Birmingham Warwickshire Archaeol Soc* 97, 57–75

Rátkai, S, 1998 The pottery, in *Archaeological Evaluation at the Church of St John the Baptist, Wolvey, Warwickshire* (C Coutts and C Jones), Warwickshire Mus Archive Rep

Rátkai, S, 2000 The pottery, in L Jones, S Ratkai and P Ellis, 112–18, Excavations at No 15, The Green, Kings Norton 1992, *Trans Birmingham Warwickshire Archaeol Soc* 104, 101–21

Rátkai, S, 2001a The pottery in *Archaeological Watching Brief of Land at Minworth Greaves Farm, Sutton Coldfield* (K Pack), LP Archaeol internal rep

Rátkai, S, 2001b Explosion Site: medieval pottery, in Booth and Evans 2001, 232 and M2:D7

Rátkai S, 2001c The pottery, in *Land to the Rear of 9–21, Greenhill, Lichfield, Staffordshire. Assessment Report on the Excavation, Watching Brief and Building Recording* (N Tavener and R Stone), Marches Archaeol 178

Rátkai, S, 2002 The medieval and post-medieval pottery, in *Birmingham to Solihull Link Main: Archaeological Survey, Excavation and Watching Brief 2002* (E Ramsay), Birmingham Archaeol internal rep

Rátkai, S, 2003 Medieval pottery, in *Archaeological Excavations at 5–19 High Street, Solihull* (S Palmer) Warwickshire Mus Rep 0341

Rátkai, S, 2004a Medieval and post-medieval pottery, in M Ciaraldi, R Cuttler, L Dingwall and C Dyer, 12–18, Medieval tanning and retting at Brewood, Staffordshire: archaeological excavations 1999–2000, *Trans Staffordshire Archaeol Hist Soc* 40, 1–55

Rátkai, S, 2004b The pottery, in K Nichol and S Rátkai, 71–96, Archaeological excavation on the north side of Sandford Street, Lichfield, Staffs, 2000 *Trans Staffordshire Archaeol Hist Soc* 40, 58–121

Rátkai, S, 2005 The medieval and later pottery, in *The Church of Our Lady of Mount Carmel and some Conventual Buildings at the Whitefriars, Coventry* (C Woodfield), Brit Archaeol Rep 389, 315–25, Oxford

Ratkai, S, 2006 Medieval pottery, in *Investigation of Iron Age, Romano-British and Medieval Settlements on the Transco Newbold Pacey to Honeybourne Gas Pipeline in 2000* (P Thompson and S Palmer), Warwickshire Mus Rep 0605, Warwick

Rátkai, S, forthcoming a, Saxon pottery, in *Country Life on the Margins Iron Age, Roman and Saxon Occupation at Grange Park: Excavations at Courteenhall, Northamptonshire, 1999* (eds L Jones, A Woodward and S Buteux), Brit Archaeol Rep, Oxford

Rátkai, S, forthcoming b The medieval and post-medieval pottery, in *The Bull Ring Uncovered* (ed S Rátkai), Oxford

Rátkai, S, forthcoming c, The pottery, in Excavations at 15, Sandford Street, Lichfield (N Taverner)

Rátkai, S, forthcoming d, The medieval and post-medieval pottery, in Excavations at Bascote: a Small Rural Settlement in Southeast Warwickshire (S Litherland, E Ramsay and P Ellis)

Rátkai, S, forthcoming e, The pottery, in *Burton Dassett; a Deserted Medieval Settlement in SE Warwickshire* (N Palmer), Soc Medieval Archaeol Monogr

Rátkai, S, forthcoming f, Medieval pottery, in Cawston, *Dunchurch: Excavations at a Medieval Grange on the Rugby Western Ring Main (Phase 1) 1999* (S C Palmer), rep for Severn Trent Water

Rátkai, S, forthcoming g The pottery in Barston Parish Survey (W Burnett and A Howrie), *Trans Birmingham Warwickshire Arch Soc*

Rátkai, S, forthcoming h The medieval and post-medieval pottery, in Excavations at Old Hall Street, Wolverhampton (R Cuttler)

Rátkai, S, forthcoming i The medieval and early post-medieval pottery, in *Stafford Castle: Survey, Excavation and Research 1978–1998; Volume II – The Excavations 1978–1991* (ed I Soden)

Rátkai, S and Soden, I, 1998 *Warwickshire Medieval and Post-medieval Ceramic Type Series*, unpubl manuscript, Warwickshire Mus Archaeol Fld Services

Rawes, B, 1982 Gloucester Severn Valley ware, *Trans Bristol and Gloucestershire Archaeol Soc* 100, 33–46

Redknap, M, 1985 Twelfth and thirteenth century Coventry wares, *Medieval Ceram* 9, 65–78

Redknap, M, 1996 Earlier medieval pottery, in *The Excavations at Broadgate East, Coventry 1974–5* (M Rylatt and MA Stokes), Coventry Mus Monogr 5, 37–43, Coventry

Redknap, M and Perry, J G, 1996 Medieval and later pottery, in *The Excavations at Broadgate East, Coventry 1974–75* (M Rylatt and M A Stokes), Coventry Mus Monogr 5, 37–99, Coventry

Reilly, K, 2000 The animal bone, in Barber and Bowsher 2000, 366–8

Reynolds, P J, 1981 New approaches to familiar problems, in *The Environment of Man: The Iron Age to the Anglo-Saxon Period* (eds M Jones and G Dimbleby), Brit Archaeol Rep 87, 19–42, Oxford

Roach Smith, C, 1848 *Collectanea Antiqua* 1, London

Roberts, B K, 1973 Field systems of the West Midlands, in Baker and Butlin (ed) 1973, 188–231

Roberts, B K and Wrathmell, S, 2000 *An Atlas of Rural Settlement in England*, London

Roberts, B K and Wrathmell, S, 2002 *Region and Place: a Study of English Rural Settlement*, London

Roberts, C and Cox, M, 2003 *Health and Disease in Britain: From Prehistory to the Present Day*, Stroud

Roberts, C and Manchester, K, 1997 *The Archaeology of Disease*, Stroud

Robertson, A S, 2000 *An inventory of Romano-British Coin Hoards*, Roy Numis Soc Spec Publ 20, London.

Robinson, M, 1988 The significance of the tubers of *Arrhenatherum elatius* (L) Beauv, in *The Rollright Stones, Megaliths, Monuments and Settlements in the Prehistoric Landscape* (G Lambrick), English Heritage Archaeol Rep 6, London, 102

Robinson, M, 1992 Environment, archaeology and alluvium on the river gravels of the South Midlands, in *Alluvial Archaeology in Britain* (eds S Needham and M G Macklin), Oxbow Monogr 27, 197–208, Oxford

Robinson, M, 1995 *Assessment of Environmental Samples from Ellesmere Road, Shrewsbury*, unpubl OAU archive rep

Robinson, M, 2000 Further considerations of Neolithic charred cereals, fruits and nuts, in *Plants in Neolithic Britain and Beyond* (ed A Fairbairn), Neolithic Stud Grp Seminar Pap 5, 85–90, Oxford

Robinson, M, 2002 Plant remains, in *Excavations at Melford Meadows, Brettenham, 1994: Romano-British and Early Saxon Occupations* (A Mudd), E Anglian Archaeol 99, 108–10, Oxford

Robinson, M A and Wilson, R, 1987 A survey of environmental archaeology in the South Midlands, in *Environmental Archaeology: a Regional Review* 2 (ed H C M Keeley), HBMCO Occas Pap 1, 16–100, London

Rodriguez Almeida, E, 1989 *Los Tituli Picti de las Anforas Olearias de la Betica*, Madrid

Rodwell, J S (ed), 1991 *British Plant Communities Volume 1: Woodlands and Scrub*, Cambridge

Rodwell, J S (ed), 2000 *British Plant Communities, Volume 5: Maritime Communities and Vegetation of Open Habitats*, Cambridge

Rogers, J and Waldron, T, 1995 *A Field Guide to Joint Disease in Archaeology*, Chichester

de Rouffignac, C, 1990 Material from vessel contents 480 and pit fill 1079, in J Dinn and J Evans, Aston Mill Farm, Kemerton: excavation of a ring-ditch, middle Iron Age enclosures and a grubenhaus, *Trans Worcestershire Archaeol Soc* 12, 54

Round, A A, 1969–70 Excavations at Wall (Staffordshire), 1966–7, on the site of the Roman forts (Wall Excavation Report 9), *Trans Staffordshire Archaeol Hist Soc* 11, 5–32

Round, A A, 1981–2 Excavations at Wall (Staffordshire), 1968–1972 on the site of the Roman Forts (Wall Excavation Report 12), *Trans Staffordshire Archaeol Hist Soc* 23, 1–68

Round, A A, 1990–1, Excavations on the mansio site at Wall (Letocetum), Staffordshire, 1972–78 (Wall Excavation Report). *Trans Staffordshire Archaeol Hist Soc* 32, 1–78

Round, A A, 1991–2 A Response, *Trans Staffordshire Archaeol Hist Soc 33*, 3–6

Round, A A, Ross, A and Henig, M, 1978–80 Eleventh report of excavations at Wall, Staffs, *Trans Staffordshire Archaeol Hist Soc* 21, 1–14

Rouvier-Jeanlin, M, 1972 *Les Figurines Gallo-Romaines en Terre Cuite au Musée des Antiquités Nationales*, Gallia Supple 24, Paris

Salway, P, 1981 *Roman Britain*, Oxford

Samuels, J, 1979 Stone artefacts, in C Smith 1979, 65–6

Saunders, R L, 1998 *The Use of Old Red Sandstone in Roman Britain: A Petrological and Archaeological Study*, unpublPhD Thesis, Univ Reading

Saville, A, 1972–73, A reconsideration of the prehistoric flint assemblage from Bourne Pool, Aldridge, Staffordshire, *Trans Staffordshire Archaeol Hist Soc* 14, 6–28

Saville, A, 1976, The Mesolithic flint and chert artefacts from Wetton Mill rocks shelter, in *The excavation of Wetton Mill rock shelter, Manifold Valley, Staffs* (J H Kelly), Stoke–on-Trent Archaeol Soc Rep 9, 84–95, Stoke-on-Trent

Saville, A, 1980 On the measurement of struck flakes and flake tools, *Lithics* 1, 16–20

Saville, A, 1981a *Grimes Graves, Norfolk Excavations 1971–72 Vol 2: the Flint Assemblage*, London

Saville, A, 1981b Mesolithic industries in central England: an exploratory investigation using microlith technology, *Archaeol J* 138, 49–71

Sawyer, P H (ed), 1976 *Medieval Settlement. Continuity and Change*, London

Scheuer, L and Black, S, 2000 *Developmental Juvenile Osteology*, London

Schweingruber, F H, 1990 *Microscopic Wood Anatomy*, 3 edn, Birmensdorf

Scott, K, 1981 Mancetter village: a first century fort, *Trans Birmingham Warwickshire Archaeol Soc* 91 (1984), 1–24

Scott, K, 1998 Mancetter village, a 1st-century fortress continued, *Trans Birmingham Warwickshire Archaeol Soc* 102 (2000), 1–55

Seaby, W A, 1992 Wishaw, Warwickshire, in Bland 1992, 116–21

Seaby, W, 2006 Coins, in Magilton 2006, 165–7

Serjeantson, D, 1996 The animal bones, in *Refuse and Disposal at Area 16 East, Runnymede: Runnymede Bridge Research Excavations, Volume 2* (eds S Needham and T Spence), 194–253, London

Shackley, M L, 1976 The Danebury project: an experiment in site sediment recording, in *Geoarchaeology: Earth Science and the Past* (eds D A Davidson and M L Shackley), 9–21, London

Shaffrey, R, 2003 The rotary querns from the Society of Antiquaries' excavations at Silchester, 1890–1909, *Britannia* 34, 143–74

Shaffrey, R, 2006 *Grinding and Milling Romano-British Rotary Querns made from Old Red Sandstone*, Brit Archaeol Rep 409, Oxford

Shaffrey, R, in preparation The worked stone, in *Fairfield Park, Stotfold, Bedfordshire, Later Prehistoric Settlement in the eastern Chilterns* (L Webley, J Timby and M Wilson), Oxford

Sherlock, R J, 1957 Excavations at Deritend, *Trans Birmingham Warwickshire Archaeol Soc* 73, 109–14

Silver, I A, 1969 The ageing of domestic animals, in *Science in Archaeology: a Survey of Progress and Research* (eds D Brothwell and E Higgs), London, 283–302

Simoons, F J, 1994 *Eat Not This Flesh: Food Avoidances from Prehistory to the Present*, 2 edn, Wisconsin

Skipp, V, 1981 The evolution of settlement and open-field topography in north Arden down to 1300, in *The Origins of Open-Field Agriculture* (ed T Rowley), 162–83, London

Slater, T R, 1985 The urban hierarchy in medieval Staffordshire, *J Hist Geog* 11, 2

Smith, C A, 1974–5 Second report on excavations at Fisherwick, Staffs (1973): ice wedge casts and Middle Bronze Age settlement, *Trans Staffordshire Archaeol Hist Soc* 16 (1976), 1–17

Smith, C A, 1977 The valleys of the Middle Trent and Tame and their population and ecology during the first millennium BC, in *The Iron Age in Britain: a Review* (ed J Collis), 51–61, Sheffield

Smith, C A, 1978 The landscape and natural history of Iron Age settlement on the Trent gravels, in *Lowland Iron Age Communities in Europe* (eds B Cunliffe and T Rowley), Brit Archaeol Rep S48, 91–102, Oxford

Smith, C A (ed), 1979 *Fisherwick. The Reconstruction of an Iron Age Landscape*, Brit Archaeol Rep 61, Oxford

Smith, J T, 1963 Romano-British aisled houses, *Archaeol J* 120, 1–30

Smith, J T, 1964 The Roman villa at Denton, *Lincolnshire Architect Archaeol Soc Rep Pap* 10, 75–104

Smith, R F, 1987 *Roadside Settlements in Lowland Roman Britain*, Brit Archaeol Rep 157, Oxford

Smith, W, 2002 *A Review of Archaeological Wood Analyses in Southern England*, English Heritage Centre Archaeol Lab Rep 75

Smith, W, 2004 *Medieval charred plant remains from Stafford College, Broadeye, Stafford*, unpublished Univ Birmingham Environ Archaeol Services Rep 84

Smyth, G P, 1994 *Medieval Moated sites in Warwickshire*, unpubl MPhil thesis, Univ Birmingham

Soden, I, 2005 *Coventry: The Hidden History*, Stroud

Šoštaric, R, Dizdar, M, Kušan, D, Hršak, V and Marekovic, S, 2006 Comparative analysis of plant finds from early Roman graves in Ilok (*Cuccium*) and Šitarjevo (*Andautonia*), Croatia – a contribution to understanding burial rites in southern Pannonia, *Collect Antropol* 30(2), 429–36

Stace, C, 1997 *New Flora of the British Isles*, Cambridge

Stanley, M and Stanley, B, 1960–1 The Romano-British potters field at Wappenbury, Warwickshire, *Trans Birmingham Warwickshire Archaeol Soc* 79 (1964), 93–108

Startin, J, 1979 Animal bones, in C A Smith 1979, 79

Stead, I M, 1979 *The Arras Culture*, York

Stead, I M, 1991a The Snettisham treasure: excavations in 1991, *Antiquity* 65, 447–65

Stead, I M, 1991b *Iron Age Cemeteries in East Yorkshire: Excavations at Burton Fleming, Rudston, Garton-on-the-Wolds, and Kirkburn*, English Heritage Archaeol Rep 22, London

Stead, I M and Rigby, V, 1986, *Baldock: the Excavation of a Roman and pre-Roman Settlement 1968–72 (Herts)*, *Britannia* Monogr 7, London

Stead, I M and Rigby, V, 1989 Verulamium. *The King Harry Lane Site*, English Heritage Archaeol Rep 12, London

Steane, J M, 1988 The royal fishponds of medieval England, in Aston 1988, 39–68

Steane, J M and Foreman, M, 1988 Medieval fishing tackle, in Aston 1988, 137–86

Stevens, C, 2005 Bronze Age and Iron Age settlement at Meriden Quarry, Solihull, *Trans Birmingham Warwickshire Archaeol Soc* 109, 1–25

Stevens, C E, 1940 The Frilford site – a postscript, *Oxoniensia* 5, 166–7

Stevens, C J, 2003 Agricultural processing: an overview, in *Power and Island Communities: Excavations at the Wardy Hill Ringwork, Coveney, Ely* (ed C Evans), E Anglian Archaeol 103, 138–44, Cambridge

Stevens, C J, 2007, Reconsidering the evidence: towards an understanding of the social contexts of subsistence production in Neolithic Britain, in *The Origin and Spread of Domestic Plants in Southwest Asia and Europe* (eds S Colledge and J Conolly), Walnut Creek, California, 375–89

Stockmarr, J, 1971 Tablets with spores used in absolute pollen analysis, *Pollen et Spores* 13, 614–21

Stokes, E and Wellstood, F (eds), 1932 *Warwickshire Feet of Fines, Volume I, (1195–1284)*, Warwick

Stokes, E and Drucker, L (eds), 1939 *Warwickshire Feet of Fines, Volume 2, (1284–1345)*, Warwick

Struck, M, 1995 Analysis of social and cultural diversity on rural burial sites in north-eastern Raetia, in *Theoretical Roman Archaeology: Second Conference Proceedings* (ed P Rush), 70 80, Aldershot

Struck, M, 2000 High status burials in Roman Britain (first–third century AD) – potential interpretation, in Pearce *et al.* (eds) 2000, 85–96

Stuiver, M, Long, A and Kra, R S (eds), 1993 *Calibration Issue*, *Radiocarbon* 35(1)

Swan, V G, 1984 *The Pottery Kilns of Roman Britain*, London

Symons, D, 1992–3 Bronze chi-rho bowl from Wall, *Trans Staffordshire Archaeol Hist Soc* 34 (1995), 1–4

Symonds, R P, 1997 Appendix 4: Roman pottery, in *The Baths Basilica, Wroxeter: Excavations 1966–90* (P Barker, R White, K Pretty, H Bird and M Corbishley), English Heritage Archaeol Rep 8, 269–318, London

Tacitus, *Germania* (trans H Mattingly) 1948, London

Taverner, J, 1600 *Certaine Experiments Concerning Fish and Fruite*, London

Taylor, C, 1983 *Village and Farmstead: A History of Rural Settlement in England*, London

Taylor, J, 1997 Space and place: some thoughts on Iron Age and Romano-British landscapes, in *Reconstructing Iron Age Societies: New Approaches to the British Iron Age* (eds A Gwilt and C Haselgrove), Oxbow Monogr 71, 192–204, Oxford

Taylor, J, 2004 The distribution and exchange of pink, grog tempered pottery in the East Midlands: an update, *J Roman Pottery Stud* 11, 60–6

Tetlow, E A and Gearey, R, 2006 *An Assessment of the Pollen and Insect Remains from Tameside, Perry Barr*, Birmingham Archaeo-Environ Rep BA–10-06

Thomas, J, 1999 *Understanding the Neolithic*, London

Thomas, J, 2003 Prehistoric pit alignments and their significance in the archaeological landscape, in *Re-searching the Iron Age* (ed J Humphrey), Leicester Archaeol Monogr 11, 79–86, Leicester

Thomas, K D, 1977 The Mollusca from an Iron Age pit at Winklebury, in K Smith, The excavation of Winklebury Camp, Basingstoke, Hampshire, *Proc Prehist Soc* 43, 70–4

Thomas, N, 1974 An archaeological gazetteer for Warwickshire: Neolithic to Iron Age, *Trans Birmingham Warwickshire Archaeol Soc* 86, 16–48

Thompson, I, 1982 *Grog-tempered 'Belgic' Pottery of South-eastern England*, Brit Archaeol Rep 108, Oxford

Thompson, M W, 1965 Two levels of the Mere at Kenilworth Castle, Warwickshire, *Medieval Archaeol* 9, 156–61

Thorpe, H, 1956 The site of the Roman bath-house at Wall, with observations on the building materials, *Trans Birmingham Warwickshire Archaeol Soc* 74 (1958), 26–9

Timby, J, 2005 Romano-British pottery, in R Cutler and E Ramsey, The Excavation of Roman, medieval and Civil War remains at Trent Lane, Newark, Nottinghamshire, *Trans Thoroton Soc* 109, 55–7

Tixier, J, Inizan, M L and Roche, H, 1980 *Préhistoire de la pierre taillée I Terminologie et téchnologie*, Valbonne

Todd, M, 1968a Trent Valley Ware, a Roman coarse ware of middle and lower Trent, *Trans Thoroton Soc Nottinghamshire* 71, 38–41

Todd, M, 1968b The commoner late Roman coarse wares of the East Midlands, *Antiq J* 48, 192–209

Todd, M, 1980 *The Barbarians: Goths, Franks and Vandals*, London

Toller, H, 1977 *Roman Lead Coffins and Ossuaria in Britain*, Brit Archaeol Rep 38, Oxford

Tomber, R and Dore, J, 1998 *The National Roman Fabric Reference Collection. A Handbook*, MoLAS Monogr 2, London

Topal, J, 1981 *The Southern Cemetery of Matrica*, Budapest

Toynbee, J M C, 1971 *Death and Burial in the Roman World*, London

Toynbee, J M C, 1996 *Death and Burial in the Roman World*, London

Trinder, B, 1987 *The Making of the Industrial Landscape*, London

Tringham, R, Cooper, G, Odell, G, Voytek, B and Whitman, A, 1974 Experimentation in the formation of edge damage: a new approach to lithic analysis, *J Fld Archaeol* 1, 171–96

Tufi, S R, 1983 *Corpus Signorum Imperii Romani, Great Britain Volume 1, Fascicule 3, Yorkshire*, Oxford

Turner, C, 1968 A Lowestoftian Late Glacial flora from the Pleistocene deposits at Hoxne, *New Phytol* 67, 327

Turner, L, 2001 Quernstones, in A Jones 2001, 86–8

Tyers, P, 1996 *Roman Pottery in Britain*, London

Upton-Ward, J M, 1992 *The Rule of the Templars: the French Text of the Rule of the Order or the Knights Templar* (trans J M Upton-Ward), Stud Hist Medieval Religion 4, Woodbridge

Vaughan, J G and Geissler, C A, 1997 *The New Oxford Book of Food Plants*, Oxford

Veen, M, van der, 1992 *Crop Husbandry Regimes – an Archaeobotanical Study of Farming in Northern England 1000 BC–AD 500*, Sheffield Archaeol Monogr 3, Sheffield

Veen, M, van der and O'Connor, T P, 1998 The expansion of agricultural production in late Iron Age and Roman Britain, in *Science in Archaeology, an Agenda for the Future* (ed J Bayley), 127–44, London

Vince, A G, 1985 Part 2: the ceramic finds, *in Hereford City Excavations Volume 3: The Finds* (ed R Shoesmith), Counc Brit Archaeol Res Rep 56, 34–82, York

Vince, A, 2002 Anglo-Saxon pottery, in S Losco-Bradley and G Kinsley 2002, 102–8

VCH, 1904 *The Victoria History of the County of Warwick 1* (ed W Page), London

VCH, 1947 *The Victoria History of the County of Warwick 4, Hemlingford Hundred* (ed L F Salzman), London

VCH, 1959, *The Victoria History of the County of Staffordshire 5* (ed W Page), London

VCH, 1964 *The Victoria History of the County of Warwick, 7, The City of Birmingham* (ed W B Stevens), London

VCH, 1967, *The Victoria History of the County of Staffordshire* 2 (ed W Page), London

Wahl, J, 1982 Leichenbranduntersuchungen. Ein überblick über die bearbeitungs- und assagemöglichkeiten von Brandgräbern, *Prähistorische Zeischrift* 57, 1–125

Wainwright, G J, 1967 *Coygan Camp: A Prehistoric, Romano-British and Dark Age Settlement in Carmarthenshire*, Cardiff

Wait, G A, 1985 Ritual and Religion in Iron Age Britain, *Brit Archaeol Rep* 149, Oxford

Walker, S, 1990 *Catalogue of Roman sarcophagi in the British Museum, Corpus Signorum Imperii Romani, Great Britain Volume 2, Fascicule 2*, London

Ward, G K and Wilson S R, 1978 Procedures for comparing and combining radiocarbon age-determinations – critique, *Archaeometry* 20, 19–31

Watkins, A, 1982 The Development of Coleshill in the Middle Ages, unpubl BA Dissert, Univ Birmingham

Watkins, A, 1993 The woodland economy of the Forest of Arden in the later middle ages, *Midland History* 18, 19–32

Watson, P, 1994 Shenstone, *W Midlands Archaeol* 37, 64

WDM, nd *Calendar of the Wingfield Digby Muniments, Volume 1.* Birmingham Reference Library Archives MSS 3888 pt 1

Webster, C J and Brunning, R A, 2004 A seventh-century AD cemetery at Stoneage Barton Farm, Bishop's Lydiard, Somerset and square-ditched burials in post-Roman Britain, *Archaeol J* 161, 54–81

Webster, G, 1959 The pottery, in H V Hughes 1959, 37–8

Webster, G, 1971 A Roman system of fortified posts along Watling Street, Britain, in *Roman Frontier Studies 1967* (ed S Applebaum), 38–45, Tel Aviv

Webster, G, 1973 Coarse pottery, in B Hobley, Excavations at the 'Lunt': second interim report, *Trans Birmingham Warwickshire Archaeol Soc* 85, 55–62

Webster, G, 1974 West Midlands in the Roman period, *Trans Birmingham Warwickshire Archaeol Soc* 86, 49–58

Webster, G, 1975a *The Cornovii*, Peoples of Roman Britain Series, London

Webster, G, 1975b Post-1st century wares, 33, in B Hobley, The 'Lunt' Roman fort and training School for Roman Cavalry, Baginton, Warwickshire, *Trans Birmingham Warwickshire Archaeol Soc* 87, 1–56

Webster, G and Hobley, B, 1964 Aerial reconnaissance over the Warwickshire Avon, *Archaeol J* 121, 1–22

Webster, J, 2003 Bronze objects, in James 2003, 289–325

Webster, P V, 1976 Severn Valley Ware: a preliminary study, *Trans Bristol Gloucestershire Archaeol Soc* 94, 18–46

Webster, P V, 1981 The feeding cup: an unusual samian form, in *Roman Pottery Research in Britain and North-West Europe* (A C Anderson and A S Anderson), Brit Archaeol Rep S123, 249–56, Oxford

Webster, P V, 1993 The post-fortress coarsewares, in *Report on the Excavations at Usk 1965–76 The Roman Pottery* (W H Manning), 227–357, Cardiff

Welch, C M, 1994–5 A Bronze Age 'burnt mound' at Millwich, *Trans Staffordshire Archaeol Hist Soc* 36 (1997), 1–16

Welfare, H, and Swan, V, 1995 *Roman Camps in England: the Field Archaeology*, London

Wells, C, 1981 *Human remains, in Skeleton Green; a Late Iron Age and Romano-British Site* (C Partridge), *Britannia* Monogr 2, 277–303

Wheatley, P, 1954 Staffordshire, in Darby and Terrett (eds) 1954, 160–214

Wheeler, H, 1979 Excavations at Willington, Derbyshire, 1970–2, *Derbyshire Archaeol J* 99, 58–220

Wheeler, H, 1985 The Racecourse cemetery, in J Dool *et al.* 1985, 222–80

Whimster, R, 1981 *Burial Practices in Iron Age Britain*, Brit Archaeol Rep 90, Oxford

Whimster, R, 1989 *The Emerging Past: Air Photography and the Buried Landscape*, London

White, R H and Gaffney, V L, 2003 Resolving the paradox: the work of the Wroxeter Hinterland Project, in *The Archaeology of Roman Towns: Studies in Honour of John S Wacher* (ed P Wilson), 221–32, Oxford

White, R H and Leusen, P M van, 1997 Aspects of Romanization in the Wroxeter hinterland, in *TRAC 96: Proceedings of the Sixth Annual Theoretical Roman Archaeology Conference, Sheffield 1996* (eds K Meadows, C Lemke and J Heron), 133–43, Oxford

Whitehouse, D B, 1960–1, A note on the pit alignments at Shenstone and Wall, Staffordshire, *Trans Birmingham Warwickshire Archaeol Soc* 79 (1964), 109–14

Whittle, A W R, 2000 Bringing plants into the taskscape, in *Plants in Neolithic Britain and Beyond* (ed A S Fairbairn), Neolithic Stud Grp Seminar Pap 5, 1–7, Oxford

Whitwell, J B, 1982 *The Coritani: Some Aspects of the Iron Age Tribe and the Roman Civitas*, Brit Archaeol Rep 99, Oxford

Wilkinson, T and Murphy, P, 1995 *Archaeology of the Essex Coast 1: The Hullbridge Survey*, E Anglian Archaeol 71, Chelmsford

Williams, D, 1984 Petrological examination of pottery fabrics, in Mayes and Scott 1984, 196–7

Williams, D F, and Carreras, C, 1995 North African amphorae in Roman Britain: a re-appraisal, *Britannia* 26, 232–52

Willis, S, 2002 A date with the past: Late Bronze Age and Iron Age pottery and chronology, in *Prehistoric Britain: the Ceramic Basis* (eds A Woodward and J D Hill), Prehist Ceram Res Grp Occas Publ 3, 4–21 Oxford

Wilson, C E, 1981 Burials within settlements in southern Britain during the Pre-Roman Iron Age, *Bull Inst Archaeol London* 18, 127–69

Wood, M, 1965 *The English Medieval House*, London

Woods, P J, 1970 Excavations at Brixworth, Northants, 1965–70, the Romano-British villa, Part I, *Northampton Mus Art Gallery J* 8

Woodward, P J, Davies, S M and Graham, A H, 1993 *Excavations at the Old Methodist Chapel and Greyhound Yard, Dorchester 1981–1984*, Dorset Natur Hist Archaeol Soc Monogr 12, Dorchester

Woodward, A and Leach, P, 1993 *The Uley shrines: Excavation of a Ritual Complex on West Hill, Uley, Gloucestershire: 1977–9*, English Heritage Archaeol Rep 17, London

Worley, F, forthcoming, Taken to the grave; an archaeozoological approach: assessing the role of animals as crematory offerings in first millennium AD Britain, unpubl PhD thesis, Univ Bradford

Wrathmell, S and Wrathmell, S, 1974–5 Excavations at the moat site, Walsall, Staffs, *South Staffordshire Archaeol Hist Soc* 16 (1978), 19–53

Wright, S M, 1982 Much Park Street, Coventry: the development of a medieval street, excavations 1970–74, *Trans Birmingham Warwickshire Archaeol Soc 92* (1985), 1–132

Wrottesley, G (ed), 1882a Staffordshire Suits extracted from the Plea Rolls temp. Richard I and King John, *Staffordshire Hist Collect* 3(1), 1–163

Wrottesley, G (ed), 1882b Final Concords, or Pedes Finium, Staffordshire, temp. Richard I and King John, Staffordshire Hist Collect 3(1), 165–77

Wrottesley, G (ed), 1883 Plea Rolls, temp Henry III. Suits affecting Staffordshire tenants, taken from the Plea Rolls of the reign of Henry III, *Staffordshire Hist Collect* 4(1), 1–215

Wrottesley, G (ed), 1884 The Staffordshire Hundred Rolls, temp. Henry III and Edward I, *Staffordshire Hist Collect* 5(1), 105–21

Wrottesley, G (ed), 1885 Extracts from the Plea Rolls, AD 1272 to AD 1294, *Staffordshire Hist Collect* 6(1), 37–300

Wrottesley, G (ed), 1886a Extracts from the Plea Rolls AD 1294 to AD 1307, *Staffordshire Hist Collect* 7(1), 1–191

Wrottesley, G (ed), 1886b The Exchequer Subsidy Roll of 1327, *Staffordshire Hist Collect* 7(1), 93–255

Wrottesley, G (ed), 1888 Extracts from the Assize Rolls and De Banco Rolls of the Reign of Edward II, AD 1307 to AD 1327, *Staffordshire Hist Collect* 9(1), 1–118

Wrottesley, G (ed), 1889 The Subsidy Roll of 6 Edward III AD 1332–33, *Staffordshire Hist Collect* 10(1), 79–132

Wrottesley, G (ed), 1890 Extracts from the Plea Rolls, 1 to 15 Edward III, *Staffordshire Hist Collect* 11, 1–123

Wrottesley, G (ed), 1891a Extracts from the Plea Rolls, 16 to 33 Edward III, *Staffordshire Hist Collect* 12(1), 1–173

Wrottesley, G (ed), 1891b The Chetwynd Chartulary, *Staffordshire Hist Collect* 12(1), 242–336
Yates, D T, 1999 Bronze Age field systems in the Thames valley, *Oxford J Archaeol* 18, 157–70
Young, C J, 1977 *The Roman Pottery Industry of the Oxford Region*, Brit Archaeol Rep 43, Oxford
Zach, B, 2002 Vegetable offerings on the Roman sacrificial site in Mainz, Germany – short report on the first results, *Vegetation Hist Archaeobot* 11, 101–6
Zohary, D and Hopf, M, 2000 *Domestication of Plants in the Old World*, 3 edn, Oxford
Zvelebil, M, 1994 Plant use in the Mesolithic and its significance for the transition to farming in Europe, *Proc Prehist Soc* 60, 35–74

Websites

Biddulph, E, 2006 *The Roman cemetery at Pepper Hill, Southfleet, Kent, CTRL integrated site report series*, in CTRL digital archive, Archaeology Data Service, http://ads.ahds.ac.uk/catalogue/projArch/ctrl
Booth, P, 2002 *Roman Warwickshire*, http://wwiaabhamacuk/research/fieldwork_research_themes/projects/wmrrfa/seminar3/Paul Boothdoc
Dalwood, H, 2002 *The Bronze Age has lagged behind…, Bronze Age settlement & landscape in the West Midlands*, www.ia.bham.ac.uk/research/fieldwork_research_themes/projects/wmrrfa/docs/Hal%20Dalwood.doc
English Heritage 2004 http://ads.ahds.ac.uk/catalogue/resources.html?eab_eh_2004
Garwood, P, 2002 *Early Bronze Age funerary monuments and burial traditions in the West Midlands*, www.ia. bham.ac.uk/research/fieldwork_research_themes/projects/wmrrfa/docs/Garwood%20txt.doc
Hancocks, A, 2002 *An overview of the ceramic basis within the broader west Midlands*,www.ia.bham.ac.uk/research/fieldwork_research_themes/projects/wmrrfa/seminar2/Annette.doc
Hodder, M, 2002 *Burnt mounds and beyond: the later prehistory of Birmingham and the Black Country* http://www.arch-nt.bham.ac.uk/research/fieldwork_research_themes/project s/wmrrfa/ seminar2/Mike%20Hodder.doc
Jackson, R, 2002 *Pits, Pots, Places and People: approaching the Neolithic at Wellington Quarry*, www.arch-ant.bham.ac.uk/research/fieldwork%5Fresearch% 5Fthemes
Mason, 1996 http://wwwuclacuk/archaeology/research/profiles/smason/smcoryl1 html (15/01/06)
Monckton, A, 2003 *Chapter 11: An archaeological resource assessment and research agenda for environmental archaeology in the East Midlands, in East Midlands Archaeological Research Framework: Resource Assessment and Research Agenda for Environmental Archaeology* Web version June 2003 pdf file http.wwwleacuk/archaeology/research/projects/eastmidsfx/indexhtml
Oelke, E A, Oplinger, E S, Bahri1, H, Durgan1, B R, Putnam, D H, Doll, J D and Kelling, K A, 1990 *Rye. Alternative Field Crops Manual, Madison, Wisconsin and St. Paul*, Missouri: University of Wisconsin-Extension, Coopertive Extension and University of Minnesota: Centrer for Alternative Plant and Animal Producst and the Minnesota Extension Service. http://www.hort.purdue.edu/newcrop/afcm/rye.html – consulted Jan 2007
Palmer, S C, 2002a *An Archaeological Resource Assessment for the Middle Bronze Age to Iron Age in Warwickshire and Solihull*, wwwiaabhamacuk/research/fieldwork_research_themes/projects/wmrrfa/seminar2/ Stuart Palmer.doc
Palmer, S C, 2006a *Ling Hall Quarry, Church Lawford 1989–2005, excavation of a prehistoric and Romano-British landscape*, www.warwickshire.gov.uk/web/corporatepages.nsf//links/42F31DEC8C968A4B80256DD400515547
Palmer, S C, 2006b *Excavation of an Iron Age settlement at Walton, Wellesbourne*, www.warwickshire.gov.uk/web/corporatepages.nsf//links/7DC9332DDA2A3D74892570ED004C4D3.
Palmer, S C, 2006c *Excavation of an Iron Age settlement at the A45/A445 junction, Ryton-on-Dunsmore 2005* www.warwickshire.gov.uk/web/corporatepages.nsf//links/D85A77DB93E2C08F80256FAC005C5A14
Pearson, E. 2002 *Cows, beans and view: Landscape and farming of the West Midlands in later prehistory. West Midlands Research Framework for Archaeology, Seminar 2: Pearson.* http://www.arch-ant.bham.ac.uk/research/fieldwork_research_themes/projects/ wmrrfa/seminar2/Liz%20Pearson.doc
Ray, K, 2002. *The Neolithic in the West Midlands: an overview*, www.iaa.bham.ac.uk/research/fieldwork%5Fresearch%5Fthemes/projects/wmrrfa/docs/Ray%20txt.doc
Wardle, C, 2002a *Roman Staffordshire: the five towns and beyond*, wwwiaabhamacuk/research/fieldwork_research_themes/projects/wmrrfa/Seminar3/ ChrisWardle.doc
Wardle, C 2002b *The Late Bronze Age and Iron Age in Staffordshire: the torc of the Midlands?* http://www.iaa.bham.ac.uk/research/fieldwork_research_themes/projects/wmrrfa/seminar2/Chris%20Wardle.doc
Willis, S, 2004 *Samian Pottery: A Resource for the Study of Roman Britain and Beyond: The Results of the English Heritage Funded Samian Project: An E-Monograph* Internet Archaeology 17 http://intarchacuk/journal/issue17/willis-indexhtml

Maps

Birmingham Fazeley Canal, by James Sheriff, 1791 scale 4 chains : 1 inch British Waterways Archive no. 6198
British Geological Survey 1:50,000 Solid & Drift, Sheet 153 Lichfield (1922)
British Geological Survey 1:50,000 Solid & Drift, Sheet 154 Wolverhampton (2001)
British Geological Survey 1:50,000 Solid & Drift, Sheet 168 Birmingham (1996)
Ordnance Survey 1956 *Map of Roman Britain* 3 edn, London
Soil Survey, 1983 Soils of England and Wales, Sheet 3, Midland and Western England, Soil Survey of England and Wales, Harpendon

Index

by Susan Vaughan

NOTE: figures in *italics* denote illustrations